WALTZ AT THE EAGLES' NEST

WALTZ AT THE EAGLES' NEST

A FABLE OF CONTEMPORARY DYSTOPIA

By

Miguel Oliveira

To my parents
To the ancestors

To my sister
And all my brethren

To the unborn

To the Earth

YOU SHALL EAT THE WEALTH OF NATIONS
AND IN THEIR RICHES YOU WILL GLORY

— Book of Isaiah

CONTENTS

WALTZ AT THE EAGLES' NEST

PRELUDE

1 - Days of Noise

Years before, through the same eyes observing the plastic bottle on the aisle shelf, Neipas had seen a vast swath of forest succumb in the fury of a rushing torrent. The waters of the flood were tainted deep with the color of the earth, and the air retched tremendous sounds of breaking wood torn from monumental heights; of giants collapsing against the melting grounds; of canopies quaking like the thunder of a million beating feathers, and mud roaring as it swallowed trunks and boughs and foliage in its path. All of nature screamed. Sometimes the noise echoed in his ears still; and the sensation of the experience shrunk his heart into the horror of its memory, which flashed yet, sometimes, in his mind.

It was, perhaps, something about the momentary failure of the intercom which brought those images and those sounds back to his recollection. But it was only a moment — presently the monotone music returned, bearing that subtle pulse in the background — and the flashback receded into the general daze filling his head. Neipas took the bottle. He placed the water in the basket (the overhead lights of the supermarket glinted on the plastic's surface as it rounded; the liquid shone crystalline for a moment), then walked along to the bread section and picked up a packaged loaf from the shelf. Then he grabbed a box of cereal and a jug of milk, and placed them in the basket. On the way out he passed by the meat section, and remembered a vague resolution he had made, that he should be eating healthier; and with the impulse he grabbed a wrapped cut of chicken breast, and finally a carton of eggs.

Amid the beeping of the auto cashiers, Neipas mumbled a timid "good morning" to the fellow in the ox mask. He was one of the supervisors — sympathetic as ever, he nodded his smiling horned head and said soberly "good morning, sir." Neipas shied slightly, his gaze lowered in the humility of gratitude; for the kind man had given him food in the past, during harder days. Without once looking up, he scanned the items, taking them out of the basket, over the beeping glass and into the plastic bag; paying then with a swipe of his debit card, he nodded bashfully at the supervisor, and left.

Neipas emerged into the airlessness of the streets, pressed with heat to the pavement and feverishly scintillating with the noise of motors, honking, steps, voices. The yawning sky was cloudless and the sun burned through it, spreading itself hot across the teetering asphalt lands and replicating itself out of the glass of windows and mirrors propagating throughout the megalopolis. The apartment complex where Neipas lived was but a few blocks away from the supermarket, and he walked with stare downcast, apologizing to the homeless who extended their hands for not having any money on him to give, passing alongside innumerable countenances of wax, half-dissolved in the thickening swelter, invariably afflicted. Aloft, the billboards dazzled with photographs of Eagles — by the apartment complex hung the golden beak and white plume of the Mayor, whose chummy grin curved over a suit tie and enormous letters.

He found the common area of his apartment in twilight, suffused with the crawling glow of rising morning. In the center, by the couch, the floor was strewn with yawning boxes of pizza and a couple of cola cans. His apartment-mate slept with open eyes staring out of his feathery mask; he breathed the sweaty air heavily, his pouting beak ajar. The shining screen on his belly rose and dropped with its oscillations, yelling loudly, filling the space through the absence of other sounds. Neipas said nothing and hoped his apartment-mate wouldn't notice him. Gliding through the blare, rustling plastics beneath his fist, Neipas opened the fridge and deposited in its chill the eggs, meat, and milk, careful to write his name on the containers with the marker. The bread and the water he kept in his own room, inside his wardrobe. He noticed the image printed on the bottle's label again — it was a photograph of an idyllic cascade towering above a sunny river. It reminded him of the river of his childhood, somewhat: maybe that's what it was.

Neipas collected his clothes and stepped quickly into the bathroom. The closed door muffled the computer screams, and the beat in Neipas' ears, streaming from his *I* out of the hooked buds, flowered in the newfound silence. Water flowed out the showerhead. The warm fumes, the jolly song in his head and the anticipation of the day to come pushed him smoothly into wakefulness. Today was the inauguration of the Axiac Zoo; and Neipas possessed one of the prized tickets for the event. The warmth, the steam, and the awareness that for the first time in a long time he had a day off work made him grow in energy.

The suppressed din of the earbuds returned to the fore of his mind as he turned the shower handle, and as he stepped to the sink Neipas found himself humming along to its tune. In the foggy mirror his shape appeared blurry and indistinct; passing a hand across the watery glass he unveiled the sight of his masked face, of his pigeon semblance — of circular red eyes, wide open; a profusion of iridescent feathers; a thin beak jutting from dilated cere, the wax of which bloomed over the nostrils and spread all underneath the plumage.

The reflection stilled through the glass, momentarily as alien to his perceptions as a gaze beyond a window. For a motionless instant, it stared... — until he recognized himself once more. At last he plunged his fingers into the wax and sculpted the drooping beak into a wide grin; and he pulled the feathers back from forehead to nape with a slick gesture of flattened palm.

Smilingly then, preened, his mask vanished once more through the edge of the mirror.

He left the bathroom into the emptiness of the common area, leading a trail of scented vapors out the door. The relief he felt at seeing the couch vacant and his apartment-mate gone embarrassed him a little. Sometimes he reflected upon how bizarre it was for two fellows who lived so close together to be so far apart. He didn't quite know why it was so. But he knew how he felt himself cringing when he heard the music and barren giggling inside the apartment upon returning from work's many grueling hours; and how he shrunk when he had to confront the dull, glowing gazes of the apartment-mate and his girlfriend, look into the skins of molten wax dangling beneath their gaping beaks, and ask fawningly if they could turn the volume down a notch. It was always awkward. The hesitation in Neipas' own voice nearly made him wince with shame. There was nothing obviously intimidating about the apartment-mate; but his conduct, which was sinister in its overt friendliness, and his constant proximity drove a bit of tension into Neipas' heart. Fortunately, Neipas was often so exhausted at night that he would fall right through the speakers' sound into sleep. But there was always somewhere some sound, some vague din, some elusive sense of discomfort. In those days the whole world lived in the noise — and yet there was something in Neipas that prevented him from getting accustomed to it, somehow.

Moving briskly after a breakfast of milk and cereal, Neipas rinsed his teeth, checked and molded the form of his visage; and, grabbing the *I*, he ensured his bedroom was locked, and went out the apartment. He strode quickly through the narrow corridor and rushed into the elevator, hoping not to see the Landlord, to whom he owed fees for late rent. He haunted the complex with his looming presence which seemed to stare out of every wall; and every second out in the corridors was an anxious race against the inevitability of being found.

Neipas flew through the submerged chambers of the *I*, floating mystically in its digital recesses. It stored many galleries, an infinitude of spaces interconnected in a wider system of large, pulsing threads, called the Webwork. The *I* was a portal to it. The object itself was small; barely the size of a hand. After all, it was but a glass; a slick rectangle with a surface of glass. It resembled a legless tabletop, upon which all things could be placed; a window, through which all things could be seen; a mirror, in which the mysteries of the soul could be known.

It was also a camera. The *I* was fitted with two lenses: the one, behind the screen, framing the gaze; the other, just over the screen, facing the stare; and it was at a perceptible change in the blurry curvature of his retina that Neipas looked up from the glass and into the window of the train, then emerging from blinkering red tunnels into the open sunlight. His eyes flinched and squinted before the dazzling expanse, the disarrayed splendor of the great metropolitan sweep, the motley spread of Columbia's biggest city, which was in those days called Axiac.

Shining colossi appeared in the distance, emanating the morning glare out of beaming bodies of glass. Here were the mighty towers of the financial district, center of the megalopolis. Giants of the age, they rose aslant in a magnificent climb toward the heights, in endless competition for growth and stature, soaring in the battle over the highest perch. Symbols and monuments to enterprise, they all loomed chief over a landscape of scrambled tar and concrete, plaster and shine, of faceless multitudes and utter confusion heaving across the vastness of a plain extending urban from mountain to sea. Yet none could challenge the central tower, prominent master among them, the tallest of all high rises, the Belab — it ascended with the fiery luminescence of a million windows to dominate all summits and dwarf all titans. The Belab, powerhouse of civilization, sank its powerful roots into the very hub of the city center; being, therefore, the exact core of the entire urban sprawl. A fervent glimmer burned on top, upon its faraway summit; an ardent sparkle, glinting at the peak of its height of shimmering glass lifted unto the heavens and above all things. That glimmer was called 'Pearl', Axiac's crowning jewel: lone flame during the day; lighthouse star at night. Neipas' accustomed stare veiled the awe he still felt when he looked at it. And before his stare was the eye of the *I* — Neipas snapped a shot; and, finding it well, he cast the captured image off into the digital pool, where it would buoy embalmed for the adulation of his peers, glancing transfixed from the edges of reality.

The train rushed into the towers' midst. Packed with anxious commuters — all, like Neipas, wore pigeon masks — it stormed headlong on tracks suspended among the dense gathering of skyscrapers pressing shade upon the earth below. Out the windows then rushed past many other windows, of a tall and solid stature, symmetrically piling into one another toward the clouds. The intercom's robotic tone announced the name of the approaching station, which read over the seats: "FINANCIAL DISTRICT (BABYLON)".

The station at Babylon was packed and in a frenzy of activity. There was the sound of steel grappling and screeching heavily as trains came to a stop; the booming noise of speakers overhead and all round rang omnipresent with announcements and advertisements; an incalculable number of bodies shuffled feet under a myriad voices sounding all at once; immense cloths dropped potently down the walls, beneath national flags glittering with confetti which powdered the space in falling flakes. Printed in the cloths were the faces of Arnold and Kruleva, the two Eagles vying for the highest perch of the land. Their masks appeared huge above the mass of heads, scattering and melding in and from all directions. In four days — general election day — one would be chosen to rule over them all.

Three trains had brought Neipas here. Waddling through the crowd, he squeezed into the last one.

A sudden shift of light at his flank made him turn his head. The train had dashed out of Babylon, and the blazing sky opened up before its tinted windows. Vast disheveled plains of asphalt, gashed with orderly streaks of white paint, rolled into the distance, with a uniform mass of vehicles reflecting the blinding sun from their roofs of steel. The eastern mountains lifted their peaks above the tar lands, their muscular rock facing the gleam, dwarfing the loops of road and the unending trails of miniature cars. Around Neipas a burble of motion ensued, the sudden progression of which coincided with a lull in the beat from his earbuds; all pigeon faces shifted sideways to capture the landscape with their glasses. Neipas did likewise, raising the *I* upon his mask. Those standing pressed against the windows together; the collective weight leaned fully on the side of the train facing the highway; and, after the pictures were taken, all ebbed back into their seats.

The lady on the seat in front had been looking at him for a while. She seemed vaguely familiar and Neipas was indecisive and awkward about whether to address her or not. Round them there was a humming silence of pigeon heads downcast, lost within the mesmerizing shine of their *I*s.

Finally, the lady spoke:

"We know each other, don't we?"

She beheld Neipas with tender eyes, in a gaze enthralling, deep of wisdom. Neipas chuckled shyly, and said, "You do look familiar... But I can't remember exactly."

"I'm sure it'll occur to us," she replied. "I'm Oshana."

"Neipas."

Their hands embraced. Oshana's friendly gaze was steady, and its firmness of stare made Neipas a little uneasy. It was a profound stare, which seemed to be peering into Neipas' very soul, hinting at its essence — for a moment Neipas looked back at it as though into a mirror, and as he glimpsed the singular plume quivering at the tip of her earring through the corner of his eye, he experienced the strange impression — a mere suspicion, perhaps

— of mutually fading masks.

"So, hum —" Neipas began. "What are you reading?" Oshana held in her lap a worn tome, bound with a thick cover.

"Not so much reading, as observing — " she said, holding it out and placing it onto Neipas' hands. "It's a photobook."

"Thank you," he stammered, surprised at being entrusted the volume. "I — I'm a photographer myself."

"A photographer?"

"Yes — well," he leafed slowly through the pages. "I want to be. This is good work."

"It has heart."

Neipas scanned the prints carefully, nodding. "It does."

"Maybe I've seen your work."

"I doubt that, ma'am," Neipas sourly remarked. "I haven't showed anything in a very long time."

Oshana contemplated the landscape as it curved toward the approaching mountain pass; and let Neipas browse the book quietly. He quickly became absorbed in the power and mystique of its images, taken in by their intensity of expression — they were made of strange compositions: all portraits, with two sitters each. In every photograph, the sitters held between them a large frame, within which gaped another photograph — that photo being the image on the previous page, within which was framed another photograph (that from two pages prior) bearing another photograph in it, which disclosed yet another photograph of the same kind, and so on successively, frame after frame, photo after photo after photo. Each picture was a reenactment of the very same composition, albeit with slightly different colors, slightly different postures, slightly different people: always two sitters, one looking back at the photograph, and the other to the front, at the lens, at the viewer. Every page arose or descended along the deepening series as its number advanced or receded. The images evolved in sharpness of definition and newness of technique — in the depths the photo became black and white, and in farther depths, the photo became a painting, then, in the farthest depths he could discern (his eyes neared the page so as to better see) engravings of some kind — and so on to undifferentiated distances. But the first page had the photographs vertiginously continuing beyond the book itself; and those of the last page, Neipas intuited as he scrutinized the amorphous face staring at him, continued too... Over the paper thus, his gaze hovered nearer and nearer, pulled by the prints' force of attraction, as if by an incantation; he analyzed the edges of the paper and of each succeeding frame, deeper and deeper; and his senses became themselves imperceptibly besieged, rounded by a silence; and he delved into them far — until, suddenly, he was hit by an awareness of having kept the volume for too long. He lifted his head abruptly among sudden noises — the car darkened as the train thundered into the shade of an underpass.

"Sorry," Neipas apologized, returning the book, somehow breathless; the train's roar and tremble along the tunnel shuffled themselves back into his senses all at once. It was as if jolting from uneasy slumber. He felt suddenly rattled, with vertigo.

"What for?"

Neipas shrugged and laughed uncomfortably. A buoyant and dewed sensation permeated the undermask. He considered he should have perhaps gone to work and not spent money on the ticket.

Oshana narrowed her eyes in a smile — delineating a steadiness of spirit, a soothing demeanor.

"Anxious?"

"(Has she guessed?) No..." Neipas looked up at her, reluctant and indecisive about what to say next — her piercing stare compelled him on, however, and he found the words flowing out his beak ahead of his own consciousness. "I guess I... I'm happy to have a day off but at the same time it's — I'm not earning anything today, you know? And," he exhaled in a flimsy attempt to scatter the strange tension gripping his heart, with a shrug of shoulders, shaping a grin, "time is money, ma'am."

"Is it?"

"Well —" he stumbled, shrugging once more, "that's what they say."

"Do they?" Her smile widened. "Maybe they do say it. Yet they're wrong. Time isn't money — but money is time, to those who have enough of it."

Neipas grinned in return; there was something about her voice, about her ways, her tranquility of conduct that becalmed him — and he said, "I guess... I'm definitely not one of those, though."

Oshana nodded sagely, empathetically; reassuringly, and as if to convey the notion that he was not alone. "And where do you work?"

"At the Belab..."

"Oh? And how is it?"

"Ah well, you know — it's ok." For the fourth time he shrugged.

"I see it everyday of course, but never went inside. Is it true?" she asked. "Do they hide treasures in there?"

Neipas chuckled sourly. "They probably do honestly. That's what they say at least," he concluded with a slight stammer, realizing he was repeating himself.

Oshana smiled. "They say many things, don't they."

An electronic blip rose smoothly, followed by the robot voice of the train. "Zoo Park Station" — the passengers gathered at once in a tight heap pressed against the exit doors, all anxious, in a uniform mold of downcast eyelids. Neipas got up and blended into the tail of the throng expectantly.

"Oh —" he began, seeing that Oshana remained in her seat. "Aren't you getting off here, ma'am?"

"No, no — farther down the valley."

"Ah, I thought you were going to the zoo too," Neipas said, looking back and forth from Oshana to the fore of the crowd, waiting for the doors to open.

"It opens today, I hear."

Neipas nodded, watching the closed doors.

"Watch out for the wild animals there, child."

Neipas laughed — somewhat nervously, for Oshana's semblance, though smilingly, had assumed a more serious expression.

"Well," he stumbled. "They're in cages, aren't they?"

The doors opened, and immediately the density of bodies streamed out from the train's slick shape, dispersing its colors and cramming its mass into the station, growing outward into the entrance of the zoo ahead. "Goodbye, Neipas. It's good to see you again," said Oshana as Neipas was dragged by the flushing tide, mumbling a clumsy farewell.

2 - Days of Light

In a moment he was out the door. Right away he was absorbed by sounds of growling, roaring and bellowing booming upon the crowd. His senses penetrated confusedly into the station and the thickness of the throng filling it, and his first impressions were of awe before the sudden noise and widening of space, and of weight under the heat, the uproar, the proximity of roving multitudes. There was an imprint of novelty caused by the sensational fanfare of inauguration. Balloons sprouted everywhere. Over and through them all came the cricketing of insects and the song of birds, and all the cacophony of dense wilderness; which was voiced — and looped — through the subtle grain of loudspeakers' orifices, imbuing the cries with a subtle synthetic tone.

From behind the shoulder of a towering pigeon Neipas glimpsed the entryway — a phallic gate yawning in the immense wall, ornately framed and flanked by long heavy curtains. Before it stood many desks and exuberant stands and displays, and many cow-masked servants walking about toward the excited beckonings of children, who shrieked through wide smiles as they held up toys made in the likeness of apes, lions, chameleons and horses, as well as clay piglets that could be stuffed with coins. The hall housing this gift shop, in which they stood, was vast. The walls afar, flat, were adorned with the silhouetted shapes of various wild animals under vague creeping vines, and vases with little flowers grew here and there by their feet. The ceiling — everyone pointed the lens of the *I* at it — was spread with a cancerous blooming of stocky roots, forming a tremendous pattern of interwoven wooden lumps glued to the top. The noon scorch beamed upon the field of heads and permeated the terminal brightly, cast out of a circle ripping the ceiling open just beyond the profusion of suspended vegetation.

A pleasant female voice thundered forth and echoed through the massive chamber. "Welcome to the Zoo Park of Axiac!" — the voice articulated each word jubilantly through its synthetic filter, pausing, rising and falling in volume with a great clarity of dictation. It, too, was part of the sound loop, piercing jolly through the din of beasts every now and then.

The horde of bodies pushed forth, monolithic, and began to squeeze like a great sponge contracting under the gate. Neipas, who hadn't advanced much beyond the train, wobbled tiny among the vast dimension of the crowd. He felt a tinge of discomfort; the heat affecting the grounds was intense, compounded by the scalding touch of the sun and the compression of many bodies of sweaty skin. A drop of perspiration slid down his face, and he worried that the moisture might disfigure the composure of his mask,

13

which he had sculpted so carefully in the morning. He took the *I* before his sight and saw himself in its glass; taking his hand to his visage he began to mold its surface of wax (a red light winked by the lens). A string of letters appeared over the mirror.

EVA: Very pretty :)

She was commenting on his photograph of Babylon. Eva's appearance in his *I* made his breath tighten; his heart deepened momentarily. An unconscious smile molded the shape of his mask. He peered deep into the glass — and the Webwork sucked him in.

NEIPAS: Thanks :)
NEIPAS: Heading to the zoo now. You should have come with!

The closeness and force of the multitude forced him to look up from the screen and place it against his breast; the space was so narrow now he couldn't extend his arm beyond the chin. He looked up disoriented, for he had forgotten what he was doing. It was as though a sleepiness had settled between himself and what he was seeing. He was by the gate; and was carried in with the flow of the seeping mass.

Beyond, a tunnel deepened and sank into many rows of escalators. Above their heads dangled lianas and the wall assumed the rugged aspect of a rock; though Neipas, who was by it, could see the texture was feigned, made of plastic. The bionic wailing of animals thickened here, and the children, brandishing new toys, clamored in even louder shrills, announcing to their parents, who hid their impatient indifference behind very sinuous grins, which animals they saw in the cavernous darkness. The multitude descended toward the revolving doors where a great formation of oxen inspected tickets (Neipas readied his own as he emptied from the rolling steps). The horns of their cattle heads lifted above the coming crowd and prickled the air as they yelled, "Stand within the lines, please! Single file, please!" again and again from swollen lungs. Neipas looked at his shoes and saw, near, a thick yellow line losing itself into the confusion of feet before him; just in its proximity was another. The pigeons rushed to stand between the lines, shuffling past one another in a delicate sidelong dance with the appearance of detailed coordination; Neipas, stepping promptly into a file, didn't rub the slightest shoulder.

The oxen, donned in pink and black overalls, mechanically ushered the pigeons through the circling gates. There was a terminus beyond, almost identical to the station they had just left. Again arose the flashy exhibits with balloons and the toy stands, and again the servants bobbed their grinning horns among the crowd. But the vines in the walls were now gilded thin, and the silhouetted shapes of beasts upon the wall were no longer black, but were now painted with the color of gold. The fat branches fastened to the ceiling were now shiny arabesque patterns. And the light that shone through them wasn't the sun's any longer, for they were underground — it was a strong electric light, not white but amber, through which drizzled some sort of flaxen powder...

There was a train at the end. As the visitors approached it the oxen organized them into rows; meanwhile the cow-masked servants distributed brochures and sold them souvenirs.

EVA: Next time mab :)

NEIPAS: And when is next time? :)

EVA: Soon ;)

He had plugged his ears to the wire once more. The music flowing out of it assumed a bittersweet tone, something primitive and hopeful stirred faintly within him. Neipas lifted his mask from the *I* glass then, and his eyes faced the entrancing sight of the grainy, gilded fog, through which the silvery horns of the workers slithered blurry and hypnotic. The cow-headed toy merchants walked about with big smiles; their horns shimmered with jeweled adornments. They wore feathery dresses. Like ghostly coats of fur they moved, sliding in steps among the multitude and into the darkness behind the stands. Children rejoiced with newer toys. Neipas, too, grew excited as he approached the train, suffused with marvel; beholding the novel view through the camera lens, mesmerized, as he shambled forth with the throng.

The train was very antique, from the epoch of settler expansion. Its sinuous, austere black shape and stirring iron bulk evoked romantic notions of adventure; its puffing was heavy, elderly, recalling the bygone times of its youth, when the land was still wild. The smoke cast from its pouting chimney filled the terminus in bursts. It carried perfumed scents — charging the inaugural scene with added mystique. Streams of pigeons filled its boxes as the oxen on the side speedily ushered in the lines. Carriages were loaded with passengers until all their seats were filled, and would then advance along the whole width of the rows of lined visitors until empty cars were facing them again — it was always the same locomotive, its cars connected in an endless chain stretching much beyond the bend in the wide station's flank. It was not long before Neipas stood in the front, being the next in order to board. He was then eased inside; and he faintly discerned the oxen over him saying, "please enjoy," upon which the door closed and the air became very snug.

Neipas leaned back into the comfort of the seat's padded rear. "Welcome to the Zoo Park of Axiac. We are delighted for your visit!" said the train's bionic speaker, voicing tones of overjoy. "Here at the Zoo Park, we pride ourselves in keeping the largest collection of wild animals in Columbia. The animals brought under our care come from all over the globe. As a matter of fact, we have at least one representative from each nation in the world! We keep animals of all kinds..."

The voice turned quite mechanical, with a didactical tone, as it hopped through the list of different animals. Meanwhile the train rocked comfortably, lulling its passengers into the monotonous song of its voice's address. Little children whispered frantic questions to their parents, whose eyes glowed in the phantasmagoric *I* lights illuminating the car (Neipas had just noticed, with some surprise, that it was now completely dark outside the window). The locomotive voice spoke ceaselessly, introducing to the hearer's attention the benefits animals enjoyed under Zoo management; expanding upon the catalogue of beasts available for view; honing in on a few individual creatures and expounding their heartrending stories, going to great lengths to explain how they were saved by the Zoo workers; using a plethora of esoteric terms to give various examples of this and that, etc. Neipas' focus had slowly drifted toward the noise in his ear, and he found himself humming distractedly when suddenly the voice of the train climbed to a volume higher than that of the buzz, exclaiming in a rising burst of enthusiasm:

"Enjoy your visit to the Zoo Park of Axiac!"

At that moment an intense flood of light burst through the glass. Neipas flinched and shied his eyes shut; before his pigeon gaze unfolded a vast span of green, grassy fields reaching mountainous distances, dotted by trees lined up in thick droves or lone upon the rolling plain. Scattered among the vegetation lay a jumble of work materials round makeshift cages, peeping in, badly hidden, from behind wooden trunks. These cages reflected the light of the sun in their steel bars as the train chugged past; inside them, Neipas was able to distinguish the faintest hint of motion, but he couldn't tell which animals that motion belonged to, for the confinements were either a bit far or otherwise very blurry. There were immense pools beyond, shining also the sun, among austere camps composed of long rectangular barracks. Yonder, farther, expanses of corn stretched athwart, like armies of myriad-armed monsters with golden heads, cloned in profuse succession to the edge of a big forest which reared its canopy in the drop of the prospect — from behind which (Neipas discerned vaguely through the *I* lens) a thin plume of smoke arose to the skies. The sun held still, scorching the earth from the distant zenith; the air appeared torpid as if in a waterless desert. In the glass and iron box of the locomotive Neipas sat in comfort and fascination, taking many photographs, brushed by the twirling breeze of conditioned atmosphere. The train's horn whistled long and joyful, to the delight of the children who gaped wide at the windows; even the adults were being coaxed by the sunny landscape out of their reverie. The avian swarm bobbed heads in every direction, sparks flashed out of their red eyes as they turned, feathers being released aloft by the motions, filling the boxed air; and all pigeons agitatedly cooed inside the carriage with much excitement.

The old machine heaved with palpitations of rail and iron, speeding up. Winding alongside the mountain rock, the tracks curved steeply onto the plateau, making for a smooth, concave stone wall that was draped with cascading banners and whose naked surface beamed as lustrous as the clearest glass. The banners, well visible from the outlying station from which the visitors had departed, hung like conspicuous landmarks over the plain, tucked beneath the ridge as they were, for they were so large — with their giant heraldic figures of eagle and lion, one at each side of the scarp, and the enormous letters announcing Axiac Zoo's opening day — as to tower as high as the most sumptuous palatial pillars imaginable, with ample grazed fields as their yard and expansive corn plantations as their moat. They billowed at the middle, in resemblance to sailcloth overhead; and the scarp itself, rising amply, majestic, looked like the inner side of an old galleon's hull fashioned from rock. A tunnel entrance yawned narrow at the bottom of its amplitude. Sitting, the pigeons all went toward it inside the vintage train, which had been the settler's vehicle when the nation was young, its pioneering and evangelist machine, vessel of the faith, enabling its wide expansion all across the continent. The locomotive seethed and puffed, exhaling rivers of smoke from its rusty lungs, and it shook, screeched and roared, sudden and boomingly, into the rock; penetrating into a gloomy terminus which ballooned sideways toward dark wooden walls. The locomotive then began to slow, churning languid, panting, its iron frame shivering — and finally, it halted with a rusty sigh.

Ox heads looked in through the window. The doors opened, and immediately they began to beckon out the locomotive's passengers, who oozed out in a thick stream clogging the vintage car narrow. They were inside some cavern. Already the gloomy chamber, outfitted as terminus, was brimming with pigeons twitching their fidgety heads, a whole parade of them crowding against the sunk walls made of tarred wooden boards, from which emanated a certain odor of pitch. Big screen displays by the tall gate ahead

17

showed animals moving around — the feed looked live — and many visitors stood by the screens immobile until the oxen finally herded them through. As Neipas went in he noticed many toys had been discarded by the entrance, forming a mound in the corner, already forgotten. Oxen eased bulky headphones onto the sides of the pigeons' heads as they stepped to. Neipas removed his own earbuds, and the music, which he had already ceased to notice, now stopped —

and a pillowed soundscape was pressed comfortably against his ears — his head was clinched by the headphones' talons. In the moment when his ears were free of sound he realized that all the pigeons were silent, and even the children were made hushed among the great crowd. They waited in a sinuous hall, narrower, amberly lit and severe in its quietude, soaring upward into overarching vaults which looked very old; intricately ribbed, the ceiling's keystones were darkly embossed with the likeness of animal faces. When the ox placed the headphones on Neipas' ears, he felt a compression in the range of sound, as though he had gone undersea; and it was as though the space itself had shrunk. The chamber's lights appeared to dim. And they dimmed further, imperceptibly; until it was completely dark.

The multitude disappeared. Neipas could not even make out their presence; and he experienced the uncanny impression not that the pigeons had vanished, but that his senses had momentarily malfunctioned. For a pace he felt vertiginous. There was an overbearing desire to stretch his hand to see if anyone was still there.

As he was reaching for the *I* in his pocket a voice spoke abruptly and dense — melodiously into his head:

"Welcome to the Zoo Park of Axiac, featuring the latest in immersive zoological entertainment! In order to enjoy this experience, it is important to be aware of a few important rules. First! You may speak, but please do not scream, yell, or shout, or raise your voice in any manner! This is important because we do not want to disturb the animals! Secondly. Please feel free to photograph, but do turn your flash off. This is very important because we want to keep the animals calm. Lastly: Please do not tap the windows! Remember! We want to keep the animals calm :)"

The voice's tone was very secretive, teacherly and paternal, and each of its syllables sounded like a gentle pat on the head. Neipas saw smiling icons in the darkness as it spoke. Faded dots danced in the deep gloom; but now shapes were emerging from the black, outlines were made sharper and forms a bit clearer. The expanse of the multitude materialized vaguely in Neipas' eyes. Another gate had opened yonder. A faint breeze came over them and the air rapidly changed, became thicker, hotter, pervaded by a stuffy scent reminiscent of a primitive age — a smell Neipas couldn't readily recognize.

scarcely had space to move and had to shamble across. Yet suddenly they stood before another large exhibit.

Beyond the glass gathered a denseness of vegetation, in a darkness beyond which it was difficult to see clearly. "Nightjars perched inside... among others," whispered the voice mysteriously. It was a display of birds, it seemed. They slept upon boughs but they, too, stirred with the screech — or something in the gloomy verdure twitched, for Neipas could see no birds at all. He found himself with eyes focused, leaning in with his beak near the edge of the glass (careful not to touch it; rapidly he retreated for fear of the throng pushing him). The voice spoke enthusiastically about the many species of birds on display, though there were none in sight. Neipas was filled with eagerness — an eagerness melding with the crowd's unpleasant bit of anxiety, made up of a vague sense that they were being cheated out of seeing those birds, which, after all, they had paid to see on opening day. Taps beat subtly upon the glass. Beneath, the children tugged at their adults' clothes, and the grown-ups arched toward the showcases and reached with their fingers, attempting to rouse the birds into motion. Neipas, moved by the same impulse, moved his face in again, a touch further, so near now that he thought he spotted the translucent ghost of his own face upon the glass surface; whereupon he distinguished, amid the confusion of boughs and leaves, a well camouflaged texture of plumes.

A reflex overtook him, and he found himself tapping at the glass. He immediately recoiled and retreated his arm, calling to mind the angry injunctions of the speaker voice; but no one said anything, and he leaned in a touch closer, and tapped the glass once more, very lightly.

The mound of disguised feathers stirred. At once Neipas thought he saw the scaly skin of a leg, thin, one of its long toes sticking out. It remained immobile for a while, and Neipas observed it closely. Not a movement; not for a few seconds of focus. Then, of a sudden, the feathers flinched and disappeared into the thickness of green. Neipas felt a pang in his breast, and a subsided tension settled in as he ruminated over whether to knock once more or not. His buoyant mind wondered, far-off, "but why did they put the birds here, you can't see anything" and as he was readying to knock on the glass with his fist, as many were already doing, he shrank suddenly under the deafening metallic voice overhead shouting "Please, refrain from touching the glass, or you will be removed from the tour!" which cut through the prerecorded talk. But the vegetation was now quaking; and quaking with increased intensity, it was soon shivering in a frantic outpour, a cacophony of exasperated cries, of discordant twittering and disgruntled birdsong booming from the disarray. In the wild swinging of foliage then suddenly exploded a chaotic tangle of feathers, a great jumble of birds squawking and cawing, dashing through, flapping wings in every possible direction; though nothing could yet be clearly distinguished from the abrupt, tumultuous frenzy. Children hopped and laughed, unruly; their parents giggled indecisively. Then, out of the center of greenery, strangely immobile amid great disorders all around, emerged a bulky bird with a large beak, approaching the threshold of its cage with little hops. Slightly bent, it faced Neipas with a look of curiosity. Without opening its maw, it proceeded to peck the glass lightly, striking it with its mandible again and again. Neipas only noticed it vaguely: the mass of visitors was already pushing him along, and he was still enduring the irritation in his nerves, tingling yet from the vibration of the voice, when they arrived at the next exhibit.

A halt, and a bright shift of light at his side, made his head turn. Beside him appeared another arena, a circular space of dry grass enclosed within another glass barrier. A singular tree rose from the trimmed span of greenery, constituted by a meager trunk and branches propagating from its head, speckled with leaves tepidly overhung, with a couple of vines dangling from the tall boughs. In the naked air sat an ape, clearly visible below the tree's faint stubble, its legs crisscrossed ably atop the branch, its flank leaning easy against the trunk. Its head was bent downward; the ape groomed a child, a baby, petting its tiny head with the loving fingers and caressing lips of a mother. The child, endearing and petite in its fragility, looked around with the marveled stare of a newborn, virgin to all the wonders of the world (Neipas, finding the scene picturesque, cute, snapped a quick photograph). Glancing down the trunk and past the tree, Neipas saw, a little distance beyond, a great ape standing precipitously before the tall tinted panes, with arms pressed against the glass dividing the cage from the vast exterior; its whole body described a straight, oblique line from ground to window, the feet standing far apart from the glass, as if the ape intended to collapse inert and completely upright — with arms flung in the air and legs stretched — and the windows had barred the fall. Now the ape stood in that position, strangely, and (Neipas noticed) beat the window lightly with the outer side of a sidelong fist. Gazes widened in a quietude of wonderment for a few moments; the echo of crowing birds rang into the gap, sounding from afar.

Neipas looked up again; and was then struck by a bizarre sensation, something possessing the tension of fear. The ape child, perched in its mother's lap, stared direct at him with a suspicious, sinister leer. Its eyes, black and opaque, had the irresistible draw of something eerie, shedding from its repelling facade a sort of mysterious pull.

The throng held a long time next to this display, proceeding only very slowly; Neipas following, with glare upturned and apprehensive, the stare of the child following him. A general feeling of discomfort got carried along —

Neipas suddenly found himself very tired — but now suddenly he flinched with fright, sharply; for one of the apes had emerged from behind the tree and hurled against the glass facing the audience.

"Don't worry!" mollified the voice, with a scientific cadence, as the tide of bodies receded in dismay. "They still cannot see you. Because it is so bright inside, and so dark out here, the glass entraps the light and gives off a reflection. The apes look at us and see only themselves, and because apes cannot recognize their own reflection, they will sometimes hit it, thinking that they are attacking an intruder."

Everyone stopped, and laughed. An entertained hubbub arose pleasantly in the darkness where they stood together. Neipas only chuckled nervously. Indeed he had been working hard lately, perhaps too much. For a while he had had the intention of changing his diet, which might help prevent these abrupt dips in energy. He resolved to do so immediately he got home. Contemplating the motions shifting by him, he perceived a certain pastor, whose pelican mask arose from the white collar gripping the top of his black cassock. He was in charge of a group of kids. One of them could not really understand why the apes could not see them, and he asked the minister to clarify. The languid rector leaned toward and twisted his head sideways and up, pointing to the top of the glass, to the light fixtures. Then he straightened his back, dignified:

"Well, little Paul," said the pelican to the child, who craned on the tip of his toes. "They think that's the sun."

Again the crowd, very endeared by the sight of the baby ape and amused by the great beast fighting his own mirrored image, grew unruly. Lights clapped above them now, pushing back the gloom; the children had either learned to turn on the flash or had done so by accident. Before the sudden volley of flares, the great ape beating at the glass started, and froze for a moment.

Then another barrage of pictures came; and the ape began to punch even more feverishly. "Please do not touch the glass! I repeat, refrain from touching the glass!" repeated the voice jarringly, many times, even as it said "Please do not use the flash!", all at once. Neipas was no longer close to the edge of the exhibit and could not clearly see what was happening. Though everyone laughed in overwhelming guffaws now, he shrank with apprehension, even with dread, sensing a noxious expectation surge to brim his innermost. He retreated; seized by a spontaneous impression that something was about to burst.

Suddenly the cacophony of birds, which had been sounding afar by the tail of the throng, erupted forcefully into the gloomy hall. The glass back there had broken and the uproar immediately rose to an unbearable pitch;

shards landed like rain upon the pigeons, who ducked in fear as the drove shot out. Wings flapped with the sound of machine guns and beaks cried great wails as they curved in flight over the heads of the visitors and thundered across the dark air. Panic broke out. Everyone jostled everybody as the voice mechanically shouted "Order! Order!" and the adults lifted the children up on their shoulders or dragged them as they ran. Neipas found himself struggling amid a great swarm of flailing bodies, and instinctively turning his head he faced the rushing stream of birds and saw a huge one already so near that it stumbled into him in the mad rush of commotions, claws bolting upon the cowed visitor, and in the next moment their flights collided with much violence. Into the cacophony of hysterical runners Neipas let out an effeminate shriek — just before the animal landed with force on his mask, stabbing it deep with its talons, jabbing it with a beastly wrath and slashing away fragments of wax in the general disorientation, flinging them away like dead layers of skin among a tempest of beating feathers, before the disoriented mandible thrust in brutal pecking, the creature's beak absolutely defacing Neipas' perfectly groomed visage; in a short amount of time it had dissolved into a mutilated mound of paste. The wax had gotten in his eyes, blinding him; the noise deafened his remaining senses; his whole body trembled in an unconscious fit of panic, his arms swung wide and frantic, aimlessly, while quivers of great trampling swept and stormed all around him.

He sensed his mind slipping away from him and his heart sinking somewhere within and beyond reach; and it was in this half-fainted state that he felt a strong grip upon his arms, his body lifting into space as if he were being carried away by a divine force.

"Sir, can you hear me? Sir, can you hear me?" a voice emerged out of the darkness, rising in volume and emphasis. All of a sudden Neipas was staring at the white ceiling of an ambulance. A screen, with a jagged chart depicting his vitals, filled it partially. His eyes were opened wide, rheumy, savage; through them he saw only a blurred vision of the confined space. His back was pressed against a mattress of some sort. "Sir, can you hear me?" the voice repeated in a practiced tone expressing serene urgency, professional and devoid of nonsense. Neipas must have nodded. "Sir, what is your name? Can you tell me your name?"

"My name? What do you mean, my name? What do you mean by that?" Neipas blurted out, delirious, before he sank back into the abyss.

3 - Days of Sickness

Parting indifferently and of their own accord, his eyes drew numbly a fullness of blurry white. Flickers of color poked the corner of them and made them quiver shut again. He perceived his chest heave closely; the profound, steady motion and sound of its climb and descent was the only tangible aspect of an otherwise small and inscrutable darkness. Echoes of vague attempts to make sense of where he was rang lone somewhere in his dormant head — they came and vanished without reply.

Noises at his flank reached him gradually. The clamor of a single voice — a wailing and beseeching coo — seemed closer and closer to him. His awareness of the sound grew and pulled him slowly and excruciatingly out of the daze. Then, a sound of steps clattering on the opposite side — the sharp clang of high-heels on vinyl. A gust of motion passing hurriedly before him. The professional and assertive voice of a female over the ceaseless cries. A flurry of steps across his head, heaving motions, a splattering of wheels.

Silence. Vague impressions stirred his senses. Little specks of dust whirled in the light and vanished about him, having barely come into being; ephemeral things among the vastness of existence, of which everything is a feast for time. Sometimes he had the impression of being at work, because he felt the odd, habitual pulsing he sometimes sensed beyond the walls. Some psychological membrane stirred yet with a vestigial awareness of it: a soft thud, coming from somewhere near, perhaps behind the door. It might have been a chance sound — something fallen — but it was too regular. It thumped at even intervals — like a heartbeat, beating in his head and breathing in his mouth. He felt very thirsty and wondered all the time why no one would give him water. His dreams were permeated with ash; dusty torrents blearing like a million goats thundering down the mountain, stuffing the air, barreling down his throat — he coughed profusely.

As his mind returned from the stupor in which it was enveloped and Neipas began to regain consciousness, an ache pierced sharply the middle of his head from the outside in. His eyelids twitched and indeed almost flapped, a sensation of thundering wings lingered upon them. But they were open, and had been for a long time; though only now did he realize he could see. Again the white was before him, opaque and complete. The color filled his vision entirely. He couldn't tell whether it was far or close. It was not quite as blurry now, though it took him a while to make out the yellow blotches of humidity spoiling its smooth progression. The flickering still acted on in the corner of his eye, though it was less jabbing now.

A long sigh of agony abandoned his motionless lips; he felt his face languishing. The headache dulled as a weakening overcame his visage. His hands reached for his cheeks. It was a nearly involuntary gesture, for he couldn't feel his hands at all. He could feel no more than his own face, it seemed; everything else was numbed beyond his senses.

Yet a vivid sensation stirred up in him as soon as his fingers touched the dried skin upon his countenance. There was something very strange about his own face, something disturbingly different.

Neipas turned his head. He intended to call the nurse, but she wasn't there. The patient bellowing in pain beside him wasn't there either — only an empty bed with stained sheets by the window. A balloon levitated atop a string tied to the rail. There was a TV hanging in the corner by the ceiling, glimmering images of fire and mobs scattering. Arnold the Tycoon emerged behind a pulpit, his blonde Eagle mask carved with its habitual triumphant, insolent grin. And again surged the flames; they palpitated convulsively, arcane: drawn by its hypnotism, which no longer stabbed his melding eyes, Neipas stared into the vivid fire and saw the moth dancing and throbbing around it.

The awareness of wires in his arms came slowly: rubber threads linking his arms and chest to a machine, which glowed and beeped lazily at his side. Raising his head (through the stiffness locking the back of his neck) Neipas glanced the wall. The framed photograph of a raised thumb mounted upon the middle of it. Then, as he craned his gaze to the other side, he caught sight of another bedstead, a drawn curtain and the vague shadow of an invalid lying in sleep.

His fingers rested upon his cheek for a while. He derived a sense of bareness from its cold touch. It roused a slightly unnerving chink in his breast, equivalent to nothing he had felt before. The fingers slid, and suddenly he was startled by the manic tremor of his lips. Why was he shaking so? — such thoughts occurred to his numbed brain with a certain casualness. The very air was suffused with vestiges of unreality. Even the way he breathed it in was different.

After an extended period lying down and staring at the languid ceiling, Neipas proceeded to remove the wires from his arm. With the utmost normalcy he rose from the bed, leaving the machine's incessant monotone beeping behind him. His bare feet touched the floor and he experienced the impression of receding gravity; all at once, for a moment, his head appeared to hover very far away from him. Neipas dangled as he stood. But he had barely noticed he had recovered from the queasiness when he realized he was already walking out of the room and into a blubbering corridor of rushing nurses, discarded stretchers and listless patients standing in wait by the walls here and there. There was a bathroom right in front of the room Neipas had just exited. He went in without hesitation.

It was a small, simple bathroom — a toilet on the left and a sink opposite, all encapsulated within disinfected white tiles. There was a mirror above the sink. Neipas, standing at the corner by the door, stared witlessly into the toilet which it reflected. There was something unearthly about this toilet. Somehow it seemed as though its hole had no bottom at all, and Neipas felt that it sank to impossible, unlimited depths. He leaned against the tiles for a while.

The mirror drew him closer. He neared it with uncertain steps, fearing steps, steps that vacillated upon the expectation of what the mirror would show. Once Neipas' reflected image entered the frame of the mirror he stopped, dizzy with the heightened sense of unreality that momentarily engulfed him.

As he faced the mirror he saw it. Neipas saw that he was no longer wearing his mask, and he beheld his real face for the very first time in his life.

He stood there for a long time, watching it, motionless. It was an uncanny visage, dirtied with years of accumulated soot piling up in a crust. His real eyes wavered with the minute twitching of hysteria. Gauzy red veins grew outward in the whiteness of the orbs; the bloodshot spheres encapsulated deep, void pupils. The lashes were stemmed at charred ends — indeed his eyes bore every indication of burning, and they gave off a slight ashen appearance. The face's pulpy skin — what could be seen of it through the soot, in its uneven gaps — was marked with creases and bumps, giving it a horrid aspect. The rest of his face was unremarkable. Neipas, in so far as he was capable of thinking in this surreal moment, thought it ugly. The sight of his face awakened only horror in him — a horror which was nonetheless small, blooming in the midst of an immeasurable non-feeling, an ethereal weightlessness that was the very stuff of dreams. Indeed, Neipas felt himself in a bizarre dream. Not quite a dream, perhaps, but not quite a nightmare either. What he experienced was something more bizarre yet, something beyond the bounds of precise definition. '*But no definition can really be definite,*' Neipas thought somewhat randomly, volleying his spirit across the dissolution of his mind.

The first thing that occurred to him to do was move his features; and so he found himself twisting his nose a little. Witnessing it move without the aid of his fingers was a source of immense awe for him, an altogether fresh experience, akin to the sudden and involuntary fulfillment of a magic act. Fascinated, Neipas continued exercising this newfound ability and he opened his mouth as largely as he could. The soot cracked as his features enlarged, and it hurt like a singe along the seams. He stretched his nostrils, then frowned severely, then widened his brow, then exposed all his teeth, then let out his tongue, then puckered his chin, then shook his nose in all directions. By and by the soot on his skin fractured loose and fell in dusty bits into the sink. Realizing this, Neipas turned on the faucet and, filling its cupped palms with cold water, took his hands to his face. Stooping over the sink, he scrubbed it with water and soap until it was clear of dirt and only looked up again once he felt it altogether clean.

Bending severely over the faucet, Neipas contemplated his real visage in its truest form. He stood silent. An immense, profound quietude burrowed into the farthest depths of his being, burying every perception. All things drew in and shushed. The droplets clinging to his naked skin were absorbed into the void. Beyond the soot, he could see clearly now the depth of it, the fealty of it. Shocked into inertia, he felt himself falling into it, hauled freely against an abysmal gale. He could not believe what he saw, and there was a pang of hurt in his breast, a dry thump in his notion of self that prolonged itself for the time he remained in the bathroom, and would linger yet for a long time to come. Yet, even with this wrenching sensation, he could not help but spot the clearness in his eyes; a mysterious depth, a profound presence staring into him, from inside him.

His chest dilated with the feeling of new air.

But Neipas became irked, suddenly taken up in an indistinct craving to get out of there as soon as possible. The compactness of the space seemed to tighten his breath. After peeing (with his dozed and droopy head far away, an infinitude beyond the hospital grounds) he opened the door — neglecting even to wash his hands, which was unusual for him — and went out.

When he emerged into the uproar of the congested corridor, Neipas all at once became hyper-aware of his exposed visage and felt a profound sense of shame. He stepped hurriedly into the hospital bedroom with a hazy intention to hide and straighten his bearings. The door banged shut behind him, making his shoulders jump in shock.

The commotion outside was muffled, immediately overtaken by the sickly quietude of the room. A smell of medicine pervaded the space. Close by the door, curtains fell around the bed and its invalid, the fuzzy outline of whom remained eerily still. Neipas circumvented the silky cage slowly; his steps rang absurdly loud, even though he was barefooted. And when he had barely cornered the drapes he halted, frozen, as his eyes caught someone standing over his own bed. It was someone huge, hovering massively over the deserted mattress; Neipas' breast rumbled with horror at the sight. An illogical dread seized him and rooted him into the checked floor for a moment. The beastly figure, who donned green plastics, looked down at a glowing tablet and poked away at it with all the fingers of his hand. He suddenly turned his glance up and straight at Neipas' frightened glare.

A reflex of embarrassment stirred Neipas into bolting upright even as he peeked behind the curtain, suddenly realizing his nakedness under the thin gown. He could not see the eyes of the form before him; he could not see his face, for it was completely covered by a surgical mask and layered on with a winding fishnet cap. He tensed. The nurse or doctor, however, looking utterly unsurprised and featureless, said nothing, and turning to his tablet again he kept tapping its radiating surface. Neipas only stared, curved and petrified. The imposing presence of the doctor-nurse shrank the space in its taut silence. Wordlessly he urged Neipas to lie down; and imperceptibly, Neipas dropped upon the mattress. He was again staring at the ceiling's blurry white.

"I'm feeling kinda strange," said Neipas — but he could no longer hear himself.

He had the impression of the doctor shouting; but his shouts were somehow absorbed by a great void, into a sinking quietude. Somehow he could discern meanings in the subtle throbs of this silence with perfect clarity, though he could not make out their words.

"Neipas, yes, doctor," motioned his lips, against the mummed air. "431999, yes."

Neipas then attempted to describe his new condition, but his resolve quickly dissolved to oblivion, as he hadn't perhaps even begun his sentence when the silence fanned upon him and asked about his insurance ("insurance" being the corporation Neipas made payments to in order to make sure he didn't have to make health-related payments if they came).

"I'm with... Health and Well-Being Insurance Services" he said, the numb feebleness of his mind beginning to fire up, heated in a rising flurry of mathematics. Would it be expensive, he wondered, and frowned. The faceless form intoned Neipas had been there 4 days.

"Four days?!" Neipas gasped in astonishment.

Yes. Many drugs were then prescribed in a dialect of names Neipas could not understand (immerse your head in water if you keep feeling weird, he heard). A moment passed. When Neipas ventured to look, the faceless doctor-nurse had already gone.

A slip of paper had been left by him on the nightstand, scribbled full of undecipherable glyphs. Meanwhile Neipas had left the bed. He stood uncertainly by it for a long time. He was alone in the room with the dim outline of the invalid beyond the curtain, from which emanated but a grave quietude. It was unclear whether the fellow was moving at all. There was little indication of it: an indefinite rustle from time to time, perhaps, though so slight that Neipas (who found himself staring at it) wondered if it was an illusion.

There was a drawer right under the wire-machine, which was still on and beeped continuously its monotone, electric whisper. In the drawer were his clothes. The jacket had disappeared; it had probably been trashed, for even the shirt Neipas had worn beneath it was shredded to mere rags. The mask and the *I* were lodged deeper. Neipas put on his clothes.

Then he took the mask in his hand.

It stared emptily out of its eyeless gashes. There was a thin mesh over them, a tightly-knit screen. Its cheeks of wax looked swollen, its beak ajar in a rigid picture of dismay. Or was it elation? he asked himself in the stillness of his breast. Mute, the slight curve at the beak's edge seemed to convey every feeling in its most zealous form of expression. It seemed enough for Neipas to blink; and the mask's stiffness would acquire a different shape. A subtle change seemed to bear its mark upon the mask's vacant features, upon that countenance that was so familiar to Neipas' contemplation. Familiar, indeed; but somehow very foreign now, too. It felt like the face of another, but it couldn't be. He looked at the pigeon mask as though it was the first time he was seeing it. Was it the first time? Was this his own face? he asked himself, in the gradual quickening of his heart.

And who was it beyond the silken drapery? As his bulging stare drifted away from the horrendous mask he wondered it; and there came a moment when a bout of curiosity roused Neipas to approach. The tip of his fingers grazed the soft fabric, but his muscles — calmly rushed with a sort of mystic languor — kept still. The room remained motionless in its quietude. Only the two enigmas of the maskless fellow and the shadow beyond the silk remained, eying one another.

Neipas found himself breathing very heavily as he stared. He found himself shocked to stillness; for he saw the invalid's countenance was hideously deformed. It was a pulp of gangrenous flesh, lacerated and burnt deep; a mess of pus festered in blisters, moist, bloated, rotten, without shape, without feature, damaged beyond the possibility of cure. The eyes lived still, gazing on from the profound recess of flayed skin; the chest swayed subtle in its shallow breathing, barely discernible under the gown. Upon the bulbous ear hung a pendant with a tuft of four little feathers, which identified the burned man as an Oyate — one from the peoples who lived in the mountain forests to Axiac's east, aboriginals of the land. His maimed lips, putrid, swollen and inflamed, were the most expressive of his unrecognizable features; they trembled and looked very scared, stuttering repeatedly in muted breaths. Neipas, tense and irresolute, neared slowly his ear; and he heard the immolated Oyate mutter a word, which he perceived to be "hook"; followed by still other forms of speech, perhaps delirious, but nonetheless unmistakably uttered in syllables which, however, rang mysterious to him, in a language he could not recognize. The mumbling, shivering flesh worked its gradual influence upon Neipas; the vision of such unbearable suffering seeped into the marrow of his own soul until the spirit twitched outward, and even the curtains seemed to stir in the dead air — the soundlessness of the place made him shudder and thump away with a fright, turning his back to the poor ailing invalid and stepping to his own bed.

Gradually, imperceptibly, he turned his gaze to the *I* which, unlit, showed his face upon its black surface. The sight was unfathomable to him. His breathing deepened, and then in surfacing it quickened as Neipas convulsed in the sudden grip of paranoia. Again he fixed his stare upon the mask. Diabolical theories rushed to his head all at once. What if it wasn't his face at all Neipas held in his hands? They might have replaced it by accident. Such mistakes are sometimes made. "All I have to do is ask for a correction," Neipas found himself whispering as he chewed a fingernail. Or was it on purpose? There was something about that doctor-nurse that wasn't normal. He cast off an uncanny vibe, his very presence was unnerving, he didn't even act like a caretaker; in his brusque way, he more reminded Neipas of a debt collector somehow.

Neipas paced back and forth by his bed as various thoughts consumed him. From outside a suggestion of sound began flowing in, by and by; a clatter of steps somewhere far-off, a distant rolling of wheels. He had sat on his bed by the time he realized it; and his gaze was again fastened to the mask before him. The bulging, lean beak receded into the youthful sleekness of its visage; the waxy skin, smooth and tender, spread under a glorious and fiery plumage; a semblance of many painted colors, the semblance of the pigeon named Neipas. It was his, without a doubt. Neipas turned it around and faced the reverse of the mask. There was nothing. Nothing but a somber hollow — the embalmed carcass of a gaze.

It was his own, and yet it wasn't the same. He sat for a long time, wondering whether he should put it back on at all. Meanwhile the chatter outside rose. The clinking of porcelain soles swelled to mad, repeated trampling; the frantic pushing of wheels would come to an abrupt halt when a heavy object slammed into the outer wall with a staggering blow; piercing yells would suddenly blast out of nowhere, sporadically, and from all directions. Startled by it, inside the room Neipas watched the door with a wide glare. A suspicion that someone could come in at any moment agitated him, and unconsciously he became very nervous that that should happen and someone would see him exposed like this. Neipas turned a blank stare toward the white curtains. He nodded shakily, darkly, to the invalid. An ominous feeling – something like fright resounding in a profound recess of his breast –

grew rapidly in him. Neipas thrust the mask into his bare face, and at once felt its waxen make surge into his true skin; the wax plunged into his pores and his every hollow, and latched into his spirit like a copious profusion of roots. Sounds intensified at once; colors were made a little paler, but less painful in their vividness; the air became denser.

He lurched out the door with his head lowered. In the corridor he took a random direction, walking it with unsteady steps. His hurried advance was halted as he rammed against someone, who promptly shouted "exit's the other way!" in a menacing shrill, making Neipas turn on his heels and nodding in a sort of respectful apology. "Take the elevator down!" the voice still thundered behind him. He reached the elevator gates, pushed a button to summon it and plunged into it the moment the doors parted. It was empty, but while he entered a large group of folk (whom Neipas hadn't seen) walked at his heels and swarmed the vast space, filling it in a moment and pressing Neipas tight into the farthest corner. His face was against the wall and he could hardly breathe. He tried to speak, but his lips could barely move and no sound came out of them. Everyone looked perfectly ordinary – jeweled bull-headed doctors sagging their shoulders after a long day of work, pigeons bobbing their downcast facades with the casualness of those whose affairs have been satisfactorily dealt with, or others nodding with the anxiety of one whose affairs are still pending. But the overall mood was tense, and there was some illegible chitchatting about something serious. Something serious that had just happened. There was a clear word about the election. Crammed up against the mass of bodies, Neipas thought — to the extent that he could think — whether they couldn't see him suffocating because he was in the most remote corner of the space, where the overhead light probably didn't reach.

The doors opened and the throng slunk out briskly. Neipas stumbled behind in a daze and as he gulped in the air he was immediately greeted by a swarm of pharmacists standing on all sides. "*Soma* helped me sleep better! Would you like a sample?" a robe-clad fellow asked as he extended a pill and a glass of water to Neipas' face ("no thanks" he mumbled in reply as he jetted past). In a complete state of disorientation, Neipas began running through the immense pharmacy, which was filled with different counters and a vast array of shelves awash with medicine and hygiene products, with gleaming advertisements stamped all over the walls and sales representatives donning a variety of suits scattered across the space. An endless sea of grins and hands holding pills stretched itself in advancing waves toward Neipas' contorted lips as he bolted out of the hospital.

It had cooled outside, though the stuffiness of the day lingered uncomfortably. The beach could be seen from the hospital grounds, which lay upon a hillock before the eastern mountains, with an open view of the shore in the west, on the opposite side of Axiac; one could easily spot the ocean from its windows. The sun had sunk well beneath the edge of the prospect. Vestiges of it remained in fading embers, spread across the limit of the seas afar; their placid stillness, reposing atop the outer rim of the waters, was similar in color to the meekly palpitating crimson alighting the sky above the very sharp, very black mountain peaks; as though a single conflagration consumed the two horizons. Darkness stooped upon downtown in the middle yonder. Equally distant from mountain and sea, its buildings rose stalwart and disheveled round the center of the megalopolis, blazing with the crimsons of dusk and deepening in the gloom of encroaching nightfall. The whole urban plain, extending in all directions out of Babylon, seemed to buoy in tones of red and amber, in blurs of gliding white, all shimmering — and from the very core of this broad expanse there lifted, quiet and noble, the great, the titan Belab. Hovering solitary above the majestic agglomeration of steel and glass, the Pearl glinted atop its faraway summit like a brave candlelight in an overwhelming wilderness, holding aloft, standing as the farthest outpost of civilization and grit against the hopeless immensitude of the universe. That most cherished symbol of moneyed audacity, the Belab stretched into the darkening heavens, culminating in a concentric mound of terraces splendorously thinning into a luminous peak, where shone the Pearl. A palatial complex of terraces and gardens — such was the Belab's summit, colloquially called the Eagles' Nest.

Suddenly, the Pearl burst open in light; the night retreated into the oblivion of space, and the tower manifested itself in full flare over the vastness of the city. The megalopolis was dazzled. Its brilliance drowned the fires at both ends of the world; its form was made clear and transfixing. The tower, the mighty tower, ascending from the fortified bosom of Babylon, from the very heart of Axiac, seemed to curve about itself, turning triumphantly, as if in a great strain toward the most highs: an inward spiral of glass and might, a contorted pillar, a spinning muse rearing the heavens; a motionless dance above the entire world. The Belab soared over all things. Somehow it seemed to keep growing in Neipas' eyes, like some manufactured growth unendingly blooming. The oftener he gazed, the more towering it looked.

Standing atop the flight of steps by the hospital doors, he contemplated everything with a vague mind. The dazzling vision of the tower banishing the evening had arrested his momentum; it deafened his senses and for a moment blinded him to the massive agglomeration of heads oozing below his feet ("Mary Virgin," he whispered to himself, mindlessly, instinctively employing an interjection common in his remote hometown). By the bottom of the staircase, where it met the roadside, an immense parade was marching down the boulevard with ferocious chants. It was a veritable swarm of raised hands, waving flags, and wide banners crowded in an obvious outpour of indignation. Thousands of pigeon masks ripped agape in shouts. Starry eyed, Neipas watched the passing protesters for a while. He was stunned at the spectacle and the whole peculiar character of the moment.

"We! Don't! Want! Arnold! We! Don't! Want! Arnold!" the multitude rallied and vociferated.

Out of choices, Neipas descended the stairs and was promptly soaked up by the pressing mass. He walked along with the inexorable noise in his ears. Looking about in a daze, he observed a confusing progression of blurred faces. Some yelled in very anger, wrathfully yanking their protest signs. Others kept a solemn stride, glancing toward nowhere and looking absolutely bewildered. A few cried; sobbed, even; wept in unabashed displays of hopelessness. Yet others, some of those who from time to time stopped to take photos of themselves, couldn't well conceal behind their outraged faces the primary motivation of just being seen in that moment, and at that place; some of them looked positively gleeful under their smartly designed signs. Nevertheless, the sense of bafflement, which swept the march in varying degrees, was common to everyone there; including Neipas, who unwittingly found himself among the throng. Their visages, progressing confusingly before his blinking eyes, all shared unmistakable signs of unsettlement. All of them felt the disquieting enigma of times ahead.

A train station neared the crowd's advance. As Neipas was squeezing out of its flank, everyone halted their steps. Cries of confusion rang up as the chanting ceased. Neipas, untangling himself from the throng as the clamor intensified, went up the station's steps and threw a glance at the head of the march. Soon he found out why they had stopped. Riot police filled the full width of the boulevard, facing the protesters in unbending formation. Their fearful helmets were in gleaming display atop their upright, powerful torsos; their gloved hands wielded maces, and ostentatious firearms gleamed strapped to their hips. Fierce horns piped out their gleaming heads, and from each of their masks protruded long funnels that amplified their voices. The chief riot officer spoke to the protesters through this, informing them of the lawlessness of their gathering and instructing them to disperse immediately. His warnings inflated ominously over the protesters.

Neipas entered the station with wide steps. It, too, was properly fortified by an assortment of law officers dotting the flanks of its entrance. Inside, a small group of folk had been made to sit on the floor of the platform, their pulses held together in cuffs behind their arched backs. A number of officers stood over them in a circle. Neipas, seeing the train on the tracks about to depart, hastened into it.

The train departed. As it progressed along the rails a disturbing mood settled between its walls and fogged its windows, growingly pervasive and hot. A sense of nausea assailed Neipas throughout the trip. Shrunken into his seat, Neipas winced and sweated. He acutely felt every little tremor, every tiny stir released from the train's frame. Every minute shift upon the tracks made him recoil; and he waned further into the seat's recess. This growing oppressive, physical agony was somewhat dulled by the aloof and anesthetic state of his mind, however. Neipas felt as if in a dream, except he retained a sense of time's continuity, the absence of which is the defining characteristic of slumber. Thus reduced to a dependence on his most disoriented and feeble instincts, he ended up reflexively pulling out his *I* once or twice. But even this he could barely muster strength for. Seeing the screen palpitate with all the bawling content of the Webwork, all the letters of all the messages, all the images and the memes, all the infinitude of simultaneous noise about everything, he only grew dizzier and turned it away. He strained the rest of the trip and heaved, then relaxed and fell into an uneasy lethargy, then felt pain again: in an contorting cycle; and all around the train was bustling with folk indifferently palpitating with excitement, busy propagating their feelings into the digital Webwork.

Somehow he found himself walking home. Groups of agitated folk passed by him. From time to time they stared at him with an expression of inquisitive revulsion. Come to think of it, many had stared inside the train, too.

His hand flung open the front door of the apartment complex, and the overhead lights buzzed on and rushed into his eyes. By this time his mild feverishness had passed; indeed throughout the whole time he had been aware of everything, but everything seemed to have a distinct aura of strangeness; there was an incongruity pervading things. Clamping and blinking his eyes, he walked toward the elevator. It was already there, the doors slid apart. And then he saw his face in the mirror. He jolted with horror.

The elevator doors slid shut without a peep behind Neipas, whose reflection stared back inside the mirror, from behind a mask that was melting at the side, its wax disfiguring into a mush precipitating off the jaw and revealing a bit of Neipas' true skin. At the sight of this his hand propelled into the wax and hastily attempted to patch it back together; a rushed set of fingers gestured in complex and skilled motions inside the paste, carving it with all the desperate passion of vanity and physical angst. His efforts were met with short reward; the wax held no longer than a moment before it began sliding off, sluggish and thick.

Someone had stepped inside the elevator in the meantime, a woman... The edge of Neipas' eye could just discern the warm plumpness of her curves. Maladjusted, he rotated his feet somewhat, and now stood awkwardly sideways — the pivoting mirror showing his face horrid, shedding off, very nearly disclosing bone. Her apparent indifference, mildly perceptible through the corner of the looking-glass, didn't factor in his numbed and mortified considerations as he inched closer to the wall. He was much too conscious of his own face trembling behind the mask and much too ashamed of his disfigurement to notice the abstraction of her nebulously eager semblance, whose silky plume, braided with strands of wavy hair, fell drenched in glass light from her *I* screen. The utter silence between them only accentuated his trepid sensation of misplacement, the offness of feeling...

The elevator shook open and Neipas shot out in a strangely energetic charge. Into the density of the carpet his shoes dug on and again in a bouncing progression toward the door of the apartment. Neipas walked in a lightness of pace and frailty of mind, stepping as if his legs moved of their own accord, as if he was detached from them and observed their sure thrust from a close distance. His hands kept pushing up his wax cheeks to their proper height and shape, handling the melting paste in between his fingers.

Neipas snapped out of this state when, feeling his hand pushing open the door of his apartment, he was startled by a potent gush of loud noise and a stuffiness protruding from the condensation of many mildly sweaty bodies; there rose a party of pigeons socializing in close quarters, swarming his small living room. They seemed, like everyone that day, to be mourning the election's outcome. There were so many voices melded in the soundscape that Neipas had the impression each fellow talked to everyone and everyone spoke at once; and though it sounded, and at first felt like a lively gathering, Neipas noticed that no one looked at one another; everybody looked at one's respective *I*. He had the uncanny experience of noticing that he noticed this (for the first time ever, he was sensible) and he sensed the bizarre realization of having observed what he had always seen. Presently Neipas, sensing the general shift of attention toward his disheveled figure standing dumb under the exposed door frame, advanced nervously into the crowd, hunched and downcast, the palm of his hand placed firm upon the wax seeping lazily between his fingers. As he dodged swiftly through the field of shoulders he couldn't help sensing a couple of sneaky glances in his direction, notably that of his roommate, who had made the irritating decision to organize that gathering in their common space without seeking his opinion. Neipas shut the door of his bedroom with an unwitting force (there had been someone inside, looking lost; "Oh sorry!") and he stood tensely still for a moment, wondering if he had made too much noise. In a swirling state of confusion he ran toward the mirror in his wardrobe and glimpsed a big chunk of wax sledding off his face just as he was turning. The sticky pulp landed on his forearms, which had automatically risen to prevent what had just come to pass. In the mirror he saw the side of his true skin revealed between mushy bits of falling goo — and it looked absolutely grim and sickly to him, the appearance of it inspired fear, disgust, loathing in his heart.

Awakened to this new image of himself, Neipas longed to sleep; standing there in swaying shock, feeling simply bizarre, he was again hit with the awareness of exhaustion, slackened all over as if he hadn't slept in days. Vaguely considering that he must go to work next morning (though it was yet very early) he undressed with all haste and, slapping back the squashy wax that had fallen from his uncovered jaw, he plunged into the sheets of his bed, being, however, careful to keep the damaged portion of his mask face up and untouched. Neipas precipitated into a restless slumber, remembering to turn the lights off just as he was falling asleep.

I

BOOK OF CURTAINS

The bus driving away from the ruins of their village had almost run over a little dove, and little Orenda, staring out the window and seeing the bird scramble just out of the wheel's reach, asked her aunt:

"Why does the pigeon only get away at the very last moment?"

Oshana replied. "Because they have to look down at the ground to eat."

4 - Axiac

In those days, History faced the horizon with blank pages; no one knew what form of suns unborn and the shadows of yet-incubating events would ink upon them. Hours melted by, imperceptible and confusing, and each minute shed from the previous with complete ignorance of its forbear. Every breast nursed great anxieties; they gnawed upon the deepest chasms of the spirit. Schizophrenic itches plagued the land. Eyes took shelter in the solace of distraction, in a downcast gleaming sleep — barely did they look up, they feared the horizon's dark maw and the somber pronouncements implied by its silence.

For those were days of turmoil. They marked the end of an age, and populaces stirred uneasy in the throes of its death. Epochal shifts coursed underfoot. Omens of storm suffused all quietudes; the air whispered prophecies of doom to those who understood its arcane idioms.

All the nation of Columbia roiled with the shock of its new leader then. Arnold the Tycoon conquered a full and permanent state of omnipresence over the streets, homes and minds of Axiac, its Capital city, when he vanquished the climb to its highest political perch. He loomed now over the whole world. From every display screen, on the facades of highrises, on the TVs nestled against apartment walls, on the sheen of *I* interfaces beamed luminous the victorious mask of Arnold, its lush eagle plume and radiant golden beak. His voice swelled and thundered over the megalopolis, made the shadows of its boulevards pulsate with the cadences of his frothing, wiry feathers; speeches of triumph ensued from the loudspeakers into the vastness of glass and concrete; his brash tone shot from earphones and headlong through the ears of the citizenry.

The national punditry was scandalized. All commentators gawked with unbelief in a vast commotion of wide open beaks. For in those days reporters were also soothsayers who squinted atop polls to tell the future — and all their predictions had come false. Mostly they had foreseen and rooted for Kruleva as the candidate of common sense and the rightful heiress to the office. Arnold was vitriolic, openly bigoted and — most gravely — indecorous and incoherent. Kruleva was diplomatic, refined, experienced. But she was no match for him. She was a representative of her class, technocrats who had ruled for decades and for too long had administered, through their abstraction of numbers, immense amounts of suffering on those beneath and faraway. None who lived in reality were surprised she lost. Kruleva and her class, who lived above reality, were Arnold's harbingers; they had dug the canals in which the worldwide torrent of hatred and chaos, of which Arnold was but a soaring wave, flowed then: a rising tide of nationalism putrefying all rivers and every artery, swamping hearts and minds across the globe. The technocrats had not a chance before the rampage. Most were sick of them. Even those who had brandished Kruleva's banner with enthusiasm loved not her, but the apparent sanity of her mask. And now all those banners, signs, flyers, flags, posters, placards, pins and every sort of paraphernalia with which they had marched lay strewn across the streets and rang crunchy under Neipas' shoes as he strolled about the mess, clapping his steps into the enveloping hush.

Neipas walked in the emptiness of a street at dawn. He hadn't slept much. Having surfaced from deep nightmares that undulated with the noise of shout and bass just outside his door, his eyes opening very wide and his breast gasping into a wakefulness of stupefaction, into the middle of the night, he scarcely perceived anything other than the descending beats of his heart for a while, descending into the mattress and beyond the rotting floor. And as time thinned out and his heart disappeared he realized — as if suddenly — that the din outside had ceased and the lights been turned off long ago. His own body, after all, had been all that sounded, and the whisper of his veins now echoed from the walls.

He sensed his numb limbs spread, facing the ceiling amply; he stared at the bleary red dot winking from the smoke detector; and he lay so, motionless, for a few hours, simmering in the lingering heat (perhaps the AC unit was broken, he dreamt). Neipas endured the ebb and flow of an insect's flight, shoring upon his ear and retreating; the rattling flow of pipes, the sudden rumbling of the refrigerator on the other side; an electric buzz pervading all things, pierced by the random spasm and blow of the AC unit; the intermittent, irritatingly sharp beep of the smoke detector on the ceiling; the tiny red blinker flashing in his eye.

He leapt out of bed in frustration and glided straight into the gloom of his apartment. Like a ghost he moved about, half-unconscious through the silence of a darkness softened by various isolated little lights: from the oven clock, the microwave watch, the orange glow over the bathroom door slumbering quietly against the walls, a computer screen looping and an *I* shining from the couch, where his roommate dozed with his girlfriend. He snored, casting grinding noises from the depths of sleep. The *I* was hers. She browsed into the Webwork, whose images were mirrored in her captured pigeon eyes so intensely that she didn't have any reaction to Neipas coming in. Going on in his ghostly stride, he opened the fridge and stared for a while. In a moment, a repulsive stench sneaked up into his nostrils; the meat, which he had bought the morning he went to the zoo, was rotten. He trashed it. He considered cooking the eggs but didn't want to wake the roommate or disturb the girlfriend, so he filled a bowl with milk and took it back to his room.

In his bedroom he made some coffee, dropped cereal in the milk bowl, and turned on the lamp, scaring away the half-light. Finding the window open (Neipas recalled then, hazily, stumbling out of bed sometime in the night and opening it) he sat upon the sill. The air came in spectrally, hovering over in its dead stillness. Windless, this air possessed but the relative chill of wider space; but it was nevertheless stuffy, retaining in its darkness much of the heat which the sunny day, long gone, had suffused into its wake. Neipas raised the coffee mug. Hot liquid rushed into his slumbering senses just as soon as the cup's rim touched his beak, scalding his instincts up into a sudden fullness of perception. Grimacing, he gulped a spoonful of milk and cereal, summoning a rush of cold sugar, injected in a breath across his brain. Then he leaned against the frame of the window, sighing profoundly — settling into the relative quiet.

He faced the window of the apartment across the alley. Reflected on it, like an apparition spirited from vague foggy lights, his countenance stared, emerging somewhat otherworldly unto his newborn view. Neipas inspected it slowly, distantly. He observed its feathers uncannily puff and contract in the tide of his own breathing. Masks regenerated during the night, deriving nourishment from sleep and soaking up the petroleum air of the megalopolis, which so fitted their essence — his mask, like all, sweated and sloughed through dreams, rejuvenating the smoothness and sheen of its surface and burying deeper all the mysterious things it hid underneath, all those things which often struggled to surface and with which it often fought in the dark. But the avian semblance looked saggy and tired then; it hadn't molted very well. It looked disgruntled, its plume unkempt (Neipas felt a remote need to shape it and comb its feathers). And his clothes... He'd been so overwhelmed by the horror of his bare face that he had scarcely noticed the pitiful aspect of his tattered shirt. He let his eyes pend downward in their contemplative despondency, their sleepless fatigue, into the mollifying indulgence of old recollections. For some reason he thought of his mother. Almost involuntarily, he reminisced little things he thought lost, snippets of mundane moments; her hand materializing in fumes, amorously sprinkling herbs over a steaming pot; the sway of her back as she bore him up and along, the almost certainly imagined thud of her heart.

Perhaps he simply felt a craving for maternal cares as he beheld his sorry state, his flimsy diet — the bowl and the cup, empty on the table now, smudged; perhaps he had been away from home too long. Sometimes his gaze would meet the *I*, which had been ditched on the bed and was still lying there. He felt a distinct — if remote, as everything in his spirit seemed to be then — a distinct undesire to grab it and check it, as he so often would reflexively during the idle moments of every day and upon every break in focused activity, no matter how minuscule the pause. He foolishly considered giving his mother a call — but he couldn't now, of course. The night was yet thick; it was prone to engendering odd whims in the soul. In a languid trance of flapping eyelashes and deep breaths, he seemed to feel his mother's herbs drizzling in ash through the alleyway as the mixed scents of charred wood, of food being cooked, and of a miscellaneous stench braiding in their levitated midst breathed into his nose; and from the bottom of the abyss between buildings, there seemed to ruminate the grindstone of the old mill; and even the gurgle of a faint river.

Having let his eyes close for a moment, and not wanting to fall asleep on that perch, he parted his eyelids and, calmly, with the resigned self-control of listlessness, he placed his glance there; and saw but the dingy narrow way and a frazzled vagrant, rummaging the discarded interior of a yawning garbage container. The chipped sounds came from his travails; the stirring water from the rumbling of pipes; the elusively pleasant smell from someone's early breakfast steaming in some other home; and the odor of burnt wood — from a place very far away. Neipas looked back up at the window reproducing his phantasmagorical likeness. Very pensive, the reflection gazed him back with an aloof stare, a far-off stare, a stare sunk in a strange face. Languid, their minds gradually drifted together in unconsciousness.

Bit by bit he sensed the presage of daytime. The gloom was scattering off very slowly as dawn flowered somewhere beyond those buildings, somewhere beyond the mountains, somewhere very far. And he sat there, contemplating the window of the edifice opposite, feeling vague impressions from days long gone.

Suddenly the window opened and a little boy emerged from it, stretching his arms out over the alley and yawning very loud. Then, straightening up, he waved energetically to Neipas, exclaiming "goo' mo'nin'!" Neipas started at the sight and waved back, chuckling in surprise and embarrassment. The next moment lights came on behind the window and a tender voice called from the deep, and the boy went off scuttling.

Neipas quickly closed his own window, shutters and drapes, and retreated into his apartment to get ready for work.

It was still very early when he got out. Outside, darkness had begun to thaw, and the dawn, commencing in the tall reaches of the eastbound boulevards, yawning just over the distant mountaintops, whispered now the night's coldest chill, something of its last breath before the sun rose to declare the day. Spontaneously deciding to take the bus — perhaps out of an instinct of material preservation, for the bus was cheaper and he hadn't worked in a few days — Neipas walked in the direction opposing the subway station and entered Ostrich by taking the street of the supermarket. Billboards loomed above him with huge masks shouting with mute bold letters. The Mayor grinned over the sidewalks, his golden beak and preened eagle feathers rejoicing in the fact of his re-election. Masks grinned from everywhere: all manner of figures overlooking the scene, donning mighty poses and fancy jewels, wielding luxury cars, wearing wealth. Neipas walked quickly beneath them all, he walked with a lowered head. Though he had lived here, at the edge of Ostrich, for at least a year, he felt still an elusive sense of oppression outside. Here there were only apartments stacked upon apartments, houses after houses; but he knew no one who lived in them. It felt as though he were huddled with shadows. The place was forever unknowable and sinister to him; he felt strange in it. Indeed, there was always a strangeness about moving in those neighborhoods, between those tenement blocks and boxy homes, with facades full of opaque windows, leprous walls bored with myriad blind, square eyes. Walking with a lowered head was assimilated behavior; he didn't know it and he didn't know why, but he feared locking eyes with someone. Without the lens of a camera his eyes felt naked, all of his vulnerabilities exposed at the bottom of their pit; and he felt always a queer tension that made him move fast. The streets were, then, but a cold extension of home: he had left it just as quickly. The roommate still snored, the girlfriend sunk still in her *I*, lounging immense upon the couch in the very middle of the apartment, absolutely indifferent to Neipas' presence, pressing him out with her absolute indifference. He felt like an outsider in the neighborhood, like a squatter in his own home.

Squeezed between the endless old shoddy houses cast across the boulevardian slums of Ostrich's edge, the horizon began assuming a pale hue of velvet, emerging into the feverish yellow blackness of city lamps that blanketed the drowsy sky. Neipas roamed out of range of the residential quarters, with its decaying splendor only barely reminiscent of bygone, prosperous days; and entered the old commercial district, stepping in between low building blocks of cardboarded windows, walls of chipped plaster, and rotting signs adorning decadent storefronts. Upon the sidewalk stuck tar blotches, dotted all throughout, all covered with the usual litter — discarded cans, rumpled carton and plastic, shattered amber glass — and the occasional flattened cardboard, upon which human pigeons sometimes lay under soiled covers, asleep.

At last the bus stop pole emerged to him, lonely under the lamplights; the bench next to it hauntingly empty with lurid colors. There was no one there.

Hearing his last step shushing into the eeriness of urban quietude, Neipas looked round upon the void street; blinked to its pallid blurs; sighed into its gaping stillness; crossed his arms, and waited, uneasy and irresolute.

He stood before the mouth of a tunnel under a bridge, into the darkness of which the road plunged cryptically. Behind him, the broad asphalt and the thin curb sloped up across a series of pools of glow. Though he had used this bus stop many times, he had never been here so early, or so very late, alone in the night yet thick. The solitude accentuated the area's evident dereliction and poverty; the silence brought to sharp relief a certain febrility of character, and the lamplit atmosphere hung breathless with warnings and premonitions. Notions of walking back occurred to him; but he had already walked too far. Anxiety weaved vaguely into his chest, as though prolonging inward the halted motion of his body; the unnoticed haste of his march persisted in the drum of his deepest veins. He kept looking from one side to the other and upward to the railing behind and over him to see if anyone was coming; he stared at the yawning bench, upon which he sensed ghosts, every now and again. Every little sound made flinch the dim tautness of his heart. Spectral nothings would tremble in the corner of his eye. The pavement elongated itself from him under splatters of graffiti and grime, and as minutes breathed on the whole landscape began to acquire faintly psychedelic contours in Neipas' sleepy and increasingly frightened perspective (by and by he molded his mask into a scowl; it was better to look menacing and somewhat insane; for a few moments he focused on his foot pattering the sullied curb).

His wandering eye chanced over that very foot — over the bit of floor upon which he stood, and which he had not yet left since he arrived. Raising his leg with a weird feeling, he realized that under his shoe lay squashed a certain bug; a beetle of some kind, a scarab. Scraps of street food (a paper, some meat) scattered strewn just by; a whole community of ants scurried and circled over it in a frenzy. Their collective writhing made it appear as though the cement itself was moving.

Neipas took one step to the side and, unattached and as it were far away from his own hands, patted the worn textile of his pants, underneath which he could faintly imagine minuscule legs crawling.

Time passed by insidiously, loopy. He found himself observing the underside of the bridge down the road near. It was crowded full of darkness; a nearly inscrutable gloom out of which only the faint outlines of a row of tents, lined up along the entire sidewalk, could be made out. From that indistinct space coursed a feeble wind dense with rancidness, penetrating his senses profoundly and surreptitiously. Faint, frail cooing breaths whispered through the fetid draught, tepid sighs of the tunnel's black gullet murmuring its imbibed afflictions, miseries, wants. Neipas' eyes narrowed heavily in their drowsiness. The underpass blurred and the gloom twinkled, stirred with dark suggestions, of the mute sufferings housed within. There were growls and meek bristling feathers in the low snore with which those exhalations rolled. There were pleas in those cooings; there was absorption in the motion of the breeze. It riveted his stare somehow. The sight, dim and insinuating, inspired fright and identification in him; diffracted recollections surfaced from its gloom; he looked at it as though into an abyss of hidden mirrors. A familiar dread of being sucked into that pit formed in him as the nauseating smell encroached deeper into his breast. Perhaps he feared one of those homeless folks withering there would surface out and confront him. How many times now had they approached him with their inarticulate cries without form or language and laid at his feet their despair beyond comprehension? Neipas swallowed and shriveled. What was perhaps most unsettling was just that part of him which understood. But what power had he?... he had barely the force to help himself. Gradually, imperceptibly, he began to pace to and from the pole, and describe circles around it as if in hopes of conjuring the bus by sheer will. He felt himself very vulnerable in that deserted place all begrimed with the stuffiness of deprivation, very small in the darkness and the pallor of sad lamps, very sickly in the grip of that stench.

Yet he didn't have to wait much longer — suddenly the air currents blew faster and hotter, overtaken by an acrid smell of rust and gasoline, the puffing of old machinery — and out of the blackness of the underpass appeared the bus. It slowed with a deep screech; its long, worm-like metal body — spanning a multitude of connected cars — heaved drawn-out puffs and came in shivers on every side; its heavy frame halted by Neipas with an unruly sigh.

He stepped into the warmly lit interior. "Good morning," the driver greeted behind the massive wheel, voice clear through the rumbling of the engine.

"Good morning — " Such were the first words Neipas spoke that day. And they burst out of him with an unfamiliar eagerness, a sudden wakefulness, a youthful energy he hadn't been conscious of or knew he possessed until the morning air filled his lungs to become words in his lips.

He quickly produced the fare and inserted the clinking silver into the box machine that separated him from the driver, who then uttered, affable and sober, "thank you" — Neipas thanked him likewise with an eager nod of the head. Advancing into the deep aisle (perhaps endless, for he couldn't distinguish the far end resting in shadow yonder) of the long bus, he chose to sit not far from the front, close to the first exit door. He sat as if tucking into the comforts of hearth and the safety of lock and insulation, all relieved; the rough bus, aglow in the cozy lights of welcoming shelter, felt as though it were embracing him against silent frosts of hunger and despair metastasizing in anonymity outside.

For a while he watched the bus driver through the top mirror, handling the wide steering wheel with the stoic rectitude of a serene and experienced spirit, looking absolutely undisturbed under the heaviness of his horns. His ox mask betrayed not a hint of sleepiness or fatigue, conveyed nothing but focus upon the execution of the driver's task; the driver presiding with his alertness over the front of the bus as a lighthouse shines over the darkness of quiet oceans. All space behind him floated in a soft liminal drowsiness affecting the few scattered passengers. One, a couple of seats in front of Neipas, rested his head against the window and slept; his scraggly feathered nape peeked just over the back of the seat and stirred along the bus' bumpy path. The pigeon on the aisle-facing bench rested his burdened, half-closed eyes upon the fluffy luminosity of his *I*. In front of him sat a very erect lady whose beak yapped soundlessly and whose stare, agape and neurotic, swerved over the aisle across the orbs of her own motionless head. Neipas beheld their masks in profile and regarded in particular, with a type of dormant, incurious interest, how the fellow smiled at the *I* from time to time, and how his grin extended into a laugh to slowly die back into an impassive expression; replaying this in numb loops as his mask dipped gradually closer to the screen and his face lowered ever nearer to the ground.

All of them tilted and shuffled as the bus' heavy frame churned forward upon its tires, and as the tall glass of the windows trembled, and the overhead lights pitched up and down in quick shudders and squeaks. Beside Neipas, across the aisle, a young woman propped her feet on the back of the seat opposite and leaned against her window. She contemplated the passing streets with close attention. Her shoes hung over a dusty, rumpled backpack; an indistinct slab of cardboard, or something like it, jutted out the top. A little notebook rested on her sloped lap, she tapped her pensive lip with a pen. Her hair, tautly intertwined with plume, was combed back into a loose hairbun, nonchalantly knotted high, facing Neipas directly. A single feather pended from her earlobe and shivered along with the creaky body of the bus. He could only see her face as a hazy reflection upon the window glass, brimming in the inner lights; he could only discern her concentrated gaze as enigmatic hollows staring into their own vague blackness. Lulled by the sight of her hairbun, erected straight atop the head, bobbing with the bus' stirrings, he dove his vision into her window and joined her in observation.

The contours of the corner shops and the endless avenues were growing in definition now. The light of the sun, which hadn't yet attained the summits of the range outlining the ragged hem of morning, had already begun to delineate the streets and to tame them with its soft glow. Lampposts were being turned off; the streetlights dissipating, conquered by the ascendant star, their pale, sickly white hue vanishing at once from the plaster of walls and the rusty entry gates of low-lying buildings. A few stragglers, lost pigeons pushing shopping carts or arising from hard slumber, wandered in the loneliness of the roadside. They dragged themselves and the full weight of their meager belongings — the few blankets, the scarce clothing, perhaps some toiletries in which to store a little dignity; and their maddened heads, which bore their debasement, their time spilt rotten upon the wastes. Their masks bubbled with groggy tar and feather, hanging low and onerous; their filth-encrusted nails clutched the handles of their carts and the edges of their boxes with a grip as precarious as their hold on life. Passing by shuttered gates unending, long abandoned, long sealed with layered shells of graffiti of signatures without name — ambling through neighborhoods long neglected like figurants against a background of crushing indifference, their slipper-clad feet trod the pitiless concrete and never produced a sound. But Neipas could see them now somewhat, emerging from the tunnels and under the awnings and out of the gutters, and again disappearing across the brutal landscape, into the edges of the glass. Sometimes one or another would climb into the bus as it rolled, stop after stop, intersection after intersection, shuddering through the rookeries of Ostrich, past myriad echoed sceneries beset with the same voiceless afflictions. Those who entered invariably shambled past Neipas into the unknown depths of the aisle — and meanwhile he remained abstracted, with unwavering eyes settled on the opposite window, watching the crumbling frontiers of Axiac pan on by.

With detachment, he discerned the flaming spires, the chimneys and the gritty sky of the industrial zone behind the shanty boulevards; between the houses he saw the oil pumpjacks working discreetly in the half-light, and in this suddenly he perceived a subtle motion from the young woman sitting on the other side of the aisle. Just then he realized how vivid their reflections appeared on the bus window, lit as it was by its ceiling lights; and that, through the glass, the woman was looking at *him*. Neipas abruptly averted his stare, taming the motion of his head so as to be as furtive as possible. In a gradual manner, with a few awkward repositionings of his body (he acted as if he had suddenly found something troubling in his seat) he turned his face toward his own window.

As he refocused his mind he noticed his own reflection on its glaring surface.

Again he saw it. He had beheld it in the spectral window opposite his bedroom; guessed it in his bathroom mirror, through the fog from the shower; glimpsed it innumerably reproduced across glossy puddles, resinous windows, the sheen of parked cars and a myriad other dull and shady surfaces on his way to the bus stop. The mask — it glanced out of everywhere. In beats and intonations it recurred, in fragments scattered and wedged in the implacable face of Axiac; flowing when he stepped near, ebbing when he stepped away. Crooked, deformed, it presented itself to him now as an uncanny motionlessness against a shifting city, a phantom hovering immutable over fluctuating landscapes, a flame ghostly suspended in a passing river. It faced him with a dejected, resigned simper; an unsymmetrical stare, manifesting, perhaps, the fundamental dissociation between the projection and the beholder. Neipas had worn it for as long as he could remember; for all he knew he had been born with it; nonetheless he couldn't recognize himself in it now. He had thought it to be his face; now he didn't know anymore. Yet it was he. Who else? he wondered at that ill mess of paste and feather, that contorted stare eying him far from his idea of himself. But though the sight pained him he was no longer assailed by the panic of the previous day; only a mild, sleepy confusion and something of melancholic curiosity affected him as he inspected the panting gap in his mask, through which he could yet see the depths of himself, his true face like a mewling wound, and as he tapped it gently and bizarrely in a rueful attempt to cover it.

What did it all add up to? He frowned into slow breaths; into deep breathing. His mask leapt from blink to blink in his tired and tapering vision, in the manner of accumulating fragments, of frames straining toward a coherent totality of sequence. He sighed; rubbed his eyes; shook his head lightly. The existential dullness that lulled him against that bus seat bubbled bit by bit with vague calculations regarding the basic matters of life and survival. Numbers broke languidly into his thoughts. His drooping beak intoned a list of bills pending sharply over his conscience.

Rent pressed him as the most urgent concern. The next deadline would close in fast if Neipas got distracted and he couldn't afford to accumulate more late fees; he had to toil extra for those he still owed, and pay it all at once lest he provoke the Landlord's rapacious leniency and unleash his wrath. Additionally, the variable price of utilities, unevenly availed but equally endured between him and his roommate, who worked from home, loomed as a dreadful unknown in the shade of all his tensions. Because it took the majority of his monthly funds, the apartment was an ever fermenting source of worry, it made him feel as though he were housed at the brink of a parapet. Of course, there was also food to mull about. Though he was employed at a restaurant, Neipas had no right to free meals and the discount for workers was risible; he was able to snatch a crumb from the kitchen every now and then, but most of his nourishment he had to derive from cheap ready-mades and supermarket sales (he ascribed the growing hollow in his stomach to his inadequate breakfast and wished he'd brought a sandwich — he thought of the rotting meat he had had to throw out that morning as the bus winced uncomfortably about him). Transportation claimed a substantial portion of his paltry budget as well. He had been considering buying a 30-day pass to save some money, but it was a gamble; it might be little worth it and he could even incur a loss, unless he used it every day without fail. But what if he got sick? The discomfort of lingering hospital airs tightened in his breast, he wasn't yet confident in the wholesomeness of his health — which reminded him of his healthcare insurance premium, the cost of which might be affected by his prolonged hospital stay, and the dues that might imply. Best not to dwell on such riling suppositions for now, however... He tapped his *I*. What else was there? Every new month brought a new installment of college debt, which the settlement money he and his sister had received, after years of legal struggle, hadn't sufficiently covered. There were also the hefty monthly fees to the Telecommunications and Webwork companies which kept his *I* attuned and functional. What else? What else?... He'd certainly like to purchase a new camera — a new apartment — maybe a ticket out of here. His mouth released a sighing, silent laugh under the mask's sagging beak — he stared fixedly at the *I* mirroring his curvy lip amid his onerous reflections. He assimilated them as added weight upon his weary soul; chains twined round his innermost heart; like an excess of gravity hardening the already burdened air laden with fumes. His mask stared up from inside the black mirror, growing larger and larger, and it seemed to crumble in digits upon the glass which was then, suddenly, glowing on. The *I* was a magical object — which, when touched, alighted and showed the hour; showed, over his face, the distillation of time in the numbers which so made him stoop. He seemed to see these numbers, he seemed to see time itself extending in shadows, bleeding into a fiery, gaping horizon that blinkered with scarlet tinges. How he wished to transcend it all, to enliven his plumes and overcome the weight of his troubles, to escape the earth and its toils and fly over the difficulties of existence, watch life with the wisdom and tranquility of distance which renders all things small... But mostly, how he wished to go back to bed and sleep, instead of going to work! He pictured the dingy walls of the restaurant kitchen with the anticipatory angst of a soul mired in the linearity of an entrapped existence — already he saw the kitchen fumes, the stove flames blinking (a red dot blinked over the screen of the *I*, beside the lens; someone was messaging him — who was it?), blinking with the anxious heartbeat of merciless labor and shrinking hopes... They blinked everywhere — amid a growing fire.

Neipas sighed. The bus grew insensible at his shoulders' lowering, and on the window, the image of his feathers amplified like an immense pillow yielding to the touch; and they spread like messy wings extending over the highway, and seemed to render the massive, shuffling bulk of the bus (as the eyelashes met) weightless. For a moment, he imagined the tires circling out of the ground, grinding nothing but air or rain. The driver unclasped his hands from the wheel and finally straightened his round back, braiding his fingers comfortably behind his head and setting his eyes upon the nearing sun — and all the eyes of the passengers twinkled and glowed in its flame as the tires spun, spun, spun, slowly, with the spirit of the winds and into the waters of the sky, as it lifted through the burning turbulence of lofty foam and sweeping clouds of ash. It shook once, and again the window opened into Neipas' eyes. His plumage rustled gently when he drew his gaze apart; seaweed in alighted glass, shell creature beholding the aquarium. He appeared vaguer. A long exhalation coursed between his lips; he sniffled. The tires underneath him had ceased grinding the rock of cratered roads and slid now upon a much wider, lighter, smoother tar carpet, which levitated over ghostly shanties, running like a skyway above indistinct neighborhoods extending on both sides of the bus as it sped north toward Babylon. Outside, everything circled, and as the tinged sky wheeled about itself the very soil of Axiac seemed to lift toward as though summoned by the imperceivable voice of its crescent motion. He beheld mystified all things blooming behind the wraith of his own brightly mirrored face.

Then the overhead lights vanished; and his mask was gone.

His sight deepened beyond the reflection into the mammoth landscape that materialized in its stead. There rose the titan towers of Babylon, glass giants looming imperiously over the highways with the glare of a million soft conflagrations. Sunlight already glimmered upon the high peaks of their magnitude, flashing like rotating diamonds; and Neipas grimaced in the brief intensity of luster before the vertiginous facade of the Financial District passed again out of the window frame as the asphalt curved. Ostrich slid into view once more. Receding under his gaze: expansive, mute, tidal glaciers of disjointed roofs breaking toward an incandescent sea, rippling at the far end of a vista of towering labyrinths of steel and great cauldrons smoking amid the haze of industrial pollution; the air turbid with flames spewed out of spires, mixing with the stir of the waters of the dock, from which stacked the innumerably vast chemical and energy plants and refineries that, dominating the skyline over the shanties, proliferated in their midst. The aircraft beacons blinkered yet on their chimneys. Against the tender warmth of dawn, their red wink resembled that of maddened, demonic, rheumy glares in a struggle against the fatigue of a full night's work keeping watch over the insomnia of the rookeries. The long tails of airplanes made of auroral embers and cooling froth extended over the bay — like dissipating garlands, festooned above it all... On the other side (Neipas turned his head and eased his gaze into the opposite window, beyond the young woman who kept staring fixedly in that same direction. The glass no longer mirrored them; it plunged fully into the landscape) the city stretched in a motley flatness of roofs — with but a few lone towers peeking out — towards the mountains in the East, marking the brink of the megalopolis: imposing, immense, they rivaled in their solemnity the haughtiness of the skyscrapers aspiring to outmatch their height. Like silent trumpets their summits heralded the sunrise, which still climbed the dramatic altitude of the range, coloring the mountaintops with the rosy waking murmurs that were softening shades everywhere in Axiac. Yet the light flowering into the cusp of the air that dawn was sickly. Neipas could detect its febrile pallor much more clearly now, as he observed the fervid eastern quarter. Sometime earlier, he had fuguedly glimpsed somewhere in the Webwork that immense wildfires had sprouted in the mountain forests up there; and indeed, there was something of flames' fulminant munching in the shivering edges of those crimson peaks.

The mountains delineated Axiac's borders in the east; the ocean swayed over them in the west. Neipas turned again to the cluttered rabidness of Ostrich under his window, running southwest-bound, and had just time to catch a final glimpse of it before the soft light of dawn was quelled from its rotting plasters and its shiny steels — for the bus, coughing up and shaky, rustling its creaky metal bulk, sneaked under Babylon's vast shade and entered its wide boulevards; the window dimmed in the shadow of behemoths, and he suddenly became aware that the bus had filled up, had vacuumed in entire neighborhoods of destitute workers and beggars on its way here. It was so abrupt a realization that he wondered if he had slept (out of nowhere someone was sitting right next to him). The horizontal chasm looked packed from end to end, thickly humid with sweat, hot with stench, full of muttering. Very near him now a pigeon languished in a wheelchair. Dressed in rags, draped with a soiled cloth in an advanced state of disfiguration — leaving much of his grimy skin bare and exposed — all precipitating in tatters toward the ground, the man inspired pity and revulsion. That same stench which Neipas so often felt wafted from the bowels of the city: it emanated thick out of the poor fellow, and it was obvious the commuters closest to him held back in repugnance, gripping their breaths; their own masks couldn't hide it. He seemed crippled with a depth that transcended the physical; something about the collapsing slant of his shoulders (Neipas could not see his face) denounced the gravity of his condition. Neipas beheld him uncomfortably, but the vision was such that he couldn't easily withdraw his perturbed stare; it roused an uneasiness of painful recollections, it summoned up old, latent fears... He turned his gaze back to the window.

Through it he saw, dyed in a pattern of tiny dots — for the exterior of the bus side was covered with ad posters from end to end, looking opaque from afar but through which one could see well if one were to look closely — he saw Axiac's Financial District laze past, with its myriad vehicles gliding into the folds of heavy shadow cast by the skyscrapers, massive, rectangular and clear-cut, occupying a vast span of land which cleared only to make way for the infinite horizons of asphalt of the crossing boulevards. Pillars crowned with brand logos, idols of the age, arose beside the tar roads. Cars most often sped hastily by, jetting through with a cutting sound; but sometimes their tremendous number grew too sharply in so small a space that they clogged it together and were forced to halt. Neipas beheld their stale, air-conditioned interiors, where pigeon heads impatiently poked the air over their steering wheels. Hugged by engorged leather seats, they all looked numb. All their eyes looked dull and breathless. It was as if all those faces had been pressed into the same cast of fatigue and disinterest, as if they were being gradually cooked or ground out of joy and care by the same machine (they only smiled when they looked at the *I*). The bus drove now on an overpass squeezed among four towers. Their insides were still exposed, their interiors full of lights, always on; their glass faces transparent. Just out Neipas' window slugged past the infinitude of other windows, of a tall and solid stature, that made up those bland faces, symmetrically piling onto one another toward the clouds. And in those windows amassed cattle; men and women with masks of bull and heifer, donned in suits, bending over machines, great apparatuses made of light.

All looked similar in their look of profound alienation; as though a stranger's soul were staring out of their eyes.

From the streets below (under the bridge — Via Sacra, the ample north-south boulevard, lengthened away from its bend) levitated a flock of balloons trailed by unmoored cords, rounding the noises and sights through their muted multicolored plastic filters as they flew... The man in the wheelchair hunched. Neipas' stare was again fixed upon his torn back. It caused him confusion, a bit of nausea, to contemplate the trembling wheel of the wheelchair firm on its axis while the world in which they were presently caged rumbled atop churning tires. A certain low grinding sound ingrained itself into the burrow of his innermost, most intimate and most secret thoughts, tickling his memory, gnawing his body contracting among the swaddling crowd. Abruptly they pressed with more force. The lengthy throng was discharged and then immediately refilled with multiplied numbers, each expecting the bus to take them to some isolated nook of the sprawling megalopolis, into the shadowy alleyways and hidden portals beneath its vast towers of glass. The young woman on the other side of the aisle arose to bequeath her seat to the arched feebleness of an old pigeon. Neipas' conscience prompted him to do the same; he relinquished his spot to whomever wished or needed it, and reared his head into the dense confusion of masks, straight into the thickly packed air, teeming with sweat, humid with stench and hot with bizarre noises uttered from demented lips trembling somewhere amid the pack. And yet, packed though they were, the wheelchair vagrant was still given space on account of the stink ensuing from his tattered body; what could he be mumbling? Neipas wondered for a moment. He couldn't know; he didn't want to know, and with a swerve of the head he tried to shove from his mind the recollections such a vision summoned. A sense of claustrophobia drew him away through the crammed swaying heads and toward the exit door. (He peeked into the *I*) it was still early... A little bell rang as he pulled the cord running along the side, coinciding with one particularly anxious heartbeat (he felt, in its ping, a presage of the call to work) and soon the bus began to slow down. He shouldered free from the jam and got off a few stops earlier than usual.

*

The air scattered free and Neipas walked a good many blocks across the openness of Babylon. Over various airy sidewalks he strode, almost at a gallop, prodded on by lingering claustrophobias and animated by a habit of racing against schedules. Various sidewalks whooshed under his eyes — many buildings vanished in the corners of his sight, until the space abruptly and dramatically expanded as he turned into the Via Magna.

He didn't notice the shift at first, possessed as he was by the abstraction of his rush; but he was compelled to slow down by and by, as he became aware of an almost vertiginous strangeness of contrast between that street as he was used to seeing it, and the street as he saw it now. There were no crowds then. Sounds were but scarce. It was still early, after all. The Via, usually so packed, so noisy, was suffused with the quietness of the present hour, which belonged to the silent cleaners; stewards of dawn, heralds of the day, who swept the urban night's litter out of civilized view.

A cool breeze glided and twirled across the pedestrian thoroughfare, breathed past the windows of stores dozing unopened, ushered along the shadowy oxen heads whose hands gripped the hoses and the rasping brooms, caressed Neipas' half bare cheeks. It felt odd. The gentle wind, carrying the tranquility of infant sunrays into his skin, stirred in him a sort of novel perceptiveness, something broadly encompassing, something laced with uncanniness and some discomfort. The very wideness of space through which the breeze coursed, suggesting a wide lassitude of time, fostered the sensibility rousing his heart to open and envelop every facet of his enormous surroundings. His pace slowed further; the path drew deep into his senses as he advanced; he watched it all, and felt it all at once pervading him. Via Magna, the massive, central boulevard cutting east to west — from the mountains to the coast, clean through the core of Axiac — flowered before him, empty; its broad promenade empty, its lush shops unattended, its copious restaurants deserted, its great advertisements quiet and giant display screens off; vacant, save for the timid presence of sanitation workers moving purposefully here and there, whose banter fell mute in the ample void.

They worked their way — sweeping and watering the grounds — toward Neipas as he stepped slowly across the pavement, all strewn with pamphlets and the scraps of political propaganda left abandoned after last night's election. Lowered over a side-building in tall cloth, like a hale and wholesome curtain, the amplified face of Axiac's Mayor grinned over the tatters of his political party's defeated campaign. He, at least, had been reelected. Widely considered to be a climate champion in those days when the climate had turned ill and mad, a liberal hero and paragon of political sobriety in those times of insanity run amok, his victory (narrow though it had been) had been hailed by pundits as a saving grace for reason and decency — though Neipas, who'd been in the hospital and therefore couldn't have voted (and probably wouldn't have voted even if he could) took little notice of such things; politicians were all vaguely the same to him.

Above him, above the billboards, highrises, great solemn towers ascended over the thin haze of dawn, drinking the heat of the swelling sun; its light sparked from the yawning heights of their summits, waking gently the sprawling amplitude of their windows (their reflections sunk darkly into the pools dimming over the floor's slick sheen). Heavens soared out of it all, pulling all things toward them like a magnet of vertical distortions; drawing to them nothing so much as the tower standing, the tower rising at the end of the boulevard. That tower seemed to erect itself higher and higher at every step — Neipas' blinking, dewy glare inevitably craning up with it.

Before the Via, there stood the Belab — the tallest, the mightiest, lord among the giants of the earth. Its godly magnitude lifted itself over all things upon the land, over the sea, the city, the mountains; it grew from the core of the megalopolis to rear into the very brim of the universe; it transfixed Neipas in his isolated walk and sensory absorption, as if he were beholding it — it so familiar to the distraction of his gaze — for the first time once more.

A vision of power metastasizing to indescribable proportions, the Belab was made up of sharp facades of clear glass which reflected the climbing megalopolis in its inhuman heights. The towers surrounding it, composite monuments of Axiac's economic prowess, mirrored it too — forming together a true labyrinth of mirrors, wherein each mirror mirrored all other mirrors in an alpine infinitude of reflections.

...as he walked past the cleaning crews, discarded papers levitated in impotent whirls like the muted gust of demonstrators in the night. Mannequins ogled his unconscious stroll across the boulevard, standing alongside eerie balloons; under gaudy billboards and glaring logos yet asleep, in unending succession, from their eyeless semblances and atop motionless poses they watched. Ghostly perceptions and unshaped musings came into Neipas' breast like whispers from afar, indistinct and mysterious, as his legs took him to the crux of Babylon.

Soon he reached it. Here was the center of Babylon, core of Axiac — Belab Square, from the middle of which arose the colossal Belab. The world gaped tremendously before its mighty feet; as if the universe itself were opening up before Neipas' steps and expanding into his heart, gradually and immensely, as he neared the majestic tower which had so captured his stare. With vertigo and breathless awe his attention progressed upward, and lifted slowly to the impossible vision of unending heights, up the continuous floors of shimmering glass finally fusing with the sky, losing themselves, evading the perception and comprehension of whomever ventured to find the summit from the perspective of the soil. Neipas inspired through mouth ajar. His nape pointed to the ground. Indeed, the top of the Belab could not be seen but from far away; there was no proof of its existence to be detected or descried from where he stood, except for the strange, unnatural gleam radiating overhead in the dim, celestial remoteness — the light of the Pearl, the incandescent Pearl beaming on the brink of the firmament.

It shined as dazzlingly as he had seen the sky erupt the previous night. Poised far aloft at the outermost borders of the planet, it was like an indelible boundary mark declaring dominion over heavens and the land. Pharos of civilizations, some called it, standing so tall as to overcome all horizons and the very curvature of the Earth. It could be spotted from everywhere (some said), crowning the distant, the sumptuous Eagles' Nest: the palatial complex on the topmost floors of the tower was almost mythical; and if it could not be truly seen from anywhere it could, at any rate, be everywhere heard — by those who mustered the sagacity to listen. Two portentous bells filled the steeple above its Ballroom, hanging each just under and on either side of the Pearl. And if it was true that no one had ever seen those bells (as it was also said) anybody in Axiac and perhaps beyond even Columbia could perceive their toll, twice every day, precisely at the beginning of the work-day and of the work-night, as it rang outbound across the shivering air into the inattentive, because accustomed, unhearing ears of the Columbidae. Neipas seemed to listen to them now in the sonorous quietude which permeated their absence, feeling the hush in his sinews as their foreshadowed vibrations.

His eyes lowered piously from the crystal pinnacles, from the ivory glow twinkling through the droplets of cascades drizzling up there, out of the streams that watered the gardens of the Eagles' Nest. Into their diffusing spray the Pearl shed its glimmer and refreshed the airs below, sprinkling the deep mesmerizingly, descending in flashing particles between the innumerable skybridges which connected the highest storeys of the towers rimming the Square to the yet higher floors of the Belab at various oblique angles; their intricate shadows, patterned like a wide net cast upon the aqueous forms of the huge circular terrain, landed softly, and glistened; landed softly beside that far-hailing light, which, fading in fervor and increasing in gentility and benevolence as it descended, settled, at last, coolly upon the ground to enlighten Neipas' captivated eyes, through which it entered, rippling across the wax and the plumage of his mask. It enchanted him. It bewitched him. It seduced him with allusions to great and marvelous things. And with the dreaminess of dimmed perceptions his gaze returned, imperceptibly, to the ground, as if reverently crushed by the sheer weight of that vision, and reposed upon the quietness of his halted feet, in stillness shod; and within which he could, somehow, feel that elusive pulsing he sometimes heard beyond the surfaces...

Tepid shades huddled round in the concrete. The sun climbed resplendent over the mountaintops at last.

The Pearl light shifted tenderly then; the glistening shadows scattered along the encroaching sunlight and into a mellow, watery shade, breezing softly, like a pervading mantle, across the vastness of the Square, mollifying the air, allaying his breast. Neipas lifted his head; and noticed numbly that the woman sitting yonder on the floor was staring right at him.

The plaza looked rather bare at that time of morning. Twelve bronze gryphons standing over twelve little fountains, and four flag poles beyond, one at each quarter stationed — with a few trash cans and stone seats disposed diagonally in between — all but made up the entire furnishings of that barren, wide yard. It was delimited by a hazy assortment of hotel lobbies, eating houses, entertainment stores, currency exchanges and machines, offices, empty lots full of mailboxes, and other miscellaneous and obscure enterprises housed at the base of the surrounding towers. Neipas didn't exactly know what existed there. He had never had the time to explore the rim of the huge area, so that the businesses operating there were blurry, faraway things to him; and even in those days when the storefront windows loomed closer, and the square seemed smaller, as if it were being inhaled into compressing lungs of glass and concrete, still he was always kept away by pressing demands of schedule and exhaustion, either in a hurry to get to work, or in a craving for bedroom and sleep. He dimly reckoned that the souvenir shops, with their postcards, statuesques, simulacra and miniature copies of the immediate landscape constituted the majority of it; for that was the type of commodities the vendors who walked around during the daytime were seen selling: parading between the crowds with waving arms and smiling horns, every limb and bone laden with flags and photo-strips, appended with whole jungles of little ivory and silvery gryphons hanging from necklaces, swinging. Meanwhile the original statues remained inert and exalted above the throngs.

Imposing monuments though they might have been, however, they appeared somewhat insignificant now, in this vastness of a nearly peopleless morning; invisible in their muteness (for the fountains were still off and did not ring) with scarcely anybody to soar over. Columbia's bold motto, which was trumpeted (IN HOC SIGNO VINCES, it bellowed) from their plinths, lingered disregarded and unread, though a few pigeons were already amassing toward the base of the Belab, looking reluctant; a few others were trudging out. The two massive boulevards that crossed the Square and the infinitude of small streets plugging into it fed the space with growing trickles of half-wakened bodies. And amid the gathering rivulets of workers streaming yet thinly, that woman who stared at Neipas — wearing an unkempt hairbun, of brown feathers and with a single plume pending from her earlobe — was conspicuous in her stark immobility. Neipas recognized her after a moment — it was the woman who had sat across from him in the bus.

She held up a cardboard, as a protester might wield a sign — but the sign said nothing. No letters, no message was imprinted upon it, but the blankness of the texture flat and enigmatic on either side. Sitting on the concrete floor in the manner of an ascetic, with legs crossed at the base of a perfectly upright torso (from which two straight arms sprouted), the woman seemed to Neipas for a moment — a prolonged, quiescent moment — as though she could sense beyond his mask what he had himself seen, just as well as he had seen it, in the hospital mirror when the mask was not there. Something (something familiar) in the intensity of her stare, which after all couldn't have lasted more than a fleeting instant, suggested the depths of an unusual discernment. It disconcerted Neipas and by the time his wits regathered he found himself moving, listening to the hollow tap of his footsteps, observing the glowing *I* hovering above the looping kick of shoes over the rolling ground. When he lifted his head in her direction again, she was already walking away — the numbers of plumbed heads were suddenly building up, and the Square quivering, astir in the expectation of pealing bells, as they coalesced and heaped toward the center, draining along desolately to where the Belab plunged its mighty weight, come from the highs to thrust into a recoiling, smothered earth; and sink to depths so remote that its reach was, perhaps, unknown to all but its unknowable makers.

Krow's Underground Restaurant nestled somewhere within the Belab's subterranean floors. Somberly, Neipas descended the staircase encircling the tower's broad base (so broad, it was said, that it would take days to walk around it), feeling every step — and within each step a beat, a small spasm, a well-known pulse — toward the gates. A gentle spray of coolness meshed into the fabric of his mask and penetrated his head tenderly about midway through. Here the waters falling diffusely from the Eagles' Nest were felt most refreshingly, tending as they did to form a thin film of spray near the entrance; its inconstant surface returned to Neipas a fluid distortion of his image palpitating in a haze without eyes or edges, gently scattering in a swarm of droplets and vanishing as he passed. The heat of the incoming day was eased immediately — the torrid sunshine, barely released from the mountains, crept fast into the shades — and upon gliding through the glittery veil Neipas entered a giant gap between two massive panes, in which he saw the hall of Belab's Floor Zero sprawling. It was a vast, slick expanse of shiny floor and pleasant ceiling fixtures lighting the space evenly, professionally; with white walls so pristinely clean and so immaculately blended with the white brightness, that things seemed to stand afore a background of uncertain proximity, either near, or fathomless. Perfectly contrasted against it (if the background existed at all) there hovered, as it were, a few couches for waiting, some coffee tables, a dignified bust with the seal of Columbia on a plinth (bearing again the nation's motto inscribed), two long reception counters like two halves of an oval partially surrounding the foyer, a row of body scanners beyond — all but blurry miniatures past that. The receptionists behind their screens, glared behind their smiles, behind big owl eyes — large watchful stares gaping out of owl countenances at the pigeons stamping on by, shrinking toward the body scanners yonder; scanners standing like a series of portraiture frames, framing plumed napes upon arched backs. Neipas laid his eyes on the lady there, the last behind the reception counter, as he neared the rectangle. It was always the same lady, everyday, though the label on her jacket bore different names and her mask assumed different features. Indeed, Neipas had long borne a half-formulated, half-conscious suspicion that all these receptionists sitting in a line were the very same individual — one entity multiplied. He passed alongside their excessive, ingratiating, slightly mischievous smiles, their immense gazes; and he walked through the whining, flashing frame; got patted down by the bull-faced security guard on the other side with the usual casualness, and continued to the broad half-circle of elevators neatly ordered along the extensive far wall. Between the elevators and the scanning area the ceiling suddenly disappeared. Space shot upward to the indiscernible reaches of the higher floors, in a continuous void save for the spiral of bridges multipliciously connecting each elevator door to its storey's entrance.

Gaining the end of the hall, Neipas pressed a button to summon the elevator. Two slabs of steel slid away from one another before him shortly after, and gave way to a spacious box, very wide and deep, though not very tall. Neipas entered; the door slid shut quietly behind him. There was no one but him inside the elevator, which was unusual — it was, perhaps, still early — and he stood wallowing lone in its subtle rumble and the quietness of his own mind as they descended into the tower's abyss. Thoughts surfaced into his daze as they dropped. He wondered if Edazima would be working today. In his despondent, half-dreamt condition, he thought of her with the profound reverence of gratitude. For it was to her he owed this job — it was she, dear and true friend, who had saved him from the cruelty of Axiac's dark corners, wherein multitudes rot and perish invisibly. He mulled upon indefinite prospects, and upon the past ever looming — and meanwhile the pipes throbbed, a moving vacuousness moaned behind the walls, and the underground oscillated with his thoughts as they sank together. The cords lowered taut and darkly.

Neipas exhaled a long, forlorn sigh.

*

Imperceptibly, the elevator had stopped — distant stirrings called him out of the vagueness into which he had sunk in bits, and he emerged into the perception of doors sliding, nearly open. Long countertops flanked him on both sides as soon as he stepped out the box, extending straight along the walls to the deep end of the narrow path. A faint malodor hovered round the dusky abstraction clinging to the surfaces. Silent stoves, quiet ovens, hushed pots and mum faucets languished in a stillness, a crepuscular stillness disturbed only by the occasional gurgling of the pipes crisscrossing the kitchen ceiling. Vaguely muscular, as though with bulging veins, and with an aspect of prolonged dell flowing with tarnished streams, the ceiling looked beset with dermal ailments corroding it to the brim of leakage; it seemed about to melt in drips onto the dozing cookhouse. No doubt it was the overaccumulation of fumes, so uncannily absent in that infant, soundless parcel of morning — soundless, but for the infrequent snore of the pipes and the ghostly breathing of a nightshift worker who remained, and who dragged body and spirit in abjection, outward, past Neipas. The nightshift laborer stood, leaning against the chipped saliences and among the desolation of pungent dishes littered about in heaps all the way to the curtain at the end of the way; a lone figure between the countertops, under a shadowy ceiling, upon the unseen floor.

The graveyard shift was just then ending, and those working it would be relieved that it was so, Neipas supposed. But there was no relief patent in his (her? Neipas couldn't determine which through the kitchen's dead glow) gaunt, sunken face, the wax of which looked sickly, pale, furrowed with inflammations; rash-like patterns teeming all over, swelling out of the bristling plumes which dwindled like charred, withering petals. It looked like that for a moment as Neipas surveyed the tiles on the walls and the sleeping lamps above the sinks, gazing here and there generally — though in truth, he couldn't be precisely sure of her (his?) countenance, for the night worker dwelt under a lowered bearing and Neipas, passing by a little bashfully, leaving but a mumbled greeting in his wake, couldn't fix the precise aspect of the eyes — which, at a glance, seemed absolutely veiled in shadow — or truly detect more than a vague outline, the suspicion of a presence almost. It was almost the absence of a face, that which he saw. Neipas had heard strange stories about the nightshift, as had all other day laborers; hazy rumors mostly, tribulations implied in vague adjectives. Whatever wasn't merely suggestive, whatever was described at length seemed too fantastical to be believed. It was said that workers went mute, then they went mad; it was said that they were subjected to physical violence; it was even said that they were bridled with shackles if they didn't perform, or locked up deep inside the tower, in special cells; and other such absurdities and exaggerations. Yet now, with what

Neipas was seeing... — but what he had seen, had been but a glimpse.

As he ruminated these and other macabre tales, the notion of something immaterial — which his imagination had somehow materialized — occurred alarmingly to his sleepy mind. He turned suddenly to face the entrance: but there he still saw, he saw clearly that elusively emaciated creature, with back facing him afar, framed in a yawning elevator; and a hand reaching out beyond the edge of the rectangle, moving very slowly.

Roaming aimlessly, Neipas somehow ended up turning into a side passage, stepping beside a flap slanted open in the otherwise uninterrupted counter — and found himself in the adjacent dish-washing area.

It was similar to the cooking area in nearly every aspect: the corridor long, the space narrow, the ceiling piped, the walls tiled and full of little cote-holes over the countertops to receive the dirty dishes from the other side. Cupboards were mounted and spaced across the top, alongside vents that subdued the saturation of smells and lightened the weight of the air a bit. A curtain draped the end of the kitchen, like it did in the cooking area, and like in the cooking area a clock ticked on above the cloth (though the times were different). The entrance, however, or what would have been the elevator on the cooking side, was here a staircase leading to the upper floor of the restaurant's backstage. Whereas the previous space was flanked by countertops on both walls, here the opposing wall was stamped with trash chutes and doors half-opening to cramped toilets and cleaning accessory closets; and the countertops lined along the adjacent wall had no stoves but were mostly outfitted with hoses and sinks. Gradually, Neipas came to, as he heard water running; some signs of activity became apparent to his senses. A couple of janitors ambled about, dishes clanked amid the silence of day's commencement. Pleasant fragrances insinuated themselves through the general foulness: penetrating scents of food being cooked. In the far end of the dully lit way, by the curtain, Janu the dishwasher bent over a large sink, from the deep pit of which rose a messy pile of dirty aluminum.

Janu scrubbed a pan with vigorous absentmindedness, the absence of mind implied in the glassiness of his stare. Thick horns stooped in crescent curve, rubbing against the borders of the wide sink, pulling further down the heaviness of poor Janu's weight. His lumped back arched down to a bristly nape, humid with sweat beads; his ears sagged as though fatigued, the stretched lobes yawning round an immense metal ring; the cheeks were made to hold their puff in strain; the chubbiness of his belly suffered onto the hard surface of the counter. The large, burrowed pan under his fat hands shook under the harsh treatment of the brush, the unbendable roughness of its bristles; pan and brush both looked, somewhat similarly to the ceiling, rusted in deep crimson blemishes; impossible to wash off but through much soap and labor. Janu seemed to forget himself in the toil of it — his usual taciturnity, which always floated on the verge of humorous outbursts, seemed much deeper within itself now.

"Hey man," Neipas greeted as he approached.

"Oh!" Janu exclaimed, taken out of himself in surprise. "How you doing man? You're early today."

"Yeah, well. Couldn't sleep."

"I hear you... Had some trouble sleeping myself last night," said Janu, shaking his head resignedly as he returned to his task.

"Everything ok?" Neipas asked.

"Yeah man," replied the dishwasher, focusing on the next sullied pan. "(Just... cookin' som' in my head)," he mumbled, and his mind seemed to wander off again for a moment, leaving only the trace of its presence on his opaque, empty eyes.

"You worried about the new president?"

"What? Nah..." rejoined Janu, reemerging from his abstraction. "I mean he talks a big game, and he probably means what he says — but dude the other guy, he's the same," he said, shrugging resignedly, as his arms circled foamy round the pan. "They're all the damn same."

"Damn," Neipas muttered offhandedly. Things retained their strange quietude, though the jet blew furiously from the crazed faucet, making a very lake out of the ample sink, a pool cluttered with rusty flotsam. Froth wound round Janu's pan, gathered in its corners, bubbled under the faucet's hissing rage. Iridescent domes gurgled and burst, the ox's sweaty arm tensed. In the fleeting moment Neipas looked up at him from the niche of his own absorption, some preoccupation seemed to weigh, to load upon Janu and force out of him extra exertion. His mask was molded harshly with the creases of inward frowns; the hair of his brow bristled in the squeeze of an uncharacteristic grimace, and a crack swept through the surface of the clay under his mask's brown fur, wet; he washed copiously and sweated; his ear flapped in the swing of the effort. A drop of hot wax seeped from the crack in the ox's clay skin, and Neipas' eye, following it, saw it dissolving strangely in that water strangely rusted in crimson; and Janu too, in his glazed stare, seemed rusted in crimson over the bubbling sink. Neipas shut his eyes forcefully. "All the damn same... Mary," he echoed Janu vacantly, taking his fingers to his brow — and then, opening his glare foggy, puffed, underslept, said of a breath, "But dude — You look off, man. Sure you're good?"

"I do?" wondered Janu, and his features relaxed as he placed the pan aside, with a sharp clatter of sound. Whatever worries tormented him seemed to relent a little.

"Yeah, you look like shit," Neipas commented with familiarity, and Janu's face, laughing, assumed its usual, its natural jovial form, well-humored in its expression of sincere humility.

"For real?" he said. "Been forgetting to attend the salon, dog — " and averting his cheery gaze from Neipas' sleepy smile, he picked up a large knife from the foamy pool; and as he passed the sponge over the blade, sighed, "I dunno... It's my sister, I guess. Just a bunch of stuff man."

"Your sister?"

"Yeah... There's this creep at her school, man. Been — creeping on her a while I guess," he stumbled, sweeping the moisture off his brow. "Preppy college kid. You know the type right. You've been. Rich parents, all full of it."

"I guess."

"Yeah, so — yesterday he tells my sister he'd rat her out to immigration police. Can you believe that shit?"

"The fuck?"

"Yeah. I mean, he didn't straight up say it apparently. But he like — implied it," he continued, polishing the long blade with additional effort, holding the hilt with a shiver, apparently unable to remove the filth smeared along the steel. "Dunno what he said exactly," he strained out; and then putting down the knife, continued, "but my sister was pretty upset about it," excavating another knife. "And she's not the type to bitch about anything, you know what I mean? Ain't good at hiding it either if she's upset though.

"I mean you know — " Janu said then, lowering his voice, dropping the knife back into the water and looking round in an instinctive gesture of caution, "you know we don't have papers. So it freaked her out."

"Mary," Neipas shook his head, rubbed the back of it. "Can he even do that, like — can she just be arrested like that?"

Slowly (it seemed), Janu shrugged — a long and withdrawn inhalation of uncertainty and dismay. The crack on his forehead tightened a little. "I dunno... Who knows, dude. I guess so. I know about people, who've been deported just like that. Outta nowhere."

Janu was one of those downtrodden exiles then numbering in the millions: migrants, who traveled from the hinterlands of the world to seek refuge and opportunity in the capitals of power. In those days, the prosperous nations erected walls (of long shadows and diverse shapes) to keep out the unwanted — most died before the gates, through which passed no sound. In silence and in droves they fell; in the seas, in the deserts, in the wastelands of the nations they perished, crowding the liminal zones of empires, swallowed in the vast indifference of empires where all was doomed to be forgotten. Some, like Janu and his family, passed — hid, prevailed, and labored quietly for the benefit of that vast economic engine that powered the civilizational machine, to which they contributed much, and from which they extracted little more than the barest life they were denied back home. But whenever that engine malfunctioned (as was nearly always the case) and blame went out in search for a cause, its most vocal engineers, perched at the top of the machine, were quick to dispatch indictments to the most quiet of its components, for their voices were adept at hiding their guilt by shouting it away from them. Arnold was such a voice. He had turned heads with his diatribes against so-called 'illegal' immigrants, calling them criminals, rapists — animals. Now Axiac expanded across the borderlands of Columbia and therefore hosted many a migrant in the underground of its hidden corners, with multitudes of them living under the blind eye of the state. Wall Street, an old slave port, had once been the main point of entry, in particular to those from the continental regions of the south. Placed at the end of a strait between mountain walls and hostile seas, it was now a fortified apparatus of razor-wired layers and high-tech surveillance barricades, almost impenetrable — forcing many to try their luck in the great inhospitable mountain areas bordering the megalopolis.

The two janitors (migrants themselves), hauled black trash bags into the chutes; down which they would tumble, toward fathoms unknown. "And if you look at this guy's maskbook page, he's like, all progressive and shit," Janu continued, induced by rancor into loquaciousness. Only his head and shoulders moved, his forearms covered in frothy sleeves and his fists made of foam molten upon the counter. "His album's full of these slogans. Posing on protests. All pro-immigrant and stuff like that. Anti-Arnold." He shook his head in perplexity. "I mean, can you believe these people man?"

"Mary... Lot of phonies out there, man."

"For real." Again his lowered snout shook, and the schism along his clay forehead seemed to deepen. "Goes on to say he's joking or whatever — I dunno, man. All I know is she wasn't happy about it. This dude's been annoying her for a while already, but... I guess the fact Arnold won messed with her too, you know?"

His hand immersed into the deep. "I mean, it messed with me too, a little," he continued downcast and mournfully; his hand emerged with a bloody grill. "Talking like that an' all. You see how he almost won even here?"

"Crazy."

Janu chuckled sourly. "Maybe not so crazy, my friend." He talked as he scrapped the ruddy grease off the metal bars — "Ain't easy for us here... But at least he says what he means, huh? Unlike those other fools. You know my dad," the soap rubbed the grates over and over and did not seem to wash, " — he got kicked out by the previous guy. All pro-immigration and shit now too!"

"You mean Shrub?"

"Nah, Clint."

"Damn, I see. That way back?" Neipas wondered, surprised.

Janu nodded slowly. "Can't even remember what he looks like."

Neipas, too, nodded — with the slowness of one peering into muddy waters, detecting something at the bottom with a dim sense of association, of remembrance. Every little bubble contained one little kitchen and a pigeon face and an ox head conversing within it — vanishing silently as they popped. Feathers rustled round his head, listless. There were palpitations throbbing and fluttering somewhere, and his beak drooped in its exhaling sigh; the nostrils snorted in various hovering scents; he experienced the comatose sensation of being outside himself. Then he shook his head — slowly, hazily, uncomprehendingly — and mumbled: "It's all fucked up, my friend."

"Just too many layers of fucked-up, man," agreed Janu. And clicking his tongue, he then commented: "Still though. How can you talk about people like that? It's..." and he shrugged, "dehumanizing, you know?"

They remained quiet for a few moments. Distractedly, Neipas observed the grill dividing the purling water in partitions and dripping lard into the pit; the smell of food sneaked into his senses, so faint that he wondered without thought whether it was being cooked on some other floor. A little beside the sink lay a crumpled packet, cookie crumbs strewn about it. Neipas had a feeling Janu was somewhat addicted to cookies; he surmised that he overconsumed them when he was distressed, which was somewhat often. There were tinges of disunion within him. Janu seemed perpetually stuck between two places, and subtly fissured, fragmented, among many psychologies — a type of malaise common to not just the migrants but to all the people of that time.

Finally Janu, curling his fingers between the grill bars, lifted the dripping metal and laid it aside to dry. He sniffed; buds of wax oozed through the clay and pasted the fur of the ox. He looked at Neipas smilingly, appreciatively; he nodded with the confidence of optimism.

"It's gonna be all good, my friend. She's gonna get her degree, get a proper job, then she'll get her papers... She's smart as hell, man. She's the brains of the family, you know what I mean? Me, though — " Janu brandished his soapy fingers and the lather sleeve bubbling up his forearm — "Nobody can top these hands, bro. You smell that?" he said very smilingly, pointing with his head and flapping earlobes to the two pots simmering a couple of stations next to them.

"I meant to ask you about it — " Neipas said, imitating his pointing gesture. Janu wiped his arms on the cloth hanging from his apron and, stepping to the pots, lifted off one lid. A very cloud of delicious scents dispersed throughout the corridor and perfumed the subterranean air. "What you cooking there man? Smells pretty good."

"My friend, this right here — this right here's history."

With a flourish of the arms, Janu grabbed a ladle and a small basket covered with a handkerchief, beneath which rested a little pile of flattened, unleavened, cornmeal bread. Dipping the ladle through the smoke of the pot with one hand — placing a plate beside the pot, and two bread pieces on it, with the other as he did it — he lifted it and spread its contents lavishly upon the waiting bread: a peculiar stew of beans eased itself languidly onto the cornmeal and the ceramic, speckled with bits of turkey dropped by spoon out of the second pot, and garnished with pepper and herbs. Janu's fingers, working over the dish, possessed all the care of a parent and the deft mastery of an artist molding a cherished creation. In quick and deliberate succession he laid the body spread, sprinkled it refreshingly, and then, very measuredly, very cozily, tucked it all in the wrapped blanket of flour.

"It's an ancestral recipe. My mom taught me how to cook this, and her mom before her, and her mom and her mom — since forever — here, have a taste of this," he said, taking to Neipas a spoonful of the fragrant stew. Neipas reflexively raised his fingers to Janu's own, curled around the handle, adjusting it a little — and, leaning the tip of his beak to the steaming spoon, he slurped. It was delicious. The stew roused his senses to a pleasurable languor, the freshness and warmth of it lulled him into the wakefulness of vitality; in a moment, it was as if his spirit, having wandered astray, rushed back to fill his body. His tongue still wallowed in the flavor, coursing the edge of his lip as Janu spoke, in the particular way he had of saying things when he cooked — with excitement and reverence: "Food, my friend, is life borrowed from our ancestors. Cuisine is a vessel of tradition, it's something spiritual man. It's sacred! We forget that, we forget ourselves... What's the verdict my friend?"

"Damn," mumbled Neipas, basking in the taste, "it's not bad, man."

"Not bad?" Janu laughed. "One day I'll be the chef of this place bro. Just don't let the chef know it."

Smiling contemplatively, Neipas wondered aloud, "What's in it?", trying to distinguish the different flavors in the mixture.

"Gifts of the earth and lots of love," sang Janu, citing his mother's refrain.

Neipas, laughing, asked, "And how's your ma?"

"Good man, same... Speaking of which, you mind taking this up to her? Other's for you," said Janu, pointing to the two wrapped breads.

"Oh — no need man."

"Bro I'm offering — don't be an ass dude, just take it."

"All right man..." Neipas assented, feeling his heart warm and the ancestral relish seep into his innermost, given to his soul to imbibe, giving him the gift of life. As the savored sensation began to fade in his tongue, he seemed to feel it still more profoundly. And for a moment he was aware of experiencing a particular recurrence of the senses; an emotion echoed across generations, reproduced now in him as it had been reprised in others and still others invisibly queued before him into the stretches of unfathomable time. It was a curious feeling that made him a little desolate as the flavor vanished for good. "She's working up in the Media Floors today?" — Janu nodded (yeah) — "For sure, I'll take it to her."

He then beheld Neipas' sad visage, and asked: "How 'bout you though, you good? You haven't shown up here a while."

"I haven't, yeah," Neipas replied, debating inwardly whether to tell Janu about the incident at the zoo. He decided against it.

"Been taking a little vacation, no?"

Neipas chuckled, molding the aspect of his mask so as to not let any of the wax drip off or make any of his uncanniness apparent. During the bus ride, he had practiced in his head, several disarranged times, the story of what had happened — for he knew of at least one person who would've noticed his absence and insist that he tell it — but he felt bizarre merely gathering the first word of it in his throat. "You could say that," he replied, quietly.

Grabbing two plastic containers from the cupboard, Janu remarked, "You're not looking too good yourself, my friend. Sure you're a'ight? Looking kinda shitty there too bro."

"Been missing my appointments at the salon too."

Janu laughed, blooming with the hearty glow and contented disposition he derived from his cooking; and then, tempering his voice with an equanimity of profound solidarity and friendship: "Seriously though... sure you ok?"

"Yeah man, just... this just fucking depressing, you know. Work and everything. Arnold now too I guess. Everything just seems..." his beak dropped slantwise in gloomy reflection, "...just weird."

"Yeah... Really is, bro. Really fuckin' is."

Silence.

"I'm a little stressed out maybe," Neipas rejoined, shrugging, "but whatever, gotta work anyway. Krow don't care about my feelings man. Gotta eat."

In fact, though the restaurant bore his name, no one knew who Krow was. No one had ever seen him. "True that my friend, true that... Say — you got a sister too don't you?"

Neipas nodded.

"You get along?"

"Used to, yeah."

Janu tilted his downturned horns, perceiving in Neipas' lowered tone his unwillingness to speak. "All right my friend. Edazima was looking for you by the way."

"Ah, she here?"

"Yeah yeah, down in the back somewhere."

"I see," said Neipas, turning to the nearby curtain. "Ok well... Thanks man. I'm gonna go get dressed."

"No worries — wait until you taste the full thing," and looking at the clock above the curtain Janu said, "You're right though shit, shift's about to start. Time jets huh."

"It's all about that hustle man," Neipas said, grabbing the two plastic containers and bumping his fist gently on Janu's shoulder as he stepped to the curtain.

"All 'bout that money money money," the ox said singing, in a humorous tone now as he rushed to pack his things. Neipas, pigeon smiling despondently behind his mushed feathers, stepped beyond the veil. A black narrowness between vague shelves filled with indistinct condiments surfaced into his eyes — various machines, boxes emitting light in the shape of numbers, with numbered buttons, hung upon the wall by the entry. Neipas pressed his digits — #, 4, 3, 1, 9, 9, 9 — and followed that (after unraveling a bit of thread through the Webwork) by leaning his I to the machine: to which the machine replied with a greeting beep, acknowledging his presence by mutedly flashing 431999 **NEIPAS** upon its little screen.

The pantry, unfolding between metal stacks, between jars, plastics, and a myriad shaded miscellanea, sometimes branched out to extremely tight alleyways from which emanated breathing drafts and sparks of snore: though the end of these little alleys was so obscure that Neipas could not see whether the murmurs belonged to anyone at all. But he knew there were closets there: closets which opened into beds. Lying on their slim mattresses were some graveyard shift workers, too exhausted, he assumed, to go home. He heard them sometimes as he came in at the beginning of his days, though (come to think of it — Neipas slowed his step at the realization) today had probably been the first time he had truly seen one of them. He beheld them vaguely now, shifting in the shadows of the icy curtains yonder, at the end of the pantry, beyond which he had never been; mere hunched silhouettes, coming into being in faded halos, dark cut-outs disappearing in the darkness of their own make. A mist of very gloomy snow peeked out whenever those faraway curtains flickered and parted. The illumination was fuzzy here, composed of buzzy refrigerators and blinkering lights dripping somewhere from the wiry ceiling or the package-shaped walls; existing dimly in the rustle of untraceable motions — of phantoms gliding about — and the invisible flutter of pantry moths. Here, in the eerie silence of these subtle sounds — bubbling in the wake of the nightshift, before the day shift began — whispering ahead of the horde of workers yet to come, just as the gas yawned and fires started to sizzle, just as the fumes began to puff, and the mops dragged lazily across the stretching floors into a halt; here now, Neipas listened quite clearly to the pulse which he so often discerned in the elusive quietnesses of this tower, beyond its mumbling walls, underneath his feet, overhead...

His eyes narrowed and deepened toward the end of the pantry, where the ambiguous curtain fell, from which the nightshift workers still languidly trickled, beyond which he had never been — and wondered without thought of the strange mysteries which it must hide.

The way to the male locker room was indicated by a bright arrow glued to one of the shelves; he followed it and stepped through the swinging, porthole-windowed door. He entered with a stealthy tread. Looking down the long corridors of lockers he saw one lone pigeon here, another one there, with no more than two occupying an entire row solitarily, wearily changing out of their clothes, wax masks drooping under their eyes. In Neipas' corridor there was no one. He walked slowly and slowly opened his locker. Inside he found his uniform perfectly folded, its aspect fresh and neat. Equally immaculate was his work-mask, which was perched in the shelf above the main partition: the hefty fur, the rigid snout, the downturned, heavy horns with blunt ends, all framed the empty eyes of the ox staring at him and into nothing.

Neipas took hold of it; he contemplated its hollow interior; and he noticed, as if he were seeing it for the first time, the cracks on its clay skin, indicative of an inner parchness of exhaustion and ground hopes. He gazed upon its outer surface: the undisguised expression of misery and crass servitude, expressed in horns crestfallen, without adornment, and in the shoddy make of its dry clay, its cheap fur, the horn made of something between nail and bone.

He undressed; his heart began to pick up pace as he did, though he couldn't understand why right away. As he was finishing the putting on his shirt, his ear caught the sound of steps — many steps shuffling on louder and closer — and of a distant bell. His head entered the mask, clay over wax;

darkness panned over his sight, as if he were spirited off the morning and sunk headlong into the night. And the bells rang more resonant, pervading the air, rippling from a great distance and across many layers of depth and height, vibrating with the growing mass of nearing feet, rustling cloth, thickening breaths; and as the fur dilated out of his outer skin of feathers and the ox head settled upon the pigeon's, everything seemed to gain in gravity, and the air became heavier; he stooped a little lower.

His sight returned — sharp.

Neipas closed the locker as a monolith parade of drowsy co-workers lumbered into his corridor, dragging shoes heavy with sleep toward their respective cabinets.

5 - Belab

A few of them opened their lockers and began their sluggish race to get dressed; others started along the same course but soon gave up the effort, eventually plopping onto the benches lined along the locker row to stare at their *I*s. Their eyes looked bleached, their gazes blank from mental fatigue and the anticipation of bodily exhaustion. Neipas gave and received a few mumbled greetings, uttered and heard as if from under blankets, as he passed by the stooping throng on his way out. He went through the pantry between the shelves, felt the transpiration of lazy and anxious, breathed cooing — a multitude of pigeons crowded up against the wall of login boxes; some were already loading out the pantry stuffs meant for breakfast cookery — and transversed the curtain back into the kitchen.

Afar, standing among the sinuous fumes already materializing between the counters, Neipas saw Edazima, holding the bovine mask with both hands and speaking in a corner with her friend Magpie. Beautiful and imposing, Magpie of sable feathers talked rapidly over Edazima's listening ear. Nodding upon the height of her dignified pose, she then lowered for a quick hug, and hastened out with a determined stride; whereas Edazima, whose sharp gaze had caught Neipas' blurry own directly, approached him at large steps and a look of agitation.

"Hey man! What's the matter with you?"

"Good morning..." said Neipas, hesitantly.

"I dropped by the hospital yesterday and you had checked out! I was worried about you, must've sent you like a thousand messages man."

"How did you even know I was in the hospital?" Neipas asked, astonished.

"I'm your emergency contact, remember?"

"Oh," mumbled Neipas, nodding distractedly, "yeah... My bad."

A silence descended between Neipas' aloof evasiveness and Edazima's scrutinizing gaze, a silence immediately filled by the rising noise of the kitchen. Operations ramped up quickly, with sounds of blowing fire and bubbling hot water, the thickening of the air into smoke, made so dense that soon they could no longer see each other. Naked arms could yet be seen flinging between the curtains, loading bits of meat, bread, sugar, salts and various ingredients on to the rolling belt stretched along the counters, from which the hands of cooks plucked them in a frenzy of synchronized motions among the chaotic droplets hissing in upward drizzles from the frying pans. Processed body parts belonging to various chicken and pigs vanished in the quickly thickening vapors unleashed by their contact with hissing skillets; little wings flexed, ground ribs shriveled; all meat wailed in a screaming chorus.

"Well? Tell me what happened," Edazima's voice spoke blurry out of the vague shape before Neipas.

"Nothing, you know – " he caught himself, watching (he thought) her mask contract into the scrutinizing features of suspicion; and then declared with some timidity that "I had an accident."

"An accident?" asked Edazima.

"Yes," replied Neipas.

"Ok, what happened?"

"I had an accident."

"That you had an accident I know already, you just told me."

"Well, yeah," Neipas gulped, scratching his forehead.

"So? What happened then?"

"I – was attacked by a bird," Neipas confessed, with an attrition of spirit arising from his own disbelief in the bizarre situation and his own bizarre sensation of self.

"By a bird? At the zoo?"

"Yeah."

"What? How did that happen?"

Neipas related the incident into the cloud of cooking scents. He began speaking, but found his voice gradually climbing into shouts as the noise around him intensified and Edazima repeatedly leaned in, yelling "Huh?!". Eventually she grabbed his shoulder and ushered him into the dishwashing area, into which the holes on the tiled wall exhaled fumes as nostrils would tobacco; and out of the kitchen through the stairway up to the backstage, where the waiters waited for the first readied dishes. There was little noise here, only mumbling — most cattleheads looked downward to their *I*s in languid stillness — and the fumes were sparser, so Neipas went on with reporting what happened. In the course of the telling one or two fellows lingered in the vicinity, performing a little distracted dance with their feet and looking absolutely aloof, though their set grins faced Neipas straight. By the time he was approaching the end of his narrative a small circle had gathered around him, the constituents of which had approached without a peep or greeting, sneaking into their presence without taking the least trouble announcing their own. Though some looked completely enraptured, others, who were holding the work-mask of full attention in their hands, weren't as careful in hiding that they weren't listening to a word. But these were the minority, most likely dragged unconsciously by the rest, trailing blindingly to the growing center of commotion; most did seem to be listening, the zoo tale being so evidently odd as to easily retain the most casual ear, and soon every single waiter was rooted someplace around Neipas, forming part of a crowded ring enclosing him. Neipas only gained an awareness of this, and his voice tended gradually to fall into a whisper; and gradually not only Edazima, but everyone else, was straining their ears in closely to listen. Their horns rubbed together with the murmur of anticipation.

Neipas wasn't yet quite done when an ox named Orassap, who had so far been satisfied with standing and bobbing his grinning head, barged in by asking, quite softly, "Wow... And what bird was it?"

Orassap's soft and drawn voice, so velvety that it sounded as though it had passed through a screen of silk, affected Neipas' thinking subtly, and yet strongly enough to quite throw him off the tale's practiced track. Neipas became unnerved, for he noticed now Orassap had been pointing his I's lens at him; he wondered uneasily whether he had been filming him, and for a few moments did not know how to react.

Presently he regained his composure; then he said, "I don't know," and shook his head as if confirming a general suspicion. A spur of laughter broke out. Confused as to the cause of it, Neipas laughed along, which charged the rolling guffaw with increased energy and made it exceedingly rambunctious.

Suddenly it died down and the waiters stood silent, looking at one another and at the floor; only the mingled music emitting muffled out of individual earbuds was heard.

Finally Edazima, who had been staring into Neipas with a perplexed expression, panning her face in a slow, vertical movement, said, hammering in each word: "That's fucking crazy." She broke the jittery quietude and that seemed to relieve some of the present elements out of a biding. The folk on the outer rim of the circle began stepping off and back to their affairs, whereas the closest wavered a little, standing there, looking out of place, and slowly liberated themselves by a sympathetic word or another — proceeding to going away with a lowered head and a hasty pace.

"You doing ok?" Edazima asked, worried.

"Yeah," Neipas said casually, but seeing Edazima's inspecting stare and the creases in her brow, he let out: "Yeah!" forcefully through with an embarrassed chuckle.

"Yeah?... You sure?"

"Hmm, yeah? Why?" Neipas asked, averting his gaze before the power of Edazima's own, chuckling coyly still.

"I dunno, you look... different, somehow."

"Different how?" (Did she notice? Neipas discreetly felt his mask and looked into the I glass to make sure nothing could be seen through).

"I don't know, just — different."

"Huh," said Neipas, looking around. "Anyway — Sorry I didn't even ask, how are you?"

Edazima peered intently into his eyes — for a prolonged instant. Then she shook her head, as if waking out of reverie; and, inserting her fingers into her mask, carved the worry out of it. "Oh, I'm all right. Been busy."

"How's the kid?"

"He's doing ok. Hating school of course, you know how it is. Says he wants to be retired when he grows up," she laughed with that abounding maternal affection which most clearly disclosed the goodness of her heart. Neipas laughed too; Edazima's cheerfulness spread like perfumed breeze, it always made him happy.

"Well, say hi to him for me."

"You should visit sometime."

"I should, yeah... Haven't seen him in a while."

A sudden profusion of muffled vibration ensued simultaneously and frenetically upon the cupped hands and inside the rattled pockets of the waiters; and all their heads sunk at once, yielding to the weight of their horns and into the light of the *I* screens. Startled, Neipas checked the digits in the glass. The backstage, where they were, was a neat loop of many little cotes, each covered with a cloth and each labeled with a number; Neipas stepped to the number assigned to him, kneeling to extract the tray from one of the holes on the wall near the ground, out of which smoke spurted abundantly as he drew away the little veil. With a quick gesture he bade farewell to Edazima, who went back downstairs to the pantry, where she was a supervisor; and he began his way up the corridor shooting out of the circular hall, walking among a tidal mass of accompanying movement. The herd of heifers and oxen marched between walls of chipped plaster, laden with a profusion of plastic plates and cups wrapped in aluminum atop trays, heavy with food and drink. Soles of polyester shoes tapped the floor in a monotonous drum. A long mass of horns swayed orderly, sprouting from lowered heads, roaming toward the elevator at the end of the corridor.

With a calm ding and a metallic ruffle the elevator doors opened to a curtain. The waiters went through. There was some confusion as the cattle amassed against the panel, each in an awkward attempt to press the numbered button. Neipas shuffled uncomfortably among the bodies until he was able to select his floor, and then retreated to the closest wall as the doors shut, pressing out the light and closing them in the black. The darkness was nearly total, punctuated only by the tiny dots of gleam emitted from the *I* screens, which lit feebly the masks of workers, waiting indifferently for their stop in perfectly upright postures and rigid smiles.

Neipas himself had been leaning neck-deep into the *I* glass when he sensed someone muttering at his side. For some time he had had a vague idea of indecision tingling at his shoulder, a vibe of hesitation coming from the ox next to him. It was the waiter called Orassap. Orassap kept mostly to himself;

whenever Neipas saw him down in Kur, he stood always at a corner with a sullen look, spying out of his *I* nervously, glancing from side to side in the hopes that someone would glance toward him. Neipas was friendly to the fellow — they had even exchanged a few, casual words once. Lamentably, Orassap was one of those pigeons who is always so eager to dispense with his thoughts that, whenever he wasn't cawing out hasty strings of words in conversation, he could be found bobbing his head furiously, as if fighting to contain the excitement throbbing in his mind.

"Yeah yeah yeah," he would ejaculate, with his continuous yank of a nod, over Neipas' words, which weakened in volume until they were completely eaten up by Orassap's overbearing eagerness. The moment Neipas' voice had become inaudible Orassap's jaw would spring into a machine-gun of cackling, expressing his belief in various garbled theories and interpretations of current events, and commenting on miscellaneous political arcana with absolute confidence in what he was saying.

Since that one time, their exchange rarely developed beyond timid salutations; Neipas never encouraged him beyond a greeting nod. His mask solidified and sunk deeper into the Webwork to avoid him; but Orassap's voice wasn't directed to him now.

"Hey," Orassap said curtly, and rigidly, to the waitress at his side.

"Oh..." said the waitress, who was called Larissa, lifting her head off the *I* as if peeking out of stupor, "Hey...!" she worked up her fabricated enthusiasm quite slowly. "Hello! How are yooooou?" She was new — Neipas had never seen her before. Faces came and went quickly in that place.

"Not too bad," Orassap exhaled with forced nonchalance. "Been busy, you know," and from then, stimulated by her minimal reaction, he began carefully into a soliloquy, stopping only to ask questions to her grinning mask, which, however, only bobbed and said "Huh-huh, huh-huh," as she slowly, almost involuntarily, drew her head back downward into the *I*. He still continued a little, for, even though she didn't look at him anymore, she still smiled — before his voice, faced with her indifference, died somewhere mid-sentence. The awkward conversation between Orassap's monotone and Larissa's bouncing "mm-hm"s disturbed the elevator's thin tranquility and made its silence even more embarrassed.

Sunlight shot through the slats on the grimy iron side of the elevator, revealing the bleak texture of the opposite wall, greasy with deep stains and rusty. They were out of the underground. As the streaks of gold crawled up his attire, Neipas suddenly perceived in himself a profound unwillingness to work, and his head seemed to grow larger, lethargic, wavering; the heavy tray pressed down heavier upon him. The sleeplessness of the previous night was digging up into his consciousness. Now the elevator would stop, and office lamplights would flash through the curtain as waiters streamed out. Neipas made his way closer to the doors bit by bit. One or two more times did the elevator stop, one or two more times did its doors part and clasp shut. Neipas unconsciously tapped his feet; sighs fertilized the quietude.

He was already by the curtain when the elevator stopped at his floor; the doors moved aside and Neipas shot out of the crammed box.

His first stop was the Finance Floor.

Neipas' sight widened up and sunk forth into an immense hall. Bells rang madly from the high ceiling, there were clocks everywhere. The hall was filled with pillars buzzing with digital lights, pillars of a strange form, stanchions outfitted with slot machines dressed up as altars. Immaculate suits stood by the machines and swaggered raptly between them; bull heads seethed over the collars, raging bulls trampling savagely, busily chasing the lights along. Their horns were decorated with cloth, embroidered with gold and laced with glittering penchants, which swayed wildly as they vociferated into screens and telephones; sometimes their horns were so adorned that they looked made of diamond. Their ties yawned and slacked onto their bellies, and their jackets grew rumpled with the elations of prayer as the day wore on. Indeed the whole space seemed a fusion of casino and house of worship. Motions assumed the raptured aspect of cult ritual, and there was such an atmosphere of clerical gravity and airy complexity, of such rabid sophistication that one felt immediately impelled to lower one's head in submission before the methodical craze of activity unfolding everywhere. In this place worked sage scribes, powerful magicians, apprenticing prophets. Like the other prayer houses imported to that land, they sold hopes — which here they called 'stocks'. Here, great amounts of wealth were conjured up and great amounts of wealth sacrificed through mysterious mechanisms, every twitch made in arcane obeisance to the divine will of the Market. Its consecrated machines, the tall columns to which the bulls devoted their frenzy, were exceedingly convoluted apparatuses, electro-telamons sheathed in glass, from which different colors flashed myriad numbers and charts — all completely incomprehensible to the untrained eye (this is how they masked their gambling) but which seemed to confer unending boons: for cheers kept erupting with glitter and champaign pops in celebration to the quivers of their lights.

Neipas passed along among the busy bulls. He could never understand anything they said, they spoke a cryptic language; an idiom of codes invented for themselves alone, and the confusion of everyone else. To try to decipher the hieroglyphs in the screens was futile. In the early days, he tried; now he simply accepted and ignored them. It was a cryptic labyrinth, this place, and it seemed to him like he walked a long time along the circumference of the tower. He walked close to the immense, cathedral windows so that he wouldn't get lost; the sunlight, touching him through the glass, alleviated the excessive chill of the air-conditioning. On the other side of him were all the cypher pillars and the rabid business-making. Beyond them all, distant, arose glass partitions describing the round format of the tower, on the other side of which were yet more machines, denser yet with more stock brokers and investment bankers and their occult movements; and beyond those, yet other glass partitions, culminating in some sort of black drape in the far horizon. It was said the Belab was made up of three great rings, divided in still three more — nine concentric circles, from the periphery to the core; though Neipas had equally heard that the tower possessed 12, or 80, or 10,000 layers at various times — but these were mostly conjectures, and in reality many configurations were possible. Some would say that, to reach the core of the tower, one would have to walk for hours and hours, perhaps days; and it was sometimes said that no one but the original builders and architects had ever laid eyes on it. Many indulged in the theory that there was a vast treasure hidden inside; though some, very few, held that the tower's core sheltered not treasure, but a vast prison. What seemed certain is that the tower was perceived to be unfathomable in height and depth, and that it had existed since time immemorial.

His *I* buzzed with instructions, directing him on where to go. Neipas marched professionally toward his client's work-station, through the ruckus of noisy caws, shouting chatters, and singing screeches arising all around him from snouts uplifted, trying not to get punched by the maze of arms gesticulating frantically above the bulls' heads. He slalomed under the ticking clocks and eventually arrived at his destination. He stepped near his client swiftly and gracefully.

"Good morning, Mr. Yemon. Your order, sir," Neipas said, very politely. Mr. Yemon was presently very focused on his work: his nostrils glued to the flashing screen, his eyes wide open and shooting in all directions. A thin trail of vapor emanated from his ear. "Mr. Yemon, sir?" The bull stock broker said nothing, but only grunted and pointed his finger to his jagged round desk, wherein he was enmeshed. Neipas promptly removed a plastic plate from the huge tray upon his upfacing palm, and all with his free hand he unwrapped the aluminum and placed it on the desk.

"Here you are, sir." Then, he bowed his ox head very low. Yemon removed his eye from the screen for a second to confirm his request for triple cheeseburger and fried wings was in order; he took a handful of it together and sucked in a wide bite. All things being checked, his eyes shot back to the screen. He produced a banknote out of his wallet and, pinching it between two erect fingers, placed it behind Neipas' lowered ear.

"Thank you, sir," Neipas said, collecting his tip. Mr. Yemon waved his hand dismissively, something like shooing a fly — probably an unconscious gesture — and spoke some indecipherable grunts into the screen of numbers.

Neipas left Yemon in his trance and bolted toward his next destination, the Media Floor. He crammed back into the mass of bodies in the elevator. The doors opened and, emerging from the packed multitude, Neipas stepped out of the veil into a discreet archive, stacked with shelves and drawers, littered with papers, disks and cassettes, with little mirrors fixed to the walls. Clerks worked in the windowless lamplight under the weight of their cattle helmets, shuffling through a maze of files to find something or other — Neipas greeted some of them, recognizing worn faces from his bygone college days. "Still feels like yesterday, doesn't it? It was only a few years ago, I guess, wasn't it?" one of his former schoolmates had recently mumbled, musing aloud to him; blinking languidly his glazed eyes.

The next division opened up. Neipas saw it cluttered full of cubicles, all of them surrounded by high walls which covered their inhabitants. The air vibrated with the blaring of telephones and *I*s shaking crazy upon tables, with rushed voices and shrieks, buttons pecked with haste and fury, all sounding together in an amalgam of activity into which pumped the melodies of symphonic music streaming from speakers overhead. The agglomeration of furniture was arranged in a labyrinthic design; Neipas wound right and left constantly, dodging busy journalists and work-stations with precision. He moved mechanically, the gears of his practiced muscles rotated automatically. It was not easy, however, for everyone here wore long tails loosened out of their suits, feathered extensions painted with many eyes, trailing all across the narrow corridors; Neipas strained not to step on any of them. He was able to do it so swiftly only because he had been there many times before. As he went he could sometimes see all the way to the towering windows, which, very high up in the upper echelons of the Belab, overlooked the entire eastern extent of the megalopolis. Journalists with peacock masks stood very straight by the glass, peering through it with monoculars shaped like funnels; scouring the horizons in search of news.

Neipas swerved into one of the cubicles. "Good morning, John," he greeted — for he knew the peacock sitting there, also from his studying years.

"Hey, dude," John greeted casually, without looking at him. His desk was decorated with a row of bobbing-head figurines, mini-mannequins of various political and entertainment celebrities. He watched the two screens before him, one of which was draped top to bottom with letters, words and paragraphs; the other flashed some sort of pornographic clip.

Neipas removed a plastic plate and cup from the tray and unwrapped the foil from both, setting them on the table; and as he performed the motions he directed a glance at the lettered screen, which beamed large the headline, 'PERSIA HAS ENOUGH URANIUM FOR NUCLEAR BOMB, OFFICIALS FEAR'.

"That true?" he asked; a lull of remembrance deepening his tone.

John replied absently. "They fear it is."

Neipas bowed low. His head descended through the air hollow and tired; something in his heart beat void. He anticipated the touch of thick paper, but he felt slick fingers petting his ears instead. "Good to see you, man. Say hi to Vera for me," John said distractedly through his peacock face, his glare still facing the flashing screens, seeing both. He always said that, but Neipas still had no idea who Vera was.

Neipas stepped out reflectively, pondering as to why John hadn't given him a tip. He had perhaps forgotten to smile; he thought agitatedly that he had let transpire some contempt; perhaps his inner semblance was so damaged that the holes had seeped through to his work, ox face. He checked his mask in the *I* — he was grinning very widely still. Then he recalled that John rarely gave him a tip; and becalmed. He glided away alongside the windows, and distinguished, afar, the Ivory Towers where he had studied, dim beyond all the skyscrapers of Babylon; and beyond that, the powerful eastern mountains, behind the summits of which plumes of smoke, erupting from forest wildfires, mounted aloft.

He paced the circumference toward the bathroom. On the way there he saw, coming toward, one of the editors, an old professor — immediately recognizable by the parrot who always rested on his shoulder. By the side of his tall, lean peacock mask lugged a portentous Eagle in an opulent suit. He had very white feathers and flashing, wide amber eyes sunken in his rotund face, from which protruded a long, hooked, golden beak. This was Moloch, the Media Mogul — an entrepreneur of extreme importance, one of the wealthiest individuals in the world, owner of that particular news outlet (there were an infinitude of outlets on that floor, many of which Moloch owned). Vexed and caught unawares, Neipas stopped and his head drooped in humility. His heart gained the weight of lead as they approached and he scooped even deeper.

They came along and the Editor, who was called Professor Moldura, greeted Neipas. "Oh, hello," (while the parrot repeated enthusiastically "Oh, hello!") and Neipas, touched by his notice even as he was engaging with someone of such importance, bowed even deeper as he said: "Good morning Professor, Mr. Moloch." The latter ignored him. As Neipas lifted his head he noticed, strangely, that Moloch, the Mogul, seemed to be addressing himself to the parrot, and not the Professor its owner. The parrot, facing in the opposite direction, looked at Neipas with cheery, glassy eyes.

Neipas rushed onward to the bathroom, without time to lose — navigating through rows upon angled rows of cubicles toward a tucked corner. He passed by the sign indicating that the bathroom was being cleaned and stepped in. Inside he found Janu's mother, Mrs. Tia, with eyes set upon the floor, which she mopped. She hummed a soothing tune, a lullaby; which fell tender in Neipas' senses, making the cacophony of the Media Floor sound, somehow, very distant. She clutched the mop in her gloved hands, and looked very much like a noble pilgrim with her concentration and steadfastness, the apron descending to her knees like a saintly vestment, her sweaty hair covered by the halo of a cloth. She looked up from her short stature, by chance; her eyes lit with recognition.

"Oh! Neipas!" the good lady said, her fixed visage transforming into the most endearing smile. She spoke some words in her native language, which Neipas did not understand, but knew to be kind.

"Hello," said Neipas sympathetically. He gave her the dish Janu had entrusted him with; and she thanked him profusely in Neipas' language and her own, touching his cheek with a tenderness that reminded him of his own mother. He had a filial affection for Mrs. Tia — though they didn't speak the same tongue, they communicated through the universal language of sincere and eager gestures, and understood each other well.

She removed two packets from her apron's hand-sewn pocket and handed them to him.

"Cookies. For my son. And for you."

Neipas thanked her as she held his free hand earnestly. She kept speaking a while, trying to persuade Neipas to eat something now — but seeing Neipas' hurry through his mask, she urged him on with a wave of hand and a big smile. Neipas said goodbye and went on, rushing to his next client.

It would be a very long day.

6 - Imago

Above the mighty Belab and the stretching heads of the towers in Axiac's Financial District, the sky, hot and cloudless, tarnished to a fading purple as the city lights turned on. The mirror surfaces of Babylon waned and vanished as electricity beamed out from behind them, revealing the imposing inner faces of those titans of glass and steel. One could see the Via Magna piercing all the way through to far Westbeach, under which the sun died in golden gray; and the lampposts emerged alit all across the boulevards. By the time Neipas left work the firmament was firmly seized by the spotlight of a million lamps from the vast megalopolis below, making the heights blind with a pale glaze. The hemisphere was tilting toward winter then, and evening had long overtaken the dwindling afternoon; despite the season, the whole extensive valley of concrete sweltered with heat, which teetered over the ground long after the sun had left the sky. Neipas, forlorn, exasperated himself under the sweat at the cusp of every pore. Despite his financial troubles he decided not to take the bus, his cheapest option. He feared the prospect of inhaling its stench, of the 2-hour ride. All he wanted was to go to his apartment, lock himself in his room and lie in bed.

Neipas opted for the train. As he walked toward the station his head swam in financial mathematics, drowning in calculations about his gains that day and how much more he needed for rent and enough food next month — numbers swung in the sway of the Tower's bells, foamed together with the drizzle of its waterfalls. He walked unconsciously along sidewalks littered with the political campaign pamphlets from the day before; slogan-words like 'HOPE', 'CHANGE', 'TOGETHER', 'VOTE', flashed from below, trampled under the mark of dusty shoes; the trash bins were bursting with these pamphlets and with the pins clamoring 'I VOTED'. By some miracle Neipas found an empty seat in the busy train — he had stayed longer at work, and though rush hour had long passed the station was yet swarming with commuters. He leaned into his seat, felt the muscles in his legs slacken and a blow of relief making his head light. Babylon Station panned out of view.

He slumbered half-awake in the Webwork for a while. His body was hoisted up by some foreign will when he perceived the next station; he almost didn't notice himself leaving until he was out the train already. There were two more trains to go. He leaned against a post and took the *I* out of his pocket.

Work became an unremitting fact of Neipas' life. The routine it demanded became ingrained in his muscles, filtered down to the very marrow of bone. His legs moved themselves. Before he was properly awake he was already running — to the shower, to the train, to the elevator, up and down the Belab's titan spine with the bulging tray pressing upon his arms and his back — all day, everyday, without cease — till, at the end of the day, his body fell upon its sores in a full insensitivity of mind.

Everyday he was in the Belab from dawn till after dusk, carrying trays full of food and drink to and from the tower's bowels, rushing somewhere within the vast confines of glass that framed the great tower's boundless interiors. Most of the time he stood in the darkness of the rising and descending elevators. Before him, and around him, only the I's rectangular glow broke the gloom in which the waiters were steeped. A restless silence reigned then, a silence full of stirrings. All day the multitude of elevators shot up and down hundreds of floors in a constant bustle, and within them hundreds and thousands of workers in silence, immersed in the vast noise of the Webwork. Music pounded relentless in their ears. Neipas, hooked to the earbuds, let them bloom into flower inside his head; his pinched fingers parted into spread wings upon the glass, his eyes dove — and he was transported. Out of the elevator, out of the Belab, out of Axiac (or perhaps deeper in; so he thought once) and into that immense, meaningless nowhere of threads and digital craze, to disperse in flight across a world of infinite interwoven caves, where every pigeon remained in its chamber and entered every other palpitating chamber all at once, carrying messages to one another; finding always no one. For all the pigeons chirped furiously at the same time; if one tried to lock beak for a second, one would hear the noise of infinite echoes cascading into the cave and overwhelm it with confusion. But no one ever dared to hush. There was too much allure in that noise, for the noise pervaded everything. To be outside of it was to be nowhere; though there was no where in the everywhere of the noise, either. Most weren't bothered by it. Everyone was steeped in noises in those days.

And yet, inside the physical elevator, where Neipas, at once, was and was not, everyone shushed, and remained quiet.

He was exhausted. It was taxing, the toil, particularly upon the body. But there was something about the grind of it that affected the mind and the spirit in insidious ways. A certain nervousness bore influence just underneath the thin fabric separating conscious will from instinct; so much so that Neipas simply couldn't think. Trying it strained him to a near spasm, and it took a great amount of effort to produce anything coherent in his head; all of which gave rise to some frustration, sometimes, but mostly a numbness which was pervasive and ready — feelings which he intuitively assuaged in the continual deep swoon of the *I*.

Outside, the profusion of city lights rushed by at a staggering speed. The train's iron cage jolted and he looked up for a second, sleepy and disoriented, trying to figure out whether he was at work still.

It was around this time that Neipas began an exchange over at the lovemaking sections of the Webwork. She was called Eva. He saw her in the *I*'s shining frame, and the sight of her drew in his heart in a muted instant. She glanced at him with tantalizing, laughing eyes. Her head toppled backward proudly, her raven hair floating down beyond her shoulders in ample curls. She smiled in natural good fun, revealing a perfect row of white teeth between the most delicate lips he had ever seen; and over her mouth she held a bough bursting full of grapes, in the most seductive pose. Another image and she was before him in full, head to knee, surrounded by the dazzle of a nightclub; she held up a glass, pouting her small beak, boisterously joyful all over. One hand reposed on her waist, which she twisted a little so as to prop up her butt; and right away Neipas ogled her breast, protruding off the side, smartly outlined in a tight top. Another moment and her mask of motionless marvel filled the *I* whole, close, making evident the perfection of her smooth skin, her silky eyes, her laughter and the endearing dimples by the corners of her smile. The sun glared behind her, and she burst in light. Neipas dreamed... He flew.

NEIPAS: Hello :)

EVA: Heyyy :)
EVA: How are you? :)

NEIPAS: Good :) And you?

EVA: I'm okk. Stressed out at wrk :/

NEIPAS: Really :(Why
NEIPAS: Same old?

EVA: Yea :(
EVA: Sometimes I just wanna quit it
EVA: But I'm taking a few days off soonnn

NEIPAS: That's good :) Any plans?

EVA: Hmmm
EVA: Not yet :)
EVA: I was thinking checking out south shore!
EVA: Have you been?

NEIPAS: Not yet
NEIPAS: I heard it's beautiful there tho

EVA: *(Picture of a beach at sunset. A stretch of glittering sand reaches for the deep horizon, disappearing into a haze sprinkled with sundust. Reddened waters penetrate its flank. Opposite the sea, imposing cliffs made pale, and without definition in their shrubbery, which hangs immobile. The crimson sky afar dominates the prospect).*
EVA: So dreamy

NEIPAS: We should go together ;)

EVA: Hahaha hold on there sir
EVA: U wanna take me on vacation already :D
EVA: We didnt even met yet silly :p

NEIPAS: Haha well...
NEIPAS: We should fix that :)
NEIPAS: We should meet sometime

EVA: Hmmm
EVA: I'll think about your case ;)

NEIPAS: Think with care :)
NEIPAS: How about dinner? :)
NEIPAS: My treat

Neipas lifted his head of a sudden. He grimaced with teeth clenched, as if wincing from a blow. Immediately he regretted suggesting this. He seemed to instinctively feel the metaphorical abyss of his wallet, and with this feeling came a slight nausea of sensation as the abyss momentarily drilled into his heart. But a sound pinged his ear, and the *I* shook. He looked down and delved back into its frame:

EVA: Well, if that's the case, then... Maybe ;)

Neipas smiled.

He leaned back satisfied. Sometimes he would come to, and for a moment he would realize he had returned from traveling in the Webwork's infinite nowhere, or that he had been slouched upon a bench, snoozing in the train. "Ostrich station," the metallic voice overhead was saying — Neipas roused out of slumber with a great inhalation of foul air and, perceiving where he was, leapt out through the train's door.

He walked mechanically to his apartment. His every move was automatic; his body knew where to take him, guided subtly by the inscrutable workings of his spirit. But his mind was blank. Flashes of color occurred to it, at times. Fragments of thoughts ruffled it out of dullness in intermittent moments as he rushed on, thoughts chiefly preoccupied with his finances and the practical affairs of life. The situation was dismal, but not unsalvageable, and the ceaseless pace of his work fomented hope in his heart. If he kept it up he would be able to pay up this month's rent and, perhaps, even the overdue fees that had been piling up from past months. After this was done he still might not be able to afford much in the way of eating, but it would be enough. Come next month all he had to do, he pondered in the dimness of his mind, was to keep working all the time. But if he kept it up, the month after that should be better.

Neipas entered the elevator and slinked his way through to his floor, trying to avoid that specter of a landlord whom he thought he had seen looming in a corner on the other side of the lobby. In a drowsy sort of panic, Neipas bolted on with downcast eyes and as stealthily as could be. He thought he heard his name being called behind him (probably imagined it) and he ignored it; then he heard it called again, louder. He didn't feel himself turning around; so it was as if the landlord suddenly materialized before him. He spotted his scrawny figure hunching sleazily before him and a sudden pang in his throat made Neipas involuntarily blurt out "Mr. Landlord!"

"Good evening, sir," the landlord greeted with his crackling monotone. His bony fingers dug into his mouth, carving a gigantic smile; neglecting, however, to mold the shape of his eyebags, which held on to their droopy, austere form. The fellow was haggard, with strangely puffy cheeks drooping out, slouched, with writhing hairs sprouting lazily from the wax surface of his mask; his lower beak lip curved and fell in a thick bulge dangling to and fro against the chin — it looked as though it might fall at any moment. The landlord would invariably wear a smudged white tank disproportionately creased at his bizarrely protruding tummy. His whole aspect was vaguely reminiscent of those neon-lit brothels nestled in the dingiest nooks of town.

"Good evening, good to see you, sir," Neipas replied, not at all aware of what he was saying.

"Good to see you too, sir..." The landlord's crackling left him slowly and shaky. The drawn out noise his beak made was unbearable to the nerves.

"Yes," Neipas nodded, after a moment of uncertain quietude. "Me too."

"Working! Is it, sir?" the landlord abruptly spouted, straightening his back very suddenly.

"Yes! Yes. I just came back from work."

The landlord nodded pensively. He was inspecting Neipas top to bottom, with eyes narrowed to a slit above their sagging, deep bags; he stretched his disturbing grin higher yet. A long time passed, and all they did was stare at one another in the meantime, Neipas lolling in discomfort, and the landlord simply nodding on without end, releasing grunts.

"Well," the landlord snorted, eventually, "it's good to see you, sir. Don't forget your monthly payment, now. And your overdue fees as well, please," he added slowly and excruciatingly.

"Of course, of course," Neipas reassured, bobbing his head as if to emphasize the reassurance. "Thank you, thanks so much."

Neipas bid his landlord goodnight and went on uncomfortably. The short encounter was enough to fill him with worries that kept him from sleep for a while. But eventually the fatigue of his body overcame the strain upon his mind. Neipas slept, to wake up to the *I*'s soft calling in the morning; and gear into the routine all over again.

*

One night, Neipas stood before the wardrobe in hesitation. His room held stiff, brittle, close about him, against four walls; it seemed to have shrunk lately. A narrow bed, a small table, a little chair, and the wardrobe he faced made up the totality of its furniture. On the floor hid a trash can and a laundry basket; on the table a lamp, an electric kettle, a jar of instant coffee, a tarnished spoon, a mug concaving smidgens of black liquid, and a bowl dusted with specks of cereal — the cereal box tucked in a corner inside the closet; there was nothing else. But for a few smudges and the lamplight, the walls stood bare; no photographs, not even a poster hung upon them. The place had always been meant to be temporary.

He had been sitting just moments before, beholding the family scene playing out in the apartment opposite. He sat in gloom, slouched in his chair, exhausted; invisible. He had been languishing into it since he returned, letting the night envelop him. In through the glass sneaked but a wan glimmer, breezed out of the streets and the window there, where he observed the patriarch flying his young daughter around their living room in an affectionate piggyback ride; her little cheek leaned onto her father's back, eyes closed and face peaceful — he didn't seem to notice she was already asleep. It made Neipas slip into old remembrances, filter down into the *I*. In the Webwork, he looked up photographs of his hometown before the incident. There weren't very many. Most pictures showed a landscape he didn't recognize, some plain seen from above, with a river of mud plastered across. One or two photos displayed rescue teams and helicopters hovering over a soggy land, an expanse suffocated under layers of brown paste; and people emerging from the heavy, wet dirt, covered thick in the stuff, resembling haunting spirits extracted by force from the deepest underground.

The canopies were shown toppled, the land drowned, the world a swamp. Among those familiar landscapes, so alien to his memory of their form, he recognized one peculiar place, pictured in one of the many photos, by its depiction of a certain tree — a fig (though Neipas himself did not know its name), huge and fallen, half-sunken in the sludge, with its spread of aerial roots veining across the mire. He remembered that place in particular because, after a certain point in time, its fig tree marked the spot beyond which he could not go; where the valley ended and the mines began. His mother had taken him there on piggyback once, back when it was but a little grove by the river. He remembered vaguely the sensation of her warm back, lulling in the oscillations of her breathing, the sway of the tender flight. The vegetation ruffled beneath them. Yonder, the river shimmered golden... Most vividly he recalled (though it might have been a different day) his mother picking up some aromatic plants and giving them to him to smell. He recalled the exact gesture — the way she brushed her hand along the plant and put her palm to her nose, and how he repeated it. He recalled the way she sprinkled herbs over the steaming pot.

Spiriting himself up from the chair, his head lifting dizzyingly, he watched his hands obscurely drawing away from his sight, gathering the shutters. A feeble lamplight glowed on.

A couple of ants strayed out from behind the closet, circling across the wall; then they disappeared again.

The wardrobe in his room was a bland piece of furniture, a simple rectangle erect upon the floor, with two drawers side-by-side on the bottom, and a door filling the top three-fourths of it, opening to its interior. The closet was lean; but its interior was deep, and could hide many things. Way beyond the hung clothes which, despite their scarcity, filled the width of the wardrobe, rested his old, broken film camera; and beyond it still, a messy heap of photographs. They had been there, abandoned to the dark recess, for a long time. Neipas had to put his head and knee inside the closet, and stretch his arm to its fullest extent to grab the photos; he had to reach so far in, that it felt like the closet went deep into the wall. He emerged back from its musty smell and sat on his bed, with the pile of photos lying in disorder beside him.

Neipas held up a photograph and looked carefully into it. It was but a small rectangle with a glossy surface, framed by a small white border round the edge. Its thin, solid make shook mildly between his thumb and forefinger.

Within the gloss were depicted his mother and father, in black-and-white. They stood a little away from the camera, basking in a campestral scene of dappled canopies tenderly enclosing a watermill, before which they posed. Foliage graced the borders of the frame, flowering into lush plants with needly leaves. The mother held on to the nook of his father's arm, shying back a little, as if wanting to run out of frame, as if trying to hide her humor; though her face was half-covered under her husband's shoulder, her bearing was entirely expressive of laughing eyes; her tilting body seemed ready to break into a guffaw; her loving nature readily conveyed in the timid posture, the soft delineations of her semblance a vision of humility and self-denial, of a kind and joyful demeanor. The father filled the picture with his regular pose of goofy dad; arms akimbo, knee bent forward, shirt open at the chest, a wide smile of glaring white teeth. He resembled a cartoonish imitation of a mariner, donning well-fitting jeans and a loose shirt, looking something like an old embodiment of romance, the very picture of an abundant will to live, to set out on adventure.

Neipas had seen his father in the *I* glass recently, only a few days before the Zoo. He would see him whenever his sister, who had stayed nearer their hometown, went to visit him in the hospice; it would be the only occasion in which the siblings spoke to each other, too. Their father, now rooted to a wheelchair, looked nothing like the youthful counterpart in the photo. His mask had hardened into something unearthly; something quiet, frozen in an incessant expression of horror. Whatever lay beyond the mask had been forever buried now. What had been, no longer was.

("Did you visit mom too?" he had asked his sister.

"Yes," she answered, behind an apathetic mask disguising a gulf of melancholy — nothing like the cheery face her brother's memory associated with her. "I took flowers, and a balloon.")

The son, Neipas, who contemplated their photograph now, couldn't remember when it was taken; but he was sure he had, himself, taken it. There were the two parents amid the low shrubbery, by the side of the river. The watermill in the background held stern, immobile; whereas it had once moved, Neipas knew. He had lain by it, listening to the methodic, creaking sound of its rotating wheel in the softness of the water drops. He had played with his sister by it, ran with her in circles round the stone house and inside its gloom of millenary reverence. Those had been good times. Whatever ills there were then, they had been forever erased in the camera's eye, and swept away from memory in its flash. For those ills, if they had existed, were little when compared to the limitless freedom of childhood as childhood was remembered. That was what Neipas recollected most clearly from those times of before, memories the photograph conjured — the distinct feeling of boundlessness, when every landscape was giant and time didn't exist. The youthful image of his parents reflected the immense wonder that pervaded all things back then.

His father had taught him to photograph — he had set up a darkroom within the peaceful, dim, stony confines of the mill house. Neipas remembered clearly the sensation, at once giddy and infinitely serene, of staring at the waters as he laid the print upon them. He remembered clearly the soothing sound of grain crushed into flour coming from the adjacent room as he witnessed the apparition of the image upon the print. He remembered clearly the expansive feeling of magic in his heart when he first saw the picture revealed in the waters.

"Son," his father had said, "we're creating the past."

Gradually Neipas was seized by a desire to photograph again, in the manner that he used to. This feeling urged him on to the roof. Stepping briskly out his apartment (calm, quiet — his roommate was asleep), he rushed to the elevator, and after climbing a few steps got off on the flat rooftop.

He was alone there. Casting his glance round him with his whole body, he surveyed the sprawl of Axiac running toward all horizons. To his west exploded the glaring lights of Babylon, with the Belab soaring into the firmament, and its Eagles' Nest throwing a beacon of glimmer shine unto all things below. To his east the mountains, severe and quiet, contrasted their black mass against the red glow of the sky beyond; a few lights from houses dotted the front of the hill, here and there. Neipas fixed his eye upon that strange red light, which flickered from some indeterminable distance. Rearing the *I* against his face, he captured a picture of it. He was unsatisfied with it — it looked duller and less vivid, the red could barely be made out. Looking for something the *I* would capture with more success, he turned to his south, toward Ostrich.

He beheld an image of destitution. The poverty of those dimly-lit neighborhoods was evident even in the darkness which crushed them. Two helicopters, buzzing over the shanty houses, cast their harsh headlights upon their slanted tops; and this would be the most prominent feature in that incomprehensible landscape, were it not for the conflagration gushing into the sky from the jagged edges of Ostrich, by the bay. It hailed from the Iblis refinery, which stirred onwards through the night and without stop, pumping out smoke and spitting fire from its nozzles in very fury. This wrathful machinery was ruthless in its toil, and made the heavens alit with crimson, as if simulating a perpetual, bloody sunset. It marked the chief nexus of an infernal latticework of factories, refineries and chemical plants; its cauldrons, spires, chimneys and pipes rising above countless other pipes, chimneys and cauldrons of steel, all churning the brew of industry within blocky, titanic shadows, out of which winked but red flares among crimson shimmers and glowing mists. Iblis' lash of fire bolted upwards over the heads of the destitute rookeries as an omen, as a threat. It held for a while, and as it seemed to be losing force Neipas leaned the *I* onto his semblance again to capture it; but he was interrupted in this, as the *I* shook and forced him away from the glass.

It was the notification of a posted paycheck — Neipas immediately jumped into the Webwork to examine his gains and verify that it was all safely deposited in his bank account.

The momentary lassitude of relief he had felt gave way to a slight tension. There was something off; about a quarter of the wages were missing. With a pang of desperation, Neipas zoomed into the small letters informing him that the amount had been transferred to *Health and Well-Being Insurance Services* to settle part of an impending debt.

In the limits of Ostrich the refinery had stemmed its flame, and held unmoving and powerful in the night.

7 - Rippling Threshold

Neipas had a recurrent dream, a dream about a tree. There in the distance, from the depths of his own horizon, grew the trunk toward the height of the sky and bloomed the canopy over the breadth of the firmament. It blossomed through twitches of lightning; ash drizzled from its boughs, for ash was its fruit, its leaf, and its bark. Tree of ash, sea of dust; through roots deep it spread across the Earth. All soil uplifted, every grain of land borne aloft in soaring rains and great cries of destruction and quietude.

Had it been shock, or the powders in the wind? but he recalled the struggle to breathe, as though the air itself were dispersing in crumbs of cinder.

*

He beheld the little cocoon, unperceived until then, stirring by the lamp beyond reach. The beeping fire detector nearby lit it with its winking red light. And he felt himself to be within a dream long after he woke up, the flash echoing the glimmer of a quiet flame. The cocoon held still — an ash flake suspended between slumber and space.

Neipas lay nearly motionless in his bed, beholding the darkness, for a long time. His breathing was profound, and at times he found himself wondering whether he had been awake the whole time or had just wakened. Feeble stirs of the imagination played upon his thoughts in the half-consciousness suffusing the gloom. Sometimes a familiar kick would rouse his breast, come out of nowhere; nauseous stirrings of worry in the half-sleep.

Some jittery instinct had hauled him out of bed. He had roamed the corridors in the middle of the night, in a delusion of dim lights, and gone downstairs to the mailbox. When he opened it a stream of letters came flushing out, a very unending river of folded papers spilling out into a pile on the floor. Neipas, dumbfounded with sleep, picked them up painfully — They were all hospital and insurance bills.

He had been trying to comprehend those charges on his account for a long time before lying down. His healthcare insurance had taken much more than usual — the monthly premium was higher; there were some miscellaneous, ambiguous 'copayment' charges which flipped him down into negative numbers; and finally the bank itself charged him because of those negative numbers, *twice*, pulling him deeper into the red. His wages brought him back afloat, but he had barely enough for rent, due soon; and the question of how he would eat after he paid that ground his mind in anxiety.

Listed among the levies were, in addition, a great number of small fees taken by many different obscure creditors with strange names. These were not names by which one would call people — they were more like codes or monikers given to machines. What was this? The blatant opaqueness and mysteriousness of it appalled him, as if some wraith had come into his life, rummaged through the drawers of his soul, taken pieces in his sleep shamelessly.

And now he contemplated those bills with a panic building up through the drowsy fog of his spirit. The violent cascade of numbers materializing out of the envelopes pushed him under completely. He had no idea what to make of them. When his father collapsed into disease, young Neipas would often hear, without understanding, how health-care costs could disrupt whole families, the toll they could impose on someone's life. In the end he didn't have to deal with his father's expenses; so he could not fathom the astronomical amounts of money that were demanded, the impact of seeing, with one's own eyes, those numbers ordered in a file, one number placed militarily after the next in a completely impassive arrangement. He sunk back in despair and disbelief. He could never have expected such absurd charges.

He slogged through his breakfast, arching under the weight of sleeplessness and concern. The cereal was as soggy as his mask, heaving and drooping from fatigue. Alone in the living room — his roommate was on vacation with his girlfriend somewhere — he gradually found courage in the general torpor. Swallowing the giddy feeling in his throat, he tapped his insurance company's customer relations department.

The overjoyed voice of a female screeched out of the *I*'s mouth:

"*Hi, and welcome to the Health and Well-Being Insurance Services' Customer Relations Department! We are very pleased to be of service to you,*" Neipas began to interject with a 'hi, thank you', but the voice kept going with no regard to him or any faltering in her overjoyment of tone. Neipas realized it was a pre-recorded message: "*Our Customer Relations' members are busy on the wires, committed to help you achieve your health goals. Please hold for the next available representative!*"

"*Your call will be picked up in the order it was received.*" Neipas must have heard this about a dozen times, first in his apartment, where about a dozen times he gave it up; and then in the drenched, rank air of the bus. The female voice greeted him again and again with its overbearing shout of joy. After she had finished a song would begin, something very rhythmic and bumpy, a waltz. From time to time the enthusiastic caw of a male would barge in to remind Neipas of the benefits enjoyed by the insurance company's customers (or 'family', as the voice said), advertising plan upgrades, discounted prices, miraculous boons. Every ten minutes it would wheeze back up and say the same thing; and when he ceased, the waltz would fade back in and progress until it looped into itself, and began again.

The bus was pulling up in a cluttered rotunda near Belab Square and the wire was still pumping the self-consuming melody. Carried up in frustration Neipas rose and was about to turn off the call as he clambered off the bus into sunshine — when he heard a voice coming in, a voice different from the repeated recordings.

"Hello? Hello?" Neipas spoke, and the voice responded. Standing now in the ample square and the teeming crisscrossing crowd, he asked it the reason for the increased premium; to which, after some minutes of research, the voice replied it was because of an outstanding hospital debt, which Neipas hadn't yet paid. The voice told him something inscrutable about increased risk.

Neipas swallowed dry, and sighed despondently. The crowd thickened about him in the square. It was hard hearing through the surrounding noises. "Ok... So, hum, what are these other charges? I have a bunch of fees on my account..."

"I'll gladly look into that for you, sir."

The voice couldn't find out what they were about, but it was glad to put Neipas through to its superior. The superior, equally unhelpful, said after a few minutes that it would be glad to put Neipas through to another department. It apologized for the inconvenience — after which Neipas spoke still to many voices, all clueless, all impersonal, all bodiless and uncaring, all of which apologized for Neipas' inconvenience. They spoke with different reverberations and the same tones, as if it were all the same robot assuming different cloths, as if the pre-recording machine were still in command of the wires.

Finally, feeling the sky brighten and the ground become insupportable in the blaze, Neipas simply hung up, maddened.

The Belab rose titan over him, and by the time he passed under its refreshing spray the morning summit bells had already tolled and the glass mammoth was awire with pulse. Within its domain the economic machine ran furious with cogs of skin and wax, paint and clay, light and shadow, in a relentless splash of velocity. Deals were made, money grown, empires expanded at every hour. The entourage of waiters ascended from the underground heat to service those creators of riches and sowers of prosperity, up and down the elevators, bending over by their side, smelling their food all day, bearing their weight all day, maintaining grin upon mask all day. Neipas' mind often sneaked away from him into the distraction of possible scenarios: many variations of hunger and homelessness found its way into his imagination.

Numbers stormed inside it: higher insurance costs, the hospital debt, lingering student debt, food and rent, rent's late fees, taxes. Did his credit score lower, and would his landlord check it and kick him out when the lease was up? Abysmal maths sunk his soul. Edazima's kindness came to mind, he thought he could perhaps borrow a little from her. But he shook the idea away, his pride dilating with shame: Neipas owed her too much already.

His worries only mounted up and he signed off earlier than usual, intending to go to his bank's closest branch, which was inside the Belab, to see if he could fix things. Flummoxed and rushed, Neipas removed his ox head, tossed himself out of his stuffy uniform and, scrambling through the kitchen's oily brume — brushing along the myriad indistinct shapes of foggy cooks — entered the gloomy elevator, navigating up several different elevators to reach the Bank.

A slick reception hall greeted him, ballooning onto blue walls and ambient light fixtures. Very modern and minimalistic, the space hosted a few odd-shaped chairs and tables, upon which rested bowls of candy. Neipas was approached by a suited teller wearing a friendly peahen mask, very poised, hands clasped and pending formally, a wide smile with which she welcomed the arriving client:

"Good afternoon, sir. May I ask the reason for your visit today?"

Neipas said that he wanted to inquire about some charges in his account. "Very well, sir," and she had Neipas write his name in an *I* tablet, and bid him wait a few minutes until he was called. Neipas sat and waited, drumming his heel. He fixed up his weary pigeon mask in the *I* glass. Other pigeons sat in separate chairs, mostly suited, aloof and silent, immersed inside the Webwork. Looking upward and about, fidgety, enveloped, Neipas took still a moment to apprehend the staggering aspect of his surroundings; he sat as if his senses were still clouded in the vapors of the kitchen, as if stewing yet in the fume, the drizzle, the pace of labor. But as time settled with him upon the seat, he first gazed, as if through the dispersing of fog, the two columns of water; there were the reception desks afar, separated from the lobby by sheets of glass and lodged into the base and center of the enormous wall; on either side, pretty statues of some Venus holding cornucopias stood a blithe watch beside the two passageways further along; one at each side of the symmetric flatness, the tall oval frames yawned into escalators which appeared to ascend vertiginously, and advance forcefully, toward some mysterious distance; then, on the extremities, the two vertical aquariums pillared the height of the towering wall, spanning floor to ceiling and, it appeared, rising and sinking even beyond — caustic motions oscillated inside, zigzagging with the fishes; and finally, between the aquarium columns and above the beglassed reception area, making the centerpiece of the whole composition, there gaped a vast glass circle, on which was affixed a massive crest, the Bank's Official Seal — an eagle clutching scales with its talons, beneath wings triumphantly spread. Behind the crest, behind the glass, there too, brimmed aquarium water.

The two Veni grinned their marble. Little founts poured from the cornucopias with a pleasant ambient purling; it seemed to set the mesmerizing, dancing rhythm to which the ripples of light swayed; in which the fish swam, floating in languid spirals up, up, up the water pillars, to and fro the round crest. One by one they emerged from the bottom and wound beyond the top in an hypnotized synchrony of repetition — Neipas thought that it might be some sort of screen, but then his gaze was drawn deeper yonder, behind the strange dance of these fishes, and it dove into the ascending bubbles: showing in the transparency of the aquarium, submerged through its waters as it were, a series of escalators, of staircases, of corridors, traversing each other at jagged angles, and varying degrees of steepness across a rising confusion of storeys, lifting a broken proliferation of well-bound precipices, alongside which bodies walked, up, down, back, forwards, bodies crossing at endless corners and a myriad angles and directions, all busy, all impassive, an army of steps abstracted and quiet in the serene tilt of the water; and he saw many strangely juxtaposed walls, and many doors of different formats opening in unexpected places — the liquid shrank, expanded, elongated and distorted everything, and all things seemed to be hanging freely and nonsensically. Neipas, who with a grimace watched and caved into his chair, presumed an impossible complexity of paths multiplying along the inscrutability of the Bank's back stage, felt unconsciously as his body sunk and his eyes rose, seeing the fuzzy lines intersecting to great depths and up great heights, the way unimpeded — carving the air in triangles, squares, rectangles, rhombii and parallelograms, shrinking the ever rising prospect (drawing away diagonally) until it became but a dot — and he, who had never seen a depth so distant, lost the horizon in a breathing palpitation of gold (gold? orange? red?) glow, beheld it panting between the ebbing shards of atmosphere, throbbing profoundly...

Quite suddenly then, he made himself upright, afraid he'd been caught slouching. Through the two oval passageways he eyed suits entering the escalator through unsuspected doors and byways, and he perceived how these initial escalators near branched out into other escalators and probably, eventually, into the bedlam of the hanging labyrinth, which he assumed to encompass a path to the very core of the tower — even to the fabled treasure of its iron bosom, perhaps. He felt that he was on the threshold of something enormous, something incomprehensible, inscrutable, and inaccessible.

At last, fascinated in the novelty of these views (for he had never been on this floor), as he completed the upward trajectory of his head he halted it toward the ceiling — far high, it, too, was wholly made of glass, and through it he could observe the underside of rich ornate tables, chairs, and shoe soles pacing about with a stern carriage. From floating suits sprouted eagle masks: their golden beaks protruding gravely, moving portentously, emitting the impression that important work was being done. The myriad translucent lights beyond the aquariums cast the ripples of its water upon the ceiling, as they did, gently and nearly imperceptibly, on the whole space; glossing over all things, parting everything in variable shards with swaying edges — like an endlessly fluid, endlessly cracked mirror. Tilting downward, Neipas even wondered if he and they all too were inside water. On the walls hung photos of the Belab, and x-rayed pictures of the Belab with mazes of intraconnected lines, and illegible blueprints. Right before him on the table rested the bowl of candy, on which he fixed his sore eyeballs for the remaining time — though he didn't take any out of a vague fear of losing the bankers' favor; he sensed that they weren't meant for him.

After a few minutes, Neipas was called up. He approached one of the desks in the glass screen, where sat a young peacock with a shiny crest slicked professionally to the side. He lifted his head from his computer and cast a friendly smile at Neipas.

"Very good afternoon, sir," greeted the teller.

"Good afternoon," replied Neipas — there was a slight tremble in his voice filtered through his sagging pigeon mask, and he was vaguely taken aback by how unable he was to contain the nervousness stirring in him.

"How may I help you today?"

"Well, um... I had some... charges on my account? and I'm not really sure what they are."

The teller grunted to signal that he was intrigued, shaping his features into an equally intrigued expression of face in the meanwhile, right brow tilted high. "I see... I can certainly look into that for you. May I see your account information?" Neipas leaned his *I* against a small strip of gleaming ruby light on his side of the counter — a sharp beep emanated from it and it turned green, as if responding in confirmation. "Thank you," voiced the teller, already studiously staring at his computer screen, in a show of determination, to get his client through the ordeal. Neipas moved his beak in the shape of a 'thanks so much,' though no voice came out of it.

The jovial teller punched his keyboard with much conviction for a good half-minute. The resolve in his eyes, taut between their focused lids, heartened Neipas and cultivated in him a hope that his predicament may be solved after all — but this feeling was promptly demolished when the teller parted the corner of his beak and clicked his tongue, shaking his head slowly; he expressed the obvious meaning of his gesture in words when he said, right after:

"Oh my... I'm so sorry sir, but I don't think there is anything I can do for you here," he lifted his glare from the computer and into Neipas' inward-sinking eyes. "The withheld charge cannot be recuperated at this time unfortunately. It was transferred to the...," he peered back into the computer screen, "the Health and Well-Being Insurance Services' account. It is out of our hands, I'm afraid," he said, making a vague motion of throwing air into the ceiling.

"Ok so that did come from them..." Neipas said, trying to contain the deepening anguish. "Um... But do you know what the charges are for? Is that specified on your end, maybe?"

"Hmm... Let's see... I'm looking here, and..." the teller said very slowly, sucking in the sharp tip of his beak before the computer screen, to signal concentration. "I'm afraid not, sir. You would have to speak to their representatives. I can also see that you were charged for a negative balance?"

"Yeah I was gonna mention, those extra charges from the bank, I..." — Somehow Neipas didn't continue, as he was awaiting for the banker to interject. After a pause he said, "What are those ones about? And why *twice*?"

"It seems like that was a mistake, sir. I'll fix it for you."

Neipas felt his shoulders lighten up a load. Then he asked, "Both charges?"

"I can only do one, sir."

"Mary Virgin — " Involuntarily Neipas took his fingers and sunk them in the corners of his closed eyes, waving his other hand as if trying to shoo away the situation. "You're charging me money for having no money?"

The teller smiled, and when he perceived that it was a real question, he said through his moving grin, "I'm afraid it's policy, sir."

There was a faint apologetic sincerity in his voice. Neipas, wavering, instinctively inferred the form of the teller behind his mask, and caught a glimpse of the fact that the young fellow was simply someone who worked there, who spoke his practiced sentences in his practiced manner under the same compelling force, by which Neipas bowed before clients and rolled out the fawning words with which they were addressed — the threat of starvation. The teller was an automaton for the Bank in the same way Neipas was an automaton for Kur during his work hours.

Yet Neipas still asked, hopeless, in a reach for the teller's masked humanity: "You can't do anything about it?"

"I'm afraid not, sir. Though you could always file a claim with our claims desk."

Neipas said "sure", more out of a confused sense of politeness than anything, and watched bewildered as the teller gave him directions on how to reach the claims desk via the escalators on his side, and via bisecting-escalators, side-corridors and oblique stairs and even ladders, through many doors and across countless halls — eventually, somewhere in the course of his monologue the teller stopped, grunted thoughtfully, and decided that it would be better if he wrote it all down so Neipas wouldn't forget. His tapping was slow, methodical, endlessly helpful and nerve-racking in that it conjured an image of sprawling labyrinths in which it was much too easy to lose one's way; and as if to confirm that notion, Neipas spied the doors behind the reception desks opening to various bifurcations and curved paths and trapdoors, leading various other clerks down to obscure basements and up unfathomable cellars elsewhere lodged.

Neipas looked up. The Eagles beyond the glass ceiling still held their endless meeting. Behind the aquariums he saw escalators multiplying with their numberless roamers wobbling austerely in every direction. He was momentarily struck by the strange variety of their forms. There were giant hogs, with immense tusks and under leashes, there, who among all others seemed most as though they were floating, flying in the waters. The teller still wrote down the way to claims (*tap-tap-tap* upon a keyboard without music); but as Neipas drew in the absurdity of those endlessly winding and convoluted pathways he intuited the futility of the effort. Right away he foresaw the difficulty of reaching the claims desk and that all the time invested in the search would be time wasted. Neipas reasoned that the money he had lost, he could recover with extra toil during those same unending hours.

Just as he was getting unnerved by the teller's prolonging, Neipas realized his friendly voice spoke, "Would that be everything, sir?"

Neipas nodded, dispirited. He never received the directions — his silence said everything.

The teller smiled a wider grin.

"Have a nice day, sir."

But in his revolt Neipas was still unwilling to give up. His insurance had taken more from him than they should, and they hadn't even covered any of his medical bills, which is what he paid them for in the first place. It was egregious — he decided to go and speak straight to their customer service desk. He went a few days after; putting it off as much as he possibly could.

The closest branch was a few blocks southeast of Belab Square in the outer edge of Babylon. There was no train going there, and Neipas was still exhausted after he clambered off the bus, his legs sore and his head heavy. He was still fighting against his unwillingness to go to the stupid health insurance customer service office and endure what he already anticipated would be an unpleasant experience; only the urgency of the situation urged him on. In his weariness he mused about taking a day off the next day, though he knew full well he couldn't skip it; for the lightness of his wallet weighed perpetually upon the back of his mind. Neipas looked round.

The neighborhood looked quite shoddy. Round the inconspicuous insurance company's edifice sprawled an unseemly mess of spray-painted scribbling upon walls of dilapidated plaster and exposed brick. Above the base of the apartment buildings ascended grimy plasterwork worn with age and lack of care, old balconies come out of it like protruding rust, some with clothes hanging from the edge to dry in the sun, others partly covered in ageing canvas fabric flapping unassumingly in the slow breeze above. These buildings were no more than 5 or 6 stories high and rose haggardly here and there, squeezed together or scattered round unevenly. Opaque trash bags lay discarded in piles at their feet, just by the side of the asphalt. The concrete of the sidewalks was shattered in many places, its blocks made uneven by the roots growing under them, of old lone trees planted at the side; a dense line of water, or some liquid, progressed through the shallow joints between each block of cement and was piling up densely in the fractures, spilling out of a corroded pipe in one of the walls. There was a bit of stench hanging just under the nostril.

For some reason it struck him as quite strange that the insurance company would have a customer service desk here. Neipas reflected that it might have struck him so because he knew that its corporate headquarters were in the Belab — he had served there a few times before. In the Belab, he remembered, the desks were made of gleaming mahogany and the glass windows flanked by very ornate satin curtains.

But here, the windows were screened with plastic and partly covered in cardboard. Inside, by the back-wall, there was only one, long desk — long enough to fit a whole union of desk workers behind — and it was presided by only a couple of busy-looking clerks; before it stood a bunch of cheap, foldable chairs, leaning back lazily and more or less arranged in a series of rows. The place was packed, and the impatience with which folk waited was thick upon the air. Over the heads of the sitting throng were light beams radiating heat. There was no air-conditioning here; that was immediately noticeable. The very breath one exuded seemed to die in the stuffiness of the space upon leaving the body.

The receptionists looked terribly busy; their owl masks were rigid under the weight of responsibility and were stressed in with astounding frowns. There were screens above them with analog numbers in red. Everyone had a numbered ticket in their hand; but Neipas, scoping the space, couldn't find where to get one. He walked to the front, passing the long line of buttocks sinking exasperated and flabby on the multitude of flimsy chairs, and still could not see it. He thought of asking the receptionists, and approaching, ignoring the dread their somber visages impressed in him, he leaned onto the desk, gripping it with both hands. None of the clerks seemed to take notice. They didn't flinch the slightest bit when Neipas appeared before them, holding steadfast in the devoted fulfillment of their responsibilities, hammering away at the keyboard with goggles gazing firm the flickering screen in front. Neipas wavered a little; for a few seconds of hesitation, no one said anything.

"Excuse me," Neipas finally began, raising an index finger in a manner of polite prodding. "Where can I find the —"

One of the clerks looked up, irritated. "Sir, you have to take a ticket and wait for your turn."

Neipas nodded eagerly. "Yes but where can I find the ticket..." his voice dimmed to a peep as he witnessed the clerk's face morph into the very form of contained rage. But he gained courage and asked again, "Um, where can I find the —"

"Sir! Will you calm down please? You have to take a ticket, and wait for your turn," the clerk insisted impatiently, with much emphasis on each word. The other receptionist never lifted her eyes off her screen and simply shook her head in contemptuous disapproval.

"Well but that's just what I was —"

"Sir! SIR! Will you call down, *please!*" the receptionist said loudly and slowly, as though an enraged babysitter berating a languageless toddler.

Neipas had just barely opened his lips to apologize when the clerk shot out "Will you calm down sir!"

"Ok alright sorry!" Neipas was already walking away from the desk, feeling somewhat choked and strained in embarrassment, as if he had just committed the gravest impropriety. He sat down on the first chair he saw empty, bending his head very low and forgetting, in his vexation, to take a ticket; it was only a moment later that he realized it and proceeded to leap to his heels — somewhat taken in a fit of nerves — lunge toward nowhere, and look around in search again. A mid-aged lady, sitting in the edge of the aisle, said motherly, "It's over there," pointing to a shadowy corner where the ticket-holder was camouflaged.

"Oh. Thank you ma'am."

Neipas glided toward and pulled out a ticket. Then he stepped back to his chair and sat on it, his body still moving inward; his feet began tapping the ground almost at once. Already he was fed up with this place.

Neipas looked up from his *I* when he heard the left-hand clerk bellow out "67!" The number on his ticket was 68; he reckoned the wait shouldn't drag on much longer. Sneaking a peek round the room he saw a gargantuan pigeon wobbling toward the reception desk, trudging his way from the very back. As he passed by, Neipas observed his static, stupefied face with some discomfort. His feathers all pasty, the wax on his face hung down from the many crinkled ripples pulling beneath his bloodshot stare, which gaped as though in perpetual dismay, its dry, dead appearance bare. He barely blinked. The sum of his vital forces seemed to be engaged in nothing except the exertion of his stout legs, now thrashing forward in a hulking shuffle; the saggy breast sunk, the wide belly drooped over his hips, his arm rolled motionless over the elbow. Only the plump lips stirred upon his countenance, and Neipas did have the impression of hearing him mutter, "my god, my god," in the most afflicted, breathless whisper he had heard for a long time. Every step the poor fellow took shed from it a vivid impression of pain. The receptionist, who never removed eyes from her screen, shouted angrily even as he approached, "67!"

"23!" the other clerk screamed out. Neipas still lifted his butt off the chair but then froze in place, hesitating between going and not going. He was still trying to figure out whether he had heard the number correctly when someone yelled from the back, "Did you say twenty three?" "Yes!" the clerk shouted back. "Ok!"

A gaunt pigeon with rainbow feathers lurched toward the desk, quickly overtaking the fat pigeon, who was still on his way there. Agitated murmurs began issuing almost immediately upon his stepping up to the clerk, and the whispered babble quickly filled the space with its noise. Everyone else was quiet. Other than the sound oozing from the desk now, only the muffled hint of music from headphones could be heard in this room. Neipas returned his gaze to the *I*; he lolled about in it awhile.

...

...

[somehow or other he alighted upon the news]

103

WALTZ AT THE EAGLES' NEST

Captains of industry to discuss climate at this year's World Market Summit

The World Market Summit, hosted as usual at the Anubel complex of venues (commonly known as the Eagles' Nest), is set to tackle some of humanity's most pressing problems

[...] Luminaries from industries as varied as defense and biotechnology will be present. Among the sponsors can be counted farming giant Penaguiar, who will host the event, and NoxxeSocony, the energy conglomerate, whose CEO recently pledged to donate millions to climate change mitigation efforts

... philanthropic efforts have achieved ... other climate funds...

committed to reaching zero net carbon emissions and promote worldwide equity through which to foster economic growth," said [...] increase of eight percent is expected between

... Investment bankers, who often use the summit to network with clients, are
[...] big tech executives, administration officials confirmed, as well as dignitaries from

... and the Mayor will also be in attendance after his reelection last month...

Larry [...] keynote speaker

[absentmindedly scrolling down, his sight landed on the only photograph: A plump Eagle, with raised jowls liquefying over his collar, smokes a long

104

pipe, and stands very erect; he talks to someone in military uniform, whose back is turned to the camera. Four chevrons decorate the Eagle's lapels (four at each side, two chevrons inverted) echoing thus all the pyramidal shapes of his suit. Above, behind him, soars the dome of the famous Eagles' Nest Ballroom, its majestic paintings curving as ample as any sky, and from which are lowered portentous chandeliers, glittering]...

Caption: *Representatives of NoxxeSocony and the Army converse at last year's Market Summit Gala*

...

Suddenly a tremendous shout ripped the barren air and sent Neipas jolting, "Six!" — it was the left-hand clerk calling. Disoriented, Neipas looked up and saw that she kept her owl gaze fixed on the screen yet. Already someone was walking between the rows of chairs toward her. She swiftly went past the big pigeon who still clumped forward with much agony and effort; and as she did the fellow stopped and rotated his neck very slowly and with difficulty to look at her passing figure. He looked shocked, and exerted himself to raise a finger in protest.

The heat accumulated quickly. Before long a drop of sweat sneaked out of a pore at Neipas' cheek and escaped swiftly down the face before he caught it.

...

EVA: I live in Golden WestBeach :)
EVA: Not sure yet

NEIPAS: There's a restaurant there a friend recommended me
NEIPAS: Right the promenade
NEIPAS: Maybe we could meet there? :)
NEIPAS: *(Picture of a colorful map of roads, a cartoonish pin in the middle)*
NEIPAS: Has good reviews

[...]

NEIPAS: Next week maybe?

At some point Neipas pulled out of the *I*, throwing his head back and shutting his vision tight. The pale brightness of the place hurt his eyes. It was like a sauna in there; he was soaked in the moisture of his own flesh by then. He lifted his fingers to his jaw and felt his skin of wax wilting, precipitously dangling off the side of his face. The *I* glass revealed to him the thin surface of plume shredding off and showing huge swaths of his real features; he noticed at once the ghastly twitches of his right cheek. Employing the whole palm of his hand he rushed to fix his mask, deftly pulling the decaying wax up and over the entirety of his visage, and spreading it thin over his jaw, his cheeks, his forehead, adjusting the beak to fit just over the nose and lips. He looked around with his sapped eyes to check if there was anyone looking at him. But no one was. What Neipas saw was that everyone else bore the same face as he.

Upon the mask of each patient was imprinted every staple of profound dejection. The parched air hovered thin, and it felt as though every patient was struggling to not suffocate in it; one could almost sense that the collective breathing was made with much difficulty. Some had big adhesive patches glued to their damaged skins, others had their legs cast and a pair of crutches resting on their lap, the older folk leaning feebly onto canes, and yet others had their arms banded and cast in plaster, hanging in as much a rigidity of affliction as the faces they had cast in wax. The ones that showed no evident damage to their bodies couldn't conceal the hurt nestling in their breast; they cared nothing for their masks in there. Most looked as if their souls had vacated their eyes, and they did not stir. A few grew and shrunk dramatically in their motion of strenuous breathing; they had the patent marks of agony upon their faces, and looked as if they had trouble keeping the life in their bodies. Neipas guessed that some of them weren't wearing masks at all. Perhaps it was so — or if they did wear them, the wax of them had been worn out of existence, and they couldn't much control how it was molded anymore, they could no longer pretend away the stuff pulping inside their hearts.

There was a fellow in particular, a pigeon sitting a couple of chairs down, who attracted Neipas' sidelong stare for a while. A long feathery beard oozed from his mask onto a muscular chest, shrunk under a massive, curved back. The powerful mass of his body looked defeated, it looked burdened with many invisible wounds. Upon closer inspection, he noticed a branded mark depicting the flag of the nation wrapped round a heap of arrows — a sign adopted by the military — upon the fellow's wrist, enveloping the needle through which blood was drawn out of him into a plastic sack at his side. Neipas contemplated his features carefully. This soldier's mask (was it a mask still? — he wondered), thinned out by years of battle, seemed affected with the dragging impact of disillusionment. He looked helpless; he looked frozen in the realization of a serious mistake. The pigeon stared toward nowhere, his cracked eyes presenting no luster; the life in them had been spirited away long ago, and the body left wondering what had happened in the meanwhile.

For the three hours (it certainly felt like that much) before he was called Neipas remained seated, his smeared teeth increasingly digging into his lips and his feet drumming into the floor at a dizzying pace. The clerks called numbers quite out of order — "40!", "89!", "11!", "239!", and so on. In a pretty regular rhythm, it seemed, the receptionists would call out, converse secretively for a few moments with whoever was called, and then launch their busily peering goggles back into their screens. The folk who walked away from the desk and out of the building looked alternately enraged and defeated.

The steady, looping pace that began with the calling of a number, followed through with chattering in frustrated mutters, and concluded in utter silence was only broken when the fat pigeon finally arrived at the desk. It had nearly been an hour since the fellow was called, Neipas having only a faint hint of a remembrance of him by then, and having almost forgotten about him in the immersion of the *I* and the swoon of the surroundings. In fact he only became aware that the pigeon had concluded his march when the clerk's voice reached his ear saying "Sir! Sir! Will you calm down! Sir!" He looked up and saw the fellow standing there by the desk, bowed, dumb, and hopeless, his old face sagging, the wax running away from his mask, the sick bloodshot eyes teary, his lower lip hanging open and floppy. The clerk just kept shouting at him, "Sir! Sir! You will have to take another ticket, sir, you can only be attended to if your number is called!... Yes... Yes, I understand! But you have to sit down, sir!" she yelled, as the fellow impotently tried to explain himself. It looked like he had lost his turn. Neipas observed with a speedy heart, a little astonished that no one would do anything about it. Perhaps that wasn't so strange, the clerk's volume of voice really wasn't raised above what's ordinary; and all things considered — with the heat and the grungy aspect of the place — it was rather contained. Eventually someone in the front row offered his seat to the poor pigeon; and he, the very image of dejection, rotated his portly torso round to sit, with the clerk still yelling "please don't forget you need a ticket sir!" behind him.

Neipas mustered some courage and leapt out of his seat, walking a few steps to pull out a ticket, then walking to the front row to hand it to the pigeon. Head downcast, he could almost feel the clerks' looks of contempt on his back. He went back to his chair and, vexed, inflated the volume of his music to drown out his surroundings and dove back into the *I*.

Suddenly Neipas' head lifted, as if on command. "68!"

He got up and walked to the desk. In a moment he was before the clerk on the left side, whom he had spoken to previously. She looked up at him from behind the desk with indifference.

"Sixty eight?" she asked; suddenly she brought her fingers to her face and carved up a very big smile.

"Yes," he responded, nodding.

"Name?"

"Neipas."

"Do you have a Health Insurance card with us?"

"Yes," Neipas said, pulling his wallet out of pocket and handing her the card. The clerk held it in her hand for a moment and, diverting her glare from card to screen, punched something into the computer.

"Very well," she said, handing back the card and stretching her smile further up, until it reached just under the sides of her goggles.

"Um..." Neipas began, always with the disorientation of perceived self-ineptitude and smallness. "I wanted to ask about some charges..."

But he was interrupted as naturally as if he hadn't spoken. "Would you like to pay your full balance with us today?" asked the clerk.

"Well," Neipas muttered, somewhat intimidated by the ghastly motion of her tiny beak, "that's just what I wanted to ask you about today. I think there's been a mistake with my charges."

"A mistake?" she wondered, cocking her head exaggeratedly to one side.

"Yes."

"No, sir," she simply said.

They remained staring at each other for a while.

"No?" Neipas said, confounded, speaking more to himself than to her.

"We don't make mistakes here, sir. At the Health and Well-Being Insurance Services company, we make sure to provide the most optimal healthcare service on the market," she said, lifting her huge grin higher still.

"Well, but look here," Neipas began, dumbfounded, pulling out his *I* and navigating toward the invoice of his expenses, then showing it to the clerk. She merely nodded her smile and mumbled "hm-hm".

"I don't understand. Are you sure? Look," he pushed the *I* a touch closer to her and pointed at the relevant numbers. "It can't be," Neipas concluded, chuckling nervously.

"Yes, sir," she said, calmly. "That's right."

Neipas felt his heart squeeze against his neck and pinched shut his eyes, completely disoriented. He opened them, and the clerk was still there with the same smile and little dots of light fluttering about her. "But that can't be right," he insisted, chuckling again. But his chuckling ceased at once, for the clerk began to shape her expression into something less nice and more intolerant.

"Would you like to pay your balance today, sir? You may also pay in installments every month over the course of..." she looked at the screen, "twenty-five months."

Neipas couldn't believe it. "But this is outrageous!" he uttered. "My insurance should cover hospital stays —"

"Sir, sir," the clerk began. "Please calm down." Neipas halted in a frigid, very upright position, nodding with head downcast, his heart beating angrily in his chest. The clerk was studying her screen. "We did expend five *mumblemumble* to alleviate the total hospital charge of *mumblemumble*," she said, matter-of-factly.

Neipas took a while to process this information, his head growing bigger in the meantime. Then he shook it, still looking at the floor, and shot out, "That's probably not even five percent of the charge!"

"Sir! Sir, please calm down. This is what your coverage offers, ok?" she said, pausing a little, her face already dropped to a near frown; but then she quickly turned her face up to a monumental grin. "But you could always upgrade your plan by the discounted price of —"

"I don't wait any upgrades," Neipas moaned, his fingers buried in the hollow of his eyesockets, his other hand waving hopelessly in front of his face. "I just want to understand how it is that this costs so much. And," he sighed, his shoulders sagging toward the floor, "how is it that my insurance doesn't cover this."

"Sir! Calm down. Please!" the clerk started, and her whole body seemed to subtly jolt back into a scowl. The clerk on the right was shaking her head quite vehemently now. "As I have *said*, your plan has covered what was stipulated *in it*. Would you like to pay your entire balance now, or would you like to pay in installments?"

Neipas sighed deeply, emptying his chest of air, meager; his beak moved without uttering a sound, trembling to intone "you can't be serious", and other laments. He was rubbing his head in desperation, as if the solution could somehow be ground out of his exfoliated scalp. Afflicted, he opened his eyes, wide and bloodshot. Through his tired gaze and out of the bleached landscape he perceived the clerk's scowling mask, her austere leer of owl; and knew there was nothing else he could say or do.

"Sir? SIR!"

Neipas just stood there. "You know what. I need to think about it," he said in a breath.

"Very well, sir," the clerk spat, immediately turning her frown back to the screen.

Neipas began his dash toward the exit, boiling in frustration, his whole being oppressed under the intense heat. As he turned away from the desk he noticed the fat pigeon was still seated in the front row; he had fallen asleep, breathing heavily. Neipas passed by the military veteran, still in the middle row, still bearing his stoic, empty glare. And as he flung past the multitude of ailed patients and out into the street he resolved, in his repulsion, that he just wouldn't pay.

8 - Lake of Echoes

Crumbs muddled the reflected sky, and the waters, once disturbed, quickly erupted in a storm of faces. Frenzied mouths fought for the bread, emerging thunderously, gasping amid a chaos of scaly bodies and quivering fins.

It lasted but a moment. The disarray of fishes little and large then promptly scattered, scampering to make way for the largest among the fishes there, who was now surfacing, and who, leisurely parting its blind lips, proceeded to suck in the bulk of the crumbs. Neipas, sitting on a bench in the Park of Echoes, chewed his bit and beheld the spectacle cynically. He said to himself that things mustn't be so bad yet — not so long ago, he recalled, he would not have spared a single grain.

The sky was a vivid blue and the sun shone radiantly, discharging a wave of heat that swamped the earth with fever. A fidgety quietude stewed throughout the wide and oscillating space. Only the crunching of the gravel path rimming the small lake broke the arid silence, of folk jogging and walking their pets; the mumbling of voices was generally absorbed by the heat. No birds sang; and everyone was too immersed in their own affairs to notice the soundlessness of the air. The treetops undulated, unnoticed, to a wind that hovered high above the soil. The grass lifted from the ground without a stir. Lone, his reflection stared from the deep of the lake; the pigeon mask appeared to him indistinct in the soft rippling, under a glitter of sunshine.

Leaning over the waters, Neipas contemplated his semblance and pondered about his life. He reflected, not by force of intellect, but through a deep instinct of feeling that he was incapable of rationalizing just then. It took the form of a vague unease broiling in his innermost, a corroding suspicion of injustice, an overwhelming helplessness. He felt ensnared by shadowy forces whose existence his mind couldn't encapsulate; whose workings seemed beyond understanding. Staring at his wide eyes staring into himself, he wondered and wondered.

Had it been true? Had it been true, that which he saw beyond the mask?

There was a distinct sense of being drained as he bent in closer to the water. He could perceive himself being sapped of something fundamental, sapped of meaning, of primal characteristics buried deep within the core, too deeply buried for his mind to reach. Neipas felt something of his essence being tinkered with; tinkered by something within and out, something strange and all-pervading; something intimate and alien. But what?

He had a misty suspicion that it was something particular about the days he lived in. There was something odd — something that induced anxiety and fright, and offered only a forgetfulness for refuge; something somehow incompatible with his nature; indeed, something intangible about that age, which cluttered, mystified, anesthetized... And yet, not so long ago the most exalted voices acclaimed the age; pronouncing it the pinnacle of epochs, they affirmed all epochs past had been immeasurably worse. Anyone could have a successful life if only one worked hard — that was their promise. Neipas had even believed it once. But his conception of success involved a kind of spiritual fulfillment, necessitating a bare minimum of material comfort which he found difficult to attain. Yet he worked hard — did he not? Perhaps he didn't work smartly enough. Yet he'd gone to university; his work possessed intelligence, sophistication, worth. It must. He refused to believe that all was relative and there were no objective standards for quality (objectivity, he felt, was applied in all the wrong places; everything was muddled). Perhaps if he were less proud... Must he debase himself to keep from misfortune, though? must he grovel? He worked hard, at any rate (perhaps not hard enough? perhaps these were but the excuses of frustrated hopes). And yet now, still he repeatedly, repeatedly wondered, whether it was all his fault.

And yet. One slip, one mistake — one accident — and already he was sinking into a debt he couldn't hope to surmount. The precariousness of his situation nauseated him; it was as if the ground was melting under his feet, precipitating him into the earth. And as these reflections worked in him Neipas involuntarily twisted his real face into the most tormented contortions and mutters, whispering his disordered thoughts to himself without realizing it, so absorbed he was in the depth of his afflictions. Leaning forward a bit more he realized that the wax of his mask was starting to drip into the lake because of this frenzy of expressions, also because of the heat; a small chunk fell in before he could catch it, and in trying to catch it Neipas pitched so far forward that he nearly tumbled into the water himself. Suddenly frightened at that prospect (for he was a pigeon and didn't know how to swim), he wheeled awkwardly and sat abruptly straight on his bench.

A butterfly fluttered across his sight, and the direction of his palpitating heart seemed to rotate with it. The quacking of the ducks (floating yonder) sounded like laughter. He swallowed nervously.

For the past few days Neipas had had the overwhelming impression that someone was following him. That fellow there by the bench, with the black suit and the top hat, face shielded by the brightness — hadn't he seen him on the train coming here? Perceiving his stare, Neipas, who had been wavering for a while, arose in a state of disorientation and stepped away from the lake.

He walked in the mollifying noon shine, his wits scattered about the heat. The jet blasting from the middle of the lake diffused in sprinkles of glitter and scraps of flash throughout the park, sowing a drizzle much too thin to cool the swelter. There materialized a rainbow in the droplets shed by the breeze from the fountain-top. A vague tinge of the hallucinatory exuded from the suspended colors, the glinting of droplets; the park looked weighed down by an accumulation of endless sunny days, mired in a sluggish cloudlessness, everything tinged by unreality, as refracted in mirage as that spectral arch sulking up there in the glimmering, sweaty sky.

On the other side of the water, beyond the towering fountain, tourists walked in bliss and smiled like convicts on parole. They looked like they hadn't breathed the open air in years. And they took photographs to look back at when they went back to prison after vacation was over; they strolled around and pointed, some even picnicked on the grass. Lake, fountain, grass, trees and the bright sunshine. Things assembled to a look of airy weekend scene, very pleasant — but Neipas was unable to appreciate it. There was a type of sleepy fog behind his eyes... a distancing from what he saw. Perhaps he had been looking at photos and screens and electric lights for too long. Nothing had wonder anymore. He had to make a conscious effort to feel it — to feel anything at all. He was insulated from feeling. It was as if he was not there; or very shrunken within himself, removed even from the surface of things. The world crowded against those round, lashless red eyes like so much emptiness, floating over a blunted sensibility that could not absorb, that could not feel, upon which nothing could be impressed; which recorded nothing definite, but the generality of existence as filtered through the dreaminess of an unrelenting fatigue. His head was but a dull slate on which things were dimly reflected. Every sight, every sound, every smell, all taste: all but a mild blur. Leafs glinted over him — as distant as stars across the universe; twinkles on the dome of his perceptions. Something of their rustle whispered. Nebulae of flies over the lake yonder writhed, barely perceptible, as one body scarcely held together, dissipating even as it undulated, buzzing silently above the water, meshing with the glitter of strewn fountain drops. Gloomy fractions of the landscape glazed over and slid off the passing cars nearby.

The gravel path branched off at the narrowest edge of the lake and led out of the park, forming into steps as it went over a hill. He felt a certain discomfort, already the discomfort of sustained exhaustion, as he lumbered up. Reaching the top, he saw, a little ways down the path, the entrance to Campus. Right away the Ivory Towers rising across imposed themselves over the landscape. They rose calmly, fantastically ornamented, spotlessly white upward, standing a formidable contrast to the searing blue: a vision that hurt his deep-breathing eyes, and Neipas, stopping at the hilltop, having gained it as one succumbs to a defeat, felt the wind touching his skin at last. He noticed a sort of glassy hum chopping in his heart, palpitating across the breeze as it passed through his transparency; and he experienced the wind's tepid breath as a tremendous sigh of abysmal hopelessness. For a moment he stood still, quite unable to move.

Walking up toward the soft windy ridge, he had felt the opaque hollowness of his hidden soul stirring. Always in the reverse of his thoughts lurked that suspicion of something missing; something essential. He felt it recurringly — and he suspected that this was not the natural makeup of existence, but that it was manufactured and all the elements that imbue life with meaning had been artificially removed somehow. What was this world, he asked himself, in which every mode of action felt fruitless and foregone; what was this world that made him feel empty inside? Why was there was no texture — no flavor to life? Every step was as if met with a toxic zephyr which peeled off his essence in bits...

He listened to the fountain dissolving behind him as he observed those immutable, immaculate towers which were to him the symbols of unrealized dreams. Before he went over, he looked back.

Down by the lake, the tourists stretched their arms and bent their wrists toward themselves, reflecting sunlight from the glass, bending this way or that, like shadow puppeteers. Looking closer, Neipas saw that most smiled before the camera and frowned behind it, perhaps recalling the limits of their parole. Had they brought their prison with them? Maybe they were like Neipas — his prison was inside him and therefore everywhere. Even as he walked around, he felt it calling, calling with a strange hum, deep and all-pervading, mumbling as he sometimes heard mutter those half-immaterial laborers that had committed their souls to the cryptic torments of the nightshift. The exit door of the prison was there, he could sense it; but it kept receding; and it receded still further. He felt as though it would disappear if he stopped running, and many times during the walk he considered going back to work; but he needed the time, he just needed the time. He needed the open air.

With difficulty he lifted his glance, casting it down across the Park of Echoes as it stretched westward toward Babylon. Out the middle of the lake burst the enormous jet of water through which the view would pierce into the financial district's high-rises; the Belab, lord among them, being the only edifice which elevated itself above the gush. It topped off into the highest highs, beyond the edges of the firmament, titan; with its crown, the Eagles' Nest, staring inscrutably from above, through the Pearl's vigilant flaming gaze.

The megalopolis prolonged itself infinitely in a blur of burning sunshine. Extending with excessive clarity in his watering eyes, it seemed to lift up in a tide and dissolve before returning in flickers through the clap of his eyelashes.

Every tower settled back down upon his angst, which he instinctively tried to unknot by swallowing. He realized the fellow with the top hat was following him still. Observing him standing down on the steps through the blurry corner of his sight, Neipas conjectured that the weird figure might have something to do with the insistent anonymous calls he had been getting lately, ringing at every hour, even in the middle of the night...

Perhaps he was being paranoid, thought he as he shook away his speculations. Again Neipas gazed toward Babylon — guiltily. He beheld it glassily, he could sense its whisper. Even now he could feel the Belab's reproaching influence bearing down over him. He felt that he should be working; he felt the fault of his debts to be his; he felt he wasn't working enough; he considered going back and working just a few hours. But his nerves were so on end, so embattled and strained that he couldn't take a step in the Belab's direction. So he turned back with an aching head to face the Ivory Towers, and walked toward them.

The path proceeded up the slope and through the ivory gate, which gave entry to the campus. It was composed of an open passageway flanked by a series of giant tusks ascending in a row; the arrangement resembled a sort of monstrous rib cage, or the horns of a sequence of bulls emerging out of the underground. Entering, Neipas passed under the cool of dappled shade. The heat seemed to shed from his skin as he advanced; his pace slowed, and his heart settled. A gradual aura of erudition became evident — it affected him to stop. There was a distinct quality in the atmosphere, something of promise, of possibility, that made Neipas momentarily feel as he felt when he first came to Axiac and stepped into this campus. The fulfillment of his dreams seemed just within reach back then. To set foot upon the megalopolis, this land of promises, realm of prosperity, was to him the realization of an intense crave to be born anew. A new life had begun for him the moment he entered into the airplane's bosom, filled with aspirations, ambitions of becoming a photographer, to do as he loved to do, and live as he wished to live. Neipas gazed upward, between the tusks enclosing in an arch, and toward the sun beyond in the remote skies, filtering through. He reflected on how that dream had faded and vanished away as reality evolved away from it.

Neipas continued onward, into the thickest shade. A long file of students was going past him now. They wore tassel caps and suits, and marched triumphantly through the ivory gate toward the park. The procession passed on jubilantly; in the density of shadow, where the students were hardly visible (above them, the tusks neared and almost touched one another) their tassels jingled and glinted. A mystique, and eerie mumblings, emanated from them.

The group seemed to be celebrating graduation, looking eager to spread the academic knowledge imparted to them through the years to every corner of the Earth. Their masks were all similar, peeping out of their collars with airs of pride and accomplishment, replicating themselves throughout the gate. Indeed the orderly line extended all the way to the end of the passageway — but as the shadow deepened to its darkest color, the queue abruptly came undone and the students crowded across the space with less organization as more and more students joined the march.

Neipas, slowing down, stepping aside, waited in stillness (with face lowered) for them to pass. He wondered momentarily: were the afflictions of penury and despair that had awaited him after his own celebration waiting for them now? Or were these the sort with connections and rich dads — with prospects assured and horizons clear? He shook such thoughts from his mind; then he carried onward to where the tusks gaped again, tingling with the hopeful mutters of the neophytes, passing under the streaks of sunlight as through the fragmented shades of his own dappled awareness, shedding fragment upon fragment toward the campus' green grounds and cobblestoned paths, nebulously dreamthinking.

Just a short distance before him stood one of the Ivory Towers. It rose from the peak of the grass field rolling itself up the slope. Scholars, wearing colorful gowns and flourished peacock faces, ambled about proudly with glasses of bubbly liquor fizzling, lifting up a genteel hubbub as they giggled at each other. Suited Eagles, with glittering beaks nodding, walked in their midst. Everyone bent their fawning heads to them; they looked important and Neipas shrunk subtly out of their way, passing along. Statues of the Past's great thinkers crowned small fountains. The sparkling water projected tepidly onto the stones; and the greats' austere eyes stared on blankly and fixedly, always at a tilt because of the field's inclination, as though they too were bowing slightly.

The Ivory Tower mounted in a series of thick rings to six floors (with an additional six underground). From within its lengthening shadow, Neipas beheld the columns of its girth, its mullioned windows and the overarching lintels carved with spirals, its bas-relief'd visages, its majestically ornate, white facade. His mask yielding to the blurriness of his distraction, he let himself stand still among the lulling, widespread genteel throng in a meditative type of aloofness. His eye rested on the windows up there, on the tinted glass flanked by gargoyles; the sky, mirrored black in it, entered it and imparted a curtain-softened brightness to the ethereal gloom inside. A hush prevailed: over the grand lecture halls, among the dusty books of the library, in the forbearing spores of wisdom and scholarship Neipas had once breathed. In the learned depths of this particular tower of ivory (which was the School of

Media), there tucked the darkrooms where he had once stood and prayed. He gazed at the black window as into the transparency of the mirror that is memory — and felt himself, tinged, steeped in soothing blackness, hovering over the waters of the chemical bath like one contemplating the wonders of beautiful skies. Deep in the darkroom, holding the photo paper with delicate tongs, he witnessed the magic of the image materializing under the rippling surface — almost always with the marvel of re-experienced beginnings, and such a totalizing sensation of completeness and absorption that his mind seemed to range the farthest extremes of the past and the wildest possibilities of the future from within the most vital depths of the moment; and he felt then — indeed nearly always, for, by some miracle of passion, repetition had not weaned away the wonder — again the soothing grindstone rumbling in the old mill, making dunes of flour out of the harvested grains as he milled harvested time into the grain of photographs beneath the stir of the enchanted waters. In the dim splashing of the lake outside (the giant fountain of which he sometimes seemed to hear) he seemed to guess the vague murmurs of that bygone river, which had so graced his childhood with freshness and song. In the sequence of his own motions he reenacted the living memory of his own self, and in the silent obscurity of this nest he could again grow freely into the child he had once been — unbound by traumas and full of promise, full of dreams. The darkroom cradled him back into happier days. It made him remember what life was — most importantly, it helped him forget what life had become. There were traces of his sister in Edazima's casual and occasional visits to what had quickly become his den, as it had been when he was a kid, when his sister occasionally, casually visited with the same kind of jesting remarks; he could even find something of his father in the overly respectful demeanor of his eccentric photoarts professor (since departed to other shores) hovering near, a sure and comforting, abiding presence — something of his father as he formerly was. The rectitude and strength of a paternal ideal haunted the quiet shadows of that sacred place; such ideals as his father had imparted him in his earliest life.

It was as if Neipas could only retrieve the withering memory of his father's earlier force and character from those chemical waters. Only here, in the darkroom, could the life be brought out of the dreary husk, which Neipas coarsely beheld every few weeks within the screen of the *I* — the absolutely reduced, mere shell of him: a grave, motionless, wheelchair-bound invalid bearing the expression of a cadaver, a shadow of a face, with rigidly dripping features completely hushed and set — moved only to an occasional mutter, always very slurred, always heavily salivated, always the same:

"*I don't know... I don't know...*" he breathed out, exhaled like a vaguely reminisced song whose tune had been forgotten; half-remembered fragments of a harmony unsung. "I don't know" — he kept mumbling that. What did he mean?...

Blinking there under the stretching shade, Neipas' head swirled in the circuit of endless questions and the confusion of a myriad half-articulated possibilities. A very bleak sense of helplessness beset him; made him freeze in very angst. Who could he resort to for aid? Who would help him? Certainly not his parents. Names arose in his mind with the shyness of interrogation marks. He even thought of the Editor, his former professor here — could he appeal to him? Many times he saw him, passed by him, greeted him during the day shift in the busy Media floor of the Belab ("Morning, professor," as breakfasts pressed his wrists and the sun, rising over the mountains, gaped through the tall windows). But no, no; no, Neipas was much too proud to ask for help and much too cowardly to seek it in the goodwill of so eminent a character. All this he considered as the gloomy reflection of an aircraft floated over the windowpanes, filling them ghostly. He'd once boarded an airplane like that, with a soul as impregnated with ambitions as the airplane was crowded with passengers. He'd seen Axiac sprawl under him, stretching from high mountain to vast sea, immense, unending, seething, shivering with the possibility of a million horizons. Those dreams had wilted, stillborn — and where was the soul now? There was but an absence in him; and nothing but.

Suddenly his breast panged, he gasped — and drew back as the airplane swelled toward him(!).

An illusion... the effect of a window opening. But there was a man watching Neipas from it, appearing, it seemed to him, out of nowhere as the phantom of the airplane vanished. The fellow had a horribly open, very wide beak; yet beyond the hideous expression, the figure startled him so because (he could swear it) it belonged to his father. But that was impossible; and he quickly realized his mistake. Still, in the instant before the figure was gone, turning back with a shudder as he drew the curtain shut, it appeared to Neipas that he wore a top hat and concealed his visage in much the same way as that mysterious character whom he had seen earlier in the park and in the train, who seemed to be trailing him somehow...

It was all but a moment; but the fleeting occurrence impressed itself unnervingly upon him — just enough for compel him to resume his walk.

The cobblestoned track encircled the Ivory Tower, from which it split in two directions — to the north (in the far extremity of which could be seen the Diamond Hills, with the Crystal Palace, seat of government, at their foot), and to the south (where, beyond the freeway, were the mid-

neighborhoods of the near valley and, after them, the destitute swath of Ostrich; tucked between the mountain cliffs and the narrow coast in the southeast, far and nearly out of sight, were the fences of Wall St, layering on deep, marking the edge of Columbia). Neipas continued beyond the tower and kept walking over the grass toward the east. The slope declined now as he moved away from the center of campus. He threw his wobbly glance yonder toward the mountains, which grew aloft as Neipas made his way down. Out of the snowless southeast peaks, muscular plumes of smoke flapped upward into a barren sky... He roamed in scattered thoughts, trying to distract the hunger which began to gather in him, hollowing him slow — he hadn't eaten properly for many hours. Already he regretted sharing even the crumbs of his meager bread with the fishes in the lake. He felt those crumbs dissolve in the water and in scale-covered stomachs; and in his interior sensed himself in a certain dissolution also, in his own deep he felt himself as strewn as the torpid rays of sunshine glimmering in the droplets of the lake fountain, whose rumble he could still hear, though he was drawing farther and farther away. It reverberated somehow in the chipped, abyssal palpitations of his spirit. Something lodged there — something malicious and foreign to him; that something which he could not locate or precisely identify. Through it, in it throbbed the admonitions of the Belab, its deep pulses underlying all things, extending under the shadow of the lake following him in sound and sensation; something like an incoming storm... ever incoming, ever brewing under the ever pending horizon. It was something parasitic — it called him back to work.

Sensing himself ill and hollow, like the husk of some boat unmoored and adrift, crewless and with sails tattered; feeling at the mercy of rapacious phantoms he was unable to see and powerless to combat; feeling steered and controlled by pervasive influences at work beyond his comprehension, he had contemplated with perplexity the seashells at the lake bottom, clustered there amid the sediment, over which his mask hovered, staring at nothing — and perceived himself dissolving in the great oceanic mire of his time. Filled with self-doubt, finding no one to blame, he could but blame himself for his woes. Yes, he should return to work; but he simply couldn't bring himself to walk back in the direction of the Belab, he kept moving away toward the smoking mountains, kept strolling, hardly feeling his steps. So enveloped, he walked upon the tended grass and past the occasional tree or statue; he walked between the Ivory Towers like a pauper wandering among the fragments of his lost wealth, or a dreamer lost amid the remains of aborted futures... But he felt abstracted from everything; and though his eyes perceived the towers and the landscape, to his heart it was all but an undifferentiated blur. He floated alongside things as helplessly and bereft of vitality as flotsam upon a stream, in a type of dreamthinking... existing as only a part of himself, hovering about in incompleteness, and moving unconsciously from sparkle to sparkle, across moments without continuity, never fully present; not fully knowing what he felt, he could grip fully upon nothing.

There was only one definite thing in the muddle of his sentiments — and that was the fear of hunger. It was the dread of the relentless future which never ceased charging at him, the horror of the recurring past which paralyzed him and starved him of hope. He remembered well those penniless, rudderless days that followed soon after his graduation, those months languishing in Edazima's couch, without money, without compass, bereft of prospects... And in a moment he glimpsed his face (he had never stopped seeing it and perhaps he was still seated by the lake staring at it) and was reminded of the graveyard shift workers he saw each morning, dragging themselves through an existence less alive than dead; he seemed to glance their masks of shadow, whose features dripped rigidly in their mold of hushed, listless fatigue.

One could make more money working that shift; but it was said it was at the price of having one's flesh and soul sucked dry, till there was no longer anything to speak of but a full, finished, joyless automaton; who would finally succumb of exhaustion, or quit. It was a place where they would skin, bone, and bowel your soul into the fragments and components of their clock, a blurry watch dissipating across the edges of fading and overworked minds.

Neipas thought of all this with the fever of guilt and the haunting shivers of anticipation. The feeling of merely thinking it was sinister; it induced chills even in that torrid weather. But the thing was already decided. That something parasitic in him made the future predetermined; the parasite precluded any possibility of decision.

His legs had meanwhile taken him to the brink of the old worship house. They ignored the slight hesitation he felt and crossed mechanically the small garden, halting a short distance before the open gate, beside which sat a beggar. A ceremony was taking place inside. Underneath the austere wooden, vaulted ceiling aggregated a small number of sheep in modest suits and dresses. The cleric in gown and pelican mask presided from the altar (behind which a sculpture of the Golden Dove hung, in a niche, over the veiled tabernacle on the wall). With his long beak the Pelican led the flock in song; their words of reverence flowed out the gates in a pleasant chorus, a unison of spiritual harmony that impressed Neipas. It called to mind his mother, and the weekly gatherings at the worship house of his childhood which she, devout of her faith, attended assiduously. He remembered well the last time he went to one, minutes prior to the mass funeral in the mausoleum near; when he snuck in alone and peeked beyond the veil mounted on the wall behind the altar, and found only a cracked mirror in a golden frame: a strange sight he would never forget.

Since then, he had gained a suspicion of these religious rites. He remembered standing low-headed among the crying women and glancing at the portraits fixed to the facades of the crypts, reproduced in rows of faces arrayed over and again, from the floor to the ceiling and all over the mausoleum walls. And even though he was in the midst of everything back then he'd felt somehow like he did now, as if he were witnessing from a distance; come to think of it (thought he), it was perhaps on that day that his withdrawal toward nothingness had begun. Occult pressures had been grinding him subtly, beneath the range of his awareness, for a very long time; sucking in his time, his youth, his vitality, his life. Perhaps it began then. Then his horizons became like the grindstone of his mill, his prospects ground to ash in the rotation of the sky, much like the wheel circled in the rolling flow of his river, which seemed to distend all the way from the park lake until here, to the toes of his steps; he seemed to feel water up to his ankles. And as he stood here stuck before the temple gates, sadly observing the devotees, a great loneliness shuddered through him; a feeling of hopeless isolation, even from himself. Looking at the congregation, he noticed their inattention, their alienation; the glassy stares of onlookers, beyond which there was perhaps nobody.

Still — listening to this song of voices now, he felt instinctively that there must be some truth beyond the ridiculous attires and the repetition of gestures — a truth buried under much distortion, something beyond the senses, unpreachable... But of what it was, his heart could only recognize unintelligible echoes; and at the moment his skeptic eyes could not distinguish much beyond a pelican preying upon the emotional frailties of common folk.

They, the faithful, looked to him with their meekness and distraction like the graveyard shift workers who shadowed him so that day, carried in the stirs of his crepuscular reflections. The Pelican walked solemnly now to the baptismal fount (the chants had ceased) and in it he submerged the base of a tall candle. So holding it, he dipped in a large bivalve seashell, scooping up a small quantity of the holy water; and then poured it ceremoniously onto the forehead of a baby who had been brought up by the arms of two well-adorned sheep (the baby itself hadn't yet a mask), one, two, three times. A small bell reverberated soothingly at each tilt of the wrist.

From the shell the water poured and streamed solemnly, magically, reminiscently, glinting the serene flame of the candle behind it...

It was a very beautiful, mesmeric ritual, and Neipas felt almost tempted to sneak into a corner of the temple to witness its conclusion — but he could not advance another step. What made him stop was the beggar sitting by the entrance, who wore a strange top hat and rumpled suit. Neipas could not see his face and yet, he was sure the fellow stared at him; he stretched his hand demandingly. Was it the same fellow from the park? Neipas became sure of it. He was sure this was the same person who had tried to reach him through the *I* several times in the past few days, often randomly in the middle of the night, and would not let him sleep. He must be some sort of debt collector... Neipas averted his stare and stepped away, with nerves overstrained by the heat and appetite.

*

There was a little path going off around the chapel that was half-hidden in the lawn's outgrowth. Neipas, taken by a vague curiosity, followed it.

The path led to an arch of limestone, erected beyond a grove dense with giant pine trees. The arch opened to a small wooden bridge, rudimentary in build, which hung old but sturdy over a creek. It led to a sort of island amid the burst of vegetation beneath which the water ran, tranquil.

On this island was a single house, built of stone. Vines twined through and out the crevices, enveloping the roughly quarried blocks in their green embrace.

As soon as Neipas passed under the arch and placed his foot on the bridge, a soothing breeze leant itself upon his bare skin. It blew soft and was neither warm nor chilly. Neipas walked through the gentle whisper of the air, toward the little rustic house.

As he was crossing the bridge the twinkling sound of chimes touched his ear; the breeze carried it, and along with it a sweet scent of flower. A serene creaking sound rang underfoot; the bridge responded to Neipas' steps with a gentle groan.

Underneath, the stream made its steady way, sprinkling the air with its shimmering melody. Neipas rested his hand on the bridge's warm railing and looked over. He lingered there for a while, watching the rivulet scintillate beneath the canes.

Then he walked slowly across the bridge, and came to the end of it. He stepped to and felt his foot crunch and shatter into a brittle earth. The sod was parched, withered; various types of grass wilted in the shaded garden, rising with a strain out of the crevices of the ground and hunching dryly, oppressed by inscrutable sorrows; some rustled near the soil, others strove for the canopies, and they all seemed to shelter different green vegetables which Neipas could not name or recognize. Strange, wrinkly trees rose from the welter and the umber, disposed in concentric circles, with open branches touching like the faithful in a quiet congregation. They roused Neipas' interest, and he approached. Out the tip of its branches, meager in the placid breeze, bloomed tiny, lustrous black fruit. Neipas neared his face to it, wondering what it was. He felt an odd sensation of familiarity. Somewhere in some form he had seen this fruit before, he felt, but he didn't know where, or what it was called.

A tranquil sun filtered through the coppice in rays, and, gleaming upon the fruit, breathed traces of mystery and divinity into the aura.

Neipas turned his head slowly; in the very rotation of his body the grove appeared to tighten closer, to shrink tenderly, to deepen in its aspect of woodland sanctum. The hush was absolute.

The little house reposed against the feral shrubbery rounding the circular garden. He began pacing alongside it, watching the thicket intimately. It was a complex wiring of thorny vines, dense and spread throughout; a grim sight, this tight wall of small daggers, bulwark of entangled vines with countless sharp needles piercing out, pointing inward. Yet Neipas discerned a small dot of bright color as he panned along; and neared still closer. Amid the chaos of thorny vegetation there nestled a good, ruddy berry, full and ripe with flavor. It was the strangest thing, he reflected in his innermost; that in the middle of this sickly bedlam of thorns, something so full of health and force should sprout. Hungry, he reached for the berry, penetrating the tangle carefully; but his tremulously outstretched finger quickly met a thorn, ramming it straight into the skin, and he recoiled with the pain of contact, groaning.

Then suddenly he turned, sensing movement behind him.

A lady appeared between the grasses; upon sage years and a very upright carriage she stood, lively of demeanor, awake. Her youthful visage was creased and a little weathered, but still it shone, mirthful and baked by the sun, the color of the earth. Framed by graying locks and disheveled aureoline hairs upwired, she smiled a very sincere, calm, imperturbable smile — an unjudging smile. From her long earlobe pended a feather that twinkled in the lines of sunshine; her plumage lustered discreetly with enigmatic colors.

"Good morning," said Neipas, embarrassed; he was filled now with a sense that he had trespassed and shouldn't be there.

"Good afternoon!" — the lady laughed. Her amicable ways immediately mollified Neipas and eased his anxiety. He chuckled. "Oh — Sorry. Is it afternoon already?"

"It is. Noon's long past now."

A basket of reeds pended from her forearm and yawned with a

proliferation of healthy hues from various vegetables. Spying the harvested blossom, his heart wondered whence that hale abundance could have come; and whether the mysterious woman could have possibly extracted such colors from the monochromatic dark green mist around them. Then — seeing her closer — Neipas thought he knew her.

At once she confirmed his suspicion: "It's good to see you again. How was the zoo?"

The lady from the train — Neipas strained to find her name in the haze of his memory; then it was puffed out, as it were involuntarily, from the hidden unconscious and out his lips: "Oshana."

"Neipas," Oshana said calmly, with a respectful, slow nod of greeting. She looked at him smilingly and tender, waiting for him to speak.

"Oh — the zoo. The zoo... Not the best day there, to be honest..." his stare became vague, eyes blurring in the fog of remembrance. He felt a hand on his shoulder and flinched. It was Oshana who stepped still closer; for a moment he had disintegrated into distraction, and had as though flown away without noticing. Flutters and splashes twitched in his nerves and he felt his breast contract discomfortingly — he felt dizzy, famished... All with one hand she grabbed his fingers deftly and, turning them upward, placed the berry she had just collected from among the thorns on his palm.

"Hungry? Come in — I'll make you something."

Neipas hesitated; he parted his lips without sound, and then clammed up. He felt some embarrassment at hearing the question and invitation. Could it be that it was obvious, that his mask did nothing to hide it?

"Don't worry," said Oshana, perceiving the shape of his heart. "You're my guest. Come in."

Touched, he uttered not a sound; but only nodded in very humility. He took the berry as he followed her inside — the flavor alone lent him strength, and pulled him a ways out of his lethargy.

The dense, cozy atmosphere of a bookstore enveloped him at once. It was homely and warmly lit, infused with an aura of tenderness and the sacral. He was quickly taken in by its mystique. The old wooden shelves, which covered the walls from floor to ceiling around the perimeter of the hall, full of old books of all sizes and qualities, had a grandfatherly air about them, an inviting immobility; it was as if they were inviting Neipas to sit, and hear the tales they had to tell. A series of trinkets and curios dangled from the ceiling or twinkled atop the shelves, lending an array of soft carnivalesque pigments and shine to the place; the pervasive shimmer deepened the holy character of its stillness. There was a refreshing earthly scent in the hovering dust. Particles drifted in the sunlight yawning through a gap in the roof, lolling in a mesmerized, powdery dance. Up there, where the sunshine leaned, vines twined out of the stone, into and across the shelves, and dispersed like enigmatic creeks, silent rivulets carrying sunlight, whispering sunlight into the gloom, whispering life. Tendrils whirled across the spines of tomes on upper shelves, revealed there in the ghostly afternoon shine, tucking in their bosom strange emblems, wooden talismans, totems: the passive faces of native gods. Vague, airy chirpings crackled from them; Neipas seemed to hear elusive notes of birdsong, the flutter of wings; and as he looked up his eye caught the contours of other winding twigs, the cushy form of a nest; the radiance framing the rim of an oval shape, a sleeping egg... And then there were yet more bookcases, shorter than the ones against the wall, running up the space in rows. At length Neipas noticed the curvature of their shelves, and how they were spread between semicircular aisles which layered out concentrically. Oshana took him between these cabinets a long way — the house had an uncanny dimension, going much deeper than its outer appearance suggested.

At the very core of it then, there opened up a snug space with an antique, round table of sturdy oak, and three chairs encompassing it, set upon a circular rug weaved in boldly graphic, geometric, colorful patterns.

"Please," said Oshana, extending an arm toward the chair, inviting him to sit. It was then that Neipas realized her right hand was tightly bandaged; only the fingers sprouted out of the straps. "I won't be long," she pursued, and retired gently from his presence with a smile and a nod, walking through the main aisle between the shelves toward a door in the far wall, which opened, slowly, to what looked like a type of shed.

Neipas, finding himself easing into the solace of the quiet library, panned his sight over the dozing, dusty languor of books and tucked erudition. There was something magical in the hush of those sage things, which seemed to quell his anxieties in the soundlessness of their murmur, appeasing even his hunger in the relaxation of his mind. Something like a spirit extended through him, stretched and inhaled. He settled well into the chair as he waited; and felt in his waiting a strange peace, a hollowing of worries, a settling unto himself and an acceptance of the present he hadn't perceived in a very long time. For the time he waited, he simply — was.

The strangeness of the feeling was precisely in the recognition of something long absent returning; a parcel of himself, perhaps. Something about Oshana, something about this place imbued him with a sense of deep trust — he didn't know why, he hardly knew the lady; though the bookstore now struck him as vaguely familiar... Gradually he found himself looking at the door yonder through which Oshana had gone.

Vapors streamed from the open passage. Her silhouetted figure paced into the fumes of a smokehouse, which already reached Neipas' senses through the ghosts of pleasant aromas. Fire sparkled in the depths somewhere, twinkling, in fiery twitches, amidst the fog it smoldered. And though the smoke rolled thick he could see things quite transparently. Over the shivery amber red glow, there hung a series of red strips, bent over Oshana's head as she passed and raised her hands up to them one by one, and from them to her forehead. Salmon. She was cooking; moving about slow, respectful, devout — as though in the performance of a ceremony. Neipas saw bells, a horn strapped to the wooden wall; he had arisen from the chair and now, looking in a little closer, he saw, farther, another door leading to another garden, a table set with pots and vegetables; and a beautiful shimmer, a swaying light of sorts, farther yet. He discerned better Oshana's voice. It sounded as though she was chanting; as though she was praying. And it seemed to him that from beyond came the gentle sounds of brooks purling, of fins flapping, of breezes sighing and the chiming of leaves; whispers of nature deep inside that shed, that smokehouse, that shrine, wherein Oshana sang reverently.

Neipas had again sat; already Oshana returned.

She carried two woven baskets, one relatively shallow and wide, the other narrow and deep. The handle of the latter she gripped in her healthy hand; that of the former arched over her forearm, which lengthened from the side of her body and hovered rigid, very straight, very poised, over the ground — at the end of it was the opposite hand, bundled in gauze, and her thumb and index fingers touching delicately in the manner of an idol or icon. There was an astute immobility even to her walk.

Neipas still made a motion to get up and help her; but she smiled and shook her head as if to say that there was no need, the load wasn't heavy. Setting the baskets on a long, empty shelf, she then began producing the contents. She magicked from one (the deeper), first, a tablecloth, which she spread deftly across the table's round wood; then she took two cups; two small pitchers; two little towels; three bowls; and finally (out of the second, wider basket, which was covered by a cloth) a loaf of bread, and the plate with the salmon; and placed them all on the table in a circular fashion.

Oshana poured olive oil from one pitcher into the smallest bowl. Into the remaining, larger bowls she poured water, carefully, solemnly, reverently, all with one hand — and then, making a gracious gesture over the table, sat.

Neipas stared at the food hesitantly; hesitating out of politeness, for he longed to consume the baked dough and the smoked flesh and to kill his murderous hunger. All suffused in mesmerism and famished distraction, he watched as Oshana washed her hand and her unbandaged fingers in the bowl of water, with her head lowered, her smile unblemished. Though now she became grave as she turned to the plate, bowing still deeper; and before she looked up she seemed to whisper a few words to the salmon laid there before them. She raised her head and saw Neipas there, staring confusedly.

Oshana laughed, tearing off a chunk of bread and eating it without ceremony. "Don't be shy about it — go on."

Timidly imitating her gestures, Neipas began by washing his hands in his own bowl of water. And saying "thanks so much" with profound gratitude, he proceeded to take a piece of salmon with his fingers, carefully placing its succulent, chewy flesh between his teeth, and tasting the flavor widely, letting it course in ruminations of growing vitality. At the very first bite he felt his energy soar. A sense of relief immediately spread through his body. At first he savored the food slowly, and relished it with deep, tired breathing; every time his fingers — all pinched, beak-like, round the vital nutriment — entered his mouth, he experienced a quiet euphoria of flavor and relief, and felt replenished. Intermittently, in the effusion of his gratitude, he would again thank Oshana, bowing his head humbly; but as his hunger diminished his appetite grew. Imperceptibly he began to eat faster, chewing the bread ravenously, progressively forgetting himself in the torpor of satiation and the haste to quell his voracity. "Dip it in the olive, it's good," Oshana suggested. He did — it was divine. Indeed Neipas was so famished that he quickly forsook his manners, and stuffed with more celerity than he could chew, on and on, restlessly (meanwhile Oshana observed him with much amusement) until his mouth became so full that he was forced to slow down, suddenly feeling quite heavy, and a little dizzy. He lifted two swollen cheeks and faced Oshana's laughing eyes.

"My, you *were* hungry."

He blushed; the reverent quietude of the library descended graciously upon him once more, with a sense of being reposing into his body with the added weight and torpor of a rushed appetite. Blinking, very embarrassed, he hid his lips with his hand and mumbled, "so'y."

"What for?" she then uttered, with a tone so full of acceptance and so devoid of judgment that Neipas, receiving it in the ample desolation of his spirit, was suddenly, unexpectedly, nearly brought to tears; he lowered his head and ate. Could he be so fragile, so mired in his loneliness, so entangled in the despair of his prospects that the mere company of a lady he barely knew could touch him so? And yet, as they fell silent, as he came in tune with the inward aspect of situations, he perceived well how beyond mere the company was; how significant the honest, maternal gestures of his companion at table were, how symbolic of a profound, unchanging, beautiful principle which he could not encapsulate within his thoughts, but whose kindness he felt softening quietly throughout his heart. His chin trembled momentarily as he held up. They shared the humble meal in silence for a while. The bread emerged, dripped golden; he tasted the wet seasoning and the pulpy crumb solemnly, as in the enactment of an ancient rite. The salmon shed its warm vapor, entering his nostrils as intimately as whispered secrets penetrate the ear, and in his soul he felt something of the secret of the salmon, of the sanctity of that food. He recalled in his sensations something of his childhood table, of the lazy gloom of the mill, where his parents made bread long ago; the mill by which the river sprinkled and flowed. Indeed the taste struck his senses as quite familiar, possessing a very old quality, as of a memory emerging from the mists of long-forgotten, infant experience.

His voice gruff, low and thankful, Neipas commented, "This is really good. What do you season it with?"

"I mix tomato seeds with the olive oil — it makes it sweeter. The flesh I sprinkle with rosemary," Oshana said. "The herb grows well by the shore, by the sea — and it's custom to present it to the dead as a sign of remembrance."

Neipas chewed slowly, ruminating the familiarity of the flavor, reflecting upon it; and he gazed unto Oshana with clearing eyes. "How do you mean?"

"It is to honor the salmon that I use the herb," she said. "To thank the salmon for my life, for I owe life to the salmon today.

"The herb flourishes up there, by the estuary of the river," she continued, "out of which the salmon goes to live, and into which the salmon returns to give birth — and to die. Rosemary grows along the banks and is there to greet the salmon at their departure, and to greet them upon return, flanking the passage gates — a frame for the beginning and the end."

Watching Oshana deferentially, he expressed, by means of an intrigued grunt or other, his appreciation for her gesture, though he did not fully comprehend it. Such devotion in the way of conduct, and the conscientious, affectionate manner in which she treated him, a stranger, stirred up memories of his mother, generosity personified, which had already been so latent in that afternoon of his mind and spirit. He missed her very much, and sensed her in the food's aroma, in the warmth of Oshana's company.

Throughout the meal Neipas had become more aware, as though, now awakened, he noticed it for the first time, of the bandages fastened round Oshana's hand — which she had not had on the train. And it was out of a genuine care and thankfulness that he asked, pointing:

"What happened?"

Her noble smile, constant and wide in its tranquility, was then somewhat tempered by a gradual wistfulness. And sighing she said, distractedly, "I can't remember," as if sinking inwardly, her voice diminished, pursuing in a whisper, "Causes are lost — too easily in the chaos of things."

Looking up again to Neipas, seeming to gather herself out of painful reflections, her smile regained in full, Oshana spoke, "I'd gone to the eastern mountains there, for the protest — when the wildfires began."

"The wildfires? Aren't they — " Neipas tried to muster some knowledge from the general haze of his recollections.

"Raging yet. Uncontrollable," she lamented. "The flames caught us by surprise... And by the time I noticed," she said then, passing the fingers of her healthy hand over the bandage, "it was there.

"It happened on that day — the day I saw you in the train."

Neipas nodded slowly, mystified; wings flapped in echoes about him.

"Weird day," he said.

Silence. Something, some instinct, some obscure and prolonged idea disturbed Neipas as he ate.

"And to you?" she then asked, as if suddenly.

Neipas took some time to emerge out of the mire of bizarre dreamthinking on which he'd been mentally standing and wading all day long, that trance of recurring fears in which he lost all sense of time. Suddenly it seemed that hours had passed since they commenced the meal; though there was yet much to eat. "What happened to you on that day?"

Neipas winced. Could she really tell? Was his mask so transparent that he could no longer hide his abysmal anguish in his countenance — could he no longer disguise his real face?

"Don't worry," Oshana told him. "Speak if you want, and I'm here to listen. But if you don't, don't worry."

Neipas wavered; yet he, feeling so at ease in Oshana's presence, recounted the strange tale of his visit to the zoo at length. Over the table flew again, now in the form of voiced recollections, that torrent of rabid wings sprung out of shattered glass; the panic of crowds, the disorientation of an atmosphere batted by the shuffling of shirts and feathers, rummaging violently through a terrible crashing of bodies, churned once more. He told the story in the exact same manner he had conveyed it to Edazima and the curious herd of Kur waiters; and in the course of the telling he wondered, as though half of him had retreated and sat at the back of his own mind — this half hearing and wondering, that other talking and remembering — wondered cryptically, if this wasn't all repetition somehow, if he himself wasn't coursing through a loop — a loop, not only of tales, but of events and even lifetimes — so that he felt bizarrely dislocated as he arrived at the end, and found himself opening his eyes in much the same way he had opened them upon the hospital bed.

Oshana listened. She constituted a reassuring vision as he came back to; and saw he'd opened his eyes to an empty ceiling no longer. The remembered, flushed haste of feathers and broken zoo windows faded into a long and deliberate silence, deep in which Oshana seemed to consider and ruminate, giving Neipas' words a wide latitude of effect.

"In truth," she said at last, "Nature cannot be tamed."

Again they had become mum, and for a while Neipas sat very still, mustering the dispersed grit of his mind, sensing the vague throb pulsing crimson in his head, in his throat, in his breast, distant. He'd stopped eating, he did not move. Gradually turning his attention to Oshana as it came back to him, he beheld with appreciation her undisturbed smile and felt his own meek lips curve under his mask. In a tone low and candid, he asked:

"You said you went to the mountain to protest. What was the protest about?"

She nodded despondently — and replied, "Against the oil pipeline they want to build under the Oyate river.

"The Oyate have been organizing for months against it. Years, against NoxxeSocony — the petroleum conglomerate," she added, confirming the glint of vague recognition upon Neipas' brow; and running a finger over the tablecloth as though over a map — "They intend to build a pipeline out of the mines of the Joachim Valley, in the deep north — bring it all the way down to Axiac, and hook it up to the Iblis refinery in Ostrich, passing under the river on the way...

"This pipeline would carry the most venomous type of sludge... Thick, viscous tar, a seething mass of it, whole swamps of toxic ooze teeming with sand and bacteria — an ocean of bitumen. If the pipe bursts under the river, and the tar spills, it would poison the stream, and the salmon, and the abundance of life that depends upon them — all whom are sacred to us in spirit and nourishment."

The described imagery of bursting pollution produced in Neipas' senses the beginning of an equivalent effect, and he felt as though a bubble which had hitherto contained and enveloped him had just emerged upon a foggy surface, and popped inward, out of his insulation of spirit and into a textured wideness — and his eyes widened further, gradually, under his gradually straining brow; so did his ears in a gulf; he took his hand to his mask in an intuitive attempt to keep composure before the hints of weirdness seeping in.

He asked, sorrowful, "But why does it need to go under the river?..."

"It does not. They could route it behind the river source — though the terrain is harsher, the distance longer, and the price, therefore — higher. And the sum of their calculations is made in the abstraction of dollars, that's their reality. The living river, the living forests, the richness of life they hold together — those are to them the abstractions, real only insofar as they can be morphed to dollars." Oshana snickered with something of bemusement and aloof disdain — "The plateau where the Oyate Reserve is, and which the river crosses, that's the easiest path for them. Whatever resides there is nothing to them.

"There's been pressure enough to make Noxxe consider the path behind the river source. Publicly, the Mayor supports this — it would be a 'compromise', that's their name for it. We are waiting to see what they do — the fires scrambled all things, we do not yet know what will ensue.

"Yet the heart of the matter lies deeper than even the sacred riverbed of that sacred river — for the entire body of the Earth is holy. What rests beneath Joachim must not be touched. It's forbidden to us, who live on the surface. To disembowel the Valley is sacrilege... What is hidden underneath, is meant to be kept underneath. For it poisons the land as it emerges and it poisons the sky as it is burned. It will rain down on us sooner or later — it poisons the very air we breathe."

After a moment of breathless quietude, Oshana inhaled, sighed, and carefully dipped a bit of crumb fluff into the vessel of olive oil; with the utmost focus Neipas watched the golden liquid drip from it slow; he waited for Oshana as she, growing distant in her thoughts, ate it.

She then spoke:

"The Earth harbors venoms in her crypts — things not meant for the living. And yet — industrial activity..." and here her voice dipped pensively; her gaze narrowing inward; "Doesn't it consist in culling dead things — to feed things that are not alive? Such things as poison life.

"But it is this that's been dug up. It's this sort of death they want to make flow under the waters."

Intrigued, Oshana had apprehended in him a certain trace of distress, the source of which she did not yet recognize. Neipas listened to her intently; with a concentration further compressed by a sort of involuntary strain. He knew well such venoms as she spoke of, and sensed in the description of the poison under her river the very poison which had once lodged in the mountain of his youth and had burst and poured over the waters of its valley. Riveted, he absorbed Oshana's words, and the sparkle of his childhood stream blinked once more, as it sometimes did, into his inner eye, flowing with the quietude of its memory.

"Ours is a world turned upside down, Neipas," she continued, looking at him, her smile yet imperturbable; gazing into him profoundly, discerning his intensity of focus. "What is meant for slumber, they've roused; what is meant to be vigorous they've numbed. What is meant to remain in the deep they've dug up, and what is meant to be upon the surface they've buried. Look at this Axiac — the trees they fell, the earth they upturned and paved with tar. Our steps fall on the stuff of netherworlds...

"They scour the Earth's vaults, forage her chambers, profane her reliquaries, sack her tombs — defile the dead. They summon the blessings of the deep and unleash its curse upon the rivers, upon the land, upon the ocean and the sky, upon the whole surface of the Earth."

Neipas felt his jaw shiver and the rustle of feathers whispering in his ear. "What do you mean?"

"Fossils," Oshana said, "are the fuel of our age.

"We light our nights with coal, warm our winters with gas, pave our ways with asphalt. Coal, natural gas, petroleum and its spawn — all are fossils. Corpses of beings that lived long, long ago...

"Over fossils we cook our food, in fossils we store our possessions, our water and our sustenance, from fossils we shape our tools, with fossils we fertilize and poison the land. And it is fossils that we feed to the machines — the machines that build our cities, that erect the towers, that feed the apartments, in which we live apart — the machines that feed civilization and whose undead heart beats in our kitchens, in our bedrooms, through our computers, our *I*s — whose thickening wires seep into our thinning veins. It is from fossils that our roads are made, it is with fossils that our paths are driven, it is through fossils that our world is shaped. Our cities are paved with the dead.

"Plants and animals of the deep past, primordial creatures whose remains the underworld folded, buried ever deeper by millions of passing years, slumbering there in the night of eons. They drew their vitality from sunlight, when they lived — as do the beings living now among us.

"The past accumulates under our feet," she said, "— it gathers power. All things grow mighty through distance, and there is much might to be drawn from the hidden depths of the ages, where the giants sleep. Where the silence is absolute. Power accumulates in silence — Silence, here is where gods are born. Though much noise is often needed to sustain such silences.

"With them, these beings of old took the power of a million suns — a million suns circling through the million skies of a young, blinking Earth. To the shadow of the deep they sank and slept.

"It is these suns that they harness when they excavate the deep — it is their power that's released, when they burn. The might of a million long-dead suns and long-gone skies — here's what powers our age. The sunlight of Earth's youth.

"But how can we hope to dig up such suns without exhuming their shadows? They come, too. In truth, the noon of industrial civilization is long past, the light quickly declines to reveal its darkness... With the scream of such revived suns comes also the silence in which they were buried. It won't be long before it swallows us."

Silence; not a sound but the chirping of birds, faint stirrings, wind in the rivulet.

"Fossils are their oblation and holocaust... It is by cremating what has been long buried that they worship their gods, their Mammon."

Neipas grimaced, very slowly.

"...Mammon?"

Very quietly, she spoke: "Wealth. Money — the object of their devotion, the source of their power. It is the center and the seed of our days. It is the cause and effect of this civilization. Its name is never uttered as loudly as its voice, which is as rife as the air we breathe here — but in its name more wars have been fought, more blood sacrifices made, more taboos broken, more temples desecrated, more destruction wrought, than for any other idol or deity. For the sake of Mammon, civilization has renounced the Earth — civilization has therefore rejected Life."

Silence — once more, silence. Her tones rang in echoes. Oshana spoke in a manner unusual, her words nevertheless pronounced with great clarity, expressed with a tone which rang profound in the hollow depths of his spirit.

"Mammon is the great parasite — he's long become the hidden lord of hosts. He insinuates himself into every space, every second, every relation, every body, every will. Gradually, he conquers every last bit of land, creeps into every speech, every sigh and every breath of wind. He rules over our lives with a command firmer than that of any other deity past — its missionaries have been most successful — no domain has been as extensive as Mammon's. Now the world's been made his altar, his feast table. Many still believe they share the meal, but many are still mistaken. Haven't they noticed the skeletons under the table yet? We are all sacrificed to Mammon — even those sitting in his throne, though they do not know it."

She spoke in a kind of trance; her voice rang deep. Her voice was so altogether absorbing as to mute within it every other sound.

"Mammon is the great puppeteer... the chief playwright. Now the world's been made his stage, where all are actors. Everything is taken to be something else. People are mistaken for machines, Nature for merchandise. Making money is 'making a living', money is 'life'. The play is 'reality'. Living by the script is 'being realistic' — and meanwhile life unravels beneath the drapes of their fictions. It is a spectacle full of lights, with many special effects and a lot of smoke — a smoke that makes the senses torpid. Many still believe the fire is far backstage — they cannot feel it burning under their feet, consuming the relics. Even those who think they control the pyrotechnics — those worshipers of Mammon — will soon be caught.

"They've built modernity on a pyre, Neipas."

Silence. Again silence. Oshana's deep tone of voice ceased, her speech without tremor yielded to the dusty quietude of the solemn shelves. She possessed a manner of speaking which gripped and absorbed his mystified attention, expressing herself in tones of confidence so intimate that Neipas felt very intimately implicated in the violent processes she described; in such a manner that the oldest, most traumatic of his memories resurged in his heart with more vividness than they had in many years. "Mary," he whispered, in a soundless sigh.

"Mammon awakens the devil in the human. Wasn't it in the bowels of the Earth that they sought him most? Isn't that where they say demons live? In truth, they sought the fire underneath the rock, and they drank the tainted water from the cleft of the rock. Dead rock is their sustenance — but the power of the dead is poison to the living, and from the stone they derive venoms.

"...Now the Earth is changing, changing because of it all. They have poured these venoms into the air, into the ground, into the water — and the Earth is slowly becoming alien. Finding ourselves estranged from the Earth, we find ourselves alien to our selves."

Her eyes lost sheen. Oshana seemed to delve into lusterless reflections.

"We are being severed from our Mother... broken from ourselves. How many today are living in a story without narrative — how many today are walking journeys without path, running without leaving their place, floating through existence without life? In truth, don't many become like fossils in life these days?

"Now the seasons confuse themselves, and the Earth assumes a moribund aspect... Everyone senses that something is wrong — but scarcely anyone feels it in their bones, unless they've already suffered it in their skin. Most haven't awakened to a sense of what's happening to ourselves, we are as if dreaming."

She waved her head despondently, ruminating upon her bread. Neipas observed her, his spirit leaning over the table earnestly, listening; the sacred whisper of the old books descended upon him, and seeped in deeper, slackening every fiber of his being. He thought he heard their leaves groan, the shelves seemed made of living wood.

"In truth," Oshana continued, "the Earth burns before our eyes, and the glare is such that it has blinded many. For now the forests are in flames and those responsible carry on with impunity."

She inhaled calmly as the soul returned to her eyes. She turned them to Neipas' dilated bleary gaze.

"Who's responsible?..." he wondered. "Do you think that Noxxe —"

Silence.

"We don't know yet," she said, "but the fire was probably set. Last year the fires began when a powerline fell — they hadn't touched it in years, too expensive to maintain, they said. They care for nothing other than money and profit, in truth, such is what they worship. But this year it wasn't intentional negligence — it was arson, I'm certain of it. The flames were calculated so that they would spread wide. It's consuming whole the land...

"I saw the fire at its conception and already it towered over all, swallowing the firs. We tried to tame it, but... Well, it took firefighters many hours to arrive. By then it was too large to contain."

She smiled still, stoic and as if impervious; but her lips were visibly tinged by sadness now. Oshana too heard the living wood of the shelves groan, and the pages of the books seemed to crackle: the tallness of those stacks became the distant height of mountain firs, whose branches trembled in the smoke and whose myriad leaves flapped helplessly in the flames. Without wishing it, she felt the smells, the noises; she experienced the faint echo of a real experience and the fresh trauma of a calamity recently lived through. Again she saw the charred skin of her brethren and sensed the heat in her own.

Her imagination was animated by vivid memory — but Neipas imagined the scene too, though his picture was but a remote approximation shaped by the abstraction of mental effort. Vague, it nevertheless palpitated with his own traumas — through which he inevitably understood every tragedy — so that he, too, sensed a certain, different forest swept by dust and traces of ash.

Meeting her eyes downcast, he asked slowly: "Why would anyone burn the woods?"

"To burn our home is one way to drive us out... There are many greedy eyes upon those forests, Neipas. And we are a threat to them — because we exist, there, in the land they crave. Noxxe is hardly the only one. Agribusiness looms even larger."

Again Oshana's finger drew lines over the tablecloth.

"There's a wide expanse of farmland next to the Reserve. There are meat farms, animal camps... and alongside, vast acres used to grow crops for their feed, mostly corn. They cram the animals in warehouses by the border with the Reserve, and by the warehouses they dump great pools of waste, driving a stench so foul that it's impossible to live anywhere near. And over the corn fields they sow all manner of toxins, seed pesticides into the ground, poison the air — which we too, breathe.

"It is a barbaric place... We can hear the animals gasp and the breathlessness of the crops from far away. We can hear them choke on drugs and pesticides. We can smell the blood and the poisons. The soil itself seems to open and render the air with screams... — Millions perhaps, of those animals, they have there... bound up and chained, all of them condemned to a life of tortures before they're shipped to slaughter right here in the city. Right under our noses — Axiac's cemented grounds are soaked with their gore."

Neipas, who had meantime resumed eating the salmon — unconsciously mimicking Oshana's motions — once again stopped, chewing scantly and swallowing timidly. And Oshana might have detected the weirdness and the introspection of guilt in his eyes, for she said to him:

"Here we sit, consuming the flesh of an animal. Who is it, though, that we consume? It is the life of a living being that is bequeathed to us — consumed by us, who are of the Earth, as we are fated to be consumed by the Earth one day. But how can you consume of one who has never lived? In truth, these animals are bred only to die — and their life knows nothing but the experience of dying. That is no life.

"The breeders claim to own their life — they claim to their death and even their birth, and the animals are never their own. They are treated like machines without soul, their existence allowed only for the benefit of their master. That is depraved — it is profane.

"But that's not all," Oshana said, raising her brow. With deliberate gestures, she took the cup, and drank the water. Slowly again, Neipas began to eat, taking each bite with the utmost respect; listening very closely as she resumed the word:

"Different farmers and different groups claim ownership of those lands, but all — in one way or another — all are affiliated to a certain conglomerate called Penaguiar."

Her distaste was obvious, as though in the mere utterance of the word she had just given shape to something diabolic.

"They claim ownership of the seed," she then said, simply. "Upon Penaguiar all in the farms depend, all are shackled to. For they hold the seed, they own the right to the seed, and now no farmer can replant the seeds of their crop, but must purchase them afresh from Penaguiar. So it is, that they came to control life's cycle of renewal and take the seat of gods."

"They gotta buy seeds every time?" Neipas said, and immediately after he said it he wondered at his own question. It had been voiced out of an instinct of experience — an experience he no longer remembered he had. His earliest youth had belonged to the country, to pristine woodland and tilled fields. The rest of his life had been urban and therefore he retained little knowledge of farming, but he instinctively retained enough trace of it to find immediately strange the concept of continuously purchasing seeds. Didn't seeds multiply on their own, forever?

"Penaguiar claims to have invented the seeds," explained Oshana. "They made what they call a 'patent', and what I call a 'patent stupidity'. In order to control they claim to have created — it's an old habit of power. To claim ownership of what isn't yours, here's how power reproduces itself.

"Now the very act of birth is levied and extracted for rent. They'd make us pay fees on every breath we take out of the air if they could find a scheme to do it! So is the way of Mammon... In his arrogance and greed, Mammon claims all things — even the claim to divinity. Here he is, proclaiming himself God, owner of life and creator of creation," she said, shaking her head with unbelief; her smile expressed a type of humored contempt. "Today, if you're a tiller, you may be sued for planting the seeds the plant begot — for only through the Market can anything be begotten now."

"Damn." Neipas rubbed the side of his head with his wrist (because his fingers were oily), wondering how such things were possible; and, taking for granted and almost natural the absurdities of those days, unable to think of anything else to say, he commented generally: "That sounds crazy."

"Crazy, yes... Arrogance is a type of madness. And there are many sizes of arrogance, but every one has at least two deceits. One lies to itself, to trick itself into thinking that its delusion is Truth — and the other lies to the world, to swindle everyone into thinking that its delusion is sane. Greed is a type of arrogance. It says to the object of its desire — 'I want this'. But always it says to itself, 'I deserve this'.

"To others greed says, 'I need it', and so it is with these words that Penaguiar comes to the Oyate. They control the farms. The whole expanse — the warehouses, the egg farms and the meat farms, even the abattoirs, even the zoo tucking at the edge of that immensitude — is under their command. They administer the farms through various shell corporations and masks — but the owners are the very same. Their domain is great and vast. But it's not enough for them. All the time they come to us, trying to seduce us with their money, to eat up more of the land — as Noxxe does. And most Oyate communities in the Reserve live in poverty... It's a constant struggle against moral depredation. A constant struggle for life."

Neipas listened fully, melancholy — Oshana commanded his senses entirely with her carriage of voice, her grave eloquence, her sometimes unusual vocabulary, even. There was a sense of reciprocity imbued in his attention. Chewing his food very slowly, he listened, and he listened so closely in part because *she* had listened to him with all her being when he had spoken; he listened with deep care because her own caring had deeply affected him. For the while he felt her woes as his own; he felt kinship that afternoon, and sensed himself implicated in the troubles of the land Oshana illustrated with her voice, and upon which he had never set foot; he candidly worried about the people she described, and whom he had never met.

"And there are still others, still many others..." she continued. "Lumberers wanting to strip the wood, real estate wanting to plant towers and mansions, tourism seeking to strip us of our grounds, mining speculators seeking to debone the soil. They want to make of the Reserve what they made of Axiac or Joachim, what they wish to make of Earth's entire wilderness: a pet, a beast of burden, or a carcass for meat, for fuel... They want to suck the life-force out of Her. They will make of Her a monster, blind and bent on revenge.

"Joachim is now flayed, a moonscape... its beauty is no more. No more rivers, no more trees, no more birds, no more animals, no more people — only machines and wasteland.

"Axiac, too, was once lush. It abounded in verdure, it was healthy. But it extended over a sea of petroleum. The tar was so abundant that it seeped out of the ground — the Oyate themselves used it to coat their boats. It attracted the ghouls. Then the face of the land was ravaged, its bowels scoured, the megalopolis built out of them. Now the underground's been hollowed out, dried up and filled with pipes... And the Oyate, whose home was here — persecuted, imprisoned, slaughtered. Most had to flee to the mountains. Those who survived."

The gravity of her words sank in through the quiet; though the meaning was too heavy to be borne, too horrible to be grasped, too vast to be imagined. "Are you — Oyate?" asked Neipas.

"Not of this Oyate. They took me in. I am indigenous to the nation of Columbia, in truth — but Columbia is made up of the many nations it subdued. My own is in the north. I was born close to the Joachim Valley, though that is not its real name — in the same way that Axiac is not the real name of this place."

"It's not?"

"Axiac is Ooxor — that's the native name of the land. To Joachim, we called Nenaan."

"Nenaan?"

"That's right."

"Have you been here a long time?"

"I left with my niece many years ago... they were already preparing to destroy everything for the new petroleum, then."

With the bare fingers of her bandaged hand, Oshana touched the cloth over her womb; deep, deep under her mask her expression was one of sorrow, and grief. Her gesture, made under the table, went unnoticed by Neipas. Four hidden feet sank mired, under the tablecloth and the dishes, in the stagnant confluence of two long, putrid, distinct undercurrents belonging to two different, two extinct rivers.

"And you? You are not from Axiac."

Neipas replied. "No... I'm from the heartlands. From a town called Minoa."

Oshana looked at him respectfully, mournfully. She nodded once, in acknowledgment; she knew about Minoa, she knew of the disaster which had ravaged it. But she perceived he wished not to speak about it — Neipas had become sullen — and said no more. For a moment she considered the young man, beholding him with sad eyes, recognizing at last the source of his ill-concealed sorrows.

At the mention of the heartlander town, however, a vague remembrance alighted upon her, which she endeavored calmly to make concrete in her mind.

They finished the salmon; the last piece of bread was ended and the last smear of olive oil scooped from the bottom of the bowl.

"More?"

"No no, please — Thank you so much, Oshana. It was delicious."

"Are you sure? Some fruit?"

Neipas politely refused and earnestly thanked Oshana. Oshana placed her hand atop his, smiling motherly. "No need to thank me, dear. It's from the heart."

He smiled back, thankful, again almost tearful, struggling once more against the surge of emotion which his gratitude roused in him. And brimming with that same gratitude, he asked — mostly unconsciously, and perhaps for no other immediate reason than to divert from his overcome state:

"You... You prayed to the salmon, and sprinkled it with herbs... That ritual — it's from your homeland?" And indeed, he still felt the soothing herbal flavor refreshing the back corners of his tongue.

Oshana's transcendental smile seemed to recede for a moment into the shelter of her tranquility and (for a moment) the feathers of her visage were like an ebbing tide revealing the gushing hearts of breathless sea-creatures...

"My homeland," she said, "is no longer. Neither is my tribe. We may be the last of our kind, my niece and I. What we used for our rites grows not here — though we, too, worshiped the salmon of our rivers."

The taste of the food finally completely disappeared from Neipas' mouth, absorbed at last beyond the senses; vividly gone. Vividly absent, gone to the subterranean chambers of his own body, the meal, flavorful and filling, triggered odd memories (odd in their unidentified vividness — like excessive sunlight casting exaggerated shadows) along the cadence of Oshana's disclosures. His mask might have suffered various permutations as he listened to her, but he paid it no heed. His being had long taken leave of his body and left it empty; had taken flight among the sense of subterranean shadows shifting solidly about him. Through the inhaling aperture of his eye he glimpsed two faces emerging from the radioactive mud of felled woods. He saw their heads wrapped in the night of first ages, rigid as old bones, featureless; and as he beheld them sprouting out of the wastelands of his childhood toward the piercingly bright sky, he felt his heart empty vertiginously in a deep penetration of despair gaping across his chestbone (the soil was meanwhile teeming with empty drawers). But Oshana gripped the backside of his hand firmer, and her presence encouraged him — the sensation passed.

Her eyes then narrowed and she looked at him deeply, leaning over the table a little; she remembered now, where she knew this young man from.

"You were a student here, weren't you?"

Yes... He remembered now; and at once realized he had come here with unconscious purpose. Something in him, discerning the familiar surroundings, trod the familiar path back to this place where he had long ago now — how bizarrely did the years pass and vanish behind one's memory in those days! — sat, and reflected upon despondencies. It had been sometime near the final semester, after Edazima had already quit; sometime before his hunger days. He recalled chancing upon the grove and the limestone arch behind the worship house; he recalled the amicable lady — had it been Oshana? — who let him photograph the olive trees and the solemn bookshelves. He vaguely recalled the calm which it gave him then; though he had never since returned. Perhaps he came to dwell on the choice between the pride of a degree and the prudence of avoiding debt; he could no longer remember. Yes, he'd come here with a purpose. Yet it had not been for guidance so much as comfort. Stuck between time and circumstance, he had no choices to be guided through now — his path was already well traced ahead of him.

"I'm gonna start working the graveyard shift," he confessed to Oshana, and to himself.

"...At the Belab?"

His bleary eyes remained absolutely fixed inside his slowly nodding head. Maybe there was no other way — terrifying as the prospect was, tired as he was already, he needed the extra income. "I see," said Oshana — suddenly Neipas felt the touch of cloth on the palm of his hand, and he came to, startled. The hand whose backside was already in Oshana's maternal grip was now enveloped in all her fingers; her bandaged, burnt palm pressed his bare, weary one.

"Do it, if you must," she counseled, gazing him intently. "I see in your eyes you see no other way ahead of you — so go. Have faith in yourself — don't let the future stand over you like this. Face it straight."

Neipas could muster no more than a tepid smile. "But I'm so tired... I feel weak, and I haven't even begun yet."

"You have inside you an inexhaustible source of strength," voiced Oshana, through her constant, her benign, her ever-tranquil smile, and she shook her head to contradict his discouragement, "Isn't weakness but an ebbing of that strength? It'll return — if the path was imposed upon you, walk it with bravery, and when you emerge, you will find yourself and your strength again... Hold fast to your will — and don't worry. In truth, it is with weakness that life declines, but it is from weakness, too, that life ascends."

"What if I never come back from it?"

Oshana held his hand a little tighter — for she saw a great fear in the depths of his eyes which he, in his existential nausea, could not himself entirely feel.

"It's characteristic of human beings," she said, "to be reborn many times in a lifetime."

Neipas nodded sorrowfully, blinked, sniffled. He had understood. It hadn't been so much the words, but the tone in which Oshana spoke them, that made him grasp their meaning. And the thought occurred then strangely to him, whether his father, half-dead, could ever be brought back to life. "I don't know," his lips said, soundless.

Oshana cleared the table. Neipas thanked her once more. "You're welcome, dear." And after she placed everything in the baskets, she said: "It comes all from the Earth. It is toward Her we must feel gratitude."

They arose both.

Oshana guided him among the sacral shelves. They walked together to the back, and the space seemed progressively larger — it seemed huge to Neipas' eyes now, the shelves growing enormously above him, brimming him subtly with wonder, and suggesting something magical in the still, vague breath of dust. Oshana opened the far door to the smokehouse, where the sunshine glimmered, scattered across the vapors and somber between walls of bare stone, and alighted upon an ornamented, musical horn, along with a small rake, sickle, and other farming tools as they hung. The crackling whisper of the fire seemed to issue out of the salmon breathing over their heads; for they curled round the beams like wisps of flame and pended out like tongues, aligned like so many laughing mouths without a body but the incomprehensible smoke through which to speak. All else was silence... Yonder, in the distant shade, there were ample bowls filled with seed, distributed across the long table and before a single candlelight, arrayed as in an altar. Then they emerged again into a garden.

Strange — this looked exactly as the garden Neipas had walked through in the front. Stranger yet — the smoke seemed to have somehow cleared his gaze, and he saw that same garden, which should not have existed here, he saw that same garden much more exuberant, much greener, haler, blooming with dewy grass and strong trees and lush vegetation out of the vigorous soil all around him. All rested serene among the blankets of the day's falling eyelid. Nevertheless he could better see now the thickets upon which (between the feral profusion of thorns) pended a profusion of closed petals: reddish petals inside which some fruit was still swelling. There was rock behind the thorns, rock stained green, rich with lichen. At the top of the rock, which formed a sort of wall like the face of a canyon, there grew great, towering pines — and half-concealed at the base of the rock lay a spring.

The spring purled beneath the thorns, his mask vaguely reflected upon its surface. It seemed to crawl hidden along the edges and down into the brook murmuring round the little island, sprouting from the bottom of the rock with a water so crystalline and so transparent that he could behold its depths, or rather its bottomlessness, churning in mysterious motions, circling in currents of dust and ember remote, nearly imperceptible. The sparks assumed varied shapes in his eyes, and at one time they seemed like a frenzied school of fish swimming, and at another a flock of palpitating birds in flight — in spirals the crumbs of the sandstorm flowed, of time strangely made. He sensed it that way. The vision was not so much a sight as it was a feeling; an intimation of tremendous violence and confusion, beneath which rested an undefinable, unutterable, unfathomable peace; a peace in the form of a slowly pulsing, very nearly motionless flame — a sun still. A peaceful sky rounded with the patience of eternity underneath it — the heavens were the seabed. It remained in the deep, far beneath the surface.

Neipas touched the surface of the spring; he submerged the tip of his fingers. Again he felt a breeze caressing his face. Here was an air that restored; here was water that restored. Here was a gentle light. Here was the Earth. Slowly the drizzling flickers eddied to its calm, yielding into the sway of olive branches spreading out of his head (he saw it mirrored in the waters). The fruits twinkled like a bunch of little lamps, like a myriad stars strewn in the placid depth of his perceptions, blinkering inside, just beyond the reach of consciousness; in a spirit allayed; a soul soothed; a being complete.

Neipas arose, calm. He turned, he looked up. The soft interlocking boughs of the trees covered the sky and flooded the garden in a soft shade; the sun was not to be spotted in the entanglement of brittle, wrinkled bark. It was no mere reflection, what he saw, or sensed. The wind, gentle, murmured back unto him the scattered fragments of his vitality, as though returning him to himself. It was a little odd to realize how close this sense of wholeness was to that of emptiness. Whereas before he shrunk and withered into his apprehensions (dissipating into a hollow despondence and a lifeless confusion — a non-feeling) before the strangeness of an alien world, now he expanded into that world and felt at one with its void; no longer with apprehension, he found himself in it, and for a moment he found in his acceptance of its opacity an echo of its transparency and significance.

Neipas gazed, blank of mind, full of spirit. Strange feeling... Oshana patted the olive tree amid its abundant richness of fruit beautifully whispering songs with the moving air; and through the quietude of their singing Oshana told him, "Look, Neipas.

"The branches of this tree bear flower, whence the olive is born. But if it rains too much, the petals stick to the olive and prevent it from birth — the very petal chokes the fruit. If it doesn't rain enough, the tree doesn't drink enough, and the fruit emerges small, feeble.

"Too much sun, and the petal burns and falls, and the fruit is left unprotected.

"You need wind so that the petals may fall — and they can only leave the fruit once it is ready to ripen.

"How fragile it is!... How unlikely... And yet it prevails — abundant. It's a miracle.

"Life is a miracle, and existence is wonder. The day we realize that — it's our highest hope."

It seemed to him that she had greeted the olive tree with a subtle bow, as she parted her reverent hand from its wrinkled, its sage bark. Before he went, Oshana held Neipas' hand too, and looking deeply into him one last time, said:

"Don't fear. You're not alone. Whenever you need, come back."

The sun was declining by the time Neipas surpassed the Ivory Tower and began making his way down its hill. He walked by the Tower, the tables, the seats, the signs, the fountains and the statues — all made of ivory fading in the growing dusk, the whole campus resembling an immense meadow of dead elephants. A very long line of students continued to pour out of this graveyard to celebrate graduation; the Park of Echoes was filled with them now, and they yelled out 'hurrah!' and threw their caps in the air. Among the graduates stood the strange creature with the top hat, the Debt Collector, watching him as he passed; but Neipas' soul was steady, encouraged, lonely no longer now; for now, at peace. Yet, as Neipas stood over the park and the swath of fake green stretching to the brink of the high-rises, he noticed a subtle haze covering the western sky over Babylon, rendering it sinister with its milky tinge; in the east, the nebulous plumes of martyred trees darkened the swooning night, foreboding.

He walked down through the park to reach the station. The water jet of the lake had ceased by this time, and the waters lay at rest, filled with caps and tassels. Neipas paced on and watched distractedly the luster of the dying sun shining from the towers. The colossal agglomeration rose to cast a vast shadow upon the eastern sprawl of Axiac, shrouding Neipas' body moving minuscule before the mighty titans of the megalopolis.

9 - House of the Anunnaki

Long before the settlers from across the ocean first moored their galleons on these shores, the people of the hills that today delineate Axiac's northern border had erected a totem upon its upmost point. For generations this totem, a tall wooden trunk meticulously engraved with the faces of gods, solemnly overlooked the vast low valley which today the megalopolis covers completely. Before many the totem had stood, motionless and grave. Through the passing epochs, the totem had listened quietly to many a dance of feet stomping the dust round it, to many a song thundered from filled lungs and wild mouths, to many a whisper breathed out of pleading lips, hushed in prayer.

Today the totem is gone. It has long been removed from its place, its memory relegated to a scarce number of footnotes hidden in the obscure depths of libraries, by where only a janitor occasionally passes with his vacuum cleaner and the music hooked to his head, utterly unaware of the existence of the totem and of the voices that worshiped what it represented.

The sacred hills have since been filled with sumptuous mansions; their heights, dwarfed by the bullying clutter of glass buildings which soar from the tons of asphalt and concrete leveling the land. At their upmost point rises an antenna.

In the totem's stead, the antenna listens. Across Axiac's valley of tar and glass rise many murmurs; a million different voices vibrate into the heated air at the same time, all the time — but most of these voices speak in a language different from that used even only a few years ago, and only the antenna (and its counterparts spread across the nation), can understand and translate them. They roam in the form of invisible waves and electromagnetic stirs spread out of digital devices — messages and pictures, monologues for the most part. The glass windows of towers pulse noiselessly with these invisible waves in an incessant rhythm, day and night, always; from them and below them the inscrutable voices lift toward the antennas, which hear them, decipher them, and speak them back into the air.

It's been said that it was the nation's founder himself who had toppled the totem — he, who gave his name to the new nation of Columbia — thus consecrating with this act his memory, exalted, to the distorting echoes of History.

*

Long after dinnertime, when the moon already approached its zenith in the pallid sky above Axiac, a silent mob of masked figures gathered deep underground to begin the graveyard shift. They came between grimy walls sullen, grave, arching their backs and necks behind expressionless, inscrutable horned masks with long bovine snouts. Neipas passed through the towering veil at the end of the kitchen. Entering the mysterious pantry, he followed through between the shelves and sought the nightshift supervisor, following Edazima's instructions and cutting through the unlit space. He had listened the frantic noises of the kitchen dim to a ghostly quietude; he had seen the smoke thin and its shadows slink out until there was barely anything but the greased tiles, the abandoned counters, the low rumbling of the ceiling pipes. Few workers remained, and the space yawned with emptiness. Kur, so familiar to Neipas' eyes as to become invisible, acquired a sense of the unknown, of stillness. He had stayed late at work before, but never so late as on that day; it felt like the crossing of some threshold had gone through him, suffused with the breath of novelty and the eerie.

A familiar stench lingered as the boiled odors dissipated out the ducts; it thickened and intensified as Neipas made way through the cold storage, colder and darker at every step. His vision sunk further in the blackening air and the only salient impressions were this smell and a constant dripping which had been born from the silence of the kitchen; but as he trod onward this dripping changed, bubbling with a scurrying of insects, and morphed gradually into an approaching beat of machinery with an undertone of instruments; into a strange, mixed rhythm to which he matched his steps unconsciously; an unrecognizable cycle of three knocks and a turn revolving in an ordered sort of distant pandemonium.

One, two three — Gaining the end of the pantry, Neipas reached another veil, which he hadn't seen in the near-darkness; and passed suddenly into a bland room with stained rust walls, where he saw the strange gathering of voiceless masks already dispersing upon dragging feet. They walked all into the gate behind them. The space was made wide by their leaving, for they were many, a whole army of taciturn bodies pulled inward by the growing rhythm. Motionless in their midst were two tall fellows in jumpsuits, who remained after everyone else had gone. One bore a smile, his fur spotted with different colors, sparkling chains round his horns. The other had a frown, was hornless, and was dressed in deep black fur. Neipas, drawing in the uncanny view of the two standing oxen — walked against his shadow in the dim, bile lighting — approached and asked timidly where he could find the nightshift supervisor.

Hearing this, the black-furred ox pointed to himself.

"Good evening," greeted Neipas. "I'm a waiter in the day shift and was told to come here to sign up for work."

In answer to this, the black ox gesticulated in a series of intricate motions of hand, and said nothing. Neipas watched bewildered his fingers move in the air; when he looked to the motley-colored ox beside him for guidance, he saw that he was observing the moving hands and nodding in understanding. And then he spoke:

"You're late," began the colored ox, "Report here at the beginning of every shift. That was five minutes ago. You shall be given your task then. Tonight, present yourself to the foreman beyond the gate. He will give you something to do."

The black ox gesticulated some more, his mask as rigid as stone, eyes flitting blankly between Neipas' lip and fingers. Only when the colored ox talked again did Neipas understand that he was translating. "Sign in and out works exactly the same way. Grab coffee or whatever you need to work before you begin," he said. "You won't be able to after that."

Some more gestures from the hornless black ox. "Any questions?"

Neipas, confounded in his new situation, could think of nothing to say. The rhythm came from beyond the gate and already interfered with his thoughts. He was directed toward it, and stepped to. The gate was a massive affair; two heavy slats of iron with but two iron rings protruding, and as Neipas walked in between he opened out to a vast city of plastics and stainless steel — sounds billowed, room expanded all of a sudden. He drew in the sight with all the awe impressed by things unprecedented. For, from the rust foyer the space increased in immensitudes, widened to such a degree that his eyes could not discern a wall in the fathomless distance. The ceiling beamed with bright lights and exposed everything to view. Very long, endlessly bifurcating conveyor belts moved from the horizon, carrying meat — infinite streams of meat, multi-limbed rivers of skin, fat, and flesh flowing methodically from the deep and pooling close to where Neipas stood, astonished, and watched as machines at the culmination wrapped up the already-processed parts round plastic and foam. Workers in strange masks proliferated alongside the meat river banks, moving through steady paces of repeated motions, all in a practiced choreography stretching in millions beyond the blurriest far.

Nearby, steps away from the river's end, a group of workers were lining up before the foreman — a short and stout fellow, with a tablet in his hand and a card hanging on a lanyard fastened round each horn. Nearly everyone discarded plastic cups in one of the immense trash cans as they entered formation. They were walking from the coffee machines on the other side of the belt and Neipas still wondered whether he had time to get some coffee too; but even as he moved toward the line, the foreman began marching from end to end, passing a word to each worker as he went. He was assigning stations to the new laborers (Neipas picked up his looping speech as he came nearer). When the foreman came to Neipas he repeated indifferently, "Experience?"

"Waiter at the day-shift."

"Station N-03."

Stainless steel posts arising from the conveyors indicated the stations. Neipas headed to conveyor N, which processed poultry. Cuts of chicken breast were wrapped in plastic in quick succession and rapid number by a myriad arms of metal, working in a controlled frenzy under the sign "N-07" — this is where the conveyor ended, and just yonder, where the plastic-aproned bodies of the workers began, he could still make out the pole and the banner marking "N-06", though he couldn't see beyond that... The conveyor merged with others, then departed, then rejoined at various junctions, making him perplexed and timorous before the confusedly angled distance. Not very eager, he tucked the pigeon's oozing wax in under the ox's brittle clay; and started along, walking wide between the streams, hoping to find station 03. Advancing into the noise, he stepped (beat, stepped, beat, step) — the way was long and winding; Neipas took a while to get there, his advance hampered by the growing shock in his eyes. A series of nightmarish visions unfolded before his riverside march... Here was an immense industrial enterprise, out the labors of which streamed the meat consumed by the entire megalopolis; supplying millions of appetites even beyond. And working the seemingly interminable line, in which the bodies of animals were disassembled into products ready for supermarket shelves, were a great many laborers, standing in boots upon the wet, greasy floor, wielding knives and saws, and wearing paper masks over their snouts, which often extended into feedbags, and inside which they ate and hid from the mixtures of stenches. It smelled all at once, in varying degrees, like chemicals, bile, blood, urine, feces — many of the workers wore diapers, and the factory's atmosphere reeked of defecations accumulated over countless overtime hours... Fluids retreated down the slanting floor (through his sagging legs Neipas perceived the floor slanting) as viscera was pulled out and slid across. Work was methodical and machine-like: a booming orchestral record playing from the walls (which Neipas couldn't yet see in the glaring whiteness of the limits) marked the tempo to which all the horned workers lifted, hacked, sliced, stabbed, sawed... The oppressive smells made him woozy, they insinuated into his sight and hazed his senses, which discerned but blurs of plunging motion and clammy noise. He felt various temperatures along the way; it was generally freezing, but yonder far, far, where the hog and steer kill zones began, steam floated up thick from the hot blood on the grounds, covering everything. Cleaners emerged with full space suits and walked aimlessly about, dragging hoses. Inspectors with immense, heavy horns weighing down their backs dotted the industrial landscape sparsely, hunched over bits of meat at stations. Vats filled with boiling fat sizzled and smoked. He floated through nauseating, chaotic vapors. Things curved and dilated in the flurry of activity; and as he lumbered alongside the dizzying belts Neipas came to the consciousness of the path twisting, and sinking, and winding into a sort of hole; he perceived the immensity shrinking at every step, and as he was forced to come nearer the system of conveyors he saw the workers more closely; and noticed now, between gaps of vapor, how many had mangled hands, or an arm amputated, or one socket eyeless... His heart puckered into his throat in fear.

Sweating and diminishing, Neipas roamed across what seemed to him a strange plastic hell, glaringly white and disinfected, with splashes of red coursing sickly through the middle, and a myriad gory chunks adrift among cutting steel. Passing him by as he went down, a procession of headless little bodies, denuded, bloodied, resembling the half-devoured child of maddened Cronos, multiplied along the hanging chains, and floated up, pulled by the legs by hooks, in slow spirals, toward that vast white heaven, to drift upstream along its soul river and be purged between indefinite, infinite lactic banks — ushered by charons with glaringly sharp oars, rustling bellies, open arms amid blazing lights...

Perhaps he'd gotten lost. There was the sign for station "N-01" below him — had he passed "03"? Neipas looked about and found himself by an entrance to a sidelong tunnel; red lights filled his eyes, revealing indistinct railtracks upon which a long train of iron cars was just sliding into a halt. Broad furs jumped out right away and hastened to unlatch the heavy doors and slide them open. Great mechanic screeches and thunderous rumbles gave way then to a very cacophony of cries, of incomprehensible wails — unhuman they sounded, unearthly in their strange composition. Already Neipas had heard it purled out of the slats of the train cars, but now the outcry abruptly exploded in the clap of metal with a blast of stink, a fetidness of urine, feces, and dread, thickening further the underground air. From the cars and the uproar a deluge of furs, feathers, and bristles came pouring out upon trampling hoofs and terrified paws, in a flutter of wings, a babel of snouts, a rasping of horns, tusks, antlers; whole parades of living chicken and swine and lambs and steer disgorged from the brimming interiors of the locomotive, with such tremendous noises, forming together such a terrible symphony of bewilderment and agony, that the walls themselves seemed to throb and shrink with apprehension. "Mary — where am I?" Neipas thought aloud, shrinking in shivers himself, as the booming tempo pounded over him and into the stomping and the perplexity of the animals. A frenzied tide of chicken twittered up the ramp at Neipas' feet and swarmed over his ankles; they were all being forced from the car by one of the haulers, whose arm operated with such robotic efficiency and indifference, and provoked such an effect of swept multitudes that it caught Neipas' notice among all that disarray. But it was the hauler's hand in particular that gripped his awareness and engraved itself upon his memory.

Concealed in falconry-gloves though it was, he could see how unique the hand appeared, in its disfigured shape — it more resembled a claw, or a hook, or a talon. Neipas couldn't make out whether there were fingers missing, but they were bent in such a tormented manner that he instinctively judged them useless. And yet, that hand would hardly stand out after the spectacle of deformities Neipas had just descended past, were it not for the association it acquired with a strange figure which was being uncovered little by little by the drawing off of chicken bodies.

In the middle of the emptying car stood a midget — a masked midget, clad in robes, clad with the motionless face of Tragedy: two little downturned crescents for eyes, one large downturned crescent for lips, and one — middle-sized, middle-placed — downturned crescent for a nose.

"Mary — where am I?" he asked the hauler, whose large bison face, with eyebrows draping its eyes and a beard falling copiously from its jowls, loomed suddenly very near him, and roused him with its breath.

"What are you looking for?" grunted the hauler in reply.

"Station N-03."

"Up the ramp to your right," said the hauler, pointing with his talon-shaped hand, and through his bovine beard Neipas distinctly made out a very wiry, very saggy dewlap bristling with shafts of plume, jostling. Already various workers were seizing the chickens and ramming their legs through the hangers behind Neipas. Their shouts sounded faint amid the confusion of bellows.

Dazed in the unreality of his surroundings, Neipas stepped back up the ramp, which curved in the direction perpendicular to that which the chicken were floating in, up through a curtain of plastic strips and into the wall ("N-02" written bold at its side). The two divergent paths lassoed, as it were, a railing-framed pit, gaping in the middle of the twilit shed which was all astir with scrambling limbs, bodies ruffling the eerie red glow. Feathers snowed languidly from the upper levels into the chasm, descending through shafts of electric light, among glitters of ephemeral dust and blood streams. And chunks of meat fell amid flaxen particles, all sprinkling without sound within the swallowing clamor.

Later, Neipas would learn that station 01 was where the chicken were unloaded and hung; station 02 was the carbon dioxide chamber, where the gas filtered into their noses to stun their brains.

Station 03 was where their throats were stabbed and bled.

Neipas presented himself to the ox responsible for Station N-03. As the hung chicken passed through, the supervisor explained to him the procedure. Training took no more than 30 seconds; when he was done, he handed Neipas a small knife which resembled a scalpel, asking, "Understood?" and walked away before hearing the answer. "Sign up is over there!" said the foreman yet as he went, pointing to the nearest wall (there were drawers all over that wall).

In the drawers he found the same plastic apron, rubber boots and gloves, hairnet, and headphones he had seen the others wear; diapers too, which he refused to put on — and a feedbag. There was also an aluminum scabbard to which, he assumed, his knife belonged. Neipas had barely heard the foreman among the noise of machines, the music, the pumping industrial din; but he had a vague understanding that he was instructed to cut the chicken's throat as it passed — "just repeat what the guy next to you is doing," was the conclusion. He approached the line timidly. Near him were other workers who hacked away dexterously, automatically, swaying vaguely upon their feet which by now had pressed upon the floor for hours. The chickens passed yet alive and curved upward over the pit, into which their blood spilled fresh in continuous flows. Neipas witnessed nervously how fast the hanging hooks moved; how the chicken, stunned, opened their beaks meekly, as if trying to force a cry for help out of their half-slumber.

"C'mon! Get to it!" shouted the foreman, hurling Neipas right into the heat of it. He stepped to, numb and overwhelmed, and swallowing down remorse and restrain he grabbed the body of a chick and sliced the neck; the cut was shallow and the blood struggled to course, trickling out in a viscous ooze; the bird's wings flapped between the toxin daze and the pain of the gash. "No! You stab! Stab it in the jugular!" Neipas, pressured by the yelling, looked alarmingly to the fellow next to him, and hurried to copy his movements. He saw quickly how it was done — the little head was grabbed between the fingers and the neck was pierced by the scalpel right over — and he jumped to the task under the thrust of screams.

Through his hands would pass hundreds of necks that night. Down his gloves ran the blood of many lives, blood pumping from living hearts. Feathered, yellow bodies streamed and pushed upon him without end, without pause, at a bewildering pace. At first, he went through the motions with fear and hesitation, but adapted himself gradually by force of pressure into the toil's mechanized beat. At first he was very mindful, and moved methodically, gripping consciously every motion for fear of cutting himself; for it would be very easy to apply excessive stress upon the bloody and bacterial knife, and pierce it through the avian throat into his own skin. At first he felt acutely the resistance of the thin wall of pulsing flesh before the penetrating blade, the delicate head and the feeble beak, the closed, swollen eyes beneath his fingers; at first he felt the quivering of each life taken when he dug in the knife. Sometimes the hen's eyes were half-open, and then Neipas sensed in himself a deeper hesitation, derived from a feeling of distant kinship to the condemned animal. There was something familiar in the heave of its breast, the dilated nostrils gasping for air, in the sad eyes staring up at him; they looked just like human eyes, hazel-colored round a black circle, suggestive of something profound — a soul, perhaps. Its gaze seemed to grip his heart; it peered into him with the expressiveness of impossible communication.

But the noise was too loud, the odors too overbearing, the beat too quick; and all human sentiment here melted in the frantic rhythm of the machine, of the line, of the uncaring imperatives of production. All he knew was he had to get through the night. The pace, which he felt quicker by the minute, was dictated in the fore by the supervisor's expletives, lashing out like the crack of a whip, "Faster! Faster!" he commanded, brandishing his arms upward like the conductor of a grand orchestra, his booming voice meshing with the demonic whir of the machines transporting and processing the carcasses; and the rhythms of the yells and the gears were in such symbiosis that it was as if the machines themselves were uttering those sounds. The music pumped, underpinning all... A long time passed. Soon Neipas would understand the reason for the diapers — when he asked to go to the bathroom, the foreman merely said the line could not stop. Holding it became really painful; the discomfort wrenched up a notch, with his mind juggling between the stress of his growing bladder and the demands of the line. Neipas withdrew into the rhythm, abstracting his spirit from the physical strain. He took solace in the fact that, at least, he hadn't taken that coffee at the beginning. And he kept going, his body aching into gear. Again, and again, and again, he thrust onward in revolutions. His own heartbeat adjusted itself to the pace.

But his vital needs would surface beyond the growing machine. It was when the discomfort reached unbearable levels that Neipas, noticing that the foreman had stepped away, tried to talk to the fellow beside him on the line. He shouted above the noise, "Do we ever have breaks!" — but the fellow, downcast, only kept at the repeated stabbing, toiling through a sort of trance. Obscurely, the sense of this impressed Neipas into a deeper fright; and it was a while before he resolved that perhaps his companion hadn't heard him, and stretching his neck out toward the fellow he yelled again, "When's our break!"

"Is no stop!" out came the muffled voice, in such a disorganized ruffle and accent that it was as though it hadn't articulated words in ages. The fear in these inarticulated words was clear, even through the thickness of the feedbag. Neipas would eventually learn that it was mostly mouthless immigrants working here. They would not speak, they could not speak; for they would be shown the boot if they tried. Droplets of fright pended in the sweaty air, mixed with the bloody stench which even the strong redolence inside the feedbag (which Neipas, too, had put on) couldn't quell. Later the poor fellow would try to clarify, "Line never stop!". Neipas would disturb him no longer. His hand stabbed, stabbed, stabbed. His wrist throbbed painfully at each squelching of jugular vein. The fright and discomfort pitched vertiginously into a panic he feared would run out of his control. The chickens assumed dizzying speeds and became a continuous yellow blur; his belly filled with swaying acids pressing out at the groin.

(He shrunk deeper into his mask. The hours flew through the blood-thick air, and all along Neipas had little consciousness of the space he was standing in. He was in a deep well, shaped cone-wise and like a sort of squeezed stadium, which, from the upper conveyors where the body parts were disassembled, rounded into a slope down which the workers made their way to their stations, and which straddled the increasingly shrinking hole. The workers were made to stand on protruding platforms by which the animals were lifted. Into the hole, and between the nearing sides of the well, the hens, arising in helix up toward the conveyor belts, dropped first their blood, and then their lives in quiet runnels, before they were scalded in boiling vats (some of their lives not having quite bled out of them by then), made unfeathered, and taken off the hanging chains. The bottommost pit yawned a couple of steps from Neipas.)

(Deeper away from body and self. The chicks would bleed down his knees, before their bodies were lifted up over that pit. In the midst of the furor, amid the widespread anguish, beyond the blurring sights and the immediate sense of repeated thrust, Neipas sometimes looked down and discerned something in the bottom. Workers loaded the panicked animals into the suspended chains. There was a mess of helpless wings. And in the midst of all this, in the crimson illuming the shed, standing by a grate beside N-02's stripped curtain and opposite N-01's railtracks, stood that odd midget, staring up, straight into Neipas' blurry gaze — standing out strangely amid the dreadful turmoil.)

(A heart pulsed in the rhythms of the plunge and the growing depths. For a moment, as Neipas stared back into that vision, the procession of industrial death in which he was enmeshed seemed to halt. His eyes narrowed, focused. His senses grew acute as he peeled the ear for what the midget might be saying to him. Indeed, Neipas felt a whispering just beyond the range of it...)

But in an instant, it seemed — within the click of an eye — the midget had gone.

[...]

The grate yawned lonely (beyond it, some stairs led down to deeper darknesses) at the spot where the midget had stood. On the opposite side of it, beyond the tunnel entrance, locomotive after locomotive unloaded thousands of screaming beasts. They clambered under the red glow which permeated the gloom and which, it turned out, was meant to calm the birds down; though they, evidently not serene, seemed to know well what they were there for.

Neipas would perceive again, as he left, the conveyors stretching to the limitless distance, beyond the fog of the kill floors, where the stunned and quiet steers, hogs, rabbits, fawns [...] were slaughtered. He could not know it then, but if he trod further alongside those meat rivers of steel to their source, he would find himself traveling channels dug through mountain rock to places far beyond the eastern edge of the megalopolis, where animals were entrapped in rusty iron cages inside immense meat farms, wherein the desperate and convulsing squeals of millions were smothered under the stuffy walls of filthy warehouses. Neipas was deafened by the pace of the line and the matching squelch of his heart; all trumpeted bloody, but if he could only sharpen his ear, he would be able to just listen, beyond the whistling of knives, to those distant screams.

But the screaming inside his own heart was too loud for him to hear anything else.

*

That night, a noiseless cry beamed out of an *I* in Golden Westbeach. It reached an antenna standing across the road a mile off; the antenna, hearing it, cast it off to another antenna, and the voice was thus echoed across the megalopolis, streaming through the head of the antenna atop the sacred hill, buzzing aloud with concentrated electricity; until it zapped to a final antenna standing a couple of blocks from the Belab Tower, and finally charged through its lobby.

The *I* shook inside his pocket.

10 - Fig Leaves

First it was stripped of will; secondly of consciousness; thirdly of life; then it was stripped of its feathers; then of its head; then it was stripped of its feet, and lastly it was stripped of innards till, so bared, it was made ready to be dressed anew; draped first in plastic, then coated in frost, then anointed with fire, bejeweled in salts and finally garnished in dressings, it was laid upon clay and glass exudingly, aromatic, spread, scattered across fractions without self, dispersed through distance and process, each piece smoking a breath without voice, ready to be stripped anew, to the bone, into oblivion...

And thus is flesh ripened to meat.

*

Something shook against his leg. His eyelashes parted and touched between heavy, deep breaths, blinking with difficulty, zoning with the languor of wings flapping in languid dreams. A cold surface pushed his cheek, trembled; with a long, sleepy sigh he drew away from the steel wall and realized he stood in the elevator. He smacked his beak; swallowed; grimaced. The rumble of the moving box continued out of his mind's slumber. Soon, heading back to bed through the shrinking spaces of sweltering platforms, squeezed between the packed shoulders of multitudes impatiently waiting for delayed, overheated trains, shuffled inside suffocatingly huddled cars, that same rumble would linger, and intensify into a continual thrusting of gears and the churn of machinery thundering on in impassive and soulless progression, throbbing in clapping lunges toward the most hidden chambers of his heart, ever louder. Already he associated with the inexorable revolving of motors the bloody plunge of knives, rhythmically, mechanically killing.

Again the *I* shook inside Neipas' pocket.

A red dot blinked over the glass rectangle now opening alight.

EVA: Hey you ;)
EVA: I'm down to meet tomorrow if you're free?

*

After a few more nights at the slaughterhouse (and endless mornings and afternoons up and down the tower), Neipas went back to his apartment — the first time in many days. He had a vague intention to rest before his date with Eva. Right away, out of fear of losing the opportunity forever, he had

156

written to her he would be free to meet.

He stumbled into his bedroom. Quickly he gripped his uniform, which hadn't been washed in days, to undress, and noticed the bloodied plastic apron was still over it. He rushed to remove it and toss it into the trash can in the corner, full of impatience and drowsiness weighing on his every cell. In a feverish swoon of mind he sensed how absurd it was to work so hard for an apartment he never slept in or went to because he was always working to keep it; then he took a speedy pass through the toilet, and without bothering to take off his shoes, brush his teeth, nothing, he, exhausted and inconsequential, simply plopped onto bed, face down, smearing his sheets with the sodden wax of his mask. His being shut down to complete oblivion immediately.

Hours later he awoke with a dull ache stiffening his muscles and a feeling of unrest twitching the ligaments. The parched staleness of his breath warmed the covers against the nose. It recoiled slowly from a bloody odor and the stench of dirty laundry which stuck to the back of his nostrils inside his head. With dazed indifference Neipas realized that a whole patch of blood had dried and hardened upon the skin of his neck. He tried to ignore it and fall back to sleep — but his nerves were fidgety again now. He tried to quell them in the lassitude of the *I*, sinking himself into the farthest nook under his boiling sheets. It was to no avail. The motion of repeated hacking and the noise of squished meat, the rhythmic feeling of flesh giving in and opening, all was replicated in the palpitations of his heart, quivering irritatedly in his arteries and lodging in his bones. It wasn't long before he gave up and sprang out of bed in frustration, nerves stirring under the labored breath heaving in his fevered body.

Neipas felt like he had dreamt through his shower. He did not feel refreshed afterwards.

Again he found himself in bed. The sun yellowed the shutters and the hidden window trapped in the heat; again the AC was not working. Neipas kept checking the time, sweltering and gnawed by the notion that he hadn't slept enough, that he needed a few more hours to regain full possession of his wits. Dinnertime was distant yet. He would stare at the *I* now and then, his mind drifting into its glowing screen, seduced by its imperceptible hypnosis of distraction — then, cursing himself, he would discard the glass to his bedside with negligent ferocity and shut his eyes firmly; and then repeat. He swayed in the daze between the *I*'s half-slumber and the inability to sleep for a long time. Neipas turned and spun in bed, from the side to his stomach, curling up and sprawling out from the center to the corner, rolling in and out of the tangling sheets. That whole afternoon preluding the date was to be dominated by an anxious feeling that frustrated the downward pull of his exhaustion. But the proximity of that hour, growing upon him, made his senses jump restlessly. Even his exhaustion was dispelled by the sheer force of anticipation; the very air became thickened with the scalding density of erotic anxiety. His mind became fully alit, ablaze with a hot swarm of thoughts which seemed to transpire out his skin in the concrete form of sweat beads.

Finally he sat up, at once weary and alert, bearing saggy eyes and a nervous breast. Try as he might, he couldn't sleep.

Roused by a ticking heart, he thrust out of bed and straight into preparations. Out in the living room he found his roommate sagging into the couch, half-buried in wet, crumbled tissue paper mildly translucent in the looming glow of a screen, which he propped up on his belly, over his comatose face. His very jowls slumped between the cushions, as if slowly repelled by the screen's twitches — which rolled photo after photo of his girlfriend — in the manner shadow reacts to light; and for a moment Neipas thought he was weeping. But Neipas was too busy to think up a word of comfort; and again he stepped under the showerhead spray, for he had already forgotten his first shower and those elusive and fetid smells still lingered. He emerged from vapors of water and cologne, wrapped up in a towel, with teeth meticulously scrubbed and mask shaped to its best possible form. Inside his room, he halted for a second. Suddenly he was struck by a vague panic. "What should I wear?" he mumbled to the wardrobe mirror, and the mask, winking, all taken up in a sudden flush of excitement, pointed him to the very best he possessed among the meager collection inside; and he dressed the anointed attire with the utmost gravity. There was still time plenty before the scheduled hour, but finally, unable to bear the compounded heat of his apartment and the vague stench, mixed in with the drowsy presence of his roommate, Neipas grabbed his keys, his wallet, and his *I* — and left.

The date was scheduled to take place in a restaurant in Golden WestBeach, where Eva lived. The area's main avenue ran alongside great bluffs overlooking the beach, and by the side of the road were various little parks and walkways where tourists and the homeless sat and lay in a strange landscape of conflated realities. Neipas settled on one of the benches by the cliff-rail. He had several hours till the meeting and sought to quell his anxieties in the contemplation of the ocean. It spread immense — a vast drape of blue undulating soft under the wind, with a thick streak of sunny shimmer flowing from horizon to shore, appearing as though burst out of the depths, as if the waters bubbled with gold. The pier down at the beach, hanging over the tide, teemed with a mass of little bodies moving between blocky stores and underneath a giant wheel and a glittery rollercoaster. All this alighted upon Neipas like a dreamy abstraction. All of it was remote, all of himself absent. He thought of trying to come back to himself with the aid of his camera, to absorb himself back into reality through the focus of its lens. But his old camera was broken, and languished presently in his wardrobe — though he still took it out occasionally, just for the feel of it. Shooting with the *I* (his fingers slipped into his pocket but emerged empty) dispirited him, so he tried to take photographs in his mind, to make still the purview's blurriness, and relegate to memory a framed image of the present; but he could not. Everything flowed by him, he could fix nothing, nothing abided under his focus.

In the shoddiness of his contemplation, Neipas photographed the air as the wind picked up over the cresting billows, scattering the wash of haze pending in the horizon. By and by it formed into clouds, and the clouds engulfed the pale sun, and stifled its slow-flickering heat; the breezes, freed from the clutches of the ray, muttered onto his skin like a soporific. His tension dropped and his eyes were made heavy, his head drowsy. The world slowly became permeated with the promise of rain; and yet the brume was still very thin, and sunlight shone still through. Rain would not come yet. Dryness kept unabated, the drought uninterrupted. But the gray sky cast now a somber sheen across the waters and upon the sands of the beach, looming mystically over the torpor of sunbathers and short sleeves, and the homeless poor lying by the trees. The declining sun bathed them together and all their lusterless shadows pended in the same direction; side by side the poverty-stricken crows dark with grime and the spruced pigeons with glowing smiles before their own cameras, the former from the ground pleading for attention, the latter, hardening their masks upon the eyes and the ears, seeing nothing, hearing nothing, ignoring all but their own reflections. Two realities mixing like oil and water. Because Neipas was so neatly preened that day — his feathers well-oiled, his raiment ironed, his appearance clean — he was often mistaken for a tourist and would be asked for a dollar now and then; to which he could only reply with an apology of sad eyes and a sorrowful shake of head. Finally, feeling guilty, he stood up; and walked about by the bluffs for a while. Soon the vast greyness darkened all around, and above the sea the great wheel lit into neon colors, blooming humid and misty in Neipas' tired eyes. A fanfare of distant voices came from the pier. The night spread warm and pleasant; it seemed to soothe all things. As sounds dimmed his spirits were becalmed. With serenity he took his *I* off the pocket and navigated its map inland a few blocks, roaming through virtual space and physical space together, following the whispers of the glass. The hour was almost at hand. When he lifted his stare, he was before the door of the restaurant.

On either side of him stretched the promenade with its cafes, cinemas and dwelling buskers and beggars. The receptionist inside took his name and the usher guided him through a gloom of candle-lit tables to his reserved seat. It turned out that Neipas was still quite early and his table hadn't been properly set up yet. Two heifer-masked waitresses got to it straight away, right as Neipas was sitting down, covering the table's wooden top with a silky red cloth, a pair of white plates and bowls and finally the napkins and utensils, all landing in perfect alignment, as if by magic.

"Good evening, sir," said a voice by his shoulder. It belonged to a gaunt ox, very young, almost a child, with small horns sticking out of his head and mask very shaved, nearly without fur. He was dressed smartly in a black waiter's attire, out of which sleeves emerged a thin hand holding two menu booklets.

"Hi, just water please," went Neipas, sculpting his lips into a clumsy, uncomfortable smile, and taking the booklets.

"Very well." In two moments the waiter receded and emerged from amid the dark jungle of candles. To Neipas' annoyance, he brought not only a cup of water as he wanted but an entire glass bottle, which he would have to pay for. It was opened and without a lid so he couldn't take it home either. The waiter dispensed its contents indifferently.

"Excuse me," requested Neipas with a raised finger a while later, after some waiting, as the waiter was walking by. "Where's the bathroom, please?"

"Straight ahead, then left," the waiter replied, with that impenetrable neutrality of conduct inherent to the dedicated professional.

"Thank you." Neipas arose and walked again among the spectral candlelights, his legs kind of bandy; he was uncomfortably aware of his every step and felt twitchy bird eyes judging him from every table. As he passed he wondered whether they could see his lips, which he felt compelled to curve and tighten into a creasy circle, flower-like, so they wouldn't shake. There were only five minutes left and he had become really nervous now. He exhaled relief at seeing the bathroom empty, and, slowing his pace just a little, approached the mirror. For the next two and a half minutes he preened his feathers and remolded his pigeon mask, trying to soothe away the distresses of his heart with his massaging, nibbling fingers. At first he was quick and rushed, but then he eased their motion. Drawing back, he considered himself more carefully. His shoulders bowed a little under an invisible burden; between them bulged his face, his mask, which could ill withhold the contained pressures struggling to find expression. The mold of feather and wax stared him down queerly. Nearing his glare to the mirror, he observed his image grow inside the pupil of his quivering eye, and saw how irritated and bloody the zone around it was. He wondered uncomfortably what ailed him so; and what was it about this date that made him so nervous. It was normal to feel a little nervous, he knew, but what he felt then overstepped all bounds of normality. Nothing had been normal anymore since that violent kiss at the Zoo — it had effected some change in him, something fundamental, which he hadn't had yet time to process. Things that had seemed tolerable to him before now oppressed him more than ever. He noticed them more now (within his eye he saw tremble endless semiopen eyes of upturned chickens and beyond them, watching cryptically and relentlessly beyond the chain, a midget). A familiar sensation itched in the recesses of his throat and he became suddenly aware that he was not alone: in the corner of the mirror he saw the base of one of the stalls; through the opening peeked, surreptitiously, a shoe.

Neipas recognized it with a start. It was the shoe of that debt collector that had been stalking him of late. With a fright he dawdled on whether he should open the door and confront him; a yell of panic swelled within his neck and almost broke out.

But then — putting his eyes under the running faucet, he decided that he was merely being paranoid. If that was indeed the debt collector (which Neipas was sure he was) perhaps his being there was merely a coincidence. Regardless, there was no time to think — Eva would be there at any moment, and Neipas returned to the table across wide steps.

She wasn't there yet. Neipas sat down. Two and a half minutes more passed, and at the precise beat of the hour he eyed the entrance eagerly, adjusting himself on the chair, expecting her appearance. Just at that moment the young waiter came and asked if he could take Neipas' order and Neipas told him to wait a little longer. The waiter acquiesced, slid away, and vanished. Neipas waited.

Another five minutes passed and Eva hadn't arrived yet. Neipas grew worried; thinking that something had happened to her, or she had forgotten. As he toyed with the fork he found himself tapping his foot nervously, and stopped himself with some irritation. The form of two red fish, redder than the silk cloth covering the table, gradually stood out to him among its weave: two red fish eating the other's tail in a revolving circle. He kept waiting, tense.

An additional 15 minutes passed. Neipas hunched over his *I* moodily. His message to her [**NEIPAS:** Everything ok? :)] lingered in the glass, unanswered and ignored. She had been online only a minute ago, he knew.

As time trespassed well beyond the scheduled minute, Neipas felt his heart stabilize and cool. The anxiety in him, sensing that it hadn't, apparently, a corresponding feeling in his date, decreased at a sure pace. Gradually, Neipas grew in an acute feeling of annoyance and even vague contempt, from which he derived a certain sense of superiority and confidence. He kept on waiting, increasingly apathetic.

It was approximately half an hour past the scheduled time when Eva entered the restaurant. The very moment Neipas spotted her by the entrance his pulse spiked with excitement. She looked round for her table with a charmingly lost manner, exuding every sort of seductive pull from her poised figure. Neipas noticed her right when she entered his view; she seemed to glow in the atmospheric shade yonder, half-concealing her in the utmost mystery of romantic beginnings. For him the span between the moment the usher began leading her toward the table, and the moment she recognized him, felt outside of time, charged full of sexual tension. When Eva rested her searching eyes upon his seated figure and waved he immediately waved back, immersing himself into the present with the focus necessary for interaction. All bad feelings dissipated instantly then. As Eva approached her smooth, voluptuous shape grew in his eyes; though he noticed (vaguely) she wasn't as pretty as in the photos. Neipas sculpted a measured smile, calm and neutral.

"Hey you!" she exclaimed as Neipas rose to greet her.

"Hi Eva! How are you?" he responded as they hugged, lamentably separated by a chair; he sensed the warmth of her cheek close to his. Their bodies parted with all normality, and Neipas felt a hit of satisfaction at having performed this embrace so well. He was emboldened, felt courageous.

"Good, sorry for being late," she said, sitting down gracefully. "Had a bit of trouble getting here. The traffic is killer in this town!"

"It's no problem!" Neipas blurted with a vivid bobbing of head, and then pulled back a little, checking his enthusiasm. "Hm, so you drove here?"

"I took a cab, actually. My car broke down last week," she sighed, hanging her bag's sling round the seat and making herself comfortable. "It's a total bummer — So I had to take a cab today, I actually just came from work. Long day... Anyway, so good to finally meet you! How have you been?" she voiced in a bubbly tone. Instinctively she grabbed the menu and diverted her look from Neipas for a second, which weakened his momentum as he was about to start speaking.

"All right, well — not much going on," he blundered, and she looked back at him. "Been taking some photos..."

"Oh yeah?" she shot excitedly, leaning forward. "I love your photos, you know."

Eva had expressed as much through text before; but hearing it in her own voice was pure elation to him. She asked, "What kind of work have you been doing?" reposing her chin on her fingers with the aplomb of a swan, and

Neipas could hardly contain himself. He was just collecting every power of charisma needed for eloquent descriptions of his craft when a voice at his flank protruded out from the general buzz filling the restaurant, "Good evening miss! Are you all ready to order?" it said.

A little irritated, Neipas signaled the waiter away with a vague "we need a bit more time," to which the waiter said "no problem, take your time" as he drew back imperceptibly into the surrounding hubbub. That Neipas had been there for too long without dispensing any money was obvious even in the waiter's polite intonation; but Neipas was too spell-bound at the moment to care.

Eva bore a sympathetic smile and her eyes followed the waiter as he retreated; then they turned to the open menu booklet. "So what's good here?"

Neipas, a bit discouraged by the unseemly interruption, tried to adapt quickly to the present demands of the conversation, saying, "Hmm..." stumbling a bit, and then remembering, "I'm actually not sure! I've never eaten here before," a touch embarrassed.

Tortuous seconds of quietude followed as they inspected their menus separately. Neipas felt very awkward. His butt shifted on the chair with uncertainty as he sought a way to make himself at ease again. Whether Eva felt similarly, he couldn't guess — he tried to; but the firm expression of scrutinizing focus she wore as she studied the menu was to him undecipherable.

The brief silence was becoming hard to bear, but to his aid suddenly struck a flash of memory and he recalled what Edazima, who had been there once, recommended a few days back; all at once he shot confidently, "Oh I heard the chicken here is delicious!" — Eva received this with slow and measured nods, still directed at the menu, and gave him a raspy answer which unfurled out her lips like a purr. "Hmm chicken sounds good..." Neipas melted.

They made their respective choices (different servings of chicken) and Eva raised her finger authoritatively over the table, looking out into some inscrutable distance. Right away the waiter slid into scene, as if her lifted finger were a magnet affecting impressionable male minds. The waiter took their orders studiously, tapping and sliding away his finger upon a tablet, collected the menus from the two guests and, ably using the hand gripping the tablet to carve out a smile, was beginning to slink backward and out of sight when Eva's erected finger stopped him again — "Oh actually can we get some wine?" Certainly, miss, what kind? "What do you recommend?" A recommendation was made and taken, and the waiter vanished into the dim ember. As the waiter's tall presence over the table dissipated it left between

163

them a sort of vacuum, an ambiguous silence echoing in their reluctant smiles. Shyly they curved their lips and stared at one another. There seemed to be an interior effort to grasp at the thread of conversation, which had been lost somewhere between the ambient noise and the candlelit shade; they didn't know what to say, and in the interim the indecision made them awkward. There were a few false starts, with heavy pauses in between.

"So —" "Some water?" asked Neipas just to say something, pointing to the bottle-full between them — but just at that moment the inopportune waiter materialized again at their side, carrying wine; in a bottle, to Neipas' consternation. He placed down the tall glasses and poured the glimmering red liquid. Eva snapped a picture of the table before they started drinking.

Already the first sip relaxed the discomfort a little. Neipas' muscles slowly unwound and his mind gradually loosened. Seamlessly they transitioned into a better flow of conversation, riding out the beverage's coziness. One line led to another, and as they progressed down the bottle they became more at ease with each other. Topics varied and things were a little random at first; eventually, Neipas couldn't tell how, he ended up asking her about her job:

"So — make-up artist, huh. Have you been doing it for a while?"

Eva nodded jubilantly. "Yep! Been doing it since I was little but really got more serious in college."

"Ah yeah? And where did you go to college?"

"At the Ivory Towers, on the other side of town."

"Oh no way — I went there too."

"No way! What year?" asked Eva — the conversation picked up from there and looped into a few more circles as they found out their years at the Ivory Towers intersected, and marveled at how they never met each other. When the dialogue curved back round to her job, Neipas asked:

"So how is it?"

"Oh I love it. It's just like... like being an artist, really. You work with paints, you make up looks... I guess it's just like any other, like anything, you know. You have your tools for your job..." she began, keeping on, and her speech evolved into an exultation of her craft. She described various techniques and transformations as she sipped down the rim of the glass, increasingly excited. Neipas listened attentively, transfixed. He observed the sway of amber light in her eyes, which shone dazzling and mysterious, the silky motion of her thin beak, finely sculpted, lean and smooth.

"You can really do anything," she went. "It's nice you know, because you can become whoever you want."

"With makeup?" asked Neipas, playful.

"Totally. The face is the first thing someone sees. It's the first impression so it's the most important."

"I don't know about that."

She laughed. "Oh yeah? And you're meeting me here why, because of my personality?"

"That's different — " Neipas shook his head, his laughter choking on flowing wine. Then, chuckling freely, he said, "we texted each other for a while first."

"But would you have texted me at all if I didn't look good in photos?"

"Of course I would."

"Huh-huh!" she deliciously threw her napkin at Neipas' mask. "Totally would... So yeah. First impressions are everything. Like, even for you males! Even you use makeup, you know."

"Not me!"

"Sure you do. Everyone's making up their faces all the time."

Neipas nodded pensively, the remark sinking into his profundities along with the intellectual wine. Just then the waiter materialized again, out of the gentle fire of candles, carrying a smoking plate on each arm. The fellow placed each in front of each, and, amicably slapping Neipas' back (the liquor seemed to tilt inside his head as he pitched forward) the waiter said excitedly, "Here you go! Enjoy!" and disappeared into the amber fog and the buzz. Before Neipas was the chicken — and suddenly he halted. The twitching in his muscles started up again. A nervous quivering trembled in his brain. It was strange, but he hadn't made the connection before that moment that he was about to eat a chicken, and that chicken was that animal he had been employed to slaughter for the past few nights. The words he had picked from the menu had been but abstraction, but now there was a sense of recognition — though the animal came in bits, chopped up, cooked, mixed in with pasta and vegetables, unrecognizable. The thought struck him that, once, those bits had been part of a body, and the body had contained a life; and perhaps that life and body had been pierced by his own gory hand.

But this, too, was abstraction, a vague bother, detached remorse; and he indulged in it but for an instant. The meat on his plate was obviously not an animal. The wine, the hubbub, the light of candles, the food's aroma, Eva's voice as she took a photo of the plate, drew him out into the present; and the first bite made him forget it completely.

"Delicious."

"Hm-hm! Yummy!"

They sprinkled and gushed different sauces and spices, and took their forks to their beaks with exceeding elegance of manner, waiting to speak if they chewed, guarding their ravaging mouths with their fingers as they spoke, following along the rhythm of the interaction, the pace of the evaluation, the synchronized dance of ages between potential lovers, and they did it very naturally, excellently. Each basked in the pleasure of the other's company and Neipas was overjoyed to find himself so comfortable in her presence. Eva looked happy as well, moving and speaking at leisure, with all the ease in the world flowing out her gesturing fingers and expressive beak. Neipas fell immediately over heels for her, and her glare upon his grew intensely curious, intimate, interested. Meanwhile she did most of the talking, and Neipas kept listening in rapture, simply nodding at intervals, sounding occasional grunts of encouragement. When, by and by, in the progression of the meal, he would pull his chin out of his knuckles he sensed they had made dents in his jaw, pushing his mouth up into a strange smile shaped like a held-up droop, and would realize he wasn't chewing properly. Eva spoke slowly, with delight, pleased at Neipas' general interest. She seemed to be speaking slower as time went, more pensively, gradually declining into a string of slur and laughter along with the wine's descent down the second bottle.

"Hahaha! Man, I gotta slow down..."

"It's all good," Neipas laughed too, all chummy.

She sighed pleasantly, weighed down in a lull by the food and wine. They had been drawing toward each other in tighter intimacy, and as if in culmination she leaned in further, beautifully, growing glowingly in Neipas' starry eyes, and smiled a smile sincere, confessing; saying: "It's a little crazy, but... You know what I wanted to be, growing up?"

"What's that?"

"An actress. Like, a movie actress. One of those actresses that are also fashion models, you know."

"That's not crazy at all," Neipas had the insight to say, smiling.

Eva laughed. "You don't think so?"

"I mean, why not?"

"I dunno! I just don't think I'm pretty enough," she receded a little, shyly and adorably, her locks of curly hair draping part of her face in the motion.

"Oh, what! I think you're really pretty," he said, and then softer, "I think you're gorgeous." — saying it with just the right softness, with the right tone, at the right tempo, and as Eva smiled and hid behind her curls with all the timidity in the world he sensed with boundless satisfaction that he was at the top of his game.

"Aww thanks!" Eva laughed, "I don't think so," she repeated, not very convincingly now.

"You are," Neipas drew a tender smile into his lips.

"But, why an actress?" he asked a second after.

"I dunno," Eva replied, shrugging. She was toying with the meat bits on her plate with her fork. "To be admired, I guess. To be liked."

"So you mean a famous actress."

"Of course."

Neipas nodded with an understanding smile. "I see."

"Isn't that what everyone wants?"

"To be famous, you mean?"

"To be liked, admired — famous, yeah, maybe. You know. Rich, too. That'd definitely be nice. Have whatever you want, live easy."

"I guess..."

Eva sighed. "Yeah, like — " and Neipas nodded melancholically, sensing a distant sorrow sprout in his distant innermost. "I guess... Yeah, it'd be nice to be rich," Neipas admitted.

At this point in the evening the chicken had satiated their respective appetites to the full. Neipas' plate was swept clean, whereas Eva's had still some scraps pushed politely to one side. Presently the waiter stole back into their presence, lifting all silverware off the table with ingenious finesse; his large grin wondered whether they wouldn't like some dessert, and Neipas, bearing a nearly equally large grin, said "sure, we can look at the dessert menu."

The dessert menu hovered over in triple-quick time. Eva and Neipas studied it; now mutually grown in confidence and insobriety, they blathered a few jokes as they went about it. Eva decided some cake composed of eggs with whip cream topping and a pinch of rum would be good to try; Neipas, with his mind's eye peeking furtively toward an imagined, depthless hole in his wallet, and knowing he would offer to pay for the whole thing, gladly accepted her suggestion to share the dessert. The dessert came transported upon the waiter's lifted palm, approaching the smiling couple with a weightless step. When he reached their table he dropped the platter with a light and quick gesture and shouted "Voila!" at the top of his lungs, which made Eva ecstatic and made her guffaw, caw, and clap. Neipas laughed also, though suspicious of the waiter's conduct. Eva took a picture and the next moment they were digging their spoons into the creamy, spongy fabric of the cake, approaching it from opposite sides in picturesque fashion. The whip cream seemed to melt the cake soft in Neipas' tongue and the whole sweet taste of it melded into his pleasantly dizzy head and his swaying tipsy senses, as if his whole body were absorbing the thing. Neipas felt himself giggle at this point, but wasn't sure if his face had giggled along or no.

"Good! Isn't it?" he heard Eva say.

"Delicious!" he replied.

Time skipped a full few minutes and all of a sudden the waiter was by them yelling "Thank you so much!" Neipas noticed, as if from far away, that the grin upon his mask extended upward to the very edges of his forehead. Before Neipas was the bill, appearing in his sight surrounded by a circle of blurry indistinctness. His hand was waving Eva away. His voice was saying "Seriously, no no, don't worry about it," and his hand was pulling his wallet out of his constricted pocket with some difficulty. It was eventually pulled out — or rather, it flew out, the final shove being so strong it sent his elbow propelling toward the ceiling — and a credit card was slammed atop the middle of the table. Neipas thought he heard Eva say "Aww thanks so much!" and immediately a vague presence approached the side of his head, disappeared, and returned with a bellow that echoed in his head as something like "Thank you! You love birds! And have a very pleasant evening!" His head proceeded to lift itself away from his legs and floated onward through the blurry wet lights and above the sitting disarray of other heads scattered across the restaurant, all of which looked at them with approving nods as they moved toward the exit. In front of him was Eva's naked back, enormous and defined in all its sensuality.

Neipas' general awareness bloomed back as the cooler air of the outdoors found him. By him was Eva; her voice resounding unfiltered, of a sudden:

"Should we call a cab? We're going in the same direction, aren't we? Maybe we can ride together."

Eva merely pointed. Neipas' bus stop and his far-off neighborhood were all the opposite way.

"Sure. That's a good idea," Neipas said.

Eva leaned on his arm, stumbling on her high heels. She put her mask to her *I* and began fingering at it. In a moment there was a car approaching the curb by them. "Eva?"

"That's me!" she said as they hunched in.

The space was small and his arm leaned against hers, into hers. His hands were tucked in his lap. The warmth of her skin rubbed onto his own made his heart pulse nervously. The vehicle rolled imperceptibly under a blur of city lights, and Eva was silent, looking out her window. Neipas looked away. No word came out of him, he couldn't formulate anything concise amid his embattled senses, struggling as they were to return to lucidity. He didn't know what to make of their silence and didn't know what to say; the expectation he felt over the imminent conclusion of the evening clogged every possibility of coherent speech. So he kept to himself, ruminating tensely in his nook against the warm skin he came to so covet, the deep respiration of the breast he so desired. A warm bulge grew in his trousers' crotch, making him tingle all over; he exerted intensely to collect his scattered focus and conceal the thing as discreetly as he could; the result was he rubbed his legs against each other awkwardly (and, in his alarmed perception, very noticeably). For the remainder of the trip he tucked himself in the most torturing of discomforts, trying to solve the problem at hand. Neipas realized in his predicament how drunk he really had been. And in the resulting, whirling confusion of his thoughts he mulled, once more, sensing that strange twitching of muscle, over his debt, over his work, over the numbers. The price of the dinner popped in his mind vividly for the first time.

The cab stopped. "Here we are!" Eva said bubbly. Neipas wondered whether he had imagined it, but the trip felt really short. He was so out of sorts at this that he didn't react, and Eva paid for the ride in the interim of his indecision, which made him feel somewhat ashamed.

Eva opened the door to her neighborhood; then, looking straight into Neipas' eyes, she said: "Do you want to walk me out?"

Neipas, out of wits, found no other reaction in him than a nod, the dazed agitation behind which he tried to conceal by carving up into his face a badly drawn expression of nonchalance. They got out into the quiet neighborhood. They had indeed moved only a few blocks northward, down beneath the bluffs and a little inland into the small basin, a few blocks from the sea. Nearby the river flowed into it, passing through the romantic canals of a well-known, artsy neighborhood. Eva lived in one of the houses in that remote street made of houses and lawns, affluent and quiet in its sweet languor. "It's my parents'," she would say in a moment, "they're away most of the year." Neipas walked her toward the brink of the house; they paced alongside one another without speaking. They paced in a magical darkness toward the lamppost in front, spilling circle light onto the curb by her lawn. For Neipas, this light seemed to possess an aura, to hold the innermost significance, the very meaning of the evening. To go beyond it was to succeed. Though — as they entered the teasing patch of glow spread across the floor — Neipas reflected that perhaps it wouldn't be so bad, at least it wouldn't be a complete failure either, if he didn't go beyond it, into her house; for at least he had gotten this far, at least he had walked her home. He had been observing his feet moving one after the other, and drooped into a philosophical mood, wondering whether it was cowardice or respect for Eva which made him think this. But, save for some fleeting thoughts, he didn't reflect much at all and his mind was just a jumble of nervous slumber altogether. He was tired, and flinched a little when the light entered his eyes. He turned his lethargic visage only slightly to admire the splendor of Eva's advance in the glow, her shimmering walk now stopping.

They were there. Eva turned her body to his and he to hers. Her lips curved into a gentle smile — suggestive. Neipas looked at her, his voice buoying in his throat in mild agitation, waiting to jump out and utter something, anything.

How things developed in the next moment Neipas couldn't clearly discern, but he sensed they had locked their glares in each other's eyes and plunged their sights deep into one another; she must've moved a step closer to him for suddenly her breasts were pushing softly against his own chest; a click of high-heel sounded; and their beaks met and dissolved into the other and through them their lips kissed, deliriously, savage — Neipas focused all his powers of attention into what he was engaged in, moving his hand with the deliberation of a drunk; very concentrated he pulled her gently toward him and set his mind wholly upon the precise motion of his tongue and the sway of his mouth round hers. He exerted himself in the effort; and when they parted, he was filled with a glorious sense of liberation and utter victory upon looking at her and seeing in her eyes that she had liked it, too.

She parted seductive hands slowly from his chest. "Well..." he began indecisively; he barely knew what he said. "We should do this again sometime."

A period of ambiguity ensued — after which they hugged. But Neipas flinched then as he noticed someone standing still at the curb a few steps away.

"What is it?"

"Who's that guy staring at us?" said Neipas, staring alarmingly at the presence under the next streetlight. And at once he realized, frightful, that it was the Debt Collector.

Eva looked back. "Oh that's just the neighbor."

The street deepened obscurely before them, pillared with palm trees on both sides of the road. From every lawn these palms sprung, except on the yard across, which stood out (very saliently now as Neipas squinted at it) by its corpulent fig tree, all leaves and no fruit, which seemed to stir slightly over the windlessness as the so-called neighbor glided into the wan brightness of the lamp beside. Neipas realized that it wasn't the Collector after all; and that, whereas he had thought the fellow was standing still, he was actually moving.

He mumbled to himself that perhaps the wine was still affecting him.

"By the way, do you have a page on maskbook?"

"I do... I'm not very active in it though. It's mostly old photos..."

"We can chat there. What's your number?"

Neipas gave it hesitantly. "431999".

Then they kissed again, longer yet. Eva went on beyond the light to her door as Neipas kept his elated eyes upon her; and right before she entered the house she turned her face round and looked at him with an unmasked expression of complicity and intimacy. He kept looking, bewitched, at her entryway and the lingering image of her smile for a few seconds afterwards.

When he walked away his heart soared into the stratosphere and his head went off to another dimension altogether. He hadn't crossed the light, but it didn't matter to him. Pacing furiously back across the neighborhood with the full excitement of youth in his thumping breast, he felt his steps so large and his head so tall he felt he could leap and fly over those beachfront buildings and dive into the highest heavens with her. Waiting for his bus on the main boulevard, he contemplated defiantly the Belab on the yonder distance, shining its dazzle from deep inland. With the flavor of her lips in his beak he felt like a god, able to tower over all towers. The ecstasy in him remained full until, very late at night, exhaustion gained over him and he fell asleep.

11 - House of Mnemosyne

Tobacco fumes spread vaguely throughout the constricted air; the smell packed to the extreme inside the closet's compactness. Neipas tried to keep his breathing shallow, but the smoke was too thick and he inadvertently drew in a good whiff of it, breaking out into a fit of profuse coughing.

"Do you really have to smoke that here?" he strained out, breathlessly.

"I really do," Edazima replied with complete nonchalance. She took another deep drag, fully immersing herself in the pleasing lassitude of the act, and breathed out the smoke with a satisfied sigh and closed eyes.

They spoke in darkness. Only the red tip of her cigarette breached it, unveiling her mask's thin snout in the firelight for a moment. Their invisibility and the narrowness of the space drew them together in intimacy, so that the conversation was made in murmurs, amid muffled glass clinking from the kitchen — dormant sounds of a work-day's end.

Edazima's voice emanated from the soft gloom in a discreet volume, yet with the same firmness that was so characteristic of her. "But yeah, don't worry about her," she said, for they had been talking about Eva. A few days had passed since the date and communication had been slow. "She'll text you back."

Neipas slipped back into the *I*, which glowed away the darkness. "It's been two days," he said, looking at the last message he sent.

"You guys are too eager. Relax. And get that thing off my face man, I wanna rest my eyes."

Neipas sighed short, and the darkness closed upon them once more. A pause ensued, the kitchen's glass and steel whispering themselves more vividly into the silence. Edazima inhaled another waft of tobacco; a small square of fire kindled out of nothing; the end of her snout cast a glow which molded the shadows into contours of brooms, mops, buckets, detergents all arranged messily about.

"Maybe she lost interest," Neipas mumbled.

"Maybe you're reading too much into it. Relax. She'll text you back, I promise."

"I dunno... Women are so unpredictable! Can't tell what's what with you half the time."

Edazima snickered. "*We* are unpredictable? Ah!"

She dragged in long, lighting up the place. "I didn't mean it like that," Neipas mumbled, chuckling inside his shirt, bracing himself with his nose dug in.

Edazima blew a fat puff onto his face. Shaking her head, she then commented, "Your gender is hopeless. Thank god I gave up on men!... Never going back, that's for sure..."

Another quietude in the blur of fire and dark. Neipas, relaxing into nebulous thoughts, took in a deep swath of air in preparation for another sigh — the tobacco rushed into his nostrils and came bursting out in coughs. "Mary!" he gasped.

Edazima waited calmly for these convulsions to settle off, then said, "And how's the nightshift working out for you?"

Neipas wavered a little. He didn't want to complain, nor did he have the fortitude to lie about it. So he said, in a venting, shrugging tone, "Bit of a nightmare."

A gap formed in the wake of these words, which was filled slowly by Edazima's profound solidarity, palpable even in the quiet gloom. Questioning him affectionately, she got him to say that they had put him down the food-line, in the slaughterhouse, and he had been doing no waitressing at all. How come, doing what? Stabbing live chicken; apparently the slicing machine is broken. Over Neipas' objections and pleas not to worry, she committed herself to speak to the nightshift supervisors.

"I looked at your hours. You're pushing yourself too hard," she said at once firmly and delicately. Neipas was then in the midst of an eruption of coughing, "By Mary, I need to get out of here," he forced out.

Edazima waited for him. "Are you that strapped for money? Let me help you out, I can lend you some. Not much but —"

"No no no —" Neipas waved her away invisibly, his throat straining to voice out the objection. "Don't worry about it, seriously. Just trying to make some extra."

As his throat was letting up, Neipas asked — still among dying coughs, and breathless; "How's the kid?"

"He's doing good. Ok, you know. I don't think he's liking school all that much."

"How's that?"

Edazima took in a whiz and blew it out rapidly. "You know how kids are. It's hard for him to adapt, I guess. I must've hated school at his age, too."

"You turned out to be a very fine student, though," Neipas said, sincerely.

"Right..." Edazima snickered. "Didn't do me much good, did it." Neipas didn't contest this, and waited through another pull of tobacco for her to continue.

"I'm worried, though. I don't know if I like *his* school. They hook them up to those machines there, now. He's in the *I* all the time. I mean, he *has* to, to do homework, apparently. I don't know if I like that. He's just too young, you know what I mean?"

"Did it get him hooked to the thread?"

"Yeah. I mean, I have to take the damn thing off his hands, otherwise he's in it all day. But then he yells and says he's doing homework, so what can I do," she murmured raspedly; her voice was made rough by tobacco and evident exasperation. Neipas threw in a vague suggestion or two — more to signal his concern and support than anything — and the conversation died off in puffs of cigarette haze. They lingered relaxedly in the silence — fondled only by the far-off noise of kitchen activity — until steps were heard near and the door opened.

Magpie entered with the light. "Smells like shit in here."

"Can you close the door please?" said Edazima, wincing.

"Not with this smell I won't."

"Fine." Edazima inhaled her cigarette — which was nearly burning upon her fingers now — one last time, and tossed it into an ash-filled bucket by her feet.

"That's bad for you," Magpie said.

"Well, I'm stressed out."

"Why's that?"

"Oh, you know," Edazima voiced into the closet's general comprehension. "How you doing, interview went well?"

"They hired me."

"Oh shit!" burst Edazima happily, smiling widely as she embraced Magpie. "How do you feel?"

"Happy to get outta this hole for now."

"I bet you're miserable 'cause you're leaving me."

Magpie laughed, lovingly sarcastic ("Uh-huh"). Her height towered over Edazima's, a very edifice of dignified beauty and unfiltered charm. She wore her lustrous black feathers, wavy locks cascading loose beside piercing brown eyes. Though she was close to Edazima, she wasn't to Neipas; and she made him a bit shy, nervous before her gorgeous appearance and imposing presence. All who beheld Magpie, craved and feared her.

"Congrats," he ended up saying, clumsily. "Is it a new job?"

"Thank you — Yeah, for a catering company. I'm gonna be doing what I do here basically, but for better money."

There was to Magpie's manner a certain mysteriousness, her self-possessed demeanor overlaid with something of a strain, her speech, her smile, always somehow on the cusp of breathlessness; things which barely anyone noticed, for she was so attractive a woman that her physical splendor concealed in its dazzle all other attributes, the natural security of her conduct obfuscating all her frailties.

"She's gonna be feeding rich folk," Edazima interjected.

"All gold and mansions from now on," Magpie quipped.

"We gotta celebrate this! I'll ask Janu to cook something."

"He a good cook? I dunno him that well. I thought he washed dishes."

"Trust me, he's a cook. And he's the best."

Magpie laughed. "All right, all right, I'll take it... What are you doing here anyway?"

"Just chatting," Edazima replied. "Guess what? Neipas here is in love."

"Oh yeah?" Magpie smiled, turning her eyes to him. "Show me a pic."

"You know what, you should mail her flowers," Edazima put in. "Ask Magpie, she knows everything about flowers."

"I don't even know her address."

"Oh? Didn't you *almost* enter her place? Stud!" jested Edazima, hovering thumb and index near each other.

"I couldn't find it again if I tried," Neipas shrugged — somewhat embarrassed — handing his *I* over.

"She's pretty," Magpie commented, holding its light up to her own eyes. "Just get her roses, they're always in season — she'll like it. Every girl likes flowers." She concluded with a shrug expressing the obviousness of her claim — and Neipas looked at Edazima, who also shrugged:

"I dunno if *every* girl likes flowers — but yeah I like flowers."

Neipas went through the days sulking in a lover's agony. A gnawing sensation of regret haunted his nerves and leadened his breath whenever it materialized into thought. Every hour of Eva's silence bit into his heart a deeper furrow, and he fell into the habit of combing over everything about the date in his memory, overanalyzing every second of it in search of flaws, of things he might have said that she hadn't liked, of gestures he might have made which she might have disapproved. He replayed every twitch. Even the kiss' every turn; perhaps he had been wrong in his perception and she had hated it. He rued the moment he gave her the number of his maskbook page; for in those days, the book of masks was considered the truthful album of one's life, a public diary of one's thoughts, a catalogue of one's qualities, reflecting one's worth. Neipas used his page in it as neither an album nor a diary, nor even a catalogue. Perhaps she had gone over it and found what she saw underwhelming. A sense of urgency arose in him — he had to improve it. More and better photos of himself, he thought, should do it. But Neipas was uncomfortable before the lens, and his reflection in the picture didn't mirror his own image of self; the photos could not replicate whom he saw in the looking glass. He considered exercising to improve his look — shirtless torsos under the mask made popular photos — but he hadn't time nor money for the gym. He thought about eating healthier, force himself to get off his diet of quick sugar, gobbled on the run. One morning — one of the few in that period, in which he had woken in his own bed — he remembered the eggs he had bought that day he went to the zoo. They were still uncooked in the back of his fridge. He opened it, with a determination to fry them in the pan long neglected. But as soon as he did a terribly foul odor ensued from among the plastic burger wraps; Neipas still, hesitantly, took one of the shells out of the carton, already greenish, and cracked it over the pan where it spread gooey, milky, moribund with a stronger release of that noxious smell. The roommate, unhelpfully, told him from his den in the couch's depths that the eggs might be rotten — all of which immediately cast a damp on his whole intent.

(He rushed out of his apartment, back to the Belab's underground).

This obsession with Eva, however, had the positive effect of getting his mind off work, off his debts — while his body applied itself with abandon, filling its time with the former to erase from its future the latter. Though he still felt the Debt Collector's ever lurking stare, it became a blur with the hours, growing distant in the flurry of drudgery as it collected nights without sleep, as he wondered in an adolescent passion why Eva would not return his messages, chastening himself for not entering her house. The fire of sexual frustration, which irritated his nerves in the exertion of their task, eventually ashened before the sanguinary character of his job and a fatigue that made him listless. His anticipation for Eva, though frustrated, was the anticipation for life, a happy prospect; and in her silence it frizzled off into a kind of depression, out of which he saw nothing but the bleakness wherein he floundered. He simply worked constantly. Toil remained the essential fabric composing the winding threads of his life. Time progressed through them, mindlessly, mechanically. Sun and moon circled about him repeatedly without ever glimpsing his gaze; for in the frenzy of continuous labor, gearing from dayshift to nightshift, he would spend days within the titan glass box without leaving, sleeping and awakening in the closet-beds of the pantry and other corners, existing in a completely instinctual unconsciousness of being. He sunk into profound unfeeling for long stretches, from which he was buoyed dizzy by chronic pains that eventually rose to plague him. Entire nights on the grind, plunging a knife through the ducts of defenseless necks, as air flowed still within them; struggling against exhaustion among a boiling mayhem of chains, saws and blood dust; hours upon hours forcing the same motion made his fingers numb and hand swollen, his wrist's muscles locking in throbs of pain. He was able to power through the sores but lived in fear of permanent damage, of losing something irrecoverable. He witnessed through his breathless, drunken perception of things the maimed nightshift workers, falling apart by bits in their struggle. Mostly mute immigrants these were, refugees who had escaped destitution or violence... Every hour bearing duress in there, toiling ceaseless under the threat of expulsion to the hells they had fled. When they removed their work masks at dawn, Neipas beheld on them the vacant, humble faces of migratory pigeons, with feathers flayed by wind and weather, by rain and claw... Combat veterans and former convicts too, toiled alongside them; all dredged out of the margins, from which no one else would save them; all fighting dead bodies to survive. All shaped out of mud.

Sometimes in their midst, in the confusion of the industrial scape, Neipas would spot the midget, standing still. And he would wonder whether the others saw this midget too; but he didn't know how to talk to them, or if he did, he feared it. He feared himself. Paradoxically, the small hours between shifts were often the scariest; paradoxically, he often could not sleep, and sensed in his thoughtless tormented mind that he might be going insane, that he was having visions, that he was sick. A great dread of disease haunted him in the dark. Occasionally, he noticed clusters of lice clinging to the chicken's skin as it hovered by on the chain; they wiggled disgustingly about the head and under his pinching fingers. And he felt lice entering his sleep, teeming at the root of his feathers, leaching through the wax into the hollow burrows of his interior, nibbling his brain. Across his closed eyes scurried the insects he often saw scurry in the shed under the pit of his station...

*

In time, however, new hopes flowered in his twitching gloom of a life, faint as they were.

Neipas was taken out of the kill floor. Because the slaughtering machine wasn't yet fixed, he thought that Edazima had some influence in the change, though she wouldn't admit to it. Perhaps he was merely bad at the job, though he suspected with a dull, sinking kind of horror, that the act of killing the animal was merely symbolic, or an institutionalized mercy since, if the neck wasn't pierced and the chicken killed at his station, it would be boiled alive in the steaming vats further up along the chain, into which it would be submerged so that the feathers would more easily fall off, and die anyway... But what use had they for symbolisms or magnanimities? reflected Neipas in the unconsciousness of feverish semi-slumber, under the dark corners of the stuffy pantry.

His night schedule was henceforth divided in two. In the latter part, he would be picking up orders and taking them around the tower, just as he did during the day. He wasn't completely removed from the meat factory, however — so that the improvement in his fortunes was only partial at first. The first half of the night would be dedicated to it. He would work at another station, at the very end of the line, as a packer: lifting, weighing, and sorting the yield of that farmed tide, that chemical river of stentorian steel, from which flesh was fished; already disassembled and plastic-shrouded by the time his plastic hands took hold of it. One by one the pieces of meat came to him, of different sizes and various weights; through the unblinking pace of industry they rushed — and Neipas was responsible for hauling them up, dropping them on the scales, noting the final number, and tossing them inside corresponding boxes in turn. Piles of such boxes were erected behind the horned workers, and were then scattered by a myriad fingers and hands, of metal and flesh both, throughout sprawling tunnels and rolling stairways, past various curtains, into elevators, down corridors, to be distributed across the cold storages of the various food joints and restaurants inside the Belab, to repose in the frost, and wait for the fire — or they might be taken beyond to vast underground depots, into deep refrigerated trucks, and finally dispatched over the highways, and to the world at large, to furnish the appetites of the numberless supermarkets and businesses and households of civilization. Kur was but one hole among thousands in that titanic structure; various paths departed from the rust foyer where the two oxen in jumpsuits waited at the beginning of each shift, and there were many such foyers, and many such oxen, surrounding the abattoir.

Neipas, ignorant of all of this, unseeing and insensible, spent half the night groping flesh through plastic, soft and artificial; half the night suspended between the weight of his horns and his burden, hauling carcasses, holding masks; half the night harvesting meat. It was taxing upon his arms, his back, his neck, his nerves. Head and knees all pushed toward the floor. His nose was ticklish, his throat parched. He still drank no coffee, and very little water for fear of having to pee during his shift. It was difficult; it was, at any rate, better than the kill floor, and he tried to allay his spirit by telling himself he couldn't complain.

There was, alas, no helping the fearful glances he still gave toward the back of the pantry, when he leaned against the shelves of foodstuffs after a long day's work, before the nightshift began. His body tilted, he was sensible, yet it felt almost immaterial, the substance of reality vanished, he leaned against shadows. A dot of red firelight, a glow of paper and fingers, hovered by — sometimes Edazima's voice gruffed something. But though he knew she was there and that she existed, doubts of a strange kind entered his thoughts, and his spirit, crouching into the oblivion of the invisible ceiling, wondered whether her existence could be sustained beyond the illusion of his own senses. He could not think. Thoughts existed in his mind, but he could not possibly think them, for, since his body could not rest, his mind slept in its stead; and all his waking thoughts were but sleeping dreams, thoughts sleeping a dream of some afterlife, through which reality was slowly and imperceptibly draining out of existence. Ghosts ruffled the air yonder upon the frigid prospect, stirring between the half-curtained mists of industrialized winters; and Neipas, perhaps himself a phantom, trod among them, and saw how those insubstantialities unpacked the boxes he himself had sealed. Stacked against coves and walls of ice, mounds of refrigerated flesh sighed vapors and whispered chill into his passing bones, meshed into the lattice of his shivering soul, became his very breath. There was frozen, dormant meat in his veins, the gore of beasts congealed in his heart. The walls echoed his heartbeat, fluttering the breast which he felt hollow. Throes of muscle-memory convulsed in the frigid, feverish darkness palling his sweating and quivering body. In slumber and in dreams, both of which soaked his waking life, he often still thought he was stabbing necks. Neipas felt blood streaming down his legs as they sunk into the crimson pit (he refused Edazima's water and shied away from her motherly glare); beneath him, the hauler unloaded the animals with his maimed, hook-like hand, amid a tumult of plumage in a red, hot, scary trench. Above him, the chickens lifted, the chickens spun, into a heaven white, freezing, numb. The midget still stared up among the hideous whirl of things. Maladjusted to the body, his soul turned nauseously, out of sync, roiling upon the shoddy mattress and amid the roiling machine, in a continuous dream of blood, excretions and bad smells, and intangible crowds all about him.

Heading to the slaughterhouse, through the pantry he trudged, through the pantry he floated. What was he moiling for again? his spirit mumbled faraway, crowded among the horned spirits laboring around it. He knew no longer. He knew only the work; Eva ebbing; his debts.

The midget stared up from the near distance still. Groaning and puffing with effort, clenching his teeth against breakdown, lost in the onerous swirl of bloodied plastics, Neipas saw that midget, standing at a distance, just upon the edges of discernibility, and looking at him in such an occult fashion that Neipas could swear the cryptic being, clad in robes and the mask of Melpomene, intended for him to follow; like the midget wanted to tell him something. Once, during a rare break — the whole chain had stopped for some reason or other, as would sometimes happen — someone, a skeleton of an ox, tall and gaunt, took him all the way down to the kill floor where the hogs were spiked. Neipas didn't know why, he even doubted he knew the fellow, everybody looked so alike in the dinned haziness of things; now the thin-snouted ox guided him through a weird silence, though other lines kept on working (everyone he passed by looked somewhat disoriented as they descended the steep winding path; the ones who grasped the situation the quickest fell into an immediate doze, others took the opportunity to sip booze; many sought frantically for a bathroom before the supervisors stopped them), and spoke some words Neipas did not understand — in a familiar manner suggesting they were indeed acquainted. They walked past mounds of pelts in an area he had never been in before. And they traversed the hiss of the vats; they alighted upon a little arena at the bottom of the well. There was quite a lot of scrambling about, pouring forth such bellows of squealing that Neipas halted in his step. Two or three pigs fumbled down there maniacally — Neipas immediately spotted the one, from beneath whose jowl spurts of blood shot onto the iron slatted floor. These were the animals that were holding up the line; somehow or other they had escaped the chutes all together; perhaps they hadn't been well stunned. Over them stood the shackler, long knife in one hand, a pipe raised by the other. He wore the mask of the deranged, raging bull — the face of a monster, seething, giggling, laughing (as he chased the pigs) with guffaws so tremendous they nearly sounded like sobs. Behind him, up on a kind of parapet, the foreman yelled and frothed with exceeding rage, hurled salivating menaces, threw his whole body over the rail in fury. The shackler below plunged the lead pipe straight atop the pig's head — whose frontal legs first staggered and hind slid confusedly, before the whole body collapsed — to the drunken spectators' general depravity of merriment. Neipas looked back. Nearby he saw pigs' bodies hung, lustrous and bare, and it somehow reminded him so much of human skin that he vomited — into his feedbag (the smell was so overwhelming he nearly fainted; he forgot he had the feedbag on, and he snorted the acids back in; he felt arms pulling him up) while the others behind him laughed rambunctiously. And in the blurriness of his gaze, there standing in the pits with the twitching piglets, he saw again the midget, looking straight at him, straight at him, calling voicelessly...

All were called back to their posts right away; these visions were so daunting that he was happy to return to his abstracted plastic-bound meat, which looked nothing like living things by the time they reached him. Moment by moment the meat flowed into the shore of his hands from the flaming distances. Moment by moment the meats kept coming, of many shapes, of diverse species, into his station; through the ravenous torrent of production they stormed — moment by moment in the boxes they were packed. And one by one they were taken by the sturdy arms of the machines and their ghosts, out of the meat factory, into the depots, and through the endless gates and tunnels and curtains into the various refrigerators, pantries, and kitchens of the underground and above, all across the land, onto the tables of regular folk; an unending supply of meat, spirited into being by a process as hidden from regular consciousness as death is to regular life. And Neipas, a regular node in the overall procedure, meanwhile no longer knew night from day, and things became a blur of whirring elevators, cold fogs, sawing machines, drums, flames in the mist, vague bodies. He was plagued by the unbearable and unrelenting noises of the rhythmic factory; rattling chains, rolling conveyors, the rustle of synthetics, the squishiness of flesh.

And so time revolved.

*

...he was too tired, on the verge of overstrain. It did not matter. He was still behind on bills; he couldn't stop.

Work at the factory in the first part of the nightshift would almost lead him to the edge of madness. The second part of the shift, serving orders up and down the tower, was easier. Though the Belab never slept, it ate much less during the night, and in these hours he often had a chance to take a break. Unlike the dayshift, in which he made money by order, here he made money by the virtue of being at the ready; and could at least doze off every now and then, deriving as much restfulness as unrest can spare, with the *I* beneath his ear to vibrate whenever an order came in.

Strangely, Orassap, the maskbook junkie, was also working the nightshift in that capacity. He made an uncanny sight in the spectral halls of the great tower — for his semblance looked nothing like its daytime version. The constantly grinning, boisterously laughing mask dissipated in the night. His eyes sagged red, still perpetually glued to the spectral glare of the *I*; his breathing was visibly slowed and his tongue combed his inner cheeks constantly as though parched from thirst. It was as though a layer of wax had dropped; and his mask thinned, something of his true face showing through.

"What are you doing here, man?" asked Neipas, aloofly, upon seeing him. They were both, then, sitting in the dimness of the kitchen, sparsely populated with but a few cooks leaning idly and quiet against the walls.

Orassap, perceiving Neipas' voice ringing on the ken of his ear, unglued his heavy stare from the *I* with some effort; and looked at him through his bloodshot, mirthless eyes.

"Oh, hey..." his voice left him as though a parcel of spirit staggering out. Accustomed to sharing every detail of his life, Orassap immediately disclosed to Neipas the tenebrous reason for being in that inhuman place, at that ungodly hour. Sighing, he told him: "It's actually pretty messed up... I was like, prescribed these anti-depressants a few years ago?... I've been taking them for like, years... It's because of this condition I have... I feel very anxious all the time, mostly... So I really like *need* them, you know... And, they just went and raised the price of the pills!...

"And, well, that's why I'm here, I need a little extra, you know... Anyway — how are you?..."

He would pause his speech to pull — very loudly — the wettest sniffs Neipas had ever heard, summoning them from the deepest strengths of his breast. Even as he finished speaking his face was already pending back downward to the hypnotizing gleam of the *I*, the glass of which seemed to draw him in whole, draining all the life-force out his gaunt heart.

"Damn man... You all right?" said Neipas — who, though moribund with exhaustion, half in swoon, found some vitality in the force of contrast between him and Orassap, who looked completely wretched; and between the lively Orassap of his memory, and the lifeless Orassap in his blurry stare.

But the nightshift held yet more bizarre wonders, some of which impressed such fright in Neipas' increasingly susceptible heart as to nearly make him faint. One deep night, he and Orassap together were summoned to serve a meal all the way up in the Bank floor. The quantities ordered resembled something of a feast. Thus they were both called upon and, roused out of their lethargy, they hauled up the heavy trays of steaming plastic in the eerily empty, huge elevator. Orassap's face appeared solely among the darkness, alit by the *I*'s gleam shooting into his veiny orbs; while Neipas, amid deep breaths of open mouth, snoozed in and out — balancing the tray in the interim with mechanical skill.

"What are you doing, man..." asked Neipas in a mumble between sleeps, noticing Orassap in the *I*.

"Oh... I'm checking app tracks my heartbeat rate," Orassap replied through a slur, his beak so close to the glass that it rubbed on it as he spoke.

They passed through many elevators. The final one opened to the dully lit, ballooning walls of the Bank's lobby, with the abandoned counter yonder before them, and the large seal, mounted on the yawning circular aquarium glass, above it. The sharp contours of the two passageways were rounded by a spectral backlight. The two Venuses were scarcely visible in the shade; though the gurgle of the founts sounded yet, as the only sound amid a very deep quietude. The fishes, the ripples of the water still swayed to its hum; and their mesmeric dance spilled in glow over the obscure lobby, resembling drunken lampposts in a city night, alighting across the floor as if through rain and upon wet asphalt. The maze of escalators was shown through.

Neipas, remembering, in the weak pulses of his memory, being there not long ago, looked up, as though by instinct; and saw above him the same glass ceiling, alit still in the same bright way, with the suited, Eagle-masked businessfolk still meeting over cigars and whiskey round the ornate table.

Neipas leered into his *I*. "Let me check the directions here..."

Behind the counter, through the aquariums, arose the cryptic maze of escalators. He had feared going in the last time he was here; but now the sight of it impressed his weary eyes to such a degree that he had to suppress, almost with physical force, a pulling urge to run back. Yet their liege waited for its feast somewhere in the depths beyond those escalators, and so he must go. They were just commencing the trek toward them when a voice in the rear saying "wait," stopped them. Neipas had forgotten the presence of the mute, hornless, coal-furred ox, who was the nightshift supervisor, and his translator the colorful heifer-head, who had accompanied them in the journey up the tower. The mute ox gesticulated through the dim lighting; and the spotted heifer's snout moved as the gesticulations stopped, producing the words, "Leave your *I*s with us for the moment, please. They will be returned to you after this assignment." Instead, he said, they should follow the directions listed on the sheets of paper which he proceeded to hand them in a little bundle.

Neipas locked his *I* and handed it over to them. Orassap, however, seemed very mired in a long, silent spell of confusion and hesitation. "But — but why?" he asked in a very dull, very sluggish tone of voice.

And here the hornless ox rigidified his features in a gloomy flash and many creases of his snout, nearing toward Orassap's lower clay mask, out of which pores strings of wax were sweated. And losing no time with translations, he spoke — to Neipas' amazement — some very slurred, dragged, masticated words: "*No Is allowed, up!*" His utterance was deep-toned, strangely accented, not fully articulated but very deliberately pronounced, with an obvious strain at coherence; and with double amazement and awe Neipas realized him deaf, and not mute as he had first supposed.

Orassap, sniffing dejectedly, handed over his *I*.

First they had to step onto escalator no. 2. Like most escalators, no. 2 was very steep. It lifted off the floor vertiginously at once and very soon the fancy reception hall looked but a faint dot in the distance; the change in air pressure could be immediately felt acting upon one's head. Gazing round, Neipas saw the immense emptiness and quietude emanating from the rolling steps sprawled across the air, leading into a multiplicity of doors of different shapes, on walls close and far in the irregular, incomprehensible structure of bending flanks and irrational angles. There were some folk still traveling those moving, diagonal corridors; and again Neipas was struck by their uncanny diversity. There were pigeons of all types here — clad in suit, shirt, denim, in near rags, tall, short, skinny, fat, female, male, in between, none, in singles, in couples, in mobs — all spanning quietly the roving distance. There were little ducks tottering up and down the steps, often by the feet of immense, giant hogs, whose tusks sometimes coiled and scratched their rotund sides.

Neipas only became aware of Orassap's uncannily speechless presence again when they were standing on a junction between four escalators, and the floor upon which they stood rotated slowly round itself, so that Neipas saw that they were still, but the background behind Orassap was moving. The poor fellow's head hung down dejectedly, in a dormant manner, though he wasn't sleeping; and he kept shaking, scratching his arms with cutting nails, scratching his eyes, starting up with hiccups (which was that sound which Neipas heard in the background of the vast quietness) and bouncing his drooping lip (which pierced under the defaced mask) repeatedly, like a fish. As Neipas was more or less thinking various thoughts, a bizarre new sensation crept up unto him. Mingling with the perpetual unease of material insecurity was a hint of intellectual abstraction, the feeling that everything he saw here — the perfect blue walls and the blue carpets, the propagation of escalators, the glass ceiling ever far — it all had a trace of fiction about it. Maybe (Neipas thought) all of it was fantasy; and in a fleeting moment of lucidity he concluded how natural it was that he would think this, for there was so much of how reality was lived in those days that bore a strong resemblance to dream.

The pathways coiled mesmerizingly, and they traversed them with a fear of getting lost. Much like the first time he came to the Bank, Neipas had the impression of sensing in the depths up there an elusive glittering, palpitating, honey-hued, in the tight horizon framed by that diagonally ascending tangle; and wondered if it could be the fabled treasure's gold, hidden there in plain sight, locked beyond a maze of impenetrable heights. His eyes blinked in flutters (two moths inside his sockets, with eyelashes for wings). Sometimes, when he saw it, or pictured it (beneath the silence, beneath all sounds over the silence) he heard some throbbing afar, very far, out in the distant core of the Belab, perhaps — as distant as his own aspirations, as far as his own self — corresponding to that aureole sight; and he contemplated it like the exit of the prison where he roamed.

Somewhere along the way Neipas realized that they had taken the wrong turn, for they found themselves just upon a tall mahogany gate bearing the sculpted inscription '*WEATHER DERIVATIVES*'. The door opened automatically before his bewildered gaze as they were carried up by the steps, and it opened with a heavy, deep creaking noise which bore a typhoon of yelling out from it.

Inside he found a rowdy scene — a room built of glossy dark wood with the decapitated heads of many animals adorning the top of its walls; and huge screens in the back, filled with numbers of many colors and satellite images: at the center of the arrangement, from the largest screen, was shown the image of the sun as an immense circle of thermonuclear fire pending in the infinite void of outer space, shining with such brightness its lava beam that Neipas and Orassap, emerging from the general dimness, had to protect their eyes, for it had been long since they had last seen the sun. Underneath these screens was amassed a group of very elegant-looking fellows with Eagle masks on their faces; they were all shouting excitedly at the screens, erupting in feral enthusiasm, shaking full of celebratory effusion. Between the wall-mounted heads jutted enormous, twisting, hollowed-out horns, called cornucopias; and out from the hollowed base ensued veritable showers of banknotes. Neipas stood there under the money rain, baffled, wallowing in a stench of perfumed cigar, wondering whether it was for this that they celebrated. He had a half-mind to turn away, but his muscles were then stunned by the vision before him and the volumes of shouting and booming laughter accompanying it. Orassap must've still been at his side, but he couldn't sense him, his hiccups remaining confined to the farthest distances of awareness. When Neipas made up his mind to just get out of there, so pressing was the discomfort that scene triggered in his breast, something very strange happened.

One of the Eagles had noticed his presence. With a pang of heart Neipas realized that one of the Eagles was looking at him, and saw that every trace in his semblance was accusatory and told Neipas he wasn't supposed to be here. Holding his stare fastened on Neipas, the Eagle lifted his finger and tapped the fellow next to him on the shoulder. In a single instant — a fraction of a second — everyone turned their heads to stare directly at the newcomer, all in unison — all of a sudden, complete quiet shut in. The money torrent halted. Neipas felt extremely visible and uncomfortable before the profusion of Eagle eyes, unblinking, their amber color gleaming wide in the crepuscular, crimson atmosphere; all at once he was overly conscious of his inadequate ox face and his 2nd-rate uniform.

The Eagle who had been tapped on the shoulder turned his body round fully to face Neipas and Orassap (everyone else remained stone still) and approached them very cautiously, as one approaches a wild beast. When the Eagle was perhaps two steps away from them he stopped and slowly raised his arm, in a gesture meant to keep them at distance, out of a curious revulsion, or maybe fear. Then he said, addressing himself to Neipas:

"Hey there, young fella... There something you'd like?"

There was something profoundly sinister in his voice that immediately inspired a fright in Neipas' breast. "Oh, um — We were actually looking for —"

"'Cause this is private property, you do know that?" the Eagle interrupted. Neipas was left without a voice to respond, so loud were the agglomeration of stares upon his face. The very heads of the animals hung wooden, totemic, macabre, gazed down censorious and lifeless.

"It's all ri'," the Eagle continued. "It's all ri'... Just make sure it don't happen agaen, all ri'? Atta boy..."

The Eagle took his gloves to his beak and drew into it a tense smile as he backed away, nodding. Neipas, paralyzed, watched as the Eagle disappeared into the multitude of unblinking amber eyes; and then abruptly turned around, taken by a surge of horror that left him breathless.

He and Orassap ran down the escalator and about the maze of suspended steps, completely lost and without direction. Orassap merely followed blindingly, blinking his eyes under his exaggeratedly curved rear. They only stopped when they passed the edge of exhaustion.

...Neipas was rambling in mad whispers. "Did you see that? The fuck was that? What was it?"

But Orassap said nothing, and kept scratching his eyes and trembling over his labored, hiccup breath.

*

They never did find the office to which the food should have been delivered. Neipas and Orassap watched as it was all angrily thrown into trash bins, as they were told the price of the meal would be discounted from their wages, in addition to hefty fees which referred to compensation for the customers' inconvenience. In the hopeless torpor in which he was folded at this point, Neipas found himself caring little; he felt but relief to have found the way out of the escalator maze at all.

As in an incantation, his mind kept muttering to his soul that it could be worse. For a little hope had flourished when he was removed from the kill floor — though the most significant prospect would appear a few nights after.

Neipas was ordered to serve at the Media Floor that night. He had been there time and again before, seeing often in that immensitude of cubicle-mazes, loose papers, long trailing frocks, blaring voices and shaking *I*s, old colleagues from his Ivory Tower days, journalists and photographers alike who aspired to impress their works in the pages of prestigious newspapers, enmesh themselves in the most powerful molders of public opinion; many of whom aspired still. In truth they all, in some way or another, aspired to be sculptors, shapers of collective minds; such was their fervent will, hidden or otherwise. Neipas, too, had considered going the news route many times, but it had been made clear to him he wouldn't make the cut — his work was simply too bizarre, his photographs too unobjective, too pretentious...

In the elevator — he waited. Orassap was not there then. He was alone. Quiet and still in the gloom, Neipas felt none of the usual, silent fidgeting and restlessness that usually surrounded him in that cavernous space. Now he could hear himself breathe. There was no flicker of the *I* in the half-light — and it was altogether strangely peaceful. Music passed through the bud. A slow tempo of string crooned in his ear. Time seemed to acquire a finer feel, as though its fabric had dissolved into spores flowing through the air, floating neither fast nor slow; hovering, simply. Neipas didn't know how many floors the elevator ascended — for there was nothing to keep mark (somewhere something malfunctioned) — nor did he know how long it took. But when the elevator stopped, he wasn't in the floor he intended to be.

Neipas hesitated, but as he saw the elevator wouldn't move anymore he stepped out, emerging into a small hall. A floor carpeted in furry scarlet, a photograph with gilded frame on each of the concave walls on the right and left, and two elevator doors on the end opposite Neipas, was all this storey had to display. Neipas was a bit puzzled at first — the influence of deep sleep had begun surreptitiously nudging him in the long elevator ride (one photo showed a tree of fire rising against an immense red sky; the other a barren plain of ice blurred by windy snows; the walls appeared to contract with a sound emanating from the quietude which was now abruptly deepened; a throb, a pulse submerged, an immense heartbeat somewhere in the depths of the tower) — and stood puzzled for a little while before pushing the squared button upon the wall at center to summon the elevator.

The door on the left opened, he stepped inside. This elevator was considerably smaller than the huge one he had left, and it was lit moodily, with a mirror on every wall. Neipas entertained himself with his reflection, mystically molding his visage as he waited and fell deeper into drowsiness (he noticed now, distantly, how he had forgotten to put on his outer mask, his ox helmet; and his pigeon visage sagged in wax, plume, and shadow toward the lower edge of the mirror, many times over).

A calm blip swelled into the silence. The elevator doors slid open, slowly, solemnly. Shaking his head violently to ward off sleep, Neipas gave a last look to the mirror(s) and shaped his mask in a rush, clearing his throat profusely. The tray quaked lightly upon his hollowed arm. His breathing had become sunken and his eyes had grown crimson; but with a surge of heart he drew a deep breath, filled his lungs with a sense of determination and vague fragrances of burnt paper and polish, spread thin the wax to conceal the fatigue consuming his real face and cover the creases under the eye, and entered through the discreet, windowless little archive. A feeble lamp illumined crammed stacks full of shelves, teeming with little drawers, some of which were open and a few of which protruded very far, brimming with innumerable papers and cassettes. As Neipas stared blankly at the masked countenances sleeping under those drawers, which hoarded article after article harking back all the way to the dawn of modernity, recording in flashes and scraps of memory the events which together weaved the threads of History — he perceived a subdued sound of moaning in some corner, a stir of metal once, twice, and again repeatedly, in even pace. Unhooking the bud off his head, Neipas stopped for a moment to try to make out what it was. This till he perceived clearly the lewd character of the wailing and panting and ruffling, which were raising in volume now — reddening in awkwardness, he bolted straight to the door ahead and walked out dizzy and brisk.

He advanced between rows of cubicles with a very straight back. His composure intact, even as sleep and the ghostly subtleness of the uncanny stole further into his mind, Neipas marched professionally as ever toward the client. The cubicles were shielded by high walls and Neipas couldn't see whether there was anyone inside them. There were whisperings here and there, and from time to time someone afar would cross quickly between rows and from one cubicle to the next. It seemed mostly empty; nonetheless the air of busy tidings, the sense of eminent deadlines, and the smell of strong coffee were evident in the moonlit space, the moonlight strange, tarnished with an unworldly tinge and filter. It was spirited through the windows afar, which uttered in also the gleam of neighboring towers, potent before the glass, rearing their luminous heads; the windows faced the very summits of these constructions which, save for the Belab, were the tallest on earth. The headquarters of major banks, main branches of insurance firms, corporate suites for tech executives — all could be spotted from those giant windows rising tall, enormous. From the walls emanated a tender mumble of string, perceived only toward the core, as if it had scattered out from the earbuds and made undisclosed, his very thoughts audible to the world round. Inner and outer melodies worked upon his dormant senses... His steps instinctively avoided the long peacock tails spread across the aisles, whose eyes were, however, closed.

Neipas turned a corner, walking round a cubicle until he reached its open side. What he saw inside the cubicle made him jolt out of the ground and he was quite forced to perform a brief balancing act so as to not let the whole tray tumble off his arms. The cubicle walls sheltered a desk, which was merely a semi-circular platform protruding off the whole span of cubicle, with a computer atop on one side, a lamp, and a heap of papers of all sorts laid on the opposite end. There were two rolling chairs nestled inside, very close to one another and filling up the remaining cubicle space. On one chair sat a Peacock dressed in suit, the shirt a little rumpled and casually unbuttoned on top, without tie. He was an Editor; and like all Editors, a parrot sat on his shoulder, eating the wax off his ear, crackling with whispers off its beak which was well tucked upon the orifice. On the chair abreast, a fellow — seemed like a journalist — who was typing furiously at the computer keyboard. His shirt was pristine, the shorter peacock tail well-tended, falling on either side elegantly, his stance immaculate as he engaged his task. But his mask was of a strange shape — like that of a funnel. The wider end covered the journalist's face, and perhaps he saw through the narrow tube of the funnel; and into each of the ears went the tubes of two other funnels, two circles expanding out at each side of the head. Into the ear-funnel the Peacock Editor whispered as the journalist kept on typing ceaselessly, just as the parrot whispered into the Editor himself. Neipas looked about him in utter bafflement and horror. He saw the interior of all the cubicles in this row now, and he saw that all the journalists in it bore the same funnel-mask, and that all these journalists wore funnels upon their ears, and that Editors sat alongside them and whispered into them in the same way that their parrots mumbled into themselves.

"John?" Neipas whimpered in, tentatively.

His former classmate John (whom Neipas guessed was the typing journalist) ignored him and kept on typing.

"I'm here with your order."

The Editor, immobile in his chair, raised only a finger and set it firmly beside the computer, then proceeded to tap that spot of the table repeatedly until Neipas, realizing with a fright what he meant, placed the steaming plate and the plastic cup there. They continued what they were doing, as Neipas stood there hesitantly. The Editor then pulled out a bill without looking at him or acknowledging him in any other way. It was a meager tip, but Neipas took it, and bowing before them, he uttered the usual rigmarole and hurried off, anxious to get out of there. He paced quickly through the row and the frenetic sound of uninterrupted typing (ceaseless tap-tap-tap on keyboards without music) which filled his ears. To deafen this noise of a thousand scurrying fingers he lifted the tune in his earbuds louder, the strings of which lashed off the windows with a tremble affecting the whole floor, and he kept onward with head downcast till he couldn't anymore. There were ashes in his mouth, dust amassing in his throat. His body stopped as though the last morsels of strength within him revolted against its motion. With his steps stopped also the string and the typings; only the pulse remained — a strange, distant throbbing. He gazed the flittering crepuscular shadows of that eerie moonshine (as the long tails of closed peacock eyes passed) and remembered the magical way his mother sprinkled herbs over the fragrant pot, and he considered visiting her soon, bring her flowers, perhaps, and a balloon. He missed her, missed her very much. His breast caved into a hopelessness, as if pushed under by the shades swelling over him as they flew by, and for a moment his sight tattered like chaffs in the wind, reality collapsed, it seemed, completely at last, and nothing existed except the strange aloof heartbeat pulsing in the distance and echoing into his own empty chest. He really wasn't feeling well; the mumblings of his invalid father trembled in the slobber of his own lip. He could scarcely go on, and so he stood, petrified, till he saw a very tall, spectacled Editor in business suit emerging from the bathroom door yonder.

Neipas recognized with trepidation his old teacher of the Ivory Tower, Professor Moldura. There were, in the back, away from the windows — toward the center of the tower — layers of encasements in veil and glass, wherein were boxed the Editors' offices. They were visible over the cubicles; Neipas hoisted himself upon his toes and watched Moldura entering his own post.

There arose suddenly a new feeling in him; it was as if he had trespassed some sort of edge and found himself staggering, about to trip. He looked on longingly as his former professor paced about his desk in the depths of that floor, behind intersecting angles of panes half-covered by curtains. Editor Moldura had always been kind to him, he remembered well; encouraging him as others were indifferent; accommodating as others scathed, as others scoffed. Neipas had long eyed that remote office as a refuge of last resort by virtue of this old association. Now, steeped in depths of despair and mired in exhaustion, he gazed that figure which was mirrored in kinder memories; and was at last moved to a determination to speak with him. It was as if he were pulled by something irresistible and painful. He had to try. Yielding himself to that resolve, strenuously overcoming his own abashment and pride, he walked through the maze of cubicles toward the glass walls deeper in, fighting the sense that he was transgressing at every step, his courage faltering at every moment. He approached that promising silhouette stirring in the twilight; dodging curtains and vitreous surfaces, he approached. Suddenly he found his hand already knocking on the door.

"Professor? Hi, it's me — Neipas," said his own voice, he assumed, as it left his beak weak, impotent.

"Oh?" began the Editor, turning. "Oh, hello, Neipas." (Hello, Nepas! — repeated the parrot on his shoulder, facing away from him.)

Neipas wavered on how to commence. He staggered frozen, immediately rooted in a painful sense of regret at having come here. With the flight of impulse he had neglected to remember that he had forgotten his work-mask, the clay ox head, and that all that separated his true face from exposure was the thin layer of pigeon wax. He glimpsed the *I* glass — and saw he was about to collapse. His semblance hadn't been molting well through those many days and nights. Teetering at the edge, Neipas found himself struggling with a pervasive numbness and suppressing surging panics.

The Editor watched expressionless as Neipas swayed to and fro. "How may I help you?" prodded he. (Help! — bellowed the parrot).

"Huuuum," Neipas began, almost jolting himself out of the mask. "Well, I'm actually looking for a change of career and, was wondering... Well basically, yes. I'm looking for a career change. I was wondering if you could help me?"

The last sentence was released in a struggle — spoken through heavy breaths, breaths that nearly sobbed — almost a whine. But the Editor seemed unfazed.

"Hm!" he piped, intrigued, as he adjusted his spectacles. "Interesting. Ok. And what kind of job are you looking for?" (Interesting! Interesting!)

"Well, actually I was wondering if, hum, if you wouldn't have a spot in your photo department?" Neipas felt himself slur a little, and rushed to correct whatever wrong impression of himself he might have provoked with a string of quick words. "I'm very versatile, and quick, and committed, and I'm experienced with photography and very passionate about it as you know. I can follow any hours, any schedule... I can be anywhere at anytime. I would be the most committed photographer you have. I — " He stopped, perceiving that he had gone too far.

His whole speech was a balancing act. Every sentence threatened to tip him over. Every word was born heavy out of his lips, jerking him toward the floor as he struggled back, to keep standing. He tried to hold firm against panic. He fought to keep standing, teetering between spilling himself before the Editor and holding himself in inside his disintegrating mask. But why didn't the Editor say anything? Neipas had been waiting for a word for a long time. At some point in the middle of this he suffered a vivid impression — impressed with a vividness so sharp it could've only been borne by reality — of being at the edge of a precipice again, and in a moment became so certain that he stood upon the platform waiting for a train back to his apartment, that he wondered which of the two realities — media floor or station platform — was imagined. Certainly the space was shrinking about him. Uneven walls or perhaps shoulders were squeezing his body; he felt crammed into a sense of vertigo and was being jostled by a growing throng toward the margin of the tracks, everyone was furious because their transport wouldn't arrive; impatient, hot, all sweated grunts, moans, shouts of exasperation (meanwhile red lights blinked in the very deep gloom of the fast-nearing tunnel). But now, after a long wait, the train's lurid glare finally neared amid thunderous screeches, shrouded in smoke, ushering forth sparks of ash that sprinkled Neipas who, constricted, scalded and swaying over the brim, about to tip over, found in him no reaction other than simply staring. "Interesting! Interesting!" the parrot still clamored, though toned down. (Almost inaudibly) Neipas groaned. The Editor mumbled something.

"Hm, ok..." A bowl of moonlit apples upon the desk. He had meanwhile sat behind it and lounged pensively on his leather chair. Neipas remained standing and curved before it, fighting his shame; he almost felt like prostrating before it, as the devout would before an altar. The Editor, in his distraction, neglected to invite him to sit down as well. But Neipas still stared, he saw that the view to the windows was unbroken from this office and that beyond the windows now pended a strange moon. It was a moon of copper, with a stain of greased black — it looked like a dime. The parrot faced it; and as it echoed the Editor's words, it spoke to it. Neipas faced it too and he ultimately realized that he spoke to the Editor's reflection in the window, and worried that this might have offended his former teacher. But he couldn't help it. He stood transfixed by the unreality of that apparition: was the moon really so colored? Perhaps it was all but an abnormally vivid dream. But no. The clock ticked resolutely — it could not be; tepid as it was, there was some sense of continuity and of a distinct fabric of the real, unraveled though it seemed.

He recalled now something he had glimpsed in his *I* in some other moment, that tonight the Earth's shadow would be cast upon it, that tonight the Earth would be aligned between it and the sun, that tonight would arise a blood moon; and he had the weird sense that no one in the entire megalopolis but he and the parrot were both awake and attent to see it.

The Editor's silvery beak had been chewing the tip of his spectacles. He said, "Have you updated your portfolio since I last saw it?"

"Yes! Of course. Absolutely, yes sir," said Neipas, nodding profusely.

"You can send it to me personally. Do you still have my contact info?" (Contact! Contact info! — shrieked the parrot.)

Neipas gasped a sigh of hope. "Absolutely, yes sir."

The Editor arose sprightly out of his springing chair. "All right, then," he said jovially, shaking Neipas' hand. "Thanks for stopping by, Nepas."

(Thanks! Thanks!) Neipas was only aware of himself nodding and mumbling "thanks so much, thank you" as he stepped out. With a lowered head and humbled posture he began moving away, eager to get out of sight as soon as possible. There was hope in his heart — and also much fear of having made himself a fool. The Editor was kind as always, but he felt the meeting had been too quick. At the same time he felt he had lingered on too long. Confusion reigned in his breast. The unearthly ambiance of the nightshift reached a dizzying pitch and Neipas was on the brink of swooning as he walked, completely disoriented, and at times sure that he was having but a freakish dream whence he ought to awake at any moment. In the elevator ride down he dozed on his feet, stirring alarmingly and with a gasp every few seconds.

Dawn had broached the sky by the time he arrived at the bottom. He had felt it through the iron shutters of the elevator, sensing in it a distant calling. Neipas knew well he couldn't take another shift. He rushed to switch his clothes and go up the elevator again to the grand lobby, whence he hastened out under the summit's refreshing waterfall into the empty square. Bloating out humidly as if through dew, were the twelve gryphons and their fountains, the tall poles and their flags, the buildings afar at the end of a vast hazy hollowness. Completely lost in feeling, Neipas didn't notice the protester with the letterless cardboard sign already sitting there, lone among the vastness of the clearing beneath the great tower. He drove his unconscious, rushing step into the protester's crossed feet and tripped on her.

"Watch it man!"

"Sorry! Sorry!" he stammered, staggering in embarrassment toward the train station.

12 - The Woman with the Wordless Sign

Shimmers spilled across the black lake. It was troubled by a chill wind, scattering Neipas' face along the ripples. Dusk gathered over the Park of Echoes, breathing a somber hue upon the silvery tusks of the Ivory Towers which sprouted from the tended grass, menacing and lifeless, flowering in the darkening air. Shadows of fish swam under the tarry field of water. They slid under Neipas' twilit reflection, in the thoughts behind his shaded mask; thoughts loaded with numbers, prospects, retrospects, all rounded by sheer numbness and disorientation. He had sent his portfolio to the Editor, and had now to wait. He didn't know if he would help him, or in what way — even a single gig, the scantest chance he could seize upon would mean everything to him, and anything, he felt, would be better than what he was doing now. Tonight he skipped the oppressions of the Belab's nightshift — he couldn't stand it anymore. The Editor had to rescue him soon. But perhaps he never would; it had been too long, perhaps. Time shrunk and widened all at once in narcotic bends. And there was Eva, too — the single breath of freshness in his life had dimmed to near silence. Time drained all hopes along. All was uncertainty; and his life seemed pending over an abysmal horizon.

Neipas waited vaguely for his face to unshatter; but the breeze moved over the dark face of the waters, unabated.

Yet the gliding air bore incomprehensible whispers. A sense of quiet magic... Neipas was drawn up and away in weightless steps. He flew under perturbed reflections — overlooking the Park from the top of the hill, he saw those blurry lights cast along the walkway shimmering to the depths beyond the windy lake surface. By his side to the east, the peaks of tenebrous mountains combusted slowly, delineated by a fire burning somewhere deep in their sleepy bosom, nearly all depleted, as though their stony immensitude were but an ember fading vast under the hearth of the sky. Before him, the megalopolis widened blotched and seemed wet, as of an Atlantis sweating with cold, feverish in its ocean of white and red and amber glows, like an impressionist dream of flames drowning out the firmament. It was anguishing. It was beautiful. His hands submerged into the blurry depths under his chin; they surfaced mystic, as if finned, as though winged, to his sight, holding up his old film camera, that abiding consoler of a lifetime — and he leaned its viewfinder up against his insentient mask.

The camera, of course, had long been broken. It had belonged to his father and it was one of the few family possessions that survived the accident; Neipas had it strapped to his chest on the very day. For a long time afterward it was as if it were his heart's eye, through which he nurtured his passions and blinded his sorrows, his young life's development shaped between the clap of its shutters. Perhaps his first use of the settlement money had been on fixing those shutters, which had grown rheumy with age — the second would've probably been on the plane ticket to Axiac. Now it was the camera's ability to take photos that was impaired. Something was faulty in the chemical process. He could still load film into the chamber, the silver crystals waited yet upon its surface, the light, to all appearances, still tossed photons into the aperture. But when Neipas developed the negative, the film showed — nothing. It was unclear, what was amiss; and there was no longer anyone to fix it. Yet the camera snapped on, and seemed to work as normal; something like an elderly head blinking at the landscape and seeing nothing, or remembering nothing. Yet Neipas still saw and, alas, could still remember. For a while he photographed the horned moon and the night. Time stilled... He was becalmed, mingling into the infinity of the machine. Then — the moment after — he was standing hesitantly before the little bridge which led to Oshana's Bookstore.

Neipas faced the little arch. From beyond it came, with the silence of scintillating stream, the sound of people; of people talking, of children playing, of song and clap filling the air. He felt shy, blocked, in a groggy mood; but something in him felt the need to see and talk to others. Something strange and profound — the confliction made him hesitate. He looked back. There was someone peeking from the darkness behind the worship house, staring mysteriously at him. Wasn't that the Debt Collector? Neipas thought he should perhaps go back; perhaps he should go in for a few hours of work; how much was it again, that he owed still — how much had he left to go? He sunk into the numbers [again]...

The sound of his name touched his perception. "Neipas" — he recognized the voice. It was Oshana's; he looked up from the *I*, into which he had been staring, lost in a thread which had begun with his debt and ended elsewhere entirely (he forgot what it was the moment he looked up). The compassionate sage stood at the other end of the bridge.

"Oh, hi," said Neipas, half-dazed, half-startled.

Oshana smiled. She smiled, a tender smile so genuine that it softened Neipas' heart at once.

"Would you like to come in?"

The little orchard was filled with warm lights and people sitting on mats — elder folk in chairs — and children running around. The thickets covered them from the intensifying wind, which whispered through the boughs and ruffled the olive branches softly, confiding a bit of chill into the clearing. Oshana interlaced her arm with Neipas', who bowed respectfully beside the wise woman's petite figure. This amused her once she noticed it, and she said, "You can straighten up, child. Don't worry — Be yourself. No need to be ashamed of anything here."

Neipas, reddening, pushed his back aloft and felt his bones crack against the weight of his own embarrassment. It was an uncomfortable feeling at first, but there was something about the way Oshana patted his arm that soothed him. An elderly woman, closest to the bridge, rose from her chair, approached them and introduced herself, welcoming Neipas to the group — in a tone so candid that he again bent very respectfully as their hands shook. And then, one by one, the elder members of the group came to greet Neipas; and then the younger ones came, first one by one, then in couples. They all looked Neipas in the eye, and every eye Neipas beheld twinkled smilingly in the pleasant evening. There was something particular about their faces, something that Neipas recognized — though he didn't know where from. It was the absence of pretense — there was a sincere quality to their gazes, a warmth; their words seemed come from the soul and not the throat; their words seemed to embrace. And finally came the children, first only a couple and then all at once — and they ran up laughing, embracing Neipas together in a show of love so moving that it shook even Neipas' sense of loneliness asunder. And even as he smiled he was somehow moved to the brink of tears by it; which surprised and embarrassed him, and he hid his feelings under the mask.

Oshana guided him through and, once he was engaged and comfortable, let him be. Unmoored among strangers, Neipas found himself strangely at ease, flowing from one conversation to the next, from one embrace to the next. The people here were in accord with nature and themselves, or walking in the process of becoming; and their words and conduct struck at once the humanity in him. These people were of all sorts and colors. Mostly from Ostrich and from the eastern mountains, but from all over Axiac too, they resembled at first a crew of outcasts, of disparate appearances — from the suited to the ragged, from the wild to the uptight — but once Neipas engaged with them who were behind the avian covers, he found something profoundly human. He suspected their masks thin; even absent (though this was implausible, perhaps impossible). They spoke of all manner of stimulating things — politics, the arts, travels and adventures occasionally, most often the anecdotes of simple lives; all, in the healing spell of companionship, temporarily numbed to the bleak components of their existence, the hardships and overcomings, the struggles. Neipas found himself chatting about his work and his own ideas about photography with honest listeners, so that he talked more and more eagerly than he had in a long time; and, listening, he learnt much himself. He flowed through the olive garden and into the bookstore, where women discoursed — aspiring politicians, running for the national assembly. They were of the community, and spoke in forceful terms against the oil refinery at Ostrich, and the plans for the oil pipeline in the east — a recurring topic, which seemed to be one of the main reasons people were gathered here today.

Neipas, then, spotted someone whom he thought he recognized. She was lean, a little unkempt, wild and scattered, pretty without paint, of brown skin and deep black feather, with a loose hairbun trailing her nape. She wore a feather earring; and was already coming toward him:

"Hey man! Don't I know you from somewhere?"

"Hi! You do look familiar..." said Neipas.

"Ah!" it occurred to him suddenly. "You're the protester from Belab Square! With the cardboard."

Even as he laughed at this, an inner sense of decorum checked him. But the protester laughed too, and he was at ease once more.

"And you're the dude who tripped on me the other day! You must've been sleepy man."

"I was a little," said Neipas, scratching his nape.

Smiling, the protester introduced herself. "Orenda."

"Neipas."

Their hands embraced softly. Orenda's hands were gentle to the touch, yet her grip was firm; a strong grip, practical. Her smiling eyes were full of soul, and were at once so bright and penetrating that Neipas found his own stare shying away from hers.

"You working at the Belab, Neipas?" asked Orenda, with a little tilt of the head.

"Yeah — unfortunately."

"You don't like it huh."

Neipas snickered, scratching his eye in a shrugging gesture of fatigue and defeated exasperation. "I fucking hate it, honestly."

Orenda smiled — a humble, earnest, understanding smile.

"Working nights?" she pursued, softly.

"And days."

"Shit."

"Yeah."

Orenda smiled once more her empathetic smile of clasped lip and dimple burrowing softly into her cheek. There was something in her manner that warmed Neipas' heart and brought him easily into intimacy and confidence with her; something in her manner that was attentive, present, listening; her eyes seemed to peer beyond Neipas' mask, as if inviting him to see out of it, and into their own depths. Little by little, Neipas' gaze really met hers — and they melded. Softly, slowly, sounds round them seemed to dim; and Neipas was encouraged to speak into the tender silence that bloomed between them.

"It's just — debts to pay, you know," he said, nearly muttered.

"I understand. And what do you do there?"

Normally, Neipas would be embarrassed to talk about his job. Not that he thought it beneath him, nor was it humiliating; it simply was vexing to him to admit to be in a place where he didn't belong, so far from where he belonged. The very uttering of it was making it take shape in concrete sound, made it real and implacable. To be this far from the path meant for him was a constant source of anxiety. He saw his dreams recede in the ceaseless thump of time; and what is anxiety but a clock pressing upon the heart, ticking poison in its every beat?

But to Orenda, somehow, he spoke about it without anxiety, shame or scruple. "I'm a waiter. Or a delivery boy, I guess. I take food up and down the tower, basically."

And yet, he would not mention the slaughterhouse. The bustle of its apparatus was too ingrained in the habitual workings of his body to be alluded to without shattering his nerves — its chains circulating with the blood in his veins, its grisly scent huffing into his alveoli, his muscles simulating with every involuntary twitch the pulls and plunges. He had to keep the psychosis of such things out of mind by containing it under the lid of a willful unconsciousness; and — at least for now — forget. Not that he didn't want to relate the wonders and nightmares of the graveyard shift: the enigma of the midget in particular. Indeed he desired it with the anguished eagerness of a madman fearing himself one. While he walked alongside Oshana earlier, his anxiety had tormented his abashment over whether to approach her with this. Hopefully later. To tell was to purify one's insanities and to be listened to was to confirm he was not crazy after all; and Oshana would listen. Yes — she would understand. And Orenda? Strangely enough (strange because he'd just met her), she, too, effected that same power of kindness and strength that roused his trust, that same accepting, affectionate manner that seemed to express the generosity of a virtuous spirit. Perhaps Orenda too would listen — and he needed to talk. Perhaps she would. No... Their acquaintance was nevertheless too recent to be broached with such topics as the possible meaning of dwarfish apparitions. Neipas shook his head absentmindedly; somehow he smiled. He saw her nodding with empathy, perceived her offering a comforting word or other; fixed, without realizing it, upon her black eyes which pierced him and coaxed him out of himself, and brought him in, into the softness of her presence, carrying as it were his soul by the hand. His mind produced this very image in a flashing thought and he laughed at himself before Orenda could say more; and instead she asked, mirroring his laughter: "What?"

Neipas waved one hand before him, covering his eyes with the other. "No, nothing." Very quickly he felt ridiculous and was trying to suppress his giggling which, however, continued to gush out of him. But Orenda laughed too, joyfully; naturally, without pretense. Neipas began to mutter apologies beneath his dying chuckle, and Orenda right away stopped him.

"You're embarrassed but it's good to laugh! There's plenty to laugh about."

As Neipas receded from his short fit he yawned, "Plenty to cry about too."

"Well — yeah, for sure. No doubt about it. But we gotta laugh to remember why we cry — you know what I mean?"

Neipas laughed again — "No," he said as he broke in guffaws, at this point amazed at himself, finding in himself something new and also very old, something at once familiar and unrecognizable. There was a good deal of venting in it; an exorcism of deep-crusted frustrations. Orenda laughed with him, at first confusedly, and then let herself surrender into a general merriment without source or reason, the very joy of laughter for laughter's sake; at the core, she knew, an acknowledgment of the miracle of being alive. What was this strange warmth he felt? — Neipas wondered, in the midst of his own laughter and the stimulating lull of pleasant sounds all around him. The elderly and the children close-by looked on and they, too, laughed — much more contained, with the exception of some children — out of sheer bewilderment, or simple contentment.

In the end of it, Orenda said, "Dude — you're a trip, man. I like you."

Hearing this as his laughter was ceding, Neipas felt a little shy. There was a sense of landing then, as of his own weight coming back to himself; and it was as if his senses meshed again into reality, the air recovering some of its oppressive thickness. He withdrew a little.

"Well," he began clumsily, sniffing in the last pulse of laughter, as he realized he liked her too. He molded his mask back to composure. "Huh — so, what do you do?"

Orenda turned up to him her smile; now wider yet, fresher, with lingering traces of laughter.

"I'm a writer."

"Oh yeah? What do you write? Fiction?"

"Nonfiction, mostly."

"You're a journalist, then."

"Occasionally. I was actually gonna say, I thought *you* were when I saw you before. I was like, 'is this guy a journalist or a tourist?'." Neipas looked down to where she was pointing, and noticed his old camera yet suspended upon his chest.

He chuckled. "Nah... Photographer, I guess. Worked with journalism students before though, when I was at school."

"You studied — photography?"

"Yeah."

Orenda smiled again that genuine grin which soothed his heart mysteriously so. "For sure. You know, I go on assignment sometimes for a local outlet," she said, "and usually I have to bring a camera and take photos myself. I'm not good at it though. Maybe you can come along next time, bring your camera with."

"Oh — I'd love to," he said, a bit timidly. "Camera doesn't work, though — unfortunately." He sensed himself reddening again under the mask.

"No, no worries, you can just use the one they lend me then. But —" Orenda remarked humorously, "why are you using a camera that doesn't work?"

Faced with her authentic curiosity, and a willingness to listen unfamiliar to his experience — Edazima being the sole exception to general indifference in his life, but when did they talk, outside the hurry of the grind? — Neipas tried to articulate that the camera was old but meant a lot to him. He explained what was wrong with it, and added that the appeal of photography was for him not merely in the outcome of the image, but in the act itself.

To photograph was not merely to generate photos — it was a way of seeing. "It encourages me to stop, and really see things. I feel like life would just pass me by otherwise. Next thing I know I'm old, I'm dead. My art is what puts distance between me and my... end. You know what I mean? It's the way I really live, my life. Life would make no sense without it."

Necessarily drawing into himself in the search for candor, he had sought inside the shadows of his mask the glitter of truth's jewel during his stumbling, hesitantly honest speech. Orenda listened near, and in the closeness of her attention he feared exposing himself too much; abashed, he sensed the face behind his feathers unveiling itself to her view and, feeling inadequate, he gradually shushed. He wondered why he had spoken so much. The very honesty of engrossment and affection this stranger possessed, and which had lulled him to comfort as in a spell, now discomforted him, and he feared disclosing his sordidness under the soft light of her gaze.

But Orenda soothed him with her eyes, her smile. Her quietude expressed her consideration of his words as she digested them with care. Coincidentally, she was just beginning to ask what type of photography he preferred when Neipas blurted in a hurry of embarrassment, "And what do you write about?", their voices swarming into each other in the air.

She chuckled tenderly. "You first."

Portraiture, he said. He was interested in the study of the visage, the secrets it expressed. "And — and you?"

In a slightly convoluted way (suddenly she, too, seemed shy) she explained that in her writing she attempted to render the unseen uncovered; the imperceptible discernible. "I write about invisible people, basically."

"Like what — ghosts?"

She laughed. "No... You're silly, man! I mean the very rich — and the very poor."

Neipas narrowed his stare, intrigued. "Rich and poor? But they're always on TV — and out there, I guess."

His comment had been made more or less in jest, made clumsily, because he didn't know what to say. "I mean invisible, not unwatchable," she replied, in her natural serenity of tone. "To really see is — something different. But you know that..." she said, her lips, her whole warm semblance settling into the smile. "I can tell you do."

There was another moment between them that made Neipas withdraw further. It was confusion, perhaps, about the nature of their congeniality, which in his boyish sentiments assumed romantic undertones and intentions; though Orenda's way was too innocent and earnest to imply that only, if at all. Lovelorn and confused, Neipas had to control the impulse to step back away from her magnetic pull or forward to meet her beautiful smile. Holding ground nervously, he mumbled something — what, he did not know — nodding in an attempt at nonchalance.

Imperceptibly they moved on in conversation — and the minutes passed by them unnoticed. They spoke for a long time yet, about a variety of subjects, in a serenity of mood Neipas hadn't felt in a while. The freshness of the experience extended his perception of time, and those few hours resting in the quietude of a new landscape, in the great calm of the orchard, felt boundless; they had the quality of eternity. How long indeed had it been, Neipas wondered, since he felt in himself? Always time passed drunkenly in the hectic flurry of routine, faded invisibly in the pace of work; and raced on, fugitive, toward the end of itself — toward his own death, which lay in the distance like a grim finish line.

But here, for the first time in a long time, he felt no anxiety; he felt no loneliness. For those few hours, at least, he was at peace.

Still, he knew; the Debt Collector, yonder beyond the bridge, still waited.

Suddenly, a single piercing cry rendered through all other sounds, and made them silence. It was the deep cry of a horn — grave, solemn, profound. It was sounded from the lips of Oshana, whose short figure stood upon a rock in the middle of the little garden.

Once the horn faded into the thicket, the hubbub returned slowly, more hushed, and the close multitude began to move. Orenda turned to Neipas and said, "You can definitely read it! It's all out there, and I want to hear your thoughts."

Neipas smiled sincerely — and Orenda pulled him toward the center of the garden by the hand, mirthfully. "But now come! The elders are gonna speak."

"What are they gonna talk about?"

"About the new ideal. Come — you'll hear about it."

13 - House of Lethe

Sunk in a gloom of blooded rust Neipas still heard Oshana's voice forming words in the warm lights:

"Fires burn still in the east — their flames consume the valley steeps and the great forest stretches... We know now they are not wild, but domesticated, and bred for violence."

Still, in the blinding nights of subterranean Belab he would see the midget in the strange despondent mask, prowling with vacant steps the hellgrounds of the slaughter factory. The dwarf would appear among the blur of hovering carcasses, passing upward by like a procession of souls toward the gates of Hades, and he (she?) would appear strangely clear in Neipas' eyes, ever more so, even as all around her (him?) dispersed further into total unfocus.

"I've been seeing things... Strange things," he had confided to Oshana that other evening. She merely bowed her head; her eyes spoke and beckoned. Neipas said to them, "I keep hearing things, and I try to listen, but I can't understand... It's always just out of range — you know?"

And he felt somehow, as he saw himself in the deep glare of Oshana's gaze, that she, in her innermost, knew.

"Things are made a little clearer," Oshana told him, with her sage and motherly voice, "if you move a little closer."

And Neipas, speaking with hesitation, said — averting his stare, "But I'm afraid... I'm afraid it could be dangerous."

To this Oshana smiled; and answered:

"There is danger in every step — and more so when you don't know where the step will fall. But if your heart leads you to step that path — follow it.

"But — beware, Neipas. Do you know your heart? Is it your heart that whispers; and do you know how to interpret its language?"

"How do I know?"

Oshana declined her head in solemnity, confidence. "If you are honest in your listening — you will know."

The sky above Axiac morphed in color as the sun and the moon performed their dance upon it. Not a cloud was to be spotted in the vast swath of parched blue; naught but smoke pumped up, like exhalations from iron lungs, out the chimneys of the Iblis refinery and the industrial zone, erect tall above the decrepit hovels of Ostrich; and the fires beyond the mountains to the east kept on raging, decimating trees in bellows of cracking bark and chasing away whole tribes of desperate folk, unstoppable on their path of destruction. Beneath the currents of smog aloft, in the wide basin, the megalopolis spread out, center of the world; and in its center was Belab Square, where Orenda stood with her banner most dawns, raising it upon the first glint of sunlight over the smoldering peaks; and from the center of the square rose the tower, deep inside which Neipas toiled day after day to make money to pay his debts.

One day of delirium, he answered the call from the deep, and followed the Midget.

His path unfolded in a circulation of dizzying hours, curling into themselves and winding off in flashes of [blank] sleep. Days, and nights, and mornings fused into one another. Neipas' mind spiraled slowly into dimness the while and instinct came to take full possession of him as time wore on. It was as if he swam through the world, as he felt his mind so sluggish and his limbs press onward constantly against their fatigue. His own body seemed sometimes removed from himself, and acted of its own accord. In an instant a bout of nerves would stir up in his head unexpectedly, and Neipas was forced to abandon whatever he was doing at that moment and stroll around in circles for a while until the tension fizzled off.

[...] He would gradually notice himself breathing very deeply, looking vacantly into nothing. He would, perhaps, be gazing into the *I*'s seductive glow in the middle of the night, sitting against a darkened wall somewhere in the recesses of the deep tower, and floating slowly, in a buoying motion outside of time, into the throbbing chambers of the Webwork, in its infinite nexus of shiny things and folk caving in an unruly collective shout echoing across the whole universe of Neipas' sleepy mind. Maybe then he would see the Midget, dim in the distance and the gloom, walking to mysterious depths, or waiting for him at their threshold. Many times in the mental tides of his wandering spirit, Neipas wondered whether what he beheld wasn't a memory; for he felt himself shrink, in those blurry instances, into his former size, beholding himself hopping about the green fields of his childhood, where he would spend days by the river... And where he would venture off, sometimes, up the rolling grass, and wait for his father at the limits of the seen horizon. And he recalled his mother carrying him aloft on her back over those fields... over those prickly, pleasant aromatic flowers she would take home to cook.

Janu the dishwasher had echoed her gesture — had he known her? "My mom taught me this —" he said, in the deep kitchens of **KUR**, over the smoking pot (into which he sprinkled herbs) — "Love, my friend, is the main ingredient for a special dish. And moms know best dude, moms know best."

Were they brothers, perhaps... It was during Magpie's little goodbye celebration that he had said it. Burrowed snugly underground, they gathered all in the brumous kitchen, squeezed between its dingy tiles, to bid farewell to their colleague who would leave them to ascend to better heights. Edazima had organized it. Every worker had been invited; surprisingly, many showed up. It was the first time Neipas saw them together like that — speaking with one another, parting bread. Traces of Edazima's cigarette smoke mingled with the aromatic fog of Janu's dish, enveloping them in a soporific embrace that made the tiny space somehow weightless in its relaxed torpor.

"That's corny as hell, man," Magpie told Janu, laughing as she ate. "This here's delicious though, that's for sure."

Indeed, everyone looked snug and numbly happy, as they ate — except, perhaps, Magpie herself, who tended to withdraw quietly to the farthest shadows of that sunless place, to stand by the exit. There was a hint of vulnerability in the way she lowered her eyes as she chewed in silence. She spoke to everyone, she spoke to Neipas when he approached to congratulate her again; but it felt like she only ever became talkative to repel her fears, and there were times when her merriment seemed forced. Something about her usual fortitude faltered, as though she was straining to merely stand, as though the vapors of that smoky air were solid ceilings and walls, solid whispers bewitching her mind into a box with the incanted threat of choking her lungs. By and by, as she grinned her humble smile she held up a little receptacle — an inhaler — and shook it, distractedly, next to her ear. She probably didn't notice herself doing it. Neipas saw her repeating this with increasing frequency as time blurred on, until, from far away, he caught her furtively tucking into a corner, and press the mouthpiece onto her lips with a big swelling motion. Edazima had once told him Magpie was asthmatic; and as he saw her drawing the fire of her cigarette and expel its toxins into that airless bunker — across the corridor from Magpie though she was — he wondered if she didn't make the connection at all. Edazima simply mentioned her lifelong friend hated the smell of cigarettes. She possessed the motherly capacity of piercing her compassionate focus beyond all masks, Edazima did, in the quest to alleviate a friend's pain — she could also be entirely oblivious, if that pain was as well concealed as Magpie's breathlessness was.

But there was something else, something more elusive, something dark and profound, of which the breathlessness was perhaps but a symptom; something hidden beyond Magpie's dignified, poised demeanor, her dazzling beauty. Neipas seemed to catch at it vaguely in her speech. In his dreamy, withdrawn disposition, he found himself wondering how he came to notice this, and why now. But it was there, beneath her pretty facade... something.

Orassap had come, too, his mask rigid in his smile, the *I* flashing before it all the time. He took photos with most and most avoided speaking with him — there were many such as he, usually younger, in attendance; and their iridescent feathers twinkled garrulously in the fog. Mrs. Tia was also present, very well-humored and at ease among the many who shared her language. At one point she came up to Neipas and held his arm affectionately — he had been aloof then, abstracted in his numbness, vacant-eyed, beginning to feel a little anguish — and, his stare focusing and finding her before him, he knew what she was saying to him, though he didn't know the words.

Edazima soon left to grab her kid from school — and Neipas, contemplating Mrs. Tia lauding her son Janu, observing them with an increasingly mournful disposition, remembered again the photograph of his mother's face. He had been often remembering it during his travails with the occult Midget, who reminded him of his mother — for the Midget, who often halted to let Neipas step in closer, stood at the very same height as her tombstone.

In those occasions the Midget reminded Neipas of his father, who stood at the threshold of some steep horizon, looking at him, waiting for him to catch up. The Midget — he or she, Neipas could not determine which — led him, in this way, down the winding steps of the slaughterhouse, following the trail of the floating carcasses, into the deep... Insects gathered near the bottom, close to the grate and the steps, before which the live animals squealed, and amassed in processions toward the upper levels, thickening. Neipas and the Midget — who never said a word — followed the path they traced, and sank further beneath.

Between the two oxen, across the factory of meat; down the well of denuded corpses hung; past the crippled hauler with the relentlessly swinging talon hands, under the red glow and over the frenzied wings of the condemned, through the little grate — into the darkness, they went. Sinking, all fell to a strange, growing, throbbing beat — that same reverberation which Neipas would sense in moments of silence. The Midget never perturbed that quietude; and said nothing, even when Neipas mumbled a question or other.

Neipas eventually realized that Melpomene's dwarf was mute.

[......] he would gradually notice himself breathing very deeply, and looking vacantly into nothing. The dimness was rancid and sepulchral, an odor of decay penetrated his face. He began to perceive breathing that was not his own (he had just passed an immense portal) ensuing from behind the barred entrance to a mineshaft. A circular glow shot from his breast. He had dwelt in great chambers underground, through industrial ruins that had every mark of old abandonment. He had trodden upon corroded floors and seen whole warehouses of defunct machinery, strewn with looms, with tatters, with suspended iron and the ruins of unfinished hulls and propellers, the rusted skeletons of locomotives; obsolete armament languished in oblivion, like dilapidated monuments to folly; furnaces would emerge from the shadows with yawning maws and the leprous skin of very degraded rust. He had walked over shards dispersed under windows whose walls had vanished — frames suspended amid a strange vastness, the limits of which he could not discern. He had seen nobody; though in the welter of a fuzzy obscurity there drew hazy proliferations of loose wires and hanging strings, from which sometimes emerged silent, motionless human shapes: statues, puppets, mannequins, toys. At first he hesitated before these apparitions, and even discerned the Debt Collector camouflaged among their stillness a few times ("I must go back to work," Neipas would suggest meekly to the blackness then). But the growing beat, the febrile vibrations of the atmosphere, and the stench leadening the air rendered all conclusions of experience null; he simply kept following the Midget. Yet now he heard breathing and stopped hard. A circular glow shot from his breast, against which both his hands gathered round an I; what time was it? — the I's dark interface glowed, conveying scrambled numbers; beyond the looping icon he saw the rusted bars, and beyond them a passage strewn with desolate mannequins and powdered bones. An open rib cage lay intact by the barred gate, resembling a sinister crib abandoned to the corner — and he thought to himself whether the breathing didn't ensue from the gaps between its coalescing waves. But the skeleton tilted before the bars, and the breathing came from behind them... Mannequin heads stared eyelessly from the hollow of the mine. Were these scattered bones made of plastic, too?

Neipas found himself following the robed mystery who floated at the farthest edge of his I's spotlight. He traversed thus deeper into thickening darknesses, treading circularly over grounds of dust and mounting trash. Tunnel walls neared him surreptitiously, diminishing the frame of an ever narrowing path which, darkly labyrinthine, branched wildly across many, many turns. The stench grew more intense, teeming his head. The beat grew louder and penetrated his skin to mesh with that habitual twitch of his muscles — as the litter piled the squirming of insects living in it amassed to high clamors. The breathings, those breathings which were like his own — a crescendo of such breathings rattled the narrowing walls of the advancing mine, until — suddenly — all hushed into total silence; such as Neipas had never heard before. And at the precise moment the darkness swallowed the Midget, a door appeared before the light.

Stone walls huddled very near. The gate looked very worn, and wrinkled, made of ancient wood, carved by the hands of a very distant epoch. It had a barnacled, archaeological handle stuck in it, which Neipas stared for some time; it seemed as if it possessed a life of its own and he braced, lest the door sprung upon him suddenly. Collarbones protruded from the arching lintel between the heads of a serpent and a lion carved in relief; the serpent was beneath and the bones jutted from its head like horns; and the lion was above, the bones flourishing from its maned chin like wings.

He covered his hand with his outfit's sleeve when he found the grit to seize the handle at last. Nothing. Any number of ways he tried at it, tinkering with it in an increasingly frantic manner; but it wouldn't budge. Notions of being at the whim of an imminent attack of hysteria occurred to his disorientation and the abrupt loneliness of no longer seeing the Midget. Scratching his own susurrating feathers he wondered; and suppressing the fright rising with his consciousness, he thought, and wondered how he could ever get out of there without the guidance of that uncanny mask of downturned crescents; and for a long time he stood in obsessive indecision under the gaze of the serpent and the lion.

Ultimately, instinctively, Neipas leaned his hand against the wood and pushed lightly. It gave way; retreating gradual with a cavernous screech of primeval hinges.

Beyond the open door it was all black. Neipas shuddered. He faced a rectangle of darkness, of a most opaque black, like a wall; a wall that whispered, for a thin cold air came from it. Neipas could deduce a plenitude of empty space extending through the quietness which had abruptly set and now acquired a strange, very restless and fidgety quality. For a long time he hesitated, wobbling upright upon the edge of tenebrosity, frozen in the clutch of a terrible fright. He even whimpered to the silence; and the silence said nothing back, closing in on itself and its odd vibrations. Behind him rose a vast, inextricable labyrinth of subterranean routes digging unfathomably through the earth. Before him gaped the unknown. The Midget was still nowhere to be found; how could he know how he got here without a guide? There was no choice.

He stepped forth.

The darkness widened into a sense of titanic dimensions; though it was so dense the *I*'s flashlight could barely penetrate it. Two or three steps and Neipas found himself in the thick of it so that when he looked back, he couldn't see the door any longer. Panicked, he took two or three steps back the way he came — then another two or three in the same direction. There was nothing; only empty space. Absolutely petrified, he stood besieged by gloom on all sides, by an impenetrable darkness rank with foul stenches, in an obscurity which seeped into his nostrils and the very pores of the deep skin under his masks. Some vital instinct forced his body onward to prevent his senses from giving in; one hesitant hand stretched in front, so he would not bump against anything; one foot dragged forth first, cautiously, before the other followed, so he would not fall; his whole body shirked, going onward at an angle. He advanced very slowly as though against his utmost fears. And it was very cold, very cold in there; he shook most horribly. The chill clawed at him and breathed into his flesh; soon he was sniffling, the tip of his nose in ice, the strength fading from him. The *I*'s light revealed a continuous circle of sandy dirt repeating at his feet, and nothing else. Suddenly, with an abrupt tensing of his muscles, that recurrence halted; suddenly, and with an immense shudder, he stopped.

Everything shook, everything quaked in a tenebrous rumble. Through the shivers of the world there rose a familiar sound — only much, much louder now. An overwhelming, tidal crescendo swelling fast onto faraway walls, encroaching into his ears and invading his body with tremors, tickling his feet upon the quaking ground and expanding into his head, his head filled double with the tremendous sound, once, then twice — in the form of a throb. It was like a monstrous heart beating out of the chest of some primeval titan. It was cavernous, dreamlike; the way it propagated made it clear that the space here extended infinitely. The boom stretched imperiously, painfully...

Then, but deadly silence — leaving everything enormous and empty. Neipas could do nothing but stand inert upon his quivering legs. Upon his perceptions the air enclosed, the shadows soaked, the stillness blew; the rancidness whispered dread into his heart. It seemed to have deepened in the wake of the noise — "What's this smell?" he asked the silence; but the silence only replied by embracing him tighter. Death seemed to waylay in presage about the darkness — the *I* revealed only more unreality and foreboding, Neipas' vacant mind whirling into the inscrutability of the dense gloom; a vague sense of someone there beside him gnawed at his frenzied wit; indeed, every time his eyes blinked the tenebrosity snapped at him, and every time his eyes opened it felt to him like peering over the brink of life.

Then, the nervous breathing, the tremulous puffs eddying about his beak ceased into the ether. He inhaled deep; for a friendly hand gripped him from below, and even before he alighted upon the Midget's sad mask he had felt the comfort of her (his?) presence. Neipas breathed easy, forgetting himself while the Midget guided him through the gloom extending vast over an earthen ground. The boom pulsed... Steps that crunched gravel faded into the abyssal hollowness the beat left in its tremendous wake. Neipas' I, held still between fingers — the back of whose hand kneaded the side of his nose — shone tepidly upon his companion who, he saw ghostly, held a rod or staff; and upon the floor, the gravel of which seemed suddenly made up of pebbles and broken seashells. A red dot beside the lens of the rectangular glass indicated the I's battery was nearly depleted and its feeble beacon about to die. Drapes, the vestiges of wires and ropes began appearing in it. Many veils drew aside before their quiet march, dropping from unseen heights in a mass of textures which felt smooth, fleshy, and heavy to the push as they brushed across his cheeks. There were layers upon layers of them; and eventually a strange luster began to shine through the bulkiness of their fabric. It was a shimmer golden and obscure, diabolic and enticing, suffusing the curtains with the muscular texture of skin; they seemed, when the light appeared, like half-transparent chests enclosing a beating heart, and felt to the touch ever more oily, icky, filthy, as their steps progressed. As they ground the long path here from the slaughterhouse, Neipas had achieved a vague awareness of the extensive slopes and stairways turning ever sooner, leading down in tightening circles, the immense spaces progressively diminishing — from which he derived the thought that they must have been nearing the inner tiers of the Belab; and as he walked now, led on by his mute guide, he perceived, through the unending succession of flapping layers, that they were moving toward its very core.

The gleam ahead grew and thickened, then faded and shushed, more and more intensely... And as the strange shimmer intensified through the curtains, ropes sprouted from the ground and stretched aloft beyond sight. The overwhelming pulse reverberated in his very marrow... it swelled and shrunk in powerful tremble, slow... — as they approached, he could already see it.

They came upon a clearing illuminated in that strange crepuscular gleam, unveiling in its twilight an old, leafless tree stretching among the upward ropes. There was a well of stone under it. The strange light, the strange shadow, the slow, uncanny absence of total darkness alighting the clearing descended from the highs — from the sky. Far, far above, in the midst of total blackness, shone an immense circular radiance, rimming a circle of the deepest dark. That circle throbbed; the twilight grew and shrunk in its booming cadence; it glowed in flares. It was an eclipse, Neipas thought; it was the notion which for his mind came closest to encapsulating that godly, unearthly vision jutting out into the soul from the very summits of the world.

"What's this?... and this smell..." — Neipas sensed it here the strongest. It had followed him out of the slaughterhouse all the way down here, as if the dying breath of the animals were enmeshed in his feathers, blowing disgustingly into his nostrils, like a repugnant tide flooding into the coves of his head and lingering long in its fetid ebb, to return in ever stronger plunges and in deepening pungencies, more and more dead; in his descending olfactory recesses the industrially cured meat had become rotten. "What's this smell?" Neipas asked once more, louder now. He received no answer.

The Midget pulled him closer to the tree — and he noticed (in the faraway perception of dreamt realities) that there was a small figurine lying by its exposed roots. It was the figurine of a woman — a goddess — broken and defaced; covered in soot, coated in ash. Behind it, an uplifted root was covered with a moldy, dusty cloth, which seemed to have served as an altar.

Neipas approached the figurine; he crouched to the Midget's height to see better.

"Who is this?" he whispered.

A certain oil lamp, set down by the idol, illumined the goddess with its strange multicolored flame, making the statuesque's decrepitude clear under the webbed shade of the naked tree. This lamp seemed made of terracotta, very old, and of a very simple design — but a vessel, a nozzle, a discus, a lid, and an oval handle, it was. Again the monstrous noise boomed, percolated his body, made him tremble all over; and the flame in response seemed to dim, seemed to hush, as if straining and nearly overpowered by the superior dark dazzle. The reverberation passed — nothing but tremors then. Indeed, Neipas now found himself shivering profusely in the silence and the cold — and turning his stare as though for aid he suddenly saw the Midget's mask very close to his. This didn't frighten him; but it filled him with a desire to ask him, or her, all the questions confusing his weary heart. After his trapped tongue unfurled, he turned his *I* to the Midget and exclaimed "Who are you? Where am I?" — but at that very moment his *I* sounded an electronic gasp, the red dot by the lens blinked and shut, its battery ran out of energy; and the light went off.

... circle on the soil. Having cleared the soil of gravel, the Midget drew lines upon the earth with the base of the staff; slow, methodical lines. These formed into shapes, and were shaped into words that Neipas, smarting his breathless batting eyes, read:

WE   CANNOT   BREATHE
WE   NEED   AIR

[the line stretched until the shadow and some kind of black viscousness oozed from the narrow—

The boom again came and again quaked; all things shook in its sound waves, the little oil lamp flickered. And even though the stone well arose a good few steps away from them under the extremity of the brittle boughs, somehow the Midget was already there by it, holding the lamp under one sleeve — it was as if time had skipped on through the rapid flickering of its tepid flame; and perceiving this, Neipas abruptly realized that he too was by the well, still crouching, having never gotten up, never walked to it. He stood up now.

"What?" Bewildered, he watched as the Midget tapped the well with her (his?) staff. More precisely, the staff tapped the lock which fastened the lid covering the well — once, twice the Midget tapped. A vague draught issued from it, well loaded with that horrible stench, unbearable — it probably originated there (I can't — I have to go back to work). The boom again came, again shook, again subsided. Into the silence the clank of the lock's old iron again resoundingly poked. Repelled by the fetid draught, Neipas turned his head away; but impelled by the Midget's iron knock and the frightful plea in his (or her) earthdrawn intimation, he approached the well upon timid feet, dragging through the pebbles, rousing the shells. (But I don't have a key) Neipas lost his voice to the swell which again boomed and filled him and, suddenly unnerved by all the twitches of his nerves and a distraught craving to get out of there, he clutched the lid upon the well; and with a deeply furrowed grimace that made his wax flow, his feathers scramble, his beak droop, he managed to open the cover slightly and thrust his gaze in at once to peek; then —

— suddenly a strange silence rushed into his ear. Everything within him drained away in a haste. Blackness overwhelmed his sight for an instant, and when the gloaming faded back to his eyes the Midget and the lamp had disappeared. A great dizziness overcame him (he held a vague notion of putrid odors swooping into his breast). Scarabs and locust and vermin emerged from under the shells and flounced about his feet. The ropes shook noisily; and the eclipse above throbbed with its rhythmic, horrendous noise that pressed out the inner sides of his head; it was growing. His every limb fell to convulsions; and in a frantic attempt to keep awake and flee Neipas toppled back, feeling his heart panic in every fiber of his beating skin — it was then that he looked up and saw that black sun between the ropes. The fiery shoots writhing out of that most dark round lashed harder and thickened into gold, a most bright, most dazzling gold (heat pressed and he felt the wax of his inner mask collide against his protruding knees as they lifted) and that light of the purest glow, emanating as though from the most radiant of treasures, beaming out of the black pit, throbbing maniacally, bulged to an intensity so blinding that Neipas was moved to gape not only his eyes, but his mouth and nostrils too; all the pores of his body opened to absorb its awe-striking and overwhelming luminosity.

The world then assumed a vague form of darklessness. All things hushed; and in an instant the gloom enveloped him again.

14 - Fevers and Frenzies, Trees of Ash

Neipas had wakened on one of the closet-beds in the gloomy pantry.

He had nimbly clambered up the tower in disorientation. As he emerged from the lobby and passed through the thin screen of spray, he plunged into a dreary haze — shadowy shapes walked in it, moving under the shifting sallowness of veiled heavens. And though the hour was well into the morning, almost entering afternoon, darkness was fast overtaking Axiac. Overhead winds blew against the sea and brought forth the smoke of the mountain. The fumes churned from horizon to horizon like a pall covering the earth; and the smell of burnt wood suffused the air. The day had become night, the sky sulphur. It vibrated with the drumming sound of rotor blades whizzing across, helicopters and spotlights hovering above sirens yelling all throughout the city. Neipas had experienced it all like a dream, dodging the ghosts in the fog with detached, far-away gliding steps toward the station.

Loud bells sounded from the Eagles' Nest. It was the end of the month.

The first thing he did after he arrived at his apartment complex after weeks stewing in the frantic routine of work was to go into the landlord's office to hand over a check in the amount equivalent to the rent, plus late fees from previous months. It was a painful detour to make, made by force of necessity and its pure instinctual will alone; for all he wanted, and every fiber of bone and flesh and mind in him desired was to sink into bed and dissolve in sleep. Already on the train he — a mere thirteen seconds after sitting — had blacked out into heavy slumber, and remained perfectly unconscious during the ride. At the edge of Babylon erupted a quick brawl between two pigeons, which emerged in shouts and devolved into blows amid the shocked and averting gazes of the remaining commuters; but even this did nothing to affect Neipas' sleep. Nonetheless he awakened right out of the machine voice's sound announcing his first stop, as though his spirit had remained aware throughout just to hear for it. Neipas arose with a start and stumbled out, not noticing that all the seats about him had been vacated — and, since he had not noticed this, he couldn't begin to suspect that it had been because of his smell of accumulated sweats without shower and amassed crusts of fetid blood upon his clothes; in the next train he was pulled more lightly into exhaustion's sway, and from time to black time flashes of the apocalyptic heavens entered his semi-opened eyes; ("what the hell is that?") a small, bright orange dot beyond the fires behind the piling smoke looked right into him from the distant horizon, through layers of fume, as he relaxed to and fro in his seat — to rouse out of slumber again. In the final train (or was it still the same train?) he stood squeezed amid many dissolving masks, and through the back-window he saw the crowds mirrored in the next car; a mass of bodies canned between the edges of a swaying frame, blinkering in the red lights of passing subterranean tunnels... He came up the staircase leading out of Ostrich's metro station and wandered into the streets toward his apartment, lightheaded to the point of barely seeing a thing in front of him, through an unconscious journey which passed by his landlord's office — who received him with his ghastly grin and authoritatively slurring words, forcing Neipas to strain to keep at attention — and ended in the utter swoon of his bedsheets, upon which he slumped with stained outfit, boots and all.

He emerged from it slowly. The air was pulled into and expelled out of his mouth in deep drags of foul breath, which warmed the sheet and tingled his noise with its rancidness. His head felt like a lump of throbbing lead, bulky at the end of the languid body, and his mind dispersed in little twinkles around his eyes. Pasted in sweat under the heat he was — the stench of it was overwhelming, and only the aroma of charred bark, still on his shirt, abated it. The air screamed outside. Mechanically he pulled himself out of bed and, peering out the window, saw a bizarre nightfall persisting over the city. He peeked into the living room and found it asleep in low lights — the roommate dozed across the couch before the computer screen, glowing and flashing with moving images. He crossed over, and taken by an urgent curiosity he climbed up to the roof to see the source of those noises. Before him then extended the megalopolis: vast, framed all in volcanic reds glowing up against the stygian sky, embers bright upon the hills. The conflagrations which had long been ravaging the eastern plateaus now perched upon the mountain peaks; they seemed to have arrived at last and suddenly, commencing now their descent upon Axiac, craving now the urbanized basin, the civilized expanse, seeking now libations of tar and holocausts new. Teeming breezes swept across the immensitude and made the air turbid, made the air struggle, made it convulse with the frenzy of helicopters circling all over the mansions of the Diamond Hills in the far north yonder, over which the flames now loomed tall; gusts swept in plumes, towering colossal and swooping deeply, smothering even the dazzle of Babylon's towers, flying even above the great Belab whose bells tolled frantic amid the pandemonium. For a few moments Neipas was held in shock, for he thought that its summit, too, was in flames. But it was the Pearl he saw — the Pearl blazing, a palpitating beacon in the infernal mist, fighting not to be strangled — until it blasted, and bled, as if dragged by a tide, into the fog of brimstone, into the glaring city, into the yelling lights of the boulevards, blending feverish with the breath of the yawning fires. And all the horizons bled which faced the oceans; and the edge of the waters glimmered with the echoes of crimson agonies. The scarlet deep, thick, canopied over the vast extent of the megalopolis, and in its encompassing immensity made everything seem small. The mountains burned, the bleeding sky seemed made of flesh; and it was as though they were all inside a vast, an omnipresent womb.

Mesmerized, he saw all this, and he saw it alongside the mesmerized stares of his neighbors who stared (mostly behind lenses) agape at the foreboding spectacle. Upon the flat roofs of his and of the surrounding buildings, and behind the closed windows of a myriad apartments, stood many, watching. The family of four living opposite his own window (Neipas noticed them as he looked around) faced the uncanny prospect — each conspicuously still among the spectators' general motion — and beheld, in their utter immobility, the bright orange dot hovering under its arch; that same orange Neipas had seen from the train on his way here. It was the Pearl upon the Eagles' Nest, he realized now... Or was it the sun? Both seemed to hover at comparable heights — two eyes cocked in midair, blinking through the veil of spark and dust. Photos were taken; apertures inhaled the fires — and here they appeared, tamed under the glass, as pictures. Though the landscape might have looked odd, the flames were yet distant. Behind him, Neipas still saw Ostrich — submerged in a silent darkness, dozing beneath the shooting flare of Iblis; it seemed to him, as he gazed out in that direction, as if the whole fume-sky spread from its chimneys — before he left, catching himself back before his apartment door, feeling dizzy. As though auguring the fires, temperatures seemed to have greatly increased throughout those many days and nights past, and even as his inner mask melted in despair, the outer facade had only hardened; drawing back inside his room, Neipas contemplated his bovine form — he had forgotten to take it out at work and now that he had brought it home he was unable to remove it. The ox was too tight about his features, glued (had his face grown into his semblance?). When he yanked it out by the horns at last, after much painful tugging and strain, he then found himself facing the sordid, grotesque aspect of the pigeon mask, with its runny feathers, its moist skin of wax precipitating all toward the abyss, featureless; his true self opening and twitching horridly behind it.

Quickly amid fleeting impressions he removed his work outfit and the sheets on his bed and tossed it all, smeared and smelly, into the basket of dirty laundry which was already bursting out in the corner. Clad in underwear he stole into the bathroom, carrying but a pair of boxers — his last clean pair — in his hand, and took a shower. The jet and wash lifted the burden of grime from his body and generally made him feel fresher; but all it did to his head was place it in a different kind of fever, it throbbing faster yet now. He went grimacing back to bed, shabbily arranging a new covering of sheets upon which he lay. Though it was sweltering and the sweat was already at the cusp of welling out again, he didn't sleep until he slid under them, for he felt exposed with his nakedness brushing against the hostile air of the room. Neipas succumbed to a feverish doze from and into which he oscillated. Images, both vivid and vague, of deep faces he did not know materialized in frail swoon, and all of them — men and women, infant and old — hung upside down and had a horrid expression, horribly frozen with gaping mouths and very open eyes almost entirely white save for a hint of iris on top, and without a mask to cover any of this. Squirming clusters of insects flashed in the corner of his sight, and Neipas would often jolt out of this hellish repose with the sensation of tiny legs crawling on him. As he frantically checked he would see it to be an itch; and the itch was incessant. Some fly kept buzzing in his ear, in and out, in and out. But he could not see the fly — the spiders kept to the corners of his ceiling, weaving their webs well out of reach; and a moth circled round the ceiling lamp, well above. And yet the buzz would not stop, the itch kept emerging in biting tingles. The megalopolis outside still screamed. Neipas tried to sleep for many hours; he felt asleep with his eyes open, and struggled to when he closed them.

But, by and by the noises shushed as the night deepened. A soft rain pattered the window glass beyond the drawn curtains. It was a pleasant sound — Neipas, wondering whether it would douse the fires, considered getting up to check. But finally what made him rise from bed was a vague worry that he had left the window open and rain would come in. He went to it quickly, wishing to be brief and return to sleep. The window was closed, he saw — but a tree was now blocking the view to the opposite building. It had perhaps grown while he was at work. Had he been away that long? It looked peculiar and familiar; it seemed very far away. Gray all, the tree grew, grew, grew, and arose on a thin and colossal trunk which reared the burgeoning canopy against the skies, and the skies stretched, taut over swelling cancerous blossoms flashing fire — circles gaped as the tree of ash parted the firmament. Its canopy grew to cover the heavens, bloating to such a degree that its fruit began to rain, drizzling onto the street and flaking sideways upon the window glass, carried by the gale; and the rain (upon closer inspection he ascertained) was made of locust. Soon these insects veiled the outer pane completely.

It happened that the glass of the window, because it was so filled with wet locust, became extremely opaque, so that Neipas could see himself very clearly. Neipas contemplated his reflection in the mirror. He found that he was mumbling some tune, and even though he was quite close to the glass — nearly touching it with his beak — his pigeon face looked quite far away. With both hands he covered his forehead and then slid them round from temple to nape, smoothing the surface of his wax skin and evening out his plumage.

He winked to himself very slowly.

Outdoors, the sun hovered at its zenith, beaming a hot swathe of light upon the earth. The sky was clear (the rain had already gone elsewhere), not a cloud challenged the bright rays bleaching the heavens. Below, the towers stood as imposing as ever they had — though today they looked somewhat colorless against the blinding shine of noon, somewhat dilapidated, too. Neipas headed toward the square with a hoppity pace, glancing with joy the smiling faces that passed by him.

The center of the square bore a peculiar aspect today. There was an enormous crater in it, as if its flooring had been blasted away by a bomb. It looked huge, giant, titanic, vast beyond belief — Neipas concluded, with some self-satisfaction and upon measured reflection, that the whole population of Axiac could fit in it. He walked down into the crater and saw a huge set of tables assembled circularly along its perimeter. It encircled a long table set at the very center. A whole load of folk was walking down the ramping grounds to the circular table and sitting down at it. Neipas imitated.

The table was covered in a white cloth, and atop it was placed a very ornate plastic plate with a chicken sleeping on it, and a tall glass with water beside; in front of the plate was a tablet, placed upright so that the screen was directly facing him. Inside the screen he saw himself throwing wild gestures with his hip; Eva was also there, with knees and hands on the floor, her mask contorted in an expression of ecstasy, her tongue out at the corner of her wide open beak. Neipas was holding the plumage at the back of her head, he was on his knees right behind her. They were both naked and had furious sex. Neipas watched this and giggled much. Looking to his right he saw Orassap sitting next to him, ogling his screen.

"Hey!" Neipas uttered, pulling the tablet toward himself. All of a sudden the tablet was gone.

"Lol!" ejaculated Orassap, parting his beak very wide. Neipas guffawed uncontrollably, cawing and shaking in his chair, cackling "Lo lo lo lo lo!" into the air above his head. In the meantime Orassap, his mask contorting into a face of extreme sadness, pushed his tablet toward Neipas. "Wanna share?" he asked. "Ok!" Neipas heard himself say. In the screen was Orassap's face, beaming to them.

The next moment they were feasting on the live and feathered chicken who somehow did not react, but Neipas choked on the last piece and as he rushed to the glass he saw the water had dissipated. It was very hot (at this moment he dipped lightly out of sleep but almost immediately fell into it again).

Looking to his left for help he saw the Editor. The Editor put his hand on

Neipas' shoulder, and it was well. He couldn't feel the chicken in his throat anymore, but now he couldn't speak either. "It's ok," the Editor was saying.

"Look," the Editor whispered, furtively, beckoning Neipas to remain quiet with his finger. He then pulled up the white cloth so they could spy a glance under the table. There was a velvet footrest, very comfortably cushioned. The footrest was the upholstered back of a midget who fed on mites. The receptionist at the Belab (it was she, not the Editor who was there, it turned out) placed her feet there and rested back into her chair, stuffing her chicken whole into her mouth.

"We found happiness," she said, winking.

Neipas could see the table at the center quite clearly now, so he decided to approach and investigate. At first he found it a bit hard to go around his own table (since it enveloped the whole crater) but — considering it rude to step over it — he crawled under and past it.

The table at center was bustling with an exceedingly rich buffet. A lot of food was laid upon wide trays atop the golden cloth and inside large bowls running across the infinitely long table. Most of the chairs were empty, though, and the few folk that sat there were in the very middle. They were all pigeons. (Are they?) Neipas looked closely. (No, they don't seem to be pigeons). As a matter of fact, they were definitely eagles, swans, peacocks, bulls and horses. Neipas recognized some of them from placards and televisions across town, from out the train window and inside the flashing interiors of the Belab. The eagles from the weather derivatives chamber were there, so was the clerk from the healthcare insurance office. Others were there, appearing somewhat blurry in the sun waves (it was really hot) and they were all cheerily drinking wine and stuffing beef into their beaks. Tuxedo-ed pigeons came back and forth to collect scraps they dropped on the floor.

"LOL!" the [right-side] clerk suddenly exclaimed, winking. The pigeons were all naked but for loincloths now. Everyone laughed, and Neipas went along, winking, though he wasn't sure why he laughed or winked. He felt the keenest desire to sit down at the table and eat a little, there was such an abundance of food and so many empty seats, he wanted to quelch his bit of appetite; but he thought it rude to ask. Moreover it was patent in the eagles' masks (he could see them more clearly now) that they would launch into some absurd excuse to say no.

Suddenly Neipas became very angry. He puffed up his chest and, savagely flinging away his mask, yelled at the top of his lungs, "Hey! Can *I* *seat* *here*?!" but it was too late. Out of the eagles' slightly open beaks and out their eyes and ears and every orifice oozed thick, slimy streams of tar; it crawled down their faces, their masks dissolved in the stuff. Neipas still considered sitting down, for there was still a lot of food and he wouldn't have liked to let it go to waste; but he thought better of it when he saw everyone on the circular table — everyone in Axiac was probably sitting there — run away frantically, screaming, trampling on each other in their panicked getaway. A dreadful yell shook the heavens, the multitude scrambled to get out of the bomb crater (are they running from the heat?).

Then, a monstrous rumble emanated from the depths of the horizon covered in infinite towers of glass, and Neipas' heart was assailed by the most profound horror, it shook and froze then, paralyzed in sheer fright. Involuntarily his face twisted into a horrid expression, and he yelled, he yelled, a long scream of pure fear, his legs were retreating rigidly and of their own accord, his fist took to his chest. He knew what was coming. He recognized the sound of it!

"We're gonna die! We're gonna die!" he screamed frantically, unable to move a muscle any longer.

The rumble grew quickly. It was the rains returning as a gigantic wave of water approaching with a thundering roar, taller than the highest tower and louder than all the dreading shouts of the fleeing populace. The crushing advance of the deluge absorbed the towers around the square as though nothing stood in its path. Beholding at last the giant waters vying for him, Neipas' heart quaked to all sides in an uncontrollable fit and his legs were roused to run like they had never run before. Whimpering helplessly, Neipas turned and sped off, and he flapped his arms in a desperate attempt to take flight — for was he not a bird? — but it was hopeless. The sun, overwhelmed by the rising waters, assumed a black shimmering form, golden shadows throbbed across the earth, and all things were suddenly very cold.

The full weight of the torrent descended upon Neipas' body with astounding fury.

*

The buzz of a fly rang in his ear, in and out, in and out. It must have been several days of this, or so it felt to Neipas when he awoke, lightly roused by a sound of belching music outside his bedroom door. He emerged in a bath of sweat, coughing and slightly dizzy, finding that he held the whole ocean in his bladder and heavy tar weighed in his intestines. The thought that the AC wasn't working occurred to him when he arose of a pull so that he could rush to the bathroom — the dead air seemed somewhat more breezy as he cut through it — but he found the door frustratingly locked; with a panic he knocked on the door several times rapidly; and, in a surreal moment which he was sure was not a dream only because of the throbbing sensations assailing him, the screeching guitars and pounding drums slaloming from beyond the door lowered in volume — and out rolled the languid, zoned-out drone of his roommate, which formed the slow words, "Yes...?". There was a venomous stretching of the vowel which irked Neipas to blow out,

"Are you almost done! Really need to go — " to which the roommate, placidly, draggedly, turned the lock and opened the door to face him with his sagging, averting eyes, his deep frustrated breathing which Neipas had never seen so close.

"Fine," whispered the roommate the slightly annoyed mumble, but Neipas had no space to notice it. He sprung right in and sat on the toilet, sinking. He bent into the cup of his hands with the force of his viscera forcing themselves out from his body; and noticed, despondently, a stiff, slightly darker blotch of fabric in his last pair of underwear.

As the fluids ran out of him — leaving a dull ache and emptiness in his head, filled by the continuous screaming of the roommate's music — he found he had the *I* in his hand... and landing into the Webwork he learned vaguely that the fires had been halted at the edge of the mansions in the Diamond Hills. Other fronts, which had been burning in the east for longer, finally put themselves out as they came upon the face of the rock in the mountain summit, finding nothing else to burn.

Neipas returned to bed and lay down. The headache had dulled and lightened; he felt but a hollow now, a draining appetite, and an immense laze. Though hungry — his stomach belched in short time — the weakness was so overwhelming he felt not the slightest impulse to get out of bed. Instead he languished there, staring at the ceiling with half-glassy eyes, trying unsuccessfully to fall back asleep. Sleep was all he wanted; to escape from consciousness completely was his most fervent wish. The itch remained incessant, popping out now here, now there (the buzz of a fly rang in his ear, in and out, in and out...), everywhere on the surface of his body; the roommate's music lingered through the afternoon and played in his nerves, so that he, eventually, rolled his body to the side in a reflex and grabbed the *I*, which had dropped beside the bed. The device faced him with its glossy dark surface, on which his mask was darkly reflected, faced him silent, expectant of the finger which would endow it light... He plugged the soundbuds into his ears and began floating in the digital hollows of the Webwork; slid into the twitch of lights...

And minutes or hours must have passed — until the glow made his eyes hurt and the music made the ache in his head rattle. His parched throat wanted beverage to quench his thirst and his muscles food to overcome their debility; no amount of distraction or strength of will could kill this need, so Neipas, ruminating in his limpness, lifted his head and gazed upon his open wardrobe. He wondered when it had been opened. The doors slanted apart; the two drawers which occupied the lower fourth of the closet were pulled out, their contents bursting over. One drawer contained all sorts of old papers, hoarded trash, pamphlets, textbooks, notebooks and portfolios from his college days; the other held tangled wires and defunct electronics, among which he kept two backup drives he still used to save photographs in. On the floor nearby lay the reason he must've scoured the drawers for, sometime during the fever between his slumbers: a box of generic pills. Sliding down to the bottom of his mattress to check deeper inside the wardrobe, he spotted the cereal carton toppled and empty. He had nothing to eat — no food, and little money for groceries after his latest expenses, and a tremendous unwillingness to get out of bed besides; so he dipped back into the Webwork to find the cheapest thing available for delivery.

(the buzz of a fly rang in...) His *I* changed hue. Some buzz rang far away from his mind — yet it trembled upon his glowing hand. Upon the glass shone a weird number; numbers that he did not recognize, but which he (instinctively) knew to be hiding the Debt Collector. He let it ring until it rang (out...) and after some very mute, extremely cursory and tortuously circular browsing through his blank eyes, he ordered a relatively cheap meal — still pricey for him, but he took the plunge anyhow, not without a flinch of dread surfacing from the empty depths of his wallet, which had well furrowed its sad way into his soul. He had to eat.

In his confined isolation Neipas had quickly gained an aversion to any contact — something that was also a result of his staring at his mask in the *I* glass, and observing it hadn't sloughed out the aspect of fatigue, and in fact had only caved deeper into it — so when the ringing of the bell sounded, he fretted irrationally over it and considered not getting out of bed at all. Finally, after hesitating, he rushed to ram his mask into proper shape. He slinked quickly into a pajama, which he dug out of the laundry basket; and went to the door, making the dreaded safari through the living room, where the roommate lounged still among an angry chorus of pukes (he hadn't gone to the door and the bell rang still). This noise made the situation even more cringe-worthy and Neipas couldn't even look at the face of the stranger standing at his door with a plastic bag holding cartons of burger, fries and coke, so sensitive he was to contact then — he vaguely wished the stranger had been a vending-machine on wheels. Stamping a final vexation upon the awkward encounter, Neipas, recalling his own experience, felt forced to draw a bill of cash from his meager stash of capital to pay for tip; which he did, painfully.

After he ate the burger and the fries, and drank the coke — all of which fed him, yet left him feeling heavy and greasy, slightly indisposed, burdened with lethargic fat and calorie from the meal — Neipas sat up in languishing repose against the pillow. His mind was left to wander freely... At first he gazed vacantly the drawn curtains of his window. He languished in the sallow marsh of numbers a while; sinking through a mental list including rent, the healthcare copay, the healthcare premium, the student loan, the public transit card, the monthly bank fee, food... And the bill for utilities hadn't even come yet. Neipas probably hated that the most, for his roommate was lavish in using up the apartment's energy, leaving lights on and faucets running without a care, which earned them penalties from the city government because of the quota on water usage — besides which, the roommate, who worked in the Webwork, was always at home, whereas Neipas was always not. He was at a loss on how to manage — he couldn't even get by on scraps from work. The cocktail of burger, fries and coke settled sourly in his stomach; he stared at the *I* for a few moments, his mind drifting into its flowing screen, seduced by its imperceptible hypnosis of distraction... Clocks ticked silently in his veins, the day passed him by. He stared for hours, let himself be drawn into the endless streams of words and imagery, carrying him through threads of connected information, a flushing cesspool made to appear orderly in the ingenious weaving of this vast digital world. It seemed to want to amass everyone on Earth in its web and glue them to it. And it was nearly successful. More omnipresent than any gods of the past, the Webwork was a drug more potent yet than the gods had been; for, like drugs and deities, the Webwork was a medium which deadened the mind and lifted the senses — where it lifted them to, and what it did to them once there, marked the chief difference between the three. It brought Neipas before nonsensical texts, frenzied videos, humorous images that made Neipas' beak curl sometimes, and sometimes he would even bend forward and look round briefly to find no one there to chuckle with him — and ads a little everywhere, framing the windows upon the houses of this virtual realm, peeping from the corners and all in bursts, all light-speed, all get and forget, threads like highways through these houses made of web, silkenful of curtains; always in the corners, the drone of some bug blinking on and on (and the numbers kept calling and the Collector kept recalling) amidst the babel. But when Neipas tired and removed himself from the *I*, he would come out feeling empty — and would feel the full viscosity of the cobweb gummed on him. There was also something of that rush of speed lingering in him after he left the Webwork; it beckoned in his innermost, promising to dispel the pasty silk. The impulse was irresistible, the allure of the *I* only became stronger, the light of it more hypnotizing yet...and again Neipas plunged into it, into the god of noise to exorcise all the quietude in him; all noise without sound, from which he left with a disturbing soundlessness which asked again for that whoosh — and the cycle would again repeat.

... whispers crackled at the edge of his dormant senses. Night had drawn into the bedroom, and a darkness had descended round the halo of the *I*. A sense of paranoia sprouted in his brain. The roommate's din of yelling metals had shushed, he slowly realized, and in his gradual realization of quietness the silence was gradually filled with other sounds, other deeply nestled sounds that encroached as his mind, awakening, loosened. Into the calm, the fridge on the other side of the wall would rumble with distant fiery clicks; the smoke alarm latched to the ceiling would beep sharply, maddeningly, suddenly every now and then — its red light flashing lone in the low sky. The dysfunctional AC unit would start up its artificial wind, which seemed to strain the place with a weird airiness, and he felt it as the occult voice of the gloom tightening round the shining glass when abruptly the *I* swerved — someone was calling — and the moth lurched into the light and flittered upon him, and he jumped up in an instant, quickly flipped the switch (the ceiling light beamed).

The bedroom was still there. It appeared starkly desolate and squalid, its walls suddenly empty and chipped. Taken by a fright as he faced the drapes, Neipas parted them to check if anyone was there — but there was only the window with his reflection in it.

He had dozed off a little without noticing; and now, without knowing why, he could not sleep, though he felt tired and weak, and wished for nothing more fervently than slumber. Flashes sparked out of the overhead lamp, under which the moth fluttered, circled, bumped, in a frenzied search for the light spring beyond the bulbed glass; the ceiling twitched as though it were snapping photos of his recumbent mask. Shadows looped over his closed eyes. A hatred of being there developed distantly in him, impotent; he went under his sheets to hide. He felt himself choking with depression; something aimless and endlessly dragging. Only the *I* and its amusements could deliver him from such torments...

Out of it, often, would shine Eva. She must have replied at some point; their flirtations continued at a gamed pace.

NEIPAS: There's gonna be a big fireworks show next week.

NEIPAS: Was thinking of checking it out.

NEIPAS: Maybe movie after

NEIPAS: Wanna come with? :)

Neipas found himself repeatedly over her page[s] in the maskbook. He flipped through every photograph, he got to know her every mask, every portrait, navigated down layers of selfies in different plumage and makeup. Again and again he would go back to it. He scoured her whole biography. Sometimes he would search in that catalogue of vanities for Orenda's page — she, too, emerged in his mind — but he couldn't find it. And even after he determined she didn't have a page, still three or four times he tried to find it.

The senses dulled. A slow degradation of the mind was taking place... the weakest, most animal, most base of instincts rose to the fore, snuck through sleepiness. His body simmered in the heat... in sweat, festering with the laze of slumber and exuding sexual impulses latent in sleep, bubbling up from a savage innermost. The Webwork offered these impulses an outlet to indulgence. He drifted, he drifted into the maze of the *I*, and in his state, vulnerable to the barest desires, drifted into the dark corners of the Webwork, where pornography thrived and mounds of bodies mixed confusedly — he lost himself in a world of latent violence, submission and domination; swollen with moaning cries.

EVA: Oh downtown? [hours later]
EVA: Not sure about fireworks might be down for movie tho
EVA: I'll let u know
EVA: :)

His deep and dormant breathing accelerated, he relaxed and subsided to a near doze, from which a warm well of sexual imagery would bubble up; as he dwelt into his sweaty mattress, into the moist underwear, he lusted for her, and lewd thoughts would pant in the hot air under the sheets, as he imagined, and touched. And he would wake up again, swaying between half-wakefulness and half-sleep, always in a listless unrest. The heat tickled his skin, making it itch. Some numbers kept calling; the moth flapped about silently. The music in the living room burst on and off. He kept sinking back into the lighted glass, into the noise of which he soundlessly whispered all his secrets (sometimes it felt as though the *I* itself was watching him back, and spoke back to him). Only once did he step out of bed, to rummage through the bottom of the cereal box, which held a bit of powdered smidgen that he proceeded to eat dry, as there was no milk; and cough back up as it clogged his throat dustily.

Languor took hold completely otherwise... He thought with horror of his father, locked in bed with that expression fixed. The smell — a strange, vaguely rancid odor floating up into his nostrils — reminded him of that time. He remembered his father (before the mirror he stood sometimes and mumbled). "I dunno, I dunno..." he mumbled in the dark; and Neipas withered, losing all strength and will; and his room seemed to shrink with him, and shadows accumulated in it. Neipas' nightmares seemed to step leisurely out of his dreams and stare at him from the corners within.

When the fatigue overdosed on the *I*, he simply looked at his hand. The lines in it: they blurred out and dispersed away from the palm.

The spiders had finished the web in the corner of the ceiling and the moth had finally been caught up in it. He observed it without vigor, empty. Still someone kept calling.

Neipas bit the knuckles of his fist, sunk his beak into the skin until it bled.

Outside, the tar ground baked under the windless air.

*

Two days had passed when the *I* shook with a peculiar ping. It had been quaking incessantly all along, lighting up with the prodding digits of some unknown caller — Neipas knew it to be the Collector, and tried to ignore it the best he could. But he sensed this buzzing to be different — and he checked.

EDAZIMA: Hey you ok?
EDAZIMA: I haven't seen you in a while.

NEIPAS: Hey! Haha I've been doing the day shift.

EDAZIMA: Have you?
EDAZIMA: How have you been?

NEIPAS: Ok :)
NEIPAS: A little sick actually. You?

Edazima showed up at his apartment later that day. She greeted the roommate with a very cordial smile — she detested him, but she knew how to wear her mask well. Her son, Martin, was brought along — Edazima had just picked him up from school — and he sat by the open window, immersed in his *I*. A good thing, Neipas thought; Edazima would have flooded his room with tobacco otherwise (she smoked everywhere and at all times, except during work-hours and in front of the kid).

She walked into Neipas' bedroom like an angel of sheer goodness. Right away she had seen, with much worry, Neipas' worn look, badly disguised beneath the messy wax; right away she noticed the smell, too — but she wore her mask well, and didn't show. The room had been sapping in gloom for days. But she parted the blinds and light was made; opened the windows and a breeze came to take the odors; and her caring manner was enough to drive the shade out of all senses. In her arms she carried a carton box stuffed with rice and vegetables, and in her pockets handfuls of protein bars; and upon the sight of these treasures Neipas brightened with the full force of hunger. He couldn't pull himself to be proud now, and accepted his good friend's gifts, ravishing the box's contents with desperation. Edazima had somehow guessed his predicament — how, he didn't know, for he hadn't made it known to her — and had brought along other boxes of food, which she had stashed in the fridge.

"Leftovers," she said casually, for she knew Neipas' pride. "Thought you might want a little. Janu cooked these, actually."

Noticing the mess, she had said, "dude, you want me to do the laundry?" in an earnest tone, knowing it would prompt him to do it. He leapt out of the bed for the first time in a long time, and in the same moment remembered his near-nakedness and the sorry state of his boxers, rushing to put those same pajamas he had worn to grab the burger, fries and coke with.

"Don't worry, I've seen naked dudes before and I'm still not impressed," Edazima laughed. She threw a sudden glance at Martin by the open window, standing yet inside the *I*, oblivious to everything around him.

This kind angel ushered in a brightening of Neipas' prospects. It was on the ground floor, where the laundry machines were lined up, that he received an email from the Editor, announcing that he had fixed him an interview — though not at the newspaper.

The Editor informed him that Eden Solutions, the same company which had just hired Magpie, "was looking for new folks". The interview was a week from then. Neipas rejoiced and glistened with hope — emboldened by the food in his stomach, he walked about in his pajamas in very excitement, climbing back up to his apartment where he made the announcement to Edazima. She received it with glee and offered to help him prepare for the interview; at which Neipas nearly burst in tears, so strong was the gratitude he felt.

As she stepped away to the bathroom Neipas felt his *I* tremble quickly and in succession; he dove in, his happiness blooming still wider.

EVA: free in a couple days if u wanna do fireworks :)

And that union of colon and closing-bracket jumped at Neipas' eyes in a little triumph. But there was something else.

ORENDA: Hey Neipas — going down to a march against Iblis expansion next week. You mentioned you wanted to come out so letting you know
ORENDA: I'll bring a camera for you

Neipas, in his distraction, had aimlessly wandered toward the freshness of the open window; for a breeze glided the streets that day. Next to him, Martin leaned quietly on the windowsill, aloof with his own lighted glass. But as he raised his head, Neipas noticed across the chasm separating this building from the next the open window of the apartment opposite. The two children of the neighboring family looked sadly out of it. A vague aunt, short and stout, wandered in the background; the parents were nowhere to be seen. Neipas knew they were from beyond the southern border and, remembering Janu, whose food had just replenished his spirits, wondered whether something had happened to them.

15 - Shrines of Opulence

Via Magna — that was the name of the main boulevard stretching east-westward from Belab Square, reaching the foot of the mountains on one end and the tip of the ocean on the other. A chief artery of enterprise, the Via was packed full of businesses and shops and framed whole in glassy storefronts (though any observer, riding east, would see its businesses progressively defunct, its shops increasingly abandoned, more and more windows locked, patched, or broken). Within Babylon, it was all pedestrian; and here it contained the most fashionable outlets, clubs and restaurants, the big houses of entertainment, the celebrated cinemas and flashy theatres, the ludic musea and curiosity shops.

At nearly all hours, and tonight especially, this path of commerce could be seen absolutely bustling with folk and noise, fluxing with confusion — particular words would rise out of the mess and fade back in as particular heads bobbed past Neipas' ear, and the profusion of bodies was so dense that most often he and Eva were either walking sideways or standing awkwardly, squeezed in, waiting for the multitude to push out; so that it was difficult to say anything to one another. There were heads and heads — heads in a disjointed sea of blurry motion and noise going, endlessly. Banners festooned over them and immense advertisements loomed from the flashing screens covering the facades of the rises above the boulevard. Their masks were splashed with electric colors and their voices pressed against jostling musics. Children shrieked excitedly among the wide hubbub; adults yapped with their beaks. In the middle of the promenade and out of the crowd, smiling, heavy-horned cattle surfaced, handing out flyers. Neipas would shake his head full of the noise of his surroundings and in confusion say nothing. By the doors, slick peacocks with suits tried to herd customers into the fashion houses, or those with aprons into the eating houses, rapidly turning from one to the next passing blur as Neipas shook his mask in the same unconscious motion. Islands would occasionally yawn amidst the river of bodies, circled by feather-foamed faces watching gaudy buskers performing, juggling, playing songs. Mannequins gazed from the margins behind stacked glasspanes; and beneath those margins beggars, some without legs, others without eyes, yet others with maimed lips, sat miserably upon cardboard, extending meekly their plastic cups to the passerbyes. All hustling for money, as it was said in those days — all struggling to survive.

Glitter snowed upon the bubbly populace from the multicolored sky. Within a detached moment, Neipas had been trying to discern the evening in it, the darkness of which the advertisements hid — when the sky exploded and suddenly Eva and everyone turned their glares up to mirror his. Fireworks popped and lit up the heights, and beaks gaped all around in wonder, and eyes widened as the flashes enveloped their orbs, blasted into their lenses, burst in sound inside their heads. The projectiles hissed out of the Belab soaring at the end of the Via like a guardian idol, an unbreakable pillar, like a paragon of solidity and might, shot out of the flanks towering over the surrounding towers and all under the fluttering Pearl, and blew up onto the night with an abundance of brightness so potent that soon night resembled itself no longer. No one knew exactly what the fireworks were supposed to be celebrating. There was a sort of conference with which they were associated, called a 'Market Summit', held at the Eagles' Nest every year, and of which Neipas, like everyone else, was only vaguely aware; yet knowledge of the fireworks was widespread and everyone amassed on the boulevards of Babylon for the occasion. The pyrotechnics boomed and shook over the city and everyone awed. A million eyes, a million lenses gaped out toward the flashing lights. They burst a millionfold across the glass facades of a myriad shrunken edifices... They filled the world in gloss. And Neipas, watching the spectacle alongside Eva who clutched tight his arm, heard in those pops the convulsive throbs shuffling in the core of the tower, in the flashes ripping away the darkness he saw the pulses of mystic dark suns, and cosmic rays of gold... He looked away. Close by, the prostrate back of a mendicant flashed in the shades of those standing and palpitating over him; his knees were pressed to the pavement and his forehead to the concrete, the sullied feathers of his nape bristling with lice. The man had his elbows upon the ground and held up a small box in his hands, the box rising above his entire being like someone offering oblations — it hadn't a single coin in it; and as Neipas contemplated the haunting vision in the crux of the multitude and seemed to hear muted pleas for help, he perceived suddenly the mistake of his first glimpse, and saw the beggar wasn't kneeling, because he had no more legs under his thighs.

The boom and flash of celestial eruptions drained away into the shifting hullabaloo, the drifting songs and blinking colors of normal activity; drained away as they ascended the escalators toward the mall, up a hill on the avenue running oblique to the Via. In the distance, the Pearl drew away and remained fixed; immovable, it seemed to pulse slowly in the vestigial popping of the fireworks' afterimage. The twitches of their memory cast fluttering shadows upon the darkening of Neipas' apprehensive heart. There was relief in departing from the sight of immiseration one so often glimpsed in the disregarded corners of the megalopolis, of people suffering invisibly; but there was dread in its lingering recollection, its recurring persistence like a leitmotif of presages upon his menaced life. He thought of the interview, looming but a few days away, and clutched to the prospect of it with the fear of one holding a fickle, final buoy. The tumult of the packed boulevard and its noises meanwhile subsided a little; or rather, morphed. And there was an unease in their flux; as though his anxieties physically bobbed in his fluids along with the changes in sound. But Eva, standing by his side — Eva unexpectedly held his hand, as if guessing his sentiments; her long, slim fingers penetrating the gap between his fingers tender, the soft warm skin of her palm pressing his; and he forgot it all in the flush and flight of his passions.

The escalator took them together to the mall at the top of the mount. The hill was called Aventine; the mall itself Capitola. Shining Aventine was rooted at the confluence of many roads. Its base bore myriad cavernous chambers dug into the rock to house whole sub-cities of cars; its steep sides of stone had been carved and stuffed in with steel, and molded, by the force of heavy machinery, into a colossal and dizzying formation of escalators streaming their way to the top. These moving stairs loaded in thousands by the day and at every waking hour. From a distance one could see a great mass of sliding heads gliding upward — from afar, the scene resembled an otherworldly heap of ants — into the monumental structure at the hill's summit. The escalators were, like the Capitola itself, flanked with tall luminous glass, out of which beamed gilded images and slogans and adverts trumpeting the virtues of the commodities enshrined within the giant shopping center. It perched up there, a massive rectangle of beaming walls; the glaring lights within projected themselves across the boulevards of the Financial District eastward, blending in with the spectacle of colors shining from the lampposts, the massive screens, the infinite number of storefronts and windows; and also to the west and all across the commercial neighborhoods stretching toward the ocean, and to the remote north over the affluent houses in the Diamond Hills; the lights of the Capitola reached as far as the districts of the southeast and their middle-class aspect of moneyed decadence. In it, one could witness a little hint of all Axiac.

"Pretty! Isn't it?" clamored Eva, as they were taken aloft.

Inside, the cacophony thickened upon them; the space closing in glaringly with its clear whiteness and sparkle. A long parade of masks floated in procession past titillating glass panes displaying an abundance of products, products multiplying across long rows and storeys arising with shimmering crystal lights. It was all imbued with a touristy ecclesiastical air, all numbed in the mesmerizing babel filling the walkways, walkways through which drifted many eyes, very open with tranced stares, sleepily directed at the showcases, in turns advancing, in turns stopping to behold the luminous windows; in a sluggish and uneven pace, lengthy clouds of pigeons swerved their heads from side to side, lifted and twisted their gazes along every direction in a languid frenzy of feathers. Above the glass-bound relics of their adoring contemplation hovered brand logos, idols of the age, summoning the flocks to their shrines to stuff their vestries. Eva, halting her stride to contemplate the floating dress and coat over the glass-shielded pedestal, made Neipas — who walked very near behind her — almost tumble upon her heels, which he avoided with an embarrassing half-dance out of the way. She didn't seem to notice, however; her eyes looked transfixed upon the dress and coat, which hung over a full-bodied mannequin standing at a pose. The mannequin looked almost real in its representation of a countenance, its cheeks and its lips, the neck beneath, the female shape of a body — even the eyes had the depth and feeling of a human, with the subtle longing common to all human eyes tucked behind the assured downward glance. An aura of glittering lights surrounded Eva, brimful and glamorous; bold golden letters spelled 'BE A GODDESS' over her upturned face. It was to this slogan that her attention was directed. It inspired in her vague feelings of wonder and want; it awakened shadowy cravings of glory and adulation in the numbed spirit of her indulgences. The dress twinkled with a million little gleams, and the coat over it was thick, heavy and imposing, with a grand display of swan feathers blooming from its back. It also looked stuffy and quite unsuitable to wear in the hot air of Axiac, but the status it conferred upon the wearer-mannequin was obvious and caused an immediate impression. It was an image of power, a seductive promise of power.

Neipas also beheld it with admiration; there was a glint of desire in his stare, too. But the yearning was different for him, for it was not about possessing the object — but about the power to buy it. He lost himself in the prospect of stepping into the store with an assertive stride, grab that coat and dress for her, and leisurely pass a credit card across the counter without a hint of worry or remorse. Eva would grin to him with the enthusiastic joy of a thankful lover; and his mask would remain stolid and self-assured in the absolute control of the face behind it. In his dwelling imagination the aspect of the mask was quite different as well; indeed, the general mood of the walkway — the endless storefront displays with their pictures of beauty and triumph, the hubbub of onlookers meshing in a droning uproar between the walls, the music blowing overhead — compelled him to dream a while and imagine himself inside all the handsome masks on the great posters and screens and mannequins beyond the myriad glasses, wearing those facades of supreme confidence, winning the astonishment of all. It was very easy to get carried away in the parade; and Neipas was easily swept up in it and transported in the alluring, dreamward dance of commerce. The windowpanes mirrored the shadows of the transients dragging over the mold of their showcases. The Pearl, through the lingering afterimage of the fireworks, still pulsed in his retina as he watched them pass; the explosions in the sky being to his benumbed discernment like reverberations of that vision he saw spasming from the dark peaks of the Belab as he stood in its depths — that golden light, that black sun. He had somehow associated them from the first with the treasures which urban fables told were kept in the tower's core. And he thought now how Eden Solutions, the catering company for which he was about to interview, did events at the very summit — at the palatial, the opulent Eagles' Nest. Not so long ago, he had asked Magpie, just hired — amidst the soot-vapored mists of KUR — how much money she'd be making there; and now the echoes of her voluminous response jingled in his memory and made him study these clothes with a real covetousness of possibility.

But as Neipas was musing in imaginations Eva decided to go in, and with a sudden step she went. Neipas grimaced with a sinking heart, disconcerted — since he couldn't buy anything, he hated being inside the stores; he felt like a trespasser. Just stepping through the front door was enough to make him giddy. Nevertheless he followed her in with a lowered head, sensing the full brunt of pennilessness even before he looked at the price tags. Eva proceeded right away to very swiftly shuffle through the files of clothes hung here and there. Meanwhile Neipas studied those bodiless torsos and limbless legs hung about in orderly rows, and there was something to the white, dazzling, disinfected air that roused his impatience and dislike. He sulked on a seat for a while. But in another moment Eva materialized before him with a whole pile of textiles over her forearm, and, beckoning Neipas to follow her, tossed a portion of the mound over him.

"Here," she said, cheery. "Let's try some clothes on you."

Neipas realized, to his horror, that what Eva had picked up was meant for him. Anticipating the nightmare of a time that would follow, he made some sort of half-hearted joke to dodge it, and even gave a tentative step back toward where the clothes had been picked up from; but Eva wouldn't budge. "C'mon you lamo!" she yelled out, to Neipas' embarrassment; which made him hesitate some more. She went as far as pushing him toward the dressing rooms, forcing his wobbly step. That he didn't want to be there was obvious, but it didn't matter one bit to Eva's volcanic enthusiasm and overwhelming will.

"This," she said finally, "would look great on you." She held up a blazer jacket with a clear bright color, fine cut and fresh, very airy, youthful aspect. It looked expensive. Neipas took it from her and proceeded to put it on, but she stopped him; "wait," Eva said as she made another go through the pile. After a minute or two she had picked a pair of trousers and a shirt to match.

"Ok, try this."

The dressing room was but a narrow stall or booth fronted by a curtain. At the immediate end of it there was a large mirror comprising the whole back wall, with a very bright lamp above it; and upon the side wall was fixed a hook rack, with a stool resting beneath that. Neipas hung the jacket on one of the hooks and plopped the rest of the clothes on the stool. Then he turned round to draw the curtain shut, making a couple of clumsy attempts before stopping to stare frustratedly at it — for the cloth wouldn't cover the booth completely, leaving a bit of a breach through which Neipas could spy the exterior and the exterior could peek inside. A warmth of shyness filled his face — how was he to undress when everyone could see him? — and his already discouraged mood was further dampened. For a while he just stood there, considering the small gap in the curtain.

Nearly the whole store was visible to him. He observed the immensity of it, with its populace of dressed-up phantoms suspended on motionless hangers and its crowds of souls masked with bird feathers browsing one another in a sort of lazy examination. Dispersed in the milky lights, customers flung to and fro in flaccid motions, and heaped upon their arms piece of clothing upon piece of clothing, moving — moved by what, Neipas couldn't tell — half-unconsciously, to all appearances, and in droves. Masks were spruced, mantles layered on, vanities fed and satiated and aroused, and much money spent; and thus the cogs of economic prosperity remained well lubricated with a steady flood of preen oil.

Nonetheless, despite all the movement — it was strange — a silence befell Neipas inside the dressing room. He realized how silly he was being as he perceived the mass of folk outside going about in total indifference to him. Even Eva, who was fiddling upon her *I* right near, seemed to not pay him any heed. It was as if the imperfect curtain veiled him completely, and the breach was visible to him alone.

So Neipas then, hesitant, took off his shirt, ruffling the feathers of his head. He faced the mirror. He had an intention to put on the new attire quickly but stopped himself short before his reflected image. Casting a glance back at the breach, and seeing everyone still shopping indifferently, he paused, with a muted breath, to behold his naked torso. It was an embarrassing sight for Neipas; especially here, under the potential sight of many. Without the concealing cloth his body looked lame, flimsy, with no allure to it. The arms, used to carrying weight, were somewhat delineated along the muscular mass; but his chest was flat, his back slightly curved, his belly slack, sleepy — a very effigy of weakness and poverty of will. Contemplating the flabbiness of his lower abdomen, a sort of itch began prodding within; the desire to become the masks outside became stronger yet.

He stared into the breach again. Those waltzing out there — they were all vapid, he knew. Within himself, he knew it well; but they all looked so good! So elegant and confident and strong, so happy did they appear under those mounds of clothes, under those perfect wax faces! Now, in the relative solitude of the dressing room, not even his own wax visage could hide the tired emptiness of his true face or the weary sheen, the sickly destitution in his eyes. In the wan glow of the lamp above the mirror, he looked an altogether feebly thing, molten and absent; and the feathers of his head, standing on end, made him resemble one of those beggars lying in the Via.

He wore the shirt Eva had picked for him: a nice, snug fit. Then he considered the jacket on the hook closely, pausing his fingers upon its fabric. It was made of fine wool, culled from many a sheep or goat in the summer days, collected, made into textile in a mill, and dyed in the toxic banks of some faraway river, then stitched up to shape by the hands of anonymous factory servants; and finally shipped, along with a thousand replications of itself, in a vast crate piled between countless other vast crates atop a vast barge floating across a whole ocean to berth at the smoky port of Ostrich. In one of its chemical plants had been made the plastic from which was derived the polyester of the shirt wrapped around his skin; plastic refined out of petroleum dug out of Earth's crust, petroleum transformed in a series of chemical permutations enacted along a lengthy yarn of machinery and process — petroleum now breathing into his pores through the shirt in the dressing room, which was also made of cotton; cotton harvested in some very remote field, picked out between sharp thorns by the rough fingers of distant peasants, wet of the sod of the land and calloused by the toil of bent backs under sheets of plodding rain, who replicated in their labor the slavering of those who under Columbia's foundational oppression brought it its second wealth. Hauled then onto huge trucks, the sullen drivers would take the load of this raw fluff to the factories where, much like the polyester and the wool, it would undergo metamorphoses and dislocations that culminated in the cross-weave of the shirt now covering Neipas' torso.

In some remote part of his spirit, he sensed the abandoned looms and the many scraps of cloth amassing in that rubbish he had seen in the depths of the Belab; in some layer of his eye he saw still the pulsating gold of its heights, and heard the boom and the Midget's speechlessly etched plea... He recalled Orenda on that night of warm lights, in the bookstore's garden. And while his mind dawdled in its lassitude of resigned fatigue, Neipas began wrapping the woolen jacket over his shoulder — slowly — inserting his arms into the felt cavities. There was a certain posture it compelled the body into, a pose of finesse, of style, even of a certain pride, and he found himself quite seamlessly with his back very straight, examining with satisfaction the renewed image of a suddenly rejuvenated self — though he realized in an instant he was no longer wearing pants (having removed them to try on the new ones) and then — it was strange but — his still-affected eye, veering uncannily upon the corner of the mirror, chanced to find the breach in the curtain behind him; and, deepening its sight through the looking glass, gazed the pigeon leer of every customer in that store suddenly fixed upon him there; all of them having abruptly stopped (he rushed to pull the pants up).

...Neipas stepped out from behind the curtain. "You look great!" Eva said. She took a photo, Neipas feeling surrounded by the general murmur of the pigeons (all suddenly shopping again) and much too ashamed to protest.

"You think so?" he simply mumbled, disheartened.

"Hm-hm," she replied, nodding her head studiously as she scanned him top to bottom. "I really do. Do you like it?"

"Well..." Neipas hesitated, looking down at himself. "The pants and the shirt feel kinda funny to be honest, but I really like the jacket." Neipas didn't really think this. He liked to see his body in those pants and shirt, they made him look better than he was; but he didn't want to feel pressured to buy them. He had to make at least a concession to Eva, however, and since he liked the jacket best, he said so.

"Hmm, ok," Eva muttered, fixated on her analysis of him still. "Yeah, maybe you're right... That jacket looks good on you for sure though." Then they stood regarding themselves for a while.

Eventually Eva roused out of her focused scrutiny of Neipas' appearance and snapped her fingers. "Ok!" she exclaimed. "I'm buying you this."

"What? No no no no," Neipas laughed, but Eva was already heading toward the counter. "Eva, wait up a second!"

"What."

"I'm not gonna let you buy this for me!" Neipas proclaimed with a nervous shortness of breath.

"Why not? I want to."

"Ok — Well, I appreciate that," Neipas chuckled awkwardly, "but I can't accept it, Eva."

"Don't worry about it. You look good in it, I wanna get it for you." It was clear this was all the reason Eva needed.

"But... You know. Haha! No, Eva, seriously," stammered the poor fellow, whose heart was quickly dissolving before the adorable frown Eva was carving upon her mask.

"Plus you need it for the interview! Don't worry about it. Here, take that off, dress up," Eva commanded with the sweetest pointing gestures, "we'll walk to the counter, and I'll get this for you, ok?"

Neipas still hesitated a bit, but it was too difficult to contradict Eva. She possessed the sort of thoughtless confidence — and the endearing femininity of her ways besides — that commands a situation from the start and compels passive personalities to quickly submit before her will. To her, things were simple — she liked how Neipas looked in the jacket and felt like buying it; that was that. She couldn't guess the pang in the pride of the man when it was affected by a sense of dependency.

Eva purchased the jacket. It didn't look great over Neipas' current clothes so they put it in a fancy plastic bag, with plume adorning the rims of it; and left the store. Emerging back into the hypnosis of blaring music and packed corridors, Neipas looked at Eva and thanked her once more, full of appreciation in his humbled voice.

"Not a problem," she proclaimed, carving up a subtle, tender smile that singed Neipas' emasculated self-esteem, beautiful though the smile was to him.

And thus, close to one another, they left the store, and rejoined the ambling procession making the round alongside the vitreous shrines which one after the other manifested the ideal of the age, the perfection of beauty, the apotheosis of the surface. Mannequins elaborate, mannequins vague, some without limb, others without semblance, all watched from the exalted height of their podiums, from the dignity of their altars as the procession passed, lulled by the incantation of noise, scattered through a greenhoused amalgam of voices and music sounded and echoed and re-echoed within white dazzled bounds; a suffusing noise, a noise all assuming, a noise so pervasive that it became inconspicuous, and into which one gradually lost oneself in merging consciousness. Minds which became noise in its seeping totality floated round the circuit, marking the tempo of industrious and inchoate hours, marching to the melting sounds as if to a hymn, relentless; the disorderly rhythm of finance's beating heart could be sensed in their wade. And the mannequins watched tall as the procession flowed, worshiped by its unending, desirous eyes; and they watched as it flocked through their gates, and proffered upon their sanctums its wealth in offering, those endless seekers of beauty and youth...

Eva and Neipas, following along, wound up at the food court on the top floor. They sat at one of the many plastic tables with their plastic trays and plastic-wrapped burgers, fries, and sodas; one among many rows of fluttering, transpiring pigeons sitting hunched over plastic meals. The court, ringed by yawning stands of scrambling fast-food cattle, was all crisscrossed by these pigeons' scouring activity, each one standing looking for a seat with twitching heads and very open, very round red eyes.

"So you live by yourself in that house?" Neipas asked over his tray, through the liquefying noise.

"It's my parents'. I tend the house for them," Eva replied. "Sometimes I rent out some of the rooms, but never for very long."

Neipas nodded and soundlessly intoned 'I see'. "What do your parents do?"

"My dad's a tailor. My mom's a dollmaker," she said, and shrugged. "I don't see them most of the year."

"How come?"

"Oh —" (she took a moment to answer, apparently not understanding the question). "They're separated."

Eva then looked at him with a clear-eyed gaze, as if surfacing from a momentary reverie, and smiled affectionately, pensively; smiled without effort and without having to tend to the mask. Her thoughts had drifted out of the heavy atmosphere of her house and into the recollection of its front yard, where they had kissed. She had been surprised at his mindfulness and self-control when she realized that despite the lust in his eyes Neipas would not be coming in — in reality, she had mistaken indecision and a general disorientation of mind for respect and gallantry, qualities rare in those days, and had come to cherish him for his enigmatic difference from the men she had been with before, all so eager and coarse; she had become intrigued by his more sensible spirit, and what she interpreted to be a certain tranquility of unhurriedness and self-assurance, which were attractive to her. The more days she waited for his text the more alluring he seemed. Even as he talked about his photography now (because she had asked) she thought about him with the absentmindedness of curiosity and infatuation.

Neipas meanwhile spoke — of longings and desires, the dream of owning his own studio, about his ambitions of travel, of collecting portraits from around the globe — and knew she was not listening. His voice melded in the noise and became babble which he no longer understood and no longer held, as he watched her mask drip, and his malformed thoughts fall in the lacunae of her inattention.

On one side of the food court gaped the large portal which gave access to the movie theaters. Before long they sat in the darkness, staring at a vast, palpitating screen, which gripped every spectator, held every silhouetted head within its ample frame. The veils had parted; and the screen deepened into a world of wonders, a place full of dangers and delights, wherein victory was assured and all things were easy — the very adversities the characters faced seemed leisurely, glamorous, the type of thing one would enjoy going through for a change, for the sake of the thrill, the satisfaction of empathy from one's fellows, and the excitement of one's self-overcoming. Neipas watched the formidable bodies and the famous visages, the chiseled faces of those stag and deer-masked celebrities, a little enviously. He coveted the ease of conduct, the power, the intelligence, the charm of those zapping superheroes, before whom life opened up in pageant between admiring crowds, before whom hardships simply parted way and under whose steps sprawled roads paved with fortune. They all in the audience gazed with varying degrees and kinds of devotion (even the scathing and the indifferent had paid homage in the form of a movie ticket), watching as one watches a one-way mirror, like transfixed voyeurs spying through a window at the object of their adoration and cupidity, as the superheroes soared and flashed, pretending not to be aware of their presence; standing giantly over the audience while their antlers branched off beyond the edges of the screen and took root in the captivated attention of every eye. The window deepened; it absorbed minds.

Then Neipas appeared before the popcorn stand — the movie had ended, the credits rolled over a nice suburban home with a pleasant facade but no interior — waiting for Eva, who had gone into the bathroom to touch up her makeup. He held the plume-rimmed bag, in which he carried his gratitude and his shame, and the weight of countless debts pulling his shoulders down as his stare glassed out. Corn popped before his unseeing eyes; popped through the noise into his heart, louder and louder.

Even expenses as relatively meager as two fast-food meals and two movie tickets — both of which he felt obliged to pay for after Eva bought the jacket — crowded his mind and deepened the gravity of his anxieties. In his thoughts he nervously envisioned the looming interview as a kind of last chance to emerge from the sea of bills in which he was currently drowning. He had to get the job, he had to. There was no other way, and it was as he was muttering this to himself that his eyes blinked with an effort toward resolution and, turning his head, he saw him.

He had caught glimpses of him all that evening, creeping here and there among the crowd. Now he materialized in full — here was the Debt Collector, coming to remind him of his obligations again; he never gave up. Neipas' rage surged from his despair — and in a sudden fit of wide-eyed madness he went to him, shouting indignantly "Stop following me! What do you want!" as his stare momentarily convulsed and dispersed to every direction, for he was frightened; but suddenly he realized he had been walking away, and not toward, the Collector — but still the Collector managed to catch up to him when he lost his orientation among the noisy throng, and somehow appeared before him now.

"What you want!" Neipas exclaimed in such a mood of exasperation that he lifted a hand to hide his face. The Collector was extremely near now, so near that Neipas could hear him hiss the words, "Pay your debts! Pay your debts! Pay your debts!" again and again, without stop, as he neared closer and still closer. And Neipas saw then, for the first time, the Debt Collector up close — close enough to actually see him. He saw the countenance under his hat; and what he saw made him gasp in horror. His legs recoiled into a backward step. His hand lowered instinctively to his breast.

He saw the Collector had no face.

16 - The Audition

Across the conference table sat a spectacled owl.

"So," she pursued, re-positioning her glasses atop her beak with one hand (with the other she adjusted the eagle mask wrapping the back of her head), "tell me, why are you the best person for this job?"

Neipas had been waiting for this question — he had practiced the answer and was ready to recite it to the tee. For the past few days he had been going to Edazima's to rehearse, seeking the aid of his good friend to make ready. Edazima, ever the compassionate soul, dedicated herself fully to the task of coaching Neipas, questioning, interrogating, examining, suggesting, revising, always present and alert, always filled with an unexplainable energy. She was a severe director. After meeting his personal quota of served day-shift meals, Neipas, mentally preparing for a couple of hours of hard concentration and intense scrutiny, would catch the bus to her apartment at the opposite end of Axiac's southside; and would find himself sitting on her couch, all jittery upon it, legs switching all over as he fumbled through his answers, stopping himself with frustration, stammering back into it, plugging his face onto the cup of his hands and dropping into the depths of the couch helplessly. Only his friend's steady encouragement would prop him up. He listened humbly to her criticism, sat still as she shaped his mask with firm fingers — and then got up again. Speedwalking by and past him, Edazima all the while tended to the demands of her household, divided between a myriad simultaneous chores: starting on the dinner, peeling and cutting a piece of fruit for Martin, throwing a heap of dirty laundry into the washer, sitting with Neipas for a moment, picking up Martin and putting him on her lap, quelling his tantrums with kisses and hugs, getting up to check on the dinner, plunging the wet clothes into the drier, succumbing to Martin's impatience and giving him the *I*, sitting back with Neipas, getting back up to check the stove; the whole time listening to Neipas cawing away eagerly his responses to potential interview questions and correcting him with a tender voice, in volume raised or subdued depending on what section of the small abode she found herself in. From time to time, when Edazima had stepped off to the stove, Neipas would interrupt himself and ask, "Don't you need help with anything?"

To which she would answer, "Nah man, don't worry. So — " and continued. She would refuse more vehemently the more she repeated the refusal; and Neipas was ultimately glad to simply sit after all those hours of toil.

But when Edazima turned round with the steaming pot, dinner ready, and a feeling of intense gratitude surged in him, so strong and sudden as to bring him to the cusp of weeping — he would feel a little bashful, bad for not helping her. He knew what she would say had he really insisted, for she had said it before — "Goodness man, just sit down! You're a guest" — and still the weight of conscience, a consciousness of debt, of an awareness of all she had done for him, would sit in him at the dining table.

The table was set between the stove and the couch. Neipas considered the cushions on which he had just sat for an hour, on which he had slept for a year, not that many months before. He recalled the first night he lay on them, how worn he was, how filthy; he sensed again the relief of his fatigued body as it slacked into the couch's comfort, his mind instantly yielding to it, into oblivion. He remembered how, next morning, he emerged from deep sleep like a stone resting at the bottom of an ocean, whose waters had drained away from it — and opened his eyes to a table, that very table, set with breakfast. Martin sat on his mother's knee, she was feeding him a spoonful of some gruel, rousing him to laughter as the spoon flew in circles toward his gaping little mouth. Stopping her giggling eyes on Neipas and realizing him awake, she called him cheerily to the table. "Good morning!" He had never forgotten the way she had said it — devoid of reproach, devoid of judgment; fully accepting, without reservation. Humbled by the loving welcome in her tone, Neipas sat, if a little embarrassed, shrunken in the precariousness of his situation. As he ate that first breakfast — feeling his energies replenish in the warmth of the meal, his mind relaxing off the strain — he promised Edazima he'd get back on his feet soon, and would stay no longer than a couple of weeks.

"Neipas — don't even worry about it. You're my guest — welcome to stay as long as you need, got it?"

And, listening to these words then, Neipas really did weep, letting shed a tear pushed out by an overwhelming gratitude, from the thickness of a strain long sustained; though he hid it by staring at his plate, petting the food.

Alas, it would be a good while before Edazima once more saved him by getting him a gig at the Belab's underground. She had been hired to work in Kur's pantry recently herself, and it was at her side that Neipas first saw the elevator doors open to its dingy subterranean kitchen, that tiled buried corridor; the interview was conducted right there by a pile of dirty pots, and he began the very day, the very minute. Then, as now, Neipas had walked along the Via Sacra, the boulevard cutting south-northward across Belab Square, from Babylon Station, passing by many roadside vagrants and refugees who extended sooted hands and incomprehensible appeals, under a smelly bridge outfitted with spikes so no one would camp there and where nonetheless folk lay and lived; then — emerging — as now, Neipas had neared the great tower with a quiet turbulence gurgling in his stomach.

Watching it inexorably rise as he approached from the south side, he'd beheld the Belab with great wonder — he had never before seen it so close. There was an immense splendor in its godly altitudes, in the cascades descending from the peak, glinting dazzlingly the light of gold. The Pearl hovered higher than the sun, like an immortal beacon shining from heaven; and the Belab's summit seemed at one with the skies. Neipas secretly dreamt of heights; something in him craved the glory of those elevations. But his reality had so far swerved from such dreams that he could never really consider that, one year from then, he would step upon the apex — that he would work there, at the crown of pinnacles — at the Eagles' Nest.

"The Eagles' Nest," the interviewer continued, "or Anubel, as it is officially known, is a luxury establishment, designed to accommodate and facilitate the gathering of high-profile individuals in the contexts of business or leisure — the structure contains private estates and houses, as well as large common areas as venues including the central ballroom, game rooms, conference rooms, swimming pools, saunas, baths, cinemas, tennis courts, golf courts, basketball courts, other courts — among others." Eden's interviewer, who faced Neipas with the owl mask and the window behind her with the mask of the eagle, sat on a very large and very tall chair, which seemed to lift up even above the edge of the table, over Neipas' head, as she spoke. "We need additional personnel for an upcoming event, held at the venue."

To him, it all came as a surprise and a shock. Her words were digested into his veins and sent his pulse into such a flight of fancy that he nearly missed her listing the job's requirements and asking whether he was fit for them.

"You would be handling high-end materials; everything you would touch, everything you would step on — all very expensive," elucidated the interviewer from the heights of her chair, and Neipas nodded along with the utmost focus, mumbling 'expensive, yeah', "— would you be capable of handling these highly delicate items, in possibly high-stress situations, without damaging them?"

Neipas fixed the lumpy surface of his pigeon cheek and molded everything quickly into a sober image. "Yes," he said. "I'm very confident that I would, absolutely."

'I'm very confident that' and 'absolutely' (much like 'well,' and 'I strongly believe') were among the stock phrases he had repeatedly muttered under his breath as he stood in the back of the climbing elevator. It was full of the kind of tension that precedes a decisive occasion, the type of occasion designed to measure one's worth, that forced one to hone every faculty of mind and body to the very best and most subtle versions of themselves. It was nerve-racking.

His chest had borne the ticking clock of expectation for days. Now he petted the jacket Eva had given him, running his fingers down the seams, as he recited his lines intimately in the corner, going along the ticking sway. Not long before, he had left his tray in Kur's kitchen shelf and had gone to change into it. At that point the smoke gushing out the endless pots was dissipating, spirited out into the vents by the ceiling. The smell of cooked meat and processed sugarcane was thinning; and Neipas' work-suit yet reeked of it. Yet he emerged out of that squalid tophet perfumed, immaculate, going without looking back at the narrow alley of stoves; and entered the elevator with Eva's jacket wrapping his anxious heart, beating hopeful and afraid.

It was a long journey up the Belab's soaring heights; Neipas had to climb through several elevators. Bodies and masks shuffled and interchanged, and their constitution morphed steeply as the lift carried on upward. Attires became better groomed, visages more colorful, beaks and snouts quieter. The space was filled in and emptied out without a peep. Peacock faces, horse semblances, even eagles, entered his ken — the supreme respectability of their suits and ties intimidated Neipas, and allured him. He kept to his corner always, at turns nervous and calm, with a queasy sense of anticipation underlying all feelings. Even as he witnessed the ebb and flow of transformations of the throng populating the lift as it ascended, he sensed him; constant, always by. Always he perceived the Debt Collector lurking still in the opposite corner, standing quietly at the edge of his glimpse; always he felt his grotesque facelessness, and often glanced inward to see the memory of a hole where a countenance ought to have been. Neipas did his best to ignore him. He kept calm, he met his circumstances staidly; he couldn't afford to succumb to his fears.

Meanwhile the elevator rose, and rose, and rose — the length of the flight was so absurd that it amused Neipas a little; generally it had the effect of subduing the hastiness in his breast. As it approached his stop, the elevator grew packed with goat masks adorned with pins shaped like the flag of the nation, which glittered very shiny under the bright ceiling glare. Shortly after, a flock of schoolchildren wobbled in with large backpacks, tailing their educator who, wobbly herself, towered somewhat nervously. They all wore different clothes and all clothes were of different colors, forming a sort of harlequin pattern across under their little heads. Their masks were, however, all alike, and the educator was busily engaged in molding them, stooping onto the children with a very agitated diligence. One of the pin-bearing onlookers, her shoulders squeezed against her neck, was very much moved.

"Aww!" she uttered. "They are so cute! Do you mind if I take a picture?" The educator jubilantly conceded, and all of a sudden all were shambling onto the walls to make room for the children scuffling about in the empty inches of space by them. Neipas, in his corner, was packed up against the mob, the affected onlooker at their head, holding up her *I* over her goat mask and pointing it to the dense agglomeration of lined up children beaming with large cuts of wax, their educator rising giantly behind them with a huge smile stapled on her face. For a long bit Neipas endured an elbow digging thick into his rib; he watched impatiently the flashes of light bursting in the box-space and disappearing at every angle, drawing up the kids' faces, their smiles already empty, their eyes already glassy.

The goats blared. "Neipas?"

Edazima snapped her fingers. Sitting across the dining table from her, Neipas had for a moment considered the same vacant stare on her son's own face, completely absorbed before his own glossy black box which flashed onto the hardening wax of his mask, whispering secrets into his receding ear. Sometimes Martin giggled to it. It was a giggle different from what Neipas remembered of that past life when he was still a student, and came to look after the baby boy and watch his crib while his mother sweated across jobs, through classrooms, to provide for the beloved newborn. Little Martin looked upward with wide eyes then, dreamy, innocent, glaring full of life's promise; beholding curiously the shiny trinkets revolving slowly over his head. When Neipas leaned in over the little railing, the baby would turn his stare intrigued, wondering what bizarre thing that could be, that head made of fingers — and when the giant drew those fingers away to reveal a face Martin would burst in such a delightful laughter that Neipas could not help but laugh himself, so much entertained that he repeated the joke again and again, over and over to the same little burst of wonder, to the same puffing of little cheeks and opening of little toothless lips, of little eager eyes narrowing with delight and sincerity, full of life.

Yet now — the child was possessed by a sort of vacancy, the glass of the *I* was become his own eyes. Whenever he was spoken to he didn't respond; whenever the speaker insisted Martin would simply nod and mumble — and he never removed his eyes from the glass. A third attempt, and if the *I* was taken away from him he would burst in a nervous eruption; his little self pitched to the brink of fury and tears. Edazima sometimes snapped at him with her own frustrations; but not that day. She let him be in his hypnosis. "Neipas?"

His eyes shrunk into focus and he lifted his head to Edazima across the dining able. She smiled — that same resolute smile with which she had first met him in writing class.

"Yes," Neipas smiled in response. "Sorry."

"Ok, let's keep going then," Edazima said, her voice ramming through the food she was chewing. "So — why are you the best person for this job?"

Neipas rehearsed the answer in his head repeatedly on the day of the interview. He mumbled it behind closed lips yet even as he waited pressed tight against the corner of the elevator where the pack of beaming schoolchildren flashed. Finally, it stopped, pending somewhere in the bosom of the great tower. The flock oozed out orderly, the educator lining them up in a long file outside as they came. As the rest exited slowly Neipas took a deep breath, making ready for the trial ahead. He followed the folk squeezing through and out.

Neipas emerged into a large, square hall. Out the few doorframes interspaced along the walls, long crowds flowed, walking across, forming many interweaving trails which bridged the departments indicated on brass plaques by the open doors. A few went along slowly — *I*s beneath their stares — most speedily, with dossiers nestled under their arms. These trails of scrambling legs (with little piglets and ducklings occasionally tottering by their feet) crisscrossed around a single sculpture at center: A roaring legionnaire with an armor made of bronze scales and the golden head of a lion, mane expanding into a flaming halo; one iron foot (a bull's hoof) upon the plinth, the other (an eagle's talon) trampling a fetal gnome made of baked clay, over which the legionnaire brandished four silver arms: one held an olive branch; the other a cornucopia; another held an elusively shaped object, a sort of rod molded indecisively between fishing cane and whip. The last hand, pulled back highest, gripped a spear. Dove wings bloomed wide from its armored back; and on the plinth from which this scene arose, was written — etched —

Quis
sicut
Deus
fecit

To the right and left were small escalators leading to the second floor, which was but a mezzanine with many other doors rimming round the square hall. On the facade of it, upon the side facing Neipas now, was emblazoned in silver caps the caption: 'MINISTRY OF EDUCATION'.

Right in front of the elevator — with the scrambling throng, pyramidal sculpture and mezzanine in the background — stood a simple wooden table. An old scrawny ox sat behind it. He wore a tweed jacket and his square spectacles hung on the very edge of his lean, wrinkled, sagging snout.

Neipas approached him. "Excuse me," he stated.

The lanky fellow raised his head feebly, drawing a smile with long, bony fingers that trembled a little. The result was a haggard grin which hardly concealed the protruding, mouse-like teeth beyond the fellow's mandible. "Yes?" he said, with some effort of his writhing voice.

"The department of aptitude, please?" Neipas felt a bit sorry for the old clerk and drew a sympathetic smile to reflect the sentiment. He'd just realized his spectacles had no lens.

"Right in front," the skeletal old ox said with much exertion, pointing a wobbling thumb backward, in the direction of the sculpture. Neipas, leaning his head aside, saw that there was a large gate beyond it.

"I see," Neipas nodded, "thank you so much."

"Have... a good day," the old clerk or pedagogue struggled through the words as he mechanically lowered back his head; his neck seemed thick with rust, and indeed the clay round his saggy jaw seemed to be cracking.

"You too." Neipas slid into one of the spoors of moving cattle, sheep and goats, trailing them to the gate in the back. Most of the crowd came in and out of it. It was a large double-door spanning the whole width of back wall, above which was fixed a discreet plaque that read *Department of Aptitude* — slowly and with the mob Neipas shuffled toward. Going round the statue of the legionnaire standing in the center of the hall, he passed close to a worn door that had one of its hinges broken off and thus hung aslant. Next to it was a plaque thickening in something like mold — it read *library*. A couple of goats and a pigeon could be seen emerging from the dust cloud fogging the interior, appearing diligent, heads down and tomes under arm.

Through the gate of the Aptitude Department there was a corridor deep and wide, altogether much larger than the entrance hall. It also looked much better kept, everything looked brand new, from the solid doors flanking the space to the complex pattern of soft tapestry under their feet. Not a whiff of decadence had infiltrated its blank walls. Neipas headed toward door #13, his destination. On the way he dodged past a great many peacocks donning respectable attires, very tranquil in their professional demeanors. Looking for the door he meant to go into he saw such captions as '5: STANDARDIZED TESTS', '3: CURRICULA' and '1: EDUCATOR EDUCATION'; "not this one, not this one..." Neipas would mumble to himself as he went. Finally he spotted his door, standing noble next to an imposing plaque reading

'13: PRIVATE INVESTMENT RELATIONS'

Beyond the door was another large reception area; its slick, immaculate aspect struck Neipas at once. Everything here looked brand new and ultra clean — there was the carpeted floor stretching its mowed fur down the sides, ending at a shiny, silvery sliding gate at the far edge of each flank; the green sofas that populated it looked brought straight from the manufacturer, so vivid was the glow of their color and so luxurious the semblance of their texture; down the middle of the aisle opening between the agglomeration of sitting, suited-up pigeons, there arched a very stylish convex reception desk, made of some glossy purple material and manned by three high-beaked peahens. Neipas walked up to them:

"Excuse me —"

"Good afternoon," said distractedly the peahen receptionist, keeping her smile upon her mask and her glare on the glowing screen before her. "Are you here for the audition?"

"Mmyes... huh, for —"

"Eden Solutions?"

"That's right" (nodding).

"Please have a seat. We will call you. Would you like some coffee while you wait?" she inquired very amicably, without, however, ever moving her blinkless stare.

"Oh — no, thank you."

"You're welcome."

Neipas checked the I — there were still 20 minutes left; he had come early enough. Looking around vaguely for an empty sofa, he inadvertently scanned the hall; as he sat, he had already discerned the brimming faces of the expectant interviewees silently gathered there, whose composure was kept up only by the sense of absolute necessity; and though their nervousness held back upon the wax pores of their masks it was well sweated under the fabric of their suits: an indistinct odor of it hid under the polished aroma of air fresheners. The aspirant sitting in front of him in particular, with his smile so exaggeratedly set, teeth so glued and jaw so rigid, and beak so shrunken, smelled of it; he seemed eager to discharge his anxiety into conversation. Some shielding instinct made Neipas look away, for he knew how contagious such tensions as those the fellow seemed to transpire could be.

"Hot day, huh," the pigeon told Neipas' cheek.

"Yep, yeah," Neipas nodded, tilting his grin from side to side. He made a blatant pretense of searching the room for something; eying, at turns, the water dispenser, the coffee machine, the framed and glassed articles or diplomas (also the depictions of two former Columbidae presidents flexing their golden chins) in the moody shade there behind the waiting, groomed, repeated pigeon heads. In a recess there was a tall glass showcase, standing like a museum piece; inside it a curtain, or cape, over which a solitary expressionless mask hovered. Neipas glimpsed all these things, until his roving eyes settled into the *I* — and kept roving inside it as he sensed the solicitous interviewee before him making tentative, shivering motions to engage in dialogue — until the fellow was called up.

14 minutes to the interview. Neipas put the *I* away and resolved to not touch it again. He called Edazima's final advice to mind. "Now just relax," she had told him at her doorstep, holding both his shoulders. "You're ready, ok? Don't think about it, don't rehearse anymore. It'll only get in your way now. Take it easy — and you'll know what to do. Got it?" The advice was the very same she had given him a year or so before, as he was about to head down to Kur's subterranean backstages for its own interview. He had followed it then, and succeeded — he was given an opportunity to place his nose above water. Now he was sinking under once more, and he felt as though he'd never ceased floating on the threshold of drowning — he wanted it no longer. In his innermost he found an artful determination, and locked in step with it. He simply let himself sag mentally (though he kept very upright in his seat), his mind fizzled out of thought; staring toward the floor his sight became blurred and his head grew blank. He relaxed. Out of sheer necessity, he let go his angst; in total command of himself, he emptied himself out. He knew that unless he soothed into a suitable inner frequency of calmness, the interview wouldn't go well.

In this abstracted state, scraps of thoughts floated in and faded out of his dormant mind. An unconscious thread was followed into the depths — he glimpsed Eva with longing and desire, in her red dress; then Orenda, with curiosity and expectation, wondering how the protest would be, the tickling forewarmth of a new experience flowering through the relaxation of his all-suppressing anxieties — he thought with satisfaction the prospect of photographing all day again, and how he hadn't truly dedicated himself freely to his craft since his days in college. The specter of Ivory Towers appeared before him, and with it the recollection of all his failures. He thought of Edazima, whose advice and encouragement grounded him and becalmed his spirits; he thought of her sadly now, as he remembered the bright young student she had once been. Neipas felt again the impression with which that girl, who sat next to him in writing class, had marked him. He saw her again raising her hand eagerly above all heads, the way she leaned forward in her chair in the library, over a spread of sheets and pages, for hours on end — perpetually overworked, piling up stress, blowing it off in cigarette puffs outside the library doors. Neipas admired and envied her capacity to work. His own natural tempo struggled always to combat lethargy — he could only be steady in the thrust of his passions; everything he didn't want to do was herculean to him. But Edazima was never distracted, always collected, always on point, drawing from an inner fount of vitality that never seemed to deplete. She had wanted to be a linguist — master of tongues and mapper of nuances, interpreter of the spirit — and she would have been the best, Neipas was sure.

So it was a shock to him when he saw her mask, ever the effigy of concentration of purpose, suddenly disfigured in tears. "What? What? What happened?" he had asked her then, as he took her in his arms. Edazima's words struggled to find voice among crushing sobs; but Neipas could finally make it out — "I'm pregnant!" she quavered to his chest. The same pronouncement had already been articulated to the child's father, a former student little older than her, recently graduated; whose answer had been — mumbled, implicitly, from behind a drooping pigeon beak — that after all it was none of his business. With a friendly tone he advised her to abort, offering to pay for part of it; and she, in characteristic manner, told him no, and pressed him to take responsibility. But he couldn't; he couldn't say anything; he could only avert his eyes. So she bolted out. When Neipas, a few days after, went to confront him, he couldn't find him; he had left, he would publicize in his Maskbook page, for a job upstate.

Yet Edazima cried but once. She wanted the baby; she was determined to finish her studies and provide for him.

The problem with Edazima, however, was that she was poor. Her parents, subsisting on a penance back home, had no money to help her with. A scholarship paid for her tuition, board, food, health insurance; but not the costs of bearing, birthing, and sustaining a child. The pace was unyielding. Her classload was too heavy — the scholarship so demanded it. When Martin was born, she had to add a job on top of that load, and it became so that he carried it almost without rest —; until she nearly collapsed under the weight. Nine months before graduation, she quit.

Neipas fingered the soft cuff of his sleeve as he recollected these things, and upon noticing his unconscious action, his stray thoughts turned in a languid blur back to Eva. Inside the stolid mask, he smiled. He felt thankful; the jacket she had bought him sharpened not only the staidness of his posture but also the soundness of his mind, influenced him into serenity and readiness. With distance (all his being was distant as though over a cushioned barrier) and some humor he thought of the old, moth-eaten coat he had vaguely planned to bring, the closest thing to business-like he had in his wardrobe. He thought with head aslant, with eyes resting at a downward angle — because, on the seat in front of him, where the nervous pigeon had been, someone else had meanwhile sat. Neipas knew who it was. A foul breeze, carrying words of cold demand; an eddying, absorbing gust issued from the gloom that was its face. The Debt Collector stared straight at him.

But he kept firm. He didn't look.

"Mr. Neipas —" came the call from the counter. Neipas nodded to himself, bouncing upon his neck in a masculine gesture of confidence-building; then he rose and stood erect, chest high. He took a deep breath and walked to the front desk. The receptionist looked up with a smile and said softly 'Your audition is in room #44 — to your right please, Mr. Neipas'. Neipas returned 'thank you' and he noticed the depth of his voice, the composure in his tone — he noticed it with empty mind and steady chest, unattached, as he stepped through the sliding silver gate into another corridor without a stir in his quiet spirit. He let himself merge into the occasion at hand; as he glided deep into the corridor he saw the photographs flanking each door as if he were a hovering ghost watching from a distance; he noticed vaguely that each picture was framed with a rectangle richly carved in gold, and the frame was so bulky as to be much bigger than the picture itself, dwarfing the photo in its grip.

There was door number 44. He collected his wits quickly, smarted his beak with a proper grin, checked the *I* mirror to see that all was right and composed. He let out a quick sigh — he was ready. He knocked.

*

"Come in please!" a studied voice filtered through the door.

Neipas opened it and entered softly. He held the interviewer in his sight, and he saw her stand up from her seat across the conference table. With his thumb and index on the corners of his lips Neipas widened his smile as he approached her; his hand reached across the table and gripped round the interviewer's fingers with a professional shake, not too firm, but very sure. "Please," she said, lifting her arm subtly toward the chair opposite, requesting the interviewee to have a seat. Neipas turned round and quietly leaned the door into the lock before he pulled, methodical, the rolling chair toward himself — and sat. He leaned slightly over the table, careful to maintain the upright posture of his torso intact; he molded his visage to an attentive, serious, receptive expression, then he intertwined the fingers of each hand into one another and settled them gently upon the mahogany table. He seemed fully collected. Neipas proceeded through the motions mechanically, unconsciously, without weight — he had practiced even this. Poised on the leather of his seat, he awaited the interviewer's word. She was studying some pile of sheets, holding the edge of one paper with her fingers and letting the remainder rest atop a neat pile of other papers. The methodical appearance of her owl mask, the enigmatic authority of the eagle mask on the back of her head, the beak of which peeked just over her downcast head (and reflected fully, dimly upon the shuttered window; she was hairless, with the two masks covering all her head, made a head of feathers) — her detachment and the elegance with which she held the thin paper roused in Neipas a vague fright. He began to feel a little intimidated. A muscle in his jaw stirred; he stiffened it, and focused his wits on the present moment, keeping close watch over her movements. Afar, a certain buzz sounded through the waiting quiet; a certain flapping murmur.

Her name was Sunai. Miss Sunai repositioned her glasses up her beak, closer to her enormous eyes.

"How are you doing this afternoon, Mr. Neipas?" asked abruptly the cold voice; her chair lifted a little as it spoke and her spectacles remained fixed on the papers.

Neipas cleared his throat. "Very well, thank you. How about yourself?"

"Hm-hm," mumbled Sunai, gazing yet the paper fixedly.

Still without removing her stare from the paper (which, Neipas now realized, was his resume) she spruced up the beak of the eagle mask, as if it were a hair bun — and said "Mr. Neipas, I see that you have been in the employ of Krow's Underground Restaurant for over a year now. Can you describe your experience working there?" Neipas' ear caught every syllable, his beak held ready. He knew this cue, and once it was enacted, he replied:

"It has been a very fulfilling experience, and it has equipped me to perform this line of work at the highest level. During my tenure at Krow's Underground Restaurant I have serviced across a variety of venues in the Belab, catering to a number of different sectors and floors, and I am proud to say that I have consistently navigated these spaces with success, delivering meals in a consistently timely manner. As a matter of fact, my rating exceeds 90%, which attests to customers' overall level of satisfaction." Neipas halted smoothly and nodded as if to close the speech. He felt a bit of accomplishment at getting the pronunciation of 'consistently' right; it all rolled out his tongue without passing through his brain, and a part of himself was aware that he didn't really know what he was saying. It was as though his voice had spoken in the strange dialect he heard round the tower's Financial floors everyday.

Sunai nodded and said, "Very well."

"And what do you like most about working there?" she inquired, studying Neipas' paper.

"You know," Neipas began, moving his fingers across his mask to sculpt a pensive expression. "I really relish seeing the looks of satisfaction on clients when they are well serviced. I really believe that we in the catering business are in the business," he stopped a moment, derailed — realizing now how Sunai really stared at him, he sculpted an even deeper thinking face and began again, careful to avoid repetition, "well, we in *catering* are in the business of making customers happy," here he caught the intended train of speech and, resuming an upright spine, looked confidently upon Sunai, "and I naturally like to make customers happy, I always have. I enjoy servicing customers and to be at the disposal of those my skills may help most — and I strongly believe my skills have developed to perfectly fit catering work," he braked with a sure shake, satisfied.

"Very well," the interviewer said again, keeping her spectacled glare upon Neipas. Her chair had slowly risen so that now she was staring a little down at Neipas, and he a little up at her. He noticed — with a flinch of the throat — that her amber eyes never blinked. "And what do you do when a customer is *not* happy?"

"Well," Neipas commenced with a rehearsed chuckle, but Sunai cut him off — "I mean, have you had problematic customers in the past, and how have you handled them?"

"Well," Neipas repeated, coughing the exact same chuckle and drawing up a casual, laughing smile. "It is rare, but it has happened in the past. I strongly believe it is difficult to avoid, having been in this service for as long as I have," he stopped, remembering that Edazima had told him not to use 'strongly' in that sentence and to cut out the last line — he hadn't been in the service that long. Mustering quickly his escaping wits, he carried on, "I believe it is a matter of asserting the exact nature of the customer's complaint and doing the utmost to ensure the complaint is addressed immediately. No matter what the customer's attitude may be, I always maintain a professional attitude and I strongly believe all issues can be resolved if that can be maintained at all times."

On this answer Neipas had derailed from the practiced track a little, and he became hyper aware of it in an instant. Off balance, he feared that the interviewer would ask for an example; the only example he could give was an awful one — it hadn't gone well with the client at all — and he wasn't good at outright lying if he didn't believe the lie in the least. Neipas had cooked a half-answer which wasn't very good, but he hoped the question would never come. Glancing at his hands he noted with relief they held immobile upon the table. A strange realization then came when Neipas looked up and, glinting, saw that one of Sunai's hands was behind her head so that the eagle mask could read his resume, while her other hand took notes. Neipas became once more aware of a buzzing sound.

Fortunately the next question wasn't what Neipas had feared; his lungs shrunk with relief. But it wasn't one that pleased him much either, and a certain angst generated in his chest once he heard it.

"I see in your resume that you had been out of the workforce for a full year prior to your current position at K.U.R," she said matter-of-factly. Miss Sunai looked down at Neipas inquiringly, as if asking for an explanation. He thought he had detected a slight tone of contempt in her voice.

"Well," he began, carefully shaping his mask into a measured expression of regret, a hint of embarrassment arisen from an unfortunate situation. There had been much discussion with Edazima about this question. She had pressed him to write down "freelance cameraman" or "babysitter" (because he had occasionally looked after Martin) in his resume, but every attempt to come up with a satisfactory explanation for that year failed. Neipas was afraid he'd be asked for clients and referrals from that period — he had none. So they settled on full disclosure; Edazima told him that he could use it as the moment in the interview when he would speak of his weaknesses, and flip them over to reveal a higher strength. Neipas was confounded by the concept — regardless, this was the moment. "Out of college I admittedly found myself in a difficult situation. At first, I took the route of entrepreneurship, but —"

"You studied photography, is that correct?"

"Yes," Neipas stammered.

"Quite difficult to make money as a professional photographer, I assume. Everyone seems to know how to take pictures nowadays."

These words might have left Sunai's beak as casual remarks about a subject she was only minimally interested in; in any case they reached Neipas' ear in the form of a ruthless question and the power of a harsh injunction. It sounded, to him, like she was questioning his wisdom over going into a field so profitless; over investing in studies so useless. His chest caught, his throat felt as though clogged by a slow throbbing lump. He let his gaze wander and set itself upon the table for a moment.

"Yes —" he forced himself to look up. "It can be tough for newly grads to get through the door. You know, competition — it's very fierce. Usually you need capital to start, which I didn't have — much of... At the time." Neipas was nervously petting his facade into an expression of indifferent powerlessness — the rigidness of his lifted shoulders, shrugging incessantly, meant to stoically express he couldn't do anything about it; lamentably, it's what it is. Circumstance had bested him. Nevertheless he saw the trail of his past, however narrowed by circumstance as it had been, littered with his own failures, festering along the unpaved road. He had failed to learn the fundamental lesson needed to succeed in the business of photography — that it was about business first, and only about photography after. The nagging sense that he hadn't learned it because he refused to never left him. He was too proud — he had avoided adding a page of his works to the Maskbook for a long time on account of his strong opinions against it, when exposure in that book of books, the most popular of those days, was crucial to rise over the vast crowd; it was the common arena upon which the rabble fought. Moreover, he abhorred what in those days was called networking, the practice of making acquaintances for personal gain — acquaintances who might someday be useful — because he found too much insincerity in it. "I hate going to these networking events," he used to tell Edazima in the winking dimness of the small dormitory pending over the court, across the clocktower. "I'm just not good at it — feels like a bunch of asskissing to me, you know? What — I have something called principles, ok," he would claim to his friend's shaking head. But Neipas would soon learn that pride and principles were luxuries not intended for the poor. The settlement money from the accident had been nearly enough to pay the Ivory Towers and put him through school to chase the great mirage of childhood dreams — but the heavy cost exacted to those who tried made follies of such natural pursuits. When he left, he had less than nothing. Neipas graduated with a portfolio he was proud of — yet with no connections that mattered and no instinct for commerce — and his initial resolve quickly evaporated upon the surging of financial realities. Within months of penury and hardship it landed him on Edazima's couch and sunk him in a depression of sucking depths. The experience left him inert in body and soul. Whenever his good friend and her growing son were out Neipas would slouch on the couch for hours, wallowing in a disorienting sense of failure, crawling the Webwork aimlessly, as if hypnotized by the flicker of the screen, slowly growing mad; he would sometimes become aware that he had gone into the *I* to look for jobs, but his concentration would quickly steal away from him again; and again he would come to with a sort of panicked start, getting up, walking about the living room with the full conscience that the living room wasn't his, carrying a chest which fluttered thick with anxiety. He would work certain gigs, on certain rare days, for a penance — but nothing stuck. He seized nothing; and he felt his head constantly underwater, bore perpetually the sense of an hour-limit approaching. He feared constantly that Edazima — who never once demanded money, never once gave toward him a hint of exasperation — would tire and kick him out.

The knowledge of dependency crushed him. "During that year of... absence," he was explaining to Miss Sunai; who had meanwhile kept silent, expecting him to go on, "I did perform a series of short-term jobs, many of them actually related to the restaurant — events and catering business. And... I really liked them, and I thought that yes, waitressing is for me. So... yeah," he swallowed. "So when I got the job at KUR, I was really happy, and I think I've done well so far." Neipas had tried to slide back into the practiced track in the course of his answer but he had stammered, faltered throughout. He dropped his shoulders dejectedly. Combing through the deep edges of his beak, Neipas had sensed the corner of his mouth twitch repeatedly as he spoke; he was very anxious about whether Sunai had noticed it, and he eyed her with a tense stare, hauling his breathing as discreetly as he was able.

Miss Sunai's eagle mask, whose chair had by then lifted her midway across the wall, studied his resume; her whole head nodded distractedly, as if biding her time. Suddenly she let go of it and her owl face drooped from the heights to confront Neipas — and though she was very far, she suddenly felt very close.

"Mr. Neipas," she said. "Please tell me what you know about Eden Solutions."

Neipas took a deep breath. "Absolutely. Eden Solutions is, a..." he summoned to his head the answer — he knew it, he had rehearsed it, "...distinguished group specializing in catering and overall set-up of high-end events, boasting a team of numerous cooks, tailors, set designers, playwrights, musicians..." he went, going on to list the name of the chief executive and year of founding.

"Very well," Miss Sunai said swiftly, gazing down into him, closer yet. Her hand returned his resume to her lap; and she pursued, leaning yet closer, "Mr. Neipas, the reason why we are hiring at the moment is because we need additional personnel for a very important upcoming event, which will be held at the Anubel — or, as it's more commonly known, the Eagles' Nest."

Sunai's description of riches in the Eagles' Nest conjured up dizzying ideas of flight in Neipas' soul. He suddenly felt the monumental weight of the opportunity before him, of the tremendous promise held in that fabled space on the uppermost floors of the Belab. The tips alone would relieve the economic strain — send him aloft well above the red, over the choking waters. But it wasn't just that. Neipas had become sensitive to the crucial fact of those days: that talent counts for nothing without connections; that connections, for one such as he, are the only channels between the talent and the freedom to exercise it. And the connections he could make there, the ears he could speak to — the very notion of sharing space with the most influential and the most powerful, breathing the very air of opulence which they exuded from their golden beaks — it vibrated with desire in his downtrodden soul; to stand upon the center of all stages presented itself as a most tempting prospect.

"You might be interacting with patrons of the utmost importance," Miss

Sunai explained. She sat on high, almost by the ceiling now, and (Neipas now realized it) the light behind her head palpitated with the flapping motions of a moth. There were two of them playing round the white glow. Flapping buzzes chipped her voice slightly, "The most important in the nation, thus the most important in the world. They are naturally very demanding, and some might be rude to you even if your service is flawless. Some will shout at you and maybe even throw objects at you only because they feel like doing so. You must withstand this and realize it is their right to do so. The patron is always — always — right. You might find yourself in high-stress, fast-paced situations, and regardless of what may occur you must be smiling at all times and always performing at the highest level. Are you capable of this?"

"Absolutely," Neipas shot with confidence. His heart was thumping and his spirits easing. He knew these cues well now, and he was getting back into the flow. "That's my job." Sunai's warnings caused no unease. He had no notion of the range of devilish possibilities and what yet lay in store for him.

"Mr. Neipas, what are your salary expectations?"

Neipas told them to her without a flinch, exuding the most firm of certainties. The number was as Edazima had advised — cosmically higher than what he now earned.

Miss Sunai nodded slowly. "Very well," she said, and the voicing of these two words alleviated Neipas' breast further.

She curved up the clay lip of her owl mask. She took a moment to re-position the spectacles atop her silver beak, then (and by this moment the chair had descended a little) said:

"Mr. Neipas — tell me, why are you the best person for this job?"

The two moths circled round the light, casting soft gliding shades onto the table. Neipas assumed the sober face of a zealous professional.

"Because I am an honest, obedient, hard worker ready to be at the full service of the most distinguished citizens of our nation."

Miss Sunai — it looked to him — molded herself into the same manifestation of approval Edazima had expressed when Neipas first recited these words to her; though in a less overt manner. Edazima had said then, "They'll buy that." Sitting at the dining table across from his good friend and her son, Neipas wondered sourly in that moment whether he didn't buy it himself.

Sunai's chair had submerged beneath the mahogany table again. The interviewer surgically placed Neipas' resume atop a second pile of papers and aligned the bunch, getting ready to stand and shake Neipas' hand goodbye. "Very well," she said in the meantime.

17 - Satanic Mills

On the day of the protest, Neipas arose from his bed without anxiety; rested. He had opened his eyes to the soft contours of his walls at dawn. A sense of calm pervaded the air, and he breathed in the sleepy atmosphere of his apartment with a nearly religious solemnity. He went out into the silence of the living room. For the first time in a long time, he found the couch empty; the roommate's bedroom door shut, with him sleeping beyond it. Neipas prepared some instant coffee, heated up a bowl of milk and mixed it in with cereal. Setting it up on the small kitchen table, he discerned indifferently the religious pamphlets spread among the empty bottles of spirits. Among them he ate.

He had a quiet breakfast. Reposing his elbow on the table and his forehead against his hand, he basked slowly in the strange, ancient tranquility which he had for so long been deprived of. He didn't know why it affected him that morning; he didn't think of it. Since the audition he felt like he had overcome a formidable obstacle, conquered a great strain, passed an eluding threshold — and was now comfortable to abandon himself to fate. Vacant and serene, Neipas played with his mask before the mirror, molding it to every expression of feeling the random flight of his fingers simulated.

A single bus took him down one of the main boulevards of Ostrich. The old chunk of metal whirred and shook over cracked tar as it drove through the rookeries, under lampposts stark against the crisp hot sky and surrounded by a desert of abandoned liquor stores, decrepit gas stations, fast-food shanties, and lost pilgrims carrying their entire possessions in life inside shopping carts. Branching from the main road, treeless streets flanked with broken cars, grassed curbs, and old houses masked with their quiet look of relative normality what the boulevard implied with its graffitied walls and its chipped plaster — the enormous agony suffusing every aspect of life in those impoverished neighborhoods. Such streets were replicated over and over again as the bus drove past, stretching yonder to an horizon shimmying with the heat of melting concrete. And cloned all across the urban swath, the oil pumpjacks after which the region was named — for, it was said, they resembled ostriches hiding their heads in the sand — continuously sucked the black blood out of a tar-shrouded earth.

Neipas observed it all through the bus window. In this way he rode toward Ostrich's core, past a landscape of neglect and destitution.

It was but a few blocks from the bus stop to the cemetery. At its gates, Neipas found a big group of people speaking to one another in muted tones, hunched and low-headed. He mingled in and navigated through the crowd for a moment, but couldn't find Orenda right away. His thoughts turned to the *I*:

NEIPAS: Hi! I'm here, you around?

But as he lifted them away (after a few further moments) from the glass, he saw her approach from among the waiting folk. She greeted him enthusiastically and in a rushed manner.

"Hey! We're just about to start. Come, we're going inside the cemetery for a little bit." And as they walked alongside one another Orenda, with a smooth tip-toe motion, raised her arms and placed a strap round Neipas' neck — at the tip of it hung a camera. "This is for later," she told him as he analyzed it, tilting it this way and that under his gaze.

The demonstration's organizers were raising their voices above the low hubbub, announcing the beginning of the protest. Feet shuffled over the concrete and onto the bare dirt of the graveyard. All voices hushed somberly. The cemetery, immense, yawned wide round the growing cluster of bodies plodding between the cedars, whose climbing leaves rose stately over the tombstones and the lowered heads of their visitors. Neipas observed the space with attention as he walked in. He perceived acutely its smells and listened to its murmurs; in the quietness of his own spirit he seized something of the essence of the place, the inverse depth of the moment. The persistent numbness which so characterized his sentient experience, the sensation of being enveloped in an inner fog, of the dissonance between his body and himself; the impression of not really being there — today, it had as if vanished. His senses were sharp. The feeling of being nowhere was in him no longer. Curious that it should be so, he thought unthinkingly, in this yard so full of nowheres, so permeated with absence.

What struck him subtly as he walked amid the mourners was the realization of how different this place was from the graveyard of his haunted childhood. Here, there were no photographs adorning the grisly tombs; the faces of the dead didn't stare out from the locking stone. Here were only letters and numbers describing the names and lifespans of the deceased, and all the graves looked the same, the orderly rows between them stretching just as evenly, and just as quietly, as the streets which Neipas had seen branching off the main boulevard on his way there. There was a sense of impersonal uniformity that softened the dappled foreshadows of demise coloring the soil; at least for Neipas, who glanced aloof at things, as he felt the weight of the camera upon his palm.

The cemetery's four main pathways branched from its central square, against the edges of which the crowd gathered in a circle. Three women and three men stepped into the empty center, and one by one they spoke of their loved ones who were lying somewhere beneath the grounds. They pointed the direction of their coffins in the vast grid of stones; they pointed multiple times. Mothers, fathers, uncles and aunts, cousins and siblings, in-laws, close friends, daughters, sons: the speakers in the circle, all of which lived in Ostrich's infamous 'cancer row' alongside Iblis and other chemical factories, had lost their families to various illnesses, tumors and cancers of various kinds, infestations breathed into their bodies by the putrescent air blown from the mouths of chimneys which arose from the refineries and plants brewing poisons throughout the area. Next to Neipas, Orenda listened solemnly to their testimony.

Opposite from them on the far side of the circle, a little boy stood holding a balloon on a string; the sight made Neipas smile. It roused distant memories of a place like this, where the dead were buried and memorialized; and of a child very much like the one yonder, holding in a similar way, with a similar innocence of presumption, a similar balloon among similarly scattered bouquets of flower. It swayed luminously, like a plastic flare, and in its motion it stimulated his recollections and their associations which flashed, to the balloon's gentle sway, from good to bad in turn; something like the pivoting of a curved mirror echoing his past. The colorless visage of his mother emerging fixed upon a rock disturbed him and guided his distracted will; he was about to raise the camera to block the surrounding scene, but Orenda stilled his arm — shaking her head to say, it is not yet the moment.

Silence was made among the chirping of birds who watched the gathering from the treetops, dancing gleeful and indifferent between the boughs, in the vivid blue sky, tall and unnoticed. A voice stirred and broke the motionless air softly down beneath. A wind whispered; and as the canopies began to sway, the voice grew to many voices who sang in mourning, in supplication to the earth and to the heavens in a tearful venting of angst and grief; a chorus so grand and profound that it penetrated the dormant reaches of Neipas' innermost, drawing out the own uttering of his spirit in song.

Two children emerged from among the crowd during the chant, one carrying a wreath, the other a candle with a long wick. In the very center of the square, in the center of the observant crowd the candle was set, and round the candle was laid the ring of flowers. Then a match was lit, and leaned against the wick, which caught flame; and the flame shone amid the quietude that was then made, descending, slowly, through the wick and into the receding wax.

"Reverence for the dead and justice to the living!" pronounced then Orenda above the lowered heads.

The silence receded into the solemn walk of feet, streaming slowly out of the gates, and as he trod out with the aggrieved assembly Neipas contemplated the cemetery yet intently. Melancholic, he observed the flatness of the grounds; and thought of how different they were from the smooth round hillocks, the soft dunes of grass of his homeland, rolling over the graves like feathery blankets for the dead, like pillows for grievous knees — or like pregnant bellies. Out of the tidal mounds there sprouted stones with faces — tombs with engraved photographs, erected hauntingly, open-eyed in their vigil — marking the boundary between the memory of the surface and the oblivion of the deep.

All subsumed under the torrent. All but the houses of worship and the mausoleum uphill — doomed to vanish without a trace.

As the crowd thickened outside a new tune began to roll out of their lips; and as the cluster of bodies thinned along the march out through the street, a beating of drums began to push upward, growing in force as the line advanced. The ones who had been waiting outside distributed signs and banners, and soon the gathering swelled into a colorful burst of floating papers and roaring songs. "Reverence for the dead! Justice to the living!" was one of the refrains, outed furiously from the advancing lips of the protesters.

"All right, now you can take pictures," Orenda told Neipas among the uproar, grabbing hold of his arm.

They were marching into the heart of the industrial sprawl. Together they walked over the sidewalks, where the roots of old trees muscled through the foundations and upended the paths, and in the middle of the roads, over concrete deformed by scalding heat and the relentless pressing of rubber wheels through the decades. Neipas leaned the glass upon his eye, and through it he saw the faces about him and the masks of anger and despondency they wore. Masks raw, they expressed, in their avian contours, sincere aches of the heart. Most of whom had come were from the surrounding neighborhoods. Ostrich, being the poorest region of Axiac, afflicted upon its inhabitants all manner of ills, and Neipas discerned through the focusing filter of his mechanical stare something of the weight they bore in their chests and on their backs. Many of them trod — those who couldn't, moved in wheelchairs — with their necks well bent, carrying the downward pull of their bodies, bound by obesity; which was a plague among the poorest here, in those days, as they subsisted mostly on the sugar and fat composing the cheapest diets available. The feathers covering their bodies were mostly black and brown: a mark of their lineage, tracing its beginnings on that land either to its first peoples, who were vanquished by the force of bullets, or those who, under the burden of shackles, built it into the economic powerhouse which it was then. And the effects of oppression across those generations were apparent. It was on display in everything, from the dereliction of the homes to the masks of the marchers and the onlookers, whose faces sweated viscous black drops, melting in tar under the sun; dissolving in the petroleum which had so seeped into their bodies as to be almost fused in with their breathless souls; oozing down round their beaks, which were battered in the effort of years pleading without being listened to. From the curbs, among the ramshackle homes, some watched as the multitude went past. They stood upon the porches and in the alleys, and some of them observed from chairs, legless or without feet; others crazed, meek, maimed and emaciated sat upon the ground. Yonder the police squads awaited. They began to frame the streets with their bull helmets in formation. Some, the legion heads, wore beaks like sirens, so as to amplify their shouts. These were the riot police. Their masks were changeless; locked in a perpetual frown, frigid in an extreme manifestation of ire. They all stood tense and at the ready.

One of the protesters who had spoken at the graveyard, an old fellow whom Neipas also recognized from Oshana's garden, was marching next to him and engaged in conversation.

"You a journalist?"

"Just photographer. I'm working with Orenda today, though."

"She a good gal."

Neipas lowered the camera gently and let it hang on the strap.

"I was very touched by your testimony, sir," said Neipas.

The man, called David, sighed and shook his head slowly. "We been trying to sort this situation for years. We complained time and again to the federal government, to the city. They know what toxins are in the air. We've had journalists come here, documentarians... You know, the whole thing. Maybe it wasn't enough. They don't do nothing — and now they want to kick us out."

"Do you live close to the refinery?"

"Right across. My family's lived here for generations now, though they had to move inland when the port start be built. Even with the money they're offering us, I can't leave. It's petty change anyway. Where would I go? It's *they* who's got to leave. It's *our* neighborhood — who the hell are they? What right do they have, to come here, poison everyone like this."

Neipas dropped his head pensively, falling silent amid the chants of the crowd.

"And the government agencies, they do anything when you complained to them?"

"Speaking empty words the most they did. And that's only when the story about our neighborhoods came out, when it start to get attention. They don't care. They don't care. Article after article, newspaper after newspaper. Did nothing. They don't care."

He stopped and gasped for breath for a bit; Neipas could almost sense the panting of his sick lungs through the surrounding clamor. Then, after a few moments walking quietly among the hymns and laments, David's deep voice emerged from the profoundities of his being to say:

"It's like it's just... a story."

Neipas marveled as he listened and beheld the man, trudging through with fortitude past the many pains of his body and soul, struggling among agonies to face up against the powerful interests which stepped on him on the amoral path to profit. He was stirred in the recognition of their supreme indifference, operating upon the living like machines, with the facade and inscrutability of machines, with the efficiency and heartlessness of machines, pursuing their objectives with untiring and cold devotion, automatic, uncaring, ruthless; callous in their expansion as cancerous blooms spread across anatomies infirm. David tapped Neipas' back and urged him to get on with his work; and, old and ailing, raised his fist and his voice in defiance of the tyrannical giants.

When they turned the corner leading on to the petrochemical facilities, the street widened and the chimneys of the plants came again into view. The great nose of Iblis loomed a bit taller than the rest, and its great cauldron bulked prominently beyond all structures; but Iblis was not the only hell to burst open upon the surface. Round it, it was all an otherworldly complex of towers, silos, pipes, all shooting upward and in every direction; all crisscrossing in labyrinthine ways, forming a grand, alien super-structure towering over the small houses. The devilish agglomeration of stacks churned up smoke and fire, making the heavens gloom and casting a thick shadow as far as the port, from which the structures propagated. Deep honks and whistles ensued from the barges docking in the concrete shores; cargo ships loomed with skyscrapers of piled boxes emerging from the dark fog. The protest's songs beat against the screaming clank of machinery, and navigating among it all, Neipas photographed, and grew excited in the exercise of his craft. His finger released the shutter in faster and faster presses of the button. His eye stared into all things through the glass. To him the camera brought out the romance in the surroundings, the dramatic and intriguing spirit of it, made things at once more intimate and more abstracted: so that he could feel abstractly the squalor and despondency of the scene and the charm of it all at the same time.

"Have you been around these parts before?" asked Orenda, who was retreating from the fervor of the chants for a minute.

"Not so close to the refineries, no," said Neipas, pointing his long glass eye at Iblis' flame. "But I live right on the edge of Ostrich so I've been around a few times. I can see Iblis from where I live."

"You're seeing it up close now. You see this row of houses? These neighborhoods going all the way down five blocks — the refinery wants to swallow it all."

Neipas nodded dejectedly, and drew the image of the houses into the camera.

"The cemetery, it wants to swallow that..." she continued. "Ghouls, literally."

"What are the odds the expansion won't go ahead?" he asked.

"It hasn't been approved yet, but city council is all up for it. The Mayor will need to sign the order and he's definitely leaning toward it. Noxxe is making big pressure on homeowners too. Those who have landlords are just gonna get kicked out. At least that's what they wanna do.

"And there's the matter with the pipeline — right now that kinda hinges on the Mayor too. If they route it under the Oyate River, it's gonna need to go through the Municipal Forest, and that's under the city's control. The whole reason the refinery is expanding is for the glut of oil coming from the pipeline in the first place. So he'd need to approve that."

"I see," Neipas said, letting the camera hang on the strap and looking at Orenda. "Are you optimistic?"

"We gotta be," she answered, unhesitating, "there's no choice. They gotta stop burning this fossil sludge. Iblis already deals more petroleum than any other refinery in Columbia. It's crazy. It's poisoning the Earth and all of us."

He looked up at the monstrous chimney and the fire raging among the shaking fumes; then his eyes tilted back down to meet Orenda's. Surely the mask must've denounced his awe of those structures of soaring steel, puffing up there like the immense immortal lungs of some god. His gaze, from which now Orenda slowly abstracted herself with a tinge of despondency, must have reflected the undeniable sense of invincibility imparted it by that towering vision.

As if to answer it, she replied by saying, with a focused and tempered sort of determination, "We must be realistic about the present — we can also be optimistic about the future. It's a tough fight, I know. But we can win." There was in her tone an underdog's fierceness of serenity, who walks with steps firm a path she knows narrow.

Neipas lifted the camera glass before his view in a reflex. "I thought the Mayor was all environmentally friendly though," he rejoined, among clicks. "Didn't he say he was gonna resist Arnold's policies and everything? Invest in green energy and stuff?"

"The Mayor?" she scoffed. "He's all talk. He's one of those politicians who says 'there's a climate emergency going on, we commit to cutting emissions' and then approves oil pipelines and oil refinery expansions all over the place. Most of them are like this. And the expansion was in the works way before Arnold came along."

"Mary."

Orenda laughed at Neipas' native interjection. "Right? The Mayor is what's called a centrist, you know — a 'middle-of-the-road' kinda guy. But you can't stand in the middle of the road when there are cars coming at you... He'll swing whichever way to save himself.

"So now he speaks our language. He talks like us, says our words, babbles all the lingo... It earns him votes, right? At the same time he's all like 'economic growth' this, 'economic growth' that — but that's delusional. There's no more space to grow. The Earth is spent — and we're just beginning to see the consequences.

"What he's doing is appealing to this side of power for votes; and winking to the other side of power, the moneymakers, his real constituency. He's not our friend, trust me... He's the most pernicious type of enemy. There's no better way to stall your opponent than by saying 'I agree with you'. He's a fraud.

"The role of folks like him is to hold the line. Draw the limits of imagination. It's their job to make even the most timid reform look crazy, right. They say, 'oh we want to do this and that, but there's this institutional obstacle, and there's a legislative bump of some kind, and the opposition, the opposition is too strong!'" she said, mimicking their speech with scornful head motions. "And whenever they can't find an opposition in the other party they find it in their own. Actors all. It's as if to say, 'you can't be more progressive than us, it's impractical — it's impossible'. In this way they're worse than the worst.

"Anyway his kind won't last. The time for indecision and half-measures, for pandering to 'both sides' — it's over. We're gonna have to go away from the center. The path must fork. When it comes to *'climate change'* [she flapped two palpitating and upraised fingers], either things change for the much better — or we're facing the apocalypse."

Neipas almost chuckled at the starkness of her pronouncement, and his mask must have not been thick enough to conceal it, for Orenda noticed it.

"Think I'm exaggerating?"

He shook his head ruefully. "No, it's just — apocalypse is a little much, I guess — no?" He wanted to say he simply thought she was joking, but he couldn't express it.

Orenda then, shaking her head slowly, seemed to soften away from the flush of clamors, the rage of protests. Smiling, she seemed to soften inward, melancholy; and her head, swaying with the downward tilt of her gaze, drew Neipas into the quietude of her intimate despair, and every sound around them seemed to hush — and it was into the hush that she spoke, "I wish I was exaggerating."

The way her eyelids rose to slowly reveal her stare reminded him of petals disclosing a beautiful black flower; the sad manner of their motion was like a hypnotic pendulum to his rapt attention:

"No, man... I really wish I was. But what's coming is — unlike anything humankind has ever seen before. Something so immense and unprecedented that... well, that it's hard to even imagine. And we've been doing a shitty job at imagining it so far, I think.

"Yeah," continued Orenda, waving her head, peering, through blank eyes that reflected a crowd, into something afar and unseeable. "I mean it when I say apocalypse. I mean the end of civilization. The extinction of humankind."

"Mary."

"Picture it with me a little," she exhorted him, looking again into his eyes. "You're gonna have to step out of yourself — or I guess, step deeper into yourself.

"Look —" sighed Orenda, "no great deluge will flood the world. No single fire will burn every forest and every city. No hand will come down from the sky and exact punishment — summon plagues and so on. No sea will turn to blood... But all these things will happen in fragments.

"*If* we don't change course, storms will come, fires will come — with more and more intensity. Of course. But the world is a vast place, you know, and most people won't see these things up close. What they'll experience will be more like a — like a drought.

"Imagine a drought for a second. Can you picture it?"

Neipas lowered his eyes in thought (and some timidness), averting them from her own as they narrowed grinningly, somewhat amused. Their brief silence pulsed with the fanning chants of the surrounding demonstrators.

"Let me guess," Orenda laughed, and again the march's sounds ebbed in the softness of her upturned gaze — "you imagined cracks on a desert floor, didn't you? You thought of a photo."

With his stare again fixed on hers, Neipas simply shrugged, chuckled.

"Right? Yet you've been living in a drought for years," she said, looking at him earnestly, intimately placing her hand on his shoulder. "It's hard to conceive. Water flows out of the faucet, there's food on the shelves of the supermarket. There's no crop field anywhere on the street, no cracked-up desert. Just the absence of rain... Sounds less dramatic than these great tempests and all-consuming wildfires, right?

"And the reason why it's harder to imagine is you can't see it," she continued, lifting her shoulders and making a sweeping gesture, pronouncing her words emphatically, "by definition you can't see it — it's just an absence. *Here*, you can't see it because our water comes from faraway rivers, and our food from faraway fields. But those rivers are shrinking; the aquifers that we use to water the crops will soon have no water. Soon we'll have to rely on water and land farther and farther away — but no soil will be safe. No stream will be immune... The poisons they're tossing into the air," she exclaimed, pointing up at the smoke-belching chimneys, "intensify the malign forces of the Earth all over. Every bad tendency will grow, and every vulnerability in all the fields.

"To those vulnerable to heat, heat waves will come. To those vulnerable to flooding, greater floods will come. To those vulnerable to fires, bigger fires will come. Plagues will come to reap the harvests and kill the animals. Ocean acidification will make fisheries perish, droughts will kill the fishes in the rivers. Fertilizer runoffs create dead zones in the waters, choking the fish out of oxygen; not to mention oil spills. Contaminants already abound. Loss of biodiversity... will tear at the threads of life. When bees die, so will much of our food. Sea level rise will bring salt to the soil and make it barren. More and more, the fields become dependent on synthetics, the way the sick depend on drugs and the dying on life support. That won't last.

"Eventually, the food and water supply, which they're straining now, will diminish. There'll be crop failures. Reservoirs with little water. And then, the farther we have to search for these things to make up for the gap, the closer you'll begin to feel the drought. These problems that seem distant now — they'll get nearer, bit by bit, and then faster and faster, until they reach your doorstep, then fill your home, then enter your body. And when that happens it'll appear so sudden, that it will be as if a great storm has come personally for your life."

Orenda stopped for an instant, seeming to catch herself in a new grim contemplation. "And there will be hunger...

"Then, it'll still be like a drought in the sense that... something of despair creeps up into you... A feeling without hope — you know? Like you know the rain you're waiting for will never come."

She said this in increasingly folding tones of decreasing volume, making Neipas (every motion made almost imperceptibly) draw nearer and nearer, so that her voice was nevertheless always clear; unlike before, she didn't have to raise it to make her words distinct from the hymns of the demonstration. She spoke beholding the Axiac River which, as chance would have it, they were now walking alongside. With hollow eyes she seemed to fix its hollow channel

— but a wide ditch paved with concrete, and little except garbage, graffiti and a runnel of polluted water within it; no vegetation save for the weeds that occasionally grew out of the seams of cement — out of which emanated a vague rotting odor. For some reason, Neipas was reminded of Magpie — perhaps because he found the sense of latent breathlessness which he associated with her stealing into his own breast upon the elaboration of Orenda's sinister prophecies and the barren spectacle of that hellish vista (he then recalled Edazima telling him that Magpie was from one of the houses teetering over those fenced, fetid banks).

"If we keep following the rule of the Market — which is the law of the land in our age — prices will rise the more supply shrinks and the farther it's sourced," Orenda continued. "That'll mean crisis. Crisis after crisis, and at every disruption they'll ramp up the use of these poison fuels for the sake of emergency, and bury everyone even deeper beyond salvation. There will be no economic fix, because everything — including economies — everything depends on the health of the Earth.

"So the day we find ourselves with less food and less water, and we keep following the Market... then many people, many, will find hunger. For an increasing number of people — and eventually," she nodded painstakingly, "this will be everyone — this will be famine."

More than ever, it appeared to Neipas as though the marchers blurred in the apprehensive narrowing of her gaze, the deepening of her respiration. She spoke no louder than the faintest of whispers, and still he could hear her:

"Masses of desperate people will form... and eventually, break out. There will be chaos. Riots. Revolutions. There will be wars, civil wars and wars between nations fighting for resources, like nothing that has come before. The law of the Market will give way to the law of Naked Power — and where the law of the Market is governed by indifference, the law of Naked Power will be guided by hatred. The new rulers will say — 'there's not enough for everyone to live; the unworthy must die' — and there will be wholesale massacre and cruelty on a scale never seen before. And meanwhile, what's called the climate crisis will only deepen, and the Earth will only become more rabid and inhospitable, as torrents of fossil fuels feed war-making machines... Seas of refugees, famine spreading and infesting more and more. Pestilence will be unleashed, disease will run amok. There will be madness so vile, so desperate, that I'm afraid to imagine... and that madness will seize the power they've been accumulating over all these glorious years of civilization. The power of nuclear bombs and unimaginable destruction... Our extinction, even *now*, is a button-click away from the finger of some maniac. So yeah," she concluded, looking back up at him wistfully, "I do mean apocalypse."

Silence settled once more between them, a quietude now hollow with tense significance. Neipas had stopped photographing. He could hear nothing. The evocation of widespread hunger and nuclear holocausts roused old associations he'd have rather kept buried, though they had already been brought nearer the surface by the sight of the graveyard earlier; he had listened to her speak like one who senses well beyond the abstraction of words their real meaning and frightful implications. And though his mask seemed unbothered as it was hidden further behind the camera (again he lifted it), her voice had meshed with the rhythm of his heart, and pulsed into it a sort of whorling unease which the act of photography could not dispel. The whiff of chemicals stirred a little vertigo in him.

"Death is at the walls, and the walls are shrinking. It's already here, coming — not in some... some abrupt disruption of the present, but by making any future impossible. By shrinking the path to it — and when it's closed, we'll be lost. Drought by drought, flood by flood, fire by fire, crop by crop, year by year, day by day, animal by animal, person by person — slowly, we perish.

"Climate change," said Orenda — very sorrowful she said it; very quietly, "is a weak pair of words to describe the unraveling of life."

For a moment she had trouble continuing, and seemed to be waiting for the strength of her feelings, so imbued in the quiet despair and muttered sadness of her words, to subside.

"Fertile grounds are shrinking, the grounds for life are dwindling every year. And where life cannot live, it seeks life elsewhere — life moves. Life runs. There's already a mass exodus going on...

"Does the future I describe... — does it seem distant to you?" The grief and equanimity in her eyes made his breast flutter as she looked up at him again. "Well then, look at the distance. Everything I'm saying is at least in the margins of our awareness — well, take a close look at the margins. Look to the margins and you'll see the future — it's already there.

"Look no further than the margins of Columbia... Just think of all the refugees crammed along Wall Street."

Wall Street — dubbed by some 'the Columbidae Bastion' — the layered system of ultra-surveilled razor-wire fences marking the nation's border, had at its founding been a port dealing in human cargo. It was now, and had been for years, the setting for yet another sprawling drama of human misery. Droves had marched to the shuttered gates of Columbia from the poorer regions of the continent, dragging on and amassing in a very tide of suffering without deliverance; languishing in tents, crammed under tarpaulin, accumulating upon the spuming fortress wall of prosperity and shoring up against its latticed neglect by the millions; millions waiting in encroaching degradation, degrading in the tumorous growth of their own hopelessness, withering in slum cities that sprawled and piled with unceasing waves of new arrivals, reliving without break the very conditions of anguish and deprivation they had fled from.

"Why do they come? why do they risk their lives to come all the way here? Now the causes are mostly artificial, and created by greed, rapaciousness and all the stupidity of powerful men. The wars, poverty, crime, hunger that are driving people away don't *need* to happen. Because the Earth is still abundant. We have enough to make sure everyone can live, and live well, and live beautifully. But that same greed is so hungry that this abundance will soon be no more, and the scarcities, the oppressions that our brothers and sisters are running from will be unavoidable — and the causes will be very real, inflexible. All life comes from the Earth — what will happen when She can't sustain life as abundantly?

"What will we do then? When our resources really shrink? When we truly have less? Will we follow the way of the Earth, care for what we have, protect what we have, sustain what we have, and share? Or are we gonna follow the way of the Market, fight for crumbs, waste stupidly — are we gonna kill each other for resources as they turn to scraps? Finish off the human race like fucking idiots?

"As the greed economy grows, so does Earth's plenty shrink — the margins are eating toward the center. The margins of *profit* are eating toward the center of life. By the time the ruthless consequences of those margins get to us, who are here, right near the center of Mammon's empire — it could be too late to do anything by then. Where would we run to?

"Because — look — it's from right here that the poisons condemning humanity and life are cast off. Just look — the margins begin out of the center."

She made a pointing, sweeping, enveloping gesture with her head — and her eyes, which had seemed to gaze the far-off, reflecting blindly the surrounding crowd, now suddenly appeared to absorb it in the full presence of their attentive stare. Following their motion, Neipas, too, looked round, and considered those marching here around him. He saw them frail. He saw them, the old dying, the young already old; he saw the very children staggering, all stamped to a smothered soil; he saw the hope in their frowning, sorrowful eyes. They marched without vigor and at the cusp of lifelessness, moved by the sheer despair of will and desire for dignity, for comfort, for a life that carries the promise of happiness and the constancy of fulfillment; longing for the life long concealed beneath the paved shattered grounds. Studying his neighbors so, eventually Neipas' gaze rested upon the fenced, moribund river, and his eyes took to tracing its path backward, slowly; and in following its path his eyes took off, lifted, and looked behind him, to see the sunless blue sky and the boulevard yawning savagely all the way to Babylon, at the summit of which the Pearl blazed mighty, supreme, watchful... from the heights, palpitating, gradually enfolded in thickening smog.

"Right from here, from the bowels of Mammon... right beneath his eye..."

The march had turned another corner and they found themselves now between the fences of two chemical plants, where a mist of putrescent odors trailed by smoke washed throughout and thickened quick amid the bodies of the throng; swarming abruptly into Neipas' nostrils and rising under his eyes, which became irritated and teary in the brimming tingle — wiggling into his throat, the stench forced him into a fit of coughing, and suddenly he found himself again inside his mask throbbing, bubbling out amid flaming throes.

"Drink this — " Orenda handed him a water container, he grabbed it thirstily and pushed it to his lips, into his gullet. Then softly and firm still, as always, Orenda said, "Here, put this on." By then he could scarcely see anything — the smoke had mantled his sight, with a texture that stirred, that writhed with motions teeming with floating arms, disembodied heads, and banners flying ghostly over the fragmented bodies of the protesters appearing here and there in the gaps — and he found himself in an instant with a gas mask in his hands (everyone, it seemed, was wearing them now) which he proceeded to put on.

His senses dimmed in the spreading cloud, deepened into the silence of the toxic dark. The world was shut out from him; and he could no longer feel anything but his own dizzying self. Yet — so enshrouded in masks and wrapped in quiet — he reflected clearly. Thoughts came clear to him. Paradoxically juxtaposed to Orenda's drought, the notion that was increasingly engendered in Neipas' troubled unconsciousness was that of a rising tide; of a gradual flood; and he imagined each foray of climate change into public awareness — the occasional, and ever more frequent, giant wildfire or storm — as a thrust of that tide inland, toward the bubble of the center, that recedes once more again for a little, and each time less: vague visions which gleamed and flinched in him as he felt the water flowing down his throat, somehow as if he were being photographed, and photographically exposed and developed, inward.

"You all right?" asked Orenda.

"Yeah, I'm all right... Mary Virgin, fuck is this place?... Stinky as hell."

"It *is* the stink of hell. That's what they're digging up — that's what they're spreading!" Orenda said, gesticulating with a pointed finger. And all at once her voice sounded much louder; again it seemed to widen against the returned flush of beating cries: "They're flooding the world with it! Building their little island in the middle, at the top — and casting death far afield. But it's gonna come back to bite them.

"It begins at the bottom, with the poorest, and the most blameless... but it's gonna eat its way up, all the way to the source, and even the most rich will suffer from it, even they will go — unless we stop them. But their stupidity ... [the sounds and the smoke grew so dense around this moment that he could not hear her] ... and generally, the movements we're seeing today are swinging with such momentum toward catastrophe that we need a massive, coherent, focused, and united counter-force to reverse and stop them..."

The dusty air then cleared; and under the particle-gleaming, scattered sunshine they removed their breathing masks. Neipas' eyes burned still; but after rubbing them with water, after wetting his throat in a few swigs, after recovering, he resumed the dialogue by asking, pensive (coughing a little still): "And how do we do that? How do you build this counter-force?"

Orenda nodded resolutely. "It takes work. We gotta build the movement, and that takes a lot of work. Fortitude. Focus. Humility. Unshakable principles. We need cool heads — and warm hearts. We need virtue at every individual and collective level. And a lot of patience... Because it takes time to build a movement — actually, not even that — it takes time to learn how to sustain it. But we gotta keep at it.

"But, well there are two main fronts of action, in my opinion. We have to gain political power as quickly as we can — and change social views at the same time. They're closely interlinked. Except one front is mainly led by organizers, and the other by artists and communicators in general, in all media — journalism, film, literature, etc," said Orenda, enumerating from finger to finger. "We have to mobilize not just the mind, but also the body, and especially, the *spirit*; and a fighting spirit at that.

"There are other tools, of course," she continued. "We gotta use everything we can. The law, for instance. They haven't been able to build the pipeline yet because we've used our legal claims to the river to stop it, among other efforts... Appealing to the law requires money obviously though, because it was made for those who have it. But there's this amazing lawyer on our side — did you meet Marlene? With the pink hair?"

"Lawyer with pink hair?"

"Yeah, like a faded pink. And glasses. Somehow she looks very lawyerly even with the hair."

Neipas considered the image for a moment. "Isn't that the one you were arguing with at the bookstore?"

"That one! Yeah we have disagreements... but she's a terrific lawyer — and a terrific person. Anyway yes, the law is a tool... But the law was mostly written to benefit the rich who write it, with some concessions when we struggle for them. Ultimately though, legal power is subservient to political and social power. What we must do is gain both — and change the law in a way that reflects a just, proper society.

"We need to get to a point where the state really represents the people. Right now, anyone can see it: the state is hostile to its own population, and subservient to corporations, which are its true constituency, its true masters. So political change is crucial — and it's gotta happen as fast as we can make it. Political power determines what's *possible* — and anything is possible, depending on who's in charge."

"What about social views?"

"Art shapes culture. I mean art here as well as general communication. Culture is essential. It frames everything. What can and cannot be done, what is acceptable and beyond the pale, what is seen and what's ignored. Our culture is especially badly equipped to even *think* about this catastrophe. We've been numbed...

"Institutions too, depend on a certain system of approved feelings, you understand? They depend on people to be a certain way — otherwise they wouldn't function. And these approved feelings are regulated by stories, they flow from myths. These days, the greatest myth is: 'there is no society, only individuals.' And also: 'there's not enough for everyone', while the rich gorge themselves on trillions in money. Right? So we must create new myths, new stories that are more in accordance with our nature, and what makes everyone happy and fulfilled.

"Much of even that is political of course. Those with power now shape the narrative. Well, they're shitty — we need to take power away from them."

"Do protests like this help?"

"They're a tool. It's an expression, you know. A protest is a manifestation of power. It's a show of numbers. Movements need to project an image of unity, in marches and in general. But it must have an actual movement behind it, it cannot be hollow — it must be an expression of something sustained, know what I mean; it must be a culmination of planning, coordination... In that way you test how coordinated you are, how committed people are, who's in it for the long haul and — and it's also just a gathering. You're putting everyone together, forging bonds. That's exactly what we need to bring political change about."

Neipas, as he listened, came to understand that protest marches, like political speeches, held the expressive power of performances, and wanted the expressive coordination of collective performances, a concentrated power flowing out of thousands of bodies. He conveyed his thoughts to Orenda — and while she did not disagree, she reiterated that it cannot be hollow; in her opinion, unless the performance reflects and expresses substance, it hurts more than it helps, because demonstrations are not meant to inspire so much as to nurture. Marches energize, she said, but they do not recruit.

Always with his head tilted and intent, raising the camera less and less now, Neipas, listening earnestly, scanned the expansive crowd of upraised banners shoving up against the veiling smog and the churning of machinery, clamoring through letters what the marching voices proclaimed in chants; he heard the drums, the trumpets, the pulse of music and the enhanced vigor of the crowd's aggregated force, beaming with the power of chorus, like in some sort of opera. "Must've been tough to organize this," he observed.

"Yeah. But it's gotta be done."

"What does it take?"

"To build? You knock on doors. Straight up. That's the first thing. Try to organize picnics..." she shrugged, laughed. "Talk to people face to face. To every member of the community. If there is no community, you create it — you pull them to the group, show them the common cause. You talk to the ones who don't agree with you, the ones who don't like you — even those — and try to bring them to that common cause. It's uncomfortable sometimes, but that's the work. Ain't no shortcuts about this.

"But you gotta know how to go about it too: patiently, subtly; always listening. You have to keep your principles steadfast and your tactics pliable, you know what I mean? One of the big problems with a lot of social movements today is they speak their own dialect — originally for the sake of technical clarity, I guess, which is commendable, but then it's often taken up just because of vanity — and they get wrapped up in what's, like, the *rigidly*, you know, technically correct way of saying things. You can't do that. You have to speak to people in their own language if you want them to understand. It's what I just said — you have to be patient and listen. Keep your principles steady, *always* — but adapt the strategy. The story is the same, but the telling must change depending on the audience.

"I mean, yeah, it ain't easy. All of it takes work, work, work. You need dedication, discipline, humility, ambition. But patience most of all. Right? Subtlety, the ability to listen... Especially to those who don't agree with you and need more convincing."

"There's a lot of people that don't agree with what you're doing? Living here?"

"Definitely. There are homeowners in the neighborhood who just want to take Noxxe's money and leave. And they can't do that until *everyone* agrees to take the money. City council was about to kick them all out with a penny to make up for it, you know, before we took them to court — then Noxxe appears and says, 'I'll offer you this much if you get outta here'. And by 'this much' I mean not much at all, but it's still something, it's still better than the crumbs city council was offering — just enough to appeal to desperation, and there's plenty of that here. We try to help everyone the best we can, but...

"So yeah. It's not just the people in the eviction zone, though. It's not only about the expansion — it's about transforming this place, make Noxxe and all the rest of these venom-cookers go away. We need all of Ostrich for that. Things are turning around, but there are people in other neighborhoods who actually support Noxxe. They say the expansion will bring jobs. And there are folks around here that... — guess the hardest to convince are those whose livelihoods already depend on the refinery, you know, who live here and work there. But those concerns are fair. You gotta eat. We have to offer alternatives. This only works if you offer an alternative. You gotta offer a vision. And only a big vision does it... At this point, only bold steps toward a concrete direction. People are ready for it. They're sick of how things are and they know something's been fucked up for a long time. They're hungry for something else. Hungry for *purpose*. We must give them that purpose."

Orenda's step slowed as her speech paused, and Neipas, following her motions, halted beside her. For a few moments they were just standing in the middle of the crowd, looking here and there, together, as the protest beat forth with the ailing and the feeble streaming by in effusive numbers, in a march that, in that instant — that strange instant — seemed so firm as to feel inexorable, so flushed with the passion of determination as to appear invincible, with its ever-ascending voices so full of spirit as to impart the sensation of a force capable of toppling the machinery against whose churn they were pushing, capable of beating it by the timbre of their clamors alone. Neipas looked down at Orenda, smiled — said, with interest, "I'm listening."

"I know... You're a good listener." Likewise smiling, Orenda stepped onward again, as if walking out of her reverie.

"We must shift the story," she then said, "turn the tide, point to a different direction: unless we do that effectively, we'll keep walking the same path, the same trail framed by those myths on which civilization is standing right now. And that trail ends in a pit.

"We'll just keep on running like crazy to that pit, trying to make sure we're not the first ones to get there, just pushing as many as we can in front of us," continued Orenda, mimicking a few shoves. "We'll just keep doing that unless we nurture compassion and solidarity for one another. 'One another' meaning, *all of us on Earth*. That's the most important thing. It comes natural to us — unless you're told that you gotta eat if you don't wanna be eaten — you know what I mean? That's what we've been told all this time. That's the great myth: there ain't enough for everyone. Even here, in the richest country on Earth! They say there isn't enough for everyone. We gotta do away with that myth. If there ain't enough for everyone is because, like, five dingbats are getting away with most of it. That's the truth. We must preach it.

"It's hard, though, because their story is easier to understand. They say, 'look, there's not enough for everyone — and look at those loafers sucking at the tit of the state, look at those immigrants trying to take your jobs — they're trying to take what's *yours*'. And what's yours is shrinking. They used to say that climate change was a hoax. Now they're beginning to say 'it's happening all right, and it'll shrink resources even more'. And less resources plus more people equals not enough for everyone. Right? So we gotta keep a bunch of them out. We must keep a whole lot of humanity in the lurch. 'We gotta care for our own,' they'll say. That's the direction we're leaning to already... Look at Wall Street.

"And many believe all this because they're angry, their lives are precarious — we believe there's not enough because we see everyone with barely enough. We look around and sometimes we see the poorest of the poor asking us for money — often enough we see crimes the poor commit out of blindness and despair. We see them because they're right there close to us. They are us. But we never see the rich steal, even though they're by far the biggest thieves. Unlike the poor, who are all around us — the rich are just an abstraction," she said with a frustrated shrug. "They're much farther away. Their stealing is much more sophisticated. To explain the ways they steal is much harder.

"They like to point to the pennies the poor get from the state every once in a while so we don't notice the millions they get from the state themselves. So we turn on each other. I have to look out for myself, because I'm an individual, and that's it — there's no society anymore. That's the other myth."

"That there's no society?" Neipas asked, after a pause — and upon a moment of reflection he said, suddenly, without intent: "I don't even know what that is."

But Orenda replied, "That too, but the myth is that we're just individuals. Of course we're individuals — but we're more than that. Like, we live in a world of mirrors nowadays. And every mirror tells us, 'this is who you are'. But we're more than the surface of our bodies. We're more than our clothes. There's depth behind that. A depth so profound that everything in the world can fit inside. The world is already inside us, but we don't look at it. You can't just see it. We have to look at the world, and especially at others, if we want to find the mirror that shows us what our depths are like... in the same way we can only have a vague idea of our bodies without a mirror. Without others, we can only grope blindingly. It's in others we find ourselves."

Neipas found that idea quite nice, and for the second time in a short period Orenda molded a smile on his face with but the sheer enchantment of her voice. "You could almost be a poet, Orenda," he said, jesting in tone but earnest in meaning.

"No vocation for that... Oshana tells me these things. I couldn't express it myself, but I feel it. If we break from others, we feel like we're not ourselves. We feel like nothing. Like nothing matters. And that's maybe the deepest impact of our days... Resignation. That's all because we're told — all because we've come to believe that we're separate from others, and that we're separate from the source — from Nature. Mother Earth.

"We feel isolated, small, scared. Threatened. We feel antsy, right? and they know it. They know how empty we feel, and they know we can get filled up with all sorts of things. We're ripe for the taking... ripe for the shaping — you know? For now, what they're trying to do is dredge us up, flatten our spirit, by flooding us with consumer products, by hooking us to machines... By trying to get us away from ourselves, right? By making us forget — numb... But that shit can't last forever. When push comes to shove, they'll begin to sell us aspirations: the idea of Nation, or God — and most of all, they will sell us Enemies — all those things give purpose, wicked as it is. 'Look around you — everyone wants what's yours'. 'Look over there — there's the horde coming to take what's *ours*,' they'll say. That kind of stuff gives narrative and focus. It strikes deeper. We don't consume it, it consumes us. And we'll be happy for it.

"That's all because such things are distortions of the truth — they do bind us to others, even though we lose ourselves in the process. But most of us nowadays hate ourselves anyway — so we'll be happy for it."

Her voice was gruff from the strain of speaking through the songs, which now rose to a unison of voices — the whole parade of protesters from the head to the tail of the march now sang a single chant with a sound that subsumed all other sounds. But Orenda, nearing Neipas closer yet, leaning onto him, still told him:

"We always have to keep this in mind: Their story — the story of the fascists, the nihilists, the tech-futurists too, right? all the masks of capitalism — is *easier* to tell, so we must be much better storytellers than they are. A good movement tells a good story, it educates people... It inspires people, it rouses the imagination. And we need a lot of imagination to see a future, a way out of this mess.

"We gotta draw up a contrast between what things are and what things can be — and the role we all have to play in shaping the world. It's not only possible, it's *necessary* to create a new world, one without poverty, without hunger, without war — it's more than possible. There are more than enough resources. We can create a civilization where nature flourishes, with beautiful cities, beautiful homes, beautiful gardens and theaters and all sorts of places for people to hang out in — we can live in community and be happy together, we can create a society without depression and all that bullshit, where people really *live* — where people carry out their lives and actually live them. So no more 'growth' — no more destruction! We have enough. Let's distribute it properly. No more mindless competition — let's flourish together, or we'll keep on decaying, alone. Let's abandon the spiritual deserts where we're languishing right now and step into a world that fulfills!... We can only do that together — it's more than possible. Come with us! Let's make that world. Let's act — dedicate our *lives* to this — it's the burden of our generation, it's the calling of our time!

"It's that vision that must win out... Or theirs will."

They had sunk deep into the heart of Ostrich, into the core of the great box-machine pumping venom into every artery and every pore. The visible organism, sprawling and rising before them, seemed implacable; its power here was apparent, titan and industrial, it seemed unstoppable in its growth; it grew deep into the bodies of people standing in its way. Beneath it, defiantly, stood now those it had injected with its poison, raising their voices against its inhuman colossal din and attempting by the force of held hands to topple the apparently unbeatable juggernaut.

They had gone all the way around the wide fences. At the end they stopped and gathered. A certain young woman of lustrous hair and brown complexion, with a flower adorning her ear, and who Orenda told was running for the nation's parliament, got up upon a makeshift platform; and with the hellish motley of pipes and chimneys as background, she spoke to the audience.

"That's my girl!" said Orenda enthusiastically. "She's running against the guy representing this area — really dirty politician, deep in Noxxe's pocket."

As they were listening to her speaking, with her voice gruff, her posture slightly arched, bearing a resolute aspect over the pulpit and jabbing the air with her finger, Orenda repeatedly tiptoed and craned her neck in an attempt to raise her petite stature over taller heads; and Neipas observed her through the corner of his sight all the while. Tuning in and out of the speech, he perceived her slim shape and careless hairbun's ping-ponging amidst the throng. He smiled involuntarily behind his myriad masks. For the first time he found in his experience of their physical proximity something of attraction and desire. Orenda wasn't the type of woman Neipas would normally look twice at, and yet she possessed a kind of inconspicuous good-looks which became enlivened by the charm of her ways, by her sincerity of conviction, her zeal of conduct, her energy and her abundance, her passion — the more he knew her, the more beautiful she seemed.

The young political candidate was just concluding her soaring speech with a very roster of aspirations: promising to fight the power of the fossil fuel industry and make them pay for all the damage they cause, and to direct the balance to building the next economy; an economy fair for all, whose benefits tend not toward the already richest. She promised the beginning of a new era, one in which the pursuit of new ideals and a new society would be the imperative; she promised a new politics of respect for the natural world, of reverence for life and responsibility toward all those under its care, so that the banes of environmental degradation, abject misery and wanton destruction can end at once and an age of prosperity worthy of the human spirit and the living race can finally begin. She promised to fight for all those ideals to the last consequence; she promised she would win.

"Lot of promises," Neipas commented as a storm of clapping boomed and floated from the crowd.

Orenda smiled slyly, detecting his cynicism; and as the applause faded and a hubbub of excited talking sparkled about them she said, "We must be ambitious. And we can't let go of our ambitions, can't be milquetoast about it. There's always a danger of being brought into the fold once she's up there — politics is rife with corruption. If she wins, she can't go there alone, but go with us, with the movement — you know what I mean?"

"Movement leaders are just as susceptible to cooptation though, so they, everyone in the movement, must be extraordinary in upholding their values — we can't let ourselves be seduced by money, fame, praise. Our struggle has lost many of its best members to those things — many under the guise of 'pragmatism' — the usual suspect. But we must be strong, we must be strength itself. There's nothing pragmatic in the way societies are being run right now."

"For sure, I'm just saying though — how's she gonna do all those things, doesn't she just get one vote? How many politicians are in parliament anyway? Even if one is honest..."

"She's not the only one of us who's running, but she's not going there primarily to pass laws — our numbers won't be high enough to pass the laws that should be passed yet. No, she's going there to be a muckraker and a bullhorn, to see their bullshit up close and denounce it to the people, to advance our ideals in the top stage, and be an honest fighter every step of the way, even if that means self-sacrifice; to defy power and always speak the truth appealingly, and widen our support with popular constituencies. She's to be a heroine, that's what's expected of her. Of course, it can't all be on her

— it's our responsibility too, we can't just leave her on her own. She'll be gobbled up quick unless we're there steadfast with her.

"But yeah, what we're after right now is not the ability to vote on laws — like, you're right, her vote would be only one among many — but to create a breach, you know, through which we can swarm parliament, through which we can grow. They make spectacle to hide truth and keep their power, *we* gotta make spectacle to uncover truth and build our power. To build a broad audience in the central stage — it's much harder to do that from the margins."

Most everyone had by then gone to meet elsewhere near, a few blocks away in an old park, for talk and lunch; and new silences seemed to arise out of the dispersal of the crowd. The mood became somber under those oppressive leaden skies and upon those cracked barren sidewalks, and Orenda spoke low, meekly now, as if she had been drawing all her energy from the people around her now walking away:

"It's gonna be difficult anyway. We have to expect many trials and setbacks. We'll be dealing with the most dangerous kind of slimeballs up there, and they won't let us win easy — they'll fight to the death to keep their place, to *our* death if we push them enough. But we gotta prevail, Neipas. The fate of humanity hangs in the balance. That's why we have to mobilize the spirit..."

Neipas listened to her silence, out of which a greater, deeper silence seemed to emerge; and into which she said:

"Our responsibility is immense, so is the potential for despair. We need the spirit. We gotta instill faith."

"...In God?"

"Yes, the God in ourselves."

She said it with a smile so tender and eyes so piercing that Neipas could not help shying away his own eyes and repeating in his own lips the tender shape of her so-tender smile. Together they walked to the old park, following the ebb of the march across the torrid streets, seeking the shade of lampposts under the noon (the organizers of the march exchanged the banners for umbrellas, under which many of the most elderly now sheltered from the caustic sunshine).

Eventually, Neipas asked about Oshana.

"Oshana couldn't come today. She's with the Oyate."

"I see."

Orenda wavered a moment.

"We found out who set the fires," she said suddenly.

His gaze turned to her startled. "I hear you... but — how? So the fires were set for sure then?"

"Yes. It was arson. One of our brothers saw them do it... He was burnt badly, been lying in the hospital for weeks — he lived just long enough to make a description...

"He said he had fixed his face, of one of the guys who did it, it was imprinted in his dreams... He said he just wanted to live long enough to tell it."

"I'm so sorry..."

Neipas felt a rising sensation in his heart.

"Wait — what hospital?" he asked abruptly.

"Northeast. Why?"

Neipas shook his head in confusion, thinking it couldn't be — the image, hidden under white curtains, of a burnt man, and of a destroyed face, surfaced to the orb of his eye from the eye-pit in a flash. But he let the memory pass him by, and said nothing.

"So who did it?"

"I mean, we have a description, and they're running IDs right now. It might be that he doesn't have a record so it'll be harder to find, and I dunno if the police much cares... But our brother was going on about how he had claw hands, you know. Like talons."

There was something in the description that made Neipas' senses flutter with recognition once more.

"Do you think it's possible he works at a slaughterhouse?"

Orenda started and gazed baffled at Neipas.

"What makes you say that?"

Neipas hadn't mentioned to her that he had worked in a slaughterhouse during the nightshift. He told her now, somewhat embarrassed; and how the wielding of the knife, slicing repeatedly through the passing corpses of animals, made the muscles rigid and the fingers inert and frozen in the slicing pose. He recalled the hauler of condemned creatures by the railroad, and how his case was particularly severe.

"A slaughterhouse... Ok, can I have you look at the description of his face? I could get you in front of it as soon as possible."

"Sure, of course — anything I can do to help."

18 - Children of the Seed

The sun had long left the sky and the night fallen upon Axiac when Neipas and Orenda stepped into the dim lamp glow of the parking lot — one of those numerous open squares on the side of the road rimmed by little stores, with the large pillar and billboard which hovered over the entrance announcing the shops therein to the passing cars. They stopped by the overnight bakery.

"Didn't know overnight bakery was a thing," said Neipas.

"It is," replied Orenda.

They entered the narrow, simple room. It had but a couple of tables and four chairs, with the glass counter in the back displaying cakes, shelves of bread loaves rising on the wall behind it. Manning the counter was a fellow with a bushy feather mustache and apron, and at one of the tables sat a gaunt pigeon with big eyebrows over the watchful red stare. Both were looking at the TV mounted over the entrance door.

"Good evening — what's going on Mannie, Iezu," greeted Orenda the counter fellow and the fellow at the table. They greeted her with a distracted 'hey', absorbed by the sports match on the TV.

"Good evening, Orenda. The usual?"

"That's right."

"Coming right up fresh for you."

"Thanks Mannie. This here's my friend Neipas by the way."

They all exchanged warm greetings and shakes of hand, and as they were all collectively drawn into the hypnosis of the game a lady came out the back door next to the bread shelves, wearing a powdered apron and a hardy pigeon mask which beamed firm into a smile when she saw the newcomers. "What's going on with you Orenda."

Orenda hugged her over the counter and Neipas was introduced to the lady, whose name was Candida.

"Bread's in the oven for you, will be just a minute sweetie," said Candida. "Not in a rush," Orenda replied.

"Is this at the Stradom?" asked Neipas, after a silent beat.

"Yeah — just up the hill," Iezu said. "Passed by it on my way here."

They fell together again in the cadence of the game, in the drawing flashes of the overhanging TV. In it, muscular bodies with steed heads raced on a green field in chase of a ball, all under a great coliseum where pigeons and horses painted with two different colors prayed and shouted. Candida watched the spectacle with a firm glare and arms akimbo; and Orenda's frazzled eyes could not be more obvious in their indifference.

"You hear how much this guy's making, Candy?" cut Orenda into the focused silence, pointing to one of the running horse-heads on TV.

"Best player in the league, though," commented Mannie.

"I think you should be making more than him, Mannie. You give nourishment. What does he do?"

"He worked hard to become the best," he replied from behind the counter, yet transfixed upon the screen glow.

"Does he work a *million* times harder than you?"

"But people wanna see him. He's popular."

"Is food not popular? Are clean streets not popular?" Orenda said, pointing to Iezu at the table.

"Orenda's right," Candida claimed definitely, her body thrusting to and fro from her akimbo arms. "Don't matter how much he work, he still just running after a ball. Shouldn't make so much while we here struggling to make do!"

"It's them market laws. That invisible hand," put in Iezu from under his enormous eyebrows.

Candida pointed fiercely at the TV. "Well I say we oughta slap that invisible hand and tell it 'bitch, get off my pocket!'" — to which everyone laughed but Mannie, who simply shook his head and continued to watch the game.

*

They climbed the street toward Orenda's place, a house on the slope where she lived with eight other girls. Behind their steps the low buildings receded as Babylon beyond them arose, the magnificent glare of the Belab piercing mighty the nightsky. The horizon was awash with the fiery sheen of street lamps; Neipas and Orenda surfaced above an immense sea of lights cloaking the tar valley, which spread flat its body of glimmering titan to the farthest reaches where the darkness of the mountains arose mute and mysterious. The vapors of Iblis and the surrounding plants darkened thick the night beyond the adobes of the hillock, between which they trekked. Their walk was silent. Its steps were infused with the lightness of the subtle breeze, leaden with the accumulated fatigue of the day, carried with the pleasant lassitude of each other's company. Arriving upon Orenda's porch, they dropped right away into the armchairs set round the table by the rail, exhausted. Orenda placed the paper bag with the warm loaf on the table. Neipas delicately set the camera at rest at its side.

"Down to eat?" she asked, reaching into the bag, taking a huge chunk, and proceeding right away to mouth it in one go.

"You wanna just eat plain bread?"

"What's wrong with that?" Orenda mumbled through the chewing: "I have some olive oil you can dip it in. I can go grab. Some sauces I can make."

Neipas shrugged, laughing. "How do you eat bread plain?"

"What — you don't like bread?"

"I like buns with ham or something in the middle. Plain bread I don't get."

Orenda downed the chunk and shook her head in her characteristic, resolute, half-incredulous manner. "All right chief," she began. "I'm not even gonna comment on the fact that you need *a corpse* inside your bread to enjoy it. I'm gonna let that go 'cause it's not really your fault." "Oh come on —"

"Na na na na na — " she interrupted quickly, wiggling her finger. "Let me finish. Dude — *plain bread you don't get?* Have you tried this? Here — take a bite. Just take one bite."

Orenda gave him a piece of bread. Neipas pinched it between his fingers: it felt warm, cozy, its fresh rigid surface yielding softly to the touch. He lifted it before his lip — "Wait, wait," said Orenda. "Eat the soft part first."

Neipas pulled the crumb out of its crust shell, from which it parted languid and soft, as if yawning and stretching out of sweet slumber. He nestled the crumb between his teeth. And he nodded pleasantly — it felt like a sponge of warm flavor dissolving in his brain as he ruminated it, melting snugly into the side of his tongue, and giving him a tranquil feeling all around, lightening gently some of fatigue's burden.

"So?"

Neipas nodded and waved his head, as one considering. "Not bad," was his verdict.

"*Right?* I told you. Now the crust."

The crust, fresh off the oven, was a marvel of crunchy taste. Neipas was quite surprised with it, and found in the pleasing act of chewing an addictive pull that made him wish to grab another bite right away.

"Right?" said Orenda, handing him another piece.

She went inside for a moment to collect dishes, and water, wine, and olive oil to accompany the humble meal. Together they ate quietly, contemplating the blur of city lights. The street descended steeply toward the drama of Babylon. Behind the houses at the slope's bottom highways scattered and blinked with little red dots and white puddles of haze, stringing a languid pulse of gleam cordoning the amber windows of the vista. Panes climbed high and low, opaque and alone. Copiously they spread and replicated across the vastness, resembling cotes, encrusted like gems upon plain walls which popped off the blurry grounds as a great mountainous wave of indistinct urban bodies. Sovereign above all else in view was the Belab, emerging supreme from the core of Babylon, rooted deep and as firm as a pillar, as though it supported the nocturnal heavens, or a mast, erected and embraced among its towers and the dazzle of the tar veins which wound and branched all throughout in a mesh of wet lights. From afar, it seemed innocuous — the skyline's meaning abstracted along its distance, hidden by the powerful radiance of the towers, lost in the splash of dormant glow underlying the buoying expanse. The silent wonderment of their contemplation inspired in Neipas vague magical theories about the landscape, where it occurred to his fancy that those lights were floating spirits roaming in search of their rightful shelters, cellar doors or escape hatches corresponding to one of the numberless luminous windows sprinkled throughout the land, dotted across the heights like the niches of unending mausolea. Like birds of lucent spectral wings the phantoms all circled round the great tower; and he mulled faintly on whether that window mightn't be found somewhere in its vertical expanse, to which all looked in search. Indeed, its Pearl glowed over all things, pulsed calmly over all things, perched mighty over all things as though it were the mustered substance of those many vagrant phantoms drifting round their ultimate aerie.

Something of his thoughts must have found an echo in Orenda's mind; or so it seemed to him when she said, reproducing in her voice the latent reflections of his heart: "Is it true? That they hide a treasure in there?"

"In the Belab?"

"Yeah."

"That's what they say. But how would I know?"

"You work there, don't you?"

Neipas laughed. "They didn't let me see the vaults yet."

A long, quiet pause spanned between them into the night. Again they nestled in the silent comfort of their chairs, resting their eyes across the dazzling expanse. Their quietude stretched relaxed for a while; completely undisturbed, until Orenda stirred it gently, wondering mutedly:

"What do you think it is? The treasure, I mean."

Somber, Neipas took a minute to reply. The Belab glued fluidly to his stare. His mind wallowed in fuzzy remembrances of impenetrable gloom and an ashy powder, rays of solid shine and a dark radiance brighter than the sun. "Black gold," he mumbled, unthinking.

"Petroleum? Why would they stash it there?" Orenda wondered, humored by his response. Then she said, pensively, "I see what you mean though."

After a pause, Neipas asked, "Why do you ask?"

"I wanted to see if you have the same idea of what it is as I do — because you've been inside the Belab, you've seen it."

"Same idea — about the treasure? What do you think it is?"

Neipas fixed his gaze on her long stare, which within its deep black circles held and scrutinized the valley. He listened to her quietness for a little; it had the kind of pondering gravity which precedes serious words. Yet she said nothing. And though Neipas was comfortable in their mutual silence, a vague sharpness of curiosity gradually arose within him, until it took the concrete form of a question:

"Why do you sit in front of the Belab with an empty sign every morning?" he asked in a low voice.

Now Orenda, too, took a minute to speak:

"The sign is empty," she said at last, "because I can't fit all there is to say into one slogan."

It was an evening full of silences, the kind that breathes with quiet words, and Orenda's company infused in Neipas a contemplative serenity that expanded his sense of time to boundless reaches; so that her short pause seemed like a tranquil, deliberate eternity.

She said: "The message is simple. The rich keep getting richer and the poor keep getting poorer, because the rich keep stealing from the poor and the poor keep letting them. That's the root cause of most problems today — the greed of the powerful.

"*How* do you fight that though? that's the hard part. For starters, who are these people? Where are they? Where is their wealth? *What* is their wealth? To have a billion dollars — what does that even mean? Nobody knows what a billion dollars means. I don't, except for this — it gives you an almost godly power... But how do they use that power? and — how the hell does that affect me? All I see are managers lording over me — and beggars, begging beneath me. What do these billionaires and their millionaire underlings have to do with me? They might as well be on another planet, so far away they seem.

"How do you understand all that — how do you fight an enemy you can't see, that you don't know, that is everywhere and nowhere at the same time? How do you stop men that are not just men — but a system? A system, like — like a spirit that possesses men and women who are willing to be possessed; the devil they sell their souls to; the devil they worship. The spirit of greed... the spirit of Mammon.

"They've built labyrinths and fictions all around us... How do you see in that fog? you know?"

Cautiously turning her head, she looked at Neipas as if to ascertain — was he listening? He was, attentively. A smile sprouted across her lips, and, twisting her beak, she glanced downward; softly, she said:

"You know, I used to go every time I had a chance, pick up a sign and go to every demonstration I could. Against oil extraction, against barbaric laws, against war. Every weekend I'd go to the Square and stand with a couple of randos to protest everything under the sun." She laughed dryly, shook her head, drew her lips over the teeth (her very beak contracted with inward intonations). "I had a sign I'd always bring, that said 'down with the patriarchy'. Nobody passing by had a clue about what that meant.

"But I was frustrated at the state of things. Angry. Desperate, you know? Knowing the pillaging, the murder, all the horror that goes on the world over by official sanction, and in complete silence... I — " she sighed, her feathers bristled in her grimace — "I'm not sure I'm making sense.

"Like, right now, for example..." Orenda paused for an extended moment, and again her eyelids, nearing each other in focus, narrowed over a gaze that seemed to blur in reflections; again she appeared as if looking very far away, to indeterminate distances. Yonder, the Belab dominated the vista, towered over every light, over every horizon, omnipresent, invincible.

"Night fell here," she rejoined, "but the sun's up on the other side of the world, shining over things we can't see. Right now, there are whole families surviving in squalor, kicked out of home because of some dam, or some forest clearing, or some mine or industrial project. There are men killing each other in wars fought for wicked interests — fought for no good reason. There are women bending their backs over sewing machines, making our clothes, probably midway through a shift that will go another eight hours, to half-starve at the end of the day. There are kids crawling into the darkness of the Earth to dig out the minerals for our electronics. In all likelihood, just while I've been talking, there was a kid who got bombed by an airplane or a drone: a little body torn to pieces, an existence wiped out, a life lost... a kid who will never again see the sunrise — never again feel — never again wake up — never again have the chance to live. All those things are happening."

Orenda had struggled somewhat to pronounce these last words — her voice, though always firm, diminishing in volume under the strain — and she was forced to pause for a few seconds. Neipas, remaining quiet, listened to her closely, closely observing her face which, nevertheless, kept as stolid and imperturbable as ever, her mask a very totem of living strength. "And why all this?" she then said. "Because it makes some powerful people a lot of money — gives powerful people a lot of power.

"We don't even need to head so far out to see. In front of our *eyes*, Neipas, just in front of our eyes, there are people hungry, homeless, afflicted... struggling to survive in this wealthy land," she said, with stare fixed upon the vast tides of liquid lights spanning the night city. "Right in front of our eyes... hidden by blocks, by windows, by the city, by... by blur," she said the last word a little breathless, as if a sudden frailty had tried to overcome her; but, composing herself, steadying her mask, she looked at Neipas with eyes hard and brows raised: "And why this? Because it makes money...

"Really. It's too fucked up. Too stupid to bear. I couldn't bear it. I still can't bear it."

She paused again for a moment. Neipas contemplated her thoughtfully, listening in earnest, saying nothing.

"I felt that I had to do something, *urgently* — so I'd end up going for anything, back in those days. You know? But I never took a second to think about if it would have an impact or what. I just did it blindly, out of despair. It's tough, you know, not to rush into things, because it seems like we're always playing catch up — things move so fast. It's overwhelming.

"Now we plan, we study, we reflect on what effect we wanna make, and we measure our success as best we can, and adapt. Today, for instance: our goal was not to convince Noxxe not to expand the refinery! They couldn't give two shits. We want to mobilize the neighborhood, convince the undecided homeowners *not* to sell — and that's why we made it a funereal procession, to try to frame Noxxe as an enemy, as evil. And it's true. Cancer grows like weeds in those neighborhoods, and it's the chemical companies fault. Noxxe is just the biggest of them."

Quiet: again flowing from the night in her ebbing words. The bread loaf rested on the plate still, for a while untouched and unnoticed. Now, half-distractedly, Orenda turned and took a chunk of it; by means of pointing gestures she urged him to eat, and both, seizing their respective fluffs — approaching opposite sides of the same plate, sharing the bread — dipped them in olive oil in turns. After some more time of a strangely natural quietude, of the lassitude of meditative contemplation in the tranquility of that porch, Neipas spoke:

"Can I ask you something?"

"Ask."

"Why wouldn't you want the Ostrich folk to leave this polluted place, though?"

"We want the pollution to leave this place — we want it banished from the Earth. What *they* want is to expand the pollution. The money they're offering isn't enough to leave the neighborhood and go live elsewhere anyway — more like just enough to get out and die. Besides, if they expand it's just gonna poison more people in a bigger area.

"Look, if we could relocate everyone while we're fighting these fossil fuels, we would. The both of us are breathing in those fumes ourselves right now, Iblis is close from here. There's more than enough money out there to move everyone within a ten mile radius into padded apartments and much more — just so happens we don't have that money, coincidentally."

A humored exhalation filled Neipas' mouth in the course of chewing and inadvertently propelled a bit of bread out of his beak. "Sorry," he masticated embarrassedly, covering his lips. She simply laughed; and he, molding his visage and composing his feathers to hide the redness in his face, rejoined after a while, smiling to her placid, infinitely tranquil smile, which had settled upon her lips in the ensuing quietude.

"You still haven't told me," he said, "about why you sit in front of the Belab with that sign."

"Oh yeah..." she said quietly, contemplatively; again transmitting that curious impression of drawing away and coming nearer at the same time. "Well, basically, it's because... how do I explain it." She chuckled, a little abashed; a hint of drowsy tiredness was manifested in her mood. "Well, these methods have their limits," she sighed. "The thing about protests, movements, legal tools, regular activism — they're ways to fight within the framework, to improve within certain parameters along the spectrum. They're ways to stop, maybe even reverse certain injustices, if you're lucky. We can say 'stop the pipeline', we can say 'raise our wages' — but you're still talking in terms of 'pipelines' and 'wages'. Which, of course, you must.

"Still, to stop, to reverse, to improve — that's one thing. But to *create* — that's another ballgame. And much harder.

"In Ostrich, we've been successful in changing the mindframe from 'let's get Noxxe to pay us more' to 'let's get Noxxe outta here'. We want to decommission not only Iblis, but all the plants in Ostrich, tax those companies, end their subsidies, and use the funds to refit the houses there, pay for health care and reparations. We wanna build parks where the factories are now and build healthy energy sources to fill in the gap — both in terms of energy and of jobs, and so on. Make sense? But let's say we're successful.

"That's difficult enough — matter of fact, it's herculean. (herculean? mumbled Neipas) I mean, it's a *very* tough nut to crack," Orenda grinned. "Ostrich has a specific set of problems, a specific history. We've managed to appeal to the neighborhood's sense of dignity, we forged really close bonds — we're like family, those of us in the movement, we'd do anything for each other. We believe that we can be successful — we have faith in ourselves, and that took time to build. Very localized time.

"But how do you spread that kind of faith across distances, you know — that kind of commitment? Without proximity? If Noxxe leaves Ostrich, let's say, would they disappear? No, right? They'd go elsewhere, and use every resource to make sure they destroy us. Probably they'd have every other moneyed interest in the world united with them for an onslaught against us, because, trust me, when they feel threatened, they're unsparing. They'll go to the end of the world — literally — to keep their power. So they'll do anything they can — and they *can* a lot — to reverse our wins again, to get back to their extreme end of the spectrum.

"What we need is another spectrum."

She looked at Neipas, smiled, and, instinctively, plucked a bit of fluff from the loaf — then slowly directing her eyes to the olive oil vessel where she dipped the bread, she withdrew for a moment in thought, eating nebulously.

"Sometimes..." she began slowly, faraway. "Sometimes I think that if we want humankind to thrive, if we want the Earth to thrive — we need a new story. New ideals.

"We don't wanna just put a few oil refineries out of commission and do away with pipelines, make some wind turbines sprout — and bam. No. We want to change the economy, the structure of society, the values that guide civilization. Restore the grandeur of Nature. Restore the grandeur of Life. *Create* a new life, one that is harmonious with nature and itself — that hasn't happened before, not to a big civilization, not for a long time, at least.

"But to do that we need to make people see that life *can* be grand. That Nature is not our enemy, not our slave, not our shopping mall or our trash can. Nature is not some*thing* aloof from us. That's all part of the myth of our age. No — life is *meant* to be wonderful. And Nature is our essence and our support. Our *Mother*.

"Seems to me like we gotta be reborn from this Mother, and become like children again, so that we learn to speak anew... I don't mean cryptically — I mean in a way that cuts through the noise and speaks to the depths, to the spirit.

"We need to inspire a new faith. A new faith in humanity — not just in its power, but its capacity for *good*. And I don't mean good like 'donating morsels to charity' good, and I really don't mean 'showing off' good. I don't mean vanity. I mean genuine kindness, genuine strength, and the power to make the world a comfortable and fulfilling place for *every. single. person* — every single life. The potential for that faith's been relentlessly attacked. Today we view ourselves as hopelessly greedy, hopeless pieces of shit, deep down. To fix that will require a connection to ourselves, to one another, and to the Earth that's been just — broken. We feel too small, we don't feel the vastness and wonder of the Earth inside ourselves anymore — the Earth doesn't spread from our feet anymore, we feel like we're always in the clouds, free falling, dizzy, nauseous... helpless. To mend that — it'll be hard, really hard. It'll take some deep reflection. It'll take a lot of creative energy. But we gotta make people see in themselves the power to shape the future.

"To create we must learn to speak anew... Learn to listen afresh. Learn to see again. Learn to feel with a deeper heart. We'll need that to reach people — to reach their souls. We can't just mobilize the body, the task is too difficult for that. And we need to go deeper than the mind. To set a vision, a destiny toward which to walk — and inspire the spirit to keep our feet steady, our eyes honest, our hearts humble — that is the task.

"That's why I sit in front of the Belab with an empty sign... It's a spiritual practice for me. A meditation and a trial. I'm trying to find that faith in myself. I'm trying to find the words that I can't write on the cardboard. I'm trying to practice my fortitude. To sustain the curious eyes, the mocking sneers, the dawn cold in my body... It makes me stronger. But that's *my* way. Just... something personal, you know? Practically, it accomplishes nothing. But we must go beyond the practical sometimes.

"We must go into the depths of the human heart and speak new words. We must learn how to decipher its language, how to listen to it. That's what I try to do... To find the center, dive into the deep... where everyone is one."

Easing from the ardor and charm of prophetic passion, Orenda's mouth settled into the contemplative slackness which follows in the wake of sighs, and took once more of the bread. Neipas observed with fascination her lustrous, beautiful black eyes, the stirring feather at the tip of her earring, the messy bloom of hair suspended over her nape, the locks cascading down her cheek. He had failed to fully grasp the last words she'd spoken; yet somehow, as with Oshana before, he had comprehended something of their meaning, with a comprehension that ranged beyond the mind — and thus, unable to rationally encapsulate a fitting question, he asked nothing, and was content to simply sit with her in silence.

He, too, took of the bread: pinched it between his fingers and brought it to his lips, tasted it as fluffy as cloudy billows clearing one's heart into heavens profound.

*

They had descended once more into a mellow quiet, having landed upon it tender, settling again in the lassitude of tranquil observation over the city lights. All the tension that Neipas had been accumulating lately seemed to fade off his shoulders among the wide enchanted comforts of the porch. In his snug languor, he sometimes sensed a bit of an itch influencing his laziness of will, urging him toward the camera which sat at rest upon the table by the plate, the bottles and the empty cups. Naturally he felt like grabbing it and taking pictures; but there was something in Orenda's posture, at once slack and contained, relaxed and steady in the simple act of sitting there and watching the landscape, which comforted him and made him want to mirror her, to share in the placid evening without interruption. Even as he often sensed that she had fallen asleep (in his own half-doze he occasionally glimpsed to his side and saw her eyes closed), what she had signaled to him at the graveyard — that, that wasn't the time or place to photograph — affected him on that porch as well. To lean the glass against his eye then would be to violate the sacredness of the moment, he felt.

But then — after a long while — a glass shook in his pocket; and the impulse to seize the *I* stole upon him so quick that he didn't have time to become conscious of it. He lifted it to his view.

EVA: Heeyyy :) How did the interview go?

NEIPAS: Not bad, thanks for asking :) How are —

Orenda's voice snuck into his sudden distraction. "Girlfriend?"

She was smiling. Neipas chuckled. "No, no... Hey by the way, do you have a maskbook page?"

"No... Screw that."

"You really don't have a maskbook page," asked Neipas, amused.

"Nope."

He gazed at her and molded his countenance to look intrigued. "Why not? Everyone has a maskbook page."

"'cause it's shit," she said simply. Neipas' laughter released her own.

"Wanna expand on that?" he said. "Isn't it a useful tool for organizing and everything?"

"Well yeah, of course it is. But we can't depend on it. At all. It can only serve as the beginning of a beginning at most... and man, on the balance it's just bad. I think it's more bad than good. Just when we need to be present, people look like they're always somewhere else now. Or more like they're nowhere. We barely speak to each other anymore. We moo, caw, chirp, tweet — whatever now, except talk to each other. We *yell* past each other. That's what it does. It's like shouting from the mouth of a screaming whale."

"From the mouth of a screaming whale?" Neipas guffawed, slacking further into his chair.

"I guess so," Orenda said, tucking deeper into her chair too, feeling the coming chill of the deepening night.

"That's so random."

"Yeah well, kinda sleepy — feeling good though..." she grinned lazily, with the raspiness (Neipas sensed it in his own voice too) of one who's long been awake and is still wide awake in relaxed drowsiness. Then she added, in a jesting tone, "I'm guessing you have a page? If *everyone* has one."

"Well, yeah."

"Suit yourself. I don't understand why anyone would want to share their private lives with the creeps at maskbook. Guess that's not what anyone's thinking about, but..."

Neipas shrugged. "I have almost nothing personal there though... Just professional stuff. Who cares what they know about me anyway? I'm nobody."

Orenda shook her head with the slowness of the dead of night. "The point's not to get to know you. It's to hollow you out. They claim to be connecting you and all but they're actually —" she paused, making a gesture of hands parting and widening with flapping fingers over her head, indicative of dispersal, fragmentation, " — you know? They don't care about you or anybody."

Neipas turned his head to her, burrowed alongside him across the table.

"Don't get me wrong, I mean — I don't really like it either," he said.

"No?"

"I made a page at first because — well I guess because everyone had one. But then I had to use it for work. To promote my photos."

"You don't sound pleased about that." — and indeed his distaste seeped all unbounded through his mask.

"No... People don't look at photos on the maskbook. They just whiz through — you know? It's nothing like it used to be. When you sat on a couch with the photographs... Or with your family, all looking at the album and sharing stories. It's all dispensable now. I don't like to feel like my work is dispensable... I want people to look at it. Really look. I want it to be special. I want it to leave a mark," he said briskly, shrugging in a despondent manner.

"How did you get into photography?"

"My father got me into it."

"Oh yeah?" Orenda said, though not in the indifferent manner with which such words were spoken in those days. Her voice carried over with interest, which she consolidated by asking, "How come?" with the active focus of a listener.

Neipas chuckled shyly. "He had this old film camera — the one I showed you, used to be his. Then he set up a darkroom of his own... My sister and I were brought up in it. I'd spend hours there. It was just kind of natural, you know." He tried to express himself, release his mind of the old sunken memories and how he felt warm in them; but, finding himself unable, he would recede into his shell of feathers and shush, feeling utterly incapable.

"Is he a photographer?"

"He was a farmer. Had a mill. That's where the darkroom was."

Orenda sensed now the mournful weight in his tone; the grieving hint of things past.

"Is he..."

Neipas looked despondently across the table, and found her gazing straight into him; he dodged her stare and looked at his shoes. "Dead? No... But it's the same, really."

"Where is he now?"

"Well, he's..." Neipas hesitated; his strain of voice died in a hopeless sigh of air. In a moment he regretted having gone into the topic at all.

"It's ok if you want to share," Orenda told him. "But it's also ok if you don't wanna talk about it."

Neipas lifted his hand to feel his mask. There was a sensation at the tip of his fingers, an impression of hearing the old grindstone circling in the depths of the mill, from the darkness of the past; and out of the quietude of the night seemed to breeze, momentarily, the soothing sound of the river sparkling outdoors, petted by the great wheel. In the shadows of the alleys he seemed to perceive his father mumbling among the vagrants, disowned by destiny and life; in the blackness extending across his sight, he seemed to see, between the dark walls of the mill, the petrified mask of his parentage, mumbling without a stir the words 'I — don't — know...'.

It took a long while before he spoke. Orenda's listening soul waited patiently.

"My dad's a cripple," he said. "Physically... Mentally... He's in an institution now."

Neipas nodded vaguely to the floor, looking down as if to hide himself as he digested his own words; his confession having stripped him of his shell, leaving him exposed and embarrassed in his sudden nakedness. He raised again his hand and touched his mask.

"What happened?"

It was a long time before he spoke; but he felt, at last, the need to speak. He had been asked about it but once — by Edazima, back in college. But he carried all the disoriented ire of adolescence in his breast then, inflamed brighter yet by the freshness of his trauma. What had happened that day was not an easy thing to talk about without his throat compressing and welling and tears bloating under his eyelids — so he told Edazima off scornfully; and she never asked again. Yet now, he felt sleepy enough to be able to remain detached from strong emotions, and sufficiently awake to render his heart to the listening, earnest, pure soul by his side.

The words left him in the form of mumbles; mumbles clear in the quiet night.

"We lived downriver from a mountain. When I was a kid... some people came. They wanted to dig a mine up there.

"It's strange, you know...? I mean, I guess I shouldn't be old enough to remember it, but I remember how things changed after that. You could just feel it all around you, in the air — the smells... just weird. I dunno — like things just weren't the same.

"They were looking for a bunch of minerals, but especially uranium. I can't remember any of them except uranium..."

The blurry lights of Axiac dimmed before his upturned glare. They dimmed until they were no more; and he spoke into the darkness:

"My parents opposed the mine. Most people in the village did. Didn't matter. The mine went ahead, and kept growing. No one liked it. Even those that got work up there didn't like it. But we learned to live with it, I guess."

In the long silences between words, the darkness spoke into him. It spoke in secretive tones; it whispered with the palpitations of chipped grindstone; through purling wheels upon a scintillating stream, it murmured. A red shone, rather distantly. Like an ethereal heart it pulsed, like a flame laughing without sound, like the sun bleeding along the river. He opened his eye into the blackness of the old darkroom and, peering into the chemical waters, he glimpsed it all flowing like a strip of film in negative colors — the land emerging alien, drained of life; his village, barely remembered, ill-forgotten, a wasteland. Yonder there he could still spot (as he peeked over his mother's nape) the fig tree, whose aerial roots were the veil, beyond which Neipas could not go.

"I remember this really big tree with these kind of falling branches, like — the area beyond that became forbidden. Taboo. There were stories about poisonous things blooming there."

Yonder, the river shimmered golden behind the draping, flaxen-powdered roots of the fig at sunset. Dust and amorous insects glinted in the sighing sunlight — blackened, bit by bit, by the encroaching uncanny forms of cinder blowing from the trucks, with a rumble of motors thundering from the forbidden zone, infusing the concealed horizon with its low, persistent noise; a noise which whispered its way sometimes into the very peacefulness of the wind, of the purling river, out of which the sun silently shone in ever darker tones; arching ever more feebly across the sky as though it were being ground against the gradual rotation of the earth, as the grindstone milled grains into the pit, where they fell in powder — scattering, denser and denser, upon the receding images in the chemical bath over which Neipas felt himself stooping in reminiscence.

"My dad used to say... He used to say that they were looking for seeds up there — digging seeds out of the rock. Seeds for a tree of ash..." his voice lowered in the strain not to shake, trying to sink again to the depths of withdrawnness. "A tree that blooms suddenly, with its own sun. Whose flower is that sun, and whose fruit is ash, a tree that... that bursts and dies in the bloom. It sows poison, and takes everything with it in the flash." He uttered all these words at the cusp of inaudibility.

"Tree of ash... sea of dust." Neipas felt himself very small. The fresh smell of his mother's cooking, the aroma of those prickly shrubs she picked up in the fields, once more tickled his nose. The way she sprinkled herbs over the steaming pot made his heart sigh; made his fading eyes turn deeper inward, to the vision of the little pool where his photographs were marinated. The sound of the wheel outside, paddling in the sunny river, again reached his ear. In the adjacent room, the grindstone scattered the light in sundust; snoring in a grainy munch, with the snarl of dying static, like a monotonic, monochromatic playback of his traumas.

"Some kid there was born with cancer..." He grimaced with recognition. "Mary, I — I didn't even know what that meant... I didn't even remember that until now." He sniffled and wiped his eye; he blew at length; and gradually his face, slackening again, reposed into the set frown of his mask.

His voice, kept lowered to a peep, breathed into the magic secrecy of the darkroom. "One day, there was — there was —" he muttered in the indecision of words to convey it. "It happened very suddenly."

In the darkroom he peeked over the edge of the cistern and looked into the pool. The paper floated inside it, peeking from underneath; and in its surface then materialized, miraculously, the image of his family inside the paper, inside the water — his father and his mother, and his sister by the river singing outside, beyond the stone walls.

"The mining people had this huge tailings pond, like they called it... All the slush from mining would go in there. It was held up by a dam carved into the slope, right into the hill. Right above the river where the village was. They kept dumping waste in it..."

The herbal perfume of his mother's vague memory scattered into a hollow airlessness; ash began to drizzle across his eye in its stead; the sun in the river under the chemical bath and under the image blinkered toward the shadow, and ever more into a deepening, increasingly totalizing quietude. His sister's chanting quelled; his father's driveling stirred. The light was as if combusting and consuming itself — as if breathing its last. Then the gleam faded, the river trickled shush, the wheel groaned into a halt, the grindstone no longer spun. Sometimes, in quieter moments, he would hear a certain sound, a certain regular sound, a slow pulse which seemed to underlie all he would ever hear. Deeper yet, it seemed as though a hum mumbled in song. That was all which was perceivable now; and the darkness was made absolute.

Little Neipas yelled into the waters. But nothing — nothing — save for the silence and the pulse, was heard.

"Me and my sister, we went off to the forest to play... We had this spot we liked, kinda far..."

Neipas and his sister had gone off to the forest to play, and ended up going very far, as they often did. Ascending the wooded hills, they soon reached a steep, bulky crag jutting over the canopies, a favorite playground of theirs for the challenge of the climb and the reward of its peak, rearing over a fabulous view of the valley. In Neipas' pocket crouched the photograph of their parents, round his neck hung the old camera: the sole material possessions that would survive that day.

That day was perhaps pleasant — it must have been, if they had wandered out to that place — the air fresh, the breeze sunny, the trees perfumed and the birds jolly with song; but he could remember none of it. The first thing he recalled was his sister gripping his hand, helping him up. They had just attained the top of the crag, and, having before them the gorgeous vista, were about to settle onto the welcoming moss to contemplate the afternoon (or was it morning? back then it was always morning) — when a dull blast, as of something massive giving way, thumped; and then a tremendous noise, diving in a murmur of collapsing giants and soaring in a terribly hastened crescendo, tumbling out of the mountaintops in the north above the village; a frightfully growing boom that whooshed, and shed into what sounded like titanic billows, a swelling tide, a wave immense, enormous, gigantic — nearing from afar, nearing quickly.

A frightened shiver had taken possession of them before they knew what was happening. First they beheld the trees toppling as if before the passing convoy of some terrible divinity, bowing in succession; then there were unbelievable quantities of mud leaping and powder belching from between the falling trunks and the quaking canopies, bursting with splinters of bark and the vast noises of an overpowering growl under the wide-gaping eyes of the two children perched above the sudden chaos. The torrent abated as it closed upon their village down yonder, but it did not cease; like a sadistic, ravenous monster it proceeded slowly, though gargantuan and already on all sides, already inevitable, to swallow the little homes, the little streets, the running people whose screams were rendered mute under the intense roar of the beast. In the instinct of dread which had entirely possessed his body Neipas took a step back, found his sister, turned his head, saw the tempest of soot approaching. The sister, slightly older and, at that age, substantially larger than him, covered his body as they ducked, and the ash swooped over them, with a density such that it blanketed the sky and all the Earth. Neipas dared peek but once out of the surreality of their panic: and between two narrowly parted eyelids there appeared the sun; a throbbing crimson circle, contracted, mad — shuddering behind a million flapping seeds of dust.

He saw it as though through a succession of photos pulsing in glass within his eye, throughout shards lodged between his mind and his heart (he had shrunken to such an extent that mind and heart leaned against each other). In the silence of the darkroom he discerned the rumble of grindstone, crunching the grains patiently in the other room as he stood there in the dark, ruminating time. He could hear still, sometimes, the river mumbling into a glassy hum beyond arcane walls; and the stone snoozing through the mysterious, distant, slow pulse.

"I guess it just accumulated too much weight, or whatever. All I know is that it collapsed... The dam collapsed, and the whole mud pond rolled down and — just took everything in its path. It destroyed everything."

The first source of his tribulations, recounted at length for the first time, muddled and upturned the very numbness in which his mind was enveloped. Probing himself with opaque, blunted eyes, his soul seemed to him very much like the place that his village had become: a valley of buried waters, of a muddled, poisoned soil, where neither streams flowed nor suns shone nor anything grew; a place stagnant; a place empty. Neipas stooped over the chemical, radioactive aridness of his being shrouded in a darkness — a darkness very much like that of the darkroom, a darkness with nothing but a past — a gloom without a future; a barren half-life. The placid anguish of his psyche found physical expression in the dimming of his senses — so that his eyes truly saw nothing but indistinct spores amid the blackness, and his ears really heard nothing now but the pulse to which those spores blinkered and to which his heart palpitated; his perception genuinely detected nothing save for the pitch-darkened waters beneath it, into which the sun and every remainder of light had died; and he scarcely knew whether he had spoken a single word at all or if he was indeed where he had assumed he was. The notion of Orenda vanished. He was alone, alone utterly. His village lay buried under his blindness. Its homes had been razed and its people crushed. Why could he remember none of them? Neither could he conceive even the contours of the village, not even his home. All had been swept up in the cataclysm thundering downstream from the mill; the mill which, strangely, was the only thing that had gripped to memory.

"Our houses were destroyed, the whole village was destroyed... My father they took out of the mud that day, so he survived, but then... And my mom... my mom..."

His mother was never found. Of her remained barely legible memories and but two photographs: one, which Neipas kept in the depth of his wardrobe, is a tiny print in which she is half-covered; and the other, affixed to her tombstone under an oval glass, protruding like the half of a transparent egg, is a small portrait without color, so phantasmagorical in its representation as to render her face almost insubstantial. Perhaps he felt it so because the tomb was but a hole in the wall of a mausoleum, a niche squeezed among the old stone compartments of other remains, all of them stacked from floor to ceiling, looking like any cabinet of drawers — this, even in his uncomprehending youth, made a mess of his grief, somehow he could not accept it, somehow it repelled him viscerally. But a still stronger reason for his aversion and fear of that small colorless photograph was the fact that the drawer was empty; the notion that, in the absence of a body, it could house nothing but confused spirits. The torrent had overflowed the town's graveyard, scrambled the bones of the dead; the old tombstones had been buried and the bones consigned to perpetual anonymity. Everyone who had ever been laid to rest in that place — forever condemned to a crushing, nameless oblivion. To sense his mother scattered across that waste, stripped of identity and bereft of self somewhere among those ruins, and to see her face as the facade of an empty mask of stone provoked an existential anguish in him that he could not begin to understand — which in its perversion was too painful to rationalize.

"Years after that my dad got sick and... I dunno. My sister thinks it's because of what happened. But I dunno."

His hand reached up to his mask; and felt its wax stiff and dry. He looked up then from the pitch darkness of the darkroom, a darkness total, and saw yonder, vaguely, Orenda emerging from the doorstep of the millhouse, as if by a miracle; listening to him with a sorrowful stare, lip held up. "We moved to the state capital afterwards. And just... watched him go little by little."

He saw the expression of mixed revolt, angst, and teary grief in her silent countenance.

"There was a big legal fight over it, and we got a settlement — almost enough for college, and to put my dad under professional care, you know. Not long after my dad got sick my sister went to college closer to home, and I — I came here."

His feathers covered his visage thickly, covered densely his frown.

"All that survived from that time was a photograph I had in my pocket — and that old camera. That's it."

*

They sat until morning. When Neipas opened his eyes from the weight of sleep, which he had indiscernibly slipped into, the brightness of sunshine blazed already upon the sloped street. A blanket covered him; another wrapped her legs. Orenda was already awake next to him, deep in contemplation, sipping coffee.

Orenda and he shared a quiet breakfast. The camera rested on the table yet; and the bread, left exposed in the night, she retrieved, returning with it toasted and glazed with jam. She was telling him how she checked out his pictures from the march after he fell asleep.

"I wish I could keep this baby," said Neipas, tapping the edge of the table where the camera was placed alongside the plate. Then, responding to the smooth roll of instinct, he grabbed the camera, admiring it with his fingers, feeling its mass and make. Almost without noticing it, he had put the viewfinder to his eye and pointed the lens at Orenda as she ate:

"Hey! Stop it," she scolded, half sternly, half humorously as the shutter snapped. Then she smiled the naturally endearing smile that so easily heartened Neipas' mood, and again the camera snapped in the rush to capture it. "I don't look good," Orenda then said, half abashed, half flattered by his gaze.

The viewfinder was lowered beneath his eyes; and gazing straight into her own, he said, with a quiet, candid tone, "Of course you do."

Both became shy, and each averted their stare in their own way. Neipas took to looking at the device's screen, and for a moment observed the miniature representation of the woman before him; to slacken the taut quiet that bound them close together now, he noted, still looking at the miniature:

"You have an earring like Oshana."

"On the opposite ear, yeah. I always wanted one like hers — this way I can say I'm the other half of her brain, like," she laughed. "Had it since I was a kid."

"You've known her that long, huh."

"Yeah — Oshana's my aunt. She raised me."

Neipas sounded a tone of surprise. Again he looked up.

"She's my mom's sister," Orenda said.

"So you're also from —"

She nodded, delicately gripping the feather pending beneath her earlobe. "From the Nenaan. I mean, from the Joachim Valley. Actually they would give this earring to all girls there when they came of age. We'd do the ceremony, and the Wisewoman — she would pierce your earlobe and... Well, the Wisewoman is gone now.

"So Oshana did it herself — she was always a little unorthodox, she probably would've done it anyway," she smiled. "She gave me my name."

Astounded to discover this affinity between Oshana and Orenda, Neipas, searching for words amongst his blooming curiosity, said, "No way... And your parents, are they in Axiac too?"

Orenda did not respond, however. Instead she said: "I wish I could give it to you," she shrugged, pointing at the camera. "Alas. But... I might have something better for you, actually.

"Hold on." She got up and stepped quietly inside; emerging, just as quietly, a minute or so later — holding a small notebook. "Here," she said, handing it over to Neipas.

"What's this?"

"It's a notebook."

He laughed. "I know what it is. I meant what do you want me to do with it, I guess."

"I'm giving it to you, man. It's a present," she said, sitting back down — and tapping the notebook cover, held between Neipas' hands, she elaborated, "Since I can't give you the camera, I'm giving you this."

"Half the pages are missing," he realized as he leafed through.

"Half the pages are mine," she replied, smilingly.

Neipas considered the little notebook for a moment. "The camera photographs the surface," proclaimed Orenda, "but with this you can search the depth under it."

Something — her tone of voice, her candidness, perhaps the graciousness of the gift — drew in his face a smile so wide that he felt the plumage of his mask spread out, so wide that he felt the sunny fabric of his mask melt warmly; and he sensed a lightness in his body so ample and comforting that he felt as if his heart intended to soar.

"Thank you, Orenda," he said earnestly. "And for inviting me yesterday too... I really enjoyed — you know."

Orenda smiled. "Me too."

There was silence as they finished their breakfast, relaxing into the advancing morning. Neipas knew he had to go, and work — but there was something in her company that unburdened his perpetual sense of pressing responsibility; her being there eased his anxieties.

"By the way," said Orenda suddenly, between the loud chewing of her gaping lips. "Bread tastes better when you smack it. Eat it with mouth open."

"Ewwww," Neipas uttered with a smiling grimace, and they laughed into the brightening shine.

19 - 3 Rules and A Poem

The piglet waddled merrily about the waiting room, strolling with a look of curiosity and wonderment under the chairs, and between the legs presenting themselves to her wide joyous stare in various forms and stages of agitation. Eventually one pair of these legs would shirk away from her; or a hand would reach down and pet her rosy head, massaging such comforts unto her that she would leap and launch her front hoofs onto the lap, ceding to the burst of happiness the caressing fingers provoked in her. The little piglet gazed now into the smiling eyes of a gentlemanly pigeon, who sported a fine mustache of very tended feathers curling upward, stylishly, at each end. Next to him sat Neipas, engrossed in the reading of a poem drawn on a rumpled sheet. They waited, all the workers, for Sunai.

Her email had alighted the glass face of his I the morning previous. The good news seeped quickly into his glare and filled his heart; he was working then, and the tray nearly shook out of his arms with the excitement of possibility, the sudden opening of prospects. He told Edazima shortly after, and she, in an effusive reaction mirroring explicitly the hidden feeling in Neipas' breast, brought it out of him. A widening unfolded in his chest, as though a change had overcome the very air; a relief spread over his slackening shoulders, they stretched freed from an invisible burden. Right away Edazima began to prepare a little farewell celebration for him. Good Janu and his saintly mother Mrs. Tia cooked for the gathering — the delicious cake their alchemy had devised being only consumed after Orassap managed to take a hundred selfies with it — and wished Neipas well with tones of unconditional friendship; most workers had once again come at Edazima's summon, and Kur bristled with their feathers full, with their tipsy hullabaloo, their masks spuming in laughter in the dirty smoke; all of which made Neipas behold the squalid subterranean kitchen with bittersweetness, as a thing already past. Time does to places bygone what it makes of eras dead — it spirits into their wandering vestiges the essence of romance, like far-off landscapes — and, full of the consciousness of it, Neipas drew out his film camera, which he had brought in anticipation; and sucked the dimness of those humid underground tiles and sodden pots onto its blind glass. Then he drew the I and captured once — only once — a photograph of the familiar place and the half-familiar throng populating it.

They waited all for Sunai. The chairs were disposed semi-circularly and faced the single door, all round a little table where a bowl of apples rested in a tidy composition. No one dared touch them. Behind the little table was an empty chair.

They had been led deep into the Education Ministry, through winding corridors of repeating doors without label, obeying the usher's direction across the paths until they were seated here, in the compact room facing the door. Portraits of great entrepreneurs hung upon the white walls, which somehow looked much too thick, as if painted over many times. Under them, droopy pigeon eyes were fastened on flashing glass; and beneath their seated figures roamed, on the checkered floor, a small happy piglet, the presence of which no one could account for; she trod sniffing about the bouncing shoes, glaring everything curiously. Most of them behind the pigeon masks, knowing not what to make of it, tried to ignore her, jutting their necks into the *I* as they indecisively waited. Scarce any motion could be discerned among them; little solitary giggles, or occasional sighs, being the only sounds accompanying the piglet's mirthful grunting. Someone or other would arise from time to time to snap a photo of self with the portraits on the wall. And meanwhile only one pair of eyes, lifted thoughtful and dreamily from a sheet of paper, observed the piglet. Neipas, at their side, withdrew his own stare into the distractions of the Webwork's dazzle.

EVA: I'm super excited for you :)
EVA: We should celebrate!

He browsed the photographs he had caught from the Ostrich march; lost himself in them, until he sensed an approaching movement at his side. A voice whispered slowly:

"Hey brother!" It came from the fellow next to him, a very well-mannered pigeon with upturned mustaches, each an oiled-up feather immaculately cared for. "Beg your pardon — don't I know you from somewhere?"

His cultivated semblance appeared familiar indeed. It was but a pending second of staring narrowly before the vague recognition flared up into concrete memory in Neipas' mind:

"You were at Oshana's bookstore the other night, weren't you?"

"I knew I knew you from somewhere — yes! Indeed I was. And you are Orenda's friend, I recall."

"Oh, I actually met her that day."

"Oh? I see," said the fellow, pinching the tip of his mustache with a flourish; and then, with a smooth stretch of hand, introduced himself. "Cesar."

Cesar was very friendly and Neipas warmed up to him quickly. There was a certain eccentricity about him that made him intriguing; commanding a sense of mystery, from which he derived a vague authority that pulled one's attention. At any rate, he knew how to augment a conversation, and, departing from Oshana's little garden, they conversed about many other things. He presented himself as an artist, "making my way through life, I suppose — though I'm afraid there isn't much consideration, in this present life, for a humble poet like myself," he said, shrugging resignedly. Neipas told him about his photography, and they bonded in their commonality of artistic purpose, speaking all in whispers among the almost monastic silence of little lights that had settled.

"What are you writing there?" Neipas eventually asked.

Cesar looked down to the paper in his lap.

"It's kind of private."

Neipas pressed his finger on his chin so as to wrinkle it, and lifted his brow to crease his forehead, nodding. "Sure."

"It's a poem for my boyfriend," said Cesar secretly, leaning in.

"Oh?"

"I'm having quite a little trouble finishing it."

"Ah — why's that?"

Neipas had further descended into tones more deeply hushed and leaned his head down into Cesar's ken of secrecy.

"Just — you know. It's quite difficult, I suppose. The ending is the most important part, I would like to get it just right, you understand."

"Sure, sure, I get you."

The poet twiddled with one side of his respectable whiskers for a minute. There was much hesitation in his manner; the wish to share whiffed through his feathers, closely pressed together, struggling inwardly.

"Would you like to read it?"

Neipas made that same face of resigned, wrinkled chin, and gave the same nod. "Sure, yeah."

Looking around, Cesar sounded still, almost inaudible, "But you cannot share these words with anyone!"

Neipas nodded slowly and confidentially.

Carefully, as one handling a relic of great importance, Cesar bridged the gap between his document and Neipas' lap. Neipas seized it just as gently. Influenced by Cesar's manner, he analyzed the crumpled paper with the utmost reverence and perplexity. Seeing that he faced page two, he began to flip the sheet — but the poet laid softly his hand upon it.

"Read only the back if you prefer to skip the salacious parts."

"Ok," Neipas laughed.

He read Cesar's poem:

and broken eggshells strewn
in shards of hourglass
glint on our bed of roses,
whose mattress sinks in the quicksand
of grainy indulgences —
all caving sudden to the black sea.

The bedsheets drop drunken
in drapes veiling away your face
and linens wash in storm
under our curtained existence.
Up there I see you! a silhouette now,
a distant shape in the whispering texture
of mirror brushing against my gaze
fogging the blood of my pen.

Salt floods my ears
Dirt swarms my nostrils
and silence fills my scream.
A quiet spilling in black letters
in a darkness echoing your name.

With seashells for fingernails
and trembling crystals for air
I rush to jot down the record of your memory.
And when I bend over my heart to write
I see you smiling already there
Smiling, always already here.

Dread possesses me when I possess
The vision of your open eyes

WALTZ AT THE EAGLES' NEST

In my own — and, barnacled, I reflect
in the hollows of my heart's cracked carapace
the black billows coming near.

And though I sense you there
I see you not.
And though you are by me now
You will be not.
And that kills me the thousand deaths
Of the death I shall die one day.

Where will you be on that day?
Where will I find you?
I question the night
Under waters dark.

But what is the night but the horizon's shade?
and what is death
but the shadow of life?

Sunless horizons...
                    Mystery.
The sea folds in blankets over the dust
where the truth sleeps.

We shall be islands in a tar pit
Tombs upon a field
Resting under withered leaves
Seeping to the core of the earth
Where the truth of all things lies
Lifeless.

These words, my love,
are the shadows of my spirit etched,
cast from the full moon
hatched behind my eyes,
whispering the sound of your voice
through every beat of my heart.

Here are the traces of my passion
Here are the ciphers of my love
Here are the words
With which I eat my lips.
Here is my lacquered heart
Burning in incense at your feet.
In ink I bleed the texture of my soul.
Unto your icon I devote all my anguish.

And I swear to you love,
Your eyes passing over these symbols
Is blood flowing in my soul's veins.
Their sound across your gaze
Wine plucked from the cup of my spirit.

Yet what shape of letter, my love
What form of sound can ever carry
The cutting pain in my heart, gashed
in the form of these lines, shaped
in the shape of this paper?
What form of life can relieve me
from the longing I feel for you
when you are by my side?

WALTZ AT THE EAGLES' NEST

The answers, like the ultimate questions
are unknowable.
For I am but a godless pilgrim
Wandering blind and submerged
in search of the kind of hope
that can only be found in answers.

Ah! Were every day one hundred hours
and every year one thousand days!
How I wish lives lasted centuries
and I lived with you forever

Were nothing able to do part
This sinful confessor
And his beloved blessed...

Take at least these verses
Of a man without faith
Elegizing a soul without hope
And a love without bounds
But death

And know that through them alone
I live still, and always
Always —
I miss you
I miss you
I miss you

Neipas arched over the delicate paper, written upon with a very deliberate hand across very thin, very elegant black lines. His heart, which had been beating somewhat tensely in the uncertainty of the wait, seemed to becalm as he read with sincere and considerable attention; and all the while a certain weight pulled down at his chest almost imperceptibly — a rectangular-shaped little weight corresponding to Orenda's notebook, lodging in the inner breastpocket of his new jacket. He had brought it with an intention of writing in it while he sat, unsure of how long it would be before Sunai appeared, and feeling a vague desire to keep his wits firmly away from the wit-scattering light of the *I* — but nothing came to mind from which to write, and even if it did, he had forgotten to bring something to write with. In the pocket of his trousers were, instead, two backup units he used to store photographs — he knew he would want to capture as many views of the otherworldly majesty of the Eagles' Nest as he could. How he would have liked to have a proper camera to accompany him on the singular experience ahead! Alas, the *I* would have to do.

The calligraphy employed in the composition of the handwritten poem was beautiful and strangely soothing; flowing cursive under his stare, the penmanship (unfaithfully reproduced here, lamentably) evidenced a certain quality of refinement, and a sensibility of spirit which roused Neipas' memory into the lulling recollection of finer eras, when he used to sit by the river, doing nothing but watching its waters course and scintillate. In the indistinct corner of his sight meanwhile, Cesar exuded a certain shimmer as well; from a very elegant fountain pen his hands danced the air with, slowly, under his own meditative gaze.

Later, after getting to know Cesar better, he would come to see that this could only be a very revised draft — he would come to realize that one with a spirit as restless as this mustachioed pigeon's could not pen those words through this exquisite font on the first, or second, or even third try. Meanwhile now, however, Neipas read the poem, not knowing what some of its words meant, the latent angst of the text brushing him harmlessly. Across the blurry backdrop of the paper he perused abstractedly — as his eyes were floating over the middle — the piglet wobbled excitedly, doubtless in search of new thrills; and hopped cheerfully onto Cesar's smiling lap. When Neipas turned to face him, he saw the poet with one hand under the piglet's chin, moving petting fingers; and another holding the gold-enameled fountain pen, which moved still in dancelike aerial gestures, with nib exposed and scrawling inkless about the open space.

"That's a pretty pen you got there. You wrote the poem with it?" asked Neipas.

"Yes. My boyfriend's gift — I go nowhere without it."

"You must really get along well," Neipas commented, a little aimlessly — which made Cesar emerge from the thoughtful absorption in which he had dived; and with a slow, wakening laugh, he asked:

"Indeed, brother. So — what did you think?"

"Yeah, not bad," said Neipas, nodding with consideration.

"Oh — thank you." — Cesar's tidy, groomed mask did not hide his sense of disappointment; the humble poet mistaking Neipas' reflecting manner for a lack of excitement, feeling that his letters had failed the spark. He turned his sad gaze to the piglet, whose coiling tail wiggled joyfully, and kept on petting her.

"I like it, I mean," Neipas rushed to add, perceiving Cesar's unveiled sentiment. "I guess maybe I'm not the right person to appreciate it, though. Just not much of an expert you know, but — I like it, yeah. I guess," he went on uncertainly, "I guess it's just a bit... what's the word."

"Grim, perhaps?"

"Perhaps, perhaps, yeah."

The poet sighed poetically: "It's a struggle. Endings have the power to absolve, or to ruin everything that precedes them. But always they cause grief... How else can I face the end sincerely?"

"This part's the ending?" Neipas asked, still holding the paper with soft fingers.

"Indeed it is. Ever changing, always anticipated..." At this Cesar brought his faraway gaze to Neipas' hands and, extending his own arm, retrieved delicately his treasured piece. "The last words... I can't help feeling a great anguish — laced with my great love."

"(Mary) Yeah well... I like it a lot though, don't get me wrong," Neipas mumbled abashedly still, with a bit of a chuckle; but a shift in the room interrupted him.

The door opened abruptly — blowing into the quietude a sudden gust of sound that spirited off all the *I* lights. In an instant everyone stood with their glasses in their pockets. The piglet, meanwhile, ran and hid.

"Apple?" said Sunai, sweeping her hand graciously over the bowl. "Please sit."

Miss Sunai took the chair behind the little table and everyone promptly followed her lead. She pressed a tablet between her hands and, holding it over the bowl of apples, studied it for a moment. Her owl-shaped mask was stern, inflexible, businesslike. The eagle countenance at the back of her head seemed like it breathed. Everyone held stiff in the expectation of her words; which her beak soon uttered, as she arose from the chair:

"Please fill in your information here," Sunai began, and wasting no time continued: "After that you will see a few documents. The first document is an employment contract, and the second a nondisclosure agreement. You may read a copy of these documents on our website whenever you wish." Walking along the sitters, she gave each a thin tablet, all of which she produced from under her own tablet in a manner weightless and immaterial, like a magic trick out of sleeve. Neipas presently held his own; and into the tablet's glass square he pressed the letters of his name, his address, the date of his birth, the number of his maskbook page — the latter of which he thought innocuous enough, though he made a mental note to censor out any photographs that might complicate perceptions, just for the time being. Once his finger touched submission, he was drawn further into a litany of alphabetical symbols comprising the contracts. They weren't very long — perhaps the equivalent of four pages. And yet four such pages, scrolled under a glass, feel interminable. It felt like a long rising wall heavily peppered with thin letters, letters which lined up in long words sometimes so obscure as to bewilder any analysis. Neipas took a good couple of minutes going over the second sentence of it alone. Meanwhile, Sunai's upturned chin, lifted well over their heads, bore an intimidating pressure upon them. The heavy silence besides — compounded further by Sunai's formal "please take your time" — compelled them to finish up quick. The pigeon sitting on Neipas' opposite side sifted through with a knowing air, nodding his head in apparent understanding. "Right here?" he mumbled esoterically to Sunai, pointing to the bottom of the scroll which had but a large button framing the words 'I AGREE', before touching it. Time seemed somehow pressing and the rest of the waiters quickly gave up the strain of reading the thing; and every time one pressed the button of compliance, the pressure of time piled up higher upon the others. Neipas soon yielded, though he hesitated a little after noticing the loose sentences referring the possibility that his data might be sold to third parties and the terms may be changed at any time. Cesar hesitated the longest but he, too, gave into the documents without understanding more than five sentences in them. Altogether the process must have taken less than five minutes.

They handed Sunai the tablets — which again seemed to disappear under her own, vanishing into her sleeve — somewhat sheepishly, with slightly lowered heads.

"Very well. Follow me, please," she demanded, and as she was about to open the door she stopped (the workers, who were in the process of getting up, froze in place) and pointed to the bowl on the little table at center again.

"Apples?"

There was something sweeter in her voice now, coaxing. Most took the apples for themselves; Neipas began reaching for the bowl as well but, sensing Cesar's reticence beside him, pulled back slowly.

Sunai opened the door into another room. Its walls were papered over with colored drawings, rough scribblings which might have been drawn by able abstractionists or otherwise zealous children. The back wall was but a big blackboard. A caged parrot hanging on either side of it clamored excitedly the words "Yessir! Yessir!" and in their fervor they seemed to be in competition for whom could yell the loudest. The volume of their piping gradually fell however, and eventually shushed, at Sunai's approach; and as she stopped, they leaned forward as if with a wish to listen. In front of the blackboard there was another little table with another wide bowl. Sunai dipped her hand in it, her fingers surfacing coated with white chalk as the workers took their seats in the chairs lined up across. The scene of chairs ordered in rows lulled Neipas into reminiscence — something about it replicated the Ivory Towers in the hidden mirror of his memory — and as he looked about, vaguely infused with recollections, he realized that his colleagues had taken really large piles of apples and were now struggling to balance themselves. They sat precipitously, careful to not let any of the fruit fall. Sunai's fingers began their silent work then, coursing across the inky wall trailed by gashes of white powder, perforating the deep black with symbols of ghostly frost. Her back was turned to them; so was the eagle mask. It was the first time Neipas faced it. He saw it, now; he saw how it really did breathe. Its shimmering beak, of a gold pure, curved upward across its gash, in a triumphant grin of culmination from its mighty hook into its crisp, white bearded cheeks; the amber eyes gazed them all who sat narrowly, held them in an ambiguous and commanding stare that exuded reproach and promise; exuded confidence and satisfaction; exuded power. The chalk lines flew in the quietude, quietness filled only by the sharp crack of bite and the muted sounds of chewed apple before them. Muted, at first, because those who ate were at first shy about the act of eating; though they quickly lost all semblance of decorum and soon threw the full weight of their masks upon the fruit as they savored through the mound of it in their laps and accustomed themselves to its sweet flavor. The avian countenance over them at once encouraged and reproached, as if goading them on with but its look. As Sunai wrote, the chalk powder released itself from the blackness; and spread across thinly, saturating the room with a fog — blurring the face of the eagle a little, as though it were its breath. With ravenous mouths the eaters gorged on their spoils, the smack of their salivating cheeks sounding across the powder haze in a savage satiating of hunger. Sunai's back held rigid, completely motionless; only her fingers and the eagle face at the back of her head moved, breathing shallow, gazing inscrutably. Neipas plugged his ears to the buds of the *I* to remove himself from the din. And yet it wasn't enough — the chewing matched the drum throb, and the chalk thickened.

When they finished, Sunai stopped; though she did not turn.

Her immense amber eyes faced them unblinking, unmoving. She pointed to the board, still with her back to them. The chalk painted three sentences on the black, and each sentence began with a number. The sitting workers, wavering, were still indecisively throwing their apple seeds and scraps onto the tall mound in the corner. But Sunai's voice then flowed out; everyone fastened rigid as authority was brought back into their presence.

Miss Sunai's Eagle Face spoke. "As you know, the Anubel, commonly referred to as the Eagles' Nest, is a place of gathering for our leaders, and others among the more valuable members of our society. In accordance with its import, there are a number of rules you must know and strictly follow." Sunai paused. The silence was absolute now; even the *I* buds closed, and shushed, on their own, inside Neipas' ears.

"First rule. You are invisible, and you do not exist, until you are needed. Inside the Eagles' Nest you will have no eyes and no ears, except to attend to patrons' requests. Likewise, you will have no tongue save for saying 'yes', 'sir', and other words we will train you to say.

"This is the most important rule. Every other rule flows from this first rule.

"Second rule: there are two main areas in the complex. The east wing (which is called the Pigeon Wing) is for general use, and the west wing (also called Eagle Wing) for private use, reserved for the patrons' private estates, deluxe services, and other such. Naturally, nothing in the Anubel's west wing may be recorded at any time or under any circumstance. Therefore, digital, Webwork-connected, or recording devices of any sort are strictly prohibited there. What happens in the Eagle Wing, never happened, as far as you're concerned. Your activity will however, of course, be monitored at all times.

"Finally — it is strictly forbidden to take of the patrons' food. Whether from their kitchen or their pantry, from their table or under their table, from their raw state to their scrapped state, you are to handle the patrons' meals, comestibles, refreshments and all their variants, strictly using the manner and methods that you are instructed, and nothing else. This rule extends to all their belongings. Nothing whatsoever may be touched without express permission.

"Failure to observe these rules may result in arrest or termination. Questions?"

Her voice ushered in a chilling silence. The chalk kept sloughing into flakes, floating across little by little; the words scattered into spores stuffing the room's air, until the haze was so thick upon the sight that no one could see anything but a granular white; and so dense upon the air that it clogged the throat, so that the silence was shattered into myriad fits of coughing.

Sunai's voice rang clear through the straining exhalations, declaring, "Very well. I will conduct you to the Eagles' Nest."

"Follow me." Arising in the deep milky fog, Neipas tottered blindingly among the huddling crowd. The powder asphyxiated him; he held in his breath and his eyes burned inside the covering lids, pressed tight together. He began to perceive a chill touching his skin. Already inside the elevator, it was only when he opened his eyes that he realized they had walked beyond the wall, which had parted at the middle. It had yawned into a spacious box. It had the appearance of a freight elevator, a sluggish, enormous thing that seemed designed to carry extremely heavy cargo. Its walls of silver steel, reflecting monstrously their image, rose high. The space was palely lit and frigid, vaguely reminiscent of a refrigerated wagon; the air-conditioning tightened up the ample space with a sickening grip. Here, the fog persisted, though thinner; lingering in the form of frost.

Icy particles twinkled in the fabric of the mist, knitting haze into his crisscrossing perspective and, by and by, crackling with a growing sound of running water into his ear; ushering into his muscles a kind of meekness, as though his vitality were being drained into the chill. The elevator had already been ascending for a spell, rattling as it lifted into the heights its burden. Sunai spoke. She was telling them about Anubel's layout and about the event that it would host. No one else spoke the whole time; the whole time, she faced away from them in the back of the elevator. None of the waiters batted so much as an eyelash, they didn't stir the tiniest muscle. The very contemplation of her back inspired a sort of quiet shiver in their hearts; the words that flowed out of her beak and swelled into the increasingly shrunken elevator (the waiters, perhaps because of the cold, kept approaching each other and formed a tight bundle as she spoke) treated them to an outsized image of inflexible power, of stunning severity. The eagle face stared them down immobile. No one dared ask a question. No one dared question themselves, either; they were all more or less numb.

The inexplicable presence of a family of ducks waddling about the grounds was somewhat unnerving, and as Neipas watched them gather about the corner, with their heads flipped backwards and bills buried in their feathers, he discerned a thin breach running the height of the side wall, by which they huddled. He noticed Cesar standing by it also and he squeezed closer in. And he saw that the sunshine poked and melded its flowing rays into the static pall of the elevator's electric light and the eerie curling haze through the breach; that the breach deepened out through the peripheral layers of the tower, and opened up into a view of the megalopolis precipitating into the depths, drawing away as they lifted themselves up into the Belab's full altitude; he saw that it faced the southern districts. The sun laid its hot noon beam onto the city sprawl. In the distance, a blotch of soot covered the flat stretch of Ostrich, from the core of which the striped chimney of Iblis' oil refinery rose to tower over the dingy houses. The mountain range peeked from the east as Neipas pivoted his heels; stacks of smoke billowed still from yonder beyond their peaks. Everything seemed like a miniature in that small breach; the immensitude like an abstract toy box, and ever more so as they slid further into the heights. They didn't feel much beyond the chill in their limbs and the slight, comforting heat of the sun by it; even the anticipation over seeing the Eagles' Nest was a distant numbness, and everything else tossed into the dormant depths of their hearts. The whole landscape shimmied slightly; it seemed increasingly distorted and runny, as if it were being watched through water.

Under blurry eyes, Cesar distractedly brushed his mustache with his stylish, glowing fountain pen. Neipas' increasingly sleepy breath took the form of vapor as it left his nostrils, and as he huddled into himself with squeezed shoulders, and batted his eyes ever slower, and sensed his chest in drooping cadence, he gained a keener perception of the silence suffusing the vast reaches beyond the murmurs of the elevator, beyond its climbing walls; and in the emptiness he found there, he heard a familiar pulse, a sound rhythmic and sustained, a vague, large, faraway throb — like a heartbeat. Was it his own? It palpitated with lightly aired quacks and the purling of water.

He mumbled unconsciously — the fog emanating from his own beak:

"It's cold. Why do they put the air-conditioning so cold?"

And Cesar, to this, replied in a whisper, "It's not air conditioning. It's because we're so high up."

Neipas dwindled and tightened into his feathers. He stared in a fading swoon at the ducks beneath him, and saw their narrow eyes inscrutable, indecipherable and set, as though frozen. Bit by bit everyone nestled closer together in that corner of the elevator; so that, when the gates of the elevator opened, they looked far in the cold's blur.

They stopped with a thunderous caw. Suddenly it was much warmer. Sunai walked through the lot of them and, stepping out, said, "Follow me, please."

20 - Anubel

They flowed out into the Warehouse Hall, where the gates of twelve elevators discharged workers into a wide semi-circular arena ending before a pit. This was an ample depot filled with boxes and sacks, both taut and empty, spread about the grounds in various degrees of tidiness. Amid all these, dazzled pigeon faces amassed and crowded thick before a row of tables manned by bulls; portentous over them, the twelve elevators formed a crescent outline straddling the edge of the arena, and their immense doors gaped with icy exhaust and pale lights blackened by the shapes of bodies marching, oozing outward. Ducks, humid from the frost, emerged out the gates along with everyone else and wobbled impassively about and between the workers' legs. Lines were shaped out of each gate and each were presided by a Sunai — twelve of them there were, exact replicas of one another. The exalted, white and gold avian faces round the back of their heads gazed yonder, where another arena on the other side of the pit stretched along a mighty railing, and from where a curious, short personage, donned flourishingly in peacock colors, watched; and with their vast owl eyes the Sunais supervised the proceedings, scanning carefully the passing workers. As Neipas waited in his line he observed the surrounding jitter of movement; he saw the masks of his companions twitching and how their feverish red gazes tended to the slated metal floor, how they already wrapped their arms tight around their torsos and arched their backs slightly, in a posture of servility, underneath the piles of boxes and sacks. One after the other they stepped before the bull. He was dressed in a black military outfit; the lapels of his jacket rigidly ironed, with insignias stitched to its shoulders; sitting in a perfectly erect pose, an unflinching stare, a stiffness of manner. Neipas, ushered by his Sunai, approached.

"ID," the military bull demanded, his eyes unblinking and fixed upon the screen atop the table.

Neipas produced his ID card and handed it over. The bull took it and scanned it over the little red-lit disk placed in front of the screen with a disciplined preciseness of movement; a dull blip sounded, and the bull took a few heavily wordless seconds examining the gleaming display before storing the card in a drawer. "Clear," he said gruffly, handing Neipas a ring with a key and a tag as Sunai at his side yelled "Step between the frame!", to which he obeyed by going inside the strange tall rectangle erected beside the table. As soon as he stepped within its bounds all its sides cracked with a sudden and powerful flash of light which overwhelmed everything. "Clear!" Sunai shouted from afar, and by the time Neipas regained awareness he had already stepped beyond the frame and was waiting by the edge of the semi-circular floor along with the multitude. Sunai stood before them all, and in a moment again she bawled, saying "Lower the bridge!" — a large rolling conveyor jutted out and the gap between platforms was connected; and Neipas stepped onward, past the final scrutiny of Sunai's owl stare, into the other side as her eagle eyes smiled their ambiguous golden grin. As he crossed the bridge he heard again the shout, he heard it many times; and saw how it erupted from the eagle's own moving mouth.

But presently another shout overtook them on the other side of the bridge. "Attennn...tion! Decorum!"

On the inner platform, Neipas and the group that had gathered were introduced to the flourished personage who'd been waiting. Everyone stopped and turned toward him, beholding with a mystified confusion the erect compactness of their new taskmaster, the Eagles' Nest steward, standing with authority in their midst. With flowery gestures of hand the short fellow announced that they were to address themselves to him as Monsieur Drrawetz or Mister Drrawetz (though he visibly preferred the former) — but first, make a line in front of me please, he said.

"... it is imperative to remember this, darlings" — the effeminate drone of Mr. Drrawetz's voice caught up with Neipas' drowsy ears, drugged mind, as he was walking — "You have access *onle* to the Pigeon Wing, and the Eagle Wing only when on the task. Don't wander anywhere else, please. It is very easy to get lost... And it is strictly forbidden! No can do! You do not have clearance, so please refrain, dears. *Pegeon* Wing — that, is it. Do not get lost, if you please..."

Mr. Drrawetz pranced along the row of them, flaunting his colors, radiant in the jade of his tail's peacock eyes, puffing up the gaudy jabot flowering abundantly from his chest, which brimmed out of his embroidered waistcoat; and even as he was saying the words above, he would throw a couple of syllables at each worker as he passed, with his chin up. "Cleaner," he told Neipas, moving along.

When he finished strolling, Drrawetz stood before them all and, after bouncing on tip-toe for a moment, brandished:

"The keys which you were given," he said with grave solemnity, "grant access to your locker of possessions. You shall store your belongings there after processing, and report back — pronto! — to your supervisors according to the positions you were given! First, do move behind the curtains for processing, dears. *Vite!*"

The mass of pigeon masks began to shuffle forward toward the giant crimson drapes behind the steward, all somewhat disoriented before the grand splendor of the novelty and expectations of what may lie ahead.

Neipas, apprehensive, lagged behind a little. Hesitant, he neared by timid sideward motions the upright figure of the Eagles' Nest steward. He saw Mr. Drrawetz checking the watch beneath his formidable beak, which was excessively curled; somewhat fearfully he gazed Drrawetz's infinitely intricate flourishes of dress, and as the sight of it grew closer it diminished his voice inside his throat even before he let it out. When Neipas did breathe it out, it was but a peep:

"Excuse me?" "Yes!" — right away sprang the response, and Drrawetz's short figure sprang up along with it, standing on his toes so erect that he almost catapulted off the floor. At this, Neipas flinched back, but then, gripping to the present, he found determination to say what he came to say, and said:

"My apologies, sir — Mr. Drrawetz. I believe a mistake was made. I was hired as a waiter, but you mentioned that I was to be a... a cleaner?" Neipas began somewhat firmly, but the firmness gradually slackened into a timidity of interspaced, sluggish words as Drrawetz sunk his pinched fingers into his hollowed, pouting beak, and spread them outward across his soft clay cheeks to form an immense, intimidating grin.

And in the meantime, he leaned closer, and raised himself on his toes to such an extreme that he reached Neipas' eye level. "My dear," he said — his tone, sour and venomous, was coated with much sugar — "you are whatever I tell you to be."

Neipas understood and, apologizing with his head lowered to the steward's asserted authority, excused himself and let his body drift along the mass sloshing through the drapes. Beyond the descending heavy cloth rose a very wide staircase. Already when he entered the Warehouse he had sensed a certain rhythmic vibration, and as he walked over the bridge it had gradually materialized into sound; but now, as he climbed the stairs, that sound, a mechanical sound of ticking, grew louder, and louder the more he climbed, until it became so loud as he neared the top that it was above everything. It pervaded and muffled all else. Tick, tock, boomed his ears, and he walked into the dazzle with clogs revolving in his brain, setting the pace of his step in one, two, one, two, one, two — beyond the peak of the staircase the space opened up greatly and he saw first a mess of towering light fixtures, giant machine eyes of radiance atop thick tripods, some of which had gel filters over them and made everything look ultra vivid and all the colors pop brightly. In the distinctness of cartoon color and under the tick-tock moved everyone, joined together in a tidal expanse of feathery hillocks. Neipas turned his head and contemplated in marvel.

The grand square vestibule had, opposite the fixtures, an immense wall covered wholly by a closet; a great, vertical plain of compartments, shelves, drawers and doors, housing jackets, ties, shirts, shoes, jewels, other ornaments. Before it, an army of seamstresses scrambled frantically, clothed in various furs, gazing through peacock masks and a panoply of exuberant plumage frothing in every direction — dressing quickly each pigeon as they came. One approached Neipas among the deep uproar underlying the rhythmic robotic thump; and, without knowing why, he said to her "cleaner!" and gave her the tag off his key-ring. The seamstress nodded and, taking the tag, retreated to the closet, to the interminable row of jackets repeating in form and color, and only changing slightly in size. As she went, Neipas looked up without really knowing what he was doing and he finally recognized the source of the overwhelming beat — fixed upon the very middle of the wall was a huge, tall glass pane, behind which hung weights and a pendulum, with a giant clock on top at the closet's peak, near the ceiling afar. He saw also, as his head kept panning upward, a relief carved out of the stone ceiling above him: the head of a cow laughing, surrounded by some letters which he was trying to read. The seamstress came back with shiny janitor coveralls and his tag. Asking (his voice was absorbed by the tick-tock) her how she knew it was his size, she responded by walking away from him and attending to the next worker; he assumed she simply didn't hear. Perhaps it had been the rectangular frame by the military bull that had taken his measurements. Whatever it had been, the next seamstress who took the tag did the very same: receding into the confines of the titan wall-closet, disappearing for moments in its immensity; and then gliding on to Neipas with shoes ready, handing them over and passing on without another word. Behind and ahead of him, a pandemonium of crowds repeated the very same gestures, moving through to the ends of the hall in a thick stream between the lights and the closet. The reverberating noise was lightly punctured by little chirping flashing all about him, and sometimes he could distinguish words articulated from such chirps (as he looked, by chance, to the side he glimpsed one of the pigeons who had been with him in the elevator, and his beak formed the sentence "Funny, I'm hungry now". He saw also that Cesar, whom he had momentarily forgotten, was also close-by and his head poked out from the wavy throng, looking on with a frowning, perplexed glare). Meanwhile he discerned a vague beat of drum underneath the incessant mechanical thump of seconds... and, under them all, his own heartbeat poking the inner side of his muscle between his neck, his head, and his ear. All beat to the same rhythm. Finally (tick, tock! rang the closet clock, untiring), another seamstress approached him and gave him a mask (on one side of the closet were the jackets and uniforms, hung up in a vast row; on the other side, mannequins with cattle faces; in the middle beneath the clock, shoes; and many other things besides in the various shelves).

"Put it on please."

Her voice had penetrated the pulsing blank noise and reached him. He gazed the mask he held.

It was shaped in the semblance of an ox. It was more artfully crafted than the one from Kur had been; from the onset, the expressions of dedication and professionalism were more accentuated. It was evidently more elegant, the lines finer and curves more smoothly sculpted. Its texture wasn't coarse as the old mask had been; the fur was soft, the clay beneath it steady. The nostrils were wider and would let in more air; the snout shorter, tighter and more sturdy in its artifice of muscular composition; the gapes for the sight wider, though the mesh covering them was more closely knitted together. The horns had the authentic consistency of ivory; but like the old mask its ends were blunted, and again, unlike the bulls' helmets, they pointed downward. Neipas gazed the mask's inner side fixedly. Its mouth and eyes gaped emptily, soulless; inside them flowed the onward river of heads already masked ahead of him. The sound of ivory rubbing and screeching entered his perception...

"Put it on please."

Neipas pressed the inside of the face against his own mask. His sight was sunk in the black; and then reappeared in that oddly crisp world of colors. All sounds were muffled, though the march of the clock sounded yet supreme. Everything at once seemed farther away. Everything — the whole confusion about him — was abstracted, and his mind calmed and focused in the gravity of the new head. Neipas looked at the seamstress, for it was at her he had to look. The seamstress held in her hand a yellow tag bearing his number — in his sudden clarity, Neipas realized that the number was the same as the tag he had been given, which was the very same as the number on his ID card and the same as that of his page on the book of masks. She leaned the tag against the soft clay skin of his ear and, with a stapler, pierced it in. A sudden thump into his mind deafened it all.

Suddenly the ticking receded into the far horizon. There was a revolution inside him; and everything switched. Now it was his heart that beat loudest, sounded among a wide silence, as though something breathing motionless upon an endless, windless lake; a silence of bells, bells tolling and spreading out among the ripple of the waters. As the heart beat beneath, so the bells sounded well above, from the heavens above the lake, from the very summit of the tower... And a voice spoke out of it clear.

"Can you hear me?" asked the seamstress. She spoke into a little mouthpiece in front of her silver beak.

"Yes, ma'am," Neipas replied calmly into the wide vastness of quietude.

"Very well," said the seamstress, and a little electronic fizz crisped as she drew the mouthpiece away. She receded imperceptibly, and Neipas was slowly swept along. A sound of sparkling jingles breathed into the lake-wide stillness as chain jewelry was placed about his horns; the only sound shed from their collective motion was a vague rumbling underlying the deep earth beneath the waters. And all the cattle streamed thus, eerily quiet in the ruckus of movement, ushered in by the supervisors to the end of the hall. As he floated along with the crowd, he turned back and held for a little against the advancing tide of bodies, slowing its pace for a second as he narrowed his eyes inside the heavy mask and tried once again to discern just what it was that the letters on the ceiling said. His face turned slowly, he strained to comprehend, for the letters formed a circle around the laughing cow head; but finally he made it out to be — as the words were sculpted in the motions of his voiceless lips — *IN PERSONA VERITAS IN HOMINEM VANITAS.*

They were herded through winding corridors, walking noiselessly upon ways padded by carpet. On one side the walls branched off into doors, stairways, and more corridors. The other wall was a long, nearly uninterrupted mirror — inside which the march proceeded under very bright, white ceiling lights. The myriad colors of the pigeon parade had morphed into an orderly sameness of outfits and faces all locked in step. All were janitors here; the waiters had split off elsewhere, so that Neipas recognized no one now. Cesar had worn a waiter outfit; and he was among them no more. At the lead walked a Supervisor who spoke in friendly tones and sympathetically winked to them every now and then as he finished his sentences. He told them — this is the Columbaria, where you will stay. Accommodation and food is provided. Choose your locker of possessions, and your key, once used, will be the only key able to unlock it. Store your clothes and belongings. Everyone should make sure to leave their *I*s too — they were going all to the Eagle Wing. Dress up and report back, he told them. The chummy Supervisor guided them along, and Neipas found himself in one of the dormitories.

The dorm was but a corridor flanked with bed bunks on both sides, stacking up to the tall ceiling. At the end, behind the stacks, the corridor split right and left; and against the wall stood the lockers. They were taller than them, and could fit many things. Neipas chose one; inside, he placed Eva's jacket and his shirt, his trousers, his shoes; he locked the locker; and entered the janitor's outfit. All joined in the same dance. Someone commented he didn't know they had to stay overnight; and someone else told them it was optional. As they walked back together, Neipas noticed, looking inside one of the bunks — the walls against which they leaned, those too were covered with mirror.

They were led through more corridors, then down some stairs.

This is the kitchen, said the winking Supervisor, as they came into a massive space with a ceiling very tall and walls extending very far lengthwise. The first thing they noticed, however, was the scent; all at once a heavy stench came over them, a stale smell of rot pervading every inch of air. Neipas flinched with surprise, and immediately checked his mask to ensure it was still on him. They walked through a wide corridor that cut though the space. On either side of it the various features of the kitchen apparatus were neatly lined up – sinks, faucets, ovens, stoves, grills, overhead compartments, dish washers, utensil set boxes, all manner of state-of-the-art culinary tools progressing into the kitchen in long rows of stations with smaller passages connecting them. The space was simply brimming with high-end and cutting-edge appliances — and yet everything was a mess. Atop the counters lay scrambled a disarray of pots and battered pans, spatulas lay discarded on the floor, heaps of knives hung precipitously on the edge of overhead compartments that were seemingly flung open; everything was dirty, grubby, soiled with muck; the glassy steel altogether filthy with mould and sticky grease and sagging bits of food melting here and there upon the counters and the floor; a gelatinous goo of a sickly color simmered upon the edge of a faucet they were just passing by, seeping down in long drops; maggots and flies strolled about the surfaces. Nevertheless, the Supervisor seemed completely unaffected and kept speaking without pause, dispensing instructions and saying that everything there would have to be cleaned in the next day or so. He rubbed his finger across a huge sink fully crusted in old grime — and tasted the tip of the finger, nodding in assent. Lot to do, he casually pronounced. Some laughed uncertainly at first; and at this the Supervisor unleashed a guffaw which made everyone laugh very hard. A human range of sound was returning to Neipas' ear; and in the unlatching from dreaminess he perceived bells among the laughter, ringing from the top of the tower and goading everyone on, setting the shuffling steps of the group. Meanwhile he, too, found himself laughing.

All walked to the inner depths of the kitchen, where a line of armed bulls awaited them. The space had by then narrowed and gotten shorter; they were in a corridor now, its walls again mirror. They made a queue. Before them, at the end of the corridor, stood imposing a long open frame. Its sides seemed to zap with sparkle. It was a body scanner, and all were instructed to step within it; one by one they withstood its scrutiny. As he waited, Neipas contemplated, balancing between the novel sensation of his new mask and the demands of the moment, their reflections scattering multifold and apart through to the inscrutable horizons of the opposing mirrors on both sides. By and by a sense of constriction took hold. Neipas had a vivid impression of the walls nearing him, as though they too scrutinized; and was conscious of the vestige of that frigidness from the ascent gripping his heart still, the aftereffect of the chill dilating his pores and weighing upon his lids.

Once he was before the scanner he heard the bull speak: "Step up," roared the bull, and he did. Immediately the air got close and his sights darkened. "Face the wall, lift up your arms and spread your legs!" ordered the bulls on the other side; and so he did. The wall was a glossy black concavity, with an ambiguously fluid texture upon the surface, from which emanated, in a snap, a streak of light that panned the length of the wall from left to right. The streak of light filled the darkness of the scanner, like the flash of a photograph; and Neipas knew that the light was suffusing itself beyond his clothes and capturing him as he was under them. He wondered vaguely whether the eye of the scanner could see beyond his masks, too, whether it could detect the dysfunction and anxiety plaguing the surface of his true face, and his breathing automatically weighed a bit heavier in his lungs at the possibility of it.

But the scanner couldn't peer under the masks, as can no machine; Neipas passed without a problem. He stepped under the Eagle Wing.

A few steps more and an entire new world, unprecedented in his eyes, opened up abruptly before him. It was a world of lavishness and riches, glimmering with an abundance of wealth and a high air of sacredness. First they were in another kitchen, much more bright and shimmering clear, though similar in form; then many more corridors and halls, draped in golden embroideries and luxurious ornamentations flashing with the color of gems fitted in statues, chests and tables, frames of paintings and other such treasures. The shock of novel views impressed itself upon his eyes so that much was passed unseen; but Neipas would have time.

Finally they emerged, as if from the depths, into an ample space bordered by magnificent arched windows. The sun shone pleasantly through the towering glass and the soft muslin curtains; through the fabric of which they could just perceive the outlines of the fabled Hanging Gardens, as they approached; and the monstrous chasm at its edge, at the bottom of which must stand the wide expanse of Axiac. The place was elegantly decorated with thrones and game tables, out of which jutted flamboyant cornucopias. Opposite the windows, immense silver statues stood godly against the walls; seven of them there were, and their proud beaks, too, were shaped like cornucopias. The ceiling was an intricate maze of rosettes and sculptures inspecting mightily upon the upraised stares. And as they collected themselves among the giant vision and looked down at their feet, they noticed there was a lot of money, in the form of bank notes, spread about the steady marble floor; especially near the tables where it was assembled in messy heaps. Uncannily these grounds, and the paper money about them, were moistened and soiled full with hardened grease, much as the kitchen had been.

All stared on in awe. The winking Supervisor let them bask in those fabled aromas of opulence for a minute; but then nicely prodded them on, for there was much to do. Make the space immaculate, he said. And the Supervisor concluded by pointing humorously to the bulls and their guns lining up around the space, telling the waiters to not get any funny ideas; to which the cattle at first laughed dubiously, and then guffawed hysterically when the Supervisor did so.

He had gone, winking his eye; and already the oxen were engaged in picking up the bank notes, stooping about and throwing them in big plastic bags as they went along. A janitor — one tall, whose corner of mouth was twisted by a scar — pulled a very long hose from the depths of some back room, which at this point slithered its lengthy neck all across the hall. Neipas began lumbering about in an inward manner, bending to grab a loose bill here and there, never fully standing, then stooping again for another note upon another measured motion; the withdrawn smile implied in his face gave his every act a semblance of reflection. He kept his eyes transfixed upon the marble floor, which torpidly offered him his reflection beyond the gummy layer affecting every step. As he went on, listening to the crummy sound of his shoes, bent and in a dizzying swirl of mind — for he was faintly aware of how much money was passing through his bony fingers — his thoughts wandered, drifting to and fro in the vicinity of a remembrance so feeble he wasn't sure whether it was based in fact or pure imagination. If it had happened it must've been a year before, for the memory of it came with the vague sense of want and sunken frailty he so strongly associated with that time. He had been in line to pay the year tax, and from his pocket he produced a wrinkled mound of banknotes as he finally neared the immense hole in the basement of the Crystal Palace where all taxes were deposited. It wasn't much — but what he could dispense. He remembered with increasing vividness the more he thought about it, of being ashamed at displaying the unseemly ball of small-currency in front of his fellow citizens; he recalled the official with the peacock face who stared him down smugly. To ameliorate the situation Neipas took great effort at sculpting his wax semblance into a flawless expression of ease and confidence, with but a hint of casual embarrassment denoting how exceptional it was that he should be contributing so little money and such wrinkled banknotes. Obviously he also did his utmost to make the notes as presentable as could be; as he waited in line he stretched and straightened the notes and piled them on his palm neatly, and one of those notes in particular stuck to his mind because it had strange signs on it, which someone must have scribbled onto with felt marker, and because it was the note with highest value among the rest.

How strange, then, that Neipas should find that same banknote here, in the Eagles' Nest, as he picked up this unruly mass of paper wealth. Yes, he was sure it was the very same, it had to be, he was growing certain of it — how strange it was that it should end up here. Neipas stood for a bit, gripping it between his fingers, beholding its razor-thin, creased paper of cheap make. His concentration wavering aimlessly, the note and the hand holding it would sometimes blur away from his sight and Neipas would catch himself staring at his reflection in the marbled floor a few seconds after.

The oxen clearing the floor quickly gathered all the banknotes into their bags. The one with the scar on the side of his mouth turned on the hose and sprayed the floor clean when they were done.

21 - The Golden Dove and the Hanging Gardens

It was shortly after Neipas presented himself for duty next morning, brow still weighty under the burden of little sleep, that his ears first perceived the music. Very faint, the melody traveled past the whispering eartags into his head, very slowly; he was already immersed in the meticulous tending of the gold when the orchestral sound, come out from the ether, blossomed into his consciousness. He eased his pace for a moment. His brow tensed up in focus and his head rotated distractedly to the side.

"Do you hear that?" he asked the janitor with the mouth scar, who scrubbed the golden statue's other paw.

At first, he thought the tune might have been coming, perhaps, from the eartags themselves. Sometimes the seamstresses on the other side played some beat or other to keep them entertained while they worked. But a subtle auditory sensitivity stirring alight, recognizing the source of sound farther away from his body, made him halt and wonder. There was something peculiar — familiar — about the sound.

The scarred janitor stopped what he was doing and angled his ear into the empty space.

"No..." he said, though he still narrowed his eyes in a second attempt to sharpen his hearing. Then — after an ambivalent deep breath — it occurred to him to pull down his lobes and widen the canal, at which point his expression loosened and let out an "Ah! Yep, yeah."

Neipas pulled down his eartag direct he saw his colleague do it; for though they could never shush its whimper, they were able to lower the volume in this way. "You can hear it, right?" "Yep, definitely." "Wonder where it's coming from."

The other seemed to take a moment to think about it, after which he bowed his curved back down further and leaned the side of his head against the floor.

"Here," he said.

Sleepy, Neipas followed his cue and put his own ear to the ground. Indeed, he found — the music came from beneath, directly under them. The tune was one of string, with but a quiet trumpet in the depth and a drum penetrating the melody subtle, beating steadily and sure. There was also a soft, hypnotic hum — something profound and angelic, suffusing all other sounds. It flowed through the warm golden floor soothing, seductive, like a song of siren; it imbued itself into the glitter of the chandeliers aloft, slow turning. It bled outward; and gradually the air itself seemed to sparkle in the notes of this melody, flowering a shimmer, entrancing the two listeners glued to the rich flooring.

"It's live, isn't it?" whispered Neipas.

The scarred janitor nodded obliquely. "I think so. Sounds like it..."

Lulled by the tune, they slid imperceptibly back into the task of massaging the golden dove's paws.

It arose over them portentous, the idol of gold. Amber deep, glossy surface solid, eternal, texture smooth and full, lush, opulent to the core; it filled their eyes with aureate shine, swooning and hypnotic; the contemplation of it, and the motion upon it, felt all like a sinking flight. The dove's sculpted skin breathed lustrous, and sometimes it seemed almost translucent. Its gleam was like flame... radiating all across the vastness round. From the Ballroom dome above them high, an oculus gazed; its stare hovered above the statue's luster with a scalding brightness (only after did they notice how heavily they sweated). Beyond the oculus rose the hollow steeple. On either side of its belfry, tucked in its corners, were the two bells; and in the glass-walled chamber above the belfry peeked, suspended, the lantern — the lofty Pearl. It glittered like some heavenly diamond. Yet the light it cast was not its own, it appeared to them, but merely a reflection from the dove's fire gold. Curved at its mighty feet, their gloved hands touched the holy body of deep amber light; and they felt as if they embraced the sun.

The very gold seemed to bathe the gardens cascading outdoors. Neipas had walked about in the shine, his steps affected by an impression that time had blurred into the far future. A quietude had set, deep. He stood inclined against the pole of a gazebo. It topped a little spiral of stairs, rising from a thickly wooded terrace to overlook the megalopolis' southern tract; it seemed hung, as if suspended, salient out of the Hanging Gardens before the crimson skies of sunset. By its flowery posts, a waterfall glimmered in the red throes of the dying sun; descending through the windless air into the immensitude of the concrete plain. Neipas' lank form stood very high above it all, worlds above. The megalopolis laid itself magnificent beneath his distant stare, shrouded a little by the heaviness of his eyelids cast downward in an awed stupor — the glass colossi of Babylon mounted in a descent under him, toward the posh flatness of the coastal villas due west; the gray industrial fields in the south were blocked out in great squares multiplying from the port, inside which a great confusion of steel meshes contrived beneath the mighty chimneys exhaling, somnolent, the wide screen of smog thinly cloaking the shanties; the rest was flattened by the great distance. Stretching away from the featureless urban blotches of Ostrich, some crop fields, ending in a small, forested peninsula jutting out into the red ocean, made up the only significant patches of green to be spotted amid the barrenness of decay and industrialization. In the opposite end of that southern coast, one could make out the layered fences of Wall Street, looking almost imperceptible, nearly unseen and completely insignificant from this altitude. Only in the east did something arise to match Neipas' height upon Earth's present summit: the mountains.

He had stared long upon those immense rocks heaving from the roots of the soil to the brink of the sky. Beyond the snowless peaks, Neipas could glimpse an enigmatic void of charred blackness, from which ensued, still, a vague fume that made torpid the horizon whence the sun had arisen. The wildfires had consumed vast swaths of those lands stretching eastward from Axiac's craggy bounds. A few days before, Neipas had looked at the sketch painted by the descriptions of the burnt Oyate man, which was supposed to represent the likeness of the arsonist responsible for kindling the flames. He recognized whom it depicted. He saw the wiry, plumy shafts dotting the saggy dewlap which flapped out the fellow's ox mask and, pointing, he identified him — first before the Oyate assembled in Oshana's garden, then before the police — as the usher of animals at the entrance to the slaughterhouse where he had worked, miles underneath his feet now, under the earth, under the tower.

The alleged arsonist had been in and out of the meat industry for many years, they later found — having been a sticker in the abattoir and making it to foreman after his disability prevented him from ever securely gripping another knife, all before fixing a job as hauler on the supplying farms — and in and out of jail for almost as long, having been arrested, on occasion, for drug possession and domestic abuse. But it was difficult to believe that his petrified hands were responsible for the devastation which had been wrought upon the forests; even with the help of other hands. Instinctively, it was difficult to believe now, even as Neipas contemplated the rough outlines of the calamity from afar; even if he did not comprehend its true extent, and even if it was but an abstraction to him. Something dormant in him felt the work of something bigger; something older; something inhuman. So colossal a fire couldn't be the creation of a mere group of men. And though he could not rationalize it, something in Neipas felt, dimly, that the conflagration had been fueled by the elemental forces of a neurotic and wrathful nature, a nature emaciated, intoxicated with the unleashed vapors of its own gastric depths; a nature crazed and uncontrolled.

But he'd beheld through the golden calm of the gardens, and all was faraway. Before he found the gazebo, he had strolled the domains of the Anubel's Pigeon Wing, ruminating the fatigue in his muscles, upon which he walked languidly. Neipas had had trouble sleeping... The dormitories were too bright, even with the blinds they had given him.

*

The Anubel — the summit of the Belab Tower, popularly known as the Eagles' Nest — was shaped like a mound. As it neared the top of its height, the tower spiraled into itself in a series of ascending garden terraces, slicing off toward the core of the structure, opening its inner rings to the heaven air; culminating in the top floor — the Ballroom — and the dome that covered it, over which rose the steeple with its bells and the Pearl, and out which sprouted, finally, the narrow spire.

The mound was parted in four by waterways which gushed from a hidden source inside, beneath the summit. These they called rivers, and the rivers flowing toward the north and south divided the Eagles' Nest absolutely into two sides — the Eagle Wing, facing the west, and the Pigeon Wing, facing the east. The westbound and eastbound waterways coursed down the middle of each Wing; though, unlike their counterparts, which ran furiously in cascades and gave no possibility of passage, their flow, beginning with majestic waterfalls, was becalmed by ducts and little canals carved all throughout the grounds, spread across founts, culminating in the open mouths of romantic statues, of gargoyles standing on plinths and cherubs holding their marbled hands, all forming a whimsical scape of twinkling springs which irrigated the air. These rivers glided with tranquility under many bridges, which they graced with the dapple of shimmering sunshine. All 4 waters cascaded off the edge of the tower to sprinkle the megalopolis with fresh spores.

The Eagle Wing had 3 great terraces, and the Pigeon Wing 9 smaller ones adding up to the same immense height. Neipas hadn't yet set foot on the terraces of the Eagle Wing, having but glimpsed their splendor, the previous day, through the windows of that hall perplexingly littered with money. He was, however, free to roam about the Pigeon Wing and its side of the Hanging Gardens, and as soon as he had his break he took the opportunity to do so. For a while he had stood watching and photographing the surreal, celestial scenery, observing the activities unfolding in the lower floors from the 6th Terrace — the open-air Auditorium — as he leaned over its balustrade. The paraphernalia of a great bazaar were being dismantled. Steel poles were being bared from their tarpaulins, which were folded and piled beneath the trees; tables were crammed in the corners, chairs stacked up, plastic structures deflated, items stuffed in boxes. It had all been assembled for the biggest event the Anubel hosted all year, the "World Market Summit", as it was dubbed: a festival where entrepreneurs, entertainers, enthusiasts, financiers, plutocrats and politicians and the general upper crust of society gathered to celebrate and honor the Free Market, one of the chief deities of those days.

All the lecturers, merchants, and consumers who had abundantly populated the Pigeon Wing's 9 winding terraces just a few days ago were now gone; only porters remained. In the effort to pack up, their masks heaved, their horns bowed, their shoulders strained under cargo, and there were multiple quietudes of weights borne in the midst of noises — of impersonally clanked metal, rustled cloth, shouted commands — disappearing quickly in the emptiness. Decorations brimmed from the 3rd Terrace all the way up to the Ballroom (earlier, Neipas had been one in the copiously numbered crew engaged in cleaning it), so there was ample work to be done.

This 3rd Terrace opened out of the large Cafeteria, where workers and guests sat to eat (during the Summit, the selection had been varied, with buffets lining across the long tables; now the choices were more limited and served by the plate at the counter). Ascending from it, the 4th Terrace lay before the foyer of the Columbaria, which housed the pigeons. The 5th Terrace, in the very middle, they called "the Lakes": much of it was but a great pond crisscrossed with beautiful overhanging bridges. At the inner end of this body of water — where the eastward river stretched tranquil and picturesque before flowing on — close to the tower's wall yonder, there arose a great concave wall of acoustic eyes, resembling a wide peacock tail, and reminiscent of a clam's open shell — whence a continuous speech was issued in a strange language that Neipas didn't quite comprehend; though this, too, seemed somehow familiar, and he listened to it long enough to pick up a few words and discern that it looped in repetition. The sound was mesmeric; it seemed to make one spread along the placid water of the lakes and blink to the rhythm of the coins glinting languidly at the bottom. A certain scent ensued through the musical words also: a pleasant aroma entering him with the subtle force of association, stimulating a sensation of recurrence, somehow, of a returned sentiment which he could not at first clearly recognize. Having emerged from the Cafeteria, and slowly made his way through the yet messy, thick terraces, Neipas climbed a few petite stairs and charming byways to enter an enormous multicolored tent, a Circus filled with balloons hovering upright, tethered to cords; resembling in their density and number an uncanny forest of yarn. The air was tinted with the many hues of levitating plastic; the sunlight stunted by the canopy of cloth. No packing up was taking place here. There was nobody; silence reigned oppressively — a strange quiet permeating the chromatic dust, a hush that snuck undetected into him to reveal itself abruptly when he was already deep inside. Tuneful whispers hummed in this silence... (just over there, the tent gave way to the bridges in the middle of the terrace, and the balloons rustled gently, with melodious susurrations, as he moved past; but his transit through this odd Circus was short and he soon forgot it — the next moment he stepped onto the bridges), he climbed the arched path over the water — and all at once, the view amplified dramatically as though the universe had forcefully ripped wide the limits of distance. His heart stilled as his feet came to a halt. Immediately before him, portentous, shown in their full pride and glory, the mountains, rising over the megalopolis at its impenetrable edge, materialized like the address and embodiment of aloof gods. But from here he could gaze still wider, still more amply than the supreme breadth of the range; his appreciation could sweep in a titanic panorama from the southern coast, into which the rookeries of Ostrich gave up and blurred away toward the sea, all the way over to the other side, to the discreet Diamond Hills, with the Crystal Palace shiny at its foot and its many mansions concealed by lush, refined shrubbery; and he could reach still beyond, faraway, farther, where the desert lands commenced and the clay or kaolin mines arose in the forms of dunes and ravines, amidst which the military bases were ensconced, and in the proximity of which they extended (it was said that a major stockpile of suicidal bombs — long-range missiles with nuclear warheads — were stored in underground silos there). He saw all of it with the amazed blunted stare that holds within it more than the mind can contain; and his mind fell numb in the contemplation of that incomprehensible immensitude. That had been the first time he gazed the vista out of the Eagles' Nest. Never before had he been so high; never had he seen anything like it. His heart contracted with the vertigo of a great awe... Then, that returned feeling: ascending from the arcane depths of his being, it took a gradual mental shape, until at last he recognized it. He was reminded of his mother — vividly so. Something about the sights, and the aromas (though not the sound, which blurred unimportantly into the neglect of his attention)... By then he was gazing fixedly, absentmindedly, at the soft rippling water under him and the stillness of the coins beneath, and, raising his head to see the concave wall behind him arching over the marble banks of the lake, he observed the abundance of needly green leaves and purple petals blossoming all around the singing eyes of the voluminous peacock feathers; and at last he spotted, in the midst of that flowery exuberance, someone. He distinguished the vague body of someone under the great peacock feathers — and it was from there that emanated the faint words he heard looping.

On either side, distant, were the long tents and the dense balloon cords, among which the terrace progressed in a curve. Below him, 4 terraces; above him, another 4. The aromatic air, the glacial height, enveloped him; and right behind his eyes appeared the printed face of his mother, trapped between glass and stone, intimated in blurry tones; and through him sighed (like a torpid compression of the vertiginous depths plunging before him) the memory of herbs scattered over a fuming pot through her fingers, strewn as petals to the breeze — a memory much vaguer than that of the photo, and yet more recurrent, more present in the obscurity of his spirit, more commensurate, somehow, with its substance. But why now?

Hazily mystified by the enigmas of his psyche, Neipas continued his way upward deliberately. The 6th Terrace was the farthest he could go. He stopped there a while. It was an ample Auditorium of many rows of chairs, with a grandiose stage arising before them, stretching beneath a sumptuous Proscenium of many rings. From behind the Stage, the eastward waterfall descended calmly; it ensued from a great bulwark of three receding tiers, which made the 7th, 8th, and 9th Terraces: together, they were called the Great Facade, a wall of splendorous sculptures on recesses, and other marvels, rising aloft beyond the Stage. The Great Facade housed the backstages and accesses to the Eagle Wing on the other side; entrance to pigeons was prohibited, unless on duty. At the top of it stood the fabled Ballroom, the last and uppermost terrace. It was crowned by the steeple where the bells hung and the Pearl shone. Neipas had stared long into it from below, leaning onto the balustrade at the outer edge of the Auditorium, completely mesmerized (he sensed ethereal intonations of grindstone in the pulses of the glinting cascade; he heard the river murmur a glassy hum). He saw that the Pearl shed no light of its own; it was but a mirror of multiple faces. But where did its lights come from? — wondered Neipas.

Underneath the Cafeteria's 3rd Terrace was an uninviting tangle of wood, where old statues stood arcane amid the shadows... The 2nd Terrace was the wildest and least tended area of the Gardens. The pantry under the kitchens hid somewhere on the inside of that level, Neipas was later told. Filled with the curiosity of novelty, he dove in the mysterious convolution of boughs — walking along a narrow path, until he came upon the stairs at the edge of the Terrace and the gazebo atop, hugging the tower wall and facing the wide southward view by the cascade.

The occult 1st Terrace, the base stretching to the limits of the tower, couldn't be seen beyond the unkempt trees and bushes. There seemed to be no access to it. It was said to be merely used for maintenance and storage; though the fuzzy distance which concealed it, and the utter lack of sound coming from the direction of it, as Neipas descended, suggested otherwise.

*

Standing in the gazebo, he looked again to the west, beyond the waterfall; afar, in the prospect, the giant shimmer of ocean rested quiet and breathed in the sun, which reared now its hot lips to kiss the outspread waters. A particular feeling overwhelmed his languid breast, containing at once a sense of smallness — for what he beheld was vast and powerful — and a surge of strength, for he stood atop it all. For the first time he looked at it from above. It was a feeling of might, a sense of the potentiality of power.

The world entire was, for a moment, cloaked in quiet.

The horizon gulped the sun; a sound like the cracking of an eggshell clicked over him. He turned round to face the steepness of the terraced altitude, he saw the beacon shining high upon the summits.

Neipas was then subsumed, possessed. Into the unbounded red expanse and the crimson sea, into the narrowness of his eyes and the bottom of his spirit, the Pearl, perched atop the Eagles' Nest, penetrated; grew; glowed; spilled, blazingly, in pure, all-encompassing light — and burgeoned deep into the falling night.

The whisperings of the eartag melded into the unconsciousness of his fading thoughts. Vague reflections surfaced and dove in his soul; memories of seeing, at the break of that endless day, the fabled Ballroom for the first time. As they were climbing the stairs toward the double trap door, Neipas had begun to discern, with building enthusiasm, the iconic features of the legendary hall yonder beyond the door's portholes. Through their yellowish tint he could already see the unmistakable chandeliers, massive, intricately ornamented, glittering in the suspended weight of thousands of the most exquisite jewels. He felt his breathing deepen.

The doors parted ceremoniously before Drrawetz's step, leading the herd. The view expanded abruptly, opening forth to the full vastness of the circular Ballroom. Neipas froze and felt his heart swell in awe. His tired sight widened large, his breath shortened to a deep panting.

His eyes, rapt, drew in the overwhelming majesty of the fabled space. It was uncanny to behold it, to have it, giant and solemn, sumptuous and powerful, tactile before his reverential stare. The Nest looked to the unfiltered eye almost as it did in photographs: one's attention was immediately drawn to the famous dome ceiling, soaring very broad, very filled with graceful, masterful frescoes whose glorious brush strokes depicted a pantheon of mythical creatures, of flaming cherubs, robed specters, muses and moirae, motley beasts arranged in concentric layers of arching magnificence. Prominently featured round the dome's oculus, were an eagle, a lion, a sheep, and a bull; from the golden beak, or clutched by the mighty maw, or coiled round the woolly hoofs or the furry neck, then descended the heavy chains of the extraordinary chandeliers with their august infinitude of diamonds dangling in much shine and sparkle, suspended in a regal agglomeration of jewels under the holy animals' benevolent gaze. The scintillating gems presided, in turn, over the enormous annular hall, over the magnificently carpeted floor which seemed to support the palpable weight of sheer opulence pervading the air about them. It spiraled wide and free toward distant alpine windows and massive tapestries rising behind elegant sculptures, interspaced in a round between the two portentous gates: the so-called 3rd Gate, leading East to the Pigeon Wing, and the 9th Gate, pointing West, down which the Eagle Gardens cascaded (the ten windows were also dubbed gates and numbered according to their equivalent positions on the clock). Chairs and couches furnished the central area, looking very tiny among the vast emptiness. These were arranged in a circle round the Ballroom's exalted, divine centerpiece — the tall golden statue of a dove, standing very stiff, with muscular claws rooted firmly to the golden ground gaping round it, the full width of its wings pressed against its fat torso, the puny head lowered, the eyes closed peacefully.

This spectacle presented itself to Neipas' growing eyes with familiarity and inspired a surging feeling of awe in his chest. In his stare there was an intense gleam of the sort of recognition that is reverent and overcome, the sort of gaze beholding the apparition of a renowned god. But there was also in it an unearthly haze, the suspicion of something very strange; and indeed he stood there more or less dumbfounded, for — even though he knew well where he was — he knew even better that things weren't as they should. The ornate chairs and crafted sofas, even they well-known to the most casual glance, were there, but they were toppled over and broken down to pieces, the feathery cushion of the couches spread in dusty shreds everywhere, all scattered and in complete disarray about the floor. Scraps of food were discarded all over the expanse — one would have to take care not to trample on a graying chunk of steak or a moist heap of caviar — and the carpet felt mucky, its softness damp, slobbered. Every surface was tainted with some sort of filth — even the window curtains hung precipitously under the load of many blotches of grease spoiling its lavish fabric. It struck Neipas as most bizarre that the golden statue in the middle was dotted with so many droppings dried white and solid, something particularly uncanny, considering they were indoors; though, upon close inspection, he could detect feces among the scraps on the carpet also, which were, however, less conspicuous, as these were generally well hidden between the fibers and the widespread garbage. As they walked carefully to the center, hardening their noses against the smell, he noticed the tiny maggots and flies scavenging the neighborhood of these spots. It would take much time and effort to clean it all up.

"Lot of work to do, darlings! Apply yourselves! Do it with joy! Decorum!" bellowed Mister Drrawetz with infinite flourishes of his arm.

Work had been tough from the very moment Neipas began working there. From the moment he began his tenure at the Eagles' Nest, exertion became almost the totality of his experience. The pace wouldn't let up.

His muscles dropped roughly into the labor of it.

Waves of dedicated movements in a sea of bobbing cattle heads swept the full extent of the Ballroom. Hundreds of gloved hands labored frictioned against the mass of fabrics and minerals compositing that wealthy vastness; upon their knees and atop every rung of giant ladders, the massive herd of workers scrubbed away with fury, in a desperate effort to erase every vestige of uncleanliness. Among the toiling frenzy ambled the vague, faint figure of Drrawetz, with an exaggeratedly casual gait and an insolent supervising manner, with a tilt of the head that gave the personage an overt air of trying to pass by unnoticed. The eyes of the laborers, buried under the hard clay of their ox and cow masks, had nowhere to look except the particular spot of filth they were tasked with washing off — they stared at their assigned blotches as though they were the only fact of life — so it was impossible to notice the smirk of mild satisfaction which the only fellow who was not glued to the floor or the wall was carving in his peacock semblance of pale complexion. The walls sweated with soap, and the gilded dome breathed hard with the chemical moistures; the very animals upon the ceiling warped themselves in coughs with the toxic fumes going up their painted nostrils.

An intense smell of bleach... But this satisfied the Master Supervisor, whose voice echoed from time to time across the openness of the space — and through the thickness of its bleach-laden air — articulating vague orders. It was clear the mask was thick upon Drrawetz; and only the intermittent glances at his watch betrayed his nervousness. His mood was perhaps affected by the continuous inspection of an eminent character looming over them all.

Perched discreetly in a balcony above the court, a portentous Eagle supervised the proceedings. His shoulders were broad, and were beginning to arch from age; one of his arms, once powerful, now atrophying, rested with fingers round an ornate cane. The white, bald head ran cleanly to a jaw covered by a dense beard of feathers, which lengthened down widely from his cheeks, in two separate wattles, and pended over the belt; his lip was drawn in a powerfully indifferent snarl along his golden hooked beak, which glistened sagely by the dappled glow of the chandeliers. The tailored drapes of his suit — opulent in its golden buttons — weaved round his torso and leaned tight on his flank like big powerful wings. His jacket white, and his shirt black round the hefty body and neck, covered the eminent figure in a display of might and authority.

Behind him stood a fellow who had on the mask of an ox: he had the bearing of an assistant, with horns very polished and well-kept, garlanded with vines and sparkles of gold, adorned with glittering silver chains round the ivory. His visage was friendly, framed wisely by the black stubble of a mustacheless, grandfatherly beard. He was taller than the Eagle, though he bent so that his head hung much lower.

"Who's that?" Neipas asked the janitor with the scar on the side of his mouth as he kept tending the golden paw.

Suckling the corner of his maimed lip, the janitor took a moment of thought before he replied, "That's the Head Gardener. He owns this place. Or the gardens, at least. I heard he's a billionaire... made a fortune with farming, or something. Don't know much beyond that."

"Harder, darlings," said Drrawetz with a snobbish drawl as he passed alongside Neipas and his colleague.

"Man there's got a stick up his ass, swear to god."

The scarred janitor was called Osir. By and by Neipas and he got into mumbling to each other, and Neipas learned that he was a veteran of the military; lifting up his sleeve discreetly, Osir showed him the symbol of the armed forces branded into his skin. "I was a marksman," he grumbled, sniffling, then wetting his scar with a lick. "A sniper, I mean ("Ah, I hear you," said Neipas). Elite, an' everything... Can you believe it?" added Osir in a trailing snicker, lifting up his sponge. His head momentarily soared in the talons of reminiscence even as his shoulders dropped back under the burden of labor: upon them, a hunched beast widened its wings (he seemed to sense it grinning in the mirror-golden surface of the statue), billowing into his limbs as they jammed and slowed with the burden of memory. He had fought on the snow-domed peaks of ragged rock, on the low-lying valleys of poppy and the dried riverbeds of distant battlefields, and had seen much, and remembered still more. All a blur, but secreting from such hazes — continuously — in his secret depths pulsed an old monster — mirrored outward in the grisly frown of his lip. The vision of a particular body — a particular dead face — haunted him.

He struck Neipas as a quiet, mysterious character, whose peculiarities were revealed by and by. Earlier, when Neipas, straining through the general exertion, mumbled that he was tired and sleepy, Osir mentioned that he had a fix; and again with effortless discretion, he pulled up his sleeve and magicked a small bottle of pills from under it, whispering a price across the golden body of the dove.

"Huh... I'm all right, thanks though."

The bottle of pills slid back up and vanished into Osir's coveralls. "Fine. Whatever you need though man — just lemme know."

Now he enacted those very same gestures; but his vision, having glassed out of his eyes, did not take a quick scan round the hall as before — his consciousness, afar, did not supervise the motion of his limb. With one quick automatic act he flicked open the little bottle and popped a pill into his mouth.

At length he regained the pace of his scrubbing — life seemed to return to his eyes, as he exhaled. "Another day, another day..." he sighed.

Neipas too kept through the toil, brushing the warm, dark sunny surface of the statue until it was immaculate, its gold pure and stainless. It flared with the gloomy consistency of olive oil; it shimmered mesmeric and undulant, as he rubbed the paw. The golden floor was very sticky, its shiny surface glazed over with a thin crust of hardened wine, made lusterless. In it, going along the rhythm of his scrubbing motion, his face appeared and shook. The reflection looked indistinct; he couldn't make out the mask. It seemed to him like an edgeless, discolored blemish, like an emptiness in the wealth of that luxurious texture, and, hiding it and pressing it with both his hands, he endeavored to wipe away the stain all the more forcefully; employing, half unknowingly, all the hopeless energy of his nerves to it — until the very image appeared to sweat in blurs (meanwhile, beneath, he heard — faintly — music).

...once, he looked up into the lowered head of the dove staring down at him; and noticed, strangely, that its eyes were not closed as he thought they were, but peeked from under parting lids.

Later — many hours later — he would stand at rest in the gazebo, contemplating the expanse exhaling alight. The night twinkles shimmered wobbly under the black sky where he was, well under, wobbly, in a sea of mellow gleam... Neipas felt again a powerful feeling — he sensed it something godly, to see everything when nothing could see him. And he felt his lip stir involuntarily into an arrogant curve; he narrowed his gleaming eyes with satisfaction before retreating back to the Columbaria to try to sleep. Back into the intensity of bright ceiling lights, beaming multifold from the mirrors.

Yonder the moonshine, right above the mountains; and right above him the Pearl had yawned into the night with white gold, the angelic whiteness of a benign and invincible beacon, glaring as if through him, as if out of him, as if from him; and he had felt powerful upon his powerful perch. Yet to behold without barriers and to see the horizon so distant and elusive (for he had stood so high up, he could discern the very curvature of the Earth); to contemplate a sight so vast and so empty, a land so small and so crushed by a sky so bereft of even a cloud, so immense in its barrenness; to gaze out of the unfathomable starless firmament and see, after all, nothing, produced a surreptitious, hollowing sensation, a gnawing loneliness eating slowly into his heart and perception. The great emptiness of the expanse had filled him with a void of his own; and his steps toward the dormitory matched the growth of that mirroring desolation, between the enclosing walls of the corridor; and he went to bed feeling as though without marrow. Keeping the ox in his head — for he was too exhausted to remove it — Neipas climbed to his bunker and eased the back of his skull into the pillow. After a few minutes pecking at the *I*, he folded his gaze; his hands pulled the blind over his eyes.

Vacant, he floated through indeterminate time between consciousness and slumber.

22 - The Museum

A vague sense of bees buzzing about his head occurred to him; he imagined they secreted wax into his ears. His sleep was disturbed by stirrings and half-dreams, ghostly pictorial fragments and perceptions evanescing out of a brightness that pushed itself against the black screen of closed eyes; closed eyes covered by blinds. And the brightness was so strong that it penetrated even the multi-layered blackness of that slumber; so that Neipas was dragged out of the depths with a long groan, awakening heavily. Right as he removed the blinds the intense radiance muscled through the slit of his opening eyes into his dull brain, and again he shut them flinchingly, looking inward to its throbbing mind. Then, recovering, he removed the ox from his head for a minute, glancing in the mirror wall aside the sorrowful aspect of his soggy, melting pigeon face; and he molded it to rights once more, as best he could.

Neipas then saw the time on the face of his *I*. It was the middle of the night yet.

He read, also, that the buzzing stirring in the radiance had been the glass vibrating upon the mattress. The red dot blinked slowly above its face. Inside it, Eva's words spoke:

EVA: I'm super excited for you :)
EVA: We should celebrate!

NEIPAS: Thank you! And we should :) Drink?

EVA: I'm downnn :)
EVA: drinks + dance?
EVA: there's a club I love on via magna
EVA: you'd love it

NEIPAS: Ok ;) Which one? :)

Pigeons and cattle masks peeped over the sheets or were delineated under them. Those that couldn't sleep dozed inside the Webwork. Neipas, after an undetermined interval of sluggish lethargy, found himself very awake — as if he had risen from a nap — and wandered the bright corridors of the Columbaria, exploring its spaces thoughtlessly, as one on a trek. Though he wasn't fully aware of it he was enticed by the vestige of some sound, a vague melody whispered from the elusive ends of those corridors; something about the air... something about the walls seemed porous. Beyond the mirror surface of the wall Neipas was replicated trudging along in the doubly intensified ceiling lights. There was something of the droning speech reverberating in the hanging gardens, and something of the melody he had heard flowing from underneath the golden dove, both strangely familiar. But perhaps it was neither of them, or perhaps it was both. There was a throbbing sound... He had the impression of the ticking clock of the Cloakroom, but as he walked in that direction he felt the beat wasn't quite so mechanical. It resembled something closer to a drum; or a heart pulsing. And as he followed it, brightly awake but unsensing in his roaming, he vaguely perceived he had progressed in a direction other than the one concluding in the Cloakroom. Suddenly he walked a corridor of repeating patterns of wallpaper, no longer cloaked in mirror, and stamped with a looping series of equal doorframes accompanied by bureaucratic plaques with incomprehensible glyphic labels at their side. Neipas went on and on.

It wasn't the plaque that halted his unconscious stroll through the doors' endless row. Neipas turned slowly and zoomed forward. Something had changed in the wall of patterned symbols which made him discern the patterns more clearly; right at the spot where he took notice of it, Neipas lifted his gaze and saw the inconspicuous door was ajar. The plaque next to it read: *Library.*

And the music — it had stopped. Its shush opened a gap of silence, through which the pulse rang more clearly now, lone; and it whizzed through the slit between door and frame. Neipas leaned his hand against the door, and pushed gently.

A light projected out harshly, assuming the rectangular shape of the door. Neipas grimaced in the sudden abundance of luminosity; for the ensuing light was yet sharper than the corridor's radiance. Once the sting of it eased, he widened his glare to the vision revealed by the open door. In wonder he saw its frame extending into a mighty corridor of shelves, filled with books, and so tall as to render the ceiling out of the range of sight, curving outward and in into similar stacks of covers and papers mounting to equally immeasurable heights. He stepped in, marveling before this strange apparition out of an ordinary door in a remote passageway.

Neipas walked flanked by orderly book mountains, towers which only seemed to grow before his advancing upward stare. Immense ladders leaned against some of the columns, climbing the heights rung by rung and finally diving in the inscrutable darkness of the far-off ceiling. Strange wailings rang from those upper depths: bats scoured the highest shelves, flying out of the ceiling and disappearing in it, dipping in and out of view in flashes. The uncanny and formidable vision of it filled him again with that fascination of novelty so alluring to the photographer's eye. Neipas sought at once to capture all the interesting nooks of the erudite landscape, to disclose all its mysteries through the glass' piercing gaze; and he walked about absorbed in its wonders, open to himself alone in the wide silence of its stacks and empty rows. For the library was silent, with a silence that fluttered only with Neipas' steps and the bats' wails — the throbbing pulsed still, but it so pervaded the soundscape that it merged into imperceptibility once more.

At the end of the shelf row the corridor broke into two others, running obliquely out of the first one. He turned.

By and by Neipas, as he became accustomed with the repetition of the advancing columns, withdrew his flashing *I* after many photographs and relented into examining the books in the shelves. He opened one, then another; but their pages were filled with words he couldn't understand, full of occult symbols, both in his language and others, and some books were but stacks of empty pages, so that it was difficult for him to find anything there that meant something to him. Intrigued and taken with the tranquil mystery of the space, his mind fogging a little in the encroaching effect of sleeplessness, Neipas began to climb one the ladders and perusing aimlessly through the volumes on higher rows. He realized that the more he ascended the less arcane the words became. Pages were slowly freed of drivel, its sentences gained clarity and he began to comprehend bit by bit as he went through into the less accessible zones of the piles.

Meanwhile — as his eyes fixed the discoloring pages — he noticed something had changed. The space had become more faded. The acute brightness dimmed subtly but dramatically, as if its initial burst had been a result of surprise at Neipas' entrance; and he saw now the space involved in a crepuscular gravity. He hesitated in his climb. He went no further, for fear of the bats — and because he saw, after the turn, a bizarre passage at the end of the corridor. He climbed down and walked to it.

The passage was circular — a perfect circle opening the wall. A steep staircase descended on the other side. On the opening's thick, gilded frame was carved the label: *CAVE*. Like the Library, the staircase was cushioned in the honey glow of lamps; its steps were likewise carpeted with patterns, as the walls of the outer hallway had been. It sunk narrow under a vaulted ceiling made of stone. The bottom blushed warmly, mellow, suggesting coffee and books, a cozy hearth. Altogether the portal opened invitingly, and appealed to Neipas' artistic sensibilities; it drew him in.

It was a simple room at the bottom, a small lobby. Round him lay a furry rug, spread across. There was on it but a single couch, and facing the couch was the painting of a gray pigeon head in profile, emerging from a black and white suit, and looking straight at him with wide red eyes.

Under the painting, the hearth was unlit. In front of him, directly before the stairs' base, gaped yet another circular doorway, bearing the same portentous label: *CAVE*. The other side was somewhat indistinct. He could only make out some vague shapes and silhouettes, possibly of more books and stacks. By now Neipas had begun to sense a little fear and weirdness at seeing no one around; for isolation is paranoia's best friend. But he still was enveloped in interest, and felt no harm could come from having a peek.

He stepped through the circle into a sort of storehouse, dusty and dimly lit, spreading austere beneath its ribbed ceiling, eerie, all embossed with keystones representing the grins of diverse animals. Books mounted in tall piles or were strewn across the thin darkness. Among them rose veils covering all sorts of shapes. Neipas stiffened his step and panned his head round; and bit by bit layers of shade peeled before his eyes. His heart slowed, and he held his breath when he saw human shapes standing quietly in the blackness. They stood eerily still (are they sleeping?) and uncannily straight. But then the gloom thinned a little more and he was able to discern the plastic nakedness of their skin — mannequins. A relief unexpectedly came over him; yet it was only then that he realized how tense he was. The silence seemed to deepen; slacken acute — again the pulse throbbed afar. Neipas still eyed neurotically those shapes hidden beneath cloths. Their immobility was disquieting; and even as he paced forth he sensed himself readying to turn back, letting his curiosity pull him on but a few steps further. Then his foot dropped down some sudden step.

He started with surprise, his very heart jumped shocked with the vibration. For his step had rung very loud — it landed with a bang upon the grounds, and the echo of its sound spread immensely across the hall and hollow chambers, disappearing a great distance away.

A quietude thickened in the trail of the departing echoes. Then — something moved. Immediately the silence bounced back, Neipas heard (completely motionless now, frozen by surprise) weird stirrings in the drapes. A sudden spasm in the heart scattered out into his muscles; the toxins of sleep blew into his brain fast; it made him turn abruptly with an intent to run away. Upon his next step the quietude was again echoed away and the moment after he shook with the force of impact. He had bumped against one of the veiled objects — which he hadn't noticed was there, and as he wondered whether the veil itself had moved to him, he heard a deep groan: it made his chest tremble and he looked all about him in panic. "Hello!"

"Why, hello."

A sudden presence towered over him. He turned his head upward the voice, which spoke from ten feet above him.

There was a head emerging from the summit of the cloth. "Why, sir — welcome," it said.

The head bore a mask of Thalia, the mask of comedy or Sock, upon its face. It was round and culminated in an upward pointy tip, altogether resembling a droplet. Its smiling, lipless mouth had the shape of a crescent with tips turned up; the two eyes, the same. The cloth descended from it like robes, descended very lean from the mask that emerged from the summit of the veil. Its smiling hollow eyes looked down at Neipas from ten feet up in the air, and Neipas looked back at them, mesmerized.

"Welcome, sir," the Giant repeated.

Neipas knew not what to say; he nodded and muttered something.

"Are you lost, sir?"

"Sorry?"

The Giant leaned down a bit.

"Are you lost, sir?"

"No, no... Just walking around."

"Very good, sir. Is there anything in particular you might be looking for?"

"Sorry?" — Neipas couldn't hear him very well; the voice of the Giant withered as it traveled the distance between its grin and Neipas' ear.

The Giant stooped down further. The lean robes widened. "Is there anything in particular you might be looking for, sir."

"Oh no, no — Just browsing, I guess."

"Ah —" said the Giant, resuming his full height. He would speak louder now, dictating every syllable with clarity, assuming, perhaps, that Neipas was half-deaf — "Say, sir. Would you like a tour, in that case?"

"A tour?" wondered Neipas.

"A tour, sir," spoke the Giant, raising his voice so that Neipas may hear.

Neipas stared into those sinister horn-like slits, trying to decipher the meaning of the Giant's words. His eyes were intimidating but incited not exactly fear. They drew Neipas to them; they had a grip on him. Neipas couldn't decide if he wanted to leave, though he felt a little uncomfortable. In any case he was too dazed to articulate his way out of there at that moment. He glimpsed into the *I* again — it was the middle of the night still — and somehow he felt it would be impolite to say no.

"Very well, thank you, thank you... I'd love a tour," said Neipas, nodding in all directions.

"Very well, sir," clamored the Giant.

With a swirling movement he turned, and out the bottom of his robes emerged a long cane, which he used to draw aside some curtains by the wall. They seemed to be back at the Library. There were more shelves of books beyond, more mannequins and objects extending themselves away from them; and some of the columns of stacks were clothed in drapes; and as he walked alongside the multiplying cover spines, Neipas realized he could now see the peak of the shelves — they were as tall as the Giant. As he tapped his long cane about the floor in sweeping motions before him, Neipas perceived, in a dull incredulity, that the Giant was blind. And suddenly he saw that the shelves were not populated by book covers at all, like he had assumed. They were now covered by glass — and the books beyond the glass were stones with inscriptions, or tablets of hardened clay or preserved wax... Therein lay scrolls of parchment, vellum and papyrus, then paper; styluses and quills of various forms rested beside them and among other such treasures. They were all scribbled with numbers and records of transactions at first. All were inscribed with the symbols of their own age... This Neipas gathered from the Giant's narration, the Giant who spoke freely about the relics as they passed them. The Giant's own robe was made from parchment — and colorless lines dotted them inscrutably. He ruffled heavily as they moved widely about the grounds.

As they began the walk, the monumental figure had presented himself as a scholar and academic. He had read all those books, he claimed, and wrote many, if not all of them. The Scholar thus guided Neipas through the corridors, through many gates and arches cloaked in veils, which seemed to widen and shrink in turn along chambers upon chambers extending in a straight line. The ceilings were always very high and white: the bats had disappeared and gargoyles of various forms jutted from the top in their stead. The immaculate brightness of the spaces illuminated a plethora of glass cases — a whole ordered forest of tall boxes of clean glass extending infinitely into the white lights afar. Within them were guarded various objects, treasures of many kinds — coins, weapons, garments, every sort of tool — from every age of the human era, hailing from the earliest dawn of the race, when wild beasts were gods and nature was absolute over all.

This is a Museum, Neipas thought. He asked the Giant Scholar whether he could take photographs, to which the Giant conceded, as long as they were without flash: and he continued to speak through. Meanwhile, Neipas' steps rang loudly still — but it was as though the Scholar's speech swallowed them and rendered them mute.

Water-clocks' liquid flow crystallized the air as they strolled through. Everything possessed a certain quality of holiness, a pristine character; like a sort of vast sanctum. All throughout, mannequins posed in the garbs of monarchs and other great men — crested with gems and draped in furs, or shelled in armor and helmet, or in suits, or other such skins. Many of these mannequin kings were damaged and headless, in which case their faces were replaced by balloons; though in some occasions an authentic wax mask was fixed to their balloon heads, fixed in the final form of their mortal countenance. The greats were depicted in paintings, statues, letters, and finally photographs. Each succeeding chamber began and ended with them... And each hall housed its own abundant collection of objects. Pelts with which the first men sheltered from the night and the shiver; stones atop sticks, with which to murder fellow men; spears, arrows and bows, and saddles, tools of conquest and domination; fragments of ancient city walls; tall pillars from old temple ruins; swords, shields, armor and chainmail, and helmets of iron expressionless and demonic; the wooden cross atop the masoned stone; stakes charred and blooded; totem poles and rows of old coins, broken chests, brass locks; printing presses; an entire ship with sail (and hidden in it, Neipas noticed as he sharpened his eye, chains and shackles); whips and gunpowder; cotton jackets and knives with ivory handles... the steam engine, power looms, dynamos, the lightbulb, the oldest cameras, internal combustion engines, the oil derrick and the pumpjack, motor cars, propellers, airplanes, guns, bombs, transistors and chips of silicon, clothes of cotton, clothes of satin, clothes of polyester, clothes and flags of every pigment, televisions of every size and computers and *I*s as the culmination of glass and sound across ages...

The glass cases were of all sizes, as tall or as short, as wide or as narrow as the object within required it. Labels bearing dates and materials were placed at the base of all artifacts; following each other in a mishmash of collages scattered across floor and walls, standing and hanging, released from their original contexts. Neipas merely watched through the lens.

At his side, the Giant Scholar extolled men and deeds with very reverential tones as they walked by. He led Neipas along the straight line, though there were many closed doors on the side, sometimes near, sometimes afar, peeking inconspicuous behind certain artifacts; doors which contained, no doubt (Neipas vaguely reflected) many secrets. He had been ushered through the chambers, which arose, descended, and were connected through various staircases. In the beginning the march arose steadily as the chambers grew in riches. The fall of the classical men was likewise marked by an oblique caving of the floors; and then, moving through sinking rooms of discarded relics, handwritten volumes and crass torture instruments, the grounds pulled aloft once more, until the steam engine materialized triumphantly amid a great hall, at which point the staircase steepened dramatically into a vertiginous climb, fogged with confetti. They had been marching a long while now, it seemed; time dissolved itself into the enigmatic whiteness of the horizons. They walked up the steepest steps yet now, where they were flanked by mannequins which wore various military and superhero costumes, replacing the old monarchs' fur mantles with glossy capes of plastic... at which point, Neipas, bringing down his *I* with a certain sadness and fatigue, stopped.

And it occurred to him to ask, "What's all this?"

"This," from on high responded the sage, "is the course of History, sir."

"This is History?" He inferred but a tale of continuous murder culminating in frivolous hedonism. There was no beauty to it whatsoever. It made him depressed.

They climbed but a bit more; and at last drew away the last veil. Neipas saw a wall arising.

With a long, tired sigh, he asked:

"Is this the end?"

"Indeed, sir. We stand at the end of History."

A vague smoke, a scent of fume pervaded the round space. The End of History was mostly empty, minimalistic. Only an immense hourglass (spanning floor to ceiling), whose sands fell continuously, stood in the middle. Out of the far wall, two immense frames were carved in relief; two arches housing two great glass surfaces, with the reliefs running inside the arches in ornate, sinuous patterns across the immense wall.

"From here, we can only regress," said the Historian.

Neipas stepped closer to the wall. Between the two arches was a relief sculpture of a serpent, with eyes shut, wrapped in a cocoon; a hood reared its head, and from it emerged the vast winding arches, which Neipas — stepping back again to analyze the wholeness of the sculpture — took to be wings, like those of a butterfly. He considered the two glasses housed under those wings.

One glass was but a mirror replicating all which had come before on their long march. The other was a window.

The first, on the left, was coated with a thin feathery texture, which Neipas, rubbing his finger on, saw was ash. The second, on the right, was flaked with thick frost. With his hand he erased a patch from the cold surface of the glass. Beyond it, Neipas saw — across a great distance of darkness — a flame burning in a tall, wide pool.

Only after a span observing it did he conclude it to be a candle, immense... The flame burned into the concave wax of the candle, flickering in its recess, sheltered by the wax and shining through it. Yet this flame mustn't be normal, Neipas realized, for though he stared into it for a very long time the wax would not wean, wouldn't melt. He asked whether it was burning at all, or what — to which the Historian replied, "Yes, sir, only very slowly. From which we must conclude that it is harmless."

And what was the meaning behind it, Neipas inquired.

"Like all that lives, sir, the flame consumes and seeks to multiply. Like all that lives, it aspires to the heavens."

Smoke left the peak of the flame in abnormal quantities — great piles of black fume emanated continuously, and even drafted sidelong against this window, though its glass was stained only slowly, almost imperceptibly. There were little spotlights on the body of the candle which shone upon the gloomy vapor, infusing it with a phantasmagoric aura — they shone strong, blindingly, like a small sun.

Neipas reared his head nearer the window. He had been, as it were, zooming in his view, narrowing his sight, lengthening his stare; and, gradually, perceived the candle more closely (a great silence, meanwhile, befell once more). He discerned letters cut into the wax in golden colors, and the letters formed the words, "*THOU SHALT*" — and these words were multiplied into all languages, carved continually round the surface of the candle.

"What's this?" asked Neipas in a whisper inaudible.

"Millenary values shine through this candle. In it shine the value of all things, sir. It is the sum of all values created thus far, this is the candle of Man. It is our most precious possession."

The parchment-draped figure stood around him like a phantom. He looked down at Neipas from the summit of his robe, through the immense grin of his eyes. Neipas looked about himself... (he sensed again the pulse, fluttering in the quiet. And in it breathed a whisper, it was very close...)

The whisper ensued from the serpent. Neipas grimaced within his leaden heart, wondered in his diffused mind; leaned his ear against the snake's closed eyes.

It uttered thus:

We triumphed.

There is no alternative

There is no turning back now

Only money can mold the morrow —

Only with power can the past be shed

Because inherited are pride and shame.

So's merit, to which wealth's bestowed.

Still, fortunes abound in the summits

and there's no shortage of ladders.

We reached the end of evolution.

We conquered the journey.

We triumphed.

The serpent expressed these words through sibilant whispers, using not so much syllables as unintelligible gusts of wind. The words, as represented here, are indeed not as Neipas heard them — but as he understood their meaning.

And yet — still, he wondered:

"What does this mean?" Neipas asked once more, but as he was looking away he saw, or thought he saw, he sensed strongly that the yonder door — one of those locked doors on the side — was open, ajar.

He looked round the circular room and saw the tall hourglass, and beyond the hourglass the round walls of the End of History, curving on each side of the curtain (and the plunging staircase and the long Museum beyond it). Twelve paintings hung there: all depicted clocks. The first clock was illustrated with perfect fidelity; the second one less so; the third still a little less; and so on in deepening degrees of dissolution and abstraction, until the clock melted, broke into flashes of light, and finally filled the canvas with nothing but glare and emptiness. Beneath each painting was a lamp, increasing in ornamentation as the clocks decreased in integrity. By the side of the 1st or wholest clock (by the side of the barest lamp, that is), the wall gave in and deepened into a silent passage — at the end of which was a door — open, ajar. There was a familiar mask eying out of it. There, there appeared the familiar mask of the Midget from the underground — peeking through, surfacing out of the slit.

Neipas saw her (or him) again, dwarf, meek and strange with that frowning mask of sadness. A rattle of chains sounded, dim; it seemed to Neipas as though he (or she) was bounded by manacles and fetters. He swallowed dry; the silence deepened, the pulse intensified with clarity. Neipas hadn't known, for the longest time, whether what he had seen in the depths of the tower had been reality or dream. For too long he had been straddling between wakefulness and slumber; and in the gap had been dropped many memories, many perceptions, as if his brain recorded and judged nothing anymore. But now he saw the Midget again, here, of all places; and wondered if he wasn't dreaming now. He had looked for her (or him) again in the slaughterhouse, but hadn't found him (or her). Without her guidance, Neipas was never again able to find that deepest of grounds to which he had taken him. Neipas stepped toward at once; but the Historian placed his giant cane before him, pressing it to the ground, making it rise in front of Neipas like the hostile seam of a gate.

"Please do not step over the line, sir," said the Historian calmly and loud, tall above him.

It wasn't beyond Neipas' capacity to simply walk around it — but even so, he stopped. He felt not the threat of violence or repercussion; but he didn't want to appear impolite. And there was something about the weight of his ox head, which now buzzed with sleep.

Neipas started. He noticed only now the eartag rang; it summoned him back to work. He looked up — but could see the Midget no longer.

23 - Keratin-weaving Tongues

Thus Neipas left the End of History. The Historian opened one of those many closed doors on the side, bidding farewell to Neipas with a slow, gargantuan curtsy; the three crescent moon slits of his wide mask leaning down very close to him. The door opened to stairs leading straight to a corridor in the Columbaria. Finding himself suddenly there, Neipas turned back to the door — and saw but the patterned wall, now doorless in its full extent. He hesitated a little, wondering where he was; but the eartag was buzzing frantically, and he rushed on through the hallway. The voice in his ear repeated:

"431999 called to Offices," said she, articulating Neipas' number in a loop. The bells of the summit rang frantically, he careered through the noise. Its echoes overwhelmed all his senses and made his hurried gait weightless, and though he scarcely felt his body, Neipas perceived all the more acutely a strange weariness in his soul. It was as though a plumb carrying his heart sank toward its innermost, pressing down agony and spreading a dizzying angst, as if its line was fastened round the throat, and pulled all his being down to vertiginous arcane depths.

He was exhausted, really exhausted. A slow confusion overtook all fast motions around him; he had trekked through all human ages and had emerged without batting a lash, unslept. Through all of it, he had kept on his heavy ox mask. The voice in his ear guided him as he went.

Neipas stopped only when he was before Mister Drrawetz.

"By the lord! What on earth took you so long?! And — my..." he widened up in shock. "He's not *even* wearing his outfit!"

Panting, Neipas stood before the master steward supremely confused. He hadn't even taken off his outfit. The winking Supervisor, who stood smiling next to Drrawetz, explained to him kindly that they had expected him to be wearing the attire of a waiter. He looked down at his janitor garments, and then quickly round the Supervisor's Office where the empty bird cages hung, frowning sleepily. The waiters gathered there were all wearing tuxedos; little bells pended from their collars; Cesar, who stood among them, shrugged helplessly when Neipas' eyes met his. Finally Neipas voiced to the two supervisors that he thought he was supposed to be a janitor. The winking Supervisor, amicable, countered this by saying he was registered as a waiter on his tablet — though it didn't matter, it was nothing to worry about. No harm had been done. There was still some time, so please do head for the Cloakroom to collect a waiter's outfit; and then on to the kitchen.

Drrawetz, meanwhile, continued indulging in his flowery outrage. "*Why* isn't he wearing a waiter!? Hiring standards these days are simply atrocious, I tell you."

Neipas left them behind and walked through the mirrored corridors into the depths of the Columbaria, alongside its myriad doors and patterned walls adorned with national paraphernalia. Then up the long flight of stairs toward the clock-cloakroom; the queasy feeling bobbed inside him in the climb. Again the immense hall of vivid colors, and the tall clock among the drawers, opened up before him. There were, again, many workers marching onward through it, mottled in a myriad hues as they went along. The lights beamed over them; the cow in the carved ceiling laughed above their horned heads.

A seamstress approached, speaking to him through the eartag. Her peacock beak opened and closed in the unsynchronized — delayed — gesture of the electronic words in Neipas' head; and she handed him the waiter's outfit.

It was a tuxedo like those the others wore: jacket black, shirt white, accompanied by white gloves and shiny black shoes. Silver garlands were wrapped round his horns as he undressed. Time was so pressing that he changed right there, and he so dazed that he scarcely minded the parade dragging languidly by. He hardly noticed the Seamstress at whose indifferent feet he laid his janitor coveralls (only now that he removed them did he realize how heavy they were; the collar in particular seemed fashioned out of iron, and the burden, which had been so far enmeshed with the fabric of muscle that Neipas had ceased to feel it, provoked now a great relief of tension as it was lifted off the back of his neck).

Stripped to his underwear, he began to enter the tuxedo garments one by one as he was handed them. Its fabric was much lighter, feathery in its enveloping touch. First he buttoned the shirt; then he tucked it into the trousers, which he also buttoned, then zipped, and belted; then he inserted his feet into his shoes and tied the shoelaces, making his way downward across his body until his beak was quite close to the floor, upon which he suddenly felt like spreading out and sleeping — a desire left unfulfilled, for, on discerning the Seamstress' extended arm in the hazy upper rim of his sight, he forced himself up through the lethargy of his head and over the weakness of his knees, stood again, and took the jacket she gave him. With head downcast and back arched he wore it. Then — for the last time — the Seamstress again extended her arms, driving her fingers to his neck. Flinching, Neipas quickly straightened his back (his every bone crackled in the contraction and the push against gravity) and felt a sort of tie being wrapped under his collar, from which hung some iron thing — a cowbell.

The Seamstress sent him off, and into the pressing crowd he spilled and rushed, sighing nervously. Overall, he felt much lighter now in his new outfit, which weighed less, much less; though the bell strapped to his neck still compelled him to lower his head a little.

Hurrying, he glided on to the kitchen (passing swiftly by the dormitory and depositing his *I* in his locker of possessions, as he dropped a quick text to Eva, as all the mirrors in the corridors showed him his new aspect), erupting through the doors in his immaculate suit — Drrawetz's frantic screaming burst upon him immediately; it filled the wide hall.

"*Vite! Vite!* To the Eagles' side!" A line was promptly formed, and the waiters mechanically locked in step with the leading Supervisors at the front. One by one they passed through the ghostly lights of the flashing scanner. As Neipas waited somewhere in the middle of the cattle column, he found himself next to Cesar again, who played with his whiskers distractedly.

"Fuck's going on?" Neipas whispered to him sleepily.

Cesar looked at him startled. Up close Neipas could see his eyes were red, beneath the mask the sunken undereye could be made out faintly; the poet hadn't gotten much sleep either.

"Oh — I'm sorry. Didn't notice you there. Good morning," he said relaxing, smiling.

"Good morning."

"You got a good scolding from Drrawetz."

"Yeah, well. First he tells me I'm supposed to clean, now apparently I was supposed to be serving tables? Good Mary."

Cesar sighed. "Kind of a shitshow, right?"

Neipas snickered.

"So what's the frenzy about?"

"More patrons came in this morning for some early meetings, it seems like. That's why Drrawetz is panicking. They weren't expected until tomorrow. And we hadn't finished training yet."

"Training!" hissed Neipas, exasperatedly.

"Yes. They have you walk up and down for hours until you get your walk just right. Bending over tables again and again, and things of the kind. You have to memorize a script and everything."

"Shit," Neipas gasped. "Why did they call me in then? I didn't do any training."

"They called a bunch of new folks. I dunno," said Cesar, shrugging and twirling his whisker tips. "I don't think Drrawetz knows what he's doing. Such a ponce, isn't he? Thing to remember is, you need to always call them 'Your Honor' or some honorable adjective like that."

The line advanced methodically in silence. All along the column, horns were motionless in the steady fulfillment of professional duty. Neipas fought sternly to keep his head still in the same manner, straining against the burden of doze and the bell.

"You look a bit tense, brother," observed Cesar, leaning sideways discreetly.

"I'm a bit nervous. Sleepy as hell, to be honest. Didn't sleep very much."

"Me neither, I'm afraid," Cesar said smartly.

"All that brightness, right? What's that about?"

"It's strange, indeed," nodded the poet. "But that's not why. I was with my boyfriend last night."

Neipas eyed him humorously. "You went home?"

"No no; he works here. He got me the job, actually."

"Oh. He did?"

The poet licked the thin furry mustache on his ox semblance.

"I'm invariously weird after a night not sleeping. And I'm often in a bad mood, except when it was a full night of good sex."

"Mary — TMI, no?"

"Not really. I didn't tell you the details yet."

"I'm good, thanks," Neipas laughed.

The both of them walked through the scanner's flash and between the row of giant armed bulls, and rushed along into the Eagles' Kitchen, where the janitors were in a frenzy of water and soap and the cooks frantic in their pace of activity; fire and heat alighted their clay masks of oxen, from their hands ensued an unbridled chorus of metal and glass banging. Drrawetz was already there, marching pompously through the stations with toes kicking the air about his breast, supervising here, supervising there, tasting dishes, and dispensing non-sequitur instructions all over. The Chef, a mellow, passive big hat, paced behind him languidly and nodded vaguely as he passed by the cooks and inspected their pots.

Breakfast dishes weren't yet ready so the waiters had to wait; the tail of the cattle line was still being processed through the scanners, and meanwhile they stood.

Neipas took the opportunity to avail himself of coffee. He stood swaying by the machine as the foaming liquid slurped itself into the plastic cup. Sugar was cascaded in; the wooden stick mixed it in. Neipas wavered a little... The Museum's dreamworld had left a vestige — it filled his head full of thoughts. He stared deep into the circling steaming flow inside the plastic cup. Tightening his breathing, he observed the coffee as it whirled into itself, like a galaxy revolving in a cosmic sea. A strange wandering of mind took him to imagine the frothy center as the Milky Way, and himself minuscule inside it, rotating along.

Neipas started. "I'm going to use the restroom, be right back," said suddenly Cesar, who apparently had been standing right next to him immersed in his own thoughts.

One sip of the hot drink made his senses squeeze themselves awake again. He pulled up against the weight of the bell and breathed in harshly all the sounds, swallowed and smacked. A sort of lethargic rejuvenation spread through his body and made his face widen with new alertness.

Yet this would not last. The cumulative toll of those many sleepless nights was well ingrained in him; he hadn't yet had time to recover, and coffee was of little help. At one point Drrawetz called all the waiters in and intoned some sort of speech — "...the cutlery, darlings, must be set upon the table with exact precision..." — which Neipas could barely understand. Already the caffeine's effects were beginning to wear off and the steward's words swam in his mind like an incantation, distilling soporific in his veins; only the latent threat in the sugar-coated timbre of the voice kept poor Neipas at alert, with irritated eyes wide open — "...this is very important, dears..." and Neipas, feeling the financial precariousness of his life storming within, sharpened his ear and heart to a strain to break through the muscular arms of drowsiness trying to subdue him to the floor.

"Decorum, dears! Be on standby, if you please... We shall be leaving any minute now! — " with this last impassioned shout Neipas jolted, wondering if he had slept and all was lost. But Drrawetz had taken his temporary leave to supervise the proceedings alongside the bobbing chef hat; and Neipas shook his head, mumbling "Mary", and inhaled harshly the fumes of the kitchen in an attempt to wake up fully.

Turning his head, he noticed Osir the scarred janitor approaching with a cautious gait.

"So you're a waiter now, huh?" said he through the lobbed corner of his lip.

"Guess so," said Neipas, shrugging, trying to hold on to his concentration to keep awake.

"Just came from one of those rooms with all that cash. S'pose that's where you're heading," Osir said.

Silence.

"Hell," commented Osir, and then asked: "What's wrong?" "Nothing."

"You look like you're spasming out." "What?"

"I can see your eyes flaring from a mile away." Neipas flexed his jaw from side to side unconsciously.

"Just kinda tired," Neipas mumbled after a while, finding no better words to describe the silent and wavering tempest assailing him.

"Coffee not cutting it?" — moving his sight to the very corner of his eyes, Neipas seemed to glimpse Osir's outstretched arm.

"Here man. I got you," Osir muttered, all confidential.

"What?" Neipas asked, meeting Osir's hand and taking it in his own, more out of vexation than anything; a small thing exchanged their hands, dropping very lightly onto Neipas' palm.

"Just take it. Trust me."

"Hm?"

"'Ts just a pill. Good stuff. Jolt you right up."

Neipas stared at him with a wondering grimace.

"Don't worry. Free of charge."

"I dunno..." Neipas said dubiously. The veteran and janitor, his scar, scared him a little sometimes.

Osir bobbed his head and placed his hand on his shoulder with familiarity. "Fine, fine... If you feel drowsy though, take it. It's completely harmless."

Meanwhile Cesar came near and he introduced himself to Osir with a flicker of his pointy mustache. But just then a great uproar ensued and once again the waiters were ushered on; with a mechanized quickness they picked up the trays lying unending on the long counter and fell back into line.

"Ready!" clamored Mister Drrawetz, scampering frantic to the head of the line. "*Marche!* Decorum!"

Again they trekked the palatial grounds of the Eagles' hallways, filled with such riches as Neipas' spasming eyes were unable to process, yet his spirit still awed at. His heart pulsed with their lockstep. And again, after a procession of chambers and halls filled with every decor of opulence, the cattle heads emerged into intimate red rooms adorned with game tables, cavernous spaces moodily lit, fitted with exuberant aquariums and sumptuous statues, shaded treasures at every corner — but in these shades now moved silhouettes, sinister forms glinting with dark sunny shimmers. Scents of expensive tobacco suffused the casino air, and through it played music. Neipas turned his head very slowly.

It was the music — the music he had heard flowing from underneath the Golden Dove. And he saw, beneath the warm light of sconces, the band.

Their faces were obscured in the elegant dimness. Their very instruments blended with their silhouetted limbs, emerged from them, made with their body one shadowy fabric; it looked, to the eye gliding among those shadows, as if the melody were sung out of the esoteric motions of their shadow-bodies. The clearer figure was that of the conductor before them, who flapped his arms graciously, flowing in ascents and descents across the air, like mystical wings. But he faced away from the marching cattle; and Neipas could not see his face.

Golden beaks glinted over the tables; pure white feathers ruffled over immaculate suits, all glimmering in the opulent ember of cigars. The cattle walked among Eagles in the highs... (Neipas strained with frightened breathing). Peacock feathers and their myriad iridescent eyes sparkled in the shadow, staring gloriously, powerful, from everywhere. Standing alongside the tables, walking from place to place, models with masks of swan emerged from titillating bodies atop naked legs, standing atop tall heels, towering over the lowered horns of the passing waiters; which were being quietly spread out across different chambers, multiplying from one to the other in labyrinthic fashion. These chambers were connected by a series of great revolving doors draped in mirror, through which the world's most prestigious reporters, its most influential diplomats, its most powerful magnates and decision-makers dallied with each other from side to side in intimate discussions.

Neipas was ushered forth into the extremities of this complex, emptying out along with a smaller group into the vast hall where the windows to the gardens arose; where, only two days prior, he had seen an enormous quantity of wealth in the form of paper notes scattered about the floor like trash. It was, as were the preceding chambers, dimly lit. Immense statues lifted, dark and sinister, over the tables where Eagles and Peacocks gambled. Out of the cornucopias (which were the shapes of the statues' mouths) flushed money, it seemed to Neipas in a curious hallucinatory fit; yet the mood was grave in this early hour of morning. Outside the immense windows stretched the splendor of the Eagle Gardens, glowing softly in its multicolored lamps. The westward waterfall flowed just beyond the towering glass, majestic and soundless. Its stream led to a bright infinity pool at the edge of the Gardens, which extended into a vertiginous drop toward the megalopolis, lying at the brink of a slowly flowering purple dawn.

The waiters were lining up a few steps from the tables, rearing orderly behind the Eagles, the Peacocks, and the Swans. Their march had ended.

"What are we supposed to do?" as they fell into position Neipas whispered to his side, struggling in the dimming intensity of his senses.

Cesar, who was still next to him, responded: "I think we are just supposed to stand still till we're called."

Stand they did, waiting over the specter of those mighty shapes moving in the thin darkness. Over yonder, in a corner secluded under the foot of a statue, limbs writhed and danced phantasmagorically, and from the thicker blackness of such motions ensued the same melodies as the waiters had been suffused with. At their head Neipas thought he discerned the Conductor, with his undulating arms gracious — beyond him, the band — and he wondered in a wild rumination whether they weren't the very same musicians he had seen time and again in every chamber they passed on their way here. He looked out the window.

"What time is it?"

"Not yet 5:30 when we left," said Cesar.

"...but how do they wake up so early?"

The poet leaned in; and secreted: "Some say they never sleep."

Suddenly the bell rang under Neipas' chin. Here and there bells scintillated and legs marched onward. Neipas abruptly stood very straight.

"Milkshake to the Nations Minister, table to your left," said the voice in his ear.

Neipas sprang forward, eying the motions of the horned silhouettes aside him and imitating them nervously. The cryptic lighting of the hall and the smell of cigars only pulled him down further into the neurosis of sleeplessness, the vague dreamworld of toxin scents he entered through the Museum.

Stepping close to those tables, however, felt to him like gliding from one dream into another dream. Neipas was affected by a stronger sense of unreality, derived from seeing, through his eyes and without filter, the faces of so many famous personalities, ones he had seen time and time again on television, on his *I*, on the facades of buildings, in posters, billboards, the big screens. It was always a breach of dimension to see personifications of fame, an uncanny rip through reality to witness in the flesh someone who had always been confined to the omnipresence of screens; as though witnessing an abstract deity come alive, come from another world.

But to see so many of these at once put Neipas positively off balance — right away he recognized the masks of two politicians who made regular appearances in News Channels as among the most prominent objectors to President Arnold's rule and which, Neipas believed, were members of the House of Law, Columbia's Parliament; and with but a slight tilt of the head he saw the Mayor of Axiac sitting close to them — the famous Mayor, whose slick Eagle mask Neipas had seen multiplied across the megalopolis' facades so many times; Reckuz himself, writer of the Book of Masks, and Moloch the Media Mogul lounged abreast, a little farther; and here the omnipresent Nations Minister with his abundant mustache sprouting in bushes above the beak, along with a few more suits, some faintly recognizable.

Neipas felt apprehensive before the eminence of such personages; but the immediacy of duty made him swallow down any sentiment perturbing his focus and stem the nervousness. He stepped fully into the mask again, regaining his presence; and stooped down gently before the assortment of mighty characters, placing delicately the exuberant glass of milkshake with the loopy straw upon the table (he had identified the milkshake among the plethora of other things atop the tray as he walked) next to the Minister, who was speaking:

"First thing we do, Jane, is, we ditch the agreement! And if they have the gall to react, we bomb'em! What other option do we gat?" spoke the Minister with little hops of the shoulder.

"No doubt, they are enemies of Columbia," said Jane the Legislator. "But that would be a slippery slope, Minister."

"Well we can't have Persia get their hands on nuclear power now, can we? Admit it, the agreement is too weak! Whenever did diplomacy with mad folk ever solve something."

"I think it's a good agreement," said the Legislator in a very reflective manner, with her finger scratching her chin.

"Jane," said the marvelously flourished Peacock across the table, draped in colorful coats of iridescent eyes, as she sweetly extended her hand to the Legislator. "It's the best for our country."

"Jane — indeed," added the gent next to her, who wore the peacock tail down his chest as a very fluffy tie. "Only think of the energy opportunities which would come from it. Don't we want energy independence for our country?"

Neipas did not know it yet — but he would come to learn that the first Peacock who had spoken was a lobbyist for ArmsCore, the nation's foremost weapons manufacturer, and the gent who followed a representative of NoxxeSocony, the most powerful energy company globally, which owned, among many other assets, the refinery at Iblis. Jane, the Legislator, was one of the leaders of the Liberals — as they were called in those days — in the House of Law, and the Nations Minister was responsible for foreign affairs in Arnold's government. The milkshake sat unexplainably undrunk next to him still, and at this moment Neipas, who was preparing to step away, noticed the Minister leering at him impatiently.

"Well?" the Minister suddenly flinched with much grumpiness, nearly bursting off the chair.

Neipas looked about confusedly and with a growing panic. What had he missed? He was hesitant to ask the Eagles — his eye caught Cesar's shape gesticulating, pointing from his face to the mess of straws wiring up from his tray; then suddenly:

"Put the straw in the Minister's mouth!" — yelled the eartag.

"My apologies your Excellency, apologies — " pulling himself together, Neipas pinched the straw with his white gloves and inserted it gently in the Minister's rotund golden beak. He felt, under the felt texture, the stream of milky sludge flowing between his fingers as it was ravenously slurped by the Minister's wet lips into his cackling gullet.

The milkshake was absorbed at once. Neipas hurriedly placed it back on the tray and took his leave as the Minister shooed him away with his hand.

"Anyway Jane," he continued. "We don't need your approval on this 'cause we hold majority in the Law House. But we could use your support nonetheless. Just letting you know 'cause we're friends anyway."

"Minister, I value our friendship..."

Neipas stepped away shaken, beating himself internally over the mess-up, and slid back in line next to Cesar.

"Shit," Neipas whispered.

"It's ok," Cesar said. "Just take it easy."

His bell rang and he sprung forth. Neipas was left alone in fear; he was afraid his slight would have consequences, that in this ambience of extreme expectations, it would cost him the job. In growing tension his mind harked back to the stress of debts constantly throbbing in his consciousness. This job was the only way out. Slying his glance to the yonder shadows he thought he saw the Collector spying upon him, and his heart fluttered anxious. His muscles spasmed and tightened, he drew in his chapped lips in growing angst, feeling his breast arising in thumps upward his throat; he remembered Osir's pill, still in his pocket. For a moment he becalmed in the anticipation of his decision. Abandoning any apprehension about the pill's effects, he sneaked his hand into his hips; smoothly, he raised his hand to his lip, and passing his palm down the lower half of his countenance, in the manner of one feeling his beard pensively, he snuck the pill into his mouth and swallowed it in one gulp. The change was nearly instantaneous.

Suddenly Neipas was much more awake. His mind, which had been struggling to keep from shrinking into the sleeping recesses of the soul, expanded rapidly outward and made him aware of everything at once; but not overwhelmingly, for his thoughts became calm, firm, steady; from one moment to the next he was able to perceive every involuntary stir in his muscles, he could pick out every subtlety of scent in the fragrant breezes twirling above the many plates of breakfast fuming their respective aromas, he could even track the minute progress of the sunlight as it inched away from the depth of the horizons beyond the eastern mounts, quiet behind him. His listening, deafened almost completely by the stresses of the job — stresses relentlessly consuming his attention — sharpened now to the point of perfection; his ears could distinguish every variation of pitch, and the stresses dissipated.

He inhaled deeply, with languid relief.

"Are you ok?" whispered Cesar, just returning.

"Hm-hm — yeah..."

He noticed the vapors rising slowly from the beautiful hanging gardens beneath the tall windows, and even through the glass he sensed their infusion of incense and the reverent character of their flight. His eyes drew away the peels of darkness in the slowly growing daylight. He discerned the bulls standing invisibly among the tables, still and heavy of muscle. He saw how one of them, standing yonder on the other side of the space, wore a nose-ring from which pended two keys; and he saw others with similar nose-rings, poised discreetly in the gloomy clearings, yet thick. Swan concubines lifted themselves arousingly among voluminous white feathers, drifting with haughty, tantalizing eyes, glinting in the suggestive shade.

He gazed, for the first time, the Eagles near. He saw the golden brilliance of their beaks, reminiscent of the sculpture of the Golden Dove itself; the pristine whiteness of their plumage, stately and distinguished; beneath the gleaming feathers, motionless and grave, their masks were made of cold clay, which they could still mold at will, which never slipped out of their control. Peacocks sat confidently among them, their individual masks replicated, at times, across the tables; as though shelled clones hovered about the hall.

The conversations between these eminent personages at the tables progressed in the heated pace of high-stake negotiations. Words exchanged above the glasses, amid delicate slurping, were spoken in good sound but somewhat subdued timbre, infusing the hall with intimate tones. The Mayor's table stood closest. With him sat his adviser, also referred to as his Right Wing; and his counselor, known as his Left Wing. With them was a Lobbyist — Neipas thought he had seen him at the Nations Minister's table, for the mask looked the same — representing NoxxeSocony. There was a Lawmaker who legislated in the House of Law, and who was a known face sometimes seen beyond glass screens. Sitting at that table were also a Corporate Lawyer and a Consultant, or a Numbers-Bird as they were named, and a PR Specialist or Spin Doctor. Finally, across from the Mayor and the Legislator was the Minister of the Environment, a politician named Salas, whose mask was faintly familiar to Neipas. To him, however, the Mayor's voice stood out among the rest because it was so recognizable. He was interested in their exchange on account of him. Neipas' ears cut through all distractions; they could discern the voices ringing through the band's melody, and by degrees he managed to isolate the Mayor's words from the general hubbub; then those of the remaining patrons at the table. Twice or thrice he was called upon to serve at it — which he did serenely, splendidly, without mistakes, without even being noticed, thoroughly professional, perfectly invisible — and he picked out the Mayor's words more and more clearly by and by, and finally he listened to entire sentences without interruption, as if the good

Mayor was speaking to him directly...

"..., you see. So these fires really protect the city's interests. Part of it is city property and we can tax on logging activity there —"

"Excuse me, Mayor," interceded meekly the Mayor's counselor, or his Left Wing, a Peahen mask wrapped in silken veils, though her feathers and eyes were a little faded. "You would have no choice but to sell the wood on the cheap, sir, if that is your intention. It's all burnt lumber, after all. Not much leeway in terms of how much the city can make, unless you would have the city fund the exploitation yourself and..."

"Yes, yes, but colleagues, that's beside the point," interrupted the Mayor's adviser, or his Right Wing, who donned a Peacock face and suit with fiery, intense irises clothed all over his neck and tie. "We can earn enough from the exploitation to fund the firefighting for next year, I believe. But what's more important is that the fires cleared the land — unfortunately it's what happened — and as long as it happened, I think we should look at it as an opportunity. Just think of the folks who will be out of a job with the forest gone — we can give those folks jobs working for the pipeline construction, and then some."

"Agreed, Monah," said the Lobbyist. Neipas confirmed that it was the same Lobbyist — or a different Lobbyist wearing the same mask — as the one in the Nations Minister's table, with the fluffy Peacock tie. "I think it would turn out well with voters, Mayor. NoxxeSocony could help expedite exploitation on the lumber."

"Surely you don't suggest the pipeline should pass through the Municipal Forest," the Mayor's Left Wing put in very quickly.

"Well, but just think of the many more miles of pipes that would be needed if we were to go around," the Mayor commented humorously.

"And just think, with the funds we would save, we could help invest in reforestation," commented Noxxe's Lobbyist.

A round of nodding circulated the circular game table, whence, among the cards and chips, piles of banknotes only seemed to grow. From the center of the table swirled ornate cornucopias, from the gapes of which blurted, little by little, such moneys, with which they played distractedly as if they were hand-wipes. Behind them, concubines flared white with their swan feathers, holding plumed flabella with which they swayed onward the still air.

Only after a short span of silence, among the general murmur and the melody, was a voice hesitantly risen:

"But the pipeline would have to go through the Oyate reserve first, in that case?" said timorously the Left Wing, and before anyone could interrupt she added speedily: "Mayor, there is a lot of public opposition to this at the moment, I dunno if —"

"Now hold on, Jonah —" the Right Wing spoke over the Left across the Mayor.

"Wasn't Noxxe considering building behind the river source?" gasped the Left Wing still in the same breath, appealing to the table.

At this the Lobbyist leaned in calmly, and the mere strength of his presence seemed to stem the Left Wing's exaltations for the minute. "Not necessarily," he interjected with all tranquility, and Neipas, piercing in his glare, noticed that his aspect had changed somehow. Over the fluffy tie sagged now, developing from his two cheeks, two faded wattles that weren't there before. It reminded Neipas of something. He wondered if it was the same lobbyist; though the mask had shifted a little the voice was still the same, and the chair was also the same.

"There's a way," the Lobbyist continued. "The pipeline could go through farmland owned by Penaguiar, my client. They are still open to the possibility as long as certain arrangements are made, as we've discussed in previous occasions. It should please the Oyate, too, since it wouldn't have to go through their reserve anymore."

Neipas, in his aloofness of mind, remembered that name: Oshana had mentioned it before. Penaguiar was the agribusiness conglomerate who owned land bordering the reserve's.

"Exactly," burst in Salas the Minister of the Environment, who spoke now for the first time. The whole time he had been sucking on a convoluted plastic straw descending from a tremendously tall vase; the waiter next to him, who had been bending over him the while, returned now to line-up, bearing the empty vessel. "Once the pipeline passes the farmland, we could hook it up to the pipes behind the Park and we wouldn't have to bother the natives. I guess they consider the whole forest theirs — but what they consider theirs or not theirs is not our business, our business is the law and the land is ours under the law — but it would be a good compromise, I think. Mayor — you should sign the authorization. Let the pipeline go through the Municipal Forest."

The Mayor's Right Wing nodded. Yet at this point the Legislator butted in:

"But, dear colleagues. That solution has been proposed before, hasn't it? It would still cost more..."

"Not necessarily. Not compared to going up the mountain and behind the river. The numbers confirm this — is that correct?" asked the Lobbyist, whose wattles had meanwhile retreated somehow.

Everyone turned to the Consultant, or Noxxe's Numbers-Bird, who had not yet spoken. He had been sitting next to the Corporate Lawyer, who had been looking here and there, eliciting translations from the Consultant because he didn't really comprehend anything; he had for so long been immersed in the business of legal documents and press releases, and was so fully dedicated to his profession that he had forgotten regular human speech. The Numbers-Bird, however, had basic proficiency in both languages, as most in that table did.

Said the Consultant, interlocking his fingers atop the table sagely, "We reworked the numbers. From the studies we have made, the savings involved in construction would be substantial, not to mention maintenance; not just in terms of pipe length, but also the differences in terrain. It makes sense. It's a much more cost-effective solution."

And, turning to the Lawyer, who strained his ear with some effort, he said: "Cost-effective alternatives compel NoxxeSocony (hereby referred to as "the interested party"), concerning the interested party's Iblis Petroleum Pipeline (IPP) project, to seek equivalent routes in pursuance of the interested party's fiduciary duty in the area of fiscal management."

The Corporate Lawyer, nodding, said: "Ah."

The Legislator in turn, juggling with the soundness of those arguments, responded hesitantly, "Well, good as that may be, the Oyate are still opposed to it. They will fight it," and turning to the Mayor — "My constituents are partial to this, Don. This could be another controversy."

"Why? If the pipeline goes through the farmlands it'll be downstream from the reserve. What can they say?"

"Well, Don," explained John the Legislator, "apparently they depend on salmon, and the salmon swim upstream. These fish have some kind of religious significance to them too, it looks like."

"Salmon?! God's sake," the Mayor exclaimed in amused shock. "How do you even know this, John?"

"I was briefed on it yesterday after those protests in my district. I went there yesterday, Mayor. The voters apparently do not like me very much. I even told them I was opposed to the pipeline and the refinery expansion but somehow I get the feeling they don't believe me."

"Why not?" asked incredulously the Mayor's Right Wing.

Neipas, who was by the table at that point, with his fingers lightly nipping the bulbous straw pumping juice into the Minister's beak, caught with his acute ear the Mayor's Left Wing muttering: "'cause it's not true."

"I'm not sure," rejoined John the Lawmaker. "Maybe it's my primary challenger. She's been saying things and I'm starting to feel annoyed."

"That girl?"

"Yes, that —" the Legislator rubbed his white feathers. "Can't remember her name for the life of me, but it's something ethnic."

"Oh please, John," mumbled forcefully Salas the Environmental Minister, with his beak still clutching the straw.

"Sir, if I may," butted in the Consultant, or Numbers-Bird. "Polls are giving you a landslide."

"And you've been in office for decades!" babbled the Minister.

"But this is the first challenge I have, you see. I'm a little... Don —" John the Lawmaker turned to him. "Her winning could be bad for you, since she is critical of you as well."

"Of me? Why?"

"Well — she claims you are not honest."

"Me! But I'm saying all the right things," the Mayor drew aback in bemusement, and looked for validation first from his Right Wing, who nodded encouragingly; and then to his Left, who waved her head from side to side timidly:

"Sir, if I may... It may be because your recent stances do not exactly match your record."

The Eagle's enormously open eyes stared confusedly, blinking with bright amber.

"And?" asked the Mayor.

"All I'm saying, dear colleagues," John the Legislator again interceded. "Could we possibly hold this off until the next election?"

The Lobbyist was swift: "I'm afraid that would not be possible."

"The election is almost a year away, John!" burbled Salas the Minister through his straw.

"But — Don," insisted the Legislator in his fear, holding the Mayor's hand. "This could trigger another controversy with the Oyate, as well as a protracted legal battle. It could bounce back to us both."

The Mayor's Left Wing seized this opportunity, holding the Mayor's other (left) hand: "Mayor, a drawn legal fight could have repercussions that we might not be able to control. What if constituents accuse you of putting the river in danger? Think of what it might do to PR! We might lose control of the story."

The faded Peahen was so forceful in her outburst that all others were quietened for the while. The Mayor thought it out, slicking back his immaculate hair of plume. All stares were fixed wide upon the crucial decision-maker, whose deliberations held the fate of the pipeline's final route in the balance. Their silence thickened — until the Mayor cut through it, saying:

"That's a good point."

There was a sudden, palpable sense of panic as favor began to tilt toward John the Lawmaker, who had begun to fear for his re-election prospects, and the Mayor's Left Wing, who had begun to fear for the Mayor's. The Lobbyist, the Minister, and the Mayor's Right Wing all looked at each other with feathers on end and golden beaks twisting, distressed at this latest turn. The Consultant whispered translations to the Lawyer.

But then the Lobbyist dealt an unexpected blow: "Mayor... I don't wish to make this unpleasant. But as you know, not approving the pipeline route here could affect NoxxeSocony's revenues. Or even Penaguiar's. They would have grounds for legal action against the Municipality."

A quietude flowed back among them in the form of speechless melody. The Mayor deliberated once more, nodding and slicking his plumage; then said:

"That's also a good point."

"But Mayor!" supplicated his Left Wing. "Is — Is that even possible? Is that legal?" she asked sheepishly.

All masks turned to the Corporate Lawyer. A great tension amassed between them as the Numbers-Bird translated the question; after which, the Lawyer spoke in these terms:

"Pursuant to article 26 subparagraph (2)(c) and paragraph (3) of the ECT of 1991, the claim may be construed as truthful and possessive of sound legal validity."

Everyone nodded in understanding.

The PR Specialist, or Spin Doctor as he was often called, had been listening attentively all the while, cunning, magicking strategies inside his mind. He hadn't spoken thus far, waiting for the right moment; but he said now in a wisely tone: "Just lie for now. If you create the perception that this is out of your hands and reaffirm your commitment to environmental causes, you can minimize the damage. There's only so much that girl can do with so little name recognition. Same for you, John. Plus — the polls do give you the victory."

John the Lawmaker, thinking a little, said, "That's a good point."

"And Penaguiar would be ok with the pipeline going through their farmland?" asked the Mayor's Left Wing, defeated.

The Lobbyist, whose wattles grew back now, responded: "As long as permission comes from the State and Municipality, discussions can begin between Noxxe and Aguiar."

Then the Environmental Minister made a final shove: "The federal government's on board. Come on, Mayor. Let's just get to brass tacks here. Look — the pipeline will bring in a lotta money. What else is there to know?"

The Mayor shrugged, smiling.

"That's a good point. I'll sign it, why not. It'll be ok Jonah, relax," said the Mayor to his Left Wing, who looked even more faded now, as he petted the backside of her hand.

"Very well," sprung the Right Wing decisively. "My thinking is we read over the bill and get acquainted with the particulars. It seems to me, though, that if it includes some provision for funding reforestation, I can't see it do much harm. The removal of Municipal Forest status and protections will have to be limited to the specific areas where the pipeline is planned to go through, too; that's important. We want to minimize backlash."

"As for the federal subsidies for the construction, we can wait to place those in the federal budget next month. I'll send the clause over to you, John," said the Lobbyist, who had ghost-written the bill himself.

The Minister of the Environment noisily concluded the slurping of his beverage. "Good work, fellas. We have no other way but to go forward on this. This'll be good for the Economy. And where else would we find the money to grow back those trees?"

The Eagles finished their main courses, and the lavish desserts, prepared by the cooks through hours of elaborate crafting, were served with much pomp as the main culinary attraction of the gathering. Business talk was suspended to comment on the rich variations of chocolate, berry, caramel, candy, and whatever else had been requested and their combinations, which the Eagles devoured straight into their mostly rotund bellies with a gluttonous appetite. The sun broke free from the mountains and the hall burst in light. The bells of the summit tolled. The smack of the Eagles' spit, squirting from their open, chewing beaks, gleamed under the pendants of bright gold dangling from the tall ceiling.

Neipas, appeased in the strength of regained tranquility, simply stood by with a dull smile in the concealed lips of his dormant brain, caring for nothing at the moment, basking languidly in the vibrancy of ostentatious wealth, in the joys and comforts of power, in the warmth of its proximity.

He watched the Eagles eat contentedly.

The night's gloom was again gathering when Neipas left the Belab. All the patrons had left the hall of game tables and the cleaning crew was entering in lazy drips the moment Osir shook him awake. He had fallen halfway into an uneasy doze behind one of the bars of those interminable red rooms in which he somehow now found himself. Seeing Osir so close so suddenly, Neipas at first pulled back, disoriented. Osir's mask looked terrible. His scar palpitated in along the length of its fleshy seam, as though boiling; and his eyes looked vacant, shaded behind a glassy screen, abstracted.

Then he buoyed from sleep on a panicky sense of breathlessness back into a full sense of himself. His head throbbed painfully in the surface, but even worse than that was the sinister, scary pulses inside his chest. It took Neipas a long time hanging onto himself before he recovered. By that time, Osir had disappeared.

Neipas had been serving in the game hall by the tall windows most of the morning, until the vapors of incense outside, rising from the lower level of the Gardens, fogged the view completely. Earlier the chef had come in and been received by applause. There had been a screech of waking children from the upper floors: some of the Eagles' sons and daughters ran to devour sweets served across the lower terrace, playing with balloons by the infinity pool and the regal hedges.

When the incense had amassed onto the glass windows, Drrawetz made his entrance and announced triumphantly that the fights were about to begin; at this everyone stormed into the inner corridors in a colorful parade of sunlight, some of the Eagles carried in litters upon oxen shoulders, their golden hooks bobbing with sparkle and glimmer in the heights, all followed by a consort of tall swans and weighty bulls, and poised peacocks dragging enormous tails full of shiny purples. Cesar, along with a few others, was taken along.

Neipas, knowing not what to do, remained still — until supervisors came to fetch those who hadn't gone with the entourage, and made them work across the smaller red casino chambers; though he couldn't remember that very well anymore.

The sky assumed reddish brown hues as the sun fell asleep under the dark sea, as Axiac's lamplights ballooned onto the opaque dome of tinged cloud. It drizzled thickly. At first Neipas thought it was but the Anubel's waterfalls sporing across; and the clouds, he thought in his dizziness, were the incense grown all over Axiac. In the train, Neipas felt the pill's effects thinning out, draining his energy and brain as they discharged out of his sweat beads, as the train's metal frame rattled tortuously upon the tracks. His head swirled so much that it dizzied his every organ, emptied them out, swooned his circuits... The things he had seen, the things he had heard in the Eagles' Nest flashed together in his head: the Golden Dove, the Museum, the Giant, the Midget, the Money; the Eagles' shady talk, the meaning of which was barely beginning to sink through. The brunt of it all only now was beginning to be felt. He looked vertiginously out the window, upon the Pearl shining misty through the wet air; he looked at it like a castaway beneath the sea, and breathed soundlessly through his muttering lip, wondering repeatedly what on earth was going on.

In the delirium, he concluded he was still reeling from the effects of sleeplessness. The nightshift, the debts, the stress of the interview, this gig, had all come so fast and so merciless... Neipas had exerted himself to the verge of a breakdown — and promised himself a few days off as soon as he got paid. Orenda had sent him a message:

ORENDA: We're all camping out on the south shore forest. Three days.
ORENDA: Do you want to come?

Already his back was on the mattress when he saw this, and immediately he decided a few days in nature would do him good. The back of his head descended toward it then; it landed upon the cushion (and it was as if his whole body also did again) as though it had dropped from the top of a chasm as tall as the Eagles' Nest.

His mind violently dove to oblivion.

24 - Oshana on Earth and the New Ideal

The cloud developed unending in muscular hillocks, whose rolling peaks faced downward, hovering broodingly over the shanties, sprouting rain upon the leaky roofs which spread from beneath the highway in various stages of decay. Droplets patted the car windows, filling the upholstered box with warmth and solemnity. Little Martin lounged quietly in the back seat, hypnotized by the glimmer of his *I*. Edazima steered the wheel wordlessly. At her side, Neipas said nothing and merely observed the panning succession of roofs, behind which loomed, all along the highway, the spires of the chemical plants and refineries, sanctums of the age. They rolled now over the river, a course of waters faded, which emptied darkly into the tar-stranded ocean yonder. Inside the car the silence was only dispersed, gently, by the occasional sound of the windshield wiper and the constant pecking drops. The coming of the rains to this land long parched affected the habitual postures and masks of its denizens: Some pigeons perched under the windowsills and tucked into their plumes, waiting till it was over. But others few, from among the children and those they called mad, spread their arms like wings and let their feathers bristle and bathe joyful. The streets were covered with snails, slugs, and winged insects with enormous legs, the type of bugs that seem to materialize out of fresh rain, latching on to every surface; the very tar of the roads glistened humidly, shining the red lights of the cars rolling upon it; and all was enveloped in a wet haze.

Neipas saw his reflection in the wing mirror clearly enough. His cheek leaned onto his fist, and his eyes peered deep into the wet glass, contemplating his mask. He looked horrible. His skin drooped in folds — particularly under his eye, where the wax collapsed into a million wrinkles; further down it hung from the jaw in a most decadent manner; and then his mouth, which gaped slightly into a black hole without teeth, and his bloodshot eyes, made him look as if he was a cadaver in the course of a perpetual yawn. He spent much of the time molding the form of his face; and sometimes, as he passed his fingers gently along his skin, he would abruptly wake up — and would have to start all over again.

"Everything all right back there sweetie?" Edazima said casually, looking in the rear-view mirror, tenderly breaching the silence.

"Yes, mom," muttered Martin's lifeless voice, infused with the lull of the *I*.

Edazima observed Neipas in his contemplation through the corner of her eye, perceiving his vague head blocking out the passing neighborhoods. She had respected his brooding mood with her silence for most of the ride. As they veered west toward the southern shores, a little peninsula forsaken beyond the monstrous agglomeration of metal and toxin cluttering the concrete shores of Axiac, the borderlands of the southeast came into view, with the massive ramparts of Wall Street conspicuous in the distance, straddled between the mountains and the sea. As Neipas turned his head to gaze yonder at those multiple, superimposed layers of fences, Edazima said to him quietly, "Everything all right?"

His mind was parted in multiple fragments, scattered in a blur. The most salient part of it thought of the Mayor. He had read in the Webwork a few articles about him. The quotes attributed to the Mayor heaped much praise upon the Oyate for being on the front-lines of the battle against climate change, and expressed regret at the damage the wildfires had wrought upon their lands. Adding to that, he reaffirmed his commitment to cutting carbon emissions through a complicated scheme which Neipas didn't really understand. Neipas, in his dozing reflections, was trying to square that with what he had listened in that meeting at the highest perch of Columbia. In his mind, the broadcast image of the self-proclaimed environmentalist bravely defying Arnold's reckless policies of tree-cutting and petroleum-guzzling battled the figure of the disinterested, slouching empty suit that he had seen and heard with his very eyes and ears. Orenda was right. And in but a few hours, he would announce to her what the Mayor would, in a few weeks, do quietly: approve the oil pipeline's passage through the Municipal Woods, and allow it to link up to the megalopolis' existing system of petro-ducts.

Neipas' heart sat heavy, confused, and vague. An elusive anguish assailed him.

"Hm-hm, yeah," he replied to Edazima, and returned his sight to the window.

Neipas' despondent manner concerned her. Edazima was hoping for a relaxing weekend in nature, perhaps even get her son keen on the outdoors (which she wasn't so enthusiastic about herself; but she thought it might do him some good, and that mattered most and above all to her). However, her tender attempts to coax the child into leaving his *I* at home proved fruitless, and now his listless slouching in the back seat made him look as boxed-in as if he had been in his bedroom; this, together with Neipas' cheerless temper, cast a bit of a damp on her prospects of a good time. The demeanor of the boys in the car was simply not very encouraging; and by and by she grew firmer in her belief that men were hopeless.

She passed her hand over her beak, twisting it to the side. Inhaling the interior air of the car, she breathed out the words, "I feel like I haven't seen rain in forever," trying to goad Neipas into some sort of dialogue.

"I guess... Long drought, huh? Read it's the longest ever in Axiac," said Neipas mutedly.

"So it's a good thing... Hey man, maybe it'll make the hippies take a shower, huh?"

Edazima snickered. She referred to those they would meet at the camp; though, lamentably, her attempt to infuse humor into the moribund ambiance didn't land. They descended back into the quietude of droplets and the wiper rubbing the glass for moments. Then Neipas, leaning against the window and the gloomy landscape, merely said, "They're not hippies."

Edazima twisted her beak further sideways, mumbling, "was just joking, jeez... God, I'm dying for a smoke..."

Rolling on silence a little more, Neipas said eventually, "You'll like them," and apologized to her, saying he was just feeling a little weird. Edazima, a very embodiment of friendship and compassion, told him not to worry; and they continued the conversation on and off, in passive mutters.

Meanwhile, the old decrepit houses devolved into huts of brick and tin strewn and disfigured alongside fissured tar paths. They began to see little plots fenced by tin boards and occupied by standing canes and little vegetables in their midst; beyond them the fields opened, the soil roared freed of concrete and widened out. These fields were mostly filled with pumpjacks, bobbing their heads tirelessly as though pleading to some deity for a fruitful harvest. The little plots of vegetables continued to pop up in their midst. The clouds parted, letting through the sun's rays which shone gloriously upon the sparkling dots of green; and the sky began to yawn from its gloomy slumber, wakening to the view of those ample grounds which had once housed endless orange groves and primeval woodlands before them. Then the pumpjacks began growing scarce by and by — and once they had cleared past the metal ostriches, as they cruised along the unhampered horizon, from which extended now but goldening dirt and lone trees, the silence was suddenly broken by a wail striking from their rear:

"Moooooooooom!"

The soundscape abruptly exploded and the car rang like a metal bull careening madly. Martin's cry pierced with such agony that Edazima, appalled, pressed her foot hard on the break. "What's wrong baby, what's wrong!" she lunged backward — "You all right!?"

Her gaze faced the image of her son pecking the *I* glass furious and helplessly.

"There's no Web here, mom!"

Edazima looked on flushed, confused.

"What?"

"There's no Web here!"

There followed a few minutes of back and forth, first coaxing and gentle, then frustrated and angry, between mother and child; and while they settled their generational differences Neipas went out the car to appreciate the prospect.

It was a fresh breeze gracing his naked cheek, ruffling his feathers gently as he leaned back upon his outstretched arms and stared up at the sky's mountainous clouds. There was a faint scent of saltwater in the gliding air, carried over from the sandy shore miles away still. The air was of a different sort here, uncluttered, free — of a sort, Neipas was conscious, he hadn't felt in a very long time. He hadn't been this far from Babylon since he first came to Axiac. Its towers rose in the far distance, shining the sunlight like beacons in the center of the vast basin, like oases in a tar desert. At the summit of it all the Pearl, crowning the Eagles' Nest, blazed solitary and remote. In less than a year, he would be back up there; though he did not know it yet.

Neipas entered the car at Edazima's urging. Her voice was much becalmed — she had sounded wrathful when Neipas stepped out — and tried to impart tranquility into her child, who wept in the back seat. "It's just one night sweetie, I promise it'll be fun..." And as they rolled forth Martin deescalated from his tantrum through various stages of infantile revolt. After several minutes he settled into a grudging half-quiet, protesting with much passive-aggressive pouting, fuming, and loud breathing over his crossed arms.

"There goes the quiet weekend, fuck's sake..." Edazima muttered. The consequent silence was punctured by sighs longing for a cigarette, every now and then. By nightfall she would have her cigarette, among the seclusion of a shaded grove; and Martin would have becalmed, and entered hesitantly and with a bit of fright into a world of new wonders which he had never experienced before.

*

Soon the road turned to gravel, and after getting lost among the unfamiliar paths, they finally entered the woods. Edazima parked the car at the end of the gravel road, where it widened into a clearing. Other vehicles slumbered there, in the dappled shade, where a pointy rock rose smooth, as if sculpted, from the core. They left the car and cast their gazes aloft. The glade was circled by huge trees, behind which were immense, steep stones, crags moist with lichen. The scene, deepening yonder into the shadow of the forest, punctured only by slender fingers of sunlight, bore all the dense mystery of rustic, primeval air. There was a sort of magical aura about it which affected Neipas immediately. The sunshine had meanwhile loosened further from its cloak of cloud, becoming suddenly very bright; the rustling canopies seemed to glow with a most ethereal shine. The smooth rock in the middle of the clearing marked the spot — they were where Orenda had indicated, there could be no doubt about it.

Recalling to mind her instructions, Neipas walked straight from the rock in the direction of the wood. Edazima and Martin followed him quietly. The soil gave in easily under their shoes, breaking at each step with a tender embrace. It hadn't quite turned to mud; the rains had but softened it. The Forest was supple and wild, satiated after these first rains. Foliage breathed strong and with relief. Trees arose gloriously upon wet trunks, which seemed to heave at each of their steps, as if inhaling the gathering breeze. Their canopies pleached, like a congregation of devotees singing in whispers, with joined hands, in an immense cathedral; a cathedral submerged in the aerial calm of spores.

As they went forth their steps were slowed with hesitation. They stopped, discerning multiple trails between the trees. Standing in the clearing and leaning against the fragrances Neipas realized, suddenly, how long it had really been, since he had truly felt the wind.

"What now?" asked Edazima, holding her son's hand. She spoke very quietly, as if wary to violate the majesty of the sylvan hush, the murmured song of the wood.

Martin said meekly that he thought he heard water. They went in the direction his little finger pointed to, step by step under glimmering sunlight, as the forest enclosed them with its shade ever closer... and as the strong trunks coalesced behind them, sighing leaves from their boughs, the air thickened with an embrace of feral aromas, scents of pine and flower hovering quiet in the stillness of a deepening charm. Breathing soothly all around them was wonder: a verdure eying them with blossoms, a somber wilderness whose trees Neipas had once known and loved, and whose names he'd long forgotten. All rested in slow and divine anonymity; everything seemed to be at peace under the shadow of the canopies, wherein only some dabs of light danced when the gentle breeze came to rustle the leaves above. It was a peace so disarming that they were again compelled to halt their march... The sound of their steps fading into the ether, a complete silence fell upon the wood — and from it again emerged, slowly, the wind's solemn lullaby, whispering through the nooks of the forest; then the chirping of birds twinkling the atmosphere with a joy of sapience and youth; and the sparkling sound of a stream, penetrating the tranquil shade from afar; all the sighed notes of the poems of the wind, humming secrets undecipherable and a wisdom that cannot be known.

Orenda had told him of a brook — that they ought to follow its course to find the meeting place. So they sharpened their ears and, continuing along the trail, tried to keep the sound of its running water within range. Eventually the path wound down into a slope and bent toward the sound. Then they glimpsed the brook crossing the path yonder, down through the towers of open air between the trunks. The stream grew louder as it ran downslope and neared; until the trail merged with its bank, continuing alongside it. They walked the course, observing the water glistening with sparks of sun in the solitude of shuttered foliage. It was a beautiful thing — a very spiritual thing, too, to consider the beauty in the hovering flight of fireflies over the stream, which in the tightness of his apartment Neipas would perhaps have found repulsing and alarming; here, in the calm of nature, even the multilegged scurrying of beetles acquired a noble character, and Neipas felt respect and even awe for all the life pervading the living flora. Here, everything was sacred.

The brook ceded into a single cascade, diving between walls of protruding rock and into a pond in a clearing full of undergrowth. The trail carried steeply down the little cliff and ended here. There was no one so they stopped, unsure about where to go next. Neipas' glance rested on the cascade, mesmerized by its spark; behind it, a languid mind, tired from the inhuman grind of restless weeks. His body, too, seemed to be soothed by the forest, and wanted to lie down in the ferns to sleep. Instead he sat by the little lake, forgetting himself and the others for a while. He stared at the rocks and the vines sprouting from the gaps. He saw they were very old; they were blocky, they had been quarried and chiseled. Unintelligible, ancient inscriptions marked the surface. It was some sort of ruin.

Edazima took a photograph quietly. Then, turning to Neipas, she asked again, "What now?"

Dominating the soundscape was the waterfall splashing onto the pond, and it was difficult to hear through it. Neipas looked about, he peeled his ears; but he sensed nothing. "I'm not sure... She said to follow the path. If it ends here... Must be around here, I guess."

Edazima began to sound a little worried. After a moment of silence she said, "but where? Wouldn't we at least hear something? It's a few people, right?"

Then, the child voiced suddenly — timorously, "I hear something..." The two adults turned to him. Martin was much calmer now, though he looked a little scared. He appeared to be in the grip of some invisible force; something unfamiliar. His little countenance was uncovered in the full vulnerability of innocence. With the mask being yet half-unformed, his face, barely touched by time, seemed expressive of a depth of human instinct yet unbound.

Edazima crouched by him.

"Which way, sweetie?"

He turned and pointed at the thickets enclosing the clearing. Edazima kissed her son's forehead; and they walked to the shrubs slowly, but even as they approached the edge the splashing pond was still loud upon their ears. Nevertheless, Neipas thought he could distinguish some stirrings in the sounds; something very faint, and still far away. He couldn't tell what it was — or whether it was anything — but a confidence bloomed in him that they should follow the murmur.

"I think Martin's right... Wanna try this way?"

The way was arduous to tread. They quickly became enmeshed in a knotty weave of branches. At almost every step their sleeves, flaps, or collars would get tangled with brittle twigs, and every motion would present a new profusion of exasperating obstacles shooting from every direction toward them. It was a stop-and-going full of dodging maneuvers; the progression being so slow as to instill a stealthy mood in them, and they did not speak. Strangely, and despite Edazima's angry semblance whenever she'd get snarled in the winding branches, they never considered turning back. The vague palpitation was becoming more distinct. It was the beat of a drum... As they stepped beyond the thick web of boughs and went along the path suddenly widened, ascended, and curved; suddenly they heard a horn puncturing the steady beat. The way penetrated gloriously under arching branches well above them, and as they paced its curve they heard the horn repeatedly, growing in intensity at each blow. They paced it for a long time, and it was as though the curve repeatedly wound out back into itself. Gradually they heard the sound of voices; soon they became very clear among the pounding drum and roaring horn, at which point they knew they were close and sped their march. Finally they heard a supreme heaving of water mass, titan — they felt the ocean, and walking the last bend, they found themselves there.

Emerging between two stately trees, which stood erect and imposing, more majestic than the richest pillars of the most opulent gates, they entered a breezy glade, glittering with the motions of a group of folk. The glade was ample and perfectly circular, rounded by an untamed alignment of wooden life, a welter of breathing leaf and bush. Beyond, yonder before them, the forest disappeared; opening vast to a glorious vision of the ocean waters under the cliffs.

The steady beat of drum spread mournfully into the tranquil air. Stepping into the space Neipas felt, almost instantly, something lift; as if the air had somehow become airier, lighter, livelier, more graceful yet. From among the gathering emerged a messy hair-bun, bobbing in their direction; and Neipas recognized Orenda coming toward them. In a moment she would meet

Martin and Edazima, who'd greet her suspiciously. The horn blared as Orenda waved her hand.

"Look who it is!" she said as she walked towards. The drum beat; Neipas, Edazima, and Martin dispersed into the group and were received with much welcome, much warmth. In the distance Neipas saw Edazima meeting Oshana, who curved to her in very respect; he wondered humorously about what Edazima's thoughts were on that cast of characters. As the drum beat marched its way through time, Neipas' ear became accustomed to it. Edazima fraternized with the group, and Martin mixed timidly into the play of the other children, who called to him again and again with much mirth.

Neipas traveled along, and the folk parted bread with him. He drank with them; and the mood in the glade was filled with merriment. The steady sound penetrated Neipas' mind, and his mind was slowly, imperceptibly, absorbed by it. It was, perhaps, that he was tired; but his eyes closed after he was already asleep under the cool of some shrub, and he did not notice himself falling into slumber — he would only realize it when his eyes parted to the starry sky.

Meanwhile his mind expanded into the universe. And its growth reached the farthest domains of outer space and the most remote stars, fueled by the steady beat.

At the limits of existence, he saw a mirror, darkly and without luster. And, transversing it, he made the journey over again.

The drum beat as it receded into the background — only the horn brought it forth again. It pulsed stronger in one push; then it stopped.

A bell sounded; the drums ceased through their scattered ringing, reverberating in almost hypnotic oscillations; and a silence spread. Neipas sat in the circle, enveloped fully in the growing absence of sound.

"Listen."

An ample halo of trees behind them rustled in the breeze. Out of the sway of leaves a mysterious whisper drifted, soothing the air. Afar rang a sound of tide, washing into the land and receding into a vastness unseen. And as the breath of wind evaporated, the sound of gliding water continued and expanded, subtly, and slowly its murmur filled Neipas' observing heart. He felt it seep into his very soul, furtively, and tranquil; and soon his spirit flowed and ebbed into the air with the gliding waters. For a moment it seemed as if the whole ocean and the entire air of the sky had leant over to him intimately, and had whispered unto him a secret. His breast stirred. A spasm moved the corner of his lip, and his closed eyes welled up.

"Open now," Orenda muttered, from somewhere in the long night.

And the sounds took shape. The ocean spread black into the prospect, ending inscrutably along the vast and mysterious horizon yonder. Over the farthest distance the moon stooped, circular and bright; it cast a motherly shimmer across the waters, and revealed the tranquil motion of pale ripples toward shore. A mystic aura permeated every sense. The firmament before his eyes was clear, full with stars, covering the infinitude of the universe with its transparent mantle. This his tranquil glance witnessed, as if it had been born in his sparkling eyes, in the moment its lids had parted to see.

A number of vague forms sat and watched the quiet spectacle in the dark. They had gathered here, in the clearings of the Southern Shore woods, to gaze the stars unimpeded. Far along the coast, the electric blaze of the megalopolis glared and blinded them to that side of the sky, so they faced the clear of the south far away from the tar-choked plains of Axiac.

An obscure length of time prolonged itself into the night, blending into the mystique of the black contours around them and the violet air, into the quietude of the wind and waves. In the calm shade Oshana took word, and spoke into the silence:

"A while ago now the herders, hunters and miners of men came and told us, 'you may no longer love the earth.'

"'The earth is a wild thing housing wild beasts. God our creator gave us such wild creatures to tame and command.

"'You too are wild beasts,' they told us. 'We shall tame you. We shall civilize and domesticate you, save you from the clutches of the earth and the demons lurking within.

"'Because the earth is vile. It is full of sin, it is corrupt, profane, unclean, a thing from darkness... We are the light coming to banish all that is earthly in you. You must reject all that is earthly in yourselves. You must vanquish the nature in yourselves, clean all the dirt, cast off all impurities.'

"'The earth is something to be exploited,' they said. 'Not something to be adored or worshiped.'

"'It, the earth, is something to be dug up and discarded, torn, sacked, penetrated to the depth, something to be violated and used. Many treasures lie between our feet and Hell, that deepest of earth's domains, its most intimate bosom. We will flay the earth. We'll tear out its veins, mine its bones, exhume and cremate the entrails — from all this filth we conjure wealth, such is our way of purifying creation and atoning for our sins, such is our hygiene.

"'It, the earth' — they said. For they saw our Mother, the Mother of us all, as a thing. She became 'it'. To them She became alien, separate, some thing remote, some thing half-dead.

"They said 'the earth is something to be tamed. Some thing to be feared, but not respected.'

"'We shall conquer it. We shall lord over it. By our ingenuity and strength of will we shall make its power bend to our command — and it will obey our command like any slave or machine...'"

Oshana, after a deep inhalation of the solemn quietude pervading the circle, continued thus:

"But no one can tame the Earth. She holds forces which may be within our conception, but not our control. They cannot be commanded — only contained. For some time. But held down under the talons of Man, Her power swells with tension; and when it is unleashed, it wreaks calamity upon all life, without discrimination or measure, without pity.

"For the Earth's forces can be terrible. They follow no concept of justice. As mistress of death, She can be implacable and blind in Her fury. Her might can be raw and unbridled.

"However, as She takes life, the Earth our Mother breeds life into being, and sustains life's existence. Without Her the air in our breast ceases, the waters no longer nourish, crops do not grow, life does not live; without Her our bodies perish and our souls along with them. Without Her, we cannot be. But She simply Is — and though we may hurt Her, we will die long before She ever does.

"For She is Life and Death, She is that from whom we spring and into whom we wither. She is Good and Evil, She is Love and Hatred, Light and Darkness, Sun and Moon. She is He and She is Self. She lives in all things. She is the frame of all things, all existence throbs within Her bounds. She extends into the outermost edges of the universe — and whatever lies beyond Her is unknowable.

"How could we be cleansed of the Earth? Nature is all that Is."

Oshana's feather swayed side to side by her ear in the mystic gloom.

"This we told them. But where there was light and darkness, they saw only darkness and chaos. Where there was life they saw only struggle... And so, my kin, did the miners, hunters and herders proclaim their ideal to the tillers of the Earth: *'Existence is strife.* Life is a burden... — Only the strongest survive it,' they said — and then added, 'Come, let us vanquish life, let us subdue nature.'

"'Such is our God's commandment, that we subdue the wilderness and mold the earth in His image, which is our own. Only in Him can we find respite from the pain of living,' they told us. 'Only in Him can we find rest. Our supreme ideal is to *be nearer to God* — which is why we aspire to the heavens. He is the farthest existence there is from earth, the most separate, the most different from earth. He is eternal, immutable, immaculate, perfect...' This is how they described their God to us.

"And still they said, 'To this God we' — meaning, *us* — 'to this God we owe a debt. It is this debt that caused our Fall from the heights.'

"But we asked them, 'Who is this God, and why hasn't He announced Himself to us until now?' And they said, 'We are His representatives and we announce Him to you. He is the Supreme Power — everything is subjugated to His Will. And We are the instrument of His Will. It is to us you must obey.'

"So they spoke from their mountaintops. These divine dignitaries arrived on our shores like shepherds to the sheep, masters to the herd, to exercise dominion over the flocks, as prescribed by holy dictum. They spoke to us perched up first atop the masts, then behind the altars, then in their balconies and in the towers of their cities, claiming that, the nearer to God, the more like God — and so they shouted, that they were His confidants, and the best fit to interpret His Will, as they directed scornful eyes to the soil beneath them — as they fell the forests and capped the mountains, so that nothing may stand higher than them.

"For the Mother who nurtured them and gave them air to breathe, food to eat, drink to swallow, and wonders to behold, they felt only disgust. Where there was life they saw only disease. Where there was beauty..." said Oshana — and her voice yielded to the nocturnal quiet, out of which blossomed the whisper of the trees in the breeze, like the ciphered words of some divinity; and her own voice of calm intonations seemed to be one with the subtle chorus of the wood, born of the wood, spoken in undulations of wind by a sprite at turns silhouetted against, and blended into the verdure breathing darkly all around. The fresh exhalations of the sea seeping into land seemed to spray the very air in which her words swam and flew. There was godliness to it... "Where there was beauty, my kin, they saw only loot.

"But again we asked them, 'Who is this God?' — and the answer has changed many times across the ages. For the Godhead — their God bears many masks.

"First they called him "The Lord", and sometimes they called him "Nation" and other times "Progress", and many other names... And in our days He is more often called "Economic Growth", "Free Markets", "Efficiency", "Productivity", and other such names...

"But the object of their worship, their god has always been the same, and his name is Mammon.

"Mammon meaning power, Mammon meaning wealth. This is their supreme ideal.

"'Fill the earth and subdue it,' said their highest voice, whom they called god. But where they thought they heard god, they were listening instead to the forbidden desire in their hearts — the will to power; the pull to greed.

"Dominion over the land and subjugation of the poor: such is their supreme ideal. And it is to the poor that they preach, 'Behold the earth — it is evil. It doesn't provide enough for all of us, so that we must fight for the spoils, and may the best win. It is only fair that the strongest get the most,' they say — sometimes. Other times they say, 'The earth is abundant — We can keep extracting forever, there is no limit to our growth. There will always be more pastures to graze, more wilds to burn, new rocks to mine, new frontiers to conquer. This playground is endless and there will always be more to wreck.' But always they say, 'We've mastery over the earth.'

"They say *the earth is dead*. It is without reason, without soul, therefore without life. Rivers and seas, soil, trees and plants, animals — these are all soulless and irrational. They are insensible.

"'Come — we will fashion our world out of these dead things. We will glory in riches and derive from them our lives.' But how can one derive life from dead things?

"Only that which lives can give life. And even when you consume the flesh of animals, it is the life lingering in the flesh that gives you life. So is the crux of the mystery of life in death.

"This we told them — and they called us heathens and persecuted us, enslaved us and murdered us. And still they said, 'the earth is dead, and with its bones we will build mountains to reach the sky, for salvation lies in the heights.'"

She shook her head with bemusement and the humor of incredulity.

"'Watch that your feet remain on the ground! lest your senses fly off from you,' we said to them. No one can detach oneself from the Earth. No one can loosen free from Nature. Even in the most remote confines of the Universe, still Nature will be there — for Nature pervades every little fiber of existence. And in truth, even their beloved machines are Nature — for everything is from Nature.

"By isolating from Nature, we escape from reality. But Reality, like Nature, is still there — everywhere — no matter if we pay attention or not.

"'And watch that you don't eat beyond Her gifts into Her extended hand! for Her ruthless fist is poised to crush us.'

"They did not listen — and still they don't listen. They've heard, maybe — and shrugged. For they've eaten well into the marrows of her wrist, sought to hollow her bones and fashion out of them their wealth, snapped the ligaments and drank of the black blood of the Earth, and drank with much thirst. And her fist is descending upon us in long, sweeping arcs, ever quicker, ever more wrathful — and they will break the most unshielded first, those most blameless — for there is no such thing as divine justice. Yet those whose fault it is — they, too, will perish. After the splurge, will come the famine.

"Are they so intoxicated that they don't notice this? Nature's myriad fingers insinuate themselves into every human ambition — they land with the force of a storm, and the gradualness of a drought — and unless we appease Her mounting fury, there will no longer be a human future.

"The heavens collapse and our very ground is shifting away — but they don't care. Does their power intoxicate them so?

"They won't stop, they cannot stop. Greed breeds addiction, and like addicts they will consume until there is nothing to consume but themselves.

"Gorge until you burst — such is their ideal.

"And this would be something to pity, and feel compassionate about — if they didn't have the power to consume and destroy so much. The fire of their alchemy burns the land, the smoke of their cauldrons chokes the skies; the scraps of their feast fall upon the ocean like acid rain; and upon our heads like thunder.

"For Mammon is a powerful god, and in truth it will be difficult to starve it of its power — but we must set upon the harsh way.

"For their ways will destroy us.

"They will destroy everything."

Silence.

"This need not be, my kin.

"We need a new attitude toward life.

"We need a new ideal."

Silence. Everyone appraised her words with much attention and respect; for Oshana was elder among them, well learned and well lived, and her voice resonated deep in and from the listening breasts of the listeners.

Into the quietude she continued:

"My kin, we need a new ideal.

"We need an ideal that *worships life* and loves the Earth its giver, the Mother of All. An ideal that finds wonder and joy in life and the Earth.

"We need an ideal that sees the holiness of the Earth and the divinity in all things. In truth, this new ideal is very ancient — the most ancient and most forgotten of all values. But humankind wouldn't have survived without it.

"These are days saturated with knowledge. But we have forgotten the way of wisdom. Science without philosophy, knowledge without wisdom — the ancients, beholding the weather, would panic. We shall again consider wisdom and honor; and fear Nature's power.

"Our generation has lost the knowledge of awe. We shall recover it. We will derive pleasure from the regeneration of the Earth — for in Her degeneration is our own. We will again find fulfillment in Her infinite wonders.

"We shall again consider the sanctity of rivers, the godhood of valleys, and the divinity of mountains, as supreme. The Earth shall again be worshiped, as shall the Skies. Trees will again be deities, every plant a manifestation of the sacred, every speck of earth the dwelling of holy spirits. From the smallest to the largest aspects of life, and the great and unknown beyond — in the intimate broadness of the world, there inhabits the hallowed.

"For divinity dwells in all life. In truth, even beneath the surface of our masks — we inherit holiness from the Earth, for we are of the Earth, and every creature in Her womb is our relative. Deep within ourselves, my kin — there live gods."

The wind whispered her voice and the very sighs of the ocean appeared to fall mum so as to listen. The contours of the trees were very still, rustling only very infrequently, as though cocking their ears nearer from time to time. Stars observed from afar, inhaling the black sky and narrowing their twinkling glare. Magic, and mystery, pervaded the quietude of wood and shore.

"Their gods — their all-knowing, all-powerful gods — are the symbols of their ideal. They're the horizon of their ambition. They were made in their image — their idealized form. Mammon the parasite is their vehicle. Mammon has driven us down this path.

"All roads lead back to oneself, and here we stand again at the beginning of the long way — and we see everything ahead of us, scorched. Many haven't noticed how everything burned in their wake, but who can claim to not have noticed now?

"We sought their ideal of power, their ideal of wealth, their ideal of heights — and here we face ourselves, contemplating our own extinction. Beyond their summit waits the abyss.

"We must abandon this path, we need to abandon these ideals. This is cause for much apprehension — but fear not. For we are all tillers of the Garden: we're not accursed. There was never any Fall: because we were born in the Earth.

"In truth the journey will be difficult, for Mammon stands lord of this age, and Mammon's servants are masters of its paths. Their heaviest tolls flank alternative ways, their thickest veils conceal all different horizons. But fear not. There are powers in you that you don't yet know — for deep in each of you, my kin, there live gods.

"My kin, we need to change the way we relate to the Earth, to one another, to ourselves. We need to change our lives. No longer can we seek the current ideals — they have led us astray. We need new ideals.

"The current ideal says — life is a race, shaped in the form of a mountain. It behooves you to climb atop the heads of others so that you may rise further toward the summit; and kick them off so that you may go even faster, with more space.

"But the new ideal says — life is a journey, shaped like so many hillocks. It behooves you to help those below you on the way up, and those above you on the way down.

"This is not easy, my kin. It requires strength to be kind, strength to carry yourself beyond your self. It requires the patience of subtlety. It requires the spirit. In truth, there is strength in helping others, and one needs nobility of character to be truly kind — it is not an easy thing. One needs to be strong to *want* the welfare of others — for one finds in the welfare of others one's own welfare. Likewise I tell you, if you draw your power from the meekness of others, you are *weak* and unworthy of that power.

"The current ideal says — abundance is good and the more you have, the more worthy you are.

"But the new ideal says — abundance is meant to be shared. Taken alone, it becomes a burden; but one that fills the muscles with pleasure. It grinds the soul to degradation, with a comforting sponge. It bloats the mind and chokes the spirit.

"In truth, the only abundance that is valiant in oneself, is the abundance of love — it must be abundant in yourselves, it must fill you so that it may spill and flow far beyond you.

"The current ideal says — The highest ideal is power; power over others, and power over nature. And the instrument of that power is called 'money' — with it comes comfort. You must seek it at all costs.

"But the new ideal says — The highest ideal is power; power over yourself, and to carry yourself beyond your self. And the instrument of that power is called 'wisdom' — with it comes compassion. You must seek it, insofar as it benefits your fellow kind through your self.

"We are selfish individuals, our purpose is to pursue our self-interest, such is their dogma. 'I must worry about myself — let others worry about themselves,' they say.

"But we say, it is in the interest of the self to reach beyond itself. Not to exercise dominion — but to seek understanding. It is in others that we find our deepest purpose, it is beyond our selves that we find ourselves. For in truth, we are not just ourselves.

"Know thyself! — so taught the ancient prophetess. To this we add, 'know thy kin, so that you may know thy self.' For in the very depth of oneself, one finds the All.

"Lo, the Earth is to us a mirror, it is in ourselves that we see Her. Beyond all Her many shapes, beneath Her myriad colors, lies the very same essence binding us all — I tell you in truth, it is beyond your self that you will find the All.

"The Earth is to us a mirror, and this is why they seek to shape Her in their image. They project power outward, so that it may reflect back into themselves — to see themselves idealized in all things. Their mansions, their cars, yachts, jets, their vast empires — but they're only weaving husks around the hollow. They need fortresses to safeguard their feeble selves. Greed is an illness, though it can infect anybody — and the wealthy these days are but invalids cowering behind their walls. Indeed, Mammon is the most comforting of hospital blankets.

"In truth, it is necessary to have material comfort. The instinct of survival responds to scarcity and danger, and the instinct of greed, to abundance and comfort. Both separate us from others, both separate us from ourselves — both make us revolt against our Mother. But hunger and thirst, once sated, is quelled. Greed, in truth, can never be satisfied.

"Today we need not feel hunger nor thirst, my kin. Nor do we need to hoard to survive. Our Mother is fruitful. She is abundant. Even now She extends to us Her boons, so that we may create a new world. She gives enough for us all.

"In Her we find sustenance, in Her we find happiness, in Her we find purpose, in Her we find each other — in Her we find ourselves."

Oshana spoke all of this with such a softness of tone that one could wonder how she attained such a clarity of reach; her words rang clear in the ears and breasts of everyone assembled, rang calmly, profoundly in the penetrating undulations of her hushed voice; a soothing whisper in the dark; a whisper into the heart, in which the heart fluttered, arrested, for every soft syllable was uttered, unhurried, with great authority.

"We need an ideal that finds the Earth in ourselves. An ideal that finds the All in ourselves. In truth, we are more than just ourselves, and the sense of our lives rests in the Earth and within our kin.

"In the most central, the deepest point in the universe of your being, there you will find the wellspring, the source of All things, the seed from which you sprout and from which every one sprouts. In the most profound degree of the self, beyond the self, you will find the common.

"Beyond our selves — into our selves, through our selves — there, we will find the cure. We will find happiness, we will find true power — we will find meaning, we will find purpose. In communion with one another, in communion with the Earth, in communion with our selves. There you will find *life*.

"*To live the fullness of life*, to seek the fullness of oneself, which encompasses the All — here's the new ideal. This entails seeking the fullness of *all* life, and the wholeness of the Earth, Life's origin and ground. Across every little speck of vitality, the whole of life's universe is mirrored. To be able to *see*, to *feel* this — here's the new ideal.

"Peer into yourself deep — and you will see the other.

"Look deep into the other — and you will find yourself.

"Seek, deep into yourself, through yourself, beyond yourself — and you will find the All. All things exist within each, and each, in all things.

"Did you hear me, my kin? Are my words clear to your ears? Do their meanings ring in your minds? It is necessary, in truth, that they seep into your souls. Don't just hear, then — *listen*.

"And it is not enough to listen with the ears either, but we must listen with all our bodies, all our senses and our minds, we must listen with our soul. It is not enough to know these things — we must *feel* these things.

"Plant your roots deep into the Earth, and hold them like arms round the roots of your brethren. Hold fast to each other and to the Earth and She, made firm, will hold you firm. Only like this will you withstand the gales that are to come.

"Berth your seed in the Spirit, stretch your roots to the very core of the Earth, to the very core of your being, and into the All containing everyone. It is not enough to know, nor is it enough to merely understand. *Love!*

"But my kin, in truth, it is still not enough to love your neighbor — it is equally necessary that you love your antipode. It is not enough to love those near — you must also love those faraway. It is not enough to love your neighbor, unless your neighborhood becomes the world. Consider the ones who hunger among us, and those afar who perish... Consider those who moil in other shores, to make the dressings veiling our cities.

"When your body is violated, it will always remember it — even when the pain is gone, it lingers. It is vital that we feel the pain of others in the same way. But for this we need much strength — for the burden is very heavy. We must have ears that listen to the mute and eyes that see beyond the blindness of the reach — and a spirit that can bear all the noise in the world, in silence.

"It is like this that we can change our lives, it is like this we change the world. It is upon our innermost, which is the innermost of every one, which is the depth of the Earth, that we will build a new world.

"We must begin by changing our values — by seeking new ideals. We must look to new horizons. And then, begin the walk — by the sheer force of faith if nothing else avails us. We must walk together, aid one another in all things, in material and spiritual sustenance both, so that no one may falter.

"And in truth, only upon new ideals can we suffer the storms, the droughts that will greet us across new paths. My kin! only upon the most ancient values can we survive Mammon's trickery and anger. They are to be a guide, to hold us steadfast on the way — a flame in the darkness, a silence in the noise.

"Let us join together. Let us remake the world. Let us worship the Mother. Let us *live*.

"Let us walk.

"Not in one body. Not in one mind.

"One soul, my kin."

Oshana's voice ebbed reverently along with the tides of the breeze; and the silence curled warm and mystic about their hearts.

25 - Bread

Over there, the children were playing; over by the foam of the tide, where the sea met their running soles, their plodding feet. The water splashed their laughter. Their salt-soaked torsos, sprinkled with sleepy sunlight, shimmered with the horizon, with distances made of crystal. With the wind their voices swam, buoyed into the ear, swept again out of range, and all the while the ocean swayed and rumbled blue beneath their hovering.

The beach was delimited by sharp cliffs on the yonder side; it was all inhospitable rock along the shore around here, and this was the only plot of sand in the small peninsula. It would perhaps be quite crowded in the hotter seasons (though all seasons blended in those days, and even now it was as warm as it might have been midyear) but it was now mostly deserted and quite wide, quite spacious. On this side, where the sand was dotted with grass and the pines began their gentle ascent to the forest, towels were laid, picnics had, conversations made between walks through the shades uphill, with a laughter softer and in a mood quieter than on the sunny seaside, where the kids leapt and sprinted.

"Over there," said Orenda, pointing in the direction of the children. "You see those cliffs? There are haunted caves that way, guarded by one-eyed giants."

"What?" Neipas laughed. "What are you talking about? You say the most random things."

"Dude I'm serious." For a while now they had been sitting together, side by side, contemplating the ocean slithering against the sky. Orenda's remark surfaced after a lull in their chat. "If you get past the guardians and the ghosts, you'll find a huge treasure, right?"

"What's that, a folk tale?"

"Of the Oyate, yeah. Anyway, the treasure's cursed — so if you die on the way out, you become a ghost yourself and you'll be trapped in the caves forever. But if you get to the exit alive, with the treasure, you become one of the guardians. So you can't leave anyway."

"Sounds like you might as well not try."

"Yeah," Orenda snickered. "You'd be surprised, though."

Together they watched the proud rock standing immovably against the sea, sloughing froth and breaking the waves, emanating golden powder. Neipas got to thinking about that hall in the Eagles' Nest with the tall statues, the huge windows and a floor full of money, half-wondering yet what all of it meant.

"No lack of treasures in this place, looks like," he commented offhandedly, and with a note of sourness that came unintended. It seemed so strange that he had been up there, that he had stepped upon the very summit of the highest tower; it seemed even unlikely, now, after the fact, as he lounged comfortably upon the large towel and observed the beach, as he felt the breeze with a sense of reposing easy in himself. Pondering vaguely, he had a sensation of having passed through a type of unreality — as through a different dimension, perhaps.

"And you?" he asked Orenda. "What do you think the treasure is?" Somehow he felt that the concreteness and tangibility of those paper notes couldn't correspond to the fabled wealth of the tower's core; it had to be something much vaster, something less trite, something beyond mere effortless imagination, something perhaps a bit more immaterial than the dazzling opulence he'd seen.

"Of the cave?"

"Oh — the Belab's treasure, I mean."

Wistful, Orenda took a minute to respond. Then she sneered, "Probably what they stole from us."

"Do you mean, from your people?" he asked, recognizing, with a mournful inflection, the history of that land.

"Well, yeah, from us especially, but — I mean from all of us in general. You and me. Everyone."

"What do you mean?"

"I mean, if they have a treasure, it's not because they just *found* it. It's not because they worked to deserve it. They stole it from us."

"Us meaning you and me?"

"Yeah."

Between Neipas and Orenda, on the towel, there sat a nest-shaped, reed basket — out of it she took first a plate with a large, round loaf of bread upon it; and then another plate from under it, which she gave to Neipas.

"Look," she said quietly. Her hand made a reverent gesture over the bread, sweeping and slow. "This is the Earth."

Neipas blinked and nodded amused, slackened in his fatigue. "All right."

"And we are humankind, ok?"

"Sure."

"The story of humankind so far has two protagonists: the powerful, and the powerless. It goes like this. Here, take half the bread, and I'll take the other half."

Neipas took the half in his hand, sitting up to face her.

"Don't eat it yet. Now I'm gonna be the master, and you're the subject."

"Why are you the master?" Neipas laughed.

"Shush. 'Cause I'm telling the story," she said humorously. "Anyway never mind that for now, I'm skipping ahead — first, let's say that we're equals. Let's go back to the very, very beginning — to the original state of things. Ok? Now we're just minding our own business, right. Maybe we were even amicable at some point. Maybe we even traded resources. Here, let's trade our breads.

"We're just enjoying our own slices and everything. Here, eat a little. It's ok. Usually it would grow back, because this is the Earth. But this —" she pointed at each bread half in turn — "is not literally the Earth. It's a metaphor."

"Ok," Neipas laughed.

"Go on, take a bite or two. Ok then I, for whatever reason, want your part, even though I have more than enough," Orenda carried on, as she was munching her bit. "I might be doing this for a number of different reasons... But if I'm the master *today*, when there's plenty of bread to go around, it's either because I just have an ambition to have it, or I want to get some oil or raise ArmsCore's stock value or market share... But I'm going off my metaphor here. So anyway, I want it. And I'm stronger than you, so I'll take it! Here —" she took Neipas' bread.

"Ah! You're stronger, huh."

"Of course I am. I'm the storyteller, remember?" she smiled. "Now I'm the master, and you're the subject. I have the power," Orenda continued, holding up the fullness of the bread loaf, its totality defaced by a few bite marks. "Because I control the resources, you see what I mean?"

"Ok."

"Look at how big this bread is! Actually, first thing I'm gonna do is a bit of PR magic, ok? Wait up —" she searched inside the basket and quickly retrieved a colorful cloth, which she placed over the bread. "Now I have even more control, you know why? Because I have the cloth now too... So I can hide my wealth if I want."

Neipas furrowed his brow amusedly and said, interrupting, "So is the bread wealth, or the Earth?"

"Hum..." she thought a little, looking indecisively behind the cloth. "Well yeah, the bread is wealth. But all wealth comes from the Earth. Anyway now I have control over it, so I can choose to share with you how much I well please."

"Why do you need to share with me anything?"

"Because, look —" she chewed on some bread. "For two reasons. First one being, if I keep eating this bread, eventually the bread will end, you see? Or... get stale, I suppose. So I need *you* to make me more bread. And even if I have more than enough bread to last me many lifetimes, the second reason is also very important — if you have *no bread at all*, you might get funny ideas and try to take the bread away from me.

"How much bread I share with you depends on what place you occupy in my society. Let's say you're a politician," she said, digging under the cloth and removing a sizable slice. "Here you go. That's enough for a nice meal, right?

"But let's say you're a regular worker, for example." Orenda lifted the cloth in a discreet, secretive manner, placing her hand in it as she looked to all sides. Then, in a theatrical gesture, a bunch of powder snowed from her pinched fingers onto Neipas' plate. "Here, have some crumbs!"

Neipas ate the crumbs at Orenda's prodding. More crumbs rained upon his plate when he finished. "Meanwhile you work like hell under the dough dust, making bread, and what I have under the cloth gets bigger, and bigger, and bigger... And you get a tiny bit more crumbs, maybe, if the times are good," she went on, scattering more crumbs about his plate as Neipas munched on the politician's slice.

Then she said, "But oh, look — This is upsetting. There's a financial crisis or something. There's some trouble under the cloth here — maybe I ate too much too fast, but anyway you don't know what exactly. You only know that Times are bad now. There's not enough bread to go around now, I tell you. So we gotta tighten up..." Orenda soughed, taking one crumb here, one crumb there. "And did you lose your job? Too bad," she continued, removing more crumbs, one by one.

"Ok," Neipas chuckled, shaking his head — something in Orenda's earnest expressions and attempts to weave a coherent allegory amused Neipas very much, and his laughter was only intercalated by wide smiling; all of it half-bordering on the edge of seriousness, nevertheless. "So why the cloth? So that I can't see how much you have?"

"Exactly. The cloth is key. How much bread do you see on the table?"

Neipas considered. "Only the part you gave me, I guess."

"Exactly... That's all the bread you see, that's all the bread you can think about. What are you going to do? Reach across this towel — and this is a long, *long* towel between us — and take off the cloth? You'd have to walk a lot, the towel would keep sliding under your feet. You don't have the time. You don't have the energy. You gotta earn your crumbs to survive. And when you don't have enough bread... You eat *yourself*. Do you understand? I guess in this metaphor you are not just you but a group, so you eat each other, and leave *me* alone. Because in the end, that's what I want — I wanna be alone with my bread and never see you, I don't ever wanna *think* about you, unless you're bringing me more. Alas I must. I can't stop interacting with you completely. I depend on you for more bread.

"But — you see? You said the part I *gave* you! But it was yours to begin with!

"Over time — over years, generations — eventually — you *forget* this bread's yours. That's what the cloth does."

Neipas nodded slowly, covering his beak pensively, listening more earnestly now.

"But in reality, it's even worse. It's more like this —" Orenda rummaged inside the basket again, and in a moment emerged with a multicolored mound of cloths in her hand. She began to lay one by one atop the covered bread. "Usually it's like this. Between you and the bread there are financial institutions, the media, think tanks, webwork platforms, the maskbook, other corporations, hierarchical structures within each one... each of those works like a cloth on top of cloth on top of cloth. And the more cloths you put on top, the more you hide the bread, the more you abstract it.

"In societies like ours, these cloths are more or less transparent — there's freedom of information, brave journalistic work that makes them more and more transparent and lets you peek under. But it's overwhelming. If I jack all your crumbs from over here, where will you go? What cloth will you look under? You know? It's too much. And something else —

"I'm holding the bread, and the cloths. You see me, right? I mean, I'm sitting right in front of you. But in reality..." Orenda held a cloth over her own face; her unkempt hairbun peeking off the top as she covered her countenance was of such a comedic effect that Neipas guffawed for a little. "Hey! Anyway," she continued, laughing. "In reality it's more like this. You can't see me now, either. And I am not one, but multiple, and I'm hiding behind cloth —" Orenda layered another color atop her "— after cloth —" and another "— after cloth.

"But it's even worse."

Orenda held up one of the textiles, and placed it in front of Neipas' face. "You become part of the fold. All the cloths hiding the wealth — there's all the ideologies, all the beliefs, all the stories that they spread and reinforce. They kinda seep into you. There's bullshit measurements like IQ to convince you that you're dumb, or GDP to convince you that making money and producing *stuff* are the most important things in life, or you make up stories like financial instruments so you forget that the bread *is bread*," she continued layering cloths before Neipas' mask, "there are myths like Mannie's 'they work hard' or ideas like Marlene's — that lawyer with the pink hair I told you about — 'it's more practical to work with the rich than against them,' et cetera, et cetera... Et cetera.

"Now at this point, you've not only forgotten that the bread belongs to you. You can't even conceive it. It's crazy to even think it."

They paused a moment for thought. Then, Orenda retook the word:

"So that's why the cloth is essential..." she stopped again in thought, for a pace. "They're like the drapes on a stage play, you know? They're the frame. And it's like any story — people will accept everything that's in accord with the premise... You need to *control the premise*. You need to *control the story*. Without it, you can control wealth, I guess — but not for long. You need the cloth to *control people* — so that you keep controlling the resources. You understand?"

They dropped slowly into an expectant quietude. Then Neipas said:

"That's pretty grim."

Again a certain, meditative silence congealed between them. Neipas laughed no more. He mulled for a while.

"Ok but... Of course none of this is fair. They're spending the bread — the resources all wrong, but... I dunno if I would call that stealing. Like, I never had that much bread in my life."

Orenda snapped an emphatic response: "No, you never did, but you're entitled to it. We all are. Because somewhere in our ancestry, we had it like that. And all our ancestry is the same — we all trace back to the same beginnings. Even if it was a thousand generations ago — it's our *birthright*. It's our birthright, granted to us by our mother Earth. A life of dignity and meaning... It's our birthright. We have enough material sustenance to have it, all of us. Earth gives in abundance — for all of us. She's the mother of *all of us*. And they take it all, they take what's ours.

"This bread —" Orenda continued passionately, placing her hand upon the cloths — "*all wealth* — all of it is taken from Mother Nature. All of it. Everything is generated from Her. And you can only expand wealth two ways — abstract it all you want but this is basically it — you either find new sources of wealth to extract it from, or you shape what's extracted from Nature differently. Otherwise you're just redistributing the wealth that already exists. And the last few decades especially have been about redistributing wealth to the top, in the form of stealing, specifically. It's been about robbing the Earth blind, extracting like fucking gluttons, taking from Nature faster than She can give, hollowing the Earth — without respect for Her who sustains our lives — with zero respect for Life.

"Look at what they do! with their fossil fuels and their madness, they're killing the Earth! They pollute the rivers, they burn the forests, they wanna dim the *sun* in their hunger for more, and faster. They keep taking and taking... for what? What are they thinking? It's *greed* that's keeping them on this path.

"Eventually — all the bread will be eaten before more can be made, before more wheat can grow. And if the bread is what the Earth gives, and there's no more Earth — what happens to us? I mean, *all of us*. Even *them*. Kaput — is what happens...

"All is Nature — you understand? Killing her, we're killing ourselves..."

Silence — the wind and the voices of the children breezed upon them and made tremble the cloths and the towel.

"They hide all their monstrosities under their veils," said then Orenda. "Everything is covered with them, *we're* covered with them, we live in a maze of them — they're all around us, they're inside us... separating us from the Earth, from each other, from ourselves — from our powers. Making us weak and hopeless. We need to learn to draw their curtains away from our eyes, Neipas. Unlearn to see through the eyes of Mammon."

...wind-stirred trees shimmered with golden, sun-shining leaves. The waves were turning green on their hunched backs, flaking showers of glimmering dust through their descent, their plunge into the bursting white of their scatter over the tide green, sea of jade. By where it clawed across the sand, the ruckus of the children had subsided, and they all sat in a circle by the water. Martin sat among them, so did Edazima and a few other adults. They were supposed to stay only one night — Edazima had to work next day — but they had been so warmly welcomed that they would end up lingering until it was too late to leave. Martin in particular seemed happy in a certain spontaneous, free way Neipas hadn't seen him be in a very long time; and Edazima, mother that she was, seemed doubly happy on his behalf. Hesitant and shy, Martin had at first blended reluctantly with the other kids, who had come urging him to join them in their play with pleas gentle, and a raw sensibility that was inviting and did not force; and now he seemed, in his quiet way, to be at ease. So they would leave in the morning, before sunrise, to beat traffic; Martin in the back, dozing off against the window glass; Edazima steering in the front, with a smile facing the incoming city. Just missing them, Cesar the poet would arrive a few hours later, and greet Neipas with his peculiar enthusiasm and a flicker of his mustache.

Orenda, surprised that they knew each other closely, would join them in their merriment, and they would bask together in the sunlight and in the sea throughout the day, and it would be all laughter between them. But that would be tomorrow; presently the conversation began to assume somber tones: "The cloth is distance," Orenda told Neipas. "Not physical distance, though, not necessarily. The cloth is abstraction. And abstraction *sets* the distance. Whatever is near, abstraction makes farther — whatever is far, abstraction makes nearer. That's not necessarily bad — on the contrary. Like, a story is an abstraction. A tale is an abstraction of what's being told, you know? It can be good to make something a little farther if it's too close — so we can look at it better. The soul is abstracted through poetry, for example. Right? Same with what's far — we can make it closer to us to see it better. Like, faraway events are abstracted through news reports, most often, or historical events through books or documentaries, et cetera.

"Now, every abstraction creates a symbol," she said. "The symbol covers whatever is abstracted — it covers a meaning. It gives it shape — or misshapes it. Some symbols reveal, others conceal, depending on how that symbol is molded, you know? It's important to know this because we're surrounded by symbols all the time. All words are symbols. We communicate entirely through symbols, and it's in the gap between what is said and what is meant that we need to pay close attention. Too much abstraction complicates what is simple and simplifies what is complicated — and nowadays we live among way-too-abstracted perceptions, you know what I'm saying?... among *their* abstractions, *their* perceptions...

"Now *they* rule civilization, and so we look at all things as filtered through *their* cloth, through *their* symbols. But their symbols represent only one thing — money... Everything is reduced to that. That's what *everything comes to mean.* We see all things through Mammon's eyes.

"And Mammon doesn't see things as they are — he uproots from things what they are, and diminishes everything to diminished symbols — to that one symbol called 'money'. How much money is such and such a thing worth? That's the only criteria that matters — and that includes human life. Everything is *objectified*, everything is leveled, right? everything is made equivalent under their cloth. Everything is priced. *Everything* is made an object, the only 'subjects' allowed are the consumer (kinda) and the 'entrepreneur'. But everything is ranked according to its cost and worth — in dollars.

"You are put on the same scale," she continued, "as any other product, as cars, dolls, bottle caps, clothes, whatever. Same with all life. It's either there to oil the machine — as worker, as consumer — or as an externality. If you're irrelevant to whatever cost-profit calculations they make, then you might as well not exist — you're so far abstracted, so distant, that you don't exist. You're a statistic at most, a casualty maybe, a number, part of a curiosity. You're nothing. You're not even some*thing*, like a product, or a worker — you're just... nothing.

"Whenever they need to choose between profit and human life... like, it's not even a choice. Life isn't even considered. Is war more profitable than peace? Then we'll make war. Fuck the consequences, the only consequence that matters is the amount of money to be made. In a society where profit is the imperative, dysfunction is the rule. Healthcare works to keep you sick longer, spectacle makes more money than substance in the media, so no one knows what's going on, everything's allowed," she said, her voice hoarse with indignation and disbelief. "Will our profits pollute the river? Then we'll pollute the river! The river and its people, they don't exist. The very basis of *life* is abstracted away and money takes precedence over — ...damn." She shook her head, she seemed flustered; her eyes gazed stern some thing faraway. "It's absolute batshit. It's crazy, crazy, just... Like... look at Minoa, right? I looked at the case files, and you know why the dam collapsed? Because they didn't invest in reinforcing it — that's it. It would've been nothing, nothing, compared to their profits — but still they didn't do it! Because they wanted to save a dime — that's why what happened happened. And they only paid settlements because that was definitely proven, otherwise no one would get anything. They sacrificed you all on the altar of money — not even sacrificed, because to them you were worth nothing!..."

She was carried away by the gales of her consternation and the flames of her revulsion, she let emotion pass unbridled through her lips; but now she stopped, suddenly, alarmingly, beholding Neipas' quiet mask deepening, as it were, through her teary gaze into a grisly silence palpable even through the hastening wind. "Holy shit Neipas, I'm so sorry... I wasn't thinking."

Neipas could not face her. He looked down at the towel, with crumbs of sand besprinkled; down at the plate, with grains of bread spread; he simply looked down confusedly. He perceived his mind hazy when it occurred to him to perceive it; he wallowed in his own soul. For a minute he did not feel the sunshine on his skin, the heat in his mask, the melting wax oozing from his motionless tongue. Without knowing it, he grabbed the cloths and bared the bread. And he stared at the cloths... He stared hard at their muddled colors bleached by sunlight, at their piled layers filtering and mystifying the deep. He stared without seeing anything. Many unrelated thoughts passed by him, as if to draw him away from his bewilderment — he thought of the eggs he had let rot, that movie he'd watched with Eva, the chicken hanging in the slaughterhouse, the banknotes spread on the floors of the Anubel.

On the sand, by the towel, one of those long-winged flies that materialize after the rain crawled along (had the wings bloomed with the water?), climbing with difficulty out of a little indentation which was, for it, a steep dune; grains of sand kept sliding beneath its little feet, returning it to the bottom — making the top forever inaccessible. Curious (whispered to his mind the random thought) — he had seen these insects before, but he had never seen them fly.

"Is that what it was?" he muttered unconsciously. "I didn't even know that — can you believe it?" He said it almost casually, almost jokingly.

He turned up his mask, and looked blearily at Orenda; across his beak he had shaped a mild grin. Then he took a piece of bread from the loaf, and said humorously, "So moral of the story is, the Belab's treasure is a bunch of bread."

Orenda smiled abashedly, rueful. "Best treasure there is..."

Neipas laughed. "Why the long face? Come on, let's eat." He spoke the words candidly, without reproach, with a certain affection, even; looking at Orenda appreciatively, beholding her with friendship and gratitude.

"Yeah..." she chuckled (very discreetly wiping her eyes). "Let's do it."

*

Over there, the kids, undoubtedly tired by now, played quieter games amongst themselves. In smaller groups, they appeared to be dealing cards, or passing a ball around as they sat, or simply looking at the western horizon reddening; one or two, lying down on their stomachs a distance from the others, seemed to be drawing or writing in notebooks. Observing them, Neipas realized that he hadn't yet written anything in the notebook that Orenda had given him; he realized regretfully that he hadn't even brought it, that it was probably still tucked in his jacket's breastpocket hanging in his wardrobe, and that it was a shame, because he mulled in ponderings he should've liked to record — he felt that perhaps the act of penning his thoughts would make them settle down, that by writing he could deepen his reflections. His *I*, too, he had left in the tent he had borrowed, and which he shared with Edazima and Martin — but he felt no desire to get up and grab it, no will to stare at the glass.

Watching the children bask calmly in the mellow sunshine and the serenity of good companionship, he wondered. Had his childhood been gifted with friends? He could not recall. His sister, of course — but who else? It was strange, but he couldn't remember a single face, a single name.

No matter — all lay buried under the toppled mountain, and there was no use lingering upon such thoughts.

"There you go, boss," said Orenda, holding two chairs. Tired of shifting the weight of her body between her knees, elbows, ankles and butt about the towel, Orenda (seeing Neipas stand on his feet too) had walked into the forest to grab something they could sit on more comfortably ("Thank you," said Neipas). Perhaps inadvertently, they each set their chairs so close to one another, side by side, that it would be enough to set their forearms upon their adjacent armrests for them to touch. But they sat, the one on the left resting upon the left elbow, the one on the right resting upon the right elbow; and so they remained for a while, beholding the vista in silence.

Sleepily, Neipas sensed the contours of his anguished, his true visage, absentmindedly touching its distant features; feeling remote from even the most intimate aspects of himself. Like a smothering hand his mask clung to him, like gripping fingers it rooted through the pores of his face into the hollows of his soul deep. His feathers sprouted from him like leaves. He beheld the faces of the children yet-maskless, beaming full with the sunlight; and he considered, how sad and tragic it was, that they were fated, perhaps, to sink under the burden of soulless labor, the stresses of moneymaking, the weight of modern urban life. He contemplated their silhouetting features as the sun declined behind their lowering voices; from his remoteness Neipas sensed a lull in their joys.

He considered his hand, so pressed with the toll of unending trays, for a moment. A remembrance of the Belab came to him calmly. Episodes of its peak flashed every so often. Why could he remember nothing of that last night in the Eagles' Nest? Only splashes of red came to mind when he tried. He could only recall (he felt it now a little) a crimson-hued discomfort — blinking hazily, painfully in his spirit — along with the fleshy scar of that strange janitor.

Neipas rubbed his brow; discomfited, he looked away. He looked yonder again.

Over there, at the end of the beach, the impassive cliff received the tired sea's caress, melting over it like a beating heart exposed, sighing old and sage, tranquil at last, slobbering like a mouth panting after the long journey. The rock seemed to acquire the consistency of a sponge; it seemed to shed droplets from its porous rugged surface, as birds shed plumes in flight, as the air flew around it; sunny feathers growing muffled with the hushing sun, the sun blushing under so many eyes. Day's end came near upon the shore. Molten gold glittered upon the great tide, and the crest of its waves rose to greenish diamond; the sea still a spectacle of jade. Flaxen haze covered the reaches; a wonder permeated the sandy shore. Spray flaked from the bending waters, progressively assuming the character of sparks over an ever-angrier cauldron — the foam plunged and exploded in tumultuous roars spreading out into the sand in spume thick; leaving in its wake, as it retreated in a furious inhalation, a sublime sheen mirroring the reddening sky upon the sand. Under the shouted command of their mothers, the last children left the water, spilling gold from their arms. Towering in the west, the roving clouds were already blanketing the crimson star; their mountainous edges rimmed in the sun's color, the landscape became pale and ethereal, the ocean muted green — undulating and plunging with tremendous force. Waters vast and mighty, they boiled in froth, roiled and scattered upon the earth — receding and rising in heaving endeavors, to and fro the infinite prospect, with grunts of simultaneous gasp and roar.

...into the depth of salty air, Neipas eventually spoke, emerging from watching his thoughts go by:

"I told you about my hometown, but you never told me about yours."

Orenda shrugged, and remained silent for a moment. Then she said: "There isn't much to say. We came because they were killing Nenaan. They were wrecking the valley."

"You came with just Oshana?"

"Yeah, my parents... To be honest, I don't even remember them. I never met my dad, and my mom died when I was very little."

Neipas took his gaze from the prospect and turned it to Orenda. For a moment he watched regretfully her sunlit, stolid, inscrutable mask.

"I'm sorry," he said. Then, in a lower volume, he added: "Sorry for bringing it up."

"It's all right."

Silence. The wind picked up and subsided.

"I remember very little of the valley," Orenda then said. "I know it more from photos than from memory. Photos on the Webwork — but I hate looking at them. I haven't looked at one for many years. I guess it's the same with my parents. I know them from what Oshana tells me... but. I don't like hearing about it."

"You don't have to talk about it if you don't want to."

"No, I mean... It's not like that. Just —"

As if to listen better to what the breeze — now again lifting — was saying, Orenda lowered her head; and with sad eyes and a sad smile she stared at the sands unfolding from their feet. The feathers of her mask swayed, rolling over her cheek and its soft dimple, the corner of her clasped lip. Hers was a reminiscent smile, thoughtful, and as despondent as it was accepting. It was receptive, and Neipas, discerning this, asked softly:

"What does Oshana say about them?"

"Well, I guess — about my father, she doesn't say much. I guess they disagreed on a lot of things, and by the looks of it she was tempestuous back when she was younger. She sounds like, kinda angry — when she talks about him. All I know is he went to work for the oilmen, never came back."

"Did he..."

They paused; Orenda inhaled the whirling breeze, then sighed:

"Die? Nah. Just, you know — gone."

"I see." Neipas kept looking at her on the opposite chair, resting on the opposite elbow and leaning on the side opposite his, contemplating away toward sunset.

"About my mom, she says... that she was kindness embodied — but kinda, like, head-in-the-clouds," she chuckled. "Super smart, super distracted. The poetic type. Loved the valley... She would go on these long walks in the mountains there, and alongside the river, on her own. She kept doing it even after the oilmen came. When it was no longer safe.

"Oshana told me she wouldn't give up her freedom for anything. That she was really brave. Didn't give a shit about anything. She wanted to do something, she'd do it. Wanted to go somewhere, she'd go. The most independent woman she'd ever met.

"So one day she goes on her trek — mind you, sometimes she would set up overnight, so it wouldn't be strange for her to be gone for more than a day. But then two nights pass, then three nights, then four. The whole village goes out searching for her... Well, all I know is she never came back."

Silence.

"I asked Oshana once, when I was a kid — 'did they ever find her?' Oshana told me that she would tell me when I was ready. I've never asked again. I don't wanna know."

Silence; once more, silence. The wind did not sound.

"...Oshana was more hardheaded, I guess. She definitely softened throughout the years though. Became more like my mother. She *became* my mother. For all intents and purposes, she is my mother. She always told me never to call her that — 'mom' — because I have two moms and she isn't one of them." Orenda laughed softly, shaking her head. "She does say I'm the daughter she could never have, though, from time to time."

After a pause, Neipas asked — his question emerging, as often happened, out of an indecision about what to say:

"Oshana never had children?"

Orenda lifted her fingers to her mask, whose feathers rustled in the blood light of a dying day. The nostrils of her beak dilated; her tongue moistened its tip; the plume of her earring stirred; her wrists brushed the side of her neck, and her hair, twined with feather, bloating with her hand, assumed the crimson hue of the decaying sun. For the first time now, she turned her head; she glanced at Neipas hesitantly, as if debating with herself whether she should say what she was about to say — then, meeting again, with red eyes, the red distance, she spoke:

"She did... Kinda. She was pregnant once, but she lost the baby."

"Oh..."

"I'm not sure if she miscarried or... Could've been because of the water that we drank. The river was already really polluted before we left... Or she did it herself — because of who the father was. I'm not sure."

Again she glanced at Neipas, who looked at her attentively; and, blinking, biting her lip, contracting her beak, inhaling and deepening into her mask, she said slowly:

"I asked her once about the father, and she told me — she never even knew his name... I was old enough to understand what that meant. And I knew Oshana well enough to guess the only thing that could've happened.

"That was when we were still in Nenaan. We then... we went away not long after that."

The night was around then closing its maw around the day, sinking its teeth into the day which bled in rusty reds in the yonder sky, crushed by the night into the darkness of the underworld. Fires were being lit up all throughout the beach. Hovering skins palpitated here and there and standing shadows walked from bonfire to bonfire. They gathered round cauldrons, watching the arms circling over with huge ladles.

"We went away after a night like this. It wasn't planned or anything. There was a raid on our village... A bunch of oilmen came with lanterns and torches, with rifles. They murdered a bunch of us and burned the houses. Just like that. Then they left."

Tucked in the corner of his chair farthest from Orenda, Neipas had his sight turned fully to her face in profile, which denounced no emotion, which betrayed, in its set motionlessness, none of the inner activity hidden behind the mask, hidden inside the heart, concealed in the refuge of her strength. Her voice, spoken in a low volume, was serene. But her words inspired horror in Neipas' listening breast. They breathed into it an air momentarily filled with smoke and screams, and he felt so much compassion for the little girl, soot still stuck under her nails, who clambered into the refugee-crowded bus (as she proceeded to tell him) that his chest felt clogged with skipped seconds — in which he sensed that nothing but hopelessness could be retrieved from a past, so present between them, which he could do nothing to change.

"But why?..." he asked despondently.

Tucked in the corner of her chair farthest from Neipas, Orenda, rotating her head in two motions, keeping her cheek on her fist, turned her gaze to the two eyes turned to her. Angled like this, her mask seemed as impassive as the sculpted visage of an idol. There was nothing in her eyes but the direction they faced. Neipas could only glimpse fires palpitating in them. Affected, he could not guess that Orenda did not remember the night she had just described, in so many words. She knew, viscerally, that it had happened; she simply retained no image of it. She remembered the bus ride very well, but everything that happened before that was a blank space in her visual memory. Despair had been choked under the force of her will — nothing but despair could be found in the recollection of those events. Only wrath, catalyzed and concentrated into determination, into hope, had survived her brief childhood; and Neipas saw the gentle eyes of that grown-up girl so intensely that he could but shy away his own.

"Why?..." said Orenda. Neipas felt her stare on his face in downcast profile, though he no longer knew if she still looked at him. "Now that's the question, isn't it..."

Silence; silence again. The chilling air stilled. With the chair, Orenda had also brought a coat, into which Neipas now tucked deeper; it was growing colder. Neipas took his fingers to his forehead. Staring at his hand then, he saw them stained with melted wax; with some sort of black oil blinkering in the firelight, the glow advancing and receding across his body.

Silence... Quietly, Orenda spoke. "Why... Because there was oil under our land, I guess. Because we wouldn't leave. One guy got arrested for it years later, you know. They grabbed him from the mental institution in the nearest settler village. He 'confessed' to it, and then he was sent right back to the mental institution he was in.

"Now apparently he had been an oilman at some point — so maybe he was part of that raid, I can't be sure. Whatever it was, it definitely wasn't just one guy. In any case, it wasn't just one guy at the bottom. Those who actually set fire to our home, those were many. Those who *killed* were many, it just wasn't possible that one person had done all that. We *saw* many people. We said that, many times... And they told us there was no 'evidence' to corroborate what we were saying. The testimony of some stupid natives didn't count as evidence, is what they meant.

"Anyway, they asked the one guy who got arrested, in court, why he had done it. Whoever remained of our tribe — all old people by that point — went there to testify. Oshana too — that was the only time she ever went back. I didn't go myself. To be honest, I didn't want to. But Oshana told me what happened... When they asked him why he did it, the man said, 'because I have demons in my head'. Apparently those were his exact words. That's probably the closest thing to the truth he could've said.

"Ultimately though... I can't understand it. I can't understand why."

She spoke; and her tone assumed the progressive character of a deepening trance.

"...What my mother used to do was dangerous... going around the wilds alone like that. But she braved Nature because she knew the Earth. What she didn't know was the heart of those men. Or — can I still call them men?

"She didn't know Mammon. No one in that village did. No one could guess the extent to which limits are trampled for the sake of money. They didn't know greed, what it was capable of. These men, they were consumed by greed and so became Wechuge, cannibal spirits, monsters."

Over there, on the beach, bodies gathered round the cauldrons; arms extended to the smoke, hands clasped round bowls. Aromas blew in and warmed the cooling breeze, tenderly rustling the flames; their tidal light reached meekly the shade where they were tucked together. Orenda and

Neipas, sitting side by side, looked both in the same direction.

Neipas' ear leaned against the sound of her voice.

"Mother Earth is the most subtle. Between the great clamors — under the clamors, always — Her voice is silence. She sings in whispers. She prophesies, and those who hear Her become prophets.

"We've built tools to interpret Her words, but we forgot how to listen with our hearts. We don't know how to heed Her warnings anymore. We must learn again, for Her omens spell doom for us.

"She told me once... that someday, we will all be gone — and all our treasures will lose their worth. All our knowledge will be forever mute. The Universe will never know the Sumerians wrote the Gilgamesh, or that we, the Moderns, weaved the Webwork. The day will come, after which no children will ever again watch the sunrise.

"But it doesn't have to be now. We can still flourish to our full potential. Many children can still watch the many sunrises yet to come, and bask in the moonlight, and witness the beauty of the world. Many generations... can still experience the magic of existence, attain the full freedom of wonder, to love. To live... *We* can still do that. We can still attain the paradise we were supposed to inherit... There's still a lot of life, a lot of life to be lived.

"We can't let Mammon destroy us."

Over there, the children made circles round the smaller fires. They shared a meal; each held one's own bowl. Much of those circles seemed to bend toward a single speaker — sometimes an adult, sometimes a kid as young as they. They all seemed to bend against the breeze, listening to tales told through the flames, crackling sparks, like feathers of the imagination shed, like wings taken aloft; like starry particles in the vast, boundless starry night.

Neipas likewise bent his senses toward Orenda, leaned his perceptions against the sound of her voice. With it, without knowing it, Neipas had been shifting his body nearer her chair, imperceptibly resting his elbow upon the armrest adjacent hers.

"Look..." she said. "I told you all this stuff, but — keep it to yourself, all right? Especially what I told you about Oshana. I don't go around telling people that. I just told you because I feel like I can trust you — otherwise I wouldn't."

It was growing colder; Neipas looked to his side and saw Orenda close, very close. He saw her cheek so near so suddenly that he felt sprout in his lips the wish to peck it. "What makes you feel like you can trust me?" At that moment, Orenda adjusted her body slightly; she placed her elbow on the armrest closest to Neipas.

Their arms touched. She looked at him.

"Well, you..."

Orenda's visage faced him close. Her chin rested on the palm of her hand, her fingers curled by the side of her lips. Her eyes stared large, black, beautiful, into his own; so near they were, that he could see himself and all the gentle fires in the world shining tender behind him. Her mask seemed to spread in a scattering of feathers and fall away. He could see her lips full — in blossom. He could sense them blooming in his breast, he could sense the whisper in their silence, he could sense their silence filling him. Over there, the world was made farther and farther away, so far away that it could no longer be heard. And the silence was taut. Its tension bound them together, and for a very, very long moment they stared at each other, ebbed into each other's eyes, dissolved; and though, in that moment, they did not move, they did not stir, they felt themselves nearer and nearer... The tense quietude, however,

was suddenly shattered. "Yo! You guys wanna eat?"

Coming over in large steps, trampling the sand clumsily, was Edazima. "Dude I gotta say, that's some good-ass soup Oshana's making. What you doing in here? Is Neipas filling your ear? He can be a blabbermouth every now and then. Don't think I didn't see you carrying the chairs for him by the way. Some gentleman, huh!"

"No," Orenda chuckled. "He's a good listener, actually..."

There was a bit of an awkward moment, an instant suffused with indecision. Edazima looked from one to the other with a wondering frown. ("What's wrong with you guys?") Then suddenly she realized the diffusing vibe between the two sitters, and she said contrivedly, "Oh — huh... I can bring you some soup, if you want?"

For a few somewhat embarrassed moments Neipas scratched his brow, knowing not where to place his gaze, half-trying to shape his mask so as to conceal his abashment, confusion, and annoyance. All of a sudden he heard Orenda's laughter, the sound of which made him blush; he massaged the feathers of his cheeks in the hope that no one would notice.

"Let's do it Edazima. C'mon Neipas! let's grab some dinner," and with these words she rose from her chair, inside which she had been so closely tucked, so close to Neipas during all those uncounted minutes under the dusk and the nightfall. She wrapped her arm round Edazima's shoulder, they walked away together; Edazima throwing back a perplexed glance at Neipas as they went.

Neipas got up much more slowly; his head was leaden with muddled reflections. Orenda's stare was impressed upon his eyes; his heart puckered round the shape of her lips. He perceived the night breeze and the pleasant warmth of the bonfires, the joyful unsteadiness of the sand under his feet, the magic fragrances; and in the amenity of things he felt an emotion for her so strong that he sensed it much deeper than the mere physical. Infatuation, perhaps? passion? even love? At any rate, their easy friendship had deepened in the awareness of profound commonality. Their first lives had both been ended by disasters wrought upon them from alien distances, and that common source of experience established between them a bond that seemed to him in that moment inextricable. And her words — what she told him, her anger spoke to his trauma, it sharpened his grievances; it seemed to have given a general direction to the aimlessness of his feelings.

He saw her over there, reaching the fire with Edazima. He saw her walk round the cauldron, unclasp her arm from her companion, wrap it affectionately around her aunt, her mother, Oshana; he saw her, a little taller, kissing the sage woman on her forehead. He saw her messy hairbun, her curvy locks, her smile. Edazima was pointing at Neipas, he noticed; and he made of pretense of looking round with a tilt of his head.

The moon rippled vast across the waves and the moths circled passionately about the fires. In a moment Edazima was at his side, placing a bowl of soup in his hands ("there you go") — then she put her arm round his:

"Damn, Casanova," she whispered, all giggly (for they were nearing the group at the fire, the giggling children). "I knew you were into some girl, but I'm pretty sure her name wasn't Orenda!"

"Mary Virgin, you're annoying sometimes," he hissed, under his friend's rambunctious laughter.

"Oh yes darling, but you wouldn't love me any other way, would you..." laughed Edazima in a low volume, making kisses in the air, slurping through the rim of her own bowl.

Neipas shook his head, smiling bashfully. "Just... eat your soup, man."

26 - Animals

EVA: it's called the Viral

NEIPAS: [having looked it up] Via Magna 26?

EVA: that's it :)
EVA: next Sat?

NEIPAS: sure ;)

[...]

EVA: still on for tonight?

NEIPAS: I'll be there :)

*

The mask was done, carved up well and proper. He left his roommate straining in the living room couch, glimpsing, as he exited, his face pressed deep against the television he had recently purchased; the wax of his pigeon semblance melting in the flashes and the shadows cast upon the dingy wall; his berserk fingers puppeteering the body of a digital avatar wandering a lush simulated universe.

The splendor of Babylon opened up before him. As the train slid in among its towers, it was enveloped in the blaring lights spreading from every lamp and out of every inch of glass; immense screens were fixed to the corners of the high-rises, images of moving heads beamed out of their giant facades overhanging the avenues and highways. The megalopolis was aflood with glow and motion — the white and red glint of a million machines clogging the tar roads — pulsing with the hectic flux of digital imagery from a thousand displays, glittering with the neon radiance of a hundred different colors, resembling threads of shining beads tossed across the boulevards, toward the haze. Looming overhead, titan and overwhelming above the enclosed heads of the denizens, the mask of Arnold and that of the Mayor — and of many others, masks endless — echoed many times over across the city heights. On the surface of huge swaths of glass their faces appeared, looking down ominously upon the proliferation of pigeons flurrying about their lives. Their beaks loomed very tall, their smiles stretched super wide into cavernous black gullets exposing themselves so vast on the giant screens that they seemed capable of swallowing all of Axiac in one slurp. And behind them, under them: windows, endless windows enclosing innumerable uncounted workers wearing the faces of diverse cattle, arching under the weight of the horns of their masks.

Through his own window, Neipas observed reality passing him by. He felt tired, listless. He had sat down with a week of nonstop work bearing on his shoulders — he'd been dropping hours at Kur while waiting for Eden to call him to his next gig, which would happen in about another week. Curving into frame, the faraway conflagrations of Ostrich's industrial zone made him think of Orenda. They hadn't spoken since their time together in the Southern Shore, and the notion of her, already growing vague, buoyed indistinctly in the meek placidness of his melancholy. Echoes of the enchanted forest and the idyllic beach struck him as distantly as memories from another life. It was as if it had all been a dream; he had slid right back into the numb nightmare that was his routine.

The glow of the Pearl palpitated at the top of the glass, on the edge of his consciousness. The flashing reds of the thundering megalopolis stuttered into his eyes a remembrance of the Eagles' Nest; brought back to his conception disjointed images of that last night, of which he remembered very little and which he was just now beginning to remember again. In fragments and frightful flickers, he saw the masks of the Eagles, as close then as the masks on the screens were large now; he saw bits of naked skin fusing with smoking meat across tables and upon platters, about the floor. Neipas wondered why his memories of that last night were so fuzzy, so turbulent — "probably that fuckin' pill Osir slipped me," he concluded in a mutter.

He shook his head, shut his eyes hard.

All he wanted now was to lose himself for a while — to relent. Orenda had given him a taste of life, and after coming back to the Belab he felt the desperate need to live, as soon and as much as he could, by whichever means he could find.

It was but a short distance to the dance club from the station, and Neipas made the walk calmly. The night city air seeped widely into him, fresh. In his *I*-plugged ear the music descended from the height of pumping beat down, at hard landings, into an ethereal whoosh of wind whispered out of the quiet alleys. Softened by this shift in the sound, he felt a prolonged sigh leave his nostrils, and let the tension in his muscles go with it; in the relaxation of his chest there seemed to rise something else from the depth, an underlying sense of vulnerability which crept up and made him teary for a moment. He unclasped the earbuds from his head and felt the diffuse noises of the city. No tears were shed. He strolled, and let the breeze dry his vision as he advanced in those great boulevard valleys renewed and cooled after the rains. The floor was wet still, blurry with the colors from the lights above; infused, in its novelty, with a sense of magic.

By and by, he let himself feel rested; he let himself grow confident. He had been paid. In a week he would be working in the McMansions of the Northwestern coast, toiling again, to be sure, but in a toil better remunerated. His prospects were looking up.

The club was just down the street now — Neipas could already see a large throng lengthening out of the entrance. His heart palpitated with expectation. Blowing the tension away in a deep exhalation, he lingered in the middle of the Via Magna, distracted by the movement of pedestrians and the homeless kneeling with trembling hands. Masks everywhere hovered...

He checked himself in the *I*, then walked alongside the queue. His leather footsteps clapped confidently against the ground, and as he trod across the thoroughfare, beneath the displays, the sound of his feet melded with the bass beating muffled and strong from the depths of the dance club. Scents of tobacco and perfume rose through his nostrils as he paced along, looking for Eva. Finally Neipas spotted her, with her back facing him, gesticulating lively, already tipsy, in conversation (she had brought two friends with her, each of which had brought companions) — perched seductively atop high heels. Neipas' eyes instinctively fastened upon the toned muscle of her calf and panned slowly up her legs, which grew beautifully toward the lace skirt in which they ultimately hid... He drew in the lecherous aroma of the evening and filled his chest with a daring spirit. Looking into the *I* again and finding the sight of it pleasing, he neared the group and said spiritedly "hey guys!"

Perhaps he hadn't been loud enough, for they didn't seem to notice him; right then they were huddling with their eyes glued to their glasses and took a moment to lift them off. Neipas wavered a little. He had even opened his arms wide in a show of complete self-assurance, as if ready to embrace all the fortunes coming to him and smash everything else with his implacable chest. Eva and her friends — in fact the whole throng in the line — turned their pigeon masks languidly and all at once to stare at his face. His heart drew in a bit, but he kept his arms apart and held tight his big smirk. It might've lasted but a second, but from Neipas' suddenly uneasy perspective it seemed as though they held their stare for a long time, as though they endeavored to peer beyond his visage.

"Oh!" exclaimed Eva. "There he is!"

Without another hint of vacillation she thrust herself right into Neipas' arms; with a flush of inner trepidation he felt the flurry of her dress, the excited smoothness of her form, the suppleness of her breasts against his rib, the curvy shape of her waist, curving — under the midriff — suggestively inward. He noticed also (or rather confirmed) that she had had a bit to drink already at that point.

"Guess what, guys — Neipas is a photographer!" she announced. And her friends looked at him with awe, moaning "woooooooow" as though before a marvelous apparition. Neipas laughed — but apparently they were serious. Requests for photos were made with many long shrills and questions such as "are you like, a professional?" were showered upon him; he took each individual *I* in hand. Through many pictures the girls posed together, facing the camera with their legs bent and hands on their knees, or standing sideways with buttocks thrown back and hands on their hips — both popular poses in those days — while their boyfriends stood awkwardly aside, or joined with grins suddenly immense. The session culminated with Neipas passionately placating their insistence that he join them (he ended up taking one picture before the lens), and denoued with everyone quietly reviewing the memories of their picture-taking from five seconds before on their *I*s.

Only after this did Eva introduce him to her friends. Neipas immediately forgot their names. They all looked very much the same — they certainly spoke very much the same way, and what they said Neipas had heard, under many guises, many times before — so Neipas couldn't well distinguish between one and the other. It didn't matter. His mind was too involved in the smells, the drunken mutter of the multitude, the pumping beat getting louder, the charged crepuscular light making blurry shapes of everybody, the feel of Eva's protruding hip, the mood containing the promise of raw youth. Plus — they were quite near the entrance already and wouldn't have to wait long, so the unsustainable small talk and consequent awkward *I* glances would barely have to be endured. Neipas had arrived just in time — on the cusp of fashionably late. He felt like a winner.

They were showing their IDs under the neon 'VIRAL' sign now. They paid the Bull at the door. Going in the beat grew much denser — the heat pulsing from the interior was instantly felt. They went down a long set of stairs covered with a thick red carpet, full width. The blinkering tunnel walls were splashed with the silhouettes of dancing birds meshing in spray paint, covered in fat graffiti letters and the stylized symbols of sound. The end of the stairs widened to a hall flanked by counters with cloakrooms on each side; approaching one, Eva took off the leather jacket she was wearing, baring her arms, her back, her cleavage; the smooth roundness of her naked shoulders lifted deliciously as she rested her forearms on the counter, cupping her elbows in her slender fingers, tapping her soft skin with her painted nails; and Neipas stood awkwardly between her and her friends yapping at their rear, feeling his desire bloom in the growing beat of electronic music. The Swan behind the desk gave Eva a number tag and smilingly she turned, clinging to Neipas as they strode toward the intensifying pulse of lights and noise:

"Have you been here before!" asked Eva in a bellow at Neipas' ear, which her beak touched lightly.

"No! First time!"

"You'll love it! It's a lot of fun!"

They walked into a wide gate of open heavy curtains and through a corridor flashing rhythmically between light and dark. They were heading into the music, which amplified steadily in volume. It grew louder as they went. Louder. Louder. Louder yet.

The dance floor opened up before them in a godly yell of bionic reverberations. It was huge; from the platform on which they stood, rising a little above the floor, they could see the immensity of it, its vastness of jumping and shaking bodies filling it to the brim. From the top and all sides a show of lights dipped upon them, retreated, flashed on and off, panned across speedily and in all colors; combined with the mammoth pulse of electronic beat, the spectacle swept the space in a craze of liquor-charged dance. "Let's get a drink!" someone shrilled into the overwhelming noise. The general vibe gave every indication that this was a proper first thing to do, and by instinct they found themselves already heading toward one of the bars, the one all the way on the other side. Eva pushed ahead, leading Neipas by the hand. The dance floor swallowed them with a powerful synthetic roar. They penetrated the thickening mass of bodies already in its maw; Neipas felt himself becoming drunk from the scented smell of sweat pervading every narrow inch of space, in a variety of degrees and fragrances, the stuff being so concentrated sometimes he felt like he was drinking it. They shouldered and slipped and rubbed their way into the heart of the wet throng and out by the bar. Vodka shots for everybody. A roaring toast, and down the throat it went; the alcohol immediately lifted into his brain and out his eyes. A long yell of joy ensued from the group. "Two red ardentes!" Eva shouted across the bar, then turning to Neipas who leaned on it she said "You'll like it!"

They had a few more drinks before diving back into the ocean of bodies, wading through toward the densest center as the music ramped up to a climax of lights and induced everyone into a fever-pitch frenzy. Everything twitched, everything flashed, every step quaked, the world blurred in laughter. Suddenly the group had been long gone and Eva was against him, swirling — slowly — her butt on his crotch, holding the back of his neck. Neipas felt her swaying hips on his hands, her skin on his wet lips, the moist heat of the multitude. The giant ceaseless boom of speakers made his every fiber rustle with fiery bang. Beat, beat, beat, beat. The lights go off and everyone cheers, whistling and shouting everywhere. Beat. Beat. Beat. Beat — wait — beat. Beat. Beat. Stop. A cavernous sound rises from the walls. Lights flicker. Noise flutters. Loud beat, explosion of light, beat quickens, everything is in sight, everyone dances. Eva's sweaty skin is glued to his collar, he heats up. Looking about in the disorientation of an overjoyed drunk, he sees the rapture of dance and intoxication, folk moving jittery and mad, skin melding into skin, masks torn off in utter furor. The lights fluttered from everywhere, all arms raised in religious symbiosis. Voices burst synthetic from every beak: "High! — flying high flying high flying high... *High!*" Beat, stir... "*High!*" Beat, shake... "*High!*" Beat, higher. "*Flying high* —" drag... hold — "DROP!" Explosion. They went crazy, broke into euphoria. His heart pumped rhythm, his head burst into a void. Another swig, a long yell.

The next moment he was deep in the cushion of a sofa in some corner, his brain swelled and shrunk to the bass, and Eva sat on top of him, her knees locking his hips, her tongue deep in his mouth playing with his in a flush of wet elation. She drew her face away and through the blur he saw her passionate, smeared in her lipstick and his wax, lustful and half-exposed.

Now he was on the dance floor again, whirling lone in swathes of fabric and feather here, in narrow intimacy with somebody (Eva?) against the wall there, buried among a wavy repetition of pigeon masks swinging about in the wet heat, and he laughed.

Now he was back on the couch, still laughing, Eva next to him guffawing too. At his side a couple buried their faces into one another's, and Neipas stared at them with a happy smirk and a slow nod, as if greeting the image of himself a moment or a thousand years ago, whichever it was.

Now he was in the bathroom before the wall-sized blocks of mirror, contemplating his reflection with the same smirk and seeing his countenance distorted into a mush of boozed-up happiness. He admired his wasted figure and bloodshot eyes ('where my bottle go? right here...') as he took a long draft of whatever was in his hand.

Now he was on the dance floor again, grinding against the whole city. Except for some stragglers dragging about lazily, everyone moved, everyone danced, everyone was crazy. It was a good vibe, he thought.

Now he was being pulled by the hand. Eva was there, and the music sounded a bit more muted. She was handing over her number tag. Time skipped a beat and she had her jacket on now, she dragged him by the hand, laughing much.

Out into the breezy wet streets where shapes oscillated along and the limp glow of lamps lent a reddish hue to the dead sky, covered by an indistinct mist that night — and into the back of a taxi where they were enveloped in one another. His fingers touched her leg and crawled up into her skirt — the sound pulsed from every corner of the dark interior of metal and cushion, into their ears and every muscle.

Then they stood in the living room of her house, and all of a sudden everything was quiet.

Neipas sat on the couch while Eva went to the bathroom. He braced himself forward, waiting, all expectation. He became quite sensible of the jumble that was his mind, and attempted to collect his thoughts with little success. Even in the silence the music seemed to beat inside his head, somewhere beneath the continuous buzz ringing in the ears. Detecting a sudden drop of energy in himself, he rose from the couch and paced in circles about the room. His mind wandered on its own; it quickly found the ravenous lust brimming in Neipas' heated body, and after only a little pacing and a wild ride of imagination he half-expected her to come out of the bathroom already naked.

Eva didn't come out naked. But she emerged into the living room like an imposing presence in the quietude, the bulk of her taut dress and groomed visage a stark contrast against the blurriness of everything else. Neipas approached her and she approached him; he perceived the deep rhythm of her breathing coinciding with his own; he noticed also that she was quite shorter now (he quickly and proudly deduced that it was because the heels were off). A tension grew as their bodies leaned onto one another. They spoke not a word — they were both keenly aware of the influence of alcohol still heavy in them at that moment, and knew they weren't capable of uttering anything beyond garble. Nevertheless the liquor dissolved in them all constrains of decorum, shame, and self-awareness; it lifted away all sense of self, and they quite naturally gave in to the primitiveness of the desire binding them into one. Amid a profusion of unfiltered laughter Eva pulled Neipas into her bedroom; he trailed the trace of her perfume, filled with the wild pleasure of living.

Time seemed to thicken and slow to a heightened appreciation of each moment. Their conjoined chests pulsed large and full of vitality at each beat. Their masks lay discarded in shreds in some corner of the room and they kissed one another with the raw flesh of one's lips gulping and nipping the other. They undressed one another by degrees, here slow and measured, here rapid and mad. Eva was lain upon the bed now, naked, the supple flavor of her breasts upon Neipas' salivating lip. He stood lustful over the bed upon which she sprawled her open arms and wide smile; she placed her feet on his chest. Eva's legs parted slowly. His eyes fastened to the bottom of them, saw the rosy flesh spread like a blossoming flower. The room swirled dizzy around him and her laugh rang sweet in his head.

Neipas and Eva absorbed one another in the sweat of penetration, swinging together the dance of living. The room embraced them with its intimate quietude and made their muted breaths of passion the only sounds to ring in the world, as if everything beyond the doors and the windows had temporarily ceased to exist; in fact the world beyond their universe pulsed as noisily as ever, as loudly and confusedly and as indifferently as always, ignorant of the intense ardor ruffling the sheets of that bed. But their senses were so completely involved in each other that they found no perception of anything but one another's body, one another's voice, one another's rhythm and beat of heart. Imperceptibly and in a near absence of consciousness one delved deeper into the other, melded further into the other's form, merged closer into the other's spirit, until there was no longer the notion of difference and disparity between them, and they had, for a few infinite moments, become one body and one spirit, man and woman, being and being made a singular existence. And so they plunged, farther and even farther (faster and faster), into the erogenous depths of one another until stimulation culminated in the maximum pitch of bodily fervor surging in both — and the illusion was slowly broken as they rolled apart onto opposite ends of the mattress...

The bare, dusky ceiling stared down into their laughing eyes and saw their chests panting with excitement, cooling away the shimmer of their glazed skins. As the breathlessness subsided and the ecstasy in their brain frizzled out Eva nudged close to her partner and nestled her head on the nook between his arm and chest. Neipas held her affectionately, drawing in the scent of her perfumed body with a transcendent sort of appreciation. Her hands hovered meditatively and playful round the shape of his nipple and he sank his nose into the messy locks of her hair.

They kept silent until Eva ventured, just above a whisper, "Did you like it?"

"Yeah," he smiled, in the same volume of voice. "Did you?"

"Yeah. It was really good."

They kept quiet for a few more minutes, basking in each other's company. Gradually, however, Neipas began to notice Eva's motions inching to the verge of restlessness — her fingers tapped his chest like they would a worn piano, in an apparent gesture of increasing impatience. This made Neipas a little uneasy; he realized that they weren't equally comfortable in their shared quietude and began wondering what he ought to say, what sort of conversation he ought to strike. Before he could come up with something, Eva spoke for him:

"So..."

"So?" Neipas laughed, bringing the laughter out of her too.

"What's up?" she said, her voice springing up a bit childish, sounding as if they were meeting casually in some cafe.

He shrugged gently. "I dunno — the ceiling?" Eva slapped his chest jokingly, rolling her eyes. Neipas turned his body to face hers. They stared into each other's eyes for a while, trying to discern each other's spirit of mind. Eventually Eva broke into a wide smile and, caressing Neipas' cheek, said, "You're so sweet."

"Yeah?" he returned in a muted whisper.

"Hm-hm," she looked into his peering eyes for another moment, then snug her body deeper into the comfort of her pillow and said,

"Did you like the party tonight? It was a nice spot, wasn't it?"

"Yeah," he nodded quietly. "Yeah, it was."

"We should do it again, you know. They're playing a Divon Venus concert there in a couple of months. They're putting tickets up on the Web next week... I think it'll be really awesome. Do you wanna go?" she asked, somewhat hesitantly and a little tense before the ampleness of his hush, which in the quivering depth of her she found a little unnerving.

"Sure," Neipas said, still in an imperceptible whisper. "That should be fun."

"The tickets are gonna be gone in, like, seconds though," she clarified in a somewhat louder tone, trying instinctively to spur the solemn mood. "Maybe I can buy it for the both of us and you can transfer me the amount after?"

At the mention of money a slight unrest began to stir in Neipas' spirit. He guessed the concert wouldn't be cheap; and though the payment from the Eagles' Nest gig widened his breathing space, he couldn't unworriedly dispense funds on such things yet. The last time he'd done so was when he bought the zoo ticket, which ultimately pulled him into the mess he was now endeavoring to emerge from. He was still too near the edge of destitution — so that he agonized quietly. Without his mask he wasn't able to veil the discomfort which always brooded within him and was now mirrored in the contours of his face, caught off guard. Eva detected it — Neipas knew right away that she had — and she said, "What's wrong? You don't like Divon Venus?"

"No no, I do like him," he excused himself, induced by his sense of discomfort to speak louder now. Then, recalling the Anubel, the hazy remembrances of which always lurked not far from the surface and had associated themselves with that perpetually simmering feeling of unrest, he said, "I saw him, you know. At the Eagles' Nest."

He spoke this without being consciously sure. But he felt like he had seen him, smoking herbs through his horse mask; he felt it with a feeling of memory imprinted in his soul such that he was certain, somehow. Eva immediately sprang up and, supporting herself upon her elbow, exclaimed over Neipas "Oh my god!" slapping his chest again, "You didn't tell me anything about it yet! You *have* to tell me how it went."

Her sudden eruption indicated that she was now comfortably in her element, which at once animated and damped Neipas' disposition, for while he liked her joyful manner he would have preferred to keep his mind off the topic just then. But into it he went, to Eva's sheer delight. He began to remember more and more clearly as he told the tale of those three days and nights; the words preceded the recollections, as they merely rolled off his lips without his mind applying itself to memory proper; he remembered more and more as he spoke. And as he crawled further in the telling his voice shrunk with increasing reluctance and fright. His increasingly shrunken mouth gave expression to searing memories of opulent lechery and extravagant debasement, memories of banknotes discarded through fire and play, and liquor-addled shouts in red rooms, drunken scoldings and even beatings, myriad unveiled demonstrations of power and greed. In the interest of accurate telling, Neipas concealed nothing — events exhaled from his tongue out of the haziness as they came — but this didn't at all temper Eva's excitement. In fact it only heightened it, and she followed the plot with growing interest and enthusiasm, the longitude of her nods ever taller and her "Huh-huh! Huh-huh!" louder and louder as Neipas' voice seemed to retreat into the black horror of his frightened chest. All while speaking, and without taking his eyes off Eva's, he followed the moth flying across the ceiling toward the shaded streetlights ushered through the closed window behind him; he observed the flutter of its wings, and in them an intimation of the stampede of feathers breaking out of the zoo window; he saw the furry texture of its body and in it a shadow of the ashes of a dead river; he saw it vanish among the weave of the curtain, on the other side of the nightstand decorated by a silently twisted conch and a pair of whispering seashells. Beyond the curtain, beyond the glass, he glimpsed the fig tree across the road lashing through violent winds as fluidly as seaweeds sway under the waters, and in their motions he discovered the dance club's electro-beat still pulsing in himself; why did the dancers struck him now so strangely? All while speaking, and without taking his eyes off Eva's, he watched the Debt Collector stand under the fig tree, watching the back of his neck through the window and the darkness. His pants lay wrinkled on the bedroom floor. The legs lay collapsed from exhaustion on the floor, and out of the pocket stared the *I*'s black mirror and broken glass; when had he broken it? He contemplated himself multiplying, gazing upon his myriad bloodshot eyes in the bathroom mirror, and saw in them the Debt Collector gazing among the dancers, behind the bar. The beat beat in him yet — he saw the lights, and remembered that he too had stood behind the bar in one of those interminably reproduced red rooms, up in the heights of civilized society at the summit of the Belab Tower, packed with busted animals — rich luminaries wearing masks very different from those they wore in public. With the latent beats surfacing the memory of that sinister place returned; he smelled wanton sodomy and brutal violence in the visions of his stinking memory following him in pulses and palpitations everywhere. The legs lay rumpled from exhaustion on the floor. Beyond the hollow legs, beyond the broken *I*, his mask lay forsaken in the bedroom's farthest corner; and from the shadow of the nook he saw his face staring at him with wide open eyes — all while speaking, and without taking his eyes off Eva's. He saw his face in the blackness of her stare; he saw himself in the pit of her leering eyes. For a moment he found it hard to breathe, finding his chest clogged with ash and feathers, feeling himself very naked without his mask. Profoundly ashamed, he grew red (in the face), bled sparks from the blink of his eyes, and sensed himself stagnant in the ash dam, stuck against the zoo window, trapped under the tower; he saw himself naked, hungry, empty, silent — all while speaking, and without taking his eyes off Eva's. By the end of it Neipas bore an expression of fear and utter vulnerability, facing directly the wonder of her beaming smile. There was something horrible about what he had seen and heard at the Eagles' Nest. Was he imagining all this? why did he only now remember it? "God that's craaaaaaazy," she would yawp between the narrowness of the walls. Eva evidently savored every tidbit with rapture; and Neipas faced this fact with a secret bewilderment. Were they normal, all the things he was now relating?

But there came a moment when Eva's hunger for gossip (which in those days was present in everyone as a distortion of the human need for tale, for context, for perspective, for a mirror into the spirit — in summary, for art) subsided and no longer veiled her eyes from Neipas' obvious distress. He had visibly diminished into a fetal curl; his maskless visage contorted into a fixed, blank whorl of profound brooding. Perturbed by this realization, Eva asked "what's wrong?" in a whisper induced by Neipas' sinister face and pose. Her lowered voice, fraught with sincere concern, soothed Neipas a little — her tone befitted Neipas' state of mind. He relaxed his stance a little; his heart softened, and in this moment of fragility he was encouraged to open it to her.

"I don't know," he began hesitatingly, noticing the shaking in his voice. He paused to gather courage and, seeing the gravity upon her face, let out a nervous chuckle. Suddenly he considered himself utterly ridiculous, and was almost compelled to simply laugh his feelings away. But, seeing that she was still listening, and wanted to hear what he had to say, he continued:

"I don't know... I've been feeling a little weird since that accident. Just... different. Or maybe not so different, just — you know?" Neipas sensed that she didn't know, that he was probably not expressing himself very clearly.

"When I woke up in the hospital... I had been in a coma for four days. Did I tell you that?" he whispered, reluctantly. His heart thumped under much pent-up tension.

"When I woke up, I went to the bathroom. I... I looked at myself in the mirror, and I... I... Well, I saw..." he decided to overcome his hesitation and ventured,

"I saw that my mask was off. I saw it was off and — I think... I think I saw — for the first time I saw..." he stopped, for Eva looked at him with a weirded-out expression. Then she laughed a bit; her body shook noiselessly with the chuckle.

"What do you mean?" she asked aloud.

"Hm?" Neipas muttered, disoriented and breathless.

"What do you mean your mask?"

Neipas looked confused.

"You know — the mask," he said with a sweeping gesture over his face, making Eva chuckle a bit more, making her tilt her head with a perplexed smile.

"What mask?"

Neipas gazed into her and tried to see if she was kidding. Then he let out, his tone reduced to a peep:

"What do you mean?... The mask we all wear." Eva immediately broke into a hearty guffaw, rolling away from him in amusement. "Fuck are you talking about?" she laughed, and speaking with a note of humored relief as she rolled back, as if having found the reason for his prior aloofness, she said, "Man... You're *still* drunk, huh." She poked his shoulder, kissed his cheek, squeezed his nipple. "You're so silly."

Neipas' face went rigid with confusion, then a sort of dismay overwhelmed him as he realized that she wasn't kidding. He scrutinized her face frantically, searching for something to disprove this. He peered into the flawless shape of her semblance, the smooth definition of her jaw, the carnal voluptuousness of her lips, the fragrant thickness of her plume, the shallow depth of her eye — until he unambiguously saw, to his profound horror, that Eva was wearing her mask even then. Her pigeon face sprouted out in a wide smile of wax, her beak protruded clearly in the shape of self-oblivion. He saw that though he had unveiled her nakedness her heart was still wrapped in curtains.

Time leapt unevenly from then on. The bedroom was now completely dark, and only Eva's mask could be seen, lit by the brightness of the *I* screen above her head. Neipas babbled a string of disjointed words now and then, and Eva responded either with mutters or overjoyed soliloquies. It was only silent again when Neipas realized that Eva had already been asleep for a long time.

END OF BOOK I

27

1st Interlude

"The face," said Eva before the mirror, "is a canvas."

She applied the pencil to her eyes as Neipas set the lights in her room. He looked down the camera's glass and saw the sofa ready, adorned with velvet mantles, out through the yawning lens. Glancing round he spotted Eva pouting to the mirror, and smiling he said to her "Very pretty." — then, turning to the curtains, he faced the sunlight streaming through the parted cloth, warming the windowpane. The surface of glass snuggled in the solar touch, embraced by the radiance of the star beyond the sky, far, far away in the void hidden under the veil of white blue, where a vast emptiness presides with the patience of immortality. A cosmic sphere of vulcan growls with fury amid that blackness, suspended in the endlessness of infinitude, afloat in the deep. In its bellowing core of a trillion multiplied screams, godly febricities and unimaginable pressures unleash at every moment a flurry of endless atoms, the fundamental ingredient of existence, racing unbridled in a frenzied elemental dance. Nuclei — cores within core — clash and mesh, are made one in endlessly repeating collisions, interpenetrating through passions so violent that their offspring are at once cast far away: pure energy thrusting out through the fire world for tens of thousands of tireless years, then launching off the edge into the void and shooting across outer space toward the sphere of land and water yonder, which circles slowly, slowly, slowly in prayer round the fire god.

The light of the Sun, long incubated in its holy bosom, takes but 8 minutes to cross the cosmic emptiness dividing the Earth from its nearest Star; it finally bursts out in majestic blueness, landing silently to spread across the sacred soil, making the little pebbles of desert sand sparkle. Upon this ancient land, desolate and mountain-fringed, a little girl sat, watched the afternoon shine in the glimmering little diamonds making the ground, and reflected.

With a stick she drew shapes in the sand. Contemplating the form of the earth, she wondered vaguely, in her infant mind, why the ground should be made of little stones like these. For a while she lost herself in the mystery of the little rocks, studying them closely, observing with awe the subtle splendor of their sheen. Meanwhile, a droning of machinery sounded overhead. A metal hawk, hovering indifferently, crossed the light of the sun and cast shade upon the girl (it, too, scouted the land). She had become used to the buzzing of these metal hawks, the girl had — she didn't understand exactly what they were, but she knew that they were menacing things and that she should fear them. She understood that the hawks took people, sometimes; though this she never saw. In her fancy she imagined that they must be picked up in their claws and taken to some nest somewhere, maybe to play with the little eaglets

— but now she was so concentrated she ignored the hawk's humming altogether, and kept admiring the little jewels of sand undisturbed. Then, lifting her head to face the expanse, she saw the extent of the plain, which prolonged itself far out; and she asked herself with much wonder, how many little stones must there be across the land! It was a thing of marvel for this little girl. And it seemed as though her young mind expanded with the stretch of the earth to cover the whole horizon, as she glanced and wondered at these things.

She sat near her enchanted tree, the shade of which had ebbed away from her; she sat near the well under the shade. The first house of the village was erected within a few walking steps. Emerging from behind it now, the girl's mother walked quickly toward her, but the girl was abstracted from everything save for the mysterious luster of the soil, which crackled in the sun's radiance. Strange, thought the girl. She turned her inquisitive stare now upward into the solar outburst (already her watchful mother was scolding her, for hadn't she said a thousand times by now she shouldn't look directly at the sun?) and saw instead the metal hawk, which had stopped and hovered now in place above her.

The copious leaves of her magic tree (shortly after) rustled with the wind and the scream carrying the dust cloud. The bird atop the tree flies; the serpent falls. The tree, too, had been facing the sun, with branches open and reverent, basking in its light, drawing supplement and vitality from that solar fusion conceived so many eons prior in the core of the heaven star, that remote explosion of divine energy, of strength long-mustered; with its life-lending force, the leaves of the sacred tree draw from inhaled air a certain molecule — a combination of atoms, bonded into a form (atoms being to molecules what letters are to words, and words being to texts what molecules are to physical existence) — a certain molecule composed of 1 atom of carbon and 2 atoms of oxygen, called "carbon dioxide"; from the soil, the roots of the sacred tree draw water, the molecules of which likewise bond to themselves the oxygen atom; and with the strength of celestial photons the magic tree synthesizes, unites, cooks these elements into food, to be stored and eaten in its bosom — and, finally, having culled from the air and from the soil, the tree gives back to the air the oxygen uncoupled and free, the vital oxygen, that which makes breathable the very air we breathe.

In other words, having swallowed of the fire of the sky the tree drinks also of the water of the soil; and with this energy and these elements, with the magic of divine existence and its wills, it makes the food of life for all those who eat; and at last exhales the breath of life for all those who breathe, being thus the constant source and sustenance of the living — and so goes the magic of life's incessant renewal. But now a powder of earth, bursting aloft, blocks the sunshine and coats the tree in shade (meanwhile the girl's mother screams). Some of its little particles, fractions of desert pebbles, latch on to the tree, its trunk, its boughs, its leaves, crumbing its body with a hue of ash (some land in the well, where it's said the profuse roots of the holy tree sprout and spread). Yet others pass onward; flying off still farther across the plain, over the mountains, between the valleys, traveling far, far away from the girl in the arid field, away from the miraculous tree and the sacred well, eventually the grains of dust land upon the distant river, with which they stream into the sea of the gulf — and from there to the wide ocean to flow along mighty currents, along which the great waters of the Earth churn.

The firmament glides on eastward, calm and indifferent, to encompass the whole planet. It soars over the oceans and over many little islands, above the big archipelagos where lush wet jungle blooms with life and newborn megalopolises rise and expand swiftly over the wilderness. Waters divine, sustainers of life whence life first came, exhale upon their shores, and inhale back into their own vastness where, loose in a great landless void, they roam freely. The expanse of tide, spanning horizons, mirrors the sun's brilliance yet more brightly than the heavens could; and the sunny scald, pressing upon the froth with its primeval force, spirits the waters upward in vapors, sprays arising like souls to cluster about the heavens. Yet in these days, the heavens are ill. The gearing skies are choked full of fumes and toxin, overburdened with the held breath and the moribund solar might of long-dead plants and creatures which had for eons been embalmed in petroleum down in the depths of the Earth — frantically dug up now, they are immolated and spouted in smoke from the untiring mouths of industries in the relentless chase of cursed treasure. Between the sky's star and the sea's own sun, such fumes amass heat and make the very air sweat. They boil the seas, affect the very winds flowing in the stuffiness. Elements acquire all a demonic temper, like one with fever. The hot ocean currents arise madly into the gusts that carve them, whirling into the skies by barrel to loom over the earth. On with the firmament, onward atop the waters they glide in the shape of cyclone, plummeting rain along wind's fury. Wrathful indeed are the gales now; joined with the might of lifted ocean, they dock upon shores and rip into land without mercy.

Beneath the mounting clouds frightened eyes stare. Great convulsions rock the land as the island folk make ready for the nearing storm. Garments flap on clotheslines as the wind rears and the sky darkens, and everyone who cannot leave stocks up and rushes to shelter. The air accelerates and batters against the island, flogging it with all the ire of many drunken gods, who hiss without cease, who drum without relent. Hidden in attics, in the darkness of corners, children whimper, their hearts quaking with fright as their houses shake in the immense scream of rabid nature. Frothing gales tear slates from roofs, violent, ravenous they toss monoliths freely into the thunderous air. Then the seas crash onto dock in bursts of spray and career through the streets and into houses, drowning floors whole, driven on by the delirious winds. Abodes collapse: ramshackles immediately, richer homes later. Wood splinters off, debris launch and scatter across the air as everything lifts with the powerful squall, arising against the hail and thunder toward the wheeling clouds. The furies engulf and chew up all things in their astounding power; and meanwhile plumes of black smoke, pushing athwart from a far-off coast to the northeast, twirl and blend with the circular winds, infusing the rains with a gorged atmosphere of ash. This pall stretches on very far over the ocean, carrying still the scent of burned trees, trees revered as gods by the first peoples of that distant land; a land they call Ooxor, and which most, in these days, know as Axiac.

At the gates of those lands a multitude wails with open arms. They are soiled, ragged, worn from long journeys across the continent. This here, before the fences, is the culmination of a pilgrimage of anguish taken by millions, a backbreaking march with death upon one shoulder — whispering against the advance, oppressing each step — and hope upon the other, pointing to the mirage on the desert horizon, to the towering beacon, to the auspicious lighthouse rising from the golden distance. They flee all from violence: violences of all the shapes violence can assume, in every volume violence can vociferate: they flee from the tension and booming snap of rampant criminality, from the growling and broken bone of abuse, from the lead in the heart and blood in the tongue; from the drawn hopelessness of droughts, from the bawling thunder of storms; from the quiet despair of poverty; they flee from the concrete prison of the soul, which is the narrowest and the most boundless of cages. They flee all from death, which chased them across the plains of suffering their tired feet walked to conquer. Whole families. Here now, standing before the center of the world, the shimmer of the great Pearl within reach, they clamor in desperation, and their cries rattle the fences of a nation. Many have realized there is no gate. They have realized there is no parting seam in the fence, no entrance to this land full of freedom and prosperity, as its great avian mask, covering every land under the sun in those days, advertised hour after hour. Some would still try to cut through — most would be broken, families separated, sobbing children wrested away from parental arms. Others, knowing that even if they passed the first barrier they would still have to overcome the second, and that after the second the third would arise, and so on infinitely, are ready to give up and return to tent to languish. But still they clamor supplicant, stretching their arms toward the phalanx of bulls frowning, with faces petrified in ire; but they clamor not to them. Above the fiery horns a platform is set, and atop the platform stands a young woman, bold, of brown complexion, wearing a flower behind her ear. She is now a lawmaker of that land. She has unseated, to the astonishment of wide-eyed peacocks, the former representative of Ostrich's chemical district, John the Legislator, so-named; and with that act had gained entrance to the halls of power and been given a voice and a hand with which to mold this neurotic age, so teeming with stifled potential, that great behemoth of peoples teetering on the cusp of something novel, hanging precipitously between dissolution and fulfillment. It was yet early to see to what use she would put her newfound powers. But many others stand upon the platform with her now and they shout with passion, "let them in! let them in!" as the hands reaching through the fences cast desperately the plea "help us! help us!". The whole of Wall Street convulses; and over its cries, elevated between borders, looms the trail of black smoke steaming from beyond the mountain peaks. The heavens flash in red and black. The sun beyond is narrow: a dot squirming among the haze.

Plumes fly in muscular spurts from the mountain forests; an epic procession of spirits levitating in the thickness of chaos, ghosts in the immaterial breath of demise. These are the specters of great millenary trees, wafting up in a monumental chorus of crackling bark, screaming out the slithering tip of flames. A great uproar develops beneath the fire; many agitated motions, very small before the towering conflagration. It is an uproar of panting breaths and water buckets carried back and forth in desperate attempts to save those titans of the wood. Warriors fight lone and brave in the midst of hell. They are the Oyate, land's primordial stewards. Less than a year on, wildfires have again arisen in their territory; and this time, encroach even deeper and spread even wider. Homes, whole villages are taken by the flames. The children and the elderly have been taken away but many women and men stay to fight the advancing blaze. All air is inhaled by the all-consuming fire. Chests heaving, throats clogged with ash, eyes covered in soot, straining across the black fog sweaty, clammy, breathless and blind, they beat back against the thumping inferno as though possessed by the very spirits of the land. Those who yell can hear themselves no longer, and the group of them disappears gradually in the foggy darkness, mute, as the flames encircle them all. No aid would come to them from Axiac, or anywhere.

Eighty of them would perish.

A silence absolute filled the grounds in the aftermath.

The forest smoldered, covered in ash.

Oshana petted the leaves of her olive tree between sad, meditative fingers, sensing with profound feeling the rough texture of their skin. That year's wildfires had just commenced, and the overhead winds ushered forth, ceremoniously, as in a sinister inaugural rite, the gushing smoke from the flaming treetops to the golden maw of the horizon, covering the wide arch of the sky with a pall of brooding colors. Waiting uncomfortably by her side was a student, a young aspiring journalist, upon whose weary mask twitched the flittering gleam of an impatient *I*. He had come to interview Oshana — the closest native at hand — about the conflict between the Oyate and agribusiness and energy interests which had unfolded with particular ferocity over the past few months. Because of their opposition to Noxxe's pipeline, the Oyate had been sprayed with chemicals, shot with rubber bullets, maced, arrested, stripped; brutally lacerated in the frothing teeth of leashed animals. The bare viciousness of financial interests had been released upon them without attracting much public attention so far.

They had held on despite it all. The conflagration that was starting up in the mountains then, however, would tip the balance of power — that mountainous weight — even further against them.

In her small garden that day, the day the new fires began, Oshana pondered upon the visitor's question. Her mind was nebulous then and she struggled to understand it. Amid the general wilting of olive flowers she saw, perched fragile and intimate, secluded upon a deeper bough of the tree, a single healthy blossom — four little petals parted from the small ripening ovary, tender rays sprouted from a nascent sun; a fragile star in the withering air. The student chafed his neck. He looked uncertain in the quietude, waiting for Oshana to say something, and his plumage could scarcely conceal the confused perplexity and anxiety simmering beneath the peacock mask. He looked marred by tight schedules, the despotism of rigid assignments, the fast approach of deadlines. The baby parrot at his shoulder insisted on pecking the side of his head. Unable to contain himself any longer, he asked again (a bit louder now, lest the indigenous matron hadn't heard him the first time), "Huh — ma'am, if NoxxeSocony has permits to use municipal lands — aren't they in their legal right to do so?"

Oshana's lip moved imperceptibly, soundless, vocalizing without a murmur the prayer in her soul. She turned her gathered stare unto the student. Already her nostrils throbbed with the scent of ash.

At length she asked him, "Tell me, brother. To whom belongs the land?"

The fidgety reporter said, "Well — to the government. It's technically public land."

"Do public lands not belong to the public?" replied Oshana patiently. "And did the public give this permission?"

"Well I guess, certainly in a democracy, the elected government represents the public in this case," commented he between pecks of parrot.

"Democracy?" Oshana chuckled sourly, sage; and smiled tenderly to the young student. "You can't worship both Democracy and Mammon, dear."

Confrontations between the Oyate and the petroleum giant had, however, subsided a little during the previous months. The Oyate had been helped, and the pipeline been so far restrained by Ostrich's refusal to let its oil refinery expand. One could not exist without the other — the torrents of underground molasses the pipes would bring from the northern open pits could not be taken in without additional processing capacity; Iblis had to grow. It had to be made ready for the feast marinating beneath the flayed soil of the Joachim Valley, a banquet of slimy, soggy, muddy vastness waiting to be swallowed up and regurgitated by industry into a plethora of different materials, into wealth. Such was the magic and curse of those strange days: the sheer power of transformation of the Earth, intoxicating the masters of civilization with delusions about mastery over nature, the most misguided illusion of control in that age so saturated with knowledge and so devoid of wisdom. This illusion was slowly breaking down by then; for the raw, invincible might of the Earth was beginning to be manifested anew — in ways never before witnessed by human eyes — in reply to the insolence of mankind.

And yet, like cynical Midases, like ghouls they pushed onward in the effort to derive gold from the poisonous relics held fast beneath the soil. The pipes lay in the razed and bored trails of the mountain forests over great fragmented distances, from north to south, in wait.

The transfiguring monster, the Iblis refinery, was meanwhile fed by massive parades of tankers at port and the dizzying network of pipes already beneath ground. Its maze of chimneys hid occult practices, advanced alchemies — through its gullets the petroleum would be poured, and flowed, like the rivers of chthonic myth, into the volcanic furnace to be boiled in the red fever ecstasy of its metallic bosom, burned, purged from long-slumbering spirits which passed, then, to the towers where they would rise, and float, and climb in spirals as in an infernal rite of passage, dissolved and separated into their disparate, most elemental parts; distilled into fractions. In the various and succeeding corridors the oil would part, dismembered at its most fundamental — to the very depth of molecule, to the very bridges between atoms — molded by cooling and heating and the crafts of science, and would thus morph into the bare ingredients to be shaped into the appliances of everyday life, as it was in those days — into fuel to power machines and animate cars, asphalt to pave roads, fibers for raiment, fertilizers to supercharge the soil, plastics, plastics, plastics; and into ingredients to be encroached here and there (a little everywhere) into the most diverse items and products, the profuse miscellanea populating modern, 'civilized', quotidian existence (the list is unending: perfumes, refrigerators, soap, shampoo, toothpaste, lipstick, pillows, film, cameras, even ink...) The exhaust, the waste, the unusable parts were discarded into the atmosphere through the belching towers and the flaring chimneys, unleashing the noxious powers of sun and air locked since time immemorial in the putrid, primordial substance, the agglomerate fossil of long-dead remains, back into the sky, released in the form of colorless gas or white plumes which Neipas could see from the beach, pumping out far along the shore. Through the fog of distance he contemplated now, as if bewitched, the misty outline of Iblis' smoldering cauldrons, and the bright flames atop the spires blazing ceaselessly, unending, more imperishable than the sun gleaming placidly upon the dismal ocean, as he held Eva's pulling hand.

(Here you go.)

"Sorry — " he mumbled as the plate landed on the table beneath him with a soft thud of ceramic, "I was distracted." Steam ascended to his eyes — Neipas pulled out of his reverie, and looking up he saw Eva in pajamas before the stove, over the frizzling sound of a cooking pan.

A vacant sigh came out his nostrils thinly, with a lingering vestige of slumber; his stare fogged up again as he observed her back and curly locks, as he watched the recurring motion of her shoulder, the lean-to and straightening of her hips. Idle memories entered his mind and vanished. Unsettling impressions lingered in their wake, mingling themselves into the overall fatigue and blankness of mind pervading his body.

Again, by degrees he slacked over the table, and once more his gaze settled upon the knife; he tried to focus in an effort to recapture the thoughts he had been ruminating moments before. His listless eye lay like a chasm in the foggy depth of steel. It split in two and blurred as he delved inward and perceived, in a hollow note, how similar his own gaze was to his father's — or how much his own eyes reminded him then of that sullen, unseeing orb, sunk into a grizzly head that seemed to shrivel and decay into the quicksand of disease more and more each passing day. Of the father's old self he could recall little; only with the aid of the only surviving photograph of life before the tragedy could he summon in his mind the idea of a strong, healthy, gleeful, protecting man. But that father he had known very briefly. He was little more than a dream to him; the memory of something imagined.

A sound of frizzling swelled onto the walls; it filled the kitchen, and into his ears increasingly rushed the accelerating noise of torrents cascading, tearing, vociferating.

Again a soft clink of ceramic hit the table. The fire had stopped. "You can eat baby, you don't have to wait for me," said Eva.

His finger, leaning on the corner of his beak, ticked upward to shape a tepid smile. "I dunno," he breathed vacantly, aimlessly.

Neipas looked at her wonderingly. Could he be a father? He mulled the possibility with some fright.

"You tired? Didn't sleep well?"

"Nah I slept ok... Bit tired though, yeah," Neipas muttered, absentminded. He prodded the omelet with the tip of his fork idly for a moment, as if to check it wasn't alive. The stirred egg burst with ham.

Eva contemplated him with a visage of inquisitive concern; her eyes fixed him with candor through the omelet's steam and beneath the planned and splendorous unkemptness of her morning mask's plumage.

Suddenly cheering up, she said:

"Hey, wanna walk on the beach today?"

That year's wildfires, which would kill eighty people, eighty lives, brought the mainstream media to the mountains for the first time since the ordeal with Noxxe began. The peacocks arrived gawking together and trained their bubbling iridescent stares upon the Oyate hard, all of them following the good story, attracted by the blood toll and its scent of sensational headlines.

The calamity represented a sort of culmination in the long struggle against Noxxe — but that wasn't all. For an old enemy had meanwhile reemerged, and the conflagrations also came to mark an apex in the almost yearlong conflict between the Oyate and the bordering farms.

The wildfires of the previous year, which had mounted to biblical proportions such that the flames had even climbed over the mountain peaks to make way downhill toward Axiac, had ignited close to the border between the Oyate's Reserve and land owned by a farming corporation called Penaguiar — specifically, the fire had begun on Penaguiar's side, burning through cropland and woodland at the border before passing on to Oyate territory and advancing unrestrained in every southward direction, then tilting west toward Axiac proper. After the fires had been put out and the land gasped beneath ash — even as some firefronts still combusted upon the far southwest, halting before the stern rocky tops — the logging companies came, with their mechanical fleet, to take the cadavers of trees still standing, naked and leafless in the smoking blackscape. Some of the proceeds from the cheap charred wood went to the Oyate, who desperately needed them; the rest to the Municipality, who assisted in and partially subsidized the logging. The very same was done on Penaguiar's land.

It was after this that the new problems started.

During the night, hefty workers bearing masks of oxen came and trod the border between farmland and reserve. They brought with them machines with which to plow the ashen soil. With industrial efficiency they sowed their trademarked, poison-coated seeds across the land, and repeated this every subsequent night, penetrating ever deeper into Oyate territory, piercing carefully the scorched darkness of their woods with silver flashlights. Their frantic labor was caught a few nights in. A confrontation ensued. When the authorities came, they sided with Penaguiar, who claimed that this was in fact their land and they were only re-planting the crops they had lost in the fire. The outrage exploding from the Oyate was met by the lifted clubs of the police and the mercenaries who, however, did not yet plunge them in as the mutual furor was deescalated before they could. Days of protests followed and meantime the oxen and their machines continued to stand on the disputed grounds — already airplanes, birds of whirring metal, were belching chemicals onto that earth — culminating in a lawsuit against Penaguiar for using Oyate land without permission. The agribusiness giant disputed this, roaring back with a counter-lawsuit accusing the Oyate of setting the fire on their crops. Controversy upon controversy piled. Eventually, the judicial court ordered the corporation cease tending to the disputed territory until a settlement could be made; and meanwhile the chemicals seeped deep into the soil, the crops rooted into the earth and populated slowly toward the lurking sun.

Those crops, which multiplied extensively across the plateau, were mostly used as feed for the immense meat farms behind the tilled land, rearing the northern border with the reserve. Here were the cornfields, graveyards of standing specters spreading in replications for miles on end. Then there were the factories of poultry and hogs — places so repulsive that their imprint could be sensed for many miles beyond, so absolutely reeking of pestilence as they were. The Oyate had long objected to their existence. Huge pools of waste festered in the open air and wafted into their domains, spreading a stench so foul that folk would often get sick from it. Despite the insular plastic drapes, between which millions of broilers were bound and choked with feed, the children of the Reserve's village closest still heard them crying throughout the neverending night; and would cry to their parents in an echoing wail of empathy, every evening, with their hands covering their ears and eyes tearful.

The chicks in those dystopian warehouses were fattened mercilessly, stuffed with haste, until their lungs nearly burst and their heart drummed with the hyperfrenzy of protein and antibiotics, their bodies so plump and heavy that the bones of their legs, newborn and brittle, snapped under the weight; fed, tortured, among wastelands of feces and the perpetually beaming, hallucinogenic lights that would never let them sleep, and forced them to eat, eat, eat — until they were shoved into crates, crammed with a million others in a confusion of panicked senses, into iron cars, down dark tunnels, damp and made of concrete, toward the deepest hells — all of which, on this Earth, are made by men — where their pulsing medicated veins would be stabbed by blade and their convulsive blood flow into metal troughs and pits, where they would die slowly, watching their life of pain run out of them senseless and cruel.

*

Oshana was speaking to an assembly of the Oyate. Just beyond the grove, the forest, dense in understory and bark, in birdsong and the scurrying of cubs, came to an abrupt halt; abruptly no more rock, no more moss, no more trunks or canopies, no more shrubbery or ferns, no more life — the earth was stripped bare. The soil overturned, upon it stood rumbling machines in broad wheels and pipes fuming patiently, and nothing more except the wide empty, blue sky arching from the desolation of a horizon peppered with blocky warehouses; only that and the ample, grim tailings pools interrupted the dismal flatness of the reach. No one could be seen then.

Breathing the silence of the sacred wood, opening her eyes to the mountain mist and the towering firs, Oshana addressed the Oyate with these words:

"To whom belongs the land?"

She let the quietude return to envelop them and aid them in their reflection; calm their souls. About her sat the battle-worn natives, the original peoples of that part of Columbia, which for centuries had endured fight after fight, defied invasion, survived genocide, preserved themselves at the brink of extinction. Most gazes were set rigid upon the bonfire, gleaming with profound shimmers of woe.

"To whom belongs the land?" Oshana spoke softly in their midst.

"At first the answer to this question was: 'To whomever settles in it.' Then it was: 'To whomever conquers it.' Finally, it was: 'To whomever buys it.'

"First it belonged to those who settled there. A people, finding the land unoccupied, inhabited it.

"Then it belonged to those who took the land by force. To enslave and murder the others, who had first settled in the land, gave those who took it by force the right to the land. In Columbia this, too, happened, and it was called 'settling' — to mask all the depravity and killing wrought out in the process.

"Finally, it belonged to whomever bought the land. Those who took land put a fence around it, and called it 'property'. They then tagged it with a price... and either kept it to exploit its riches, or prostituted it to others to do the same."

Her voice yielded once more to the quietude. The silence became so grave as to infuse the very breaths of the circular group upon the air, and the air was as if dissolved; all things made weightless in the slow lull of rumination — the very crackling of the flame in the center seemed to withdraw into the timber of the burning wood, to find shelter for its dancing reflections; and into this silence stole, by and by, the low, distant rumbling of the machines waiting in the field beyond the last trees.

Some allies and friends of the Oyate were also there. It was to one of them that she turned when she retook the word: "We all deserve our place in the world.

"We all need to be alone sometimes — and only in solitude can we be ourselves without reserve. And really, we can scarcely find a deep religion to others unless in solitude and the silence that dwells in solitude. Because only there can we find ourselves — and how could we find others without finding ourselves first? We all need our privacy, my kin.

"Only in private can we be our own. Only in our secret places can we ready ourselves for others. All of us need such places, my kin.

"We can be our own in places like these, and because these places are extensions of our own, they are our own. Our home is ours. It is the place to which our body can retreat, so that our mind can retreat to the body, and where the soul roams free. Everyone deserves such a place by the virtue of living — and in truth, our Mother has reserved such a place for each of us, because She has given each one of us Life.

"What else is ours, my kin? What else can be mine alone? My body is mine alone. All the sustenance it needs, is mine alone.

"If I take fruit from the tree, it becomes my own — and if I take of it, it becomes me, and I become it.

"And if the tree is of my home, so the tree is also my own. It is my own, in the same sense that my children are mine, and I am their mother — I am theirs as they are mine. So it is with the tree. I am the tree's as it is mine. It is my duty to take care of the tree as the tree takes care of me and my own — and this duty is sacred. For the tree, too, is my relative.

"A home can be my own, and to those to whom my home belongs, are also my own, as I am theirs. A tree can be my own to care for and feed from.

But, my kin, who in the world needs a whole forest?" — Oshana opened incredulous arms and shook her head, smiling; and some along the circle laughed with her sudden gestures and her words.

"No single person needs a whole forest for sustenance. Certainly no one needs a whole forest to be alone — no one is that *immense*, though some like to pretend they are. With a whole forest, one can only exploit — take more than one needs. And no one needs a whole forest to find solitude — but one may need a whole forest to hide in.

"My kin, this is why they need whole forests, this is why they need to own the whole land. To exploit, and to hide — such is their greed, such is their guilt."

(Only a few weeks after, she would tell the student with the peacock mask, whose ears his baby parrot cawed into and pecked, as they stood in her little garden by the bookstore, right by the Ivory Tower, close to the foot of the mountains, "This land we call campus — it was once a village. Did you know that?"

"Hum — vaguely, yes, I think," said the interlocutor.

Oshana loosened her fingers delicately from the olive flower — and performed a subtle gesture, of bowing her eyelids and her head in the utmost respect and reverence. Then, turning mournful eyes upon the student, said:

"What of the children that were massacred here? Is the land not theirs? Or does it belong to the shareholders of the Ivory Tower?"

And at that moment Oshana's stare pierced into the youth's very earnestly, with a force of rectitude and honesty such that made his breast tremble with human sentiment. The baby parrot slowed its motion, looking to the sky as it slouched toward the ground).

Oshana would lower her eyes whenever she spoke. As she stopped, her sight rose again to meet her companions, and the feather hanging from her ear waved subtly. Her stare settled upon one of the Oyate — one of the eighty who would soon die.

She spoke:

"Nothing is truly ours. Property can be owned forever — this is why it's passed down to one's descendants, because they are an extension of oneself. But one is much more than the descendants — one is also one's ancestors, and the brethren of those ancestors, and the brethren of those brethren. In truth, if we follow the stream of our lineages, we will find the very same source.

"My kin, our own lives are leased to us — we can only give it to our descendants, in the same way that our ancestors gave it to us, in the same way that the Earth gave it to them and gives it to us every moment — but we cannot hold on to our lives, because they are not our own; not ours alone.

"Because our Mother gives us our lives every single moment. Without air, without water, without food, without the operation of our organs, the blood in our veins, the activity of our cells — how could we live? In truth, whole worlds conspire to give us life at every moment."

Cloaked in dappled shades, the grove tucked from the sweltering sun — now inching to its zenith — undulating with mystic vibrations as Oshana's voice once more faded to the vast quietude of the mountain. The small fire palpitated in the inward gazes of the congregation. In the canopy-cast cool and the shelter of verdure, the ant climbed the tree, the worm weaved silk, the spider its web between treetops; the moth slept; the bees were still.

With a glint of her eyes Oshana nodded to the smiling woman near — a sprightly girl with a sad, determined gaze; the gaze of a strong and suffered youth — who would soon perish in the flames.

"My kin — the land to the Earth belongs. Those who tend to Her have a right to Her care, because they know the truth most elemental, unmasked by law or deed of property — that we must protect the land, for the land protects us.

"The land belongs to no one but Her," Oshana told in a near whisper, setting her finger upon the soil — "And therefore, the land exists for the benefit of all.

"The land belongs not to us, my kin. *We* belong to the land. So is the truth.

"It's the most elemental of truths, and the most well-forgotten of all truths. This is because," said Oshana to the gathering, "we no longer see the divinity in the Earth. For how could we treat a deity like this?

"Let me tell you how divinity left the land — "

And she began to tell of the lifecycle of the western gods.

Soon, the little grove on which they sat that day would be swallowed by the fire along with vast swaths of forestland that the Oyate protected.

Orenda would tell Neipas about all of it afterwards. As he stepped upon her porch he saw her eyes, distant and absorbed, glaring at the dimming sky with the worn fixedness of a long held obsession. It had been a while since Neipas had last been with her, a good while since he had attended one of their meetings — his being so busy with the new job. He saw her now like a long lost friend, faded, as though from a past life; and greeted her with a certain awkwardness, as if sensing in her a changed character, as if she were someone altogether new. She did look more somber than he remembered her. There had certainly been some awkwardness between them since he had started dating Eva — whatever might have caused it on Orenda's part, however, she shaded under the smile of her own mask.

But her look now was different. Contemplative — mournful. Undisguised in its sorrow. Neipas had just heard of the tragedy. In the wake of the conflagration's cease he came to her, to check up on her, and to pay his respects. In the course of that evening she would tell him a great deal about the intricacies surrounding the conflict between the Oyate and Penaguiar. She would tell him it was their fault — they had set those fires directly, she believed.

But who exactly *they* were was unclear. The croplands and the meat farms in the plateau, she found, belonged to or were leased by either Penaguiar, or its subsidiaries, or affiliated corporations more or less related to it. Some farmers managed the rearing warehouses, others the fattening compounds, while others owned plots of farmland which they sprayed with Penaguiar's mutant seeds and with its affiliate company's pesticides; this motley crowd supplied services to the company and its affiliates as contractors, renters, or serfs, indirectly — and much more rarely as employees. They would buy the seeds from them and sell the resulting crop to the meat farms, whose ownership either had significant common shareholders or were part of the same umbrella corporations, which themselves hid under the shadow of other umbrella corporations: all superimposed fictions upon other fictions in a multi-layered game of shells. Orenda had traced their kinship through the line and found an overarching pharmaceutical company of distant parentage, under which all those myriad affiliates and subsidiaries and legal entities ultimately hid, called KL Fraben. Resting her tired brow on her knuckle, she told him how that company was based in a distant nation, its chief executive faraway. She could not reach the leader of Penaguiar's local affiliate either. He hid behind multiple anonymous fund owners and convoluted walls of PRs and HRs, behind an army of suited peacocks, and spokesfolk with an infinitude of staring eyes and mouths and open fans covering the back-works and gears on which those corporations ran. The artifice crusting over them was impenetrable. It was difficult to ascertain who they were really fighting against — such was the nature of the titans of those days. They were everywhere and nowhere at once. Meanwhile, national and local authorities cared nothing for the Oyate's plight, and they only had themselves to resort to.

There was anger in her voice, but it was not a fighting anger. It was anger moribund; burdened with the weight of hopelessness. She looked withdrawn, tired; shellshocked. Her eyes were glassy and mute.

Neipas asked softly:

"You really think Penaguiar set the fires?"

"Yes, of course."

"But why?"

"To do what it did. Destroy our land so we get out of their hair. So they could keep what they took."

"And... they would risk killing people? Do you really think so?" Neipas asked hesitantly.

Orenda shrugged. "Fuck knows. Yeah —" she nodded with certainty — "yeah... They're maniacs. All of them."

She sipped a bit of strong, hot tea. The air had gathered an uncommon chill.

"I'm sorry," whispered Neipas, his voice unsure and half-caught in his throat.

She shook her head slowly, in utter unbelief.

"All of them died — trying to save the land," she muttered with much difficulty, under a disoriented scowl, evidently struggling to abate the weeping in her tone, trying to hold down the shivering of her breath. Her mask became gradually fixed in a show of fortitude; but only after a long period of silence could she continue:

"Eighty people... Eighty lives..." whispered Orenda at length, all the time moving her head in the same slow, baffled motion of incredulity. "One life taken is a tragedy out of all proportion, you know? but eighty is... How do I even describe it? It's impossible to even conceive. Really, it's..." She held her breath in the perplexed search for expressions that would convey the totality and the depth of the loss — and, not finding any, she sighed frustratedly into the closing sunset. After shaking her face a bit more she sank it into her hands. "It's all so fucking stupid," vented she, lost in the stranglehold of grief.

Neipas could find no phrases of consolation, nothing that would make the reality of the tragedy less real for Orenda; though he himself wallowed in a sort of fatigued abstraction insulated from all pleasures and horrors of the world. Orenda emerged from her hands sniffling, and turning her set gaze to face him for the first time she said with strained outrage, "They acquitted the arsonist a couple months ago. Did you hear?"

He looked at her wonderingly. "From last year's fires."

"The guy from the slaughterhouse?"

"The very same," Orenda said. "They couldn't find anything... And the only witness is not only a native, he's also dead."

Neipas avoided her stare, gazing at nothing over his pending lip. Into the abrupt quiet surfaced the memory of the Oyate in the hospital, of his charred skin infested with pus and horrible blisters, the soiled bandages, the labored breathing.

"Sorry... I didn't know," he said.

There followed a long mulling silence, during which the megalopolis, extending above and below them, buttressed against the sieging night as it came, yawning all in soundless blasts of light, insinuating itself into the lulling porch. Again the great urban vastness blazed aglow with tones of red, white and yellow, and at the very peak of the jagged sprawl a mighty beam gaped, like a beacon atop a world ocean of molten tar — like a manufactured sun.

"What's been going on with you?" Orenda's voice asked through the quietness. "You disappeared."

He replied slowly, mollified by the dusk and various layers of fatigue, "No, just... Been having a lot of work lately, you know?" He was being sincere, but work wasn't all that held him. It wasn't only the time that labor stole, so that he had too little; it was also that space was too vast, too tangled, too inhospitable. The sprawling insatiable architecture of the city, the great distances and the onerous means of transport made it difficult to live up the time he had. Whenever time was free — space imprisoned him. The megalopolis itself erected barriers all around him.

"What are you doing now?"

"Same thing. Mostly gigs in the Northwest now."

"In the sea mansions?"

"Yeah... You wouldn't believe how trashy those folks are though."

"Trust me —" she snickered. "I'd believe you. Not liking it?"

Neipas shook his head, and with his fingers drew a drooping beak. "Just saving up to get out of it somehow, you know... Pay my debts and everything. They're sending me back up there in a few days though," he said, pointing to the immense beacon light suspended over Axiac.

"To the Eagles' Nest?"

"Yeah... Three day summit."

Silence.

"And how are things with Eva?"

Neipas shrugged. "Going ok."

They looked at each other for a moment; and suddenly — in the mysterious swell of his heart time seemed to skip a whole beat — Orenda asked, as she scratched her plumage, "Want some tea by the way?"

"Sure sure, thank you. I — gotta go soon, though."

"No worries. I'll be right back."

She returned with the steaming tea the very next moment, finding Neipas within his *I* [**NEIPAS:** I'll be back soon ok].

"Here."

The tea flowed pleasantly down his throat, distributing throughout him a lassitude of relief. "When are you doing the Eagles' Nest?" she asked.

Neipas told her, and she said, "I see... Anyway yeah — I'm going to the mountains tomorrow to join them. Wanna come with? We could find you a ride back before the summit job..."

"I can't... I have prep for the summit tomorrow. Rehearsal..."

Silence nestled once more between them, and remained so as each drank their tea. Neipas suddenly felt really tired. He felt like sinking into the chair and sleeping as he fixed his glare upon the Anubel's Pearl; all the while he remained, however, very conscious of Orenda's presence by his side. Her feather earring swayed lightly on the corner of his eye even as Axiac soaked into his head. Contemplating the city and its sky from her porch, the world seemed to him made of fleeting and unreal substances, of dream-stuff barely glued together, assembled dissipations about to vanish into the waking eye of an Almighty Sleeper.

Orenda nodded and smiled despondently; and as if not a moment had passed she said, "that's ok. I appreciate you being here. I really do."

The world seemed enveloped in the aromatic vapors of her tea.

The vast wheel circled before the reach, whose spokes curled into the fumes which dominated the horizon upon the shore, and where the sight, lost in the landscape's growing vagueness, could only guess a few contours of factories among the giant haze of dissipating forms. A long succession of whispers and sighs instilled itself into Neipas' void stare, whose eyes blinked to the cadence of the wheel's turning as the sea edge gasped and strove at his side, endeavoring obstinately toward his naked feet. He felt as though the very prospect were attempting to tell him something. How long had he stood there unmoving now, trying to decipher its message? wondered he as Eva pulled him by the hand.

"C'mon, baby. You sure you're ok?"

They turned away from the pier to face the deep immensitude of beach extending northward. All along the running shore the ocean clapped and soughed, very tranquil, very appeasing, stretching to a haziness of distance whose ethereal perfection was marred only by the looming shadows of faraway bluffs. They strolled between the rearing spume and a wide arc of shells strewn across the high tide, and the further they advanced the better they could distinguish — enveloped in the goldening vapors of the prospect — those cliffs of the Northwest, wherein tucked, concealed by the jagged rock lifting from the coast, the mansions of the bottom-tier rich — actors, athletes, celebrity journalists and crafty marketers, musicians and managers, some producers, a few politicians, and other entertainers. These were quite visible and even conspicuous to whomever drove along the highway there, perched impossibly upon the rocks, all buttressed with incomprehensible profusions of roofs and balconies, like animate fortresses watching arrogantly those passing beneath. But as the road curved into the ravines, valleys and desert plains of inland Columbia, the beach continued, eventually barred to all access and to all scrutinizing eyes, to where private stretches of shore lay, pristine, at the end of private roads leading to private communities of opulent real estate. Here were the holiday houses of the oligarchs, masters of the flock, which were rented for most of the year to their proteges and immediate subordinates, the various multimillionaires — the outer walls — who wore the friendly masks of their empire. Majestic and immense, the waterfront properties supported a large workforce of grass-mowers, dog-tenders, toilet-cleaners, banquet-servers... — Neipas had been an occasional element among their lot for the past year, at turns assigned to an event here, a party there, according to the needs or whims of supervisors he had never seen. The pace was difficult, the very commute to these places strenuous — they were veritable enclaves at the outermost edge of the city, hard of access to anyone without a car, and hard to find. Neipas' journey to work involved very long walks and various buses which had a wild frontier aspect and were as rare as oases in the desert — and carried the forlorn waiter to the beginning of a day of many grueling hours standing, often by the grainy sea, bearing only his stuffy mask for protection from the parching sun. For hours he would stand obediently and swelter, without recourse to break or bathroom, suffering mute indignities as he smothered the protests of his body and stooped, again and again, over white canopy beds lined up along the sand, upon the white feathery mattresses of which the wealthy frolicked, glib, inane, flat before the wide nothingness of an ocean which to them was but a vague backdrop to the numbing abundance of life's pleasures and exertions.

Bending over the cackling drinks, ever beneath the close watch of the sun's ever-open eye — dissipating the horizon in sways of mirage, scorching — Neipas would often feel himself to be a mere shadow of someone who had never existed, a mere dream barely incarnated and long-ago miscarried; he contemplated his gloved hands and the serrated horns at the corner of his sight, damming his exhaustion in the reservoir of a stagnant mind, and felt himself half-dead, delivered unrealized into the river mouth of vicious fates, left to dwell in the mire of its delta; his senses and organs drifted scattered in the breathing motions of the sea. And when he looked through the brume of his past toward the spring of childhood he spotted, sometimes, himself — very tiny and very vague, a mere speck of film grain — imagining a mythical future upon the grassy margins of a dead river. The child that he had been (now dead too) would never have dreamt himself bowing with hefty loads before the rich and bearing a heavy ox head and a face of furs under scalding sunlight. There had been a kind of fascination at first, a feeling of reverent deference to the glamor of those houses, the gated properties and the exclusive soirees under the warm glow of festooned lamps and vast barbecues at the poolside, with the fresh beach breeze suffusing the air over the lawns; and the masked dignitaries plastered with pigments and bloated with plastic, vaguely famous, as Neipas was told, enjoying the benefits of young wealth in the ceaseless self-scrutiny of their fans through ever-watching *I*s — their audience, constantly there. But he tired of it quickly, as he grinded further into the uneven routine; and soon began to nurture a vague, almost involuntary scorn for these mottled harlequins, as he watched them — day after day, bowing and bearing — lounging in the absurd lavishness of their seaside abodes. It was their attitude of smug aloofness — perhaps. It was certainly, partly the fatigue of the job, but there was also a sense of dehumanization which encroached, somehow, into his moral sensibility as shifts were shed and days piled on. Eden, the corporation that employed him, was different from Kur in that he spent whole days in the service of specific patrons rather than rushing from one to the next, and the feeling of being regarded as a thing — an animal at best — seeped much more deeply with the prolonged interaction with these folks, who would never look at him, who'd never address him except in issuing orders, generally with a sustained arrogance of detachment so blatant as to drive him into resentment; a gradual accumulation of anger. This wasn't always, strictly so — but even when those horse, swan, or deer glares pointed to him with anything resembling acknowledgment, even as their snouts opened to him for anything other than to paraphrase "obey", and even when Neipas was given leave to articulate himself without bending, still there was a glaze to their stare, a vacancy in their voice, a peculiar rigidness of demeanor which would induce Neipas into extreme caution, and a vague sense of fright that would eventually cause his horned head to lower anyway... There was always an indubitable wall — a platform of ascending steps, as it were — between him and them, that much was clear; their masks scarcely tried to hide it. Neipas was their inferior. A pet, at best — or a beast at worst. He was but a prop; a machine of convenience. To someone who'd once been free, and had dreamt only of wider freedom, it was a degrading experience; less so because there were many others with which to share the burden, but indeed, it was humiliating to him, nonetheless. Yet he endured the sense of debasement. He carried on with the pride of hope and the resignation of need; the need to survive, and the hope of emerging from the hole of indebtedness and resuming, at last, the path he was meant to take in life.

(He dropped a few coins on the alms basket placed before the conch busker's feet). Neipas often chagrined himself for feeling the way he felt — and felt that he ought to feel gratitude instead, for in fact, he earned more money now and was better able to keep apace with interest payments. Soon he would be able to buy a camera and proper equipment, and save enough to afford time for his craft: to rent a studio too, develop into something self-sustainable, perhaps even travel on expeditions to exotic reaches later on. Only such prospects kept him on his feet. He was tired — tired of the very tiredness and lingering exhaustion of his body and mind. That he was forced to effectively live with Eva — for her house was much closer to the distant Northwest shore — and sustain an increasing weight of dependence (she would even drive him to work sometimes) didn't help matters either.

She walked ahead of him, every so often bending down in foggy motions; even at that short distance Eva seemed altogether enveloped by the mist of spores blown from the waters, and acquired in her steps a dreamlike quality which Neipas observed carefully, contemplating as if from very far away. They had walked upon those sands many times together by then, they had stood, hand in hand, within view of that ocean as the fireworks of the new year glittered upon its black waves. Seasons passed by them under the same sunlight, with but gradual variations in its daily length, with little change in the febrile weather except, perhaps, through the occasional, slightly colder breezes at night. For months now she had received with excitement the tired reports from Neipas' work — for she knew about these millionaires and their relative fame, much more than he. Neipas thought deeply, sourly as he watched her carefree stride. They walked on the smooth soil, between the tides and the stretches of sand dappled with a multitude of steps beyond the belt of shells clustering along. Step by step their feet caved into the wet grounds, clay of the ocean, disturbing its unbroken form, before the waters slid in to shape it aright again. It shone sleek in the tepid sunshine, beneath the sun glare which once witnessed the first ships arriving with lifted banners of canvas, under the peace symbols of which brimmed intentions of plunder and the fervor of gold and new riches... It had been just beyond the vapors which Eva and Neipas faced, their first mooring — docked before the extensive reserves of clay of those cliffs which, once exhausted, gave way to the wealthy mansions and to the vast military bases beyond, housing in the hollowed wake of the once-rich world of grottoes and caves their myriad suicidal missiles and suicidal armies; where once the rock teemed with the inconspicuous life of a billion little beings, it was now flooded with the deranged intents and fantasies of powerful nations.

"Look at this one," said Eva, stopping; showing Neipas a beautiful cornucopia of a shell, with 8 coils winded, as she held it up, and took a photo of it. She had a full collection of such seashells in her home. Neipas smiled a sad smile; and kissed her cheek to disguise it.

At this they slowly drew away from those waters stretching without margin, that unending river covering, like a vague mantle, the innocent years of Neipas' existence from which he'd fallen, as a fledgling clambers down from its nest. Each step waded and bled across it — the river was thick in his veins that day.

Meanwhile, the smoke grew insidiously and yet imperceptible — from the horizon to the south and the north and even the mountains west, to smother the very Belab, the shining Pearl, and even the declining sunshine as the fires sizzled afar...

*

"First they lived in the womb of the Mother, and so existed inside all things. They were unborn, and thus still unnamed.

"Then the gods were delivered," said Oshana, "into the minds of men. They moved each to their assigned places — and though they were now separate, they still were everywhere.

"But then," she continued, "they sought to unmoor from the Earth. They wished distance from their Mother, in the manner of thankless children, or children afraid. So they moved into the mountaintops and to the skies beyond — because canopies are still too close to the Earth, whom they began to loathe, and fear, and hate. And where trees culminate in an embrace of open arms to the Sky above and the Earth below, mountains rise into a flight, as if desiring to flee the Earth. All their might fathers into peaks, which point to the Heavens — this is why the gods moved to the mountains.

"All things grow mighty through distance. And though the peaks are coldest, they are also the last to whom the sunlight bids farewell before it departs, and the first to be greeted by the sun when it returns. Light and frost made the gods very 'awake' — and so the gods thought they could see better than those who had remained below. They thought they themselves were the light — and they became cold in their hearts.

"Still they descended upon the Earth, for they missed their Mother. They were petulant and often played masters in their youth, but the Earth, like any good Mother, received them with open arms. The gods of light raved and stamped and made much noise with their tantrums. And She, like any good Mother, was patient. Often they tried to subdue the Earth, and still the Mother loved them.

"Less and less then, though, did the gods descend to the Mother. More and more they remained on the mountain. And bit by bit the divinities left the Earth."

Into her pause flowed the crackling fire, casting fading sparks to the distant sky.

"Gradually the gods became one God — and the one God, too, was everywhere. Yet still, He was distant, remaining in the mountaintops and in the skies beyond. And the one God was still these many gods — he was the Jealous God, the God of Armies, the God of Truth, the God of Light, the Living God, the God who is Three Gods and many other gods besides. He was a very angry, very judging God, he only descended from his sky mountain to issue orders, pass laws and proclaim judgments, and He was the first to see the Earth the way machines now do, in binaries — good and evil, light and darkness, male and female. But He Himself was many. He was even the God of Love later in life — for age softens even the most furious tempers. This God — a composite of all self-exiled gods, a unity of separate powers — was most successful in subduing the Earth in our souls.

"Some now spread the rumor that this God is dead. But don't these gossipers know that the lives of gods, like the lives of mortals, linger beyond themselves?

"His corpse is animated now by the true object of Wechuge adoration, the true god of their worship, whose name is Mammon. Mammon has always been a god among many, but at last he proved to be the strongest: all of them died and Mammon is the only one that stands now. Mammon has consumed them all.

"Mammon is not the god they pretend to adore, who they say is everywhere. No — Mammon is not everywhere, but it ambitions to be. It wants to grow, that is its chief desire. It wants to grow until it encompasses everything. It wants to grow until it subsumes, until it subdues all things.

"For you see, Mammon cannot coexist with the Earth. But it cannot exist without Her. It can only thrive by stealing from the Earth; but it can only be sustained by Earth's graces. It can only live by killing the Earth that nurtures living. So it is a suicidal god — a god who hates life.

"Mammon is the great measurer, the tailor of reality. He assigns a number to all things in his great hierarchy of worth. But how can we measure the value of something that's worth everything?

"How can we measure the worth of rivers, how can we measure the worth of forests, the worth of mountains — the worth of water, the worth of food, the worth of shelter? How can such things be quantified? In truth, one cannot do it without quantifying life — without cheapening life.

"'That life is worth such and such, and this life is more valuable than that life,' is what Mammon says. 'Everything is relative, nothing is stable,' is what

Mammon teaches. To Mammon, there is no such thing as 'truth', and reality itself is a fiction to be commodified.

"Mammon is the great alchemist. He takes everything into his domains and turns all things into abstractions — so that all things may be ranked according to his laws, his whims. He mystifies all things, between all things he places borders dressed in pretty curtains. Mammon severs water from rivers, food from land, life from nature, worth from value, reality from sacredness, present from past, past from future... Cause no longer has any connection to effect and madness rules his domains. He unmoors and desacralizes all across his domains, whatever fastens to him unattaches from the Earth. And his reign is vast — it covers the land, it covers all beasts, it covers human bodies, and it is nearly at the threshold of conquering the human mind completely. But there is one last frontier for Mammon — the human soul.

"In truth, the human soul cannot be quantified — therefore it must be abandoned. Only then can Mammon conquer completely — but Mammon is a suicidal god, and for him, victory necessitates destruction.

"Nature was the first to be conquered by Mammon's ministers. They came dressed like the disciples of the one God. In truth, the one God was the most successful at subduing the Earth, because he represents a composite of all deities, and is the unity of all western gods. But Mammon is the parasite of gods, and within them he has hatched his egg. Mammon is the parasite of the Earth, and when it destroys Her, it will find no more hosts to conquer. Yet the Earth is much stronger — Mammon will perish before She does, but not before he takes us with him, if we continue to feed him.

"Behold, we all live in Mammon's dream, and unless we act, we'll all die in his sleep."

Her eyes open, her senses wide, Oshana felt the soil with the palm of her wounded hand — the bandage was off now, the sensitivity returning, the burn healing — breathing in the air, of smells of forest, fire, and machinery mixed; and she spoke:

"Mammon is a relative of that God who once said, 'let men rule over the fish of the sea and the birds of the air, over the livestock, over all the earth'. But he has nothing to do with the god who said, 'Love thy neighbor' — for a loving neighbor does not impose upon another.

"'Love thy neighbor,' this said the god who wandered the Earth, the god who had a human mask, the grandson of the one God. He was a prophet and a prince, and came to redeem the mistakes of his lineage. Hadn't the one God rejected the tiller? But his own grandson was born in the house of bread, and his first crib was the trough of herbivores.

"He preached differently — he spoke of love and mercy, and he spoke against Mammon. And though he still spoke about extraterrestrial rewards and punishments, and though he was confused in his speech, still his heart was righteous and his intent pure. His words were well-meaning. But few listened and instead they killed him, and even his own disciples didn't listen, and still they crucify him on their altars and everywhere. In truth, those who profess to follow him are the ones who understand him least. And today, some of the worst monsters name themselves after him. They, the hypocrites, wear a mask in his likeness and bear his mantle. Still they resurrect him, so that Mammon may consume his spirit and eat his liver.

"This grandson of the one God had such weight in life, that when he died and thrust into the Earth, he broke History in two. Such that he became the center of History — but now we approach another center; a crossroad of two paths. This center breaks into a choice.

"There is the path of the Earth — and the path of Mammon. My kin, I tell you — that unless we tread the sacred path of the Earth, and stop trying to set our feet upon Mammon's sky — unless we begin to walk upon the Earth, we are fated to remain forever still, forever forgotten, *under* the Earth.

"My kin, we need to learn again the oldest, the most fundamental of all wisdoms — we need to learn how to recognize the sanctity of life and existence, we need to learn again how to see the sacred in the Earth."

The canopies chanted and chimed in the lifting breeze; the wonder of the wood was made manifest in the hallowed sounds and the environs' living splendor. For a prolonged moment Oshana closed her eyes; and receiving the air, she smiled. All those round the circle listened to her voice, to her silence, coursing through the song of Nature, with all the devotion of their attention and all the serenity of their being.

"It is unfortunate that this venerable god — despite his qualities — still often disdained the Earth. But who can blame him? It is difficult to revolt against one's ancestors, and more difficult still to liberate oneself from their influence," she said.

"My kin, in truth, we need to return the sacred to our sense of the Earth.

"What is the sacred? The sacred is a passage — and a mirror. We need to find the sacred in the Earth and in ourselves again. We need to bring our gods back from their mountains. We need to rediscover the divinity of the land and the immanent godhood of Nature.

"In truth, this is anathema to Mammon, because Mammon seeks to gain ownership — that is, absolute command — over all things. That is his way. But one cannot absolutely command the living — only tools and machines and dead things can be commanded. Therefore all things must fall inanimate, everything must die at his feet.

"Indeed, to 'own' the land one must desacralize the land. And it was only when the sacred was extracted from the Earth that Nature could be dammed, mined, and burnt. The sacred, my kin, is life.

"My kin, in truth I say — that unless we learn to see the sacred we will be blind to the pit already enveloping our senses — we will fall into that pit at last."

*

The smallest seed splits — and in an instant there blossoms the sun, flowering in fire, fading gradually into a trunk that climbs, climbs, climbs aloft... The canopy covers, it burns the whole sky. Its fruit is poisonous — it spreads in spores of venom and kills everything near. It's a tree made of ash.

"The seed of this tree," *said once Neipas' father, pointing to the mountain,* "is what they're looking for up there."

Day by day, time went inexorable.

(The murky waters of the canal showed in caustic shreds Neipas' mask) Side by side, they walked, in a leisurely pace, by the little manmade river canal, over its tawdry arched bridges that sought to imitate, in a cheap, decrepit carnival style, the ancient cities in that romantic continent of the settlers. Eva held Neipas' hand in one of her own; and with the other she gripped the *I* up to her studious gaze. He trod by the waters and glimpsed his reflection here and there treading along with him, hung limp toward the sky and precipitous, about to fall up, headlong (like a suspended fruit beneath the brittle bough) into the circle of white fire blazing from the depth of the shimmering liquid firmament, spilt.

Eva halted vacantly — perhaps to photograph something — and Neipas looked down to face his mask.

The little murky river looked back at him with his own eyes. It was frothed with the texture of his own feathers, swaying the cloudy scum of his own memories; his own soul was brimming with them today (the river looked stagnant and filthy; there was a rotten stench, as if it were clogged with bodies). Through the river's eyes he could see his father's; his presence abounded, it seemed somehow, in its mulch.

(Already the smoke flowed over the turbid canal and the ash mixed with its waters) That day dwelt in him a recurrent fear — which he endeavored greatly to consign to the oblivion of his unconscious — that the illness which plagued his father would come to afflict him too; that the toxins of his river contaminated not only the immateriality of his memory, but ran also in the tissue of his brain.

Neipas had watched his father wilt, and hollow, for months, for years after

445

the mountains collapsed upon their valley. The first change was as drastic and abrupt as might be expected. But (Neipas) the child could scarcely notice it with the overwhelming impact of the shock, which had thrust implacable and tremendous into his little body and inexperienced and vulnerable senses, violating without warning or mercy the sanctity of his innocence, the purity of his youth. It was only after the all-pervading, deafening shiver of distress winnowed out that he began to see his father — or the strange vestige of him that remained.

It was in his mother's absence that he first noticed him. There was a ghostly trace of her in the grave quietude which his sister, once bubbly, elated in her calculated silliness, now put on as she assumed the head of household's heavy mask; yet more starkly, her absence seemed to soak thick the white, frameless, portraitless walls of their new apartment — their bareness seemed to reflect the very silence of her voice. She was no longer in their ears, nor was she in their lips. The food tasted different. Now it was ordered and ready-made; packaged; labeled; no longer culled from those fields, peppered with herbs picked from the side of the river... (for the fields had been buried and the river itself, perished) The father, he fell into a morbid sort of lethargy, a brooding inscrutability of blank gazes, gazing blankly toward nowhere. He looked thoroughly stunned. He expressed himself by barely audible mumbles, and over time became as good as mute. Day after day he sat in his chair, contemplating the silver wedding ring which he now wore round his neck; his fingers rounding continuously, almost obsessively, its circular shape. The other hand would lift the weight of an *I* to his empty stare again and again. Whenever he got up (this became increasingly rarer) he slouched markedly, like a man whose foundations had crumbled, held up by nothing now but an occult trace of life which seemed to continually weaken against the attrition of still air, in the dissolution of crawling time. Neipas had the impression that his soul was being drained to the mysterious place where his mother's had gone. He witnessed, with a deepening sense of anguish, the degeneration of his own father — into a pathetic, dwindling man, whose motionless twitchy days were wasted between a ring and a glass. He watched helplessly as his father roved in the idleness of the *I* and seeped into the tangled intoxications of the Webwork through days and nights without sleep. He gazed long and discreetly, peering deep with photographic eye and spiritual eye near, indeed so closely and so profound that he seemed to discern the very unity of his father's being severing, the molecular structure of his father's intellect breaking down as the net of lights enveloped him tighter and tighter, twitchingly weaving across the missing bonds of his fading mind — as he searched (for what? perhaps for culprits amidst the fog of debris that was become his existence; yet the blame in this affair was as fleeting as scattering birds, as inaccessible as the life under the crumbled mountain, as receding from his grasp as his own mind... everything, as irrecoverable as grain after the milling; it was like an intrusion of ghosts or demons into his reality: the tragedy had presented itself as a deed without doer, a sin without guilty, a crime without punishment, a suffering without deliverance, a thing without sense; smoke). Deeper and deeper into the mesh of glows the father searched for what he could not find — and thus gradually lost himself in hopelessness, impotence, and anger. Indeed he only seemed to remember himself after he slapped Neipas — a teenager by then — in his sudden outbursts of fury. There was hatred in the way his palm slammed against the son's cheek: it was that, and not the violence of it in itself — not even the fact that there was no apparent reason for it — that really stumped Neipas and made him weep and scream in clamors of despair. His sister remained as quiet and as indifferent and insensible as ever — her mask mirroring the sedate form of her soul. The father meanwhile, receded, sank in the confines of his chair, being slowly consumed by a futility of rage — here was the animating force keeping him alive, the only thing that sustained him as his depression aggravated, as the illness intensified. A tree of ash had sprouted in his heart, propagated roots through its arteries, through long years... his veins already fully suffused in venom, when it bloomed and took flower in his soul it breathed in all possibility of voice; and eventually he became as silent as stone, except to pronounce the cryptic words

(‘I don't know’)

"I don't know," Neipas' lips molded voicelessly, behind the beak of his pigeon mask. Eva would sometimes gaze worryingly at his crestfallen brow. "Maybe you've been working too much baby..."

They walked by the little artificial river. Sometimes he would open the wardrobe in his bedroom and excavate from its depths that single picture, of his parents laughing in clumsy poses, standing in the grove by the river, by the mill. Peering through the only surviving photograph into his past, Neipas saw in the grainy texture of his father's stare the bygone reflection of his own, of mariner's eyes thirsty for the river and the freedom of the oceans, fascinated eyes hungry to explore all corners of the world and witness what may exist of wonder in its inexhaustible vastness. Dreams these which were embalmed under the muddy refuse of a radioactive mountain, mutating in the disease of years much as matter mutates in the decay of atoms and the past in the contemplation of the present: dreams that made up the only heirloom his parents could leave him, toward which he strove, as he fought to excavate himself from the stifling traumas of the recurrent past.

He strove for those dreams; soon, he would have his own studio, money to travel — and in the meantime he had saved enough to rent proper lighting equipment and start a new project, of which Eva would be the model and muse — but to get to where he wanted, he would have to keep working. And so he kept bending, and the glasses of spirits cackled under him. From under the rigid brow of his clay mask, he observed. Neipas would watch their ways and their lifestyle, carried out among the gaudy, plush opulence of the Northwest seaboard, and as he himself assisted in their gourmet-drenched soirees and the decadent inebriation of wealth playing out across the gilded coast, he would sometimes reflect on Orenda's words, spoken to him in the peace of a sandy shore on the opposite side of the bay ("They sacrificed you *all* on the altar of money — not even sacrificed [...] to them you were worth nothing!...") — and wondered, whether these peacock-masked princelings, and the horse and deer-headed royalty fattened on prosperity and prestige really had anything to do with the calamity that befell his early life and ended his parents'; had it been they who tore him away from the dream of that grainy photograph, through which he saw all things, and from which he had emerged into the light of day and the heat of present reality?

It seemed far-fetched — their aloof masquerades couldn't feel farther apart from the predicament of his homeland and Neipas told Orenda so when he visited her.

She lowered her heavy brow, and contemplated the grass on the sidewalk between the balusters of her porch. "They may look rich to us," Orenda then said, "but they're only employees.

"They can create and maintain power — but they don't hold it. True power hides *behind* them.

"You know, Oshana once told me," Orenda said, recalling an afternoon at the bookstore's little garden — sometime last year, perhaps, as she helped her aunt harvest the olives ripe on their branches, ever dwindling in number — in which Oshana told her, "Celebrities are to the mighty today what gods were to god-kings in their time: masks and justifications. All the rest of their army — their lawyers, lobbyists, politicians," Oshana concluded, beginning to gather the olives on the cloth extended at the base of the trunk, "— those are god's royal priests."

"And where are these god-kings?" Neipas asked Orenda.

"There," she answered, pointing to the shimmering Pearl above the megalopolis, "for instance — at the Eagles' Nest."

He elevated his grainy stare from the photograph and lowered it from the Pearl shine as he heard the sound of a conch playing on the margins of the canal — and Eva prodding him, saying "Look, baby!"

She pointed to a gathering crowd on one of the little arched bridges. Before their huddling feathers stood — against the arching rail — a teenage boy bearing hefty downward horns and crisp fur in a very upright stance; his hands held a large conch, which the boy presently played.

"So pretty," said Eva, admiring the spiral form of the conch, as she wound her arms around Neipas'.

She had a whole collection of shells at her house, stored in the middle drawer of her nightstand. All of them, she had found. The one she was most proud of was a bulky affair of beautiful patterns, out of which the ear could listen "to the sound of the ocean."

"I'm the queen of shells," Eva told Neipas, once, on a walk. "I find all kinds."

Eva bent over the faucet — to wash her skin before the shoot. The mirror disclosed a featureless blur of abstract colors, looking at her, without eyes, from behind the foggy glass. Orienting her motions by those of the nearly shapeless figure, Eva automatically applied to herself the powder, mascara, and foundation of her beauty and being — very slowly this time, much more methodical (perhaps distracted) than usual. Something troubled her.

She noticed the water was still pouring and closed the faucet quickly. It ran toward the drain in spirals; making gurgling murmurs down the pipe as Eva watched absentmindedly — petting her womb — for long after the waters had gone and the mirror made clear.

Her house had many empty rooms; more vacant compartments than one would have guessed from looking at it from outside.

"Why are your parents never here?" Neipas had asked her once.

"Oh — they're divorced," Eva replied.

She entered the obscurity of their (her parents') empty bedroom, recoiling with distaste at the dusty silhouettes of the two mannequins by the window and of the dolls spread about the mattress. The closet at her side — a deep compartment, a very pantry of a place — had all the provisions she needed for the photoshoot. ("Oh — my dad's a tailor, mom's a doll-maker"). On one of the adjacent rooms, Neipas prepared the lighting equipment and the set. A vintage dressing table stood against the wall, and soon Eva would layer on the more intricate patterns of her makeup before its oval mirror — she came to like the furniture piece so much that Neipas would help her move it to her bedroom downstairs (they were on the second floor and Neipas peered at the other side of the roadway through the window, which was always closed because Eva feared bugs might fly in) the very next day.

"Do you ever rent these out?" he asked her in regards to the unoccupied rooms.

Eva nodded absentmindedly. "Sometimes... People come and go."

Her own parents made her pay rent — so as to teach her "responsibility," she said. It was an old house, and the occasional chipped plaster at a corner or lifted woodboard concealed under the rug denounced a vague aspect of decay; clearly the rent proceeds hadn't been used much toward maintenance.

Neipas peered at the other side of the roadway through the window, which was always closed because Eva feared bugs might fly in. The very asphalt of the gap dividing the street seemed to crackle in the excessive heat flooding the land. Drenched in sunlight, being slowly overtaken by the creeping shade of the fig tree rooted into the lawn of the opposing house, the faceless Debt Collector rose its occult physiognomy in the direction of the window where Neipas was framed, through which he observed. A momentary hesitation overtook his mood, as his spirits, in a vulnerable moment of contemplation (as he thought of adjustments to the set), receded to the mathematics of the equipment's rental costs — he stirred. His eyes shuttered and flashed the blinding sun as it penetrated the window's glass.

Turning round, he considered the triped alienoids standing lean and tall over the room, with gaping rectangular eyes for heads — linked to wires, connected to the grid, awaiting to be charged with the power of light. These were expensive to purchase, expensive to keep for even a day. But Neipas' prospects were brightening, he considered, nodding his head. In a few days he would begin preparing for the 3-day Summit at the Anubel — rehearsing lines and motions, training his mind and body for the task; the work would be arduous, he heard (many times — but it was also handsomely paid) — which would culminate in a splendorous gala at the Ballroom, in the very peak of the Belab; a banquet, and a waltz.

A few days afterwards — after the wildfires had quelled — he would gaze the Pearl beaming atop the fabled Ballroom at the top of the world, inhaling the vision thoughtfully from Orenda's porch. "They're in the Eagles' Nest, huh..." He recalled sourly the Mayor, the Ministers, the Lobbyists he'd seen there the previous year. Dimly and frightfully he remembered the Museum, the Midget shackled and the looming Giant; that world of nightmares and money strewn across the floors like so much refuse, in the midst of abundance; the twitching, turbulent splash of rooms red and crimson, the laughing decadence, the disordered memories of degrading, drug-fueled labor. The very notion of the Eagles' Nest haunted him subtle; made him feel uncomfortable, made him sense a type of creeping nausea.

"I mean, they meet there occasionally... Show themselves for a bit from

mirror. She lifted the eyeliner once more; and muttered half-consciously.

"The face is a canvas... You can paint anything into it."

Still a nauseous feeling persisted inside her.

Neipas turned on the floodlights.)

Eva walked over with naked breasts, with the plush serpent wrapped round her like a blanket. She was just then settling down upon the lavishly arranged sofa, before the ogling scrutiny of the high-tech camera and the lighting equipment Neipas had rented.

Neipas stood steady behind the miraculous device, focused. He placed his eye upon the viewfinder, window to that stage of mirrors and prisms that is the world beheld in glass; and through the lens he saw Eva's naked torso pass in glazes of torpor, and sit. Looking out through the camera lens was to collect himself; to come back into himself. He had long felt unmoored — his whole life, perhaps; only the lens gave him some sense, some anchor, a form of seeing which tethered him to reality. The lens focused what is scattered and untenable: the present itself.

His fingers adjusted the aperture, widening the circle of it, yawning core among a receding spiral of blades; fixed his gaze, slowed his breathing, spoke some words unconsciously as he penetrated her visage, her body with his eyes. He looked at her with an ardor of desire, as if for the first time; for she, behind the new makeup and lighting, looked like a different, new woman altogether.

Eva reached into the bucket placed before the sofa; she sprinkled rose petals all about her body and the cushions.

Then she leaned back. Her head tilted toward the backrest — slowly. Her lips pouted, like a beak; and spread open, seductive, like a blossoming, carnal bud.

Her eyes narrowed between the black eyeliner. The irises flared, smiled; her pupils contracted, inhaled; they drew him in.

He breathed in, focused his attention. As his eye pressed the viewfinder and saw her through the lens, framed, regal, supreme, lascivious, naked, he tried to quell the distracting pulse swelling under his zipper. His thoughts flashed. In a moment he would go to her, yielding entirely to his lust, and plunge into bottomless pleasures, joys wild, noisy, of flesh pounding flesh, of sweat, saliva and moaning, pumping secretions seething, smacking, sucking, groaning; sheets wrapped up in blissful strains. He beheld her powerful, arousing; in a moment he would hear her satiated laughter. Yet in the very moment before the glass drew in her light, he would glimpse — in an instant of absolute transparency, very fleeting and almost illusory — he would see in Eva's eyes the same longing, the same anxiety and sorrow — the same emptiness he saw in the eyes of everyone else.

And yet, her lips smiled — and time stopped.

In a moment the shutters would part, the light would flood into the box and impress the very moment into their minds; the memory of it to be etched into its surrogate fabric.

His finger leaned upon the button.

....

....

Click.

II

BOOK OF MASKS

"Reptiles once ruled the planet, but they never claimed the land as real estate," said Orenda.

"Who do you think will be next? After us."

Orenda surveyed the urban landscape calmly.

"Birds," she said, "and insects."

28 - Eagles' Nest

The image propagated far, far across the digital threads of the Webwork. It was of a man on a shoddy raft afar and beneath, floating along muddy waters. Over his head a strange mask, multicolored and beaked — like that of a pigeon. It was made of wax and it melted in the sun, dripping onto his shoulders and dragging down the naked torso. The eyes staring out of the mask looked vacant, glassy. They reflected the chaos without sentiment. The sun shone up with unearthly, pale hues out of the waters; and out of the waters emerged towers with many broken windows.

The pigeon-man on the raft was lone in the vastness of the flooded boulevard.

Miles aloft, atop the highest tower, hundreds of cattle-heads swayed and strained among the noise of rubbing metal and the quietude of garden shrubs. The sky was cloudless under the full moon; the picture had not yet been taken. Cords stood erect everywhere, and the balloons tied on end had the moon inside them, trembling from the rub of motion underneath. The Hanging Gardens bustled with activity in the dim, mystic colors of its lamps, which shined soft beneath the Pearl's tall and mighty glow of gold. They were behind schedule and time pressed on with ceaseless shouts. Steel and wooden poles mounted, shining cloth, tables, frames, screens and gadgets installed, all rattling among the sweat and breathing of cattle faces as it was built. Yet even among the general ruckus and the relentless pressing of Drrawetz's stare and shout, Neipas, exerting his forces, couldn't help but sense the wonder of the celestial gardens; and in the total abandonment of the toil, his mind and soul were sometimes transfixed, transported by the aromatic smells and the suggestion of majesty in the black shapes of the trimmed shrubs and canopies, the soundless forms of statues, the height of fountains glistening against the stars. The estate stretched in a slope of terraces and confounded the eye with its vastness — the garden limits below and above, wherever they were, suffused themselves with the vertical ebony sky — slowly covered up by the market booths emerging in the night.

But presently Neipas lowered his horned head again and drove the nail into the slopped grass as he heard Drrawetz's nervous voice near. "What are you doing! What are you doing!" he repeated countlessly in a shaking voice, brimming with threatening undertones. Round them worked the carpenters and the masons, the florists with their floral arrangements, the technicians in glitter, the cleaners and waiters with soap, the cooks round steaming fragrances, the landscapers about the sculptured bushes, scurrying. Bull guards enormously overlooked it all; and the Head Gardener, propped majestically against his cane, stood quietly above them in the distance. Magpie walked among the mess and, beautiful and imposing in the serenity of her voice, spoke to Drrawetz, who was agitatedly reproaching someone bent beneath him, and got him to calm down. Silence was made among the ringing of hammer and nail, and the ruffling of flying drapes; and soon the steward's tremulous voice rose up to agitated shouting again.

Neipas had seen Magpie among the crowd in the cold, grated elevators. In the squeeze of bodies they had spoken, sleepy and nervous, to while away the time. As the elevator climbed the Belab's spine in a lumbering ascent to the summit, they mumbled to one another among the flashing of I glasses — subsiding into the Webwork themselves after a time. Before their conversation died they conversed animatedly about Edazima. Magpie was happy to see someone she recognized. Though she didn't know him well, Magpie had always liked Neipas, because Edazima had always liked him. For a bit they bonded in conversation over her, extolling her virtues, her gruff cigarette humor, her kindness — until they fell into an expectant quietude. Their shoulders pressed, and in his proximity Neipas discerned how her exhalations produced a wheezing sound; and realized how she labored to tame her breathing so it wouldn't be noticed. The moonlight, streaming sidelong through the deep breach on the wall, revealed the trembling steam of her breath, materialized in the thickening cold. It was as though her breathing disclosed something of an inner state, which was otherwise walled off; for she stood completely immobile in her regal bearing.

Soon the grated gate opened, and the multitude of rickety pigeonheads streamed out into the Warehouse Hall, full of sacks inside boxes lying about in the corners. Out the twelve elevators an entire army of workers, clad yet in sleep and in every color of attire, came and amassed closely across the circle. Neipas saw many faces, many masks, some of whom he recognized. Afar, vague among the myriad, hunched Janu the dishwasher — whom Neipas was surprised to see. Osir the janitor, Cesar the waiter, Simon the florist, Amurad the cook — and many, many filling the throng. Beyond was the bridge which led to the Clockroom, where the seamstresses adorned the drapes and distributed the masks, and before the bridge stood Sunai, stolid, straight, impassive. There was only one of her now.

She welcomed them, eating an apple. She listed the rules and handed them scripts; and then she lowered the bridge. On the other side, Drrawetz waited with a large grin, rubbing his hands, swaying fidgety upon the edge of his toes.

The pigeons walked silently across the chasm.

Neipas' mind was cloudy coming in; his head full of Eva. His breast reeled remembering the last time they had spoken, just the day before. The fight between them had been timid, the volume of their voices contained; but the words contained in their voices were full of venom, and penetrated each other's skin profoundly. Amid the general ruffle of the Columbaria dormitory, subdued by drowsiness and the timidity of the *Is* alit, Neipas regarded the jacket Eva had bought him. He thought of her longingly, with a clutch of the heart, full of anxiety to get out of there and fix things. Yet, staring into the *I*, he couldn't bring himself to reach out to her across the thread — it was too soon. He mulled over whether it'd be best to wait until after the event, until he could speak to her personally, to her eyes, without another screen of glass between them. The three days before him presented themselves giantly. Drrawetz, in the Columbaria's Office, trumpeted up the importance of the Summit to its highest pitch, as he had been notching toward for the past few weeks. In his tongue, it almost, somehow, sounded as though their lives depended on the event's success. The expectation had mounted to such weights as to make his heart droop in a leaden pull. Neipas felt nervous; he wanted nothing more than those three days to pass quickly.

He hung Eva's jacket inside his closet of possessions (vaguely he noticed the little notebook Orenda had offered him was still inside the breast-pocket) and placed upon himself the ox head.

His breath deepened inside its fur, his neck arched under the bulky horns; thoughts were muffled and made distant inside. Drrawetz was calling them to the Gardens.

The herd of oxen marched — Seamstresses came and pierced eartags into them as they filed out.

Once all preparations had been made, the workforce drained exhaustedly onward to the Food Hall, en masse, for breakfast and rest. All sat; Neipas with Magpie, Osir, and Cesar in one of the small plastic tables. They ate languidly. The space became mostly filled with expectant silence, underlain with murmurs of nervousness. Windows on the farthest flank opened the view to the Gardens; and they could see the southern heavens yonder clearing away the night in preparation for the sun's birth. With the star shroud disappearing, it seemed to Neipas, obscuringly, as if some veil were being lifted to expose him — the Sun's ascent ushered in the entrance of the Eagles and a toilsome day attending to their needs. Their incoming figures, imposing and powerful, loomed large in the collective imagination. Even Magpie, who in the eyes of many was a pinnacle of composure and serenity — even she seemed nervous. There was something different about her, too. Neipas, sitting in his plastic chair vague, brooding, could sense it. Perhaps it was that he had never really seen her up close, but he felt that something had altered; something beyond the mask, perceptible if one observed with attention; though he couldn't tell exactly what it was.

Eventually, like others, they took to small talk in an attempt to tame time's approach. Neipas mentioned Janu, whom Magpie had occasion to talk with briefly in the Gardens. He had felt a surreality, even through the general surrealness of sleep, at beholding the friendly dishwasher there, at the top of the great tower. It was like a sudden jump of compressed time; one moment in the dingy kitchen of fried scents and oily air of the underground, and the next, together before the gates to the most lavish complex ever built over the Earth. Janu was apparently a cook now, Magpie said. He had told her that KUR's nightshift supervisor had found him at the pots after hours, tasted what he had made, and liked it. He was hired to the nightshift and made second chef straight off, after which he went through a number of jobs in upscale restaurants along the western shore, before being hired by Eden Solutions and recruited back into the Belab as one of the assistant cooks for the Summit.

Neipas threw a general glance round the Food Hall, trying to find him — but most cooks had been summoned to the Eagle Wing already. They murmured around other topics. Cesar would throw an occasional quip about Drrawetz, to which Osir would cheer and nod.

In the lull they fell into their *I*s, and sneakily Neipas stole into a snooze.

The silence in his head was now absolute. Eva whispered, and the rivermill paddled softly in the waters. But a great rush crammed the distance — there, between the trees. It resounded with a toll of bell...

He awoke. The bell's echo dispersed heavily over their heads.

"That's the 15 minutes," mumbled Osir through his scar, lazily, as he stared into the *I*.

Neipas grumbled sleepily. "Anyone want coffee?"

"Hmm nah," said Cesar. "Not much of a coffee person."

"Yeah I'll take one," Magpie said.

As Neipas rose he reflexively reached into his pocket, and flinched, for his *I* was not there. He looked back, a bit alarmed. "Did anyone see..."

Osir was holding it. He looked at the gleam with a glassy, distracted glare.

"Hey man... I think that's mine."

"Hm?" Osir looked up vacantly. His expression was perturbed and it grimaced, as if he was emerging from a dark place, back into light. Mechanically he reached into his pocket, and produced from it his own *I*. His scar twitched.

"Oh... Shit, my bad. They all look the same. I saw it on the table, and just kinda took it."

"No worries."

"You should put some barrier on it man, so people can't enter. I guess I should do the same too," added Osir, taking a pill from a little bottle.

Neipas had just left the coffee line when the 7-minute sign sounded. First the same bell, ringing aloft, at length; and then another one right after, curt but more powerful yet. He handed one cup of coffee to Magpie and when he took the hot liquor to his own lips it shot through the sleepiness of his veins at once, loosening the weariness of his muscles, widening his eyes, expanding his senses.

"Guess it's time," said Magpie as the bells sounded again, at the same time now, godly and commanding upon their ears. It was the call. The entire mass of workers arose from their seats with a quake of dragging chairs, and marched out in an orderly formation of tumultuous noise, a long rumble of one thousand feet shifting along with profusions of animated twittering and mooing crowding the air. The massive herd drove on to the lockers to change to proper attire once more. In a loaded silence of muted heads they passed through the drapes, and they made a line through the scanners as the bulls looked on with frowning gazes tall, rigid in the steadfastness of duty. One by one the livestock passed through the whirring frame, which flashed into their sparkling suits again and again, tirelessly. On the other side a whole team of Seamstresses and Makeup Artists stood in alignment and ready to prune the cattle, fixing the clay under their furs into the proper expression, tidying their ties and pins and eartags, polishing their horns with oily cloth and adorning them with gilded flourishes. And on they went, goaded on by Drrawetz, who tapped his foot and checked his watch convulsively as he muttered soft and tremulous admonishments to the passing workers to try to make them go on faster.

As the file of workers was made scarce Drrawetz began to recompose his own mask. The team of Sculptors huddled about him and, holding three mirrors before his faces so as to cover every angle, they spruced up his collar and molded his peacock mask into a perfection of professionalism. The rest spread orderly out the myriad ways; hundreds strong, with barely a peep. Neipas followed a group to collect the trays of drinks and snacks already prepared in long rows in the long kitchen, which shone of steel, immaculate, immense.

They were taken along new paths into a vast atrium framed in tall mirrors, called the Hall of Portals. When the steward of the Eagle's Nest emerged into it his visage was solemn, collected, full of purpose. The entire workforce assembled in the giant hall, surrounded by the perfumed glamour of the interlocked and gleaming carvings which twined their way up the silver walls. Forming in concentric circles according to their occupations — managers and supervisors toward the center, set designers, technicians, florists and decorators, waiters, alchemists, cooks, janitors and all else toward the rim — they all stood facing the colossal candelabrum of diamonds pending from the ceiling to touch the carpet lightly. In between the gates, mirrors spanned the height of the hall likewise, and inside them the circular formation of cattle heads and black shirts was reproduced in a confusion of reflections extending and replicating themselves to infinity.

"Decorum, dears!" clamored Drrawetz at the conclusion of a few words. Yokes and bells were placed upon the necks of the workers. The weight upon them thickened, their breathing became heavier and prolonged, calmer, the vision narrowed and focused, sounds sounded farther away.

Two great entry gates opened between the mirrors at each side. From one ensued, humming low and rhythmically, breezes of white fume, through which came priestly fellows wrapped in robes, donning masks of pelican, and holding thuribles from which the smoke streamed; and there were peacocks with luxuriant suits of very long tail who swayed fans and diffused the mist, spreading its disinfectant aromas. The nebulous landscape whence they emerged had the air of an opulent bathhouse. And yonder, far along its deep corridor, Neipas discerned the light of a flame atop a shadowy form; the flame burned atop a great candle, it seemed to him. His ear perceived (or he had the impression of) a strange palpitation throbbing from that distance.

But the waiters entered the opposite gate and quickly lined up along a sumptuous, wide passageway extending from six ornamented elevators, which were called the Anubel Gates. These great doors stood imposing, with an air of ancient, eternal firmness and authority. A staircase of class and aplomb unfolded outward, so that the ground rose slowly from the gates. It shone clean its ivory; alongside it concubines, with naked legs and masks of swan, waited in photographic poses. At the base of the stairs, flanking the newel heads, rose the giant statues of two gryphons. And at the depth of the corridor, in the Hall of Portals now behind the row of waiters, had appeared, unnoticed and as though out of nowhere, the orchestra.

The silence was absolute. A great sense of expectation and anxiety suffused the air, coursing every breath. Unconsciously Neipas strayed his sight from the rigid formation of equal heads pointing in the same, single direction; and he found his eye upon the orchestra yonder, which was far enough that he couldn't discern their faces very well. The conductor faced away from the cattle with arm raised and ready.

There was something about the configuration of the orchestra, or — an emanating feeling, which Neipas, swooning into distraction, tried to distinguish with narrowing eyes. Again his ear perceived the throb.

The conductor's arm dropped suddenly, and an army of trumpets blew out in force. Drums — and Neipas turned his head in an instant. The elevator gates opened ceremoniously. Inside, one by one, were revealed vast padded chambers housing whole entourages and chairs of throne, adorned with various species of riches. Choruses and strings ensued from the band. The Eagles sat in the center of their elevator chambers, with Peacocks of many colors and Swans and Horses ruffling feathers around the entrying diplomats, high officials, executives of the tallest perches, decisionmakers of the gravest consequence, lords over civilizations and masters of the universe. Power assembled before the sight of Neipas' humble eyes — and he extended his tray in preparation for its passing.

In a crescendo soared the horn of trumpets, exploding into the full sounding of all the suite's instruments and all the range of voices. The bells sounded together, one, two, three times, stirring the air in triumph.

The Summit had begun.

29 - Pidgin Market

The Summit Bells rang quickly and without delay, and all at once the Market was astir with great palpitations of voices and steps. Its sounds fell and dispersed over the deep megalopolis beneath; the bright dazzle of the Pearl, shining atop the summit, spread into the long sky.

The Hanging Gardens were filled with crowds. Tents, festoons, glitter, music, a panoply of voices and colors revolved in the tended greens, psychedelic rainbows of balloons swirling all about, tied to strings or loose in the air, covering whole trees as they got stuck in their flight. Schools of little children shrieked among the forest of legs and cords, marveling in the chaotic contemplation of all there was to see; and the adults swarming along the booths swerved their heads from display to display with grave nods, commenting with one another in knowing tones. They took glasses of liquor from the waiters as they came along with extended trays and sipped with serious airs, stopping here, stopping there, pointing and nodding with their pigeon masks all the while.

"Excuse me?"

"Yes ma'am." Neipas balanced the tray laden with tittering glasses of expensive drink as he rotated upon his toes. The liquors ruffled above the outstretched palm of his hand, which strained beside the horns of his ox head with the shape of a clean stump, growing like a suspended bough from his curled wrist. He faced a suited woman of tightly wound pink feathers, beside whom stood a child, a little girl, looking up from the summit of her short height with bubbly eyes.

"Hello!" said the little girl, waving her little hand.

"Hi!"

"It is vewy nice to meet you. My name is 'oobie. That is my knee name! What is your name?" asked the child, swaying herself from side to side. She spoke every syllable slowly, with the airs of someone being tested; and lowered her head smilingly when she finished, as if expecting approval in the answer.

The pink-haired peacock lady whispered, with a smile and a wink, "I think she means Ruby."

Neipas told the little girl his name, laughing. "Your daughter, ma'am?"

"No, actually I found her wandering around by herself, she says she doesn't know where her parents are... Wondering if you could help."

Neipas nodded very much. "Sure, ma'am. Let's see..." He clutched his ear between his fingers, pressing the eartag further into his skin.

"Yes, 431999," said a passive, robotic voice inside his head.

"I have a little girl here, says she's lost?"

A moment of silence followed.

"Hold on, I'll send someone to get you."

"They're going to send someone, ma'am," said Neipas.

"Good... Will you be ok, dear?" Ruby, below her, nodded energetically and the tressed locks of her hair dangled before her closed eyes. "Is it ok if I leave her with you? I have to attend a seminar upstage in a few minutes."

Neipas looked at the bright-eyed child and sensed the weight of the tray, fearing the added responsibility of tending so small an existence in that chaotic wood of bodies and things, pulsing stirs and noises.

"Sure," said Neipas, bowing his horns, "that's no problem."

"Ok... Listen, do I know you from somewhere?"

Neipas beheld the kempt pink head, and peacock face protruding softly from it with a studied expression, looking very professional behind squared spectacles. Indeed, he had the impression he'd seen her before, perhaps with a different mask.

"You're Orenda's friend. I've seen you in meetings," she said conclusively.

"Yes..." Neipas said slowly with narrowed eyes, trying to find her name in his memory.

"I don't think we've met, though."

At this moment, out of the mass of bodies emerged Cesar, who had seen them from afar. He touched her shoulder with a side bob of the head.

"Marlene!" the poet called enthusiastically.

"Oh hey! Good to see you."

"What are you doing here! You look fancy today."

"I'm speaking at a law seminar..." explained Marlene the lawyer, looking back with some anxiety. Then she looked at Cesar's mask, his curled mustache and his horns. "Are you working? I have to go upstage but let's eat together after."

Cesar agreed. Noticing Neipas' presence, standing there somewhat awkwardly with the bubbly child already beside, holding his hand, singing voicelessly and swaying from side to side, the poet asked if they had met and, without waiting for an answer, he introduced them.

"I'll see you guys around," said Marlene, and she disappeared in the maze of booths to make her way up the Gardens to the Auditorium. Ruby asked Cesar his name, and Cesar gave it to her with a wide smile. But he had to rush out — he and the little girl traded goodbyes with jolly waves of hand, the poet smiling and the girl laughing timidly, and he went out at a quick pace, followed by the tickling sounds of his tray. Neipas and Ruby stood waiting in the little square of shaded booths, in a glimmering twilight under festooning cloths, the tissue of which glistened with the colors and sway of overhanging balloons. The grass beneath their feet was flattened by the stomp of a million steps; not a blade of green had been spared. A miniature pumpjack model stood for display in the middle of the otherwise bare space.

They waited a while — Ruby held Neipas' hand and mummed patiently, swaying the flowery edges of her pink dress — until there was a buzz in Neipas' ear.

"431999, come in," said a robotic voice in his head, a little different from the one that had last spoken.

"Yes?"

"Why aren't you moving?"

"I just called in about a lost child? About five minutes ago?"

"What? Just keep moving. You said you found a lost child?"

"Yes, she can't find her parents."

"Keep moving. We'll go to you."

Neipas and Ruby walked further into the crowded, large garden terrace. They waddled through a shaded row of booths selling cars and motorcycles, treading upon trodden green paste strewn with bits of glitter until they emerged, slowly, into a sunny glade sprinkled unevenly with statues and shrubs, where barbecues sizzled upward in steam over masks. An enormous pig had been impaled with a stick and circled now over a fire. Many hands reached into Neipas' tray and eased the burden of the bubbly liquors upon his wrist as he and Ruby climbed a coiling stair onto the next terrace, according to Neipas' planned circuit, going up along creepers in the walls and tangled balloons which radiated the filtered sunlight with their colors, and away from the smell of meat, charcoal and gasoline. Ahead of them opened a great hall of tents bustling with hullabaloo.

They roamed in and out of stairs and pathways wide and narrow, vibrant and confused, through exuberant groves and draped corridors. The Market was rapt among a great labyrinth screened with veils of different colors at every passage, a great rainbow world of big smiles, a carnival of glee. Its loopy trails were alive with counters and bizarre displays of all sorts, overwhelming the senses with its variety of sights and noises. Smells of food, cologne, plastic and stenches of rubbish and sweat thickened the crowded air. From their tables, merchants advertised what they were selling; and they sold everything that could be imagined, extracted, or made. Perched in booths of endless shapes these bovine masks performed with much adornment and flair, much pizazz, announcing loudly the miraculous benefits of their wares. Their outfits and ornaments were varied; but their bovine faces differed little, the mold to which they had been pressed being the same — that of smiling, dancing facades of salesfolk. Commotions of different multitudes shored upon the booths, and crowds moved erratically in reaction to the merchants' performances, often swinging in single great masses from one booth to another. There was a dizzying number of amusements, pulsating with shrieks among carnivalesque decorations in areas small and large. Next to fair vitrines selling foods and plush toys, buskers danced about, clowns and pantomimes with spiky hats and jingles and fire-spitters with phoenix masks. Effigies of the festival deities — "The Economy", or the Golden Dove, and its prophet "Industry", the Silver Eagle — to which the Market paid homage, arose everywhere in the form of balloons and inflated mannequins.

All this entertainment attracted many children. Consumers of all ages, the smallest were as little as Ruby and the biggest even taller than Neipas. Adults and children together rejoiced and indulged in the glorious profusion of commodities — there was something for everyone. The children sometimes wore masks, imitating the adults; but the masks were not yet their faces. Generally, the semblances of the youngest resembled those of grow-ups only vaguely. They were mostly shapeless, and innocent, with eyes big, admired and mystified at the existence of things.

Much money was spent here, and the Market throbbed happily in the healthy stuffing of the Economy. Gaiety beamed with gilded shades from the top of the world. Such was the Anubel's Pigeon Wing: the other side of the Eagles' Nest, meanwhile, stood veiled beyond Bull guards and scanners, silent. Its joys were more secretive.

It was a constant push and pull through the crowds. Neipas' burden was constantly lifted and refilled as tides of hands swept the cups on his tray, and almost immediately a swift ox would emerge from little mirror-fitted gates in the terrace walls, beneath the vaulted galleries, with more cups for him to carry. Neipas assumed they came from the kitchens, which were connected to the gardens through various passages; interconnected labyrinths hollowing the core of Anubel which, some said, were so complex one could easily get lost in them.

Ruby observed the Market's wonders with great admiration and surprise all the while. She would ask eagerly what was this and what was that, and Neipas, flushed with her great insistence, would make explanations up whenever he didn't know. The child trailed him without complaint or care, holding his fingers firmly and skipping joyfully alongside whenever there was enough space. Only when rides came within view did Neipas really struggle (frequent bouts of "ca'ousel!", "look! look!" and "yay!" would suddenly break out from below Neipas, at which time Ruby plucked her hand out of his arm and leapt away merrily) and was forced to jog after her, balancing the shaking glasses. He watched a little fretfully as she waved her arms from the carousels and tilt-a-whirls. Sensing the omnipresent lurk of Drrawetz' temper and power, he worried about being reproached for not moving, and the longer he didn't move, the more he was afraid of repercussions. He couldn't afford to lose his job.

Ruby watched raptured a show of marionettes about chickens, and Neipas was nervously considering calling the Seamstresses for help when his ear buzzed:

"431999?"

"Yes?"

"Hi, what did you say the kid's name was?"

Neipas thought a little, for he had forgotten; he peeked into his head through the noises.

"Ruby."

A pause, a holding silence. The Seamstress seemed to whisper something away from Neipas' ear.

"Ok. Why are you not moving?"

"Well," Neipas said with veiled impatience, "I'm trying to make sure the girl doesn't get lost again. Could you please send someone to pick her up?"

"Just keep to your circuit. Keep moving. We'll go to you."

Neipas prodded Ruby gently and she went along at once. She was uncomplaining in her contentment, and her endearing little nature often made Neipas smile, despite the pressing stresses of his labor.

Following Neipas' circuit, they delved into darker recesses in the thick jungle of things, through veil after veil, into spaces where squares gleamed before dazzled eyes... They walked through a maze of stunned faces before flickering screens in the gloom; and here the noise ceased, and everything was a whisper. The world inside the glasses was lush and exuberant, pulsing with digital magic. Even babies played with the *I*s, their faces open with stupefaction. They went slowly... Finally, they arrived at the red drape.

He had to go through there — it was the last stretch, through which he would access the butcher shops at the beginning of the circuit. But beyond the red drape there was a peculiar space. It was synonymous with the one they were in now, but aglow in a soft crimson color. Its screens flashed with pornography. Other lewd displays abounded also, with special, hidden rooms in the walls of the terrace's limit, in the arcades leading to the Anubel's interior. A lot of money was made there, somehow; the gleam of gold scintillated from the floor, as if it were a crop growing out of that earth. Here before the drape Neipas hesitated, and wondered. He vacillated between decisions. After all, he had seen folk of all ages there the other times he had circled through, casually walking about in the shadows of the crimson light. Everyone looked indifferent, and so everything looked normal.

But he looked at Ruby's bubbly, smiling visage. He thought of going in and covering her eyes the while. But he couldn't; it felt wrong, just wrong to take her there.

"Maybe we can go around," he mumbled to himself.

Neipas made a different turn, and they followed a path called "Aesthetics". Beauty products were sold here, massages and wax creams peddled enthusiastically along with jewelry and all manner of shiny trinkets. There were entrances flanked with chimes, bells and cloth, overarched with awnings that shaded narrow tunnels, leading into deep twinkling stores full of mystique, where masks were sold. Mirrors were affixed everywhere in the corridors here. At the end they walked in wide and curvy passages filled with slowly blinking lights, which painted the topping cloths in blots of rainbows (very tall, silent mannequins adorned with plume and scarfs stared at them from the flanks); and suddenly Ruby jumped in an elated fit.

She was pointing her finger somewhere even as she kept jumping. "Look Nepa! Look!"

He let himself be led by her energetic rush into a place called Tents of Idols, where celebrities posed for display. In one side there was the sports booth, where Neipas saw children and grown-ups alike gathering before a famous athlete. Even Neipas, who didn't care much about sports, had a sensation of unreality and even pride at seeing, live, this face which populated so many screens and billboards and whose name was so exalted across the whole nation. He sat in a sort of throne, holding a golden ball, with horse mask thrown up so that the muscles of the neck could be beheld. The crowd lined up before him; and one by one they would go to him, and kneel, and kiss his golden boot as they dropped money on the basket near. Then, the admirer would turn his or her face upward and the celebrity would sign his name on the admirer's forehead, who would then hold his *I* aloft and draw a photo, so that the moment could be witnessed for all posterity. Finally, thanking the idol profusely, this worshiper would step away, elated that he got to look directly upon the face of the deity. Here was where the gurus of masses, leaders of herds, flounced their bodies for the admiration and devotion of their followers. Wandering among the crowds everywhere were journalists and enthusiasts with long eyes made of lens, watching everyone in gulps, through convulsing peacock eyes, drawing things onto the surface of their glass stares. They massed here with most intensity. And indeed, all attendants of the Summit took photographs, and every angle of every moment was captured by every lens of every *I*.

Ruby had gotten a singer-actress to sign her forehead and she was very happy. Neipas glimpsed her countenance of deer — a stag waved his gloves at her side — and recognized her from a movie he'd watched with Eva.

Then they moved on, passing along children masked as their favorite heroes. There were signs at the crossroads of walling cloths indicating which paths led where, but the meaning of their labels was often unclear, even occult, and not helpful in the least. Neipas chose his course uncertainly. Flanking them on the next path were many electric screens and television frames, popping full of jagged charts, digits and formulas whose function was incomprehensible; though a great many oxen and pigeons huddled about them and watched the numbers with much excitement and furor. And as they went deeper into this maze of abstractions the oxen in suits got shinier and their forms loopier, their behavior weirder and weirder. Pretty soon Neipas and Ruby were quite lost. Off to one side, where the trail widened and rounded into a clearing, they heard a loon with spirally horns claiming they could shrink the sun and whiten the sky and that it was a brilliant thing to do, and a great gathering of pigeons amassed to hear his words. It was space beaming with gadgets, glass bottles and frothing concoctions; and above the berserk salesman, who wore a white lab coat, hung a banner clamoring triumphantly "SCIENCE FINDS, INDUSTRY APPLIES".

Neipas avoided those crowds and stepped the opposite way with haste. Quickly they reached a crossroads with four arrows which contained nothing but hieroglyphs he couldn't comprehend; and he mumbled some jargon when Ruby asked him what it meant. They turned into a shady aisle. Strange bulls with suits inhabited it, and they were bulls of a sort Neipas thought he had seen before, somewhere down the tower. Mostly these bulls spoke in cryptic dialects, though Neipas could understand some words every now and then. The mood was hectic with waggling of papers and foaming snouts. Shouts came from everywhere. "Shorts!"

"Bonds!" "Stocks!"

"Efficiency!"

"Premiums!" "Futures!"

"Options!"

"Solutions! The best solutions sold here!"

"Value! Stockholder value! Best stockholder value! Here *only*!"

"Hey? Pal!"

One of the merchants was calling Neipas. It was the solutions merchant — he approached.

"Would you like a drink, sir?"

The merchant didn't say anything but right away he took a cup of bubbles from the tray and drank it in one gulp. Meanwhile Ruby looked at the empty booth (the table had but a laptop) with fascination.

"What ah you selling?" said the girl in her bubbly voice, swaying side to side.

"Hm? We sell solutions, obviously."

"Hmmmmm... Solushons..." Ruby twisted her little nose and reflected on what to say next. "Ah! I know! I know! So, so... you have got problems!" she said with much effort and thought, triumphantly concluding her sentence.

The merchant eyed the girl suspiciously. He gaged her interest with calculation, and seemed to be trying to determine whether she could be part of his target audience or not. She seemed too small to have buying power... But, he thought, even though appearances are everything, they sometimes elude, and he was in the business of eluding appearances — he'd be remiss not to probe.

"Well, yes, ma'am," he began, addressing the girl directly and ignoring the waiter. "We sell solutions to problems. But if you don't have problems, we can create problems. We have a wide portfolio of problems for sale as well, and discount packages that include both problems and solutions."

Ruby received the words magnanimously and looked up at Neipas with finesse and a smile swaying side to side, with the calmness of something accomplished. They walked away wordlessly and the merchant continued to stand behind his booth. Not a moment's confusion shaded his expression; right away he recommenced belting about his solutions.

But little Ruby swiftly took to asking every seller she saw what they were selling, employing the enthusiasm of something she had just learned to do. Already she had scampered on over to an interesting cubicle on the other side where she began parlaying diplomatically with the two manning peacocks. She asked the first of them, wiggling her tresses: "What ah you selling?"

The two merchants were half-twins, that is to say, two halves of a whole. The mask of one was painted in shade on one side, and the mask of the other was its mirror opposite. They were the Merchant of Dreams and the Merchant of Doubts — among the most successful merchants in those days.

"Why," began the Merchant of Dreams with a vast grin, leaning copiously over, "I trade in dreams, little one."

"Dweams? Like when it is sleep?"

"Oh no, my dear," the merchant chuckled gaily, with his fingers over his snout. "I mean dreams as in, *objectives*. Life goals!"

Ruby looked to Neipas in confusion. "Huh??"

"Oh my dear, I mean money, of course. Great treasures and..." he went on with theatrical, sweeping gestures. Dramatically then, his fingers reached under her ear, and emerged out swiftly with a glinting coin: "...and all your desires fulfilled!"

Ruby's mouth gaped with great awe. Triumphant, he took a glass of champagne from Neipas' tray and downed it in one long slurp.

"Wow!" said Ruby.

"Meaning, dear, that if you work really hard, you can have a lot of these! If you just believe, there is much more hidden in the secret chambers of this tower..." and at this the Merchant of Dreams raised his finger and launched into reciting verses:

"Atop the tallest tower
Mums a twinkling sound.
A whisper of deep power
Drapes treasure unbound.

Squint and you will hear
Glinting in the grail cup
Hurry! Lest it disappear
Work hard, climb up!"

The merchant bowed ceremoniously.

"My gran-daddy has a lotta those!" the child then declared (hiding her incomprehension of the words with some effort), pointing to the coin which the merchant had flaunted through the recitation.

"Oh! Indeed!" the Merchant of Dreams exclaimed, suddenly becoming much more fawning in his manner; and even his partner aside him, the Merchants of Doubts, who had been sulking with crossed arms all this time, neared with some interest. With much flourish the Dream Merchant inquired if the little lady would be so kind as to open her mouth.

"Aaaaaaa," did Ruby, and deftly the merchant produced a silver coin from under her tongue. The child stood again open-mouthed, completely floored with wonderment. And then suddenly, she went "ih-hi!" with a sprightly and charming little giggle.

Neipas momentarily forgot his work, intrigued and amused by these tricks. "Do you think the treasure actually exists?"

At hearing the waiter's voice the Merchant of Doubts abruptly stepped to, grunting: "Hmph! Such treasures do not exist! Do not believe in fairy tales. It's better not to elude yourself, after all. Like this, you are guaranteed not to be disappointed."

But even as he prattled, the Merchant of Dreams winked knowingly.

"Any more questions, lieges?" asked he.

"Hmmm..." Ruby thought a little. "How do you make money?" Ruby slowly inquired and Neipas laughed at this. Suddenly, however, his ear fizzled again with static.

"Oh, little miss, not to worry — I make a lot of money."

In Neipas' head the voice spoke "what the hell are you doing in there, 431999?" — and apologies ensued out of Neipas' mouth, nervous explanations that he had lost his way. Ruby was by now hopping toward the Merchant of Fears, but Neipas, who was by now more comfortable with the child, hurried her along. The Seamstress tried to direct him through winding ways up and down the draped terraces and groves of the garden, alongside mirrors and smoke from various displays, spaces of every light, through noises loud and dim, sounds melodic and screechy.

In time, they stepped onto the tulip-strewn banks of the East River, which coursed through the middle of this side of the Hanging Gardens. They went down the central stair through which it flowed, with the Auditorium and the Great Facade looming immense behind them, and gained a clear view of the labyrinthic mess of the Market, plummeting below them into the wiry, thorny woods of the lower terraces, and then beyond to the edges of the tower, spilling into the megalopolis far beneath. The mountains yonder, to the east beyond Babylon and the outer highways, still smoldered from the chokehold of the extinguished fires; their ancient stones faced quietly the flashes of great noise and excitements, the rumblings of raptured multitudes in the Eagles' Nest. Neipas led hopping Ruby down the steps. On the way, close to the aisles, they glimpsed the Bazaar of Careers, where aspirations were traded. Owl stares manned the stands. Many children huddled there, and the oldest among them approached the booths with hopes of renting themselves, receiving, in return for toil, the reward of change and adulthood. Their worthiness was measured right here — and the gravity of the place could be felt in the very breathing of the crowd, affecting the air profoundly.

The Seamstress ordered Neipas take a turn into the labyrinths on the fifth terrace, the core of which was dominated by bridges over a beautiful lake. Before the river continued down the terraces in a single long stream, its multiple affluents spread soft and languidly across this lake, from the depths of which (on the yonder bank the terrace wall receded into a concave, acoustic shape; it was feathered and colored like a peacock's tail, sprayed with what seemed to be a myriad eyes) rippled a profound reverberation, a voice whose sound pervaded everything. Various pigeons and their families were leaning contemplatively over the bridge railings. Little plops, here and there, broke from the water surface beneath them.

"Why are they t'owing coins?" asked little Ruby.

"For good luck."

They entered a great domed tent. It was a broad playspace encircled with a curtain of red, white, and blue stripes, called the Circus. Thousands of rope-like cords, pulled taut from the ground by the force of balloons attached to the upper end, gathered densely here, so that the ceiling was made entirely of balloons of all colors. It was like walking in a forest of strings. The sunlight filtered through the balloons and the air was filled with refractions of hue. Normal perception seemed to be altered. Sounds were different — though this place was nearly as crowded as the rest of the Fair, where the noise thickened the atmosphere to a palpable heat of sound, here the voices of the folk sounded far away, echo-like, abstracted; dreamlike. The broadening of space couldn't account for it. Perhaps it was the influence of the strings, for whenever Neipas touched one, a little note sounded — something eerie and unearthly, nearly inaudible, more like a whisper. He had heard something like it before... The canopy of balloons in the summits of the cords quaked chaotically, and below, the colors moved like phantoms over the crowd. All over children ran with toy guns, and adults ran with glasses of spirits, with multifold palettes of harlequins guffawing and bouncing about; they all threw eggs at the circus animals trying to squeeze through and particularly at the apes, and at the pigeons masked as apes.

Neipas knelt and placed Ruby atop his shoulders. He waddled through the multitude with one hand holding the tray, now empty, and another upon her knee as she held on to his horns. There were a few stands with legumes and plants, and flowers; suddenly, scents possessed an earthly tinge, as though some deep wet soil had spirited its breath all the way up to the top of the tower. Medicines were put for sale just beyond; health merchants and insurance peddlers walked about zealously in their suits and white coats.

Through the health markets they would be able to reach the butcher shops under, where Neipas' circuit began. But just as Ruby pointed astonished toward the Bug Seller, whose myriad bottles and flasks trapped a pandemonious catalogue of insects, a sudden and alarmed buzz rang in his brain.

"431999! What's the name of the kid with you?"

"It's Ruby."

"Ok... We're looking for a kid named Flora. Just in case, be on the lookout, ok?"

"Flora?"

"That's my name!"

Neipas looked up at her. Suddenly his horns seemed to weigh thicker and pull down. He lifted her from his shoulders and placed her on the floor delicately; then confusedly asked:

"What?"

"Floa is my name," she said with a wide, bobbing beam.

"I thought your name was Ruby."

"'Ooby is my knee name," she clarified.

"Knee name?"

"Yes, not my '*eal* name,*"* she said with emphasis, "my knee name".

Neipas puzzled over the swaying tresses and tried to unwind the mystery of her bubbly words.

"Do you mean nickname?"

"Yes, 'oobie is my knee name," as always she dictated every syllable slowly and methodically.

"So Ruby is your nickname and Flora is your actual name?"

Ruby patiently explained, swaying her braids didactically: "My 'eal name is Floa bu' my gran-daddy calls me 'oobie.'"

"Mary..." Neipas muttered in frustration. Petting the child and quelling his anxiety, his fingers then ascended to his long earlobe when, to his horror, he beheld Drrawetz emerging from the teetering throng. The steward was followed by a portentous Eagle — the Head Gardener, who was trailed by his bearded, mustachioless ox Assistant, as well as his guardian Bull, titan and muscular over them, potently carrying two glistening keys which pended from his nose-ring. They strode straight for him.

Drrawetz's growing face sunk in feathery wrinkles of great ire as he stepped closer. His silver peacock beak already shook with mumblings, which Neipas could read as repetitions of "what are you doing, what are you doing" menacingly emitted from the full despair of his anger. Behind him, the imposing Gardener, pacing forth with his opulent cane, his commanding wattles and thick beard of plumage, stared with a piercing look, impassive in its consciousness of authority. After tossing a fleeting glimpse of disgust into Neipas' petrified eyes, Drrawetz molded a quick, overtly fawning smile.

"There you are, you little naughty!" he said with strain, turning to Ruby, pressing his hands to his bent knees.

But the child, at this, frowned very severely indeed. Standing on the tips of her toes Ruby belted petulantly, "I don't like *you*!"

Drrawetz straightened up immediately and turned to the Gardener with a solicitous, almost supplicant grin, an obviously feigned giggle. The Head Gardener laughed but didn't look at the girl directly or addressed her (the Assistant behind him smiled tenderly at Ruby, obviously endeared to the child) — instead turning to Drrawetz, and saying calmly, "Come on, let's take her back to her grandfather. Begin practicing your apologies," he said, the laughter already dissipated and gone from his stare.

"Yes, Head Gardener, indeed, I do apologize, it's my responsibility entirely, you are certainly correct, Head Gardener, I will strive to improve and continue meeting standards," stammered Drrawetz with repeated curtsies and a mournful visage, with his gloved fingers wading through the substance of his expression. It was extraordinary how deftly he sculpted his mask of cold clay.

"What's your number," the Gardener then demanded, turning abruptly to Neipas — who instantaneously lowered his horns.

"431999," he said promptly, taming and concealing behind his masks a great surge of fear.

The Gardener contemplated him for a moment. Then, reaching under his giant wattle, he pulled out a banknote and placed it behind Neipas' ear.

"Thank you, sir," said Neipas, bowing lower.

"I notice an accent on you. Are you from the heartlands?"

"Indeed I am, sir."

"Mary Virgin, I knew it. I'm from Doris. What's your name?" the Gardener demanded, in a tone mixing sternness and familiarity.

"Neipas, sir."

"Good. Pleasant to see a fellow heartlander," said the Gardener, and immediately turning he motioned his entourage to move on, and began walking. But as Drrawetz pulled Ruby's little hand she sunk her feet into the soil and shrieked from the deepest profundities of her little self, wailing and crying in an agony of torture, her face suddenly awash in tears and her mouth open wide to the clothed skies. The Gardener then voiced impatiently, "Kasim, could you?" at which his Assistant, with his fatherly beard, leaned down fatherly-like and smiled to Ruby. His mollifying eyes seemed to produce some effect; the child becalmed, touching the vines garlanding his horns curiously. Delicately, the Assistant picked her up — and the entourage was off. Seeing them depart, Neipas still caught Drrawetz' look of scorn toward him; and Ruby's little face, bobbing over the shoulders of the Assistant Gardener, waving her little hand in farewell.

Neipas stood there a moment, reeling with an indistinct feeling. The Gardener's strange tone of familiarity, issued from his powerful, hooked, golden beak, was intimidating; it possessed an ominous tinge, an authority laden with threat. His very manner had impressed Neipas, and the feeling would linger on for a while; the Gardener inspired fear, somehow.

Turning his head with a relieved sigh, Neipas saw Cesar's silvery ox countenance walking among the wavering pigeon beaks scouring the booths. He winked at someone.

Approaching Neipas, he commented, "Drrawetz looked mad. What was that about?"

30 - Masquerade

The summit bells rang repeatedly and in rapid succession. Its vibrations spread and fluttered down across the Market veils, rousing away the drowsy quietude of the Gardens and ushering in at once a flurry of noisy activity; it was as if the sudden din of voices had emanated out of the bell sounds themselves. So the second Market-day began. Trading could then commence, and suddenly a feeling that there was no time to be lost pressed everywhere — every Merchant yelled from behind a counter, every Politician clamored atop the stage, Pigeons scrambled through the aisles and pointed their beaks in all directions — for the Market's freedom must be exercised and grown, lest it be lost.

Inside the Columbaria the ringing of bells had already sounded long before. Neipas had been yanked groggily from his sleep. Heavily, he lifted the blinds from his eyes as the brightness of the dormitory rushed to get inside them. Grimacing, grunting, languid, he sensed stirrings in the mattress above him and all over the space, the beginning of motions which began slow and increased in tempo as the hectic bell shook and punched drowsiness straight out of head's nerves. The Supervisor scurried among the bunkers and pushed some buttons on the wall. The bell stopped. "Everybody up?" asked the Supervisor, with the voice of someone still asleep. Neipas turned away from the aisle and faced the mirror inside the cote, which covered the whole wall. He saw his pigeon mask through a screen of blur, and he saw how it looked droopy and tired, and how its wax was moist, descending in folds from the base of his eyes like it wanted to peel away from his face. He checked his own state of mind from a distance, then he checked the time in his *I*. The sun hadn't yet risen from the horizon beyond the windowless dormitory. His muscles sored with the scars of toil, his head ached from the lack of rest; he had been made to do clean-up the previous night and hadn't slept more than 3 hours.

Bodies were plopping down from the shelves and amassing toward the door. Neipas climbed down heavily, merging into the outgoing throng; in the Food Hall, Osir gave him a scorching cup of coffee "with something special — jolt you right up" (sleepy, Neipas clinched the cup with hesitation, remembering the effects of Osir's pill; the janitor told him to keep eating to avoid bad symptoms) and Neipas awoke fully, jittering; the acrid beverage shot into his head that same moment, forced his eyes open and pulled his skull back by the hair.

His heart beat strangely the rest of the day, and it was in a state of inner trepidation and throbbing veins that Neipas braced himself for the long hours before him. He was pushed headlong into the grind by the drumming of the summit bells, headlong into the noises and smells of the Market labyrinth and into the winding pilgrimage across its trails. That morning he had a different circuit. They had also given him a tray of snacks to serve, in addition to the tray of alcohols, so that he had one loaded tray rattling upon each hand (there was a shortage in personnel, a Supervisor had mumbled). He staggered along. In the beginning, he had to stop every few minutes to put down one of the trays and unburden himself of some weight. The two were too heavy for him to carry. But these stops were fleeting, and he would hoist the load again the next moment; he couldn't break for more than a moment, lest the Supervisors catch him motionless and he incur Drrawetz's wrath. Neipas felt his influence in the works, had the impression that today's labor was harder and that it was because of him — though, when he spotted the chief steward later, perusing his watch at tip-toe, the fellow was exceedingly cordial. He wore his mask very well.

One of Neipas' transit stops was the 6th Terrace, which housed the Auditoriums. The main Auditorium, which topped the Garden's middle levels at the base of the Great Facade, was something magnificent to behold. Above its Stage rose the colossal Proscenium arches, which were lodged into the Facade towering above the Markets, as if they were a portal into its opulent and stony interiors. A silent waterfall cascaded from underneath the Ballroom on the summit in a majestic descent of heights, gracefully setting somewhere behind the Proscenium to continue its soft glide beneath the Auditorium and down across the Gardens. Its stream twinkled with the fiery sheen of the great Pearl above, coursing the air in its hypnotic sway. The arches of the Proscenium were 9-fold, sinking into the bowels of the Facade bulwark, and they were golden, with many carvings; they had a general appearance of superimposed shells. Heavy curtains descended from the deep heights of these arches, under which sat now three figures. Lit in the glow of lights, two Horses sat at opposite sides of the stage, debating. In the middle, more toward the back, sat the Journalist who moderated the debate, wearing the mane and visage of the Lion. This was Editor Moldura, Neipas' old professor in the Ivory Tower. Neipas had already seen here a few times in passing and never failed to lower his head in profound respect and gratitude. His parrot perched upon his shoulder and ate at his ear as he moderated.

They discussed what they called the Persian Crisis. The Lion had asked the Horses the best way to solve it, and two opinions jostled one ear each. On Stage Right, facing the left side of the Auditorium, a case was made for sanctions. "A pressure campaign is what we need to make them capitulate," said the Horse; whereas on Stage Left, facing the Auditorium's right side, airstrikes were favored: "Targeted strikes are quicker and more streamlined.

It would be a more efficient tactic," said the other Horse — both were Legislators, each representing one of the two dominant political parties. The Editor nodded with pensive considerations at both propositions, and the audience on each side nodded in turn. Reflective pigeon heads proliferated through the terrace, underlit with the glimmer of *I*s. Stepping up into the terrace from the stairs at a margin of the Auditorium, Neipas could glimpse the wings of the stage behind the drawn curtain of the fore, and he saw that in the shade there was a small audience of Eagles on thrones, and that they, too, nodded.

Somehow things got easier as morning circled past dawn. They either refilled Neipas' burden with lighter weights or he simply grew used, or numb, to it. Osir's occult drug seemed to be thinning into its intended effect, too. The frantic pumping and squirming in his muscles eased, first into his innards — which made him fly to the bathroom in a panic, carrying chanting trays in little hops (his ear steeled for a reproach, yet no one said anything) — but then it seeped even further inward, into his very soul; it stopped, and his spirits became settled. It even seemed as though, as the sun lifted well free of the mountains in the east and shone softly upon the gardens, that he became more animated. Energies grew inside him mysteriously as he geared into the motions. By degrees the weariness wore off and was replaced by an adrenaline which lubricated his muscles and accelerated his thoughts. He noticed the Stage only when he passed by it for the 11th time. And every time thereafter the spectacle upon it was different; gradually he discerned the long tables of Academics, Lobbyists and PR Professionals extending from the pulpits from which the Politicians spoke, donning Horse masks to the audience; these scholars petting the oculi of their peacock feathers, mumbling sage advice to the Horses whenever they broke their speech; and he realized how they painted their furs in different colors each time he went by — sometimes pink, other times black or brown, according to whatever most pleased the pigeons...

Each cattlehead was in charge of one row of seats, alongside which he or she would traverse with trays of snacks, fast foods, sodas and alcohol for the audience members to pick up in passing. Neipas walked through one of the front lines, whence he could see the orchestra pit. He should have been near enough, but he couldn't spot the orchestra itself. Though he couldn't lean over to peer and make sure, the gap looked to him enveloped in total shadow; it seemed very deep. The orchestra, nevertheless, had to be there — Neipas could hear it. A long whisper of string, and a hum of voices, emanated from the pit like a gentle gust; like breathing. As he became aware and attent to it, his senses were as if absorbed, and all other sounds faded into its farness, all other sounds became whispers. To the melodic hums the Eagles beyond the drapes gesticulated their beaks; to its intonations all in the audience and all upon the stage nodded, slowly.

He experienced again a similar sensation ruffling from the balloons and their ropes. Whispers, stirs and throbs exhaled from their touch. Out the pandemonium of the Circus he emerged, out its forest of strings, out the maze of curtained hallways into the Circus and back from corridors which he roamed repeatedly, corridors made of veils, sometimes opaque, sometimes transparent, corridors of multiple colors, with passages between them also covered in such cloths — so that the eye could pierce the roving multitude through a haze of colorful layers interposed across a thousand depths, in a great confusion. He began to feel as though the Market was half-organic; as though it breathed. Perhaps it was the effect of Osir's drug, but he came to perceive the pigeons, whom he would see revolving round the trails in blending mobs, again and again in mechanic paces, as gears in a kind of clock, or threads pumping in a circuit. Out the Circus now he surfaced into the beauty of the lake and its bridges.

Something in the shimmer of the lake, something in the greens flaking its marble banks made him recede into vague abstractions of memory. The sun beaming from the waters reminded him of his mother, somehow; called to mind her printed image. Something in the bright ambiance summoned the distant, elusive recollection of her. But what he experienced was a memory of feeling, and it was too faint for him to grasp intellectually and wonder what it was in that landscape that made him feel it.

Afar the reverberating voice from the wall of many eyes, whose concave words Neipas could still not quite understand. As he slugged through the crowds there, he heard a tour guide lecture, pointing to that wall upon the outer bank:

"That is our Chief Economist," explained the suited ox cheerfully. "He interprets the will of the Market. It's a complicated job — for the Market is everywhere, and It speaks in mysterious ways, by means of signals. But to understand It is to understand ourselves," the tour guide then said, profoundly, "because the Market is the maximum expression of our rationality, and It is what makes us who we are. So teaches the Economist."

And back up the terraces Neipas went. He walked also through some of the other, smaller auditoriums round back, for there was an area inside the Facade, at its very base, which the public could access. There were big posters by each of the doors, depicting colorful pictures and crafty fonts, which spectacularly announced the events inside. In one of the posters he saw Marlene the Lawyer's name — something about environmental law and the markets. In a corner, a large Bull was selling tickets to a fight in front of a large and curious throng. Neipas walked about the theater lobby until his trays were empty, restocked, and then went back out and round the main Auditorium, from where he descended the central steps, over the lake and along the river, to plunge once more into the Market and the swirling beholding of its many pleasures.

By late morning the effects of Osir's special coffee were wearing off. Neipas began reeling with clenched teeth behind his mask when, quite suddenly, the Seamstress in his ear called his number and simply told him to take a 30-minute break. Already another ox was in position by him and picked up his trays. Neipas felt relief landing upon his muscles as the weight, which by then had become a part of his body, was delivered from them. And then he went, alight, out of the labyrinth and down the terraces, rushing off to the Columbaria to take a quick nap. He strode past the lobby into the corridors, along its mirrored walls and under its glaring lights. On the turn to his dormitory, across the corridor leading to the Clockroom, he nearly barged upon a tangle: an intimate scene unfolding quietly in a nook.

He saw Cesar pressing someone against the wall and kissing hungrily against the other's shy reticence and muffled laughter. They embraced and kissed in turn, madly, like lovers long lost. Narrowing his eyes in a drowsy moment of suspension, Neipas recognized who it was — it was the Head Gardener's Assistant whom Cesar kissed. Shaking his head against sleep and dream, and suddenly feeling like he had transgressed into the privacy of a bedroom, Neipas rushed off before they could see him. Briskly, with the efficiency of a model worker, he stepped before his closet of possessions and extracted the *I* from it; programmed an alarm so that the *I* would wake him in 15 minutes; climbed to his shelf without bothering to remove the ox from himself and (not putting the blinds, so as to moor himself to the shallows) dropped instantly into the depths of sleep.

31 - Magpie

The sound of bells shook in the same manner as in the morning; but whereas in the morning they had felt like a crazed death toll, they sounded now like a holiday melody, and landed upon Neipas' heart more lightly, as a sort of softening hand upon his breast.

The second market-day was over. It had been arduous, rampant with accelerating activity. Since waking from his nap he had been working inside, within the huge conference halls; serving lunches at first, and then scurrying between the immense pavilions with beverages of all sorts upon his hand, drinks of all colors, like a hurried alchemist peddling dubious mixtures. He had paid Osir for his special morning coffee but refused a kindly discounted second dose; he settled with a triple shot of the regular strain to get him through the rest of the day, and with the liquid scintillating in his wrinkled brow he pushed through fatigue all afternoon long, for hours. Neipas seethed in a silence of deep breaths. His steps locked onto the path with the stimulus of racing, competing against a schedule felt in his bones, against the feeling of watching Supervisors, against the instinct of Drrawetz's dislike; goaded onward by the dizzying noise of the closed interiors and the influence of the drug. It wasn't wholly mechanical — his circuit would change frequently so he'd had to keep his wits about him. He could never predict any next moment with certainty. Many times it wasn't clear what he should do, except that he should keep moving as much as possible and be flexible as required. It was chaotic, unstable, oppressive under Drrawetz's scattershot lead. His dizzying supervision led to an extreme general mood, charged with stress; yet they all raced onward, clay visages only growing more firm in the heat of toil. But the 3 days of the Summit were nearly over — indeed, all volition and sense of faith were moored upon the relative shortness of the gig.

No more orders came — he could relax. Exiting into the Gardens, Neipas, sore of muscle and mind, sought refuge from the lingering twittering of the pigeons and the muttering of the merchants now ending their shifts. The prized merchant cattle emerged from behind the booths already wearing pigeon faces and so merged into the crowd, indistinguishable from the rest but for the subdued silence they held, a languidness of exhaustion. There would be more for the pigeons — The Market, in reality, never stopped. The summit bells simply signaled the conclusion of the day Markets and the beginning of the night Markets. Now the crowds would increasingly seep into the deep of the complex, into its ceilinged mazes, its mirrored labyrinths, to indulge in all the hidden pleasures which money could buy. Commerce of hard drink, bazaars of sexual innuendo, trading in dreams — these enterprises, always running, profited the most during the night.

There were, beyond the Market pathways, in the very edges of the Pigeon side of the Hanging Gardens — by the meridian rivers running north and south — a few nooks where quietude and peace could be found. Neipas recollected walking such paths the year previous; and so he roamed down the vast terraces after dinner, through the tangle of tents and their chaos of tended greenery, into the very bottom of the soaring stairway where the stacked floors abruptly sunk into a darkness of trees, thick bush and thorny stems; where fragments of statues lay in ruins, strewn soiled across the wood, patiently colonized by moss and cobweb, climbed silently by insects of all kinds. Neipas navigated its stillness without wind. The Eagles' Nest was covered with a thin dome of glass which shielded it from the harsh elements and filtered the glacial temperatures of that elevation; a shield immaculate, spotless, invisible but for the skyward balloons which, freed from their ropes, leaned against it in their flight. They hung motionless aloft, afar, and eerily over all the masks.

Shades were slowly amassing over the fading light beneath the canopies as the Earth tilted away from the sun. Out from under them Neipas entered the little hidden plot below the gazebo, which arose dramatically, like a solitary minaret jutting out the entwined mess of boughs and puffed mounds of treetops. As he ascended the steps to the gazebo he spotted someone leaning sideways against one of its posts. A back, clad with waitressing attire, faced him motionless. Down past the nape cascaded curly locks of deep black, meticulously tended between glistening dark braids of pigeon feather. It stood in a dignified, upright posture, meditative, sage, absolutely still before the giant expanse sweeping the reaches far below and far away from the tower. Neipas stopped. The sound of his steps ceased, and the rush of the southern waterfall replaced them in his ear; the waters rumbled languidly in the empty air, echoing the lazy, yawning end of day. He hadn't noticed someone was there until he was at the very top of the stairs, and he considered turning back, afraid of intruding upon the observer's solitude.

But then very suddenly — in such a swift movement that it made him start — the person turned her gaze to him. Neipas confronted Magpie's alerted stare, which pierced into his own startled eyes with a forcefulness of intensity. She held it for but a moment: but it was a stare so wide, so intense, so penetrating that it impressed itself profoundly upon his memory. It was one of those moments that become etched to the soul, expressive as they are of profound human feeling — Neipas would come to remember it later as a perfect image of the mysterious power of the hunted.

Her gaze becalmed, but only gradually; as if the recognition came slowly to her. She turned back to the prospect without a word. Neipas stood still and undecided for a while.

Finally he took hesitating steps toward Magpie's enigmatic back, as if irresistibly seduced by the mollifying deep blue of the landscape beyond it. He approached carefully, and leaned slowly against the railing, still wondering if he should turn back and leave her alone.

"Hey," Neipas greeted in a muted tone, as if careful not to disturb the silence.

"Hey..." Magpie replied in a softer tone yet, almost in a whisper. Her voice, unveiled to the tender evening, was without judgment or annoyance. She was too enveloped in the broader view and too withdrawn in her own reflections. Her indifference was almost welcoming. It was enough to make Neipas stay; and his body gave in, too fatigued to move from there now. He joined Magpie in her silent contemplation.

She surveyed the ocean which spread immensely in every direction, from the low-lying beachfronts of Golden WestBeach, through the great industrial operations of cranes and boxes and ships docked at Axiac Port, to the caged greenery of the southern shores, and all along the mountain range running southeast over the thin strip of coast extending beyond the border from the old bay by Wall St., which had once been an entry port for slaves and a market of humans. From that extreme altitude, the vast waters made even great Axiac appear small. Magpie's eyes flashed with the rippling of the cascade at her side, with the softness of the sky softening the flow, with the glint of the Pharos above. Their gaze reflected outwardly her inner despondency. Tracing her stare against the land-bound tides faraway, she ruminated on landscapes hidden behind the horizon, lulling in vague possibilities. But after a long time fixed upon those magnificent horizons, her sight inevitably tended, as if pulled by gravity, downward toward Ostrich.

Before their very feet were the rooftops of Babylon's towers, suspended amid thin screens of smog. These monumental edifices propagated in all directions from the Belab, standing invincibly against the rest of town like a disheveled bastion of glowing orange, of beaming glass quickly disintegrating into the grimy blotches of shacks and broken houses of the southern sprawl, the dereliction of which was obvious even from this height; for it was collective and enormous, the visual marks of poverty clear upon the urban plain. From the very core of it, and proliferating all the way to the port, tall chimneys rose tall, lone in their conspicuous height among low-lying abodes; and from them churned huge clouds of smoke, trailing into the air in a great continuous puff, covering those neighborhoods dark with its pall. Tongues of fire stretched and licked the waning sky from the middle of the industrial zones — they burn always, thought Magpie, they burn always. Their flare would survive even the sun, like sacred flames devoutly tended to by the religious of the land, never to be extinguished.

The light of those flames coursed behind her eyes even as she averted them, even as she turned her stare to the waterfall flashing the dying throes of the cascading sun. Even as she glimpsed the horizons due west, still those flames scintillated inside her eyes. It was as though she were bound upon the concrete of that plain, Ostrich her home: somewhere in that stain was the little house her parents had left her, and which her grandparents had left her mother before them. But what was Ostrich to her? A jungle of cement where the ground hemorrhaged tar and the understories were made of cardboard and broken glass... A ceilingless prison, pressed beneath a sky made of ash, a sky solid and very low, like a lid; under which proliferated a maze of squalid streets, where people steeped in tar languished, poor, burdened with the legacy of servitude, scorned for centuries for the darkness of their feathers. People hungry — Magpie had known the fear of hunger even when she was a child. She recollected the sepulchral stench of home, suffused heavy with strain, the relentless tension of poverty which snapped with frequency, lashing out with the force of screaming... She felt an indefinable trace of those endless bus rides to school, the convulsing noises of the classroom, the way those streets stretched from barred windows as if they were melting under the sun. She recalled, in a recollection of feeling, all the days swallowed in the general squalor of existence... stretching through the calendar etched in numbers to her soul, to that very moment. Her eyes floated again to Ostrich.

From that highest of summits, Magpie regarded the so-called rookeries as tidal rubble dredged from the wider sea, like an ample swamp washed out of the waves; the lights of cars already alighting upon the highways were like currents of drifting refuse. The molten asphalt swung...

"That's the refinery right there," Magpie began in a gruff but clear murmur. "The one they want to expand."

Neipas was going to say 'I know' — but, because of some vague fear of sounding condescending, he stopped himself and didn't say anything. Instead he looked at her, nodding lightly, as if to affirm the same thing; and then, captured momentarily by her untamed beauty, his gaze stilled upon her. A glint of the sunset glow splashing the megalopolis rested atop her eyes and cheek, and the rest of her face was involved in a delicate shade which lent it a mysterious quality, a penetrating sense of enigma. Her visage was chiseled into straight angles and soft edges, her black skin of feathers glowed somehow even in the shade, and so did her locks of curly hair in the most charming manner; a manner encapsulated in her round, hazel-colored eyes, expressive of an innocence that was often hidden beneath the intensity with which she neared her lids, eyes focused and alert all the time. But now she looked at Neipas with the full roundness of her eyes, and he felt as though he witnessed her at a moment of tranquility, when she was at her most serene and unguarded; and the sight of such eyes made Neipas a little nervous, so beautiful they were, so gentle and full of contemplative feeling. Magpie took Neipas' gaze as a sign of attention, and felt comfortable in his silence. It was as though he told her he was listening; and the quietude softened her, and encouraged her to speak as she gazed out again:

"It's been there since I can remember. When we were kids we played around it. We even snuck into it a couple times. The second time we got found, and we never tried to sneak in again." Pause.

"Anyway, I never minded it much. It was just there, you know. Just this huge thing with chimneys behind some fence. I didn't associate it with anything," she chuckled — "I actually kinda liked it, when I was a kid. Fed my imagination and everything... I guess I spent a lotta time in my head.

"I dunno why I have this kind of memory, but I remember a lotta stuff from when we were kids and I remember the first time —" dwindling pause; Magpie narrowed her eyes, regaining a bit of that intensity of stare, though vaguer, more vacant than usual, reminiscent — "I still remember the first time I realized the... — you know. What that thing actually was about."

Magpie looked at Neipas tentatively and, seeing that he looked at her and listened still, turned her eyes to Ostrich and began again:

"Me and my momma were sitting on our porch... this one night. My dad was in prison at that time. Anyway, we were just sitting there — my momma had this old rockety chair, and I was sitting on her lap — the chair was like up and down," Magpie gestured the swaying motion by bending her pulse under her flattened hand, "up and down, real slow... She was telling me my favorite story, that she must've told me a thousand times before — about this mermaid, you know," she chuckled, "but anyway, I was almost falling asleep when all of a sudden — woosh," her hands joined and parted in something suggestive of explosion. "Out of the chimney comes out this huge... — this flare, you know. Just a huge flame. Tall like the sky... Lighted up everything in a second and I jumped up all scared. There was this terrible noise with the fire — like a roar, but, also like a slurp, or something. I dunno how to describe it. Like —" and here she tried to emulate the sound; but nothing could impart to Neipas the experience of that apocalyptic noise ripping asunder the heavens, screaming out from the very bottom of the earth, blooming aloft like some infernal tree, making skies aflame with crimson and revealing that the night was made of flesh, that it throbbed in womb-like palpitations. "But anyway, after that, came this smell..." a click of the tongue, her face twisted momentarily with disgust. "Damn. I swear to God I still feel it to this day."

"Momma rushed us inside... She put me to bed, I think. I can't remember much of what happened after the smell, but I remember momma was coughing a lot. The smell stayed on for days... Until these officers with masks came to the hood, and we all had to move for a while. I still dunno what happened exactly. Wasn't for long, you know —" Magpie shrugged — "couple months or something."

"But momma was sick already by then. She always had issues with breathing... and she was always a little sick all the time. But it got much worse after that smell. Momma had to stay in bed all day and couldn't stop coughing. One day I went to her and saw her nose all bloody. I can't remember if this was at our place or my uncle's — that's where we stayed a while, when the officers told us to leave. My uncle lived a few blocks away and even there we could smell the... — you know, whatever it was, from the refinery.

"I got sick from it too. But then things got better and we got on back to our house. Momma got better, I got better. And for a while, it was all good."

She paused. The sun was nearly upon the horizon then, and the tranquil orange of the heavens shimmered in the waters and softened the sights all across the vast outdoors; it was as though the light caressed the view, and made everything calmer, infusing a vague sense of magic even into this fabricated air they breathed.

"But then — I dunno how long after that, but it must've been a while — momma got sick again. Real sick, and real quick too. One day she couldn't even stand up, and then she died that night."

Magpie paused again, abruptly. Her voice was very calm; she narrated her story very calmly, level, staid, as if she were relating the most casual of occurrences. Her mask was stiff and transpired no strong feeling. But her eyes had narrowed to their usual intensity of concentration, they faced the vast prospect as though it were an adversary approaching threateningly.

A silence deepened between them, and the wax on Magpie's brow slid a little in the meanwhile, giving her countenance the appearance of a severe frown, driving an uncomfortable wedge into the former peacefulness of their shared quietude. Neipas, not knowing where to look now, wandered his gaze about the terraces, somewhat at a loss. Then, bothered by the silence, he said something for the sake of making sound, and a little to get Magpie out of her sombre mood; speaking more out of impulse than thought: "I'm sorry."

Magpie eased her stare slowly. Mollified by Neipas' condolence, she retook the word:

"Momma was sick all the time, all the time... I dunno if it was that smell that tipped her over, you know. But I know for sure it was that refinery that killed her. Dumped all sorta shit in the river, too. Everyone was sick all the goddamn time. I remember," she said broodingly, nodding slowly — "I remember... I began hating the hood from that point on. There were all these other problems, but damn — that smell, it's what made me really wanna get outta there, you know. It was like a turning point for me. Fifteen years gone by, and I'm still there."

She sighed in calm resignation. "I just wanna leave. I wish they'd lay off and take the money from Noxxe. I mean I get it, but..." And she shrugged helplessly, shaking her head.

After what felt like an extended period of quietude, as the Earth sunk toward the deep gloom of the universe, Magpie turned her head from the deepening reds of the horizon and looked at Neipas enigmatically, as if expecting him to say something. Neipas, soaked in an uncanny feeling, asked her:

"Do you mean your neighbors should take the money and leave? So the refinery expands?"

"Yeah. I mean I get why they don't. It's shit money and they can't go anywhere else in this city. But we'll get kicked out anyway. Might as well before they kick us out by force, and without money."

Pause.

"And you? Where would you go in this city?"

"Nowhere. I just wanna go as far the fuck away from here as possible."

Magpie had again turned her eyes to the fading distances. She didn't regret telling her story, recluse of soul as she was; but she wondered now why she had opened up to Neipas in that way. Perhaps it was because the gazebo was so calm, peaceful. Inside Ostrich, the world had seemed to her like a torrent rushing toward a waterfall, against which she must constantly struggle. But here, all things lay as tranquil as a lake. Ostrich itself looked innocuous. The realities of it were flattened by the distance. In that tucked perch in the hidden heights, they stood as though upon hallowed ground; in a berth of confessions.

But Neipas, progressively uneasy in their soundlessness — there was an edge to her calm disclosures which had made him so — brought out of himself a few words:

"What happened after..." he stammered. "You know."

"After momma died? I went to live at my uncle's place till my dad got outta prison. Then I moved back home," and as she said this her fingers tapped the rail nervously, unconsciously.

"Did you get along with your dad?"

"We had problems." She moved not an inch as she said this; nothing but her beak stirred. Her hand gripped tightly now, in a casual and perhaps practiced manner, the base of her jaw and the lower half of her face, as if to prevent her mask from spasming and dripping off. Her eyes kept steady; but suddenly something in her voice, and in the oddity of her conduct — something in Magpie suggested the sinister nature of their relationship.

"Anyway," Magpie continued, taking the initiative to ward off the silence and the disquieting sentiments which had suddenly penetrated it with memories stirred from the deep, invoking an aura latent with screams and blood-soaked lips. "I get it... I'm pissed, you know, but if they don't wanna leave, let'em stay then. These rich folk don't gimme money for my house, they gimme money for being here and feeding their rich asses. Then I get the fuck outta here. Not much longer."

The day was at an end. Afar, the horizon blushed as the sun kissed it, drawing the star's loving warmth slowly into deep watery bosoms. Magpie leaned forward on the rail, looking through the Eagle Gardens beyond the cascade to the west, where the ocean spread the distances and covered the world like an immense, wind-swept mantle whose end is fastened to the horizon line. The hour tucked in under the sheet of ocean and the mantle of sky, and was drowsing to slumber when the Pearl banged alight above them, jerking it awake to the mechanical fascination of the sleepless city.

"Gotta go," Magpie said quietly, straightening her attire and placing her head into the heifer mask. She had been working in the Eagle Wing — she told Neipas, with thinly veiled distaste — and had been called upon to work that night, though she didn't know where to yet. She left. Neipas stood against the rail and watched the yellow-laden, electric sky of Axiac's night for a while. He wasn't called anymore, and soon he turned round and walked through the somber woods, which were very dark — and back into the terrace stairs. Strangely, he was faced with a dim immensitude — there were no lights on upon the Gardens.

A burly shadow materialized suddenly at his side. It was a mass of towering and solid black, on the summit of which rose a sort of crescent shape, with two very high, pointy tips. Neipas flinched upon it.

"Are you working?" came a grunt from the darkness. It was a Bull Guard standing before him.

"No," Neipas said with a firm tone of voice, carrying none of the startlingness which momentarily tipped him off.

"Do you have a ticket for the fight?"

Neipas stood in confusion, blinking and grimacing. His eyes cleared up to the view of a few twinkles of light here and there, streaming about the terraces; alighting, it seemed, faint figures of pigeons — a sort of procession of them being led in a line.

"If you have no ticket," lowed the Bull, "then what the hell are you doing here? The gardens are closed off for the night. Go back inside."

The harshness of his words alone did not convey the unwarranted aggressiveness of his tone, which was laden with latent threat; in that sudden, unreal blackness Neipas felt for a moment that he would be punched.

"Sorry," he said, and he heard his words as though they had been said by someone else. He pulled out his *I* and climbed two terraces up to the Columbaria with the help of its spotlight. He felt the Bull's stare in the darkness behind him. Yonder above, the strange little gleams converged slowly through the clothed passageways.

Deep inside the bunk bed, Neipas, who had so longed for the night to satiate his need to rest, couldn't sleep. Somehow disjointed thoughts of flames shooting up, somehow mingled with the fountains of the Hanging Gardens, kept appearing in his mind. He thought of Eva and the last time they had spoken, the stinging argument they had had, the venom in their words; he thought of Orenda's words in Ostrich and her sombre prospects, the doom pending over their heads, the stacks of smoke surging above the peaks of the eastern mountains; and these thoughts interchanged and mixed together uncontrollably in Neipas' increasingly fraught state of mind, growing frustrated with the inability to sleep. But he couldn't sleep not because of these thoughts — it was something underneath, a nagging feeling of unrest that lurked all about his body. He struggled mentally with it to much frustration, for hours, never leaving the bedsheets' increasingly uncomfortable enclosure.

Nevertheless the mind eventually, surreptitiously gave in to the exhaustion of the body; the frustration faded into dormancy, as did all else. And just on the cusp of sleep, it seemed to Neipas that the flames dominating his dimming consciousness were swept off by a great, slow tide...

Meanwhile great fumes churned from Iblis, and ominous clouds neared the horizon.

32 - The Hall of Games

Something poked his brain. A little noise stirred by it, as of a fly buzzing very deep inside his ear. The sound lifted his eyelid with a titanic effort — and somehow he mumbled numbers with his dormant lip, wet with thick exhalations.

"431999?" — distracted, Neipas had forgotten to remove his ox face.

"Yes, yes?" he babbled.

"Are you available now?"

The strange question sounded like an affirmation. Neipas groaned with heavy breath, said "Hm-hm — yes, hm" — for there was nothing else he could say to that voice in his ear — smacked the foul taste of his own tongue, and rotated his body of boulders to the edge of bed, lifting the blinds from his bloody eyes; and the brightness of the dormitory dove at once into the reddened whites and dilated pupils, stinging and perforating into the core of his head, exploding in a throbbing ache.

Neipas went away grimacing, going along with a little team streaming sleepy from the dormitories. Cesar walked beside him with closed eyes and beak ajar. They made their way unconsciously down some steps of mirrored corridors, zapped by a thousand suns of electricity shooting out from the ceiling. Neipas noticed the bright contours of the Food Hall and one or two blurs sitting lone in an immense desert of tables and chairs. He woke before the sudden figure of Bulls standing at the sides, enormous by him, and saw a row of horns being formed over the rattling of their guns, coalescing toward the deep frame of a scanner.

"Mmmmmmmm!" Cesar moaned with a tight grimace upturned. He stretched, yawning loudly. "God! What time is it?"

His voice croaked, it spoke through his nose. Janu, breathing in thickly the kitchen steam, looked over to the oven clock.

"It's late."

"Fucking shit, man," ejaculated the poet, frowning sleepily. "Honestly. A man can't even sleep anymore."

Neipas approached with two little cups of coffee. In the diminished awareness of his squinted eyes he chuckled, dimly, distantly thinking how very humorous it was to see Janu and Cesar, who were both all smiles all the time, with such grim faces.

"You taste like shit," Cesar mumbled to the coffee, convulsively pinching the upturned tip of his mustache.

The coffees were for him and Neipas — Janu, in the fury of his activity, was the most awake among them. The good cook scrambled amid clanking metal and jets of fire, his sweaty, chubby visage veiled in steam blown away out of the pots, intent over the large stove spitting upward rains of boiling oil, churned up scents of meat bubbling fervently in the rush. Before Janu's quick, gloved hands, juices were soaked up in pans and raw meat shriveled over the flames, rices yelled up water in the pots, spices scattered in smoke, blood sizzled. It was a massive fiery chaos which Janu mastered, as though he were a deity presiding over the creation of worlds. The thing was confounding to the sleepy heads around him who contemplated the work like it was the expression of some divine mystery, something incomprehensible to mortals.

"Smells good," said Neipas.

"Hopefully it tastes good too, man," Janu responded without breaking concentration. "But who knows — palate of these fools 's different my friend."

A great many cooks were engaged in the same scramble. The ruckus of batting silverware was reproduced hundredfold across the Eagle's Kitchen, stirring the majesty of stainless steel shimmering immaculately and immense, among beeping of machines in the aisles and over the ovens and stoves, under the piped ceiling half-sunk in shadow high up, over the great surgical basins of water and piling dishes. Afar, by the exits and entries, hung lavish paintings which seemed to impart the importance of that space. They all scrambled skillfully, wearing focused masks of bronze fur under white hats. Like Janu, many wore pajamas under their white aprons. The Chef sauntered quietly along the aisles, peeking in at station after station and carrying on.

Neipas scratched his furry nape. The weight of his horns made his head ache slightly now, after a full day wearing them. He waited along with a small army of other waiters who simply stood fidgety aside. Somehow the scene recalled to his mind the idea of an old factory warehouse, where thousands of hands rushed with booming sounds echoing up toward ceilings of crisscrossed beams. The pipes above him seemed to pulsate with the life of veins.

"Voila, amigos," Janu said, giving a last squeeze to the lemon. "It's ready."

In the end, all the disarray had yielded was a handful of gourmet dishes, which, though they looked infinitely flavorful, were petite in portion.

"That's it?" asked Cesar.

"That's it?" Janu repeated in incredulity. "You got some of the tastiest grub on the planet right here dude. I'd let you have some but my chef's looking."

Neipas, Cesar, and other waiters who approached now collected the dishes and arranged them skillfully onto their trays — the arrangement was checked twice by the Chef and then by the Supervisor, who winked.

"All right my friends," Janu finally said, inhaling a sigh of relief and smiling earnestly his usual smile. "I'm gonna sleep. Good luck."

At the kitchen's exit a small team of Makeup Artists fixed up the workers' faces with hands, paint, powder and ornaments as they passed. Drrawetz waited for the cattleheads outside. When they came out, he didn't speak, but merely rotated on his smiling heels and walked forth, leading the formation. He didn't look the least bit sleepy; his mask wore the same countenance of wakened and over-dignified, dandy servility as always.

There were corridors cloaked with ornate wallpaper and paintings, after which they entered a sumptuous space aglow with crimson and scented like many cigars. Music bloomed full and soft into Neipas' ear — what he noticed first was the band nooked in the shade of a corner, with the piano by the wall of red velvet and violins and flutes by its side, under a sconce of warm light. Their features were occulted in shade, they moved with the immateriality of shadows. Before them, with back turned to the entering waiters, the Conductor gestured widely, with the span of a bird's wings; slowly, with the tranquility of a god. Naked legs with swan masks trolled about between the tables round which vague Eagles lounged, smoking and puffing fumes with laughter. Their beaks glimmered golden in the moody dimness. Drrawetz approached them gracefully and greeted with deep bows, while the grinning, winking Supervisor directed the waiters into their places with swift hands. A few cattleheads remained. At the urging of the Supervisor, Neipas and Cesar walked on with a few others through this casino suffused with pricey brothel airs, awakened now by the opulent stimuli floating about their noses and ears. They seemed to walk in a curve, through many revolving doors wafting golden aromas, in and out of intimately luxurious rooms dimmed in reds, upholstered with furs, fitted with all the comforts of wealth; finally stopping in a cozy parlor, at the end of which were a series of tables veiled by thin shutters. Ingrained in the padded wall was a lavish aquarium, inside which swam red fish; and all around unbodied taxidermies were mounted on the gaps between the sconces.

They took position before the silken shutters. Elusive shadows moved upon their fine texture, mingling in the vibration of various soft radiances, broken through ambient lights into multiple mirroring forms that meshed as they stirred. Flames burning in a hearth were discernible from their palpitation. The ambiance was somewhat romantic, posh. It smelled of cigars and comfort, money, tremendous opulence. Perfumes from the concubines tingled the air seductively. It was as though they inhaled gold through the nostrils and the ears. Glasses clinked with buoying ice, even the laughter sounded rich. And there was the music, too — the band was also here. They were similarly arranged and played the same symphony as all the orchestras in all the parlors they had passed by on the way there, with the Conductor (was it the same Conductor?) facing away from them, in the farthest corner.

Neipas had been instructed to look straight forward at all times and move as little as possible. The imposed motionless quickly became a strain; inside him, the strength of the coffee receded before sleep's advance, and he felt the vitality in his muscles abandon him slowly, his torso wavering a little, his knees trembling; his breathing deepening; his eyes becoming vaguer. Now and then cowbells, with which they had been strapped on entering the Eagle Wing, jingled beside him, and motions ruffled back and forth. The vision of shiny objects and smoking suits blurred, and the orchestral music mingled with the mum of a distant song from long ago, which his mother used to sing to him by the river.

Suddenly he felt a pinch in his leg and a jolt clamber up into his head, and his eyes widened, startled and pulsing with accelerated heartbeats. Miraculously — by the miraculous force of hard training — the tray in his hand hadn't stirred the slightest bit.

"Wake up!" Cesar whispered forcefully and exasperatedly, in a tone of quick breaths that suggested he himself was struggling. But then at just that moment the bell in Neipas' neck rang — his action was automatic. He stepped forward at once toward the tables.

"Duck for the Minister," said the voice in his head, and Neipas glimpsed into the tray with an anticipation of nervousness, checking to see if he did know which of the many little dishes in his tray had once been a duck. He thought he spotted it, confirming it with a certain buoyancy of sight and feeling that left him not too sure. But he hadn't time. The concubine slid aside the shutter, and the next moment Neipas stepped into the intimacy of a table ensconced between drapes of silk, lit by hearth, round which sat the Minister of Nations, whom Neipas was to serve, with two Lobbyists, a PR Specialist, a Think Tank Analyst, and one of the Legislators whom Neipas had seen on stage the morning previous. There was also a peahen wrapped all over in exotic veils, staring out of them with protruding, intense, bilious eyes. She petted a golden egg on the mantelpiece.

Only when Neipas was very close did he distinguish the individual words they spoke:

"Well which is more humane?" the Legislator, who had sat on Stage Left in the morning, put to his audience. "Murder by starvation, or by bombing?"

They laughed. Into the roaring Neipas slid gracefully and, stopping next to the Minister, greeted with a deep bow, according to script. "Your excellency," he said.

"Come on now, let's speak seriously," said the Minister to the table, ignoring Neipas.

"It is a serious question, Minister," defended the Legislator. "How is it going to affect us in the polls?"

"Don't worry about the polls, Jon. They're as unpredictable as the weather now," said the Minister, who gestured to Neipas without looking at him. Neipas made a little flourish through the air with his empty, gloved hand, and reached down into the tray. "We can't simply chase the polls, Jon. We have to shape the polls."

The PR Specialist, pinching his chin and making an expression of reasonableness, put in:

"With all due respect, Minister, but the push for airstrikes isn't being well received by the public. We'd rather make the process more streamlined too. But the wars in Mesopotamia were a public relations disaster. The numbers were a very bad look," argued the PR Specialist.

"Nonsense, Jonty," argued with a sweet voice one of the Lobbyists, emitting a little giggle. She was very flourished in layers of colorful coats, with exuberant eyes weaved in puffy shining plumes — this was ArmsCore's lobbyist. "Strikes are good for business, and what is good for business is good for the country."

Neipas picked the gourmet bit of duck with the finesse of a surgeon. He lifted it off the little plate but, seeing the Minister's beak opening, he waited — though the Legislator retook the word again first:

"But sanctions sound much better. No newspaper in the nation would connect it with any such thing as starvation, isn't that right Jonathan?"

The Think Tank Analyst nodded. "I would definitely agree. Time isn't ripe for bombing. Unfortunately there's a perception that strikes would quickly escalate to a ground invasion, which is a no-go at the moment."

"Well how do we fix this perception?" asked the Minister, closing his beak now a bit. Neipas took the opportunity and maneuvered his hand toward his mouth, which he opened now again; Neipas gently inserted the mushy, saucy meat into it, and the Minister took it and smacked it slowly, savoring it as he thought. "Hm."

Neipas would wait for him to finish; meanwhile other cowbells came and went across the layers of silken drapes on either side.

"Anything that is associated with dead troops right now is a no-go," the

Think Tank Analyst continued. "The problem here is that Persia is depicted as a big threat, and it's difficult to square that with the idea that quick strikes will solve the issue — The public perceives that won't pan out, again mostly because of the Mesopotamian war. On the other hand, sanctions just sound like something connected to the economy, like bond markets. No one knows what they do."

"It is slower, but it will end up accomplishing the same result, Minister. There's a strong anti-war sentiment right now."

"War might kill troops, but it's good business," the Minister said as he chewed. "You can have, say, 3000 troops dead, but if we can make a million times that in profit — It balances itself out, and more."

"It's just rational," agreed the arms Lobbyist.

"That's a fact, Mr. Minister," said the Think Tank Analyst. "But as you know, we can't spin it like that while the media..." but Neipas was gradually losing sense of the sound as he stepped away and entered the surreality of his leaden heart. Again he traversed the shutter and joined the line. Somehow what he heard had at once the effect of waking him up and pressing him deeper into a dream state. But just as soon as he dismissed it all as mere words, his bell jingled again.

"Duck and caviar for the Minister, and duck for the Lobbyist," said the voice.

Which Lobbyist? Neipas approached once more. The table waited for him now; the Eagles all beheld his approach in silence. Neipas felt his breath thicken, his chest pulling him toward the cushioned floor. Had they guessed the reaction of his heart to their conversation? He noticed now the composition of the table, outspread with cards, chips and mounds of banknotes which plopped joyfully from a cornucopia. Bankers at other tables would sometimes rise and yell out numbers. His sight focused.

"Have a taste of that duck, Johnny," said the Minister, pointing to the second Lobbyist, who hadn't yet spoken. He wore a most gossamer, long peacock tie.

"Hm. Wow," Johnny the Lobbyist said as Neipas' fingers were still inside his beak. "You're right, Minister. It really is exquisite."

"Hmm. Damn," the Minister mouthed between smacks.

"Can I have a taste of the creme brulee?" asked the Analyst, and Neipas obliged.

"Madam," said the Minister, addressing the peahen wrapped in exotic mantles, who was still playing with the golden egg. "Would you like to try the foie gras?"

"Oh, yes! Oh oh oh oh!" blurted out the peahen, suddenly reaching into her mantles and producing a stack of bills which she puffed upon the air, to the joy of everyone sitting.

Neipas' tray was cleaned out. He bowed deeply to the table in thankfulness, said "your excellencies", and turned to the line. But as he was walking back his bell rang again. "C'mere," he heard the Minister say behind him.

His heart sunk and his deep, sleepy breathing was cut short. Perhaps because of the fatigue, a dizzying sense of paranoia assailed him and it was as if his feet intended to plummet through the floor into the bowels of the tower; he felt nauseous. Maybe he had done something wrong. He had a fear of those beings in Eagle masks and suit, of their immense power, their ability to crush and obliterate with mere words; they frightened him even more than Drrawetz.

"Your excellency," Neipas asked with the tranquility of his servant mask.

"That's all the same cook?" asked the Minister. The vast amber eyes looked straight into Neipas above the feathered mustache, fastening him with the oppressive force of authority. Their extreme broadness insinuated all the confidence and lunacy of power.

"Indeed, sir."

"And what's this cook's name."

"Janu, sir."

The Minister nodded slowly, wrinkling his chin. "A beaner, huh. They can cook good, but this is something else." Everyone around the table nodded in agreement.

"What's wrong?" Neipas was by Cesar again, who whispered at his side.

Neipas gazed weirdly at the shutters, upon which he saw the admixed outlines of the eagles gambling, laughing, squawking. After a moment he mumbled:

"I just heard..." — but the Seamstress' voice interrupted him, shouting metal in his head: "Silence! Please refrain from — "

"You must whisper so they don't hear," whispered Cesar.

"Nevermind," Neipas sighed.

But the poet seemed to have perceived his meaning.

"Brother. You hear the most fucked-up things up here, I know. Here their mask slips... I feel horrible working for these yokels, but what can I do? The body must eat. And unfortunately the times don't agree with poetry. Whatever. But what I hear I tell Oshana and them. Here they don't know —" Cesar said this almost inaudibly "— because I'm discreet. And you must be too. Otherwise they would've vetted you out."

"Mary..." Neipas voiced, exhausted, dizzy with shock and slumber.

"And the things my boyfriend tells me... They're even worse."

A memory of last morning emerged in Neipas' thoughts.

"I think I saw you with him yesterday."

"I saw you seeing me with him. Way to ogle. You sure you're not gay?"

Neipas reddened behind his expressionless ox mask. Cesar laughed mutedly. "Just kidding."

They were waiting. Janu must have been pulled out of bed again, for the Eagles had swallowed all his dishes and ordered more in bigger quantities. Neipas held expectant with his empty tray, anticipating the refill. After a few moments he gulped a strong rush of cigar air, straining to keep awake; and after a painful sigh, he whispered:

"So how did you come to date the Gardener's assistant?"

"His name is Kasim," Cesar proclaimed earnestly, with some severity. "And he's not just an assistant. He actually manages the pantry and really does all the work around the gardens."

Neipas, breathing in, asked again, "So how did you meet Kasim."

"Long story, brother. But I will tell it to you someday," he said in a smiling state of reverie.

"Did you give him your poem?"

"Not yet... I know. I take forever."

"You didn't finish it?"

Cesar deepened into silence.

Said the poet, "I am not worthy of him, nor are my words."

"What?"

"I dunno if I will give the poem to him. I have a new ending, it's just... not completely sincere."

"How come? What's the ending?"

"Because he —" Cesar breathed, "He is kind. His love is pure. He wants a family. Children. But I. I'm a scoundrel. Look — I see other men!"

The words flowed abruptly, in a shamed hiss. Neipas turned his head with a start and glimpsed Cesar's rigid posture and immobile mask. "But if you love him?" he whispered after a while, barely knowing what he was saying.

"You don't understand. I can't help it. It's my addiction, I suppose." He shrugged helplessly. "I feel guilty — but mostly it's because I don't feel as guilty as I should! But I love him. I do, I do. It's just..."

Only Cesar's mustache stirred, slightly, as he spoke by means of whispers, whispers nearly inaudible.

"I was raised by a very religious grandmother," began Cesar, and Neipas, for some reason, found himself holding in a fit of laughter when he heard this. "Don't mock!"

"No, I... Sorry. I'm sleepy, man."

Cesar continued, "She was very devout. And she was widowed very young, you know, so she had to care for all her children by herself. My grandpa went because of a factory accident... As sudden as can be, you know? And, well, a couple of her children died after him. They were poor, you see, she didn't have the means.

"So this put the mania of death in her. She's still kicking," he said mutedly, and as if with pride, "but it's still all she can think about. And even when I was a little boy, you know, she would talk to me about death and death. I swear. How that's the way we're all going. I've been expecting it almost since I was born, brother. You understand how that impresses a child? Now there's not a single day I don't think about it. It's always in my mind, somewhere..." slowly the poet shook his head, very slowly he spoke, "Ah... What's there in the afterlife? Nothing, brother, not as far as I know. Kasim seems to believe there is, he keeps saying we'll be together even then, but... As much as I want to believe, I can't. But oh!... How I want to, how I want to... It's my fear of dying, brother. I know it. The poet pierces all veils, even one's own. Shit," at this he stopped abruptly, with a start. The eartag had picked up his speech and yelled inside his ear. He collected his bearing and his wits; and only then did he take word:

"I'm afraid to not live. It's my fear that makes me lie to him, and makes me hesitate at the idea of commitment. A poet can lie, yes, poets lie best... But the poetry cannot. Not to him. No. This new ending is no good. Verses must speak with the force of confession, or not at all."

They shared a moment of silence together, filled by the sounds of expensive glassware, the lull of tender music, the ambiance of wealth.

Finally, Cesar said: "Sorry — I'm sleepy too. But it's true, it's true."

Neipas panned aside his eyes and saw him still, immobile, yet.

"Can't wait to get the fuck outta here," whispered Neipas after a long pause, knowing not what else to say.

Cesar nodded slowly.

"Today's the last day before tomorrow, brother."

Janu's food finally came and, at the frantic blare of bell beneath his chin, Neipas advanced beyond the parted shutters, where he was received with a mix of impatience and elation.

"I'll have the maps drawn for Noxxe in a couple weeks then, Johnny," Neipas heard the Minister say to the fluffy-tied peacock Lobbyist. All Eagles and peacocks raising their glasses then, the Minister concluded, addressing the peahen with the feverish stare and the exotic, ornate wrappings, and who still clutched the golden egg:

"Here's to you, Madam. May we see you restore freedom to Persia. To democracy!" and even before the exalted official finished speaking his golden bill twisted with great unconstrained laughter, which simultaneously broke freely from all the sitters.

"Yes yes! Oh oh oh oh!" cackled the peahen, showering the table with banknotes.

Some time after, as Neipas was feeding them, Drrawetz entered and made himself announced: "Dear excellencies! I apologize for the interruption. I should like to bring to your notice that tonight's main event is about to commence."

The Eagles walked into one of the side gates — camouflaged in the wall's deep red — which slid away to reveal what looked like a padded elevator fitted with chairs. Drrawetz accompanied them with a large grin. The cattle, herded by the winking Supervisor, walked out the side and up labyrinthine staircases which turned in all manner of directions. They climbed up and down, turned left to right in a swirl of patterned wallpaper. Neipas could barely feel his legs. From time to time the wall would open through a tall window, and out the glass they could glimpse the Eagle Gardens. They saw that they were rising to the upper levels, for well beneath the sills now extended the middle terrace, under which the bottom terrace stretched in mazes of hedges into the edgeless pool at the tower's brink. The westward river flowed softly into its glowing waters, beyond which the megalopolis, appearing far and deep as in the bottom of a colossal chasm, radiated with the force of a billion lights up into the night.

In a sudden — and it felt as though wind rushing through a tunnel, without transition or accommodation — they were again amid the noises of clinking glass, again inhaling the fumes of cigar, scrambling among a bedlam of naked legs in another red space lit by many candles in sconces glowing upon furry green tables and pillowed thrones. It formed a wide ring round a pit, and the two halves of the ring were divided by a wall on each flank. On this side Neipas saw again the Minister, sitting at a table with Johnny Lobbyist, who was already rising. But Neipas wouldn't stay by them. The Supervisor directed him and Cesar to fetch drinks at the corner bar, and then sent them over to one of the tables, instructing them to serve the beverages as requested.

Neipas dove deeper into the sense of surreality and dream when he saw, sitting at the table he waitered, the famous mask of Reckuz, the great tech magnate, that generation's most powerful entrepreneur — the creator and owner of Maskbook. It was as though he had materialized out of billboard paper, stepped out of the many flashing glasses which reflected his semblance, into reality. But this reality had a thick sense of fiction for Neipas.

The space was a veritable gathering of elites and galactic personas, rulers and masters over civilizations, and the sense of unearthliness among them was palatable in every breath.

Eagles were animatedly crossing from one side of the gallery ring to the other through immense revolving doors. Neipas saw Johnny the Lobbyist on the other side now, speaking to a portentous Eagle face, rotund, mighty in his carriage. The Eagle smoked a very long pipe and acknowledged the Minister on the other side of the pit with a raised hand. From his finger sparkled a blueish glint, as from a sapphire gem. His eyes wavered lecherously, leering at the naked legs passing by, whose masks served him drinks with straw and gave him little kisses when requested. Neipas soon learned who the Eagle was — This was Baron Noxxe the petroleum tycoon, chief executive of NoxxeSocony, possessor of the Iblis refinery and swathes of oil-steeped land.

"That's NoxxeSocony's chief?" asked Neipas, to Cesar who had told him.

"Yes, and that right there, you see?" mumbled the poet, nodding discreetly in the direction of the Head Gardener. "There's Kasim's boss. He's a horrible fellow. He's got dealings with Penaguiar, did you know?"

"Does he?"

"Yes. Kasim told me so and Marlene told me so. He's a sadist, Kasim lives in fear of him."

Neipas threw a quick worried glance at him.

"He likes to beat people, I mean," said Cesar.

Neipas gazed with dread through the smoky twilight and across the pit to the formidable personage, with his portentous carriage, his magnificent bearing, and his expressionless Eagle semblance as he stomped his cane slowly, but emphatically, against the floor over and again; as he waited for the event to begin with contained impatience.

The orchestra was also here, their music played everywhere. Swans and peacocks lit cigars. Bankers stood above everybody and shouted numbers, "239! 11! 89! 40! 23! 67!" — Here, too, the tables were wide and furnished with cornucopias from which money streamed like water out of a faucet. Cards flew from side to side. Banknotes traded hands and even as one handed out money he still didn't have any less as his pile only kept growing, for which reason there was much laughter in the Eagles' beaks. But now there was some momentary confusion in the midst of it, as there was so much money in a particular table that it spilled to the floor and over the feet of one of the oxen, the one they called Lou the waiter. There arose a big uproar because of this. Drrawetz came at once and met the Eagles' outrage with many smiles — and Neipas thought he might indeed be dreaming, because the steward's face switched to a picture of pure wrath as soon as he turned to poor Lou, in an instant so quick, he thought it couldn't be possible. It was a vision of horror and hellish distortions ("is that his mask or his face?"); it was quick drunken air flooding the brain and heart. Drrawetz grabbed the waiter by the arm as the Eagles demanded an explanation for why Lou had touched their money — a promise of violence hovered about. In the mess of it all, Neipas took opportunity to turn to Cesar:

"Where the hell are we?"

"This is the Hall of Games... Part of it is in the House of Finance, but it goes through many of the Houses... I don't know exactly where we are."

Neipas grimaced in shock and awe.

"Mary! Where's all this money coming from?"

"It's other people's money." — the poet almost whispered it.

"What?" the uproar grew as the money kept flowing and spreading across the floor, and the peacocks scrambled mad to catch it all.

"All the people's money."

A bell tolled heavily from below, once, twice, three times — and orders to hush were issued from every wall. All leaned over the pit — and only now did Neipas, approaching, see that there was a sort of arena at the bottom of it. This arena had two opposite gates; and the rest of the encirclement was made of glass. Behind the glass were many pigeons, sitting in a kind of sunken theater auditorium and staring up in expectation. It didn't look like the pigeons could see them up there in the galleries. Waiters served food and drink among the rows — and Neipas saw, making the circuit round, Magpie. Her mask of heifer glimmered impassively with the adverts shone upon the pigeon spectators.

A Banker slithered through the tables, hissing: "It's almost starting! Make your last investments now!"

At last, the gates of the arena were opened. The first contestant emerged — out came the bullhead, face propped forward on the culmination of a straining, muscular neck. Its nostrils were open wide, fuming; its eyes narrowed in concentration under a furrowed brow, tensed with accumulated fury. From the other gate stepped its adversary — the stallionhead, soldier and athlete, donning an Olympian suit of wings and noble poise.

The competitors faced each other. Columbia's hymn was played, to which the two fighters and the spectators in the glass pane below stood in formation to sing.

Then — silence. The stallion lifted high a thick cloth. It glimmered a myriad flashes of gold, and rushed away in pulses the darkness round his feet.

The fight began with the toll of the bell hanging above the arena. At once the bullhead charged toward the winged stallion, lifting dust high; but suddenly it stopped and emitted a painful wail, dropping heavily to its knee and hand, casting its wide nostrils of impotent wrath to the distant ceiling, whence the Eagles watched. A chain clasped to its ankle, Neipas realized. He noticed, also, the sunken mark of a brand on its bulging neck. The stallion hit its head with a punch, forcing it deeper down. The bullhead of lustrous dark hide and silver horns, of proud and ancient race, lay prostrated, castrated and helpless under the raining decadence of laughter from gilded beaks, and the glare of transfixed pigeons beyond the glass, and the mocking neigh of the stallion, who stomped his hoofs.

The stallion taunted the bull-ox by flaunting the shiny cloth, provoked him with his agility and freedom of movement. From time to time he would leap forward and slap the bullhead, which would throw it into such a frenzy of powerless rage, shaking horns, furious and exasperated bellows, that the Eagles would erupt in delirious guffawing; and the audience of pigeons tensed in expectation. So it went — the bull-ox thrusting up against the limits of his reach, crying with pain as the chain strapped him strong; and the stallion jumping nimbly about, striking with slaps when he had the chance. But these were meant as taunts — the first definite blow came only when the bull-ox was tired.

First the stallion removed a feather from under his wing — it slid out easily, as though from a sheath — and the feather looked abnormally sturdy, with a rigid shaft. Carefully he approached the ox, who panted with face downcast, nostrils blowing against the dirt. The stallion hid his arm under the dazzling mantle — the feather, borne like a knife, held in his hand. The noise dissipated; silence, expectation mounted in the galleries and the auditorium beneath. The Eagles leaned farther over the rails. The pigeons had come to smear the wax of their faces against the glass, and even some of the cattle among them stopped; only Magpie ignored the spectacle, and kept walking her circuit as if nothing out of the ordinary were happening.

Swiftly the stallion's hidden hand rose, plunged and struck the bullhead, who grunted and bawled in an explosion of sudden agony. Its jaw was hurled to the dust and a jet of blood spit from its mouth and spilled outward, muddying the earth crimson. The Eagles yelled hysterically in a long and continuous guffaw; the audience of pigeons burst into cheering and excited jumping, clapping, arms thrown up. Some of the cattle in the upper galleries and in the lower auditorium, carried away by the general emotions, did the same behind the Eagles and among the Pigeons; while the rest watched in horror and bewilderment. Neipas looked at Cesar in a confused state of unease, and he looked at him sadly, averting his stare from the arena. They were too far to see the trembling in Magpie's lip; who, however, continued to walk her circuit and serving drinks, looking downward.

The fight would continue for a long time...

33 - Pulsing Walls

Repeated blasts hit and spread out into the bright racquetball court. The sound made it tremble whole. The court was immense — its earthen walls stood an immeasurable distance away from each other and reared colossally up into the far ceiling. In the middle of it was Reckuz, the great young entrepreneur, Writer of the Maskbook, looking to Neipas' eye like a miniature in the vastness of empty space. He ran to and fro, clad in sportswear, with very short white shorts and very high white socks. Attached to his mask was a cube covering his whole head, and in his hand he held a geometric shape — with a thin tall cylinder handle, which he clutched, and an oval attached to the top of it — that resembled a racket. His arm had some sort of wiring coiled up around it. Reckuz swung it back and forth.

Barely a moment after he plunged his arm wide, that explosive sound boomed into the emptiness; as of a ball hitting the wall, with the force of a cannon. Then he held up in a stance of preparation as the ball-hit sounded again (somehow not nearly as loud now), after which he ran to swing his arm once more.

There was no ball, however. It existed entirely in Reckuz's eyes, fed to them through the cube on his head. Its sounds blasted out of speakers, resounding into the court like explosions. There was a kind of godly effect to it. The sight of the entrepreneur's arm swinging into the void, followed by a boom so tremendous as to rattle the chest, had the appearance of cheap fiction, too: the cubic court being like the inside of a huge television, wherein a skinny wizard summoned the divine forces of an electric air.

Reckuz's opponent also was invisible — a body of pixels running and swinging its racket against the pixel ball in Reckuz's mind-representation of the court.

The lower corner of the court was partitioned with transparent glass, inside which there was an office with a big oblong table. Around it sat a group of Eagles, leaning over their computers. They drank out of red plastic cups and donned lax clothing, with ties loose over t-shirts, beanies upon their feathered heads, bandannas around their beanies, and green cigars jutting out of their beaks. Cattleheads stood at the corner with trays of drink and food.

In the very back of the court, Neipas stood holding a small tray upon which rested three cups and three jars. One of the cups was tall and thin, the other short and wide, and the last one of medium height and width. The glass jars contained water, lemon juice, and soda. Neipas held them in perfect balance and stillness, observing quietly Reckuz's wide movements upon the giant court. From time to time he would pause his game and beckon Neipas to approach. Neipas would, serving him the beverage of his choice — which Reckuz would drink, showing his appreciation by nodding his head breathlessly.

Then Neipas would recede to the back again, where he held still in a line with two other oxen. The one to his right held an empty plate on a tray, and the one to his left held a towel, also on a tray. Later the waiter to his right explained to Neipas that Reckuz needed to see an empty plate so he could remember he was on a diet and encourage himself to keep going.

In the time between Reckuz's pauses Neipas simply stood, waiting. He had come directly from the Hall of Games into Reckuz's private Estate in the 3rd level of the Eagle Wing and hadn't been given a moment to rest yet. His mind wandered off at times, and though there was something in his body now that didn't let him relapse into sleep — it was, perhaps, the uneasy feeling which the arena spectacle had left him with — he became enveloped in a sort of sleepy trance. Random thoughts floated inside an empty head. Normally, in such a state, one's worst instincts are given space to arise within the soul, and the vague feeling of loathing he bore gradually took shape in the remembrance of Eva.

A failed photographer. That's what he was, she said. With a single mumble she had summarized the entirety of his person; Neipas, sensible, couldn't help but feel truth in the venom of her words. In that moment their profound differences, profoundly contained, burst out in hushes; it felt like a sort of culmination. It had been months of papering over their incompatibilities; months of becoming at once dependent on and alienated from one another; of pulling apart even as they came together. They had never argued much, generally preferring to avoid confrontation.

But that last fight felt like turning some indelible bend, now unturnable — it was all darkness behind them as they fell back to silence. Somewhere in himself, Neipas knew the fault wasn't entirely hers. It was, perhaps, mostly his. In a petty lash of anger, he had pointed out to Eva some apparently essential flaw in her body (almost in a whisper) knowing how much it would hurt her. And it did, profoundly — because Eva had been raised to bind her self-worth with her physical appearance. He could sense her very breast contract in shame, in nervous anxiety, and in rage.

Had he said it first, or was it her; who had said the first word? Neipas couldn't remember anymore who had, or why he spoke what he did. He didn't linger on it; he felt too spiteful to admit any blame.

(Something of what the Eagles had said ruminated in the recesses of his spirit. But he was powerless and tired — and fearful of this place. All he wanted was to get out of there.

The boom vibrated with reverberations in his head. As the night deepened further outside, its sound deepened too, and took the form of strange, fleshy throbbing; as though something were answering Reckuz's swings from beyond the ample walls. He had heard it in the Hall of Games too, down by the arena — a profound, carnal pulse.)

Neipas was jittery, sometimes the nerve behind his eye flinched uncontrollably. He winked and waved his head round, but only a little, being so adept at wearing his mask by now that he looked no more bothered than a cow did among a hundred flies. Orenda once joked that cud-chewing cows chilled too hard for anything to trouble them. Or something like that. 'It's a good point,' muttered Neipas (sleep filtered up into his consciousness like a slow powder streaming in sunlight).

The powder was suddenly dispersed — Neipas widened his eyes with a jolt, his heart leapt into his brain as he felt a sudden movement in front of him. The two oxen on either side of him gave way as Reckuz charged toward Neipas with his racket held back like a compressed coil; it sprung madly and hit Neipas in the face.

Reckuz himself was startled by the unexpected contact — something had put itself between him and the ball. He yelled in despair, "What happened! What happened!" At once the Eagles and cattle inside the glass partition came out running and gathered around Reckuz to make sure he was ok. Meanwhile Neipas groaned on the floor a few feet away, by the back wall. He had moved in time to avoid the full impact of the blow, and had stumbled skillfully away so that the jars would not break anywhere close to the entrepreneur. Alas, he lay amid broken glass and a mixture of water, soda and lemon juice; the ox with the towel approached hesitantly, evidently wondering whether he should use it to clean up the mess. He was quickly rescued by a janitor and a Supervisor who ran to the spot, and in a moment more janitors joined in and cleaned up things in a haste. The ox with the towel, still hesitant and sleepy in the path between Neipas and the crowd, resigned to helping Neipas get up. Neipas himself felt very tired and tempted to simply lay back down and doze on the spot.

It took a little bit for the disarray to subside, and Reckuz to remove the box from his head and realize what was going on. For a while still he checked himself to make sure nothing was missing. And then, as if following an impulse, he approached Neipas with unusually large steps. Neipas saw his bald head and famous robotic, baby-like Eagle face become larger until it nearly filled all his sight. Words rolled out of his mouth very rotund, very fat. His beak was tightened into a pout of oblong shape; resembling, in this way, more a cartoon blue canary than a white Eagle.

"Oh! I'm so sorry! Oh! I'm so sorry!"

It was bizarre — it didn't sound like an apology so much as a recording playing. Neipas imagined there was simply a computer, or another box, behind that Eagle mask. Of course, Neipas didn't let himself be out-apologized; he professed infinite regret to the great young entrepreneur, saying that he himself was to blame, he should have been paying attention, he should have stepped out of the way. It wasn't Reckuz's fault, he assured — Reckuz was just exercising his freedom and going about his business.

But those words, too, came automatically. Behind the contrite eyes of the ox, Neipas' pigeon stare was red and glassy.

34 - Preparations for the Last Night of the Summit

Even though Neipas was too numb to care about anything at that point, still there was a tinge of fear polluting those inner spaces beyond thought and even feeling at the sense of Drrawetz's approach. He couldn't rationalize it — he was too tired to produce thoughts — but behind the lassitude of muscle and mind he knew Drrawetz would blame him for what had happened with Reckuz and fire him for it.

Thus it was like the intervention of divine goodwill when the winking Supervisor, pulling him aside, told him not to worry about anything. The incident would be kept from Drrawetz's knowledge — after all, Mr. Reckuz didn't seem to mind. "I'd already won anyway," Reckuz said out of his baby cheeks, laughing with his oblong pout and a wide open stare (there was something obscure about the entrepreneur's friendliness that frightened Neipas). Beholding the Supervisor's nods and smile of understanding, Neipas felt his heart warm, and he thanked him sincerely. It's ok, said the Supervisor, go on — Neipas was free to take a long break, get some sleep.

Escorted by a duet of Bulls along with a few other cattleheads, he climbed down the labyrinthine stairways and crossed into the Pigeon Wing through the kitchens again. He still entered his dormitory, placed the ox mask in his closet of possessions and dawdled inside the *I* for a bit; but then, instead of climbing to his shelf, he thought he'd have some breakfast and went into the Food Hall. There was no one there yet. He grabbed a loaf of bread from last night's basket and went out into the Gardens. Outside, there was a breeze blowing; the heavens near were charged with a deep blue that was progressively brightening — like a giant person awakening, yawning immensely in the sweet languor of dawn. This breeze ruffled the canopies, infusing the air with the scents of trees, which were gently roused awake; willows teetered, bent, as if preparing to stretch their rugged torsos. Their fragrance widened Neipas' senses — He thought things strange, for he assumed Anubel's outer glass never let in any wind.

Impelled by the whisper of the sky, Neipas walked down the sleeping booths. He found the old trail to the gazebo and climbed the slope under the breathing pines. But just as he reached the bottom of the stairs he saw there was someone there already. It was the Gardener's Assistant, the Pantrykeeper, Cesar's lover; Kasim.

Under the little gazebo he knelt, facing the rising sun in the east. Kasim's eyes were closed, and he whispered inaudibly. Some form of ritual was being performed; he took his hands to his eyelids and moving lips and passed his fingers down across his face. It was a solemn vision; he seemed to be whispering into the innermost corners of his own being. He arched his back until his forehead touched the ground — his lips moving silently all the while. The sun of morning, the sun of tender gold, peeked out of the mountain summits and stretched softly its ray of light onto the pilgrim's cheek, as if in a caress. Prostrate, the man kept whispering, lit in glow by the newborn star.

The quietude and solemnity of the scene touched Neipas' heart, softening it. For a while he observed the man in the morning radiance, absorbed by the force of some mystic, inscrutable pull; there was something alien and true in that vision.

As though by instinct, then, at the tug of a nervous stimulus — a desire to rescue the beauty of that moment from the washing tides of time — Neipas reached for his *I*, resting in his pocket, and framed the gazebo and the man within its sights. A click: and a copy of the tender sunshine and the strange worship was drawn into its glass, to be encapsulated forever outside of time.

The hour sounded with tolls of bell announcing the last day of the Summit. There remained one more day and one more night before it ended.

He awoke with a sore jaw and a dull head; as Neipas came to consciousness he perceived the low grunt muttered out of his mouth. With effort, and at great length, he arose from bed. The dorm-bell's incessant ringing worked him into a sort of sluggish irritation, with his nerves palpitating at the frantic speed of the noise under the lassitude of his tired body. He tried to fix his face before the long bathroom mirrors, where pigeons and oxen were engaged in brushing their teeth over the trough. His cheek swelled where the racket had struck. A bit later, a Supervisor came with a new bovine face for him to wear, for the old one was ruined.

Neipas' pigeon cheek trembled as he covered it with fur and clay. At breakfast Osir, seeing him sloppy, offered him a piece of his alchemy — but Neipas refused grudgingly.

The wind had gone. In its stead the air was moved by the tug and push of the Market's many voices. Such noises assailed the solemn procession of horns walking up the Garden's central stairway, in a show of numbers so dramatic that many of those on the flanks of the stair would turn their heads as they bought and sold, as the workers passed along. Their day would be spent setting up for the Summit's gala, its peak event, in the Ballroom. The orderly herd marched up toward the Auditorium. Neipas, in their midst, maintained the straight posture he was wont to maintain, and as his gaze was fixed upward he saw the profile of the Great Facade growing and rising over the top of the stairway. They reached the 6th Terrace; and the Facade assumed its complete form. With the Stage and the framing Proscenium at the base, and its balconies of receding width, the Great Facade resembled a strange, hatted titan head with an open mouth and myriad gazes.

It bore airs of ancient fortification and modern luxury hotel. The Great Facade had many windows of many different shapes — rectangles, circles, slits — and one had the immediate impression of eyes staring out from behind their curtains. The windows' shapes were repeated and the order mirrored and replicated, presenting a pleasant and refined design. At even intervals there were niches, wherein would stand statues of great Men carved out of bronze, marble, ivory, and gold. Their poses were identical. Head high and noble chest puffed, one boot placed forth. In the outstretched hand some sort of staff — a torch, or crook, or crosier, or scepter, or sword, or firearm, or, sometimes, a chisel, stylus, quill, or pen; and in the other hand, retreated, a pearl, looking as though it had been retrieved from the interior of the recess which, at the top above the statue's head, was shaped like a shell. At their feet were inscribed names, and sometimes dates. Linking windows and statues were salient floral rows, in the midst of which protruded the faces of animals — by the feet of the Men were often animals, too, chiefly the eagle, lion, bull, and serpent. The towering structure culminated in the Ballroom dome and the crystal Pearl shining atop. It had three levels of courtyard, which were the three upper terraces of the Pigeon Wing. Though they were accessible to no one but the Eagles and their security apparatus, they would hardly be spotted there. Instead, it was rumored that they would look out of those windows to spy upon the swarms of pigeon and cattle with those ample eyes that could see very far.

The herd advanced through the Auditorium and over the steps above the orchestra pit. Here Neipas, taken with curiosity, broke poise and turned his head to look down the chasm. It ran down concrete walls to great height — and then it was lost in darkness. He still could not see the band; the pit looked without bottom. And yet, humming melodies emanated from its depths, wafting up rancid, with a strange thickness of pestilence...

Such sounds accompanied Neipas as he walked among the workers. The melodies rattled his nose... Beyond the Auditorium, beyond the Stage they went, marching through curtain after curtain after curtain under the Proscenium's descending rings. They left the noises of the terraces behind them. With each succeeding curtain the Market's din seemed to leap a great distance, until it sounded like a great clamor issued from a far-off land. And with the diminishing of those noises grew the melody of the orchestra, and the ruffling of the cloth sounded like chimes as they brushed past the veils. Even the quality of the air seemed to change; the sound of their own steps distanced themselves from the ears... Strange contraptions appeared in their flanks — and attires, masks, other props. Ropes hung shadowy, humanoid shapes emerged faintly amid languorous winks of machinery. It extended all alongside the vastness of the curtains which seemed to lengthen to infinite darknesses, across unseen heights and distances... The melody buzzed between each curtain... something inside him snapped lightly, and he experienced the uncanny sense that the rings were themselves scanners feeling beyond his masks, like eyes piercing into the soul...

The Proscenium descended in a slope along its many rings. Its deepest ring was shaped like a lion's maw and framed a large gate (a carved relief protruded from the gate's surface, depicting two men, each laid atop a cloud, whose arms were outstretched toward one another. Their fingers touched). A bulky army of Bulls stood at either side, motionless, erect, with machine guns at the ready. In their stillness they looked as rigid as the statues of the Facade.

The shortest among them — their leader, it looked like — stepped forward. Drrawetz, who led the herd, shot up his chest and in a theatrical whirl his hand was taken to his forehead in salute.

"Greetings, commander!" he clamored emotionally. The thick layering of his mask could not conceal the admiration in his contained smile, the subservient tremble at the corner of his lip. Drrawetz seemed elated to be before all those guards and so close to their guns.

The commander said nothing. Turning round, he motioned to the bulls closest to the gate. It was opened slowly, with a portentous screech of hinges and the roar of heavy brass echoing greatly. The arches sparkled gold all around them.

Drrawetz nodded gravely to the trailing herd. He lifted his head high, dilated his nostrils wide, and threw back his shoulders; flourishing his peacock semblance, and the jabot in his collar, he walked with bobbing head and the stride of a military official, kicking up the tip of his boots. With this the chief steward conveyed the weight of the moment, meant to impose upon the herd a corresponding weight of discipline. Orderly, with steps matching the exactitude of machines, the herd marched. They entered.

It was at first a lobby matted with a fresh green color, embroidered with flowery patterns of gold on the rugs and the walls. Sumptuous sofas reclined in the center, encircling shiny mahogany tables, with a great tube of glass in the back for the elevator, vintage-looking with its worked golden frame (a little boy, wearing the mask of a peacock, stood next to it — he seemed to be the operator) and a counter, also of gold, encrusted with warm lights (behind it, three swans in suits of velvet). The herd didn't linger. Drrawetz took them behind the counter, where they followed the corridor into a deep side-elevator. They rose, keeping formation. Finally they exited out the other side, up a set of stairs and out through a hatch.

They were in the Ballroom. It opened up immense, majestic, unbelievable in its great opulence. Again Neipas had the uncanny feeling of being inside a photograph. Its immense chandeliers seemed to have materialized out of digital frames, the glazed carpets unfurled and enlarged out of an *I*, along with its grand tapestries, the giant windows, the glorious statue of the Golden Dove.

But the colossal activity already underway quickly dissipated that illusion. Rows of oxen and heifers knelt prostrate upon the grounds, locked together by long yokes. Groups of ten or more scrubbed the carpet fur in coordinated movements, in an advancing dance presided by many overseers. Tables were carefully placed in the areas already cleaned. Florists were at work over the tables already set, decorators flourished the curtains, polishers brushed and waxed the statues, the mirrors and the windows were cleaned by entire multitudes of specialists, and the set designer, Drrawetz, leaped at once to oversee the operations with a flowery voice of iron.

"Dears! Lot of work ahead! Stay sharp!"

He proceeded to hop about in all directions, the crest feather growing from the crown of his head dangling back and forth. Another, very tall peacock with a long train approached the waiters, calling himself "the master of ceremonies". He guided the herd through a routine — for the event would be highly choreographed, and by the middle of the afternoon Neipas would know all the paces for the gala, who he would be serving, all the proper procedures, all the correct ways of moving. It was daunting following the frenetic steps and detailed instructions of the choreographer, made even more so by Drrawetz's sudden creeping in, looking straight at the herd's progress with a fixed, anxious stare. He was evidently very nervous. Drrawetz insisted in managing every little bit of action, everything had to be registered under his eye. His conduct was so scattered that contradictory orders were issued and workers were berated with yells for following them, so that it created a stressful mood of trembling nerves, quick breaths, erratic motions. The cattle stared the millimetric area to which they applied their herculean efforts with anger, and they bore upon their backs the demanding heaviness of the lordly air, moving frenetically toward a goal whose point they forgot, their eyes growing red and teary with a frustration culminating from what seemed endless sleepless nights.

The monumental frescoes gazed at them from the recess of the great dome, motionless and divine in their heaven, and watched their domain transform. And through the chaos, the kingly venue was made ready.

Toward the end of the afternoon, Neipas walked to the towering windows looming over the Eagle Gardens' terraces. His aspect stood in contrast to the golden aspect of the glass; he looked lone and discreet amid the agitated motions still underway behind him. But the frenzy was unwinding slowly, all preparations done; a general lassitude of fatigue befell, spreading through the gathering silence. It was an hour of quietude, in solemn hush after a noisy, toilsome day, and a queer feeling of accomplishment seemed to pervade the deep air. For the first time, Neipas had the space to really observe that side of the Anubel; so he contemplated carefully. He walked to one of the open windows so as to see better.

It was a vertiginous feeling; the vast gardens spread widely underneath him, in great stacks of carved vegetation enmeshed with gold and silver, brought up to these tremendous heights by the sheer force of tremendous wealth. From his feet cascaded three monumental, sumptuous, glimmering terraces. The upper Gardens were laid at the base of palaces, whose roofs gathered in ornate clusters of myriad styles beneath the Ballroom. He could spot their portly gates and luxurious balconies, ample and airy, fitted with quaint vases and strewn with scented flowers. They opened regally over the lower terraces. The terrace in the middle was a confusion of bushes sculpted to human form, magnificently lavish fountains, and a variety of wide spaces — in its immensity lay a golf court, helipads, outdoor lots with shiny automobiles, and other marvels. The bottom terrace was a vast profusion of hedges, in the midst of which tucked many intimate delights, little walkways under pergolas, lakes with comfortable lounging chairs at their banks, pleasant orchards. Just beneath the Ballroom, the river flowed and winded tranquil, glamorously sparkling down the gardens.

Beyond and monstrously under this splendor lay the megalopolis, the great Axiac. Neipas had an ample view of its entire west-facing coast, from the Southern Shores all the way to the Diamond Hills in the north. His stare had pivoted in that direction, taking in the suburbs and their immaculate aspect. Lording over it all were those hills at the northernmost edge, with the Crystal Palace, residence of Columbia's leaders, at their base. The hills concealed mansions in the clean bush, and their masters hidden within their white walls, within the tall panes through which they observed. Beyond the hills, Neipas saw a great desert; it was populated entirely by expansive army bases, industrial-military sprawls, entire cities of weaponry.

And framing the great expanse, the ocean; its waters hugged the curvy shore that sieged Axiac almost entirely. The urban landscape looked like an island of mountains and sea, all tucked in and comfortable in the enjoyment of its great wealth, all its complexities flattened and irrelevant in the extreme heights whence Neipas contemplated it. He was so high up that he could faintly discern the round aspect of the globe; he felt his head reared the stratosphere and it was as though the whole wide Earth rolled before his tall eyes, as though his own eyes were set on the face of a colossal deity. For a few moments he held in his eye all of Axiac, all the world. Neipas felt its immense reach expand his own chest. There was a sense of accomplishment in the general slack of fatigue; a proud feeling that the end of that toil was very near.

Within himself he sensed a strange feeling of power, too; the colossal megalopolis, stretching under him, looked like a colony of ants, all within grasp of his hand.

Turning his gaze inadvertently, he saw that Magpie had stepped near him. She beheld the prospect with a hopeful air. Sensing his sight upon her, she looked at him.

"Evening," she said.

"Hello."

"Last night. You ready?"

"As ready as I can be, I guess. You?"

"Just waiting to get paid and leave, honestly."

Magpie beheld the horizon wash with eyes intent, gaze sparkling the sun's glare in the wish to meet it; reflecting a feeling of anxious longing, a depth of prolonged feeling.

"Hey, I — I think I saw you at that event last night? The fight?" asked Neipas.

Magpie nodded slowly.

"Yeah, I was there. It was a strange thing. They blindfolded me and everybody before taking us there."

"Blindfolded? Really?"

"Yeah... Dunno why. They're crazy. It was right after I left you in that gazebo, actually." Magpie shrugged. "There was like this flush of light in my eyes, and then total black. And this intense smell of rosemary. They made us walk, walk, walk. Took off my blindfold and I was there."

"Rosemary..." Neipas mumbled in ignorance, vaguely recognizing the word; but not knowing exactly what it was.

"It's a plant. Aromatic," Magpie said knowingly.

Neipas nodded in the silence, smiling, tired. He sighed.

Magpie asked, "So what are you going to do after this? Are you gonna keep working for Eden?"

"I dunno...Maybe. I haven't decided yet," said Neipas. "Get some sleep first. And you?"

"Nah... I'm out. I'm going... Somewhere far from here. Just waiting to get my money and get out. Been saving for it."

They kept silence between one another, and in the solitude of their own selves they watched the vastness together. A wide pathway ran through the middle of the bottom terrace, in between the two mazes of hedges. The westward stream ran in it serenely, merging with the Infinity Pool at the very brink of the tower. Magpie stared intensely upon the edgeless pool, and the ocean which seemed to spill from it; the ocean seemed an extension of it, as though the tower birthed the waters, laid flat upon their immensity; shining vaguely, yonder, with the blinking lights of Golden WestBeach's pier fairs. In the inner end of the bottom terrace's pathway, tucked into the tower and opposite the Infinity Pool, white steam lifted out of the open gates of the so-called Temple, which yawned enormously before the great mazes. Magpie was very still; only her fingers tapped the railing subtly, and her foot the floor. She saw the sprawl expectant, as if on the cusp of something she had been waiting for a long time.

The wind lashed again, stronger now, blown from the west, bringing with it the cold scent of those altitudes.

Magpie spotted it first, in the horizon. After staring at it for a minute she pointed yonder in its direction:

"What's that?"

But by then Neipas had seen it, too. A great, mountainous mass of dark clouds rose from the southwest and mounted sideways in a great swath toward the sun. It was still far, very far; but it was clearly broadening out of the limits of the Earth inexorably, ominously.

"I dunno..." Neipas mumbled uncertainly.

A crew came to close the windows, and just at that moment their eartags shook, summoning them to the lockers beneath, wherein they had showers for the workers and special outfits for the gala. It shook frenetically even as their gazes remained locked in the brooding enigma expanding across the distant skyline, cordoning off the boundless vista with a titan churn of fumes.

Neipas stirred out of the reverie and stepped away suddenly.

"Well — should we go?"

Magpie nodded slowly, her eyes yet transfixed upon the wide prospect. Then she, too, with head downcast and thoughtful, went.

35 - The Waltz

Silence.

Not the faintest sound fluttered the atmosphere, which hung still and undisturbed in the tense chest of all workers.

Neipas stood firm by his assigned chair. His feet rooted into the richly layered carpet, and out its exuberant fur sprung his body, stiff in the manner of a lone tree atop a small island. Planted in that sea of pelt were many other islands and their lone trees clad in suit, expectant of the wind that would sweep them to motion.

They had all bloomed to at precisely the appointed time; at precisely the scheduled second all were in position, standing ready and motionlessly waiting by their tables, all of which spread adorned with a choice arrangement of sumptuous china shimmering under the thousand twinkles of light dangling from the four chandeliers. Painted forms surveyed the scene from the ceiling whence those chandeliers sprouted; birthing their florid chains the eagle, the bull, the lion, and the lamb; and the wheeling pantheon of mythic creatures and shapes besides looked on impassive, inscrutable, breathless over the wash of horns above the carpet, soundless over the fiery glow of the Golden Dove. The tables were positioned in concentric rings around the statue, which, indifferent to the deferential presence of the waiting waiters, kept its eyes closed and its back bowed... Through the towering glass windows afar (Neipas caught his glance sneaking a peek, and immediately corrected himself to face and look straight forward to the gate, as per instruction) the sky, choked, flushed, and about to lose color, pressed on close. It hovered in wait and bled. Silent.

A breath of distant melody would soon suggest itself into the senses.

The vast extent of the Eagle Gardens rested in a similar quiet of immobility. Even the mammoth cacophony of Axiac, far below, could not disturb it. Not the slightest peep survived the ascent to those heights; all sounds died along the climb. An immense group awaited on the deep of those gilded terraces: from the Infinity Pool to the Temple front, a large consort of dignitaries, exalted journalists, sports celebrities, celebrated actors, and streams of musicians and dancers in the flanks awaited with glares set on the fuming gates ahead of them. None spoke. The silence was complete but for an occasional, quaint breeze sifting in upward twirls about the ear.

A flick of the wrist set the play in motion. Soft undulations of harp string emanated from the orchestra then, as if rippling directly from the

Conductor's subtle gesture. The melody drew a long line of peacocks and pelicans out of the fumes of the Temple — their ceremonious steps accompanied by a gradual, soft, stately tapping of collective drum, their motions tinging with the occasional ring of triangles. They puffed incense from their thuribles; they wore intricately laced robes, priestly garments with capes so wing-like and so lengthy as to trail across the floor far away from their feet. A second set of drums heightened the volume and might of their percussion, rising as the bodies of the bulls first shaded the white fog. Great apparatuses grew from their laden shoulders, and as these became clearer to the view there sounded grave horns — and then, triumphant trumpets. Out of the profuse vapors and the powerful beat emerged litters — very tall litters, towering stacks of pillows and pillowed thrones, upon which were seated (beyond silk curtains) the misty, regal figures of opulent Eagles. Borne by poles and bull muscle, flanked by rows of swans wielding immense flabella (ruffling the smoke with which their whiteness blended), some of the majestic litters carried nothing but mounds of gold and jewel sparkling among a profusion of embroidery and textile, haughty and aloof as the music swelled victoriously, soaring in glorious crescendos as their treasures were conveyed up the great steps.

So the parade commenced, driven on by the mighty thumps of the orchestra. It was a massive fleet beating upward, upstream, counter to the flow of the westward river, marching alongside its courses and under the cascades sprinkling the shine of the golden hour. The sun faced directly the backs of the rising fanfare of Eagles, bulls, swans, owls, peacocks and peahens, steeds and mares, stags and deers, pelicans — a panoply of masks following solemnly the orchestra's grand row of trumpets, of drums, of cymbals, of chimes; the players were but mysterious hooded robes, from whose facial chasms protruded immense horns and long pipes blowing savagely, somber, war-like. The chorus wore the masks of all types of songbirds, trailing (in an uproar) cockerels whose red wattles vibrated raucously, whose cries boomed harmoniously into the highs and whose voices were tossed to the skies whose confines hung near. The cacophony hauled up the steps to the Summit deliberate and inexorable. Dancers swung and spun with shimmering mantles and threw confetti joyfully out of great baskets; there were jugglers and fire-spitters; the colorful entourage led piglets on leashes, with parrots singing passionately along atop journalistic shoulders. And from the sides watched every clan of wild animal: elephants scraped their ivory upon the tended greens and rabbits observed from their diminutive heights, every single one of them bound by some means. All, all coursed the terraces and mounted the royal stairways and elevators up toward the expectant, massive gate of the Ballroom, following the Conductor who, afore the march, walked backward across the myriad steps and waved his arms furiously.

Neipas' heart stilled suddenly, bracing itself, and though hardly a stir was to be detected among the workers, one could almost guess the stiffening of muscles preparing for a succession of coordinated movements. All could sense the tempest of sound beating up the ascending path to them: it intensified in the ear, and it was as though the gate swelled...

In the distance (scurrying up from one of the hatches) appeared a small figure, noiselessly breaching the silence with its little hurried movements. It was the Chief Steward, Monsieur Drrawetz, a tiny speck in the immensity of space — he halted, and presently lifted his hands to this neck, keeping them rigid, cupped, nearly touching one another. Then, in a sudden flurry rushing through his puny body, Drrawetz jerked himself upright and tip-toed, and clapped. The quietude shivered — and with a mighty rumbling the gates opened, blowing in an explosive symphonic gale of opulence, of exuberance, of splendor and dancing cloths, of towering litters, of cackling eagle beaks peering through curtains embroidered with pure gold. Much happened at once. The crimson sky deepened under the streaming horde, and the last gleam of sun faded through the gate. As the star cooled into the horizon deep, the golden statue of the Dove intensified in color, became, as it were, more golden; its arched form radiated gold, it emanated light with such intensity that cries of awe resounded through the sounds of the parade; and a beam of white coursed through it, through the dome's oculus and into the Pearl alighting and spilling over the distances, onto the gardens and the skies. Neipas placed the tip of his toe lightly behind him and took a swift step back, pulling the chair out elegantly; every single waiter did as he at the same precise moment — a collective shuffle of retreating chairs and bodies, of sounding bells in the intensity of unison motion, thrust up into the marching music. Its boom penetrated slowly the giant hall, immense.

The gilded crowd had, meanwhile, thinned. Horses, deer, owls and peacocks — masters of sports, screens, gates and the media — all the lower dignitaries of the capitalist machine remained in the lower terraces of the Eagle Garden, already seated. The Eagles, they descended shining from their mounting litters now, accompanied by the swan concubines while their armed bulls regrouped round the perimeter of the vast space. And the whole orchestra filed into a corner of the Ballroom completely steeped in darkness... On and on the whole long parade of musicians was absorbed into the black, dozens, hundreds of them marching in one by one until the very shadow seemed to pulse with the accumulated notes of their music. Only the

Conductor, whose back faced the ample Ballroom, remained visible. For the rest of the night he would be gesturing to that pool of shadow, from the arcane depths of which flowed melodies. There they also laid down the litters and the regalia; all of it disappeared.

The patrons' royal air seemed to herald a change in the very atmosphere as they came in; and the hearts in the breasts of all waiters swelled nervously before their advancing presence. The firm clay of Neipas' ox mask let transpire no astonishment; but he did rock a little inside with awe. Here were, in lavish and unabashed display, the hegemons of the age. Most of them Neipas had never seen or heard about. But he immediately perceived their power; and, in a sudden flash of lucidity, he understood the point of it all. Luxury, comfort, wealth — *power* — were the sense of it. Deranged, stupid as it all was — their mere words compelled multitudes, their commands were law, their whims priorities among the fates of existence. To be wealthy in those days (perhaps in all days) was to be a god upon the earth.

Neipas, maintaining his soft grip on the back of the chair, watched motionlessly as the lords unmounted and neared.

Presently he sharpened up, still without moving an inch. Here came Mr. Moloch, the Media Mogul, approaching the table, guided by a swan who, halting by Neipas' side, curtsied gracefully and made a sweeping, theatrical gesture toward the chair. Moloch was an old Eagle with very puffy cheeks half-burying a small yellow beak; the underskin of his eye sagged toward a flappy jaw, revealing a bright red sludge of flesh just beneath, full of little veins shredding the whiteness of its orb. The plume atop his head was uncannily sparse, dappled with irregular bald spots.

"Very good evening, Mr. Moloch," Neipas said in a very genteel manner. "It is an honor to stand before your illustrious presence, sir. My name is Neipas, and I will be your host for the evening. Would you like a beverage to start?" he concluded, articulating each word out his beak with a mechanical eloquence. The swan stood beside them at attention.

"Wine. Finest you got," uttered Moloch with a deep, rough gargling voice. He stared at the intricately woven tablecloth with a concentrated frown, and seemed a little out of breath; his eyes never met Neipas'. Neipas said, "Very well, sir. We possess an exquisite collection of wines. I shall — return presently," faltering a little because he couldn't recall whether he ought to have said 'shall' or 'will' in that line. He stepped up to the swan so as to be placed at her side with symmetrical exactitude, and once this maneuver was performed, they both bent their spines very low — making their heads parallel to their respective groins — and retired with a very dignified appearance about them.

Neipas and the Swan scurried away in different directions, the latter taking her place at the periphery of the table, melodiously swaying the flabellum, and the former dashing straight toward the cellar with a very stiff walk, holding his fists firm abreast his waist. From the tables dispersed now a great rumble of activity, with some waiters jetting coolly to the kitchen and others heading in the same direction as Neipas, so that a great number of them merged about the hatchways at the same time; and as soon as they stepped under the trapdoors all semblance of composure was promptly abandoned. They all began leaping down the stairs like mad, clawing into each others' faces to push ahead and bellowing ferocious caws in a desperate effort to obtain the wine bottles and return to the side of their guests in as efficient and expedient a manner as possible. Neipas himself was caught in the confusion and his immediate impetus was to thrust down the crowded slope with all the force in his body, his muscles bulging outward in a sudden great strain to hurry, coerced forward into a rage by the mess of bodies erupting on the steps. When he was a few steps out from the bottom he simply jumped the distance, regretting it very much mid-air (his face braced for the impact — he landed clumsily and, in the rush of things, pitched himself forward for a few meters, bumping against streams of running legs). Now in the crepuscular brick vault, Neipas dashed directly to the depths of the towering racks to find, by the far wall, the collection of Chateaux du Pouvoir bottles, which they were to collect if asked for the 'finest wine in the house'. Another waiter — Neipas couldn't see who — fought him for the bottle for a few seconds, when Neipas, in an instant of clarity, let go of the bottle and hastened to grab another one in the rack by him; upon which he took to his heels again, attempting to overcome the fellow who had just stolen his Chateaux by grabbing his jacket and throwing him on his back. Up the stairs there was again much disarray as the waiters felt no scruple about climbing on top of one another to be the first to return to the Ballroom (all this because of the sleepless stress of the past few days and the manic allure of huge sums in tips; Drrawetz had driven hard into their heads the point that every second late meant fortunes lost). Amassing in the room under the hatch, before the last set of steps, they checked their masks and made sure their grins were perfect and their suits immaculate — then the waiters pushed their horns out professionally, emerging with wine bottles perfectly balanced on the palms of their gloved hands.

Spreading out into the refined hubbub, they walked elegantly between many august characters. Through Neipas' eye passed mighty executives, investors, politicians, generals, monarchs, emirs and chieftains of the highest prominence. Powerful oligarchs from across the globe crowded the Ballroom, filling it with the air of their consequential words and the weight of their gilded breaths. There was the lady of exotic veils and bilious eyes Neipas had served in the crimson room: the leader of a cult from Persia, he would come to find, who sought to rule that nation under the patronage of Columbia's Eagles. Yonder he glimpsed Bezitos of the Silicon Jungle, king of the commercial threshold between the digital Webwork and palpable reality; Bezitos the hopeless romantic, or 'the slave driver' as he was otherwise known. He was the richest among the rich of those days — and so infamous for wearing out his workers, for being so villainous as to be almost cartoonish in his greed that Neipas averted his eyes with much fear. Close-by piped Reckuz the Maskbook writer, who sat next to the Head Gardener and near Larry the Data Tycoon and Sobs the Prophet of Tools, who, along with Reckuz and Bezitos, made up the core group of tech luminaries of the age. There were also arms dealers, pharmaceutical executives, real estate magnates, insurance and banking capitalists, leaders from all industries upon the Earth; and many others besides... He passed close to Baron Noxxe's table, blurry from the smoke of his long pipe (amidst the opulent stenches of which glinted his sapphire ring). Neipas was supposed to serve him that night, but he had been swapped by Magpie for some obscure reason; she was there now, next to the oil tycoon, and poured him his wine while he eyed her with an attentive, sidelong stare.

At Neipas' assigned table sat, besides Moloch and his two adult sons, the Minister of Nations and his family: composed of his twin, the Minister of Borders, and his brother's wife the Heiress, beneficiary of a large fortune from a sprawling media empire (second only to Moloch's own), as well as from a global sugar-processing giant, both of which her ancestors had founded (she was also, of course, a recipient of rents from numberless shares in countless comparable conglomerates). The Heiress was a silent, if commanding presence. Her tiara reflected the Dove's light dazzlingly, casting a potent halo from her head and somewhat softening her relentless frown; she sat stiffly and radically upright, observing the sacred rules of etiquette with all the sternness of royalty; the very shape of her beak and her pinched nostrils, which gave her the appearance of someone perpetually about to sneeze, were the very staple of aristocratic bearing. The exalted personage was there accompanied by her chaperone, who stood respectfully behind her chair. There was also her cousin the Minister of Energy — an infamously gaffe-prone official who wore a cowboy hat and boots, with sunglasses to conceal the glassy imbecility of his fixed stare. He frequently smoked a pipe which, no one but him and his personal servant knew, had only water in it.

Most of them at the table conversed animatedly — the Ministers' bluster mingled over the porcelains, and Moloch's sons occasionally gruffed a few sentences into the mix, to which everyone nodded approvingly. But whenever Moloch the father brought himself to raise an arm, everyone at the table fell silent. He did this usually when he approved of a particular remark one of his sons had made, proceeding to pat the crown of his feathery head; which invariably brought out the undisguised resentment of the other son, whose smiling mask suddenly caved into a frown of raised hackles. The Mogul and the Heiress spoke least, barely anything. The former communicated chiefly by means of grunting, and the latter by sniffling; for every word from their beaks was a pronouncement which bound up everyone with the force of law, and every slightly louder breath shushed them all. The Ministers were but vassals — lesser eagles, nearly peacocks — to these two, one creator of, and the other heir to dynasties. Their words had the weight of empires. For they had money — an infinitude of money — and their very bills uttered riches.

"Anyway I don't like mixin'," the Minister of Borders was saying, venturing a deferential glimpse at his wife (Neipas, who had but vague knowledge of his patron's power, slid to the side of Moloch. He poured the wine with much care, holding the base of the precious bottle with the tea towel).

"The filth cramming our borders... we must deal with it," continued the Minister. "Now with this climate change business, we must have a handle over resources. Gotta shut'em out. That's the angle."

(Neipas tilted the bottle's tip at just the proper angle so not a droplet of the wine hopped over, filling the tall glass to no more than a fifth of its height; this he did according to script and even felt proud of himself for how seamlessly he pulled it off).

"You're right, Petey. And now with the Persian menace, we might have additional crowds trying to ram down the wall. We must hold."

The Minister of Borders, having obtained his brother's approval, chanced a peek at his wife. The Heiress bowed her head, diplomatic and taciturn — and the Minister, encouraged, nodded with much energy.

From the shadow corner flowed sounds of piano and violin, glazing every mutter with a refined sparkle. Neipas bowed down deeper and with infinite deference he asked, "Would you like anything else for the moment, Mr. Moloch?", to which the Mogul simply replied with a dismissive wave of hand.

"Very well, sir," Neipas proceeded to say, very composed. "Appetizers shall be served shortly. If you should require anything, I am at your disposal. Please do not hesitate to summon me at any time." With this Neipas bowed still deeper; Moloch grumbled something then, and Neipas, unsure whether he meant to articulate something, arched his horns gently and with some hesitation inquired, "Pardon me, sir?" and the old Mogul simply enunciated more grunts, with additional firmness and waves of hand to shoo Neipas away — to which the waiter reacted immediately by saying "very well, sir," bowing submissively once more.

("Say, Richie, how's the stockpile of nuclear..." one of the Ministers was mouthing, but) Neipas stepped away as the Energy Minister commenced blabbering about something, and he made off to the kitchen at once.

The ruckus had swollen to feverish levels there. When he passed through the hatch leading to the kitchen, Neipas wondered how it was that the noise wasn't audible from the Ballroom; strangely, it wasn't audible at all until he passed the trapdoors, and the abrupt burst of sound was a shock that made him shudder whole. There was a lot of yelling and angry gesturing, folk running from counter to counter, scraps of lettuce flying about, flames jetting into the scorched ceiling. The most dramatic aspect of the scene was perhaps the uncanny difference of posture between the chef, who walked calmly by the cooking stations and approved everything with a knowing grin under his tall hat (he walked in weird inebriated circles), and Mr. Drrawetz, standing frantic at the fore of it all. He gesticulated with ire, had worked himself up to a tremendous pitch of agitation — his face must've been so hot the mask had melted off it completely, and was now but mush hanging in flaps from the jaw, like the densest and most unclean beard to have ever sprouted from a fellow's cheek; his face was bright red and the poor steward seemed to be fuming from his ears. Neipas saw his mouth move cavernously, as if it intended to swallow all the cooks and puke them back out, so as to discipline the impertinent fools proper ("impertinent fools" — yes, Neipas was sure he heard him say that. He neared him, and considered the steward's exposed face for a moment. He was as much pigeon as the rest of them, or — indeed — Neipas confirmed it with near certainty now, that the steward barely wore a mask then. All the feelings of exasperation, rage, anxiety, and outright panic that were apparent in him showed themselves unfiltered, pure in their expression, with no vain sense of self or fear of judgment to distort them — the pressing deadlines completely overwhelmed those instincts in Drrawetz's overcharged heart). Suddenly the eartag shook and the cowbell rang frenetically upon Neipas' neck — it was Mr. Moloch requiring more wine.

Neipas promptly stepped back up into the Ballroom and was at Moloch's flank in triplefast time. He performed the usual dance ("would you require anything else, sir?", grumble, "very well, Mr. Moloch Your Honor, please do not hesitate to let me know, I shall be at your disposal and appetizers shall be served soon", grumble and concluding bow) as he caught words flowing from the table:

"And how does the President feel about going in on Persia, Paulie?" one of Moloch's sons asked the Minister of Nations.

"Well he's reticent, unfortunately. Base doesn't support it, as you know. I think your assistance would —"

Neipas was darting — never losing the composure of his walk — toward the kitchen to fetch the appetizer dishes when someone beckoned to him from a table near, "Please! Please, waiter. Here, please."

"Yes, sir?" Neipas took a wide step to the verge of the table. He looked right at the gent, a mid-aged Eagle with a portentous chest and beak lifted quite high. Neipas' heart rustled when he noticed that Bezitos sat at his table.

"Young fellow," started the Eagle who had summoned him. His voice was uncannily frail, in a posh sort of manner, for an Eagle his size. "Please. Would you procure for me a fine bottle of your finest scotch?" he was already turning his head back to the table as he finished the sentence, leaving Neipas babbling the practiced track with the usual scripted lingo ("it is an honor, sir —") and he went to collect the scotch at a glide, just short of a sprint, for he was already nearly out of time — the appetizers were scheduled to be served in just a moment, and if they weren't all served at the same time as according to script, it would be a catastrophe — Drrawetz might be moved to fire him on the spot. So Neipas thrust through racked nerves, with every wiring fired up and trembling, straining under the thickening descent of deadline.

"Thankee, m'boy," squeaked the gent and he turned quickly to Bezitos, who leaned his pinkie haughtily against the corner of his beak.

"It's an honor, sir," said Neipas with a gasp and a bow, and his body was spinning out when he was once again stopped.

"Hey —" ...It was the Head Gardener, on the table next. "I notice an accent on you. Are you from the heartlands?"

Neipas stopped for a moment. Cesar, who had been serving the Gardener, retired in a rush, gesturing his horns to Neipas as if to tell him to hurry also.

"Yes, yes sir."

"Ah. I knew it. I'm from Doris. What's your name?" demanded the Gardener, once more.

"Neipas, sir."

The Gardener produced a banknote and placed it under Neipas' bent ear.

"You look familiar. Go on," said the Gardener authoritatively, immediately losing interest.

"Thank you, thank you so much, sir — " already his legs had brought him near the hatchway, distances away from that central cluster of tables by the Dove — He entered the kitchen.

Someone was shouting with a thunderous might of voice; it rang out against every wall of the space, this monumental, dreadful roar. Taken aback, Neipas looked around quickly in an attempt to ascertain where it was coming from. "Is every body here?! Is every body here?!" boomed the unworldly voice which was gradually dimming out the kitchen's lingering hubbub. Everyone shushed now; in the middle stood Mr. Drrawetz, with the chef wavering to and fro at his side, wearing a dull face. The steward looked absolutely beside himself, with every nerve bulging out of his skin, every muscle straining away in all directions, the wax and clay of his masks bemixed and seething, foaming with wrath; his fists hung quaking against his flanks, his whole body trembled, bulgy neck deformed by strenuous weights of frustration. Drrawetz opened his mouth to an unbelievable extent — it looked as big as his entire head — and left it like that for a second. A terrible sound emerged between his gaping teeth...(and it was only then that Neipas realized that the voice from before really was his).

"Is every body *here?!*" he thundered after a long scream. A thick chunk of clay was dangling from Mr. Drrawetz's mandible yet.

Mr. Drrawetz glimpsed at his watch, drew a vast gulp of air in through his nostrils, and calmly said: "Every body is here. Good. Listen up, dears. We have one minute to collect the appetizer dish! and two to serve it to our illustrious patrons in the Ballroom. Waiters!" he lifted his hand in his characteristic, ballet-like style, and gestured pompously toward a steel shelf full of small plates, "you may find the appetizers at my side here, courtesy of your cuisine colleagues. Pick them up! and do better than your very best, dears! Be graceful, be classy, be solemn, if you please. Decorum, waiters! Remember — this may be the most important moment of the evening. Upon the serving of the appetizer, our own Mayor! dears, shall emerge into the Ballroom," he hoisted up both hands, as if lifting a great weight, "and rise onto the pulpit! A string of most illustrious speakers will follow," Drrawetz swung forward dandily here, "culminating in, as you know, the President! of our great nation! darlings, who will grace us with his words during dinner," here he chuckled gravely, twirling his fingers about the steamy air, "Anyhow! Time is short! You know what to do. To work!" and he walked forth, triggering a great rush toward the shelf as waiters grabbed their respective plates with much haste. When Mr. Drrawetz was nearly by Neipas he made a swift gesture upward and over his head, and in a moment his peacock mask had flung back and pasted itself onto his face. In a moment his immaculately courteous smile once more flashed from his clay visage, and any trace of stress or lack of self-control had completely vanished.

They all seized their plates (a few paces before them the cooks scrambled — Janu's long earlobes dangled frantically, his nostrils panted furiously through smoke) and went back into the Ballroom to line up behind Drrawetz and before the concentric tables. The steward clapped high, exceedingly polite in the execution of the clap.

"Madames et monsieurs! The appetizers," he announced, bowing his head almost to the carpet. Immediately the cattle marched forth in very coordinated, light steps. Neipas neared his assigned sir, saying, "Mr. Moloch," and laid down the plate in front of him very delicately. The gesture was simultaneously replicated by each waiter in the room; all servings performed without flaw. Shortly after this, Drrawetz, as master of ceremonies, announced the Mayor of Axiac — who rose over the applause to the summit of a towering litter, which had been left by the open Gate; so that he faced the Eagles in the Ballroom, and loomed over the remaining guests in the lower terraces of the Eagle Garden, all of whom turned their ears up to listen:

"My dear colleagues," began Mayor Don, brushing his oiled hair with his fingers, with pomp, "and venerable guests. It is an honor to stand before you tonight. It is an honor to stand before you here, in this distinguished institution, mark of stability. It has been with us for as long as History can remember, in one shape or another. Regimes come and go, systems come and go — but this place always remains as the pinnacle and axis of order, it prevails above all the turmoil which may rock underneath it..."

His speech rolled smoothly, sweet and impassioned, into the attentive ears of the exalted audience; and meanwhile everyone nibbled. Among the choice appetizers were so-called hors d'oeuvre, which consisted of mollusks — oysters and the like, slimy carcasses still housed in their shells — which were meant to be slurped; making the air courteously filled with much saliva inhaled underneath the words and the music.

The Mayor descended to the roar of claps, the hall and the gardens swaying with infatuation over his eloquence. One after another, illustrious men with avian faces rose to the pulpit atop the pillowed mount, announced one by one by Drrawetz. Powerful Bankers went up, as well as Executives of every type. The remaining guests snacked on their foie gras and caviar mush, and sipped their lavish wines as they listened carefully, and with pleasure, to the voice of power replicated through different timbres — being, as it were, their own voice, reproduced before their ears as in a sonic mirror...

This short period of speeches marked a lull in the evening, through which Neipas kept replenishing Moloch's wine, running but once to the caves to reap another bottle. Later in the kitchen, the same fury of activity pulsed over the burning stoves. The dinners were just about finished; the cooks scrambled to get them atop plates and under cloches (steel domes) as quickly as possible, and meanwhile the waiters were being called upon to help, for everything seemed to be behind schedule and the mood was one of tense haste. Neipas ran to the side of Janu, who worked frantically across two stations, over a great profusion of flaming kitchenware; for he was cooking two separate dishes, servings of duck and turkey for the Minister of Nations, who had become a great fan of his food, and for his twin the Minister of Borders, who was now trying it for the first time.

"Just finishing up," the good cook panted over the fire. Neipas stood in wait, tapping his toes to the beat of Drrawetz's fanning roar, which grew dimmer as he observed the fat leaping in uncontrollable hisses from the frying pans. The gas flames blew so loud that it was as though the spirits of the turkey and the duck themselves, burning over them, were screaming.

"*Come on!*" but the pressing demands of the moment, manifested in Drrawetz's rage, stomped out their voices in an instant. Neipas came to as the steward yelled at his ear, and Janu began matting the birds with sauce as his assistant flung caviar around the edges of the refined porcelain. They all worked furiously and in silence, stressed, their heads boiling with mute intensity. Everywhere there was the sound of meat splashing and clanking china, running fervent under Drrawetz's yell of "quick! quick! quick!" It was indeed quick, and Neipas' face under the ox sweated wax by the time they were done. He had just enough time to fix his visage in the mirror and tuck in the melting wax before Drrawetz shoved him forward, shouting "Pick up your plates! Let's GO!" with a voice so close and so monumental that it seemed to blast wide Neipas' eartubes. The severity and might of the steward's howl still drilled across his brain when, in a state of utter confusion, he grabbed the duck plate and rushed out the trapdoor along with a multitude of scrambling bodies squeezing him on all sides, all amid shouts of "Decorum, dears!"

The lights were dimming as the enigmatic, mighty Minister of the Treasury came down from the pulpit (his spectacles flashed as he turned his head — like a flicker of short-circuit before the moody shade crept in again). By then a sort of enthusiasm had mounted about the tables as the wine, mixed with the supple refinement of the appetizers, worked its influence. Talk of profits and praise of the Market gods made everyone happy and giddy, the music coming from the corner in shadow exuding an ambiance of amenity and prestige. Meanwhile the waiters hurried on and spread orderly across a line of horns, stopping in flawless unison. On Neipas' forearm rested the plate covered in the cloche of stainless steel, and it held completely steady, though Neipas sensed acutely a vague trembling in his muscles. His legs, rigid, spasmed invisibly.

Drrawetz hopped in front of the waiters and announced, with open arms and very jolly: "Ladies and gents, exquisite patrons, quaint guests — the dinner!"

Prompted by this, the waiters sprung to their assigned tables at once. Neipas neared Moloch and leaned the plate onto the tablecloth with all due finesse, saying "Voila! Mister Moloch," and removing with a swift pull the plate's cover (the big mound of roasted duck appeared amidst scented fumes). Then, taking the bottle of wine, Neipas asked,

"Wine, Mr. Moloch?" to which the Mogul grumbled in confirmation. Neipas poured the Chateaux du Pouvoir into his glass.

From beneath the plate Neipas produced another plate of the same size, though a little deeper and more ornate. He placed the empty plate beside the first plate, the fat duck atop which was bustling out the edges. He proceeded, then, to remove a pair of latex gloves from the pocket of his jacket, and put them on over his regular white gloves. He dug the fingers of his left hand through the glaze, the grease, the meat and into the entrails, and gently grabbed a chunk. Finally, he put the flesh in his mouth, chewed it, and lingered a bit on its succulent texture; then he spit the gummy muck of it onto the palm of his right hand. With very surgical fingers, Neipas grabbed the chewed meat paste and placed it strategically upon the empty second plate.

Neipas repeated this operation until nothing but bones were left on the first plate. To finalize the procedure, he gathered the caviar with one scoop and delicately plopped it into the middle of the duck goo filling the second plate almost entirely. Moloch, who by this point was quite nearly finished with the second bottle of Pouvoir, burped loudly and demanded more. Neipas placed gently the filled plate before him and removed the china topped with bones and oil, as well as the bottle, and hid them swiftly behind his back. "I shall be right back, sir," Neipas said, and stepped out.

He fastwalked dizzily down the steps into the cellar after quickly dropping the plate and the bottle in the kitchen. The cavernous space, filled to its twilit depths with endless rows of shelves, which shot up to a ceiling covered in thick shadow, looked empty, and there sounded nothing but an ominous quiet in the vastness of its vaults. Neipas didn't slow his step, dashing straight to the far wall for another vessel of Chateaux. On the way, he thought he could discern vague shapes of bodies in the dusky vicinity. One or two or maybe three, he thought he saw, and they seemed to be lying upon the stone floor, motionless by the racks — he was sure he heard breathing, too. But Neipas did not stop for a second and it was swiftly that he collected the wine he had come to fetch, a wine whose grapes had been culled in the stepped mountain hills of distant regions, by local folk who wore bonnets round their heads in hot autumn days; who by the hundreds journeyed the terraced steeps in their toil, and for many days labored; and who pressed their joyless feet upon mounds of grapes inside great pods; hapless because, whereas the rite had once marked a period of festivities, now there was a fellow watching over their work; and they wouldn't eat any of the grapes they had reaped.

Neipas halted for a moment, struck by an obscure, uneasy sentiment. Under this strange feeling, drawing his senses momentarily into a sort of weakening void, he perceived again — or he could swear he did — he saw more lying shapes spread down about in the dark, and wondered. But his collar began to ring; he rushed out.

"Sir, I have obtained the wine," Neipas announced, bowing. His bell was ringing impatiently even as he said the words.

Moloch turned his wrinkled Eagle head very slowly to look at Neipas. It was the first time their eyes met. The waiter saw deep into the orbs of the Mogul — and he glimpsed, for only a moment, the contained rancor, the quelled sort of spite simmering in the watery depths of Moloch's coal pupil. It was uncanny, but Neipas could swear he saw the eyes laughing too — mocking. Had Neipas taken too long? The undisguised appearance of these eyes instilled in Neipas a sense of self-debasement that made him want to shy his stare away; but he kept firm.

Moloch relaxed — it was as if Neipas had imagined it, for it was indeed very quick — and directed his glance to his plate. Then he pointed to the glass, mumbled something which sounded like "pour" or "please", and Neipas obliged immediately.

"Would you like to have your dinner now, sir?" Neipas mumbled very secretly, because the table had meanwhile assumed a very solemn quietude; for the Heiress spoke.

Moloch guzzled his wine and nodded. He pointed to his glass once again, and Neipas poured him more.

The topic of conversation seemed to have shifted to the Oyate's Reserve and the natural beauty of its valleys. There were certain interests which had long sought to take hold of the territory for the sake of its visual splendor alone; interests either connected to a desire to extract dividends from tourists, or stemming from appreciators of natural wonder who appreciated it best when they owned it, and could ogle it in private and at leisure. About the matter, the Heiress was presently making the comment, "What on earth makes those savages think the land is theirs anyhoo?" said she with much gravity into the circle of reverent silence. "Absolutely cockeyed, I say."

A few moments passed in anticipation.

But the Heiress would say nothing more — her Chaperone began to feed her, and her husband the Minister of Borders took the word again (hesitantly at first), agreeing vehemently and with increasing enthusiasm. Neipas had by then removed a linen napkin from the pocket of his jacket — with much care, and a certain detached gesture of affection, he laid the napkin on Moloch's chest and tied it behind the fat bulge that was the back of his neck. Leaning over with all the delicacy one can hope to muster in this type of situation, Neipas picked up the silver spoon with the very tip of his fingers and dipped it sideways into the pasty meat on the plate. The mushed duck was thus scooped up and taken to the Mogul's waiting, very open mouth. The old Eagle snapped his beak round the spoon. Neipas then slid it out, deliberate and measured, and watched as the spoon returned to the open air with a shining screen of spit on it. He noticed it in private, kept the nausea swaying in his throat (nausea which was lightly stirred and fanned by the wind of the flabella) to himself, and simply kept feeding Mr. Moloch, who, in between scoops, would down in one gulp all the wine in his glass. Whenever a chunk of meat was seen to be smudging the corner of his beak, Neipas would take the napkin to it and very carefully wipe it for him. And so the dinner was a succession of lifting spoon to tongue, setting it down, rubbing greased mouth, pouring wine, and picking spoon back up again; the napkin was bombarded with spots of grease by dinner's end, its white fabric soiled beyond the cleansing powers of any soap. Neipas kept his head down and empty throughout. The nauseous feeling wallowing inside his neck settled somewhat in the mechanical nature of the gestures he repeated; though it lingered in a diluted form, bobbing persistently with the motions of flabella, nonetheless.

Mr. Moloch clicked his tongue, making clear the excess of saliva filling his mouth, and snapped his beak open and shut many times. As soon as Neipas removed the napkin from his chest, the Mogul's chin tottered down to it and bulged with muted grunts and smacking, wavering in an undecided state of encroaching inebriation. The bottle of Chateaux was empty. "Would you require more, sir?" asked Neipas — to which Moloch simply fingered the glass.

As Neipas was crossing the Ballroom toward the cellar, he saw in the distance, peeking out of the hatchway to the kitchen, Drrawetz's legless torso gesturing wildly with inward wavy arms, like some sort of malevolent plant sprouting out of the furred soil. The profusion of horns seemed to be coalescing toward him. Neipas headed there with rushed steps.

"Put down the dishes and grab drinks!" hissed Drrawetz to the dish-laden cattle as they neared. "Be on standby for dessert. Hurry!"

The last speech was about to commence. Neipas rushed into the kitchen and racked the duck-blooded, greased porcelain, glimpsing the cooks straining in the meticulous preparation of dessert as he went out. Then he scrambled to the cellar to collect another bottle, battling with an onward hail of waiters as he careered to the end (tripping multiple times on the strange shapes lying on the floor) and they all surfaced into the Ballroom with a collective jingling of bells, poising beside their masters delicately; the last drop of wine landed in Moloch's glass just as the lights, already dimmed, went off.

Darkness breathed from the eye — every shape became murky. Inside, nothing, save for the Dove, glowed; the music, which had never stopped, faded. The monumental windows were pressed against the night of an unfathomable outdoors, whose bottomlessness was sweetened in the Pearl's mystic gleam spreading far, spilling inward in the shape of windowpanes, with the softness of glass. Nothing but it, nothing but this light shone in the vast extent of the Eagles' Nest now. Most of it hid in the shadow of a very dense blackness; and inside it a quiet commotion of bodies held still, expectantly. The silence was total...

At last the lamps encrusted in the walls flared up, beaming intensely; the chandeliers lit feeble at first, but then their lights grew, grew, grew along with a quickening play of drum sounding from every side. By the end of it, all thousand lights dangling overhead dazzled so brightly as to make the sight an indistinct vision of fervent white, into which all figures were blurred and flooded.

Out of this unicolored chaos the steward's voice emerged with gushing reverence:

"Ladies and gents, the President of the Columbidae, D — C — Arnold!!!"

The drumming sequence culminated in a dramatic clash of cymbals; all the trumpets erupted, and the lights shifted, softening everywhere and everywhere inhaling, concentrating all their intensity on the towering litter set before the 9th Gate — a tall, bulky, giant Eagle ascended solemnly the pillowy mound, steeped in spotlight and waving proud at the raucous ovation below. The ruler of Columbia perched upon the dais... Everyone was standing now; every ox, heifer, swan, horse, peacock, every owl and every Eagle stood and clapped with enthusiasm. The industrialists in the Ballroom flapped their hands together, and many seemed to have trouble keeping their feet on the ground, swaying here and there, as if balancing themselves upon the deck of a ship or wavering on the cusp of flight (Neipas, who found himself clapping ardently along — the treasured wine bottle had been carefully placed on the table — could observe them sweating liquor out their glowing plumage; applauding swans did not move their flabella). Arnold raised his haloed arms. Behind his eminence flew that magnificent cape, the glorious flag of the Nation, flapping now to an artificial wind that had been set up especially for the purpose, flapping like a titanic wing lifting Columbia to its most exalted heights. Raised before the gate, it veiled the sight of those in the lower terraces of the Garden to the back of the leader — it would be from the glorious motions of that hallowed cloth that all those beneath would hear his voice...

The orchestra climaxed in an explosion of drum and trumpet, its triumphal blare caving into the applause as the audience crescendoed to hysterical blissful cries, whistles, caws; the lights blazed and screamed to their maximum power —

(...then dimmed slowly). Then everyone fell quiet amid clapping flickers dying... and there was only the very soft, nearly imperceptible murmur of string as audiences awaited expectedly. The Eagles stretched their feathers and their ears, swaying upon their toes; the others, in the lower terraces, looked up at the flag with emotion and attention. For the President was about to speak — and his words meant money...

Having soaked all that ardor into the voluminous fur of the blonde lion mane — symbol of the Nation's supremacy — framing his eagle mask, Arnold began happily chanting his litany from on high. It was a lively ramble which praised himself and, by implication, the Market God which he served and embodied, of which he fashioned himself the incarnation and ultimate prophet. Arnold, heir of fortunes and magnate of land, towers and city blocks, was the boastful epitome of the age, a thorough expression of the core values of those days: for he was a partisan of contest and a champion of victory, and he thrived on the idea and perception of both notions; the necessity of vanquishing one's competitors and adversaries — for the sake of money — was a core motif of his song, which flowed from his beak imperiously askew and smiled down everyone's ears with the sweetness of the accompanying harp.

(*money[...]money[...]moneymanyprofitsgrowth*) Indeed, the President was, like those gathered in the Ballroom that night, a rapacious, amoral capitalist — and if he wasn't liked by some, it was only because he didn't hide it. Arnold's mask was the accurate, unabashed representation of the spirit of the epoch; his was the great countenance, vaunting without shame all the glory of his wealth and exhibiting in pride the sordidness of his greed. All beheld his smirk, his visage; everyone saw how clearly his mask displayed the great hatred and stupidity that had been festering latent in the heart and veins of the Nation. The ugly face of the age made some of its defenders uncomfortable; they liked to keep it hidden, even from themselves. Yet even those patricians who grimaced at Arnold's uncouthness with the aspect of degustating a turd were but pretenders; in their depths their dislike was feigned. Other politicians envied him his position, perhaps, and those inimical journalists who were in attendance were perhaps genuinely appalled by his demeanor, which they found a little unpalatable — but they all played in the same orchestra, they all chanted the same opera, and antagonistic as some might have sometimes seemed they all spoke the same song, like counterpoints in the same grand polyphony involving all humanity in the same neverending fugue. Crass though he might have been, Arnold was a great trickster, and his art was to entertain — and spectacle was, above all, profit, which in the end spoke deepest... At this point in the evening some of the cattle began to feel dizzy: exhaustion manifesting itself, surely. It was a sensation of immaterial waters or spirits buoying inside them, from their chests to their heads and vice versa; the flabella stirred weird breezes into them, and the sound of string curling under Arnold's incantation insinuated itself round their necks with the consistency of a hum and a whisper, with an effect such that it seemed to take control of their breathing — the melodies breathed air in and out of them, at their own rhythm and whim; and one, then another, under the stifling horned masks began to suffer from a certain humming nausea.

Nevertheless all, like all the rest, listened carefully to the President now — because his words meant money...

And they were apparently worth a lot of money, for when he was finished with the first part of his carol everyone reveled, everybody was roused to a fit and a frenzy. The Eagles and peacocks and pelicans and owls and horses and deers and bulls all burst in cheers, the whole cascade of garden terraces beating up with euphoria. There was a tremendous agglomeration of very wide smiles — even the few frowns of discontentment were seemingly struggling against an impulse to grin; a couple of the attendants (Drrawetz among them) were even weeping, shaking their heads with much emotion. Some Eagles engaged in the violent rocking of their chairs, stomping their feet inebriatedly upon the tables (their pounce shook the humming sound underneath the music, which fragmented into a strange, deep throb among the noises), others whirled and already they spun and danced in very excitement. The mood was one of supreme ecstasy and booming elation — for Arnold had spoken passionately of all the magnificent wealth he would extract from the soil, which meant (to the understanding of all but the cattle) everything surfacing from it and everyone pressed against it. Days of unbridled prosperity would follow, he promised, and declared that under him there could be no limit to their might.

Wines were poured like libations everywhere. The Chateaux flowed gently from the mouth of the bottle, the bottle was held firmly by his gloved hands, he gazed out of his ox mask seemingly unstirred, absolutely focused on his task — and yet his mind, his muscles, his heart convulsed strangely in the deep throb which seemed to pulse under the buoyant tunes and the flaring lights, the overall strange sway of things... There was breathlessness under the raucous noise of the patricians; under the downcast horns.

Moods were again drooping to an expectant silence, now giddy with winking and many drooling smiles — again the music, which had momentarily arisen in a clamber of drunken instruments clashing, hummed down and lullabied in hypnotic ululations. The President raised his arms (his mane lifted a little over his tie); he was about to sing again.

Vested with the power of the state now, Arnold the Tycoon considered it appropriate to extend his patronage yonder beyond the august confines of the summit for a moment. The President began the second part of his speech by mumbling about 'our fellow Columbidae', to which the response was widespread laughter. Then he mentioned something vague about human rights, and there was much guffawing, and every earnest nodding was sprinkled with intermittent chuckles. Arnold gave a sly grin to his audience. Proceeding, he began extolling the ideals of freedom and democracy upon which Columbia, that great country over which he now presided, was founded; that great sprawling empire, that nation so bloated with struggle, so flooded with conflict and nausea, so dizzied by movements and counter-movements in the grand tidal dance of dialectics, so embattled in the war between its subjects and its masters, the powerful many and the mighty few; so misshapen in the clash between ideals and reality, between those who used the ideals as a facade to hide behind and those who sought to mold reality to fit its mask, that one could not gaze seriously upon the face of this kingdom of illusions without landing the eye upon its many malformations and incongruities, the many abysses marking the gap between ignored reality and the professed aspirations — about which Arnold grumbled now. At all this the audience laughed in increasingly hysterical volumes (some rolled over on the floor, the whole landscape seemed to blur in their mirth, the tipping teary lights); and the President smiled along, though his grin seemed a little confused. Those who were paying the most attention noticed how visibly his aspect had changed, how starkly his stature had diminished, as he muttered; the locks of his blonde mane were grizzly now, and he stooped over the pulpit very meekly. Even as his beak moved, he seemed to molt, and change colors... Was he sinking into the pillows? He tripped on a word, scratched his head, opened his arms — his eagle face amusingly contorting — and let them hang in a most senile manner; he appeared more and more clueless, and so debilitated one almost felt sorry for him. And yet the looks of satisfaction upon the masks of this audience of emperors was undeniable. Already they had begun drawing away from Arnold as the strings scratched and the music grew and the yelling swelled deliriously, pivoting, dragging the lights with them, leaving the President in the half-light as he squinted and strained, standing there bobbing his lower beak, mumbling incoherently (the cymbals clashed and the very tuba snorted to comic effect). His mask looked suddenly perfect in its representation of besieging decadence... an amalgam of hypocrisies and sheer stupidities, of all the sins of that nation sovereign over the age, a mask piled with bizarre concoctions layered on like the erstwhile titles of long-fallen kings. Here was the symbol of a decadent age and a crumbling empire; an icon approaching its meaning.

The music, which underlay all sounds always, was growing again (*hahahaha!*), retaining still the mesmerizing lullabied quality pervading this second part of the President's declining speech, and retaining in its climbing pomp the sensation of chopped throbbing and a fragmented hum; it veiled Arnold's mumble like velvet, very soft and very calm (*hmmmmm*). For a while now (the violin's bow scratched across the inflamed nerves of the cattle and drumsticks rained upon their skin) the overall movement of the Eagles, who, in their increasing drunkenness, had been drifting away from their tables by and by, had tended to spiral toward the Golden Dove, round which they gradually coalesced (at first very disorderly, shoving each other out of the way — all among tables dragged and chairs toppled, amid shouts and hullabaloo — but now the melody, grown in volume and softened in tone, whistling and trotting in prelude to the waltz, guided them to become organized and talk, like Arnold, in grave mutters). Driven on by the shifting tides to whirl round the sculpture, dragging the Swans whom they had haphazardly seized, the Eagles floated all with the refined music and assembled in the Ballroom's inner ring, against the glowing Dove's white gold. Flutes breezed and oboes whispered, violins and cellos marched delicately, in expectation; every so often a clarinet would glide by in a quiet. And in this quiet, this rumbling hush of tubas and clopping drums, the rich (in an uncanny show of coordination among the roiling liquor) arranged themselves in pairs — Eagles and Swans, forming a perfect circle round the Dove... In a frail absentminded motion, still perched upon the pillows, standing at half the size he had stood in the beginning, Arnold tremulously lifted up a piglet — and it was then that someone bumped against Neipas and he came to.

The silence was made total a third time. Again all sounds were breezed away, felled and dispersed. Yet the throb stirred beneath the quietude, beneath the deafness, and under the skins underneath the masks it pulsed like the reechoed echo of some distant reverberation. At the periphery of the scene stood the waiters and ushers, quiet, still and stone-faced; no emotion transpired from the professional posture they held, no stir disturbed their bovine masks; they held decorum, as instructed. Neipas watched bewildered behind his snout's professional cover. Having stood next to Moloch's ebullient bursts, he marveled, having only a feeble grasp of the tremendous interests being discussed and celebrated in that otherworldly space; though his intuition caught well the arrogance, brazenry, and detachment which pervaded every word, giggle, and clap.

All around a darkness fell (nobody made a sound). President Arnold stepped down from the dais and wobbled about, shaking many congratulatory hands; here and there an important-looking Eagle would pat him on the head, grinning with grins curving from eye to eye. The oligarchs drank unrestrainedly, twisting themselves backward with laughter (and still there was no sound) and Neipas, beholding this after a long, alien period of wavering glows and sinister words resonating in his mind, seemed to wish to shrink under the towering figures, take cover before the dark prospect of their unseen shadows. The lights, the sounds had made him dizzy; an uncanny feeling overwhelmed him, pushed a lump up his throat and he had to strain to stay put; he suddenly noticed that he felt very scared, and that this fright had been building secretly through the evening, throughout the last three days, from the very beginning of his life.

(The throb pulsed in his muscles, in his brain) Moloch had long departed the table along with the other guests, all of which were poised in the circle along the Ballroom's inner ring. With perfect elegance one and its pair neared and joined hands, clasped fingers round shoulders and pressed them upon waists. In the lower terraces, guests arranged themselves in smaller circles. Male with female, male with male, female with female, the pairs shrunk into the bodies of its elements; slowly stomachs pressed against bellies, hair brushed on plume, blotched cheeks touched cheeks.

It was such that all Eagles were enveloped in the glow of the Dove, bathed in the only light now shining — and all the cattle stood inside shadows. Neipas beheld the faint shapes of beasts on the ceiling. Vague, he contemplated the darkest corner, where the band stood (motionless; total silence had befallen the darkness. And still the throb pulsed and trembled in his muscles, in his brain, in his fleeing spirit; it flowed down the roots of his masks, screaming in the hollows). In that corner, only the Conductor could be spotted, with his back facing them, his arms tucked silently as he presided over the gloom; the darkness seemed to take shape into something slick, gooey, pulsing, with stretching arms... but this was a momentary impression. When Arnold raised the piglet, so did the Conductor his hands: the waiters were made to move, and in a sudden rush of silent activity they collected dishes, napkins, little snacks, whatever lay upon the tables. Someone bumped against Neipas in the dark, pulling him from his reverie, and at once he grabbed Moloch's leftovers and, in the dark, stepped hastily toward the kitchen. The prelude had again begun to play (Neipas breathed feathers nervously) and as he went through the hatchway all lights burst open behind him — the silence blew up (*!* into a collective blast of horns, trumpets, trombones, tubas and raging timpani trampling over cymbals and bassoons and clarinets and flutes and cellos all undulating drunk with the pulse), the orchestra performed a fierce, boisterous, violent version of the Kaiser Walzer, booming the melody over volleys of drum — and all revolved feverishly to the tempo, and as Neipas looked back before the trapdoor closed over his head he saw the Ballroom devoid of fur and horns; absolutely flaming with white plumage. The Eagles, now lone in their Nest, waltzed vigorously round their Golden statue. Round and round and round they spun, and spun, and spun, wrapping themselves in the swathes of their own spinning, in the flame of their own feathers, in golden light, curling through evolutions and revolutions in the great waltz of their laughing masks. The carved gold shimmered tall over the circling body of suits and faces; the patrons danced with glee round their totem, beaming smiles of pure ecstasy. An exuberant joy of wealth and triumph exuded from their motions, performed with a flawlessness such and a perfection so uncanny, with noises so diabolical that it felt as though the carousal was the enactment of some timeless rite, reproducing in burning hypnotic waves the ancient summoning of a primeval, bestial god.

"Hey!" a supervisor yelled behind Neipas. "You coming or what?" Neipas rushed away from the trapdoor. The kitchen was enveloped in a final fury of activity, and Drrawetz was livid. He pushed, slapped, and kicked anyone standing in his way as he vociferated with ardor every pent-up frustration in his roiling breast. The cooks rushed the complex preparations of the desserts and the waiters hurried to pick them up.

"My God," gasped Cesar, going by. Through his neck oozed melting wax, seeping from under his bovine head. Afar, Magpie ran out through the exits, away from the Ballroom. Janu gave two elaborately flourished sweets to a heifer. Neipas picked up his own dessert and sprinted up the steps and out the hatch.

The light in the Ballroom seemed suddenly so intense that Neipas was forced to squeeze his eyes shut as he went in. His walk was irregular, he was being pushed around from all sides, round him the Ballroom swam and he felt as though he himself was drifting and losing balance; his feet felt strangely distant from the floor. He strained to collect his wits and straighten himself up. All of a sudden (and now he found himself wondering whether it had been like that since he had gone out the door) he was moving with a perfectly upright gait among a formation of perfectly aligned waiters heading toward the tables. Many of the Eagles were seated already, waiting with severe faces, but others bumbled about in dancing steps yet, on chairs and under tables (those spinning round the Dove tripped on each other and laughed under a drunken rendition of Khachaturian's festive, rambunctious waltz); and as Neipas approached his own table he found Moloch wasn't there. The Heiress munched her dessert ravenously from the chaperone's hand, and presently collected herself on the back of oxen coming to pick her up. And again the lights dimmed — fireworks burst violently and brightly in the sky right beside them, every inch of space seemed to convulse between light and dark with confusion. Drunken clapping and yelling ensued. Seeking Moloch, Neipas was drawn to the edge of the Ballroom on the side overlooking the Pigeon Gardens, where a denser group gathered and the fireworks blew stronger.

Down there he saw, to his surprise, the wall of a myriad eyes from the deep end of the lake terrace — he saw it moving. It was an enormous, open peacock tail — and it walked across the waters on an elongated platform. So the Chief Peacock came, striding from its perch. It turned around and faced the Ballroom, to much furor. The echo of its song reverberated onto the Auditorium, where the pigeons gathered in enormous crowds and waved their hands in concert; and the Peacock bowed decorously, its immense tail extending upward down below, in the shape of a great semi-wheel, in the form of a vast, fabulous fan or shell.

Noises everywhere. (Yet blood pulsed inside his brain and in the ears of his heart among and under the pandemonium, and the shouts around it were shushed by its hastening command. Something beyond, yonder beyond that great confusion of stimuli, in the very lowest terrace, caught Neipas' attention). He sank his eyes further into the cascade of gardens.

[...]

What he perceived there, he didn't exactly see. He spotted but a glint of something; but his soul told him, somehow, it whispered to him what it was.

Neipas saw there, looking up toward him from the lowest level of the Hanging Gardens, beneath the Ballroom, beneath the Auditorium, beneath the Lakes and the thorny woods, beneath the 8 terraces — there, at the very bottom, he saw the Midget from the Slaughterhouse.

He saw the Midget in chains, he saw the Midget facing him with the mask of downturned crescent slits — he felt the Midget calling him (and still that infernal pulse sounded!) with its voiceless immobility, up here near the summit of the heights, as he had once been called down near the bottom of the depths.

But he stepped away from the edge by the force of a pull. Someone, a shaking Eagle face slapped him repeatedly. "Didn't you hear me calling, boy?

Didn't you?" yelled a pulsing beak. Neipas staggered away with his dessert and cried apologies, his senses thrown into confusion. With the lamps again off, the raucousness was only illuminated by the explosions in the sky and consciousness was battered in a hail of noises and pulsing lights. Reckuz of the Maskbook wrapped his arm round his neck as he passed. "Don't worry, man," said the voice of the tech tycoon, loaded with the rancid breath of alcohol. "Don't worry, man," he repeated, pressing his weight heavy upon Neipas' back. "Don't worry, man. Don't think about it. Lol, man! We care about you, man!" and he released him, walking off somewhere.

The music resounded with the explosions. A voice screamed in Neipas' ear, commanding he find Moloch. And the Eagles' Nest was at this point a monumental disarray of inebriation: Eagles ran about and turned tables downside up, knocked out on the carpet, swallowed pricey bottles of the finest wines whole and smashed them, played golf with table legs and crumbled banknotes, and even ate the banknotes in laughter... Some still waltzed round the Golden Dove — but mostly they stumbled and fell about. Neipas, bewildered, imagined himself suddenly in some extravagant madhouse. He was somehow able to find steadiness amid the turmoiled state to which he was quickly succumbing; and still went about suave, in almost dancing steps, sporting the professional semblance he was trained to wear.

Yelling, jarring sounds of breaking glass thickened on in his ear. The patrons had spread into the recreational spaces and the various estates of the Anubel, making the cattle scatter across its vast, majestic halls propagating down endlessly from the Ballroom. As Neipas was stepping out (having made sure Moloch wasn't there) he ducked at the firing of a gun; his heart charged into his throat and ballooned in a surge of fright. He turned his head in all directions in a frantic attempt to ascertain where the shot had come from — but he saw everyone proceeding as usual in the laughing, merry gathering of suits.

It was difficult to keep composure. Neipas descended the stairways toward Moloch's palace, and as the steps precipitated beneath him the collective grasp on reality seemed to blur even further. He felt as though time flowed well outside of him, as though it couldn't affect the heights of the Belab's highest floors. It seemed like that night had been running on for a long spell, like it had begun many centuries ago, like the waltz had been rounding since time immemorial. Neipas really felt this for a moment, he felt it as though it were palpable fact. In his frenzied run down he perceived the megalopolis as a vast ocean of blinking lights, billowing hither almost to the height of his stooping over these altitudes... (Yonder he saw Arnold's helicopter leaving, filling the air with concentric waves; the President had an appointment in some foreign nation, but the Ministers in attendance would stay the night).

His wits dispersed into the noise as he wandered about, increasingly disoriented and outside of himself. In the first terrace, blustered with majestic facades, he saw the Editor, his old Professor Moldura. Neipas must've spoken a few words to him. "Mister Moloch?" said the Editor. "Put in a good word for me. Wink." He did not actually wink, but rather said the word and stumbled away.

Casting off that strange encounter as irrelevant among that uncanny night of visions, Neipas carried on into the outer courtyard of Moloch's estate, seeing the inebriated Bulls asleep at the gates. As Neipas sped deliriously through the pools, saunas, baths, giant balconies, sports courts, bunkers, lawn rooms, theatres, libraries, golden-platted game rooms, opulent offices and meeting rooms, as he dizzied deeper into the Eagles' world of luxury and extravaganza, he witnessed scenes of rabid intoxication, wanton cruelty, overt debauchery. He saw a small group of Eagles punch and kick a waiter into the ground, right in the middle of a corridor; they had yanked off his ox mask and took turns wearing it as they beat him unconscious, Neipas noticed as he passed by them, scared out of his mind. He had seen a triplet of them fondling one another in the Infinity Pool by the tower's edge earlier. Now in one of Moloch's inner gardens, bearing a massive mosaic depicting Romans upon Sabines, he saw a massive orgy, a mountain of limbs, a lewd spectacle of moist skin mounting up on body. They ran naked in the halls, with beaks wide open, and some wept as they fought each other over trinkets. Money bills rained from cornucopias, wealth poured from the gilded walls as Neipas scrambled about, disoriented, through manic velvety laughter.

The hidden magnitude of the Eagles' Nest baffled him. Neipas seemed to walk over convulsive carpets in an endless curve, through many revolving doors wafting golden aromas, through diamond-studded gates which were opened by owls holding the pole on each side; out into palatial halls, across which luxurious tables stretched beneath massive mirrors and chandeliers. The music boomed all the while; the orchestra, descending over the Gardens, had evolved into a titan birdsong voiced from a winged demon.

But — dwelling frantic the gilded halls as he may — he could not find Moloch.

...deep in the Media Mogul's estate, Neipas suddenly found himself lost. He was just beyond the inner garden with the mosaic of the Sabines. A corridor stretched and curved widely beyond his sight with multiple closed gates on either side.

There occur, in the course of one's life, acts whose cause cannot be traced back to reason: events which are triggered without decision, by an occult, unconscious impulse whose source is absolutely indefinable, hidden forever behind the natural incapacities of science and introspection. They begin in the lull of other demands — in the gap between sentiments and the void of intellect; perhaps in the general yawn of indecision — with that impulse pulling one down a little trail which, appearing suddenly before one, connects with the sense of life's main road only much later.

There was nothing that could have cued Neipas to turn the corridor deeper into the palace. There was nothing to rouse his curiosity. He went on without the least idea why, swimming in the general fluidness of things.

He knew from Cesar that the Gardener's palace was inside, or beyond, Moloch's own estate. All the Eagles' properties were connected, co-existed within a complex labyrinth of mirrors and corridors, which, some would say, linked all the way to the Pigeon Wing and shored out in the very Pigeon Gardens; though the connecting paths were so winding, so confusing, and so inscrutable that none could hope to trespass them, unless perhaps with a guide, which cost fortunes; lest one become lost in the mazes.

Neipas hesitated with that fear. But it was then he heard, faintly, the voice of the Gardener himself; and he carried on a little further, enticed now by a keen sense of interest. One of the massive, ornate gates on that corridor was only slightly ajar. Neipas dared not peek into the open slit nor even pass in front of it. Instead he stood in the corridor, indecisive with fright, and bent his ear toward the door. The indistinct mumbling was shaped to clear words as his hearing neared the gate; and he heard the clear words molded in the Gardener's voice:

"The refinery is your problem, Mr. Noxxe."

A deeper, resounding mutter responded to this statement; though no words formed out of the muffled sound with enough distinctiveness.

"No."

Vague, guttural mutter, laden with consequence.

"No one will know. The Oyate will yield in the courts..."

He was interrupted.

"They don't have the resources to win the case or to investigate. The meat farms are not operated by us. He's not our employee, no one can connect him to me or to any of our shareholders. Not even he can. Moreover, he was acquitted — it doesn't matter..."

A sharp pang sank deep into his heart. Neipas looked in very carefully: and he saw, sitting at a triangular table in the middle of a large room, the Head Gardener, Baron Noxxe, and Maskbook's Reckuz, who threw his pointy eyes to every side with puerile eagerness. Around them (on the walls) were mounted the heads of stags, and glassed shelves stocked with guns; strange, heavy-looking cut-outs rotated midair, hung from the ceiling; a single map covered the giant wall on the far end.

There was some muted laughter.

"We have weathermen working for us. They had the know-how. Once they knew the time to start the fire — the rest was easy, as far as I'm concerned."

Neipas sprung back away from the slit, and the blood coursed in his brain so loudly, palpitating with the orchestra's song resounding in the corridors, that he couldn't hear for a while, and for a while he found himself all in a panic about whether to step away. But he controlled his urge to run for long enough to hear, beyond the fading pulse of inner shock and confusion:

" — pipeline, Noxxe. Come on, now. I'm risking much more than you are. Mary Virgin. It's going through my land, is it not?"

Another muted grunting, humorous, and a childish giggle.

"That's why I'm signing the deal, isn't it, Noxxe."

A type of mucous laughter ensued, which rolled into a collective guffaw; dense, smoky, contained, opulent. At last Noxxe, perhaps in an attempt to make himself heard above the amusement of his companions, spoke louder:

"Very well, dear fellow. You're right. The way to make money — is to buy when blood is running in the streets."

The next moment — as though time had tripped and pitched forward several minutes — Neipas was again running in immense, shimmering spaces, empty and pulsing only with screams. His eartag shook uncontrollably. He hadn't time to process, he hadn't time to feel. Somehow he ended up having to cater a lot of desserts; the number of waiters seemed to be somehow diminishing through the night. He traversed with much fear as he passed by many visions of unbridled violence and sex writhing in the halls of power.

Yet working he kept, impelled at all moments by Drrawetz's angry shouts, which seemed to blast omnipresent in those halls. Neipas toiled beyond the limits of strain, through the locking of his every muscle. It was perhaps only the lash of Drrawetz's despot tongue which thrust him on.

Among the last memories Neipas had of that night was of standing next to Moloch's collapsed body. He had either returned or had never left — for Neipas found him at his table in the Ballroom. The Mogul pressed his white cheek against the tablecloth, though he kept the same lucid, no-nonsense expression on his visage; and he slept, though his eyes were wide open — and snored with noises of angry lion. Neipas had in his hand a Chateaux du Pouvoir. He took a good swig of it, straight off the bottle. It was very potent; his body, exhausted, relaxed at once under its own weight. Neipas recalled liking it very much.

Then he remembered waking in the dark — his eyes were open wide but saw nothing. Out of his mouth was cast a loud, continuous scream; his lips were stretched far apart — his whole face widened away in panic.

Someone covered his mouth; he released a moan, and shushed. His chest burned; his throat billowed; he shook all over.

In the dark he distinguished Osir's growing face. His pulsing scar approached Neipas very near and whispered, "shh..."

"Quiet... We're all trying to sleep here."

Osir removed his hand slowly, and Neipas, filled with horror in his heart, nodded quietly. Looking about, sweaty and trembling, he realized he was in the wine cellar, and that the inert bodies of cattle were lying asleep about him. He looked vaguely to the racks of wine bottles ascending to the black above him. His eyes were still very open; and it was with the vivid fright still in him that he succumbed to exhaustion again.

Silence.

36 - Styx ashore

Faint stirrings fidgeted in the corners. It was an indistinct shuffling about, and it roused Neipas confusedly out of the heavy darkness of a dreamless sleep, back into existence. His legs sored. He opened his rheumy eyes to another darkness — they were already open, very wide, when he realized he was awake — but this was a restless black, with motion in it, unquiet with whispers and mumblings. Suddenly a door opened in the heights and electric light spilled across the stairs. Neipas grimaced and groaned mutedly; everyone began speaking very loudly. A ruckus came from above, accentuating the immediate confusion. The light flickered as a great many bodies passed by and shadowed the door.

"What's going on?" panted Neipas, in a sleepy mutter — though he was well wakened.

Whether someone responded to him, he wasn't sure. But by the time he was out in the stony gallery outside the wine cellar, wavering with disorientation, he somehow knew that a sudden and dramatic change in the weather was the cause of the commotion. Neipas didn't grasp this right away, being in a state of bemused perplexity; but his senses, dormant as they were, perceived the general anxiety in the growing throng coalescing toward the Food Hall, and half-unconscious he bumbled along with the mass out of the Ballroom, watched by Bulls and their machine guns. The Hall was already quite full when he arrived. Neipas noticed the clock at 3:30am before turning his eyes to the collective point of focus. Everyone watched the televisions on the pillars, all in anxious quiet. Those who couldn't get in backed out into the Gardens, and those of them closest to the terrace's balustrade stared out in undisguised tremblings of awe. In the far distance they saw the giant palm trees of Ostrich's boulevards swaying like mad beneath a brooding sky, their large rotten leaves flying; the patchwork of houses shook in terror. The moon shone tranquil near the towerhead, which rose clear of the hissing, broiling winds; but under the Eagle's Nest, celestial fumes were assembling in a rainy fury; lights blazing from its windows spread atop the clouds of golden pale, amassing in a rush.

From within the frames of the TV a suited Lion spoke and elucidated. A hyperstorm off the coast, which had been projected to miss Axiac's shores by many miles, had abruptly swerved in its direction. Through the week past, its tornadoes of wind and water had razed whole archipelagos, taking homes and lives in its gust. Families cowed in their ramshackle abodes and lost everything. Despair, the peculiar contraction of chest and mind that is characteristic of unassailable loss, the crushing hopelessness before widespread death — such maligned sentiments swept and caved into the land. The islanders, already burdened with the plight of poverty and the constant anxiety of peeking hunger, were the first to suffer the ire of altered nature. For miles and miles of earth and sea they stood, by the thousands, lost among debris.

The suited Lion inside the TV told of no such details. Somehow this devastation of biblical magnitudes warranted no more than a dispassionate tone of mild concern. Indeed, the destruction wrought by the storm had been conveyed in lukewarm terms so far, the tally of the damage presented as abstract math with no more gravity than classroom formulas. Mostly the main media had no time for it, shrouded as it was in the daily circus of political clownery. Barely anyone in Axiac knew or cared about it.

But the storm — which was called "Styx" — quickly rose to the prominence of pagetop headlines, just as soon as its direction changed. It still wasn't taken seriously. Newsfolk took it with glee and mockery, cawing ready-to-wear phrases ("buckle up folks!", "make sure you wear a jacket!", "better buy an umbrella!"), pinching their grins upward in a sly gesture of their hooked little finger as they tilted their heads to the side and shook them a little.

The tip of Styx first blew a slight breeze into the megalopolis as it arrived the previous afternoon; which was a welcomed change to Axiac's windless air, for whoever noticed. But the sway of it grew, and as footage of houses flying in sand-shored coasts in the night, paired with reports of the comparative damage gales of such speed would make to impenetrable, unvanquishable Axiac spread viral through the Webwork, citizens, at first amused by the rare rains, began to feel a slight trepidation; then these rains grew into an outpour carried by accelerating winds, and the slight trepidation morphed up into a hesitant state of panic; illusions of safety gave way to premonitions of doom speedily; and ultimately the contained panic swelled, rapidly, into a frenzied effort of evacuations as belated, sudden official warnings shouted their way into the ears and eyes of Axiac's death-fearing citizenry. In a scramble folk got into their cars straight into an infinitude of traffic lines in booming hyperways, or swarmed into supermarkets to fight for all the supplies they could get and hunker down in wooden-barred, steel-reinforced fortress homes. A frantic and crazed motion of millions rocked the vast cityscape in preparation for the sudden tempest.

Neipas himself had seen something about it in his *I* in the morning, but he had taken it like most others — with indifference. Seconds later he had forgotten about it. Like most in Axiac, he was unsuspecting of the weather's power, and if he were to give it any thought, he might have thought a little rain couldn't hurt — it might be a good thing, after so many years of drought. But the scattered reports of the storm's effects in the islands, and now the compounded testimonies to its strength from scientists and victims, quickly amassed to form a coherent story about a murderous behemoth come. Gradually it instilled a sense of fear, then panic, within Neipas. And once he learned to dread the tempest, his first thought was to call Eva. But already the *I* couldn't make a connection.

There was a way. Landline phones were set in the far recesses of the Columbaria, from which one could reliably make calls. Others must have had similar ideas, for already there were motions in the throng toward the phone booths, a felt general desire to reach the world below. Anticipating a pandemonium breaking out soon, Neipas slunk through the gathered multitude of bodies and hastened to the phones.

In the gilded halls of the topmost floor of the highest tower, shielded from the deep night, the Eagles reflected. Many were awake; for the most astute among them never slept; the most powerful never blinked. Already they had begun deliberating. Cushioned into their thickly padded chairs, from which they molded the rules governing societies and the hopes of common folk, warm in their meeting rooms of glossy ebony and fabrics of heavy opulence, lit dazzlingly from sparkling lamps atop ornamented bureaus, the Eagles debated in secrecy, patiently, many miles away from the ground and safe above the gathering storm. They had heard of it with interest. Immediately their collective mind, perpetually lustful of profit, jumped to calculating how they could extract gold from the raging rivers the deluge would bring. The Eagles spent the night arranging, organizing, designing; and they waited for the morning, when they could dispense their wealth in the celebration of their ingenious plans and wonderful opportunities ahead.

*

Hours mixed into one another in a night that was growing narcotic, full of fidgety sleepiness.

Neipas contemplated the shape of his hand. The fingers were outstretched, and callouses sprouted mildly from under their roots; the skin fastened tight and firm, soft to the glance, coarse to the touch; rugged lines cleaved across the surface of the palm, dashing painterly strokes suggestive of dynamism, action, flight; potential. It was a human hand, his — perennial tool of the human mind. Twitchy gestures of his fingers recollected the feel and weight of a camera. In his head played the snap, that sound encapsulating the moment into frame. He had worked so much of late, bearing dishes, serving food into the wealthy beaks of his superiors... He contemplated his hands both. Were these the tools of *his* own mind? Were these the executors of his will?

Neipas stared into the *I* on his hand. Through it, he read Eva's voice.

EVA: heyy
EVA: i'm sorry ok? :(i shouldn't have said what i said
EVA: (i was really hurt tho)
EVA: (w the things u said)
EVA: let's talk about it k? :)

EVA: call me

EVA: ...

EVA: ?
EVA: ok like you should at least respond
EVA: :/

EVA: wow
EVA: are you really not going to respond?
EVA: ok then

EVA: Asshole

EVA: hey...
EVA: i'm sorry :(is everything ok?

EVA: miss u :(

EVA: omg
EVA: [Video: Interior of Eva's apartment. The camera points to the window, which rattles violently - like bars clutched by a prisoner struggling to break loose. A strong whine of wind whistles through the gaps. Everything else shakes. It's a wrathful gale coming on, mounting all its force against the house.]
EVA: where are you right now
EVA: pls reply asap!!

But Eva wasn't there now. She had been yesterday — but Neipas had worked all yesterday.

He was very tired. His thoughts swam widely in the stupor. He hated his job. He wondered whether he could just drop it. No; a tension within him ordered that he wait. There would be a time where he could break free, he believed; he would just have to keep his head down, amass some money. Perhaps his most recent photo project would land him new gigs. Perhaps he would soon be able to make a living as a photographer, and finally be who he wanted to be — finally be himself.

But he couldn't drop out for now.

Such were Neipas' reflections in his current, placid state of suspension. He sat on the floor, in a long line, waiting for the phone. A row of horns wavered to and from the wall, balancing between them similar thoughts, perhaps. Neipas might have been surprised by the amount of landlines apparently still around, but mostly he felt nothing; all he had seen and heard the night previous swam like a vague dream in his mind; only his muscles held the solid recollection of it. Was it normal, all that had happened? But he could think nothing of it. From time to time he dozed, and found himself coming to, not knowing he had slept. When he saw the queue of folk stretching from the phones at the end of the room he thought of leaving; but a sense of obligation, guilt, and hope that the line would move quickly, made him stay. The telephone room was but a very long and very narrow set of walls with a glass booth at the very end containing two phones in it. The round lights beaming at short intervals from the ceiling, which rose very tall above the row of heads, produced a mollifying effect, so strong they were, and enhanced the drowsy restlessness of the tight space.

NEIPAS: baby! I'm so sorry. Are you ok?

NEIPAS: I was working all day :/

NEIPAS: Sorry I probably forgot to tell you

NEIPAS: :/

NEIPAS: I want to talk about it :) I'm sorry too… I shouldn't have said what I said. I'm a jerk sometimes.

NEIPAS: I'm worried about you

The line seemed interminable; Neipas must've been there for many hours. There was yet enough space for Neipas to squeeze back down and out along the queue, maybe; but this he wouldn't consider, though truly he wasn't very adamant about calling Eva anymore. Pure concern for her welfare wasn't what triggered the impulse to call her, ask how she was, if she was safe, ready. Something about the unreality of the situation warded off any serious worry.

He had no doubt she'd be fine. The sense of obligation and guilt, too, had vanished with time. Languidness, drowse, and a vague notion that he had invested too much time already and it would be stupid to leave now, were all more immediate reasons to linger and wait. A yet stronger, deeper reason was the fear that Eva would throw a fit if he didn't call. Expressing his love for her — in the form of concern, in this case — had become a matter of course, expected conduct.

But there had never been any love between the two. Their relationship evolved through attraction, infatuation, friendship, and settled finally into bored, mutual comfort. Not love, that profound willingness to give oneself to another. It hadn't begotten anything as deep as that — such was the way of most romance in those days. Time together had made them distant, and at the same time brought them closer, more used to each other. It wasn't good or bad, what existed between them. It was mostly just vacuous, and a little off. Their incompatibilities were subtle enough, but not so much as to be undetectable; indeed they were profound, fundamental. Eva's constant need for validation tired Neipas. Neipas' artist aloofness exasperated Eva. Neipas felt she was a bit inane. Eva thought he was a little boring. They almost never fought, and when they did, they tip-toed their grievances around one another — expressing themselves by means of slightly displeased tones and silences cloaking venomous meanings; being "passive-aggressive", as it was called in those days. But even this was rare. Their relationship was marked chiefly by inaction.

Nonetheless, they appreciated each other's mere presence. Everyone needs company. And indeed, shallow as it might have been, their relationship was grounded on basic human affection and companionship. That affection existed, even if dulled by loveless monotony; in the end, they liked each other despite it.

But after months of sameness, something changed. It became toxic.

The terminal drama had its conception in the ruffled sheets of Eva's bed. Neipas had been spending quite a few nights at her house because it was much closer to the northwest, where he had been working. This became more and more usual; they practically lived together after a while. Over time he brought a few things over — clothes, his photo projects and albums. And it came to be that he began to feel guilty over staying there. He didn't know if it was because of Eva or himself; but always he had the feeling he was intruding, had the suspicion that she didn't want him there. He offered Eva to pay for part of the rent, which she refused — out of spite or kindness, he didn't know. Sometimes her mask was so thick as to make her inscrutable, and half the time he didn't know what was going on inside of her. Neipas grew frustrated, blaming himself and Eva in turn. He shrunk into himself, became petty. And she, in response, became petty too. One day it broke into a fight — an overt fight, where Neipas shook his head almost in a panic and cry-yelled from general fatigue and frustration. Neipas was conscious he was to blame then. It was stress, it was the relentless pace of work. The stupidity of it all exasperated him — he had to make money to pay rent for an apartment he could no longer live in because it was too far; but he could live nowhere else because it was too expensive. Downtrodden, after nerves had cooled he neared Eva with head downcast, muttering apologies.

NEIPAS: baby?
NEIPAS: Let me know as soon as you get this

But it was in the reconciliation that their end began. It was clear that it had to be consummated. They had been celibate for a while now, tired of each other's bodies; but there was no better way for them to express reunion than in the union of skin. From among the heat of kisses Neipas scrambled out to begin a search that quickly turned frantic. There were no condoms to be found. He hadn't bothered buying any for the past couple of weeks. So he, indecisive, wavered silently between safety and the prospect of Eva shrugging and saying 'ok' to his failed manhood; and finally he said, "Do you want to try without?" — He regretted those words ever since.

Eva didn't much care, so they did it. From the get-go Neipas was nervous, which influenced his performance a great deal. It was a very delicate balancing act, trying to fulfill the mental need to please her and restrain the physical urge to discharge what his organs had been brewing for at least two weeks. The nervousness stimulated his muscles beyond control, and his ego had no grip on his body's functions at all. He tried to hold himself in as much as he could, but finally he succumbed to the imperatives of evolution — he pulled out at the last moment in shame, not quite on time — and the very stuff of primal life pumped out of him uncontrollably, onto her skin, onto the bedsheets, through his fingers.

It was the worst orgasm in his life. He couldn't feel the lassitude of muscle spreading across him through the thickness of embarrassment. Eva kept repeating "it's ok baby, it's totally fine" with a sweet voice and much petting; but that did nothing to placate the sense of worry and total failure. It was stress, it was the relentless pace of work. He wasn't himself, he thought. His mask spilled to the ground and lay spread, powerless and empty, completely defeated.

Almost immediately, Neipas' head spun with the paranoia of consequence; and this feeling — this premonition, almost — only grew in his heart as the days went. Eva did the pregnancy test as soon as she could. She went in nonchalantly; and came out with as much nonchalance.

"It's positive," she said to Neipas' waiting posture.

Neipas nearly fainted. "It's positive!?..." he blurted breathless, digging his fingers into his melting forehead.

Eva's mask held its calm expression of complete unconcern. To Neipas the sight of her was uncanny and incomprehensible. He couldn't bear it; he walked round and round Eva's small room in a stupor of thought, dominated by a mayhem of emotion revolving within every inch of soul in his body.

Eventually he sat down — and only after a good few minutes of staring into the blur of his vision did he say, "What should we do about this?"

Eva sat with him now, her cheek on his shoulder, looking blankly into nothingness, as Neipas was; though — unlike him — there was no wildness in her stare, no grip upon the moment, no desperation; there was only a glassy tranquility, a sinister abstraction of being. Neipas could explode — through his mind passed all the moments Eva panicked about the most trivial things; he wondered wildly about the source of this strange calm now, and almost fell from the couch when Eva shrugged and said "I dunno", so suddenly did his heart drop.

In his disorientation bloomed a rage toward Eva and her tranquility. Her attitude seemed stupid to his exasperated senses; and she, as the bearer of his coming child, seemed like a burden; instinctively he placed all blame upon this burden, and, getting up, burst. "How can you be so calm about this?" he yelled dryly, gesturing short of breath. Eva simply shrugged; and Neipas, peering hopelessly into the inscrutability of her mask, resumed his circular walk about.

At some point (time bent round and through his head confusedly, it could've been a minute, it could've been hours) Neipas had gone into Eva's room and then come out to see her in the kitchen with a wine glass against the tip of her beak, and the same blank, pensive expression of apathy.

"I'll just take a pill. I don't get why you're stressing out about it. Chill," said she, with a cold shrug of enormous indifference, taking a sip of crimson.

Eva spoke with the clarity of a solution — and it was just what Neipas, in his boundless panic and indecision, craved in that moment — but, if her words were clear in their meaning, her tone was equally clear in its cruelty. They couldn't support a child, of course — the very thought of it made it immediately obvious — and neither could Eva support a pregnancy. Hers was the only solution for them. Truly, he had only been waiting for Eva to say it, for he didn't have the courage to express it himself. When he heard the intimate craving of his heart explicit in Eva's beak, he shuddered with throes of cowardice; with relief, but also horror. There was something horrible about it — even in the stupor involving him, he knew — but they had no other choice.

Neipas faced his disfigured mask as different sentiments battled for supremacy — the guilt over the necessary abortion, the financial strain of it — and underneath it all, the feeling of impotence and self-disgust. It made him shy away from Eva further yet.

It had only been a week — exactly seven days — since Eva had swallowed the pill and the little clot of potential life had gushed out of her womb. And now Neipas sat in the long queue, and in the long and narrow space, in the phone booth room, in the bosom of the Eagles' Nest, summit which overlooks all things. The lights overhead had dimmed, and the lined herd of cattle waited, crammed in the stupor of crepuscular shapes fuming heavily. Neipas was next up. He lifted himself out of crouching amid the general creak of stiff bones and stepped heavily to the glass booth, from which a blank-faced cook with crazed eyes and a gaping lip was emerging.

The air tightened and pressed upon him as he shut the glass. Behind him, on the other phone, a waiter sat straight, facing the opposite direction. This waiter was very still, only his shoulders stirred in their breathing, hands rested upon his knees; the receiver remained untouched. Neipas grabbed his own receiver with the slowness of a hazy deliberation, and with a careful motion he placed the earpiece against the side of his head. The plastic tickled his ear — a dreamy sound reached him from far away, like a continuous whisper of chaffed wind, like a distant and melodic hum. Neipas dialed Eva's house number (how did he remember it?) — he anticipated the sound of her gruff voice sweetly — but by then it was already too late. Outside, the somber storm brooded already over the whole extent of Axiac. Its gush of rain poured furiously against the plains of concrete, the walls of glass shook uncontrollably before the force of its winds. The demonic push of the torrent had made quick work of the megalopolis' moribund infrastructure; powerlines had tumbled like cards upon a table, energy plants had flooded to overdrive and fizzle. All communications were cut off; and all waited for the storm to pass in panic and isolation.

Neipas must have sat on the booth for a long time, for when he removed the earpiece from his head and turned his eyes to the side there were many bovine faces pressed against the glass with obvious looks of impatience. He was a bit surprised upon seeing how many could fit in that tight and crammed space outside the booth, then a sound came out of his mouth reflexively:

"Doesn't work."

"What do you mean doesn't work?" someone asked in an uncanny, whispered tone of secrecy.

"I mean the phone doesn't work.

"I mean I dial and it beeps, but there's no one on the other side anymore."

The lines are cut off, someone proclaimed from the depths of the room yonder, and all the faces turned and clashed horns in a disarray of motion; the herd pushed itself out of the room in a sleepy wave of confusion, leaving Neipas alone in the booth with the waiter on the opposite side, who remained completely motionless. For a while more Neipas sat, empty, vacant, hollowed, as the ground beneath him rattled and the electric lights above fizzled in and out with a frying buzz; the tittering of heavy glass sounded cavernously from the great halls of the Eagles' Nest amid a profound silence left in the herd's wake.

Quiet. Neipas stared at the small, rectangular space upon which his feet rested. The booth could fit no more than the exact width of his sitting body, but Neipas, exhausted and dull as he was, didn't notice the discomfort of maintaining the same position inside that tight space. The waiter in the other booth — he seemed like no more than a plume of hair on top of a suit — faced away and kept inert; breathing, but otherwise not moving.

Only when Neipas' eartag shook, abruptly commanding his attention, did he rise and squeezed himself out of the booth, already in a hurry. The other waiter, motionless yet, remained.

37 - Gales of Flabella

A sombre quiet commanded over the halls of the Eagles' Nest. Neipas heard his steps echo from the marble, wobbling the still air like a specter hovering through a wall. Retreated deep inside their palaces and their soundproof chambers, the Eagles made no audible sign of their existence; and yet their presence was felt. The mess from the night's festivities seemed the work of some unearthly beast, an invisible demon — fields of trash immense and widespread, with grime deeply encrusted into the grounds, and vague scents of toxicity pervasive and lingering. Filth proliferated into every corner of the great sumptuous spaces of the Eagle Wing, and there was a general feeling that it entered the body, festered in the throat and the aching chest, and filtered down to the very soul.

It was a sickly feeling, and soon Neipas felt quite unwell from it. A vague nausea settled in his throat as he passed through hundreds of fellow workers rubbing water and soap across the rich floors, under the sped-up intensity of Drrawetz's oversight. The steward seemed to never sleep. His yelling rang from every wall, echoed in Neipas' head with the intensity of a million distant voices. He spotted him as though in a dream, walking with feet well raised above his head, stomping it with steps that boomed across the corridors, looking downward at the prostate janitors with arrogance, frowning at his enormous watch. By him Osir scrubbed with a frown, fuming under the weight of the yoke. Neipas trudged along the caravan of cattle heading into the Heiress' Palace, bobbing his head and straining to keep awake in a breathless swoon of mind and inconscience.

He had seen Janu in the kitchen. The cook looked mystified for a moment, but his smile, carved out of clay, hid the marks of premonition which shaded his brow. Conversations about last night filled the sleepy soundscape. It was all idle chatter — and yet, there was a palpable suspicion hovering in the general atmosphere, an impression of something wrong; that what had happened the previous night had, at last, crossed a line; a profound boundary of universal character, between basic decency and inhuman disregard, tolerable condescension and wanton cruelty. And yet, when Neipas asked, in a secretive tone, "Was that normal?..." — most shrugged, or giggled in perplexity, or exhaled nervously, and said "like what?", "what do you mean?" or some such reply...

Only Magpie wasn't quite able to hide her discomfort. She was evidently unnerved — looked at the verge of tears, even, sometimes; Neipas saw it, he was sure he saw it, through the haze of his own stare. Neipas thought it very odd, for she was usually the most self-possessed of them all; but he hadn't the mental or spiritual strength to conclude anything, and he had to pick up his tray and go.

They passed under lofty gates, they were led through opulent corridors filled with conspicuous paintings, in which various aristocrats stood in all manner of dandy poses between ornate frames of a dense gold. They walked toward the inner gardens... the passageway was involved in a burlesque spectacle of rabid colors and dance, a confusion of cushions and persian mats proliferating across the grounds beneath raised bodies bearing diamonds, in all hues of sparkle, under festoons of crimson silk hung over the ample space while the dancers and accompanying harlequins with swan and peacock masks moved about in chaotic sweeps of cloth everywhere. The ceiling rained flaxen powder. They walked through the height of the din, the orchestra cramming the halls. Bows trembled upon tense strings, a drum beat loudly in Neipas' head; the Conductor sang with arms raised... And even though Neipas passed very near them, between them, yet he was so exhausted that he couldn't discern their faces through the fog.

Screeching of wild animals in slow motion: the gardens opened up, an extravagant blooming of dull green powdered with glitter. Just above them the sky was beginning to gain color. The servants held lions and giraffes, elephants and boars on leashes and the clanking of chains reached the ear as if from afar. Among the sofas there was the wide gaping beak, monstrously open, of a child — the Heiress' son — and out of it was emitted a ceaseless and intolerable screech. There was a great commotion all around it, the Heiress' chaperone and many servants tried to temper the scion's tantrum with shiny gifts. Pillows and pillows littered the grass among the shrubs, of deep green and red hues and gilded embroidery, all shining, and sofas wherein lounged patricians drinking wine. Sovereign among them was the Heiress, reposing upon a throne of gemstones and furs, surrounded by swans and peacocks bearing immense feathers which they waved slowly, up, down, up, down (Neipas entered the cozy breeze of swaying plume)... He felt his head near the grounds as he bowed, and his arms were raised and offered the tray of delicacies to the modern monarch. They stood at the command of her hand. And as he rose, he saw. The villas and the estates of the palaces had walls enclosing their inner gardens, all along the giant terrace; but here they were by the side of the northern river and they could see the whole extent of Anubel's drop into the chasm of the air. Beneath the Hanging Gardens of Belab's peak the storm gathered and thickened with the massive fury of overwhelming indifference. The river cascaded freely into the darkening clouds, as though fertilizing it with blessings. And the patricians, sitting comfortably in their eden of pillows, observed attentively from above, for a moment halting the progress of their idle chatter; resembling gods, gods atop the mount, witnessing the marvel of their creations.

Beneath the stormy mass, hidden from their view, the broad unconcern of elemental forces plummeted fury upon humankind in swathes of rain and wind.

Neipas had to stand until all the food he had brought with him was gone. He rose his head from the tray with a slow motion and a blurred vision, brain-numb. With a short muted sigh from his caved and breathless chest he straightened himself, feeling the watery crimson in his eyes. The space sparkled with the swaying of jewels and the languid movements of the servants, who would come to grab plates and feed the mouths of the Eagles and wipe their beaks. Sounds of salivation slobbered the air wet. Droning sounds... Sometimes the Heiress' child came over and jabbed him on the calf, and Neipas succumbed to his knees. No reaction from anyone. Hot in the cheeks, he would watch confusedly as the Scion sunk his chubby hands into the plate and gorged himself savagely, spreading food all over himself and Neipas' arms as he smacked the cakes and candy aloud, between puerile mumblings and great clanking of jewelry; he would stop only to frown, angry at his inability to eat without stop, and would screech through the chewed food in his open beak. Muscle spasmed as his spit landed on Neipas' indifferent mask (the next moment he was up) and the storm churned beneath. Hours seemed to pass and the sun had not yet risen; as the sun ascended it got tangled in the thickness of the haze. The melody of the orchestra, the dances jingling with sparkle, the clinking of chains, the screaming of scions...

The windlessness of the air was stirred by the hedonistic chaos. Neipas thought of Eva in her house. He must call her. She'll throw a fit otherwise. But Neipas, full of hunger now, for he hadn't eaten for many hours, sensed his attention waver and his heavy, droopy gaze descend toward the tray of food. It looked delicious, all of it. Its aspect infused in him a mix of emotions, chief among which was appetite, fueling the general sense of disorientation clouding everything.

(Eva) Words of the storm morphed into worry. An impulse almost overcame him. He needed access to an *I* and he was sure the Heiress had one. Surely hers had more power, surely it could reach Eva. Could he ask?

His head swam into the imagination of this scenario for a second. But he was too hungry and senseless — the impulse got hold of him and he stepped forth toward the Heiress' chair. Nearly overcome with emotion, somehow his voice managed to penetrate the dense fog in his throat and come out.

"Excuse me," Neipas breathed just above a whisper, meekly.

There was no reaction from anyone at all; not a flinch — they all kept going at their business. Neipas, hesitating, took another step toward the

Heiress, approaching the rear of her throne.

"Excuse me," he said, a little louder now.

Neipas thought he saw one of the servants, who was then passing by, throw a quick glance in his general direction, not quite setting eyes on him. But he quickly concluded this was an illusion — in reality, no one had looked at him.

He was not speaking loudly enough, perhaps. Again he stepped toward the Heiress; and was within arm's length of the chair's back frame.

"Excuse me!" he yelled. Everyone stopped.

The first voice he heard was of the Heiress' son — a shriek that blasted his eardrum to shatters. It made him flinch and breathless, he shut his eyes in a tight grimace. Right away the chaperone approached him — Neipas heard his steps growing loudly (the soles of his shoes rang severely) fast, and he saw the shocked gazes of the Heiress and her patricians — they looked incredulous, outraged, livid — before he heard the chaperone snarl "how dare you" as he grabbed him by the arm with a choleric pull. Neipas' head snapped back; he experienced the sensation of emerging from warm water and thrusting into the freezing air in a sudden shock; his heart thumped and he opened his eyes.

He found himself with his chest empty of air; he was gulping a surge of it into his nostrils. He was farther away from the Heiress now, where he had begun; it seemed like he had never left. He held wide his burning, confused eyes. The sights unblurred slowly. His alarmed stare perceived the space: by the wild animals in leash, a group of servants scampered about mounds of shiny trinkets, bearing calm faces and full of agitated motions; the orchestra played still in the corridor; all around, the Eagles still lounged on their sofas and the Heiress reposed upon her throne, her little heir sulking deep into his, puffing and grinning, making weird noises. Neipas' tray was now empty somehow, the food all gone.

For a while he kept very still and quiet, discreetly numbing, weathering the startled tempest in his breast — wondering if anyone had noticed, and questioning whether he had fainted or fallen asleep, or what had happened... but everyone around him went on as usual, and seemed to pay no notice. He let himself settle, his tense features relaxed a little under the perpetual rigidity of his ox face. And when he gained enough awareness and courage, he quietly approached the chaperone.

"Pardon me," Neipas said. "The food has all been eaten. Can I be dismissed?" The chaperone, who didn't seem to take much notice of him, merely looked over to where the Heiress was. The personage waved her dismissive hand in a general manner; and the chaperone, particularly, repeated the gesture to Neipas.

He marched out, glimpsing the clouds underneath like a hellish mirage covering the horizon. Most of his colleagues had scattered out of there already. He left along with two others through the music, and they wandered disoriented and blank-minded, empty of soul, in the dizzying corridors of the Eagles' Nest. As they walked back to the Pigeon Wing the Summit bells tolled dreamlike above the weather, announcing the end of the 3rd Market-night, the end of the Summit. They rang together, the two bells, once, twice, three times; rang with the authority of absolute law, absolutely undisturbed by the tempest, absolutely unaware of its might.

On the way to the dormitories they saw a large commotion taking place by the Supervisors' Offices. An enormous group of folk (all the workers, it seemed) were gathered in a mass and raised their voices loud in anger. Facing the throng, Drrawetz waved his arms agitatedly, trying to lift his yell above the collective ruckus as everyone coalesced about his shrinking form. His mask was all discomfited; he looked frightened. Something serious was brooding, a vague promise of violence hovered bloody in the air. Neipas approached to find out what was happening.

38 - Et Tenebris in Lux Tenebret

Out of all droplets in that jittery sea of masks, the first he recognized was Osir's. Neipas approached him through the haze of his sight. Osir (who stood at the outer edge of the crowd) lowered his head, which had been craning above the rest in an attempt to see what was happening up front, and looked at Neipas.

"What's up man," Osir greeted his colleague with a languid nod. He seemed somehow slowed.

"What's going on?" Neipas asked. He unconsciously hoisted himself upon his toes and lifted his head, trying to interpret the significance of the disarray with a vague side-to-side motion.

"Everyone's freaking," Osir explained. "Drawetz told us no one can leave today."

"No one can leave?"

"Yeah, think so. 'Cause of the storm, he said. And he was trying to get us to keep working apparently, because of clauses in the contract or whatever... I dunno, that's just what I heard; just barely got here."

Osir's head alternated between Neipas' left side, Neipas' right side, and the mass of bodies against which they stood. Once, he looked straight at Neipas, and even as he looked at him it was clear he did not see him. His particular motion mimicked that of the general crowd — sleepy, with a somnambulant edge just underlying — though there was something calmer, more satiated about Osir's manner... his eyes were foggy, wrapped up in a new level of high; his scar did not twitch (thought Neipas as he perused the crowd and observed its faces). There was a savage edge patent in the semblances of the multitude; their eyes were monstrously open, shot filled with a lunatic red lividness; their masks in shambles, wax and clay spread messily about their neck, their limbs, and their hands, into which they sunk and shook their heads. Their whole conduct resembled that of a crazed addict bereft of his drug. Folk breathed heavily. Everyone was expectant, in the outer edges of the crowd all quiet.

The empty bird cages round the Office swung vaguely, nearly imperceptibly as they hung. He glimpsed Drrawetz shriveling beneath them and under the mounting voices of the workers.

A yell broke out of the crowd very suddenly — Neipas was violently roused out of the semi-reverie into which he had swooned — followed by a disjointed, collective bellow (a long *moooooooooo*) swelling out as the mass of bodies began moving on Drrawetz. Pushed onward in the dense march (meanwhile a great number of workers had joined the gathering and amassed

559

behind him) Neipas looked all about himself in utter confusion. There were a million deformed cattle rattling horns, making a frightening noise of rubbing blade amid bellows of protest, of desperation, of wrath. Flying into a panic, a sharp fear of the advancing herd, Neipas tried to turn back, pushing against the heavy multitude that pushed him. But it was impossible; and, fearing a stampede of boots upon his meager body, he let himself be swept in with the crowd as he heard Drrawetz's cries of impotence increasingly drowned in the growing upheaval.

Meanwhile there had been another shift. The pace of the crowd quickened — it seemed that Drrawetz had escaped the circle of rabid oxen that enveloped him — and all of a sudden Neipas found himself running with everyone, moving rapidly out of fear of falling and getting stepped on. It was all confusion and generalized panic; all ran, all sprinted, though Neipas didn't know where to. He hadn't the time or temperament to think about it in the furor of breathless panting; every time he tripped his heart would leap into his throat and his head hazed with horror; as he sensed the rushing swarm seizing him his muscles tensed and his instincts heightened, and his entire body geared entirely toward the purpose of survival. All moved onward in a craze, and though Neipas could not feel it, he himself opened his mouth madly, his nostrils fumed wide, his limbs palpitated in anger and his head shook convulsively.

The herd emerged in a burst out into the dawning Gardens and climbed the steps like a mad river rushing upward. With the running and the progressive widening of space, the mob had dispersed a little and Neipas noticed he had quite a bit of room to move about freely. Nevertheless, perhaps due to the heat and frenzy throbbing in him still, he kept on sprinting with the rest, running in the throng's flow, ever faster, ever louder, screaming with all the might in his lungs. Toward Drrawetz sprung the wrath of sleepless nights and accumulated frustrations, the whole weight of horns, clay and yokes borne aloft out of rage and without thought. The herd crashed headlong into the seats of the Auditorium, trampling over the rows and squeezing through the aisles without a moment's pause, and all together in a coalescing rush they ran above the palpitating chasm and climbed onto the stage as one throbbing mass of delirium. Trumpets blew furious pestilential winds from the orchestral abyss, the colossal curtains parted swiftly with a great exhalation of air; and the crowd slowed — then suddenly stopped.

They pressed together in a dense mass, body trapped against body without an inch to move. A wall of military bulls barred the passage — Drrawetz cowed at their feet, holding firmly onto the shiny boot of one of the guards. The bulls pointed their weapons at the cattle who, faced now with a long row of gun barrels, convulsed in total confusion, with some in the front trying to turn back and those in the back intending to push through, and the ones in the middle moving in all directions, creating a tidal swirl of disorientation from which emerged panicked bellows, animal noises, pandemonium. Neipas swung to and fro between bodies, nearly losing balance, and suddenly he felt a blow to the rear side of his head that sent a sharp jolt into his brain and filled him with anger. Before he knew it he was punching in all directions, clutching fur hard, pulling horns away from their heads with all his strength and the full blindness of fury. Everyone in the crowd did the same; it was a tempest of swinging fists and noises of knuckles hitting bone, panicked cries and enraged throttles sounding off between bleeding gum. A sound, a voice, blended with the yelling and it grew out of the mess. "Stop! Stop!" — amid stomping feet and screaming and the whole weight of the herd pounding against the surfaces it grew, it grew into many voices. The tide of bodies swung all in one direction and toppled over itself and all trampled atop each other in a sudden desperation not to get stuck under the horrified thunder of boots.

"Stop! Stop! Idiots! We'll fall!" — The voices were referring to the bottomless orchestra pit, whence a wind ensued furiously, imbued with the screaming of civilizations; and just then a greater shouting arose and Neipas fell into the cascade of weights and noises. He fought for his life and punched and kicked upward madly, he sunk his teeth into fur, clay, plume, wax, skin, into flesh, and ripped furiously; blood squirted through clenched teeth and flowed down quivering maw; and while some revolted against their exhaustion, nerves twitching, heads boiling with rage, muscles pushing against an inexorable swirl of confusions, yet others were giving in to fatigue, and seemed no more willing to do anything but to succumb to their fate.

Suddenly the glare of the stage lights broke off with a bang. A great cry rose and subsided; the Pearl softened. Only the soft light of the new sun shone upon them now, just above the clouds; and it seemed to becalm the herd. Imperceptibly, without a clear transition, the fighting stopped. Neipas found himself able to stand, and he was standing still upon his throbbing bruises, quiet among the equally still mob.

They directed their eyes to the edge of the stage, where folk coalesced worryingly about something and scattered slowly as a team of medics tried to penetrate the mass. The bulls retreated a few steps and gave the workers some room to breathe. Neipas was pushed back along gently, along with the rest; and like the rest he tried to discern what was going on.

Someone lay by the orchestra pit. Someone who was hanging halfway into it, with torso bent backward and arms pointing numbly toward the darkness. Neipas couldn't see the face. "He's dead," someone mumbled, and similar mumblings rippled in various tones across the quietening crowd.

They pulled the worker up by the legs so that he would not fall into the pit; and it was then that Neipas saw, hanging from the waiter's breast-pocket, Cesar's beautiful fountain pen.

39 - The Sun Maw

The undulating shade of the trees sheltered them from the heat. The day was feverish; under the blistering touch of the rays the seas sparkled and all lights seemed livid.

"They're moving ahead with the pipeline. The Mayor's signing the permit."

Orenda's voice rang into the fresh sound of a nearby spring. It sprinkled Neipas' distracted ear with its husky intonation, such as showers from a far-off fountain carried downwind. In his present absentminded state, Neipas couldn't grasp the drama unfolding behind her words or the alarm implied in her voice. It all sounded as distant as his mind now felt from his body... Among the light shade and the cool air, it breathed, with the gleam of the sun dancing warmly about his face as the foliage above fanned and whispered a coastal freshness, a scent of ocean on to the tip of his ear, the spiking hairs upon the back of his neck... Here, it was impossible to believe that the shade of this canopy and the embrace of its bark weren't invincible and eternal.

Neipas slept. Orenda leaned against an adjacent oak a couple of steps away, by the cliff; she perused the horizon vaguely. Faint, uneasy notions mingled with horrible pictures in the recesses of her mind; all was possessed by a hollow sentiment, an emptiness, a feeling vague and far. The immensity of the ocean, that rippling drape of blue extended over the earth, came to her withdrawn stare as if rolling out of a dream. Reality abstracted itself from her; the force of her determinations, clashing against the might of wealth and the incomprehensible wickedness of greed, retreated into herself with a tremble; a fright, and the creep of hopelessness snuck into her heart, and she, stolid, tried to draw from the ocean the strength to steel it, to shield it from the full brunt of a reality in which the basest among us perch at the nest of rule, where the sheer irrationality of gluttonous profit triumphs over the necessity of survival and the imperative of a good life; in which the few — and the vilest — subjugate the rest.

"A new pipeline will kill us all," she said to the approaching sound of steps behind her; and she felt intensely what she said. "Are they just crazy?"

Orenda had already recognized the soft crunching of fallen leaves and dust, had already identified the source of the calm, wobbled rhythm. Oshana stepped between Neipas' tree and Orenda's; she felt the rugged bark with the tip of her fingers, in a delicate, reverent gesture; then she placed her hand upon it intimately, contemplating the swaying canopy aloft.

"It didn't kill us yet," breathed Oshana in her steady tone of voice, expressive of the tranquil steadfastness of her spirit. "We have to keep on struggling — for the right to life — as long as we live."

Orenda said nothing. Her eyes kept firm upon the shiny horizon; they seemed focused between the neared lids, discerning, but without luster.

"There's something to be gained from loss. We gain ourselves, and the depth of our determination. It's what we must always shelter ourselves in."

"Wise words," Orenda snarked.

"They are wise words. Your gramma used to say them," Oshana replied in a smiling voice. "She also said: the depth of our determination is deeper than their pockets."

But Orenda said nothing. The sky, vast, gazed at her with the tenebrous quietude of a resting titan. Its blue was so vivid and clear, so immaculately without cloud, without break, that it seemed tepid and vacant, indistinct; inoffensive. It seemed, in its flatness of tone, to have neither beginning nor end, and to be neither close nor far. There was a deadness to it. It was with a silent might that it rose from the bottom of the ocean into its vague form of innocuous space without depth, without shape. There was a tension, too, in the immensity of the firmament; something toxic and faint hanging about them, in wait. Her imagination, perhaps — so she thought — but, yes; beneath its flat tranquility, she had the impression that the sky veiled a pending anger in its vastness —

something about to collapse upon them.

"We're out of time!" she uttered from her trembling lip, sobbing; and now her eyes shimmered full, horrified.

Oshana remained still. She, too, faced the horizon, and squinted at the vast gleam which proceeded from it; a large river of gold sprouted from the ocean, extending the sun about the waters. Its radiant fire sprinkled the waves alit with shine — the whole world seemed to sparkle before them, full of embers waiting to reignite.

The sun had inched closer to the end of the earth, and the horizon began to soften with the nearing heat, awash with a faint crimson glow.

"Don't worry," Oshana spoke, in their ancient language, after Orenda's weep had subsided into somber, mute breathing. "We'll see."

"We'll see, we'll see... We'll see, says the blind one," Orenda responded silently, after a pause. "Gramma used to say that too, remember?"

Oshana laughed heartily. The horizon ushered in a chill, heralding the incoming night. An increase of activity behind them announced that most folk were packing up and readying to leave. Cesar looked sadly toward the trees where they rested, wondering, with a hesitant pinch of his mustache, whether he should walk up and say farewell. Orenda's sinking eyes, her mute lips agape, her lumbering away wordlessly, all her manner denounced the paralyzing sorrow constricting her bosom when the poet told her what he had heard the Mayor speak in the gilded halls of the Eagles' Nest — this was about a year before he died in its folding heights.

Cesar thought best to leave her alone; and walked away from the grove.

Neipas remained in his barked nook, sleeping in the fig's embrace. Orenda, calmer now, considered his repose.

"I wish I could sleep like him," she said.

"Do you?" wondered Oshana, approaching him quietly.

"Look," Oshana pursued, pointing toward his quaking eyelids, the hidden shaking of his tucked lip, the drop of sweat crawling down the moistened, pasty waxen mask. "It isn't as it first seems. Look at the disquiet in him. He's not at rest."

Carried in the gust of this rising chill — the far breath of approaching darkness — Neipas traversed alien landscapes, roamed deeper into unsettling dreams.

He walked in a forest (was it this one he slept in now?). A spectral view arose before his frightened steps. Beneath his feet, ash — ash extending far beyond the reach of the eye. Ashen dust ascended, like breath out of a corpse, from the stomping of his shoe. Barren and still was the earth, and from it arose ghostly sticks of charred wood, emaciated, and erect toward the heavens in deadened repose. The sky was thick with a somber gray; smoke filled the air, lifted out of the burnt land.

Neipas walked in swelling awe and horror. As thousands of dead trees drifted before his eyes, amid the hanging fumes he spotted (he seemed to see) gray silhouettes with strange shapes scattered across the distance. Then he (thought he) saw one such silhouette in front of him yonder; it was motionless; and he walked forth to meet it. The vague contour gained definition as his eyes wandered further into the mist; a form grew in the receding shade. It was the statue of a fleeing goat; an effigy of pale, speckled marble. Neipas reached his hand for it; and pieces fell upon the touch, pieces of dust scattered into the smoke. At this point he had the impression of smell, of cooked meat. Piercing his hand into the ribs of the animal, he felt its hot, blistered skin as it disintegrated about the thick air. And in the entire extent of this forest such animals proliferated; there were millions and millions of them, an endless confusion of sculptures of ash, of burnt animals of every species upon Earth and the Skies. Everything here was dead. Everything upon the entire land was dead; everything upon the planet. (No), not everything. Amid the flakes of ash filling the earth, insects flourished; scarabs, spiders, roaches copulated and multiplied quickly over the lands. Neipas himself was neither dead nor alive, nor was he perhaps dreaming. The shock of seeing that infinitude of charred flesh might have plunged him aloft of this nightmare; the sight of horror in the animals' suspended faces, running away from the conflagration that had finally consumed them, made his heart pound with a tremendous quiver.

But all of a sudden he came to the edge of the forest. Where it ended, Belab Square began. It was different, however. The multitude of spiders had weaved giant threads shooting all across the air round the tower, making the space dense with silk. Millions of people were trapped in the web; bodies hung upside down, obliquely, in every position and contortion of head and limb; the bodies seemed in decay, and all were still and seemed asleep. And the threads propagated all from the tower, whose shape was erected monstrously amid the haze, and dissolved itself in the haze, and blended in ashen powder, its core thinning like an accursed trunk and summit spreading like a blooming canopy; the whole fading and omnipresent structure pulsed, and in its midst pulsed a dark sun rimmed in flaxen gleaming.

As Neipas abandoned the burnt woods, the fumes dispersed and the blue of the sky was revealed — and he saw that the sky was the ocean, and the waters extended over the heavens. In it a plague of godly magnitudes propagated, in the form of a swarm of flies, locust, and moth which formed a black mass dominating vast upon the firmament, and they presided over all beings alive and dead. Petroleum then rained — very quickly it was pouring from the dark and blue waters — precipitating to the ground whence it had been torn. The tar soaked the land with its muddy substance, and the web disintegrated in its final descent, freeing the people trapped wherein.

All were upon the ground now; all were stuck in the tar, perhaps (no one moved). Only one fellow — well-mannered, suited up, donning a very respectable eagle face — rose from the immensity of mush swelling from the earth, which bubbled up, ever higher, until it nearly drowned those who knelt in it. Immediately upon seeing him, Neipas flapped his arms frantically in a desperate attempt to take flight — but he too was trapped in the oil. The Eagle took something from the inside of his suit jacket (Neipas peeked a holster) and, cackling uncontrollably from its open beak, he lit a match.

Oshana and Orenda waited until the sun touched the horizon before they spoke of leaving. They had been in silence, watching the change in colors that came over the prospect, the solemnity of red and orange assuming the range. The spectacle of existence and the wonders of reality touched Orenda's heart, and she settled in a calm; tired, she felt the anticipation of hope upon her spirit, and knew she'd be ready to retake the fight the next morning.

"Maybe we should wake him up," she breathed into the long quiet of crying seagulls afar.

"Yes. We should... Let's take him to his home. Everyone else left."

"Hm-hm," Orenda nodded. Neither moved yet.

"He's been sleeping for a couple of hours now," said Orenda, and after a pause she pursued, "you know he works with Cesar?"

"Cesar the poet?"

"Yes. At the eagles' nest."

"I knew he worked at the belab, but you say the eagles' nest?"

"That's what he was telling me before he fell asleep."

"Hm," Oshana muttered contemplatively, her gaze fixed yet upon the distance. "Cesar is a good man. They are good men both. Better than they think they are."

When Neipas awoke the sun was sunk halfway into the end of the ocean. The distance was all a fiery crimson; as though an immense fire ravished the deep. A queasy sensation of unreality was retained in Neipas' startled mind, and the interrupted dream seemed to pervade the vastness yet. In his blurry and confused eyes, jolted from the darkness of sleep, the sunset horizon appeared like the open mouth of a titanic beast, like a boiling maw foaming blood and seething with building wrath. The view, sinister and macabre, mingled with the horrible images of his dream, of the entire world burning in flames that rose heaventall from an earth steeped in oil, and spread throughout the land, sparing nothing in its advance. His eye didn't see clearly out of the recent slumber, and burned in it still was the image of the Tower, that giant shape made vague by the dust, gaining a distinct form in the towering inferno. Dream and reality confused themselves in bright teary reds, calm; in the dream it had been as serene as this, for no one made a sound — those who opened their mouths had no voices. Everyone died in the fire.

In the transition between dream and the crimson sky of sunset, Neipas seemed to grasp a sort of faint revelation — but the impression of it never reached his consciousness, and soon it was gone. He fell asleep again in the back of Orenda's car, and dreamt no more.

40 - Embalmment in Shrouds

They buried Cesar that same afternoon. Wishing to make the ceremony discreet, they chose for it the small plot under the Gazebo, which was hidden beyond the winding, thorny greenery of the lower terraces. Nevertheless, many came and watched, though most did not know him; they were there for the spectacle of it, driven by curiosity, horrified and fascinated by the stampede that had killed him. A crowd of pigeon masks clustered and lengthened in succession, disappearing into the dappled shadows of the wood. Everyone gazed wide-eyed as Cesar's corpse was brought in on a stretcher, his head covered in wraps; apparently the face had been badly trampled in the confusion of boots. He passed under the eyes of many low-headed workers, still donning their heavy cattle masks and their yokes and cowbells, affected by exhaustion and a sense of unreality, of numbness. A strange taciturnity reigned among them; a mood both mournful and aloof; a general indecision on how to react, perhaps.

The makeshift funeral was presided by a popular Priest, a peacock who donned the mask of pelican very contritely. He waved his laced sleeves dramatically toward the crowd; it was rumored that it had been him who called all those spectators, from whose midst popped many *I*s drawing photos. Scouring those masks in disorientation, then looking up toward the Gazebo, Neipas unconsciously expected to find Cesar's boyfriend Kasim, whom he had spotted praying, just yonder atop the steps, barely a day ago; a day made of ages. Next to him, Magpie visibly struggled to control her breathing and was forced to use her inhaler a few times. Marlene the Lawyer stood near, quiet and aghast. They watched as Cesar passed beneath them with face wrapped in shrouds, to be veiled wholly and forever under a little, hidden patch of dirt at the top of the world — a little plot which would be called "the graveyard" by its inhabitants from then on.

Many were wounded in the stampede. The most serious cases were rushed to the infirmary, where a team of doctors and nurses cared for them. In the end, Cesar was the only fatal victim.

Neipas took the *I* to his ear as his sister called him. Her worried voice filtered through the electric mouth of the small mirror — she wanted to know if he was ok, Axiac was all over the news, looks like the storm is severe, looks like it may destroy a lot of the city, they say it's something unprecedented, that no one could see it coming (Neipas chuckled sourly at this; meanwhile he had turned his eye into the *I* glow again).

It was only after the call that he lifted his head. He had heard her words but listened not to her meanings; his speech had been composed of mumblings ("yeah" — "I'm not sure"), he was far away; shrunken and as if drunk. He looked up now and still he was far away, and he processed the distance through a thousand eyes seeing between reality and himself.

[Snow in the northern capital, plagues along the silk road, Columbia sanctions Persia and ice in the poles crumbling into the sea, record number of refugees, camps and dancing songs, the jubilee of the Horse athletes, talking masks, smiling masks, masks with open mouths, masks with no eyes, the things and things and things and things and things 00100001010011101111111111].

And the *I* kept feeding the mind...

The whole morning he spent inside the Webwork's glow, hypnotized into a thousand fragments. By the end of it he forgot himself and almost forgot Eva and everybody; amid the general mental exhaustion his concern receded into the dormant soul.

He had wandered past many heads like his own, each bowing before his or her *I* across the whole space of the Pigeon Wing — in its Dormitories, in its Food Hall, in its Gardens. Everyone was off work and waiting. Since no one could leave, the Eagles wanted the workers to keep on working through the storm. A small committee of the cattle had been more or less elected to negotiate new terms — as everyone had had enough of Drrawetz' tyranny and the grueling amount of hours they had to grind through. None in the committee were supervisors; the workers had chosen from among their ranks whom they thought best fit to represent them. Among these was Osir, who was at that time in one of the conference rooms, negotiating with the new Chief Supervisor and his team.

All in the worker herd were called to a general meeting in the Food Hall. That supervisor who winked perpetually and spoke to them encouragingly had been promoted to the top position to succeed the maligned Drrawetz. From atop a table, the new Chief Supervisor explained to the herd the new rules governing work, which had been agreed upon after negotiations with the workers' counsel.

First of all rules: no one had to abide by them. One could drop out, if one wished; their contracts' duration had expired. Whoever wanted to could stay and sign a new agreement. Pay would be increased. No more random call-ins — the workers would be assigned specific shifts, one per day, with large resting periods in between. The demands of the work could drive shifts into extra hours, the Chief Supervisor admitted; but those potential extra hours were covered by the new contract and would be paid for. As soon as a shift was declared over, he said however, all should feel free to turn off their eartags until next morning (some stood in amazement at finding out it was possible to turn them off). There were questions, and the Chief Supervisor answered them patiently. He deflected whatever didn't have to do directly with the workers — there would be a briefing for everyone later regarding more general matters — though he did say the elevators were out of commission, so it was impossible to leave until the storm ended; but more details would be disclosed soon. He seemed very candid, sympathetic, energetic; and he wore the mask of the ox like the rest of them. Everyone took a liking to him, and they all signed the new contract.

The big briefing was held in the Auditorium. Horns rose from the stairways behind the fidgety heads of pigeons who amassed anxiously. All turned to the stage, waiting with nervous stares under the shade of the Great Facade. Beneath the steep cascade of steps, trees and tents, the fields of clouds extended to cover everything. Many had the sensation of standing in a ship sailing in an interminable ocean of fumes.

Finally, a set of oxen rushed in from the stage wings and set up pulpits and microphones. After a few minutes, a crew of Journalists stepped out of the backstage. Editor Moldura, Neipas' former professor, was among them. Rising to the pulpits, the Journalists solemnly placed on their peacock heads the Lion mane and face, symbol of the nation, voice of its people. They stood solemnly before the soundless crowd — and even their parrots were quiet in the absolute silence. (But as he strained his ear Neipas seemed to catch a faint, deep pulse emanating from the clothed orchestra pit).

The Editor began by tapping the microphone. "Hum... (Is the mic on?) Oh — Good afternoon, everyone." He nodded over to the Journalist at his side.

The Journalist cleared his throat and, nearing his jaw to the microphone, proceeded to explain the situation. He repeated what the Chief Supervisor had said earlier. The elevators were not working and, since they were the only way in and out of the complex, it was impossible to leave. No one questioned this curious architectural arrangement, which was explained by the fact that the way to the base of the tower was too long for stairs, so all emergency exits were carried out by flight. But no one could fly out of there either, the Journalist reported. According to sources, the storm was bad. Very bad. "How bad?" someone yelled. Apocalyptic, something unprecedented. It stretched on for miles and the vast expanse it covered was being absolutely plummeted by wrathful torrents of wind and water. Communications towers and powerlines across Axiac were being felled by elemental forces which the Journalist, suddenly bombarded with questions from all sides, was having trouble describing.

"Yes, basically —" he explained, "according to sources, all communications in and out of Axiac are off. We're not really sure why yet but it looks like it has to do with failure of critical infrastructure..." A feeling of stress swept through the chairs of the Auditorium, and after the word 'off' was uttered out the pores of the microphone everyone stopped listening and frightened murmurs arose from the audience. The Editor spoke into his own mouthpiece and bid the spectators "please, folks", gently telling them to be quiet.

Silence was again settled in the Auditorium and the Journalist, clearing his throat, continued. "But it may not be all bad," he reported, vaguely gleeful as he balanced himself on his toes. All patrons were welcome to remain in the facilities and make use of all its services. They had food, board, and all necessities. The Anubel was running on powerful backup generators, so everyone still had access to electricity and to the Webwork; and for an extra fee they could also make use of the spas and saunas of the 5th floor, as well as a variety of other amenities (he added in small letters that "aforementioned necessities would also imply small fees") — and they could ride out the storm in comfort. Moods relaxed a little, though worry pulsed through the Auditorium yet as thoughts about their peers beneath the storm roiled over the crowd. Neipas saw many checking their *I*s convulsively, among them Janu the cook; he seemed to be trying to reach his family.

The session lasted a while — in the meantime more chairs were set up on stage, and a series of guests, interviewed by different journalists, came and went to speak about the storm, how it was serious, how it meant nothing, how it was an omen of rough times to come, how it might actually be a good thing — with entertaining breaks in-between, so that by the time Q&A time came everyone was very much dulled out. There weren't many questions. Most of them were frivolous, mingled up in whole speeches that led up to nothing; though there were two questions that roused Neipas' attention in particular (he sat on the balustrade in the back, supporting himself with his arm around a big vase sculpture) — the first one:

"How long will the storm last?"

"We do not know at this time, unfortunately."

And the last:

"Do we have enough food for the duration?"

"According to official sources, the food stocks would last for years."

Everyone was satisfied at that point.

41 - Noxxe

Given the choice between permanent shifts, Neipas chose the morning's. He was transferred over to a new dormitory where only morning shift workers slept, so that the others might doze as long as they wanted without the alarm waking them. Neipas himself went to bed very early before the first day of work above the storm; his eyes were covered by blinds against the lights, and his mind sunk black into a kind of stupor, adrift in roiling nightmares long, before seeping into true, restful slumber.

*

Baron Noxxe's palace resembled a fortification built in the golden age of the caliphs. Its surfaces were intricate with starry patterns replicating themselves across, cut with elaborate passages and porticoes, doorways the shape of oblongs with many pointy tips, framed with graceful curtains embroidered with gold and leading to inner courtyards round pretty little fountains, or inner gardens of hedges whence ensued the laughter of children and smells of picnic. It was said the Baron had a fascination for the middle lands of the Orient, birthplace of wealth, civilization and empire. The decor of the magisterial property derived from those far regions; the opulence on display was dazzling, nothing like the tackiness of the seaside megahouses Neipas had worked in for the past year.

"Goddamn," whispered Osir, nodding appreciatively with his glassy eyes and skewed corner of lip, breathing in the pleasant gilded air. He led the group as Supervisor for the first time. He — and a few other workers — had accepted the role in the negotiations between the workers' committee and the Eden Solutions officials; though he had accepted it quite unwillingly. He would shed the weight of the title by joking frequently — his own authority displeased him. Now, however, he was quiet, oppressed by the weight of opulence, much as Neipas and all walking in that procession of lowered horns were. The Bull guards, flaunting their own horns proudly, watched them as they passed.

As soon as they crossed a gem-studded gate, the walls became bare and the children's sound ceased. They went through a corridor sparse, interspaced with bland paintings of past chairmen of NoxxeSocony.

Osir knocked gently on the door. Four seconds, and it unlocked with a sharp click, then opened slowly of its own accord.

On the other side they beheld an unbelievable sight — Neipas had to suppress the gasp. The ceiling of the bedroom soared above his head and the floor projected itself into walls very distant; the space was immense, of an unreal vastness, and he couldn't believe those walls fitted within the physical boundaries of the Anubel's narrower upper floors. Nevertheless, save for its colossal dimensions, the room could be said to look very simple. On the wall through which they had entered, and above the door, a giant screen was mounted, much larger than anything any of them had ever seen in a cinema; indeed it was bigger than they could imagine possible. And then, there was a bed — and the bed was the size of a whole field, a whole stadium could have been built to frame it. Far away from the waiters, at the end of the bed, a single mound arose from the otherwise perfectly smooth, blood-red covers. It was the Eagle waiting for his breakfast, leaning onto giant pillows of feathers.

The cowbell rang under his chin. Trying hard to contain his astonishment and maintain a semblance of normality, Neipas bowed low and began the long trek around the bed. He flinched when he noticed no one came with him, but he kept walking.

It felt fairly like a hike, so many steps he had to take to cross his path. All sort of wild thoughts and dreamlike feelings passed through him as he marched by the flank of Bull guards stationed by the walls; as Neipas beheld the Eagle growing closer, a suspense of fear intensified and consumed him. He remembered the last time he had seen the Petroleum Baron, eras ago now it seemed, in Moloch's estate, the night of the waltz. That waltz had been such a bombardment upon the senses, with so many claims upon the memory, that Neipas had naturally been kept from thinking about it by some instinct of sanity and self-defense. Now with the sight of Noxxe in his fixed stare, his mind searched his soul — which had lately retreated deep within and out of intellect's reach — for the memory of the Head Gardener's words, words addressed to the Baron. He had spoken of fires. What had he meant? The Gardener had spoken of the Oyate, he had implied complicity with the arsonists of their land. Cesar had told him the Gardener was involved with Penaguiar. Perhaps Orenda had been right; perhaps Penaguiar had the fires set. Was Noxxe in on it too? Perhaps there was some conspiracy afoot.

Neipas' heart fluttered with these questions; his mind felt to him too dim to bring them to any conclusive answer: their whole conduct seemed to him so cruel and stupid, so beyond the grasp of belief. His thoughts frizzled. All the rest of the waltz flashed in buoyant sparkles, like vague reminiscences in the midst of slumber. The dance, the wheezing gale, the orgies in the golden gardens, the violence and the noise, all the demonic swings of crowds popping under the incessant fireworks, all cascading down the terraces with the lulling melody of the Peacock and its thousand eyes... He recalled seeing again that strange shackled being from the slaughterhouse, from the underground, way below — By Mary, had he actually seen that strangely masked Midget? Neipas began to doubt the impression of his own senses had any grounds upon reality (if there was any such thing still) and knew no more whether his thoughts corresponded to memory, dream, memory of dream, or complete and total imagination... Meanwhile his body kept moving on its own. Outside giant windows (only one had shutters open) the fumes from the Temple in the bottom terrace puffed up meditatively, like exhalations from an old locomotive. In the titanic screen on the wall, a series of numbers and charts — the type one would associate with stocks and the overall accounting of profit — flashed in front of a black background. Baron Noxxe watched these numbers intently from his bed. Ostrich's popular resistance against Iblis' expansion, the Oyate's protests against the construction of the largest transnational oil pipeline in the world through their lands in the east, and the steady decline in global oil prices had sent the value of NoxxeSocony Corp. stock staggering downward. Developments in Oyateland were cause for hope. All legal permissions for the pipeline's construction had been granted and the wildfires stifled any protests that may have carried on, which had the double advantage of clearing the forest for building and saving on military contractors to watch and remove protesters if police needed aid. The nuisance to the east was nearly dealt with. Troubles at Ostrich would be tougher to overcome, but the force of the law was on his side and could be employed against the masses in those rookeries. And there was the storm now too...

Most disconcerting was the slump in oil prices, because it made those investments worthless in the first place. The pipeline was needed to bring in the extracted sludge from Joachim Valley in the far north. It was an inhospitable alien zone, where vast fields of tar the size of nations lay exposed under the hot sun, oozing toxic stenches and fumes of charred soil, all of it waiting for drills and pumps and the whole force of the latest industrial machinery to come and suck up the dark blood of a dead earth. There were continental loads of it — worth billions. But it was a type of oil that was difficult to process, a heavy crude oil mixed in sand and clay, costlier to extract, harder to refine; and with the price of oil so low, the cost of producing was higher than it could be sold for. The prospects were profitless for the moment. No matter — the Market would turn things around in time. Doubtless, Arnold, his Ministers and Legislators, all wardens of the state would soon grant the cash he requested. The Minister of Energy was an old chap; and the Minister of the Treasury had been Noxxe's subordinate but a year ago. The Lobbyists under the Baron's command — many were former Lawmakers — were actively pushing for the invasion of Persia, for there was no faster way to drive up petroleum prices than war upon petroleum-exporting nations. He had only be patient. Riches lay in wait just under the ground, Noxxe needed only wait for the moment most propitious. They were his for the taking. He had worked for that company his whole working life, since he was but a youngster forming yet his perspective upon the world. The Baron had grown in it, he had grown to lead it, he had grown to become it. The company's success and worth became bound up with his worth and success, with all the drops and rises that entailed the progression of such an enterprise. Evidently such wavering flights were made always in the highs and never at the level of ground, so rich the company was. But it was imperative that it grew richer yet; he had that obligation toward his shareholders, his very honor was dependent on the success of the task... As the Baron ruminated, he regarded the approaching waiter with suspicion. What in the devil could be taking him so long? Sat atop his perch at the head of the bed, Baron Noxxe puffed and waited.

Neipas was at last concluding the long path around the bed. At its upper edge he stopped and, once again, bowed.

"Good morning, sir!" he greeted very loudly, for the Baron was still somewhat far away. "It is an exquisite honor to serve you this morning!" Baron Noxxe faced him with his Eagle mask. His visage was like the apparition of an ancient deity — stern, and impersonal. It impressed Neipas with fright as he placed both his knees upon the mattress and began dragging them along, to cover half the width of the bed toward the Baron's location on the pillows in the very middle. To cross the interval between the edge of the bed and those pillows required a series of elaborated maneuvers and the utmost concentration. Neipas, being upon his knees, couldn't touch the covers with his shoes either, all while holding the bulging tray. As it was impossible to support himself on his knees only, and with his feet up, he had to place his elbows on the mattress and move upon elbows and knees. The trip lasted an eternity. It racked his nerves and ate at him to the edge of despair, but somehow — by some unknown source of calm within him — Neipas managed to hold his composure. The surface of his skin twitched and trembled spasmodically by the time he arrived; but the mask covered it.

Bowing, his forehead sunk into the soft mattress, and his butt lifted along with the tray as it was presented to the powerful executive — it was reminiscent of an offering in a rite of yore, of a sacrifice to an old god. Here was the mighty Baron now. His white face, golden beak, fiery amber eyes, and portly torso were easily distinguished from afar; but now that Neipas was so close, he was able to see the very rotund belly shaping the form of the covers over it, and he could smell the stale reek of the Eagle's breath as it oozed out of wheezing lungs. In his proximity, Neipas discerned the decadence and rot of this fellow.

It was an infinite relief to him when the Baron signaled that he wanted to be left alone and would not require assistance in eating. He did this by a dismissive wave of his sapphire-studded hand, as if shooing off a fly — but to the waiter it was bliss. Neipas placed the tray solemnly on the Baron's belly and, thanking profusely his pittance of a tip, proceeded to make the excruciating way back to the edge of the bed upon his knees and hands. Neipas receded into the mammoth landscape, traversing the room's length; walking slowly, as he had to, and with decorum.

"Thank God I gave you that pill," whispered Osir as Neipas merged back into the team, laughing with his defaced mouth. They went out through the corridors of the palace to serve the other Eagles, who awoke now among their jeweled sheets.

*

Neipas slept. A sensation grew in his sleep. It was a sensation of consciousness, a vague perception of the darkness embracing him. The darkness was heavy, it was dense; but yonder, beyond the thick of gloom, he thought he spotted a light quivering. It quivered blurry and almost imperceptibly; perhaps it wasn't moving at all. By an indistinct levitating motion, the light became — both slowly and suddenly — closer to him. And in the light Neipas saw, distant and shadowed, vague and tarnished, as if he were seeing it through a very old mirror — in the light he saw his own mask, and in the torpid inconsciousness of his mind he wondered whether he was wearing the semblance of the ox, or that of the pigeon, or that of the self. In his sleep he wondered whether he slept truly.

It was the light of the *I*, and what he saw was how the *I* saw him; a red dot blipped above the glass, growing and shrinking at short intervals. Someone spoke to him across the Webwork.

It was Eva. There was some trepidation in the numbness of his spirit, but before he properly realized it his fingers had already moved into the glass, unveiling her message.

> **EVA:** *MESSAGE NOT DELIVERED. PLEASE CHECK YOUR CONNECTION AND TRY AGAIN.*

Again Neipas saw her clip, the recording from inside her apartment. He watched her window tremble violently, as though from cold or fear, rattled and drowned by the howling gales. He noticed that Eva said something before the clip ended; something which he couldn't understand. The sound of torrential wind overwhelmed her voice.

There was the same message from Edazima; none of his texts had gotten to her. In a pulling depth of torpor he wondered what had become of her and the kid.

Neipas replayed the rushing torrent from his childhood; the catastrophe that ended his past life. He heard again the roaring sounds, the screaming rains. The forest titans succumbed once more before his horrified wet glare. Looking into the mirrored wall of the Columbaria with wide, blank eyes, he observed vaguely how unwell the wax had molted. It drooped tiredly, with a look of despondency and madness, and it seemed livid in the overwhelming brightness of the dazzling corridor.

42 - Cesar and Kasim

The storm clouds extended like a veil over the earth. Its expanse spun peacefully under the Gardens and produced no sound, like a thick mantle over the deathbed which muffles all voices. Little news arrived from the world beneath it. Sometimes the Journalists and Analysts, up on stage, would vaguely describe statistics about Axiac, statistics measured in damaged property costs and the numbers of mortally wounded, and they wore serious masks which made everyone nod pensively.

In the meantime the Market and the Merchants continued their activity uninterrupted. There were many trinkets to be sold still and therefore no time could be lost. The bells rang with abandon in the mornings and in the evenings, ushering the pigeons into different cotes of comfort and convenience. Wines flowed freely and delicacies were abundant. The children ate many sweets, and with time the adults learned to appreciate the sweetnesses of their candies too. Life was good and nobody could complain.

Still, sometimes — but this was rare — some pigeon would break into a wail and wonder loudly about that universe far below them. Such demonstrations were quickly put down with many looks of scorn. "What," said one of the Academics, triumphantly approaching one of his audience members, "how can one complain? Behold these charts — notice how the rates of survival have dramatically improved in the past 200 years! Fatality rates will likely be much lower proportionally than they would be then." But incidents like this were easily forgotten — and everyone delved into the drunken mazes of Market booths so that everything could be forgotten quickly.

Work continued. Every morning Neipas would emerge to work his shift — and more and more he was appointed to work the Eagle Wing. He was good at keeping silent and invisible, and the Chief Supervisor seemed to like him. Every morning Neipas would leave his *I* in his locker of possessions and pass between the buzzing frames of the scanner into the opulence of the other side of the Nest. He served all types of important personalities. Ministers, lawmakers, judges, monarchs from exotic nations, famous artists and editors and opinion-makers, prominent economists and marketers and executives, chairmen of important corporations, owners and masters of industry, rulers of empires... The bulk of the apparatus of cattle-made machinery geared toward serving their needs. There were breakfasts, lunches, dinners, snacks, drinks of all sorts at every hour. Cleaners and decorators moved about all the time, for the premises were to be kept spotless and beautiful at every moment. The majesty of the Eagles' Nest must be brought to bear; the Eagles' comfort and pleasure was paramount.

In those days Neipas would often wake very early, long before the bell rang. It was as though the blinds were no longer enough to keep out the strong glare of the lamps. He felt them pressing into the blind-cloth, like an animal seeking shelter from the heat in the deep darknesses of his eyes. The light scratched his skin and made him itch. It possessed and roused him, made him stir with little tremblings all over. Little by little the very touch of the sheets irritated his skin; and he could do nothing but get up through the ache, breathing deep, swallowing dry, with rheum gluing the lids of his eyes. There was a restlessness assailing him always. It was torment; that though he was always tired, he could never rest.

Fidgety sensations drove him to seek the open air of the Hanging Gardens. The heavens in his midst were waking up slowly, bearing the serenity of dawn. Neipas walked up among the fading stars, consumed in tones of violet, calmly spirited away with the scents of waking flowers. The Market dozed still in the Gardens, always with one eye open; a few merchants already walked about, preparing their wares with shouts which rang like mumbles, swallowed by the general silence. Their masks conveyed the infinite patience of oxen. And the pigeon head of Neipas passed them in a quiet agitation, stirring to itself, seeking a place to be alone. Instinctively it headed to the little gazebo on the 2nd terrace's isolated hill.

When he passed the forested area and he began the climb up the narrow stairway Neipas stopped; the feeling he should pay his respects to Cesar took over his senses. He circled back and walked past the stairway into the yard beneath the gazebo. He halted some distance from it. By the poet's grave was his lover, the Gardener's helper.

Kasim lay prostrate by the humble tombstone, honoring the soul of his lost half, which had been whisked away in the shouted wind among a stomping of hoofs. The kneeling figure was framed in the tender glow of waters; the river fell just beyond him in a sleepy rush. And yet, even where he stood Neipas could hear, carried by the quietude of dawn, the tremblings and sobbing of the mournful worshiper. He wept, wept, wept uncontrollably. Over the terraces and the storm clouds Kasim cried for Cesar, love of his life, who had been taken in the inexorable flow of time beyond the great cascade, never to surface again.

From the patch of grass before the tombstone sprouted flowers, and from amid the flowers rose a string fastened to a balloon, erect and quiet under the canopy which brushed the gazebo; all quiet in the windlessness. All the elements listened to the wails in silence. Without voice. Senseless — as if the very air had succumbed to the death which had taken the poet.

A rainbow then appeared among the goldening droplets, as though materialized from some spirit world made visible by the sunrise. The air twinkled with the mystic light of the Pearl. Against the background of tranquil sky ascending from the clouds, the scene was moving, picturesque. The exotic prayer and the dramatic lighting appealed to Neipas' sense of aesthetics. It was beautiful. It stirred his soul with a profound sense of the immateriality which binds all life; something incomprehensible and, because of it, restless. Neipas watched the man, but not for long. He was taken by an anxious impulse common to those living in that age; and he placed the *I* glass between himself and the vision. With a motion of his finger the scene materialized in the glass; held beyond the chains of time.

As he beheld the photograph behind the screen a voice called out to him.

"Hey —" Neipas looked up, startled, at the mourner approaching with quick steps. Immediately Neipas sensed a panic in his voice that jarringly contrasted with the peaceful sight embalmed in the *I*'s picture.

"Did you just take a photo?" asked Kasim, stepping up very close to Neipas, abruptly stretching his neck to catch a glimpse of the *I* glass.

Neipas reflexively dodged the sudden approach. "Well I —" he began, taken aback. "I saw you there and it was such a nice composition... Sorry, I couldn't resist." — he babbled for he knew not what to say.

"Can you please delete the photo?"

Kasim beseeched. There was desperation in his voice.

"Can you please —" he reached over to Neipas in a breathless and weeping jab, trying to take the glass from him.

"Ok I'm sorry! I'm sorry, ok?"

Neipas deleted the photo before Kasim's staring eyes. Reaching the glass, the mourner rubbed his finger on it a couple of times to make sure no more photographs had been captured. A couple of pictures of the Gardens flipped inside it.

"Ok thanks," he said abruptly, through contained tears — and walked away quickly, sniffling.

Neipas stood alone over the red clouds.

He was ashamed, his heart made heavy with regret. He felt like the sleaziest and most immoral of photographers, like the gossip merchants and pickpockets that were called paparazzi in those days. He brooded over the violation he had committed. Foolish, Neipas had trespassed a holy sanctuary of intimacy: a hidden place where love and grief can express themselves without shame. Filled with shame himself, he stood, his heart grimacing. That feeling nailed him to the grounds of the graveyard for a while until finally, glancing sorrowfully at Cesar's tombstone, he strode away shaking his head, mumbling pejoratives at himself.

Soon, the summit bells rang, and the Market-day revolved to another beginning.

43 - The Garden on the First Terrace

At the end of one of those days, Neipas found himself near the Library. He remembered he had been there once.

He must have been following some tune. Only now that it had faded did he notice it (had it been in his earbuds?). It had contracted to a mute, hollow sense of a pulse, a deep sound from somewhere beyond the walls spreading wildly away from him.

He had been out deep in the hollow threads and chambers of the Webwork, floating along its submerged currents. Far away he had been; shrunken and as if drunk. He looked up now and still he was far away, and he beheld the view through a thousand eyes seeing between himself and reality. Vaguely, he processed where he was.

This was one of the most remote areas of the Columbaria. For a long time he had roamed its vast corridors, walking very fast, storming into an unconscious of muscle and mind and straining himself out of fatigue, into numbness. In his march he passed by many doors, thousands of doors, an infinitude of doors facing mirrored walls, walking alongside his pigeon-masked reflection for miles of corridors replicating endlessly into an unending horizon of strong electric lights.

Now the walls were coated in mirrors no longer, and were instead covered with wallpaper dotted with strange glyphs. Next to him was the plaque reading *Library*. The pulse sounded beyond the door, which faced him ajar.

There was no one else there. The silence was absolute save for the strange pulsing sounding from somewhere in the confines of the tower, which, in its very vibration, only deepened the quietude. It was as though a sound swallowing all sounds, a mere pulse of silence. Neipas quickly felt surging within him a certain fear. He had emerged from a world of noises and convulsive twinkling; and the sudden absence of sound was eerie. This soundlessness only deepened further and was as if pending, as if the Anubel held its breath; he felt as though a yell might suddenly break out of nowhere at any point. Ill at ease, he looked about himself. From the corridor was cast the sterile and uniform white glow of the lamps, permeated with the fumigated air of hospital. The silence sounded out of it — and the pending yell. In the Library's door he detected the throb; it pulsed almost melodiously; far off.

(What time is it?) It wasn't yet late and Neipas decided to enter the door, which opened again to an immense flash of radiance; which then subsided and widened into the fantastic towers of shelves crammed with books. He walked again among them, again along its curvy paths, watching mesmerized the moths flapping their wings among the shelves, crawling between the volumes, between the myriad ladders shooting into the dark ceiling. This time, Neipas did not stop to peruse the tomes. He was possessed by an urge to walk on — for he had remembered the Midget in manacles in the depths of those spaces, and determined to find the occult creature once more.

The Library assumed a deeper tenebrous aspect the more Neipas walked through it. His mind was blank; but he was well awake now. When he came upon the circular opening, he faced it without surprise, as though he had followed a familiar path to it; though in reality he had gone through the corridors without knowing where to turn. He read once again the inscription upon the opening's gilded border as he looked up: *CAVE*. Slower now, Neipas stepped beyond and entered a stairway of patterned carpet, running steeply under a stone vault and glowing with cozy, honey radiances. He passed still slower the small lobby with the couch, the hearth and the painting depicting a gray pigeon with enormous red eyes. And with the utmost slowness — a feeling of caution dominating his motions — he traversed the circular doorway which bore down here the same message as the passage above: *CAVE*.

The pulse still throbbed afar. Neipas followed it and entered the dusty, dim storehouse space, and again he was greeted with the dark outlines of veils, book piles, and the human shapes of mannequins, which again made him stop with fright. It was as though he was living anew an experience from some past life. The memory of it was hazy and distant, but his muscles retained the essential reminiscence of all the steps he had last taken. His toes slithered forward under slow, profound breathing. Again they came in contact with the verge of a sudden drop; and they descended very carefully.

Stepping lightly on the floor made the chambers reverberate lightly; and he recalled awakening the Historian the last time he was there. He remembered the uncanny Giant, his blind mask of smiles atop a mountainous robe of parchment, his ghastly tour of History. Instinctively, driven by some profound guide of unconscience, Neipas took off his shoes and met the floor with his socks, and trod — lightly, very careful not to disturb the dusty quietude of the glassy space. Something still stirred behind him; a sound of wooden clatters beat against the hard ground: but Neipas swiftly sneaked out, silently upon the soft fabric of his clothed feet, away from the range of the blind Historian.

Neipas passed the curtains into a renewed succession of shelves, witnessing as he went the babel of languages on the spines of books, and stones and clay tablets, and sheets of animal skin out of which letters bulged in relief. Some of the stacks were covered in raincloth, and through their breaches peeked yet more mannequins...

Following the heartbeat sound, by and by he came into the melody of water-clocks, passing under gates and arches and a myriad veils. Again he traversed the marvels of the Museum, again he traveled the course of History. Up and down long steps and through long corridors, past an infinitude of glassed artifacts and relics and labels with numbers and names, past paintings and sculptures filling the halls chaotically, past the mannequins clothed as kings and other great Men — plastic statues expressionless and balloon-headed — through myriad colors, lights, confetti hazes. He didn't dare touch any of the side doors or any of the treasures housed within. In the wide solitude of exhibits he felt himself trespassing, and so he roamed through quickly, lest the Historian should discover his presence. Once more he descended the long steps into the darkness of the Dark Ages, musty and filled with crucifixes and stakes, and obscure codices smelling of dust; at the end of this Neipas noticed a toppled totem, out of which the stair arose again, steeply and dramatically, gathering in vividness and color, growing gaudy and irreverent with its effigies of superheroes and suited, smiling masks.

Finally — applying much exertion in the final climb — Neipas reached the End of History.

He faced the two ample facades of glass. One a mirror, the other a window. Between them the relief sculpture of the serpent wrapped in its cocoon, out of whose hood formed the two golden arches and sinuous, ornamented bulges, its majestic wings. Neipas walked past the hourglass in the middle, past the meaningless sculptures; he walked toward the windowed wing and cleaned a swipe of frost off its surface. He looked through it; and he saw again the strange and immense Candle of Man, its great streams of black smoke far out, the carving on its towering bulk forming the words *"THOU SHALT"* in every dialect. He noticed how the flame swung gently above a wide font of lucent fluid. Mesmerized, Neipas observed its palpitations and wondered whether the wax had weaned at all since he last saw it, about a year ago then (beneath the Candle he could now see, pulsating with the fading daylight, wide marble grounds; at the very edge of the window he thought he spied a sort of altar and a giant book); and he listened to the whisper of the serpent beside him and to the swelling glow, which pulsed slowly at the sound of the distant throbbing, now much closer; sounding as if directly from the fire...

On the side, far, the door out of which the Midget had peeked stood wide open.

Neipas stepped outside and, still fearful of the Historian, kept walking along on his socks. He looked about him. The trees were soothed in the suggestive glow and air of approaching dusk. Yonder, the sun had already sunk beneath the clouds, and though the sky softened, the light had not yet touched the horizon. He didn't see the Midget. Nevertheless, these woods attracted Neipas and, desiring not to go back to the oppressive atmosphere of the Museum, he decided to walk around a little.

He wandered the spurs of undergrowth. Here the vegetation was quite untamed, left to develop on its own. Trees and shrubs of all varieties grew out in a tangle inside the manufactured air. Their roots swallowed directly from the irrigation system set up underneath. Pines dropped from the needle-tops and were left upon the grounds abandoned; fallen apples were strewn across the lush grass, and other fruits besides mixed into the panoply of color. Neipas picked one of the apples. Surveying the crust of it, he turned it round and saw that the other side, that which touched the ground, was horribly moldy, infested with fungi that almost seemed to move in Neipas' hand. In repulsion Neipas dropped the fruit and wiped his hand on his trousers with a few quick strokes. Upon closer inspection, he saw that the leaves on the ground and all around him looked chewed, filled with holes and spots, leprous. There was something unearthly and prehistoric about the vegetation. A general appearance of ruins. Though the green here developed freely, still it looked contained, faded, hunched. It looked bound by limits that Neipas could no longer see; and he was surprised that, though he kept walking forward, he could not reach the edge of this terrace. It was as if the terrain grew before him, faster than he walked. Suddenly tickled by this idea, Neipas resolved to run until he reached the edge; and so he did, but he became tired before he arrived.

Though the first facade of these woods looked healthy, its depths were filled with flowerless dirt and leafless trees of dead bark, with an increasing amount of trash littering the grounds — plastics of all shapes. The deflated skin of balloons proliferated. Oily, thick black substances gushed from the exposed roots of these sullen trees and spread among the stained rubbish. Strange spores emanated from fell trunks and filled the air with a noxious fog. He could see the clouds afar, beyond an uncertain edge, but still he could not reach the outer bounds and the braiding tree corpses confused the path. Irked and a little frightened now — for it was getting dark — he walked straight back the way he came. Under the reddened sky he wondered, panting and shaking his head among mutters, where the Midget could have gone.

His walk sped through the thickening spores and it quickly turned into a run. The vague panic in Neipas' breast was turning concrete, the suspicion that he wasn't in a normal place took hold. He ran until there was no more breath in his body. He bent over his aching ribs, swallowing the stench of the air. His hands went into his melting mask, through the sweaty droop of his feathers. Neipas was sure he had walked back a longer distance than he had gone in — and still he could not reach the healthy part of the woods. Still all manner of plastic rubbish littered about his feet. Wondering wildly about the impossibility of it all, as soon as he recovered Neipas yelled for help into the drawing night.

But now through the weeds he thought he saw (as he looked up from the blurry ground) the inner limits of the terrace, just up ahead beyond a pile of trash. Hopeful, he sped toward it in a stride. But the gates to the Museum weren't there. Only a wall — and though he walked round it, still he could not find the entrance. The wall sunk into a narrow ditch filled with wet leaves and rubbish, from among which peeked disjointed parts of mannequins, dressed in rags and wired with sparkling stones. Where had he gone? Neipas was sure he had walked straight forward, and back the same way... He wondered how walls could exist where just moments ago were doors.

Topping the wall he saw the tangled, spiky overgrowth of the 2nd terrace; so that he knew he was beneath the Pantries and the gloomy verdures leading to the Gazebo; he was in the lowest ring of the Pigeon Wing. The lights and sounds of the Market streamed mystically through the thorns above. He balanced himself over the gully, pressing his hand against the wall. Night thickened behind him as he thought over what to do.

Eventually, as in a reflex, he took his *I* out of his pocket and drafted a message to Osir the Janitor Supervisor, explaining his situation and seeking guidance. But here, he saw, he had no connection to the Webwork. He yanked up his head in frustration and it was then that he saw the Midget, over by the wall ahead.

"Excuse me?" Neipas approached; but upon his first step the Midget turned and walked away, sounding the clack of shackles that bound her (or him). "Hello? Excuse me please!" The wall sunk into vaulted galleries and the Midget swerved quickly into them. "Hey!" Neipas followed her (or him) into the arches, led through the thick air by a noise of rattling chains, across a little bridge spanning the widening ditch; he dove headlong and strode through the galleries, in and out of the deep shadows of the columns, toward a distant sound of rushing water which grew greater and slowly overwhelmed the mumblings of the Market above. The path curved along the tower's shape; the chains beat among the water and the nervous breathing in Neipas' lips; and though Neipas would sometimes sprint in an attempt to catch up, the Midget was always out of reach, just over the bend and almost out of sight. He thought he was dreaming; when he stopped, so did the sound of the

Midget, whom he perceived always just over the bend, and almost out of sight. The ditch kept widening — it filled up fast with litter and bubbly refuse from the rivers. The woods to his side had assumed the form of standing shadows, resembling an assembly of ghosts arching over some victim. His eyes tricked his mind with hallucinations. He thought he saw trees walking, boughs flexing with unnatural motions, and shrubs swaying amid the movement of mythical creatures, of standing dark hooded shapes and winged lions and serpents with human faces who watched. Neipas fled with abandon, employing all the might of despair in a chase to catch his sanity.

The Midget disappeared completely beyond the bend and Neipas' heart was filled with panic, panging and swelling up into his head and every vein. He charged his run with his last strength. Yet, the Midget was gone but a moment. Round the curve he (or she) stood, and after an endless trek Neipas was suddenly able to cross the distance between them. He stopped before the little figure, recovering his breath.

After he had drawn in enough to spare, Neipas asked politely, between gulps, "Excuse me — I'm lost. Can you help me?"

The Midget, with her (or his) tragedy mask, stood in irons; an uncanny figure, somehow he (or she) inspired trust in him. The Midget had stopped near two doors. On the wall opened the door to the Museum and the End of History; and at the galleries' end stood a glass door covered by a hanging rug, now lifted by the Midget's staff, which he moved with a soft clatter of chains. Sometimes the clouds would arise and spread across the woods to envelop everything in fog, making the trees ghostlier and the apparitions more vivid. So they lifted now, spiriting the eye with an aura of mysticism, blurring the gates. As Neipas ceased panting he discerned again the sound of rushing water — one of the river cascades was very near.

The Midget opened the glass gate under the rug-curtain. Immediately a strong wind rushed in through it, a chilling draught suffused with droplets. The fog was momentarily dispelled and Neipas gazed out.

Beyond the gate, the gallery continued into a narrow set of stairs descending into the tempest; the clouds puffing up and down continuously, Neipas was able to spot the narrow passage which they covered. This platform straddled the wide circumference of the tower and seemed to pass under the waterfall cascading down into Axiac, the waterfall belonging to the southward river beside the Gazebo. This meant he stood on the border between the Pigeon and Eagle Wings.

The rivers formed an impregnable barrier between Wings, but in this strange place, between the sky and the tower, it was possible to walk under the waters.

Neipas, wits scattered in the humidity of the night fog, looked into the door to the End of History with the intent of going in and taking shelter there. He shook with cold, the winds blowing through the glass gate were frigid. But he looked down and saw the Midget still bore her (or his) staff and his (or her) shackles, still pointed to that opening leading down to the mass of clouds.

"What do you mean?" Neipas asked, though he knew. If he went through there he could reach the Eagle Wing, and in fact, even as he asked he felt in himself the desire to traverse the path into it. There was curiosity and something of obligation in him — he wondered vaguely what secrets he might uncover therein if he were to look upon it without the weight of the ox head pulling him down, without staring through its cumbersome eyes. Perhaps it was the desire to walk free of supervision in those golden halls, so immense and so often deserted, with so little people to occupy them. Perhaps it was something more profound — the vaguest allure of mischief and power moved his breast too — but the wish for it, surfacing now upon seeing the path, was acute in Neipas' heart.

He was afraid too, for the real danger lay tucked away in his pocket. In it hid the *I*. If he was caught with it in that space where the most powerful dwelt with their true faces, without veils behind which to hide, naked in the remoteness of the heights under the blinding sun — the consequences were unthinkable. To the Eagles' den no remembering eye could turn.

"*Nothing in the Anubel's Eagle Wing may be recorded. Recording devices are forbidden. No Is allowed! What happens in the Eagle Wing, never happened. Breaking this rule could land you in jail for trespassing...*" Sunai's stern mask had told their souls.

But even as he mulled on his fears, Neipas thought of Cesar trampled in the wrath incurred by the unbending discipline of Drrawetz; he thought of what he had heard from the Head Gardener, about the Oyate and those sacrificed in the fires, about Noxxe and the infirm inhabitants of Ostrich, about Orenda and about the raging rivers of his lost childhood.

The Midget pointed no longer. But Neipas could feel, even through his (or her) inscrutable mask of perpetual sadness, the wish that Neipas walk that path. He still held his two shoes in his hand. His suit was soiled, the shirt clung to his torso; he unbuttoned it. He pushed his wet hair of feathers back. As he gained possession of himself again, he lifted his fingers to his face and fixed his mask before the *I* glass. His jaw gained shape, his eyes consistency. His heart calmed itself. The mist thickened at his side until the woods disappeared altogether.

Then he stared at the Midget. "Who did this to you?" he asked, pointing to the manacles; but the Midget did not speak. Assuming he (or she) was mute, Neipas lowered the *I* and presented its surface, compelling the Midget to touch upon its catalogue of letters. The Midget only shook her (or his) mask; touching the glass made the letters appear and vanish immediately. The mystic being's fingers produced no effect upon it, as though the Midget were immaterial. Gazing unto him (or her) below him, Neipas took this calmly, as if it were some arcane confirmation. He then unhooked the *I*, so that it would not connect to the Webwork; and tucked it back into his pocket.

Still he looked to the Midget and, though he knew they could not communicate, he asked, "Was that the core of the tower?" for his mind was filled with the memory of the throbbing dark sun, the strange vision the Midget had led him to in the tower's bosom, underground, "What was it we saw?"

Night fell — the Pearl blazed alit, high above.

His unconscious entertained the notion of some golden treasure hidden in the tower's center; he recalled the great flash that drowned his senses, its overwhelming dazzle. He ruminated such things vaguely as he stood before the opened glass door, slowly suffused by the wet draught, steeling himself in its chilling embrace.

Moved by the breeze of the spirit into a flight of faith, Neipas soothed himself to the decision. He resolved to go.

After some time, Neipas still asked, "Who are you?" — but the Midget would only describe an oval with her (or his) chained hands.

44 - Faces in the Fog

Neipas walked down the narrow staircase, along the tower's long circular shape. The air lifted up and trembled as he descended toward the storm clouds, it moved with a penetrating cold that rattled his bones. The very blood inside his veins shook and his heart contracted. Wobbling, he stopped; and teetering with hesitation, he huddled about himself and looked back up the steps to the gazing Midget. Neipas stared into her (or his) occult mask of tragedy, of Melpomene, with its droopy gashes of dejection, and felt the inscrutable semblance whispering words of encouragement.

He was afraid, but he knew he could not turn back; for the decision had been made, as though by an irresistible force outside of himself and, at the same time, deep within him. He felt that force compelling him on like inexorable destiny. Neipas paced down the round curve toward the bottom, feeling the winds grow chillier and more treacherous, and the clouds gradually thickening about him as he sunk further to their midst. The gazebo became visible up the mounting walls yonder as he turned; Neipas gazed its shape of minaret outpost and the moon crescent above it being veiled by the clouds, until he could see no longer.

There was the narrow passageway at the bottom of the stairs, flanked on one side by the tower wall and by a fence on the other. The fence was all that separated him from a colossal drop of miles down the face of the Belab, down to the far urban sprawl consumed and ravaged by tempest. Now blinded by the thick whiteness of the vapors, he proceeded with both hands upon the wall. In the beginning of his trek he was merely suffused with that dreamlike quality of uncanniness; his mind numbed sightless by it, his body moved simply by soul's command. The winds spiraled about the wall deviously, mostly calm, but often blowing with bursts so sudden as to force Neipas into a halt, his mind straining up, fraught in alertness. Such bursts raked his spirit and made him very afraid. All sense of shelter disappeared as he advanced and the winds picked up gradually, and, unable to see his own feet, he began to feel as though he walked through the open air, suspended, pending from a great altitude.

Little by little he was overwhelmed with vertigo. The motions of the air swelled into a howling gale that rattled the fence with terrible violence. Neipas even moved into a jog in an attempt to outrun the weather, but fear quickly took hold of him, and he became very dizzy. For moments he still tried to go on, tottering in great trepidation; but soon he held on to the wall, pressing it with all his body, closing his eyes tight and clenching his teeth, unable to take another step. He was at the mercy of the elements now. The wind blew against him furiously, choking him cold into the wall. The chain-link beat and shook against his face, swirling rains came and went in great droves. He must've been by the southward river; though the noise of the gale was so strong that it drowned the sounds of the waterfall. The enveloping haze moved with terrible speed and in a confusion of directions — it was all Neipas could see, if he peeked. He felt in the grip of a million great, powerful hands which intended to crush him slowly against the concrete or drown him in the crazed showers. Incantations of hatred seemed to sound through the tireless scream of the air. Again, between deep breaths and moans of fright, gasps of panic, Neipas looked back — for the second time.

He gasped breathlessly from shock, he gasped as though emerging from deep waters, inhaling a great rush of air between his open lips. Neipas beheld a hallucination.

He saw her standing in the fog, he saw his mother. His eyes, wide open now, gazed upon her. Not the image of his mother upon the tombstone, not the shying visage in his safeguarded photograph. No. There was no separation in time or distance of abstraction. She stood *there*, before him; he could sense her. The present moment was suffused by the presence of her memory, the memory of her presence made actual, made physical. He could not see her face well in the rushing haze; in the chaos of sensations he could only discern a vagueness of shape, yet he knew it was her and he knew she, her spirit stood there draped in flesh. Neipas' lip trembled in incomprehension. It was her. It was as though the storm had summoned her from the dregs of the mud-drowned river, as if its force had washed away the stifling tailings, unburied the past from the depths of the trauma; and brought her aloft, here. It was her — His mother stood there before him, in the passageway between the hard wall and the chain-link fence lashing rabidly against her, in the furious wet gale beating and choking them. The showers drove on without relent.

Yet she was calm; motionless. (She looked at Neipas with a smile of encouragement), saying, "Can you hear that?"

And the air was silent.

"This is where Gods are born."

He even wondered whether it was rainwater or tears flowing down his cheeks.

Neipas sensed his mother by him, slowly sprinkling herbs into the fragrant pot. Yet the voice he heard was not hers — it was Oshana's, to whom the words also belonged. For Neipas could no longer remember his mother's voice.

A breath of life whispered among the clouds. Neipas found a warmth in his chest, rising from a secret recess in his own depths of being. His chest swelled against the gale, and he breathed in the storm. Screaming into the ear of God — moved with a strange sense of purpose — he continued on, embracing the wall with his arms and with his back, but with eyes wide open against the ire of the winds.

Yet Neipas had still to pass under the waterfall which divided the two Wings. It came upon him in the general blindness of the storm as an impenetrable barrier; he became submerged in the fury of the river, which, moved by the might of the storm, pushed against the tower like a barrage of water-bullets, without compassion, without stop. His eyes were forced shut again. Overwhelmed with the sudden added weight upon his chest, he rotated upon the wall with difficulty and pressed in with his shoulder. He lifted his shoulders high and his forearms covered his face against the hail. Strangely, the wall seemed to sink, as if receding against the forces of the wind; and its surface became rugged and felt like rock, as if the storm were molding it in the attempt to penetrate the depths of the tower. Neipas pressed and struggled along the sinking wall — but it was too much. He stopped for a moment and crouched, sheltering himself against the battering of rains. And its river beat relentlessly against the rock... It was too much. He couldn't breathe; he was losing consciousness; he was drowning.

(And he heard flames in the waters... He thought he spotted something appearing among the density of haze and the narrowness of his grimacing eyes. Through the waters he thought he discerned the surface of the rock next to him; and the surface of the rock glistened in their rush, the caved wall plunging into a great chasm, a quivering, pulsing abyss facing him like a drenched mirror, like the bubbling surface of an unruly lake; and in it he thought he saw his own, true face. He gazed it maskless and horrendous. In one hand he held his pigeon countenance, he realized, and in the other still his shoes. The chasm throbbed.

The heart of the tower pulsed deep.)

Amassing the rest of his forces, Neipas pressed up against the rock and thrust along, digging through with all muscles straining, pushing away and being pushed against the rugged surface of the indented wall, floundering and rolling on with yells.

But finally he emerged on the other side, breathless, his consciousness on the edge of succumbing.

He staggered onward, and in the meantime the wind eased a little. Though he was dazed and hurt he could now hear the river descending normally as he went away from the wall. At last, Neipas arrived at the steps on the other side and climbed them toward the Eagle Wing. He was drenched, beaten up, exhausted; his chest ached and he was chronically short of breath. Once he had climbed enough to lift himself above the storm, he sat upon a step and let himself slacken against it. He recovered his breath with difficulty, tired drawings of wheezing air. Then, little by little, he rose, stiff all over, and clambered up the steps. A glass door stood at the top.

The air petrified; once more his nose touched the disinfected, alpine atmosphere of the Hanging Gardens. A warm glow spilled from the top of the wall. It was different from the glow of the Market, cooler, thinner, more refined; and though the air was barren, it bore scents of a finer quality, without the rancidness of carnival meat. And so, he knew — he was on the Eagles' side.

Access to the Gardens could be gotten through ladders mounted along the wall — the stairs did not continue up the platform and onto the terrace as they did on the other side. Neipas leaned up against one of the ladder's rungs, and reflected.

He was in a terrible state. No one could see him, for they would know right away that he was not where he should be. And where could he take shelter in that flood of light in which the Eagles bathed? There were tall hedges flanking the central path connecting the Infinity Pool to the Temple colonnade, and the trails between those hedges served as corridors leading to the entrances and all other sections of their bottom terrace. Neipas would start there. He breathed deep, numb. His spirit was all involved in insensibility, a type of psychological self-indifference which precedes all bold action. He put on his shoes and his mask so that his hands may be free. He checked that his *I* was not damaged, for, though it was waterproof, the journey across had been violent in the storm's whirling bosom. He fixed the aspect of his pigeon semblance in its glass so that he would be less conspicuous; he buttoned up his shirt; and he rested still a little more, for his chest panted and his ears gurgled with the rush of water.

Then, he climbed.

*

The Gardens were filled with fluorescent golden flakes hovering about in circles. Afar, in the center of the terrace, the Eagles bathed in the Infinity Pool at the tower's edge, all between a great entourage of cattle, swans, and peacocks fawning over them, each in their own manner; soothing tunes flowed from the band standing near. Neipas — climbing to the terrace side — dove headlong into the hedges, which rose right in front of him.

He walked through shaded paths, across quaint fountain squares, under pergolas embroidered with vine and alongside rows of magnificent statues who gazed over his march behind eyeless orbs of marble. He moved only in a general direction, guiding himself by the colossal walls of the terraces peeking above the hedges' height. Yonder he could see the westward cascade, falling gracefully into the fumes from the Temple, which hissed, as though sighs from scalding fonts. But it happened that as Neipas advanced the hedges became taller; and soon they became so tall as to cover the complex all the way up to the Pearl. Suddenly he found himself in the midst of flecked green walls bordering paths that winded confusedly, seemingly turning into themselves, as all corridors of hedges looked very much the same, without any marks to orient himself by.

He was soon quite lost, turning in all directions, aimless in that monotone confusion of sights without horizon. Over and again Neipas entered the same little topiary square: a space framed with shrubs which had been clipped to resemble immense heads, monstrous sculptures with lunatic smiles and eyes that stared at him giantly. In a whimsical reflex he looked up at the sky, vaguely intending to guide himself by the stars, though he didn't know how — and neither could he try, for the stars were all covered in the golden dust filling the Garden skies. Between corridors of garden greenery, hedges strewn with flower and lumped with thorns he went, diving into a disorientation such that he began to fear for himself.

The clipped leaves were full of whispers and steps, but he saw nobody; it was full of the permeating melody of the orchestra; and many times, as he stopped without knowing where to turn, open-eyed, listening to his thumping heart, and noticing the motion in his lips, he wondered whether it wasn't himself who was whispering.

He became careless; Neipas seemed to roam for hours and hours, and eventually he began to discern the sky clearing over the gold flakes alighting the hedge-tops. The sun would soon rear its gaze over the clouds. His legs were already catching into a run and his nostrils muttered rushed regrets, nervously panting; his beak cursed the confounding maze; and his whole being panicked, for there was not much time left before his shift was to begin.

Again he entered the square of bush sculpted to the shape of heads, and stopped to rest. His heart pounced his ear as he bent over himself, out of breath as he wildly considered screaming for help; but then, through the drum of his pulsing veins, he heard voices. Voices clear. The mouth of a ghoulish head rustled with murmurs.

Filled with fright, Neipas chanced a peek over the little curvy bend round the devilish face. He walked in a narrow lane between tall, sinuous bushes. And as he turned under the sculpted shrubs he caught the words in the voices. "Kill the savages!" — it was the distinctive timbre of the Minister of Borders.

Neipas crouched into an intersecting path edging to a sharp bend, which turned into a little plaza of sand and stone rimmed with statues of fat warriors tottering on pedestals. The height of a mesquite tree reigned wherein. The mesquite had little lamps pending from cords tied to the boughs; looking like upside balloons. The Minister lounged in a large sofa underneath, and by the moment Neipas glanced over he looked asleep already. His head bobbed, though he had one eye wide open; he embraced two swans on either side, violently squeezing one breast of each, and the discomfort they felt was obvious even through their graceful masks; they tried to part loose with gentle movements, but the Minister would not let go. A smell of booze and vomit permeated the tended perfumes of the hedges. Round the mesquite tree stood the Minister's entourage: two guardian bulls; two peacocks, staffers of the Minister; the two swans; and three oxen. The oxen stood and bore the weight of their trays, laden with drink. The peacocks, who wore ties dotted with oculi, sat on the empty edges of the sofa and worked furiously with their fingers, looking extremely busy inside their *I*s. The swans next to them bore their discomfort as the Minister who gripped them mumbled words in his sleep; and the bulls, erect with their machine guns, laughed heartily.

Neipas felt the *I* in his breastpocket; and the glass was warm upon his heart, whispering into it the urge to photograph the scene. It was what he had come to do, and the conscience of his purpose intoxicated him momentarily. The vision of the inebriated Minister suffocating two girls would make a good picture. But he couldn't do it; he was much too frightened to expose the *I* to the open air and turn it on them. He could easily be seen.

"Fuck'n bean'rs and their donkeys," ejaculated the Minister from the sweetness of his dreams, and the Bulls rejoiced.

Presently one of the peacocks rose from the sofa. Never taking his eyes of his *I*, he announced: "Minister, you are scheduled to go to bed by this hour."

To which the Minister of Borders replied, seeming to half-wake up: "Ain't gonna let no tonk tell me what to do!" — and at this the Bulls broke out in laughter.

"I am not a tonk, sir," said the peacock calmly, fiddling yet with the *I*, as if confirming in the glass that what he had said was a fact.

The guards helped the Minister out of the couch. He released the two breasts with much reluctance, pinching them so hard as he was coaxed off that one of the girls screamed in pain — a scream so sharp it sent a tremble through Neipas' chest. He shrunk into himself a little at first; and then, relying on the confusion which amassed about the Minister, he peeked in. He saw that mustachioed, bushy, white-feathered head which was so often broadcast from between big frames being lifted up in a state of near unconsciousness, the noble and exalted face drooping ridiculously, like a buffoon's. The powerful Eagle, twin of the present Minister of Nations, had himself once been a notorious high-secretary in the powerful Nations Ministry of a previous regime, and oversaw many a massacre in far Mesopotamia from the comforts of his office couch — with great advantage to his career. His beak had issued casual sentences dictating the deaths of thousands, and now Neipas witnessed that mighty beak drooling like that of any common drunk.

They carried him away. A mix of emotions flustered Neipas, and for moments he was pinned down by fear; but he was made to move by the urge to act and the need to rush as the day commenced above him. Hastening on, he caught up with the entourage by following the soft rattling of the key-ring pierced to the nose of the Minister's chief Bull. He trailed carefully, at a distance, guided by the clinking taps of the Bull's keys. Their march was at first wordless, but at a new burst of pejoratives from the Minister the Bulls erupted anew in laughter, and the mood became outright jolly at once. The Bulls were loosened by the boisterousness of their master, and their thoughts flew freely in a torrent of wine out their mouths. They became excited, the guard with the studded choker most of all. He had been recruited from the ranks of the Frontier Patrol, the watch-force that shielded the extent of Wall St. along Columbia's vast border against the migrants from the destitute nations to the south; he presently bragged about his exploits during his time in service.

Though Neipas didn't hear much over the loud beat of his heart, the Bull's words were sufficiently clear, belted cringingly in the soft quietude of dawn. "We hunt them down..." The collared Bull boasted of things he did to the people he caught crossing into Columbia.

"She was literally squealing!" said the Bull, amid laughter. "They're like animals, I swear..."

In the heart's flux of turbulent feeling arose repulsion and revolt against the Eagles and their goons. The rushing torrent of Neipas' childhood washed in blood through his veins. All the intimate contempt he had been entertaining for these sovereigns over peoples, these devious tyrants, gathered up in an instant. He sensed the rot and tragedy flooding Axiac, Columbia, and the World. And now he was here, here where he could see them and hear them in their house beyond all veils, Neipas felt like one facing the gullet of leaking sewage, the retching pipe overlooking all sacred wells. In a moment he sensed the source of most evils in their beaks of gold.

A decision was made between the hard breaths of nervousness that set the pace of Neipas' trail. It was too risky to bring out the *I*: someone in those gardens could see him, and the feeling that there were eyes everywhere never left him, like an ill presentiment. It wouldn't do to take photographs; and to bring out the *I* to film was even riskier. He would not record images — instead, he would record sound.

Removing the glass from his pocket quickly, Neipas turned on the voice recorder — the remembering ear of the *I*. He hid it promptly, and kept following the entourage from afar, trailing and recording their voices, keeping sight of the oxen which were last in the file.

Wet to the bone yet, exhausted, Neipas gnashed his teeth and set his brows in a furrow, straining along, until he saw the labyrinth's exit. The Minister of Borders and his entourage traversed the Garden plot into the Temple grounds. Neipas himself held up, cautious of the open gap between the hedges and the complex, and tried to make sure no one was passing over before he crossed. Then he rushed out at a quick step... but presently he stopped.

In his agitation, he hadn't seen them — walking from the edge of the Garden along the colossal terrace walls, which were the facade of the Temple, three staffers from the Treasury Ministry halted and looked at Neipas through the tiny, sunken eyes of their masks. They were spectacled, alienoid creatures with long legs, dressed in peacock gowns out of which ensued immensely long trails of feathers, dotted full of colorful spots. Two isolated crests sprang from the bald crowns of each. For a while pigeon and peacocks faced other, the latter eying the other suspiciously. Their crests swayed as they cocked their heads. Neipas' heart stopped (the *I* in his breastpocket seemed to beat in its place, as if wishing to be found); he tried to utter a sound but none left his rigid beak. He quickly took stock of his unkempt appearance; though he worn his uniform, it was damp, and he had neither the bell in his collar nor the ox mask on his head. His brain raked for excuses as to why he was at that place looking the way he did.

However — to Neipas' fortune — they were Economists all, and like most Economists, they were myope and could not see the world very well. They could not interpret Neipas' bizarre and solitary apparition before them, and so abandoned the subject in proud confusion, dismissing the weird-looking waiter as an anomaly in the system.

Neipas went over the remaining yard, heart rushing. He hastened inside the Temple's fumes and the wet air of aromatic odors. The haze here was thick and he was again blind, but he could hear springs coursing, the melodious sound of tranquil water; it appeared to be some sort of bathhouse.

He had to find the kitchen and cross to the other side — but he had never been here and didn't know the way.

The wax slid disastrously off the pigeon mask as he went through the bath fumes which hid him. Blurry silhouettes occupied the space alongside; otherwise he saw nothing. He knew his shift was about to begin, and so went about aimlessly and in despair. Yonder, the only clear thing he could see was something like a flame, dancing and palpitating among the vapors, very far away; and sumptuous statues flanking every step, emerging from the fog like white shadows, smiling with golden adornments about their limbs. Every now and then he spotted saunas and pools emerging from a momentary clearing of the fog. He had a vague idea of where the kitchen was situated inside the Eagle Wing, and knew he had to go upward. His only desire was for a stairwell leading to the upper floors; he thought of nothing else.

The sun shone over the storm clouds outside and filtered in through the fumes. The Market bells pealed. "Ohmygodohmygod" Neipas stammered to himself as he sped. A door appeared to him amid the fumes, and unthinking in his rush he made straight for it, without a moment's hesitation. His fingers had barely scrapped the handle when he heard a voice behind him.

"Neipas?"

He turned, stunned and confused; his mind had at once halted, but his jittery body was dragged by the impulse that had thus carried it along, and still tried to open the door, striking at the handle frenetically multiple times. It was locked.

"Sorry," Neipas gushed.

He rooted to the spot, overwhelmed by the loudness of the mental clock ticking in his head and the consequential loss of his wits, driven to the winds and scattered among the sweaty vapors; he was pressed down by the pressures of his obligations and the financial stability on which they depended. What if he were fired and stranded there above the storm? Worse — what if he was found here with the recording I and put in jail for trespassing? For a while — it was impossible to say how long — he was unable to say a word, and just stood there. He didn't recognize the woman before him at first.

"What are you doing?" she spoke again. It was Magpie's voice; though it wasn't Magpie's face before him.

She looked different. Her mask was so absolutely plastered with paints, her natural beauty so covered with decorations as to make her unrecognizable; her curly hair, entwined with white feathers, hung loose onto her shoulders; she wore a white bathing suit, a one-piece with a bundle of plumes blooming out the lower rear, and her long legs jetting out of the bottom shiny and naked; from the white collar above the cleavage pended a little bell. Magpie's black skin was molded into the semblance of the swan.

"What are you wearing?" Neipas blabbered, perplexed and strangely amused, forgetting himself for a moment.

She stammered voiceless for a moment, looking down about her. "The Chief Supervisor told me to wear it..." she said, visibly vexed and uncomfortable, not at all like herself. "I dunno! Quit looking, man!"

"Sorry."

Neipas had barely seen Magpie since Cesar's funeral, for she had been assigned to the nightshift — so that he was shocked to see her like this.

"It's these fucking creeps that want us wearing this. They're creepy as hell. I swear to God if they lay one fucking finger on me..."

"Mary, have they tried?"

"Fuck, Neipas. What's wrong with you? What happened?" she whispered quickly, cutting into his speech and pulling them down into a tone of secrecy. Neipas looked about himself too and suddenly became aware of his situation again.

"I need to find the kitchen," he said with a renewed strain of agitation. Magpie's scrutinizing, narrowing stare seemed only to constrict him, he felt himself out of breath in the clammy steam; and in the squeeze of his throat, his voice popped out: "I'm not working right now..." and he leaned over, opening his breastpocket to disclose the *I*. "Need to get to the dorms..."

"The fu-- did you steal that?" Magpie shot, alert, looking from side to side and quickly scanning Neipas' ruffled state. "You know you're not supposed to —"

Her vexation promptly vanished into sharp conduct; she pulled him quickly. "C'mon, follow me."

Magpie guided Neipas through the dense humidity. She appeared like a mound of white feathers at turns dispersing and amassing in smoke. He followed her, traversing the halls at a walk, the deliberate pace of which drove him to near lunacy as he tried to restrain the maddening impulse to run tingling all over his nervous body. He could scarcely see anything in the blinding whiteness of this strange place. His steps puffed with the sound of faint dreams from the marble; he wandered in the tormented feeling occupying his heart, enlarging itself across the space as he shrunk in the possibility of being fired or found out... Surely he was already late. The Chief Supervisor seemed more lenient, but rumor had it that Drrawetz still called the shots from the backstage. Perhaps he'd be blacklisted forever and thus condemned to poverty, homelessness, hunger. Or incarceration.

Fingers sunk in his arm and he jolted. "Come inside quick," Magpie said, pulling him into a sort of theater dressing room full of cosmetics and paints spread in front of a large mirror. There was a swan sitting before it, contemplating herself with dull eyes as she plucked the feathers of her brow slowly, one by one ("Don't worry about her," Magpie mumbled as Neipas stared bewilderedly).

"Wear this —" Magpie gave him her waitress shirt and jacket as he blunderingly removed his own — "C'mon, hurry!"

Though Magpie was his height, her clothes clasped upon his torso tightly and clumsy, uncomfortably. Only when he held up his own shirt did he notice it was sticky and filled with blotches of some black, viscous substance; it emanated the rotten egg odor of tar.

"The hell did you do that?" Magpie wondered with a grimace as she molded Neipas' mask, resorting to paints, powders and all the cosmetic tools upon the table.

"I was out in the rain..."

She fitted his collar with a bell. "Look — I dunno what you're up to man. Just keep me out of it, hear?" she told him decisively. "The stairs will be to your left, there's no missing them. Go up two flights and you'll be in the kitchen."

Morphed, Neipas took his *I* out and put it in the breastpocket of Magpie's jacket, which he now wore.

"What about you?" he asked, without knowing what he meant himself.

"I have a spare. Go on, hurry up! The bell's rang."

Neipas stepped toward the door, which hissed with smoke, and mumbled many gratitudes. "This will be over soon and we'll get outta here," Magpie still mumbled vaguely, breathlessly, as he left.

He climbed the steps in a hurry. The kitchens were bustling with cooks and fire, sounds of water bubbling and ringing steel. Emerging quickly into the immense space, he stole toward Janu's cooking station and, opening the cupboard, he placed the *I* in a little nook inside it. He still saw the hour flashing upon its glass: late, bone-chilling.

The casualness of his motions concealed compounded fears aggravated throughout the course of that night; and though he didn't feel it, sleepiness began to make itself heavy upon him. He arose.

"Jesus, dude," Janu breathed as Neipas crashed against him. He'd just come back, and Neipas almost made him topple a plate of raw meat as he got up.

"Sorry, sorry," trembled Neipas.

"What are you doing here, man?"

"I got up late," he mouthed, looking from side to side aimlessly. "I'm so fucking screwed!"

"I thought today was your day off."

Neipas stopped. He looked at Janu with livid eyes, teary with exertion and fatigue. "What? What day is it today?"

"Monday."

The loud crash of pots and flames spewing receded into a soundlessness of background.

"Oh," whispered Neipas, breathing deeply, blinking convulsively. Inhaling the kitchen airs, he said, "You're right."

The good cook was already back at work over his station. "What happened bro? You look nervous or something," he said as he beheld Neipas' wax face disintegrating.

Janu himself looked discomfited. Constant worries had been gnawing at him since the tempest began, all rattled to the point of strain in all the free hours spent in the Webwork trying to contact his family. Still, he went through the motions automatically, and his ox mask twitched only barely above the cooking fumes.

"No... I'm all right. Thanks, man," said Neipas vacantly. "You?"

Janu shrugged. "You take care of yourself my friend. Get some sleep or something."

Bearing a weighty neck, with head down-turned in a posture of servility, Neipas walked to the scanners, stood between the Bulls and the Owls lining the exit. He was nervous — but none peered beyond his mask. In their routine inattention, no one noticed he wore his regular pigeon face. Safely on the other side at last, he moved through the Cafeteria, through the glass panes of which he saw the sky blazing; and went along until he reached the Columbaria where, long wakened to early morning, the blare of alarm bells still sounded.

45 - Of Scions and Swine

On that particular morning, Magpie stood by the Infinity Pool, in a line of Swans which flanked the watery edges of marble. Out from their feet stretched the amplitude of the Gardens. In the distance yawned the Temple beyond the colonnade, standing center, at the base of the House of Finance. They were in the lowest tier of the Eagle Wing, and close to them was the drop; the infinite pool stretched into the open air carpeted with clouds. It was dawn yet. In the pool reposed the eagles, contemplating their domains. The field of clouds was beautiful at that hour. The tops were covered by a dull red at first — filling, like blood spreading under sheets — which then turned brighter, until it exploded in the blaze of the surging sun. The tower's long shadow stretched suddenly over the hillocks of white fume to the west, stretched far beyond the horizon, as far as the eye could see.

Magpie breathed deeply in the serenity of her disciplined temperament. The sky above her was limpid. Through the corner of her eyes she perceived the rosemary's blooming flower, and recalled those afternoons from long ago, when she traveled alone to the dry shores of the south beyond Ostrich, in the seaside preserve where trees still swung in the open wind; a magic realm so close to her neighborhood, and yet so ruthlessly beyond its byzantine, flattened walls of tar. She had never before breathed clean air. It was then, perhaps, the first time she breathed. Standing in the Southern Shores, little Magpie had contemplated the southernmost horizon like the distant beacon from a dream. How many times had she skipped school to go there afterward; and how many times had she saved on bus money to buy books about trees and flowers? A vague ambition was sown in her; and she imagined herself a biologist, or psychologist, or priestess of some sort, dedicated to exploring gently the great mysteries of that green azure... amidst nature, where she felt as though she had found herself.

But it was not to be. She was scolded badly for missing school and for dreaming impossible dreams; and slowly retreated to the entrapments of cement, ideas smothered under clouds of pollution. Magpie did eventually buy a book on plants, already an adult and with little time to read it, with the vague intention to study the mysteries of faraway, fantastical nature. For there were no trees in Ostrich; the derricks and pumpjacks stood as their sordid replacement.

She noticed the bedlam panoply of vegetation sprouting from all colors in the Eagle Gardens; all seasons mixed, all bloomed at once in a strange effect of spilled paint oozing and blemishing. Rosemary, tulip, poppy, dahlia, narcissus, snowdrop and cactus mixed unnaturally with everything else in a mutant sort of landscape.

*

The *I* lodged heavily in his breast-pocket, leaning against the beat of his heart. Its weight overwhelmed everything else in Neipas' consciousness, its presence crowded his thoughts. The pocket was shallow, and the top of the *I* rose subtly out of it (he thought). Was it visible? If he made a sudden motion, would it jump out? Neipas stood dead still. An unpleasant itch frothed under his skin and his throat began to sore again (he had been chugging pills — bought at discount from Osir — to keep down illness after the soaking he took). His hazy stare dropped toward the jacket. The fabric was so thin — the *I*'s rectangular shape was slightly distinguishable, a very small bump in the otherwise immaculately smooth texture. Would they notice? Neipas adjusted this way and that, by inches at a time, in a contorted effort to ensure the invisibility of the mirror glass. Sweat broke out on the side of his neck; his chest palpitated against the deadly object (a vague suspicion that the *I* would record nothing but the might of his heartbeats gently pulled him into psychic depths — he could be risking himself for nothing after all); his breath was made shallow with nervousness. His back wanted to arch under the weight of perceived stares. Predators glanced from every corner. He felt vertiginous and at the verge of being caught.

And yet, his mask betrayed none of his distress. His feelings were kept secret under a stoic ox stare, fixed sharply upon the needs of his attendants, who conversed round the wide, draped garden table and the lavish meal on top. It had taken Neipas a couple of afternoons' shuteye to recover from the strain of sleeplessness he had bore for days on; and it was only after he felt in full possession of his faculties that he decided to take the *I* from Janu's cupboard in the Eagle's kitchen, sneak it into his pocket, and hit record, so that the confidential sounds of the Eagle Wing would be drawn and embalmed in the glass. Though his courage faltered, still he did it; but now he stood there close by the great and powerful, and regret toyed with him.

On one side of him extended the Eagle Garden's middle terrace, full of portentous tables. Lampposts the shape of winged fish arose from the perfectly tended grass; out of the fishes' open mouths ballooned globes of light, and in the orifices of their eyes burned little flames; a Horse-masked athlete looked at them mystified and somewhat awkwardly as his Eagle owner flaunted his muscles to investors standing round them; Eagle-masked impresarios seemed to be trading Horses all throughout the yard. On the other side spread the wide facade of one of the many restaurants and recreation parlors of that terrace. The Game Halls stretched all across, up and down the complex, with its many delights. Restaurants, casinos, opera houses and other fine entertainments proliferated through the interiors beyond the three-story massive front which rose above the terrace. The westward river flowed down in little fountains upon it, sparkling at that hour with the color of champagne and sprinkling a pleasant melody throughout, mingling with the calm orchestral tune.

The area where Neipas stood belonged to a peculiar restaurant. All its cooks were Bulls who worked there year-round and were trained in the art of preparing living animals from the moment of slaughter. Wild beasts were allowed to roam about under the control of leashes; and, whenever pointed to, they would be killed, and finally prepared in front of the patrons.

Eagles and peacocks took breakfast at a table overlooking the Temple's hedge gardens. The clouds propagated beyond the edge of the lower terrace beneath, churning slowly in a powerful, dense mass of fume. The Spin Doctor looked down at the hillocks of smoke with vaguely meditative, distracted airs.

"Don't look too good, huh," mouthed the Mayor's Adviser through the mound of chewed salmon stuffed in his golden beak.

"Hm," mumbled indifferently one of the Bankers.

"Esteemed colleagues," began John the Lobbyist, speaking on behalf of NoxxeSocony. "We must look at this as an opportunity. The storm's impact will benefit our interests. Whatever it destroys, we will have the power to rebuild. And we can do a lot of good."

The Consultant, who sat at the opposite side, turned to the Corporate Lawyer next to him. The Lawyer looked somewhat confused and the Consultant said to him, translating, "Weather complications present favorable conditions for profit maximization."

"Ah," exclaimed the Corporate Lawyer, nodding with satisfaction.

At the table were gathered a group of powerful mutual interests. Representing NoxxeSocony was John the Lobbyist, who had been a Lawmaker until last year; the Corporate Lawyer; and an Economist, or Noxxe's own Numbers-Bird. Representing the State was the Minister of Energy; the Mayor's Adviser, known as his Right Wing; and a Legislator, whom Neipas recognized as the one who had sat on Stage Right, facing the Auditorium's left on the 2nd day of the Summit. Sitting there also: a public-relations Consultant; a Think Tank Analyst (the Spin Doctor); a Maskbook Engineer; and a Defense Contractor representing ArmsCorp. Among them sat three Bankers and Financiers — so that there were thirteen in total sitting at breakfast.

Neipas was just then sliding a spoon out of the beak of the Corporate Lawyer, who wore many glasses, a whole cluster all at once in his peacock eyes — eyes so large they resembled owl glares staring out of his face, neck, and shirt. Some of these eyes were magnified so as to discern the fine print on the sheet he was looking at, others to see across the table and distinguish friend from foe, yet a few others just to look smarter. He listened attentively to the conversation and seemed frustrated at his inability to understand common speech, for he had been a Corporate Lawyer for a long time; he was so deeply mired in the dialects of agreements and contracts and laws that he could no longer communicate in the common language. Thankfully the Consultant, who had once been a Corporate Lawyer also, did the kindness of interpreting.

The Minister of Energy, donning his sunglasses atop his beak, replied slowly, "What are you suggesting, John?"

"Well Richie, that's precisely what we'd like to discuss, you see," John the Lobbyist, who wore the eyes on his neck in the form of a tie, said diplomatically, sticking a finger into the air. His peacock mask resembled Noxxe's eagle countenance: his whole bearing exuded Noxxe's persona, he represented him perfectly.

"Indeed," added the Legislator.

The Legislator and the Lobbyist shared a special affinity with one another, for they had been together at the House of Law, the legislative branch of government, as members of the same party representing different districts of Ostrich. In those days districts were but abstractions on a map; lines over paper. And the success of a politician depended on how well those lines were drawn, so that these legislators were not only writers of laws, but also artists of cartography. Jack, the Legislator, was not as charismatic, nor as good of a deal-maker as John the now-Lobbyist was; but he was a better cartographer and scholar of law. He molded his own district into the shape of a salamander writhing through different neighborhoods and gobbling into its own stomach only the homes of voters who were most likely to vote for him — particularly, those in Ostrich who would rather take Noxxe's pay-out and leave. He regained his seat in the House. Jack the Legislator was obviously in favor of the expansion of Noxxe's Iblis Refinery; and so was John the ex-Lawmaker, but in the effort to retake his seat he found it necessary to tell his constituents he would fight "tooth and nail" to stop the Petroleum Baron's efforts. Voters must have seen through the mask (or the map lines were not properly drawn, as he argued passionately in private). His seat was usurped by a young activist — from Ostrich, of all places, which caused him great consternation.

But the sourness of defeat did not last long. John's eloquence and connections were recruited at once by the lobbying firm which had NoxxeSocony as its most important client, and he molded himself into the job without trouble. The principled Lawmaker was taken to the great revolving door; and came out the other side a conniving Lobbyist. He had more power this way. In representing Noxxe, he wore his mask, and had influence over the metabolisms of both industry and government.

"Chances are," John the now-Lobbyist continued, "the refinery is completely flooded by now, and there's the possibility that the chemicals might spill all over the Ostrich basin. The basin itself will be flooded to the brim, Jack, Richie. The neighborhoods will need rebuilding."

"True," concurred Jack the Lawmaker.

"Funds will need to be allocated."

"That's right."

"It's an opportunity to put those funds to good use, Jack," put in the Mayor's Right Wing. "To rebuild Ostrich into something new."

"Hm-hm. Following."

The Lobbyist rejoined. "So far the refinery's expansion has been jammed by Ostrich's residents. With the storm, there are no more residences. No more residences, no more residents. See?"

"Ah!" clamored the Energy Minister, finally catching on. For a while now, four figures had been traversing the vast lawn of the estate. The one furthest in front was very short, the one behind gigantic. They approached the table and Neipas, in his torpor of mind, only now registered that they were the little Scion (son of the Heiress and the Minister of Borders), accompanied by his tuxedoed Butler, as well as the Head Gardener and his Bull with his nose-ring and keys. The child's cheeks were puffed up with anger. "Uncle!" the air exploded out of him. He addressed the Minister of Energy, who was the cousin of his mother the Heiress, and borne out of the same family wealth.

"Just a second, dear nephew," said the idiotic Minister with the sunglasses beneath his cowboy hat. "Mr. Noxxe is speaking now."

"I! Need! To! Speak! Now!" the child heir screamed in increasingly louder bursts.

The Eagles and peacocks at the table laughed pleasantly.

"That's a fiery little fellow, Richie," commented the Defense Contractor humorously.

The Minister looked torn for a moment, vacillating between the great portent of his table companions and his nephew's anger.

"Mr. Noxxe, Jack, do you mind?"

"Not at all, Richie," replied the Lobbyist.

The Minister turned to the little Scion. "Yes, nephew?"

The child's whole frame filled up before he spoke: "He's a stupid!!" the child boomed with the full rage of his little form, pointing furiously to the motionless Chaperone beside him.

The Eagles and peacocks laughed leisurely, amused, apparently, with the child's cuteness. The Minister, hearing their approval, turned to them momentarily and laughed with his beak toward them.

"You mean he *is* stupid, dear nephew," corrected the Minister, smiling approvingly.

"Derp!" yelled the heir, punching the Chaperone's leg, who stood as still as a statue.

"Well. What seems to be the problem?"

The child Scion crossed his arms and buried his chin into the fold; his jaw compressed into many creases of waxy skin.

"He doesn't let me play with the gun! And I'm bored! Gardens are BORING! What are the flowers *for*, uncle???"

"Sir —" the Chaperone attempted to interject, but the Scion blasted with a panicked screech right off — "Shut uuuuuuuuuuuuuup!!"

Much approving laughter. The Minister, even as he laughed, turned to the Head Gardener confidentially. "Has he been behaving?" he whispered.

"Of course, Richie. He's a precious child. Very smart," said the Gardener.

The Energy Minister nodded proudly. "Dear nephew — come on now. Let the Butler speak."

The nephew sunk his nose into his furrowed arm with mumbles of utter contempt. Neipas had the impression that the kid's little devilish eyes set upon him for a moment; and he felt his own throat flinch, a little panic filled him as he sensed the *I* slipping over. But he did not move, and as the Scion deviated his eyes erratically side to side and away from him, Neipas calmed down.

The Minister's arm made a bestowing motion toward the Chaperone. "Well?"

"Sir — I meant to say, the master would like to play at the shooting range. I only thought it best to ask your permission first, sir," explained, deferentially, the Butler.

"Ah... Yes, let him do what he wants. That'd be ok, wouldn't it, Mr. Head Gardener?"

"Without a doubt, Richie. I'll make sure preparations are made."

"Thank you, sir," said the tuxedoed Butler peacock, bowing low.

Before he walked away, the Gardener — and now Neipas was sure — threw a definite glance at him, and seemed to inspect him with a moment's scan. Neipas' heart bumped.

"Can I have a machine gun!" — They stepped out, the Gardener and his Bull, the Scion and his Chaperone, bearing always a very rigid uprightness as they began trekking back across the lawn. All at once the child's wrath vanished from his mask — his cheeks deflated into their regular chubbiness and he waddled away jubilantly, with arms outstretched and making crude airplane sounds.

The Eagles and peacocks at this table and the tables nearby laughed genteelly again, and seemed well-humored. At the conclusion of the exchange the Consultant, remembering the Corporate Lawyer beside him, turned to him and summarized what had happened — "Externalities."

"Ah," said the Lawyer.

"Good kid you got there," commented one of the Bankers.

"Well," said the Minister, and he leaned over the table in a manner of secrecy, placing his fingers flat beside his beak. "Good genes, I suppose."

Everyone laughed. The meeting resumed in good spirits.

"As I was saying, Jack, Richie," Noxxe's Lobbyist rejoined, "we'd like to discuss the rebuilding efforts, not just concerning the refinery but also the surrounding area, you see."

"Hm —" nodded the Legislator, slurping his whiskey. "So you would propose relocating recovery funds for the expansion project?"

"Exactly. We drafted a bill that would grant us a bump in subsidies targeted for this specific thing."

"That might be dodgy, though, with the Liberal majority in the Lower House now. Specifically, the new members..."

The remembrance of the young activist who had defeated the now-Lobbyist John passed through the table.

"Well you're a Liberal, Jack," commented the Minister, endeavoring to be helpful.

"Understood —" explained John the Lobbyist, "but it's not direct, you see. Part of the funds go to the City, and the Mayor already has an order ready to fund the expansion as part of the recovery works."

"You spoke to Don already?"

"He's in favor of the expansion," said the Mayor's Right Wing. "He can't let on too much, but the rest of the city chamber agrees too."

"They were convinced by the prospect of us suing — not expanding clearly hurts Noxxe's profits, you see," said the Lobbyist ("indeed," said the Mayor's Right Wing).

The Corporate Lawyer had been all the while turning his head from speaker to speaker with all his eyes very narrowed, enveloped with confusion. "Just a moment," said the Consultant, holding up one hand, and he turned to the Corporate Lawyer to summarize: "Withdrawal of residential personnel around the Iblis Petroleum Refinery (IPR), belonging to NoxxeSocony Corp., would present substantial opportunities to increase the physical size of IPR's facilities and enhance its processing capabilities. Hereinafter, governmental proposals to that effect will be put forth to permit the execution of the aforementioned project."

"Ah. Comprehended," the Corporate Lawyer nodded with joyfulness, with a little jingle of his many glasses.

Orchestral music floated softly, and all around wild animals groaned in their various ways, pushing the air out their throats against the grip of collared leashes. In the background, along a line of trees at the edge, a team of burly oxen were at work setting up a massive apparatus. A great cubic structure of rusty iron was hauled through the grass, carried onward by the force of their push. The box housed three stories of tiny partitions bound by iron grates. These were what were called gestation crates in those days, and little piglets were locked within. Shackled in the extreme narrowness of the crates, the piglets squealed frantically and squirmed, jolting side to side in a madness of hopelessness.

Inside this restaurant's kitchen they stored, in a separate compartment, long shelves keeping an array of countless butchering instruments. There were knives — but there were also swords, spears, arrows, handguns, semi-automatic rifles, automatic rifles, sniper rifles fitted with amber scopes. This had to do with the restaurant's particular service. Besides choosing the type of meat to be prepared from the living animals wandering about, the patrons also had leisure to choose how they would be prepared; which included how they would be killed. From time to time one of the restaurant's special Bull cooks would call for everyone's attention; and all would turn their heads to witness the chosen animal's execution, applauding with great glee.

From that stock, a weapon was chosen for the Scion. Some paces before him the piglet cages were set. Round his chubby head they put earmuffs, upon his eyes a set of spectacles. A table was placed in front of him. The child Scion, accompanied by his Chaperone with the peacock mask, bubbled with excitement as the Bull, so giant the kid's height barely reached his waist, imparted upon him some preparatory "things to keep in mind". The Gardener stood right behind them.

One of the cook-bulls brought a machine pistol, which was placed carefully in the child's arms.

"Got it. I will whip the votes easy. And so — how much will you need?" asked the Legislator to the table, wondering disinterestedly how much money they would have to take from the common coffers.

The Economist present, or Noxxe's Numbers-Bird, had spoken nothing so far. This was because he, like the Corporate Lawyer, had understood little, and would understand almost nothing until it was translated into numbers.

The Legislator's question, however, he was able to understand. In response to it the Numbers-Bird twittered digits unfurled at the head of a trail of many zeroes, like the eyes of his long peacock tail. He blinked his myopic eyes, cleared his throat, and licked his silver beak at the end of it. The Bankers confirmed the numbers with large smiles.

"Well, Mr. Noxxe — John. Feel free to send the bill to my office and I will put it up," said Jack the Lawmaker, finishing his drink with a noisy, gurgly slurp.

"Very good," replied the Lobbyist, satisfied. The Minister of Energy nodded approvingly. Back yonder the Gardener's Bull shouted instructions at the Scion's tiny muffled ears, rotating his chubby shoulders in a soldierly manner.

"Very well," said the Consultant. "We will prepare a campaign to promote the expansion's economic advantages. We already have articles and op-eds ready to push the narrative. We will also begin focus tests on the Market right here to gage consumer-audience reactions. You," (addressing the Think Tank Analyst), "could start discussing strategies of communication with news outlets and we'll coordinate with the Conspiracy and Doubt Merchants here and across the Webwork together."

"Yes. Worries about weather and climate may arise, but we have partnered with scientists and opinion-makers that are willing to thwart those claims," the Analyst said proudly.

The Think Tanker certainly had nothing behind his mask, Neipas was sure; he was like a vessel of oily ideas, floating in an endless ocean without people. Sometimes Neipas would look up at a sly, and see, beyond the complex facade's great windows, Baron Noxxe himself looking on to the storm horizon.

"And I," put in the Defense Contractor, "will make arrangements for securing the site ASAP. We're already working with Reckuz and Bezitos on tracking," he said, and the Maskbook's Engineer, a surly, skinny, bald peacock, nodded at this. "My team is ready to be put in place as soon as there are conditions, weapons loaded. In case the residents try to loot the neighborhood."

The booming voice of the Gardener's Bull was still sounding over across the lawn when the first shot mummed it. It came off like a sharp crack, followed by a rapid sequence of resonant air-punches quaking frenetically. All sounds were subsumed, except for the orchestra's violin, which kept playing and played rapidly, and the panicked squeal of the piglets which pierced through the loud gunshot noise in desperate pleas. The Scion's elated screech could be heard too; and in the meantime the Gardener had fled and all the Eagles and peacocks hid under their tables and wailed with fright, while the waitressing cattle watched horrified and confused, bending their necks and their knees. Shot after raging shot blasted. Lead pierced and ripped flesh and organs with thunderous rushing fury, screaming in bursts of blood splattered across rust; and the little piglets, gored thus out of life, ceased to squeal long before the erratic noise of the clip ended.

The sound of bullets spread and vanished into the sunlight. The violin played still, slower now.

Yonder, the Gardener's key-bearing Bull squirmed and moaned before the gory shelves of dead piglets. He had been hit in the hands by a bullet and lay now upon the grass in agony. The restaurant's wild animals bellowed uncontrollably and tried to gallop, but their handlers pulled tight upon their leashes and stopped them violently. Louder than everything else, the child yelled still, he writhed on the lawn; and all soon discovered that his uproar was not one of elation, but of pain. Out of his beak ensued a great bellow of tears, and the water streamed down his round cheeks. The tuxedoed Chaperone stepped forth to pick him up. He laid the Scion's head on his shoulder. Apparently, the child had cut his finger when the gun's slider thrust back, and the recoil kick was so potent that he fell sideways at once; in the initial burst he had shot all piglets, pierced holes all over the crates, and as he fell one of the bullets blasted through the Bull's two hands as they reached for the Scion in the reflex to hold him.

The kid cried and cried, rabid with pain — and only calmed down when the Chaperone placed the Scion's finger in his mouth, rocking the burly eaglet up and down. The little heir was soothed, and his aches tempered amid much sniffling. The Minister his uncle stood more or less nearby, with arms akimbo and an air of vague preoccupation. As he came back the Eagles and peacocks laughed, chummy and well-humored, sitting now after hiding under their tables, their masks betraying none of the dread they had shown just seconds before.

"Good aim. He's going to be a great politician someday," said the Defense Contractor, whose own son also had a high position in government.

The Minister nodded happily, sitting down. "Takes after his uncle!"

They all bobbed their heads at each other in agreeable manners, very much content. The waitressing herd kept stuffing food into the patron's mouths, petrified at heart. Neipas felt the throb of the *I* more heavily than ever, and the very sole of his shoes felt leaden, intent to sink into the grass and through to the darkest bowels of the great tower. And the *I* — the *I* listened to everything all the while.

"Well. Back to business. We should wrap up."

Everyone looked at the Minister of Energy.

"Oh!" he bumbled with understanding after a few seconds, his sunglasses and cowboy hat tipping forward a little. "I'll do whatever permits you need, just let me know."

The Corporate Lawyer then reared his avian head over the table space, and, making a flourish with his hand, declared: "Conditions are satisfactory and proceedings estimated to develop within the bounds of legality, according to clauses 12J and 34B of the Energy Freedom Act, as well as clause 60b of the Municipal Infrastructures and Factories Act."

Everyone in the table nodded and understood. The Consultant, compelled to translate and flourish anyhow, added:

"Like my grandpa used to say, 'Crises are like mountains. They're not meant to be avoided, or walked around, or climbed over. They're meant to be mined'." And turning to the Corporate Lawyer, he said, "Vexing circumstances could increase shareholder value if proper actions are taken."

Glasses were lifted for a toast.

"Here's for Oil and Progress! To Iblis!"

Beneath them, the clouds of storm churned with monumental slowness and cosmic indifference.

46 - Ear in the Inner Breast

Days passed and meshed blurredly above the clouds. The summit of the Belab buzzed with punctual activity, the hours within its halls and gardens ticked orderly with regular motions acted everyday without variation. Every day went with the same normality. And yet minds wavered. Staring down from the bounds of the upper troposphere, distracted gazes contemplated a extensive world of billowing gas mountains and began to forget the earth. The routine schedules made nights succeed days quickly; but the incomprehensible landscape made it seem as though time had stopped and would not go on. The fields of cloud stretched on beyond the horizon and there was nothing but fumes beyond the gardens. In the intimacy of their hearts, hidden within many layers of wax, a secret belief developed that the Anubel was really an island, and the clouds the sea. Its tides churned, labored spirally with the pace of millennia. They began to believe that the Market was all there was.

Magpie gazed over the vanished horizon, the prospect shrouded in pall. Neipas hadn't seen her since the night he snuck into the Eagle Wing and hid his *I* in one of its kitchen's infinite cupboards. He beheld her now from the base of the stairs leading to the little gazebo, stoic and beautiful and still, looking yonder with eyes the color of the dying day. Neipas had gone there with the intent of leaning on the gazebo a while; but now he hesitated. There was something about the glint of Magpie's stare, visible even from the bottom of the slope — a type of sadness, a hint of despair, misted under glassiness withdrawn — that made Neipas feel that he should leave her alone.

She would appear, later on (perhaps days after; though there were calendars and clocks marking the time all around, inside the glass of every *I*, still time moved imperceptibly) in the Cafeteria at breakfast. She sat alone at a table and Neipas joined her, and at length Osir, Janu and Simon the florist did too. There was a discolored gash on the surface of her skin, by the eye, where it swelled and twitched; the crust of paint atop it couldn't conceal it, and was beginning to crack over the strength of the wound. Nevertheless, Magpie ate slowly, silently, unperturbed. No one asked anything but everyone glanced. Sometimes an uncomfortable quiet would settle in the breaks of the languid conversations between the rest of them; Simon, most unsettled by the gash in Magpie's face, kept trying to shoo the discomfort by means of inconsequential talk. Somewhat unthinking, tactless, he took to relating how, in the night previous, he had witnessed one of the infamous events in the Arena, deep in the Hall of Games. The florists were often ordered to arrange buckets of petals for the fights; petals which would be ultimately showered upon their victor.

There was always a succession of brawls of different types, following one after another till dawn. Invariably, the final show would be a savage tussle between the two strongest fighter-oxen — last night the current champion, Simon told them, had vanquished his opponent once more. The winning ox resigned to receiving the petals and the effusive cheers from above as always. Yet then, he turned his horn stumps and laden neck toward the window, whence the spectators beheld him with wonder, with pigeon beaks agape and plumage flurrying with applause; and no sooner did the ox touch the glass (Simon, who was close by the window on the other side, described the fighter's mournful expression) than a squad of Bull guards stormed into the Arena and pulled him away, subduing him with so rough and senseless a manner that Simon was shocked. This had all happened but hours before, he said, glancing at Magpie.

A silence of tense nodding ensued. Osir then spoke, holding the foam cup close to his lip:

"Yea," said he, taking his habitual pill from his little plastic bottle, swallowing it with the coffee. All looked as a thin stream of it dripped down the corner of his beak, over his flinching scar; and waited for him to continue — "I swept the arena once. Everything went to this hatch in the middle, petals, blood, dust and all... It took a while. Only me, a broom, a mop, and two buckets. I was the only one working. Besides those guards watching me, I mean. There were at least six of them, just watching me clean. They looked tense. You know. Ready to jump at me any moment."

"They're pretty aggressive sometimes, huh," Simon mumbled, nervously.

Osir sipped from the cup and fixed his gaze darkly upon the mirror; a bizarre mood set in between them, and Simon, Janu, and Neipas tensely spied Magpie, who ate still at a deliberate pace. The uneasy quietude thickened all breaths over their table as they worryingly peeked at her injury — until finally she said that she had hit a door; and said nothing else. Shortly after, she left.

They were all convinced a Bull had done it. Rumors of abuse from the guards and small anecdotes of harassment had been circulating the Pigeon Wing, all culminating in a particular incident which became the source of much controversy. Osir himself had witnessed it, and he related to them now the story of the janitor who hadn't heard the guard calling and got pulled by the horn into the ground and kicked in the ribs until they broke. Four of them sat at the table and listened to this, silent and forlorn. Myriad apologies ensued from the Eagles, endless statements of outrage, calls for reform, promises of punishment clamored from the Stage into the Auditorium, reported from the beaks of the Journalists and the Editors and their parrots.

The Ministers, and in particular the Minister of Borders, to whose legion the Bull belonged, entrenched, however, stating that the janitor was to blame because he was in an area he wasn't authorized to be in. Osir recalled in his mind the scene and saw himself standing before the memory, as if looking at it through the lens of a camera. It struck him quiet at first; it was like the memory of a memory. Like a reminiscence of the war — so far back in time now. At first he did nothing, perhaps because the sight was familiar and normal to him. It was a while until he intervened and called the Chief Supervisor and the Medics.

They ate by the mirror wall, as always; and Osir looked at it with hollow eyes as he ate, seeing through the haze of remembrance his own defaced mask and the thing pulsing inside, peeking through the pores.

Neipas contemplated his food with a glassy stare, petting it with the knife. Another certain kind of discomfort had been spreading gradually among the workers and the pass-holding pigeons. There were emerging suspicions about the food; whispers that there was something different about it. But such discussions were kept at the margins and easily dismissed. Upon close inspection, they found the food tasting the same.

Nonetheless, it was undeniable: there was a sense of paranoia germinating through the air and within the unreachable depths beyond the masks.

All of a sudden Janu spoke:

"A guard threw a bottle at me the other day."

His voice punctured timidly a silence that had formed among them in the meantime. He smiled in his usual humble way, and spoke calmly.

"Wait, what?"

"For what?"

The other three looked at him in shock.

"I dunno. Maybe because I was eating cookies. I dunno man."

He shrugged and smiled, as if admitting a mischief.

"It smashed on the wall next to me and like, I felt the glass prickle me man. I just looked around and saw him standing there. I dunno what it was. I didn't say anything".

An instinct of self-preservation had made him assume it had been an accident, and move along without a word. He had just stepped out of a meeting where he had cooked personally for the Minister of Borders, who was so pleased with the meal that he promised Janu one wish that he would attend to personally. Flushed, Janu confessed to being very worried about his family. And the Minister bid him say their names; he would make sure to find their whereabouts and situation. And so Janu the humble cook walked out the gates with a sort of submissive elation and hope, which was confused by the sudden violence whooshing in beside him. He turned at a glance; and spotted in a moment the monstrous uprightness of the stud-collared bull, casting smoke out of his wet nostrils. Janu's heart quivered and he felt cowed behind the ox mask; neck strained forward as though under a yoke, he simply left.

It wasn't clear what had compelled him to speak out of his introverted self. He looked around the table, smiling and nodding slowly; perhaps looking for validation of some sort. Osir nodded also, but in the distracted manner of one who isn't listening any longer; and the others knew not what to say, so after a silence they mumbled:

"That sounds awful man."

In those days, Neipas worked intensely, and was mostly assigned to service in the Eagle Wing. He possessed the most important quality demanded of the waiters — he was able to be invisible — and the smiling Chief Supervisor favored him. But he also had days off and time to rest. Though the work and conditions were as hard and stressful as ever, the Chief Supervisor's soft rule and sympathetic treatment mollified and even encouraged the workers. No one missed Drrawetz. Sometimes the former steward would be seen brooding in the distance of the Eagle Gardens. He had gotten a happy job polishing their talons... yet from the look in his eyes it was clear he seethed, and craved the old power.

Whenever he could, Neipas took the forbidden ear of the *I* into the depths of opulence, the ear to capture the gilded voices of the Eagles and Peacocks freely let loose. It was always nerve-racking, but by and by he developed a method.

Janu's mother, kind Mrs. Tia, had once taught Neipas how to sew a patch pocket. So he bought a pair of scissors, pins, needle, thread, and fabric in the Market; and every night, after dropping his uniform in the vast laundry and collecting a fresh outfit from the Clockroom, he would tuck in his bed shelf and sewed a pocket inside the jacket, on the inner part of the breast, to hide the *I* there next morning. Every day after his shift he would store the *I* in the depths of Janu's cupboard, in the Eagles' Kitchen; and every day he would remove the pocket before dropping the jacket for cleaning.

Hidden safe in his inner breast-pocket, the *I* listened to many words sealing many deals and schemes of theft. And, above everything, it captured the scornful tone with which the Eagles referred to the rest of the universe, the immense indifference and derisive contempt with which they regarded their subjects. Neipas heard the most diabolical things uttered from those beaks gifted with education of the highest level, with privileges of the highest comfort. Here, they were at home — and they wore their true masks freely, without fear.

The *I*'s battery-life would not last long, however, and soon it became necessary to recharge it with electric vigor. There was no way he could do this in the Eagle Wing without being found, so he had to return to the pigeons' side the same way he had taken the night he was led through the Museum's woods by the shackled Midget. Neipas thought of it and worried for days before he acted. He decided to move out at the end of a shift, and simply walk through the hedges, with his ox head atop the worker tuxedo and eartag off, keeping to himself as best he could. Just then, his *I* still had a bit of life left.

Toward the end of the afternoon now he went among the green walls of shrubbery, through its shaded paths, past its quaint follies, along its ornate trellises embroidered with thorns and along its flowery ponds, from the midst of which mute statues beheld his march with eyeless globes of stone. He strolled through a particularly remote patch on the way which made him stop.

It was a grove of trees of a very strange kind. Above the sturdy and crooked trunks bloomed the canopies, and the canopies were encapsulated inside thick cocoons. They looked like grisly cotton candy atop uncrafted sticks, wrapped in plastic, like furniture, or embalmed like museum pieces, like ancient tombs... Like nests. Approaching carefully the sinister vision, Neipas touched the fabric; and he saw that it was silk; the trees were enmeshed in cobweb. The sun, directly yonder, flowed phantasmagorically through the dense weave of fluff. A subtle breeze passed over them. It was eerie; but beautiful. It was a singular vision, something he had never seen before.

He looked about him quickly. There was no one. The upper terraces were nowhere in sight or hearing. A sudden craving to record what he saw, a sudden desire to frame it and encapsulate its magic, took hold of him; and so he took the *I* out of his hidden breast-pocket and raised it before his sight. Before him the grove spread with spectral wonder, the choked leaves of its canopies clustering against the reddening skies in plea and embrace, progressing forth in circular motions. It was a strange image of calm, a sight irresistible in the eyes of a photographer, and enough to stir the sensitivities of any artist. So Neipas placed the *I* atop his sight and prepared to shoot the ethereal scape.

His heart stilled. Click — and in that same moment his heart sprung into a frantic beat as Neipas lowered the *I* and fumbled it back into the pocket of his pants. He hadn't time for anything else. Right as he shot the picture he spotted forms blackening the sunny distance, turning the bend and walking in his direction. In a sudden panic he rummaged through his mind and searched for a decision; should he turn back, or keep walking? — and in his indecision he kept still, the rumbling of his heart nailing him to the spot.

It was the Head Gardener who was coming.

47 - The Eye of the Storm

Kasim the Pantrykeeper and Gardening Assistant followed close behind the Head Gardener. Towering bulky over their lank shapes was the Gardener's powerful Bull. They appeared to Neipas' eyes as sinister blots over the sunlight, nearing with demonic intents, shushing the breeze.

Neipas acted with instinct. His fingers thrust into the outer mask to ensure it held the deferential look of a servant and the impassive manner of a professional; and he ascertained the inner mask did not seep out in flows of wax. Though he couldn't well weather the rocking inside him, his body stood erect, and, placing his hand formally over his stomach, he waited. Before the ambling shadows gained definition, Neipas heard the sound of metallic rattling. As of a chain of keys repeatedly scrapping off each other in sparks; and his heart quivered at every beat.

Finally they were there. Neipas lowered his horns with his whole back. The Gardener nodded and tapped his cane, the Bull kept staring firmly forward, his hands wrapped up in gauze, keys flashing from his mighty nostrils — Kasim, who was burdened with picnic chairs and a folding table about his limbs, glanced at Neipas and then fixed his stare away with some nervousness — and they passed.

Relieved, Neipas eased slowly back into his walk. His nerves slackened as he heard leaves crunched underfoot a distance behind him — but now the Gardener's voice was sounding. Neipas still took a couple of tremulous steps with vain hope; but the voice sounded again, and it was calling him. His heart bulged in writhing blood, injected with sudden dread.

"Mr. Head Gardener, sir." His voice came out entirely regular, clear, stolid. It was the mask which had spoken, and it denounced nothing of the juddering underneath. He greeted the Eagle, the Bull, and the Ox with a deep bow.

"Taking a walk?" asked the Gardener. The Bull stood at attention behind him, enormous.

"Yes, sir. I'm on break at the moment," he said without thinking, and immediately he feared the Seamstresses would still be listening.

"Sure, sure," said the Gardener, as if in passing. He looked about himself, nodding contemplatively. "So, how do you like this?"

"Oh — the gardens, you mean, sir?"

"The Gardens," he said with a long, absent nod. "Yes."

The Gardener gave off a vague air of seasoned explorer with his ornate cane and feathered wattles, and the upright stance along the golden buttons of his black shirt, wrapped round his broad torso, implied an aged sort of aristocratic sentiment. He emanated authority. His very presence was intimating; it belittled Neipas, rousing an instinct to bend submissively before him.

"It's very beautiful, sir," replied the unnatural voice of Neipas' mask.

"Yes... Yes, it is. It took a long time and dedication, a long, long time. A lot of craft, you know. And a lot of money too, of course. But here it is."

The Gardener fell silent and contemplative again. He nodded admiringly at the glade of web-wound canopies.

"This happens to be my favorite part. Do you see these trees?" the Gardener pointed. Without waiting for an answer he took a few steps to enter the unearthly, silky shade of one. "They came from the Land of the Pashtuns, or somewhere nearby. It's a wonderful thing. They had a great flood in that country a few years ago... Whole populations of spiders climbed to the canopies so they wouldn't drown, you see. Once the floods receded — and it was a long time before that happened — the Pashtuns found the trees all wrapped up in silk.

"It turned out with a beautiful effect. They look like cocoons, don't they? Or like nests that grew to envelop the tree... Mary — Once I saw the photographs, I knew I had to have them. So I had a couple flown here.

"It struck me that there's a wisdom to it. The earth is dangerous and unsanitary. Our nests will have to conquer their trees before they conquer us. We'll need our own cocoons to survive someday.

"We'll need to overcome nature. That's what I mean. Only those that climb above it will escape. You can see... — " he trailed off, nodding.

The Gardener spoke with the inspired mysticism of a poet. His voice, murmured but clear, seemed to sprout from the profundities beyond his effortless mask, out of the confident authority granted by his white, avian face. He patted the tree's bulky stem with his cane and beheld the canopy with pride.

"Yes, quite a thing. I only brought a couple of these in the beginning, but soon all the trees around them looked like this. I'm not entirely sure how. Then I expanded the whole grove to make it look like this," said the Gardener, turning back into the vastness of the orchard. "Fascinating, isn't it? It simply flourished here."

He looked with a distracted glare toward Neipas, with vague eyes turned inward; and nodded pensively. Neipas, who had somehow regained his cool as he heard the Gardener speaking — in his stillness and immersion, he forgot the *I* resting in his trouser's pocket — had sensed a strange feeling of confidence spread within, as if the confident voice of the mask had whispered its power inward too. When the Gardener's head leveled and his stare focused, Neipas at once perceived he had been waiting for him to speak.

"Maybe it's the type of air," said Neipas, calmly.

A pause, and the Gardener padded the tree wonderingly. He nodded again — slower now, darkly, as if surmising a malicious significance in Neipas' words.

"Hm. Perhaps," he said.

Then, suddenly, as if snapping out of a daydream, the Gardener asked, "What's your number?"

There was nothing particular in his tone, but the abruptness with which he asked tipped Neipas a little, nudging him off balance. The Bull stood inert close-by, and though he looked rooted to the spot and Neipas himself hadn't moved it appeared, somehow, that they were nearer together now. Kasim was further back, and he too was still; but in a different way, with the stillness of one containing internal shudders.

"431999," Neipas replied with a respectful bow.

"431999..." repeated the Gardener, nodding slowly. "431999, what are you doing here?"

Neipas' heart skipped a beat.

"Sir?"

"In these gardens, I mean. You know you can't walk here without a supervisor."

Neipas felt the corner of his lip twitch and his entire being prayed that the mask had concealed it. His mouth opened but it produced no sound, and trembled even more.

"What are you doing here?"

The repetition dropped in his ears like a dipping bullet. Veins swelled in the brain. Suddenly his mind was blanked with noise; his body stood vaguely tremulous as his spirit contracted to an atom; he struggled deliriously to keep both linked. But his mask of docile ox, stooping beneath the horns, betrayed nothing.

His voice sounded from a distance — "I apologize, sir" — the voice of someone else, strangely calm, uncannily cold, mechanized; his hearing had retreated behind the shield of clay deep into the recesses of his being, and cowered in the darkness, frightened. It seemed to him that his *I* vibrated in his pocket.

"I — I confess I didn't know, sir. I walked here from service at the terrace."

The Gardener nodded slowly, menacingly. Neipas hadn't noticed it before then but suddenly he realized that the Bull had somehow moved behind him. Neipas sensed him ominously near; he anticipated heavy hands crushing the bones of his shoulders or breaking the front of his neck at any moment.

"I believe you, 43199... —" the Gardener pondered, craning forward his narrow eyes, not for a second removing them from Neipas. "What's your name again?"

"Neipas. Neipas, sir," he quivered, and now the quiver had entered his voice.

"Don't worry, Neipas. I safeguard this place. It's sacred — I must be a good custodian, and make sure nothing slips. You wouldn't object to a little pat down, would you?"

"Sir?"

"Would you?"

Neipas had no choice.

"No, sir. Of course not."

Neipas' spirit shrunk to nonexistence and his mind wavered in a delirium. Though his body stood firm he felt himself falling endlessly, as though he had been thrown out of the tower; his head was full of thunderous clouds.

"Kasim, could you please?" said the Gardener, finally looking away from him.

"Master? Me?"

"Well? You, Kasim. Look at his hands," meaning the Bull's, whose hands were bound in bandages. "Search his breast-pocket first."

"Very well, master," stammered Kasim with some difficulty, and approaching Neipas shyly, courteously, he bowed his horns and lifted his fingers toward his breast-pocket.

"No, Kasim," the Gardener put in, interrupting the movement. "I mean the *inner* breast-pocket."

Behind his mask, Neipas stared at the Gardener with shock; and Kasim with confusion. "But, master. If I may, there is no inner pocket in these jackets."

"Search," the Gardener insisted.

Kasim neared yet closer, and as he did Neipas saw fear blazoned in his eyes too. Timidly, Kasim pulled first one, then the other lapel on Neipas' tuxedo jacket, and peeked inside the sewed patch pocket. There was nothing there.

"Well?"

"Nothing, master," said Kasim.

"Let me see."

The Gardener took one step and, leaning upon his cane, craned forward as Kasim gently showed him the open, empty inner breast-pocket.

"All right," the Gardener uttered magnanimously, "Go on."

Neipas rooted firm to the grass; his heart pumped in every fiber of muscle, from brain to under the toenail.

Yet his body was stolid; his mask unmoving. Stirrings everywhere under it, but the surface was still. The certainty of firing had overpowered him but he held off yet against the prospect of prison, or worse.

Kasim patted his body from top to bottom, clumsily but thoroughly — as he knew he was being watched. When he touched the *I* in Neipas' trouser pocket the whole gardens seemed to crumble underfoot, sounds of bursting wood and rushing rivers came tearing up from the earth's utmost deep. Neipas felt his legs falter and had the mental sensation of tripping. He was doomed.

He waited — but Kasim said nothing.

"Well?"

"Hum... Nothing, master. I cannot find anything out of the ordinary."

"Very well."

The Gardener smiled at Neipas amicably, suddenly adopting a different tone of voice. As he shifted Neipas suddenly realized the aggressive tinge accompanying everything he had said so far.

"I hope you don't mind — Nepas. I'm in charge of these Gardens, and they are sacred. All precautions must be met, you understand."

They looked at each other.

"Of course, sir," Neipas said; he heard the tranquility falter in his fake voice, and felt afraid again. The *I* was almost dead and he was sure it had trembled now; he dreaded, with profound terror, that the Gardener would hear it. But he wasn't close enough to Neipas.

"Ne — Nepas, correct?"

"Yes, sir." Neipas didn't dare to contradict him.

"So tell me, what's the reason you sewed a pocket to your jacket?"

If Neipas passed this test and answered the question to the Gardener's satisfaction, he would be safe. He didn't hesitate now — as though the miraculous outcome of the frisk had lent him strength. All the divine powers of improvisation rushed to his aid and suffused his soul, which spoke for him without flinching, without even his control, through the professional immobility of his ox mask:

"Sir, to be honest... It's just that I stand for hours on end during my shifts and I am not allowed to eat during all that time. So I — sometimes I sneak a little food to snack on here."

The Gardener simply looked at him, expressionless and inscrutable.

"Say, Nepas, where are you from?" he asked suddenly. "I notice a tinge in your accent — You're not from here, are you?"

Neipas was surprised at the sudden tone of familiarity and wondered if the Gardener really didn't remember him.

"No, sir, indeed. I'm from the heartlands."

"Mary! Let me guess — Minoa."

"A little outside of town, sir," said Neipas, smiling.

"I knew it!" exclaimed the Gardener, lifting himself on his toes. "I'm from Doris."

"Ah really, sir," Neipas said between professional impassivity and friendly enthusiasm. "I've been there many times. Nice place."

"Oh come on," shot the Gardener before Neipas had finished articulating the words; there was a sudden impatience in his voice that made Neipas shrink. There was a sudden spasm in his thigh, and the glade paused; a swelling flared up in his head and he felt the *I* vibrating again.

The Gardener kept on:

"You don't really believe that! Nothing but a whole lot of mud and flies... I liked Minoa, though. Very idyllic. The accident with the tailings dam was unfortunate."

"Yes, sir," said Neipas as sounds of a furious torrent sounded afar inside his head; a certain discomfort inched up in his throat.

"Indeed..." the Gardener looked about him, and then, addressing Kasim — "Let's settle here, shall we?"

"Next to the tree, master?"

"Yes. Set up three chairs please."

Kasim picked up his load and ambled toward the tree, unburdening himself carefully. Neipas automatically stepped in to help him, happy to disengage from the Gardener's talk for a moment. As they unfolded their chairs they exchanged furtive glances. Neipas couldn't interpret the eyes of the other ox mask, and the mystery of general intentions made him nervous, eager to leave. The Gardener paced about the glade around them, examining the silken shrouds of the canopies with his cane.

The table and the three chairs were set. The Gardener and his Bull approached, and the Gardener slid upright into a chair as Kasim spread the linen cloth over the table. The Pantrykeeper removed food from the basket — cheeses and ham, bread, wine — distributing the items fashionably. Once this was done the Gardener, clearing his throat, made a gesture toward the table. Kasim sat; Neipas and the Bull stood still, and a chair remained empty.

"Join us. I know you're hungry —" the Gardener retreated into his memory for a short moment. "Remind me your name?"

"Neipas, sir," he said, and he trembled inwardly at the prospect of stepping that closely to the Gardener; surely he would hear if the *I* vibrated once more.

"Neipas! Please," the Gardener rejoined, motioning generously toward the empty chair. Neipas complied, as he knew he ought to do. He stepped near, and sunk his head lower into the spory, choking air of the glade. His chest seemed to be made heavier as it dipped.

"Always happy to see a fellow heartlander," began the Gardener. "We were going to eat up in the estates, but I prefer to be here. It's quiet and I like the isolation."

The Gardener took the bread loaf and, seizing the knife, cut half for himself; then he helped himself to the ham and the cheeses, drawing great quantities to his side of the table, and as he did so he requested that Neipas serve him a glass of wine; which Neipas did, having to bend over a little awkwardly and impotently as he wasn't used to do it sitting down.

"Well? Help yourselves," instructed the Gardener.

There was a moment of hesitation on Neipas' end, whereas Kasim sprung to action immediately, taking hold of the loaf and parting off a slice, spreading cheese on the crumb and laying a frond of the light-colored ham on top. Neipas followed his lead tentatively. The usual smoothness of his conduct as a waiter contrasted with his stiffness of motion now he sat at the table and wielded the blade. He felt something in the sturdiness of his ox mask falter.

"Don't be shy. Eat."

There was something unseemly in the act of eating in front of an Eagle. Opening his mouth felt like a transgression; so he made the gap between his lips just narrow enough to fit the piece through.

They ate in silence and Neipas simmered in extreme discomfort. He tended to fix his gaze down upon his plate, looking up only in glances. He chewed slowly, handling the meal with one hand only; he pressed his trousers beneath the table in an attempt to shut down the *I*, or so that its vibration would not be noticed. Before him, and behind the Gardener, the Bull's uniform of vivid red streaks bulged from the languid shimmer of the glade, rimmed in glow. The guardian stood at attention upon his corporeal mass, motionless and obedient, a hard wall of muscle ready to bend over and break bone at command. Veiled by a deeper shade, Kasim appeared meek and muted, inscrutable for the moment, eating. And though he daren't peek, Neipas felt the eyes of the Gardener intent upon him, he felt the weight of his stare and his chest compressed slowly between the thinning air of spores, in a torture of expectation.

Eventually he looked, and he saw the Gardener's narrow eyes fixed on him; contemplating, evaluating, judging. Neipas returned his stare with the stare and the smile of his own mask; and, feeling the oppression of the situation, enduring the unbearable weight of the *I*, he quickly felt compelled to say something:

"So, hum — is this all yours, sir? The gardens? Did you make all of it?" Neipas more or less blundered this, but in a calm tone; internally anxious to diffuse the tension.

"The Gardens and many of the facilities were reshaped to my taste, yes. They shift according to modern tastes, whatever modernity means at different times."

The Gardener took a sip of wine and for the first time since he had sat down drew his eyes away from Neipas. "But I don't own the Eagle's Nest," he said.

"No one person owns the Eagle's Nest. I'm the most recent caretaker, and it's a great honor. But the Eagle's Nest has been here since the beginning of times, and there were others before me."

Neipas nodded shyly; the Gardener nodded slowly. The silence settled and sat uncomfortably in Neipas' chest again; and again he sought to dispel it.

"How did you become the current caretaker — if you don't mind my asking, sir?"

"It's a long story," the Gardener said, but it was obvious he intended to tell it. He took another sip of wine.

"I began by herding sheep. My father was a priest and we didn't make very much." He paused and chewed long on a bite of sandwich.

"Your own farm, sir?" asked Neipas into the unquiet silence.

"No, no..." — The Gardener gulped the rest of the wine at once. Whenever he drank his eyes would look up to the canopy; and the silence ensuing was almost as uncomfortable then as it was when he stared straight at Neipas. But presently his intent gaze returned to the waiter ox; and he continued, speaking as he ate:

"I was just a hand. I had to feed the sheep at dawn, take them out to pasture, shear the fleece in the spring, whatever else there was to do. Clean out the barn. Select the lambs for slaughter. Slaughter them myself, sometimes."

Parallel memories alighted in each of their minds, in each of the four present. The sensation of living flesh pulsing in their hands and blood coursing feverishly through their fingers stirred them for a moment.

"It was hard work, but I didn't mind it," the Gardener continued. "I liked it sometimes. The work itself, I mean. I liked working with the sheep. Of course I hated cleaning the barn. I hated the smell of it. And — I have to confess — I hated the mistress of the farm. I always wanted to be my own boss, you see.

"So I saved up, little by little. It was tough. Let's just say my father wasn't the best minister," the Gardener chuckled sourly, "so we would go hungry sometimes.

"But eventually I managed to get out. I invested in the stock market. That's where I first learned gardening, by the way. I planted my seeds here and there, watched what grew and what didn't... And harvested when the right time came.

"Money is the best kind of plant, let me tell you. It grows fast, you see. Nowadays it doesn't even need land, and the more you have of it the faster it grows, the more sun it gets, and the less you need to work. It grows and grows; it almost harvests itself.

"Anyway, I ended up buying the farm I had worked at. The sheep farm. I expanded it. I bought cattle, swine, poultry. I grew to be one of the top providers of meat in the nation. And I made a lot of money, a lot of money. Stems beget branches beget fruit. I expanded into related enterprises: agribusiness, and then pharmaceuticals. Timber also of course. Advertisement. I'm starting to invest heavily in geo-engineering... I'm telling you now, that's the next big thing. The next frontier. Soon," said the Eagle, pointing to the hedges in the direction of the tempest, "we will be able to control even the weather. Kasim — please."

The Gardener had finished his meal. During the course of it Neipas had strained to keep his pace adequately; not too fast so as to not appear indecorous, but fast enough to finish at the same time as the Gardener (to continue eating after he was done would have been a travesty of good form) — and kept his hand pressed upon his pocket under the table always, holding choked the throes of the *I*. At the same time, he strained faintly to subside the unruliness of his emotions; as the Gardener spoke, the distance between mask and self widened deeper.

Kasim rose and began packing up the dishes and scraps. Now only Neipas and the Gardener sat at the table.

"Things come to you if you're ready to seize them. I grew, I climbed... Now I live here, and safeguard the top of the tower. I designed the Gardens to their current state and I tend to them. Gardening is something I went into meantime, while I grew — as sort of a pastime. But really I've been designing gardens all my life."

Kasim had cleared the table.

"Well," the Gardener rose, and Neipas anxiously got up with him, taking great care not to bump against the Bull as he moved round. He could almost feel the great oscillations of his powerful chest, and the warm fumes of his nostrils. Kasim rushed to collect the two empty chairs and the table.

The Gardener had occasionally drawn his eyes away from Neipas during his monologue; but they were now fixed upon the ox semblance of the waiter again, focused. Kasim had concluded his work and the quiet tones of the glade settled fresh upon their ears; for a moment.

Below them the clouds heaved with deep intonations.

"Success often begins when you step somewhere you're not supposed to, Nepas. Especially for those of us who come from where we come from," the

Gardener took a step toward him. "It's always best to have backing if you're caught, but — don't worry. Technically you're not supposed to be here, but it's ok."

The Gardener took another step. Neipas shook, and dominated the impulse to step back as every inch of his body went into a fit; he strained and held on with all his might.

But already the Gardener was walking away with his entourage. He waved as he went onward the trail.

"Always good to see a heartlander!"

The *I* shook convulsively one last time inside Neipas' pocket — and went off.

The sun had sunk into the clouds underneath and the color of the sky above was rusting. Shaken, Neipas sneaked out of the Gardens, climbed down the ladder and opened the glass gate into the hidden platform bridging the Eagle and Pigeon Wings which hovered narrow and precipitously upon the air, straddling the tower wall. Yet providence favored Neipas; for he journeyed just as the eye of the storm enveloped the Belab.

Neipas stood over the eye. No wind troubled his passage. The air was unruffled; the abysmal view clear. Neipas stood over the eye, and he faced the massive wall of the tempest retreating from him, churning slow; and beneath his feet plunged the abyss along the mighty face of the Belab, down, down to cosmic depths. Stare widened in awe, his senses pierced the worldly drop, opened titanic underneath, resembling the moving gullet of a colossus. The spinning walls cascaded dramatically toward the remote, fluid Axiac; they looked to him like the ash tree of his nightmares, the titan ghastly tree rooted in heaven, blooming in the maelstrom; growing down into the depths of tar soil, worlds beneath his wide gaze, gaze wide with horror.

It was Sunday then, and the firmament was nearly moonless; the glare of the Pearl dominated the airy dusk widening into far reaches. Neipas had the impression of seeing the mountain peaks surfacing through the tempest yonder, draped in dark snow, as of a slumbering god about to shake off the dew of ages from its colossal mind. He was closing the second glass gate when the eye vanished and the second wall of the storm overtook the Belab. The whole Eagles' Nest convulsed abruptly then, everything began to stir and tremble mightily.

Neipas shut the door with strain, entering the Pigeon Wing — a great rattle of chains beat upon his steps, and immediately he saw, lying before the Museum doors, the fetters which had bound the Midget.

Standing there confusedly a while, feeling the heart inside his chest tremble with the teetering of the altitude, he beheld the chains and remembered suddenly to take off his shoes so as to not awaken the Giant Historian. All shook in mad drunken sway, and the bells pealed feverishly; it was as if the whole structure of the Belab intended to tip over and collapse. He hastened through the Museum doors, staggering in upon his bare feet; he faced the End of History and its two mighty fronts of glass, swooning hazy before its carved serpent of closed eyes — he stared bewildered upon the mirror showing the entire depth of the Museum, and had the impression of someone behind him, perhaps his own reflection replicated in the shiver — when it happened.

The lights disappeared. Neipas flinched, his heart panged; in a panicked moment he assumed he had gone blind. It was but an instant.

Suddenly all came still. Voices came floating to him ghostly from far away, voices of confusion and protest.

Neipas shambled forth in the thick darkness.

48 - Fiat Tenebrae

"Once," said Oshana, and her voice sounded from the invisible tide beneath the cliffs, whispered from the dark foliage of the forest, "darkness ruled the night."

All forms became ghosts after dusk. They molded the imagination and commanded the soul, blanketing the spirit, rendering the eye blind.

"In the absence of light, the universe was sound. Noise without body. Spirit without vessel." One's own invisible steps upon the earth were acute upon the senses. One's own sense of presence was profound, felt; mystical. Whispering black trees and invisible beasts rumbled low. Gods waited in the black foliage beyond the edges, whispering the breath of life through hungry maws and mighty teeth. They stirred the senses with primordial frights, sharpened the instincts.

The night was sovereign and tyrant over the hearts of men.

"The first victory against darkness," said Oshana, "was the taming of fire."

*

As the blackness filled everything of an instant, Neipas experienced the physical sensation of falling. It was as if he had momentarily lost footing in sandbanks plummeting undersea — his knees collapsed, he staggered forward, and he would have tumbled altogether if the palm of his hand hadn't found the wall before him. His heart panged, he had the impression of his head swirling and diving in a spiral. Putrid smells pumped up his nose and blew into the very core of his brain; and his ears were filled with a throbbing movement along which his breathing bulged and shriveled, bulged and shriveled...

He could see nothing but black. The Museum had disappeared. Neipas hovered in pure darkness, the deepening ocean had swallowed the End of History. He stopped and tried to recover, breathing deep, pressing the glass wall hard as though it were the only proof of continued existence. Gradually his spasming muscles stilled; the throbbing faded, the stench vanished. By and by he becalmed. He waited with head downturned in anticipation, sure that the power would return soon.

Whereas there had been sound just before, a sudden quietude befell; the gloom seemed to deepen further. Neipas strained his ear. For a while he could only hear his own breathing drawing air from the dense shadow and expelling air back into its confines; and nothing more. His own mind dispersed slowly in the darkness, and he felt the inclination to lay down against the base of the glass and sleep. But he stood a little more, waiting for the power to return.

Bit by bit he came to realize the cadence of breathing beside his own. Its rhythm broke from his own. At first he thought it was the Midget — but it couldn't be, because it came from right beside his head. Neipas reached into his pocket. But the *I* was lifeless; it could not cast light. He stood, petrified, against the sheer unreality of the gloom, the feeling of wide open space and the sense of eyes prowling in the shadow, of presences lurking. His own smallness before the infinitude of an invisible universe occurred to him. There were little sounds now; and in here all little sounds were magnified, and all were signs of danger. An indefinite fear began seizing hold of him. Yet he waited, sure that the power would return at any moment.

After much time standing in growing fright and indecision his body wavered, to and fro slowly, unmoored in that endless ocean of shadow; and he began to tremble. The breathing next to him blew spectral into his ears and whispered in his heart. It trembled, too. It was a sibilant whisper, a voice from the deep. Its presence quickly became more palpable and Neipas almost braced for sudden contact, a hand on his shoulder, a push. There was someone — someone very near him now, very close. Panic began to take hold of him.

For a moment the whole world tipped over; the ground lurched and the air shook. Nausea and vertigo overcame him, his muscles twitched with anxiety and an impulse to run indiscriminately possessed his every nerve. His heart exploded with the first abrupt step as he pitched; but just as it began, it stopped. His breast drummed, his breathing quivered through his gaping lips. Yonder, behind the cold wall, he could see, very faint, the glimmering of a flame.

Neipas felt a hand from below, holding his own. And he becalmed; for he had felt the grip of that hand before. It guided him through the darkness. His cheek parted from the wall's cold surface... Neipas felt himself gliding across endlessly open skies, obscure heavens whose sun had been drowned in tar. He was taken down steep invisible steps, led by the patient divinity; and even as they descended he felt his head pushing aloft, very far from his feet across the black air of submerged spaces; up many steps again, very slowly and for a very long time.

Something in the air changed and he felt the grip of the hand from below no longer. It must have left him sometime during the walk up those steps, and in reality he became aware that the presence hadn't been with him for quite some time already. Neipas stood in the darkness frozen. He saw dots of red light blinking languidly in the walls.

Eventually he began sliding along on his own. He drifted away from the Museum and along the corridor of the Columbaria toward the dormitories, having gained some sense of where he was. The craving for isolation and silence he usually felt was replaced by a pressing desire to hear a word of clarification and comfort. He longed to hear a friendly voice, or at least a voice he could recognize and anchor himself upon. The tenebrous unvision in his eyes corresponded to the state of his heart as of late — unmoored, unfamiliar, confused — and it made him feel the secret despondency of his breast in its full reality. The sudden darkness, and its absolute solitude, made him feel sick and afraid.

(A very faint sound reached into his sleepy head from afar – it had the character of electric wind with some beat sprouting out of it. Just then Neipas took his hand to the sound and found the eartag dangling from his earlobe. He pressed it back in — through the static played orchestral music, pervaded by a deep, angelic hum — lolling in the mellow pulse of it a while. 'Wasn't the eartag off?'. He was sure he had it turned off. In the humming he discerned the form of words whispered, sung, undulating: numbers repeating in a loop. His other ear held outward, vaguely anticipating other forms of life as may be found lurking in the dark.)

On the one ear whispered the music, turned down low; but on the other ear Neipas could perceive no more than his own steps falling nearly muted on the floor. His feet felt as though they landed on nothing sometimes, and sometimes the ear that listened for them heard other things, a bit of wind, a murmur of some sort. Neipas would stop startled, feeling someone's presence (it wasn't the patient divinity, it wasn't the Midget; was it the other shadow, had it chased him?). His lips would voicelessly mutter a "hello?..." to check — after a moment he concluded there could be no one but himself.

And yet his empty ear occasionally perceived vague, ghostly rumblings in the nearness of its ken. These strange sounds mingled and confused themselves with his own steps, and Neipas, in the general indistinctness of things, could not distinguish which was which. The blinking red dots, which he interpreted as having something to do with the power failure, only enhanced the sense of mystical paranoia. He deviated from his senses; at times he wondered whether he wasn't actually sleeping. It was only after a long, long time — it seemed to him, but as he snapped back into reality he had the strange sensation that he had just begun walking — that he recognized noises which were clearly not his own. He quickened his step and advanced largely, with head between shoulders, one hand on the wall and another rummaging the shadows in front. He sped up; but even in his accelerated pace it seemed to him that the darkness had lengthened the corridor for a tremendous distance, for he walked for a long time yet in absolute nothingness.

(There's a light yonder).

As Neipas approached he saw that there were many lights gleaming upon a multitude of shadowy shapes moving about in agitation, movements squirming twofold before and beyond mirror walls. One of those lights beamed on him straight, and from it emerged a voice:

"Who's that!" — it was Osir the Janitor Supervisor who spoke. "Neipas? What are you doing back there?"

"What happened?" spoke Neipas out of his mental fogginess. The sounding of his own voice injected some sense of presence into the air, blowing away feebly at the gloom of his own perceptions.

"The lights went off, just like that," said someone behind Osir.

"Huh," mumbled Neipas, spacing out further still. Then, regarding the conversing bodies — some of which had swollen eyes and lingered about in underwear and pajamas, while others donned work attires, with a few still inside their ox heads — he noticed his own reflection on the mirror wall. It was almost translucent in the ghostly lights; and there was that red dot blinking. He reached for the reflection; and when his fingers touched it he perceived that the red dot was beyond it, beyond the surface of the mirror. He tilted his stare subtly and frowned a little; then added: "Yes I know, but do you know how it happened?"

"No. I was just getting ready to doze off," replied Osir. His scar looked positively fleshy and the deformation upon his face horrible, protruding with carnal glints and casting heavy shadows upon his features as he looked into his *I*. "We were trying to find the panelboard... No one knows where it is."

"Do you have connection?"

"Not here."

But not two seconds had passed after Osir said this when the lights turned on again. There was a collective motion of heads and open mouths panning upward then, as though the ceiling had opened to reveal cherubim come down, bathed in heavenly radiance. All at once they relaxed and looked glassily at each other. Then they began resuming whatever they were doing before the darkness came – some dwelt in their *I*s a little, others scrubbed their feet along back into the dormitory – until they stopped again at the sound of Osir's light slurping, and voice.

"Wait up," he said roughly, raising his hand as he dunked into his *I*. "Special meeting called in... Cafeteria. We're all supposed to be there in thirty minutes."

A few mumblings of protest ensued from the general crowd, but they came so weak as to not pull Osir's attention in the slightest. Osir himself didn't seem pleased. "Goodness sake. What's this about now?" he wondered aloud and grumpy as he stared into the *I*.

The little red light had disappeared. Neipas reached for his image in the mirror again, in a total blankness of mind.

He shook his head, and decided that he had to sleep. Now that the mighty lights were on again Neipas wanted no more than to return to darkness; to close his eyes and faint upon some mattress somewhere. He wanted familiar voices no more – the drowsy presence of his fellow workers irked him already. Giving in to mental fatigue, latent feelings of irritation buoyed to the fore of his mind and affected his nerves. Neipas looked at the sluggish bodies staring out, and felt acutely his hatred for their stupid masks. He wanted listen to nothing, to nobody. "See you guys there," Osir said sluggishly as he walked off.

But the angst about some vague punishment — Neipas didn't know anymore what exactly it was he feared — led him to walk to the meeting in the Cafeteria. He entered it groggily, joining the throng congregating round the tables. A mellow buzz of muddled voices rose amid the glut of *I* lights and lowered horns. Some sat, others leaned against something, and almost no one stood straight. It was late; and the general exhaustion from the preceding shifts' work was palpable in the stuffy air. The nightshift workers wandered in the Auditorium above, whence microphone voices boomed out into the night skies, telling the assembled pigeons what would soon be told to the cattle in the Cafeteria. These voices were momentarily interrupted, for the lights went off again, and a great collective wail of shock arose everywhere. About the flanks, spilling into the Garden, horned heads were teeming with anxiety, as those who waited there looked out to see the storm still stretching to the furthest confines of the world. Time had done nothing to it. Nothing seemed able to abate its sustained power — and they were all trapped there yet.

A vague premonition pervaded the common mood, embedded itself in the lull of the tired room. Whatever the Chief Supervisor had to say, it couldn't be good. Neipas, like all the rest, was mildly afraid of it; not fully afraid, or consciously afraid, because the bodily fatigue overwhelmed all other feelings at this point. Whatever it was, he simply wanted to lie down and sleep.

At precisely the appointed time, the Chief Supervisor arose from the crowd, propping himself up and standing upon a table (the lights had been turned back on in the meantime). He lifted his arms high and wiggled his hands a little in an appeal for patience and attention. Then he rubbed his hands together and looked around the room as he commenced to speak.

The Chief Supervisor began by apologizing to his audience. It was late, he knew, and they were all tired after a full day's work. Some were even woken from their sleep, which he apologized for with particular emphasis. He took the opportunity to apologize for other things, and expressed his desire that all know he and his team were doing everything in their power to make things better for all of them; furthermore he said that, should any complaints arise, please do not hesitate to voice them to him personally, and he would do his very best to ensure individual grievances were addressed – and so on. By and by he softly inched to the point. More apologies for the lights going off – the technicians had been promptly dispatched to inspect the backup power generators, and had lamentably returned with an unfortunate report. Simply put, power was depleting. Running out. And with the storm going outside, there was no way to replenish electricity to the full, so they would have to ration it. Lights and power were to be kept on in the Pigeon Wing during essential hours, he said. He couldn't tell them exact figures regarding the number of hours yet, and didn't clarify what he meant by essential hours, but he would be sure to inform them as soon as he knew. A few recommendations too: do not charge your *I*s and other appliances until batteries are fully drained. Turn off dormitory lights if you're leaving and no one is inside (many nodded at this, agreeing that it was necessary; though no one knew how to turn off the dormitory lights or indeed any of the lights in the Columbaria). Quickly and in small letters he added that it may be necessary to subtract a small fee from allowances for the privilege of using the electricity — etc. The Chief Supervisor then concluded by diplomatically apologizing in advance for any inconveniences the situation might cause, and opened up the floor for questions.

The audience of blurry-eyed bovine and pigeon masks answered with general mutterings. Inwardly, many stirred with a provoked sense of urgency. Through the collective intellect coursed remembrances of small indignities, workloads insidiously heavy, isolated mistreatments, generally vague and intimate oppressions. Neipas himself scrambled within his head to find the questions to ask, because this seemed like the proper moment to ask them before a long and turbulent time arose between now and his next chance to voice himself. But he was so tired... He considered whether it wouldn't be best if he simply approached the Chief Supervisor when he felt a little more at ease; perhaps the next day. Besides, the presence of that massive agglomeration of bodies around him made him feel nervous, apprehensive about raising his voice. He couldn't find anything to ask for now, at any rate; delirious instincts loitered about his soul, unable to find expression. And so it was in the minds and spirits of others.

No one asked anything, and as he called off the meeting the Chief

Supervisor thanked everyone for their understanding.

49 - Fluorescent Gloom

In the East, the sun surfaced red and bled its color all over the cloud fields, spilling its rays through them and upon them, as though fertilizing them with the ichor of its solar veins. Hills of crimson and shadow swelled under the Hanging Gardens. To Neipas' heavy, sleepless glare, the sun seemed like a giant maw drinking up the vapors of the Earth; as though to cool the stygian heat it had amassed in the volcano of nether hours.

The Anubel itself glowed in the young sunshine illuminating the weary faces of its Garden dwellers. Teary eyes glistened in the tender light, half-closed, fresh off disquieting dreams. The terraces and their stairways were packed with lying bodies, from the shadow of the thorny woods at the bottom up to the very seats of the Auditorium near the Orchestra Pit. The beaks of the pigeons were tucked in their still dormant chests, breathing tranquil; and the cattle walked about, lumbering heavily, and hauled their arched horns among the cloths and drowsy cooing.

Sunrises multiplied across mornings. Many wondered how much time had passed.

Attendance of the outdoor Markets surged immediately after the power outages began, especially during the day when sunny warmth suffused the grounds and the bright, pleasant shine made the tents and the cloth mazes bristle with carnivalesque liveliness. Nevertheless, in those early days many were still drawn to the charms of the chaotic marketplaces in the inner halls, where lights ran on supplementary batteries and the world was made of fluorescent shapes. Tour guides made a lot of money then, leading throngs in with flashlights ready, down long corridors and trails which, being bathed in electricity, would suddenly plunge in darkness. It was all part of the excitement: and indeed, the myriad advertisements that had popped up around these tours appealed to the adventurously daring, showy character of each mask.

Yet certain rumors surfaced in the nightly period, whispered in terraces glazed with the warm glow of lampshades and the beam of tall light fixtures upon tripods, as the unfathomable insides of the Anubel gleamed in neon shadows; abounding rumors about theft, assault and unthinkable violences committed in the abrupt invisibility of those infinite spaces; about folk lost in them, never to be seen again. Journalists and Market Analysts did their best to dismiss such tales, but their efforts could not abate the growing fear of walking inside the complex, where lights could erratically go off, seemingly at random. For that was the worst of it: not knowing when the lamps would flash shut. The sudden quietude was unnerving. More than a quietude: a moving, throbbing silence, which immediately impressed upon one the consciousness of hostile presences lurking near. Though the tour guides continued to make light of it and tried to cheer up their flocks, the complete unpredictability began to play upon the nerves, gnawed one's confidence insidiously, made breaths tremulous... It instilled in hearts a slow dread, a crawling instinct of paranoia which took root deep, festering, spreading inaudibly; and which took command of one's senses before long. Though there were large spaces where dimmer lights powered on yet and music still boomed, the vast and long passages in-between would suddenly become alleys of darkness, suffused with a shadow so thick as to be tactile; it breathed; everyone feared being caught in its midst. A ghostly surreality drowned the mind as one found oneself in a gloomy world of languid, red flashes. Much of the Columbaria, the conference halls, the cafeterias, restaurants, gyms, bathhouses and every chamber sunk deeper in gloom, and even during the day the vast interiors of the complex, cold and distant from the sun in their depths, came to resemble unventilated catacombs, moldy and thick with the unreality of palpitating blackness. Wide gaps converted to nothing...

Many simply abandoned the interior of the Eagles' Nest. The majority even gave up their own rooms and their cotes and slept crammed in the comparatively small Gardens. Mats and mattresses were brought out to the terraces and to the windowed halls where the waning moonlight still fell, soft. They left the choking gloom to the view of open skies.

Evidently, the Market followed its consumers, for it was in its omnipresent nature to be wherever they were. Inner daytime Merchants brought out their booths and set up shop in the Garden, stuffing its grounds with their numbers. The terraces became very packed then. Music blared from speakers to hide the general discomfort as everyone huddled in the mazes, basking, under the sunlight, in the Market's myriad dulling pleasures. Every effort was made to create a festive mood of delirium. The Great Peacock of 1000 Eyes chanted more ebulliently than ever, reciting the arcane edicts of commerce gods, all in droning tones that suffused every movement, every thought, every atom of existence in those Garden terraces hoisted aloft above the tempest. Pigeons dropped more coins than ever on the Peacock's lake, placing all their sense of faith in His pronouncements. The Market became the prime solution to all ills (as always). Anxieties gnawed the collective spirit — but there were plenty of paid distractions to dodge such feelings; and many variety of pills on sale besides. Electricity was unreliable — but there were sellers of generators and batteries to fix such shortcomings. Everyone flocked to them, and long lines formed before those booths renting power outlets for consumers to charge their *I*s; many spent entire days going up and down those queues, living entirely in their Glasses and in the Webwork; and the Merchants in the vicinity profited immensely. Revenues went up, up, up. The Market Watchers, with their snouts fuming against the screens, horns quivering, jubilantly watched the jagged lines of charts ascend in delirious climbs. Sometimes the terraces would shake suddenly amid all this, and in the beginning everything would stop when this happened. Fear clutched at one's throat, clogged up in a silence of tension... Indeed, the grounds always trembled a little since the power outages began; and no one knew why. It caused much general consternation — yet there were comedians and masked clowns aplenty to put minds at ease, and eventually everyone got used to this. The Market housed all remedies in its effusive and serpentine bosom.

Soon, even the infamous Night Markets emerged into the Gardens, where once a quiet atmosphere of romance had reigned after sunset; and quickly the terraces ascending from the clouds became so thoroughly thick with bodies it was almost impossible to move. Those Merchants brought with them their lights, run with the charge of 1000 little batteries of electricity; their neons of sinister rainbow shedding gleam upon dreary faces, ecstatic, screaming, weeping. And the Night Merchants brought with them their noise, so that all had trouble sleeping; even the thicker blindfolds and earmuffs now sold by the reams did not help very much. Their alcohol flowed abundantly. And from the very depths of the tower came out, eventually, even those trading in sex of all kinds, dealing in the most deeply hidden dreams. At first those cloaked Merchants hid under the red drapes beyond the digital labyrinths of flickering screens; but soon, without many noticing in the general mess, those secret spaces brimmed and their red veils were rendered, and the sordid commerce underway inside became more or less open for all to see. Meanwhile the Day Merchants, witnessing from behind their gloomy booths all the hands exchanging neon money, became Night Merchants too and learned to never sleep. They entered in competition so that all were confused with one another, and gradually the Night Merchants became Day Merchants too.

It was around then, in the feverish lights of the new night, that Neipas realized their masks were not only made of feather and wax, fur and clay, ink and paint; but also of light and shadow, noise and sound... A sort of merry forgetfulness proliferated in the drunken rainbow of flowing heads. The noise was ceaseless, and both children and adults screeched in the shake, in fright, in pleasure, in expression of all emotions swaying from second to second — so that adults and children resembled one another more and more. The children's masks rigidified; the adults' deformed.

Meanwhile the Pearl continued to shine its light, unabating, constant above them all.

In those days Neipas slept very badly. He still slept in his dormitory, and the lamps, beaming on randomly during his slumber, induced writhing nightmares. (He breathed in the tree of ash...) night meshed into day deliriously. Time passed quickly during the day and slowly during the night, and imperceptibly always. The moaning permeating the spaces disturbed him. His head throbbed at the sound of something which sounded from the silence, something which sounded beyond layers and layers of darkness, in the deeper tiers of the tower depths. Something he thought he had heard before; a pulsing; and which he sensed had always been there, in the background. But he didn't know yet what it was.

His time was largely spent in the Eagle Wing, where he continued to labor at a relentless pace; though he was only too glad to work there and escape the madness of the Hanging Gardens on the side of the pigeons. Indeed, he was almost thankful to bear the ox head, emblem granting him passage to that spacious realm of luxury and comfort which, though he could not feel, he could at least behold, distant from the claustrophobic ruckus and trembling silences growing among the tightening crowds. He would find himself in the Eagles' casinos, where they dallied most often in those days, dispensing their tremendous wealth in the enjoyment of games and varied pleasures. Night and day looped round each other and mixed, confused; and since the Eagles themselves never slept, nightly events stretched into the day and continued nonstop; so that the arena fights succeeded one another forever. Often did Neipas stand witness to the bacchanalia of that arena, with its prodigious flows of money gushing through the faucets of plenty in the galleries above. He saw the absolute euphoria of their golden beaks yelling, the ecstasy those violent sports generated among the privileged strata. Blood flowed besmirched with the golden shimmer cast from the surrounding boxes, the galleries rising enthusiastically from the pit, and savage battles proceeded in succession before Neipas' shaded glare, throbbed in his invisible gaze. Meanwhile all laughed joyfully; swimming in cigar, waddling in banknotes and under forests of naked legs. The air smelled like expensive wine and tasted like gold all hours round...

It was throughout these days that he, along with many others, noticed something strange. Often he would work in the windowless depths of the Eagles' complex, where the lights were always on and bright. Indeed, the lamps shone invariably, unfaltering, upon the richness of their embroidered tapestries and through their deep curtains of taffeta and other fine silks, gleaming in their golden plates, in their glossy woods, their refined glassware and their translucent ceramics, twinkling on the tip of their laughing beaks.

They shone still, unfailing, upon the dust and the blood of gladiators in the game halls and flashed from the sonorous petals descending upon the arena; they alighted still their money. Their conference rooms stood as bright and private theaters as moody. But now the workers began to realize, too, that the lights were always on even in the places where there were vast windows and where the sunlight streamed in amply and aplenty. Some of them began whispering to one another, "Is that normal?" and "Should they not be rationing, like us?". And they could not find an answer.

On occasion the Chief Supervisor, who had promised specificity regarding schedules for power outages, would make some vague references to the matter, but no straightforward answer ever came. Then one day, they were told that all unnecessary expenditures would be cut; and the lights in the Pigeon Wing (the interiors of which workers still had to traverse, in one way or another) had been mostly off since then. But the fact that they were still kept on in the other side of the Anubel confused some in the cattle. Later, a few of them would go to the Chief Supervisor to ask for clarifications, half in protest; and the Chief Supervisor clarified that it was all normal, going on to explain that if the Eagles do not have lights, they cannot work, and if they cannot work, they cannot make money, and if they cannot make money, the cattle would not get paid either. Besides, he said, it was so normal that their contract even had a clause predicting such situations. The workers nodded wearingly, for they were tired and the Chief Supervisor spoke a lot, in his sympathetic way; and became convinced of the logic of all of it.

"What time is it?" Neipas asked Janu.

"Hm?"

Janu lifted his head. His eyes confronted Neipas, very open and glazed, without recognition; he breathed heavily, in the manner of one sleeping.

"I don't have any battery."

"Oh," said Janu, inhaling a long, dense knot of atmosphere. "Yeah... [he looked back at his *I*] It's late, my friend. It's late."

"Oh."

Neipas sat next to him and slouched into the chair, assuming Janu's own posture. He let his dazed head sink. "Hey..." Janu said after a while, drawn out. "You remember Orassap?"

"Hm-hm." Neipas had been staring at the glass of his own *I* for quite some time now, contemplating his mask on the black mirror, dead of light, lusterless and empty.

"Look at this," mumbled the cook. Raising his glass before Neipas' eyes, he showed him a photo of Orassap, their old colleague. His rambunctious avian mask grinned down to the lens, which pointed up to the distant skies, to a soaring background dominated by a spiral of clouds circling the clear blue; the vista wholly cloaked by the dramatic walls of the storm stealing upon his turned back. Orassap wore his habitual smile of pride and unremitting glee, absolutely idiotic in its feigned totality. It was a good picture. The angled perspective wedged a sort of daring pathos into the beholder; Orassap's practiced grin, borne out on the edge of this apocalyptic background in the exact same manner as in all other situations, almost made him look heroic; seeing him standing fully upright before that wall about to crush him, one could almost envy the turmoiled ignorance of that constant irreverence of being. Janu swiped to the next photo.

"Fuckin' idiot," muttered Janu, shaking his head. Neipas remembered the storm's eye under him. Crunching sounds rubbed the air about them as they snacked on cookies.

"How did he get Webwork connection?"

Janu shrugged. "Dunno... Some people seem to have."

Neipas blinked slowly. Janu kept swiping indifferently; Orassap got folded along to the layered depths of the digital queue and forgotten.

"Did you hear from the fam?" asked Neipas.

..."Nothing yet, my friend. Just those texts from my sister..."

Neipas clicked his tongue in tired, empathetic, impotent exasperation. "Shit... Did the Minister say anything?"

"Nothing."

... "I'm sorry."

"I dunno what to do..." Janu breathed in between cookies; and after a while he added, inscrutably, "Honestly man, I dunno if I'd rather be down there or up here."

Having lightly perceived he was still moving as he took notice of his step touching the floor, Neipas stopped. He blinked in the darkness — he held his eyes very wide, as if it would help him see better — and stretched his head into the sound, rotating in so that his ear faced forward. For perhaps some time now he had been guiding himself by touch along the glass wall, where the red dots winked upon him — when he heard, out of the wobbling silence, the sound of someone vomiting. It came from near; from the bathroom a few steps away.

Magpie could see nothing and even the darkness roiled about her head; she was dizzy and felt the whole world shaking and waving about, as if perpetually about to collapse and sink under. She felt claustrophobic inside her own mask. Her whole being felt encased in the invisibility of her sufferings, entrapped in a little box; bound by shackles of insidious character and at the mercy of turbulent seas, realities made up of shifting surfaces and stormy depths — she felt a kinship of experience to her forbears, who had been brought to this land of Columbia chained in the floating dungeons of slavers, crammed by the thousands into the tight recesses of naval catacombs. Her sensible, delicate nature was being ravished by barbarous forces much more potent, violent and numerous than she could defend herself against. It made her sick to the soul. As she lifted her tremulous lips from the ken of the toilet, she pushed up against the very weight of that rancid air involving her in an intoxication of nightmares; dark, convoluted, confounding — and felt without exit. Verging on a panic attack, she hastened to turn on the light of the *I* and suddenly faced the speckled mirror, panting toward her smeared face and hairtips drenched in filth; "Magpie?" Neipas beheld her like one would a phantom, her gorgeous black visage floating in the air amid a darkness pressing from all sides, scourging and ravenous. (He witnessed as she scrambled in agony for her inhaler and pressed it against her lips). Her mask looked like a sort of cadaver of her face; gaunt, sunken, hollowed and caved; undead, with heavy ridges under her eyes. "Magpie?" Neipas called her again, very afraid — for the incorporeal head had said nothing the first time, hadn't reacted to him in the least, and at once he became suffused with that sense of the supernatural which overtakes one among the confusion of the senses in the face of the unknown. His whole being sensed he was really before a ghost.

He saw she was crying when she turned her eyes to him suddenly. "What happened? What happened?" Neipas breathed reflexively, feeling his lips askew, agape and stiff with horror as he faced again the intensity of that enormous, haunted, tearful stare. The next moment her eyes were covered up by a quivering beam of light suddenly forcing itself into his own gaze; he pressed the lids shut, tight together; and Magpie's voice reached him as though from a distance, amid the light's noise: "Huh? Fuck are you? This is the girls' room!" her voice wheezed breathless, strained out with much difficulty. She didn't recognize Neipas' mask — his hand partly covered it — in the shivering interplay of white light and deep shadow, the convolution of falling horns and myriad fingers, as she pointed her *I*. Again she heard her name called, and she shuddered at the recognition.

Neipas had already backed away by then, had given a step back out of the door and stood aside, because Magpie had admonished him for entering the bathroom. In the end, she realized who he was — fleetingly — but, steeped in shame and in the hastened desire to be alone, she dove into the gloom (the *I* light off) and fled without a word.

After charging his *I* (after an hour standing in line and paying a fortune to use the merchant's power bank) Neipas receded to the gloom of his dormitory one night. Haunted by an indefinite restlessness, he stole out of his bed three times to go to the bathroom, and found the corridors illuminated with as much brightness as he was accustomed to seeing them. The misty surprise at beholding the space lit stroke his eyes blind. Over and again he would coil in his bunk for as long as he could until he could not hold it anymore, and would lift out of bed frustrated, climb down the ladder, and traverse the mirrored corridor in a heavy hurry, rushing to go back to sleep; struggling with a crushing drowsiness weighing upon every step. In the somnolence of his comings and goings in and out the dormitory he mingled notions in his head, and for a moment he thought himself at Eva's house and half-expected to find her lying at his side as soon as he turned. But there was no space for anyone else on that narrow bed; all he found was the chasm which led to the next set of bunks.

It was the third time he awoke that night. He stared into the inner mirror of the shelf for a long time, bobbing and jerking his head. In those days, Neipas almost always wore the ox. He hadn't beheld his pigeon face in a long time.

Soon he would find himself gazing into his *I* and listening to its whisperings. He faced it with puffy eyes. An impulse to talk to Eva took him there; for a while he swept through their photos and memories (he was always very careful to not enter the Webwork, lest the Eagles find he had been recording them; and resisted the temptation to open her Maskbook page) then, imperceptibly, he rooted the soundwire into the *I* and plugged the buds into his ears; and he listened to the things he had recorded in the Eagle Wing.

The recordings were often disappointing. Unclear. Voices were spoken in dialects he didn't quite understand and laced with differing noises. They had a bizarre palpitating quality too, breaking off and coming back, as if they were streaming across the Webwork, as though made of digital matter. And beneath all those voices and all the dispersed sounds of music and dishes suffusing the recordings, there was that strange, constant pulsing, that bizarre throb... He heard it somewhere in the distance, beyond the walls, always; so that he didn't truly perceive it anymore, it had merely become part of the silence and the foundation of all the Eagles' Nest's sounds. But he listened to it now blooming out the earbuds with a ravenous character.

Lately, he had felt that pulsing most intensely when standing over the arena; and especially during its peak event. Ox and ox wrestled viciously then, battered one another in crazed lunges, brutal and inconsequential, wild; and in the end, when a victor emerged from the broil (Neipas realized that the arena was slightly caved, slanting into the circular hatch in the center, toward which the dust tended and the blood oozed) — total silence was made. A tension of anticipation formed. The shivering of the tower could be felt. The Eagles stretched their twinkling fists over the pit, and everyone — the waitressing cattle, the watching bulls, the spectating pigeons beyond the glass — awaited the direction of their thumbs. It was then, it was in that wait, it was in that silence that the palpitation throbbed most vividly.

The thumbs had jutted upward last time: and noises erupted, cheers broke out, petals rained upon the vanquisher.

To reach the casino galleries above the fighting ring, Neipas was always made to pass labyrinthine ways — he did this many times, and gained an increasing, basic sense of the Anubel's inner layout. And though he doubted his bearings very often, he deemed that the game halls must be near the center of the tower, and the arena somewhere near the core of those game halls. As Neipas watched the growing savagery of the fights — in its many shapes: ox vs ox brawling, horse vs horse racing... — he mulled. Yes — here, he could hear the strange throb perhaps more clearly than in other places. It pulsed strongest, and there was a convulsion almost of pleasure at each hit, at each punch, at each crack of bone. Even through the chaos of the crowds above and below he sensed it, for now that he had learned to hear it in the quietude, he could sense it in the noise as well, even amid the far sounds of the orchestra. The throbbing palpitated beyond the melodies of the band and beyond the arena somewhere, beyond the jarring revelry of its surrounding crimson halls, beyond the labyrinthine corridors, the luxurious chambers, the delicate curtains and tapestries, all the convoluted layers of their wealth. It palpitated deep beyond everything. When Neipas stopped and became conscious of it, he remembered feeling the same sensation and the same vibrating sound that day he had first followed the Midget into the lowest depths of the tower, beyond the meat factory; that day he saw the dark star shining in gold above him. Had it been a dream, all of it? Yet he had seen the Midget again — here. At the summit of it all (*We can't breathe*, the Midget wrote on the earth; the letters flashed in Neipas' mind time and time again).

Neipas had never again returned to the Museum where she (or he) inhabited, though he often thought about it. But he feared the dark bowels of the complex; the Museum in particular was completely plunged in black, and no one dared going in its direction.

He'd been feeling weak; some have been saying there was something different about the food, and maybe it was true...

Yes, the voices in the recordings were often unclear. But there was more than enough to make out, much scheming and many proud boastings of countless crimes to be unburied from those sounds, much damning evidence in both word and tone. It was all separated and disjointed, sometimes barely legible, but with the proper work, that agglomerate of words and tones would yield proof of the Eagles' true character — perhaps it would change things.

As he listened — when he was almost falling back asleep — Neipas was hit by a sudden sense of emergency. He had to make backups of those recordings — down in the locker of possessions he kept two storage drives he always carried with him to save his photographs; pushing up and overcoming sleep, he got out of bed and, grabbing the drives, he hid them under his shirt, goaded by the unsettling brightness into a queasy superstitious mood. He climbed back to his shelf, up past the laboring breathings of others, *I* glasses snoozing, winking here and there.

Neipas sheltered under his sheets and made the backups there, tucked; and slowly, as he watched the little machines working, he fell asleep. In his troubled dreams he perceived flashings of light tapping his dusty eyes, like sudden implosions in his heart, ushering darknesses and more implosions and so on until the end of time...

He awoke with the Supervisors calling. He opened his eyes; outside the sheets it was completely dark.

(In the depths of his bunk blinked that strange red dot, from where his mask had stared back at him but a few moments before).

Descending from his shelf, he dragged himself to his locker of possessions; hid the backups within; and sealed it tight.

50 - Island in a Tar Pit

Now the mound of terraces, mounting steeply from the clouds, was so crowded that it took Neipas hours to traverse it from end to end. He struggled against the turbulent tides of hedonistic consumers after a day working in the Auditorium; and was taking so long in the attempt to reach the Columbaria that he eventually gave up and, tired, lay down by the lake, under the shade of one of the many crisscrossing bridges hovering its waters. The noise and fluorescent lights assailed him — the coins spread across the lake's bottom glittered demoniacally all night — and he dozed uneasily.

The only period of quietude was at dawn, when the sky sloughed its velvety black cape away over the softening cloud fields and everyone slept. Only the distant drone of the Economist, the Great Peacock, sounded over the crowd's dreams. He recited his arcane verbiage upon the lake's banks of marble, yonder on the far side; his immense open tail, fan-shaped, arched like a shell, swayed its iridescent eyes hypnotically, all surrounded and framed with delicate herbs of spiky leaves and purple flowers. For some reason obscure to him, every time he passed through that place — and through the Circus and its forest of strings near, whose fastened balloons seemed to whisper strange melodies as he touched their ropes — Neipas remembered his mother; felt some lingering essence of her person seeping through his image of her, that haunting portrait lodged in the tombstone. He had dreamt of her that night, and awoke unsettled.

With the sun not yet risen above the pall, and the air still dusky, Neipas lifted the *I* above the sea of lying bodies ascending against him, and drew a photograph. He felt a momentary sense of control; even as the picture affirmed the reality of packed sleepers, it also mollified the hellish discomfort and the anguish it provoked to the naked eye. There the terraces stood beyond the glass screen, frozen, small, between his fingers. He felt something resembling command over that vertiginous scene. It was reassuring.

The Columbaria was only one terrace below. Its gardens spread with veiled mazes, brimming with people, from the edges of the stairway, whose deep steps were also populated with lying folk multiplying so far as beyond the lobby leading to the dormitories; multiplying far down the steps, up which emanated scents of breakfast already sizzling from the Cafeteria lodged in the next lower terrace; multiplying into the very contorted shades of the woods in the terrace beneath that, where the marble staircase yielded to gravel and earthen pathways, to the base of green-tinged statues who, mute, overlooked their sleep. It was toward such shades that Neipas waddled, stepping carefully on the scarce empty spaces in his long descent, very arched, muttering timid apologies as he looked down; for many slumbered with one eye wide open and stared up at him.

Beyond the forested zone of Terrace 2 Neipas reached the stairwell under the little gazebo. Beneath its dome he saw Kasim the Gardener's helper, praying in the soft light, prostrate against the horizon. Framed in the tender glow which swallows the stars, the softness preceding sunrise, he looked as if summoning the morning. Neipas respected the quietude of his worship. Turning the bend under the stairs, he walked to the graveyard, where he paid his respects to the poet.

Neipas was surprised by the soft sound of crunching leaf. The soothing flow of the waterfall bloomed into his waking spirit. He had fallen asleep beneath the tomb's tree; now he raised his head, and saw Kasim a little distance away.

Neipas inhaled sleepily, awareness lagging; his senses sharpened slowly. "Good morning," his voice said. And the Gardener's helper answered likewise. He knelt mournfully and placed a flower before his lover's grave.

When he rose, he turned and spoke. "Your name is Neipas, isn't it?"

Neipas, who had been solemnly watching him grieve, smiled humbly and nodded. "Yes. Nice to meet you." They shook hands. "Kasim?"

"Yes."

Neipas bowed his head a little, respectfully. "Kasim — I've been meaning to talk to you," he said, giving form to the vague intention which had brought him there.

Kasim bowed in the same modest manner.

"Me too," he said.

Without another word, he turned to the grave and whispered a prayer with eyes closed. He walked away slowly after he finished, observing silence, solemn. Neipas followed him; he felt strangely calm, soothed by dawn.

Once they were by the base of the stairs, Kasim asked, "Have you eaten?"

"Breakfast? No — not yet."

"Follow me, please."

Kasim led him along the wall, away from the stairs, until they came to a service door nearly overgrown with creepers. The Gardener's helper produced a chain of keys from his pocket and opened it.

"Please wait here."

Neipas saw that the door opened into a long corridor ending at another door; beyond which there were long shelves, stretching yonder onward.

"Where does it lead?" Neipas asked Kasim when he returned, holding in his hand a couple of wrapped sandwiches.

"To the pantry. This floor belongs to the pantry."

"Ah, that's right."

Kasim closed and locked the service door. Then they walked back the short way along the creeper and thorn-strewn wall to climb the steps to the little gazebo. Up there, Kasim removed the plastic from his sandwich and, before he took of it, he lifted the bread above his forehead, pointing it to the east, closed his eyes, and whispered — and Neipas discerned the tune of a strange, distant language; he seemed to be sounding it in thankful prayer. Neipas watched, fascinated. When he was done, Kasim looked at him, a bit shyly, and nodded.

"Bon appetite," he said.

They ate in silence for a while, leaning upon the rail, overlooking the clouds. Neipas glimpsed Kasim through the corner of his eye. The Pantrykeeper's mask seemed at turns dense and stolid, or transparent and constricted; like he was struggling to hold something in his heart that longed to be released.

"Please," he finally said. "Don't tell anyone you saw me pray like this."

Kasim spoke softly, with glance downturned and shy, and in the voice of a timid youth; a voice contrasting with his portentous frame, and the fatherly beard which rimmed his jaw, a tended trail of plume meeting at the chin, without a mustache atop the lip. Above it protruded a snout which twisted from time to time, as if in doubt; making the garlands round the ivory horns jiggle. He spoke with a noticeable accent — Kasim was evidently from somewhere far away, far beyond Columbia's borders.

Neipas didn't immediately understand the reason for his request but, unable to articulate his incomprehension, he said nothing. There was still the toxin of sleep dulling his intelligence; and instead, he muttered in response:

"You know my secret."

Moments passed in silence, and meanwhile the clouds swelled with the push of the ascending star under. Neipas seemed to be gathering courage, looking for the right words to speak; as if broaching the subject wrongly would compel Kasim to give him up to the Gardener right away. Neipas had difficulty swallowing his bread.

Finally, he strained out:

"Why didn't you give me up?"

Kasim took a while to say. He lowered his head over the railing — he took his gaze away from the horizon whenever he spoke.

"I'm not sure. Maybe... Maybe because Cesar mentioned you a few times, and because he spoke well about you. Or..." Kasim shrugged. "I am not sure. I must have other reasons, but."

His timid voice subsided, and he looked up, yonder to the brightening distances.

"Thank you."

Kasim looked at Neipas for a second, then back to the cloudy hillocks; and he lowered his head again. "What were you doing?"

Neipas breathed thinly into his constricting chest. He couldn't muster words; he was a little nervous and struggled to find in his mind an explanation. Neipas tried to sharpen his thoughts and intellect, feeling in himself a general inability to measure consequences and make rational decisions. By instinct, he wanted to place his trust in Cesar's lover and mourner; he longed to share the burden of his lonesome task. Indeed, Kasim had known and said nothing. Only he the Pantrykeeper, Magpie, and the Midget had any knowledge of Neipas' predicament, of what he was doing. Of these, the Midget did not speak, and Magpie did not want to speak about it; and, sensing in Kasim a discreet companion in the vastness of his solitude, Neipas — instinctively — took a chance, and told him:

"I was recording their meetings."

Kasim kept still — he didn't react. His horns were lowered over his intertwined fingers, above the railing gleaming soft the softness of dawn. The garlands involving their ivory pended gently in the drop, pointing in a subtle sway to the graveyard, to Cesar's tomb below. He appeared immersed in a tension of clashing sentiments.

"Did you record the Head Gardener that night?"

Neipas looked at him perplexed. Kasim heard his silence and pursued in a vacant tone: "Of the waltz. I saw you."

"No..." Neipas mumbled with glance downcast, absentminded, unconsciously tapping the railing with his fingers. "No. I didn't." He hadn't had the chance then — and neither had opportunity since, nor heard the Gardener speak of the wildfires again.

After a long, long period of quietness — during which Kasim swung lightly to and fro over the rail, one moment casting his stare down sharply into the drop toward the graveyard, the other pulling back and gazing the horizon — the Pantrykeeper spoke, in a subdued, secretive, calm tone. Weighing each word, slowly, he said:

"I saw him once — the Head Gardener, I mean — I saw him beat a cow to death. With his cane."

Neipas winced. "Mary... Why?"

Kasim shrugged lightly, gazing downward sternly, rubbing his brow — as if there were no answer, or the answer were too horrible to utter. "He scares me. God alone knows..."

Neipas sensed his fear, even through the impassive ox mask and the garlanded horns, borne heavily and dutifully. And in his fear, in his tone of voice, Neipas felt an enmity toward the Gardener; indeed, Kasim didn't hide it.

"What involvement does he have with Penaguiar?" Neipas asked at once.

"He is the Chair."

Neipas breathed in tremulously; all but Kasim and his own thoughts blurred out. "...Did they have anything to do with the fires... in the mountains? Do you know?"

Yet downcast, Kasim nodded. "Yes. He ordered them himself."

Neipas' glare blurred and blanked widely; his hand rose to his brow in shock, penetrating his plumage unconscious. The feathers brushed in between his fingers profusely but didn't tickle his senses in the least; he became dumb, deaf, and senseless for a moment.

"But why? Didn't the fire start in their land?"

"By the hogwash pools, yes. But they knew the wind. They knew the flames would blow in the opposite direction. Some of the foremen in the pig farm started it."

"Mary! So!... But why, man?" Neipas repeated, pressing his nails savagely into his waxen brow, into the melting paste, dissolving in the fever of his incredulity.

"Because they want to grow their land. They want to grow more feed, so they can increase the number of animals. That is all," Kasim said simply, in his heavily accented, timid voice, staring to the leafage spread underneath the gazebo. "And because he can."

"Mary Virgin — that's crazy, that's — He actually ordered it himself? How do you know this?"   `

"He is my employer. I work closely with him. He is discreet, but — you learn things if you are always near to a person... And yes, well — I am not sure if it was his idea. Surely there were other people involved. But the decision passed through him and he had a lot of authority, from what I know."

Fingers interlaced the railing fiercely, grasped them maniacally. Under the irate plumes and the receding wax Neipas recalled Orenda's tears and how she was right; he recalled the tombstone photograph, the mausoleum walls, Oshana's words and Cesar's death, and the Oyate in the hospital wheezing among burnt, bleeding flesh and pus. "What does Noxxe have to do with this?"

"With the fires?" Kasim said vacantly. "Nothing. But the situation is useful for them. The indigenous people are out of the picture, and now they can build their pipeline in that territory. It's because it's much cheaper for them. In exchange, they pay Penaguiar rent, and sell them fertilizers with a big discount."

"Fertilizers?"

"Yes. Nitrogen — I even believe this was their first product."

Neipas watched the clouds for a moment and tried to extract some reason, some sanity from their opaqueness; sometimes it seemed to him as though the spiky peaks of the tallest mountains in the range glanced charred above the billows.

"But what if the oil spills? Don't the farms use water from the river?"

"It would not matter to Penaguiar. Their water comes from reservoirs in the mountain, from many dammed rivers."

"Mary..." — and, after silence — "Did — did Cesar know about any of this?"

"No, no. Of course not. I never told him anything. It would put him at risk."

They stood there for a while, immobile and quiet. Neipas stared at his toes, chewing on his lip, letting the pigeon mask seep unkempt; lost in a murky sort of introspection and knowing not what else to say.

"Be careful, please. You could face serious consequences if they find out you recorded them."

Neipas sighed mutedly, heavy: a slumbering exhalation. "Thank you."

Then after a while Kasim, looking yonder to the rosy distance, said:

"May God help you."

They watched the horizon spreading above the railing as it changed color. Again, they did not speak. They had long finished their sandwiches, and each twiddled distractedly with the plastic wrappings in their own manner. Beneath the railing and under the dead still foliage, Neipas could just make out the humble stone of Cesar's grave, the flowers and the balloon floating motionless alongside. Almost reflexively then, he voiced into the stillness, the expectant hush anticipating the coming morning:

"I'm very sorry about what happened to Cesar... He was a good man. With a kind heart," Neipas lamented softly, sincerely.

It was another while until they spoke again. The clouds became rimmed in molten gold; they veiled yet the rising sun, and their brightening air caressed their cheeks with soft hands of newborn god, soothing their hearts. It was then that Kasim, inhaling the insulate air of Anubel, said:

"Cesar had a pure heart. May he rest with God in Paradise..." — and here the emotion welled up his eyes, and with a sniffle he suppressed it. After a brief quiet he retook the word:

"And I'm sorry," he said sternly, "I am sorry for yelling at you the other day. But you did not have a right to do that."

Neipas' cheeks reddened in his mask, and his very plume swelled with shame as he recalled his invasive photographing. Kasim continued, returning to the shy softness of his voice:

"Please, do not tell anyone about what we had together. Cesar... he told me you knew."

"Of course," Neipas said very softly, in a tone remorseful, earnest, with words which seemed sourced from the depths of a sincere soul and which, released thus into the silence of the young sun, entered and dropped far into Kasim's sensibilities. They were again quiet, and Kasim became comfortable in Neipas' silence; it was, he felt, a listening silence. The Pantrykeeper was moved to speak more.

"I'm sorry..." he began, looking down over the railing below to the poet's eternal resting place. "It has been many years... I..." Kasim struggled to articulate his sentiments at first. He looked at Neipas, and saw that he listened patiently. The sun hoisted onto the cloud fields slowly; the Market noises had not yet begun.

At a loss for words, Kasim, feeling himself in an indefinable bond of secrecy with Neipas, his lover's friend, resorted to gestures. With a relenting breath he said to Neipas, "I will show you," and, drawing away his jacket, he lifted up the side of his buttoned shirt to show him a mark upon his brown skin, a large lump of discolored, dead flesh forming the shape of a circle, pressed with hot branding iron.

Neipas grimaced with shock, pity, confused repulsion. "Mary!... Who did that to you? ...Was it —" suddenly lowering his voice — "was it the Gardener?"

"They did this to me in my homeland. I am lucky to be alive," said Kasim. "They did it because... because of my orientation... But I cannot help it! This is the way God has made me. Can the clay argue with the potter?

"And they said I blaspheme against God. They said I worship the devil," he shook his head many times, incredulous at the impiety of this. "This was when the war began... When your country came to mine."

"Are you from —" Neipas began, but couldn't bring himself to express what he had guessed; for in those days his nation, Columbia the great, unleashed its powerful, moneyed war machine upon countless peoples.

"I am from Mesopotamia. I worked for your military there, because I speak your language well. To survive. And then I escaped. I came here, to the land of acceptance... the land of opportunity...

"They said in my country that here, if you work hard, you can be successful, no matter who you are or where you come from." Silence.

"I am here. And I am doing what I love to do. To plant seeds, to watch trees grow... To tend the ground. Manage everything. It's what I love to do. But even here they harass me and discriminate me... Not so much because of my orientation here, but because of my God! I do not understand."

Kasim said all of this very matter-of-factly, with his soft, temperate voice, rocking sagely against the balustrade as he talked, looking down, more or less in Neipas' direction now — talking with quiet, wearied, subdued indignation.

"It was hard for me in the beginning. It was very hard. I wanted to return to my family and to my country, even though I knew I could not. It is not the same anymore, anyway... What Columbia did not destroy, Columbia took. Took here... And my family — my sister, my niece... They did not let them come here like I did.

"But then, I met Cesar." — and only the sound of his name formed in his lip and the whole memory of him shook his throat, and he faltered. "He... I am sorry. I'm sorry."

Kasim struggled not to weep, averting his glance away from Neipas, who felt a chill of emotions coursing through his spine in response to the poor widower's grief. Tentatively, he reached his hand over and grabbed his shoulder in earnest solidarity.

"It's ok. It's ok," Neipas said in consolation.

When Kasim turned his gaze to face the sun again he smiled tearfully, laden with the waterload of sweet memories. He nodded to the star, encouraged by the gesture of Neipas' friendship.

"He gave me new life. I don't know how to say it... in any language. He's simply... he's simply..."

The Gardens' keeper straightened himself off the railing and looked at Neipas directly with his smiling eyes teary.

"Look," he said, reaching into his breastpocket. "In the last time we were together he left his notebook in my room. He's always so distracted," he laughed, and the tears began to course as his lip trembled.

"I'm sorry," he said, containing himself with a sniffle. Out of his breastpocket he took a piece of paper. "I was looking through it after... And look. He was writing a poem for me."

On the paper Neipas saw the handwritten verses of a neat typographer, neatly written with a pen's thin nib. Some of the lines Neipas recognized; he had read them before. But the final stanzas were different. His eyes landed on words of a more intimate nature too, and he averted them, unsure now whether he should have looked. Kasim didn't notice it — he read the poem to himself line by line, shaking his head slowly at places, as if still putting up patiently with Cesar's fancies.

"He was a libertine," he said, "but I loved him!"

Kasim cried, he sobbed painfully. He felt fully in Neipas' confidence now, as if speaking to an old family friend. It was evident he was dispensing with sentiments which had been corroding him for many days. Neipas put his hand on his shoulder encouragingly.

And when he calmed down, Kasim said:

"He had this obsession, I don't know why — this obsession about speaking his last words. He wanted his last words to 'encapsulate the whole experience of his life'," Kasim said mournfully, "and he wanted them to be special and remembered. That's how he said. And I say obsession because he said it many times...

"I wonder, what his last words were... Did he get to speak them? What did he say..."

Kasim's eyes had dried and, as if by a last push away from angst, he inhaled the widening sun and straightened himself up to his full height just in time, as if by a perceiving instinct. He looked at Neipas with a sad and thankful glance. Yonder, the sun pulled itself over the ledge of the fumes with an explosion of brightness, and the Pearl, which had beamed dazzlingly all night, faded and glowed its undulating sheen onto the clouds beneath. They both knew the poet hadn't spoken his last words, the way he had wished.

Before the Market bells tolled, the Gardens' keeper still said, weary, trembly, "It's been very hard for me. It's been very hard."

51 - Imperium Columbidae

The *I* glass illuminated Janu's face — he was lit in pallor, distressed, distractedly crunching cookie after cookie after cookie in a corner of the dark Cafeteria. His mind flew in stormy tunnels, scouring the interconnected threads of the Webwork.

Earlier that night he had cooked before the Minister of Nations and the Minister of Borders his twin, both of whom were chewing mutton. One of them lounged in a magisterial couch at the farther end of the hall and scrutinized an old rifle, fondling it studiously as he smacked the meat, his beak flashing noisily in a crazed pace of bulging and deflating. The Minister conversed animatedly with his spike-collared Bull, pointing the gun's barrel this way and that with much excitement, now and then getting up and fetching another weapon from one of the immense glass-paned wardrobes as an humble waiter chased him to and fro and stuffed meat chunks into his mask, which was always snapping ravenously. The other twin, the one closest to Janu, sat at a triangular table, in a puffy chair, and ate broodingly.

Kind Janu wore a large surgical mask over his snout; a bulbous chef's toque covered the crown of his head — veiling his horns — so as to prevent his brown fur and plumage from soiling the food he was preparing. His face gulped in great upward wafts of aromatic smoke. Salts, peppers, lemon, various spices and the choicest of meats sizzled on the grill, seasoned to perfection in an alchemical dance and frizzle under the magical hands of the immigrant cook. He had been there for hours already. For hours he and a crew of assistants had been scrambling to keep up with the Ministers' insatiable appetites. A team of oxen kept coming in with raw mutton fresh out of the slaughtered sheep, running from the depths of the pantries to the upper reaches of the Eagles' Nest, wherein lodged the State's palatial chambers (which tucked somewhere beyond Moloch's Estate), occupied in those days by members of the Conservative Party. The Ministers chewed very loudly and very thoroughly, sucking in as much juice out of the mutton as they could before they swallowed. Janu's meat was delicious. It had become a sort of drug to them. They kept eating and eating and eating.

The Minister closest to Janu didn't seem completely satisfied, however. A foul mood creased his brow. His obsession with Persia weighed upon his thoughts; his dreams of carnage kept being frustrated by stubborn pragmatisms...

Beneath the puffy plumage bristling at the top of his golden beak, words were muttered. "Hell. I don't get it."

One finger drummed the table of ornamented ebony at which he sat;

another petted his feathery mustache with convulsive taps. The Minister's glossy, lion-leather shoes patted the deeply upholstered floor impatiently. The table, triangular in shape, was a little lopsided because it sunk into the pillowed ground, tilting along with the Minister's head and bobbing slightly at the rhythm of the shoe-sole's puffy tap sound. The hall shivered slightly; though none but the cooks noticed it. Decapitated stags gazed from the walls, their antlers branching into the open air above their heads; and beneath their dead lips, ajar and incredulous, colossal wardrobes of towering shelves boasted a whole armada of guns, all encased in glass rising precipitously and teetering with the movements of the folks in that room. Tall paintings of dandy aristocrats, monarchs and revered conquerors posed in the spaces between the portly closets. The farther wall, yonder, was but an enormous, giant world map. From time to time, robed figures with pelican masks came, holding thuribles, and puffed smoke upon the paintings and the glass panes housing guns, hazing the lights, a hundred of which beamed very brightly out of the nooks of the gilded ceiling. And there were shifting shadows gliding over the space — from that ceiling hung a sort of installation made of sparkling paper cut-outs shaped like countries; all were separated, like a map shattered along national borders, and spun slowly from rods.

Janu's mind floated with the scents in which he was enshrouded; for they summoned old, cherished memories. The Ministers had said to him, "Cook whatever you want." — and he obliged. He requested from the pantrykeepers all sorts of exotic sauces and spices from his old homeland. Down in the pantries, it seemed, they had all imaginable ingredients, and after half-an-hour navigating that labyrinth of stored flavors they brought everything Janu had asked for. The condiments harked back to fragrant meals outside the abode of his childhood, under the Ceiba tree; reminded him of his mother calling them to the table when he and his sister played in the arid shrubbery. Later, he would be told they were very poor, and that they had to leave after the crops began to fail and the city to encroach upon the land. But he could not remember being poor; his memory had only kept the good times, retaining in his heart an affection for that place he only barely remembered.

Sometimes, when wiping the sweat off his furry brow, Janu would look up to the installation of cut-outs and see the outline of that place they called his country, that place he never really knew. The northern edge of it was shaped like the southern limit of Columbia, the form of whose borders loomed largest among all the cut-outs, in the very center of them, unmoving; all the rest rotated around it (Columbia's cut-out was, unlike the rest, made of black glass). Mentally drawing away from the frantic toil his muscles had by then geared to mechanically repeat, Janu reflected in his soul about his grandparents. In their childhood days, those shapes would have been cut differently. The land over which he stood now, above which his feet reposed, many feet above its grounds, had been their home. Axiac had been their home and their grandparents' home before it was theirs, and before it was theirs it had been the home of their great-grandparents and so on back till before the beginning of History — countless generations before Axiac became Axiac. Then the settlers came from the vast ocean... Hovering above the waters, streaming up from the horizon, they flew with immense bloated veils, bearing blood-crosses, gazing yonder from the deep recesses of their eyes, like specters. Penetrating into shore, the settlers shed the blood of natives and injected their own blood into their lineage. If Janu were to trace the expanding paths of his genealogy, he too could find himself somewhere on the castle-strewn hills of that distant continent across the land, across the ocean, whence the settlers had come. But most of the trails of his past led right here, to this place now called Columbia; the most immediate tracks led a short ways down the basin, where his great-grandparents and their children had lived until they were driven off the land in times of economic depression; off to the south.

For two generations they remained, until their offspring, Janu's mother, returned; though she came not like one who returns home — but with a bowed head, sneaking under the gates they had built during her forebears' exile. So Janu today stood, with head bowed under the opulence of his conquerors, an immigrant in his own land.

For hours he stood, working without stop. He strained without rest to keep up with the Ministers' ravenous appetite and insatiable demand for meat. All that time the lights were on and beamed strong upon their heads, too, so strongly that they thinned the grill fumes levitating all about him. It was like so across the entire Eagle Wing. The lights shone all the time, day and night, sunlight or no sunlight. By contrast, the Pigeon Wing had become sunk in a perpetual thickness of night. The crescent moon cast a thin, eerie gleam through the windows of the Cafeteria, where Janu's face would later be obscurely revealed in the light of the *I*.

Neipas approached it, waddling in from the Garden's Market, where he had worked the whole day among the thick mass and maddening noises. With wide motions of his arms he drew apart the thickets in the forest of strings, listening to the strange whispers rustled out of the cords, the sound of balloons rubbing with a mystical ring overhead. Neipas thought the night was making him hallucinate; perhaps it was the snoozing of the sleepers beneath his feet. It was the darkest hour, not long before dawn. He had been looking for a place to lie down for a while, but the sleeping crowds were so numerous that they filled all empty spaces, and they spilled over to the deep dark of the interiors, into the mumblings and motions of ghosts. The looping drone of the Great Peacock sounded from the lakes and scintillated in the air like water, mixing with the winking of *I*s shining from the ground here and there; fireflies glowed drowsily inside flasks in the Bugs Display, in the near distance. By and by Neipas made his way to the Cafeteria, attracted by rectangular dots of white light hovering in the air, showing ghostly faces of sitting cattle and birds. He sat in the usual table, above which levitated the bodiless semblances of Janu and Osir, floating in the pale gleam of their *I*s. They were both engaged in fidgeting lazily with its glass surface. The unguarded expressions of the cattle were marked by resignation and anxiety — an anxiety which was kept at bay only by the grueling intensity of toil or the mindless languor of the Webwork.

Janu's leg had been bouncing nervously under the table for quite some time. Neipas lifted his sleepy eyes from the nook of his arm, where his head sheltered, and, looking up, saw Janu's beak fully inside the *I*'s lit screen, his torso contrived in a coiling pose over the table. In this moment Neipas perceived, too, that Osir rested his chin upon his hands, fingers enveloping his cheeks above the empty plate. Neipas himself was hungry, though he dreaded the journey to the food stand, which would have to be made over all the bodies sleeping on the floor. Osir contemplated the windows abstractly, with sleepy eyes. His gaze panned imperceptibly toward Neipas (Neipas could only see the vague contours of his visage in the dark).

"'S goin' on man."

Neipas could distinguish the motion of his crooked lip even in that gloom. Silence settled in their midst and prolonged itself into a general state of numbness. They were all exhausted, and yet none could sleep. It was due to the heavy dosages of coffee and pills, perhaps. The fidgety high that filled them with energy and restlessness had worn off, and lowered into a wakefulness without vigor, a thorough depletion of strength. The slightest of movements required a herculean effort; and so it was that most would abandon the distraction of the Webwork (all but Janu had done so in their table), resigning themselves to staring blankly into the inscrutable paleness of space, full of sitting shadows and the silence of diminishing *I*s, going off like candles blown.

In the circle of shadowy forms round table, Janu's contrived semblance was the only defined shape. His *I* shone brightly with stress and worry, casting stark shadows across the face, deep shadows, full of ink. Into the Webwork Janu injected that ink, writing, shouting with letters of desperation — he tried to contact his family again and again. But nothing could pierce the storm, and nothing could reach them.

Janu had been in a constant strain of anxiety since it had began. The *I* light took to his eyes his sister's words:

SOFIA: Lot of traffic out of Axiac
SOFIA: Everyone's trying to get out
SOFIA: Weather's already kinda weird
SOFIA: (*Video recording of the highway entering the mountain range. Beyond the railing a field of grass with a few trees, dotting the distance; they swayed back and forth to an irregular but strong wind. Beyond the field, the mountains rose, expanding in a row away from the road and into the horizon; above their peaks big clouds amassed, graying the skies and darkening the air. The eye of the camera turns to show the line of cars stretching beyond sight into the mountain pass. The sound of frustrated honking dominates the soundscape. Their mother spoke above the din. In their language she expressed concern for the weather and pointed to the skies.*)

Two hours later she added:

SOFIA: There are agents inspecting documents...
SOFIA: OMG mom's with me
SOFIA: Hope they just let us pass omg

That was the last Janu knew of her.

Janu's mind was in a flurry of thinking, his heart enveloped in lead. Steeped in excessive vapors, he considered talking to the Minister, that aloof figure sitting a few steps in front of him, across the immense and rising chasm of privilege and power.

The Minister finally said: "That's enough. Good job."

That was the last thing he said before a long period of quietude. Janu turned off the fire; the cleaners came to help move and scrub the grill. The Minister closest to him reclined in his extremely comfortable chair, and he ruminated the meat juices still sousing the back corners of his tongue. They were very well seasoned. They had accumulated in his mustache over the hours and now he licked it and savored it slowly, thinking. He contemplated the cut-outs, beholding the shape, the abstraction called "Persia". It was just a piece of cardboard.

Every ambition must find some purpose to serve; even if only as pretext. Together, the need for purpose (or, the need to serve: for even the most egotistical actor needs an audience) and the will to power — that is, the desire to make reality mirror the ego — project the self into some ideal.

The Minister was bound by an ideal — the idea of "Nation" — with which he wound up the essential stuff of his existence. He was part of the nation, and the nation was he, its servant and master. And the nation was inextricably linked to notions of hierarchy and domination. No nation develops unless over another. Nations existed but by a series of confrontations in a ceaseless competition for supremacy; were but players in a concrete chicken-eats-chicken game. One must eat to not be eaten. Resources were perhaps abundant; but supreme power, and all the advantages of comfort and praise inherent, was limited. The top of the pecking order was slim. The throne was too narrow.

Persia was a threat. It was a threat to Columbia's hegemony, their birthright. It was a threat because it did not conform. Because it was defiant of their authority. But he would make Persia bow. He would make it. He would have his war, whatever the cost. He had staked his pride on it.

The Minister was no sadist (thought he in his musings). He had some vague notion that there would be something called 'deaths' in the unfolding of activities, and that their unpopularity prevented his war. But the war would be over quickly. He was the strictly pragmatic one; realistic in the face of difficulties. They had only to drop a few nukes to show force. Often he had advocated for deploying the strongest of nukes, those that drew power from the very foundations of matter, to show the full extent and awe of their strength... For only the excess of force is the proof of force. And only the unequivocal display of Columbia's unparalleled might would make Persia yield quickly and prevent wider violence and more deaths. In the end, he was no more than a pacifist, brutally realistic, freed of la-la notions.

To be sure, he had staked his money in too. The Minister possessed shares in the arms corporations which would profit from the destruction and oil companies which would gain from its exploitation. But money wasn't what drove him; he didn't measure his self-worth by his net worth — like many others he personally despised. Money was but a symbol. It was a consequence and measure of success. It was not what he worked for. The true reward was in the act... He worked for the betterment of the nation — mirror and embodiment of his ego, vessel of his glory. Not just for his own sake, no; for the benefit of his family and those he cared about. All extensions of himself. He devoted his life to them too.

Why else would be work so hard? He was always pressed for time, his life an ongoing stress... But why was the cook approaching? What was this annoyance, interrupting his reflections?

Meekly, with boundless hesitation, Janu removed the surgical mask, freeing his mouth to the open air, carrier of voices; and felt its tingle tugging at his afflicted heart. Ceaselessly he was invaded by the premonition that his mother, who had no legal mask and no papers and was therefore not considered human within the borders of Columbia, was taken and tossed back to the destitution she had been born into and escaped from, torn from her family and all she loved. Janu's whole being shook and rattled with the possibility. He had shot a barrage of messages to her and his sister across the Webwork — nothing came back, maybe they never got them — he raked every bit of news, every little report, for a mention of his mother, or at least a mention of why they were inspecting documents at the mountain pass out of Axiac — something to appease his mind, something to hint at his family's whereabouts. For days and days he searched — every moment he had free, he searched; every moment between the relentless toil of cooking, of sore arms and stiff back, of yelling in his ear — and he found nothing in that dizzying Webwork labyrinth, nothing; and he despaired.

But here, a few steps across from him, was the one who had the power to know what happened; and the power to influence what would happen, with mere words. The Minister of Borders had promised him he would look into what happened to his family; and for days — weeks now perhaps, perhaps months — Janu had waited in angst, and he was at the verge of bursting. He needed to ask.

Janu stepped forward toward the powerful Minister, with his hunched figure, his bashful temperament. He parted his lips and drew in the thick atmosphere of pillows and opulence.

Someone spoke loudly in the rear. The voice swelled into shouts, expanding into the silent, invisible vastness of the Cafeteria like a transgression — Neipas' breast squirmed in discomfort. It kept growing in volume until someone yelled "Shut up!"; and, like a spell, it gave way to renewed silence.

Neipas, leant against the mirror wall (inside which a red light blipped lazily) and staring blurredly into the swaying gloom, voiced in a muted tone:

"Has anyone seen Magpie by the way?" — not knowing what profound impulse had pushed the whisper through his lips.

She had been gone for a long time. No one had seen her in days. But the only response they could muster was a slow pan of the head. The tacit assumption was that she must be working.

After a long while, Janu dropped his *I* on the table in a sort of weary exasperation. "Ain't workin'," he mumbled, and joined his companions in gazing vaguely the blind distance, tired and wild eyed. They remained in silence for a long time more. Neipas and Osir sat motionless in the complete exhaustion of their bodies; Osir looked stunned, as if something troubled him into inaction, something obscure. He moved very seldomly, stirred only to take pills from his little container through his crooked lip.

Only Janu couldn't quite keep still. He would shift in his chair, he would lightly tap the table with his fingers, and would lean back, then lean forward after a while, then scratch his head — all with but brief pauses in between.

Eventually he thrust himself onto the back of the chair and, taking his hands to his head, grunted a pained sigh of frustration.

Janu stood open-mouthed before the Minister sitting languid and stately at the triangular table. He had just realized he had very nearly made a grave mistake. This wasn't the Minister of Borders — it was the Minister of Nations, distinguishable only by the mole on the forehead, enfolded only by the tuft of feathers round it; whereas his twin's mole sprouted from the chin. The cook stood awkwardly a step from the Minister; and improvising he spoke:

"I hope you enjoyed the meal, sir," said Janu in his coarse manner.

The Minister of Nations blinked his livid, beastly, lashless amber eyes; and mumbled vacantly, waving his hand in vague dismissal: "Yes, yes, excellent..."

Neipas turned his head very, very slowly. He blew soullessly into the darkness: "What's wrong?"

Janu gasped low: "! — shit, man. I've been fretting over in the kitchen about the storm for days, my friend. I know nothing about nothing. Can't even sleep. Don't hear nothing... What happened to my family?..." he whispered this softly, meekly, the last words even more so.

"The storm?" (The storm...) Neipas had been enveloped in such a daze, soporific in the luminous depths of the Eagles' Nest, and so buried in windowless halls for days, that he had forgotten the storm. Other worries, increasingly vaguer, had been gnawing at his core with increasing intensity, even as he seemed to be pulled deeper into a wakeful sleep. There was a storm outside unleashing devastation upon the earth — but what that meant, he often forgot, and then sometimes remembered again through an obscure anxiety, the source of which had receded into an oblivion of memory progressively larger in his mind. His eyes had grown used to the clouds. His glance hovered over the tempest many times, of course; but even then — though they battered the megalopolis with furious winds — from above, the clouds seemed suspended in a perfect brooding stillness. The eye of the storm moved only very slowly, as though scouring the flooded vastness now wholly submerged in black.

Janu took a pack of cookies from his apron's big belly-pouch. He ate them nervously. He ate them by the loads with crunching chewing before Osir's indifference and Neipas' tired staring. Neipas perceived his own hunger. He craved the cookies and waited for a while for Janu to offer them; but the cook, who would usually share them full of goodwill and without hesitation, was too obsessed with his worries to see anyone or anything. So after a while Neipas, too proud to ask, gave up and, nearly overwhelmed with weakness, hauled up the impossible weight of his body and strained through the Cafeteria, making the journey to the distant stand, carefully stepping in the little dark gaps between the lying shadows sleeping; he would soon arrive at the plate of gummy edibles which (they felt) have been slowly becoming stranger and stranger...

The Minister of Borders was still enjoying the refined quality of his own nourishment when Janu took the first step toward him. He was the twin on the farther side of the Hall, a few steps of immeasurable distance away from the cook. The exit stood to Janu's left nearby. They'd already been dismissed and it felt like an immense transgression to cross the hall to talk to the Minister; already the Bull of the Minister of Nations, a former mercenary, directed his gruesome glare toward him threateningly. But Janu must try, he must.

Separated by mere meters of felt now, Janu and the Minister of Borders had always been bound together over a distance of many layers, a profound chasm of widening shadows descending in a cascade of dwindling privileges, from the wide, gilded perches of power and comfort into the dark recesses of poverty, of want, of desperation. The Eagles at the top spoke; and the pigeons at the bottom suffered the consequences. From their lofty outpost, a few, powerful, molded the confines of the rest: far away, far far away from them, out of reach of touch, voice, or eye, beyond plea, beyond appeal. But Janu was so close to one of them now, so very near: the one who had promised to search for his family, the one who had irrevocable power over their fortunes. If only he could incur his favor, if only he could rouse his goodwill! Surely he had a beating heart like him, a soul capable of compassion. And he had promised, he had promised. Look: the Minister has hands, exactly like those that Janu uses to cook for him. With them he joyfully brandished the guns' collection, picking up one by one and aiming them all over the place with an almost singing glee. The exalted immigration official celebrated the lavish new funds provided for the wall at the frontier (he and his Bulls guffawed drunkenly; between the convulsive trips to fetch weapons from the wardrobe, the Minister simply stood awkwardly, swaying, delivering droning litanies on his knowledge of warfare). The Minister was a fervent defendant of the idea that mere fences were not enough to defend the homeland from the swarms of the poor and the meek looking to mooch on national resources. No — a border, shape and essence of a nation, must be *manifest*. It must rise strong from the very root of the land. It must stand as a bulwark, with the solidness of concrete, as the stern guardian face of the national spirit, to vet everyone who requested passage into *their* land.

Janu walked alongside the dizzying array of guns mounting aloft and spread along those massive shelves. Here were the instruments of their exploits, relics of conquest, tools of their success; tools of expansion, behind which countless conscripts and patriots alike — their instruments of flesh and bone — had murdered and perished. All on their behalf, all for their power and leisure. He walked nervously under the spinning nations and upon the bouncy carpet, afraid he would trip. The Minister's Bull, eying with unveiled disdain, was the first to notice his approach. His spiked collar twisted menacingly; his weapon jiggled instinctively. Then the Minister of Borders, caressing an arquebus, lifted his empty eyes and he, too, saw the cook: a sort of blurry brown sack, chubby, bent humbly with its hat in its hands. The Minister recalled, vaguely, having made a promise of some sort to it. He had been feeling magnanimous when he promised to look into Janu's family, for the House of Law had granted the funds for the concrete wall that day (funds which the President had just signed off on — construction would begin soon). But now he looked at Janu, with his immense bored earlobes and sweaty cheeks, and felt repulsion; a strong distaste at being reminded who it was that cooked his food.

The Minister of Borders loved his country; loved it to the point of deriding, and even hating whomever didn't belong to it. He loved it, not with the staid, rational, sophisticated veneers of his wife the Heiress — also a staunch patriot — who cloaked her racism in various ideas of space limitations, concerns about resource depletion, passion for wildlife conservation, and a certain, missionary zeal founded in mystic, imperial myths of uniqueness. No. The Minister loved Columbia with the unbridled obsession of a fanatic. His drives were more visceral and much more vague; but sincere. His whole being had been forged in the fiery discourses of patriotism, of exceptionalism, of innate superiority. All frailties of his human essence were drowned in the godly invincibilities of the Nation, with which he fused his soul and to which he joyfully sacrificed his identity. And there was an idea of purity irrevocably linked with anointed Columbia, an ideal of virginity reserved for them who earned Its inheritance; a cleanliness and perfection spoiled only by Its enemies, parasites who strove to feed off Its riches: filthy hordes from obscure, marginal sewages outside and festering corners within. A nebulous fear of impurities was the Minister's chief feeling. He simply felt an intuitive disdain for those brown folk, whom he considered too numerous and too dirty, he nourished disgust for their grimy clothes and their snotty children, which looked teeming with lice, indeed they all looked riddled with disease, their soiled, swarthy feathers looked infectious and probably convulsed with all manner of pathogens. His whole frame was prickled by their alien talk; he considered them stupid, for they could barely speak his language and he hated their accents when they tried. Still — they were necessary vassals and needed to be placed near to a degree, under control. Near. Near with their hands, their eyes, their voices, near, within reach of his perceptions. But the Minister could never recognize in them any commonality with himself. For when he looked in himself, all he could see was Columbia: a powerful God who commanded him, whom he served, and to whose image he aspired; a virginal Goddess, much adorned in shiny wrappings knitted with idle words like "freedom" and "democracy", whom he sought to master. He loved his country.

But his love was sick, and his malaise old. His illness had to be sunk and muddied in the venom of "Nation" and its superior high. But at bottom, it was made up of self-loathing, its most profound source. Godliness was its aspiration. And bloodlust, and run-of-the-mill racism, were its expression.

The Minister was but a confused mishmash of weakling's anger: exactly the same drive that, at the core, animated his twin brother.

Janu bowed lowly...

"Sir? Excuse me... I hope you wouldn't mind my asking, but — have you gotten the chance to look into my family's situation?" he began, mustering his best words and the most polite, deferential tone possible.

All looked at the cook in frowning stupefaction.

Everyone was shocked at this ox's impertinence. For Janu had broken the most important rule: He had spoken without being spoken to. This was terribly annoying; he interrupted the Minister's excitement, and now the Minister was forced to waver his attention between the slack gun in his hands and the meek cook humbled before him. Admittedly, though, the dishes he made were too good to dispense and, because he feared the immigrant's treachery (for he cooked the food, after all) he refrained from being unpleasant; and, with his mind scheming on how to dismiss him, instead laughed aimlessly:

"Sure! Sure! Ha ha!"

And he said no more. Janu, perplexed, waited still for an endless, extremely awkward moment; and then responded meekly, with a bowed head: "Thank you, thank you, sir."

He felt a sharp sting in his heart as he heard the Bulls' laughter behind him when he left. For hours afterward he replayed the Minister's words, the Minister's tone, the Minister's laughter, and tried to decipher their meaning. Eventually he concluded they meant absolutely nothing.

Staring emptily out to the shadows swaying in the darkness, Janu withdrew into a gnawing lethargy, sunk slowly into a pit of hopelessness. He faced the receding sky with increasingly crazed eyes. In and out he would drift, from sleep to wake; and there was almost no difference. Osir, who had sat by him this whole time in total silence, communicated through a voiceless tug, through a considering glance. Janu, noticing Osir sitting with the reclining pose of one listening, drew the stuffy air in through his nostrils; and it roused his brain a little. He perceived himself beginning to speak:

"This world ain't fair," he began, and after shaking his head in anguish he continued:

"They would be nothing without us. We feed them... We wash their homes... We make them comfortable... They got rich off of what they stole from us. And they keep getting richer off our labor...

"We were here first. And they're trying to kick us out?" His soft speech, spoken into the vastness of silence, was permeated by movements of head, resigned, gesturing great impotence.

Suddenly, as if in a release of pent up frustration and anger, he grunted in exasperation, "I hate those fuckers," he whimpered in shaking, powerless breathing.

Neipas was just then coming back, indisposed with the bland taste of that food in his tongue. Osir said nothing, but he listened. A tense silence spread slowly across the vacant darkness; it was as if oozed from Janu's silent face, from his fastened beak and wrathful nostrils. All sat straight in their chairs and leaned forward, listening to the silence of his lingering anger.

But the tension in the quietude dispersed with time, and disappeared. No one spoke for a long time. Janu resumed eating cookies; calmly at first; then more and more nervously. His face was palely lit of the *I* again; all others were submerged in the fatigued gloom.

The silence was momentarily disturbed by Janu's *I* plopping solid upon the table. "Ain't workin'," he mumbled again, and the darkness closed supreme upon the table, shrouding Janu's head and all the preoccupations, all the angst it held.

Dawn flowered languid outside the massive glass fronts. Inside, all senses were yet steeped in pitch.

*

Her beloved son had sent her many messages of tenderness and worry.

But his mother would never see them. The messages had gotten to the I, but she would never again hold it, and would never again hear from her son.

She lived through the worst of horrors. Taken, handcuffed, shoved and yelled at, pushed away from her daughter by demons of twirled tongue whose growling she could barely understand, she was crammed into a small room with a hundred others, pressed against the inner walls of the concentration camp by a weight of crying bodies. For weeks she did not shower. She drank from toilets and washed herself in their water. She ate the same plastic food repeatedly, watched by guards who hated her and looked upon her like an animal. She witnessed the humiliation of men under them. She lived with the stench of bodies unwashed for weeks, and the smell of urine from diapers. She saw humanity soiled in dirt and teardrops, soaked in waste, she saw people ailing in fevers and succumbing to disease with none to avail them. She witnessed the plight of mothers, mothers wailing for their babies who have been taken, taken, taken by those demons with the flashlights.

Now Mrs. Tia sat on a ledge made of brick, sat next to a mound of sand and a mound of rocks, in the hills over the slums; far, in a place she could not recognize. In her hand she held a letter. And the letter shook and was wet with her tears.

She would never again hear from her son. Her son, her dear Janu, whom she so dearly loved, would never speak again.

He had died, the letter whispered; the letter told, spoke out of that ill-omened land of promise and madness, the lost paradise stolen from her and her kin.

52 - Nature and Its Discontents

The Eagles kept cushioned in all the lush pleasures of their wealth. Day by day Neipas saw the opulence of their gardens and all the comic figures strolling about it, guffawing, padded in abundances of leisure and comfort. He beheld all the Emirs, Sultans, would-be Kaisers and all manner of prominent corporate chieftains and exuberant oligarchs from all across the globe still basking and feasting as the multitude on the other side languished in the darkness, and the workers, burdened with the horns in their heads and the loads upon their arms, buoyed over in stygian seas of coffee (and other substances). Yonder the fumes of the Temple, lucent in glaring lights which were always, always on, puffed in bursts; and in the pathways between the hedge labyrinths, a sort of different marketplace was set up one day. It seemed the sports market season was on; and business could not stop, so the big entertainment tycoons traded athletes with horse masks here, at the top of the tower; and reams of banknotes changed hands before Neipas' impoverished stare. He was strangely hungry. And he saw myriad oily fingers clutching the bodies of the Swans, who often (Neipas saw this whenever he served in one of the balconies of the upper terraces, and gazed out) hid in the shrubs, and shirked from contact whenever possible. Deep inside, the arena fights continued and grew more savage; the contestants roiled in blows ever more vicious, blood squirted in fiercer gushes from clenching fists, the drunken effusion of the crowds intensified. And he witnessed how the pigeons wept when the victor of the final match was showered with petals, how emotionally they pressed their hands against the circling glass when the Eagles waved munificent thumbs over the ring, as they endowed boons upon the winning ox — for the fighters (Neipas was made to understand by the branded marks on their necks) were convicts of some sort, and the champion was released whenever the Eagles commanded it by pointing their thumbs upward; or would otherwise continue to fight until this happened — as the orchestra sounded melodies and the throngs screamed.

And the storm kept on spewing rivers under its deceiving, bending shawl. The clouds stretched beneath the Anubel in eternal immobility, and the multitude of eyes, red, twitchy in the burrow of pigeon masks, beheld them like an indelible fact of the landscape. They took for granted that the storm would last forever. Most had forsaken the clear consciousness of a world beneath the clouds. It was simply too bothersome, too frightful, and increasingly too abstract to think about. As suns upon suns passed over the tower, a sense of general stupefaction came to rule over the Hanging Gardens, and in that state of numbness a new fervor for consumption arose.

They purchased to forget, they consumed to forget, they lived to forget. Axiac survived in their heads only as a blurry notion of blurred edges, something illusive and with a vaguely menacing character, a realm of phantoms lurking somewhere under their feet. Laughter and inconsequence reigned. Space and time spun themselves into a delirium, out of sequence. Electricity zapped in and out erratically. All consciousnesses melted as the pigeons passed days and days in those mazes grown bloated, unbearably full and with no more place to grow. Woes were suffered in the overall solitude of the indifferent crowds; there was grief, but all grieving was lost among their excited shouts. Seizures of panic and bouts of claustrophobia moaned unregistered among the overwhelming clangor. Sometimes Neipas witnessed, in dark corners, grown adults crying upon their terrified children's feet.

But the ecstasies of noise slowly gave way to silence; a burdensome and ceaseless silence deepening, pulling down with it the fluorescent lights as batteries and portable generators depleted; so that the terraces began to flood with widening pools of black. Carousels and other amusements became silhouettes in a haunting stillness. Even *Is* faded into brooding gloom, no longer did their glasses alight abundantly under the night sky. For the Webwork increasingly became more difficult to access. Great crowds huddled round the access devices still functioning — and yielded small fortunes to their owners for the privilege. Indeed, many were losing their money very quickly. Webwork deprivation and economic insecurity caused much anxiety; it was as though some spiritual foundation was being taken from them, as though becoming unmoored. Their pigeon eyes became redder — and glared very widely, the Market all a swarm of livid, fidgety gazes which seemed to roam in darkness even during daylight. Without Webwork and almost without money, without reference or bearings, they were increasingly left feeling blind, naked, and maskless. As the moon waxed, it revealed by bits the weary faces of the packed garden dwellers, their blood-shot eyes blinking in the remote depths of their sockets. The sunlight disclosed their grimy feathers — for they were afraid to go inside, to that airless crypt where few still slept, to bathe. Naturally, shower-renting businesses materialized, seeking to satisfy the latest popular demand — cramming the space even more. Lured by the Great Peacock's song, these enterprises were at first set up by pigeons trying to make money, as they saw the enormous profits the Merchants accrued; and were then either bought out, or copied and summarily crushed by the Eagles, most knowledgeable in the ways of the Market and most capable of swaying Its divine will; and who ruled them all from beyond the myriad gloomy and impassable corridors of the Pigeon Wing. Long lines formed before these new improvised showers. Others bought soap and washed in the eastward river — until the guards began to forbid the practice.

The worsening lighting provoked all manner of fugues, instilled vague fears; the ceaseless growth of the Market — growing so stuffed that great piles of things were tossed to the lower terraces deep, as far as the Museum gardens or even overboard — pushed them all into stressed manias. But the fact that the tower shook incessantly brought many to the outer edges of sanity. They all lived in shivers; and began to nourish strange beliefs. That the tower would collapse. That rainwaters were rising all the way up to the Eagles' Nest. And at first such theories were laughed at; though all felt like they inhabited a ship adrift in tides whenever the Gardens moved noticeably under them. Rumors that the electricity had been damaged by foreign saboteurs made many nervous and suspicious of everyone with a peculiar accent or browner tinge. Some began to say that the storm itself was caused by nebulous terrorists; others claimed that the storm was a mere hallucinogenic-induced vision and that the cooks put drugs in the food or in the water. New psychological malaises poisoned the collective mood. Gangrene of the mind, they festered slowly...

The Merchants of Doubts and the Merchants of Fears made fortunes in those days. The pigeons bought more feverishly than ever, so that they might assuage their nervousness. Though some effort was made to ensure panic would not spread among them, the profit bestowed to gun sellers skyrocketed. The sale of calming pills proliferated. More Bulls patrolled the grounds.

"Who is to blame for this?" was the question that began to give shape to their angsts. Signs of discontent were generally confused by all the different theories of guilt circulating the Gardens, theories which generally either pointed to vague conspirators or, more generally yet, to the government.

Once, during one of the afternoon seminars at the Main Stage, Editor Moldura, Neipas' old professor, presided over a roundtable in which various Eagles and peacocks — government officials, analysts and thinly veiled lobbyists — participated. They spoke on the subject of Ostrich's rebuilding:

"Oil is the cornerstone of our economy," said the Minister of Energy, peeking at his notes. He wore his usual cowboy hat and boots, and smoked his little pipe. Underneath his shades beamed a supremely moronic grin.

From the packed Auditorium watched somnolent stares, mostly above sagging eyebags, sometimes beneath frowns. Many dozed in the chairs they had paid to sit on, in the brightness of the sun, under umbrellas — another booming commodity — for it was uncomfortable to lay on the floor and no one wanted to sleep in the darkening corridors of the Market at night. The drone of the avian guests onstage imbued the motionless air.

From the wings of the stage, Noxxe's regal visage watched stern, listening carefully to every word, observing from the shade under the fanning of flabella.

"...before anything I would like to ask you very generally about your feelings toward this," the Editor was saying. "Scientists are calling this the type of storm that only happens once in the lifetime of a species..."

"It is devastating, Max," the Mayor remarked, reclining gracefully against the chair, back erect, molding his chin into a wrinkle of concern. He poked the air before him with his fingers as he delivered the words, "But we are resilient. The citizens of Axiac are resilient and they have a strength like none other. We will get back from this, and we will have the city running normally in no time, I can assure you."

A few scattered claps ensued from the drowsy crowd.

"And what is your plan, Mr. Mayor, for Axiac's recovery?" asked the Editor, with the parrot at his shoulder eating from his ear.

"We intend to make sure we minimize damage as much as possible, Max. Which is why industry is pairing with the local and national governments to help those in need," the Mayor replied.

"That's right," added the Minister of the Environment, waving his hands. "We're joining with government in a philanthropic initiative to aid the storm's victims and provide them with food and shelter and rehabilitate those who've lost their homes."

"Industry is donating thousands of dollars for reconstruction as well," added the Lawmaker still further.

The Editor bobbed his head very earnestly, with a sort of very serious frown concentrating all the significance of the journalistic profession, and his parrot nodded along as well.

"That's very interesting," he commented, lifting his thoughtful beak from his thoughtful fingers and molding a very thoughtful face. He was readying to ask a question but was cut off by the Legislator, who said, "It's a wonderful initiative —"

"Especially," the Editor rejoined quickly, "especially considering the losses to business, which must be quite substantial."

"Quite substantial," concurred the Analyst.

"Very much so," reinforced the Mayor, sitting between the Analyst and a Lobbyist for the utility firms, who picked up the word after him:

"Yes indeed, there is significant damage to the grid, powerlines down, stations flooded — and the rain is still falling," said the utility Lobbyist's peacock beak. "Ostrich is completely under water. But we're planning to turn the lights back on in folk's homes as soon as the storm goes away. Local and national authorities will help with reconstruction to make sure of that," (the

Mayor, Ministers, and Lawmaker lowered their heads in recognition of what was said). "By withdrawing unnecessary regulatory burdens we should be able to get services back online as soon as possible."

"What about the lights here!" clamored a sleep-deprived voice from the Auditorium which, however, resounded weakly in the general vastness.

"We're writing up a stimulus package to energize the economy!" blurbed suddenly the Minister of the Treasury, who hadn't yet spoken. The dozing pigeons were startled by the way the Minister's voice squeaked and his beak pouted, how the right lens of his spectacles winced convulsively and his left shoulder shrugged ceaselessly all the while. It startled everyone because he had been so inconspicuous when he was silent, but now he spoke they noticed the berserk twitching of his whole frame, which was offputting and scary even. "We should be able meet GDP growth projections with the stimulus plan outlined in ASA! (aka Axiac Stimulus Act)."

A quietude spread among the nodding heads of all attendants. Noxxe, in the wings, upped his chin regally and petted his sapphire ring.

The Editor, nodding along, cleared his throat and followed up, addressing Jack the Legislator, who represented Ostrich's Industrial zone, "Energy suppliers have taken a heavy toll as well," he affirmed in an inquiring manner, calming the Treasury Minister's crazed antics for the moment.

"Yes," replied the Lawmaker, "significant damage to refineries and even pipelines, some of it structural and difficult to rebuild. Mind you though, necessary security precautions were taken to avoid spillage of any kind. With ASA, we're demonstrating support for citizens of Axiac, all citizens of Columbia, and industry in a bipartisan fashion. Columbidae come first in our mind. Their energy needs must be met." — and the Mayor nodded diplomatically, and everyone seemed to be in agreement, nodding masks along — until they turned their heads to face the Auditorium.

"We have no energy and no fuel here! The lights are still off!" ensued a yell from the crowd.

Immediately after: "How will you rebuild the city if you can't even manage these facilities," asked someone at the microphone, which somehow on, even though Q&A hadn't yet begun — the calmer voice boomed tremendously into the stage and made the panel momentarily shudder. ("Shut up, you crow! We're trying to sleep!" cawed a disgruntled pigeon, however, sitting in the farther right margins of the Auditorium — using the pejorative term "crow", usually applied to folk in the Ostrich rookeries, because the pigeon standing in the aisle before the microphone had swarthy-complexioned feathers. A small tussle developed).

A defiant edge formed sluggishly from the crowd, rising from the dissatisfaction of days without energy, hours in queues and among packed throngs, and excessive costs to use electricity and other basic utilities draining wallets generally. Voices now picked up and swooped up in demanding tones, and the Editor, as if picking up on the uproar now just beginning, asked:

"You know, I was reading the stock market index earlier, and I found it very interesting — NoxxeSocony stock has actually been going *up* for the past forty-eight hours. How do you explain that, with such a sizable portion of their facilities underwater?" — the Editor's parrot squawked confusedly.

"Well Max, the ways of the Market are inscrutable I'd say, but it generally works to the benefit of everyone involved," explained, mystically, the Minister of the Environment. He was named Salas — a known crook, who had managed to escape prison through the payment of various little fines throughout his career. An ex-lawyer, as a politician he became an expert in the drawing of maps; and he mostly drew lines fencing off vast natural tracts for industrial exploitation. Deft and soulless, the fellow had had a visceral dislike of trees since he was a little child, saying that they harbored too many bugs. His unfortunate chinlessness, which hours at aesthetic sculptors had done nothing to smooth, was rumored to have come into being because he recoiled so often in disgust of things.

Salas wasn't the most astute or eloquent politician, however, and his justification had little impact; noises of protest continued to ensue and grow from the Auditorium. Crowds began to huddle and amass, many, having heard the ruckus there, climbing up the steps to see what was happening.

"Any particular course of action you have in mind? Could investors be anticipating the expansion of the Iblis' facilities in Ostrich, and the oil pipeline advancing? Does ASA fund these projects?" — the Editor's parrot leapt up and down his shoulder.

"Well yes now," mumbled the Analyst quickly, and deflecting he added, "NoxxeSocony always said they would not expand the refinery without the permission of that community. And we're gonna do everything we can to help them transition."

"So the community has given you the go ahead," asked the Editor in a challenging tone as the shouts of the audience, demanding answers, racketed up.

"Well Max, everything is flooded," responded one of the opinion-makers/ lobbyists in a slightly incredulous manner, the motionless equivalent of opening his arms and shrugging his shoulders. "Our own derricks have tumbled! But we will help the community with whatever they need. But we must be pragmatic."

"The storm is a significant hit to the economy and an expanded refinery helps the economy Max, we must recover fast and keep on our course of growth!" squealed suddenly the Treasury Minister with an abrupt writhing of shoulders.

"Plus, it would benefit all Columbia and really further us in the cause of energy independence, to be able to extract and refine such large quantities of oil in-house," said the Minister of the Environment.

"When will the lights be back on!" shouted someone from the thickening Auditorium. "And what about our families! What about our families down in the city!" someone else clamored tearfully. And amid the lifting shouts (already the Bulls were emerging watchful from the backstages) the Editor leaned forward and prodded:

"Indeed, Minister, but if I may interject — many activists, and even some newer members of the House of Law counter this by saying that the type of economic revitalization you're advocating for will ensure more storms like these, more often and with more intensity. Is there any validity to their claims, in your opinion?"

Deep inside the burrow of his throne, Baron Noxxe adjusted his bulbous torso in dissatisfaction. Neipas was close-by, next to the dishes along with other cattle, and witnessed all this from the wings of the stage. He had a good view of the Orchestra Pit and could see relatively deep into it, and sometimes saw some light shine, and pulse, from the bottom when he looked yonder; glimmers blurring into the glinting hypnosis of Noxxe's sapphire ring. Wine had been flowing freely into the Eagles' throats and it was beginning to produce its effect; the Baron was visibly frowning, his mind buoyed in a somnolence peppered with the sprinkle of voices.

The Analyst, feeling Noxxe's stare, countered passionately: "I'd say they are naive. Look: it's reality we're talking about here. We get off fossil fuels and the economy stops. Understand? And that is because the economy rests on these fuels. It is the basis of our growth. Without them, we have nothing. We simply need oil!"

"Turn the lights back on!" — shouted many, and a chant began to form.

The Editor, meanwhile, turned to the Energy Minister, who hadn't yet spoken: "What is your opinion on this, Minister? You're responsible for the energy supply —" and at hearing this the uproar rose to a feverish, almost maniacal pitch. The crowd seemed ready to climb onto the stage.

And here the Minister of Energy, heir of old-money, finding himself unprepared, grinned his smile of malleable idiot and, suddenly straightening himself in his chair, peeked once again at his notes and repeated (now into the microphone): "Oil is the cornerstone of our economy."

But just then, when the ire of the pigeons ran highest, the Mayor suddenly lifted himself from his seat and opened his arms toward the

675

burgeoning crowds pressing now from the very depths of the garden terraces. His assuaging gestures made them, with some patience, yield a little, and becalm.

The Mayor directed himself smoothly to the audience. With his diplomatic smile, his impeccable getup and his immaculate hair of feathers, he spoke thus:

"We realize you are hurting, and we understand we have a lot to improve on. There have been many shortcomings — and trust me, some shortcomings have been my own. But listen — the world is messy. There are ambiguities. So you can't just keep yelling at folks once you've highlighted an issue and brought it to their attention. That will only delay things. The way to resolve issues is through dialogue and compromise," he dictated these words with his mask tragic, understanding, hurting, compassionate. "Listen, we are setting up a bipartisan taskforce to look into the causes of this problem and fix it. We are working as quickly as possible. Trust me, we will solve this issue. But we must be pragmatic and patient in the way we dream, because progress progresses incrementally. We must march with our values and stand up for good. That is why we must invest in energy security and independence, so that our ambitions can fit the shape of our democracy. Trust me. I am with you, and may God bless Columbia."

The audience and the Editor acquiesced before the graciousness of the Mayor, who brushed back his hair of shining feathers. Moldura's parrot, who had been conducting itself with effusive motions — probably on account of the audience's roar — settled.

Pensive, Neipas withdrew to the backstages, following Noxxe's entourage. Editor Moldura's performance inspired in him a sense of confidence. He already held his old professor in high regard and profound respect — all sentiments founded upon a debt of gratitude. But he perceived a certain defiance in this interview which made him look up to the Editor even more. He viewed him with trust.

He ruminated with horns bowed as he delved into the depths under the Proscenium.

Moods were tempered by the Mayor's intervention that day; and yet whisperings of resentment kept on blowing about ominously, presaging an escalation of some sort. Many of those whisperings began to be directed toward the Eagles, as more and more were becoming very displeased with the contrast between their quarters, which were more and more time without power and helplessly sunk in all manner of darknesses, and the quarters of the Eagles, always bathed with light and full of sparkle, full of glitz. More and more pigeons were becoming aware of that contrast, and their rage grew by the hour.

They were growing aware, too, that something about this arrangement was decidedly not normal, and began to call it by a name: "Injustice". Some — few at first, then many — began to stand in the Auditorium with placards and then march up and down the Gardens in protest. Days of commotion came then. Hope and despair suffused the revolting throngs as they chanted furiously to the skies. Above them all, above everything shone always the Pearl atop the tower, which some still looked upon as a sign of hope; yet which others, those crying "injustice!" on the Auditorium and atop the steps, came to view as a symbol of oppression.

To all this the Merchant of Doubts — whose commerce was growing in those days — would say: "But there's always been injustice, therefore injustice is normal." Besides which, the Eagles upon the stage wore different masks everytime, of different colors everytime, of different shapes and animals, and they did this ever more skillfully. Sometimes they even let the protesters climb onto the stage and protest from there. And all this would confuse cattle and pigeons — it was difficult to know who to blame and who they were protesting against, exactly — enough that most quit demonstrating. The clamor of these protests, moreover, was largely swallowed up in the raucousness of the Market; and it seemed to annoy some who, tucked safely in their prized Auditorium seats, refused to budge from there, no matter how stiff their muscles and how intense the need to discharge their fluids, and, filled with disgruntlement, kept shouting pejoratives at the activists. Sometimes their confrontations were severe. The Eagles, spying from the windows of the Great Facade, made very merry with this infighting. They scoffed — they did not yet fear the protesters. Their number was not enough to storm the Eagle Wing; and, even if they had the strength to overcome the scanners and the Bulls, they weren't enough organized amid the general pandemonium, and would surely get lost in those aimless mazes bridging both Wings, if they tried.

And in the meantime, things did get better (it was important to placate tensions before they really grew). Gradually, lights were turned back on; and power in the Pigeon Wing stayed on more frequently, and for longer and longer each day. The Gardens deflated, slowly became more spacious as pigeons returned to the comfort of their chambers and the cattle to the constancy of their dormitories. Collective energy revived. The crowd began to relax.

A special event was being prepared especially for the benefit of the Summit workers and attendants. A grand feast was scheduled, and it would celebrate the pigeons, including those who wore cattle masks every day — this feast would be for all of them. It was even said that the Eagles would serve the pigeons themselves. Rumors bubbled in every utterance about how luxurious it would be; rumors spread about by PR specialists as they propped up hype for the event with 'organic marketing' techniques; and everyone rejoiced in the anticipation the more was known.

Things improved rapidly. It was confirmed the feast would be held in the Ballroom. For the first time, many of the pigeons and cattle would step beyond the Stage, into the luxurious back-halls and secret terraces of the Great Facade — all would, for the first time, step inside as guests. The event would take place in but a few days, and the Eagles' Nest, its kitchens, and halls and rooms of both its Wings were again abuzz with lively activity.

*

It seemed like Neipas heard something different the night before the feast, besides the throb in the ubiquitous distance, pulsing through the walls. There was a great shuffling of weights beneath him; subtle, because it came through the thickness of ceilings, and because it was done secretively, but it was there, below him; perhaps in the Cafeteria or the Kitchens, or even further below, in the Pantries.

He fell asleep hearing this sound, lying sluggish in the nook of his shelf and trying to see his mask in the darkness of its mirroring depth. But he could only see, where his head should have been, a strange, blinking red dot.

He sunk into unsettling dreams...

53 - Feast of the Pigeons

There stood he, before himself, beyond the glass. The hall behind him dazzled; outside, the terraces cascaded in dim, moody glows. His incorporeal image hovered in buoyant lights, phantom among phantoms, as Neipas faced the Ballroom windows. The translucent wall brimmed his eyes like an aquarium filled with the springwater of dreams. Masked in white feathers, his beak shimmering golden through the pane, he beheld the royal, Eagle visage that was then his face. Clothed in amber eyes, he saw more widely, his senses gripped deeper. He reclined calmly into his floating body.

The feast began with a steady beat of drum. A fashionable rhythm of guitar swam across the Ballroom as the pigeons entered through the main gates. The Golden Dove greeted them from the center, standing mighty, bright, towering above everything. Circular tables had been disposed in a square shape, set very widely along the edges to cover the whole perimeter of the vast hall. Upon these tables lay napkins, forks, spoons, knives placed diametrically on either side of a gap for the plates — all set up in genteel and immaculate arrangements. Another group of square tables ran circularly between the wide round tables and the Golden Dove, and upon which every variety of alcoholic beverage could be found. The pigeons entered in a slow drip, as though intimidated. For the first time the immensity and glamour of the Ballroom opened up to them, welcoming them as guests. As they sat, some kept silent, timid, and subservient, while others quipped jokes in whispers, laughing in a low tone to quell their nervousness.

There were many workers among them. Workers and pass-holders alike were given personalized, tailored suits, prepared on the hour by Seamstresses who measured them and stitched up the choicest fabrics for them; along with glitzing golden watches, which were a true delight, especially to the workers who ran about everyday to meet erratic deadlines and who now felt like they had a command of time — for it was framed by gold upon their wrist, pulsing under their veins' beat. Finally, they had been given Eagle masks.

At first, most felt quite strange wearing them. No one knew what to think or expect. It was uncanny to be there, in that sumptuousness, sitting; even uncomfortable for some. Neipas tapped his foot under the table and looked out the enormous windows, which the Eagle-masked pigeons all faced, having their backs toward the Dove and the liquor tables. Outside, the Hanging Gardens were soothingly lit, the extent of their varied green romantically shining in amber under the night. Beneath Neipas' table descended the Pigeon Wing, and directly under his feet the beautiful Facade terraces and balconies spilling into the Auditorium, with the lake and the

Great Peacock chanting upward to the Pearl and the Market tents sunk in shadow well below. There were the Venus Groves down in the 7th tier above the Stage, its fountain waters dressed in warm colors of light; the 8th tier's stone plazas with their magnificent sculptures, immobile and mysterious, glinting silvery under the quarter-moon; and the glorious carved shrubberies of the 9th tier rustled by the artificial wind of flabella, waved by servants hiding in the shades as the pigeons took pictures. Neipas observed them leaning with awe upon the crenelated parapets, admiring the haughty statues on the recesses, trying to peer (without success) into the heavily draped windows on the massive walls. They were entirely free to wander those terraces and the Ballroom that night, yet still could not step upon the Eagle Gardens on the other side. They could contemplate them, however — they could gaze upon them as patrons, from above. The view conferred a certain sense of power; and as the night progressed the pigeons would grow into the masks they were given, and become comfortable in partaking the largesse of the great masters of the earth.

He saw some folks were coming in. The music changed.

A thrum of saxophone schmoozed into the tune, spreading a lax vibe throughout, loosening the collective muscle. Into this walked a long parade of waiters, holding domed plates, wearing swan masks and swimsuits with transparent frocks whose tail dragged elegantly on the fur carpet. Eagles marched at their side. They sported casual attires — turtlenecks, unbuttoned shirts without tie, chino pants, sometimes jeans — and they nodded and waved diplomatically, with big smiles. Neipas was turned back in his chair, holding the backrest under his arm, and watched the spectacle unfold with wonderment and some suspicion. Clapping arose over the music.

The swans spread in a choreographed manner. One of them approached Neipas and laid the plate gently before him. She removed the cover swiftly, revealing a dish of what appeared to be grains with a side of minced chicken and legumes; all looking and smelling deliciously. "Have a good meal, sir," the swan said from behind her mask. Neipas tensed a little, sharpening himself. Her voice — vacant, professional, direct, soulless — sounded familiar. The twisted muscle of his neck spasmed slightly at the same time, for in the very moment the swan took the cover off the plate there ensued a jubilant boom of trumpets, ramping up the symphony to something very joyous and fun-sounding.

Neipas looked around. He realized that the orchestra played from behind the open gates, quite close to him, tucked in within the circular frame of the Ballroom but outside the square format of the circular table group at which the patrons sat with the foods. The faceless Conductor, facing the deep shadow of that corner whence the music flowed, seemed to stare at Neipas with the back of his head; as if there were eyes hidden amid the silver hair. There was something discomfiting about it and Neipas withdrew his gaze. Pigeons with eagle masks all about him, sitting, some a bit tense, afraid to eat, shy about it; uneasy in the immense gap between their old and their new, temporary masks. In the open space between the food-laden tables at which they sat, and the tables with drink behind them, Eagles walked about and uttered phrases like "please, enjoy!" or "it's fantastic" generally onto the heads facing the windows and into the air above them, ample and topped with the painted dome where the great pantheon of beasts and angels loomed with ample jaws. Neipas himself felt strange before the plate. Spying his illusive reflection on the spectral glass, he tried to grapple that indefinite feeling bothering him —

— but an Eagle passed by him. "How are you enjoying your meal mister!" sounding vague and probably not addressing Neipas directly, but he took it to mean that he should start eating. He turned his body and attention back to the food.

Neipas ate the grains, ate the roasted chicken and legumes in the amiable torpor of the music. He found himself eating faster and faster, taking in greater chunks. It was delicious, really very nice. Strange — he hadn't noticed before how hungry he was. As he chomped through his meal with a lowered head more food was set upon the table — cake, fruit, shrimp, candy, all a nonsense mix of varieties — and during the course of dessert some pigeons, comforted by the settling of warm food in their stomachs, rose from their chairs and helped themselves to drinks at the other tables. Between the food and the beverages they sometimes stopped to converse with the Eagles, who entertained them with the distance of a tutor and made the pigeons excited and hopeful by their patronage; all around creating a very cordial mood. Meanwhile, through the orchestra bloomed the angelic voice of the Conductor, levitating, bouncing from wall to wall on wings.

Neipas poured a glass of wine for himself and walked to the windows facing the Eagle Wing. He noticed how different, how composed his gait was, how self-possessed: the trimmed suit's embrace bound him to heightened norms of conduct, the respectable cuffs steadied his hands, made him feel at once grand, loose, and focused, whole: powerful. Upon the window materialized his new avian head, and he contemplated the intermixing of glass and self as he indulged in sullen, philosophical drinking. Beyond himself now spread the Eagle Gardens, sparsely illuminated tonight, its true richness concealed. The Infinity Pool stood out afar, at the edge, shining neon rainbows morphing their colors every now and then. Neipas tried to peer beyond it — but he couldn't. He couldn't see the storm. The mellowness of the night, of the music and the space gave him the distinct impression that there was no storm beyond all those tended shrubs and trees, beyond those lamps of soothing color; that he wasn't trapped at the top of a tower. He felt, warmly, that there was no horizon beyond that cozy landscape.

He gazed over the reflection in the window glass, where all their transparent forms were hovering atop the mysterious and alluring outdoors; flying over all the heights, mighty like deities with solar faces. Imperceptible, he suddenly found himself focused in his own stare, his amber eyes. And he wondered. Oppressive thoughts came to him, and he stood increasingly small in the vastness under the colossal ceiling as he beheld the pane, as he sipped his wine, as he remembered, mournfully, his true face hidden beyond all the layers of mask. Who beheld his image through his eyes?... In that emptiness between image and sight hid, perhaps, the truth of who he was.

He thought of his parents, he thought of their photographs. He thought of Cesar, the poet, silenced upon the stage. In the long run, Neipas concluded, he himself was no more solid than the floating specter in those lights. Time rendered all things immaterial.

...How long had he been there? How many days had it been? How many weeks? How did he get here? Surveying the glass, he saw the pigeons smiling dreamy grins; common folk standing atop the world, schmoozing with captains of industries and presidents of conglomerates, with state officials and emissaries of all the nations and empires, with prominent arms dealers, generals and other warlords, with mighty bankers, rulers over the captive fates of billions, arbitrates of destiny, molders of lives... All seemed pleased, but weren't they all angry yesterday? It afflicted him to realize that time passed in snippets, from scene to scene, from daze to awareness, in cuts of film. Life rolled like a movie made of stills, a slideshow of photographs. Neipas noticed he had somehow taken the decanter of wine with him. He kept pouring into the glass, slowly.

He was halted in his reflections by the nearing figure of Reckuz, whose oblong Eagle mask stole up to his proximity and said "Hello!"

"Oh! Good evening, sir," stammered Neipas, caught unprepared, and he was already beginning to stoop and bow when Reckuz interrupted him:

"Ho! Ho!" he cackled with his strange bionic laughter. "No need to call me sir!" His smile frightened Neipas.

"Sooo — how is it going, man?"

"Good, sir, good — I mean, Mr. Reckuz." "No need to call me sir!"

"So, are you enjoying the food, man?" asked Reckuz's offputting grin.

"Very much so — thank you, thank you so much," replied Neipas with wide, respectful nods.

They nodded at each other for a while.

"To you, sir," Neipas finally said, raising his glass timidly.

They drank together in this awkward fashion for a bit. The party carried on — the swans went about serving snacks, and the Eagles and eagle-masked pigeons hung out fraternally, consuming from the endless supply of alcohol. A few peacocks and owls hovered about here and there. The drink loosened the mood, and whatever stiffness of conduct there might have been on the part of the pigeons relaxed, and soon everyone was altogether chummy with everyone else; it wasn't very long until loud guffaws began breaking out of the crowd here and there, nonsensical yells of amusement ensuing. Neipas and Reckuz, too — quiet, shy creatures both, in their own ways — began fraternizing in more comfortable terms. By and by they came to the topic of the Maskbook (evolving naturally into it, since Reckuz, it turned out, was fond of speaking about himself). Somehow Neipas disclosed that he was a photographer, and Reckuz seemed to find that interesting (he nodded with very open eyes and beak slightly agape to let Neipas know he found it interesting) — for the Maskbook, the entrepreneur said, was also an album of photos. So what was Neipas' experience, Reckuz wondered, with the platform that he himself built? Neipas thought instinctively — he was tipsy enough to wish to be frank, but not drunk enough to not fear offending Reckuz by telling him he didn't like the Maskbook (these thoughts lived mostly in his swimming heart, and only a few flashes buoyed to the surface of his intellect) — though he didn't think for more than a second. The alcohol tipped him over, and he said words. Reckuz was shocked when he heard Neipas saying he didn't use the Book all that much. Why didn't he? — Reckuz asked, interested (with the interest of a zoologist observing an undiscovered species).

Neipas reflected with his swaying head — a little longer this time. His fear of Reckuz's power, of the power of his mask, which gave the entrepreneur hierarchical superiority over the waiter, made Neipas timid and cautious. Nevertheless the alcohol, making him warm and cozy, gave him such an urge to express his feelings, to be sincere, to have an honest conversation — and Reckuz seemed so very interested! So he spoke his truth, though slowly and cautiously, watchful of Reckuz' s reaction at every moment:

"Well — to be honest, I can't really look at Maskbook as a photo album... I hope you don't mind me saying that." — Reckuz didn't seem to mind and kept on nodding idiotically, cawing "huh-huh!huh-huh!"; a vague impression that Reckuz wasn't listening passed Neipas' mind, which only gave him encouragement to keep on — "A photo album is something intimate, in my opinion... I remember when I was a kid, the experience of flipping through the pages of an album with my family, you know. I remember how we'd all sit together looking at the same, physical thing. All focused on it, all sitting around it. And every photo, you know, every photo had a story. Sometimes an epic story," he carried on with a chuckle, transported into the tender charms of remembrance — "and we could spend, like, half an hour staring at the same picture, analyzing it bit by bit, while my parents told us the story behind it. We would bond like nothing over it. Could be about an old family member, or a place that looks different now, about this and that — about a past we could not live but were witnessing, right then and there — you know? And that's what fascinated me about it, and what fascinated me about photography — that you can capture this one, fleeting moment, and look at it, and make it stretch for a long, long, long... Almost an eternity. It's like bending time!

"Anyway —" Neipas rejoined, checking his growing enthusiasm, "I don't think Maskbook replicates that type of experience. I don't think it can. I hope you don't mind me saying that... But when you're looking at photos in an *I*, or a tablet, or a computer — all of which were built for single use, by the way — you're looking at it alone. And even if you weren't, there are the tabs, and the prompts, and the comments, and the ads, all this just busying the space around the picture, and even if the picture is full screen you have... I guess you still have the promise of all those things in the background, you know, the stimulus. The urge... do you know what I mean? — All these things apply to professional photobooks online too, and that's why I don't use it as a — well I guess not professional, but more than amateur photographer — hum... Ah, and that's why I don't really use Maskbook that much as a photographer, either." — he paused for a bit. As he caught up with his thoughts he unconsciously realized something while looking over Reckuz's shoulder and seeing that swan who had served his plate.

"So what I think you're encouraged to do is to flip through the pictures as fast as possible to keep that stimulus going. You don't really go into depth with anything. And 'commenting' is not like talking. It's more like shouting to a wall that's slightly interested. Like talking to an altar, you know? All't wants is to be complimented. All surface, you know? All masks! All pretend. Sorry — I hope you don't mind me saying this. But I think it breaks people apart more than brings them together. Because nobody's talking to nobody."

In the course of his monologue Neipas alarmingly felt himself sobering up; but at the same time he was growing bolder, so he stopped for a second to drink more. Meanwhile two more Eagles joined the little discussion — which would have cowed Neipas, perhaps, were it not for the absence of the sentimental filters felled by the torrent of wine. Moreover, Neipas was able to glimpse himself and his glorious avian visage and golden beak in the window glass as he spoke. The Eagles approaching were Sobs, the Prophet of Tools, and Larry, the Data Tycoon, the very greatest of the age, and they leaned their ears intently with glasses half-raised in refined manners. Their fingers took notes in their *I*s, automatically, without need to look. Reckuz himself listened still, though with brooding contempt — which he couldn't well hide, and Neipas couldn't well discern beyond the watery veil of wine marinating the back of his eyes. They all listened, interested in the way a businessman scans an untapped audience; as though scouring prey. Even Reckuz, despite his anger, took notes.

Neipas kept talking: "And there are other issues, of course," he began, drawing breath right out of the wine glass. "There's the issue of privacy, which is really, really important for me man. I mean," Neipas gagged, chuckling in his stupor. "— what you do is create a vacuum, or whatever — that's probably not the right word, but — you create this vacuum, you know, and you tell folks, 'Hey, put all your photos here, put all your thoughts here' — like a diary too, right! So Maskbook wants to be a photo album *and* a diary. But a photo album is something *private*! And a diary is *even more* private! So those pictures and those thoughts aren't being shared with family, or friends — well unless; ah..." — Neipas chuckled drunkenly again — "unless suddenly we found a new definition for 'sharing' — we should probably call it 'bragging' most times I guess, or something — and; ah — for 'friends' as well... So if those photos and those thoughts aren't meant for family or friends, who are they meant, to. Well — to you, man! I hope you don't mind I say this," he added, checking himself momentarily — despite his words, his tone had been tempered and respectful throughout the monologue (save for that last outburst): "You're the ones looking, using I guess, that photo album, that diary. You're the only ones really using — I guess eating up, you know, all those intimate moments. You're the eye at the bottom of the vacuum..." Neipas mumbled, nodding slowly as he felt a hand pulling at him, appreciating the poetic correctness of what he had just said. "Nice... That's just business, I guess."

His body was somehow removed from the proximity of the three tech impresarios. Neipas had kept drinking through his speech, and all the while Reckuz — who had been sipping his alcohol, slowly upping his buzz — bloated in his growing anger and vexation, even as he took notes, listening to Neipas and staring at his babbling face with twitching beak and cheeks, and an increasingly sweaty brow. (Neipas thought he saw, as though in an hallucination, a glowing red light behind the entrepreneur's mask). The other two resumed conversing, disinterested, as they sipped on their glasses with cool and refinement. The music had become more intense yet; someone spat drunken verses really really quickly.

"Hey man, calm down a little all right?" admonished Osir, who was pulling Neipas away. Neipas frowned at him, wavering, absolutely perplexed with the enigma of Osir's dancing scar. "You know what I'm saying, though? And then they sell those photos and those thoughts...—" "I got it man. Chill.

"What's wrong with you guys? Goddamn it — that cook Janu even came in from the kitchen and started blabbering on with the ministers... Did you see him? Needed three of us to pull him out of there.... They're not your friends dude! They're your bosses. Ok?"

Osir's scolding put a sort of fear into Neipas' chest. It stirred his heart, making it rebel against the buoying sway of drunkenness commanding his senses. Neipas stared firmly at nowhere for a bit, very stiff, mumbling "Ok. Ok. Ok." as if planning his course of action. Osir watched this bobbing mess with yellow eyes and mouth opened stupidly, and muttered: "Jesus."

"All right man," Osir broke out, shaking his head suddenly as though emerging from a spell — he had been observing Neipas' intoxicated antics for a minute, popping himself a pill in the meantime. "I'm gonna step away for a bit but you pull yourself together; you hear what I'm saying?"

Neipas didn't hear, though he was thoroughly immersed in the problem of pulling himself together. Gradually he clawed himself to the solution — first, a cup of water. He should get a cup of water, he concluded. That's what he did (he was very careful not to step anywhere near Reckuz's range as he returned to the drinks table, where he found — with much difficulty, as it was all a very rainforest of booze — some water). Then he navigated through the stumbling crowd a little aimlessly; a continuous "hmmmmmmmm", as one does when thinking aloud, rung inside the full space of his head as he went about, searching for the elusive solution for pulling himself together — water hadn't done it. He was driven up by a vacuous panic about being fired; a strong impression of having messed up throbbed in him.

He roamed for a while, and eventually made the unusual move of crawling under the food table with the intention to hide. That same moment he concluded the idea was ridiculous, maybe, and crawled out to the other side of the tables. Still with the impression he should probably be discreet, he squatted low, placing his arms on the table and his chin on his arms, looking in at the festivities. Waveringly he observed the revelry in the center of the Ballroom, waiting to sober up.

Inside the square of food tables the feast rolled into an increasingly extravagant hullabaloo. Under the festoons of confetti and string suddenly flying across the air, and the music bombing down into the eardrums of everyone, eagle-masked pigeons drank, chomped, stumbled, laughed, yelled — and occasionally, a few, more contained, conversed amicably between themselves and with the Eagles; the Eagles which, whenever free, prodded the pigeons on and encouraged them to keep stuffing themselves with chow and liquor, wearing exorbitantly large smiles all the time. (As mentioned in the sentence before this one) some of the eagle-masked pigeons were more contained and collected than the bulk of the crowd rapidly sliding toward generalized mania; most of these were Supervisors who had been instructed to not get inebriated so as to not hinder the task of supervising. Some of them pressed their advantage and adulated the Eagles, gripping at the perceived opportunity of advancement with near despair. Others kept to themselves. One of those supervisors was Osir, who would recount to the janitors after the party:

"...I guess I can't really describe it to you right now, it was such a mess the whole thing, you know. There were guys falling down, hugging the execs, spilling drink all over the place, Christ, even puking at the end of it. You went up there, you saw it — it's a mess. It's hard to describe, but... but yeah, there was this guy singing and screaming on the mike too — think it was one of us, or maybe not, I'm not sure; might've been that conductor actually [...] Money showered like glitter... Everybody was going mad. Seriously. It was unreal [...]

I thought everyone was going nuts."

Neipas watched and heard from the perspective of the outer side of the Ballroom looking in. The party amid tables unfolded in its ruckus and inebriated uproar. Bit by bit his tipsiness wore off, leaving a queasy hollow in its wake. He began to feel mildly sick, but held. Mostly a feeling of dullness overtook him, slowing his senses; and he kept there, looking, as the dizziness made him want to keep still. He observed passively. At one moment his eye stopped and focused on a particular swan-waitress as a pang of recognition struck him again. It was the same swan that had served him his meal earlier. Tall high-hells, long legs, lustrous dark feathers and hazel eyes beyond the mask; and that voice, too. Though dressed in blazing white now, painted in a very psychedelic rainbow of suggestive allure, though in a disguise different from that she usually wore — Neipas knew her. He narrowed his eyes and sharpened his wits. In a discreet moment she took air from an inhaler; and he knew who she was. She was Magpie.

"That's strange," Neipas mumbled, with a vestige of liquor still dancing about his brain. He had thought that all waiters were to participate in the feast — as guests. Raising his chin subtly, he wondered why she was working, then. And in a flash of clarity cutting short the drunkenness, Neipas remembered the last time he saw her, remembered that it had been a long time ago already, remembered that she had disappeared completely.

But a new development broke into the debaucherous progressions of the jamboree all of a sudden. The noise soared to fever pitch. An adolescent Eaglet in a lax, tieless suit jumped onto a table holding a microphone — he had just been talking to the Gardener (who had watched Neipas with interest while he talked to the three tech magnates) — and the Eaglet's puerile voice boomed into the vast space the next moment:

"Ave! Even in crisis, we thrive! Even in the midst of catastrophe, we grow! And we expand! Ave! We are invincible! Cheers, friends! Ave! [the Eaglet reached into the inner pocket of his suit] — Let's dance!"

The Eaglet's hand flung out and a shower of grains flew into the air as the orchestra erupted into the 1-2-3 rapid tempo of a frantic waltz. The grain landed on the fur soil like a rain of pebbles, and most pigeons threw themselves prostate upon it, and they kissed the ground, pecking hungrily at the grains in a berserk rush to devour as much as possible, bowing to the Eaglets who laughed atop the tables. The voices of all birds sounded all at once on top of one another in a chaos unimaginable and ruthless; simultaneously the Eagles coalesced in a circle round the tables and spun the waltz round and round them. A few of the eagle-masked pigeons — those most shrewd, or perhaps most foolish — joined the Eagles in their dance. The eagle masks of the rest fell in the grains and were eaten.

"Praesto! PRAESTO!" The place was in a tremendous uproar. Loud music and a confusion of movement broke everywhere. Presently Neipas noticed a Bull grabbing Magpie's arm and bawling something into her ear, after which she tried to walk away, and immediately had her arm pulled again. Then she walked with him toward the far Gate into the Eagle Gardens. Neipas frowned, disturbed upon seeing the obvious discomfort in her semblance. He got under the table, decided to follow them.

Its legs veered and dragged as a whole heavy mass of bodies bumped violently against the table. Neipas plunged through and at once found himself among the mess of heads licking the floor rabidly, shoving each other's faces into the coating of grains, and sometimes sticking their teeth into their neighbor's skin. A mad hand seized Neipas' forearm, making him slip and lay spread on the ground for a second. He fought and rose to his feet, but not before tasting the bit of grain which had rushed up and sprinkled his mouth. He realized that it wasn't grain — it was but crumbs of bread. More crumbs showered upon them now as the scion Eaglets climbed atop the chairs and joyfully threw them in the air laughing, laughing, laughing.

His feet waded through the marsh of heads and the dancing Eagles, peacocks and pigeons. Eventually — after a panicked hustle — Neipas reached the Gate and, rushing through, closed it behind him; and all the loud chaos of the waltz was muffled.

54 - On the birth of Nations

Neipas stilled. He sharpened his ear, leaning it into the sudden darkness. The Pearl shone indifferently above the Eagle Gardens; its light did not land upon their grounds that night. Their terraces were barely lit, but slowly the gleam of lanterns afar seemed to reach meekly this nook of hidden green, and Neipas' eyes accustomed themselves to the obscure surroundings. Meanwhile a moving sound of rustling landed upon his ear. He followed that sound, carefully.

He followed the whispering of shrubbery through spiral staircases of stone lit in meek violet and statuettes and fountains dressed in red glints, and orchards with blooms of flower bleeding color out of the twilight, down toward the Temple's moonlit haze afar — the demonic pulses and song from the Ballroom, deep, infernal, retching, trailed and descended with him — all through the thick of foliage, he followed the stir of leaves into the ornate back-door of one of the Palaces. The inebriation was so generalized at this point that even the Bulls were asleep at the gates... and besides, Neipas wore the eagle mask. He went through. As he delved further down a sort of rancid smell ascended; as if the perfumes clouding the Gardens had vanished, overwhelmed with the shouting winds of alcohol. It was a stench he had often felt before.

He found himself crouching at the verge of a hidden grove. Yonder, a tiled wall and a window with a view to the flashing pool of infinity.

Within the grove was standing Magpie, perched tall atop her high-heels; and beneath her height a peacock, at one side, and a Banker, the Mayor, and Baron Noxxe, all surrounded her. They fastened lecherous stares upon her figure. Magpie stood very straight and dignified; her eyes firm forward and countenance proud, while the three Eagles salivated about her like vultures upon weakened quarry.

"Please, sweetie" said the Mayor in a lowered, dense voice, scanning Magpie top to bottom; his hand pointed to a small assortment of chairs and a table, with a couple of canopy beds adjacent. "Why don't you come sit down."

"I'm fine where I am, sir," Magpie answered, keeping her chin up. Her voice bore the same confidence and firmness that was so characteristic of her; but it came with a slight quiver. Neipas' heart wrenched upon hearing it. She was scared, he knew.

Baron Noxxe had been nodding all the time, evaluating Magpie hungrily, with a villainous air. The sapphire ring glinted as he reached his oily hand into her fingers, and she reacted immediately with a flinch, pulling her hand away fast. "Please don't touch me," she said sharply — but the quake in her voice was more discernible now, and her proud chin trembled.

The petroleum sovereign uttered a dry laugh, and commented, "she's got moxie, this one. You're right." The slime oozing out of his beak manifested his lewd intentions toward Magpie, who stood there, unmoving, tall yet.

"C'mon sweetie, no need to get worked up. Just relax. It's ok," said the Mayor with a disturbingly soft voice, and a forced smile that quivered in his mask of power, full of lecherous desire, full of want. "You know what I mean? [Chuckling nervously] It's ok."

The Mayor reached out his hand to hers; but before he could touch her she drew it away, saying firmly, "No."

"Oh c'mon," broke in the Banker, drawing a little closer to her. "Do you think we're paying you more just to wear the outfit?" Again the Banker tried to touch her hand, and again she drew it away, saying, "don't touch me."

Magpie's voice trembled more noticeably yet now. The middle of the grove shone with the sparkling white colors of the swan; her dark semblance high enough to receive the gracing light of the half-moon, where the firmness of her expression fleetingly dissolved into a shudder of fear. Abandoned to the mercy of the three ghouls lurking in the full shade beneath her, she resembled a sort of immaterial goddess, craning her neck beyond the known reaches of life; a being graceful and dignified, a being sacred, and fragile; all her life gnawed by parasites and now haunted by vultures. Her face seemed an inked depiction of wild beauty, and her body a fine sculpture of nature's charms; her fragile form, within the reach of their filthy talons. Behind them in the crepuscular glint, the tiled wall depicted the foundational abduction of the Sabines stretching on either side of the window.

Silence — heavily suffused with the tension of their greasy stares. Their chests gasped up and down, avid. Their glutinous eyes were stuck fast to Magpie's body; the creepiness of it all made Magpie tremble with increasing intensity, and Neipas cringed. He thought to interfere, but lacked the courage just then. He set his body at the ready to spring up, however — with the intent to move in as soon as they touched her again.

Magpie finally said: "I'd like to go." And though her voice was serene, her throat convulsed visibly as she spoke the words.

"It's all right sweetie, c'mon," said softly the Mayor, attempting to reach her shoulder; and now she pulled away more forcibly, taking a whole step back and bumping against Noxxe's huge belly, which didn't budge. Startled and aghast for a moment, she said, gesturing this time, "Seriously, let me go!" and she kicked her long leg a step forth, trying to break out of the siege encircling her. She began to walk away, but the Banker seized her wrist.

"Just a moment sweetie! Calm down!" — and Magpie, trying to pull away from the forceful grip, saying "Let me go!", was herself pulled violently and, tripping on her high heels with a frightened and strained gasp, tumbled onto the grass.

"Why are you being so hysterical?" mouthed the indignant Banker.

"Let me help you," said the Mayor, extending his hand in the direction of Magpie, who trembled shocked upon the grass. But the Mayor's hand didn't help her; instead it touched the floor, and the Mayor knelt, pressing his crotch against Magpie's head, covering her eyes. Her limbs shot up in revolt, but the Banker seized her legs and the Mayor her wrists, and pressed them against the ground; meanwhile the Baron unbuckled his hide belt and pushed down his suit trousers, revealing an erect penis pressed down under a ball of hairy fat. It dripped with sweat; and his beak salivated with grime as he descended himself upon Magpie's restrained body. "No! Stop —" she was muffled.

The Mayor covered her mouth. She was completely smothered now; all the motion out of her was the convulsed quaking of her chin and the muscles of her gripped limbs, struggling in panic and desperation. The oil tycoon pressed upon her legs and the Banker helped him strip her; they did it quickly, with lunatic violence. And so it was that her dress of sparkles was torn from her, and Magpie's silken skin of ebony was laid bare to the elements and the lecherous stares of the slobbering vultures. Her breast, falling to the side, was at once grabbed by Noxxe's oily hand; and as Noxxe seized her and lay his overwhelming weight on top of her, the Banker drew away to sit at the nearby chair. The bloated petroleum king, spreading his fat wide atop Magpie's thin, helpless body, adjusted himself clumsily to penetrate her — and as he did she convulsed and moaned painfully, she screamed tears through the Mayor's clutching fingers, and every fiber of her trembled with repulsion. The Mayor trapped her with his weight, and one of his hands covered her mouth; the other scratched his chin as his head nodded thoughtfully. The Banker, in his chair, felt himself under his trousers, beak slightly agape with appetite, with half his tongue leaning upon the corner of it; banknotes jutted out of the pockets of his ruffled pants. The peacock watched at the side, impassive; he looked oblivious as to what was going on.

Neipas witnessed all of this absolutely petrified with terror. He was still in the pose of stand-by; but his body never sprung up. The indignation and disgust at this scene, so completely vile, so absolutely profane, so profoundly evil, made his heart jump and his body stir. But he held, and held, waiting until it got worse to intervene. He thought that perhaps Magpie could save herself, and needed not his help; that it was perhaps unnecessary to do anything, that if he stepped in he might get into trouble he could avoid — for he was still deeply conscious of his words to Reckuz earlier in the night. He thought that perhaps he might even make things worse. So he waited. The feeling that it was unnecessary to intervene gave way to a sense of futility as he watched the situation get worse — the Eagles were too powerful, and how could he stop them? He was only one, too. What could he do? What could he do? — The question repeated itself in his mind.

Yet upon witnessing the repellent vision of Noxxe, naked in all his wickedness and filth, tear apart Magpie's garments, Neipas felt his own muscles tremble with fury and indignation; but a sudden sight held them to inaction. A little beyond the grove, hidden amid the far trees, he thought he saw — blanketed thinly in shade, shape emerging indistinct — he thought he saw Reckuz himself leering in with wide eyes, stroking himself in the protection of the thicket, with the other two tech execs studiously lurking at his side, taking notes. Neipas thought he saw this, and he thought they would see him. His mind was full of possibilities of repercussions; his soul, filled with paranoia and fear. — *And what if there were bulls hiding in the bushes...*

So Neipas snuck away from the shrubs, dodging his eyes from the sight of Magpie violated, desecrated, destroyed. He went away brimming with shame, feeling ignoble and pathetic; chagrined red upon his own cowardice.

Magpie lay pressed against the dirt as Baron Noxxe raped her; the entirety of her body and soul besmirched, injected with the venomous fluids of their depravity.

And Neipas left her there.

55 - The Pantry

Dawn had just begun to flower upon the skies above the tempest when Neipas was led down to the Pantry. He had been waiting in the kitchens for an assignment... standing in a corner, uniformed and at the ready, waiting for the food to be cooked, waiting for the eartag to buzz. He had waited in vacant anticipation, held erect by the coffee high alone; the liquid jittered in his every fiber, his muscles were sustained by it. The kitchen looked like an enormous, primeval cavern full of phantoms and voiceless spirits. Its ceiling lights blinked dimly above the intermittent flaring of shooting flames, which revealed the bovine snouts of the cooks. Janu's ghost appeared before him limping, moving busily round the pots and pans of his station, dejected and sweaty before the swelling and shrinking fire, filled with red glows. Out of tacit agreement, they did not speak. The entire Eagles' Nest found itself in a sinister disarray, with the feast's hangover dragging itself through the narcotic day and evening into the next night, carried in the torpid heads of the pigeons, in increasingly psychotic perceptions of reality straddling fiction and dream. The clean-up was carried out languidly, at the pace of hallucinogenics; planes of food scraps were swept together into mounds before brooms, and thrown out by the pile.

Only later would Neipas learn of what had happened to Janu. Despair, fueled by liquor, had driven him to step into the Ballroom and approach the Minister of Borders. The cook plead insistently for his mother and sister, who he was sure were not well — a presentiment which had always been with him, only the drunkenness had lifted it to the fore and totality of his senses. He had just seen in the Webwork that border guards had been rounding up immigrants fleeing the storm... At once Janu was taken out of the Minister's presence, and was afterwards seized by the Minister's Bull who, mad, inebriated and abandoned to his hatreds, slapped the woeful immigrant and threw him down the stairs amid shouts and cruel laughter.

Neipas waited. He waited quietly in his corner, holding the feeling of what he had seen that night, under; holding it down as it wrestled in the depth of his sedated, unconscious heart. He waited for quite a bit, until his nerves got the better of him; at which point he began pacing nervously about and gnawing at his fingernails. In a moment his breathing quickened and suddenly he looked like he was about to have a panic attack. His whole body seemed ready to revolt against him.

When Kasim the pantrykeeper called his name Neipas nearly jumped out of himself. He hadn't used any particular tone of voice, he acted quite regularly; but Neipas felt so irritable that the barest stimulus made his guts lurch and twitch buoyantly with hysteria.

"What's wrong?" asked Kasim as they descended the stairs to the deep Pantry. His tone of voice denounced a certain nervousness now.

Neipas deflected instinctively. "I dunno, maybe it's the coffee... I'm all high-strung."

"I see," Kasim noted absently, closing the exchange.

The pantrykeeper's mask appeared stolid, and his ways as composed and collected as ever Neipas had seen them in public, away from the poet's grave. But as they approached the imposing Pantry gates, Kasim let off a hint of agitation in his walk; the manner with which his shoulders bobbed was weird — shaky. Neipas could vaguely sense that he was keeping silent because he feared the growing quivering in him would shake his voice.

The gates parted with a cavernous screech, echoing into the huge space inside. Neipas contemplated the deep and colossal shelves multiplying without end to the sides. It had a bizarre resemblance to a library; a dreary, impersonal library of boxes. Kasim led him through the Pantry — a whole world of shelves, cavities on the walls, mounds of cans, and farm pens in the deep, bustling with the squealing of exotic beasts, where mute workers washed and perfumed the animals to be sacrificed. The workers were mostly equipped with screen meshes over their masks, and wore long aprons clean and bloody. They greeted Kasim upon his passing with silent, distant bobs of head; there was a strange feeling of agitation in their motions, in the shuffling and reshuffling of boxes — boxes upon boxes, which were so easily picked up and tossed that they seemed empty — and an uncanniness in the strange immensity and increasing disorder of those spaces. Neipas' perception of it all was vague. Through veils and plastic curtains he was taken, and through storage rooms upon storage rooms, under airtight locks, circling past successive sectors of foods until they arrived at a large, heavy door at the end of a warehouse space filled with piled-up sacks. There was a line of winter fur jackets hung up on the wall by the door.

"Put this on, please," said Kasim, handing one of the heavy coats over to Neipas.

They entered a pale blue vastness, permeated with frost. Neipas immediately put his hands round his own arms and quivered. The chill was piercing — he hadn't felt this cold in a long time, perhaps ever, and the frigidness cleared up his mind with a new sort of neurotic high. He felt about to faint, and maybe he wanted to, but his body stiffened up against the gravity of exhaustion; his eyes burned wide, his teeth clattered, his heart pounded and his lethargic senses strained against the discomfort. He flung the hood with the thick bison fur over his horns and shrunk, breathing fast.

"What are we doing here?" Neipas asked in a breath.

Kasim's agitation was obvious now. His hands shook visibly, though not from cold; he wiped the sweat off his melting forehead every few seconds. He looked around nervously as though to check if there was anyone that could listen. Heavy glass partitions formed into rows between wide aisles, storing a variety of frozen packages — of vegetables, fruits, meat, fish, butter, bread — under bright blue lights. Yonder at the end of the aisles the space opened, and there, blurry in the frosty haze, decapitated carcasses hung by hooks, inert. Their form shaded the distance gloomily; theirs was the only presence in the quietude. In the aisles there was no one.

Kasim recited something in his native tongue; a sort of quick, supplicant prayer. Then he turned around abruptly.

"Neipas," he whispered. His eyes — the mask, which hadn't lost much of its composure yet, could not conceal it — were wild with anxiety and shot in all directions separately.

"What? What's wrong?" Neipas asked, alarmed. Kasim's apparent unraveling affected his own rattled nerves right away.

The pantrykeeper opened his beak, but only a trembling breath came out of it. It was a very timid sound, and yet it penetrated the gelid silence very sonorously with the cold puff that emerged with it; it was a very image of fear. Neipas looked around in a paranoiac motion of head, with very open eyes. The shelves stretched until they met the bloody and flayed, headless cows, strapped by hooks of steel; motionless, sinister, and so far away they were lost in a hazy cold of alien blue. The reaches of it seemed to move slowly... Neipas turned his enormous eyes of paranoia toward Kasim again.

"What's wrong? What's wrong?" he asked again, in a frenetic whisper so low as to not be audible even in that vast quiet.

"Look!" whispered Kasim agitatedly. "The food is almost gone!"

Neipas looked. The shelves seemed pretty well stocked. Packages, containers, wrappings of every sort filled them. Yonder, where the meats were stored, entire beheaded cows hung grimly in the arctic mist, pressing tightly against each other and beefing up the distance in a curtain.

The discrepancy between what he saw and what he was told befuddled Neipas to such a degree that it soothed the shakiness in his temperament a little. He stared at the shelves for a very long time, confused.

"I don't get it," he finally said. "There's plenty of food."

"No no no no," shot Kasim with a frantic shake of the head. "Please, look."

Kasim pointed, and then, rushing to the freezers, he opened one of the glass doors and removed a couple of boxes. "Please, take a look." Holding the packages under his arm, he pointed in to a very deep shelf with nothing in it.

"Look," Kasim continued, opening another door and removing a couple of packages from a shelf. There was nothing behind them.

"And what's more," said the pantrykeeper, "Many of these boxes don't even have anything inside."

Neipas grimaced, taken slowly aback with perplexity. He opened one of the doors himself, looking about; and he saw that after the first three boxes, which filled up the front, there was nothing. He opened one of the boxes — there was nothing inside either. The glass-doors seemed pressed with packages which were there for no other reason than to be facades; props to hide the massive void stretching within. An ill feeling took hold of him, and, impelled by instinct, Neipas crossed the aisle toward the hanging beef at large steps. His hand seized the bulky loin of the carcass, and pushed; it drew aside easily.

Beyond the veil of meats, the space was wide and outstretched. Raw beef hung here and there — but scarcely, like hanging trees in an inverted forest, with ample gaps in-between.

Neipas was shocked preemptively, even as he struggled to consciously grasp the significance of what he saw.

"What — It's like this everywhere?" he gasped.

"Not everywhere, no. God be praised. There is still a lot of food scattered around. But we are low, very low on stock. I don't know how long we can last this way.

"Believe it or not, the largest quantities are here in the freezers. The refrigerated stock. That is what has been keeping us afloat. I've been decreasing the quantities little by little, and so far no one seemed to notice... But this will not be for much longer."

"Mary... I thought something was different about the food! It's the quantities?"

"There is something else," Kasim said, worried. "This food has been restocked two times. There are items here unaccounted for in the inventory."

Neipas contemplated the pantrykeeper through a narrow and glassy stare, confused as to the meaning of what was being said.

"But how could they do it, with the storm outside? This is why I think," Kasim said and he stepped nearer, lowering his tone of voice, "that they have a secret stock."

"A secret pantry?"

Kasim nodded gravely.

"I know the layout of this complex well. On the other side — do you see?" he turned his glance to the end of the corridor momentarily, to that far blur of winter blue. In the horizon after the sparse forest of corpses, the barest shade of an exit could be made out. "Beyond there, you can access a corridor watched by guards. It leads to *their* pantry.

"I know every store of food in their side too. They have been taking from here everything that is quality. And they partly replace it with these foods from this other place — I do not know, exactly where it is from."

"Wait, what? They've been taking food from here?"

"Neipas, you have no idea. If I told you, maybe you would not believe me. But — their pantry is even worse! All of it is gone! So that is why we must replenish from this side. Everything left that was quality was squandered... in that feast.

"And — God forgive me! [Kasim repeated it in his native idiom]. Part of what they gave you, we had to gather — from their scraps!"

"The fucking crumbs — " Neipas let out in shock. "Holy shit man! How's it possible? They're like a hundred times less than we are."

Kasim shook his head in despair and exasperation. "They take everything in huge quantities, and throw most of it away. It's madness, it's madness. I tried telling them again and again... But the Head Gardener will not listen. They think the food will last forever. They think they are invincible. There is no limit for them."

He said all this in a whisper, as if in fear of defiling the oppressive gods of that place. Neipas reached back into his memory for something to grab on to.

"But, but — Just a short time ago the journalists said the food stock was all good. Just a couple of days ago or something." And indeed, the journalists had claimed it from atop the upper stage of the garden terraces. They updated the pigeons regularly about such logistics as those, and it had become so routine that the majority stopped paying attention; though Neipas, with a lingering instinct borne out of his days of hunger, kept attentive to such things.

"Yes," said Kasim. "But they did not actually come down to check the stocks. They were merely told that they were plenty."

Neipas exhaled "Good Mary," taking his fingers to his forehead.

"But Neipas," and now Kasim neared with intent, secretly and intense, as if pitching toward the point. "Their pantry, just beyond there... It sits above the Temple in the bottom floor. And I am sure... Neipas. Have you not heard it?"

He said this very gravely, his voice loaded with grim undertones.

Neipas sunk his whisper very low to follow Kasim's into the depths of secrecy. "Heard what?"

Kasim lowered his voice yet deeper, so much so that he was inaudible to himself:

"The pulsing. Am I crazy? No... I heard it. I know it."

"What?"

"There's something... I know there is... Something in the middle of the tower. Haven't you heard it, at night? Like a heart, beating..."

(The throbbing...)

Neipas had heard it. His head nodded with a perturbed expression, slow, vacant, and tired.

"I swear to you, Neipas. There is something in the core of the tower."

"A treasure?"

"Sustenance is the treasure of treasures. Maybe... And in the other day, Marlene — Do you know Marlene? Pink hair..."

"Marlene the lawyer?"

"Yes."

Neipas waved his head indecisively. "Not well but I've met her."

"She was good friends with my Cesar..." Kasim pursued, nodding gravely. "Marlene — She knows their language. She can understand what they say. And she told me that she heard them talking about a bunker... A shelter of last resort. And what they do, makes her think they are hiding something like that.

"Neipas. Please, think with me. There is no possibility of rescue for them. I know that. The storm reaches so far that nothing can fly out of here. And I think they are not stupid. I have warned them multiple times — they know the food is getting scarcer."

"And?"

"They simply do not care. But when the food here... What do you think will happen when the food here is finished? They have no more that is worth taking from here. They will probably lock themselves inside their bunker, and survive from the secret stock they have stored — until the storm ends. They will not share it with us. We will be locked out, and starve."

"And you think this bunker is in the center of the tower?"

"Yes, I do."

Neipas stared blankly into his scattering wits.

"...Maybe we can let everyone know about this, maybe together we can do something," he said.

"And go up against the guards? Provided we are believed."

"They sell guns in the market."

Kasim looked at him startled.

"And — what? — you want to have a shoot-out with the guards? No no no. That would be a massacre," he answered with a shudder.

Kasim seized his arm with intention.

"Please, listen carefully to what I have to say. We still have time, but we must act preemptively.

"Their pantry is above the Temple. I hear that sound most clearly there, in the silence... I am sure, I am sure the entrance is through the Temple.

There is a big curtain there, in the inner chambers — have you seen it? I swear to you, I have probably seen every corner of this complex, except perhaps the private estates, though I know their outline — but under no circumstances am I allowed beyond that curtain. It is a complete mystery to me.

"I want to know what is behind it. Neipas, if perhaps we can get access to it, we can..." Kasim seemed to struggle with repercussions; he fiddled with his index finger, probably fumbling with decisions inside his head.

"We could make sure they do not lock us out. And they do not starve everyone."

Dazed, Neipas strained to bring his mind under control, strained to think, strained to understand. "But —" the cold froze the progression of his confused speech, seemed to clutch at the deep sides of his tongue. He stalled for a second (the summit bells rang dreamily, afar) — "how do you know this bunker is there?"

"I do not. But we must find out."

Neipas' mind wavered and he recalled, for a moment, that the dark Museum sprawled in the floor under him too, under the Pigeons' Pantry. He recollected the Midget, the underground, the dark sun pulsing.

"Neipas, are you in a good standing with them? I cannot approach the curtain. But if you can work at one of their meetings there, maybe you can take a look behind the curtain and tell me what you see."

"I'm not sure..." Neipas wondered, remembering his brazen monologue to Reckuz. Then his mind resourced to Osir's prospective help. "But maybe I can find a way. Huh — Do you have any money?"

Neipas explained to him that he could maybe get Osir to assist, but that it would cost. Kasim nodded without hesitation.

"Sure, sure. Please, take this —" Kasim removed from his pocket a wallet, and from his wallet a small bundle of banknotes. "Do you think it is enough?"

Neipas considered the money in his hands — then he shook his head to ward off the amazement and confusion at the general situation.

"This doesn't make any sense. This whole situation... Are you sure about all this?"

Kasim seemed to think it over, juggling reflections in his bobbing head. "I am positive there is something hidden inside the tower. I can almost feel it. And... Everyone knows it, Neipas. Everyone. Yes — they must hide something there. They must hide their true riches there. Yes," he nodded almost deliriously. "Perhaps what is said is true."

"And what does Marlene think about this?"

Kasim exhaled deeply, with fatigue. "That it is a fool's errand. That is what she said. That I cannot do it like this."

"How come?"

"I don't know. She just said... I don't know. She has a feeling. She is thinking about what to do.

"But we must act. Once the food on this side is finished, they will move. They will take their families with them and the best of their guards. But this place will turn to hell quickly."

"Wouldn't they take you with them?"

"Me? No... They won't waste their food on me. Besides, my services will no longer be needed. Surely there are no gardens there and they will not need me to manage their pantry. I will be expendable."

The pantrykeeper looked from side to side, almost neurotically. "They will blame me for this. I know it. Even though I tried again and again to warn them, even though I told them to consume less, to slow down, to ration... Still they did not listen! They only wanted more and more. And in the end, I will be blamed for it...

"I'll be lynched!"

He wiped the molting sweat off the pulp that was now his masked forehead, off the waxen semblance which had become entirely discomfited — a mushy confusion of paste. His throat pulsed nervously and his cheek was possessed by spasm. Neipas withdrew into the unreality of his tired body and absent mind.

"Ok," Kasim managed to force out of himself, restraining his pulse. Then he sighed, "Please — let me know what this supervisor Osir says... Neipas, thank you. Please, do not say a word of this to anyone."

"Of course."

Kasim and Neipas stood silently for another moment, before hurrying out of the Pantry's biting chill.

56 - Sol Invictus

Neipas did not see Osir at dinner. He ate in the crepuscular Cafeteria, which dimmed as the clouds swallowed the sun; and in that twilight he sat, chewing with difficulty, without energy. The plate stood meekly under him. He beheld it carefully. He held his heavy stare for a long time, breathing deeply. The portion allotted to him might have been less than before, but at any rate it seemed sufficient. It spread across the whole plate. He wondered, then, why it was that he felt still so weak, still so devoid of nourishment, even as he took of it; it was as if the food was laced with some sort of light narcotic. He ate broodingly — hiding some of the food in napkins — and went to bed early.

Power had been failing frequently again. Although Neipas had been sleeping in the gardens of late, that evening he decided to venture into the deep gloom and try to find his way to his dormitory, so that he could store the food he had taken in his closet of possessions. Walking behind the light of his *I*, he stopped by the bathroom on the way, and there he saw Osir. His outline darkened the thickening dusk, standing before the mirror; he stared deeply into the darkly surface of it, with wide red eyes and the scarred corner of his lip, which he petted with his tongue, twitching lightly under a heavy breath; he seemed to be struggling against something inside him. In his trembling hand he held a bottle of pills which, after a while, he swallowed, with the help of the water which he lowered himself to the faucet to get. Neipas had already called him twice by then.

"What?" Osir turned abruptly, snapping out of his reverie in a twitching movement of bird head.

"Do you think you can get me an assignment at the Temple?"

Osir did not ask what he wanted this for, though he wondered; and only said "maybe, but it's a hard ask." Neipas gave him money.

"Give me a couple of days to see." Osir sniffed — "Do you need any pills? Supply's running short but I can still get you some," he said.

"No, no... I'm all right."

*

Far to Axiac's northwest lies the Joachim Valley. Deep under its grounds rest seas of bitumen, vast swathes of thick petroleum lodged in subterranean darknesses of sandy quietude. It emerged through a process borne from fathomless time, beginning through ages of the deep past, across a distance of eons. Millions of years ago, the Joachim Valley lay under a giant ocean, where little creatures imbued with primordial life flowed in the currents

701

revolving across the young planet. Upon dying, their lifeless bodies descended to the bottom of the waters, profound and devoid of oxygen, and sheltered under the young earth. Countless of these organisms were delivered up to the motions of the great sea and came to rest in with the depths which took them, amassing, over succeeding epochs, in ample fields of silence, layering the anoxic crust of the netherworld.

Elemental forces collided along rifts breathing out of the planet's core, pressing together godly mights, sculpting the face of the Earth. Through ages the buried corpses became wrapped up in gathering piles of matter and heat as the Earth, with the patience of divinity, molded itself into paradise. They rested in their shifting cemetery for millions of years as these tellurian powers drained the vast sea away from the land and exposed it to the sun, which nourished it slowly, breathing new life into its uncovered surface; and out of it plants and trees grew, and rivers swept in, and mountains arose as the tectonic steppes shifted and turned with the pulse of ever-reborn life, ever revolving in its womb.

And under the trees, lakes, and mountains of the lush boreal forest which that valley would become, the dead ancients still rested. They had been transformed, tilted like rocked infants with the epochal sway of the planet across millennia; embraced in the heat of their compressing forms. They had become conjoined, molten, unison, peacefully nooked deep within a shelter of rock among water, clay, and sand — they had become petroleum.

When the new race of dominant life stepped upon the valley, they christened it 'Joachim' — after the grandfather of their god. They felled the ancient trees and laid bare the earth, unveiled it once more to the sun and made it parched; rendered the virgin wilds to waste, made rancid the sublimity of air and killed all life teeming within. They sought the vast crypt which the earth sheltered, for this new race fed upon the dead.

Machinery hordes stood ready to sack the primeval tomb.

Miles and miles away, in the southeast, a storm shrouded the urban coastlands. From the great field of clouds spread across the sky only one thing emerged — the summit of a tower. Up there, miles above a flooded city, billionaires with eagle masks discussed, with very sober tones, the riches to be pilfered from that ancient soil (they spoke enthusiastically about "creating shareholder value"). Boundless vaults of shale waited to be disturbed by an army of ghouls.

The Temple breathed irregularly, its fumes clearing and thickening at turns. Here the sight unveiled to show statues of marble, wearing penchants of gold and glittering in diamond; from the fog appeared Juno Moneta, burdened with heavy adornments, with amber jewelry deep; Sol Invictus' emblem encrusted upon the wall in relief, flaunting his icon of violent power, whip brandished in hand and rays bursting out the head; Mnemosyne peeked from behind veils and from the white shadows mysteriously, disappearing in smoke. Much emerald glinted in the fogs. Herbal, aromatic scents possessed the nose, sedative, levitating in increasingly aphrodisiac tones with the soft reverberating melodies and drugged giggling of swans, whose torsos were delineated in the mystique environs, curvy, naked, as they trod further in.

The gates frothed like the mouth of a smoldering cauldron when they entered, and from that moment on they penetrated a volcano of narcotic vapors, imbued with the sense of magic and power. A fire burnt somewhere in the distance.

The Temple was composed of a series of octagonal chambers, each of four sides opening to another chamber, the other four adorned with all manner of ornamented walls; often fitted with mirrors framed with spectacular sculptures of deities, muscular and stern, wise in their regal indifference of irisless eyes; and these mirrors were so directed that they pointed to other mirrors in other chambers, and reflected one another far across the haze and the bending paths, in endless refracting duplications. Each chamber had slightly differently angled and slightly differently sized walls. Each chamber a bathhouse, each made of marble, each enveloped in fumes, filled with perfumed toxin, confusing of the sight and senses. Each seemed built to a vaguely different purpose. Led by the winking Chief Supervisor, the workers carried in a monumental cake on a litter, mounted all with candles, glamorous; Neipas was among those who bore the pole pressing their yoke-laden shoulders. Apparently they were to serve at a very important meeting — they advanced deep into the House of Finance, chamber after chamber, passing through multitudes of laughter and cigar in a fathomless circle without center; as though shedding through the raveled cocooning of capitalist structure, exhausting, intoxicating; traveling through the intricate multi-hub maze of stock markets, bond markets, hedge funds, private equities, investment banks, leveraged buyouts, structured finance securities, derivative securities, futures, forwards, swaps — here is where they paid homage to all that mythic wealth, made of make-belief stuff, in this steamy maze of languages where the lords of human capital hung clotheless; enshrouded in the haze where they hid their sins. Neipas felt weak; his mind distressed — close to delirious; he imagined the cake spoke to him sometimes. Since the Feast, they had been given portions of pastes and something that tasted like grass. No one said anything about it, and most were slow in detecting their own physical deterioration; but Neipas knew the truth of things, and felt it acutely in his bones.

The pole was unloaded from his shoulder; they were far inside the Eagles' den now. They stood in the deepest chamber, before Kasim's forbidden curtain.

With the vapors and mirrors, it was difficult to make out exactly where the curtain was; though Neipas could discern it, because it shimmered with flashing glints from the fog. It descended from a pole of heavy gold up in the distant ceiling; and a tall peacock perched upon it, and the curtain was his tail, unfolding from his majestic glittering poise. Yet the peacock's lights shone in myriad replications out through the confusing haze, and it was difficult to distinguish reality from reflection.

(A vague fire burnt somewhere nearby. It came not from the candles dotting the towering cake, it was but a single, great flame; of essence different. But it wasn't the sunlight; for they were too far inside, and no power of mirrored repetitions could overcome the dimness of the deep. And it didn't come out of the lamps lighting the chamber. It was something unearthly, something familiar...)

At the center of this division arose a fountain or jacuzzi, portentous, enormous in size. Nine layers high, the centerpiece lifted in a series of animal head carvings evolving in a spiral, each gushing in a continuous stream to the head beneath — ox heads gaped at the bottom, and an open-winged griffin stood at the peak. The naked Eagles sat outside the wide circular rim in puffy executive chairs, black in the whiteness of fumes. The rim, spacious as a table, was vaguely shaped like a series of bent backs, headless or with heads folding into their torsos, and arms taut on either symmetrical end. Here was Noxxe, and further down his Lobbyists, next to whom sat the Mayor and his assistant; there were two Legislators and the Ministers of Energy and the Environment, and in between each member sat Bankers with grins pushing back their masks with many creases. They conversed among themselves with serious faces and their voices scattered into the drips of steam. Swans reared their soft feathers behind them, attending to their every whim; some were massaged, others whispered to mysteriously. The usual entourage was also there, the pairs of bulls, their suited peacocks, and inscrutable aides with owl masks.

Neipas was the Banker's liege that morning. Following the usual proceedings, the oxen spread the various breakfast dishes — meats, cheeses, fruit, cereal, sugar, candy, slices of cake, glasses of juice and wine, scents of flower and a snug morning feel mingling with the bath perfumes — across the rim of the fountain. As Neipas tucked the flourished bib under the Banker's chin he noticed with a start that Magpie was among the swans standing behind the Oil Baron. There was a visible gash on her upper lip.

A voice was released from the griffin-sculpture's marble beak — it seemed outfitted with a speaker, and the waters stirred as it spoke, initiating the meeting. As usual Neipas picked up utensils and fed the Eagle in his keep, alternately taking forks and spoons to his mouth, which opened monstrously over the bib.

The Griffin changed its voice as different Eagles moved their beaks (it was necessary to conduct the meeting in this way because they were so far away from each other round the giant fount). They were talking about Ostrich. Their language was cryptic, but Neipas knew they were talking about Ostrich. Iblis. The pipeline. Joachim. And dollars; there was much mention of numbers of dollars punctuating their incomprehensible babble, which grew in excitement as time wore on. Magpie seemed to glance at Neipas who, nearby, was engaged in the same task as herself. She was but a more or less defined blur in Neipas' tired sight and he couldn't make out her expression (only the gash sinking her lip into her disfigured skin). But; it could be his imagination, he thought. He could vaguely discern her general motion as she fed Baron Noxxe, who was lifting his chinless semblance to speak:

"Iblis will process the bulk of crude supply in the west," the Griffin said with Noxxe's voice, but Neipas felt too feeble to comprehend anything. Ostrich's importance. The oil in the valley. Dollars. There were two or three waiters from Ostrich there, but they all stood beside their respective Eagles and fed them, all isolated from one another; Neipas couldn't see them well. The tempest inhaled souls below and the chaos opened fronts of opportunity for enterprise all across the megalopolis (as the excitement grew the inscrutability and gravitas in the Eagles' speech diffused). They spoke in legible ways now, and as the wine flowed so did a certain crudeness of spit. Louder and louder they spoke. There was much enthusiasm about Ostrich specifically and how Iblis was going to gobble it all up. Iblis, the breathing money-maker, icon of their might over the earth; engine capable of breathing in its sludge and flare it into power, motorized lung of the great box-machine, Axiac! It could now grow — in the wreckage, there was plenty of space to build.

On top along the surface of the rim, where they sat, rested a row of papers, which the Bankers spied greedily with greedy bloated eyes, their elastic grins huge. Presently the owls wrapped ties round their necks and let them pend down their bare stomachs. The agglomeration of billionaires picked up the pens with their talons.

The paper was a classy affair especially prepared for this occasion, weighty, thick, textured, letterpress printed with a glyphic serif type and an off-white color. The cellulose pulp of which it was made derived from wood cut out of the Eastern Forest beyond the mountains, taken from inside the borders of the Oyate Reserve by clandestine loggers. It seemed to be impervious to the humid air, for the steam did not wet it. Pens hovered over the paper tremulously, over the straight line indented under the drape of hieroglyphic font. What the paper was, in fact, was a contract for the loan of funds to NoxxeSocony and associated contractors from Private National Bank; a potent injection of money to get the operations for bitumen extraction, pipeline installation and refinery expansion started and finished quick. Though the cattle could not understand them, its words seemed momentous; like they held the fate of thousands, of millions, of everyone.

But suddenly Neipas, who had paused feeding the Banker on account of his speaking, noticed he was making gestures. Even as he issued his pronouncements his finger poked the fountain-edge with increasing frustration, again and again, and then it would point to his own talking beak with wringing jerks of his wrist. The sound of the Banker's finger badgering the marble was what alerted Neipas, and he promptly sprung up and back into service, picking up fork and spoon and inserting them full into the Executive's mouth. It was incredible, but indeed there was not a millisecond of interruption to the Banker's flow; his speech went on undisturbed even as he chewed and swallowed the mounds of food that Neipas kept frantically pumping into him at his demand. Most of the breakfast went unconsumed, nonetheless. Food catapulted from the Banker's beak and landed all over the rim and on the water as he blabbered on; and Neipas grimaced inside his dutiful mask, thinking he'd be the one who would have to clean it up.

They laid pens upon the paper and wiggled their arms. Sounds of scratching in a tense silence — then came the owls pointing with their skinny fingers to the paper. The Eagles spit on where they pointed; saliva made of hot wax flashed out of their golden, pouted beaks; and finally the owls, with little hammers, stamped seals upon the contracts. There were then great effusions of tongues twirling, savage, in release; the Griffin yelled in frenzied ecstasy. The need for a suitable celebration was quickly agreed upon. Champagne bottles popped and confetti materialized in the steam all of a sudden. Candle-flame vanished into steam and the towering cake was dissected, stuffed into their frothy beaks. With their shoulders the oxen lifted the chairs in which the Eagles sat, the nakedness of their bodies indistinct in the effluvium of fragrances, and deposited them in the fountain amid joyful shrieks; into which torrents of alcohol soon poured, all melting into bacchanalia of drunken indulgence and debauchery. Blows of laughter and festive yelling stirred the fogs and in a pinch many swans and some peacocks were pulled inside the fountain and water arose and splashed everywhere.

It was a madhouse built with gold. (A fire burned nearby still. Did it burn from the angular walls, in the sweeping mirrors? Or did it glow before him? It was impossible to distinguish reality from reflection. A shimmering formed undulating slits in the intoxicating fog — symbols, glyphs, letters, forming a very garble of mystifying codes — but among them Neipas discerned the message *THOU SHALT* blazing through the smoke). But of a sudden a great stir, affecting everyone, overwhelmed their voices and silence was again made. It had felt as though the tower itself had shaken; but though powerful, the tremble was only momentary, and presently they had recovered, blaming their collective imagination. Noises boomed in orchestral bursts, melodies shouted from everywhere.

In the confusion Neipas stepped out next to the refreshments table and pretended to wait for the eartag summons. This was his chance. He sharpened his attention and tried to perceive the veil. At the same time, he tried to look for Magpie among the bedlam. It was difficult to ascertain even the size of the space, where the replicas began and the original ended, and with the steam and the heat it was hard to know where things really were.

And then he perceived a sort of movement — a purposeful motion in the generality of aimless craze, directed to a single path. Neipas did not know where it started and which of the myriad motions was true; but an instinct made him follow it in the direction of the orchestral sounds. It was the walking motion of two bodies, one short and one very tall and bulky; and as he followed one of their versions (hesitantly, for fear of hitting a wall) the melody grew nearer. His eyes narrowed and strained. And then he saw the band emerging through the mist...

The orchestra spread along its members and instruments, and all their backs faced him. Behind them all was the Conductor, whom Neipas had the sensation was staring right into him (the movement of his head followed his walk); and yet he still could not perceive his face, for the steam hid it in puffs of fume...

There appeared the logo of Sol great upon the wall, and laughing Plutus holding a caved mirror; on the left flashed the blazing glimmer; on the right fell the peacock's shimmering tail. The two figures penetrated its curtain. Neipas was sure now. He hastened his march behind them and, looking round him and finding no one — the steam was dense and shrouded the origin of all those noises — he stepped to and plunged his head into the veil, which was made of myriad folds; and he felt its fine texture of reed sprouting with delicate plume, a plume painted with many eyes, whence glitters of gold shined. He parted the fold — The view of the other side appeared to him clear.

There was a vaulted stairway studded with gems of all colors, diamond, ruby, sapphire, jade, onyx, amethyst; all the crystal wonders of the underground. At the bottom of it was a big door, resting within a frame shaped like a serpent's maw. And before the door he recognized the bald head of the butt-naked Treasury Minister, and beside him his key-bearing Bull. The Minister's hand held the key, which he inserted; and turned in the lock.

A moment passed — in which they must have been trying to push the door, which looked heavy — and then it opened; Neipas could not see anything but thick darkness inside, which swallowed the two bodies in an instant.

He peered in, with an instinct to go through — but now Neipas jolted and retreated from the curtain. Someone had hit him and pulled him back. He gasped, unsure if it was by accident — perhaps a stray body wandering the diffuse Temple grounds — or if it was intentional. Nevertheless it shot much fear into Neipas' heart, and at the same moment his eartag shook and the voice twittered into him, instructing him to fetch champagne and pour it on the fountain.

Chaotic noises and the general disarray of motion made the watery haze tremble. Neipas rushed to his duties through the accelerating music. His muscles remembered the path which he had walked, and he traversed it again through the thickening steam, arriving at the refreshments table where he saw, on the other side, appeared from smoke, Magpie. Neipas wavered for a moment — she appeared quietly, wiping with a cloth the edge of the fountain, where Baron Noxxe, now lolling near the fountainhead, had been; and with the voice in his ear cheeping again Neipas was pressed into grabbing a bottle of champagne, making his way quick to the jacuzzi near where the Bankers waited with upturned beaks, pouring its contents on the raving crowd of billionaires and consorts splashing deliriously in the warm pool. Then he stepped back and circled round, drenched with the waves of liquor-stained water which spilled in droves out of it. Suddenly he stood facing Magpie.

"You ok??" he asked exasperatedly, in a sort of breathless gasp. His voice came out secretive and rushed from the airlessness of his chest.

Magpie leaned over the fountain, one hand supporting her weight and the other cleaning the surface of marble in circles. She didn't say anything at first, or pause in her movement in the least. Neipas stared at her with bewildered eyes. Apart from the deformation of her upper mandible, which — seen closely — turned out to be but a scratch, she looked the same. Her swan mask bore that same serenity so peculiar to her, her features still fixed in a rigidness of purpose, eyes narrow, lips tense, face full. For a moment — a moment that seemed suspended in time — Neipas assumed that somehow he wasn't there, that Magpie couldn't see him, that he must be dreaming. His eyes bloated, and his breathing stilled heavily. The space in the chamber seemed to disperse away from him, and all of a sudden everything went quiet; so quiet he could hear his own breathing very clearly. Neipas realized how exhausted he was (how much had he slept since he entered the Belab?) and how it all felt like a dream to him; his senses buoyed in some kind of semi-reality; all the time. Something quivered.

(Had the room shaken? But no one noticed). Raising his head in a start, he looked quickly about the bathhouse and saw shadowy forms scrambling. Then he turned his glare to Magpie again — and this time he noticed something different about her.

She leaned over the fountain still, one hand supporting her weight and the other cleaning the surface of marble in circles; and she toiled industriously. Yet the steadiness of her movements was breaking down. Neipas could see her lips beyond the rough mask, which was dissolving slowly and inexorably; and he could see that she had to bite the inside of her mouth, which twisted, to keep them steady. And what he had seen was more than a scratch — Her upper beak was really cut short, deformed... Her shoulders quaked weirdly in the motion of her work, looking as though she were working in the freezing cold. The hand supporting her weight pressed upon the fountain-edge — its fingers tapped the marble alternately, visibly; the back of her hand, and her wrist, seemed to strain under the weight of her body, and trembled visibly.

Neipas reached a hand for her, touching lightly her trembling shoulder.

"Magpie..." — she turned with a violent start, roaring "Don't touch me!" with a gasp of ferocity and fright, flinging away his hand with her forearm, which she held now in front of her face like a shield.

"Magpie!" Neipas looked at her in shock. "It's me!"

Magpie kept her forearm up, as though bracing herself for a blow; her strong mask was rigid in a threatening manner — but she trembled still and, though she hid it well even now, she felt terrified.

"It's Neipas!"

Only by degrees did Magpie lower her forearm; and even then, she did it very slowly. The swan mask had shed off and lay disfigured on the fountain-edge. She bore, beneath it, the pigeon visage of lustrous black feathers. It was molded like the semblance of a prey under siege, tense, ready to spring up and attack. But once she realized who it was, its features seemed to fade. The cheeks relaxed and gave themselves to weariness, quivering as they lowered; and her eyes, so beautiful in their opaque, glossy black color, and so profound in its depth of strength and purpose — her eyes seemed to collapse into a watershed of despair, if only for a moment. But Neipas looked upon her with much fright.

Her beak was missing; her voice escaped through a gaping chasm in the lower side of her mask.

When she recognized him, she turned her face away slightly and raised her forearm even higher above her brow — as if expecting to have wings pending down from it, with which to hide — before she steeled herself again and lowered her arms, straightening up her posture.

"You ok?" Neipas asked again, in a frightened whisper.

"Yes," Magpie answered forcefully and in a bizarre tone of formality. And though it was noisy, her voice pierced clearly. Everything seemed to quieten around them.

He cast a hesitating glance off the side. "Are you sure?" he said. Magpie shrugged.

There was a suspended moment of silence between them as they gazed at one another. Neipas forced himself to pierce through the blurriness of his own tired eyes to really see Magpie's. He held his breath; with an enormous strain he focused his sight. In front of him Magpie stood with a completely hollowed aspect. It was obvious she struggled to keep herself steady, to hold her countenance firm.

"You ok?" Neipas asked a third time — it came out of him automatically, reflexively, involuntarily. Time bent uncannily around them and they weren't aware of how much of it had gone by.

Suddenly (after how long they could not know) Magpie's expression of strength fell apart and the gaping pit which was her mouth clammed shut in wrinkles, quivering uncontrollably; a breathless sob came out of it and tears slid down her face.

"Don't look at me," she averted her gaze and inhaled a deep, thick gulp of moist air. With obvious strain she pulled herself together again, wiping her eyes and reshaping her mask. "What do you want?"

"Nothing," replied Neipas, not really knowing what he was saying. "Just wanted to see how you are."

"Well I'm doing all right, as you can see," Magpie said through the pit, stiffening her forehead in a nodding frown, feigning indifference.

"Where — where have you been lately? We haven't been seeing you..."

Magpie said nothing.

"You know, the Chief Supervisor said that we can sign out of this if we want, at any time... if you want — whatever they took you to do..."

She looked at him incredulously, tear-eyed. "You think I can sign my way out of this shit?" Neipas didn't know what to say. He shook his head indecisively and flexed his shoulders in a helpless, somewhat stupid manner.

"I dunno — why not?" "You serious? I sign out — then what? You think they'll just let me go? I'm branded already. They'll keep me right here... Then what do I do? Where do I go?"

Her tone progressively faded down to a mere whisper as she spoke; her last words were but feeble puffs. She was breathless. Speaking more than a few words was a strain to her composure. Magpie could only hold herself for moments at a time; the characteristic ferocity, firmness, and sense of purpose were in her voice and manner still — even now she intimidated Neipas with her fierceness — but it was as though she had to muster all her strength lest it all broke down. She stopped again to recover. The oppressive sprain within her heart was powerful, overwhelming. "Where do I go?"

The chasm shut in folds as she fixed her mask. Lifting her chin in the dignified manner so particular to her, she said then, "I need the money. So fuck it — I'll stick with it till we're out. Then I get my paycheck, and I bounce.

I'll go. I'll go far away somewhere."

But Neipas stood there hesitatingly, trying to find words. He felt pinned between his concern for Magpie, imagining the hells in which she must have been imprisoned under Noxxe, and his sense of obligation to help somehow, obligation not only toward Magpie but toward himself as a Man, too, an obligation to defeat his own cowardice and his shame — and his fear of the Eagles, the crushing consequences they could wreak, as well as the perception of his powerlessness before it all.

He mustered courage to stammer some words out: "Magpie... I know... What Noxxe and the Banker... And the Mayor — God."

Neipas grimaced, furrowing his brow under the weight of his own nervous breathing. "I followed you and... I was worried, I —... And I, I saw... I saw you..."

He could speak no longer. It felt somehow as though he were the one who had been violated in the most humiliating, degrading, and filthy manner; for he shook and his whole being was pervaded with trepidation. Meanwhile Magpie had retaken her work, and her face regained its serenity. Her beak had grown back, though shortened and deformed, in her pigeon semblance. A silence lingered between them for moments. She cleaned the fountain-edge in circles... but then she slowed — and stopped. Then she turned to him again, and Neipas saw the revolt in her expression, the eyes brimming with water under a frown of exasperation and misery.

"Then why didn't you do nothing about it?" she said. The pent-up anger was palpable in her breathing. Full of battered might, she held her wet stare in Neipas' own; and the sight of that wounded, proud glare was so inflicting upon his frightened soul that he averted his eyes from hers in shame.

Magpie's expression relaxed into a resigned sadness. She resumed working. "You men are all the goddamn same."

Neipas' ear had been buzzing for a while; and the voice inside it had meanwhile turned to screams pounding his brain.

The rest happened very fast.

The band stopped playing — all but the drum, which beat deliberately. It beat a familiar sound, a sound of throbbing, deep, and distant; spreading from afar out into the marrow of bone. Then the curtains — all thousands of them — opened swiftly; and out came a giant swine, with mighty tusks the size of an elephant's, with bristles quaking and nostrils dispersing the steam with great exhalations. They brought in the mighty boar wrapped by the noose and bound by rope. He was led on by the spectacled Treasury Minister, whose Bull held the leash. The orchestral sounds erupted all at once.

First they grabbed guns and shot it. The boar wailed in pain as lead penetrated its flesh and quickly overwhelmed its senses. Once its sides were drenched with red cascades and the boar's powerful semblance teetered toward the floor in a swoon, its step faltering, the Bulls strapped hanging ropes around its rear legs and, pulling the ropes forcefully toward the ground, lifted the giant body of the beast, and while its hoofs were held aloft they came in with long ladders and knives and butchered the pig down the middle, and a torrent of blood came pouring forth from within its gaping belly. "Wine!" they yelled, and the Eagles set about bathing in it and drinking of it unrestrained; and by degrees Neipas realized, with his horrified stare, that golden pellets emerged from within the blood as it spread. Red banknotes also...

"More wine! More!" came the yell, and it was followed by the sound of a big bang; suddenly his vision was shrouded by a black drape. A great wail of protest and delirious laughter arose — then the world seemed to tilt and quiver, and the air was sucked short.

"Hey..."

Only now did Neipas notice the silence. Everything was very still now. Everything was dark.

Clocks wound for long.

"Can someone fucking turn on the lights!" the authoritative voice of a Legislator boomed into the quietude. A shiver of fright rang through it.

There were many stirrings in the darkness, sounds of activity, whisperings of something being done.

But the lights did not return.

Demons prowled, and the breath of ghouls blew disoriented in the black.

57 - Hunger

Sitting upon the towel, in the spread of beach before the sunset, Neipas and Orenda contemplated the reddening tides, which flared up in a last gasp before folding into the gloom of night. They shared bread; Neipas masticated very slowly, tasting its simple, invigorating flavor with particular appreciation, feeling the nourishment coursing his body, mind and spirit, suffusing him with its energy. Orenda had asked him something. The calm breeze of day's end tickled his ear, sensible and deep, with silent whispers of memory.

"It's difficult to describe," he voiced mutedly into the graceful air, remembering his days of hunger. He remembered that time well enough; he remembered it all too well. The sensation of it was imprinted in his flesh, the reminiscence dwelt in the marrow and had been made part of his very soul. To his senses returned the feeling of languishing on a couch that was not his own, the general feeling of humiliation, the weakness of body, the complete disorientation of thought and slow despair of feeling...

"Yeah, I guess... yeah. It's difficult to describe," he confided in Orenda. "There's nothing close to it that I've felt before, you know...? Like, people might say they're hungry, many times a day, maybe. But that has nothing to do with hunger — it's just appetite. People might even fast; but they know they'll break the fast soon, and eat. It's not knowing that really gets you. It's the constant tension... you know, of not knowing if you'll have enough to eat next day. That never leaves you. It puts a... a strain, on every decision you make; a heavy strain. Heavy," he nodded, downcast, wrestling with the turmoil of his memories and the feelings they wrought, "heavy, really heavy... It eats you from the core. Degrades you slowly." Silence.

Orenda, watching him with all the attention of care, placed her hand on his shoulder; but he couldn't bear to look at her. He felt an elusive sense of shame and the words came to him painfully; only Orenda's devoted listening, and the profound respect which it conveyed, could make Neipas speak.

"I never wanna go through that again," he whispered, meekly, after a while.

*

The plain of white, puffy hillocks stretched to all ends and beyond every horizon, nearly motionless, resembling pure foam stilled in the course of time. Mighty, swelling clouds curved like strangely tilled fields, inclining in a demonic march toward that inscrutable pit afar. It was like a tranquil current suctioned by a mystic whirlwind, a maelstrom drawing force from the dark sky, divine sculptor, mother of all fears. The round aspect of the universe pushed down upon this new Earth. Its boundaries sniffed the summit of the Belab, edge of a vast, limitless, black, inscrutable reality expanding to distances unknown. From it beamed the single, supreme light above the clouds: the Pearl, sole outpost of existence, beacon atop the last watchtower shining to a gas-choked, desolate, empty world.

The Pearl glowed lone over the clouds. It shone above them all in the hanging garden terraces, and all looked up at it as a divine sign, as the third eye of God eminent among the skies, even over the radiant sun and the waxing moon; night star, ruler of their fates. The whole Eagles' Nest succumbed to darkness. Both Wings found themselves without power, and for a few minutes (before the torches were finally set aflame) all four rivers flowed invisible through their grounds.

"If the Pearl still shines," confided Kasim with a frightened voice, "then there must be something powering it. They said the backup generators have enough power to last for months — yes, even privately they said this. Neipas! This is proof that I am right."

Neipas had just told him of what he had seen in the Temple's inner chambers, beyond the peacock's curtain. He reported the sight of the giant boar brought out from that veil. Kasim stood before him speechless for a while; and mumbled that he had never seen such an animal, and of such prodigious size as Neipas described; but he did not doubt his telling for a moment. The pantrykeeper divined that there must be a hidden area in the center of the tower, a bunker full of riches yet powered by the backup generators which, he admitted, he had never seen with his own eyes either.

"What do we do now?" whispered Neipas in a corner of the Columbaria, by the mirrored wall.

Kasim summoned God in his native tongue. "We need to move quickly now, we need to enter that gate. A crisis is upon us. Without energy, all the refrigerated food will rot. The lights are off even in the pantries now."

Neipas shivered, though it was not cold, and as he spoke he had to contain the quaking in his voice: "All the food's refrigerated?"

"There is plenty of canned stock. But — you do not understand. I have seen what people do when... The *perception* is what matters, and once everyone knows — Even if it were not mismanaged... God be merciful! I cannot think of the consequences. They might even move it all to this bunker, and leave us here with nothing."

"Fuck," Neipas' fingers clutched his horns and he saw his vision blur and swim with despair. "But —"

"We will need to drug the guard with the keys, Neipas," Kasim told him urgently.

"The Treasury Minister's guard? They're hard to spot..."

"No no, not necessarily. Some of their personal guards hold two keys, have you seen? One is made of silver and another made of gold." Neipas nodded; his obscure shape flashed with the red gleam blinking inside the wall. Kasim went on, "I have noticed the silver ones are all similar, and I am willing to bet that this key opens that gate. They should all have access. I — I have access to the Head Gardener's personal guard, I know their schedules well."

Neipas looked fixedly at him, lit dimly in crimson, with straining eyes attempting to gather determination. "So now — what?"

"This Osir," whispered Kasim, very low. "Do you think he can — to drug the guard? We just need him to sleep for one hour, at least one hour."

Neipas blinked widely and inhaled deep. "I'll talk to him... I still have some of your money — Can I use it?"

"Yes, of course. Please hurry."

Night was heavy upon the firmament, and the immense and convoluted terraces were dominated by dancing flames and the shadows they cast; phantoms of all shades spirited between cloths and veils of every color. Indeed, the insulated air of the Anubel was stirred by the agglomeration of nervous breathing as the pigeons moved about; though everyone moved really slowly, every step charged with dread, laden with caution, with huge eyes — and by the relentless shaking of its grounds, which always trembled slightly and sometimes lurched, seizing every throat and hurling every heart violently inside each chest. Sounds of vomiting ensued sometimes; it really felt like being adrift in a massive ship, and indeed, the belief that the storm waters were arising to the very height of the summit grew into a near certainty among the generalized paranoia taking hold. The voice of doomsday sayers ruled atop the perches and even upon the main stage of the Auditorium, where pelicans listened to confessions and labored to assuage anxieties in its seats, lit under the ghostly light of the Pearl above... The droning chant of the Great Peacock sounded encouragingly as always in the background, suffusing every breath with the dictates of the Market who (as every Merchant echoed) would save them all.

Food prices soared abruptly, and Neipas went to nibble on the scraps he'd been storing in his locker of possessions since he met Kasim in the Pantry. He entered his dormitory in very fear — his senses guided only by the spotlight of the *I*, the battery of which he endeavored dearly to save. All night, without batting an eyelash for sleep, he looked for Osir. Very nervously he sought the Janitor, even to the moment when the clouds began to gain color — he could not even contact him, now with the Webwork wholly cut off, and could not bring himself to wait in the long lines before the few booths which still supplied access — and though he looked all night, he still could not find him.

WALTZ AT THE EAGLES' NEST

The Eagles buried their shoulders deep between the opulent arms of their thrones. Already, they experienced the first symptom of hunger — the fear of it. Though their relative sufferings were thickly padded in mountains of velvet cush and swarms of workers still attending to their every need, yet their egotism and greed was only heightened by the madness of their fright. Their tremendous arrogance overwhelmed all hesitations and pleas for caution and moderation, and even though resources were at a limit they still insisted on preparing a third feast and ball, a third waltz to celebrate the locking of funds to finish Noxxe's pipeline and expand the Iblis refinery, among many other such schemes and achievements. So they ordered the cattle wipe the Ballroom and adjacent spaces, which were still messy from the Pigeon Feast, and prepare for renewed festivities. The workers complied; and carrying the weight of their yokes upon their necks they passed through the immense curtains of the Proscenium beyond the stage (where the gloom was deepest — and red lights winked slowly) and ascended to the very top of the tower's summit.

Mr. Drrawetz had meantime returned to the rank of Supervisor. No one knew when this had happened, for it happened so imperceptibly that, once he was there, everyone just took it as if he had never left; there were some perplexed mumbles about it in the dark confines of the Cafeteria, where there was suddenly a dearth of nourishment and every meal had to be paid for; but everyone was so numb that none complained. That morning, Neipas was assigned to the janitor team, along with many other waiters — for many janitors had fallen ill — with Drrawetz at the head of the march up to the Ballroom. To Neipas' consternation, Osir was not there either.

Bent severely under the weight of the yoke, and pulled down by the load of his horns, Neipas now rubbed the luxurious carpet and felt the thinness of his breathing. His mind was strangely empty. On his bare forearms, moving vigorously — then very slowly — in a circular motion, he noticed the wavy light of the Golden Dove reflected, playing upon his skin, the straining muscle, like the sunshine cast from a lake.

Neipas was bound to a row of other janitors all clasped by a common yoke; which he presently removed from his neck. He got up, deliberately, very, very slow, as if surfacing from the immense tide of prostrate, fanning bodies. The rest carried on; but Neipas stood as though hypnotized; he stood there still, and gazed upon the swaying gleam, the fiery shine of the Golden Dove, which in its arched pose, its pose of dignified submission seemed to spark with the glint of flames. He frowned deeply in wonder; above, the myriad characters of myth — the lion, eagle, bull and lamb, the angelic littlets and the sinister robed forms — stared, and the caved dome seemed to deepen; and it, too, stared at him like a narrowing eye, as he stared at it; like two

716

abysses contemplating each other; one aloft, another beneath. What was it that affected him so? This uncanny feeling of withdrawal and abstraction, of distance from himself, the general impression that all was dream stuff... He had been feeling like this — for how long now? Not since the bygone days of childhood, when his mother culled aromatic herbs, had he...

... a ruffle at his shoulder roused him from his distraction a little. He looked over. It was Magpie passing, bearing a stolid posture, a general air of vacant steadfastness. Perhaps she was working — Neipas thought so for a moment, though she wasn't carrying anything on her. But there was something particular about her gait — something off about her; more so than what Neipas had seen of her in recent days. He said something to her, but she didn't seem to hear. She kept walking, and passed the 9th gate to the Eagle Gardens. Neipas watched her advance attentively, affected by a sense of strangeness enveloping Magpie; he tried to determine what was off exactly, what was different.

Magpie looked scrawny now, emaciated. Only a few feathers remained upon her decaying body, sticking out haggardly at uneven intervals across the head, which was mostly bald; those few feathers had an awful charred aspect, and often only the shaft remained. The wax had largely fallen off, though some of it still glued to her face in moisty bits and deformed, shriveled patches. The former luster of her mask, gone, revealed now a moribund skin, pale and cracked dry, sunk into the fissures between her bones. Her eyes, just recently so beautiful, so full of purpose, so firm in their gaze, darted out of her head manically, lost, watery and liverish, without any life in them. Rivulets flowed along her descent across the stairs, sometimes the flow crossed her path. Her reflection would stretch at her feet, cast like a shadow across the waters, nearly as featureless as a shadow. She saw herself bled across the waters; her image refracted, scattered, deformed; she saw the mask, which she knew she could not remove; and she recognized the face behind it. She resigned herself to it. She let herself sink in it. It had been too many years (centuries?) fighting. In her childhood Magpie had somehow connected two different narratives (the first one she couldn't remember what it was, but it was told her after her father scolded her in their backyard, which faced the concrete, fenced and fetid banks of the Axiac river; and the second her mother had first told her one night, to console her about something, she remembered — it was a fairy tale about a mermaid who wanted to leave the sea) to conjecture the world as an immense river. This river has an end to it, yonder, very far — some land at the top of the stream, an island perhaps, where people live in peace, where the trees whisper cool gusts and the flowers sway tranquil, and the sun shines soft on them everyday... Otherwise, the river has no margins on either side (once, Magpie imagined land existing beyond the horizons she could see; but this was impossible...). The current is stormy, surging downward in this tilted world — in it Magpie swims, pulling herself upstream, upward toward the island where she could lie down and enjoy, finally, the gifts of sunlight. But behind her, a monstrous roar sounded always, the noise of mighty waters plunging against sharp rocks, boiling far below, in the depths; a giant waterfall, making a descent half the world's height. She must keep onward against the current, without a moment's rest, and mustn't succumb to the lurking fall, for she, unlike the rest of them, didn't have wings to fly back. If she fell, she fell forever! And she went on, toiling for fear of the pit behind her, ambitioning the island yonder which, it was said, even some crows had reached, and where all are given wings to fly.

Magpie retained this abstraction into her adult life; she found the imagery apt for the realities of the world, and it helped her cope with its brutality. Her childhood mind — like most, perhaps — had the potentialities of literary genius. But in her life there was no outlet to develop that potential. There were no books to be found in the growing destitution of her home, nor was there a will to be mustered from the fetidness of the Axiac river which pressed disease and weakness into their bodies; nor was there encouragement to flex the creativity inert in her heart amid the dereliction of her schools which, instead, hardened it — the destitute teachers, holders of that sacred duty, being helpless against the revolt of infant poverty raging degenerately all about them. She could have been one of the greats, one of those enshrined in History's pages, beyond golden letters... She could have been a Morrison, an Austin, a Dickens, a Cervantes — An Ellison! A Zola! She could have been a Shelley, a Pessoa — Thoreau or Arundhati! Or maybe a great inventor, Skłodowska or Archimedes, or a great leader of the folk, a d'Arc, a Zumbi, an Amaru, a Tubman, a King, or a Queen and Sovereign of her own life... She could have been Magpie — but she never had a chance. Mired in a bog ruled by men without care nor mercy, she could toil as much as ten beasts of burden everyday, she could exert herself to godly extents, but there was no getting out. She had been thrusting against the current for too long... For too long had she directed her gaze toward that golden island, toward the sweet sound of those voices which seemed to encourage her on from afar, telling her to keep swimming, to keep trying... But now — just as she thought herself near the far shore — she felt herself losing strength. It began with a suspicion that the earth had vanished, that there wasn't a horizon any longer. The tempest stretched as far as the gaze could reach. There were no longer horizons for her to behold, no longer prospects to contemplate in the foresight of her mind's eye, no longer islands under the sun, and all the islands there were lied within the heaven-shore of the Eagles' Nest... Her eyes sparkled with the flow of a stream descending beside her on the steps, and she knew she stood somewhere, upon some vague rock, some reef; but it wasn't her island, it wasn't her land (already the waters were rising to her knees again). It was all but a heat shimmer, a cruel mirage, and now she could only see her island-dream waft up in smoke; and nothing else. Now, at the summit of the world, only now at the peak of society did she see it, did she hear clearly beyond the current raging all about her and the roar of the waterfall hunting her behind — those voices weren't of encouragement, they were mocking her! There was no sanctuary for her, no firm earth upon which to set foot. And now that she had caught a glimpse of the top, now that she saw the substance of land, now she had stepped out of the current — or so it had seemed to her, for just a moment — the stream had finally sapped her energy, her every bit of will, her every possibility of happiness, every hope, every aspiration. If this is what awaited at the top of the river, if this is what the island had to give... she would rather resign to the pit.

Magpie crossed the 9th gate and stepped into the sunlight, in which she found no joy; the faint breeze lacerated her face and burned her eyes, which teared up, but didn't blink. Holding her march steady, undeviating, she descended every step of the terraces, walked the pathway between the hedges, and entered the infinity pool. The Eagles in it stopped suddenly. For a long moment they remained very still; not a breath left their gilded nostrils as they observed this ragged and filthy crow swim in their waters, passing calmly through them; they were held and constrained, disgusted, nervous, knowing not what to do. Then, at a snap, an upheaval rose among them. They yelled at her and shoved her and pulled at the few feathers and hair she had left — even now! — but she didn't seem to notice any of it. Magpie passed beyond all the Eagles and, at the pool's edge (there was a collective murmur of awe upon seeing there was an edge) she hoisted herself up and stood.

A furious gale rushed into the Gardens as Magpie opened the glass door. The ire of the storm penetrated the Anubel frigid, lifting, for a moment, all its veils, chilling its every corridor and chamber, scattering the vapors of the Temple and disclosing the flaccid nakedness of the Eagles within, making the crowds of the Market wail and its mazes tremble, gushing waves into the Infinity Pool where the Eagles stood frightened with gaping maws and quaking lips, whimpering for the Bulls who were already rushing toward. The webs of the hedge trees were spirited away; and its branches, revealed to the skies, were shown eaten.

Magpie gazed firmly the storm, churning violently beneath her. Her mind was empty, her body relaxed, her decision made. It wasn't very long until she let her body topple beyond the edge — she fell into the depths, plunging freely and disappearing into the clouds round the tower.

The horrible sight entered Neipas' stare in a screaming shock. He jolted and shuddered, and rooted to the spot in a panic, before starting at a run, wild of mind, mumbling confused syllables from his trembling lips. He wasn't yet fully clear of the Ballroom when Drrawetz hopped into his flank, hissing savagely that running was forbidden here; Neipas halted immediately at a reflex, with his heart churning loudly in his throat. His legs failed for a moment and the whole universe seemed to collapse around him in a sombre yell of horror. Only after Drrawetz, livid beyond belief, picked up his collar and straightened him up did Neipas discern the reproaching stares the Eagles in the pool and gardens directed at him, as if his little run had caused them great inconvenience; they looked almost shocked at his conduct. The Gardener had already shut the glass door and the air was again windless. Confused, cowed, oppressed, at once fast-breathing and breathless, Neipas managed to shakily ask Drrawetz for permission to rest — ("Get out of here and pull yourself together before I lose it with you!").

Neipas bore the throbbing dread inside his chest as he scampered toward the dormitories. Everyone went on as usual — but Magpie was dead, dead!

Somehow he was able to feel a small sense of relief when he opened the door to a dormitory room and found it empty. Neipas went inside a closet; and for hours he did nothing but shake and weep, mumbling in panic, "dead! dead!"

58 - The Market Corrects

An expectant crowd gathered in the 6th Tier, the Auditorium terrace, filling all its seats, cramming its aisles, pouring onto the wide stairway. Red eyes flashed in the searching heads emerging from the head-sea pushing toward the stage; disquiet gurgled in the general motion as they waited for the announcement of the new rules. Food prices had risen suddenly and dramatically, triggering a rapidly escalating crisis. Everyone was on edge.

Up on stage materialized the figure of a Journalist, Analyst and Academic, whose avian mask said (as a parrot pecked his ear):

"Fellow Columbidae[...] Market fluctuations are an unavoidable component of commercial dynamics and natural law[...] We are happy to announce the opening of interviews[...] and opportunities to join the labor pool[...] Productivity is the central purpose of a healthy economy[...] We remain adamant in our promotion of individual freedom and free Market values[...] Wealth and happiness are gained through hard work, as everyone knows [hahaha]..."

The peacock spoke thus as he fanned himself with his colorful tail, and comprehension was made even more difficult by the windy, static noise of the ruffle pouring out the mike. Various translations circulated among the crowd. The interpretation that was most widely accepted was that "if you don't work, you don't eat", and so the pigeons signed up for the interviews in desperate droves. Those already swimming in the "labor pool" were notified that the current would be sped up. The Chief Supervisor informed the cattle that "free" meals would (lamentably, he regretted) have to be terminated, which in practice meant they would have to spend the whole sum of their earnings on the now-ridiculously expensive food, and join the massive lines stretching from the few cash machines which still worked (*No card payments accepted*, read the handmade signs up on the Market booths). Drrawetz, regaining a modicum of his old power as one of the many Supervisors, expressed pride to his weakened crew at the general fact that "handouts" were finally over. "One must pull oneself up by one's bootstraps," he would enunciate (a ridiculous saying current in those days. Neipas had never actually thought about it, but now he perceived that what they meant was, pull yourself up by *their* bootstraps as the boot lifts — to avoid getting stepped on, and launch yourself that way to a higher perch).

Cries of owl emanated from the gloomy edges of the Columbaria as lines of job applicants trailed into the Warehouse Hall, where Ms. Sunai sat beyond the bridge and interviewed the pigeons one by one. Torches illuminated somberly the pits of boxes and sacks and the stern walls where the unfunctioning elevators rested in a lifeless, darkest glimmer at the end. Along the corridors were torches too, flames moving over the heads of peacock masks, who gave consultations and personal advice for interviews for a fee, and long pelican beaks, who prayed for the pilgrims trekking to those inner recesses in search of blessings. Indeed, in those days the peacocks and pelicans exercised great influence over the crowds. Disoriented, aimless, and in increasing despair, the pigeons sought their wisdom and guidance. Two general schools of thought come to dominate the zeitgeist. The Peacock taught the pigeons to practice rationality and be austere, to worship the Market, King of the Earth, in service of the self in this world; whereas the Pelican taught humility and servitude toward God, King of the Skies, in service of the self in the incoming world; and the weary pigeons bobbed their heads wearily.

A revolution of efficacy took hold. Many pigeons were hired and made cattle, and many cattle — those who fared most poorly in performance reviews — were stripped of their work-masks. Those who were left jobless would be quickly shunned. Pigeons with higher proportions of black and brown feathers became the majority of the unemployed now; gradually they were pushed into the gloomy interiors, into the perpetual darkness of the Columbaria, which most — the pigeon in their rooms and the cattle in their dormitories — had left again by then. The Pigeon Gardens became a little emptier and more spacious. Bowed, lusterless horns came to dominate the slant of terraces, aligned in long, slithering rows ascending from the Cafeteria and the booths selling food. Great gatherings amassed round big fires upon which the last pigs were roasted. Torchlight was almost the sole source of illumination now, and the Gardens, the myriad layers of cloths and the towering trees palpitated in the night. Days were still normal for a while; everyone wore smiling masks and worried about what others thought. But nights made everyone fearful; for the air assumed a somber weight, and breaths were laden with the tension of hunger which clutched slowly, first their hearts in premonition, then their minds in anticipation, and finally their stomachs, their muscles, their whole beings in experience... Whereas before one could feast at leisure, and fatten oneself at the pace of will and largesse of wallet, now it became normal to eat only two meals per day; not altogether wholesome meals either. All were forced to ration — food was expensive and said to be running out, money was short and fast depleting.

Later, attitudes that were considered unseemly of yore would become commonplace. The most astute — the unemployed pigeons, forced into astuteness by their newfound situation — were the first to notice the fruit trees in the Gardens, and began to cull nourishment from them. This drew the ire of the cattle, who considered this stealing; and the force of the bull guards was unleashed upon those pigeons who, brown and black and furthermore stigmatized by the weary mark of darkness, inhabitants of the deep Columbaria, were oppressed into a situation of forced squalor. Then the remaining workers began to eat from the trees — for a short while, until one day they found all the fruit gone. It had been all taken by the Fruit Merchants and was now available at their booths at discounted prices.

As to water, there was plenty of bottled quantity to go around yet. But the merchants here, too, took advantage of the situation, and made it very expensive; so that many began to drink of the unfiltered water of the eastward river flowing down the terraces.

The fountain gushed serenely beneath the Pearl in the meantime; its waters fell softly behind the Proscenium, flowed quietly under the Auditorium and spread from the open tail, the fan of 1000 eyes of the Great Peacock, who droned Market edicts ceaselessly, all day, all night long... blooming from the lake's outer bank, which fluid spilled out of the gaping maws of stone of gargoyles, from the little fountains, brought to those fathomless height by colossal pumps draining seas from aquifers deep under the earth, many distances beneath them all... the Belab drunk it all up into long gullets thrust into the Anubel's pipes and ducts and airy cleaves, running through every cranny of its sumptuous halls and gloomy depths with springly sounds...

Again the sun shone very hot that day. It made the head throb. In the beginning it was so bright that he had to close his eyes, but gradually it cleared, and he breathed tiredly. Deeply and breathlessly. The
waterwheel paddled in the river, and for some reason there were no trees around the mill. And there was no grass upon the ground; the earth was bare. And the wheel paddled. The sound of it was the only thing he could hear, and it absolutely filled his head, which pulsed to the rhythm of it.
"Neipas"
His heart pumped very strong.
"Yes?"
His fingers reached beyond the surface of the stream. There was no feeling in it. When he took the fingers out, they were bleached.
"Hey, don't go in there. It's dangerous," he warned.
His father stood next to him at the verge of the stream. He looked at him, and saw they were the same height.

"Look here, son," the father said. Somehow his head was descending, and Neipas had the distinct and bizarre impression that his father was transforming into a midget, the thought of which made him laugh (the laughter that came out of him was unfamiliar), but the next moment this laughter was overwhelmed by a gasp of panic. His heart jumped when he saw his father's legs sinking into the earth.

"Dad!"

Neipas seized him desperately, holding his arms tight around him.

"It's ok, son."

Neipas pulled very hard. His teeth were clenched and the veins of his neck jutted out as every fiber of his body strained and exerted. The earth seemed to be dredging into the river. The wheels seemed to paddle harder. A sound of motor emerged behind them. Then Neipas felt his own feet sinking in, too.

"It's ok, son," the father kept repeating.

But Neipas kept pulling, and pulling. His head made mad involuntary convulsions in the struggle. A yell broke and stretched long out of him. Then panting; he slackened, and his eyes opened very wide and angry, his lips stretching to the sides and teeth clasped furiously in a savage grin of wrath.

"Don't do that again!" he lambasted. But then everything happened very fast.

Suddenly there was the quick screeching sound of a door opening. Magpie left the mill and moved to the river with very large steps.

"Stop!"

Neipas ran after her with an outstretched hand; and he was about to reach her when her body simply dropped headlong into the river, and she was gone. Neipas too almost fell; and he had to balance himself on the edge. The river had also gone. It had sunken at once into a chasm without bottom, which extended to the farthest reaches of the horizon.

A toothless maw of unlimited gloom. Lo: a smoke rose from it fast. It was the tree of ash, puffing wide into the black skies.

His heart started and he woke up. A weary ox face stared at him suspiciously.

"The fuck are you doing in my closet?" the ox spotlight grunted breathlessly.

Neipas said nothing. He felt very dizzy and startled, and he stumbled out of the closet, pushing the weightless fellow out of the way. Next thing he knew he was wobbling about in the corridor. The elongated box shape of it spun, as though he had thrust breakneck into the interior of a spinning wheel in motion. His heart beat frantically inside his neck. Vaguely, he noticed — the lights were on. He entered the bathroom aimlessly and saw the horridness of his true face reflected on the mirror, wax sliding away from him into the sink. His mouth opened to the fullest and released a frightened whimper; and the next moment the world switched to shapeless black.

He sat haplessly in the gloom of the food hall.

Neipas became listless and sickly; the shock of Magpie's suicide lingered in every pulse of his soul, in every breath of his existence. He fell into despondency, into shifting sands of lethargic hopelessness. His mind had gone. His body still worked, somehow; it moved like an automated machine. But he instinctively avoided Kasim, whose sense of urgency had only increased; he wished to make a move through that ghostly curtain to the core of the Anubel at once; but Neipas felt, without thought, that it was hopeless.

Neipas chewed his food — he regained the old habit (from his hungry days) of eating very slowly, chewing long, tasting all the nutrients of every bite — and ruminated in his soul.

Completely sapped of energy, he stared into the invisibility of space. His eyes, bound by darkness, were very wide and empty, devoid of life. He looked at Janu (though he could not see him) sitting on the opposite side of the table. Simon the Florist sat beside them. Outside, afar, the waxing moonlight gleamed and swayed with the subtle rumbling of the ground, and the teetering of torches, the constant glare of the Pearl.

Simon's voice breathed into the ether without vigour:

"Why would she do that"

Neipas' chin and lip quivered with terror. He could feel his eyes watering up. "I dunno... I dunno..." he shuddered breathlessly.

"She wasn't like that. She wouldn't do that," whispered Simon in a sort of mystified incredulity.

"Why would she do that. What drove her to this. Why?"

And Neipas could only say, trembling, "I dunno... I dunno..."

"You saw it?"

Simon's voice came out feebly. Neipas couldn't see him, but he heard him sniffle, and imagined him holding back tears.

"Why? Why would she do that?"

Neipas whispered beneath the perception of the ear, trembling convulsively — "I don't know!... I don't know!..." — but in his soul, he knew. He knew.

Silence. A heavy, morbid quietude filled the universe.

"It was them," Janu suddenly broke out in a whisper, of breath choked with impotent rage.

Later, Kasim would find him. He approached Neipas' meek, muzzy figure and clutched his shoulder intimately, lowering his head in a confidential mood:

"Neipas!" he whispered fiercely. "I heard them speak. They are speaking urgently about 'the vaults'. That they must protect the vaults at all costs. I heard the Gardener say that. I heard him say that they must make preparations to go there."

Neipas scratched his nape irritatedly, and breathed at gasps and in a tremulous manner. He felt immensely tired.

"Have you found this Osir? Do you have the drug?"

"No... I don't know, I looked for him but — " Neipas shrugged, downcast.

Kasim caught his own head and whispered hastily in his native tongue. "God help us! Do you know anyone else...?"

"...Pharmacies in the Market?"

"No, sleeping pills are sold out. I checked," said Kasim, and it was indeed so — all stocks had been depleted, for insomnia was a common ailment among those trapped in the Anubel in those stormy days.

"The Infirmary?" Neipas panted.

"I checked also. Please — "

"— but who knows if he even has it —" Neipas breathed in-between, talking through the heavy breaths of his nose, generally mumbling and overcome with a desire to sleep.

"— you said this Osir can supply anything."

"I don't know where he is. Kasim. I don't know if I can do this"

The bulky height of the pantrykeeper rested in black and red contours in the Columbaria corridor where they spoke. For a long moment, it said nothing; but merely rested the weight of his hand upon Neipas' invisible shoulder.

"What do you mean?"

"I don't know. I don't know. I don't think I can. Ok?" he sounded as though he were not awake; like a moribund mumbling out of nightmares.

"Please," Kasim said resolutely, not as a request but a steadfast insistence meant to snap Neipas out of it. "Please, I need your help. Let us do this now. Where do you — Neipas!"

But Neipas was already walking away from him into the darkness, disoriented and instinctual, bumping against the languid red dots winking, on, off, on, off, on, off, on, off beyond the walls... — the sounds of their conversation having vanished altogether from his consciousness as in a dream.

59 - Moonshine

Something was obviously troubling Janu the cook, for his pigeon mask displayed signs of wear in its molten surface, with grinding anxiety pressing its marks upon his face. Somehow he looked much older as Neipas, who reclined fatigued into one of the plastic chairs of the Cafeteria, contemplated his worried, still expression of half-lunacy. Janu's eyes were very open, and even in the faintness one could see the blood filling its whites in veins.

"What's wrong?" Neipas asked in an exhausted murmur, a murmur so low that it didn't penetrate the heavy silence that permeated the hall.

They remained in quietude. There were three of them sitting at the table: Janu, Neipas, and Simon. A plate of food lay in front of each, and yet they were so sapped of energy they were unable to muster any to eat. They languished in their chairs, breathing shallowly the stifled aroma of the steaming dishes. But their senses were dulled, and they could smell nothing; and their eyes saw nothing. The whole place seemed drunk with sleep, already submerged in dream. Moonlight delineated the horned shapes of a thousand exhausted heads, motionless or bobbing in droning circles. In Neipas' gaze things buoyed softly.

His head dropped and his eyelids fell. Beside him rose (furtively) a figure of powerful stature. It inched toward his chair, and stood close by him for a few moments without moving.

Finally — after what seemed to have been a lapse of awareness — Neipas' face started up and his eyes looked widely to the figure, who towered over him with a broad visage as he himself sat despondently in the plastic chair. All of a sudden Neipas lifted from the chair, but not with his body; his mind soared to the shadowy figure who turned around and brought Neipas inside him. They walked together decisively between the tables and went into the corridor.

"What is it?" asked Neipas' mind, looking at the mirror.

"Atone your debts," replied the Debt Collector.

A loud bang made Neipas jump in the plastic chair. Suddenly there was Janu's face before him again, but a dramatic change had deformed its shape; it was now agape in horror, the blood-shot eyes vast and the lips quaking terribly; he rose from his chair, as if drawing back.

With his heart imploding in quick bursts Neipas turned to see what had happened; and he saw that the inner doors of the Cafeteria had opened, and a file of murky shapes marched aggressively among the tables. It was a phalanx of bulls which penetrated the hall with their powerful bodies of armor, carrying heavy weaponry across their swelled torsos. The dense formation advanced methodically and inexorably. Isolated sounds of protest were heard, but these were quickly muted down in an unidentifiable sound, which sounded like a dry thump of metal upon bone. Mostly no one moved.

Only after a few moments of internal confusion did Neipas grasp what was happening. As the formation marched closer he saw that it lodged a group of Eagles in its midst; the moonlight delineated their shape feebly, caressing their figures with a mythical, ethereal glimmer of purple. They donned perfectly ironed suits and were wrapped in ties which hung down without a wrinkle, professional, accomplished, prestigious, divine.

The formation suddenly dispersed and the huge shapes of the bulls spread through the shadows with guns and gear clanking in their wake. They were setting a perimeter, as they called it, around the hall, besieging the pigeons, most of whom sat in their helplessness and confusion, watching curiously from the bottom of their chairs (some kept at their *I*s and didn't seem to notice) as the perimeter was set, and the spectacle was readied.

Then it unfolded. In the vagueness of the night, and in the weakened perception of Neipas' drowsy mind, what happened next was imperceptible and he noticed it only by degrees. He didn't realize fully what it was until it happened to him. Suddenly the stature of an Eagle stood behind his shoulder — he could sense the authority in the stance, and the heaviness of breathing scalding his neck made him freeze in terror. The Eagle leant over him (Neipas looked straight forward and only glanced the brilliance of the golden beak in the corner of his eye) and a bulbous, hairy hand emerged before his sight to lay hold of his food; made into a fist, it proceeded to stuff itself into the lustrous beak, which scintillated dizzyingly as it opened and chewed. The Eagle went but another one came, and Neipas, pinned to motionlessness, gazed through the whirl of his exhaustion at another hand, this one rimmed by a shining watch of silver, grabbing his food in the same manner — with the crushed paste of meat oozing between the closed fingers of the fist — and masticating it by his ear with the same sounds. And this Eagle went, and another one came, and so repeatedly until his plate had but crumbs upon it.

The Eagles sauntered through the rows of tables and ate of the pigeons' food, until all had but crumbs upon their plates. Neipas watched them as they did this to others. The excess of food hung moist about their faces, and smeared their lip in a repulsive way; much of it would drip and plop into the ground, which quickly became littered and sticky, as they tried to stuff in as much as they could. The sound of munching was intensely audible, it filled the room. It rung horribly in their heads and filled them with vertigo; the smack of saliva and insatiable breathing mixed in an agonizing display of gluttony. And yet, the Eagles somehow maintained an aspect of supreme respectability, even at this moment. Their suits remained immaculate. The appearance of their masks kept superior and smug — as it had always been. From afar, that noble semblance of Eagle, calm and collected, had always showcased such a measure of self-control as to leave one in awe.

But now Neipas gazed a trace of their true aspect in the moonshine. There were no spotlights to hide their faces; no media machine and its myriad layers of angular mirror; and the sun of daytime, through which millions toiled in utter absorption, shone elsewhere, and didn't blind his eyes. Thus for a fixed span of time, concentrated, motionless — Neipas saw the Eagles as they were. Their bearing of respectability was practiced, and was all surface. Right beneath it their souls twitched with emptiness — an enormous vacuum of insatiable hunger, so powerful as to swallow up all humankind. He could see the desperation with which they snatched food off the plates; and the way they smacked their mouths showed the degeneration of their kind. There was nothing noble about them. They were but degenerates and thieves, delinquents of the most cunning sort. Their privilege hid the sliest form of thievery the world had ever experienced. And so they were the most successful of criminals — the sort above the law, the sort which makes the law.

Two or three pigeons fought, and were promptly shushed by the near sight of muzzles pointing at them. The rest did nothing. Some shuddered in fear of what would happen if they did something. Others didn't seem to mind it at all, and bowed their heads respectfully, with honest smiles, as the Eagles ate their meals. But most didn't even notice that their food was being stolen. They remained enveloped in the glare of their *I*s, flashing selfies.

As the operation inched to its conclusion, a quietude seemed to close upon the space once again. The Eagles and their bulls left the hall differently from the manner they had entered it — in complete and utter silence.

60 - Dreamthink above the cloud

It was only the next day that most pigeons noticed that they were hungry. "Something happened," some would whisper, worried.

Others, more perceptive, would say, "something's been going on for a while now."

But only a few grasped what was really going on. At first, they were quiet in the immense quietude of the Cafeteria. They were so quiet as to be nearly nonexistent in the thickening darkness, and the moon faded from the windows as it penetrated the clouds. Their masks were drained of silver and filled with ink, merging with the throbbing silence of the gloom, the slowly pulsing, closing gloom. Janu, motionless in his chair, muttered voicelessly, "what the fuck just happened, what the fuck just happened," with trembling lips over, and over, and over again.

Neipas sat speechless and unfeeling. He might have fallen asleep a few times, over the course of indeterminate time; he would come to sometimes and realize he was there, where his body was sitting over a plastic table, and discern the existence of his own mind. When Osir, materializing somewhere in the vicinity, arose from his chair, years could have gone by.

Osir voiced calmly: "Let's talk to the Chief Supervisor".

Among those who had grasped what was really going on, there were a few who had heard Osir's voice, or discerned his intent, and followed him along. There were only a handful. The rest, feeling alone in their understanding, remained where they were and by themselves tried to command their indecision and despair, knowing not whom to speak with. Neipas, following closely behind Osir, seemed to sense something of this sentiment and, as if by a force of divination, bid the little group wait as they got to the doors and, turning round, announced:

"We're going to talk to the Chief Supervisor!"

His voice roused the muscles of rigid cattle out of their tense dormancy. By the force of some collective unconsciousness the workers began to stir, to rise, and to move, and soon a commotion of feet spread dizzyingly throughout the dark hall. In droves they went. But still many — perhaps still the majority — by fear, ignorance, or indifference, stayed.

They made their way through the corridors as a monstrous monolith of revolt, a whole shifting field of rattling horns increasingly mad and enraged. Osir the janitor marched in the front, followed closely by Neipas the waiter and Janu the cook, who limped in the pace of one escaping a growing abyss. Neipas walked so close to Osir in the darkness that he felt him becoming increasingly riled up as they marched on. He could hear him rattling inside his head, with a trembling which coincided with the shaking of pills in his hand. Osir took them twice, by the mouthful; but the acceleration of his breathing was not be slowed by chemicals. Behind him the silence of marching feet swelled ominously. Neipas sensed Osir's step hasten with his breathing and watched as he stormed into the Head Office of the Columbarium with a whole squall of bodies in his wake, thrusting in as violent gust, and heard as his meager chest opened up like flash and his breathless voice boomed out like thunder, *"The fuck's going on man!?"*

Before Osir's outstretched arms of outrage the Chief Supervisor retained all tranquility. He faced the mob of workers with nods of understanding, calm, standing but a little arched forward in a sign of humility and solicitude. The Head Office, which was populated with little bird cages hung about the air, receded gradually to a tired silence, out of which bloomed the soft twittering of the little caged birds — who shook the metal of their pens with little hops. By then Osir's arms had lowered and pended dormant by either side of his waist; he moved only his shoulders with deep breathing. Only then did the Chief Supervisor speak. The first thing he said is that he was open to listen and improve, and please inform him what was perceived to be amiss.

The Chief Supervisor was a darker and featureless silhouette among darknesses. Neipas observed the outline of his face as it listened to the workers' concerns. It was very calm and understanding, it nodded patiently and with sympathy. Occasionally it hummed "hm-hm" — slowly, to show the talkers he was listening. And then Neipas heard as the Chief Supervisor clarified the situation: It must have been an issue of miscommunication, he explained, as the new policy should have been divulged in advance. Unfortunately, elucidated the Chief Supervisor, food stocks were low, as some might have noticed, and so the Eagles were regrettably forced to withdraw a percentage of the workers' rations. Of course, they were free to eat freely before the Eagles stepped into the Cafeteria. Another stir predicting the abrupt break of violence rustled the crowd, but again the Chief Supervisor, ever serene, anticipated them. There was no reason to be concerned, he clarified. All would be ok — what was needed was the right perspective. The food hadn't been 'taken', it had simply been recruited — voluntarily, the Chief Supervisor added as a sudden twitch of pre-motion rippled through the mob. Lest his fellow colleagues forget (by fellow colleagues he meant the herd hunched before him), the Chief Supervisor reminded them of article 19.27J of the contract they all had signed, which stipulated clearly that the Eagles possessed all items of property in the Eagles' Nest, and they had a right to hold a percentage of the herd's possessions as interest and collateral. The right to take food from the cattle was also very clearly written.

Besides, the Chief Supervisor concluded in a tone of humor and camaraderie, if the Eagles didn't eat, they wouldn't survive — and how would the workers get paid if they didn't?

This last point made the oxen pause half in reflection, half in confusion and indecision. And — Had they really signed into that? But yes, they had — one of the assistant supervisors was ready with a paper copy of the agreement to show them. Horned heads cluttered in to analyze it in the shine of an *I*. Faced with that document, which didn't look so very bulky that they could complain it was too much to read — in fact, it was merely ten pages of very complicated prose, punctuated with hieroglyphs which they pretended to understand — and seeing the assistant supervisor's finger point to the pertinent article in the text, the oxen said nothing. After a careful reading of it, they all agreed that there could be no doubt of the article's meaning; it corroborated what the Chief Supervisor had said.

"Christ," Janu exhaled out of his teeth. With matters clarified, the group of downtrodden livestock left the meeting, broodingly. This time, they were not happy, and most were not convinced; yet they didn't know what to do about it.

"Hey," Neipas muttered, approaching Janu. The good cook stood in the corridor, staring at the wall with moistly vague eyes. "You ok?"

"My friend," Janu began, but he couldn't continue; for his voice was already shaky as it left his lips. The darkness had thinned a little. Janu's mask was so deteriorated that it could scarcely veil the constriction of his face, which seemed to hold so much tension, so much oppressive weight, as to make the very pores of his skin twitch under the emotional burden he felt.

"I dunno what's going on anymore," he whimpered, nearly without breath and at the brink of tears. He held the water upon his eyes with clenched teeth, drawing in a deep gulp of mucous air and making his face rigid. With the contrived motions of a struggler he reached for his mask, and with his shaking fingers molded it to appear a bit more controlled, more collected, more stable. "Christ, my friend," Janu muttered, breathing out a long sigh of fatigue and disorientation, and quaking his head side to side.

"You ok, man?" asked Neipas again.

Janu shrugged somewhat helplessly, but then made himself strong as he approached Neipas very near. "Neipas," he whispered, "don't you think that's weird?"

There was still a bit of wobbliness in his voice; it was obvious that he was straining to keep it under control. "What just went on here, you know what I mean?"

"I think the whole thing's been weird since the day we got here," said Neipas in an even lower whisper, pulling them further into a ken of secrecy. It was tinted with fright and despair.

Janu nodded slowly. "Maybe even longer than that."

They were really close together now by the wall; red dots blinked in its glassy surface. Around them the murmurs of the throng had dispersed as the cattle dragged themselves away toward the gardens. Osir had long gone. It had vaguely occurred to Neipas' dormant consciousness to speak to him, but a faint idea that it wasn't opportune and a general lethargy of futility made him remain quiet inside his deep-breathing, dreamlike, hovering body as they walked together; next thing he knew, Osir vanished again.

"The food's almost out," Neipas whispered almost soundlessly, saying it more to himself than anything; as if it were his unconscious speaking directly. His eyes were blurry, foggy, as they faced the wall; his neck was bent in prostration.

Janu but gasped a muted breath, unable to say a thing, not knowing what to say. "..."

"What's gonna happen?" Janu asked finally — in the lowest whisper yet, though everyone had gone now — he asked it reflexively, more to himself than to Neipas.

"I dunno, I dunno..." came the empty, undecided murmur. "But we gotta do something."

"Can we do anything?"

There was a long pause before Neipas voiced, in a vacant whisper:

"I dunno."

The next night the Eagles came again, and no one knew what to do but sit still.

*

But on the third night, as the bulls broke coolly through the twitchy spread of shadows round their hips, one gloomy shape lifted itself from the expanse; and just then the grave hush was rendered by a tussle of furniture and bodies and a sudden shout that cast shivers into the numbest spine in the crowd. "Tha's mine, dog!"

Horns and plume turned cautiously. Yonder they spotted a Bull looking down at a small figure, whose vague upturned head stared from the level of his chest. The Eagles had already left; but a great disarray erupted as the squadrons at the procession's tail, flowing outward, returned and scattered again throughout the Cafeteria with shimmering motions and thundering rattle. They besieged the standing, diminutive shadow — someone boomed "Calm down! Hold still! Sit!" — and the small figure, stirring down toward his seat again, froze mid-motion and then, slowly, stiffened his knees and stood erect once more. The silence vast, total, immersed all attentions in its deafening tenebrosity.

"That's mine," the diminutive shape repeated, lowly, timorous, quivering; one could feel the immense strain of overcoming through the nervous air, inhaled deep by all quivering nostrils in the hall alike.

All beheld the hunched, chubby, short figure of Janu the cook standing before the towering and powerful physique of the Bull with height twice over his. Steam inked down the silverlight. The spike-collared Bull, servant of the Minister of Borders, growling smoke, held in his burly hand Janu's pack of cookies. Through eyes scornfully bemused the Bull stared down the immigrant with his tribal earlobes, his sweat glistening in the moonlight, his bulbous shapes heaving in the rhythm of his respiration, full, deep, availing his lungs of every weight of air they could store among the wide mix of fear and courage imbued in his breathing soul.

All upturned, pointed horns loomed high round the downcast, sawn-off stumps bearing upon the cook's bowed head. The air was strained with tension. Breaths stilled as the atmosphere stiffened, and the motionless pose of the Bull seemed to swell in the anticipation of a blow; the general certainty of violence shrunk every pore, made feathers ruffle, made hairs bristle. All watched nervously. Suddenly —

the Bull lifted his hand and everyone jerked; stifled moans could be heard agitating the darkness. Then there was a meek flutter of plastic — and loud, crunchy chewing. The Bull had grabbed a handful of cookies from the pack and snorted with a coarse, disdainful giggle as he ate.

"Better watch yourself — dog," tossed the Bull, letting the pack of cookies drop onto the floor.

The bulls left in a deliberate march of jingling metal, giant, imperious, commanding, almighty. Janu himself had kept still, holding his fingers strong against the pouch of his apron; he held on to his body with all the strength of his will and forced himself rigid and steadfast; all in him kept motionless but the spasming muscles beyond the control of spiritual fortitude. Neipas, sitting by his side, had watched it all listless; absolutely overcome with the abstraction of unreality suffusing him at present. He mulled now. Beholding the only silhouette left standing among the jaggedness of shadows afar, he recognized Kasim's lingering form; the pantrykeeper had stealthily remained in the Cafeteria, stealing himself away from the Eagles' presence after witnessing them impound the workers' evening meals. Neipas thought of his design like a sleepy blur in some remote distance. What held him from action was not fear, but that distance of abstraction; that foggy padding between his every perception and reality, that haze of being. He didn't believe they could succeed in breaking beyond the Temple and he barely believed there was anything to be found there at all. He couldn't muster the life to believe. He felt himself bound up with the image of Magpie dropping — simply dropping, like a weight already dead! — from the edge of the tower; and it was as though his soul had been whisked away into the clouds with her. All his mind was Magpie, all his energy drained into her image. The blunt of trauma, the experience of helpless witness and the consciousness of his own cowardice had made him succumb to all predatory, whispering doubts within himself; he felt like he was nothing. He couldn't bring himself to do anything. Quite simply, he had given up.

He realized he was biting his knuckles to keep himself from crying. Sniffling, he called Janu. "Hey man." Janu's audacity before the Bull had stirred him enough to sense a feeble need to act. The shivering cook chewed slowly his cookie — and (seeing Neipas' waving hand in the shine of the waxing gibbous) Kasim was already approaching their table.

"I wanna introduce you to someone," breathed Neipas to Janu.

61 - Mosaics

Neipas thrust abruptly, awakening from turmoiled dreams with a weight dense in his chest.

A silence of deep breaths arose.

His eyes opened to the stuffy darkness, stirred by his palpitating heart just minutes before the alarm was to trigger off. He felt clammy, found himself whorled in sheets. An impulse to get out of there immediately assailed him; his soul was wrenched by a desire to run into the open and breathe in fresh air, but — he hadn't yet properly realized what was going on or where he was (he panned his head from one side to the other in utter confusion) when the cloth parted and flashlights filled the gloom, blasting into his sidelong gaze (which he shuttered flinchingly) and a sound of sirens wailed robotic in their ears, pulling everyone's red eyes awake. Around him he felt the motion of sleepy bodies dragged out of bed slowly. Following their movements, Neipas pushed his body away from the sheets, compelled by a powerful and invisible force pressing counter to the whole weight of his will, which was desperate to get out, get out, get out. The faces being lifted away from their pillows were tumorous with shadow and nearly stripped of their masks, which sagged molten out of their skin in swollen blobs, tired, shapeless, crushed and inhuman. It was a horrifying sight, powerfully lit by the white beam swamping the room.

(431999, wake up, 431999, wake up) Neipas' dejected heart was made heavier yet as he dressed. As he entered the ox mask (and as he placed it on he realized he was already within it) it seemed like it constrained the air even more than usual.

They had brought the bunks out into the Gardens and spread them round the sinuous woods of the 2nd Tier, placed them in rows and covered them in tarps; there was much more space to walk about at night now, with the cattle sleeping in stacks. As he left the plastic tent Neipas spotted, through his heavy eyes, the outline of the gazebo and the darkened blades of grass against the still dark sky, where Cesar slept yet his perpetual sleep. The delirious moonshine was fat upon the wood, permeated with the Pearl which kept beaming afar atop the dramatic mound of terraces. They palpitated in torchlight above the 2nd Tier. Passing under the upward flames, the workers climbed the heavenly ziggurat steps to the Cafeteria where they were given a few minutes for breakfast before the shift began. Most didn't eat anything. Above them — one level up — yawned the entrance to the Columbaria, sunk in darkness; where most crows, the jobless, the already-penniless and hungry, dozed in squalor, and languished.

Neipas kept working. He had to. Food cost more than his wages now and he had to be strategic about what meals to eat and which to pass; but he would starve if he didn't work.

The Chief Supervisor greeted everyone by name after they passed the checkpoint. He faced Neipas with an exceedingly pleasant smile as he left the scanner, and even bowed his head a little in a show of deference so humbling that Neipas could not help but repeat his movements, except he would smile even more servilely, his head would bow even lower. There was something about the Chief Supervisor's amicable ways that made one feel grateful to have such a superior. The cattle liked him — for he didn't have to be nice; he was nice because he chose to be, they would say. The weight in one's heart didn't dissipate, but it was tamed momentarily, ignored, almost forgotten. The Supervisor's smile and readiness, his fraternal wink, his amicability made the livestock want to work well, out of a sense of obligation to him. Faltering at the job made one feel not only afraid, but guilty — he was so very friendly, after all.

Spurred on by this softening of heart they (the new workers in particular) walked into the Eagle Kitchen and sipped their coffees, encouraged. Neipas drank also, he drank it hot. Everyday it had to be hotter for him to feel the effect, more scalding to the tongue; painful though it was, he knew he wouldn't have a parcel of energy left to stand if he didn't have it. But he, used to the grind, found that multiple hits of coffee did little; and growing unconvinced of the Supervisor's good intentions, deepening into a sullen mood by the dragging lethargy and slowness of his body, which the stimulant barely affected, he heard nothing but a distant ringing, beyond which echoed occasional voices, steps, the clatter of dish in a kitchen which was visibly emptier by then. Many of the cooks had fallen sick, too weak to get up; some already swooned with pangs of hunger. By his side — as Neipas looked down and saw his own elbow sliding on the tabletop — he gazed a cook breaking egg after egg after egg into a wide bowl, staring with glassy eyes to its ascending bottom; bulls, and the Chef's headless hat lurked near to ensure he didn't eat any. Neipas picked up the tray of breakfast, the weight of which bore down against the whole vitality of his being, and sapped him of spirit altogether. His head was a ball of hollow ache; a glass snowdome in which he himself stood, small, naked, and shivering. He seemed moved only by that same indelible force; the very same force that forced him to rise from bed every morning of his adult life. At times he reasoned this force to be the fear of hunger. Yet he was hungry already. And yet he was afraid still. He, like many, had chosen not to take breakfast, and waited for lunchtime when portions were bigger at the Cafeteria — expensive, but still the cheapest option. He only drank coffee. It spurted repeatedly into his empty stomach; it was the only sustenance still free-of-charge, the only thing which still flowed abundantly to them.

They headed to the chambers of the Heiress. Neipas would be charged with giving breakfast to her child; a sorry task he anticipated with sheer dread.

The troupe of oxen and heifers was much more meager than usual. There were but four of them — Neipas, Lou the waiter (who had been fired during the Summit, but was then, recently, rehired), and a waitress called Marianne, as well as a supervisor. Lou held his eyes firm and stance rigid, though his cheeks were evidently sunken; Marianne's posture was meeker, the fragility in her more apparent. It was obvious she could not hold the entire burden of her tray and the supervisor — marginally more hale than they — carried a tray of his own, and loaded some of the items she carried onto his own strength.

The crockery teetered slightly as Neipas marched alongside the few others, all of whom were quiet. The familiar sounds of clanking china, hurrying soles of shoes echoing upon marble and sharp lines of dialogue cutting the air amid all this were sounding across the corridors; the daily bustle continued and often it seemed as if nothing had changed. Tables were set and breakfasts served, floors and walls rubbed, porcelains glossed, chandeliers waxed, statues polished, suits cleant and dried. Cattle toiled through their routines with a particular hollowness of mind; a sort of painful sucking out of their vitality invaded their bodies, the presage and feeling of hunger. The specter of it shadowed over all.

They passed a big hall, full of crystals; a bright glare of morning filled Neipas' eyes and made him wince. The sun stared the windows straight and its light filled them with a blinding radiance; it streaked into the space full and shadowless. Yet it was a radiance of morning, and it was soft, and made all surfaces sparkle. In it toiled the cleaners who formed a long single row across the hall and lay prostrated upon the floor, scrubbing in sweeps in a single collective succession of motions, all of them bound together by a single yoke for ease of coordination. The yoke seemed heavier upon their necks that day; they had to exert themselves more to perform the same movements; and every movement seemed to hurt more; and reality seemed somehow more distant from their minds. Drrawetz loomed over them with his screaming echoes — (Vite! Vite!) which sounded very far — his flowery jabot, his domineering, dandy march in circles around them. Neipas, transfixed and dull, heard the summit bells ringing dreamily and felt the sun palpitate in the windows, light blowing warmth through his flowing veins, the throbbing in the walls pulsing stronger at each step; he passed, and the herd of janitors kept at their unison toil with ritualistic exactitude, their foreheads against the floor. Faces frowning, snouts made of clay bordering the marble, sniffing the toxic rancidness of detergents — Neipas hadn't recognized Osir's own mask as he stared, breathing deep and intense in its utter absorption. The scarred ox arched under Drrawetz' yelling supervision, having been demoted as soon as Drrawetz was made supervisor once more; Osir's twitching eyes peeked at those mirror images of himself multiplying under the yoke and scrubbing in furious sweeps, straining against the shell of plastered wine; and their prostration recalled to his hidden mind memories of the war — of the time he flew Columbia's colors in far-flung regions of the world... The very moment they stormed into that oriental temple and saw all worshipers there, lying forward over their colored beards in that stance of devotion and piety, had become ingrained in his mind, as would a photograph upon paper; before the sound of gunshots but a second after.

Sunlight splattered upon his bare forearm, where the branded tattoo of the nation's flag wrapped round a bundle of arrows, army's emblem, swung to and fro over the majestic floor; inside which his face snorted and wheezed in reflection, fogging the underside mute, wetting the stone over his irate scowl and maddened creases; and oftentimes in his exertion he closed one eye, burning and teary from the detergents, and sighed atremble, grimaced in pain, grunted mutedly; and gazed beyond the marble through the tunnel of his reflected eye, in the depth, in the black bottom of which pit he saw his palpitating heart flushed with the secretions of poppy afar... He dove into the crater of his shuddering stare like sight through a scope; like poison through a needle — and saw the poppies like graves under which his brothers-in-arms lay, quiet and still, the unfathomable shoots spreading like a conflagration, where those brown kids burned silently and stared aghast at the sun. His reflection assumed a livid, almost deranged aspect. His lip, gruesome and askew, had never been able to smile again since that day, and yet the horrible monster in the reflector laughed —

(Far above the opium flowers of Pashtunland...) That had been the day his lips were defaced by a cut of rebel blade thundering upon him in desperation, and as he contemplated the gloomy mirror he licked that wound, that scar rooted deep, entwined in its intimacy with the fathomless arteries of his heart. His open eye quivered over the pinched nostrils, the irritated flesh of his defaced flank throbbing always. He felt it with his speechless tongue and held his breath. How many times had he repeated that gesture, he wondered quietly; in the silence over the running trough of the dark bathroom, he was transported by memories of war into the physicality of the scope, to the days when his open eye was the barrel of a sniper rifle and his jutting tongue the gun's trigger; when he exercised judgment and delivered death from afar. He popped one of his pills and saw that the bottle was nearly empty.

It was then he heard a voice, shaped in an accent which immediately roused suspicion in him:

"Osir — That's right," he said in reply. "Who wants to know?"

Kasim faced him with his exotic appearance of tanned plumage twined with garlanded desert flower. His shape came out in frothy contours in the gloom of *I* lights; Osir looked fixedly at those big eyes starting out of that brown face. "Please," said Kasim. "I was indicated to you — I would like to purchase some sleeping pills. Of a strong variety, if it's possible."

Osir studied the stranger's feathery jaw beard, his solicitous expression, his starting eyes framed by thin, very brown plumage, the firmness of his stare troubled by orbs deviating in opposing directions languidly — blinking and snapping themselves back to focus — as if mirroring Osir's own swooning state. He petted his scar disdainfully, glimpsed at his own pill bottle, nearly empty. The kind of pills he needed were different from those Kasim sought and much harder to obtain. He feared sleep, sometimes; through sleep reached him nightmares.

"You need sleeping pills?"

"Yes."

Osir shrugged. "You and everyone else, pal. Dunno if I can get 'em."

"Please, it is very important. Neipas referred you."

"Neipas? Oh — sure..."

The veteran considered the foreignness of Kasim's black eye-bags, vaguely irked by his thickly accented insistence; and felt the monster fever in his head for a moment, hood over him and growl upon his shoulders. But he was tired. A feebleness sat upon his brow and dulled his prejudices. Nothing mattered, he pondered vaguely. A sadness of old, much-ruminated guilt affected his temper as he stared at the misty bathroom floor.

Osir asked despondently:

"Are you Pashtun?"

"Mesopotamian."

Silence.

"Ok. Give me a day or two."

Kasim asked him the price. Osir named it; ballooning the number quite a bit.

"That much?"

"Law of the Market, buddy. Demand is high and supply is low... It's a world of junkies, man."

"Ok, Ok..." Kasim said. "I will get the money. Give me a few hours."

Neipas swallowed the parched, sugary flavor filling his mouth as he squinted in the brightness (didn't the sun rise in the east? he wondered).

The sun burning in the panes quenched behind the walls as they penetrated the complex; the shadows danced heavy, spongy upon their brocaded surfaces, and fires crackled in braziers lodged ceremoniously in the corners. Everything trembled slightly around him, and with the fatigue wearing his mind it was somewhat difficult to keep his balance. The shadows throbbed; and the throbbing bled in his ears as he walked; more strongly as they walked in. The group, laden with its procession of trays heavy with food, marched through sparkling shrines, discreet golden aeries, huge private auditoriums, halls lit by ad screens and populated by executive chairs, private museums housing precious relics and outlandish trifles, opulent salons mounted with heads and spiraling stairs where the smell of oil and blood floated vague in the atmosphere. The fragrance of freshly cooked breakfast floated up from their bosoms all the while, marinating about their nostrils, affecting their minds like a weak hallucinogen; how uncanny it was to be starving and yet have such foods upon one's arms! In an indistinctness of feeling they glimpsed the opulent assortment of dishes, adorned with fresh flowers and a scent of morning lavender, sprinkled through with colored petals and sugar bits upon the edge of the plates.

The Heiress' palace was tucked away beyond layers of staircases, entrenched beyond puzzling corridors lodged between the myriad gilded, crystallized walls of the Anubel. The paintings hung upon the last passageway stared them down with scorn. Generations of monarchs and the royal bourgeoisie, increasingly abstract, seemed to behold these sons of peasants from the shelter of well-kept, ageless canvases and frames of gild; tilting their noses toward the top in a gesture of zealous conviction in their own superiority. At the end of the corridor stood erect two bulls and an owl, flanking the gate to Her residence. Their eyes seemed to burn with a seething contempt; their guns held menacingly upon their arms. They said not a word to the nearing livestock as the doors opened and the herd of waiters entered.

Neipas walked between the portentous gates with his aching body and his dormant head. Inside, he faced the same burlesque spectacle of rabid colors and dance he had witnessed before. Festoons of deep crimson silk were hung across the ample air above their heads, and a confusion of cushions and persian mats proliferated upon the ground beneath raised bodies bearing diamonds in all hues of sparkle; while the dancers and accompanying harlequins moved about in chaotic sweeps of cloth everywhere. After many passages and chambers, where fire gleamed soft upon the rich damasks and breastplates in their cabinets and on the serpentine tapestries around them, they filed past the orchestra playing — all its musicians faced the covered walls — in the alcove before the Heiress' exotic garden (fast violin string tugged nauseously at their nervous hearts and) They stepped out into the hapless sunlight. Servants held enormous feathers and swung them up and down methodically. There were various reclining thrones under the swaying plumage scattered pleasantly across; and some perfumed fruitless trees cast additional shade. Upon the sides lounged tigers, fastened with leashes; yonder an elephant and a giraffe grazed. A hamster ran and squeaked by Neipas' feet. Sounds of children playing... Some kids running about; one nearby sat alone and tapped a large fishbowl. A little distance from the drowsy felines, tables of foods, myrrh, jewels and all assortments of luxuries stretched, closely attended by a team of dandy oxen, vassals of the Heiress' court. In a corner the remaining members of the orchestra played fine, quaint notes of organ and soft drum. The back of the conductor's head observed the workers passing, raised, phantasmagorically still. The throbbing pulsed stronger; rhythmic; overwhelming... Anxiety gradually commanded him, and his nerves teetered with the swing of excess coffee in his veins. His stomach felt weird; felt floppy. He sensed the mask inside his ox mask fluid, felt its feathers seep, runny — as though all about to melt down into the shuddering neck. Sounds mingled with echoes in his head. A screech, a particular movement flashed at his side. Some small shimmering form blipped toward him — a swaying blue and golden yarns. "Nepa!"

"Nepa!"

Little arms clasped his leg. Neipas froze with surprise, his senses sharpened abruptly; only his throat quivered with the fear of falling. He looked down. The child, about three years old, who had been playing with the fishbowl stood under him, hugged him with a disarming smile of closed eyes and swaying tresses. "Look gran-daddy! It's Nepa! He's my fwiend I told you!" the child hopped away eagerly toward one of the princely sofas. It took a while for Neipas to recognize her — it was little Ruby, whom Neipas had taken under his caring wing on the first day of the Summit.

How long ago had it been now?... he wondered duped inside the fog of his mind. Weeks? Years?

Ruby cruised cheerfully to the consortium of tables and sofas scattered genteel across the orchard. In its very center was the Heiress, all surrounded by servants waving flabella. She reposed on a *chaise longue* of thick paddings, wholly upholstered in opulent velvet, with golden framing encrusted with gemstones. She lay upon her elbow, head raised royally. The avian features of her mask were extravagantly magnified; her large bill had only seemed to have gotten larger since Neipas last saw her, her cheeks more bloated, sucking in the pouted beak; and her body was much plumper — as though she had never left that sofa while everything else was going on, and had just kept on eating. Clad in furs and lion manes, a sumptuous crown round a bonnet of extravagant swan and peacock feathers, she pinched the upper end of a small balance, on one plate of which rested a mound of pellets shimmering, and on the other, a mound of roses; and she gazed studiously to where the scale tipped, which, in her hands, was the plate of shining beads.

Hers was a vast garden of baroque contours, full of flourishes, topped everywhere with resplendent vases whence voluptuous flowers bloomed. Mosaics covered the recessed walls between stuccos of arcadian fancy, reminiscent of pastoral Edens. Marbled cherubim smiled with blind eyes; cupids, vague putti and other winged sculptures of mythic infants hovered in motionless dancestep, holding joyfully dispensing cornucopias atop the soothing fountains, their bending waters drawing gracious shapes of idyll. The grounds spanned the marvelous balcony, suspended between the great hanging porches of the adjacent palaces and open above the cascade of the Eagle Gardens in its highest terrace, just beneath the Ballroom. These balconies projected from the mansions' sumptuous facades at different heights and into different lengths, shading tranquil patios lodged in the nooks of vine-covered walls, all in a quietude of ornamented stone and porcelain springwater. Effigies of Mars (chipped, made to appear like old ruins) arose here and there on the balustrade limiting the Heiress' balcony garden. Upon luxuriant couches over the grass within lounged a number of majestic notables: Ministers, Judges, Executives, Generals, Kings and prominent Bankers and other chieftains of the business world affecting all peoples, sipping already on drinks and snacking on appetizers. Yonder, the Gardener conversed with a prominent Magistrate; sitting by them was Moloch the Media Mogul. The Mayor just beyond, with all their key-bearing Bulls standing abreast with flaring and shimmering nostrils watchful. Close by the Heiress' side lay her husband the Minister of Borders, and their child in his little throne; and his face made a very intense frown. He looked as though he was on the edge of throwing a fit; an eventuality which the Heiress' butler, standing by him, seemed very much aware and afraid of. And before them, just on the other side of a little fount, bulging in his immense weight, scratching his puffy cheek lightly with his sapphire ring, sat, on a magisterial sofa, the tycoon to which Ruby ran. "Gran-daddy look, it's Nepa!"

Baron Noxxe petted her hair with a heavy smile of uplifted, protuberant brow. "One moment, Ruby," he said without looking at her, and continued his languid address to the Heiress and her husband. Little Ruby crossed her arms and pouted impatiently, "Bu' gran-daddy!" and already she was leaping back toward Neipas, whose strained awareness was divided between her flailing, growing blue dress and the Seamstress' voice in his eartag.

Ruby was nearing merrily when one of the peacocks who lolled about the grounds stepped in front of her. "Miss Flora," he said, addressing the child by her real name. "Please. It does not behoove you to speak to waiters."

"Bee'oove?" Ruby said with much amusement, and laughing she began to hop toward Neipas again when again she was stopped.

"It is ugly to speak to waiters," clarified the peacock. "They are not your friends, Miss Flora."

"Not my fwend?" the child said, taken aback. Then she closed her eyes and shook her head resolutely, smiling in a cute play of tresses, "Not t'ue."

"Miss Flora," insisted the peacock, who was her tutor; and then confidentially he told her, "They are ravenmen and will take you away if you do not behave."

Ruby gasped astonished, and frowned in the most incredulous expression of outrage Neipas had ever seen. "No! Not t'ue!" and crossing her arms she said, "Nepa is not a boogie!"

"Ruby," the Baron Noxxe called. "It's time for breakfast."

"Breakfast will be served now, Miss Flora, please do sit," insisted the peacock, ushering the child on.

"Yoowe tupid! I want Nepa!" said she, stomping her foot — but as she then tried to step round the peacock he nimbly blocked her path. "Miss Flora, if you would..."

"Flora, stop talking to the ravenman," called Noxxe, half-sternly, half in jest, half laughing amidst the Heiress' snobbish giggle and the sycophant cackle of her husband.

"Huh?" Ruby's bubbly face deepened to a confused frown; she covered her lips with her tress, and swayed her blue dress in slow contemplation. She didn't yet realize the presence of their masks and their difference in importance; she didn't yet know she must look down upon Neipas. "Flora!" Noxxe called impatiently now, cold — and the child let herself be led to her seat in doubt, wondering; she settled, puny, with swaying legs, on the couch on the other side of the little fount.

The waiters stood in the back by the entrance; additional small teams had joined Neipas, Lou and Marianne; most hadn't eaten yet. The supervisor was telling them something (Marianne looked very weak as they received their instructions).

Marianne shook visibly. The supervisor made a gesture and they marched forth, already exhausted, in the glassless solarium, in the frail sunlight, to serve their dishes. Once more they entered the airy breeze made by the oscillating giant feathers and bowed before the Heiress. Neipas' head drooped into the hollow of his neck and the tray rose above it, pressing its entire weight onto his wrist and forearms. Inside the mask he grimaced with a sharp pain, trembling with the strain of the effort; his inner waxen visage squirmed and bubbled; it was so excruciating that it quickly threatened to overwhelm his forces, and he was just about to rise when a clatter of silver and glass crashing sounded beside. With an alarmed start he got up and looked over. Marianne had dropped the loaded tray and all its contents, producing an uncomfortably loud rumble; it all lay spilt on the rich grass carpet now, and Marianne scrambled desperately to contain the damage — whispering half-crazed all the while "Oh my god I'm so sorry, I'm so sorry, I'm so sorry...", and trembling with faintness.

"What the devil is wrong with you?" admonished the Heiress harshly as soon as the burden of the poor waitress collapsed out of her. The Minister of Borders snorted contemptuously. At the same time their child burst out laughing, disfiguring his frown momentarily to make fun of the poor girl, at whom he pointed with unfiltered cruelty. It was but a short break, for the next moment the child Scion was back to frowning again, and Marianne shook with terror, looking completely emaciated with her sunken cheeks and jutting scared eyes, bony limbs, frail complexion, sickly — maskless — semblance. The strain to keep collected was all too evident. Marianne tried to clean up fast, but the supervisor acted right away: approaching her at once he secreted something in her ear with vigorous angry movements, and nearly frightened out of consciousness she hastened to get out of there, weeping and quivering.

The supervisor was equally quick in apologizing to the Heiress and to everyone present, and a thousand apologies he did offer as the patrician's private horde of servants rushed to clean up the mess. The lawn needed specialized treatment — a swarm of kneeling bodies coalesced round the fell tray in a fraction of a second. Neipas watched their frantic work, mesmerized... He was shocked somewhat — confused — and dislodged, as it were, by what he had just seen. He saw the spread food being scrubbed up and plopped into a discreet can of trash.

Next moment the supervisor was clapping his hands right near his face, rousing him. "Set up, quick!"

At once Neipas sprung to the task. His tired limbs being mechanized to the motions of the toil, he moved up to the little table close to the Heiress' son and placed down the tray, prepared the dish, removed the plate, stepped to the child's side with a thousand flourishes.

"Sir," Neipas began, addressing the child with a deep bow (feeling a bit weird at this). "Your meal."

The child remained resolute in his tight frown, which pulled all the fat of his features toward the little round, bulging nose. It was a sight to despair at. His little slit of an eye turned on Neipas with a concentration of pure hatred in it such that no one would have thought possible for a little boy.

"Sir?" Neipas insisted, very softly. Already one of the Heiress' private attendants had neared, and awaited ready with a velvet napkin to wipe the child. Neipas waited too, holding a spoon of mushy cereal flakes in the air. But the child kept on pouting and frowning intensely. He didn't seem to want to eat.

The Heiress' main butler leaned himself forward. "Master," he said very respectably. "If you please, master. You must be fed."

But the kid wouldn't budge. His crossed arms only seemed to tighten and dig deeper into his torso, and his skin further slurped toward his brain along with every facial organ. Neipas glanced at the butler expectantly, knowing not what to do.

The butler tried again: "Master," he said softly, and again with supreme respectability. "Please, master. You must be fed. You must eat."

The butler held on leaning in for a bit, awaiting an answer. None came, and meanwhile the Scion's frown only sunk deeper in. Finally, the butler straightened up decorously; and, rotating himself in a manner vaguely reminiscent of a military private, he trod softly round the little fount to the Heiress, which he seemed to wish to consult. He waited for her to conclude dispensing a few words to Baron Noxxe, sitting opposite. Respectably and with discreet pomp, the butler then leaned toward her ear. Meanwhile Neipas kept motionless, gripping the silver spoon suspended in the air. His attention again blurred in the wait — recurrent flashes of thoughts surged in his mind.

On the other side of the grass mat, the punctilious butler presently removed himself from the Heiress' exalted presence; rotating his body gently, he hovered back toward the throne where her child lounged and puffed, and before which Neipas waited with the spoon and the private servant waited with the napkin, frozen still. Again the butler positioned himself on the side-rear of the much cushioned chair. Clearing his throat (and discreetly checking the state of his mask) he tilted himself in once more.

"Master," the genteel butler began. "Your progenitor wishes to inform that a present will be acquired for your possession, provided you accept to be fed."

The child kept his beak clasped for a moment, and his frown tightened still further to monstrous and really indescribable proportions, before he mouthed: "Is it the War of the Pigeons game set?"

"Her Excellency's words were, 'Whatever the Master chooses.'"

The Master seemed to relent a little; his frown relaxed a bit as he mumbled arrogantly, "Told you I wasn't too young, derp!"

Neipas glanced at the butler in expectation. The butler signaled to him with a tactful nod, so Neipas focused his mind now. His hand, which held the spoon, approached the child's beak very carefully; but when it got close to the beak the hand slowed delicately to a stop, for the beak still did not open.

Neipas glanced at the butler in poorly disguised desperation, but the respectable peacock was already on the issue. He leaned in and simply said, softly: "Master."

The Heiress' son opened his pout a little, doubtfully, grimacing as though he were being tortured into it. Neipas' hand reared in the spoon, which entered the small beak with much difficulty; it was a herculean task to exercise the precisely correct amount of force so that he could slip the mush of cereal into the pampered child's moneyed mouth and not annoy him in some unpredictable way.

However, to Neipas' great relief, the boy seemed to like the mushy paste; and so he drew away the spoon easily, and took another scoop as the private servant wiped his gilded lips with the velvet cloth.

Neipas kept feeding the heir with automatic motions of his trained arm. By and by the child vanished from his awareness; it was difficult to hold attention. He hadn't eaten a proper meal in a long time — how long again?, he wondered. Time itself seemed to lose sense in the hollowing out of vigor caused by hunger. He felt very weak. The life in his eyes was drained slowly as his sight gradually turned inward to his soul. It was in an increasing commotion. A panic, building up toward the entirety of his being.

He saw Magpie. He saw her again. She was a little farther away, and her body dropped limp beyond an edge and into a monstrous chasm full of smoke. The shock of what he had seen lingered in him very strongly, and he kept seeing its image, he kept witnessing that moment with as much reality as if she was indeed throwing herself off the top of the tower again.

The first course was served. Now came the chocolate mousse, which the heir licked his beak at as soon as Neipas held up the silver spoon with it.

Magpie had looked so scrawny, so debilitated, so drained of life and devoid of soul; so altogether different from the strong, vigorous and steadfast woman she'd been, the beautiful girl so spirited, so full of will. So unjusticed, violated, destroyed... Her tenacity before all the obstacles of her station in society shattered, and all of her broken in body, in mind, in spirit.

Neipas was mildly roused by a little force tugging at the end of his hand. He was pulling the spoon out of the Scion's mouth, but he bit it in; he seemed to be licking every little bit out of the silver, relishing the treat.

The spoon was pulled clean — a film of spit glistened from it. Next and last dish would be fruit.

Neipas peeled it vacantly. His eyes were empty, glassy.

Magpie died. The image of Magpie's body succumbing into the chasm was as though seared into his mind; it kept repeating in it and he saw her dying over, and over, and over, and over, and over, and over, and over, and over, and over, and over, and over, and over, again...

The pampered heir was making an ugly face. Neipas extended the fruit out to him. The heir did not seem to like the look of the fruit.

The child heir did not want the fruit. And Neipas could not get over that vision which seemed to have been burned into the fabric of his mind, cursed to retain it and repeat it forever. The beats of his heart mounted up to a slowly swelling panic.

Hidden in the grass among the flowers on the base of the fountain, a spider shed its silk and weaved its web. The hamster nibbled on a found crumb (inside the fishbowl). Meat was brought, upon platters, for the tigers whose stripes swayed gentle in the dappled shade, enormous jaws yawning, eyes falling back to sleep. It was brought in mounds; what sort of meats they were, Neipas didn't know, but in his stupor he conjectured they might be storing the last remaining carcasses in salt, or something. The sun opened above them, glistening in the waterfalls, peeking in from the hypnotic light of the Pearl in the tower's peak; opened like a giant's eye staring from the zenith of the world, subsuming all under its blinding supervision. The orchestra's melody still animated the air; the dancers yet whirled about; there was the raspy murmuring of the peacock reading to little Ruby as she was fed quietly and dejectedly, and listened to the constant 'rrrr' the peacock tried to teach her as he taught her how to growl, and sneer; sounds of chewing everywhere, everywhere disturbing every little atom of air; and conversations droned among the burble of fountained water...

"I wish to acquire that land, Mister Noxxe. It afflicts me profoundly to see it under the management of savages," said the Heiress with her dragged, dandy voice of pinched nostrils. "They let everything burn to ashes."

She nodded poshly, and a broccoli was removed from her plate of vegetables and placed delicately between her lips. Her consort the Minister of Borders chewed quietly, looking timidly, deferentially sideways at his patrician wife, and waited inside his mute mustache. Noxxe, before them on the other side of the little fount, nipped his cufflinks and sniffed his sapphire rock, massaging it with the ridge of his bill.

"The reserve is government-protected land — and not for sale, I'm afraid, Madame."

The Heiress placed her gloved fingers on her breast and bobbed her head in a very dignified manner. "Everything has a price, Mister Noxxe. Petey?" she looked at her husband — and the Minister of Borders nodded profusely.

"What are your plans, Madame?"

"I wish to build a wildlife reservation in the area. I must say, Mr. Noxxe, that I do not agree with your installing pipes under the river, and am hoping we can arrive at some compromise for a different route."

There was a break in the conversation then (Neipas realized the ground shook still — even here it shook) as the two magnates, the oil-baron and the fortune-heiress, ruminated their delicacies, in the silence of sprinkling founts, with much refinement.

"It's too late for that, Madame," the Baron rejoined.

"Can you not blow some mountain and steer clear of the river?"

"We have considered that solution. It is too costly, Madame. We must be practical."

(Across the little fount the peacock teacher growled:

"RRRRRRRRR!"

"Huuuuuuuuh," replied little Ruby; still young, still innocent, still human, yet unmolded in the ways of her class.)

"I could assist with the funding, Mr. Noxxe," said the Heiress, speaking gravely, the weight of her immense wealth thickening her every utterance.

"Much too impractical, Madame."

Silence.

"..." voiced the Heiress with a royalty of tone that floated high above all heads. Her quietude had the bearings of moneyed admonition. The atmosphere steeled. And his husband the Minister of Borders held his breath nervously, anticipating her wish to dispense additional words.

"Madame, the pipeline runs downstream from the reserve anyhow," said Noxxe preemptively.

"I am concerned about the impact on the salmon, Mr. Noxxe. It is an important species for that ecosystem, don't you know."

Laughing, Noxxe followed, "And what would you do with the natives, Madame?"

"It isn't a matter that concerns me. I suppose some place would have to be found for them."

("RRRRRRRRRRRRR"

"Huuuuuuuuuuuuh")

"Indeed, my dear wife!" slipped in the Minister of Borders, fervorously, suddenly finding a niche for his opinions; he looked very eager to participate in the discussion. "These Indians belong to that ilk of breeders trying to mooch off national resources... To put them in charge of resources at all is a scandal in my view. They're idlers. *And* uncivilized. Have you seen, Mr.

Noxxe, how they paint their faces? I would say this: they either assimilate properly, or we cast them off. That's what I think."

After chewing, Noxxe pursued — ignoring the Minister — "With all respect, Madame — but it's not worth the trouble. Pretty though it may be, the land is just a bunch of dirt. Rocks and dead matter. Salmon, trees... They don't talk, Madame."

The Heiress lifted her glinting, golden bill.

"Some things are worth preserving, Mr. Noxxe. It is our land after all."

("*RRRRRRRRRRRRR*"

"*HUUUUUUUUUUUH*")

The ground shuddered — lurched suddenly, as though a feeble beast in an effort to shake off fetters. It cut across the air; and even the patricians there seated halted for an instant; all time stopped — in that static moment of teetering glass, the slightest doubt formed in their hardened sense of supremacy, the slightest fear — before they continued on, eating. The next moment it was as if nothing had happened. The Scion frothed immobile in the intensity of his frown and Neipas held still the fruit; only his insides shivered.

It was noon; they had been there for hours already, and even as breakfast was ending, lunch was already being served (more meat was brought atop shimmering platters; wine flowed and sparkled) — on Neipas' tray the knife's steel flashed sunlight, and as he leaned in mystified he saw his mask reflected dimly on the blade's surface, wavy, dispersed. Taking momentary stock of himself he realized how very uncomfortable he was; how much his round back ached; how much his heavy horns weighed upon his sleepy, exhausted head; how much his strained wrists trembled. His throat felt clogged; his stomach seemed to flap a little with discomfort, damp, increasingly unsolid with coffee and no food (the uneasy need to rush to the bathroom was coming on). The little fountains stung his ears; to the point that they sounded like insects buzzing in his fraught nerves, scattered across the whole length and depth of the Heiress' orchard from end to end, from balustrade to balustrade, atop which replications of Mars Ultor perched, leaning drunk upon bundles of rods strapped to axes. Beyond them the air sunk to shaded patios; where, lodged just below, within view in the near railing, one could spy a discreet mosaic recalling the epochal abduction of the Sabines, who were sacrificed for the birth of the most lingering of empires. Beyond its wall spread the remaining Gardens, descending in enormous, concentric terraces — into the profuse fog of the Temple, and the yonder Infinity Pool at the abyss' edge, where Magpie discovered the summit of the world was the height of Babylon and nothing lay further; her last stand before the maw of her destiny, her portal to — what? Where had she gone?

He held the fruit before the little Scion making an ugly face. He was hungry, hungry...

During the progression of the meal, Neipas retained a peripheral awareness of a phenomenon happening around him, which he processed, as it were, in his subconscious. Feebly he noticed the way the patrons were eating; and he noticed how the Heiress, her guests and her inner circle of advisers and attendants — peacocks with mostly leeched visages, thin and sleek — routinely discarded bits of food into large vases of gold. In his present state this was incomprehensible to Neipas and quite confused him; so he left it to the side, drawn into the misery of the lingering shock and the vision which it flashed unto him.

But this practice would abruptly surge to consciousness and send a jolt into Neipas' clouded soul; he was pushing the fruit slowly toward the heir's beak when his vision cleared; the Scion's face seemed to be disfiguring again in an expression of dissatisfaction, and all at once a monstrous scream blasted out of him:

"I DON'T - LIKE - THIS!"

The childish screech thundered with anger into Neipas' rattled soul, pervaded his famished bowels; penetrated with an authority derived from generations of accumulated wealth, reaped by a dynasty of agrarian tycoons, slaveholders, sugarcane planters; big industrialists, bankers and arms manufacturers, chemical producers, and finally retail giants, all rollers in huge investments and sovereigns of hidden kingdoms larger than the mightiest nations, accruing unimaginable riches across decades of theft. This petulant child was but the latest fruit in a family-tree of coiling, incestuous branches; imbued with the power to toss Neipas into destitution if it pleased him.

But the Scion flapped his wing like a frustrated eaglet, featherless and impudent. General attentions turned in their direction, but only slowly and lazily; for it seemed that such fits were common show.

In a swift and stealthy motion the butler stepped into Neipas' flank, appearing suddenly next to him like an apparition. With a flick he removed the fruit from Neipas' hand. "Can you not see?" he snarled.

Neipas was confused and didn't know what the butler was talking about. He held the fruit up to Neipas' face quickly. "There is an indentation. Master cannot eat this."

He couldn't see anything. The butler pointed at it — "ah yes...", Neipas mumbled, out of sorts; there was indeed the slightest indentation — and in the same moment the butler threw the food in the trash.

"It is your responsibility to notice such things," he hissed, then a little louder he commanded: "Please, a new fruit for the Master." Neipas suddenly came to; a feeling of outrage swelled up in him. He stared at the insolent and snarly face of the butler with anger and disbelief — how could he throw out such a perfect piece of fruit when so many of them were hungry?

He vacillated for a moment. Magpie died in his mind again in a flash. He was unable to move for a second, and still thought of reaching his hand into the trash vase and gobbling the fruit.

Every circuit of his mechanized body seemed to fizzle and become unwired. His nerves snapped.

A great shuddering came unto him. Unable to contain it, his hands grasped the sides of the tray in a tremble; and in a sort of mad seizure he lifted it, and hurled it to the floor by his feet; an outsized clattering of silver and breaking porcelain boomed from the impact and rattled the air for a while. All stilled; all shushed in its wake.

Everybody was turned to Neipas with open mouths. The dancers halted in their dance, the servants ceased in their serving, the Heiress and her cronies stopped eating, the golden dust vanished from the air, the orchestra shushed. The waiter rooted to the ground, petrified, his eyes very open and wild and wavering madly, his fists clenched at the end of stiff, stretched arms quaking nervously. He stood like one possessed, pinned frozen to the floor by some demonic force of gravity and outrage.

The profound silence sucking in every breath in the wake of the noise, was shattered as a great, inhuman shout released from Neipas' gaping beak:

"Why would you do that!"

He looked down with glassy, blind eyes; and he seemed to see with detachment and desperation his own expressionless face and horned head lying shattered on the ground. It spread in shards, some of which had fallen into the little fount by them. The clay became lucent in the water; and he saw the shards reflected myriad fractions of little selves.

Godly plumages sniffed at him; blue glints and gold sneered coldly. The broken air twitched and glinted with awed clamors from rising beaks everywhere. Even little Ruby looked across the spray with shock, stared tearful, aghast, scared into Neipas' unrecognizable, monstrous visage; and the Heiress' quivering son whimpered.

"Mommy!" the child wailed. Gasps and exclamations of unbelief ensued from every corner; the heavy sprint of the bulls could already be felt upon the velvet.

Neipas, wide-eyed and crazy, was pulled back violently and hurled out of the Palace in a moment.

Everything after that was a blur of fear and unconsciousness. The only remembrance he could solidly grasp afterwards was being brought before the

Chief Supervisor.

The Chief smiled and was very understanding. He apologized for how things had been lately. He was very nice. But still he said:

"You're fired.

"Please keep within the Pigeon Wing. Every other part of the complex will be restricted to you."

62 - Forest of Yarns

By and by he began to see disembodied masks in the darkness. Famished and cavernous, their puckered heads floated in pale halos, suspended amid a very oppressive, very heavy gloom. They appeared dreamlike, muddy, ambiguous; resembling rough sketches drawn with pencil on spellbound papers. Portraits of destitution, they were; his brethren in poverty, twins in affliction, refracted copies of his ailing soul. Gaunt and colorless. Quiet. All was quiet when Neipas saw them; a very eerie, very deep quiet. As he floated forth in the dizzying experience of hunger, he felt as though he were roaming the unlit exhibition of some haunted gallery, where the etchings, bearing a circular frame of oppressive pallor, a yoking nimbus, seemed somewhat alive; and all the other spectators were ghosts.

The unnerving silence of the hovering heads, sieged in black, was horrible — but it would give way to something even worse as the *I*s, having no electricity to feed on, would die, and no longer give light. The bodiless masks gradually vanished; with them faded the quietude of discolored glow. In its wake came a fullness of night, and a darkness that whispered. A scarlet, winking darkness; a darkness perfect...

All things became sound in it. All nothing but mutterings and steps ringing ghostly in the void. Often Neipas would call out timidly as some noise without body would brush him by, and no one would respond — all steps without feet, moans without a mouth; sometimes screams. At times distant yells reached the ear, out from beyond many thick shades of darkness, in places unreachable. It roused the heart with horror. And often he would feel the invisible touch of a passing hand; even in the friction of his own shirt against his skin he felt that hand...

Even when the crimson lights blinked, he saw no one. And the knowledge of a hundred invisible, starving maws hovering all around him in the black and the spectral red gnawed at his sanity.

The entire vastness of the Columbaria turned into a murmuring opera of horrors. It was like walking among phantoms; enough to drive anyone crazy.

Once more, Neipas experienced the sensation of constant tension, of relentless fright derived from deprivation. He had but little food left to go on now; and scarcely any money to buy more. What he did have did not satiate him. His body, weak, languished in the cradle of his frail mind, where naught but feverdreams dwelt in that final and unending night of the soul. Most hours he would exist in a febrile state of trepidation beneath sheets, or

wander the thick blackness by some instinct of bodily necessity — in vague
search of a bathroom, or a doctor, or food, or he didn't know what. His
intellect was often coiled in raving mathematics, counting the time blowing
past, in which he did not work, nor made any money. Random and torpid
dream-thinking all the time — flashes of Eva, Orenda, his family, his photos
in his head — Magpie dropping into the pit, faceless Cesar at the verge...
The nearly constant nothingness, punctuated only by dizzying spells of glare
— and the ruffling, the stirring darkness thick with unknown voices... Life
descended into a permanent terror. But how does one describe this terror, the
terror that festers in the heart when the sight is wrapped in gloom, when one
does not know where one's next step will land? It is impossible to accurately
describe, as are all such things. Neipas was thrown back into the experience
of the primordial fears of Man.

He was afraid to die; he felt, really, that his end was near. The cold choke
of mortal dread made his heart gush and his throat falter, made his
consciousness drunk, made his eyes scream; his breath tremulous at every
moment.

There was a red dot blinking in the dark.

What is it? — Neipas asked himself. He approached.

Walking up to the (small) red dot he found that he could click it. His hand
went to it, and pressed the red dot in.

(It's turned on now) before his seating figure — suddenly he was seating
— there was a vast field of snow and ice. The soil was enveloped in a
crepuscular whiteness and the air suffused with a nighttime chill. From the
horizon emerged a colossus of ash, resembling a tree of thin trunk and an
enormous canopy expanding to cover the whole sky; like a growing cave
engulfing the arch of the world. Indeed this tree of dense fumes rooted into
the ground and sunk into the heavens, spanning the entire verticality of
existence. Thin haze beyond the dense ash lifted, ascended continually.
Neipas' legs were crossed. Between them was a burning candle — it was the
candle of Man, and millenary values, the sum of all things created thus far
shone through its flame.

But Neipas turned his head slowly. Behind him stretched another
landscape, one very different from the immensity of frost staring at him.
Behind him the sky was ash no more — no, it was quite clear, very blue; an
uncanny, milky blue; nearly white. The sun presided over it, and the shafts of
its heat boiled over the surface of the earth. A desert of diamond sand — but
lo, afar rested a vast body of water. The water was very still, shoring up into a
grove of reeds, whence Neipas saw emerging a small herd of cows. They
were 8 in number, and very meager; indeed emaciated, thinned to the bone.

Their flaccid hides dug deep into every cavity of skeleton, which protruded out of their hideous shape. Out the waters came the herd — meanwhile Neipas sensed the approximation of some presence (walking from afar toward him). Even though it was so far as to not be yet visible he knew that it was an Eagle — a bloated Eagle in a suit. With this presence a sinistrous fear blossomed in Neipas' heart. At the birth of this fear he tried to rise, and found he couldn't; and the 12 cows (four more had emerged in the meantime) ate the reeds, but the reeds did not feed them — and one by one they fell on the ground of hunger, lifting dust off the land. And this dust covered the sight like the powder of spring, though it was without life. In the powder of the desert and the haze of the snowfield Neipas felt approach that presence, and the fear in his heart grew proportionate to the presence's approach. He could see it now — it was an Eagle in a suit, who, though far, advanced at large steps. Neipas opened his mouth large to scream at it; yet no voice ensued. He kept trying, and he strained. He felt the strings of his throat nearly snap and break apart. Meanwhile the Eagle came closer, and closer, and closer, and closer, and closer, and closer, and closer ("Stop! Go away!" — Neipas' voice exploded out of him in a supernatural roar of spirit). Neipas' fear culminated and he rose endlessly.

He was now inside a little house, which he didn't recognize right away, though he would conclude, much later, to be the watermill of his childhood. Before him was a window, and in it was the hot dust of the drylands and the swelling waters; and behind him another window, beyond which the cold fog of the snowfield and the colossal ashen tree. He saw the candle of Man no longer, but he felt no alarm at this, for he felt it still there — it was inside him now, and it was his heart, burning slowly. The presence approached still, and it came toward both windows, nearer, nearer, nearer, nearer, nearer, nearer, nearer.

It came toward both windows through layers of violent rain, which, however, fell upon the panes quietly; with the quietude of snow and the wrath of tempest. Here rained the speeding fog of ash passing like a pall over the earth; there the glittery dust. Here black, and there white; and both snows were made of locust and moth driving on against the glass — all without a peep.

The presence came nearer (Oshana's voice was at his side. It spoke unto him, "after the splurge will come the famine". But Oshana's voice came not from her — at least, it looked not like her. Opening and closing her lips atop an eerie motionlessness of body was his mother, and she was ashen and wore a mask of stone. She sat on a wheelchair).

The presence approached. Neipas saw it out of the windows. He saw it clearly now. It wasn't the fat Eagle in a suit — he could see that now, who it was.

It was the faceless Conductor of the Orchestra who approached. Or was it the Debt Collector?

It was almost here. Neipas panicked, and out of fear reflexively turned to his mother, who had stopped speaking Oshana's voice, and Oshana's words. She leaned forward a little and blew into his heart. The flame vanished. The candle of Man went out, and suddenly it was all dark again.

Neipas jumped out of the pillow. His startled eyes gaped into darkness, so that for a long time he felt that he was dreaming still. But by and by he sensed how much more palpable the sweat upon his body was — the distinct sensation of reality, faint as it was, gradually affected him. He was awake.

The intense toil had exerted his every nerve to the brim of rupture; after he was fired he made his way unconsciously to his dormitory and landed on some bed that wasn't his. He couldn't muster the strength to climb the ladder to his shelf; his bones seemed to dismantle and his muscles collapse upon the mattress like fell rags from a vanishing scarecrow, his legs suddenly discomfited like a crumbling house of cards; wax mask disfigured and pasty, it smeared itself spread all over the pillow, and in that state remained, half-dead and open-mouthed, for hours and maybe even days.

Waking now in the foulness of his stale breath, Neipas smacked his dormant lips and opened his pasty eyes. He found his fingers shivered as they touched his wet brow; his clothes glued to his body. His head throbbed, he felt frail... He was very hungry; he should go out to the Gardens and eat at some point (thought he, deliriously). The weakness of his instincts led him to seek a general solution in the lit mazes of the *I* and its Webwork.

NEIPAS: Hey

NEIPAS: You there? :)

NEIPAS: I'm starving

NEIPAS: My minds spilling

NEIPAS: You there?

With one hand he checked the pocket of his work jacket, which even in the heat of his fevers he wore. Hidden there was the cash Kasim had given him. He still had some food he had stored; and some food Janu had given him earlier; but it was very little, and satiated even less. Adrift in his own mind he resolved, with a drooping frown, to go to the Gardens and use the cash to buy a wholesome meal. Onerously — the listless weight of his body bearing upon him — he removed the jacket, and extracting the money from it he buried it deep in his trousers' pocket.

He arose with a feeling of indisposition in his stomach. It growled and its contents became as if dissolved, sending a dizzying spell up into Neipas' head (in a sudden wild rumination he thought it sounded like a structure of moisty paste collapsing). He lifted his *I*: it was early still, not yet 12. Casting its light toward the door, he tottered out of the dorm room, reeling bent and clutching at his belly.

He lowered the *I* to open the door. It felt heavier, somehow – as though it were pushing through a wall of water – and he pushed it outward with some difficulty. Its rectangular frame resembled the opening mouth of some geometric monster; within it, the darkness was so palpable and dense, and imbued with a silence so heavy and total as to induce a sense of steep vertigo in Neipas' head. "Where is everyone?" he whispered to himself. It was something unnatural. The corridors should have been full of folk at this hour. Not even sounds could be heard anymore; all held dead still. Gloom and quiet reigned together, and for a moment as he stepped out into the airless black Neipas even wondered whether he was in the Pigeon Wing of the Eagles' Nest Complex at all; or whether he had been kidnapped by some ungodly force of the obscure, and transported to an alternate realm where sights and sounds did not exist.

A refreshed lurch of his stomach roused him out of these reflections, and he hastened toward the bathroom, raising his *I* to see. Even the *I* could scarcely pierce the darkness; its light didn't stretch very far; the outer edge of it was blurred and grainy, as if in the midst of a black fog (and why does everything feel so heavy?) Neipas himself had to force his body through it, feeling a counter push of windlessness, a resistance of some sort in the emptiness of space.

Neipas was undoubtedly in the Pigeon Wing, however. Here was the bathroom. He entered its sharp putridness — noticing quickly with a fright the ghostly mirrors and the dust salient in them – and directly swung open the door to the toilet. Holding in his bowels with a strain, he still took care to cover the seat with toilet paper before he sat on it.

A thunderous racket then blasted out from the stall, echoing into the quietude of the empty bathroom. Inside it, Neipas sat, feeling awash with relief after a final swirl of dizziness. He bent forward and put his face in his hands. Feeling the last remnants of physical agony dredged out of his stomach, Neipas looked forth with swollen eyes into the darkness, breathing in deep. He lingered a while then, momentarily distracted by an impulse to check his *I* (but the Webwork was still down). He sank the *I* back into his pocket and rose to use the toilet paper. A sudden sound – of a click, and the bathroom door screeching open slow – made him stop.

Steps. They rang deliberate – one, two, three; then they slid in a turn, and stopped. The stall door in front of Neipas' face rattled suddenly, sending a jolt of horror into his heart. He winced with fright, and in this he took a moment to bellow out a muted "occupied!"

He waited.

Sounds of vomiting faded in from the darkness of silence; very faint at first, then louder, and louder, till they pitched to just under a scream and filled his nauseous head.

Then – nothing. There was no sound, no sounds but that of the deadened silence which brought the very groan of Neipas' internal organs to the range of his ear. He waited, holding a rather vexing position: knees forward, toilet paper clutched in hand, trousers rumpled at his ankles. His nerves jittered anxiously. "Hello?" he called. But only the quietude of the thick shade responded, closing in immediately, claustrophobic, on his dissipating voice.

Neipas rushed his business, checking its progress by the light of the *I* (somewhat embarrassed in this too, ultra-conscious of the *I*'s stare as he shone it onto the soiled paper). Then, in a besmirched solitude, he stood hesitantly and in fear within the narrow confines of the cubicle, sharpening his ear in a bracing anticipation of something sudden springing upon him.

Nothing came. He opened the door carefully, lifting the light of the *I* as he did so. It shone into the phantasmagorical mirror; beyond the speckled and stained surface of which he saw himself. (He checked the bathroom corners, he alighted all stalls; there was nobody.

Slowly he turned to the mirror.) The glass resembled the positive of a photograph, with the profligate stains of dragged shape brought out to bear upon the sight, whereas these would have been invisible under the overhead light; the absence of which rendered everything else to this bizarre blackness sieging and pressing upon Neipas' body, insinuating itself into his mind. Upon beholding his reflection his breast suffered a mild thud. His mouth agape with awe, he stood paralyzed, watching horrified his maskless face.

(Where's the mask?) Horror spread slowly in his veins, in the manner that ink sinks into the stillness of water. There was Neipas' true face, again beheld after so long a time. What had brought it back from the depths of its veil? Had the waxen semblance been so far sweated, its features so far ground up as to dissolve altogether? Neipas stared hard at the abysmal appearance of his visage, contemplating with fright its fealty of form; the feeble, fragile form of a weakling. Was this indeed what he was?... But his mask couldn't be lost.

He looked — and in a second he found it. It was in the trough (but how did it get there?). All in a trepidation he rushed to lift it out; yet, before he placed it on, he looked up into the glass once more.

Neipas didn't know what it was that compelled him toward that ghastly mirror. Curiosity, perhaps — though in his innermost he sensed the action of some sort of moral force, a triggering of innate consciousness. He stared into his uncovered visage. Unsymmetric, rutted, sooted and sort of twisted; bare — and yet there was a peculiar shine in the less grubby parts of its skin; a nobility in the fundamental frame of jaw bone. A very mess of contradictions — again he found himself rubbing violently the soiled surface of it, as streams of watery soap descended between his fingers and merged into a coiling river down his forearm, dripping loudly into the deep trough.

Yet he halted. He drew away his trembling fingers as a buzz grew in his head, the far sound of bells; many tiny flies groaning within him. Abruptly he stopped, for he feared seeing again what he saw in the hospital — he dreaded the vision of his true form, dreaded facing with his eyes what had been half-shrouded in his mind since that day when, shrouded in white gown, he'd gaze through them the horror of unshielded faces, the inwardness of ailed spirits.

Neipas beheld deep his naked eye. He saw the deep blackness of the pupil sinking into his secret profundities; and from this mystic core, this crater of mystery, spread a mist of color, hazy and dusty, propagating like a cosmic explosion — the beginning and the end of the universe contained in his very eyes. All becalmed; for a moment all was silence. In the pupil — and in the mirror inside it, which it saw — Neipas witnessed trees sprouting from very green fields, from mossy rocks and clear springs, stretching their boughs to the heavens in a profound yawn of waking. And then he saw, upon blinking, the very same landscape — devastated, scorched, overtaken and consumed by flood and flame. Rushing torrents puffed fumes of ash from their frothing smolder, bilious and gray. The day was as dark as the deepest night. Soot, aerial and drifting, drizzled across the breadth of existence; and a hail of embers broke aloft, whirling with the substance of parched waters; and great toxic waters poured from earth and heaven. Vague shapes of bodies staggered from the mounting chaos of elements, and from the conflagrations birds took form, spreading their wings in the struggle to fly; at once succumbing, without strength, to the ash, the bubbling sea arising to meet the burning sky. Flood and flame blended in a tormented sigh of fumes, snuffing in its poisonous breath all remaining life, and he felt its ash blooming into the infinite depths of the opaque blackness of his eye — as it widened, and swallowed everything.

His whole face twitched with fright as he leant into the pigeon mask, being soothed progressively as the wax seeped into his pores, whence bloomed out a healthy set of feather shafts, full of plume. Checking quickly his regained visage, he placed his hands under the faucet.

And his hands he washed — with eyes closed.

Out in the dark corridor he heard a few whisperings, some steps. But he saw nobody. Dots of dizzy light floating in the black and red, a tiny buzz of flies deep in his ear, assailed him, bit his brain with tiny pats... Moths materialized quietly and flitted by the *I*. Wearied and heavy with trepidation, Neipas hurried back into his dormitory, wherein he saw, unveiled from the shadow by an *I* light, someone sleeping on the bed he had been in.

Out of wits, he moved to the opposite bunk, finding the bed there empty. He entered it, clothes and all; and penetrated deep beneath the sheets, where he coiled in a confused and stressed state of mind until, many hours later, he fell back asleep.

*

Gazing on with opaque, glassy eyes which reflected nothing, Janu the cook shattered eggshell after eggshell and observed the translucent fluids accumulate and flood the bottom of the wide bowl into which they were tossed, twitching with the fervid palpitations of the giant cooking hall alit in fire and flashlight.

Kasim, the pantrykeeper, roamed the kitchen with an uninterested visage; he neared Janu's station gradually. He navigated the edge of the tabletop with a casual walk, sensing the cook's uncovered throes of fright and nervousness; and saw how firmly he gripped his belly pouch, as if in convulsing pains. Discreetly — even within view of the chef, the supervisors, the bulls; for he knew how to wear his mask well — Kasim stepped right up to Janu's chubby, arched figure of flapped earlobes and labored breathing, as if in passing; and said:

"We do this at dinner, tomorrow, before the games. Are you ready?"

Janu bobbed his head as in a jerk, trying to be as confidential as he could under the weight of nerves and all his worries, as he watched the albumen mount up the bowl.

"Why so many eggs?" Kasim asked in a mutter, aghast, as he walked away.

"That's how much their cakes take man."

A bit later, Janu would go to Neipas' dormitory, where he now lay infirm, ill, and tell him of Kasim's plans to break into the Temple's far gates next day. Janu left him some food he had managed to smuggle out (Neipas had, for the past couple of days, been living off the scraps he'd stored in his locker of possessions, which, besides providing him no nourishment, were nearly rotting); and then left him to his fevers, in agony that he could do nothing else for him.

The bulls sealed all passages connecting the Wings only a few hours after the cook crossed back into the Eagles' side.

*

Once, it had been customary to have the Cafeteria's overhead lights on at all times. Not now. The canteen, its small tables crowded with arms, its squeezed chairs, were all made visible by a weak luminosity shone from the tepid, lusterless glass of the windows; it was suffused with a daytime obscurity very different from the overpowered white glare that made the canteen a flat, glossy and shadowless print of sterile blocks akin to a factory of dystopian fancy. Now there were shadows, unpronounced shades cast from the tables and the figures slouching over them, cast away from the windows in the pale light of day. The contrast between what he saw now and what he was used to seeing made the Cafeteria appear much bigger, and the clanking of dishes ring more remotely, as though into a farther distance. Everything sounded more silent. The vibe was languid; the aspect and echoed noises of the space sank into some chasm left by his mind's absence, and permeated his limbs, dissolving the stiff adrenaline that kept them going and making them yield into the fatigue that had been lurking under every step. He leaned against the counter a little.

When he realized he was awake, Neipas was already moving between the glass walls of the corridor, between throngs of shapes made up of deep shadow and crimson glares emerging from black folds. Sounds had been floating in his buoyant mind well before he removed himself from the sheets, billowing at each landing of step, shrinking at every lifting of foot, heavy and bereft of feeling, and without sensing anything as he dragged his feet out the door. He scuffed forth, behind half-closed eyes bearing the weight of their lids, in and out of thick breaths puffed from the upward-facing nostrils of his beak, fluttering the dejected lashes of his tired gaze. The choking stench made the air thicken and tremble like jelly; the smell alone gave a solidity of existence to the nothingness all around. It made him taut with an alertness, grounding him under, grinding him, fraught, keeping him from yielding to the desire to faint. He braced constantly for something sudden lunging at him from the darkness; always on guard, his nerves wretched, worn out, working twitchingly in the billowy, watery bottom. The tiny arteries of his temple teetered along with the ground. Nothing seemed to be able to hold still, nothing seemed steady; he couldn't help but feeling the very collapse of the tower was imminent.

Roaming the sonorous hallway full of the hungry and the sick, he witnessed their moaning take flesh as he approached the lighted Cafeteria. The neurotic high diffused as he entered it. Neipas stared for a while between his arched shoulders, blinking very slowly. Without its blaring lights the Food Hall looked less artificial, more material, more tactile; and at the same time more distant. It had the texture of dreams; tactile like a canvas tinged with pallor and vague shapes; and he gazed upon it as one gazes upon an unfinished, abstract, or decaying painting, uninterestedly pondering on what would be there, or what was there, or what had been.

He passed by the sitting and lying mob of visible moribunds languishing in the sickly light, walked past many pigeons of charred feathers and cattle with singed furs, all of them famished. In one of the back tables, Lou the waiter sat with Simon the Florist, on opposite sides, both emaciated; both rested with their foreheads against their forearms, their faces sunken. Then he surfaced into the gardens, into the palpitating sunlight; he merged into the stream of horns flowing thick through the Market; he saw the pigeons, smeared with soot, dirty in the corners, between tents, between the colored cloths, begging; he spied many bowls with no alms between cupped hands sprouting from already-tattered sleeves; and he glimpsed adults dozing with their thumbs in their beaks. Children and all the young crafted their masks and teemed anxiously before the Career booths, which still operated, even as the food quickly depleted. The food was quickly depleting... this everyone knew. So how was it that stocks seemed full everywhere else and the Market was still brimming with trinkets? Snouts still shouted from the stalls.

(*Up in the central aisle of the Auditorium some oxen were setting up a projector on a tall tripod. An immense crowd was already assembled there. In fact the dense stream of herds on the lower terraces all tended toward the 6th Tier, where the Auditorium was. Their sights were all upturned to the Stage, upon which stood a Flag, a Pelican, and a Peacock*).

There were some fat oxen prancing about with machine guns. Ensconced in grimy nooks, the so-called crows — the unemployed, the outcast, the penniless, the mostly brown and black-feathered pigeons shunned to the darknesses of Anubel's interior — didn't cower at their passage anymore. Rather they twisted their heads and uncontrollably sunk their beaks into their feathers, pecking themselves obsessively, the way an addict would scratch himself until he bled. They had grown used to being harassed (he noticed the spikes placed here and there to impede the jobless from loitering). Encroaching hunger withered everyone...

(*If any bird were able to fly up to those suffocating heights, it could behold what appeared, from a distance, like a mess of festive grandeur. A summit in disarray: full of bubbly crowds, with tarpaulin rows flashing, the glittery trees jutting out, the glimmering fountains coursing out of carved stone, the carnivalesque rainbow of hanging balloons, the gravitas of the statues in the niches of the Great Facade; great receding, ascending, concentric terraces culminating in that majestic palatial facade overlooking a wide lake opened in the very middle of the staired mound, with a shell-shaped, flowery wall of eyes in its deep bank and a gaudy circus flanking it on all sides. It resembled a quarried rock displaying a concave heart of petals, a yawning mountain powdered in every tint, roiling with confusion. Voices projected from the Stage nestled under the Facade and over the Lake. Swaying bodies gathered in the lower terraces by the Cafeteria. They were feathered and disheveled; and they also began to lift their voices).*

With swollen eyes and labored breathing Neipas roamed the mazes, looking vaguely for something, he didn't quite know what (He walked to his last meal. Clutching his pocket he felt the money Kasim had given him, and his hand closed round the banknotes, his eyes wavering with fear he'd be robbed. His heavy, downward gaze blinked constantly, it struggled against the blur. His fingers sunk beyond the money, deeper into the pocket where he kept the scissors... A flux of thought rushed to his febrile pulses. Even now all debts came to his mind. He felt the presence of the Debt Collector in the mass, everywhere — even now. His debts (even now they haunted him), the punishing vestiges of his days in college, of his days in the hospital, of his days in the world; the toll of stepping upon the hallowed ground of the Market which, in its fullest extent, was everywhere. With faltering, shivering strength, he restrained the impulse to pull out the scissors and stab at the multitude choking him). One hand was in his pocket; the other gripped a sandwich of Janu's, gripped it very tightly, for it was the last bit of food the good, humble cook had given him; gripped it as though it was the final claim upon his life; and his jaw circled very, very slowly, his teeth chewed each bite to the last... The drowsiness was overwhelming upon his mind. He kept

jolting. It was as though he was born into every moment; he came to again and again and could not remember how he got there. There was no continuity in time. The progression from moment to moment was severed at vague cuts...he lost himself, again and again he ceased to be (very frail grip to all pasts, to everything preceding him). He was at once new and weary, and no one... Neipas hummed something through his nostrils, in his labored breaths. Noises everywhere... Grotesque masks replicated themselves a swoon fever of a landscape; the sunken corridors full of wandering eyes, livery, wavering, lost, searching desperately for some understanding, for explanations, for deliverance and relief. He slogged on to the 5th Tier, up and down vague steps, through the Circus (*floating amid the string-fastened balloons thick, in the corners shed by the plastic ovals... as he brushed the strings Neipas heard whispers, many whispers sounded from the ropes, like chords from phantom chimes, like breathing harps. The lunatic screaming, weeping and laughter of the horned attendants sounded very remote, very distant as they watched a magician holding aloft a birdcage ["This is Jahgowa," he explained amicably to the awed children and adults, all cross-legged before his motley hues] and as he covered it with a cloth. He removed the cloth — the bird was no longer there ["Woooooooow!"] The noises were neurotic, deranged... gushed from people who had gone over the edge of insanity)* into the Lakes and its overarching bridges. Neipas saw the glinting streams of the artificial river; it had begun to assume a pale color; a faint reek held stealthily about it, to be picked up by the more sensitive nostrils. The adults would swim in it nonetheless.

He gained a wide view of the bridges, crammed with bodies; of the Lake, shimmering with raining coins as they wailed supplicant; and of the Great Peacock at the far, marbled shore, with his concave tail of iridescent stares surrounded by ample bouquets of purple flowers and sharp leaves. He sang yet...

Notes of music, like whiffs of fragrances, hold memories — Was it the Great Peacock's chant that reminded Neipas of his mother whenever he passed over the bridge here? He seemed to feel her dropping aromatic herbs upon the pot, a pot holding all the sweet waters of all musical lakes... Over the railing he looked, and he beheld his reflection under, dim and turbulent upon the surface of the water. His pigeon mask was a mess, a disarranged bob of drooping feathers and flaccid wax; it hadn't been sloughing very well; it wasn't very well fixed.

("The Market is a very old God," hissed the frightened Tour Guide nearby as he explained the current mood of the Market, cowering somewhat before a horned gang of hungry, disgruntled consumer-workers, "He's capricious. Full of whims. Bipolar and fond of drink. Look how He oscillates. My, how He stumbles downhill! But have faith! He will come roaring back upward. He always does...")

Neipas looked over beyond the edge of the Eagles' Nest, onto the clouds beneath. Nothing but barren, insubstantial waves filled his eyes, opaque tides beyond the heaven-ship muting, under puffy folds, the private afflictions of a million lives. *(Two terraces below him, the mass of wiry, grimy, tousled plumes kept growing by the Cafeteria doors).* The ground shook.

The whisper of the strings hung still in his ears *(and irritated livestock pressed toward the Orchestra Pit. On the stage stood a gowned Pelican and a suited Peacock; and above them on the Great Facade the heavily draped windows stirred, a little from the tower quaking, a little from the waterfall gleaming, and a little from the rush of people on the other side. Preparations for the arena fights that evening were being made. No cattle or pigeons could attend; though the fights would be screened up on the stage, for which the projector was being set upon a tripod in the middle of the Auditorium, where distressed oxen and heifers congregated, mumbling intentions of revolt.*

And the Pelican preached thus to the horns, "You are the Light, a Light besieged by much darkness. You are the Chosen, the vessels of our Lord, the medium of His glorious action. Ave."

"You, Columbidae workers, are second to none," added the Peacock, "but you are being crushed. You're being swindled. Beware the faceless mass waiting for handouts. Ave."

But their words did not readily abate the dissatisfaction of their audience; it did not quench the hunger. Words of protest and rage began to mount; but then the sagacious orators, always very perceptive, and with a clear sight of the lower terraces, spotted the pigeons gathering outside the Cafeteria yonder and with a sudden and shocking jolt pointed to them, clamoring, "Look! Look! They're eating!"

Furious, starved, made mad by fears of malnourishment, the livestock turned their heads in dismay. Already the Bulls were making their way with raised bludgeons).

There seemed to be a general direction to the flow of mesmerized bodies, which Neipas had been following, as one follows toward the hollow of quicksands, or yields to the strength of the mire: toward the Merchant of Doubts and Dreams on the other side of the Lake, the Tents of Idols, and the Auditorium beyond, on the upper terrace, where a gowned Pelican and a suited Peacock gesticulated to amassing horns. In the ample openness over the bridge Neipas gazed up. The fiery gleam of the Pearl struck his eyes with the admonition of sunshine. Then (as he opened his eyes again) he beheld the Great Facade, immense; hazy, he saw the shell-shaped recesses, the niches afar with their imposing statues, all guarding the bulwark with their regal poses, their one outstretched hand, the other held back, as if hiding something; he saw the windows between those statues, heavily draped, mute and confidential. It seemed to him like they fluttered a little. He thought it was, perhaps, the glimmer of the waterfall running down the Facade — he had never seen anyone in those windows.

(The guards fell upon the gathered pigeons with the whole fury of their authority. They all stumbled down the various steps and paths, crumbling disjointedly into the thorny, sinuous, garbage-stuffed woods of the 2nd Tier, and perhaps as far as the Museum gardens of the 1st Tier... They tried to fly away from the blows, but could not).

Neipas barely noticed the turbulence in the lower terraces; there was some added jostling, perhaps. It was only when he crossed to the other side of the lake and he entered the cords again that he realized their heightened intensity, as he listened to them again, as though they whispered screams from some depths faraway. Then, before he perceives it, all other sounds wane — reality recedes to oblivion. The balloons rustle multicolors upon the sight. Strange whispers in the fore of his mind... Everything retreats.

Among the density of strings, Neipas looks back.

Above the pale furs, the hollowed eyes and the bobbing horns, up through the concentric rings of the revolving terraces and between the sumptuous statues in the recesses of the Great Facade, among all the draped, black windows: he sees someone beyond a window glass, by the waterfall. Someone tranquil, dignified. He eats Janu's last crumb from the palm of his hand. The Great Peacock sings, the Pearl shimmers, the skies resound and the Anubel throbs deep... Everything shakes.

It's Magpie he sees at the window.

(Her mouthless visage opens and clams — what is she saying? He narrows his eyes...)

. . .

(I can't breathe!)

. . .

I can't breathe

"*I can't breathe,*" said the balloons. "*I need air!*"

At once all sounds returned in a flush of stimuli, in a torrent of gushes. Drums befell him. The crowds stomped. Screaming rendered all hided eardrums. All at once Neipas remembered the Midget in the depths of the Anubel, in the forsaken Museum sunk in darkness.

Deep in his pocket he held a pair of scissors, the ones he had bought to cut the lines with which to sew the patch-pocket into his waiter jacket. He had kept it all those high-strung nights, afraid he'd be jumped by the ghosts roaming the hellish darkness of the Columbaria — he had no money for guns.

Neipas cut two of the balloons — twice a whine broke sharply, like that of a severed violin or vein — and staggered, wild and unsteady, toward the Museum.

Lights frazzled on and off as he walked the deep Columbaria. Rows of beggars stretched glaring and moribund in the corridors — then vanished.

[. . .]

(*The projector on the tall tripod blasted light onto the wide stage. Everyone stopped...their languid, half-asleep, bewitched stares turned toward.*

The arena appeared in the glow. Two fighters stepped onto the ring).

63 - The Darkrooms (Trail Of Visions)

Over the bluffs and among the murmuring boughs, Oshana told them:

"We spoke across the flames. Civilizations were forged in such fires.

"And we spoke to the flames. It was then we began to worship."

They gathered all in a circle, round inside the grove, supervised by dark, spectral giants, the tenebrous bodies of which shook with whispers, whose distant crowns nodded in mystic sleep. The ocean breezes lifted frightful auguries in their glide. Ancient suggestions pervaded the air, and the sinister gaps between the trees seemed to shelter lurking, watchful gazes.

"The night made the soul retreat to the senses, and the body cling to the soul in fear. It found itself whispering. It whispered, because it spoke only to the most sensitive ears, only with the most secret pleas. It whispered to the night."

It was to the night that we first began to expand; and the first child of nature we sought to conquer in our advance. But we never did. "Chased by the flame, the darkness fled — inside.

"It was in the darkness that we learned to pray."

*

I. The End of History

Neipas clambered across the gloom-sunk corridors of the Columbaria, clearing a path through the porous layers of darkness with the I's flashlight. His head swam through the black tides of air frictionless, moving fast and deliriously down toward the Museum. The dry, plastic thud of the two balloons followed him. Along the way, wide eyeballs flashed blank as feathered ghosts stared on from the corners, from the mirrors, by the beeping red dots...

Wobbling, Neipas reached the portal beyond the Library shelves, and on the circular lintel the letters 'CAVE' jutted darkly; and again at the bottom of the steps (CAVE) where Neipas removed his shoes, balancing himself against the light trembling of the universe. He received the cavernous halls of the Museum and breathed in its disinfected dust. Colossal monoliths of cloth, ancient mirrors of stone, sacred relics from dead cults, old weapons washed of their blood, contours of mannequins standing mute — among pictures of mute gazes cluttered thick across the walls — and all the old objects collected and displayed contextless and alien in that immense shop of yesterdays appeared in the dissipating dark and were consumed again by it as Neipas passed along. His hand wrapped his mouth and nose, hiding their agitated breathing under its pressing palm, and his socks slid over the marble with susurrating sweeps, stealing forwards to the two mirrors at the End of History.

Up the royal steps he struggled, and strained until he arrived, breathlessly, upon the great final wall. The *I*'s beam scoured the fog of black. The darkness moved in sidelong swirls, and pressed — Neipas could feel it — against the light, against his back. If the Midget was there, the gloom shrouded her. Only a vague, strangely shaped flame blushed very far, dim beyond a foggy pane of glass. The electric light-cone landed on the sinister surface of the mirror beside, where the dust accumulated, compounded in a thick crust; interrupted only by the deep clefts (which were already being coated by flakes of ash) which spelled the cryptic message: *We cannot breathe, We cannot speak, We need air.*

"Hello?" Neipas whispered. The two strings ascended from his hand and disappeared in the darkness. In the perceived immensity of the concealed space he felt not a stir. The immobility of an occult emptiness pervaded his senses and made him jittery and nervous. His head ached yet; his throat dissolved, bilious and acid. The trembling of his breaths grew more precarious, nervous and neurotic, the drops of sweat pending from his brow and jaw shook at its feverish rhythm. Again he grew in the perception of his own feverish rhythms, the pulsing ails of his internal body filled his ears and overwhelmed his mind. His head swung lightly, back and forward, over the edge of swoon.

Suddenly he felt a hand from below gripping his own. Startled, Neipas released the two strings and the invisible balloons lifted them up toward the distant ceiling — but as they dragged across the floor and left it, the Midget seized the cords, and held them on. Alit spectrally in the dim flashlight, he placed a finger upon the droopy crescent of his sad mask, turned upward to Neipas' pixelated, twitchy stare; walked quietly to the shadows, to the edges of the space; and with the vessel in her hand she poured olive oil in lamps which had been set around the space, and lit up a flame in each. The oil glittered in soft amber flashes in the palpitations of the fire, which grew to fill the space in warm, mysterious firelight; and the vast hall materialized slowly, taking shape in the amassing glow and the dispelled shades. There appeared the portentous hourglass and its unending sands flowing from ceiling to floor. Gradually revealed along the rounded walls were the sparse nonsensical paintings hanging (hanging clocks melting, disintegrating, scattering). And immense before his blinking eyes, Neipas beheld the haughty serpent, tamed in stone, made visible in the golden oil fire, looming between its elaborated wings. Both were glass; one a window, beyond which burned steadily the

Candle, afar; the other a mirror reflecting all that came before them, the entire linear corridors and all the staircases of History stretching through gateway after gateway, between veil after veil — which Neipas gazed with hard-set brow, contemplating the looking-glass through a thousand vague layers seeing between himself and the distance (his were eyes gazing through many other eyes across the length of History) until the Midget finally drew the curtains shut.

An aura of mysticism swelled warmly with the flame, numbing Neipas' senses pleasantly and easing his distress. He watched as the Midget pulled down the ropes slowly, and solemnly untied the balloons; he gazed as the Midget placed both balloon tips upon the downward crescent lips of the stoic mask together, and sucked the air out of them at once — the swollen oval withered.

Everything stilled for a moment. The silence deepened further.

Then, suddenly, the Midget began to speak; Neipas receded shocked into the yawning emptiness of the cavernous chamber. There were many voices in the Midget's voice, male and female both, ensuing from the bobbing mask of downward-pending smiles. They spoke many languages, languages from all quarters of the Earth and languages long unspoken, dead and living he spoke them; in the same breath they uttered Akkadian and Urdu words, Etruscan and Aramaic, Kalkatungu and Portuguese, Tongva and Kikongo. The sounds unleashed from the mask proliferated across the End of History with whispers and babel, incomprehensible to Neipas' ears, and he heard the Midget without understanding and looked at him/her horrified. Fearing the Giant Historian would perceive the building ruckus, he shouted out as the volume mounted: "Stop! He'll hear you! What! What!" The voices only grew, as if uttered from a spirit of ascending height billowing into the vault. "I can't understand," Neipas repeated many times.

"Who are you?"

The Midget ceased. Her/his head panned up to Neipas solemnly, his/her robed sleeves touched, together. Pending, quiet.

Then, the Midget spoke:

"We are the voice of those whose voices Hist'ry silenced."

Neipas watched and listened open-mouthed, bewildered, in awe. The sounds of a man and a woman were voiced together powerfully, divine, ethereal, out of that inscrutable being in mask and robes.

"Neipas," said the Midget's voices, *"before you rises the opaque portal, which they call 'The End of History'. Much lies beyond it, hidden.*

"Lo. Have you listened the serpent's answer?"

The Midget pointed up, bidding Neipas to consider the end wall. He did so without feeling vertigo. There must have been some sort of medicinal quality in her/his voice. It had a certain healing influence upon Neipas, and soothed his heart, relieved his body and senses of their pain. The dancing flames cast shades from the saliences and edges of the ornate patterns in the arches framing the two mirrors, playing about as if molding them, bringing out their shape, making its overall form clear. And with the shift and dance of light and shade, and an attentive stare, Neipas noticed now that the two arches depicted not wings, but were really two vast *ears* whose orifices comprised the mirrors.

The Midget approached the tall, snake-headed cocoon between the mirrors.

"Listen to what the serpent affirms. It hides a gate. It hides a lock. The key to it is a question."

As they stepped closer to the stone relief the shell of dust glowed with the pressure of the glass beneath. A calm, sage, and seductive voice flowered out of it, and again said the words:

```
Because inherited are pride and shame,

so's merit, to which wealth's bestowed.

Still, fortunes abound in the summits

and there's no shortage of ladders.

We reached the end of evolution.

We conquered the journey.

We triumphed.

There is no alternative

There is no turning back now

Only money can mold the morrow —

Only with power can the past be shed

Because inherited are pride and shame.

So's merit, to which wealth's bestowed...
```

The Midget, turning to Neipas, said unto him:

"The serpent hides the gates. The answer to opening them is realizing the right question; the key is knowing the question to which the serpent answers, and asking it aloud."

"And what is the right question," asked Neipas.

"It has many forms, and can be shaped many ways. But one of the ways to shape it, in your language, is this."

And the Midget, approaching the cocoon between the ears yet closer, spoke the following words:

"If merit is rewarded with success, and the measure of success is wealth, how is it I

was born poor, and you were born rich?"

The mirroring glass erupted with light, piercing itself forcefully into Neipas' vision. He shielded his eyes with his hand and closed them; meanwhile a foul wind ensued from where the mirror had stood; it fell in shards, and the dust which it had supported scattered like toxic powder across the room. It rushed into Neipas' lungs and he coughed profusely.

As the dusty spores spread, stifling, the eyes of the Serpent, which had so far been closed, opened with a wide glare.

II. Catalogue of Vanities

All but one of the twelve oil lamps had been lit. The Midget seized it and fixed the handle round the top of his/her staff. Then she/he gave the 11th lamp, sitting amid the glass shards, to Neipas.

They entered the open ear, and were immediately faced with wall-high layers of a solid material which, however, they were able to chip through easily. It melted when Neipas leaned toward it the flame of his oil lamp.

"What's this?" asked Neipas.

"Paraffin," answered the Midget.

Neipas bobbed his head a little.

"Paraffin?"

"Wax."

They dug through the wax and, once clear of it, found the ear tube coalesced into a passage leading to a circular portal; a sort of window lodged in the shadow wall. It was framed with a silver ring, adorned with a relief of loops winding into one another, and on which was carved the inscription: *CAVE, CAVE, DEUS VIDET.*

"What does that mean?" asked Neipas, looking up, alighting the message with the serene flame.

To which the Midget replied:

"Beware, beware — God sees."

Before they took another step the Midget still told him, *"Abandon the lamp where it was. 'Tis powerless in the gloom before us. Go back and leave it to its place."* So Neipas did, and returned to the portal.

They pushed open the window and passed through.

They moved into a shadow so thick even the *I*'s light had difficulty penetrating it. The darkness sloped down a series of tenebrous steps, and was gradually punctuated by a myriad dots of blinking color that twinkled independently, hovering in the black air everywhere and emitting no glow beyond themselves (and as those little lights grew in number the gloom about him amassed, so that he could no longer see the Midget by whose hand he was led. This darkness had weight, and exerted pressure — the *I* faltered under, flickered a few times, went out quietly; fading very mutedly, as though doped into sleep). Low electronic moans sounded, neutral mechanical whimper resembling the purr of cats. There was the sound of fans blowing cold conditioned air also — from somewhere, everywhere. The unnatural breeze seized Neipas gradually, first by making the breath artificial in his nostrils and then by sneaking its frigidness through his shirt and into the pores of his skin. As he descended among the blinking, purring lights he saw that they were discharged out of tall boxes connected by wires. There were rows and rows of them. They whispered to him all manner of murmurs and blew cold synthetic breath onto his mask as he passed; inhuman, incomprehensible, the boxes puffed and purred low but frenetically, and seemed to be working fast; Neipas had the impression of innumerable thoughts running through the machines, as if they were concerned with comprehending the entire mind-load of humanity.

Even before they stepped into the sea of blackness on the other side of the strange window, Neipas had heard it — as he had heard it many times before. The sound of a melody afar, blowing soft from the lights; a softly pulsing melody. The volume of its tone grew slowly. Silken brushes touched his cheek as he passed. They seem to be walking through soft veils, which covered their faces and rose across their skins with a tingling, nice, soporific feeling. As they traversed the veils, a vision of something afar was made more and more distinct; something distant, multicolored, and blurry, which grew in his sight at every step.

Neipas stood still; his heart swelled and halted its beat. He stared out in awe.

The melody resounded soft. It was but the sound of a glass harmonica, stretching itself slow across the darkness; and the voice of an angel filling the walls.

They must have arrived at the end of the steps, for the ground was now flat. The space had endlessly widened on all sides. And before him rose now a wall of gloom, out of which shined screens. These screens illuminated the space only very tenuously; and covered an enormous expanse, towering above the darkness and multiplying sideways and upwards until the eye lost them. (The melody soothed Neipas' swelling breast with spores of mineral and crystal... It rang ethereally in the dark. The angel sang; behind the voice's hum a deep, slow, colossal pulse throbbed.)

Inside the screens were images. Some remained motionless; others flickered and changed, and moved. Though many images appeared nearly the same, all were distinct from one another; the entire spectrum of color radiated and glimmered from the screens in chaotic disorder. There were many of them, many, many, many, an innumerable quantity of them replicating across into horizonless prospects.

"Everything that can be watched," said the Midget, *"can be seen here."*

Neipas took a step forward. His foot landed with a particular echo, boundlessly outstretched, resembling the sound of a droplet fallen into a quiet ocean. The step blended and disappeared into the celestial euphony of oscillating glass. That hypnotic melody of sparkle lulled his troubled heart; and yet a fear remained lodged inside, contained within a shell of hesitation, permeated with the mysterious intonations whispered by the music. Looking down, he beheld the glow of the screens mirrored in the dark floor, spreading infinitely away from his feet.

It was inexplicable to him, and the sight seeped into him with a hollowness that overwhelmed. There was no processing of it, no interpretation he could make in his thoughts or in his spirit, of what he saw.

He walked alongside the screens for hours, and still could not find their end. He could never see their top. The lights confounded him, he was assailed by the sheer quantity of pictures, distracted into a sort of hypnosis. For a long time he kept walking and knew not what he was doing. The Midget accompanied him, calmly. A few prismatic duck shapes waddled along; gliding yonder, vague, in the changing watery glows that covered and infused their figures, as he roamed.

By and by he sat. A long time must have passed before he took stock of his bearings and emerged into himself again. Shaking his head, as if to ward off the mystic discomfort the images bore into it, he sat in place, on the floor, for a while, rubbing his eyes, turned toward the dark floor — gazing the vague shimmers reflected in it. He felt as though he were hovering over a starry ocean of blurs; all alone in a universe of liquid pixels and gloss, fathomless.

He could not perceive the boundaries of that fathomless place; so mesmerized, Neipas did not realize that afar — very far, in a nearly invisible remoteness — hung clouds, entrapped in the windowpanes of a tower.

Neipas raised his head again. The infinitude of shine and flicker rose titanically above his eyes...

Streets of people coming and going. An intersection of waiting cars. A playground. A kitchen corner and a child fiddling with an *I*. A suited pigeon with mask inside a computer. An open book upon a desk. Gunshots and explosions. Animals grazing the prairie. Airplanes and robots. Showy marriage proposals. Sex faked, sex forced, sex voluntary, sex for money, sex for fame, rape. Castrations and beheadings. Babies laughing and wildlife yawning. Bodies falling and leaping and running and jostling and brawling.

Much dancing and bodies swinging, many disembodied talking heads. People killing themselves, people murdering people. Little windows, little squares of people, a city of frames, a civilization of bars, a sprawling prison universe, a graph sheet where each mathematical cypher was a face masked. Many trillion moving maws. Masks, masks, masks; masks copied and multiplied across the whole stretch of existence, everywhere. All and everything palpitated in the lights.

The most vile things were bragged about; every happiness feigned; and whatever was genuine, had been stolen.

Here stood the entire immensity of civilization in its fullness of chaos — absolutely silent before his multicolored eyes; with but a throbbing pulse, throbbing dimly somewhere beyond it; and a song of oscillating glass and the voice of an angel insinuated into the depths of the soul... All noises, hummed in its unending dispersion. All the pretty and the awful, the horrible and the trivial, all stood side by side in equivalence, in a mass indifference; everything leveled, everything trivialized, everything abstracted.

"What's all this?" Neipas either mumbled, or whispered, or thought — to himself, for he had forgotten the Midget's silent presence at his side. Yet the Midget answered him:

"The tar that held the walls of old Babylon is the same tar with which light was first trapped in glass. It sprouts from the foundation of this civilization — its bedrock. A heart of stone. An island in a tar pit. The sun-clock, round which these days wind, and all days have wound for centuries now."

But Neipas, for moments nearly insensible (barely feeling the Midget's presence) did not fully hear her/his voice. He whispered to himself, "it's the Webwork... isn't it?" he whispered to his reflection, staring up at him as from underneath the waters. He saw his reflection dark, featureless; for an instant he thought he glimpsed it maskless, and out of the contours of his true face emanated the unbounded glimmering lights... and as he returned his stare to the universe of screens rising over him once more, he seem to see in all its partitions, indistinctly, his own self... (for an instant).

Mystified, he kept staring. He felt as unsubstantial, as immaterial as the Webwork, where all humankind roves and grows mad. Here it stood before him in its full extent, ablaze in all its rabid derangement and stupidity... The *I* had but one glass, one window, through which he could advance through its unending layers of curtains — though he could only peek into one chamber, glimpse one cote, skim one page at a time; impulse drove him feverishly from one to the next, all calling to him repeatedly, relentlessly replicating themselves to infinity. But now he beheld it all, all at once in its contemplative sum; and — strangely, perhaps — the vision filled him with a sublimity of wonder.

But gradually some shape, which Neipas could not, for a long time, distinguish from mirage, took prominence over everything else. The figure seemed to emerge from the universal extent of lights, gliding out of them with a sinuous, seductive gait. Long legs, naked, grew from the swimsuit; their feet met the floor with pointed heels; and she rose over all, gorgeous, sensual, with voluptuous breasts, full lips red and piercing eyes, black, drawing his accelerating heart in an invisible pull. His breath deepened out of his open beak.

"Eva?"

She turned and walked back toward the screens. "Magpie?" Her luscious hips rose and fell in suggestive motions, her rabbit ears pointing to the skies powerful and assertive, turning this way and that. Neipas arose with fluttering breaths and, swallowing nervously, followed her. Rose petals were strewn across the grounds. They walked at an even distance from each other, until the wall of flickering screens grew to encompass everything — there was a particular screen which rose out of the ground, and was a little different from all the others: nothing but pure light came from it. It was the entrance to a sort of burrow, the edge of a cave. A peacock with oily, unwashed feathers and a simple t-shirt sat at a table covered with red cloth and a microphone atop, smiling widely inside the screen by the hole. There were many, in fact, in the various screens round the entrance, smiling and speaking with gestures, inviting him in. The silhouette of many women stood against the light inside, which had drawn further into the cave.

Neipas stirred, to step onwards; but the Midget's hand seized his. *"It would be a grave mistake,"* said he/she. *"For many have lost their way in this path. Many forgot themselves inside. No. Your path is another."*

Already, Neipas could distinguish — yonder, far beyond the lithe and seductive shapes — the thorny contours of the deeper cavern, which secreted sweet poisons and intoxicated the wanderer with indulgences and distractions, with unwavering certainties and maddened hatreds. The peacocks had in the meantime assumed demonic expressions, and hurled shouts and insults against Neipas.

"Come. If you are to see the truth, you must hover above these lights. Screens were not made to reveal; but to hide."

She/he pointed upward again. Neipas again looked up, but now with the dizziness of one who had stared into the sun. He closed his eyes, and saw behind his eyelids many flashes of undistinguished color hovering about in the diluted black. Once he opened them (*"see?"*) he saw, ensconced in the shadow between the screens, lenses; camera eyes immobile, nearly imperceptible. The lens were concave; that is, curved inward. They were immense. Peering deeply, Neipas was able to perceive gaps in their core; passages.

"If you are to see it, you must wear the legs of the learned and have clear eyes on your head."

"What do you mean?"

"Go to the Historian of Official Hist'ry. The scholar of giants. Then, come back to us."

Immersed in the headspace of dreams, though he was wide awake, he grasped the logic of the Midget's words and understood their meaning. Deep into the trance of self and its surroundings, Neipas returned to the End of History, where the oil lamps yet shone and cast flailing glimmers to the sketchy and soulless paintings, revealing their livid ugliness. He opened the curtains to the stairway; and, grabbing one shoe in each hand (he hadn't yet put them on his feet again) beat one against the other three times. The echoes shot through the stairs' corridor.

Out of the darkness below an enormous shape was delineated. It plunged titan into the hall, robes billowing forth, pouncing its long cane upon the hard floor.

"Who," clamored the Giant through his smiling mask, "disturbs the quietude of History? Ghosts must not be roused, dear guest. If you would please — make yourself known!"

The last few words were shouted in the manner of a threat. Neipas had slunk into hiding before the Historian's arrival. He had left his shoes where he had clapped them; and now he neared silently, sliding atop his socks. The blind Giant stood very quietly, with his head up, trying to hear.

"Dear guest, to be sure — you have come in the wrong door. There is no exit, and the entrance is on the opposite side."

Neipas was almost upon him. He neared very quietly... For a while there was total quietude. "Make yourself known, imbecile!" the Giant shouted thunderously, filling the halls of all the Museum.

It was then that Neipas took hold of the edge of the robe of parchment and pulled down with all his might, so that he felt himself drop through heights, vertigo soaring up through his throat. Neipas ran back and continued to pull the cloth. The Giant toppled at once, without weight; as though he simply disappeared. Beneath the robes lay a pair of wooden poles. And, once Neipas was able to take stock of himself again, he saw the truth of it, that the Giant History was no more than a pair of stilts and a mask.

Before he left, however, Neipas inspected the mask lying on the floor, bearing still its wide smile of upturned crescent. He found, beneath it, an old, rusty key; and stored it in his pocket.

He took the stilts and abandoned the robes, and came back to the fullness of the melody, into the humming angel. It made him want to sleep and yet, at the same time, he felt quite awake. The Midget awaited him.

"This was but a first step."

"I found a key. What's it open?"

"You will see. But not yet. Keep it."

Neipas contemplated the heights, in the darknesses of which the lens hid. He began to prepare the stilts and, in a conscious moment of lucidity, he looked into himself and considered amusingly his own state of soul, how calm he was in that particular situation.

"Will you help?" asked Neipas — to which the Midget lowered his/her head in affirmation.

Neipas set his feet upon the saliences of the wooden poles. And then, propelling himself forward with a swing, and with the Midget's surprisingly vigorous push, he was lifted into the air; and then all the dizziness in the world rushed into his senses. He tipped, and felt on the verge of falling from a great height — the horrid image of Magpie flashed before his eyes again, and he gave a shout which left him meek (the air had fled his throat in that first gasping moment) — and a vision of hallucinations unfolded before his eyes. As Neipas took giant steps forward the wall of infinite lights receded and was flattened beneath him. The screens extended before him like a flickering land of faces, beaming in a craze of alternating colors. They extended out, round, into a pitch-dark horizon beyond, and it was as if he suddenly stood over the planet. The eye of the lens came to meet him in mid-air; his body moved out of instinct — his feet left the stilts — for a moment he hovered in mid-air (his heart panged and shot adrenaline into his brain) — and stepped onto the interior of the lens.

He stood bent, wide-eyed and sweaty, feeling the great pulses of his heart filling his throat bloody. He seemed to be on a sort of platform over the globe of screens, with grated flooring, like those he'd imagine aloft over the stages of theatres. Beneath him, well beneath him, the Midget stood in a screen which showed nothing but black — he/she appeared miniscule, in fact invisible — and in his hand Neipas held the two, intertwined cords which had once held balloons; which descended like a rope into the chasm. Neipas asked himself, amid the chilling delirium, how they could have gotten there. The Midget, worlds below, held the other end.

When she/he spoke, it was as though the Midget was next to him. *"Pull us up."*

Neipas pulled up the cords, steady as a rope now they were fastened and intertwined, until the Midget stood beside him in fact.

III. Judean Tar

They beheld the vast world of lights beneath their feet, extending far beyond the reach of the eye into opaque black distances hung over horizons awash with gleam, like a myriad megalopolises joined together and replicated over and over again. The lights crammed into immense clusters, blinking out a carnival of color spectra at every speed. Often the glow moved in giant arteries flowing between the clusters; serpentine highways of raging glares; coiling circuits of blinking colors; frenzied rivers of light. And between these there were vast pools of utter blackness; in the sheen they obtained from the cities and highways of shine they appeared to possess a kind of immense viscosity.

"What is that?" Neipas asked the Midget.

"*That,*" said the Midget through her/his two voices, out the waning crescent of his/her frown, "*is a world abstracted, so that it looks fake to the ears. They call it 'the digital', for it's molded by human fingers.*

"*Do you see? Those lights are people.*"

In an intermediary layer, between them and the world of cities beneath, there hovered an extensive field, stretching over the lights. Though it was very far, Neipas could see it clearly, for the ground he stood on could be looked through, and it magnified the things below. The field was made of masks; avian masks, and it stretched also to infinitude. He had the impression of pigeons flying in mazes; labyrinths of circulating radiance.

"What are those?" Neipas asked the Midget.

"*Those,*" the Midget replied, "*are the inverse of the screens you saw. They are faces, through which the people below look beyond the screens. They call them 'hosts', because they house parasites.*

"*Do you see? All those faces put together — they made it arable land.*"

Neipas knitted his brow and twisted his beak with his hands.

"To plant what?"

And the Midget answered: "*Stories.*"

The viscous pools by the lights seemed to Neipas like a series of oil fields sleeping; with fires bursting from them, fading into them, propagating and shrinking across their infinity (flying...).

"*Civilizations rise from them; and the spread of its roots is defined by them. But the soil must be made fertile for this.*"

The lights surfed over that placid ocean... Seen through the transparency of the soil of upturned stares, the soil of masks, they seemed to weave gleaming threads in their wake, they seemed to make thin silk of their paths. The vast pools between their flight were as smooth as glass; their dark sheen possessed the consistency of glass, and the silky threads in their midst appeared suddenly like cracks in a shattered glass surface. But as he squinted, Neipas said to himself that perhaps there was nothing there after all — yes, he became more and more sure as he observed, as the lights leaned against his eye and throbbed inside his head; indeed, those were but lacunae between the threads of a massive web.

"Where's the spider?"

The Midget answered, *"Unbounded by place.*

"Its reflections are as numerous as the shards of its shattered web glass… every lacuna a pit where you are mirrored."

The lacunae seemed to him then like immense empty stages full of muted screams… cells…

"Your reflection wrapped in silk."

Now Neipas looked up onto the prospect before him. The space was made up of many dim compartments, silent with a silence permeated with the low whirring of machines. Little red lights blinked occultly from the blackness without distance at their side. Neipas stood on grated flooring, underneath which bulged the lenses, which magnified the worlds below.

"What is this?" Neipas asked the Midget. "Where are we?"

"This," replied the Midget, *"is a library of minds, a catalogue of vanities, and a market in which such things as may be found here are bought and sold; and many things besides.*

"From here the land beneath us is molded. Its fruits are culled and stored here.

"Come together. We will walk through it."

The Midget had wound the two intertwined cords round her/his staff, their many coils descending from the coarse lamp whose oval handle hooked the very top. Next, they entered the window before them, the label of which read,

PLOWING ROOM: *Something must have happened when they passed through the window. The layer of lights and the layer of masks, which had been below them, stood now before their eyes, and the grating of the floor-wall-screen expanded over the lenses so that they could see them still more clearly. Translucent, bionic hands reached down into the land of masks and revolved it at will, by force, with subtlety and without. Neipas beheld the process with horror. He could see it closer now. The masks were molded and disfigured into pulp and shard, so that the lights shined through like little crystals, like minerals from the depths of a wide cave. Coppers, tins, silvers, glass — many treasures seemed to glisten under the tilled soil. Holding their gaze forth, the Midget said, with his/her two voices:* "This is where they appropriate, this is where they dispossess. It is the beginning of a cycle, discernible throughout human hist'ry. Behold —

political realities begin with violence, though some violences are more subtle than others.

"This is the beginning of power. The process repeats in downward spirals; and we are nearing their end," *concluded the Midget, as she/he and Neipas walked through the compartments. They descended a stairwell, and entered a window with a label which read,*

FERTILIZING ROOM: *Here, Neipas witnessed something extraordinary. The darkness of the space shed and spilled in rains of droplets and powerful cascades down across the revolved fields, drenching them with a sort of tar, which was cast over again and again. A smell of fetid resin and defecation filled his nose. Below, the glistening crystals were covered. The bionic fingers tilled the oils, molding them back into faces as they hardened to wax. Facing the vision, the Midget spoke thus:* "This is where their exploitation begins. Political realities grow from fiction to fact by the force of battering and repetition. They are solidified and reality itself is pressed into its mold. Resistance is quelled by force or conniving — to such a degree that all become blind to alternatives. Look — a veil is placed over the eyes of the populace.

"They come to believe it all inevitable. Exploitation becomes a law of nature," *concluded the Midget, as he/she and Neipas walked through the compartments. They descended a stairwell, and entered a window with a label which read,*

SOWING ROOM: *Ropes, or threads, connected the eyes of every mask to the upper world, where Neipas stood beside the Midget. Flashes of powerful spotlight were thrown into the fields, spotlights with the form of various images and symbols, either motionless or succeeded by other images. They were accompanied by booming sounds of clapping. The glistening crystals were brought out, and shone brightly now through the contrasting black. Little spiders crawled on the ropes, crawled down by the millions into the emerging lights behind the masks, and little eggs were thrown haphazard across the soaked stages. Neipas looked awe-struck at the teeming plague streaming on the cords. Peering in closely, he saw that the effusing clapping was meant for each mask, particular to each; it came from the translucent bionic hands, who also had their thumbs up. The Midget told him:* "A gradual process of alienation takes shape. Their seeds are planted in you, so that you become miniatures of them. You are tricked. You come to worship them because you want to become like them, and grow to reach their perch. And you check your progress every day in the glass. Today's exploitation has your consent. Though indeed, no true consent is possible; after you are hollowed out of soul and filled up with restlessness, no true consent is possible. You too, have checked your progress in the glass. Have you not aspired to wear their mask? Have you not aspired to grow to their height?

"Look — their ideals seep into the populace," *concluded the Midget, as she/he and Neipas walked through the compartments. They descended a stairwell, and entered a window with a label which read,*

HARVESTING ROOM: *This space was still darker than before, and Neipas began to have the impression that this room was really the same as the last and the ones before it. Below, the lights were the dimmest they had been. Out of the tarred fields the ropes hauled up the masks, and from the masks hung mannequin bodies. They were placed standing, orderly, in the room, in the manner of a silent and motionless auditorium, all facing the same way, away from where they came. Now they were closer, it became clear that the masks and mannequins were wrapped up in strips of cloth, perhaps to protect them from the tar. These rags were unwrapped by machines, and presently the floor moved and the quiet mannequins along with it; taking them along also. Said the Midget:* "This is where they extract. Illegitimate power is rooted upon that supreme principle called 'violence'. When all fails, physical might is their resource, though there are many softer shades of might and many gradations of force beyond it. However, it matters to know how to direct their power. For this, they need knowledge — or rather, knowledge without understanding, which you call 'information'. They have always extracted from nature, and always they have extracted from human bodies. But this epoch has bred new crops. Behold, now they extract from human nature. See, how they cull the spirit from you?

"Lo, it is your greatest danger. The time of the last men is nigh, unless you stop it," *concluded the Midget, as he/she and Neipas walked through the compartments. They descended a stairwell, and entered a window with a label which read,*

IV. The Bridge

Neipas and the Midget stepped out — and for the first time Neipas could hear the sound of his foot under him; as if the very air had receded from his ears and now slowly returned. They stood upon a bridge. It was suspended over an abyss of unfathomable depths, indiscernible in their tremendous distance; it was made of glossy silicon and wobbled under their feet. His legs teetered slightly over the vibrating melody of voice and angelic glass flowing from the deep, all-pervading. A foul wind rose distinctly along with it, carrying a stench he had inhaled many times before in his comings and goings through the tower. As for sight, only vast contours, vestiges of immensitude and gigantic emptiness all around could be made out. Otherwise Neipas perceived nothing.

It was then that, as if blossoming from the remoteness of his senses, a glimmer sprouted yonder. It was at first like a droplet in still waters; which then rippled, and swelled, and became immense. Before them widened — and arose, and sank — a colossal, convex wall made of endless panes of mirror; an awesome, godly prism flashing with numberless twitches of motion. Behind it, and through it a titan, dazzling light swelled — and subsided. The throbbing sound poured airy and dreamlike, deep, soothing in its immensitude, overtaking all senses as it bulged; and the heavenly tones from below heightened to a quaking crescendo which overflowed the spirit in its expansive totality. In the mirrors — which lifted well above, and plunged well below the tower, and stretched in all directions till the stare lost them — Neipas saw what stood behind him.

He beheld the sight of sights; and it was incomprehensible.

As he was enveloped in gloom once more, Neipas heard his own breath shiver; the vision hovered in his eyes; their retina twitched and even when he shut them he could see it, gray and ghostly, like firm haze pressed to the blackness of his inward grimace.

"What was that?" he whispered, but even as his mind endeavored, his spirit already knew. By degrees he discerned the shape of the glass idol before him.

It was a face. A vast face; a face with one hundred eyes one hundred times multiplied; its eyes were the mirrors, propagating in deep infinitude among a void still greater. *"This is the Googol Machine,"* said the Midget, *"that feeds on dreams."*

Again the light sprouted and intensified, soft, warm, ethereal; and again Neipas saw, reflected in those eyes, what stood behind him.

He turned, and looked up; awe widened his lips and thinned his breath. He faced bewildered and overwhelmed the great wall from which they had emerged. Concave, it followed the immense arch drawn by its opposite, losing itself to the shadow of the horizons and the deep. It was entirely made of squares; and in those squares were people.

There were thousands, millions, billions of them. A chaos of sensations penetrated Neipas' dreamstate and assailed him as he attempted to decipher what he saw.

It was a sort of hive. The walls of each square were made of wax; each was as narrow and shallow as a cage. But all were glossy, glowing with the honey color which the mirrors spilled delicate upon them. On the yonder side they faced each their screen — for this was the reverse of the wall of screens Neipas had stood mesmerized before — and pressed their faces against the pigeon-faced wall tender, pecking gently with their lips; and on the nearer side, facing the mirrors, their eyes peered dazzled into the infinitude of reflections (squinting Neipas suddenly realized, horrified, that each person had at least six heads and twice as many legs; each of their twelve ears were plugged to flashing wires) as they leaned against the soft texture of the golden comb; and their faces pressed against each of the remaining four sides of the shallow cube to stare into the next person, who stared also into them.

Each one laughed; and each one cried; each one smiled and each one frowned. Each wore many clothes; each inhabited many masks. In them existed all feelings at once, and all of them existed in a great confusion of destabilized perception, an apocalypse of the senses roiling through the massive vertical crowds.

Again the light shrunk and faded out. Again all was suffused by the silence of the angelic chant. Without Neipas perceiving it, they had been walking slowly across the bridge making passage between the great hive and the fathomless Googol, thin among the vastness of the hollow tower, hanging amid a cosmic void. Neipas was taken by the Midget's hand as she/he led the way with his/her staff of winding strings; and when the mirrors came alight again he noticed the numberless wires, cords, tubes, great pipes and other bridges spanning the vast gap all above, below, and around, connecting the Hive to the Googol. Flashes ensued from the suspended threads now and then; mute beams of light coursed them fadedly in the darkness, nearly imperceptible because of their speeds. Above them could be just made out — beyond the density of wires and structures — the wide arch of the gap opening up against the starry sky. There was the glint of golden arches over the edge; and as Neipas glimpsed it, he realized they stood inside the Orchestra Pit.

Angels sang with putrid gusts. "Wait," Neipas pleaded softly. "What's... What's that, behind us?"

"Do you not recognize it?" asked the Midget; and indeed, Neipas did recognize it. He stared at the hive with much fear, for he feared finding himself somewhere inside; yet he couldn't stop staring.

"They know no rest and yet they sleep, are of one whole but exist along a thousand rifts within themselves, at once unbroken and shattered, ever split, ever anxious."

They bobbed their many heads and pecked their tender waxen walls as they stared at the winking channels before them, at the people next to them, and especially at the people below and above them; and at the eyes of the Googol Machine, where they could see themselves and everyone at once, confused, deformed, wonderful in the mishmash of swollen mass. Their boxes pulsed slow and golden, and in their fluid calmness resembled mechanical wombs; from each ensued a thread, plunging from each person's navel to the Googol Machine, and from the Machine to the navel.

Neipas and the Midget made their way across the bridge as it curved; it branched out multiple times but the Midget kept them steady in the onward march.

"Mary," said Neipas mutedly, barely feeling himself speak. "What's this smell..."

Replied the Midget, *"'Tis not yet time. You are not ready to know. And even when you know, still you will not be ready to feel. For none can ready to behold that which lies beneath this tower — none can behold its foundations without burning oneself. But the time will come when you will know."*

They crossed the bridge as the honey dawn flowered above them, entering the mountainous wall of mirrors through a lipped cleft (*"Come"*) — and

into a dark and twitching passage, at the the end of which a window opened, by a label which read,

THRESHING FLOOR: *There was no light whatsoever here. Mannequins stood orderly across the infinite and were taken along the moving floor. Many, many mechanical hands hovered from the web-like ceiling above them. As the mannequins passed, the machines seized each head one by one, plopped out the top, penetrated it, and took from inside an oval canister (an egg?) which was then placed on a rolling line to the next compartment. Neipas watched the immensity of the enterprise at work with much awe and bewilderment; thousands and thousands of machines undertook these operations in unison upon numberless plastic bodies as prolific as the spiders they had hosted, all in the blindness of the thickest gloom. The Midget said to him:* "Behold the future. Watch now their new power. The self has been a sanctuary since Humankind began; perhaps since Life began. There are many who fear they will know everything about you, they will be able to read you so far as to reach your very self, soul's chamber, sanctum sanctorum of the essence. Yet 'tis not how it will be.

Lo — what they want is to hollow the self; there is no longer *you, Neipas. Only a void to flood with their tailings. Have you not perceived it? Have you not noticed the plastic seeping into your senses? In truth, the last men are already among us. They hide behind glass. Whether they triumph,* **it is up to you, who live***,"* concluded the Midget, *as he/she and Neipas walked through the endless floor. (Imperceptibly) now they ascended a stairwell, and entered a window with a label which read,*

WINNOWING WELL: *The faint band of crimson radiating yonder from the window's slit lit up in a depth of red as they stepped in; the whole space glowed monochromatically with it. They climbed a spiral staircase going round a huge silo filled with machinery. Here, frantic machines twisted and opened the canister-eggs neatly as they flowed up the winding disassembly line; film rolls were produced from these canisters, which were then unfurled and hung on lines, or wires, which moved orderly toward the distant ceiling into the next compartment. The husks were discarded as the film inside was extracted* *and were let to fall upon the yawning floor, a large pit fitted with a powerful fan that shredded the rain of canisters upon contact. It cast a fierce gale, blowing the characteristic stench of the deep underground mixed with the odor of chemicals. Its force was overwhelming, the noise it produced overbearing, strange sound resembling the mechanical hawking of snipes. They rushed out through a side-door into a mirroring silo; and suddenly found themselves well above the ground — though they were perhaps still in the same place — and Neipas watched with astonishment as the stretched strips of film flowed upward by his eyes — and, inspecting them nearer, saw that the frames constituted only two forms of content. Negatives, on which was etched the number '0'; and positives, on which was displayed the number '1'. The phantasmagorical red glow shined through the transparent strips.*

The Midget, bathed in crimson beneath him, spoke: Many have tried to tame the soul — and those who succeeded derived from it their power. Yet they have all failed over the long term, in some ways less, in others more. Soon there will be a new paradigm. Those rising in power today say, 'there is no soul, there is no free will, all volition is illusory.' The masters of today say: 'There is no society.' The masters of tomorrow say: 'There is no individual.

There is only data. You are an aggregate of behaviors — you are but specks in the flow of information, and soon we will control the dam and hold all canals. You are events in time, you are dispersed through time, you are everywhere, you are nowhere, you are everyone, you are no one. There is no you anymore.' *Behaviors, events, data: to them, such words suffice to describe reality. The very stuff of your existence is residue... You are digital spores flying in their currents, to be molded along their tides. It matters not if this is true. They strive to make it true.* **Whether they succeed now depends on you, who live***," concluded the Midget as they were about to pass beyond a window by a label*

PROCESSING CATACOMB : *[FLASHFLASHFLASH] Here, the red glow was interspersed with powerful white flashes beaming on every few seconds. Long strips of film were carried on lines shooting all across at fast, constant speeds, while hasty machines, wielding lenses and blades, peered closely through each frame, then cut certain pieces off and rearranged them, placing one here, another there, distributing them throughout the crisscrossing lines above[FLASHFLASHFLASH], overseen by another set of machines which would clip frames off and superimpose one atop the other by the thousands or perhaps millions, forming dense bundles that were taken to the heights there — a glass globe lodged into the dark ceiling, round which rose terraces of circularly disposed seats, as one might expect to find in a classroom or stadium. Teams of scientists, engineers, and crowds of squalid microworkers in shapeless swimming masks sat before the electric glows of digital interfaces [FLASHFLASHFLASH] All arranged concentrically, they resembled a cult gathered about an idol; and over them stood arching apparatuses, massive, leaning over the* *glass globe — they were reminiscent of cranes with one huge lamp for an eye (Neipas thought they were enlargers). The wires took the superimposed frames of film, negatives and positives piled neatly in succession, and placed them before the globe, which seemed to bear water (the crimson glow swayed mystically across floating dapples) and under the arching apparatuses; the lines stopped — and a white beam swelled out of the eyes of the apparatuses, drowning the mollifying red glow, the concentric swimming masks, and the crisscrossing bands of film in light, making a powerfully blinking noise[FLASHFLASHFLASH]. Once unblinded, Neipas' twitching eyes gazed up beyond the marching strips of film crisscrossing — the globe rested far above him, and the priestly scientists, engineers and microworkers all sat upside down.*

The Midget told: The masters of the new age seek to frame all things in their corral. They pave all paths. No longer will there be a 'side of the road' — for they will have dug all woods and made abysses of them, so that to stray, is to fall. And they call the miming horizon above the flat line, full of white blinding suns, by flattering names like ' the future'.

This future will seduce you, it will hypnotize you, it will speak words like 'justice' and 'autonomy'. But these are but other masks. The same symbol may veil numberless meanings — so can one meaning take the shape of symbols innumerable. Beware — beyond all the glitter of their speech will throb the same aberration, the same cancer that is greed, said the Midget as she/he pushed open a sudden door in the crimson gloom with his/her staff, and they entered the

STORAGE VAULT : *Soft mechanical groans purred into the corridor between the tall black boxes; the red light blinkered calmly. Red, darkness, red, darkness... It was cold here. Neipas perceived the cold in his body and realized he had been completely senseless throughout the journey — that is, he had suffered no physical sensations up to now, when only a chill reverberated through his spine and exhaled from his skin, but had only felt immaterial and abstract, all emotions roiling mute in the level of the subconscious. Only now did he perceive he really was awake and he regained a sense of his physical form. Turning to his side, he opened one of the tall, glossy boxes — driven by some desire to know — and saw inside the storage tower, strips upon strips of film hanging limp from invisible ceilings, replicated in rows upon rows, on and on in such fashion to depths very far away. He closed the door, swallowed dry. He followed the Midget across the sterile corridor blinkering with the red glow and blips and flashings of light from the boxes, shivering slightly, and observing mystified the occult figure bearing his/her staff of winding cords.*

The Midget said to him as they approached the steps:

"You need to choose what kind of creatures human beings want to be. Will you be as they want — passive machines, behaving animals?

An era is about to pass. How will you emerge?" said she/he as they stepped through the hatch.

V. The Hive

Into focus gathered, by degrees, a chaotic image of endless cords joining, splitting, connecting in nodes and shooting off in all directions, all around them, pulsing the form of an all-surrounding net proliferating in a sudden vastness of space. Neipas looked at his feet; and saw himself hanging downward from the floor, with a sky of unending shards beneath his arched, faded pigeon visage of blooming and withering plume. His eyes rolled slowly into the canthus. At his side, the robed Midget looked on impassive, absolutely inscrutable behind her/his dejected mask of crescent frowns; his/her staff shot into the floor and seemed to fuse with the confusion of thin cables.

Behind them surged the almighty eyes of the Googol Machine. Towering and supreme, it lifted and expanded beyond discernible limits, colossal above them and abysmal under; plunging magisterially through the reflective floor, which glittered soft and rippled subtle, vaguely watery (Neipas felt his toes slightly damp). They were on the other side. The wall of eyes appeared transparent, and presented to Neipas his own image translucent, vague, ghostly, scattered and reproduced across all panes of the expansive surface; beyond, before them boomed the horrendous vision of the Hive, which came now in full view as the honey glow sprouted and grew, resonated and overwhelmed everything. The throbbing pushed inside him and stretched his spirit until it rendered; the cavernous glass and the cherubic song swelled into his notice as the volume of those sounds rose to godly heights — and subsided (Neipas' heart sighed and fluttered as the mighty pulse deflated). A tender vestige of music survived as the dazzle and the throb dissolved into nothingness. All came still.

Yonder through the eyes he looked. He could observe the Hive more closely, as if endowed with a zooming sense of sight capable of approaching far and retreating at will. The bridge they had walked on crossed the chasm and curved beneath them. Wires, pipes, ducts and all kinds of connecting structures spanned and multiplied throughout the caving openness of the abyss. A cord was projected from every chamber of the abysmal honeycomb — from each of the disjointed people inside, connecting each navel to each mirror-stare on the Googol. Once the cord plugged into its mirror, it would break into a thousand shoots on the other side, connect with thousands and millions of others and lose themselves in the intricate vastness of their multiplicity. Through these cords, thin as hair, dim flashes traveled with inhuman velocity: out the navel, into the mirror, and throughout the network in myriads.

"That, too, is a Market. Every one lives behind one's own stall," told the Midget as Neipas saw them inside the burrowed cells of the wax comb with their heads straining apart, gazing upon the flickering screens and ogling their neighbors, incessantly staring at the mirrors where they could contemplate their image and everyone else's, incessantly grooming themselves and incessantly smiling, incessantly laughing, incessantly pouting and crying and frowning and twittering, all the time slouching with 120 frenetic fingers and standing suddenly straight before the flash. *"Spectators and performers all. By these mirrors directed... Watch closer. Into the pith."* Comprehending only on a subconscious level, without knowing why Neipas gazed at the navel whence the cables shot. Beneath the multiple heads and above the multiple feet, in the crux, the core of each prismatic cell, inside each navel: therein lay a *child;* a miniature person, a baby almost, tucked in a fetal curl. Neglected, neither heads nor hands nor legs paid it heed. The legs moved everywhere and made the torso buoy as if on the surface of the sea; and the hands tended to the bird-masked walls relentlessly (between applauses and thumbs), shaping their waxen make, and their bloodshot stares stared constantly — at the walls, and through them. Incessantly writhing, cultivating effigies of themselves, those in the hive seemed to strain upward and melt slowly. *"Behold how they mold and shed, and strive to gain wings; behold how they market themselves."* The forgotten child in the navel secreted wax and honey through the wire coursing in light through the mirrors of the Googol...

"Is this to be the culmination of humankind? Lo, nigh is the time when humans must decide what kind of creatures they wish to be.............."

Behind them — through the porous wall — came the mesmerizing glow, filling all with tranquil amber, filling all with dazzling gold. Pulsed the sound... (the throbbing filled the universe with a glassy roar of angels and sucked it of all sound (and Neipas sensed it bulging into the Hive yonder as his eyes widened and his ears yawned agape) and perception).

"What's that?" (with latent discomfort he had turned around), asked Neipas after the omnipotent glare had receded. Out of the general blackness before him he discerned now a solid form, a glossy sheen blacker than the pervading gloom. It was something enormous — a monumental idol of pure obsidian. Its texture glinted vaguely with the flashes from the labyrinthine entanglement of cables rendering the air. As Neipas became accustomed to the darkness the jetting lights seemed to grow brighter, and gradually he could see more clearly; and he saw, standing out of some indefinite wall in the near distance, at least four such statues, interspaced at great lengths — they arched forth giantly, and from their dizzying pinnacles they overlooked the golden hive; the slow, collective, gargantuan twitches of which reflected darkly on each of the statues' opaque, glassy eye. That single eye was the only discernible feature of the great overarching apparatus, besides a coiled sort of horn protruding from its vague mouth. *"The Augur,"* explained the Midget, lifting her/his staff of winding cords. *"Silent mage and oracle."*

The expansive multiverse of cables and flashing wires all around them tended to conflate into the open horn-mouth of the singular Augurs, plunging to the interior of their massive, alien countenances. Neipas saw the surface of their eye-glass parted in an endlessly complex matrix: a mirror of jittery hive cells, wires and unending silica, beams of lights coursing them at indescribable speeds. *"With the glass it reads; with the lituus it listens."*

The golden light began again to swell; and before it overwhelmed and blinded everything in rippling honey glow, Neipas saw defined the obsidian giants replicated along a horizonless bare wall of wide convex shape, ingesting the infinite little flashes, staring without cease the Hive walls whose masks and people were being pleasantly covered with the recurrent pulse.

Again Neipas felt the acute sense of dream, the weightlessness of things; as if he were inside the Webwork, outside himself. Thin lines hung airy and taut, ethereal, everywhere; and everywhere was here... Little sparks by the trillions every second, lashing subdued and relentless through an omnipresent network of fiberglass. *"Behold the new fishers of men and women,"* remarked the Midget with a sweeping gesture of the staff.

"I feel really dizzy," said Neipas, wavering vaguely. Underneath him the floor was so clean and the reflection so immaculate that it looked nearly as real as he.

Don't look down then.

"What?"

The ground beneath you does not exist.

Neipas' body seemed to drop; and his heart soared and thrust into his throat, pushing out a terrorized scream as he flailed his legs; a roiling nausea overwhelmed his senses and he grabbed on with stiffening muscles, and when his fingers tightened toward the palm he found the Midget's hand already there, holding his. His expanding eye breathed in. They floated in a cosmos of neural streams, spread far, into the farthest reaches of existence, pulsing like veins in the hallowed body of some primordial deity, pulsing with the hues of light hanging in a deep blackness. All vibrated and tussled, the lights coursing through the glass arteries sang... Its sparks glimmered like stars in the infinitely branching currents. They flew thus; his toes pended downward toward the unfathomable, his beak agape with awe, and the Midget next to him drove them on by movements of his staff, which stretched to the unseen deep in endless coilings of cord, infinite, as if touching the mystery of the unexisting soil far under. Here and there among the streams flashed and dissipated shapes and figures: of himself and countless others flying in and out of arcane dimensions, incomprehensible.

Yonder, the Augurs hung in nothingness. Neipas and the Midget flew toward one of them, floated toward the gaping belly, open in the form of an oblong passage, which soon grew before their eyes; and before they entered Neipas read the inscription written in an arch over the lintel:

AVE AVE, DEUS SUNT!

*

Time here unfolded in a fluid continuity, melting towards — or away from — the senses; like time flowing in a dream. And as though Neipas were awakening, his perceptions gained solidity by degrees, emerging, surfacing from the submerged world into which he had imperceptibly swooned, back into an awareness of place. The first thing he noticed was the stench. Here — wherever he was now — the air was scentless, yet a dull putrefaction lodged in his brain in the very depth of his nose; retained (Neipas recollected it now) from the soaring gales of their flight.

The second thing he noticed was that his feet touched the ground.

VI. The Augurs

He was in a place which resembled the End of History in almost all respects. It looked about the same size; it was circular; it gave passage to a long, wide corridor which was very similar to the Museum, with arched entryways and glass-cases all over — except the glasses contained nothing, there were no artifacts strewn about, and the passages were all perfectly level, the path straight and stairless; nothing hung upon the walls, for the walls were sunk in the most complete blackness. Instead of the clock paintings of the End of History and the oil lamps underneath, here 12 Augurs jutted from the wall — they assumed the form of towering obsidian falcons, standing at attention in a pose of austere, ancient pagan deities. On each of their statuesque countenances, one eye was trained upon the center of the floor, the other up toward the center of the ceiling. Substituting the hourglass, a half-sphere bulged from ceiling and floor both. The half-spheres were made of glass also: and through them could be seen a nebulous motion of cloud-stuff, and nothing but. The deep end of the circle, where the Serpent with two ears would have been, was blocked by a brooding shadow, very dark; exuding the sensation of profound angst, of emptiness and danger, like an existential black hole out of which the angelic murmur still oozed, resonating in Neipas' nausea, as he came to. There was unease and curiosity in the sight of it. The sound of it trembled in Neipas' disorientation, his sense of self eddying yet about his body, trying to fixate itself at its center; he found himself with hand upon his knee, bent, and tremulous. The discomfort made him turn away from the shadowed deep of the hall and toward the corridor. Bit by bit, it gained definition in his view.

Meek crimson lights blinkered in and out of a darkness that was near total. The corridor extended indefinitely; he could not make out its end.

Neipas leaned closer. "Where are we?" he asked the Midget, who stood still at his side; he hadn't let go her/his hand.

"'Tis where they foretell the future."

Wrapped up in a gauzy shroud of mystique, Neipas opened his beak and breathed: "What future?"

Then, forgetting himself and his question in the immediate absorption of the moment, he perceived tepidly his already advancing step, pushing slowly in — goaded by the urge to draw himself away, away from the black hole in the limit of that inverse End of History increasingly affecting him. His eyes were gliding through the blinking lights the next instant *(The projection of their project, elucidated the Midget —)* They blinked rapidly and evenly across a lengthy extent, the extremity of which Neipas could not yet discern.

A single red lamp flashed always between two archways; the interval between each archway was always the same. Neipas crossed that interval once, twice, thrice, multiple times. Onward legs vanished in darkness and reappeared into deep crimson beneath his sight again and again. He didn't walk too fast; his pace was fixed by some unconscious imperative of motion, his haste checked by the impression that the elusive edge of the corridor yonder was curving slowly as he went on, passing under the vaulted entryways again, again, again.

"That which is past and that which is to come race to one another," continued the Midget. *"The present future's but a permanent becoming — of never being."*

Neipas bore a queasy sense of premonition and avoided looking down at him/her. Beyond the scarce, empty glass showcases of equal size, equally and evenly populating each sectioned hallway, the walls stretched and deepened, and seemed made of darkness; a darkness that would plunge and recede at the clip of the red lights blinking on and off, on and off, on and off — and a darkness which, persisting on the sides of his path, emanated a pulling aura, an eerie sensibility of desolation and unfathomable airiness, as of a spacious pit. It felt to Neipas like a gulfing sponge, exhaling abyssal airs; and he avoided looking at it as he moved. The whole platform felt suspended somehow, bordering on a precipice, as though it were a stage or a bridge.

"'Tis why you seek oblivion," said the Midget.

Despite everything, however — the walk was strangely soothing. There emerged a kind of steadiness through which he flowed, a continual torpor in which the effort of the march disappeared; his legs even seemed to vanish beneath the hollowed cloth of their trousers. His mind integrated itself into the rhythm of the glide, as it were. It was even entertaining. There was humor in the contemplation of his passing through the blipping glow, and to watch his reflection splashed crimson on the transparent glass of the empty showcases, and the mingling shades projected from him and swallowed by the plumbing blackness at turns — it amused him with a dulling, nonchalant, sort of intoxication. He floated, as his myriad reflections were floating.

"Are we almost there, you think?" asked Neipas of the Midget.

The horizon kept curling, it seemed — very slowly, progressing imperceptibly in the interval between red flashes. But now he was becoming aware of a shift in the way his mask was projected in shadows and reflected in glass; it was strange. From the corner of his eye, he saw himself vaguely multiplied in mirrored images, and as he passed one and another by in succession, he noticed that the crimson form of his moving body materialized more weakly at every blip, progressively fading — until it nearly disappeared — then abruptly regaining vividness again. He also perceived a bizarre mismatch between his movements and their reflection on the translucent panes; the reflections acted a bit before he did, somehow. He was out of tune. This realization induced him to try to match the pace, and for a while the movement of the body replicated through successive glass surfaces, and the movement of the legs beneath him, locked in sync. [......] But he was becoming anxious. His sense of space was uncanny, it felt dislodged. There was the looping dissolution without vanishing of his unendingly succeeding repetitions among the crimson pulse, and he still couldn't see the end of the corridor; by and by he realized that his heart fluttered with the rhythm of the quick lights, in palpitations edging toward panic; simultaneously, the heart accompanied the flurry of the reflections' loss of vitality — and sudden jolt; he felt the strange sensation of recurrence sweeping over him over and over again. He traversed those stages between two incertitudes, always in a state of anticipation, always one step beyond himself, always expecting to find something just over the bending end; now it curved fully, and perhaps it would bend enough to find him, he still hoped — vainly. Finally the vague shadows of his motion, rolling on like succeeding waves of frail gloom upon the red floors, began to slow. The mismatch between image and reality grew.

He slowed down — slowed down...

Neipas stopped — yet the sensation of movement continued. The red glow blinked across the infinite. As though he himself was spreading into the hollow glass boxes, his unthinking mind witnessed its reflections escape from the ghostly surfaces of glass, as it were, and hover about the space twitching continually in its longevity of red and black. Fragments of the body — a leg, an arm, an ear, a mandible, a nape — flashed in and out of existence in the crepuscular gaps where the lights intersect and enter one another. Fragments of people were strewn about the air; half-beings composed of flicker, with the substance of a flash, spawned in the instant the light flares and disappeared the moment it vanishes — existences replenished by electricity this, and even the bare skin of the torsoless limbs beneath the cloth and the radiating bones underneath the skin sometimes flashed in the accelerating spectacle of phantasms. Neipas had had the impression of spotting the fragments as he trod, but they always disappeared just at the moment he opened his own eyes from their own blink, and in his eagerness to relieve himself of that nightmare ride he simply kept walking... Now he wondered if those flashing bits were his own or not; he had the impression of seeing (Magpie? Eva?) others walking along the receding corridor but (Orenda...?) could never be sure. His eyes winked and twitched repeatedly.

Now he closed them; he covered his eyes with his hands. He felt the oppression of wide dispersion and sensed himself broken and unexisting. For a while the fragments twitched behind his eyelids and the vestige of surrounding motion assailed him still. But it halted.

All of existence was felt to vanish then, and silence fell upon him, and permeated his detached senses.

Almost involuntarily he had turned around, away from the direction he had been heading. He no longer knew why he was there; if he had ever known. The sensation of hunger returned, and he thought of checking his pocket for Janu's sandwich, which had been eaten; in the gesture of looking for it he removed his hands — his eyes saw.

Neipas faced the spiritless gloom of the inverse End of History. The Midget stood before him; not at his side. She/he looked as though he/she hadn't moved, and Neipas hadn't advanced one step beyond the threshold. The whole time he thought the Midget had been at his side; though indeed, his/her reflection had never been projected on the glass panes of the empty showcases.

Turning only his head, Neipas saw, through the corner of his eye, that the deep end of the corridor was again flat and out of reach.

(Matter moves through space — and time, through matter. Do they not?)

Brought to pains in the certainty of his own lunacy, Neipas, inexplicably, took a few steps backwards, again immediately mired in the serial flush of red-black blink. He never quit facing the End of History as he drew away now. Again through the corner of his sight he glimpsed the reflections losing vitality at each beat, then suddenly jolting once more into vividness, as he moved in reverse. Pixelated fractions of people snapped into being and vanished with the light. Then the archway came over him, the lights went out; and the next moment, the light flashing on again, he saw himself back before the End of History's circular hall, as if teleported there (the shrinking Augurs were suddenly giant again). He tried again, stepping backward, retreating away from it; and as soon as he stepped beneath the arch, he was again before it. Again he tried, much more slowly now, with the reversed advance of his echoed motion — winking, glimmering in the glass panes of hollow boxes — parted from himself in growing asynchrony; slowly again he stopped, and now with eyes wide open he beheld how the corridor, at each blink, moved, and his reflections, too, kept moving in loops, discontinued from himself. The corridor jumped little by little at each flash; until he stood again at the threshold before the hall. Neipas was receding forward through an unending recurrence of progression — the very same progress mimicked in fakery across unlimited loops. He pleaded to the Midget with his eyes, but the Midget said nothing. One final time then, in a rage of madness, he moved backwards, at a run now — nothing. The inverse End of History, retreating, snapped again suddenly before his eyes. Beyond the 2nd archway he could not go. The first two archways marked the essential frame of his action: everything beyond it was but repetition and simulacra. The rest was unattainable. The end of the corridor was out of reach (whatever that end was, though Neipas cared not for it; he wanted to escape, not to attain); forever out of reach.

Crouching, Neipas covered face, mask and view once more in his hands. His eyes were shut tight behind his fingers. He heard the feathers rustling on his shaking head like something apart from him, though not very far, sounding through an electric filter; as though they were a turbid pack of pigeons breaking away into flight, and then, turning the distance, rushing in a frenzy of beating wings through him.

"*Time rushes in gales, torrents, thunder. 'Tis the river upon which life roams. To blunt life, one must dam its flow — and numb the spirit thereby. Is it not the compression of time which they seek? Here's oblivion — in time's dissolution. And there is no oblivion like that of the machine, which cannot sleep; which can't but dream.*

You're held stagnant in the dam, the constant present, into which the past continually flows — yet you are spilling through the floodgates — draining into the abyss," said the Midget and Neipas, opening his eyes to look at her/him, found himself already standing — the Midget under him, pointing with his/her staff to the darkness at the deep of the circular hall, the inverse End of History, where the Serpent would have been. *"Motionlessly rushing — within the machine's bounds, thou art.*

Many have tried to crush the self — they've learned and would rather you forsake it, to roam without cease in relentless and unceasing becoming, driven by anxious winds."

Neipas winced and, turning his breathless stare to the Midget, grimaced wonderingly. There was something like the feeling of wax squeezed out of the pores of his incorporeal skin as they puckered into deepening frowns.

"What?" the question left the beak jutting from his slowly melting plumage, but Neipas had, in his torpid discernment amid the dreamlike succession of events, understood. One gliding step after another took him into the proximity of the shadow wall; out of which the angelic hum serenaded still, beautiful, hypnotic, oppressive, totalizing. It instilled a pendulous and nauseating wobble into his floating sense of self. And as he entered the deep gloom the crimson colors followed him, so that the darkness dissolved before his advance; and he could see now, through them, the stark outlines of the obscure wall... There was, like in the End of History, an immense pane of glass — one rather than two; a window. It was framed by an immense stone relief: the image of a Lion's maw, a mouth clutching and framing the rounding Serpent that eats itself; the Serpent circled the glass. The window, lodged broadly between its stone scales, was also a mirror; it was filled with water on the other side, water clear, pure, streaked with undulating, slightly palpitating moonshine, spilling dappled gleam onto the End of History's twin hall, mingling with the hazy fumes of its spherical center.

"Do you see the horizon? Lo, a day shall come when all centuries dissolve in ash.

Yet will you let the generations run their course — or will you rob all future life by your folly?

Fear not. Look," spoke the Midget's cryptic voices behind Neipas, the crimson blink washing away the gloom and swinging back, tipsy, as it mingled with the lunar shimmer of the waters. Grains of sand whirled by in the manner of a languid day's snow; fish that were either red or were mantled in red colors flew among the serpentine sway. Neipas watched, mesmerized. A sort of ticklish sensibility blew upon his nape; he felt the Augurs eying him intensely with their perpetual stares, into their computing, irrational minds. He was again conscious of his hunger; again he thought of kind Janu, who had thought of him and fed him.

His outstretched fingers, the palm of his hand pressed the glass. Its surface was lightly coated with musty vapor; his hand swept across the damp film, very slowly, as his brow furrowed, too, very slowly, upon the strange sight unfolding before his eyes. The sweeping motion of his hand left no sweeping mark in its wake. It was another picture of discontinuity; lacunae between the fingerprints, as if they'd been pressed on separately in a successive rhythm of lifting and laying. A misshapen palm appeared spilling over the surface, and the five fingers became fifty fingers as they brushed across the mirror through creeping time. The mark looked like a screaming mouth under many eyes; or a wide flame hovering over firewood; or a fanning tail widened over a peacock. Through the blots, Neipas could see, in a perfectly mirrored image, the very same place where he stood; he saw his back facing a window similar, or equal to the one he stood before now — the Midget's mask stared directly into him.

Neipas leaned closer to the (*click!*) waters made red by the winking lights. He saw on their vertical surface his own nearing mask; glass-bound, it was distorted and gathered in the shimmering sway of their moonlit streaks. Neipas' wits again scattered; now into the photons of the crimson lamps. His consciousness dispersed in the hypnosis of the liquid mirror reflecting into remote depths.

A river valley of quiet trees and village-dotted fields lengthened from the crimson glass; disappeared in the dappled gloom; and appeared again; for a moment he thought he saw behind him (his parents, flashing on and off, on, and off)... —

The black crater of his red eye amplified like a gaping maw vacuuming all things.

Wind lifted and roused the fields in a growing flurry of sand-crumbs. The river in the valley sped; from the cavernous distance floated a strange, featureless silhouette, nearing him slowly. It came from the horizon, it had been the horizon. Meanwhile the lights blinkered,

on — off.
red — black.
red — black.
red —
       black.
(tick — tock).

A sudden dread gripped his heart and Neipas stepped back, already falling; the floor behind him was receding and the corridor stumbling into a steep cascade; he felt himself diminish as he regressed and out of his nostrils blasted the yell of a frightened child, his lips parted uncontrollably in a muted scream of horror and his eyes enlarged in convulsions upon the deepening mirror as it (the silhouette grew in size and rammed against the glass which) shattered and let the waters burst out in a violent torrent rushing toward the yonder deep, thundering toward the half-sphere which had ebbed afar and broke now wrathfully with coughs of ash, ash overwhelming everything; and the pouring waters thrust into it and rushed into Neipas' gaped mouth and open eyes and into every pore of his body as he fell backwards —

"Neipas".

He came to. Though his legs teetered and his feet wavered in their contact with the ground, Neipas hadn't fallen; he held on to the Midget's staff standing immobile and secure, with but the hanging oil lamp clanking lightly at the top. His throat and his senses still shook with the impact of that real, horrendous dread.

For a long time he stood upon tremulous feet. He had seen the face of the silhouette uncovered and clear as it beat against the glass. The face was lifeless; as if it belonged to a corpse. The face was Janu's; Neipas had the distinct impression that it was his, though now he second-guessed his perceptions in his tremendous confusion and shock.

Neipas took — but who can say how long time takes to flow between the edges of the mind? — and after those moments had come to pass the Midget whispered, her/his double voice coursing thus through his/her inscrutable visage:

"Come. We stand near the center of the path."

The red lights had ceased blinking. The corridor was now aglow in the lunar shine flowing from the aquatic window; the end of it revealed itself. It was the counterpart of the circular hall upon which Neipas and the Midget stood, another copy of the End of History, bearing, at its depth, the relief of a Lion's face; from whose stone cheeks fell a mane, like a tattered curtain, draping a circular entryway.

They walked into the straight corridor; and would move under 13 archways, through 12 passages, to get to the yonder Lion. Throughout, Neipas felt somewhere in himself — distantly, vague — the impression of shivering, though he was not cold. By and by he stopped, and knew instinctively that it was so; but it was not only he that trembled, the inconstant ground upon which his feet lay wobbled too, and so did the structure underneath the ground, which seemed to him then like a great composition of brittle twigs, a giant built upon sand, about to slide off. Inhaling a tremulous sigh, holding firmer to the Midget's hand, he carried on walking with eyes half-closed.

But before the trek was ended, a vague curiosity compelled him to look sideways to the mysterious walls, which had shed their darkness cloak; they were naked walls, half in shade still, lined up with simple doors. Absentmindedly, Neipas observed them as he passed; and then, remembering the Museum, he opened one of the doors and peeked inside.

There were piles upon piles of mannequins, stretching on in blinking red lights and into the deep shadow of unperceivable distances.

VII. *The Book*

The stairway bent outward in a long curve along interminable steps. Neipas' legs climbed, its muscles tightened and slackened over the way aloft, unnoticed by the head, separate, wholly dismembered from the mind. They climbed through the thickets of hanging ribbon, the dense atmosphere somewhat damp and slimy — endlessly thin layers of celluloid rubbed on the skin of his neck — as if digging through the lion's humid mane into the furthermost darknesses of its cavernous spirit. The Midget's oil lamp, unlit, perched atop the staff, swayed with gentle taps by his ear.

They emerged into a sort of antechamber steeped in gloom (as were all spaces through which they had traversed) — with but feeble, vermilion lamps over the doors, hanging still and spectral. The strip-curtained entrance through which they stepped was but one of twelve replicated in a half-circle along the black wall. In the center there opened a downward staircase. In front of it was a rectangular passage, shimmering dimly — the Midget led Neipas to it first.

The very sound of his steps perished upon the invisible floor. His stare widened, the lids of his eyes drew far apart, slowly, as they entered; and the blackness of the iris became an aperture absorbing the sinking view, gaping with the deepening awe of its texture.

They stood over a book. It was a giant book, an open book whose gutter was as deep as a valley and the black pages as wide as savannas in the night, rising midway like immense hills and curving in like waves, the tip of each cosmic sheet meeting in a swooping sky; two pages perpetually on the verge of turning. They stretched on, unending, like a parted sea whose tide froze in the motion of returning; like an iconized heart, like the cupped wings of a swan blooming from a quiet lake. The seam ascended in an arch across the galactic ceiling. It was a universe of vellum bounds; glimmering an infinitude of stars, a text which, through a squint of the naked eye, seemed composed of digits or musical notes. The starry script kept crawling, seeping up the pages very slowly; like the rotations of celestial shimmer. All of it was written with light projected from the core between the pages — the center of the gutter afar, opening like an immense, beam-shedding vulva.

Said the Midget through her/his inscrutable tragic visage, *"Here's the Book of Masks."*

(The Book of Masks?) They stood on a type of theatre box, in a sort of convex pod over a ridge which held the lower edge of the Book fixed under. Neipas perched like a mountain over the sweeping tome; like a bird surveying a wondrous landscape; like bewildered eyes over cryptic pages.

A binocular telescope was perched by his ribs (he had not noticed it while he grappled with the awing nature of the lettered vale spreading on all sides). Through its lenses he could study the contents of those titanic pages; for such pages had been made for machines to read, and human sight needed to dive through multiple layers of glass and mirror to discern their meaning. He leaned in against the instrument (he had to stoop in order to look through, though fortunately there was a velvet cushion for his knees under there); and with spirit numbed in sways of mystic wonder he understood that the Book was a list of people; and perceived at once its incomprehensible complexity. On it were billions upon billions of names, numbers, facts, desires — secrets. The deep mirror of all living upon the Earth.

As Neipas drew back confusedly, he noticed two objects on either side of the convex platform. On one side of the scope rose a rectangular glass, vertically disposed — a black mirror affixed to a tripod. On the other was a similar surface placed horizontally, and from it beamed red numbers [ID000008].

From the tall mirror the following text was emitted:

```
#: ID000008
NAME: NEO JADE PIGEON [test]
DATE OF BIRTH: UNKNOWN
VITAL STATUS: ALIVE
DATE OF DEATH: TBA
EMPLOYMENT HISTORY:
— Freelance Contractor, Cleaning
    Services (Janitor)              @ EDEN SOLUTIONS
— Freelance Contractor, Labor
    Supervisor                     @ EDEN SOLUTIONS
— Freelance Contractor, Cleaning
    Services (Janitor)             @ EDEN SOLUTIONS
— Storefront Salesman             @ TERASOFT INC.
                                  (Via Sacra 68 retail)
— Marksman (Sharpshooter,
    Sniper), Sgt.         @ COLUMBIDAE ARMY, REX BATALLION
```

```
    — Rifleman, Private              @ COLUMBIDAE ARMY, BOVIDAE
SQUAD 110
    — Student                              @ 100011010010
    LIKES:
    — Hallucinogenics
    — Medicine
    — Spiced food
    — ? 00
    SEXUAL ORIENTATION: TBA
```

FEEDING HABITS: [this was the bottom of the page; with a rub of the finger the text scrolled down and across Neipas' eyes flowed streams of disjointed information]

Neipas realized his *I* was glowing. Upon its black surface a circle (not fully formed) coiled endlessly upon itself, chasing its own tail; his finger touched it, and he was at last able to access its digitized contents. The machine seemed to be drawing energy from this place.

With the image of Janu's carcass ramming against the glass yet impressed in his general sensation of experience, he searched for his page on the Maskbook and, seeing its number, he typed it on the horizontally-placed device by his side; and thereby beheld numbly as the telescope turned. The vertically-disposed screen on the other side of the box showed him Janu's information now — his full name, date of birth, employment history, likes, dislikes, familial affiliations, movies watched, webpages read[...]

VITAL STATUS: ALIVE, Neipas read with relief; then, unconsciously, with mechanical fingers he typed Magpie(whose final moment replayed ceaselessly in his soul)'s page number after he checked it in his *I*.

The telescope pivoted in the quietness of astral blackness — zooming in at a section of the Book headed ID161900.

He began to scrutinize its contents through the lens. Magpie's section, like Janu's, recorded many things: her name, birthday, likes/dislikes, fears, desires, an infinite plethora of attributes. The little dots of light upon the dark vellum clustered to form images — unfathomable collages of photographs replicated in orderly rows, and still frames of records, and phonic scripts expressing sound — of voices, of laughters, of all manner of utterances — through symbols he did not understand. That section of the Book alone, but a speck among the starry constellation of its page, seemed interminable in the amount of information it contained. For fear of losing himself Neipas stuck to the top (Magpie's numbered chapter name), and saw, for instance, that under **MEDICAL CONDITIONS** were listed **Asthma, Gastric Reflux** and others; that under **DESIRES(professional)** was written **Become a biologist/related** (which Neipas had never suspected — and there was a long list besides) and under **INTERESTS/HOBBIES** such things as **Nature, Plants, The Outdoors**. Under **VITAL STATUS** he read the word **Alive.**

Perturbed by this incongruity ([how can it be] he thought) Neipas typed another number on the horizontal panel and roused the scope to move once more. He sought Cesar and saw that his **VITAL STATUS** was in fact **Deceased** — and vaguely concluded that, perhaps, Magpie's status simply hadn't been updated.

He typed another number.

"Beware," warned the Midget, *"for it is easy to lose oneself in these pages. They were composed for machines... and they turn seekers into machines."*

But Neipas was too strongly compelled by curiosity and too vulnerable to its seductive power in his present state of psychic suspension. He explored the Book ravenously. He discovered deeply held secrets of people known and unknown to him; secrets unknown even to them. He saw that even people who had never made a Page in the Maskbook had a Chapter in the Book of Masks — his mother **[Deceased]** and his father **[Mentally Incapacitated / Physically Incapacitated / BY —]**; he found that **ORASSAP** was **DECEASED**. Neipas discovered that he, Cesar, and even (to his shock) Edazima and his sister took nude selfies; and so did **EVA,** some of which he had never seen (or at least didn't remember). And upon seeing her nudes, old and recent, upon the open page, abreast of the lifting tide of all other printed souls, he started in a maniacal search **[NAME: Eva AGE 26 VITAL STATUS Alive BIRTHDAY LIKES DISLI010010010000]** to find out whomever she had sent those photos of her body to through her list of **AFFILIATIONS[........ / — ID 343456 (friends) / — ID431999 (relationship) / — ID488009(friends) .... — ID0210203(.) ....]**, digging crazily through the bifurcations of that boundless array of privacies... And he found his stare over her list of **DESIRES(personal),** studying them idly — ever more intrigued as the secret whisperings of her innermost life were revealed to him — until he read (further down) **become a mother.**

(What?) His eyes lifted from the glassy scopes, feeling a knot of unease in his throat, fastened with the stranglehold of all that information. He felt enveloped by the whole mechanical, magic apparatus, effused everywhere, in his very marrow...

"It's nonsense this," mumbled Neipas. "I don't get it."

Spoke the Midget: *"Never has a generation been more lonely. And never have the lonely been so alienated from their selves. Sliced into little boxes and in a prison away from the self, looking at oneself from the outside, this generation has no recourse but the black mirror into which they whisper all its secret ails... But they listen behind light cast from the glass, and the more you tell them, the more they know, and the more they know, the further they can control you. The more they can herd you into their planned future."*

"But what I read it's — not everything's right," Neipas said and indeed, even in his own Page/Chapter (which he too had scoured) there were mistakes both slight and large.

*"The Googol, the Augurs are not perfect, nor will they ever be. They are machines. They can only read machines with exactitude, **and not unless you have become machines yourselves will they ever succeed."***

Neipas gazed wistfully the bizarre, tunneling prospect; standing very still in his own roiling feeling of vertigo, waiting for the nausea now billowing through him to pass.

Once it did (how much longer after was impossible to tell) he heard: *"Come, we are almost at an end."*

They left. The oil lamp atop the Midget's staff clinked softly in Neipas' head as they descended the stairs in the center of the antechamber. At the bottom was another dark corridor, ending in a slender arch of pointy tip, with a little light.

This corridor was flanked by waist-high tabletops running across its whole length; burrowed in them were rows upon rows of slightly different pigeon-face molds.

VIII. Mammon

They left through the slender arch of triangular tip and Neipas felt as if he were traversing great distances with his stride. Having crossed the tight gloom of the arch he found himself staring at a giant head.

It hovered well above him; hanging like an immense corbel supporting a balcony extending from a wall made of shadow — where a steam-enveloped light smoked tepid through a golden, smile/horn-shaped slit. Only half of the head could be seen. From between two deep pits — the nostrils — descended in a dramatic inward curve the folding cleft sinking into a monstrously wide, lipless mouth; the chin beneath protruded, then rounded down into a concave wall which bowed in all the way to the floor. And the half-head's mouth had a tongue; it was made of some kind of paper and it fell, like a long scroll, into a hole burrowed in the core of the veiny grounds — the floor altogether choked with a mess of tubes and wires emerging from that hole, and spread all about. This tongue rolled into the mouth infinitely; as it slid up between the ground and the colossal slit, the tongue was subjected to taste flashes of shimmer, bursting upon it with demonic vigor and leaving characters printed on it.

This intense shimmer (Neipas turned to face the path from which they'd come; the pinched ridge of his beak pressed shadows against the manufactured air and a thousand clones of himself spilled and hung back in the motion), swelling and bursting upon the paper tongue, surfaced from the fold of the Book of Masks' joined edges — which, on the outside, formed a long cleft parting the top of a titanic head. Here was the suspended head's missing half. Tilted downward, it sank into the floor; the ridge of the nose emerged from it, and the wings of the nose pressed spread against it as if sniffing the chrome soil. The ridge lifted between two closed, colossal, slumbering eyes. The lustrous, browless forehead rounded into the flashing cleft ascending in a long arch, perfectly dividing two halves of a crown cascading sideways — the arching covers of the Book of Masks' opened pages.

All the paths they'd crossed extended from the back of this head; and they had finally emerged from the indentation on the tip of the dipping nose (under the scrolling tongue, the protuberant hanging chin above was likewise clefted, triangular).

"Whose head is this?" Neipas heard himself ask.

"This," answered the Midget with both voices, *"is Mammon.*

Mammon their god, Mammon their mirror. Mammon the hoarder, the thief conjuring from the summits and the deep. Eater of lives. Destroyer of worlds. With glee it bestows; with indifference it ruins. Amoral, it aspires to consume all things... It requires no less than the sacrifice of the entire world, for the benefit of its own cravings and delusions.

Mammon is lust. Mammon is gluttony. Mammon is greed. It is the foundation of all vices — to take from the other, to the detriment of the other. Even the noblest of hearts chills at its touch. It takes with smiles of gold, it whispers to the soul with its teeth — as it devours. All but its desires — are but abstractions and mere dreams.

Behold — the deity remaking the world in its image! In truth, Neipas, all their gods are but masks of Mammon. Maker of the age, it is... All today live inside its head."

Neipas listened with his heart, with lips sealed and mind silent. He reclined into the returning tranquility of his spirit (the unfeeling sense of unreality had meanwhile reemerged) and calmly focused his gaze.

Turning to the ascending ribbon, wide and alighting with glyphs, Neipas asked, "And this paper?"

Replied she/he, pointing staff to the drawing tongue: *"'Tis the Book of Profits — Oracles' scroll. The script behind the End of History. Money... With it they can predict the future. And they can predict the future because they can **will** it. Such is the nature of power.*

Above there, sits their Temple," the Midget pursued, lifting the staff higher still, *"House of Mammon. This scroll is the writ undergirding their power, upon it rises their mountain. It is the foundation of this very tower. All the gold, all the glass, they are but facades; and even beyond the cement and the iron, this place is built of paper.*

Its foundations are steeped in ink, they lie in a bony darkness, they bleed shadows... But you will come to know, what spreads under your feet."

Neipas, stepping closer, saw that the scrolling tongue was weighty, thick, textured, letterpress printed, peppered with a glyphic serif type and an off-white color, soaked with light; and all its letters were numbers...

Neipas beheld the polished idol standing before and behind him, in front and above. Powerful flashes emerged and bloomed from the top of Mammon's head to burst upon the rising Book of Profits; but there were also faint glints palpitating upon the smooth surface of its unburied cheek, flickering vague golden tints, and forming strange characters, letters, words.

He began to absorb now the rest of the space, isolating it from the preeminent head. On either flank, jutting from both walls — somehow shaded — arose the bust of a cherub. Both cherubim shimmered vacantly, brass-like; enormous, as were all things in this peak of the world. Each statue had four heads. On the left (as he faced Mammon's chin aloft, away from Mammon's forehead on the ground), the Cherub's neck sprouted first the head of a Peacock, then a Stag and an Ox, and above them an Eagle. Beneath its neck was transparent glass — worn like a medallion — and behind it pressed thick sand, or silt; or clay.

From the Cherub on the right jutted first the head of a Pelican, then a Horse and a Pigeon, and, above them, a Lion. The transparent glass medallion in its breast revealed a column of wax; it palpitated with glints of flame, casting particular shapes into the room where they stood; and those shapes formed words. Neipas tried to read them on the surface of the clay opposite. Many of the words — and even many of the symbols which formed them — were incomprehensible to him. They were inconstant, and shivered. Slow drips of melted wax oozed over the symbols; but among them he thought he discerned a familiar maxim. It palpitated behind the wax and began to shine through the glyphs vividly.

He stepped closer.

"'Tis the Candle of Man," spoke the Midget. *"Their values shine through it, in it shines the value they ascribe to all things. It is the sum of all values they have created thus*

far. It worships Mammon. 'Tis another of its many incarnations.

For too long has the Human flame burnt in its bosom, coursed down its wick," she/he continued. *"It shall soon consume itself, lest we supplant the fuel whence it survives."*

Staring widely at the tower of ancestral wax, Neipas discerned words in its fabric, which palpitated with the meaning *THOU SHALT* gushing into this glossy sepulchral chamber of mechanical dark chrome and wondrous glow... From the candle's base propagated a rushing tide (motionless) of molten wax. Obscure figures, whose faces Neipas couldn't well see, scooped it up with shovels; and a Pelican paraded round the great cylinder waving a thurible and filling the great hall with fume, accompanied by a Peacock (his acolyte) who waved ceremoniously, like a fan from side to side, a wad of bills. Squinting, and sharpening his ear, Neipas saw, and heard, a waterfall beyond a gate, far in the distance of the hall.

His foot lifted squelchy from the ground. Staring deeply into it, he gazed his shoes half-sunk in the black floor, which was covered not only in darkness; it was also soaked in a gooey substance of petroleum. Pipes and wires bulged out of it and sneaked across in all directions. There stood barrels oozing inky, viscous matter, and tall black boxes messily arranged. Crates, sacks, casks were stored here and there, and ropes wound atop and between them, among hooks, knives, weapons, musical instruments and various props veiled and unveiled with curtain and plastic, all steeped in tar. Yonder, in the large concave burrow beneath Mammon's chin, hung darkly a whole wall of avian masks — worn on Mammon's neck, as it were.

Now his ear took stock of the sounds within; as if sound had been drawn back to his senses by the present attention of his eyes. First there was a buzzing, like the droning of flies. Then that buzz grew to resemble the zap of flowing electricity and motor spurts, and with the sound Neipas noticed the slight tremble of the scattered black boxes and the discreet pipes running all over.

"Are these the backup generators?"

"Yes. They drink the burning nectar of the underworld. It must keep flowing, it must keep burning, for these machines to live their deaths. All this you've seen upon this trail cannot stir without such fluids."

...and from under the powerful belch of combusting oil emerged a deeper sound; a resounding swell, a gigantic pulse. It made all things tremble... It throbbed mighty behind them — beyond the Eagle Cherub with the medallion of clay.

There was a sort of porthole amid and between the Cherub's four heads. Stairs — curving toward and then away from the statues to accommodate their shape — led to the balcony over Mammon's nostrils.

Neipas and the Midget climbed the steps on the right side of the room, by the Candle, following its height. The stairway flattened into a landing about midway through.

He looked through the porthole at the nexus between the Lion, the Pigeon, the Horse, and the Pelican; and he saw fire. An ungodly column of smoke spouting and pulsing into the sacral hall forming a great arch round the Candle; a pillar of inky fume serpentining from the deep of a wide basin of wax, indeed so vast in width as to resemble a basin, a giant's chalice, on the bottom of which an immense pool of colorless fluid — vaguely tinted red — palpitated under a grand, multicolored flame twitching aloft, as if with open arms and supplications toward the unseen ceiling (*"The human flame,"* said the Midget).

...they resumed the climb until the staircase flattened again, mere steps from the balcony. There was another porthole there — through which could be seen another set of steps: of immaculate ivory, between walls draped in velvet and lit by braziers.

(But the throb pulsed from behind him. It had grown; and swelled to fill his soporific breast; to overwhelm the pace of his heartbeat.)

Now having climbed into the gloom of the balcony seated on Mammon's suspended lower face, Neipas fixed his gaze upon a curious crescent-moon (with both tips upturned) shape on the shadowed wall, from which a tepid light, gilded with smoke, peeked. He looked through and saw the spiraling fountain where Noxxe had signed the contract; the last place he heard the voice of living Magpie — the Temple's last octagonal chamber (and his eyes became Plutus' smile on the back wall). Marbled bodies adorned with gold flinched with the light of flames. The insignia of Sol Invictus could be spotted just at the crescent's corner.

Below them, the pit whence the Book of Profits arose seemed to gurgle; heave with muscular convulsions, something reminiscent of a bare, swallowing gullet.

He lifted his hand from the railing and, still thoroughly suffused with that sense of dream — which pervades all forays into the ineffable depths of reality — floated on, insensitive and weightless, to the opposite side of the balcony and the set of stairs on the left side of the chamber. Mere steps under, the stairs flattened into another landing and another aperture, shaped like a porthole, opened in the wall. Through its glass he saw another set of steps which he recognized instantly, with the alienated sense of recognition so common to dream-thinking.

The walls were bejeweled. They were encrusted with the most precious minerals, decked with the sparkling treasure of earth's bosom spread throughout the flank like stars of rainbow — amethyst, onyx, jade, sapphire, ruby, diamond (the pulse bulged; it hummed and chanted a bulbed incantation in his head).

Here was the passage beyond the perched peacock's veil, leading to the gate framed in the maw of the serpent, which Kasim and Janu would soon try to break into; which (according to Kasim's theory) would lead them to the vaults where the Eagles hid their secret pantry and (according to Neipas') to the fabled treasures of the tower — to the very core of the Belab.

But now a gradual unease slithered into his mind as it thought of Janu. The vision conveyed in the glass of the inverse End of History haunted his benumbed spirits yet, and as he descended the steps further he felt returning to him a sense of his body, of the pulse and revolutions of his internal organs, together with the pressing swell of the throbbing beyond the wall, ever louder — immense and overbearing. He could perceive the source of that sound was very close. The stairs flattened again at the next porthole (at the nexus of the Cherub between the Eagle, the Ox, the Stag, and the Peacock) and he again stopped.

Neipas leaned his open eye against the porthole, which widened into the size of his face as he neared. Within that nautical frame he saw a dusty, barely discernible picture; a sort of dark wooden deck which by degrees was revealed to his stare through layers of darkness that ended, yonder, in a tall, tattered drape. In the middle there was a wide vase (or urn) or fountain, into which a continuous, thin stream fell from the ceiling — along with a soft rain of petals and dust. It was hard to see anything else; the sight deepened only to further darkness, hinting depths hidden. Yet something in him could still discern a bit farther... With the widening of his eye he heard more amply the beat of the throb — and the sound of a great body of water flowing. A vague aura of dock and seasalt tickled his senses; he could almost perceive a sandy shore yonder beyond the darkness, a vague watery glint.

"Is that the core of the tower?" he asked.

"*That is a path,*" spoke the Midget in reply, "*which leads to it.*"

"Is —" Neipas began, swallowing dry as he felt his body returning to him, "do they really have a treasure hidden there?"

"*They have much hidden there,*" told him the Midget, "*treasures and destitutions, triumphs and guilt. There is to be found much of what is to them everything — and a whole vast emptiness besides.*"

Neipas, slowly regaining a sense of material weight, plunged another glimpse into the porthole and realized upon looking at the dripping stream that it was blood — and upon spotting the falling petals that "(but) that — that must be just under the arena," he said, calling to mind the remembrance of the strangely cult-like, violent brawls in the pit under the Hall of Games.

"*You have felt the cost of their wealth in your own skin. But you are not yet ready,*" broke in the Midget authoritatively, making Neipas turn. "*Still you aspire to their* *height, still you desire **their** freedom — therefore their power. Still you must shed the face of Mammon.*

*You merely seek to replace the **mask**. But it is necessary to forsake the head of Mammon. Still you must learn the substance of their fortunes."*

Before Neipas' shimmering stare, bewitched by an odd premonition of rising momentum, the Midget produced from the hollow of each of her/his robe's sleeves a string of glass beads. From one sleeve emerged silvery glass; from the other golden.

"Give this to the boatman to cross," said he/she, handing him the golden glass, *"and this,"* as she/he bestowed the beads of silver, *"to return."*

Neipas took the beads, all wrapped up in the mysticism of the Midget's words; then —

He flinched as a very loud and abrupt sound twisted in his ear, of a key turning in an old lock. His ear was leant against the porthole's foggy aperture; and he hastened to turn his eye back to it. There was an ample rustling as the tattered drape moved and arose.

Neipas had some difficulty seeing what it was at first. But by degrees he began to see that it was a slender mound of feathers... lifting into the emptiness, and tilting forth in a ghostly stride toward the closet-like protuberance at the edge of the musty chamber — the other side of the serpent maw gate. The mound of feathers slouched in slowly.

With horror Neipas saw a single, giant eye emerge from the feathers' peak; it leaned against the keyhole, and stared.

Taken by this, Neipas hurried with muffled feet up the steps to the porthole above, where he could spy the Temple's curtained, bejeweled stairway. What he saw was an entourage of musicians in front of the gate, with suited backs facing him — the orchestra, with the enigmatic Conductor at its head and a key-bearing Bull at his side.

The gate opened with a tremendous roar of hinges blasting into the general silence of the Temple, heightened in the cringing billow of the pervading throb. All except the Bull entered; and the Bull, suddenly turning, seemed to fix his irate gaze upon Neipas who, feeling his heart thud and expand in an instant, ducked, and hid. Sweating, short of breath now, and with panic pressing at his throat he crouched down the steps to the porthole below, opening amid the Peacock, the Stag, the Ox, and the Eagle... and witnessed as the spectral mound of feathers, the giant eye, pulled back the door to let in the orchestra.

"The eye only admits those of their class. Power alone is admitted."

And Neipas beheld still how the Conductor, shrouded in a vagueness of foggy pitch, plunged his gloved hands into the urn and smeared himself with the blood within; one by one the musicians of the orchestra did likewise, and one by one they paraded through the yonder layers of darkness into the shimmering sandy waters and the throbbing beyond, into the core of the Eagles' Nest.

Neipas' head was crowded with alarmed impulses. "They're gonna try to break in, they're planning to steal the key," he told the Midget in a hushed, hurried breath, thinking of Janu and Kasim. "The key doesn't actually open the gate, does it?"

"The key is but a knock. Only the eye can open the gate."

Lost to disorientation for a minute, he beheld the wall of masks underneath the chin of Mammon, their varied expressions, their exaggerated smiles and hyper-distorted grimaces, the richness of their textures, the gold, as he felt about his mind for thoughts as might occur to him; and as he reflected his way through the confusion of feelings presently besetting his soul.

"Can I cross from here?" he wondered.

The Midget said nothing; there was nothing to be said. Neipas could sense no way to the other side here (he knew he could not break the glass of the porthole and that he could not fit in it until he diminished much more in size); he could sense but Mammon's head flashing, the Candle of Man glinting, *THOU SHALT* pulsing in his veins, the tongue scroll, the portholes — Janu's death in the lunar waters; Magpie's fall into the tempest; Cesar's bruised arms dropping in the Orchestra Pit, his unseeing eyes glaring the golden Hive and the glassy Googol beneath, his lifeless lips bereft of their words — and a great dread and agitation swelling from within the most sensible confines of his spirit.

"I — I gotta warn them!" filled with a rushing panic Neipas arose and rushed down the steps (the candle gleam covered his passing body as he fled). He knew where he could enter now, he knew where to go — the entrance lay behind the arena.

But how to reach the arena?

IX. *Apokalypsis*

Taken up by a sudden rush of anxiety, Neipas sprinted down the bending steps and with outstretched arms he thrust against the black window-glass (suddenly blocking the pointy archway on the tip of Mammon's nose) violently swinging open into a burst of cries on all sides; insect swarms roiled amidst hanging strips of film, flew and scurried confusedly before Neipas' abrupt intrusion and made the multiplying layers of film glisten and jingle with the motion of a million little bodies. Neipas didn't stop, he ran onward in a frantic drive to outpace hunger and beat back death in the primordial race of time; he barely noticed he ran inside one of the black boxes now and that the Twin Museum had somehow vanished in his rapid coming to, possessed by a crazed instinct to get out of there as he absolutely was. In his mind flashed repeatedly the image of his opening the black glass and a density of bugs scattering, the feel of it, again and again it pulsed in his overheated brain and out through his squirming eyes even as his legs sped away from the black glass, through the jungle of hanging film clicking infinite pictures into his hurried glimpse, and these seemed to deepen the sound along the blinkering of red lights... All things sank inside him; the writhing gales of moths and bees and the fleeing seas of scarabs and roaches blackened out before his throbbing vision; and at last his hastening, famished breath became the only perceivable thing in the entire world.

But the loudness of a push bar and a large door opening echoed into his senses and made them stir and grip the external world. His body pushed through, pulling him along, his mechanical legs geared lone and furious and freed of volition. The sound of their footsteps arose to the perception of his ears; he was climbing a blocky iron stairwell, in the shaft of which tattered drapes and masked mannequins hung suspended, limbs fastened by cords, spinning slowly; their lifeless glares inspecting Neipas' ascent as he rushed his way up the steps and in and out of the red lights, out and into the darkness, until he came to the door at the end of the stairs.

He was in some backstage corridor, moving alongside red upholstery and doors labeled with names; he entered one of the dressing-rooms and ran past the flashing mirror into a huge studio behind, filled with props and a thickness of dust immediately stuffing his nose, the whole space trembling with a hammering noise that reminded him of Reckuz's racquetball court (and even as instinct pulled him further away and revolved itself out of thought he knew the court stood on the other side of the facade wall); he was running in a tunnel which had dropped and presently boxed all around him having left behind a classroom full of parrots in rows of cages suspended before a big screen, a screen uttering phrases and showing glazed delicacies (all the parrots wore funnel hats), beyond which a sudden thud to Neipas' breast made him stop.

He paused in his breathlessness, his body rigid. He noticed himself; and in but a moment all he'd seen in his maddened flight swarmed to his mind and he processed it all at once.

It was not fatigue that made him halt. It was the sight now before him, which pressed the awareness of moment back into his scattered sense of place. Suddenly he realized where he was.

One of the golden arches of the Proscenium widened above him, and the ground under his feet was the floor of the Stage. He stood in darkness. All around him, props; vestments and masks and ropes, theater machinery. Dots of electric light winked meekly here and there. Nearby, one of the heavy drapes fell heavily and spread ostentatiously its regal folds.

Now he moved more slowly, with a keener sense of his steps. His hand held the door behind him, the door at the hidden margins of the deep Stage through which he had come, and which, he knew, would be locked if he let it close again. Frightened — with a renewed perception of fear making him hyper-conscious of reality pressing upon his skin — he stared at the Bull posted just ahead, with back turned to him; and receded slowly back in.

With deliberate, careful motions, he sneaked through the hallway, past the parrot classroom; realizing that the lights were on and how exposed he was, he proceeded with extreme caution into a stairway, going by a vague instinct of direction and making sure that no one saw him; he took glimpses at his *I* glass, now glowing again, and fixed his unkempt and miserable pigeon mask by degrees, in case someone caught him walking about there (he knew he should not be here), though he was painfully aware of how begrimed and unpresentable his attire was then (it still occurred to his fear to look in the dressing-rooms for new clothes, but his exasperated nerves would not let him).

Two floors down he went. Neipas made a tepid calculation toward the Columbaria, into which he hoped to find an exit: instead he found himself in yet another passageway he had never been in before, spaced with stately and confidential offices and meeting rooms. He advanced almost by tip-toe under ensconced cornucopias, alongside deeply wooden walls; sensing presences round all corners, endeavoring to tighten his very breathing. Through the slits of slightly open doors he spotted Seamstresses monitoring dots and numbers on black screens, whispering through microphones; and in the carelessly shuttered room before the final door — a marvelously padded, small auditorium — he saw Reckuz and his accomplices and lackeys. Therein sat (all the seats were thrones) Larry the Data Tycoon, Sobs the Prophet of Tools, and other tech luminaries; the Head Gardener and an Airforce General convened within also. And he saw, horrified, Reckuz without a mask — for he spoke to them earnestly.

Before a beaming screen, surrounded by upholstered walls lined up with the disembodied, stuffed, laughing heads of animals, Reckuz giggled with his mouth and stared with his motionlessly glassy gaze. His face was bionic: lips yet flesh, but in his eyes pulsed electronic digits, and across his iron forehead rolled strings of digital letters. His mask was in his hand; restless silicon fingers held it.

Neipas must have stopped before the door, through which he could behold this uncanny abomination, for a moment at least; for he had time to feel the horror of what he saw and to try to dismiss it as an illusion, a hallucination — before he slid away incredulously, he still had an impression of glimpsing the Gardener turning his back and peeking at him through the corner of his rolling stare.

Neipas entered the door at the end of the corridor. The image still haunted the inside of his obsessively blinking eyes at white flashes when he finally realized what the door at the end of the corridor led into. Perhaps because of the incomprehensibility, the unreality of it, he took a very long time to perceive that what his unbelieving eyes stared at now was far more consequential, far more grave, and far more unbelievable.

He advanced through a dark hall of rather vague contours. There were rows of comfortable chairs; the space resembled a theatre. A formation of slowly pulsing dots of a red color stood beyond and, in front of those dots, a glass-front. Beyond the glass a corridor lengthened, and masked people, masked with animal faces, stumbled to and fro in it.

Neipas knew that corridor. He knew it very well.

The masked people in it couldn't see him, he realized. He realized it only after a long time of staring incomprehensibly, grasping feebly at understanding; and with the realization came a sonic wave of terror which drowned all sounds and all perceptions and nailed him to the very spot, trembling, open-beaked, wide-eyed, blurry-eyed.

The dark auditorium in which he stood was walled by glass on all sides but one — behind him (where he had entered). The spaced row of blinking red dots stood along each glassed wall: the red pulses came from recording cameras, mounted on tripods. Before him Neipas saw the corridor. To his right and left, confounding stacks of shelves mounted on the other side of the glass, shelves with mattresses and bedding, beneath which beamed labels bearing a number and a name. People lay and languished inside these shelves. It was a dormitory.

They had been watching them, monitoring them, studying them the whole time.

A narrow set of quiet, carpeted steps led to a platform over the dormitory, a platform of equally soft flooring, upon which his shoes landed noiselessly. From here he could glide to the other auditoria where he could observe the other side of that dormitory as well as other dormitories, and he could step over the corridor, walk alongside it and spy its different sections. He could see through the mirrors of the bathrooms, and he could gaze onto faces — miserable, famished, unsuspecting faces — gazing into their reflections and unknowingly looking at Neipas without seeing him, as he stared at them without being seen. Mesmerized, completely outside himself with nausea and unbelief, he went so far as to lean his beak against the glass, staring fully into the vision of a man making deranged faces at his own image mirrored upon the other side of the glass, in a room filled with the power of dazzling lamps, suffused with the treachery of obfuscating lights. Neipas watched the man's sunken eyes and his fingers pulling their under-crescents, opening his breathless beak widely, grimacing to the point of strain and defacing his mask by punching the wax of it and scrambling its feathers madly in sudden bursts — thinking himself, in all moments, alone. Moving on, unable to bear seeing this, Neipas walked along in a trance, afraid to grasp the deeper meaning of what he saw, teetering between discernment and withdrawal, toward and away from awareness. He stumbled vacant, stopping only when he stood on the other side of his own dormitory.

When Neipas beheld his Columbarium from the hidden side, it looked to him like a sort of Mausoleum of stacked niches; drawers, poultry coops. And under his own bunk-bed-drawer he read in electric letters the epitaph,

431999 NEIPAS

...he faced it like an enigma which, already solved, remains fully beyond understanding. His body tensed and slackened at once, and all the faculties of his mind strained and languished to disparate directions in the incongruity and dissociation rendering apart his restless and motionless being. Only his soul, perhaps, only his innermost lay still, yet at rest, in that moment.

But the general shattering afflicting him coalesced into consciousness truly only after his eyes had drifted to his locker of possessions. They'd been fixed upon it for a while when a pang of realization punched his breast.

Immediately he hastened on. He did not know where he went; his intention being to get out, he also did not dare return through the backdoors of the secret auditoria which led to the office dens and meeting chambers of the overlords directing the whole surveillance enterprise and production. From auditorium to auditorium he navigated, alongside the one-way mirrors; chancing, sometimes, upon owl-masked technicians sitting in those watching chairs, taking notes, not noticing Neipas' presence as it passed through the concealing darkness upon muffled footsteps. Finally he came upon a larger staircase, rising alongside the staircase which led to the Clockroom. A few standing mannequins swarmed him in the stillness of gloom then (he glimpsed innumerable giant laundry machines and spinning textiles and dizzying mantles flashing in the corners of his eyes) and he emerged out of the vast closet, under the hall's giant clock.

Its hands were still; and time itself seemed motionless. There was not a sound — only that of the southern waterfall near, beyond the Warehouse Hall and the broken elevators at the Anubel's exit. And there was, too, no color; all the vivid, flamboyant hues which had so brightly invaded his fascinated stare when Neipas stepped in here for the first time — a year before, already — had faded to a dull, dead gray.

Now on the other side, he sped alongside the mirrors with the rocking conscience of a million eyes staring unblinking beyond the glass. Over him the lights fazed in and out, and the red dots of winking light emerged and vanished at turns. Crowds of the destitute, of the hungry groveled upon the ground, stretched their hands aimlessly as he rushed by, wept and tore their bleeding plumes in the sheer madness of growing starvation. Seeing all and sensing none, Neipas plunged breathlessly into his dormitory and battered against his locker of possessions, fumbling the keys and struggling to open the narrow door with his trembling hands.

There was the jacket Eva had given him, still floating from the hanger. Underwear and socks lay strewn beneath it, mostly unwashed now, soiled with the scarce crumbs of his long-eaten food. He put his head inside and looked desperately at the depths of the locker — which he had neglected to inspect for so long now in his consuming worries — where he had hidden the backups containing the voice recordings.

But they were no longer there. Someone had taken them.

The Eagles knew.

64 - Solarium

They ate the meat ravenously. The glinting hook of their beaks sunk into the flesh; its tender bits burrowed and accumulated in the drooling crannies of their teeth. "Hm," they commented, as they devoured. "Very special — kind of tastes like veal."

"Yeah — ..." the other mumbled nasally, through the smack — "you're right... tastes like squab."

Janu looked on from behind the grill as the Minister of Borders and the Minister of Nations sat at the scarlet-drenched table. The soles of his feet shivered upon the padded floor of the Hall of Games. He held firm his apron pouch under one hand, and let the other wrench, pull and flap automatically over the fire and the grate; he felt the parched craving for sugar in the rear flank of his tongue and the hollow of his forehead, and gazed nervously as the Ministers savored the glazed meat with all the calmness of assured authority. But their tranquility was feigned. The confidence of their stubborn frown veiled a faint shudder of foreboding; for the ground shook with frightening throes, and their Bulls had been drawn away by an immense commotion then rocking the Pigeon Wing of the Anubel. No one knew what exactly was happening; but the picture of a seething rabble storming through their gates was easily suggested in the atmosphere's fraught cigar-haze — and meanwhile the very tower seemed intent on toppling. Something of the turmoil lodged in the Ministers' sealed innermost crept to the surface — Janu could detect it in the slightly faster munching, the slightly shorter breaths of their chewing; even as their speech flowed through the slobbered mush with the same breezy arrogance as always.

When they fell asleep, Kasim and Janu stripped the two Eagles off their garments and masks to place them upon themselves. Lone in the discreet booth behind the shutters — the serving oxen had been sent away as soon as Kasim stepped in, and the guardians bulls had already gone — they beheld with astonishment the evolving revelation of the Ministers' unmasked forms. Out of their trappings, they were so monstrously diminished as to appear unexisting, like hollowed sleeves snoozing across the upholstered crimson leather where they lay. Janu in particular couldn't help but freeze upon the sight of their true faces — something uncanny and indescribable, at once wrinkled and babyish; tiny, their heads resembled shriveled fruit — and, blinking, he wondered if the drunken glow were playing optical tricks on his scarlet perception.

The Ministers' velvety cloth rubbed down across their feathers of mostly brown tint like palls. The magisterial masks fitted them ill at first. Only by straining their chins up did the disguise cover them completely, from brim of neck to edge of nape, and they found themselves wrapped in many layers of padding. Things became dim and remote under those mighty semblances.

Kasim became one Minister, Janu the other; and with their new personas they traversed the crimson rooms — through the turmoiled clouds of cigar, under the opulent sconces and the decapitated heads royally borne, by the aquariums encrusted in the pillowed walls, where the water swayed scarlet and strange fish swam red, lightly twitching, slightly pulsing... — a shadowy multitude of silked and skinned curves rubbed by, floating along with the hum of melody softly breezing from pitchy corners; completely arcane, the musicians seemed to whisper admonishments unto the two moving masqueraders, telling them with the voices of invisible, watching glares that they could see through their deception. In their nervousness, Janu and Kasim even heard cowbells jingle hypnotically under their chins, denouncing them, as they walked without words.

They passed myriad gilded, revolving doors; and finally, stepping into the abundant sunlight descending upon the Eagle Gardens (suddenly all remote sounds neared them in profound quietudes), they made their way down the regal steps curving to the bottom terrace — toward the Temple gates.

*

The sun ascended golden from the clouds, which for many days had shrouded these coastlands of glass and concrete and driven into them cascades of rainfall. Shaped by the forces of a gale whose breath did not cease, the storm vomited torrents in a dizzying rage and drowned the world beneath; water and wind together wreaked destruction upon the megalopolis, and everything solid crashed and melted before their push. But above the billows of the downpour there floated a garden island whose dwellers had forgotten the existence of the world. A large procession took place upon its steps, between palm trees and the flame of torches. From the clothed stalls which ramped along the margins ensued a great babel of blathering, grunting, mooing and twittering of many different dialects, setting the grounds atremble in a low, rumbling quake. From the middle of the procession rose a litter, carried aloft over the eastern river (flowing down the steps), and between whose curtains could be seen the head of the Horse. The heavy poles transporting it rested upon the strained, yoked shoulders of many pilgrims. Peacock and Pelican priests led the parade on either side, holding thuribles and tossing puffs of incense fumes to the sides of the central stairway, from which a crowd watched in tears, out of the Market corridors.

A row of cows, oxen and bulls standing upon their hide legs followed, their horns decorated with flower, vine and gilded beads and rings, and their steps trailed with the ringing of bells pending from their necklines. On the Pelican side the followers walked somberly and with lowered heads, their bells producing sorrowful tings, heavily swinging in unison melancholy; and behind the Peacocks the ringing lifted in chaotic hurls, mixed and asynchronous, for the cattle on that side danced uncontrollably. There were stirrings of great fronds and splashes of wine. When they passed up through the lakes of the 5th Terrace a great ruckus arose as the crowd rushed to throw coins in the water; and the booming voice of the Wall of 1000 Eyes swelled aloft in prayer. All were in a craze, for the followers of both schools had come to venerate the Horse as a saint or demigod; making an altar out of the Main Stage and a church out of the Auditorium, up toward which the procession headed, and in which they finally faced the uplifted new deity as He tottered onto the dais and pronounced the words 'IH-HA! IH-HA!'. Moved by this, the cattle and pigeons bobbed their heads tearfully; and lo, some began to turn to sheep and others goats, and all longed to be domesticated and scrub their noses in the alpine grass of those Gardens.

Marlene's pink hair stood out dimly in the crepuscular, amassing tide of heads drifting in the cloth labyrinths of the Market. Soggy and fuzzy, it pushed along like a slothful torrent of mud; its very slow movements up the terraces seemed to presage abrupt shifts of intensity, like a cracked hill pregnant with tension presages the landslide.

Neipas chanced upon her among the general sleepy rush against time; approached her with the stride of a legless ghost, barely feeling the crowd. Unthinking he panted to her, "Excuse me, do you remember me?"

Marlene the Lawyer flinched at the touch upon her shoulder. She turned with an enraged visage. Her face of degraded peacock was livid, her eyes febrile, sleepless, her brow straining. She was much thinner than the last time Neipas had seen her.

Marlene tried to blend into the moving throng and averted her gaze, tilting her head away from Neipas, as if fearing a smack. She did not recognize him. He was at first disoriented and disheartened by her reaction and let himself lax into the seeping flow of bodies, blurry himself into the vagaries of his dull mind.

But then, moved by some pull of the heart, Neipas called out: "Marlene! It's me Neipas, Cesar's friend, friend of Orenda."

Marlene turned once more.

Her eyes had regained some of the liveliness of old, though they still looked worn and weary, ground-up; and she stared at him with an inquisitive squint, trying to frame him against the remaining mob and isolate his face in her crowded memory. Finally she nodded, swaying and adapting herself to the throng's flow as it oozed on all sides of her.

Moments later they stood by the terrace wall, under a shaded, arched arcade. Beyond a little deserted store in a corner recess, the passageway was blocked by a glassy panel of lusterless mirror; and Neipas, afraid there might be ears lurking on the other side of it, spoke to Marlene in low tones:

"I need your help. I need to find Kasim."

"Cesar's boyfriend?"

"Yes. I know he's going to try to break into the vaults. He told me you knew —"

Marlene shook her head wearily, with the frustrated resignation of prudence witnessing folly. "Will he actually do it?"

"I need to warn him —" Marlene scratched her tired feathers as he said this, her cranium pushing up against the thinness of her skin, of her plumed, wax forehead. "For all I know he is in the Eagle Wing right now. They locked the gates so I... You didn't know?" asked she as she saw Neipas' melting countenance. "I told him it was a mistake, I told him."

Neipas preened his mask on the mirror with the deranged gestures of fatigue and despair.

"Do you know how to enter the arena? In the hall of games?" he asked as he stared into the mirror still.

"No... I've been to one of the events but they blindfolded me on the way — Why? What does that have to do with this?"

Neipas shook his head, breathless. "Nothing."

Marlene eyed him scrutinizingly, her shoulders slouched a bit, very much unlike her former bearing; now pressed down by accumulated shocks and destitutions.

"Sorry — what's your name again?"

Neipas looked at her, bewildered, and for a paused moment he failed to understand what she meant.

"Oh — Neipas."

"Neipas — you don't happen to have any food, do you?"

"No..." he lamented. "I'm sorry."

Marlene smiled wistfully; and said aimless: "Just checking."

They stood leaning upon the arcade, in the shaded recess of the terrace wall, silent, contemplating blindly the ceaselessly fluxing throngs on the other side of the Market booths, all horned heads passing lowered under the Merchants' increasingly deranged antics. In the black nooks between stands, soiled crows huddled and begged in humiliating prostrations.

Suddenly a thought sprang out of Neipas' saturated memory. "Listen!" he began half-crazed and Marlene twitched with abruptly alert eyes. "Do you know Professor Moldura, the Editor?"

"I know who he is, sure... I've met him briefly here, once or twice."

Neipas produced his *I* in a rushed motion of confidentiality. In his mind throbbed the missing backups and the foreboding nature of their disappearance; in his accelerating heart breathed an urgent fear. "I have — certain files with me," related he in panted whispers, "that I need you to give to him — and to Orenda."

Marlene the Lawyer frowned. As he bid her to approach, she did, quite suspicious of this maddened pigeon who, however, was among the few vaguely familiar faces in that cloudy sanatorium of shapes. He leaned his beak into her ear — and almost of one breath he hissed to her the whole tale of his recording the Eagles.

"What —" she began; though she understood what Neipas had said — Neipas, whom she stared wide-eyed now, never stopped talking: "If I'm caught I need you —" (drawing her away from the mirror panel) "— I need you to give the recordings to Orenda and to the Professor."

Greatly becalmed by the burden of the task — giving her an anchor in the shifting grounds affecting current reality — she nodded; she had grasped, in her immense mental presence, everything at once, even amid the flush and hurry of events, even hungry as she was now beginning to be. "Ok," she said, and taking her *I* out of her blazer's pocket she continued, "Here — give me yours. I'll copy the files over. That way we'll both have copies."

"If I don't get out," gushed Neipas in his messianic lunacy, not fully conscious of what he said, "give this to them."

"Ok, Neipas — don't worry." At this moment the sunlight burst from the clouds, onto the terraces and the pilgrims on the stairway to a great wail of emotion and the overbearing toll of bells.

*

Kasim (masked as the Nations Minister) waved a wad of bills in the same solemn manner he had often seen the priests do it. Janu (as the Minister of Borders) walked tensely at his side. The sun beamed fiercely upon the Eagle gardens in its descent west and everyone flashed in a scramble about them.

Earlier, they had stolen the silver and golden keys of the Gardener's key-bearing Bull, who was off escort duty on account of his injured hands — and they carried one each now, Janu the silver, Kasim the golden, in their pockets. The guard's big mask had leaned upon the table where he dined alone, asleep from the drug they'd slipped into his meal, as Janu and Kasim moved his snotty nose-ring until it unclasped from his nostrils — and removed the precious keys it fastened. The cook watched with lurid eyes the handgun on the Bull's waist; and the pantrykeeper, sensing Janu's fear and rage, said firmly, "Don't. Please, let us make our way to the Ministers. It is almost time. Here are the pills — I will meet you there in half-an-hour."

A little nervously he watched Janu leave to make sure he didn't take the gun.

Donning the bouffant ministerial semblances, they stepped together into the glaring visibility of sunlight. Behind their mighty masks, they sweated, drenched with anxiety; for the very gleam of the waterfalls flowing down the Eagle Garden and its towering, terraced facade, made them sprinkle and shine, it made them vulnerable to the least attention of all watchful notices... Besides, their body shapes barely resembled those of whose identities they had borrowed — they were well aware of it. One was too short, too chubby, and limped; the other was too tall and too lean, moving with an awkward gait that was too obviously trying to be stealthy. But Janu was the most conspicuous of the pair, going on with an unnatural posture entirely dissimilar from the Minister he impersonated; his chin tucking instead of jutting, his shoulders bending instead of swelling; his hands constantly feeling his bulging stomach, the shirt taut upon it under the suit jacket. They trekked thus strangely down the steps, toward the bottom terrace where countless royal gazes bobbed upon propped bodies, dallying about in the protection of burly and menacing horned guardians.

And yet none among the guardian bulls, none of the peacocks, the owls or even the Eagles noticed their deceit. As soon as they emerged from the Hall of Games they caught themselves in the midst of an uncannily vibrating air, bombarded with ephemeral reverberations, vestiges of distant uproars unfolding on the other side of the Anubel. Unreality pervaded the soundscape which was more characterized by the stillness of the Eagles and their vassals than the noise whispering from the Pigeon Wing. Everyone acted normal; though their voices ensued more mutedly. Kasim and Janu floated through the palpable uncertainty stemming from the suggestion of clamoring throngs jingling the ether, floated as though drunk, guided by instinct. And as they reached the bottom of the stairs and turned toward the Temple gates they contemplated, rising over the flaming Pearl, an ominous stack of smoke; as though the storm clouds had wakened off their stationary flatness and yawned — and would soon, calmly engulf them. Remote clicks jolted the atmosphere; but then, as if seamlessly, Janu and Kasim found the fragrant vapors of the Temple enveloping their eyes as they passed through the gates. No one stopped them. The bulls here stood stiff upon their positions as usual, but — Janu perceived it with one nervous glimpse upward — their stares looked different, moist and glassy behind the rigid features. A hint of surfacing savagery tainted them; it made the cook all the more scared.

And as they looked back through the fog, the sun shone like a threatening, deep-orange gaze, all-seeing...

*

Neipas struggled to pierce through the bedlam of amassed bodies. He sought Osir, whom he recalled had once, a lifetime ago, swept the bloody dusts of the arena. He found him by a Pharmacy in the shadiest corner of the Market, where bodies roamed in the darkness; his *I* light chancing upon his face hiding among a million others.

He was looking at the distance through the blurry scope of his glare. From there could be seen, between the gloomy mess of tents, the clouds afar. Osir faced them like one before a landscape of enemy giants, all immaterial. He felt an incessant itch — a spider crawling under the surface of the skin, upon the brain... reminding him (with little pokes) of his brothers-in-war, whose lives got sucked into the needle. Licking his scar he mulled on how to kill enemies as titanic and incomprehensible as those — it would be, perhaps, like fighting with gods — and noted vacantly how uncannily blue the sky arched above him.

"There's fucking nothing dude," Osir said simply.

Neipas lost no time. Desperation rushed a whole string of speech out of him, in which he told Osir in frantic whispers all that was going on and beseeched his aid. He asked him how to enter the arena as they left the whispering chaos of the crowded dark Market and continued on in a wider area where the brightening sunlight flourished.

"So that's why you all were asking me all those things..." said Osir — the single pill inside his bottle rattled as he shook it. "There *was* some kinda gutter in the arena... well —..." Evanescent flashes in his mental haze spoke to him, in dim siren tones, of hope; perhaps — thought he — there were pills to be found in those secret vaults the wealthy held, that would quell the preemptive shiver in him; the surging malevolent thoughts; the gnawing of the monster that lived in his memories. He was, as were all, savoring the incipience of desperation, and thought nothing of stealing from his bosses that which should be his anyhow. It was their fault... And he was tired of polishing their golden toilets. "All right... Look, they blindfolded me before we went, so I don't know. I suggest we go around and find out. C'mon."

After a brief moment of reflection then — Osir swallowed the last pill in his small plastic bottle.

First they went toward the Merchant of Solutions — having to walk over the eastern river and across the procession, which seemed endless; streams of bovine and sheep-masked zealots kept joining the tail, emanating out of the terrace of thorns in the bottom and as though materializing from all the way down in the Museum, huddling in tightening masses on the Auditorium (as he strained to pass Neipas still asked himself "Is that normal?" amid the torpor).

They came to the Solutions Merchant and asked him, "how do we get to the arena?" He made a quote. It was expensive; but — to Neipas' surprise — Osir gave him the cost (which was all the cash he had).

"You're in luck — you came at the off-hour. There's a lot of folks asking for solutions these days, often there's a big line... Give me a moment," said the Merchant, sitting at the table and grabbing a pen. "Sorry — the crisis forces me to resort to primitive tech."

He jotted something in longhand across the whole length and height of the sheet. Within a few minutes he was done, and he handed them the product of his labor.

"Huh??" grunted Neipas, looking bewildered at the sheet.

"What's this?" asked Osir, grimacing.

"It's a detailed map in writing, a set of instructions on how to arrive at the arena."

There were definitely words that could be made out on that sheet of paper; but they were written with letters so ineligible it would take days to decipher the whole document.

"Could you write this more legibly?" Neipas asked.

"Surely. We have premium packages which..." and the Solutions Merchant went on to explain that he could write more legibly for an additional fee. When they protested, he clarified that they were paying for his time, and that drafting the document in a way they could understand it would take longer; this is the best solution he had for what they had paid.

"Fuck this," mumbled Osir as he stepped away angrily. "Where could we go next... Shit by the way, I'm out of money."

Neipas, however, still had part of the cash which Kasim had given him. Next, they went to the Merchant of Doubts, who was lately rumored to know a lot of things. He had become one of the most successful sellers in the Market in those days; they found him speaking to a great crowd amassing before his booth, there to hear him advertise his products. The Dreams Merchant, who had once held a booth beside him, had since declared bankruptcy and closed shop. There were rumors that he had gone into the gloom of the interiors to live with the crow[d]s...

They listened to the Merchant of Doubts speak (he seemed to be replying to some query or protest):

"My friends," he spoke — "Everything is relative."

"You must look at a situation in a given context. If looked at carefully, everything is justified.

"Everything can be bent to your will. Therefore everything is possible.

"My friends, everything is relative. Even morals! To tell you the truth, there are many possible meanings for the word 'morals', and even the word 'truth'.

"You must follow good morals and be true. It's our highest ideal.

"Climate change? Humph! But hasn't the climate always changed?

"Climate catastrophe! Everyday there is bad weather somewhere. If were to lose sleep over that, then we would be sleepwalkers forever. Always somewhere there will be bad weather.

"Storms, droughts, famines! My friends, always somewhere there have existed storms, droughts, and/or famines. We shouldn't sleep any the worse for it.

"Why worry? My friends, to tell you the truth, life is meant to be enjoyed. If you spend all of it worrying, it will pass by you.

"Enjoy life, and stop worrying — that's our highest ideal."

After the pitch, some in the audience scattered and turned to the procession (which was unfolding right next) for reassurance; but most formed a line to the booth, which Neipas and Osir joined and where they waited for a while. Osir meantime went around to ask if anyone knew how to enter the arena (taking some of Neipas' cash with him), leaving Neipas to unravel in anxiety. Having heard much and learned nothing useful, Osir came back just as the heifer in front of Neipas was stepping away.

They asked the Merchant of Doubts, "Do you know how to get to the arena?"

To which he said nothing, making it clear he required payment. They gave him a banknote. "Ok."

To which he replied, "Maybe" — and made a ping-pong gesture which implied he required more payment.

"The fuck?" mumbled Osir, and he looked at Neipas' hand, where he weighed the meager pile of banknotes still in his possession. "How much?" Neipas asked.

"Maybe it depends? Whatever you can pay, please," said the Merchant of Doubts, and each word was employed with a different tone from the one preceding it, so that they weren't sure if he was solicitous, or angry, or mocking. Neipas gave him another banknote, parting with it painfully.

"An entrance to the arena exists — *maybe*," the Merchant told them; and though they waited a little, there was nothing more forthcoming.

When he realized this, Osir became infuriated. "And what's the way to it!"

he exclaimed, but the Merchant wanted more. Neipas held him back and calmed him down, calling to his attention the papal bulls close-by — for they stood on the edge of the central stairway; besides which, there was an evident anxious vibe exuding from the queue behind them.

*

"Praise be to God," mumbled Kasim in his own language, ascribing to divine providence the coincidental fortunes of lax security and distracted moods. "No one saw us."

"Fuck's happening on the other side? I think I heard gunshots," Janu's voice trembled in the language they held in common, stirring the fumes.

"It's ok, it's ok," answered the pantrykeeper stoically, firmly, encouraging the cook in his steadfast attitude to keep going without thought, speech, or hesitation.

Kasim and Janu walked through the Temple's octagonal chambers; dressed among the naked, among Eagles wrinkled by vapor, age, and decadence whispering to each other askance in the tucked corners of their spas. Rumors of riot abounded in the haze; fright sullied the incense scents. It bubbled out of every steamed mask, its odor could be felt emanating from even the most haughty magnate. Perhaps it was the fact that everyone was slowly becoming equal in the delirium of terror that no one noticed the two blatant intruders passing through in shivers. The marbled floor yet shook, often jolted in violent convulsions. Yet the Eagles still did not believe, as the pigeons had begun to, that the powers of the Earth could ever topple them; they dreaded only the rabidness of the crowd, which they checked obsessively and endeavored with fervor to keep under control. They ascribed the tremble of the floor not to the living soil and the rains — which to them were but dead things — but to the ever simmering ire of the rabble.

And still, aloof as they were in their apprehensions — still they did not show it. They were still too wrapped up in the illusion of security bequeathed by their perches; too invested in the fantasy of absolute power. Any slight whiff of dissent had been easily blown away for decades. Nothing would happen, they assured one another. Their regal masks sneered stern.

The Bulls and Peacocks blinked unconsciously in the steam. The Owls, those, they watched with closed eyes. Janu and Kasim walked past them undetected and without wavering they reached the peacock curtain of reed and shiny feather, then accelerated their pace between the rainbow of gem-studded walls and soon reached the maw-framed gate.

Kasim placed the silver key in the lock and turned...

*

They (Neipas and Osir) stepped out onto the other side of the Market corridor. From there they could see the ascending march very well, that great slow mass of horns and woolen furs, that herd of pious workers streaming slowly up to the Auditorium in hopes of listening to the wisdom of the Horse clamoring atop the stage. Above the deity arose the Great Facade with majestic terraces solemnly quiet and dark, with its statues of the Greats staring down upon the wailing crowds. One of its windows, framed with rich adorned carvings, looked at Neipas with its inscrutable glass covering the mysteries lying inside.

"Magpie..." he contemplated that window upward the stage, where he thought he had seen Magpie as she was forced to become. "Magpie... Magpie was in the arena" (what'd she say again?").

Neipas' soul wandered back in time, through half-forgotten memories... his eyes roamed the confusion, looking for the gazebo on the perch which was, however, concealed from view. He beheld the Pearl undulating the flame of the sun, filtering it dreamily — somehow the star had already wound behind it (the sky slouched with somber colors then). Contemplating the magnificent entrance to the Ballroom beneath it, Neipas recalled standing against its balustrade before the Waltz, when the foreshadowing sense of leaving the Eagles' Nest gave rest to his scalded, tired nerves; he remembered Magpie at his side, eager to get out of there. He remembered how they watched the storm's approach without understanding. And, vaguely at first, then more sharply, he remembered what she had said. She had mentioned feeling the redolence of a herb as she was ushered to the arena...

"The rosemary!" he panted; the thought hit him with the impact of a breakthrough.

Immediately, his instinct led him to fetch his *I* in a forgetful impulse. He intended to ask the glass what rosemary looked like; but there was no connection to the Webwork. Disoriented, he asked Osir, "Hey, do you know what rosemary looks like?"

"Rosemary? What's that?"

"The plant, it's a plant I think."

"Ah. No. Why?"

Neipas' initial high at the remembrance fell into a sore despondency of hopelessness as he realized that, even if he knew what the plant was, he wouldn't know how to look for it in that chaos of garden immensitude. He sunk his fingers in his head of plume and pushed tremulously. "What? What?" Osir demanded. Magpie died before Neipas' eyes again; holding down the panic, Neipas explained that Magpie had been in the arena's auditorium before, and, though also blindfolded, she had felt a strong scent of rosemary as she went in.

"There's a plant seller by the lakes. C'mon," said Osir, already on the move.

They made for the bridges over the lake, where the Great Peacock of 1000 Eyes still preached and coins still rained in splatters upon the surface of the water over numberless grimacing tears. They traversed with great difficulty the bulging mass gathered there between the intertwining balustrades, struggling for hours squeezed between throngs of masked pilgrims and penitents. Seeping below them and beyond above, and all around, climbing from the precipitous bottom of the terraces in a supreme ascending effort, the sluggish mass wailed ebulliently "Ave to the prophets!" or, "Ave to the profits!" as their masked heads strained upward in sobs; a very horde, thick with cymbals and drums which were added to the sound of cowbells, crossing now upon four limbs the grand stairway to the upper heavens. Bleating maws trembled inside fluffy coverings. Chaos and rapture dominated that triumphal march of hope and despair, as the paraders prayed for money and manna; pleading, in sheer horror, for deliverance from those frightful throes of the ground, delivery from inconstancy, delivery from hunger; the very waters of the river lapped between the flanks as if intending to escape. From the ebbing lake, fugue, glints of aquatic light soared and rippled upon the multitude passing through the bridges, over the stairs. The refractions snaked along the numbing voice of the Great Peacock, quivered with the jelly-like pop of falling coins... And once more as he hovered the lake, even in that fever of stimuli, Neipas — even as he strained on the verge of delirium — remembered his mother, an intangible flash of sprinkled herbs arose in reminiscence through him... Why? Many times did he slap his melting mask of hanging plumes with the impression of hallucination. And all the white frantic palm leaves swung all around, and the crowds rocked to, involving Neipas and Osir in the turbulence of their craze. Yet finally they were able to cross; and arrived shortly at the small greenhouse market, whence plants grew in the twilit dampness.

There was a great crowd here; they had to endure another lengthy line before the Plants Merchant. By far the longest queue was, however, the one in front of the exuberant Bugs Display, where entire nations of insects buzzed and reproduced inside great glass flasks and tubs under the intense glare of special lamps. The Seller of Bugs had been "making a killing" in profits, someone had told Osir; for he was selling the crawling and flying creatures as the cheapest food on the Market.

"I ate one of those mashed-up, myself," mumbled Osir, matter-of-factly.

They almost shoved away the ox in front of them as they stepped to the stand at a running pace. "What's a rosemary!" blurted Neipas at once.

"Would you like some rosemary?" asked the Merchant of Plants, bearing an enormous grin on his mask.

Neipas understood. He gazed down at the bills mournfully. "How much?"

The seller cited the price of a twig of rosemary — as much as Neipas had at that moment.

"Fuckin' A, man..."

Neipas gave him all the money he had; the Merchant reached back into his boxes and gave him a plant soft to the touch, with leaves shaped like vague needles, faded green; and pressing it gently against his nose, Neipas felt a scent which came to him across from memories of a very distant past; which emanated from the revived pulses of a bygone life.

There the river glinted sunlight... There the wheel turned lazily. His mother touched the rosemary and moved her fingers tenderly across it; she took it to her nose. "Smell it, Neipas. Isn't it nice?"

Rosemary strewn over the fields, sprinkled over the perfumed smoke from her fingers...

His eyes wetted at the recognition. Swallowing dry, his features were made rigid.

"Wait..."

"What? What is it?" Osir asked, but Neipas was already making his way back through the cloths and the crowds toward the lake.

Upon its banks, he saw it. The throbbing he felt most deeply here, the weird gurgling noise embedded in the booming, hypnotic intonations of 1000 Eyes, the uncanny remembrance of his mother that surged in him so often in that place... There, in the narrow marble round the terrace leading to the Great Peacock, sprouting out the cracks, framing the eyed feathers, he saw it in great bursts of violet and green — rosemaries.

"It's behind there," Neipas mumbled. "The wall of eyes hides it."

*

Kasim and Janu stood before the maw gate. The key had just turned, but the gate seemed stuck; though they pushed, it didn't budge. "Is it stuck?" again Janu asked anxiously through the Minister mask, which could not fool the feathered guardian gazing through the peephole on the other side.

The shiny veil behind them swayed and breathed vapors — it stirred with the confusion of many motions...

*

Right away they had set along to the most remote corner of the Market, wherein tucked a small shop selling masks — a small shrine, in truth, lodged into the wall of the terrace, in a narrow tunnel full of sparkling trinkets glinting in half-light, and at the end of which rested an altar table with a bowl atop, holding coins, banknotes, checks and credit cards as offerings, placed between incense sticks and candles and before a small oval mirror. Neipas and Osir, who had immediately concluded they could not approach the Great Peacock the way they looked, entered, stepping on the woven mat flanked full of objects and under the awning, from which pended wind-chimes, suncatchers, bells, cloths, pendants and masks of all sorts rotating slowly in the air. They sought the semblance of the rich and powerful. Inside, the noises subsided a little; between the mess of piled trinkets, and the hundreds of empty masks staring at them from the wall, scintillating sounds of clinking rang softly with the tremor (they noticed better, here, how the ground shook steadily, at an increasing pace); and the empty masks seemed to whisper above all the hushed sounds...

Luckily the shopkeeper was not around, for they had no more money. They moved quickly. Picking the most expensive and therefore most credible masks they could find from the wall, they leaned up against the little altar and gazed into the mirror.

As Neipas entered the Horse mask, he felt himself change; the very lighting of the place seemed to alter. The equestrian visage, which extended down to the chest, made his neck muscles swell; he sensed in himself a contained power of voice he had never thought he possessed; and he felt hunger no more then; the snout and lips, which stretched into the open air, projected a natural contour of power and superiority — it compelled him to lift his chin to contemplate his mighty jaw, and he released a low quaking nicker of fumes between a beautiful, lunatic smile.

"What are you doing? let's go..." — but just then a motion disturbed the wind-chimes — they guessed the shape of someone by the entrance — and they scattered instinctively. Neipas stepped quickly into the open closet beside him; Osir crouched behind the altar.

It was Drrawetz who entered.

From the inky shadow inside the closet, through the slit of the door ajar Neipas witnessed the former Master Supervisor hug the walls and weep. Drrawetz embraced the masks, placed his cheek upon them, wore them and growled, yelled, and cried furiously among the clinking of trembling things piled all around in muted colors. He seemed to dance and hum deliriously as he advanced through the narrow shop-tunnel; until he arrived at the altar, before which he fell on knees, sinking his face on the bowl of coins where he wept uncontrollably, his gulping sobs doused in the gilded shine. "Why! Why did you leave me!" he whimpered, lamenting the fact that the Eagles had closed their gates and left him on the outer side.

This went on until he lifted his head suddenly (shimmering circles stuck to the disfigured wax of his face, coins poured out of his beak as it drew away from the bowl) — he had felt a motion and realized he was not alone. Abruptly Drrawetz stumbled to his feet, shouting agitatedly, "Rascal! Thief! You're not supposed to wear that!" and even as he was stepping back and pivoting into a run Osir leapt from his hiding spot and thrust his hand toward the escaping steward. "Motherf—" Osir strained breathlessly as he seized the steward's mouth and pulled him seething. Drrawetz tried to yell and his feet squirmed in panic, his jabot frothed frantically in the scuffle. "Help me man!" Osir grunted through the exertions of his slobbering scar as he struggled; Neipas stepped out of the wardrobe at once and, under Osir's direction, pulled strips of cloth out of the many hanging from the ceiling, and with these they strapped Drrawetz's legs, arms, beak and eyes as they suffered blows from his flailing limbs; at last Osir shoved into the closet the writhing and blubbering body. He wavered a second, shaky and out of it, as if holding down an emerging seizure.

"Let's go."

"Shouldn't we knock him down or something?" asked Neipas breathlessly, fearing Drrawetz would escape, dreading that he had been recognized.

But Osir said nothing. His muscles trembled from the effort of subduing a living body; his temple twitched with remembrances of wartime, the clock of which never ceased ticking in the old warrior's soul, marking secretly the pace of his heartbeats, the speed of his poisoned blood coursing through gorged arteries. Inside him lived a monster; it whispered in pulses... Osir felt it now wakening, sinking its teeth through the clutching nails of his fisted hand, his shivering fist as the mollifying effect of the pills waned.

"Let's go," he merely repeated in a mumble.

They emerged quickly from the shop and were soon steeped in the tide of crowds again. Into the noise... into the tumult of bodies they melted; but something had changed. Unlike before, the sea of bobbing horns began to part before their advance. Many looked at them in astonishment; and gradually a great commotion arose as the cattle asked the horse-masks for autographs, while some whispered to others, wondering who they were; to which no one had an answer, knowing only that they were famous.

Quickly they became the focus of every stare in the Market (all of them sleepless, eyes jutting out of deranged grinning faces). Neipas and Osir heard nothing; they didn't even feel their feet touching the floor. Gliding through the center of attention, they were as if possessed by a spirit that was not theirs...

They each grabbed a torch as they came within view of the Great Peacock, the Wall of 1000 Eyes, that open fan shaped like an arch, like a half-dome which projected the sound of the preacher's voice powerfully into all ears. There was a big commotion when Neipas and Osir arrived at the bridges. "Look! Look!" yelled the cattle and the sheep. Wails of awe and adoration soared from every mouth and made the gardens shake all the more, made every leaf and blade of grass, every cloth and glass surface quiver mad.

And then there followed a great, befuddled silence as the procession finally stopped — everyone looked wide-eyed at the lake as the horses waded through its sacred waters, over the glittering coins...

The shower of money ceased as all movement halted. Only the preacher had not stopped its deep sound, proceeding with its ever-looping litany: "The Market is everywhere..." the great primordial Economist repeated. "And He speaks in mysterious ways, by means of signals. The Market lies at the heart of all animals..." — and all in the cattle, all the goats and sheep and all the pigeons still beheld the dazzling eyes in wonder and confusion. Yet it became clear to the two who advanced through the waters that the Peacock's true voice was but a feeble squeak, a meek babel of words which meant nothing.

(They noticed for the first time that there were fishes in this water; they nibbled at the coins; they nibbled at their legs as they passed. The torchlight mingled upon the surface of the lake with the mellow glows of a declining afternoon).

Osir and Neipas neared through the shallow lake; they were closing in. They found themselves in range and finally they saw the Grand Economist's actual size — tiny, minuscule in the midst of all that iridescent plumage and all those deceiving stares. The Great Peacock, who suffered from severe myopia, couldn't very well discern who they were in the diminishing light of day — he saw but two Horse masks wading in the water, and though this was irregular he thought not much of it. But once they hopped out of the lake and onto the little pier the rest of their bodies emerged (starving fish clung to their legs and were shaken off as they stepped to quickly). The Peacock swiftly evaluated the monetary value of their wet clothes, sparkling dirty under the torches; and, adding it all up, concluded the two were not who they pretended to be.

They dashed at the preacher. "Papa Mammon! Papa Mammon aleppe!" shouted the Great Peacock, wailing a primal cry of alarm and fear. This bizarre creature, descendant of Plutus and Argus, had fallen into a decrepitude of ages. He appeared drunken, demented, far removed from his noble lineage. His tongue was confused, long had he forgotten the language of his forbears; and whatever words he spoke he spoke with the lucidity of a record player. Now the High Priest of the House of Mammon shrieked and shook, panicked at this sudden clash with blunt realities. Neipas and Osir tried to pierce through the arch of eyes as a great revolted commotion arose behind them. They tried to clear away the thicket of reeds and plume and get to the door they spotted already on the other side as the thicket cried and shook convulsively. It was very dense and they began to fear they'd be trapped; the heat from the flailing torches lashed on their faces, already some of the feathers had caught flame. Many splatterings of feet on the water as the Peacock's followers rushed to save their guru; but they, who wore ties, were slowed by the grip upon their necks, which pressed upon their breath; a gunshot sounded and panic thrust to fever pitch as yells of dread erupted among all. "Stop! You'll shoot the teacher!" someone's scream sounded among the chaos of screams. The agitation in the waters advanced closer to the perception of the two struggling horses who strained with frantic flails of arm through the forest of eye-quaking feathers and shafts. Already there were steps upon the pier.

Just then Neipas cleared through (a rush of fragrance closed upon him as he plunged), drawing a great and desperate breath of air; turning blindly he saw Osir stuck and pulled him out with the supernatural force of adrenaline-charged muscle. They sprinted like mad through the squared walls of the corridor, with a world of shouts and sheer insanity seething behind them and seeking their blood. They ran out of their senses — at the end of the corridor they found the hidden auditorium. They dashed down the aisle and were halted by the glass barring them from the arena just beyond, the dusty arena plummeted at the bottom of a tower of gilded galleries, and the ruffled screams exploded through the corridor into the auditorium from just down the passage then, running feet of a million furies clamoring "Grab them! Kill them!"

"C'mon! C'mon! Before they see us!" Osir and Neipas removed the horse heads and plunged their hands into those masks of skin and fur; they punched the glass frenetically with the hardened muscle of jaw and teeth and were able to get through bloody, storming in through rains of shards — at the center of the arena they promptly found the trap-door, hidden in the dust; they pulled up the ring which fastened it and entered the pit in a scramble, disappearing from sight; and locked the hatch above them straight.

All their maddened chasers found was two soulless and bloody horse heads by the shattered glass at the edge of the arena.

65 - Terrarium

The air thickened at once and closed in about them, made hotter, dense, stuffed with primitive scents: smells Neipas vaguely recognized. Osir and he came to through blinking eyes; all their senses dull, they had a sense of having been transported here in the abrupt shift of perception they experienced, as though realizing they were far away from where they had just been, long after the previous moment. They found themselves in a low-ceilinged space, standing on a harsh rusted floor littered with hay. The hatch just above their heads was perforated with square-shaped holes, like the trapdoors on the decks of those ships the settlers had come into those lands in, long ago. It was shaded in flickers by the searching trampling of the masses above — whose sounds had suddenly ceased.

This silence was only perturbed by their own breathing. Here was a sort of barn... And as they settled into its serene, remote, fluttering obscurity, they began to perceive other stirrings, vague twitches in the darkness spreading from their immediate ken. Neipas leaned out his torch without speaking a word. The flame gave form to the shadowy movement — ... Neipas clamped his hand round his beak to smother its screaming.

There were people sitting there... They donned oily rags and were scrawny, some severely emaciated, at the deeper stages of starvation; and though their heads vaguely resembled those of pigeons, they were featherless — the skin bristly and full of burning rashes, as though the plumage had been torn out violently; hot tar oozed from their boils; yet the most horrifying feature of their aspect was their beaks, which had been maimed severely, so that they seemed not able to speak — and their eyes, which stared with supreme indifference behind a moisty filter, and with a lifelessness so uncanny that Neipas felt his arteries freeze bloodless as he saw them.

He turned to Osir with eyes full of horror; but Osir only pressed his finger to his lip, with gaze wide and alert; clutching Neipas' arm, prodding him onward.

They were standing on another hatch, which on opening revealed a spiral set of ladder descending into tenebrous unknowns. They went down slowly into the darkness, into air stuffed with wood and hay. The glimmer of the flame licked the reaches, where further platforms hid, narrow in the heights — there were cages and pens in the downward walls; stables. Inside them were bodies of men with horse heads — very old, decrepit, withering in the gloom; eating ravenously from troughs. Osir, transfixed, stopped his downward climb for a moment and reached out his arm farther. Neipas above him halted too; shuddered, said nothing. There was a particular man

Osir recognized. He had been known once — had been very famous, a long time ago, though he scarcely looked the same any longer — and now, stripped of his glories, was relegated to that place. Osir stretched his neck out a little, very gradually, so he could look closer at the pen. Through the quiver of the flame came the entire horrid form and motion of the man unveiled. Osir mulled soundlessly.

"He's eating money..."

Through narrowed, confounded eyes, they saw also those strange featherless creatures perched upon the narrow platforms, replenishing the troughs by the bucket with banknotes collected from among the scattered hay.

Rung by rung they neared the bottom. The torches alighted the grounds from above, revealing, slowly and in palpitations, a large fountain stagnant with blood and petals; and the giant, looming shape of a densely feathered creature, a bizarre, towering heap of plume — a lean monster, inhaling the rusty atmosphere in deep asthmatic swells. Osir landed carefully, without noise; his hand shot up in a brusque military manner, ordering Neipas to stop. He lifted the torch high above his horned head. The expression of strained surprise carved itself into his face, frowning widely, as he evaluated the apparition before him. Then he took his finger to his lip, and gestured Neipas to come down by careful sways of fire. The feathered mound breathed by the door, like a trimmed shrub filled with the spirit of air. It turned slowly — the next moment it had risen ten feet over their stares. "Don't move! Stay where you are!" hissed Osir (curiously, Neipas saw his lips move but heard nothing), but the creature faced them in its full monstrosity, and (as it bent down) out the tar plumes they saw emerge an enormous, bloodshot eye which was double the size of their own faces. Propelled by impulse and fright Osir staggered backward and thrust his torch forth into the feathered eye, which set off in flame and across sudden jabs of light sizzled, and crackled to the ground, covering the air with the stuffiness of many feathers aloft.

Stunned though they were, they lost no time to approach the gates, made of two simple doors in a protruding cube, resembling a wardrobe. Neipas looked through the peephole and beheld the strangeness of Kasim and Janu adorned like the twin Ministers, struggling to pry open the maw of the gate. Neipas and Osir parted the doors each at his end, and gave entry through the threshold to the other two. Their Eagle-laden faces were astounded before the ox and the pigeon whom they recognized as Osir and Neipas; both of whom touched their own lip with finger, and bid them come. Neipas spotted Janu with relief for an instant, as he entered clutching his belly — but all sensation was then immersed in a totality of silence as the gates closed.

Within them pulsed the fire's upward ebb, shushing their minds to perfect muteness; they floated in that pulse, winding, wordless, soundless, corresponding in its pace to the cryptic glow there, shining in golden flickers at the end of the corridor, calling to them...

Neipas neared the fountain at the center of this cellar barn, pointing at it to the others; and, plunging his hands inside, palms cupped, shell-like, he dabbed first his countenance and then the rest of his body with blood and petals, as he had seen the Conductor do. By means of gestures he instructed the others to do the same.

The blood of the fount dripped copiously down to a concavity burrowed into the harsh floor at the base, then flowed up a gutter rushing ahead. Soaked in the viscous matter of life, the four went along and followed the bloodline coursing through the grounds along the deepening barn.

Immense pens flanked them as they moved through the dark, musky tunnel. Side by side, the cages were replicated in cavernous shadow, continuously straddling the path, and it was as though the wall had maws with slick tongues; vast tongues hidden in the black. Through the bars they could see, if they squinted, the thin-haired, pinkish fur of giant boars; they were linked to tubes by which they were fed... A slight trepidation of leg muscle somewhere afar made Neipas perceive, faintly, that they were climbing up the (downward) slope; the blood coursed up the ramp through the gutter dashing alongside and glinted the torchflame in sparks of carmine.

Eventually, they alighted upon a sumptuous veil over an archway, from the lintel of which protruded the bronze head of a lion.

The sense of firm soil under their feet, already vague, completely abandoned them as the floor melted into a damp silt; out of the darkness they shored, emerging upon a sort of beach where the sand shifted and sunk very slowly, pasty with the thickness of clay. It culminated in a shoddy sort of dock — a small pier flanked by two statues of lions with hoofs and human faces, smiling cryptically above square goatees; staring away at a vast maelstrom, presided by a flat sky of leprous rust from which leaked various slimy, languid drops; a rabid maelstrom circling round an immense pillar ahead, sinking into the dripping ceiling above and into the waters below, roaring with a pervading, mute scream — a loudness of quietude... The air was lit by a strange sourceless light of pale, fevered hue.

Along the back edges of the dock lined the stalls holding giant swine, whose wet snouts slobbered upon the bars of their cages and whose maws, connected to tubes, opened monstrously and without sound. Rushing from the dark passage between the pens, the passage whence the four had entered, the blood flow clefted and burrowed through the sand and discharged into the water. They hastened their step lest the sinking ground swallow their feet, making their way to the grim shack next to the dock — but a cubicle made of wooden boards, resembling a phone booth. Neipas knocked on the door (no sound).

The flimsy hovel gaped with a tremendous, secretive yawn — revealing a figure, fully robed and hooded, sitting on a stool inside, with an oar held upright (here's the boatman). Out of his pocket Neipas took (as the others looked on) the string of golden beads the Midget had given him, and extended his arm; then, out of the boatman's dark hood surfaced an enormous ear, twice as large as their faces. Amid the sinuous valleys of skin and above the pending drop of lobe opened a black, bottomless, widening hole, and Neipas (he witnessed aghast, dreadful from inside his body as it moved naturally and undisturbed) reached his fingers thither, and let the four pearly beads drop into the ear canal. The boatman arose and led them to the pier with oar in hand (hand concealed by sleeve, fingerless; and ear tucked back in the darkness of the cloak) as they followed wading, ankles dipped in soggy clay). The small boat there was but a halved husk, a shelly, egg-like thing made of weaved reed and soaked in pitch. By the water now, they could well see how it gurgled with the strain of crowding weight; clogged with garbage, it circled in a diabolical parade of rotting plastic, beneath which red fish hovered on, dragged.

With the oar the boatman unfastened the rope.

They set off; the boat was so constructed that Kasim, Janu, Osir and Neipas were forced to nook on the round bottom and the boatman alone, standing at center, could gaze (eyelessly) over the edge; so that they did not sense the violence of the current as they navigated to the yonder shore. Sometimes the droplets trickling from the blighted ceiling flicked Neipas' upturned nostril and flowed down his beak to seep into his tongue (the slimy drips had the flavor of milk). All the rest of them stared widely, glassy, to the round hollow depth, tucked and hunched, vacant; and the waters shifted unsounding beneath them...

Suddenly the boat rammed into solidity and Neipas' head was shoved against the side (something in the deep soundlessness cracked and the boom of a throb erupted in a synthetic scream; Neipas' torch, which had sweated fevered wax out of them, vanished in their midst, and for an instant they all disappeared into the boatman's limitless robes). They all lifted of a pull and clambered onto shore. The human-faced lions grinned at them from either side of the platform; and expanding beyond them, the sand thoroughly soaked in the bloody fluid that lapped into shore here, making a treacherously shallow bog of sanguinary clay (a few lipless, featherless stragglers, scooping, collected it into buckets). Spurting and gushing out of the whirl, a stream of that mixture of blood, milk and tainted water coursed further, shrieking quietly through and past the palisade of reeds rising at the end there (pulsing with crimson gleams) which Kasim, wading vigorously in front, parted like curtains as the boatman shut himself on this side's shack. Neipas looked back quickly before he went in. From here he could see the whole giant circumference of the tower. No, not even the whole circumference — as they stood in one of the inner rings, hedged between the more slender terraces of the summit. The full circumference could never be seen; it would lose himself beyond sight and range, unfathomable Belab... (Neipas moiled ahead, in dreamy vagueness).

Beyond the reeds — another dusky, damp, humid tunnel. From the sides of it, out of clefts emerged skinny mouthless children with faraway eyes, dusty, soiled with deep earth, covered with blisters; their naked, dark skin all coated in white dust. Their bony arms, cupped against their famished bosom, bore mounds of ore and cinders; their legs releasing, as they ran out of the breaches, miasmas of toxin and the writhing clambering of insects stirring onward through the shadow.

Ahead, hot-red colors rose and subsided. They traversed the dark corridor and inhaled rusty odors of a dying air, entering imperceptibly a hell-world of forges and furnaces where the featherless, debeaked and ill, stood before the blazes laden with thick gloves and aprons of leather and hide peppered with black dust. Wheelbarrows loaded with coal were taken to feed these extreme heats, lifting noises of mechanized trampling and revolutions amid the continuous roaring of fire. Mounds of sand and stone laid in great piles stirred and sprinkled the air. Things reddened and faded in smoke, sizzled, screamed. Here they warmed the baths in the Temple, perfuming the vapors with incense; and engaged in many other, inscrutable tasks among whistling steam. Shovels, hammers and tongs were the chief instruments; and some wore long, long beaks, with glowing orbs of molten glass at the tip.

The blood glimmered like lava here, lashing forth up the small gutter, scintillating with the mysterious quality of embers. All those who labored looked at the four who passed by with eyes incurious, uninterested; distant, as if glancing over from another world.

(as they ghosted on Neipas replenished the torch-head at a kiln) Up stairways of Tophet they climbed, spiralwise, involved in occult numbness, through chambers of iron and wood progressively blacker and colder. Pipes slurped the gutter's bloodflow, entering the ducts frenetically as though from exposed vein into enclosed body; and Neipas perceived rabid multitudes of scarabs and spiders crawling along, over swarms and rivers of ants filling the round surface of the dispersing pipes, whereas locusts and moth swirled close about them and hopped here and there, as though they were all part of a great pilgrimage or parade of vermin round the frenzied pipe-path — the insects (and this could only be noticed if one really looked) were bursting from every little crevice on the walls. Janu, Osir, Kasim, Neipas together passed through various veils of cobweb as the air thickened with powder and dust, acquiring the consistency of ash, heavy and ancient. They were as if entering the bowels of a primeval tomb: the featherless and the tarred came and went by them through these iron corridors, appearing in various shapes as they zoomed past; and the four came thus suddenly to a factory-like hull, topped with a net under the ceiling, on which many such bodies writhed. A profusion of machines proliferated beneath, operated by these slaves of myriad forms — the light here, weak, fed mostly by the scattered fire of anemic candles, alighted them somberly — there were the elderly strapped to wheelchair, and the infants suckling on the dry teats of their mothers or wailing, as the women shuffled their arms hurriedly in convulsively revolving motions; dreamless boys, scantly men, sat with them at unending rows of endless tables, and with them they soldered, drilled, fitted, fastened, wiped, and polished glossy metals and black glass, assembling machines out of myriad little pieces and at inhuman speeds; their heads hanging under their swelling backs, orbs flittering vacant over the unending deluge of stygian tabletops, fluxing mechanical organs across over rolling carpets, ribbons of pitch moving beneath their blistered hands without rest... — they labored under (Neipas saw this and still he did not believe it) the supervision of tall, wide, almost square robed figures; and out of their hoods emerged parted lips, immense faceless lips; the bottomless pits of screaming mouths onto which were fixed giant, monstrous, ticking clocks.

There stood by a large gate at the end of the factory hull, with a cobra head protruding from the silver lintel. In a flash it emerged onto their sights. Occasionally, a single, immense lamp fixed somewhere at the top, flickering in a colossal struggle, swelled in an buzzing yell of soundless light, which they but heard in the corresponding flutter of their hovering hearts — by which glimpses of bugs were revealed in their squirming tide, teeming the cobwebbed pipes on the tarnished walls, hurrying along. Pallid radiance flooded the space brightly, crisscrossed it in the shadow of the net and of the bodies incised in yarn. Then they could spot the lurid reaches of the factory; and witness the crazy multiplication of assembly lines as if the limit of the factory neared and drew away by the booming and withering of the big industrial lamp. All things shivered in suspension for a moment. Yonder on the far edge, beyond infinite hustling arms, those whose fingers had been sanded useless gazed out of the barred windows into the Gardens below...

Clearly now, the horrid pallor of the laboring workers was unveiled to the four splaying gazes. Many wore surgical masks over their debeaked faces; many others showed their lipless maws without disguise. The sweatshop slaves were injured by many deformities, the babes already loaded with protruding bellies and skull heads of stretched skin, some noseless, fingerless, others marred by halved heads; all glared indifferently from the enigma of inscrutable distances, as if from beyond a portal of sensory abstraction, in absolute mute silence, as they passed; and as they went, Neipas kept wondering (if these are bodies without souls, or souls trapped in bodies) — as the electric lamp once more fizzled, and he beheld them across the vaporous air of tapers.

At the center of the operations sat great contraptions, a circle of a great many looms; at the core of which arose three big spinning wheels. Three creatures covered with hooded shrouds of plume worked at each one. Three twin sisters at the first wheel spun the yarn to be weaved into veils and curtains. The other three, at the second wheel, spun thread that would be woven into money. The first sister spun the yarn onto the spindle, the second measured the emerging thread with her rod and allotted the fabric into portions, and the third cut the threads with her shears and loomed them into form. Great quantities of fabric, mostly silk (for the curtains) and cotton (for the banknotes), which was loosened into the air and hovered about in fluffs among the mechanized workspace of the factory below the generalized writhing of the bodies caught up by the overhanging net, were carried to the spinning wheels in wheelbarrows by workers entering from the yonder gate; while others took the finished textiles and paper bills the other way, or inserted the money crumbled up in spirally rolls, into sucking tubes on the walls.

The third spinning wheel was an odd apparatus, whence great flares arose to overwhelm the candle lights and make them tremble, and subsided into them. The great wheel, bearing 12 spokes, spun a lump of clay which the first sister, of face shadowed by her feathery hood, molded; shaped it into heads and masks. The second sister used the frantic spindle to make fire (a strange silver-colored flame) and harden the shape of the mask into something definitive. A great many looked bovine — oxen and cows — others, much fewer in number, like peacocks, swans, deers and stags, and horses; and a very great few like Eagles. Finally, the third sister, who seemed the oldest, as she was shorter and more hunched than the other two, bore a scale; and she placed the finished mask upon one plate of that scale, and a feather on the other; and she wrote down the results in a book.

Then the masks, too, were carried away.

Kasim, Janu, Osir, and Neipas navigated to the yonder gate. It opened and closed easily and constantly with the ceaseless ins-and-outs of the featherless workers as the cobra on the lintel looked on. Beyond it lay a wondrous sight, like nothing they had ever seen before.

[They faced a great hall.] Quite suddenly the floor broke into a myriad different paths, though they couldn't discern this at first; because every single surface — the floor, the ceiling, the walls — were made of mirror. Moreover, those surfaces were twisted, concaved, joined in all manner of bizarre angles. All surfaces reflected off each other in an infinitude of replications and tangled deformities. Their eyes drew in the sight of themselves expressed in all possible shapes at once: stretched, shrunken, bloated, with small head and long legs, with wide necks and loopy torsos (twisted in spirals, dispersed in ribbons, squeezed (etc. etc.) The flame of their torches alighted the galaxy of personas in demonic, laughing dances circling impossible bends. And the slaves of the vaults moved out of the mirror labyrinth with fabrics, and came in with money. Kasim pointed and his lips described some notion ('this way,' Neipas understood).

In one mind they understood the perils of that path and that they could not go in without aid. So they turned back a pace — and walked, together, into the range of the nine sisters at their spinning wheels. There was a cluster of yarn clews at their feet (we will use this). As they neared they saw the inscrutable depth framed by the cloak hood, mired in black, and could not see whatever lied beyond it, or whether anything lied beyond it. Meanwhile, with the spindle's flame glaring the industrial lamp grunted feverishly, and still they only saw nothing. Kasim was the first to seize hold of the clew — by the spinning wheel of money. Then

the three sisters arose in a pull so sudden that the four intruders froze in place. All sounds suddenly stopped; only now did they notice how long and pervasive the noise had been. The factory still revolved furiously — but though the threads churned and the minerals shimmered and the sparkles fizzed, yet they made not a peep. The oldest of the three approached Kasim — leaning toward in her hood, out of which emerged a giant nose with wide, gaping nostrils. And they closed in upon Kasim's petrified, upright torso, surveying its scents with great dilating pulses and low, roaring exhalations. Neipas' hand was upon Kasim's chest, brought there by a sudden reflex, telling him not to move. The great nose [twice the size of their faces] inhaled the blood-soaked clothes of the pantrykeeper in great pulls, with great sucking whiffs. And out of the chasmic sleeves of the cloak came fingers, long and tentacle-like, and they rubbed against Kasim's body and felt his avian semblance covered with Eagle; Neipas, too, felt the slick and viscous fingers slime the skin of his hand. Kasim had by that time given the ball of yarn to

Neipas, and he had passed it on to Janu, who stood beside as petrified as they all were. Around them the toil had not halted —

— and bit by bit the sounds returned to fill their ears and consciousness. The lamplight subsided. The nose receded into the chasm of its cloak, satisfied with the reek of plasma; and the tentacles disappeared into their sleeves, deceived by the Eagle semblance, and thinking Neipas' fingers were Kasim's own. The four retreated slowly toward the gate as the three spectral shrouds of plume sat back at their spinning wheel — back at producing money.

Janu unwrapped the thread through the labyrinth of mirrors, and the rest followed his limping tread, hand on the shoulder of the one in front. They came upon many dead ends but were able to retrace their steps by tracing back the line. They climbed up and down winding steps of different shapes and sizes, clambered up slopes all made of glass, through hardship and the mental vacuity that came with the all-pervading, constant, unbreaking noise (though as they advanced they perceived that the noise was dissolving into palpitations, into beats, into throbbing, into throbbing). Blood coursed now along chinks carved on the floorside, or the walls, or the ceilings; it was impossible to know which, none dared try to touch the flow — exploding into many streams, it ran upward freely along with them, and many insects, made swarms of infinitude by the infinitude of glasses, followed. Whenever they saw one of those maimed slaves rushing unhesitant along the path, they knew they were on the way to the core; to the vaults. The debeaked seemed, somehow, to see the way clear. Neipas thought (or the reflections whispered unto him — Look. They don't recognize themselves in these mirrors).

The trek was so long and difficult, made through surfaces so irregular and confusing, paths that merged into themselves, curves that looped into mid-air and disappeared, structures which made no sense, that they walked on the brink of giving up, always. But they were always a little outside of themselves, just enough to be unconscious of the strain of their bodies and the exhaustion of their minds, as if their souls spilled onto their companions and merged with their steps; as if they scattered onto the soundlessness of the noise and the void [and into the confusion of images].

Near the end, they fell without feeling it, and lay along the glass though they thought themselves still walking. They had encountered many dead ends; there was no path to take. This was the farthest they could go. (It came to be that the parade of ants, spiders, centipedes and moths, roaches and locust, were passing before Neipas' withdrawn glare; and he saw the trail they drew. The blood and water streams came from beneath a visible chink in the mirror there — a movement of foul air also). Neipas pushed the mirror.

There was a kitchen here.

The electricity ran, though faulty. It lighted up, endeavored and flickered, and fizzled out. It revealed tiled walls (perhaps this is some sort of hospital). On the stainless steel bed lay someone — a body, whose sloughed off skin and mask had already been removed by the workers. The body, it seemed, had belonged to one of them, one of those slaves. It appeared that he had been one of the gladiators who fought upon the arena; for his rib was lacerated and purple, stained with blood dry; the ox mask and its ornamented horns were set beside the plucked-out face, which without its features looked much more emaciated. The other two, standing by him, wielded knives, and were already engaged in cutting him up — always, always bearing that same visage of soullessness and indifference — and the four, upon entering, saw them inserting the blade into the open gap between the deceased's maimed beak: out of which they removed a tongue. The blood flowing freely from it spilt onto the gory floor to join the upward stream. They opened a vent on the wall and dropped the tongue inside.

Neipas saw Janu's semblance widen with shock, then grimace — then expand again in disbelief. His lip stammered soundlessly (*that's — that's...!*) as he realized that was where the eagles' food had come from. That was what he had cooked — and eaten.

The cook felt his arm gripped and pulled away. His expression was closed, wrinkly and teary, endlessly perplexed in the confounding shock of an unbearable revelation (that's — that's — that's where their food...!) The tiled, surgical floor of the morgue continued beyond the plastic curtain. They crossed a series of dimly lit foyers, and filthy hallways whose walls seemed to move and dissolve in rust before their passing sight. Crowds of the debeaked slept on the hard floor. Women, girls with bald blotches on their wounded scalps wiped the ash with brooms of straw; some of them — covered in a bedlam of paints — approached them, opening their toothless mouths without lip, blinking their eyes without [*what?* — Neipas seemed to be dropped backwards into water as it struck him that it was the absence of *life* that those glares most brandished] as they fled horrified. The flame gasped, like fish out of water, frightful, timid; as though it wished to tuck into the comforts of the torch-head's tightly wrapped, waxed cloth. They moved in unison, as if to a mystic instinct of synchrony, as though they could feel each other's landing steps and pumping hearts; ran slowly to account for Janu's limping, glaring vacantly, savagely holding his belly as if in pains to stop the hunger from spreading. Finally, they

came into a great hall. The overwhelming quietude, which never stopped in its all-consuming flatness, lowered in tempo here, as it widened into the abruptly larger space [...]

It was a sort of gloomy bathhouse. A vast silvery hall, it circled round a thick column at the middle: a broad, sturdy pillar which supported the ceiling and separated it from the floor. From the circumference, at the point of contact with the soaring top, there spread veiny, stocky patterns of root-like stone, carved reliefs hanging menacingly overhead. Silkworms hung by thin threads from up there, and the ceiling was thinly coated by a swaying ebb and flow of foggy cobweb. The column itself was delineated with slithering carvings, crowded with high-reliefs protruding from its stone. Imposing statues, thrice the size of they who approached now, stood one at each quarter. There was the Ox facing South; the Dove in the East; the Eagle toward the West; and the Lion to the North. From each of their stony maws flowed a prodigious cascade, which then thundered onward through deep canals that would, finally, flush the water out the walls — and into the Gardens on the East and West. And as the waters rushed out fourfold, four fluids flowed to-ward, and into the column, in four lines between the quarters. Entering from the Southwest, they first saw the torrent of hurried blood stretching to pierce the column's base. In the same manner, in the Northwest afar, they beheld a steady ooze of glimmering honey. From the Southeast flowed milk; from the Northeast, petroleum. All the liquids penetrated the stone and disappeared beyond its sinuous round surface. It was as though the pillar was sucking in all these disparate fluids and morphing them into the gushing water, which, however (as they approached in the torchlight) seemed to be tinted now with a sort of purplish hue.

The day was dying cold inside the vast chamber. Two of them circled round the east, the other two round the west, through which the rosy light of the languishing sun filtered. Approaching the column, they beheld in all their might the portentous sculptures emerging from it. All had men's bodies, except the Dove, whose head stood atop the body of a woman; all stood upright, arms flat upon hips, backs erect and embedded into the pillar — and with each of them was Mammon, of austere stone, sculpted into different poses, assuming the shape of a human-faced vulture. Mammon stood upon the shoulder of the Lion; snugged in the shell-shaped palms of the Eagle's human hands; with its talons of myriad fingers, shaped like spiders' legs, it gripped the Ox's horns and stood upright atop its head; and with them Mammon clutched the Dove's body between many coils, and kissed, with pointy lips, the Dove's human rib. Each vulture bore the impassive, indifferent, dreaming head of Mammon... Sarcophagi stood lined up round the pillar, between the four statues. Their inscriptions spelled out revered names, champions of the human order and harbingers of civilization, industry, and wealth; some the age of millennia, others more recent. The insect-breeding stone of moss which covered the bodies inside was the first thing the running waters touched. Its droplets, leaping in bounds over the canals, hushed among the all-consuming noise of quiet sound [...] There was a calm here, ebbing out of the nightmarish intensity of the factories and sleeping-houses whence they'd come. The waters sparkled, and the stone shone softly in the streaming sunlight and the undulations of the Pearl near, made together bloated and bright on the western sky. There were windows shaped like portholes on the East and West. The Western portal opened the view to a desolate cascade of immaculate greens and whites, tinged blood-red in the drowsy sunlight; motionlessly trimmed shrubbery, and shapes so still they could correspond to frozen bodies, thawing slowly in languid solar radiance. The torchlight palpitated against the Eastern glass — and through it, conflagrations raged, flames bloomed before the night gathering out of the clouds, overtaking the Market terraces in their commotion of tents and stalls. They looked out the eastern window (for they desired to walk through the shadier area as they went round the pillar toward the yonder gate) to the Pigeon Gardens, and saw a great disarray of masses churning well beneath them, bodies pushing and pulling among those flames — yonder trees, and patches of grass scintillated ablaze, with great motions of panic all about. Yet despite the chaos, none of the noise pierced the stone perch from where they gazed; it was fully enveloped in the silence of its own ceaseless noise. Fusing in lockstep on the other side then, the four of them stepped on the platform over the outflowing river and came to the exit, before the gate — under the lintel with the protruding head of a golden calf. Neipas lifted his arm to clutch the handle. The very air seemed to press down on his limb; the whole thing seemed too heavy. With the heavy, ring-shaped handle (which came out of an eagle-head's beak) in his hand, he knocked the brass against the immense gate three times.

It wasn't the sound of the brass knocking that entered the silence; rather, the silence palpitated, pulsed and shook with the knocks in great sonic vibrations, and the floor itself convulsed once, twice, and again — the gate opened solemnly, with all the majesty of its carriage, and as it did the ground began to quake again and did not stop. Up a narrow winding stairway, circling widely round — and finally, a hatch. The torch was put down; then the sky burst before forty pushing fingers.

The world exploded into a vast panoply of vivid colors.

They faced a mountain, or a pyramid. It was very steep — and it was made of wealth. There were avenues of crystal jagging upward; the trees spread in jewel and lamps hung in glittering diamond; a river of honey coursed lazily down the sparkling slope. Gold ingots made up the uncanny structure of regal houses, which mounted up to the summit in an accumulating heap. Everything looked disheveled and incomplete — either still under construction, or already in ruins. The city's peak (still far above them) reared up against the ceiling, and all around the mountain they could see nothing but blurry white. An escalator coiling round the mound made a cleft between those messy hills of things, the only discernible way up (the crystal boulevards were too steep) in that tumultuous clutter. A very parade of crawling, jumping and flying bugs trailed up the whole extent of it. Lights emerged flickering from the piled riches. The air and ground shook. As they went up they beheld treasures, of many commodities — wardrobes, beds, clothes, hanging wires, windows, houses — but also rocks, trees, whole fields ingrained in the aluminums and plastics and irons, and people, both eagle-faced and pigeon-masked, stuck in-between; some struggling to get out, others sleeping. Buzzing lights seemed to emerge from *I*s lodged within. The silence palpitated in beats. There were luxurious rooms and living spaces beneath the washing machines and other things — perhaps these were the bunkers. Adults played in the chambers under those great bedlam piles and giggled with the weeping children.

The abundant, exuberant vividness of colors and motions dimmed as the escalator took them through a tunnel; and all they saw were flashes of electronic light. The shaking tilted and convulsed stronger, as if the whole tower had turned into a beast trying to unshackle itself from the ground. The sonic reverberations of mystic quietude, drowning their heads, intensified. Suddenly Kasim grabbed Neipas' shoulder and peered into his eyes with a scared expression of extreme alarm. He seemed to say something. (The bulls! The bulls!) but the immense silence swallowed up his voice, it had no influence upon the air whatsoever. The pantrykeeper gesticulated convulsively toward the way they came. The others looked on too, Osir with a rigid look of concern and Janu with a glassy, wide face of shock which he had fixed since the morgue-kitchen. Kasim leaned his beak onto Neipas' ear (I have to go! I must try to stop them) but Neipas understood nothing, he perceived nothing but the perception of that loud quietude. Neipas was given the golden key hastily [as he gave away one silver pearl to pay the boatman for the passage over the maelstrom]. Drawing his wide stare away then, Kasim — with the clumsy, unfitting garbs and mask of the Eagle Minister still worn — turned round in a sprint and clambered down the ascending steps.

Drowning in... The somnolence spread like slow powder to fill his hollow mind. What was it he wanted? (Yes — I'd like to sleep) and the distant possibility that he might not wake up stood distantly in the horizon — at the top of the great heap had been erected vaulted gates, barring entry to some fortified stronghold. They spanned a wide circular path, round a moat filled with viscous, bubbly and steaming oil covered up by a density of many twigs and white feathers. All bridges were raised; all except one, which lowered as they passed. The Minister's mask that Janu wore seemed to stir in recognition; and it was as though the bridge had somehow acknowledged the mask's identity and power. The round gate beyond presented itself to them like an enigma, full of patterns and contraptions and gears, full of bizarre and convoluted mechanisms upon its steely surface.

But there was only one lock, which eventually they found — and they possessed the golden key.

The golden key turned in the lock and the wheels and gears writhed and coiled in a receding manner, the silence revolved with mechanic pulses. The strong gate backed away (it felt surprisingly light). As it opened seven other doors opened also behind it, and Neipas, Osir and Janu traversed the distance of their span.

At the vault's entrance there was a curtain of aerial roots, which pended down from a fig. There was a glass pane before it, which they opened — then they parted the roots. They parted them (a wind blew upon them in bursts) and finally they saw it.

The air was immediately dense and hot; and smelled of synthetic dirt. The stuffiness of that closed atmosphere quickly loaded their breaths, which had the effect of making their distant spirits descend a bit closer to their bodies. The ceiling was crossed by serpentine sets of beams, from among which sunk lamps of dull, violent glow. It came in and out with the long heaves of the silence. The whole perimeter was encased in glass (except the far distance, which glimmered strangely). There were vased stretches of dirt all into the depth, from which grew plants resembling dismal limbs of infants in the sinister light. Behind these plants rose shelves.

All the shelves were full of fruit.

Janu and Osir ran gesticulating toward the shelves, drawing countenances of relief and joy (yes! yes! he was right!). But it was a withdrawn, deficient joy of stony eyes and beaks askew in starved grins. They took up three apples.

Immediately they set on drowning their hunger, plunging their teeth into the fruit, sucking every bit of juice and saliva out of the bite. Everywhere there were boxes filled with seed. Vines round the vague walls bloomed with blurry grapes; there were wilted leaves strewn among banknotes in the corners. The immense fig behind them wrapped its trunk round some other wood, which looked a bit decayed, a little rotten — it was (Neipas approached gliding slow as he took a second bite) a dead tree, which the fig had wrapped round. The carcass of an olive tree it was, made hollow. Neipas looked inside — it was crawling with insects which ravaged the dead wood. They trailed a path out of the fig —

(What's that over there?) Neipas seemed to sense his own lips moving but wasn't sure what they said. Yonder he saw two bodies walking into the depths

847

of the vault, into a sort of shimmering distance. He thought he saw the Collector — and the Conductor of the Orchestra besides. (Are they?) As he bit the fruit he finally realized it — though the fruit had form and texture, though it bore feel upon the teeth and tongue, still (strange) it had no taste, and was bare, without substance, without energy or nutrition. It passed through him; but it didn't satiate his hunger in the least.

Neipas dropped the fruit and approached the shine.

At the end of the terrarium was a bulbous covering of plastic, or fingernail — or eggshell — pulsing with light. It resembled the skin of a balloon. The stitches gave way — he entered — and closed up behind him again. Albuminous fluid spilled soundless at his feet.

Floor of glass shattered underfoot, giving in softly to the weight, like a crust of snow. The torch flame blew forth in rage though there was no wind. The bloodstream poured in from the stitches of plastic skin, flowing into the yawning chasm in the core. It commingled with something like milk; spread all about over the glass, which was full of pebbles of gold, glinting bright like the sun, daubed with blood whence they emerged. A large black stone protruded from the pit, and out from its top blew upward jets of flame, a continuous and immense fire whose extreme heat stuck at once onto Neipas' whole skin; petroleum gushed in great bursts from the rock. Titanic prismatic spotlights rose upon a pole from the giant flame, though they emitted no light. The circular ceiling was made of gold, and the gold was as transparent as glass; and through it could be seen the fur grounds of the Ballroom, spiraling broadly into the middle, where there was an aperture; and in the aperture perched the Golden Dove and it, too, was of transparent gold. The golden sculpture bowed down and stared through the glimmering ceiling with vast, angry eyes; its open beak oozed honey, anointing the flame glimmering golden from it; its talons coursed down like roots to involve the prismatic pole and envelop the gushing rock — whose firelight blasted through the gold into the crystal prism above, through the Dove, and beyond the Ballroom's oculus into the Pearl, reflecting and propagating its gleam from the highs into the farthest corners of the world... Well below, Neipas gnashed in sweat. The brightness and feverish heat quickly overcame his senses and vanquished every bit of will and wit in him, so that he felt perished, somewhere beyond death. He had long let the torch drop. He fell to his knees and pressed his hands to his ears, for out of the globe walls, which were poked with orifices like the pores of skin or those of loudspeakers, there rolled a continuous scream, a single scream which broke into many voices, something drowning and total; it was a noise of voices; a sound of sounds (the sound of all voices — something hummed into Neipas' spirit). Though Neipas wasn't conscious of it the ceaseless scream lashing out of his gaping mouth joined those chaotic pleas as a plague swarm of moths rushed into the flame from the air and a million other insects crawled or fled from it over the pebbles and the blood ground. Myriad petals seemed to ascend toward the Dove as his eyes narrowed and fell. Beneath, yonder beneath the glass and the stone, something huge and horrendous writhed, into which petroleum, wax and gold-blood dropped, and that something monstrous and unconceivable pulsed, pulsed, (pulsed, pulsed, pulsed...) pulsed.

Into the black stone was carved an inscription which read (in gold):

'EGO SUM PETRUS ET SUPER HANC PETRAM AEDIFICABO MAMMONAM MEAM'

On either side stood the Conductor and the Collector, waving each one arm, as if directing the rising agony of the cries mixed with the frenzy of the orchestra and the accelerating hum and the fastening throb beating in a craze; the other hand held a torch, one pointed up, the other downward. He saw them. He saw them. They had no hat or wig now. He saw them clearly. His stare laid upon their faces.

But there were no faces. There was but a pit where the faces should be.

The sound of all yells soared to an unbearable pitch. Neipas felt the air coursing his throat in rushing flames as his lips parted to their largest extent to cover the whole face and all existence.

The spotlights were turned on in a thunderous and blasting beam of white light that flooded his eyes, mind, and spirit — and the world went off in lights.

*

Neipas removed his hands from his ears and stared at them for a while. He saw their palms were stained with black oil, and as he laid his fingers upon his ears again it seemed they were secreting this type of fetid tar. A lingering sense of piercing rancidness hovered deep in his nose and flittered in his brain. Aloof, he felt the texture of his wax visage, made a mush, deformed by the extreme heat — he saw the countenance of a monster in the glass of the shelves, and that face without shape, too, bled tar in between lumps. He was back in the glass-bound terrarium. His own deep, sleepy breathing, the weight of his eyelids, the blurriness of his vision, and the meekness of his insides and senses emerged to his notice.

Osir and Janu stood near him with perplexed glares. Osir's assumed the character of accepted resignation, and his brow wrinkled with simple sadness. Janu, however, stared out with the glassy delirium of one who took the shock and was absorbed by it; so that his lips muttered without saying anything, and his cheek trembled by his blinded eyes. They, too, had long realized that the fruit did not feed, did not satiate, did not kill or even appease their hunger; and yet the wild craving of starvation led them on, to eat into the core. Now they stared out like stone upon nothing.

Osir was the first one to speak.

"It's rotten."

Janu, ceding abruptly into fury, threw the fruit onto the floor, which burst with a rush of writhing maggots dispersing from its core and releasing an unbearable stench.

"I can't believe it! I can't believe it!" Janu kept panting.

"Damn…" whispered breathlessly Osir, in disbelief. He looked about with the air of supreme fatalism, remotely teary-eyed, as one who had given up; he shook the empty bottle of pills next to his ear.

Neipas was approaching Janu with an emerging intention of calming him down. He was being worked up to a state of awareness by the influence of the situation and its urgent demands; a desperate grip upon life pulled him on. The sound of uncanny silence had stopped, and so had the screams; though now he heard everything far, and he neared the good cook as he panted and shivered, hyperventilating himself into an overwhelming panic. But just then the ground tripped with a quake again and shouting blasted from the walls. Voices called out from speakers, addressing them, ordering them to show themselves and surrender.

The shouting jostled Neipas and impelled the frightened gasp out of him — "It's the bulls!" From the speakers he could almost feel the impact of their muscular march stepping upon the shaking of the ground, landing the full weight of their powerful hate-fueled bodies intent on breaking Neipas' meek frightened own.

"We must hide…" With his breath tremulous and cheeks stirring in dread, Neipas turned quickly to the other two.

He saw, horrified, Janu — one of his hands supported the weight of his grief-laden body upon the shelf; the other held a gun.

Neipas furrowed his brow, shaking all over.

"What are you doing? What are you doing?" he whispered dreadfully under the panicked trembling of his breath.

The gun in Janu's hand quivered profusely, its make clattering faintly.

Neipas neared — very slowly, as though approaching a sort of apparition in a dream, as though facing a dangerous maniac, or an animal — he neared Janu's dreadful, ghostly, blank eyes, filled blind with horror and wrath; until he stood very close to him, eye to eye. Neipas caught the sound of his faint, trembling whisper; so very faint that he didn't realize its meaning until he could touch the very breath of it — "I'll kill them!... I'll kill them!" he repeated, over and over.

Neipas breathed with his shuddering lips, almost inaudibly, into his ear — "Janu...

"Put down the gun...! You're gonna get us all shot!"

66 - The Vaults

Janu's eyes were glassy. He was overcome with the intensity of feelings warring deep inside, drawing in his entire being, consuming him. His face looked suddenly shrunken, gaunt and livid. The mustache of the Minister whose face he wore bristled and puffed under the dew of his stare, muttering, quivering in a breathlessness of growing agony. It was as though the hunger, strengthened by the shock of seeing such abundance of nourishment — and then finding it uneatable (finding itself fooled, finding but despair in the trickery of its own impressions) — had decided to prey on its own host. The poor cook looked as though he was being eaten from the inside.

"Janu?"

Neipas himself spoke through a thickening haze of delirium dissipating every power of mind. It took an immense effort of self-control to keep his stare on Janu's soulless eyes, to root his feet in before the slow transformation taking place before him. The starved cook held the gun aloft, close to his chin, with a trembling hand and the hollow gaze of a maniac. For an instant Neipas thought he'd shoot himself; meanwhile the bulls' shouts grew louder.

"Put the gun down man... Put the gun down man..." — Neipas felt his voice ache in his throat, but he didn't hear it. He breathed the words out from the unconscious. His legs shook, and his whole force of will was required to not give in to the impulse to run blindingly out of there.

And Janu repeated his words into a deeper soundlessness... "I'll kill them. I'll kill them..."

The bulls kept approaching.

He had limped his way half-consciously down the garden steps, arisen with leg stiff and aching from their midst after being tossed like some worthless thing out the gate. He had looked up, teeth gnawed, lip atremble, and seen only the silhouette of the spike-collared Bull wavering in inebriated laughter, leaning against the hinges as he stared at the darkness of the terraces into which the brown cook had vanished; then returning to the Feast of Pigeons in the Ballroom. With eyes set and blind in their drunken fury, Janu traversed the little patio walled by the Sabine mosaic and stumbled under the Columbidae banners leading into the Map Hall, where the shapes of nations spun heavily from the ceiling and the vast wardrobe of guns spread wide open... The dread in his heart was steeped in alcohol and rage, he could scarcely sense its throbs and screams bubble under the muting influence of the roiled liquor; so that he walked among the tottering Eagles unperturbed, walked among the crowded suits and jeweled magnates as they played and fondled courtesans, pointed guns around, drank profusely, ate of the choicest delicacies. Janu noticed the faces of the concubines with a clarity which cut through the center of his all-peripheral senses. He saw them beyond their swan masks. He saw that they came from faraway places, from the exploited corners of the world, foreign of country, culture, and class. He saw how absolutely terrified they all were.

Janu took a gun from the wardrobe and stored it in his apron pouch. He had borne its weight and felt its metal in his stomach all the days since then.

The Sabine patio's shade stirred mysteriously as he limped back. Janu looked closer. A girl lay there curled, arms round her legs tucked and straining chin upon her knees, crying, crying. (Magpie?) He asked her what happened. A breathless heave, a suffocated effort was her response (inhaler! my inhaler!) and suddenly he found himself gaining consciousness of his own deep breaths as he scrambled to find the inhaler; the next moment she had it, she drew in the spray of life.

Again he asked (what happened?). Sitting at her side upon the grass he listened to her sobbing, and at length, over the course of the long night, her story came out in suppressed whispers, surfacing and subsuming into tears again and again.

As the narcotic's influence waned, Janu's sentiments grew sharper and the indignity, squalor, and horror of everything happening around him seized his lungs, his heart, his throat, wrinkling chin, shivering lip; his eyes welled up, and they wept together until the day broke and the feeble light covered them.

Suddenly Janu came back to his eyes, and Neipas, too, jolted out of dizziness at once. They felt the grip of Osir's hands on their shoulders. Amid the booming yells his calmness was uncanny, like the sudden apparition of a different reality. In his palpitating vagueness of head Neipas wondered which of the realities was real.

Osir's voice likewise sounded from a remote area of the universe. "We gotta get out of here," he stated tranquil.

The bulls had come in with riot masks, and their voices shouted from every wall, frothing with the fury of deep hatreds. Pure wrath was unleashed upon their ears, shot into their hearts — without cease; the whole place quaked with the noise.

Neipas found himself following Osir, keeping a wrenching awareness of Janu and the teetering gun behind him. They were descending the mounds of things and stumbling down the rolling steps amid the swarm of climbing bugs; strangely, the escalator bifurcated into several paths now and they roamed amid confusing heaps of pillows, lost themselves in the attempt to dodge the incoming guards' ire. But Neipas was eventually possessed by a fear that Janu, in his madness, might shoot him. A strange sensation of air warming on his skin took possession of him, and he felt himself becoming aware of Janu's uneven steps, Janu's shallow breathing, the shaking sweat off his neck, the steely rattle of the loaded gun and the menace of a bullet leaning back into the firing pin... Janu munched on cookies maniacally, the crunching was audible. Reflexively, Neipas' eyes would glare back slowly — and even the overpowering shouts seemed to distance themselves in the intensity of focus and nervousness about the famished cook.

It was a long time until Neipas realized that Janu hadn't been there the last several times he had peeked. "Wait. Wait!" Neipas whispered loudly, tapping Osir's shoulder. The noise suddenly pushed back up into a maximum level of volume and pressure; the shouting beat at their brains with physical force. "Where's Janu?" Neipas exclaimed louder now, almost in a scream. They had wandered the vaults for a while, perhaps blindingly, enveloped in mounds and mazes of piled-up riches (whence catapulted the seething voices of the bulls).

"Where's Janu?" Neipas repeated. Osir looked about; but the disappearance of the cook didn't seem to disturb his aloof serenity.

A myriad mirroring surfaces reflected confused perspectives around them. Ornamented metals sparkled into the deepening oblivion of their replicas, sieging with towering heights the many little figures of Neipas the waiter and Osir the janitor, meek and humble among crushing quantities of vain wealth.

"Where's Janu?" Neipas' infinite beaks motioned voicelessly. Shouts of angry authority hurled from every surface and oppressed the little figures. Even the metals vibrated in the boom, sometimes as though the boom issued from the very pores of their reflections. Osir kept looking around with an aloof air. Looking into him, Neipas saw his eyes empty.

Silence. Suddenly they focused their hearing and sensed no sound. Neipas turned to Osir's furrowed brow, gazed worriedly into the hollowness of his narrowed glare. Then, without moving, he looked beyond him; and saw, emerging from round a wardrobe in the depths of a glass, a boot.

It could be anywhere. The mirrors revealed corners otherwise inaccessible to their sights.

Neipas' first instinct was to duck and whimper a low moan of fright. He seized Osir's wrist, pulled him down and, staring widely, he tapped his finger against the tip of his own beak repeatedly. From between his shoulders he stared out and surveyed; he saw boots in the mirrors no more, but here a new perception reached him in the quiet — a stealthy sound of heavy steps.

Motioning frantically and soundlessly, Neipas moved along in a crouch.

Osir followed him close. Keeping his head low, Neipas strained to maintain a hold of himself as he thrust through the chaotic sights of replicating shimmering and the confusion of seeing himself in all angles at once, all about him in reflections of every color and rust. The pace of his own breathing was slipping out of his control, he felt himself choking. The heavy steps sounded in and out of range, but no one spoke. Perceiving a secluded nook amid the pile of things, Neipas sneaked in.

They crouched and waited in a fever of anticipation. Whenever the steps sounded Neipas would hold his breath. In the strained motionlessness of his own body he could clearly discern the agitation stirring inside it; his heart palpitated with punches at his throat.

Time passed. Though the steps seemed to be always within range of hearing, sometimes far, sometimes closer, there came a period when Neipas realized that it had actually been silent for a while. And yet he sensed the presence of the bulls still prowling about the space. All faculties still in his possession told him they couldn't have just abandoned the search. The bulls knew of the intruding oxen; and their presence there was intolerable. Fear, an encroaching sense of exhaustion and hollowing hunger, paralyzed Neipas.

He lulled with deepening breath. Many hours seemed to have passed, Neipas thought as he regained awareness of himself sometimes, before he faded into a dormant nonpresence again. Always an anxiety pressed or gnawed at him.

It was somewhat gloomy in here.

Osir had sat calmly atop a chest covered with black and white textiles. His stillness was eerie. The janitor stared forward fixedly, vacantly, with soulless eyes, taken not by the madness which had possessed Janu but by something slower and more insidious. He seemed to be in the midst of a battle against rising physical sensations. The pill bottle had been taken out of his pocket, he held it; and from time to time he would turn it upside down and shake it over the palm of his hand, as if expecting a pill to drop — but the bottle was empty. Osir would do this many times over. Bit by bit, he began to shake.

Neipas checked the time in his *I* — it (time) was, to his surprise, still moving. There was a little table between him and Osir, and after (a few seconds? many hours?) some indeterminate period of time staring at the glow of the *I* he set the glass deafly upon the table.

The nook was a mess of furniture, textiles, toiletries and small heaps of gold dust. By his feet Neipas noticed a little case of cosmetics, with a palette of make-up colors on one side and a mirror, with framing lights, on the other. Soon he was looking at the mirror.

The feathers of his pigeon face were pasted with black sweat, glued to the molting wax underneath. Its messy plumage lumped about his jaw and chin, sprouting from the wax in decadent and unkempt clusters. Tufts sank into his cheeks, which seemed hollow; gore soaked the disheveled crown of his head; its wetness (dried upon the surface) felt like it seeped into the brain somehow. The lower lid of his eye sagged, limp and sickly; the eye itself twitched involuntarily, irritated, with a bloodshot intensity. He stared deeply into the crater of his pupil — it was sinking into the remotest profundities of his soul, and the dusted iris widened tremendously, extending unbridled and furiously to cover the entire universe of all that exists.

Always the anxiety pressed and gnawed, always it bit and chewed. Osir, in front of Neipas, kept still and flipped the empty bottle of pills again and again.

"You look old, Neipas" — it was not Osir who had spoken, nor was it Neipas' reflection in the little mirror; it was the little make-up kit Neipas held in his hand. "You look old, old," it repeated.

"That's true," whispered Neipas, secretly.

"Time doesn't stop," said the mannequin in the shadowed corner. "Wrinkles amass about your eyes. Your whole skin sags; it aspires to the dirt. Your kind aspires to the dirt. It's too weak to face the sun."

"What do you mean."

"Pull yourself up by the bootstraps, pigeon!" said the little make-up kit with energetic motions, for now the kit was opening and closing like a mouth. "Why so agitated? You have choices! Change your situation! Quit lazying around, you!"

"But I work hard."

"You do!?" — the make-up kit flapped bewilderedly in Neipas' hand. "Then how are you in this situation? Thief! Look at how low you've stooped, man! You didn't work hard enough..."

Neipas rocked back and forth in the gloomiest corner of the nook, beholding the mirror in the make-up kit nervously. The anxiety overwhelmed him, pushing his internal organs shrinking in a painful retreat to the recesses of his spirit. All his fiber trembled, all he wanted was to run blindly and scream, and cry; instead he whimpered, paralyzed by dread. Osir, in front of him, finally moved.

"Why so agitated?" asked the mannequin. "You could have been a successful photographer... Why did you have to be such a stuck-up? Why didn't you get on the ladder like everyone else? Do you think you're better?"

"No, I — just... I just wanted to be true to myself..."

"Good work! Fucking snob! Uncompromising fools like yourself never get anywhere... You're unrealistic, pigeon!" said the make-up kit.

It was his own reflection now who continued (he did not feel his mouth move and yet it moved inside the mirror): "Maybe you wanted to fail. Lazy ass. And now the dreams of your childhood, which you used to dream by the river, are dead."

Neipas nodded melancholic, with water in his bloodshot eyes. Osir had leaned forward on his chest, plunging his eyes into the *I* light. Meanwhile, Neipas began to whisper:

"The river... I remember the river. I used to sit on the side of it for hours... Just watching it flow. Just watching. The waters passing, and the shimmer, and the rocks under it, the fish — the water was so clear. It shone with the clearness of crystal. Beautiful, beautiful, beautiful. I would stare in wonder. And the flowers (what were their names again) swaying in the river bank, the canopies breathing wind above me. And there was the sound of the wheel, kissing the water. Everything was so calm, so pristine...

"I could observe everything for hours. Just sitting there, just... being, you know? Taking in everything. The wonder, and the beauty of it all... Watching, feeling... Being.

"Being," his voice had gradually grown tremulous, even as his body becalmed in the comfort of reminiscence. The sound of the flowing river sprinkled peacefully in his ears; but already a brooding noise was stealing behind it, a thunderous rumble coming from the distance. He spoke these words to — whom? (Through his pores were voiced runnels of ink; he imagined his voice translated to a page — words were but abstracted pictures, he thought) and in the meantime a certain intention was building up inside him, a desire to see the old river again. The anxiety clutched, made it impossible to be still.

"Being... Isn't that what we're called? Human beings? But I haven't been able to do that for so long, so long... I can barely remember... I — " his voice was but a whimper now. "How long has it been... since I've been? I..." The water in his eyes broke out and rushed down his cheeks, effacing his features deeper. The river was mud now, it was toxin, it was dead.

"I..." Neipas choked up, and trembling he said, "I don't feel human anymore!"

Reflexively he reached for his pocket, brimming with weeping desire for the lost days of childhood, for the lost peace of the lost river. But the *I* wasn't there — he forgot he had placed it on the little table; but it wasn't there either.

Osir had it.

"What are you doing!" Neipas hissed with a gasp of fear. Osir didn't react. In a surge of nervous emotion Neipas got up and pushed Osir's shoulder — though he was too weak now to make the push as strong as his agitation. "What are you doing!" he repeated, taking the *I* from Osir's hand.

"There's connection here, man," the janitor stated calmly, unfazed, though his hands trembled; he was drooling through the corner of his lips.

"Mary! Oh god!" Neipas moaned, growing in despair as he saw the *I* was connected to the Webwork. He felt the eyes of the Googol light up, bearing his image.

Right away he unplugged the *I*. "They're gonna know we're here!" he said, or thought — already he had given himself to the anxious impulses goading him on and was sprinting aimlessly through the maze of things. The walls suddenly exploded with thousands of replications of his likeness, running, running, running, running away and towards one another and in all directions up, down, horizontally, vertically, obliquely, in all colors and all manners of distortions all at once. Skinny Neipas, fat Neipas, Neipas compressed and expanded and with a million arms and without a head, scrambling across a space of self-multitudes.

Two simultaneous events halted his sprint. He crashed against a mirror (all worlds were mirrors now) and everything vibrated dizzyingly around him; and as he was getting his bearings, he thought vaguely he had heard a gunshot — the sound of a fired bullet, somewhat distant.

Then a sharp boom made him start. Another gunshot, released like a powerful explosion across the halls — really close now. Shaking from head to toe, half-delirious, Neipas took a few steps, and came into a bend where he saw it.

Two bulky towers of armored muscle standing over what looked like a sack: the image, refracted and distorted, propagated endlessly through the glass. They clenched machine guns over protective heavy gear and riot-masks and helmets on their bovine heads. All round the floor lay a mess of crumbs dissolving into a pool of — something like blood, spreading slowly and viscously from their boots and out of the sack. Neipas couldn't see what it was exactly. It was tattered, vaguely human, resembling a bedraggled doll with deflated limbs and a disheveled appearance. One of the bulls (the spike-collared one), having unsheathed a large knife, now crouched over the dumped and violated thing; while the other (the one with the keyless nose-ring pending from his exposed nostrils) propped it up with his boot and let it drop back, again and again. It swayed heavily as the guardians fiddled with it — the squatting bull now pulled back in an effort, and seemed somehow to be flaying off the skin of it.

Neipas, spying round a bend of the mirror labyrinth, was petrified, made rigid with the clutch of horror. The thought that it could be a body lying there suddenly occurred to his distressed imagination. Though he was immobile, indeed unable to move, his entrails were revolting frantically and his heart seemed intent on punching a bloody hole through his throat. His veins swelled with rushing red rivers flooding every corner of Neipas' being; the blood roared in his ears, and the vision in his eyes penetrated him with the force of an imprinting trauma. Before them flashed Magpie dropping from the tower. Cesar's limp arms and shrouded face. An overwhelming dread of meeting their fate thrust, rooted, tussled violently through Neipas' buoying gaze, which foresaw the act of his own murder mirrored thousandfold in the endlessly reflected pools of his own blood; his nostrils quivered with the sensation of his hunters' imminent approach.

Already Neipas' body was drawing away from there; but in his hand he held the *I*, out of which some occult force surged suddenly and made him lift it up to his eyes, get the *I*'s lens ready... unthinking, he snapped a photograph of the grisly scene.

He couldn't know if it had been because of this — but as he snapped the shot the Bull with the nose-ring turned, and, through the messiness of reflections, looked straight at Neipas. The mortified waiter faced a moment of indecision — it was impossible to actually know where they were. But then all at once powerful shouting boomed out of everywhere, thrusting itself with full fury onto him; and when he came to he was running, his own image breaking out across the walls and quaking with the uproar. Shots rang among the noises of wrath; there was the sound of glass breaking afar, and then two unbearably loud bursts with shards falling all over Neipas' body. He ran like a maniac, fueled by despair with the charge of a thousand Olympians, maddeningly clinging to life through the twisting surfaces, coiling reflections, confusions of shimmer and the thunder of hatreds pronounced from every vibrating direction (the voices were like the mirrors, replicating themselves endlessly over each other, so that they sounded like a chaotic army of millions), bruising himself, lacerating his clothes with gashes, slitting his limbs bloody and pushing through succeeding limits of pain in the desperate escape from death. Until he faded from the walls.

(Breathing throbbed in his ears and gasped tremulous into his deflating heart. Fingers from below twined with his own, and now guided him across the path; and for a moment he was becalmed, for he had felt that hand's touch before. Two threads writhed forth between the turmoil of images, ascending and descending the lean tower/staff by his side as they revolved in the looping motion of a double helix. Where his feet should be, the double threads now were. He/they glided across in a wind of breaths.

Yet the hand had already gone.)

Through an unconscious process of desperate action Neipas managed to escape the labyrinth. He had only the vaguest idea how. There was no energy left for thought or awareness of himself. There was no time. Suddenly some kind of cloth collided against his frantic thrust and he recoiled in a scramble for a moment; when he opened his eyes Neipas found himself in the factory of beakless slaves, who kept working, and paid no attention to his passing. At a run he saw, once more, their relentless toil, their bent backs over the rolling carpets, over the moving tables, their maimed fingers putting together mechanical puzzles. He saw once more the furnaces, the starving children coated with dust, the frightened brows, the indifferent brows, the hollowed brows. Again the same dim gazes, whose souls flared somewhere in a distant continent.

With hurried knocks and rickety breaths he summoned the boatman in the coastal shack, the door of which opened to reveal an enormous hooded ear. Neipas fumbled the string of silver beads out of his pocket — and as one almost fell out of the broken cord, where one bead was missing, it occurred to his hastened mind to leave beads for Janu and Osir to pay for the passage back. He tossed two beads onto the soggy ground, and lodged the last one in the deep pit of the boatman's ear. Through the palisade of reeds they went then, and out over the amplitude of frothing waters circling this inner ring of the Belab, which Neipas, shivering under the great noise of the current and the ravages of the dripping leprous ceiling, crossed, tucked in the hollowed shell of a little tarred boat. He gaped frightened at the abyss of the boatman's giant earface inside the deep hole of its hood... until he landed scrambling on the sucking clays of the outer shore, where he fell headlong, the draining sands all over his mushed visage.

The giant hogs squealed frantically and rammed their snouts against their cage bars as Neipas sped past; the fountain dripped blood and petals into the gutter still, and the guardian lay in tattered rags upon the dusty floor. With atrophied muscles straining, the veins of his neck jutting, and the pulpy wax oozing, boiling onto his shoulders, he pulled the heavy double gate on the closet-like entrance open.

The screaming, which had chased him through echoes up until this point, ceased. Nothing but a wobbly silence filled his ear; it bore down upon his soul. Fraught, bleary, Neipas proceeded with caution up the royal steps and between the bejeweled walls. His toe stumbled on some clinking thing. His blinking gaze interpreted a shard — some ceramic, a bit of hardened clay stuffed with plume, the corner of a beak flowering with mustache. It resembled Janu's ministerial mask (the image of his lunatic heaving and gnashed teeth still bobbing in Neipas' mind). Had he escaped? — mulled

Neipas swimmingly as he climbed. With terror numbing his fingers he reached for the eyed curtain, tail of the perched peacock. The very first moment's slit between its reedy folds exhaled a puff of vapor into his peeking eye, gaping wide and quavering all in tiny veins. The fumes were sufficiently scattered for him to see the great fountain and its spiral head. The darkness itself was softened by some sidelong palpitating light; and in it there was no one.

Indeed, the octagonal bathhouse's vapors were much sparser than the last time he was there. Neipas crossed it, navigating at the tip of his stiff, outstretched neck, behind jutting eyes, runny mask dissolving in the heat pulling down, down, dulling... There was the fountain edge, where he had last spoken with Magpie. The emblem of Sol Invictus raged in mute stone close by his side; various gargoyle lips gaped at him with soundless screams. Plutus laughed his marble grin from the wall, held the caved mirror between a profusion of cornucopias and (farther to the sides) two arches. One of the arches was covered by the peacock's plumage curtain; there upon the high pole, motionless, silent, eternal — it gazed and saw nothing. The other arch (on Plutus' left) was open, and it gave passage to a descending stairway, and to a candle.

Already upon the final bathhouse, upon the last chamber of their Temple he saw it; he saw, as he had many times seen, the Candle of Man.

He descended the ivory steps — amid the dark braziers — into an immense sanctum.

There it stood.

It was a colossus; a giant tower of wax, godly, terrifying; its round body glistened with the words THOU SHALT in every idiom known to History. Before it arose the object of its worship: upon the grand wall, a vast extent of glimmering scales reflected the words in various hues of gold... Each of these scales a mask — together, the masks assembled the form of an enormous, open-winged dragon. Upon the peak of its shimmering golden body perched its blank, indescribable face — a vaguely human face — a face of facelessness. It was an effigy — an idol.

Mammon.

The vast circular sanctum was clear, no vapors clouded it. Behind him, some distance afar, a great opening let him gaze a waterfall, beyond which stretched the clouds, the open air. A deep quietude abated him to a state of diffusion; at once aware and distant of his beating heart. Everything stilled as he absorbed everything.

The ground shook slightly.

Among the fume-shrouded arch atop the stairway, where Neipas had entered, which palpitated by the candlelight, with its pulsing words, there appeared the silhouette of a crescent, a crescent with tips pointed up, a crescent atop a head, a head atop a body, horns, a bull...

His breath snuffed out and muscles locked, still Neipas found himself running, found himself looking, like a spectator, through his eyes as they shivered frantic toward the waterfall. (BOOM!)

([a reverberating...] BOOM! BOOM! BOOM!) His legs plunged into a sudden stop under the crazed tolling of bells, his head thrust forth as he regained his balance. Storm clouds wheeled just beneath his feet and billowed up and down. He had emerged into the crimson sky by the dim bleeding cascade, and stood on a narrow pathway leading along the edge of the tower; the unending tempest, blooded by the already buried sun, filled his senses (BOOM! BOOM! BOOM!) The infernal noise made his brain pound and he literally couldn't feel himself think or move as he clambered away from the northern waterfall and up the steps of the encased platform — a platform similar to the one he had walked to cross from the Pigeon to the Eagle Wing of the Anubel, though this one was shielded from the tempest by glass, and faced north, where the Diamond Hills sheltering the abandoned residences of the wealthy lay vulnerable to the scourge of the storm. Neipas rushed through a door and hastened again into the tower, finding himself in the crepuscular, deep, vaulted storehouse filled with veiled boxes and mannequins, and ceilings full of beastly faces, where Neipas had first met the Giant Historian; the floor echoed and thundered with each plunge of his sprint, and with the reverberating bells the whole infinitude of space seemed to tilt and vibrate in the wide sway of sound. He never stopped, stretching himself beyond all limits, dread stretching the natural capacities of his starved physique, running and running in the darkness with but the light of his *I* to guide him through. His existence was all instinct; and instinct, that divine animality, drove him toward the Columbaria. He left behind the circular portal (CAVE, it clamored on the lintel) and the small lobby with the hearth and the pigeon painting, and scrambled up the stairway into the dark corridor to the dormitories.

He found himself panting over a trough in the bathroom; the next moment he stared at the mirror, beheld his shoulders heave in deep shrugs. He was a mess — his clothes were torn and caked with blood, his mask made mush. He tip-toed to his dormitory, next door — changed his clothes in the darkness, still panting — and returned to the bathroom to fix his visage.

Someone was coming out of the stall just as Neipas entered. He could barely see anything in the gloom and did everything by the light of the *I*. Vague reds blinked. Two faucets ran soundlessly in the dark (deafened by the roiling of the bells), one by Neipas' side and another under him.

Things revolved like a dream. It seemed like a long time had passed when

Neipas, in the process of carving up his damaged pigeon mask, turned to the other faucet, which was still running (he perceived it was, even through the tolling). A question had vaguely materialized in his head and it sprung now almost involuntarily out of his beak:

"Hey, where is everyone?" he yelled. Indeed, the corridors had been completely deserted.

A strange and unknown voice spoke over the running faucet: "They're staging a trial up in the Auditorium! Someone was caught breaking into the other wing."

The bells and both faucets stopped; and all became the silence of dripping drops.

67 - Trial

Above moon and sun, sole under the overarching universe, there stood a single beam of white light. It mounted fierce atop a terraced mound surfacing, like a stairway for giants, from a tidal plain of clouds, ascending to the pharos holding back an ever looming night. It rose like a triumphal fist in defiance of the vicissitudes of mortal existence; a lofty, regal outpost of survival among the crushing inscrutabilities of life, a celestial fortress guarding against the siege of dissolution lurking in every second, menacing the possibility of every breath — a sun that never dies. A pearl shining in an ocean of darkness — the fumes underneath propagated like sand upon the seafloor, outspread over mute, forsaken burial grounds in a desert made of silence and dream stuff...

Holy summit of a drowned mountain, it made the night tremble with its clap of pealing bell, ringing incessantly in the heights; gathering round itself, with summonings of flapping bronze, a congregation of ghostly shapes. There shored and massed the cloak of fumes, its hilly contours revealed by the light. The mantle was infinite; it was as if the smoke of Iblis and all the vapors of the sky had accumulated there, lain beneath the shining nest in prostration, praise and worship, expanding from it, cast from it, into the unseen horizon and to the very confines of the world.

In its terraces, human beings with animal heads crowded. Tired, grotesque faces crowded darkly, gazing upon a stage with eyes drowned in pools of gloom beneath ridged brows.

When the vast curtain was first parted, the Stage and its Proscenium frame resembled a black, toothless maw suspended in the act of inhaling, perpetually about to speak. Within it could be seen nothing; its open immensitude was sheltered from the beam of rising moon and of arisen Pearl in the topmost Summit. Then they brought up torches, and the first thing these torches alighted upon the stage (beyond the lusterless ivory of the livestock who carried them) was a slick vermillion cape, which glistened darkly in reply to the palpitation and shiver of the flames. There was a golden glint also: hooked and bowed, with sibilant, flaring nostrils.

The Stage assumed form with the mounting flames, before the attention of a multitude of stares, whose eyes, tucked beneath the ridges of tired brows, all hid in impenetrable shadows. Black burrows beholding a large black maw — dark hollows between cheeks and foreheads splashed in the sheen of intense white Pearl, animated by the spurring flames of torches standing over, waving vaguely from side to side. The ground trembled and everything rocked in a fanning of noise. Heralding judgment, the bells rang even more rabidly, more feverishly, more maddened than ever they had for the Market; as though in the delirium of a drunken auction. Their vibration subsumed all senses in its totality, everyone remained petrified in its sound; everyone was still, in it; and beneath it, all was silence.

The bells swung over a tottering descent of naked terraces, where a mess of cloth lay strewn in toxic moistures, where the trees had toppled or stood leafless and singed, where the shrubs were no more than crisp and mangled skeletons; the stones were charred black; from the angry shocked mouths of the gargoyles, from the little founts, in the clogged lake and through the gutters, the water of the river flowed thickly and slow, with the density of bubbly scum, in a comatose hush. An uproar of motions had broken out quickly after the first gunshots popped in the crowded gardens. Just as Neipas and Osir crossed the Great Peacock's lake, a group of crows was limping meekly out of the Columbaria, all ragged, hungry, and desperate, holding up their hands in protest and pleas that all remaining food be made free and equitably shared, lest they all starve to death. The Bulls pounced them at once. The procession, already breaking, was scattered. There were fistfights and scared children crying and running in all directions. The most maddened among the crows, in response to the gunshots hurled at them, produced their own weapons, which they had long ago bought; and began firing blindly, under gnashed beaks, glassed eyes. It was utter chaos: torches fell and flames conflagrated across the tarpaulin streets, thick with fuel, soaked with veils, doused with hatred; and feet sped and trampled upon feet in the flight to the frigid darkness of the interior, where everyone that could escape hid in the non-presence of the thick, silencing gloom.

Now they had all resurfaced, and stood with unseeing heads, in a daze; the terraces behind them were emptied of clutter, and one's gaze could pierce as far down as the bottommost level — the Museum gardens — where mountains of discarded appliances arose, flushed from the burnt woods of the 2nd tier which previously concealed them. No one knew, or wished to think about, whether anyone had died in the violent pandemonium.

Some had... Their bones hid among the garbage piled in the exposed bottom terrace, End of History's yard.

Their flesh had already been snatched away.

Sneaking up from the back, Neipas beheld a turmoiled sea of heads spanning across mottled depths. Its harlequin colors paled in the overwhelming Pearl light. The bells had stopped, but its vibration persisted in the air of murmurs, into which he dove, densely. He swam through the tide of sound till it quietened. There was motion upon the Stage.

The satin world of clouds behind them birthed the full moon — it shone upon the nude terraces of the Anubel, softening the starkness of the Pearl and the deep shadows it cast. Every seat was occupied, though most were standing, and the aisles were crammed with bodies. The ones with pigeon faces, the most wretched among them, watched with lurid, bloodshot glares from the very back; their fidgety masks peeked from the balustrades at the foot of the statues in the Auditorium's perimeter. Further ahead, over the seats and in aisles thick, there emerged a confusion of moaning wools and of ivory and silvery horns in various stages of degradation: rusted, battered or broken. In the front rows sat (behind a line of armed papal Bulls) an array of luminaries: mantled Horses and Stags with heads lifted and solemn; expecting with royal airs the beginning of proceedings. Pelicans sanctified the Stage by tossing smoke from their swinging thuribles. In the shaded depths up there, peeking between the fringes of the curtains, stood large-eyed Owls, watching. And above, high among the majesty of the Great Facade, in the garden terraces suspended behind the ramparts, the Eagles lounged comfortably, and discreetly observed. Bull horns peeked over the merlons of the battlement; the muzzles of their guns projected through its crenels — ready, tense between the soft, subtle red lights winking over the lenses of recording cameras.

The great Auditorium, the vast terrace was absolutely full; it seemed like everyone was there. All their shadowed eyes were fixed upon the Stage.

A court had been set up upon it. At center was the bench where stood a vermillion-robed figure, the Judge, whose beak leaned against the ear of a Peacock (to Neipas the props had an appearance resembling one of the stands of the Market — perhaps the pulpits, tables and chairs, which indeed looked a little charred, had been taken from there). Close by the bench was a little table with an *I*. On either side and in front of the bench was a pulpit; no one stood behind either pulpit yet. And suspended above the platform was a tall, wooden stake.

Strapped to it, aloft — a mere shape in the distance to Neipas' eyes — stood, upon a very narrow footrest, Kasim. His arms were tied behind the pole. His toes held suspended over the drop.

His head lowered, he looked like he hung in the air — perched with folded wings upon some invisible twig, sleeping.

Curtains kissed one another in folds behind him, towering high and immense over the scene.

Neipas dug his way through the dense crowd, attempting to see better. He was in the midst of the murmuring now and it was as though he walked deep into a spell. The dizziness grew in the incantation of mixed voices; hunger carved its teeth in his brain with little jabs. Neipas saw the Peacock with whom the Judge was speaking leave his side, and take position at the little table by the bench. Neipas' voice asked who that was, and someone — perhaps addressing him — said that he was a reporter, charged with minuting the judgment.

Now the Judge, perched behind the stand, placed solemnly on his round bald head the lion mane, symbol of Justice. He waved his head a little, perhaps to make sure the wig was well fixed — and, pursing his long beak, he looked out of the enormous amber eyes with largesse, and subsequently frowned and pounded the hammer upon the drum, gawking "Order! Order!". Everyone went quiet.

"The counsels may take their posts," said the Judge. At this, an Eagle emerged from the back-stage and took the pulpit to the right of the Judge; and a woman with a pigeon mask climbed up from the auditorium, and took the pulpit on the left. It was Marlene — her pink hair faded, her face unmistakably haggard, still she was able to retain her dignified, professional aspect, the neatness of her ironed clothes setting smoothly upon the thinness of her limbs and bony shoulders, her strained disconcertion well disguised under the composure of her practiced mask.

"Dear constituents," began the Judge. "We are gathered here today for the trial of Kasim the pantrykeeper, for the crimes of conspiracy, terrorism, theft of property, disobedience, petty treason, identity theft, and violation of private property. The venerable Minister of Justice will take up the prosecution. Miss Marlene offered to take up the defense. We will start with opening cases. Order! Order!" concluded the Judge, pounding the hammer, as in the meantime the murmuring had shyly begun to rise again.

Silence was made. From the Judge's table was lifted a thick tome, the Book of Laws — a Bull held it solemnly as Marlene and the Prosecutor, each standing on their own side, placed their hands upon the cover.

"Do you swear to tell the truth, the whole truth, and nothing but the truth?" inquired the Judge.

"I do," they both swore in their turn, returning then to their respective pulpits.

Silence remained among the crowds — a watchful silence, a waiting silence, it was. Kasim stood above everyone, an enigma hovering in cryptic, gleaming shadows amidst the air, under the arching golds of the Proscenium; alien, his well-defined contours were mostly steeped in darkness, with but the red fire to light him from below. High, still, bowed — thus he perched above them all, his figure wavering, with the palpitating glows of the shifting flame, between power and vulnerability, between menace and innocence.

The Minister of Justice, Prosecutor, was the first to speak:

"Your Honor, dear constituents. It is with lament that I address you here today. The defendant stands trial for some of the most heinous crimes predicted by The Law. Conspiracy against the nation. Theft of property. Violation of property. Treason against his master, disobedience! The defendant broke into a Temple! His conduct is monstrous, an outrage. An affront to everything we hold dear, everything we hold sacred!"

The Prosecutor went on at length, describing the main beats of Kasim's plotting — his impersonating the Nations Minister, his breaking into the Temple to steal its items — coloring the narrative with dismayed interjections and facial contortions conveying the unbelievable sordidness of his actions. Point by point and in detail he revealed the sins of the accused, repeatedly throwing, amidst all this, the not-so-subtle suggestion that Kasim had somehow conspired (with nebulous foreign accomplices) to instigate the riots which had so defaced the Pigeon Wing and battered its inhabitants. Upstairs the bulls cheered — and there was scattered clapping among the audience when he was done.

Next up was Marlene the Defense Attorney:

"Hum — Well, to begin," she checked herself a moment and somewhat goofily veered off track. "Your Honor, dear constituents." Then she was silent, trying to gather her wits. Marlene had suffered secret and profound realizations in the Eagle's Nest. She had lived its 28 days in deepening agony, spying sights which seared her eyes, surviving experiences that rendered fundamental beliefs. She had seen beyond the mask of the Eagles and what she saw shocked her into a crisis of conviction. Hunger gnawed at her capacity to focus now. She searched deeper within herself.

The audience's murmuring had meanwhile filled the silence. The Judge summoned order with shouts and a hammer, and order imposed quietude onto the auditorium again. Neipas, among the mass, felt the restlessness of its compressed weight, charged with a brimming need for vocal articulation which was quickly working itself up into expression again. But in the interim Marlene spoke again, saying simply:

"My client is innocent of all charges. I hope to prove that to you."

"Order! Order! Order!" shouted the Judge, for the audience had begun again. "Very well. Let us commence proceedings. The Prosecution may begin."

The Prosecutor questioned Kasim. While his voice was magnified by that of the microphone, Kasim's was barely a peep over the silence of the great crowd, which strained its myriad ears in an effort to hear.

"It is true that you broke into the Temple — which you knew to be forbidden — did you not?"

[...]

"You were in charge of food stock, is that correct? You were in charge of the pantry throughout the scarcity of food in the Market — were you not?"

[...]

"Don't you think it's a bizarre coincidence that the riots began *just* as you were breaking into the Temple? *Just* as the violence was beginning?"

[...]

"You are from the east, are you not?"

[...]

The questioning ended and the mumbling rose up again, now full of questions asking 'what? what?'; apparently he was the pantry-keeper and had mismanaged the food stocks badly. Everything was his fault. He orchestrated the riots so that he could sow confusion and steal whatever it was that was stored in the Temple. He was a thief who tried to loot the treasure inside. He was a terrorist, it looked like, who intended to wreak havoc. He was a foreign spy who had infiltrated the highest echelons of Columbidae society and he had been plotting everything from the very beginning. Echoes spread and refracted across the mist of babbles. In reality no one really understood what the accusations meant. No one knew what was going on. But the pigeon floating there over the torches looked suspicious — see how threatening his face (lit by pulses of fire from below) looks? Some were already sure he was guilty. Neipas froze in his advance and hunched amid the multitude; had Kasim mentioned his name? bubbled in his lips the question as he heard the mumbled words of their flinching nostrils, the nonsensical drivel of random disconnected phrases buoying in that seasick nightmare.

They were all starving and none could think. Between their animal heads and their selves they were all shrouded in silent masks of darkness — untethered.

"Quiet! Quiet!" shouted the Judge, beating the hammer again. The audience shushed. "Defense — please state your case."

"Your Honor, constituents of the court," Marlene began. Her voice, though still feeble, sounded more composed now, as though she had dedicated the time of questioning to collect herself.

"Before anything, I'd like to give my client a voice, your Honor."

"Well? He has a right to speak," the Judge responded annoyedly.

"I mean, your Honor, I don't think anyone can hear him. Can someone get him a microphone, please?"

There were mumblings of agreement among the audience and the microphone was somehow arranged against the grumbling of the Eagles.

"Good evening, Mr. Kasim," began the Defense Attorney. "How are you feeling?"

"I have seen better days. But also worse ones," he replied.

"You'll get through this, Mr. Kasim," she said sympathetically, humane; and then locked in back to tone — "Mr. Kasim, just to reiterate — is it true that you entered the temple vaults without permission?"

"Yes."

"Thank you, Mr. Kasim. About the two other persons detained in connection with this incident, hum... Janu the cook, and, Osir the janitor. Do you know them, Mr. Kasim?"

"Yes."

"Were you with them in the vaults?"

"Yes."

"Was there anyone else with you?"

"No."

Tiny among the vast crowd Neipas, afar, was experiencing a strange mix of emotions. His nerves were racked with the anticipation that his name be mentioned — and now he becalmed. But he wondered about Osir's fate with guilt, and forebode Janu's with horror, afflicted as he was by the uncertain circumstances in which he had left them — and by the knowledge, now, that they had been caught.

By degrees he regained his step amid the crowd, and through them he advanced closer to the stage.

"Whose idea was it to inspect the vaults, Mr. Kasim?"

"My own."

"And why was that?"

"To take the food stored in the vaults and distribute it to the rest of us. We are hungry."

The mumbling started again and rose instantly in volume. Vivid nods of agreement shook the crowd; and the beginnings of an ovation were heard just under the hammer boom, which was currently sounding. "Quiet! Quiet! Quiet!

"I will have order in this courtroom!" the Judge roared jugularly. Once the agitation becalmed he said: "Defense — continue."

"Mr. Kasim, was there any particular catalyst for your decision to inspect the vaults? A turning point that made your situation so unbearable that you simply had to do it?"

There was a pause — into which a stillness of expectation subsided, and the billowed moonshine alighted upon the perched man hanging over a multiplicity of scrutinies, half-shaded eyes. The man, in the secret intimacy of his soul, prayed; and he endeavored serenely against the weakness of hunger and the strain of his fixed position, gathering his fortitude into coherent words, before he spoke them:

"I made my decision long before I did something," said he. "Food stocks were decreasing quickly. It was easy to predict, what was going to happen — I saw it coming long before I saw people malnourished in the corridors. Many have been dying from hunger. Surely, some have already died."

A somber rumbling of anger stirred through the crowd. It crumbled of its own as the audience focused its ears to listen. There was a suppressed heave of exasperation in the body mass.

"I tried to warn my employers many times, but they did not listen," Kasim concluded.

The voices of the Judge and the Prosecutor bulged in their throats, hesitating to emerge into the great silence that was then made; and Marlene, standing in the middle of the great Stage, bowed her head gently. She then, gently, asked, "It would be helpful if you could give us more context — generally, as to how you knew the food would run out so quickly, and why — and so forth. And — could you describe your experience up until the moment you entered the vaults, and what you perceive the experience of your peers to have been?"

"Your Honor, I don't see how this is relevant," said the Prosecutor.

"Indeed, Miss Marlene, what is your point?" asked the Judge.

"Your Honor, The Law states that circumstance and intention have a bearing in determining whether conduct is criminal or not, and how severe a crime it is if it is indeed a crime. That is what I'm trying to determine."

"Miss Marlene..."

"Let him talk!" someone shouted from the audience and a clamor soared above the shout. The hammer exerted itself to quell the sound.

"Quiet! Quiet! Very well, Miss," the Judge said impatiently.

Kasim spoke of those days. He described hours of grueling toil without rest, and without joy, while their masters lounged among the riches.

(The Prosecutor countered. You had plenty of resting periods).

But the work continued even then, relentless in the mind. Kasim told the audience of their hunger, and in the telling they felt it deeper yet; it sank into their souls with the gravity of an important realization, with the weight of significance. And they hungered, Kasim said, while the Eagles ate and wasted. "We were treated like animals in one way or another. Sometimes like pets, sometimes like beasts of burden," he said. Kasim was a natural orator, gifted with a poetic instinct — a talent perhaps derived from Cesar; yet he was also naturally a man of action, with none of the doubts and insecurities of poets — and he remained motionless and serene throughout. He related to the audience the state of its own maladies and diagnosed their source. In their growing nervousness the Judge and the Prosecutor tried hesitatingly to stop the account many times, but the vast audience's desire to listen was too strong to suppress. Kasim spoke at length, and finished with the words, "We could have had food for much longer. Much longer. But they always wanted much more than they needed. And what they couldn't eat, they threw out."

When he was finished, the Defense Attorney asked him:

"How would you describe their reaction when you warned them about their excesses?"

"They did not care."

A single yell was released from the crowd beneath, followed immediately by an uproar of indignation from all mouths. A vague intention to climb the stage was forming among the moving heads; the bulls lined up across the front rows and standing behind the ramparts teetered and even the mighty Judge hesitated before pounding the hammer.

"Order! Order! Quiet, please," he said finally. The commotion subsided only with great effort; the Judge had to pound the hammer multiple times.

"Mr. Kasim, do you know for certain that there is food stored in those vaults?"

"I have a high degree of confidence, yes."

This time the Judge anticipated the rabble's stir and was already smashing down the hammer when the first note sounded.

"SILENCE! God's sake."

"Your honor!" the Prosecutor interjected, indignantly. "There's no proof of this!"

"Your honor! My client meticulously logged the inputs and outputs of stock in the Pantry. I submit to your consideration Exhibit A1, which shows not only the input of stock from an undisclosed source, but that these inputs were made to make up for massive quantities of food being taken from one Wing to the other — that is, the food reserved for the Summit attendants was taken away, as my client related."

With immense formality, Marlene produced from her jacket a neatly piled stack of papers and handed it over to the Judge, who fingered the upper tip of it (the rest was curtained by his mane).

"This proves nothing," retorted the Prosecutor, "and anyway these transfers, if they did happen, must have been approved by the pantrykeeper himself."

"Under his employers' orders, Prosecutor!"

But the Prosecutor shot fiercely, "Is there proof? Very convenient this piece of paper coming from the defendant himself, by the way!" the Prosecutor tossed to the audience with a sideways motion — and a few of those watching from the fringes agreed with bellows, while the remaining onlookers gripped their snouts and beaks indecisively.

"Are you saying there is no food inside the temple vaults?"

"I certainly cannot confirm that," averred the Prosecutor. "The Temple is private property. And the contents of private property is the private business of the proprietors. We provide for everyone here."

"You provide —" Marlene gasped in shock. "Oh but that is flatly false, Prosecutor! This is ridiculous. All other parts of the tower are cut off — where else could these inputs have come from? Tell, is there or is there not food in those vaults?"

"I don't own the vaults, how should I know what's inside them? I don't even know if they exist. I don't know if this piece of paper you presented has any basis in fact," said the Prosecutor.

"Prosecutor, anyone working in the Pantries would be able to confirm the authenticity of this document," said Marlene, looking at the crowded audience of mingled masks for aid and witnesses.

"Miss, the contents of the vaults are irrelevant," the Prosecutor was quick to add. "If they do exist, whatever is inside is private property."

"Do you not hold considerable amounts in the vaults yourself?"

"Your Honor, this is absurd! How is this relevant to the case at hand?"

"I agree, Ms. Marlene," the Judge interposed, knocking the hammer. "Please keep to the point."

"Your Honor, it is relevant —"

"I'm not the one on trial here!" bawled the enraged Prosecutor.

For the moment the audience had quietened, entertained by the heated spectacle. Neipas pushed onward through the field of bodies.

"Anyway it's my turn to speak now," the Prosecutor snapped, his head unhinging from his neck in a flap.

"The defendant trespassed on private property. That matter is settled," he began. "The Law says that is a crime. Now we need to determine the severity of the punishment. Mr. Kasim! You claim that your motivation in committing this crime was a certain deficit in nourishment, is that correct?"

"We are dying from hunger!" — Kasim's voice was audible but it rang weak over the audience. His microphone had been cut off and already the hammer pounds sounded, stifling any reaction from the confused spectators.

"Quiet down! Shush! Hush!" roared the Judge, brandishing his lion mane and plummeting the hammer from on high.

"The defendant's claim is false. I will prove there is no reasonable justification for this hideous crime. Your Honor, I would like to call my first witness," the Prosecutor said.

The trial's first witness was the Chief Doctor, MD. The Doctor's voice was very reasonable and mild, very responsible-sounding; it was like a soporific that immediately mollified the mood of the crowd. There was an initial assertion that was clear — the Doctor had examined several sick patients, and those who perished died of natural causes, not hunger. He related postmortems, using smart words which many masks nodded to but did not understand. Meanwhile there were other physicians in the audience; and some protested, while others cheered. Those who cheered were much lesser in number but they were just as loud — somehow they had obtained microphones. After this there were many questions and answers, very technical and incomprehensible for the most part, but the claims that malnourishment was generally not an issue were intelligible enough: claims supported by science. The protests shrunk to weary and muted grumblings while the cries of support only grew louder.

At the end the audience was worn out; and everyone knew it was because they were tired of being there, though many had also forgotten it was because they were hungry.

"Your Honor, will you not let me question the witness?" the Defense Attorney protested, with fatigue in her voice, as the Chief Doctor walked behind the drape. Somehow this slid by ignored and the trial continued.

But as the Prosecutor was about to retake the word Marlene snapped. "This is ridiculous! Of course we're all hungry!"

"Will you dispute the science, Miss Marlene?"

"Didn't you hear! Most scientists were protesting these findings! Your Honor, may I call a witness to the stage?"

"With respect, the case is clear enough, your Honor. I think we're ready for the verdict," argued the Prosecutor.

Before the Judge's hesitation the crowd began protesting. "Order! Silence! Shush!"

"All right, go on," said the Judge to the Defense Attorney.

A physician was called from among the audience, and he rose to the stage to dismiss everything the Chief Physician had said. Though his words were decisive and incriminating, his tone was tedious and for a moment afterwards a silent confusion reigned in the Auditorium.

The first voice to arise was that of the Defense Attorney. "So you see, your Honor, my client was justified in inspecting the vaults, for the public interest."

"It's private property!"

"It is not, Prosecutor!"

Broad silence. Everyone was taken aback now. Marlene's voice had erupted with such anger that time itself stopped so as to listen.

"What? Balderdash!" the Prosecutor protested and the auditorium laughed (the Prosecutor extremely confused as to why).

"I will prove it to you. The property of the vaults belongs to everyone here."

A mumbling pause ensued between deep, intermittent quietudes then. There was general befuddlement; and there was deep reflection in the auditorium. Evidently the great majority of those in the crowd thought that the disparities between them and those watching from behind the battlement above were unjust; that their bosses were wasteful and undeserving; that, if there were indeed food in the vaults, it should be given to the workers, and to everyone; and that, though everything inside belonged to the Eagles, it was unfair if they did indeed take from the Pigeon Pantry into their own. Though it was the secret wish of many that the vaults be broken into, though it was their conviction that its contents should be taken and distributed fairly among all, when it came to confronting the realities of the matter, they dared not make a step in a direction that would accomplish that. The Eagles had given them jobs, fed them, housed them; and upon the whole treated them well. There were worse things. From inside their masks the pigeons, the cattle, the goats and the sheep checked themselves and their situation, and many didn't find the confidence to blame the Eagles; perhaps it was their own fault, they tended to realize. Things were tough and unfair, but in the end, they, too, had been wasteful. Even beyond this — they worked there, they saw what the Eagles wasted, they felt it coming; they should have done something while there was time. But to go into the vaults now and take of another, was to break a taboo of basic morality — and so it was strange for most to hear the Attorney claim that what was in the vaults was, in fact, theirs too.

They listened closely.

"Your Honor, may I follow a line of inquiry with the prosecution?"

"God's sake, Miss! I can't allow for such nonsense on court!" the Judge, who had been stricken with unbelief at the Attorney's words, said impatiently.

"Please, your Honor, I —"

"I believe we have enough evidence for a verdict," the Judge began, lifting the hammer. But the crowd, for moments hesitant, was beating back now against the Judge's words, fired up with curiosity about what Marlene had to say. A palpable anger rang in the clamor, a fiery demand for her right to speak. Again it was felt a tendency of that huge tide of heads to push toward the stage; an early phase of intention. The bulls wielded the threat of their guns, and a confrontation between the hammer's knocks and the audience's tumult ensued.

At last the audience won. The Judge, weary and frightened, tapped the hammer and mumbled, "Sure, all right."

"Mr. Prosecutor," Marlene fired immediately. "There is something called 'stealing', is there not?"

"I don't see the point of this."

"Is there something called stealing or not?"

"Yes!" roared the Prosecutor angrily, by this point thoroughly repulsed by her voice. "That's what your client did. Right."

"Very well," continued the Attorney, ignoring the Prosecutor's latter words. There was surety in her voice now. "If someone steals something, does that something become his?"

"Of course not."

"Of course. And would you concede there are various ways of stealing?"

"Sure...?"

"For example, if I point a gun at you and take your possessions, that's clearly stealing."

"Clearly."

"If I go to your house and take your possessions while you're asleep, without your permission, that's stealing."

"Sure."

"But if I took what I stole and invested it — let's say I invest a thousand dollars I stole and make tenfold. Are those ten thousand mine?"

"Technically if it could be proved the invested amount was stolen —"

"Are those ten thousand mine, or are they not?"

"Well no, they wouldn't be."

"And if I — just a couple more questions, your Honor!" Marlene gesticulated, detecting the Judge's twitches of impatience — "if at this point I, having almost completely dispossessed you, still keep hold of your possessions, and offer to give them back to you little by little in exchange for ransom? Is that not criminal conduct?"

"Sure, though I'm not sure what type of ransom that could be if the victim is as dispossessed as you claim. Defense, where is this going?"

"There's much that can be taken from someone which cannot be taken in one go, Prosecutor... Just concluding now," said Marlene quickly, directing herself to the audience. "Let's say that now you have nothing but your home with yourself in it. You do not know who stole from you — for you were either asleep when I came, or I wore a mask. You do not recognize me when I come to you, and with my loot multiplied, I buy your home (provided I simply did not shoot you and took it). Then I rent it back to you.

"You strive to buy back your possessions, but they have all been sold off by now. What is returned to you is similar — familiar, and strange. Copies.

"You recognize the clothes in your drawers, but they no longer feel like they're yours. When you pick them up, you feel a very faint, very strange smell — and you can just make out minuscule blood droplets sewn between the weave.

"You suspect there's something wrong. But what? The portraits on the walls feel like they are watching you now — like they have ears. The wardrobes have eyes and all the mirrors are fake...

"Month by month you must pay the rent on your home, and day by day you endeavor to buy back your possessions. But you were born very wealthy and even if you endeavored all your life, you would never recover what is due to you. Your only hope would be to rob, in the same manner you've been robbed. But then, you would have to begin by robbing something from yourself which is most deeply yours, something that only you alone can take — and would possibly, never be able to get back.

"But let's say you don't. Soon again, you have nothing to purchase with but your own body and, in the same way your own home was rented to you so must you, too, rent your body if you hope to live.

"So much time passes that you forget you have ever been wronged. Indeed, you feel all the time that something is wrong. But what?... And as your possessions are returned to you — foreign to you, strange to you, no longer truly yours — your home becomes strange with them. And as your rented home feels strange to you, so your rented body and your rented being, which you must rent to survive, feel strange to you.

"Your home and body come to feel like prisons, which I, warden and owner, thief and proprietor, command; and whose commands you must obey if you hope to recover all this that you've lost, and that you forgot I've taken.

"Tell me, Prosecutor. Is any of this licit?"

In the wake of her words fell, once more, a deep silence. It was a silence of contemplation; a silence of incomprehension; and a silence of recognition. It was a silence as deep as the universe opening just above them, a silence reaching as deep into the depths of the soul as the universe reaches the depths of existence. The Pearl shone mute over the heads of the crowd and pointed to the zenith of black velvet. The Moon shone on their napes, rising fully out of the clouds, and into the strange figures standing upon the stage. The Stars, finally unveiled in the dark horizon, circled slowly round the unfathomable dome of gloom with profound, inaudible groaning — the sound of an infinitude, stretched through eternity, echoed in all the hearts of all the fragments of existence.

All eyes faced the moonlit actors and contemplated their own quiet, moonlit spirits. Kasim above them was now wholly bathed in silver, dressed without shadow, gracious, heroic, saintly, prophetic, pure. Neipas, nestled in the vastness of slacking shoulders, beheld him like a martyr offered up to malevolent gods; a sacrifice to bloodthirsty beasts. The personages on the stage hung still over all the glares like otherworldly apparitions.

The Prosecutor snarled lowly and with contempt.

"That's a ridiculous proposition," he finally said.

Marlene snarled back. "Is it? But did I not describe the way of corporations which profit from war, such as arms companies, energy companies, real estate and agricultural enterprises and whoever else needs to control territory that is not theirs and will not be given away freely? Doesn't ArmsCore gain its wealth from the misery of those maimed and slaughtered by its weapons? Did NoxxeSocony gain its concessions in Mesopotamia by other means other than violence? Isn't Penaguiar taking Oyate land by force right now? Do they not all steal at gunpoint?

"And did I not describe the way of chemical corporations, who pollute our waters and our air slowly, stealing our health, our future, our lives, without our knowing it? And the private equities who profit from them, and the health insurance companies and pharmaceuticals who sell us our own stolen health back with interest? And the banks in the middle of it all, who skim off our wealth, and sell it back to us with usury? And the politicians corrupted by them, who hand our wealth to them as they distract us with gimmicks and clever tricks? Are they not stealing from us in our sleep?

"Did I not describe those who despoil the Earth and deprive us of its gifts and wonders — and sell them back to us in the shape of lousy, useless commodities and barren cities made of oil and glass?

"Really, am I not describing our nation, whose land was paved over the blood of its natives and its towers erected from the sweat of chattel and indentured slaves...?

"Did I not describe the way of tech companies, the new powers! who, after societies have been broken and atomized, sell us counterfeit, machine versions of the 'social'?

"And don't these all invest in this way the wealth stolen and thus multiply it, gaining still more power over us?

"Thus we come to depend on them. What belongs to us naturally, they own. Even our means of survival — even *food* — is theirs.

"There is only one thing we can offer to buy back the things we've been deprived of — our bodies, and our minds. It's the only thing we own which we cannot fully, willingly give; and so we must rent it. They too, depend on us — but they have more power. We must work for them and multiply *their* wealth — until we ourselves are no longer ours. And if we don't...

"Really, did I not describe the way of all modern enterprises, which put to you the 'choice': 'work, or starve'? Are we not born into a massive labor camp called 'capitalism'? Isn't that what our home has become... Is not our labor forced — would we choose to do it had we the real choice? The method of coercion is different — it's the threat of starvation — but it is coercion nonetheless.

"And look! Regardless of everything, we're starving!"

"Blasphemy! Nonsense!" shouted the Prosecutor in trembling ire, "This is a free country. No one forces you to do anything! This has no foundation whatsoever in reality!" The Judge also, behind his table, clutched the handle of his hammer as he eyed the visible trembling of the ample throng.

"Are you not thieves of land, labor, and life?" Marlene's voice blasted out of the microphone with supreme indignation and rage. "Is not the wealth of all those I describe the wealth that's stored in the vaults? This wealth, this food, was stolen — therefore it is not theirs. On the contrary it is ours — who sow, harvest, prepare and serve the food.

"How can my client be punished for trying to collect what is his, and to distribute among everyone that which is everyone's?"

She spoke to the audience, from which arose a thunderous clamor of raised arms. The tower shuddered with their cries, and even the sky trembled with the awe of the uproar booming over the clouds.

"Your Honor!" clamored the Prosecutor exasperatedly. "This is all nonsense and beside the point. It is clear the criminal stole and trespassed! I think we have enough to rule a verdict!"

"Very well," said the Judge, wiping his nose on the mane so as to cover his face. "You are quite correct. I will stand for this charade no longer! I rule the defendant — guilty!"

"What a mockery of a trial! There's not even a jury! This is supposed to be a Democracy, for God's sake!"

"It is a Democracy! It is!"

"My God, what charges is he guilty of then? All of them!? Is not the point of this trial to seek justice, your Honor??"

"The point of this trial is to apply The Law, madam, now calm down!"

The Bulls were already gathering upon her, but Marlene turned swiftly and gesticulated with desperation over the crowd. "It is your Law that should be on trial then!" but the microphone had been cut off — to escape the Bulls she hastened to the bridge hanging over the Orchestra Pit, which pulsed light feverishly, and shouted, "My kin! Trust the evidence of your senses! Trust the feeling in your bodies! You've been raised to believe that if you work hard, you will succeed. That those who've succeeded are successful because they worked hard. But you've all seen it! you've seen how they just lounge and talk, and we're the ones bearing the weights, we're the ones serving them, we're the ones who sweat and work hard! And look! Which of us is starving?

They took from your plates to feed themselves!" bellowed the defense attorney as the bull-helmeted guards seized her and muzzled her with their crushing fingers, pulling her to the ground under mountains of pressing knees. "Stop! Stop it!"

The audience was riled up by the sight of Marlene being grabbed so brutally and erupted in shouts of protest. Already they were surging onto the stage; the flocks pushed from the back and the herds from the middle of the crowd, hauling with them the Horses and the Deer in the front seats. Neipas was dragged along with the sweeping cries in the maddened advance; but held his pace, firmed himself and let many bodies seep by his flanks. The Bulls were clubbing folk as they climbed with all their fury — yet they were soon overwhelmed. The multitude filled the stage quickly; someone had removed the Judge's wig and already they were preparing to pull his Eagle mask off.

"Look! He's bald!" they said. The Judge cowed red and without authority as they laughed at the hilarity of the situation. They trampled all upon the stage now under a myriad shapes of animal mask — bleating Sheep and Goats, mooing Cattle and cackling Pigeons. The Horses and the Deer, caught up in the middle of the revolt, tossed vague slogans of support as they slunk toward the sidelines and the backstages for shelter. Meanwhile the Prosecutor had been picked up and was being tossed about by a thousand gleeful arms, the festive motions of which belied and presaged a sinister will to rip the lawyer to shreds... Long had they suspected they had been wronged, and that vagueness of suspicion began to take concrete shape now in the frenzy of the escalating swarm. Nebulously they recalled the dark nights when the Eagles came to steal their food — they had long known it — though it was all musty and blurry in their doped minds. All let themselves be possessed by hunger. Even those who had eaten, starved — even those in the working livestock who still had some means. For they had all been fed with food grown in the Eagles' secret terrarium; and even if they had stuffed themselves, still they would be starving, and even those whose stomachs revolved with those foods walked with hollowed spirits. Collectively there was a growing desperation, carried through the stringent noises to a boiling pitch, and everyone was driven together by a madness of conduct.

At least two among them were striving to thrust their hands into their squeezed pockets where they kept their guns. Everything wobbled and roiled in the furling mayhem. Lone above them all, Kasim stood a quiet observer, as if atop the crow's nest of a ship braving through crazed oceans, shattered by conflicting tides, rising in wrathful waves of gale.

But then, all at once the giant curtains before them parted — in a motion so rapid and colossal, with such flair and so imposing a swish, that all halted for a moment to look at what the majestic cloths revealed.

68 - Judgment

The public, that great quiet shout, found its voice and spoke. Protests emerged from the chaos of lips, and bodies pushed through in outrage against the Eagles' power and oppression, their seductive witchery. A wild realization of their own hunger, the general awareness of injustice, made them swarm in an outpour of their own pent-up, disoriented anger — which found a nebulous target in the figure of their absent masters. Indeed, none but the shirking Judge and the cowering Prosecutor were to be seen upon the stage. Yet still the crowds climbed and rushed widely across the platform, all possessed with a directionlessness of hope and a latent faith that they would become replenished just by stepping up on that altar where their sated, gluttonous gods would occasionally appear to be listened to and adored. With cries like incantations they whirled vast — till the curtain-wall opening abruptly behind them made everyone stop.

Light flooded them all. Suddenly the massive cloth was open — it parted so abruptly that the crowd was surprised back to silence. A high podium materialized among the glare, and upon it stood the Mayor.

He revealed himself to the disgruntled mass in an all-white, coatless suit. His golden beak was no longer hooked; it was shorter now, tucked in, humbled; it smiled with fatherly understanding. White feathers covered his head, smoothly combed back. His eyes blinked innocently.

The Mayor wore the mask of a dove — a perfect pigeon — presenting himself with open arms, like an envoy of divinity appearing miraculously among the common folk. "Fellow citizens!" he exclaimed, extending his arms farther out to embrace them.

The dazzle twinkled and pulsed and moistened the dry, hard, wide-open eyes teeming all over the stage. "I've heard your cries, fellow Columbidae — I've listened to your pleas," the Mayor pursued with bowing magnanimous gestures, "and I feel your pain. We face the biggest crises of our lifetimes today. A storm rages our beloved city, our home, our treasured Axiac," pointing with casual theatricality yonder toward the clouds — some followed the motion and spotted the blurry incandescent, dim, apocalyptic landscape which all had forgotten — as if introducing to the crowd's notice the fogginess of their thoughts — "Who could've predicted it? There are times in life when the unexpected happens, and it is in times like those that the true character of a people is revealed. Our character has been tried — and it is as great and as noble as ever."

The Mayor dipped a couple more platitudes into the wavering ears of the throng before proceeding to point out to them that, actually, things could be worse. "You are hurting, my fellow Columbidae. I'm hurting too. But think about your brothers and sisters there under the storm. Think about how blessed we are to be living in these beautiful gardens, think of your own perseverance that got you this far, and *lifted* you above the storm. Listen — Mistakes have been made. We all make mistakes. We're human beings, just like you. But trust me when I say that I am suffering from those mistakes as much as you are. I share your pain, fellow Columbidae. I hunger as much as you do — "

The combed seductiveness of his words seemed to quell the crowd's animus for the moment. They appeared in the stagelight all, half-alive, numb, bruised and in tatters, blinking empty glares. Suddenly it seemed like every color of the range had flowered into that brightness. The court was filled with all the vividness of hues, dappled mottles in the light, an immobile harlequin made up from the greens of the florists' attire, the crimson of the bulls, the blacks of the cattle drove and the smeared whites of the waiters, the iridescent rainbows of the pigeon plumes, the rusts and stripes of the jesters and the multicolors of the stallions, the vermillion of the Judge's cape, the haloed gloom covering Kasim hung between stake and a slow throbbing spotlight; all the myriad pigments of their many clothes and skins. The luminosity shimmered mystically and mingling and stirring shadows were cast tall on the towering veils. The Mayor's hypnotic intonations rang pleasantly into the mob, inside their hollowed spirits, like a reassurance. They mustn't give up hope, kernel of the Columbidae spirit. To them the gifted orator said that change is just around the corner and that together they will persevere — they were too strong to succumb to those who'd seek to divide them! he clamored, while within view of his feet Marlene endeavored to stand up among the wiry tangle of famished bodies; and as she rose she saw him between two horns of a bullhead, the Mayor behind and above a discreet row of guards half-mixed with the crowd.

Somewhere in their midst, the Book of Law still glowed, golden, tepid through the mixing shades; the lectern upon which it rested still stood.

Hemmed in before the Stage — still some distance from the Orchestra Pit — Neipas gazed upon the strange scene unfolding beneath the sinister rampart of the Great Facade. He narrowed his stare heavily. Having held back among the pushing mass, for fear of the Stage's exposure and for fear of exposing his pulped, blood-tarred visage, Neipas had now a much wider view of the scene than those who stood within it. He saw, arising above it all, the shadow-cloaked pole; and Kasim, barely discernible in its midst. The pantrykeeper overflowed with the darkness cast by the powerful spotlight behind the stake to which he hung bound. Through the confusing distance separating them Neipas could just make out the occasional fidgeting of his slippery feet, which stood bare upon a small plank protruding from the stake; he could just discern the slight wobbling of his tired head in the weakened moonshine. Behind the tall mast and under Kasim's suspended height, the dove Mayor perched before his congregation, framed by a soothing angelic halo that made his wings sway in heavenly intonations, his voice ring in divine breezes of white shirt.

Looking up to the Facade's terraced battlements, Neipas thought he spotted some indistinct shapes... observant, shadowy forms spying through the crenels.

They watched the audience — mostly jobless pigeons filling the auditorium now — from above, and through the cameras (blinking languid red lights in the Stage wings) they saw the dazzled agglomeration of oxen and cows, sheep and goats, stallions and mares, stags and deer, swans, peacocks, owls, bulls. They contemplated as Marlene stood up and perched straddled on the shoulders of the livestock, a meek, pink-haired mask struggling to overcome her own fatigue. Breathing in long and deeply, she waited for the Mayor to finish and then spoke, straining to lift her voice and propagate it to all in that vast assembly of ears:

"You imply my client incited the riots," Marlene charged hoarsely — for the Mayor's speech had been full of innuendos and nebulous references to 'those who would divide us' — "but on the contrary, he acted to *prevent* the riots, which were but the predictable outcome of this deplorable situation."

"What's that?" the Mayor replied, astonished; scratching his chin thoughtfully. "I implied no such thing! Listen — I defend that investigations be made into this, and naturally I'd like to see those responsible brought to justice. But since the crisis began in the pantries, we should begin by investigating those who work in the pantries, don't you think?"

"Yes, maybe we should start with the pantry owners..."

"Which, as you pointed out," nodded the Mayor, with a raised finger and a lifted hand, "are all Columbidae. And you are quite right when you say that we must protect our interests. Now would we act against our interests? Would anyone?"

Hovering masks pivoted side to side, quietly.

"Of course not!" exclaimed the Mayor merrily, parting his fingers into his wax semblance to draw a smile. "But obviously something went wrong," and now his doven mask drooped; suddenly he looked very serious, "no one starves voluntarily. We are hurting. My fellow Columbidae, something went very wrong here, and we must look into the causes of what happened. Now, it's simple — the food was badly managed. Who did the management?"

The various animals upon the Stage glanced at each other in undecided ponderings before all eyes settled toward Kasim — whose feeble moonlight was already beginning to shed — suspended in growing shadow over them, jagged, bearded, exotic, unkempt, strange. Marlene protested repeatedly but she could not make herself heard over the Mayor's rhetoric, amplified by the microphone's boom as it was; and even when he paused, still she scarcely made sound even as she strained and shouted, as if the very almighty spotlight subsumed her voice...

"Now I'm not accusing anybody," the Mayor followed, lowering the corners of his beak into a drooping crescent, shrugging, "because managing can be tough. It takes a lot of responsibility. But the food was supposed to last many months. Have we been here that long? [the question seemed to be rhetorical though in fact, no one knew] Fellow Columbidae, management was negligent at best, and at worst...

"Think about it," said the Mayor, and suddenly he appeared among the crowd — without anyone noticing it he had shifted, and now he wore the head of a rainbow-colored peacock. His voice still pervaded the whole Stage and spilled to the Auditorium — "All I'm saying is, there are those who hate our freedoms and our way of life. Studies have shown that benevolence can breed resentment. And Columbia, and Axiac in particular, and its people are the most generous of benefactors — there is no one more committed to the principle of freedom and democracy than we, and we like to spread our gifts across the world (What are you getting at? Marlene demanded, still perched atop shoulders which were sinking slowly in weakness; her voice dimmed as she merged into the crowd). Still! there are those who would do us harm and seek to divide us. And to divide is to conquer. We must not let them, my friend. We must stand united." Having walked through the crowd, he now emerged on to the brink of the stage — over the auditorium and the orchestra pit — as an ash-colored ox.

"We must rise up against the elites and our enemies and be very careful: there could even be spies among us... Look counsel, your Honor, I don't agree with you on anything," the ox Mayor said, addressing the Prosecutor and the Judge who had slunk behind the discreet phalanx of Bulls near the backdrop, "but I'm old-fashioned and I cherish the old-fashioned values of cooperation and bipartisanship. So I concede your point: if whoever was in charge of the pantries at the core of this crisis entered the vaults *at the same time* the crisis erupted — I mean, it's a *strange coincidence* worth looking into, don't you think?"

Meanwhile, bizarre rumors circulated among the gathering, whisperings (ɪ mean how do you even account for all that grub being gone?) growing (who knows what the hell they even do down there) ever (I heard they sacrifice the food to exotic animals in these rituals down in them pantries and they season the food with the blood of children) louder.

With a frantic dash Marlene climbed to the platform where the Mayor had stood, and took the microphone — which was already off. She sensed everything plunging out of control and in the heat of despair her voice raged over the furs and plumes and wools, "Pantries that *you* and *your* ilk robbed!"

"Miss, are you accusing *us*?" the ox Mayor replied quickly, incredulously, with open outraged arms embracing the stage crowd and circling so wide as to even encompass the auditorium. "Do you hate our country?"

"What? No no, what are you saying?" Marlene shouted with all her might, with much panic through flaring aches in her narrowing throat as she beheld a swathe of sleepy, enraged masks turn toward her disapprovingly. "I'm talking about the rich! The rich ate all the food!"

"What rich? So you're scapegoating job creators now? Look! here's a fire-breathing radical anarchist *lawyer* — now *that's* rich!" laughed the Mayor, and whereas some giggled disorientedly, those in the thickening fringes guffawed with reverberations of hysteria, through stretched, open mouths. "Don't you remember how they organized a feast in your honor?" — and indeed, they now remembered, and bobbed their faces meekly — "If it wasn't for enterprise managing food distribution, no one would have anything to eat at all — it would be total chaos!"

This seemed like a sensible general proposition to most listeners; and into the widespread nodding the Mayor continued discoursing with the utmost speed and confidence "Don't listen to these fearmongers with their bugaboos! What we need is a return to normality, not radical, untested nonsense. No more malarkey. We need stability. We've got to build back, build *better* — and I guarantee you, my fellow Columbidae, we are strong enough to defend ourselves from dividers who would derail us. I will protect Columbia from every attack, seen and unseen, everytime!" (**You** say yourself that you — you the rich! managed the food !! ... Yet before the Mayor's rapid molding of circumstances Marlene's protests fell feeble, powerless. She was no longer convincing; her mask looked somehow different, somehow more eccentric than before (had someone put that mask on her?), very unkempt, messy, somewhat unreasonable and even a little deranged; her pink hair looked more pink than ever, and so flaringly disheveled in its accentuated lunacy that she suddenly appeared quite creepy; her beak opened exaggeratedly large in its exertion to be heard, expressing itself in shrieks hushed by the pouring light through which Neipas, beneath, could sense the throbbing of the core and all those horrible screams siloed within it... The floor shivered and nerves sharpened in excruciating agony — the light began to morph: into an image).

886

Tumultuous shudders rippled over the stage as heads turned and voices rose. Discussions broke out regarding Kasim's guilt and the mystery of so much abundance vanishing so fast; debates developed in increasing volumes of incoherence and noisy convulsions. Those who had known from the start that Kasim was to blame for the whole situation endeavored now to convince the rest of their verdict's truth. With them trotted masked peacocks, who tried persuasion by means of whispers; and robed pelicans with increasingly daring yells, increasingly more overt in their ardor, chastising the heathen looming from the stake there — all deputies of the Judge and the Prosecutor, who had had time to recover during the Mayor's speech, and had reconvened behind the Bulls, by the backdrop, in the blinding light. Parrots pushed along atop shoulders. Those who still believed in Kasim's innocence, meanwhile, did not try to persuade anybody; instead they quibbled with one another, resorting to bizarre performances consisting of crowing and flapping their wings to try to leap over the others, in an attempt to show who among them advocated for Kasim most purely. Many of these screamed all at once, but those who screamed together resigned themselves to chanting tepid slogans at the folks in the middle, denouncing every maculate word; and all of them troubled themselves with smoothing every little crease in their jumbled masks (whenever some wax was missing they would tear it from another mask) — being so involved in this that in the wide roiling of the mass they were pushed, without realizing it, to the fringes of the stage and the brink of the orchestra pit as the other group consolidated at ever more frantic shouts toward the center. Marlene had disappeared, swallowed by the crowd. All was confusion and everything was enveloped in smoke, as the pelicans threw fog from thuribles into the eyes of the crowd and swung chains at them. The light refracted as it transformed... Music sounded mystic, electric from the background. And all the others in the dwindling undecided middle simply gawked as the fog overwhelmed them and blinded them into submission.

The Mayor himself (suddenly he was a Swan) continued his speech even through the noise; he had never stopped, though indeed many had ceased listening and many looked at him warily, with some suspicion now. Knowing something of the Mayor's true essence, Neipas was able to peer through his mask of plasticine — he had seen how the Mayor had trembled with fear in the beginning, trembled with the unceasing quake of the ground and the rumbling of the mob; though he was again calm now, if a little tired and old. Some around Neipas in the thick flock of smelly pigeon feathers were eager to pin their faith on to the smiling, jovial and decaying official, for the Prosecutor and the Judge scared them with their ill-omened glances. They saw the Mayor perched at the threshold — flailing his white swan arms in the white haze like some holy spirit of the waters, luminous in the refracted light of beams and torches — as the last rickety barricade between them and the others on stage. An impetus to flee was gaining force in the auditorium despite the Mayor's appeasing grin. All in the auditorium kept mum as they sensed the tide turn against Kasim and rise in a crest of madness — they felt it could well engulf them in its ample fall. Their masks dissolved in groanings between their fingers and they pecked themselves in the schism, too absorbed by their own hunger, their own fears — for they knew they could be next. Indeed, they were sure...

From below they watched the drowning noise...

But everyone shushed now as the fog dispersed and they saw the light transformed.

Now, upon the flat background, there loomed an image — a giant photograph, spanning airy from stage grounds to proscenium arches, high, colossal, consuming all horizons — like a malevolent influence behind all things unveiled.

Neipas frowned — slowly, very slowly, in a contraction of his innermost — as he recognized the photograph splashed threateningly on the ironed drape.

Everyone stared at it — with glittering eyes, with blurring eyes, with frowning eyes. On the pane appeared a photo of Kasim. He was prostrated, praying, worshiping his god with forehead against the ground, perched in a minaret gazebo under a vast blue dome. It was the picture Neipas had taken the morning before the Waltz (long ago now) upon the break of a full day he had assumed would be his last in that place; so long ago that he had forgotten about it completely.

There was nothing adulterated from the original photograph: it was presented just as it had been taken, without cropping, color modification, darkening of hue. What had changed was the size — augmented, every pixel in it bloated to gargantuan amplitude — and the circumstance. The texturelessness of it too... hovering as it was above those stares, presented as pure colored light, without mediation, without the restraining bounds of glass — like a mighty chromatic deity, a ghost. His face, swollen to inhuman proportions, rose well above all their heads like an imposition; like looming flames — it was as if the colossality of it showed the demonic potential of that hovering figure there... The photo exuded diabolical suggestions, and insinuated itself into the imaginations of the audience as something foreign, strange, unusual; unsettling. The sordid meaning of it, no one knew; interpretations mirrored and bent through like so many prisms in their minds. But it depicted an uncanny rite that no one practiced. No one upon the stage acted that way.

There and then Kasim's face seemed to change before the eyes of the beholders. His very beard, mustacheless and fatherly, looked menacing — a fashion of terrorists and fanatics. With the nocturnal figure of Kasim perched, wearing beard wild and unshaven, sweaty, in clothes stained all over with blood glinting sinisterly over the torchflames, the image of his strange soul projected large and giant over everyone made him look like a beast in shackles; a contained danger. The image, conveyed in so dramatic a manner, so charged with nefarious associations by years of propaganda, materialized like a supreme and irrefutable proof to the chaotic throng. No one could dispute it, for no one knew what there was to dispute about it except the accusation it implied; which none at that moment, before the crushing consensus of argument synthesized in that light, had the fortitude of spirit to do.

"The world is a dangerous place!" someone proclaimed generally into the silence; a mantra then repeated, like a series of relays, by the various parrots hanging about. It was the Prosecutor. Everyone glared vacantly, either confirmed in Kasim's guilt or resigned to it. His culpability was inevitable; for it was much easier to blame the unkempt, dirty, blooded alien above them than an impersonal, abstract "rich" no one could see (everyone was tired, tired). And hadn't he bungled the pantry's management, hadn't he poisoned his masters, stolen their keys, sought their possessions like a thief? The last gleam of moonlight slid from all the faces of the auditorium as the great, floating lunar circle hid behind the Pearl...

Neipas stared at his own photograph with horror, much horror; he stared at it through wide, blurry eyes. His teeth sank into the bleeding lip pulped beyond the mask.

*

The vision of placid wrath and desperation materializing dimly beneath Kasim resembled, to his tired perceptions, a night of stars ablaze, in tranquil fires; all under him little specks of glass multiplying, twinkling each with the glitter of torchflame. It transported him thousands of miles across remembrances until at last he stood over a pool mirroring sleepily, sodden, an orange sky that palpitated; a sky where there was no night.

Kasim stood again in the nightless land whence he had been born. Flames raged unceasing atop spires all around, fanning the sun in deadly vibrations of heat and banishing the darkness with despair; banishing the silence with gluttonous yells of licking flame. The sweltering air hung with the stench of tar, a constant whiff of rotten eggs, of aborted futures; walking against it singed the skin, and the very leaves of the trees were curled and tanned. Sometimes it rained, but the only rain there was was made of oil. Many times had Kasim heard his forlorn father lament their ruined garden. Their beloved crops, the beautiful desert flowers — all wilted and dead. Nearby, the great ancient river, nursery of civilizations, groaned under pounds of sludge dumped into its sacred waters.

His family moved to the royal city after the eldest brother died of cancer. Even today Kasim could summon to his senses the image of him in bed and the shock of seeing him so: his nimble, athletic brother, reduced to a skeleton with the thinnest cover of skin; his mouth gaping wide, horrible... Upon the face of his corpse was imprinted the last effort he had made in life, that of struggling to find air in the overwhelming putrefaction suffusing all things, battling to hold the life in his narrowing lungs. Another of his brothers perished on the way to the old capital; and Kasim recalled, too, as if the moment surfaced abruptly from the tide of epochs into his sense of the present, his mother's weary look, her aimless stare, which no longer cried, her fastened lips no longer screaming. Four of her children had died by then; the grief had but taken in more weight, and deepened to places beyond reach, beyond expression.

Yet the family, in the face of all the grimness of reality, took shelter and found strength in God.

The move to the royal city, old capital of a kingdom long extinct, had been made at a great cost. Yet, after much adjustment and accentuated deprivation, the family's patriarch managed to get a job at the palace's vast gardens, where he would often take young Kasim. There, in the shade of sumptuous palms, Kasim discovered his passion and path in life: he learned to commune with plants, to recognize the miracle of fruits, the majesty of flowers, the teeming wonderful existence of botanical life — the minuscule awes of nature. They settled into an existence of minimal comforts — without luxury, but without hunger either — and those were among Kasim's happiest years.

Happiest years, short in number but infinite in the perceptions of youth, which saw also the most profound inner turmoils in Kasim's blooming soul. For it was then, in those gardens, that he discovered his own homosexuality. He found it slowly and fearfully in the attraction for an older man who worked security at the palace. Soon, and barely realizing it, he was drawn into a romance developing secretly in the cool shades of the parapets under the bright desert sky. The nights no longer flared, but they were soon permeated with a buoying fright — of the security guard, who revealed himself manipulative and commandeering; and of all the security guards of the mores of his society, over which a cruel dictator ruled and people like

Kasim were shunned.

The burgeoning toxicity of Kasim's secret affair seemed to burst into expression when the nightsky began to explode with many suns shining and fading in the spreading detritus of the city. His family huddled in dread and saw the convulsing air as it flashed again before their eyes, as though in recollection of past days — as though gazing snapshots from their nightless village.

Bombardments had begun; another war with Columbia had started.

Strange soldiers paraded through the main avenue with their pagan masks lifted haughtily. They occupied the palace; and though they let Kasim and his father stay, every official and every security guard and gun-bearer was expelled and dispersed. Time moved very quickly and events rolled into a blur from them on. But three events in particular stood in Kasim's memory with sharp clarity, of the remaining time in Mesopotamia before he fled to exile.

The first was of an old woman in his arms, her black veil soaked with blood oozing from a stray bullet wound; pumping and drenching Kasim's skin, as a shopping basket and a great many fruit lay strewn at his feet.

The second was of a mob sprinting after him — with his former lover at its head. The security guard had joined one of the new militias along with other ex-members of his disbanded political party, ousted from power; and after Kasim broke off their closeted relationship he denounced him as an infidel for his sexual aberration and a traitor for working with the enemy invaders in the palace. The guard didn't want him dead, however; humiliation was sufficient. So they tore Kasim's clothes, beat him and branded him with a cattle iron, abandoning him, gored and swollen, in a filthy alley somewhere in the poorest area of the city.

Kasim fled the next morning. He presented himself at the Columbidae military base in a nearby town, where his sister lived. He knew well the language of his invaders — it was spoken across the global extent of their nation's hegemony — for he had studied it during the numberless hours spent with the books and films of the palace's library. Having gained the knowledge and practice of its foreign words, having learned to flex his tongue to embody them comprehensibly, he was given a job as a translator. Little did he recall of those days — all a cocooned mishmash of sitting at tables between two endlessly varying masks (of the investigator and the scrutinized), perforated by sounds of explosion — but it was then that he was confirmed in his suspicions about the Columbidae. They brought not blessings as advertised. No graces from the sky whence they'd come, came along with them. What they sought was not the liberation of a people from tyranny but the abysses beneath the surface of their land: infernos excavated from the innermost deep, and the wells through which their fires sprung many feet high. The museum lootings, they ignored; the turmoil in their wake was accepted. They sought the rich black blood of the earth, promised wealth of their religion — a type of satanism to whose god all of Kasim's brothers had been sacrificed — which was the common religion of all despots (masked and unmasked alike) in those days, whose church spires blew flames and sanctified the air with the poisons of the soil.

Over the fumes spewed from their spires now, perched (tied) atop the center of the world, he recalled the third reminiscence from those days, which stood clear in his memories. It was from the week before he left Mesopotamia.

It was years into the war, and his mother and father had already died (one shot, the other cancerous); his sister, Fatima, had just given birth. Kasim, floating over the course of his life as he hung against the stake, recalled walking between the rows of hospital beds in the nursery. He recalled, as if she hovered over him, his newborn niece. A ghastly cleft disfigured her little face, ripping from nose to throat; and her little hands were like the talons of a pigeon, three long fingers sprouting monstrously from the wrist, maimed and deformed. That poor baby, innocent of all sin, suffered from the first from the most horrible ailments; and so did many newborns in the eerie silence of that nursery. Their little bodies were stuffed with the uranium used in munitions — fully loaded with the toxins of war, greed and stupidity. Kasim's sister, like their mother, did not cry. Her visage appeared weary; her spirit was too far buried under accumulated sufferings to surface into her eyes.

Yet they, in the face of all the grimness of reality, took shelter and found strength in God.

Kasim promised Fatima he would come back for her — but it was a promise he could not keep. After years in the refuge of a neighboring nation, where he matured deeper into an adulthood of traumas silently borne, Kasim finally gained admittance to vaulted Columbia, lord-nation of the world; an unwelcoming place, where people like Fatima and her daughter are shunned. He tried relentlessly, but could never obtain the necessary papers for them to come.

Sullen, worn into a stoic demeanor, he carried through life with a quiet type of determination bearing little purpose or conscience. He found steadiness in the keeping of plants alone, and in the silent observation of nature's wonders, unfortunately so scarce in Axiac's tar-walled world: that, and his surviving family, sustained and drove him onward. There were moments of private happiness in the mute companionship of leaves and boughs, stems and blossoms. But he wouldn't know joy in the promised land of opportunity till he met Cesar.

A smile came over his blasted lip. Cesar — to merely look at him was, to
Kasim, to widen all vistas and deepen all horizons. It was something of a
vertiginous feeling that possessed him when the charming Columbidae first
spoke to him; a feeling which would repeat itself in endless variations
everytime they saw each other. Cesar's vigorously romantic view of life and
his conduct — his every moment had a lightness to it, his very walk an
essential quality of dance — injected into Kasim's own life a sort of energy
and a gentleness that made him look up from his plants and consider the
vastness of the forest. He had long clammed over his own bud, curled inward
to the indiscriminate gloom; but Cesar's sun, carver of shadows, made him
blossom, and let the starry light sift through.

Kasim rooted himself to life — something altogether new. He fell in love
for the first time. With Cesar he felt comfortable enough to shed his shell of
taciturnity, comfortable enough to settle, to speak, to confide, to become
himself in his presence. Cesar was a good poet, if not in letter, then at least in
spirit — and like all good poets, he knew how to listen. He knew the art of
opening every door of his being in welcome and wait, silently, for the other to
take shelter in it. Kasim did — in Cesar he took solace, into him he brought
traumas, within him he disclosed his wounded soul bare. At times he feared
the jealousy of God, whom he felt himself abandoning whenever he exposed
himself onto his lover's innermost. Yet then he would admonish himself for
his lack of faith, and his piddling idea of God; and recalled that in entering
Cesar's soul he did not draw away from God, for even Cesar, too, was in
God. Even Cesar the unbeliever, the infidel.

"God?" Cesar laughed with a somewhat impudent nonchalance, and a
tinge of mockery that irked Kasim as they lay in the hammock in Cesar's
room, as they so often did. Kasim parted his feathery beard from the fur of
his lover's chest. "Who's this God? Ah, my love... If only He could whisper a
word of comfort," he would say mournfully, contemplative, to himself more
than to Kasim; and then concluded in a louder, dismissive tone, "As it is
though, I've never met him."

Kasim would grow angry in such moments, not because of the words,
which were inoffensive enough, but for the blasphemous tone with which
Cesar molded God's name in his beak. Still, eventually the faithful refugee
would lean his ear back upon the poet's open heart, wherein he took refuge
and drew force; to which he applied his kissing lips and into which he
whispered his spirit, hovering placidly like a wanderer in search of its own
mirror. In the amplitude of passions which made up Cesar's romantic soul he

sought the essential surrender of self which precedes all true faith, wishing to make him see God as they curled tightly in the intimacy of their hammock. But there was much he could not access — beyond the many hallways and open chambers of Cesar's bosom, Kasim found many closed doors, and often realized himself in the guest house of his loved one's soul, pleading sorrowfully to opaque windows.

The guesthouse became, nevertheless, his safety and his shield against the vicissitudes of his new country. Bigoted eyes often glimpsed askew at him. An irate bull-cop once made him lie on the ground and cuffed his wrists because he read of the Holy Book on a bench in the Park of Echoes (Kasim could find no other explanation, for indeed he wasn't given any). And as he tended to the gardens of the rich (Kasim, like Neipas who in the present moment stared at him strapped to the stake and cleaved an unconscious path through the frightened auditorium, had worked on the seaboard mansions of the northwest) he was treated invariously with either suspicion, scorn or condescension, or a bizarre friendliness whose very smiles were frigid and sinister. It was to Cesar that he vented, in his quiet mood, all the tension which all of this built up in him; it was because of Cesar that he felt this tension so acutely. For he rooted himself to living like he had never before and through the poet he learned, as he had never before learned, to love life and fear death.

Was he himself losing faith? Kasim sometimes wondered. In his most intimate he sometimes questioned whether to draw closer to Cesar and to tether himself to life was to unmoor from God. He wondered if he ought to break from his poet. But no — even in Cesar he saw God — and what a gift it would be if Cesar could see Him in himself too! Kasim endeavored in his patient love to make him see. What else could he do? As he contemplated with vacant eyes the orchestra pit, he called to heart the time when Cesar took Kasim ("his friend") to meet the morbid, pious grandmother who had raised him; and found himself confronting his father, red-cheeked and ever-drunk, who was also there to visit. The mother introduced herself meekly, one eye always on the father who, sunken in the couch before the TV, and without once directing his gaze to them, muttered finally: "You're fucking ahmeds too now, you degenerate?"

At this Cesar held tight Kasim's hand — to Kasim's surprise, as he watched astonished the contempt in the father's eyes — and said "Know yourself, dear father! It's your hatreds that degenerate. Just look at what it's doing to you — what I do is love, and love regenerates..." saying it with all the air of having fumbled words long mulled over, long polished and long practiced — his fingers trembled between Kasim's and he spoke with hesitation and some shame. But then his fingers stiffened and his hand tightened its grip of Kasim's own; and in a burst of spontaneity he declared, "And if you wanna know, I love this man and I will marry him one day!"

"Why you fucking faggot —" and the father looked at them, and rose heavily, steaming with hot anger. Cesar stepped between his swelling bulk and Kasim, never letting go of his hand, never loosening the grip (with his free hand he parted his own mustaches repeatedly, nervously) — and with a voice tremulously firm he mouthed, "What? Are you gonna hit me again? Huh?"

Beneath him now flashed the ghastly, huge eyes of the deer, the horses, the swans, the sheep, the cattle; all lit in the demonic palpitation of the torches, unnerved by lack of sleep. Flames drifted in their glassy stares with the drunkenness of Cesar's father's bilious gaze, with the same inconstancy of being. The flittering darknesses of the proximity gained the whole expanse afar, swallowed even the light of the Pearl, which seemed to recede and fade in the insidiousness of their power. Yonder below, beyond the gesticulating Mayor and the auditorium's shadowy sea, the lake rested still, without ripple or glimmer. Fish had sunk dead and their corpses decayed slowly into the seabottom of coins; on the bridge over it, the Great Peacock stood watching the proceedings of the above terrace with his myopic gaze, his thousand open eyes dressed in gloom. Still further down, deep, Cesar's body rested beneath a clump of earth above the clouds, out of sight. Kasim's eyes wavered again in the direction of the Orchestra Pit, by which brink his lover had perished — trampled, bent backward, with dying glare toward the bottom. Had Cesar seen the deep as his head fell over the edge? Did he speak his last words? What were his last words...?

Was he afraid in his last moments?

Had he begged when the Angel came for his soul, did it seek shelter in his body still, was it violently torn from him? Did he suffer?

He asked God these things in his prayer, Kasim did; and the Pit shimmered strangely as he looked at it. The heavenly languor of the hammock pervaded his muscles. Within, in the embracing nook of it, he often watched Cesar as he curled his mustache contemplatively; sometimes for hours on end. The recollected feel of it made Kasim droop in an exhaled grin of resignation. He closed his eyes, and again he was there; caressing Cesar's heart, which boomed, Kasim could hear, underneath the stillness of its chest. He opened his eyes and saw the lower ridge of Cesar's human lip, the delicate, fleshy hillocks rising and curving toward the combed waves of hair. Pinched between fingers, his mustache was slicked over and over into swooping upward edges, polished like a blade; a horn growing out of his mute thoughts...

The bland ceiling entered his eyes and the eyes of his grandmother; both stared up at it with wilted, sunken cheeks.

Shadows had inked the bedroom. A religious icon hung above a sinuous headboard, and among the many photographs on the bedside table was the one surviving photograph of Cesar's grandfather; black and white, impersonal, as dead and as wordless and mute as he was. On the bed's edge, little Cesar curled and stared into the long window, at the wet lights of rainy outsides. His grandmother ruminated her sorrows; thought of herself newly widowed, recalled the image of her husband's coffin upon the center of her living room. His face was exposed under an oval pane, bandages covering the top of his head, where the saw in the lumber factory struck and sliced. Her eyes were fixed. There he was upon the shadowed ceiling: his eyes shut under a pane of glass, leaving naught but the sight of his dead visage, their many children and the prospect of penury to remember him by.

Lying stiff in the center of the bed, she told her grandson, no older than six then:

"Oh, but death, you know, it's like a dream when you're sleeping... The body stays here and the soul goes here and there..."

But little Cesar never dreamed. Sleep was but deaf, dumb darkness to him. Even then, his maturing instincts nurtured a great fear; creeping horrors fed by the words of his crepuscular grandmother. Even then he dreaded his own insignificance and littleness in the infinite extension of the universe; he felt himself but a speck of sand in the monstrous, tidal enormity of existence. Even then he regarded time as a shifting ground beneath his feet, precipitating him into an abyss in the maw of the horizon.

"I'm afraid... Afraid to die, my love..." he would confess to Kasim in low tones many years later, with difficulty. "It's just — just..."

Hanging over the ground which Cesar so feared, they remained thus for hours, perhaps, in a quietude of inexpressibility. Words floated about, just beyond their pod, just beyond reach; delaying their way to Cesar's lips.

"We go to God when we die," whispered Kasim to the silence of his lover's heart, pruning its feathers. "We will go together, my love."

And he would feel Cesar's chin brush the feathers of his own head as it moved, slowly, side to side.

"I thought you said god was everywhere," he chuckled, mournful. "Nah... We will be eaten by the ground..." muttered then the poet vacantly, trance-like. "Only our words survive. That's the only part of ourselves that stays."

Kasim grinned wistfully. "Only words?"

"That's the only part of ourselves that survives," repeated Cesar. "You know — they make up the story. Words. Symbols of the soul... Only symbols remain. And the last words — they're the most important. Because first words sustain — they keep you listening. But..."

"Last words linger," he continued mutedly. "They give the lasting impression. Last words carry the story beyond the ending... You see? Only through them can you keep on living."

What had his last words been? Tied to a stake, standing on a short, narrow footrest upon slipping and trembling feet, Kasim reflected that only God could know the last words uttered by the poet's lips, his body, his mind. Only symbols of words could be consecrated to the memories of the living — and Cesar had left his last symbols as heirlooms to Kasim's undying affection. The last words of his last poem — the last verses of his lingering heart. Those were his final utterances as the poet would wish them, consoled Kasim thus his noble spirit.

Neipas scoped out the luminous maw of the stage as the fluid droves moved toward final deliberations. The Judge spoke. Once more he read the charges leveled against Kasim and asked solemnly that the crowd act as jury, invoking multiple times the holy principle of democracy. And Neipas ploughed through the auditorium now with long arms, moved by a hollow impetus and by every sense made vague in hunger. His breast panted with a rush to do something; but his eyes grew blurry in his powerlessness. They roved the walls aimlessly and settled on the battlements of the Great Facade, where sitting shadows loomed; through the crenels of which the Eagles watched from under nocturnal veils, bathed in night, invisible. They lounged upon cozy thrones. Spaced across great distances, in the high terrace above the Pigeon Gardens sat all 5 Ministers of State present (with the exception of the Prosecutor now upon the stage, the Minister of Justice) — there was the Minister of the Treasury, gaunt and spectacled, and the chinless, nature-hating Environment Minister, as well as the Minister of Energy with his cowboy hat and sunglasses; and there were the Ministers of Nations and Borders, mirror likenesses of one another, scowling equally with rage and desiring great suffering upon Kasim. Among them reposed the Heiress, Media Mogul Moloch, Reckuz of the Maskbook, Larry the Data Tycoon, Sobs the Prophet of Tools, Bezitos of the Silicon Jungle, Noxxe the Petroleum Baron, prominent Bankers and Legislators, important Lobbyists and Lawyers, Generals and Warmakers, eminent Chieftains and Diplomats of wealthy foreign nations, and the key-bearing Bulls, fortress walls of flesh and metal and safeguards of treasure — all avatars of the diffuse might governing the destinies of all living beings in those days; an almighty structure seeped into every fiber of reality, made up of beasts of arrogance and covetousness presiding over the end of the world. Among them and of them too sat, somewhere, the Head Gardener, chief pastor of the Anubel, leaning over his opulent cane. Kasim's boss; he contemplated attentively the spectacle of his subordinate's trial. Chair of the sprawling, powerful Penaguiar empire, tycoon of meats and land, great industrialist of agriculture, lord over the houses of slaughter, feeder of civilizations, he saw through his circular, vast amber eyes, one fixed upon the muddy auditorium under the parapet, the other set upon a framed glass in which the trial on the stage underneath played through camera lenses. A cold, practical man who had hired Kasim on the merit of his talents, without the least vestige of bigotry muddying his sagacity, he now delivered him without the least compunction to the disoriented wrath of a starving throng.

For it had been him, the Gardener, who had first suspected Neipas' subterfuge; it had been him who had Neipas' *I* taken from his closet of possessions; and it had been him who suggested using Neipas' photo of Kasim, now still amplified monstrously over the stage, as a way to steer the masses...

The masses whose time to vote had now come, began, in an uneven wave, to raise their hands. All but a very few were being lifted over the stage. They were too tired... Too numbed for revolutionary notions, though desperate enough to be roused by them temporarily. Marlene's effort had been futile; no matter how true her words, and no matter how intensely that truth was felt in the audience's famished bones, still she was striving against lifetimes of indoctrination and walled horizons of perception; and she had little time. All these Summit attendants, who had thus far lived comfortable lives (those most experienced in suffering were buried somewhere beneath the clouds or, at most, gazed with twitching eyes from the black auditorium), sought, was a return to normality — a normality which the Mayor represented. And the allure of that known normality was too powerful against the strangeness of truth shown by Marlene, who surfaced now at the brink of the Orchestra Pit after having disappeared somewhere in the crowded depths of the Stage; and with her remaining strength and all the force of her empathy and despair she pleaded "Stop! Stop! What kind of proceedings are these! Final arguments haven't been made yet!"

But her voice withered promptly in the unstirred bodies of the populace. Already a cloth was being placed over the Judge's eyes, that he may pronounce his judgment. The heretical image of Kasim shone even more brightly. And from the magisterial curtains' folds which flanked it emerged roosters in suits, holding instruments, and rising musical sounds began to fill the ear. At first everyone thought they were mannequins in the background — for the whole time they had been there, in near perfect stillness — and now from among them stepped a single hooded figure, whose face could not be seen, holding a torch at the end of a raised arm.

The Debt Collector.

"Stop!"

Kasim smiled faintly, appreciative of Marlene — friend of his dear Cesar... His love, who used to hold him tightly in the hammock; whom Kasim watched as he petted his mustache distractedly.

Cesar looked at him; and his eyes cleared with the sunlight.

"What?" he asked, with a tranquil visage, bared of all masks.

His mind numbing away from the body in its sufferings, his soul already distant in its flight, Kasim saw, just as well as if he were in front of him, the upturned tips of his mustache rise with his smile. He saw his lover seated at the kitchen table, appreciating with devoted eyes the beautiful fountain-pen Kasim had gifted him; he saw him scratching reverently the paper under its nib, covering it with his arched back and his enfolding arms whenever Kasim drew near ("You can't look, my love," Cesar would say, blushing.

"A poem should not be looked at until it's ready," he said.

"What poem are you writing now?" asked Kasim.

"You will see.") And his eyes cleared in the sunlight, flared in the sunlight, deepened along the great depth of his unfathomable spirit, through the unending chambers of its domains, throughout the soul's suddenly transparent kingdom — well beyond the guesthouse, Kasim seemed to glimpse, for a moment, his innermost form.

After Cesar's death, isolated, desolate in the oppressive opulence of these airless heights, Kasim would often ask himself with a great dread whether his lover had, in the end, accepted God; whether it was possible that God the All-Merciful had taken pity on him and admitted to His realm his unbelieving soul. Having lost Cesar in life, would Kasim find him again in death? Had Cesar, in the end, accepted God? Had Cesar, at last, seen Him?

Now, the poem seeped out of the reincarnation of that very first paper, having grown throughout various papers and innumerable drafts to be finally read, years after and altitudes above that first draft sketched under the brand new fountain pen, by his mournful eyes; his eyes which saw in remembrance the sunlit depths of his lover's eyes, the innermost shapes of his spirit.

Was God to be found among those shapes?

Kasim thought of the poem's last lines... Were they sincere? Was this its last draft?

Had Cesar, perhaps, spoken his last words to that unfathomable, divine silence beyond speech, beyond sense, beyond all symbols; was he at last able to listen to that silence untouched by any word?...

Kasim saw him now, before him, leaning his elbow against the table as he twirled his mustache, creating his poetry; he saw his sunlit eyes against the translucent fabric of the angelic hammock, and saw the clarity of his wonderful soul; and he knew then, he knew that Cesar, having known the magic of reality, knew the divinity of creation, and could but know the existence and the marvels of God. Yes... Cesar knew.

Kasim smiled. Yonder... Wasn't the sun rising over the mountains?

Kasim took shelter and found strength in God — Cesar was with him still. They were one, they had never parted. He would be with him in Paradise.

He knew God was Death as much as He was Life — and all would be well.

The uproar grew. Marlene directed herself to all crowds and even appealed to the fearful auditorium whose mass squelched and masks dissolved. "Can't you see they're trying to scapegoat this man!"

(*"I love this man and I will —"*)

"That's not a man!" yelled someone in the upper crowd, "It's meat!" and suddenly those who had begun at the fringes of the auditorium repeated from the very center of the stage *"Meat! Meat! Meat!"* and a great ruckus erupted, the parrots mimicked their shouts, the goats convulsed in crazed bleatings of approval. The Eagles licked their golden chops with their scarlet tongues as they studied Kasim's strapped body with gluttony, his very veins already seasoned in oil... The rabble of empty stomachs gathered expectantly. Some shrugged resignedly. Kasim was to them a full abstraction even as he waved before them; if not meat, then at least a ways to eat, somehazyhow — to eat, or to sleep already, was all they wanted. Behind them, Marlene found herself wholly voiceless now, all but wordless air emerged from her straining throat. But even she had to make an effort to care in her overbearing fatigue, amid all that noise; until finally she relented, and covering her face she turned away.

All hands were up.

The verdict was clear. The Debt Collector approached the stake with his torch. The vermillion cape arose. The executioner was about to act.

"Burn him!"

But at this Neipas sprung out of the crowd with a despairing shout:

"Last words! Last words! Let him say his last words, please!"

He was wild-eyed, crazed by the utter madness swirling about him. His voice trembled on the edge of cracking, on the edge of weeping. The hunger beat. Kasim, turning his body, seemed to recognize the voice, but said nothing. And the crowd fell silent; a faint whiff of doubt blew through the assembly, and the dirty moor seemed human again to some, for a moment.

The leonine Judge and the Eagles found this interruption annoying. It had given the mob pause, space to wonder. But there was no doubt Neipas' cry had produced an effect, and there was no option for the Judge but to beat the hammer and say "Very well! Do you have any last words?"

"Yes."

Kasim, drawing for the last time the breath of life, expelled it in verses — and so recited the last lines of Cesar's revised poem:

Take then the loving letters
of a man inverted — converted
to a hope without bounds,
serenading a passion of faith
and a devotion undying.

Wonder... In your eyes
I behold the future.
I see the truth.

I see now, life unending —
and know that in our love,
We live still, and we live,
evermore,
eternal.

I am here
I am here
I am here

And at the last verse he broke into a recited prayer in his own tongue, tearful declarations of faith which none could understand; and which, in the minds of all the animals there, confirmed his guilt beyond doubt. Kasim's last words suited perfectly the poetic soul that spoke them. He had spoken as someone who had submitted to his fate; the clarity of his voice reached Neipas' ear like an incomprehensible enigma, like sounds from another world. He couldn't accept it. In his deepest he felt a conviction, he had to do something.

But he stood there, shaking with fright and horror. The feeling of impotency was overbearing. It was all too much; his eyes widened, welled up with tears, and though his lips stirred no sound emerged from them.

Wordlessly they said, repeatedly, "what can I do? what can I do?". The Judge rose from his throne! And again he said "burn him!" as the flame touched the base of the stake, all smeared in tar, and shot toward the feathered body of Kasim yelling with excruciating pain, a searing wail which quieted all other sounds. All lips sealed, all breaths shut, as the audience watched wordlessly the burning of a human body. It was a silence of every feeling — passivity, resignation, confusion, indecisiveness, pity, outrage. And the silence continued under the searing noise of the man dying in the hot fire, in the blinding light. Even before Neipas covered his eyes he could not see Kasim among the brightness.

Then a great stir beat the structure and the whole Market shook as trumpets sounded, and everyone twirled and mingled in a confusion of yells and fear, broken waves thrusting into all directions everywhere. Suddenly they found themselves fighting for air among the tangle of crashing bodies. Tides of nausea billowed up in the collapsing weight of the frenzied audience, a rush of vertigo swept through their heads. Many felt they were drowning and all sped to the depths of the stage where they could hide from the rising flood which had finally come to claim them — the tower was finally going to fall.

Then everything settled... They arose blurry and feeble as if from the detritus of a dream. Imperceptible shouts began to emerge as heads peered out over the lain:

"Storm!..."

"...the storm...!"

They had trouble making out these sounds. Only by degrees did it become clear. Eyes and more eyes looked yonder at the dawn, at the extremity of which rose some mountains, on the foot of which appeared a city.

"The storm ended! The storm ended!"

The air was cloudless.

69 - Fate of the Oxen in the Labyrinth

It began with a certain numbness, taking hold quite quickly. Before Osir noticed it, it had already seized possession of his body and mental faculties. The numbness was followed by ringing in his ear, which grew slowly to overwhelm all other sounds, made distant, remote, surreal. In a blurry instant would come an otherworldly sense of physicality; he felt bizarre inside his own skin, out of place, absent. Finally, his body would return to meet its sensations. It would grow in rigidity; he would feel hot, a bead of sweat sprouting from a pore in the forehead and sliding down into his eye uncomfortably. He was slowly dominated by shaking, beginning at the tip of his fingers and spreading throughout every inch of his body. And with the shaking would come pain — a lot of pain. A pain which burned his insides with acid and grew slowly in sharpness and intensity, slowly..., slowly... slowly becoming the entirety of his existence, all he could perceive. In the nook, buried within the edgeless immensity of the vault labyrinths, Osir trembled and endured in silence. He no longer acted consciously. Moved by the spirit, he summoned his deeper will and strength. He met the pain in various stages; sometimes he tried to contain it, other times he withdrew himself mentally; or he tried to diffuse it with a sense of acceptance, diffusing himself into it, relaxing into it. But as the physical strain became unbearable Osir sought to distract himself out of it. Reflexively he picked up the *I* on the table, thinking it his — it looked just the same. And he stared down into its dazzling light, down the sparkling pit with sounds of glitter chimes and his nerves were unwired and twitchy, he flew through many digital threads and glided over many pages and saw nothing — but even the mere movements of his finger and the flashes into his eyes helped him through the climax of suffering, when screaming conflagrations swelled inside his creaking chest, his cracking bones.

By the time Neipas ran away the pain had eased a little (Osir noticed vaguely that Neipas was no longer there and wondered where he could have gone). With the progressive relaxation of his muscles Osir realized that he had been there a very long time now, so he dwelt out of the nook, with some intention of finding the way out — but from the start this feeling felt aimless and futile, resigned to the fact that the bout of pain would come back, and stronger. When the gunshots boomed across the corridor, he barely noticed them; and with the shouts raging from the walls the pain returned.

When he came to, he was on the floor. He had fainted this time, he realized in a surge of clarity. With a struggling groan he rose, now aware of himself and the dizziness biting his brains, and stumbled through the vaults, which were quiet now, eerily quiet, as though filled with the silence of ghosts. He walked meekly alongside the walls and among the riches until he noticed something on the floor, atop the carpet, by a fishbowl. A gun.

Osir picked it up, thinking that it looked familiar. He saw that it was loaded and he kept on walking, clutching it alongside the hip. He hadn't held a gun since the war (flipping the bottle he felt no pills. The

signals in his brain signaled

the want for pills).

Must be someway outta this fuckin' place. Osir rushed through the carpets. His elongated figure was reflected on the golden surfaces of teapots, among china of delicate porcelains and ivory vials; his maimed lip spilled across gilded surfaces in runnels of poppy sap. Silk fabrics hung from the ceilings, into which the wall of riches stretched, embroidered with glittering thread into rich patterns of flower, winding onward to all directions from stem to petals and from amid the petals stems burgeoned into endless leaves. Some corners were dominated by dangling cobwebs, weaving soft drapes over the textiles and the china — no human eyes had lain upon such nooks in a very long time. Their antiquity and decadence spurred haunting recollections in the vicinity of Osir's perception, traumas pumped into the pulse of his gun-holding fingers and out through the flashing eyes hovering away from him. The pores of his reflections exhaled whispers from the hideous folds and curves of their brass skin; the scar throbbed and slobbered. Blood secreted from his memories, and his monster chomped through blood-lips out of mirrors spreading dim.

His body dropped onto pillows of satin. The relative comfort of the landing, into which his body lulled in velvet colors, was soon overwhelmed by another surge of agony which yelled like a blowtorch up his thorax, compressing the cavity, squeezing his heart; melting his throat hot from the inside; Osir grimaced, furrowed his face deep in the struggle to endure. Grunts sparkled out of his gnashed teeth.

He didn't faint this time. He emerged from the torture panting and trembling, light-headed to the extreme. He kept his body tender against the velvet satin and closed his eyes. The pillows were very comfortable...

The arid desert mountains faced the cloudless sun with a pose of enormous crags. Sometimes the drops were steep, and the earth was hard and hostile. It crunched beneath his boot. There was gravel and dust everywhere. Clank of automatics and marching boots; he marched in a file of helmets. Who was that fellow with the long red beard and the turban wrapped up round his face? Osir greeted him effusively, and with the other hand he drew his handgun, just in case.

(Hey — do you see that?) someone said. And the dyed red beard said, *watch out!* He pointed into Osir's chest with his brown finger, but already Osir was running among the opium poppies in the valley below. He was chasing someone. Where was this someone?

He awoke with a rumbling stomach, drained of all energy, extremely dizzy. He was so detached from his own senses he couldn't feel the parchness of his throat, his thirst. Some elemental instinct of survival made him rise with a long, weak, weary sigh; and he couldn't even feel the gun in his hand. It, like his mind, was weightless. But his body, his body was heavy. Too heavy... He dragged it along, along the walls.

There were some crumbs on the floor (why were there crumbs on the floor?). Osir knelt and scooped them up onto the palm of his hand, into a little pile. His mouth pecked and stuffed into the palm of his hand, and smacked the crumbs (cookie crumbs) The cookie crumbs made a trail on the carpet. Osir followed it — it led to the place where the floors and the walls and the ceilings were made of mirrors. He saw his body at all angles at once, scooping down to collect crumbs and eat them. It was amazing the clarity of mind these little crumbs gave. Hunger can be tricked by morsels, he thought. But hunger can't be tricked long.

Osir followed the trail of cookie crumbs and he munched madly on them. For a while then the cookies ceased, and Osir sucked from his hand as much vestige of flavor as he could as he kept onward, aimlessly looking for more. In the mirrors the monster gnawed at his bloody fingers and drooled in muttering laughter. Osir's neck oscillated profusely — his pores tightened, sweat secreted and spilled, like poisonous sap from unflowered buds; the presage of flaming agony tingled already, distantly, upon them. From time to time, he reached into his pocket and shook the little pill bottle next to his ear. He could hear nothing. Little empty bottles reverberated thousands of times into depths all around him. And then,

suddenly there was a profusion of cookie powder scattered in heaps and spread across the ground. Osir swept them up with his arms and, suddenly slower, decided this was futile and slowly ate them up straight from the ground. He exhaled like an ox as he munched. But then,

(what's that over there?)

He rose, and stood over the pool of blood. A gradual realization restored in him a suspended sense of mental acuity. Slowly, he wondered about the origin of this crimson stain, spread and dried among the mirrors. His features hardened; his eyes narrowed, bit by bit. Osir exhaled a breath dense and pensive, out from the profundities of suppressed memory. A sense of deja vu pervaded him with its uncanniness. The glass was shattered under the blood stain, where the body had fallen. In his eyes (for he saw his eyes myriad and multifold in the shattered glass beyond the blood stain) Osir saw the scene repeat itself — the blood shrank till it was only his reflection and the cookie crumbs at his feet, which were gravel on the foreign desert; and the body landed with a puff of dust. Underneath the muzzle of his gun the body resembled a perforated bag, but it had an uncanny quality to it; at that proximity, it looked almost human. Osir saw the ear and brown cheek of a face. A circle of blood propagated sluggish and uneven from under the body, the back of whose grimy shirt was punctured by three holes. A brown cheek, the corner of a lip. Osir pushed the body with his boot, and it turned heavily, like a loaded sack; exposing, under it, the gooey, fresh blood muddying the earth wet, shining darkly under the cloudless sun. The body beside the blood pool was soaked, the shirt absolutely drenched with it; it soiled the cheek of that face, one side of which was brown, the other deep red and teeming with the texture of gravel crumbs.

Osir furrowed his face deeper, slowly, slowly, and his heart furrowed along with it, pensive, doubtful...

It was a boyish face, and it had belonged to a boy no older than fifteen. The boy looked at the sun with eyes bereft of soul, with lips shut in a matter-of-fact expression; as if the sunshine itself had scattered the life away from the body. A boy no older than fifteen... Osir had killed before, but this was the first time he had seen a dead face, made dead by his bullet. (And where was the boy's gun?)

Osir stood over the blood staining the glass of the mirror labyrinth, and his soul ruminated upon the brown face of a boy in a distant desert. He felt behind him the swaying of the opium fields, erect ghostly in the windless air.

But the blood under his boot had belonged to another brown boy from another land, the same land which the tower stretched down under Osir's feet to touch.

The blood on the glass under his feet had belonged to Janu.

*

To witness those endless shelves of food lifeless and uncared for, to bear testimony to such unimaginable levels of negligence was, to Janu, something like a limit-breaking indignity. It drove him out of his senses with rage. A feeling of despair paralyzed him, all knotted in a realization that the Eagles were not only brutal, sociopathic degenerates, but were also incompetent in the wide confidence in their own invulnerability. It was the understanding of the blind hubris and arrogance of the masters which made him panic. How could they have hidden such tremendous amounts of food stock, enough to feed the entire megalopolis for months, while the herds of workers hungered; how could they have failed to care after it? Perhaps it was not merely arrogance, but sheer stupidity, pure inability. Or maybe it was pure malevolence; the desire to enact suffering. What was it? Why? — Janu asked himself repeatedly, with increasing despair. At any rate, it was unjust. Justice was so severely violated, and in so many ways, so brazenly and wantonly, that Janu grew almost blind with the will for revenge, to set justice through violence. He fumed and trembled; through the mind of the humble cook coursed images of gore and domination, scenarios where he exacted punishment with a sadistic glee befitting the crime of the punished. "I'll kill them, I'll kill them..." he repeated, desiring in his delirium to pull the trigger and blow off the subjugated head of the collared bull...

The crippling pain in his leg and the sheer exhaustion which he had to battle through only made him more mad. In the effort of moving, and absorbed as he was in his raging thoughts, Janu tended to look down, through a filter of absent blurriness which he, himself, often did not see. (At this point the seething yells salivated out the walls, pulsing insanely (and through this his heart quivered madly and made him crazy)). His limping made him slower than Neipas, and bit by bit the distance between them grew; through the turning of curves and crossways Neipas was soon out of sight, though neither he nor the maddened cook would notice it for a while.

"Neipas?" Janu breathed out his lips. "Neipas! Osir?" and as Janu found himself completely alone he called with a long shout, the very last breath of which was released into an abrupt silence. The yelling of the bulls had stopped (had someone been caught? had anyone been seen? had he been heard?) — immediately, out of fear, Janu ducked, and sought refuge among the satin pillows. Hidden deep under the cushions, the humble cook watched with sweaty, nervous eyes; he attempted to control the rampant pace of his own breathing. The metallic rattle of the gun sounded by his ear and wormed its way into his brains, making him more nervous still. Holding his breath didn't work — it would come out in whimpers through the nose. He wanted to close his eyes badly but knew he shouldn't. In a rack of nerves he waited.

To calm himself down he began munching cookies from the pack he had brought. One cookie went after the other — the sugar rush, ceaseless, lulled him by degrees. He waited.

Janu waited for a long time. Nothing happened.

Bit by bit the softness of the pillows drew him in — a comforting sensation of security emanated from the cushions, the sugar; the general quietude dulled the sense of danger. Bit by bit, munching cookies, the good cook emerged from the mount of pillows and wandered out through the maze of riches.

He wandered, and wondered, for a long time, through turns and twists carved out by the sparkling piles of treasure. But he couldn't find his way out, and it seemed that as time went the things around him began to take a life of their own. Janu heard whispers. The objects, it seemed, had been whispering for a very long time, but only now did the hushed sound of their voices reach his perception. What were they saying?

In one hand Janu held the gun. He had stopped eating — it wasn't practical to eat from the pack without both hands free. The craving was there, but subsided, buried under a renewed sense of danger, a reinforced fear. A long time had passed, and there was no exit. And what were those whispers? What were they saying?

By and by, he entered the labyrinth of mirrors. And all was glass around him.

His image broke into every surface, shattered into shards, scattering into interlacing depths. By this point Janu had regained the impression of a lurking presence stalking his movements. He felt hunted. His imagination, perhaps — perhaps derived from the enveloping objects and their glittering whispers. His reflection beheld him from the glass now. His aspect was unkempt, haggard, mucky. His earlobe yawned lifelessly, it yawned into a scream of silent despair, of hopeless fright, of an elusive sort of entrapment which had besieged his whole mature life — a life ripened too soon, as all lives such as his were prone to become. It was a choking sense whose elusiveness now gained concrete form, becoming physical in the occasionally cast sound of approaching steps... Janu's ears trembled with its traces, and his eyes were confronted from all sides with the Minister's Eagle visage, which he still donned; from all sides it stared into him in the accusatory gaze of hostile authority and command. It was muddied with blood; the whiteness of its feathers defiled. It made him stop. And the dread besetting him was not appeased by the consciousness that it was not the Minister who stared thus from the walls, that he looked nothing like him, that he could never look anything like him, for the mark of poverty and the stigma of caste were beginning to bubble out, in dark tints, through that visage. The mask, by which powers over the fates of nations were conferred, looked increasingly stained with the pasty wax of Janu's inner face. The very mustache dripped black over the tarnished beak. Color of soot, color of the earth — he saw the brownness of his face, made browner still by the soil and sweat griming it; the brownness which no molding of the mask could conceal. He saw the gun jutting stiffly from the end of his arm, quivering by his leg. And he knew that he couldn't have that gun in his hand. A lifetime of living at the edge of hostility, beyond which the frowns of authority stared always with hating eyes, had taught him that he couldn't have that gun in his hand. He'd be shot, without hesitation. It wasn't a defense, a protective shield, or any kind of weapon for him — it was the glaring sign of a target.

Janu paced backwards as he sensed the gradual approach of the lurking presence, as it acquired a sense of materiality — and inevitability. The mirror labyrinth ebbed away from his retreating steps; bit by bit its glassy nakedness was covered by carpets, curtains and shining things, and the oblique starkness of his multiple duplicates was, little by little, dimmed into the many little mirrors of a myriad polished golden and silvery surfaces. Seeping from the sides until they rounded the whole orb of his eye, moneyed objects glided ahead slowly, wrapping his sight like blinders; until his heel touched a clinking artifact. It was a circular piece of glass — a fishbowl — upon the velvet. Carefully he put the gun down (his hand was warped in the reflection) in the corner by it. Then he walked forth again slowly, and ate; tried to calm down.

Again his likeness entered, through an infinitude of reproductions, into the manifolded depths of the mirrors. The horns began to sprout, bloodied, out of the soggy feathers of the Minister's mask; their weight compounded into his brain, splitting his forehead of clay through which his face of wax oozed, leaking toward the ground toward which he hunched miserably, feeling strange, strange, strange, alien, even from himself, alien... Always alien in his own skin, an immigrant in his own country; forever an outsider in his home. His ancestors were from the fertile lands of Ooxor, now the megalopolis of Axiac; he had grown up not far from the border himself, born but a few miles out on the wrong side of the fences, the wall, the iron drape — on the side to which the muzzles pointed with gaping stares. But even inside Great Columbia, Great Axiac, he lived behind a border, he himself was a walking border, an edge between safety and harassment, normalcy and violence — as were all his brethren who had been kicked out and all those who had been brought in by force, and all the brown and black plume in the world which came with aspirations of flight, with aspirations to lift from the dust, to soar. All of them, living borders — on the other side of which were scornful stares, staring constantly. Janu himself had seen into those eyes; he had gazed into the eyes of the bull-head and seen human hatred. To those eyes, Janu's mask — the mask of the ox, the mask of humble servility — was his face and his due. To them the brown, grimy visage — was grease; dirt to be cleaned up. In the settlers' eyes Janu's face was but a speck of mud, a sludgy droplet from the wider mass of filth pressing against the nation's levees; a great rabble of the impure, the infected, the unwashed. The collared-bull's dislike for them was visceral and born out of centuries of unendingly renewed hatreds, incestuous in their spread across the unconscious mind of modern civilizations; hatreds finding their root in a will to power and its stem in the pleasure of using it. And the collared bull enjoyed using it, he relished the exercise of power — particularly its physical variety and violent expression. Without the feeling of remorse, the application of physical power, of violence upon another, can become the biggest rush. For the bull there was no remorse — in his eyes Janu and his ilk were but empty sacks, soulless. He saw in Janu a thing, an other, an alien, a mere pigeon... His abstracted and indifferent vision removed the guilt; and his mask, his uniform, his flag, with which he bound up his deepest pride and identity, removed the responsibility and provided the justification. And the automatic that came with the uniform and the flag — the totality of the mask — provided the kind of power he most craved. The very grip on it was a kind of kick. He pointed it along the depth of his eyesight, determined, focused, professional, with fury contained, like a tethered beast anxious to be unleashed, as he walked furtively beside the trail of crumbs...

Janu brought his crafty, delicate, culinary fingers to his corroded mask, through which seeped a widely gaping and horrified face...

He became a whole shivering mess as he trod deeper into the labyrinth, aimless and frightened. His mouth was thick and parched full of sugar. Eventually he ceased munching as his nerves worked on him and his fear attained command over his body. He would stop for a minute at a time and stand there, grounded by a swelling premonition. The fright shook his every limb and made him raise his arms. One hand held the pack of cookies. He walked with raised arms through the labyrinth, sensing the approach of the lurking presence. He nearly wept with nerves, but there was still an inkling of hope in his heart — the exit had to be somewhere. Maybe, maybe, if he were caught, he'd be taken to it; out of the maddening labyrinth. His every reflex prepared to beg for clemency.

Then he saw it — a boot.

When the trail of crumbs lost itself in the glass, the muzzle saw it: In the multiverse of mirrors, a hunched, bloated figure, a brown blot filling a misshapen suit (an unkempt sack). Janu saw them too; the presence finally materialized in the glass. He waited, he waited, he waited as the million arms coalesced around him. The muzzle sight was trained on the convergence of targets, narrow in its focus, wide in the discernment of the passing images of various forms, replicating the short, brown pigeon in the melting mask... The muzzle found the figure with its back turned: through the riot mask a shout was issued, and the figure moved abruptly; the muzzle exploded in a flash, and from it the booming sound propagated and filled the vastness in an instant.

Janu felt the shout enter him and quaked; the next moment there was a sharp boom and in an instant he was down on the floor, as though he had been shoved by a truck. The impact was such that it knocked the scream back into his throat; his lung swelled with the shove, he didn't even feel his body crash onto the ground. The first sensation was of overwhelming confusion and dizziness. Then, as the agitation dropped vertiginously, he began to hear the gasping of his own breaths and the sound of steps growing nearer. A sharp and burning pain on his upper back made him wince and cry; the pain spread, his heart palpitated with panic; his vision blurred. The pain grew sharper, excruciating, intolerable; he was pinned down by it, he was trapped (he was rooted to the floor by the agony sprouting in blood out of the lodged bullet); and as he gasped for breath, as he lost strength he saw, coming round the edge of his sight, a boot...

Voices far off.

The pain subsided somewhat, relieving itself into the glass, the cold surface of which he felt now on one of his cheeks...

He breathed still, but weakly. The vague consciousness that he should be struggling faded itself in the lull. He felt himself falling asleep, fading with open eyes.

The boot stood immobile before him, like a colossus made of hide and strapped with ropes. In the mirrors he spotted a million blades...

*

It was a copious, exaggerated amount of gore drying at Osir's feet; it was as if the victim had been purposefully bled. He wondered (nauseous)... This was, perhaps, the accumulated flux of many murders and endless sacrifices.

The brown boy hadn't had a gun — but by the moment Osir realized it he was already dead. He hadn't been the one he was looking for.

The boy's face had rounded to the shape of his eye, forevermore contorted to the recurring form of his memory, masking his warped gaze — through the dead stare of those soulless eyes Osir had seen, from that moment on, all things. All those he had killed prior, they had been but blots, pixels in a wide abstracted field — and then that visage appeared to him as sudden as though he had been plunged through the scope's glass across the distances it so cruelly bridged. His (that anonymous boy's, whose name he never knew) had been the first countenance to face him so, with the mute judgment of death's stark, horrible, horribly empty aspect. Shockingly, at the turn of the empty body, there appeared the face, full; and there solidified in his senses the realization of reality and its brutal moral truths, finding condemning expression in his repulsed sense of humanity. The boy's features were the most legible in his mind, because of all this; the rest had been merely swept up in a tidal blur of massacres and mutilations, dozens of faces mingled in carnage, through the fluxing masses of chewed skin of which the monster grinned, gnashed teeth, clenched brow.

The poppies secreted grievous sobs, cries of revolt. And by the time he returned, the men of the red beards — all the other prostrated worshipers — lay dead inside their temple (all their faces wrapped in soaked turbans). Whomever he had been looking for (but who, after all, was he after?) had perhaps fled.

The monster grimaced, blood driveled between its teeth as they pulped Osir's flesh behind the looking glass. Osir stared at it straight; it stared straight at him. Opium discharged through the sides of his scarred lips. Accusatory, the light vanished in inexorable succession into the blackness of the eye which drew it; it was retained only in gleams of painful memory [...] until the void grew to encompass the whole being and all the accompanying senses. ...what was life to him? It was but a black hole and a draining ache, a barrenness without horizon. To feel was to be hurt; to wake was to bear the burden of existence and memory anew. There was no relief forthcoming — the boy was forever dead — and without it, how could there be anything else?

Osir walked away from the blood pool after standing over it for a long time, ruminating with his soul. Whispers befell his ears. He walked among ghosts of past landscapes and past selves, haunted by the stillness of the opium poppies. He walked in the scent of the flower, in the swamp of its secretions, its spell of sleep. Whispers of gunshots and yelling... The pain came back excruciating. He couldn't bear it anymore. The monster in the glass screamed at him. He couldn't bear it. In a last despairing attempt Osir overturned the bottle, shook it vigorously against the palm of his hand — but there were no pills and nothing to avail him. He shoved the bottle furiously against the teetering wall. The monster laughed and screamed. His chest burned, his throat choked, his head churned with shots of cannon. He couldn't bear it, not anymore.

Raising the muzzle of the gun against the monster's head, Osir grimaced with a wide grin of clenched teeth, and pulled the trigger.

The boom sounded across the labyrinth, lifeless and full of objects.

70 - Capita per caput

Neipas dipped his mask into the bobbing of the stairway-descending mob, let yield his languishing energies to the tired flow seeping through Columbaria's gates. Like the eye of a colossus the sun peeked over the mountains, and, like the eye of a god through which all mortal eyes see, on opening it revealed the whole wide extent of a landscape hitherto concealed from every gaze. Just at the moment his toes slid off the top stair, and as his chin sunk abruptly, his sight plunged into the blurry confines of newly unveiled depths: Bright, shiny, cloudless, the gaping pit beyond Anubel's edge staggered between trembling jerks, hedged in and shimmering between the multitude of plumed heads, glaring monstrously, unfamiliar, hellish, dreadful in its chaotic amplitude. The vision of it induced vertigo; and the numberless feet plodding in its direction trod down very cautiously indeed, the waving heads above them sustained on shallow breaths and a pure instinct of self-conservation alone; their minds retreated somewhere beyond sensitivity. The stench of charred flesh lingered in their nostrils and floated down the steps with them. No one dared look back to the Stage.

Disoriented and instinctual, Neipas contrived to blend in with the exodus, and match the tempo of its downtrodden march. His psyche squirmed full of anxiety and a furious eagerness to run out of there, his will strove maniacally toward the elevators in the Warehouse Hall, whose doors now yawned open; his legs, trembling to hasten ahead of the throng now coursing to their dormitories to grab their things, were leashed by Neipas' sense of prudence alone. To submit to the crowd was to seize control of himself. Every instinct of his felt that the Eagles were on the prowl for him — and he had the premonition that, if they caught him, it would be the end. He couldn't expose himself.

Yet most of the Eagles were, at that point, boarding their private helicopters, which populated the various helipads and vacant patios and groves of their Nest in a dizzying, ringing succession of whirling blades, making the terraces of the Anubel's west-facing side resemble a warped colony of steely dragonflies and waltzing wings. The flying vessels lifted in clamors of synthetic whirr, casting windy, mechanical shrieking into the heavens, and were off beyond the Belab's immense drop into the shattered expanse. Some of the humanity remaining deep underneath their Eagle masks, under the facade of implacability, must have been affected by the apocalyptic sight as they hung on the precipice of a megalopolis absolutely ravaged under the bright skies; a wreck of battered concrete and broken glass stretching on to the farthest distances, bloated outward into a vastness so immense the eye could glance nothing, absolutely nothing, else. Some of that humanity — in some of the Eagles, perhaps — might have been stirred by this vision of utter devastation. Numerous press releases published after the fact claimed emphatically that it had, and that the Eagles would do everything in their power to clean up the damage. Whether they were frankly munificent, or rather masked themselves in the mischievous cloak of charity, we'll never know. What is certain is that they entered their helicopters, one by one, and left, soaring above the cataclysm, bound to the intact comfort of far-off mansions — and that, regardless of whether soothing strategies of magnanimity accompanied them or not, all, like scavengers over carrion, glided over Axiac with thoughts of profiting from its destruction in one way or another.

They left behind the tower, which elevated storey upon storey of vacant windows of cracked, broken, or vanished glass, peaking in a crown immaculately preserved, though shaken; wherein a huge herd of fatigued heads and drooping masks endeavored in preparations to leave. The helicopters' thumping noise kept slashing into the Pigeon Gardens, and into the corridors of the shadowy Columbaria, which was uncannily devoid of clatter, shouts, busyness; the herd marched through in perfect order, menacingly silent. Suddenly — upon the last slice of sound — the lights blasted on over those heads swarming the corridors, and in unison their eyes shut in sluggish, exhausted motions. There was no other reaction. No limb sped up its pace, no lip murmured. Only Neipas' heart seemed to audibly flutter in the new visibility; and his neck strained down deeper, his pigeon semblance blotched more widely across the anonymity of the masked throng, in his struggle to be inconspicuous. Once inside the dorm, he was quick. He opened his closet of possessions and put on his jacket in swift, shaky motions. His arms slipped unfeeling through tunnels of wool, shoulders of cloth bore upon his shoulders. Then he gradually stepped out again, mixing his form with the mass wobbling sluggishly to the exits. All streamed out of the infinitude of doors and coursed down the corridor.

Neipas blinked profusely his blotted eyes. He wore the jacket Eva had bought him a year before, though he was barely conscious of what it was — he could've forsaken it, were it not for the necessity to follow the herd's flow.

...Slowly, very slowly in the mushy traffic of advancing bodies, they went. Trapped in the midst of this dense multitude, as he made efforts to keep away from the mirrored/windowed walls, Neipas considered (with his photographic instincts roused in the slowness of his progression) the faces around him. They were very many, and all looked embroiled in some stage of degradation. Some had a hint of strength in them yet; but others were completely devoid of anything, in every sense dumb and soulless. It was like walking among the dead — there was no pulse to the motions of that collective evacuation. No one said a word. There was no sound but that of deep, drowsy breathing, and shuffling feet.

Through and above the profusion of bobbing heads, Neipas saw, towering over the height of the march as it slanted up the steps to the Clockroom, the bulk of military bulls overlooking the proceedings. Their masks looked lively and fed, presiding over what seemed to be a shifting field of graves by comparison, with photographs of the departed stamped upon the top of stiff tombs carried by a dull landslide — watching with inspecting eyes the slow march, as if standing on the banks of a muddy river of vestigial will. It crawled forth and stopped, crawled forth and stopped; at the very front (out of view) folk were boarding the elevators, which they filled to the very brim. The elevators stuffed, their doors closed, and those who couldn't get in waited — and so it went on at a pace so slow as to be excruciating for Neipas. Random thoughts passed through his tired head. They were thoughts of everything — the image of his old camera, a recalling of his father in a chair, a faint consideration of what he would do outside and whether it was cold, his apartment, a TV, the film he had wanted to watch in theaters (was it still out?), a remembrance of Eva wiping her body with a towel — thoughts with but vague connection to one another. But then he checked himself, and stiffened his countenance — he had to focus. Carefully he would pass his fingers over his mask, molding it slowly to what he thought it ought to look like. It was an ordeal. The wax dripped through his fingers in a sodden and dispirited mush, drooping in the extremities of the long grind, so tired, so tired, so tired, it was.... (But what if they can tell?) He labored to his last reserves of strength into removing any sort of mark that might give him away, but he was too afraid to look in the mirrors and his *I* had run out of battery, so he could but wonder in his distressed ignorance, how, how was the utter chaos of feeling miring his soul expressed in his semblance then?

He didn't know — and so, trembling, he merely walked with his shoulders up and head low (not too low, so as to not attract the attention of the watching bulls and supervisors), as if bracing himself; and waited in the sluggishness of the mass, avoiding the bulls' glare, feeling his *I* grow heavier and heavier inside his pocket, inside his heart. He as if carried lead — so heavy were the voices contained within the glass — feeling already the burden of the convict. (But I can't give up)

...

[time passed above him...] Round him widened the sensation of bodies, over him the sensation of space. Finally they had reached, after many upward steps, the Clockroom. Its amplitude contrasted immediately with the compactness of the corridors. But why was it that the crowd, already too slow, was slowing down still more — why was it stopping? Neipas felt despair at the perception of this and, unthinkingly, dared lift his head.

The lights standing on towering tripods still swamped the huge vestibule in cartoon colors, the wide loud closet still faced them, the clock still churned and the pendulum still swung. Atop a dais (a box from the Warehouse Hall yonder) set up beneath the clocktower, the Mayor stood clamoring "Fellow citizens of Columbia!" — A thick ring of faces gathered about him, halting the progress of the march. Listening through the bombastic thump in his ears, it was soon apparent to Neipas that the Mayor was but stringing festoons of disjointed syllables and generally babbling nonsense, availing himself of buzzwords like 'justice' and 'democracy' to win over the favor of the clogging crowd. His voice pealed along the ticktock — his arms swayed in the cadence of the pendulum; and Neipas could plainly sense the beating of Belab's heart under the throated voice of the speaker. He could discern it plainly now. Behind the confident grin, the professorial cadence, the pondering gesture of scratching the chin as the elegantly combed head nodded thoughtfully — there was something of arrogance; as of a sly bandit, proud of the audacity of his deceit. He waved his arm right and left, right and left, and the frozen masks followed along... The Mayor's voice gradually blended with the orchestra of heavy breathing and shuffling feet sweeping the long corridor, with the mechanical ticking thundering in the brain's veins, blurring all together into a soundscape of dream. It seemed that Neipas could hear the musical band afar; the sound of drum resilient... His head wavered — unconsciously soaring, its eyes faced already the ceiling where the sculpted cow grinned and guffawed; it seemed to bellow circularly the letters round its head, *VANITAS IN PERSONA VERITAS IN HOMINEM* (Neipas' beak dropped as it wound these words soundlessly); and as he blinked, his head, which had for a moment craned above all others, was already facing straight the tide of feathered masks, through which (close to him) a military bull mumbled something to the side of his own neck, with vigilant airs; he seemed to spy glances upon Neipas from time to time. Neipas himself ceased to hear or see anything clearly. The whole force of his instinct directed him toward a single purpose, one desire only — to get out of there as quickly as possible. He could no longer withstand the tension, no longer could resist the grinding of his spirit, he could no longer wait. In a struggle he lurched (as discreetly as possible) through the crowd, and strove away from the agglomeration of mystified listeners spreading thick from the dais to join the flow rounding it. He backed off into the tide of moving cattle and pigeons as he observed the bull's eyes observing him, following him. His jaw trembled away from the attentive gaze, and his eyes drank the wobbly vision of still blurs under one single gesturing blur, under a pixelated clock. The seamstresses there had gone, and cattle masks and heads were simply dropped about, uncared for; they were trampled on and crushed into bits of clay, and soon the marbled ground began to feel grainy. Neipas felt himself shifting along, as in a beach of wavy quicksand, toward the wider ocean. And though all heads bloomed in feathers now and there were no heifers nor oxen in view, still cowbells jingled mystically in his mind, as if they still moved beneath the myriad unfurred chins. Their movements affected the nostrils; the stench of countless unshowered days stewed in the closeness of the pack...

Yet — presently the numbness and the disquiet eased, space opened up. As it neared the stairway to the Warehouse Hall the flow seemed to be pulled by the sheer force of imminent relief. Suddenly Neipas felt as though he flew, as though he soared down the steps! Between the heavy drapes he moved at the pace of flight — there were the elevators, right there! So near, so close now! Just beyond the bridge... Presently the gates were shut — but he eyed them, he eyed them anxiously, inching himself a little closer through the dense pack of weary, beaten bodies, as though he were diving through a wall of tar. He heard his name. Multiple Sunais ushered the crowd and herded it into queues as they crossed the bridge. Their Owl stares seemed to engulf everything; a nausea of fear assailed Neipas, which he tried to quell with the hope of confidence while he tended his mask. He heard his name being called again. The sound voicing it irritated Neipas and initially he paid it no heed; he ascribed it to a fiction of his afflicted instincts.

The gates — they were opening now! As they slid apart it seemed to him like a pool of light emanated from the interiors, bathing the waiting crowd with its warmth, enticing him with the promise of freedom... Once more he heard his name — the sound of it affected the nerves behind the eyes, he felt almost like crying. He forced himself to ignore it and went breathlessly with the flush; teary-eyed, flummoxed, anguished, he saw the open gates of the elevators nearing.

"Neipas." — someone grabbed his arm. He tried to force himself out of the grip; but then he felt his arm clutched again. "Neipas!" His head swooned; his breathing came short. He felt vertiginous, free-falling, too weak...

He turned. "Yes?" — gasping, on the verge of tears. It was the Chief Supervisor. Even as he saw his winking grin he turned again, reflexively, toward the elevators. He stood at the end of the bridge now. The doors were still open...

"Can I have a quick word with you please?"

Neipas barely perceived the motions of his own body, which endeavored still to inch toward the big rectangle of light swallowing mounds of heads, receiving them in its warm maw... "What," mumbled he vaguely, through the knot in his throat.

"Can I have a quick word with you?"

The Chief Supervisor had slowed his progression. Many passed him by on their way to freedom. If he could only thrust through now! — he would still have time to reach the doors. "Neipas."

His breathing weighed heavily upon his meager chest. The Supervisor still held his arm, and he hadn't the strength... Sunai had begun to turn her stare in his direction. The *I* inside his pocket pulsed like a raging heart (Maybe, maybe I can still reach it).

He watched in frail despair as the gates closed, clasping upon the vanishing light.

Suddenly it was as though it got colder; Neipas shuddered.

"Quick word?" insisted the sympathetic Supervisor, letting go of Neipas' arm.

"Sure, sure..."

Neipas muttered without sound.

"Can we talk out in the gardens?"

So said the Chief Supervisor, ushering him with little taps on the shoulder, as Neipas watched the elevators shining farther, the luminescence their gates opened to, getting dimmer. He was guided on like an invalid, passing through the hundreds or thousands of moribund masks awaiting deliverance; anticipating, numb, the fresh winds of the outdoors; expecting to leave the tower — if not forever, then at least for now.

*

The Chief Supervisor escorted him up the Gardens with mollifying pats on his shoulder, assuring him that all was all right, telling him to not worry. "I got you," he told him amicably, with a wink.

Neipas was ultimately brought to the Ballroom; wherein sat waiting, regally, the Head Gardener.

71 - Meat

They had walked the somber silence of the Pigeon Wing, through vacant corridors, the empty kitchen and its vast and spectral solitude of motionless pans. All the while followed by a Bull, they went back into the piercing radiance of the Garden terraces, with its broken aspect of flotsam run aground. Sunlight, diluted through the canvas of toppled tents, beaming off poles jutting athwart; the upright stillness of trees, scorched leafless, arising like ghastly masts; the pandemonic heaps of miscellanea strewn across; the few balloons yet lifting, iridescent, from the disarray of ropes winding throughout the circus, and hanging down the shimmering lake; a very jungle of debris, traces of a strange battlefield; all left abandoned — the lot of it made the Gardens seem like a sinister exhibit, a grim memorial to the vast wreckage deepening under the tower as they climbed, and as the Grand Facade ahead of them arose. The chasm made for a most unnerving sight. Used to the dulcifying reach of puffy cloudiness as they were, Neipas' eyes contracted in pain and blinked copiously, violated by the intrusive brightness of a flood burning with the reflected power of a million suns. The dazzle felt abrupt somehow in its violent newness; as though an essential curtain had been ripped from the floor of the world in a great, cruel revelation of reality. To Neipas' tired eyes it could be nothing more than a painful blur — impossible to process. And yet he could not stop looking back at it; even though he could not truly behold it.

The Chief Supervisor still patted his shoulder encouragingly. Underneath him, the air deepened; and there were smells of metal, there was a stench of whirring melodies — and a honeyed pulse filled his shirking gaze (then, darkness). In the suddenly audible, soft groaning of the wooden floor he seemed to sense a million absent steps and the enigmatic stillness of Cesar.

Deliberately now, Neipas turned his head. For he knew he was being taken past the Stage, which he didn't wish to face; he turned his gaze to the depths of it, sunk into its shadows of arched rigging and blinking glows, only as soon as he walked past the stake (the bells rung dreamily then, as if very far).

The stench lingered; though he never knew if Kasim's scorched cadaver still hung upon it.

Neipas was brought before the Gardener.

The agricultural tycoon sat comfortably in a padded, royal chair set in the wide-open gate, facing west over the Eagle's side of the Anubel. A long shadow prolonged from his feet; softly cast out of the waking sunlight upon his mighty figure, it spilled onto the august stairways and cascades gracing those hanging gardens, which were, even then, so immaculately preserved. The three sumptuous terraces opened up before Neipas' glimpsing eye, colossal and clean, expanding in tremendous contrast to the sprawl which, beyond the Infinity Pool's pristine edge, flushed in debris about the gorged ocean. Even from those heights, the devastation wrought by the storm was evident; though it was still too far, still too indistinct, for Neipas' numbed perception to grasp with acute feeling. As he approached, his senses were much more fixed on the short table beside the Gardener: it gushed with an abundance of meat, cake and fruit, a burst of culinary wonders. A copious bunch of grapes hung off the side, overflowing from the profusion of nutritious color that brimmed the top.

On the far side of the table stood a small mirror. Round in shape, it was ornamented with many clustered faces of a silver sheen, staring out of the frame with gaping mouths and hollowed eyes. The motionless explosion of food was reflected upon the glass, which mimicked also the Gardener's hand sinking into it, and retrieving the succulent bits of different delicacies, and stuffing them deliciously inside his satiated, ravenous, hooked beak. Drrawetz, who smiled with genuine pleasure, stood beside him now, and gently wiped his greasy lips with a cloth after each bite. The steward's face did not stir out of this pleased expression for even a moment; only (it seemed to Neipas) his eyes managed to deviate themselves from the task for a split instant to hiss a contemptuous glance at the approaching waiter.

"Mr. Head Gardener, Your Excellency," began the Chief Supervisor his announcement, bowing. "I bring Neipas, the waiter, to your presence."

[...] The Ballroom, vast, seemed to doze yet in the fresh clarity of morning. An overwhelming sense of dispersion permeated the immensitude; everything seemed, in contrast to a few hours before, more exposed. Something elemental had been torn open, vistas had been created out of sheer haze; the world extended much farther beyond them now. It made Neipas, even more than earlier, feel very small; dislodged; and unbelonging. Standing in that ample richness of space, he did indeed look as he felt; something like a blotch of gloom oozing upon sunshine. He resembled a very scarecrow, draped as he was in the now-musty woolen jacket and the bloodied, tattered rags of his uniform which, unlike most others, he had forgotten to remove in his rush. His mask was disfigured in the sodden misery of all his exertions, smashed in the grind, sagged by the toil, wrinkled — as though he had worked so hard as to have worked his share in life already, and had simply sped to old age as a result.

So silent was the Anubel, so numb, that the airy immensity acquired a recluse, intimate, and oppressive closeness — urging Neipas, dim in the western verge of the grand Ballroom, to diminish further into his fatigue. (Something throbbed under his feet)

For a bleared stretch of time he thus stood. The Gardener did not yet speak. With one hand, he ate; keeping his gaze upon the prospect, he ate in a languid pace, thoroughly relishing the opulent meal, chewing and slurping in ruminating motions of circling jaw. With the other, he tapped his ornate, wooden, ivory cane; on and off the carpet, breaking and reconnecting with the long shadow that ascended and descended, ascended and descended, ascended and descended, in mighty pulses, down the Gardens and beyond; again and again in tortuous repetition. The cane thumped through the fur into the wobbly marrow of Neipas' skull; like a phantasmal stirring spoon; like a poking fork; like a probing knife. Thoughts of murder sallied through his starved mind — if he were alone with him, perhaps he would do it, perhaps he would thrust his fingers into that warm neck whose jowl waved with the food passing behind it — but he was too weak and too afraid; and the Gardener's Bull stood giant and furious close-by. (One, two, one, two, one, two, one, two... Somewhen between beats of cane something had shifted. Could the Gardener read his mind? for now he noticed the Gardener's mask turned toward his face and the Gardener's vast engulfing glare swallowing him whole). Neipas abjectly curved his neck. His veins throbbed. For eons he waited, and the sun did not move.

(One, two, one, two...) A voice reached him finally: from very far, growing within him painfully, or as it were pulling his consciousness into the strain of the moment.

"It's ok," began the Gardener, keeping motionless in his chair. "No need to be anxious."

Neipas fought tremulously against the push of gravity. Looking slightly up now, he found himself standing awkward and dizzy, out of place, a short distance from the Gardener's looming throne (Neipas perceived that as the Chief Supervisor stepped to the side he winked, chummy, and even now nodded in encouragement —), swaying a little upon his aching feet. He swallowed dry, repeatedly, convulsively; his lips then parting for air, withered and chapped, gasping as though emerging from the ocean deep. A stone lodged uncomfortably inside his breast. He felt his heart beat frail upon the summit of his throat; the back of his mouth sizzled with an unbearably acrid itch, but his parched tongue could not reach it. The feebleness of his starved belly spread and drained in every fiber of thought and vitality. His head — nauseous. His eyes red, moist, sickly; burning with the horror of recent memory etched.

"Do you know why you're here?"

Neipas tried to focus his sight on the Gardener, but he couldn't. He nodded, but not in affirmation; it was, perhaps, a faint attempt to shake the weariness off, to make the blur sharper, to clear up his head. It didn't work. He felt, in desperation, the solidity of his pigeon mask slipping away from his face.

Even as he nodded — slowly, mystified — he whispered shakily, as in a cold sigh, "no".

But the Gardener said sharply, "Yes you do."

Neipas' chin coiled and stiffened, his cheek trembled in nervous convulsions; a tear slid from his wet, empty eye; he sniffled. His wet nostrils fluttered, inflamed. A great unrest seemed to rise within his soul, spreading like poison, and making it succumb — all the pillars upon which his being rested its foundations were felt to crumble. This was it, he thought.

"Your *I*, please."

By and by Neipas, automatically, as though controlled by another mind, reached into his pocket; and slowly, very slowly, extended his arm. The *I* seemed to greatly weigh down the palm of his hand, and he could feel the smoothness of its surface so sharply that nothing else, for the moment, seemed to exist. The mighty Bull (his keyless nose-ring billowed menacingly close to his neck) took it. Neipas' glare snapped before his frightening presence, and he saw Drrawetz suddenly rushing in with a long plastic thread whose end could not be seen, and plugging it into his *I*, which was without battery. A tiny red dot then appeared above the glass; and the glass alighted with electric glow. The Head Gardener took hold of it. Soon the voices of the Eagles streamed out from the device — scoffing, arrogant, triumphal. Neipas sighed a tremulous breath, swallowed air; convulsed with the effort of standing, as if trying to quell surging throes; he cleared his nose and, gnashing his teeth and straining under his chin, tried to mentally clasp onto something, anything; tried (but it was futile) to remove himself from this dream; willing it, feebly, to halt its progress into the nightmare it was becoming.

The Bull seized his wrists and tied his hands with rope behind his back — without violence, however, without rush; calmly. Neipas didn't resist.

Their terrifying voices kept streaming into the monstrous vacuum of the Ballroom. After focusing on the glass and his own roaming fingers for some time, the Gardener's stare rolled toward Neipas and kept fastened upon his scared, meager shape — whose bashful eyes would occasionally risk tilting up slightly — with a gaze that didn't really discern, and an absorption that didn't really contemplate, as if he were looking not at Neipas but at nothing.

His meal continued uninterrupted; he listened, and ate as the Eagles spoke, and guffawed, and chewed in jubilee. This lasted for a very long time. Meanwhile — while their recorded utterances aired out in electrical sparks — Neipas suffered. Extreme dizziness, pervasive discomfort, twitches and throes percolated every floating fiber of his being. Wafts of stench (which were probably his own, for he hadn't showered in days; he could feel his own filth marinating the nooks and folds of his body) lifted to his nostrils and lowered back into the fuzziness of the ground. Whatever extended beneath his stomach had evaporated; he could scarcely feel his legs, and the pressure (pulsing) under his feet was vague and faraway. His head was as if swollen with vacuity; flashes of nothingness, like quivers, spawned inside and nothing else. Vestiges of muscle shivered somewhere in his ken.

"Don't worry," bloated the Gardener's croak unexpectedly, after a span of ages, saying, between the laborious smacking of a great chunk of flesh: "I'm curious. Didn't we give you a good job, housing, a pretty nice salary, free meals? You live in one of the richest cities on the planet. You served in one of the most prestigious venues on the planet. You can't say we didn't treat you well. It could be much worse. So — why? After all we gave you."

Neipas only swayed upon his feet, his head oscillating dizzy, too weak to say anything.

The Gardener kept glaring, and from amid meaty chewing insisted, "Why did you record our conversations? You're working for someone, aren't you? Look at me."

His avian orbs were giant, colossal, overbearing. Neipas trembled. Again he noticed that their stare didn't quite meet his own, widening glassy onto some ghastly nowhere. The sun's indiscriminating light twinkled in the Gardener's venomous eyes, intensifying the amber lividness of their glare.

He had stopped eating. The full gravity of his voice sounded out of his cavernous beak: "I'm talking to you." The menacing tone penetrated Neipas' consciousness sharply and made his breathing deepen and quicken. He could feel himself apologizing, mumbling sorries beneath panicked gasps, slurring, at the cusp of tears, "I'm just hungry, I'm just really hungry..." Yet his own speech seemed remote from his shivering lip, almost nonexistent; his own motions as if belonging to the body of another. The voice was reduced to a raspy peep, his windpipe being parched from thirst. He exerted himself enormously to speak and his breathing deepened further still. His chest seemed to have shrunk and the skin felt as if it penetrated between the bones; he panted intensely. He smacked and pursed his lips and licked about his face, feeling the wax — altogether molten and disfigured by this point, it was but a sodden mass without shape or pattern.

The Gardener resumed his meal in a deliberate slowness of pace, casting sounds of pleased salivation loudly into Neipas' throbbing ears. Drrawetz, at their side, rubbed his hands sheepishly, with a grin so excessively servile, and so immense in its servility that it nearly tore through his chinked eyes; the smile was his whole face. Whenever the Gardener finished chewing he would promptly collect the white cloth hanging from his apron and wipe the grease off the tycoon's lips, doing it in the most sincere exultation of feeling.

When the Gardener finished he said, "You can have some," and with this he grabbed a random handful of food from the table and tossed it onto the floor, by Neipas' feet. He grabbed another handful and did with it the same; and then again, studiously, indifferently. The prisoner, tied-up, stared down at the meal mounting beneath him with intense feelings of humiliation and craving. "So? Eat." Mechanically, vacantly, as the Gardener stopped, Neipas knelt and bowed prostrate upon the ground. Having stood on his feet for so long, his entire weight yielded gratefully to the carpet and his lips pummeled drunk into the strewn blur of leftovers; salivating onto the furry soil as they gaped and closed upon one another, struggling breathlessly to mouth as much as possible. It didn't occur to him then the indignity of his pose, the humiliation of his position already forgotten. All he could feel was relief. He pecked, and gobbled, and slobbered and struggled clumsily as juices poured from the side of his beak, all smeared in the bizarre panoply of flavors mixing round his tongue. He ate ever faster, and with great hurry, as he felt his vitality deplete. He ate until he no longer could. Finding himself lying along his side, with his cheeks pressed to the floor, panting, he tried to get up; and couldn't. Though his body slackened in relief it was far from satiated and the strain of the pose had quickly overtaken the energy gained from the nourishment. Still, he had returned to an acuter sense of his flesh. He felt the ache upon his knees, the hardness of his back which he unsuccessfully attempted to straighten. He remained thus, lying yet; eyes downcast aslant, lips knotted in a growing sense of scorn. He could feel the Gardener's stare directly upon him.

"Are you feeling better?" the Gardener addressed Neipas' head. The question was asked with no particular tone, without reproach nor compassion. His voice was simply mechanical; aloof. Neipas couldn't bring himself to say anything.

"Well?"

The carpet then drew away from his face; Neipas felt himself lifted by two powerful hands, and as his mind spirited back into his brain he saw the Gardener's Bull taking a step back from him, and found himself again before the Gardener's throne, standing on his knees.

"Why did you record our conversations?" the Gardener asked once more, but Neipas found himself physically incapable of speaking; he tucked dormant inside his deep-breathing head, very close, very heavy, unable to project himself out. Some fingers raised his chin, and he beheld now the tycoon's gloved hand cupped under it, brimming with grains in the hollow. His beak dropped of its own to it — perhaps from no volition other than the succumbing to physical weakness — and he ate upon the Gardener's palm. Lifting his sight and gulping, breathless, he spotted at first indistinctly, then precisely, the feeder's other hand, holding between the tip of its fingers a long slab of rib, and a tongue which, judging by their motions, were intended to be taken as they hung. He felt again a stench; nestled now behind all the preservatives and spices, emanating from the depth of the cooked, tender meat as it jingled suspended from the Head Gardener's gloved talons. Suddenly, the pulsing and writhing which had been rearing against Neipas' overcome legs and feet and nerves found in his memory a matching image and sound: that of the pulsing thing at the Golden core of the tower, the unimaginable clamor of screams thundering under the neurotic Dove; then, the mouthless, featherless, tarred servants or slaves in the alien factories there; and the dead fighter's body being sliced upon the table, flayed through the twitching glows of a grimy kitchen; Janu's horrified gaze; the ignoble trial, the burning screams of Kasim.

Neipas shook his head. The Ballroom gyrated and tipped slightly; he felt on the edge of swooning again.

"Vegetarian? Fine," mumbled the Gardener, placing the slabs of meat back on the table. Drrawetz meanwhile, weighed down by insufferable fawning, drooped with a large tray of water in which the great industrialist of flesh washed his hands.

"Why did you record our conversations?" he rejoined firmly.

Lifted by disdain, Neipas' eyes arose and he looked toward the Gardener's eyes, which, blurry, looked past him.

"I know you had the wildfires set."

The tycoon's gaze blurred further in the shining amber sunlight; slowly he deviated it, nodding pensively. "Hm. I see." But the powerless rage in Neipas' heart was only building, its frothing crest rising to fill atremble every pore of his skin, and he muttered in tired, incoherent tones, out of frustration and helplessness. The Gardener heard nothing of it and asked, somewhat meekly, without conviction, "Where did you hear this?"

The Gardener, custodian of the Anubel, considered only the possibility of failure on the part of security forces, either flesh or machine, as he mulled for a while on how Neipas could've sneaked his *I* into the Eagle Wing. He had forgotten — perhaps he barely knew about — the existence of the neglected basement of that castle of palaces, its Museum with its own maze of exits and treasures. But promptly he turned his uncanny and unseeing gaze back to Neipas kneeling beneath him, groveling clumsily as he adjusted his hurting knees, unable to get up. "Help him," ordered the Gardener.

The Bull pulled him to stand. Though they ached, there was more strength in his legs now, and his feet held more firmly upon the ground. But his head still lowered with dullness, so low that, though the Gardener sat, Neipas still felt much shorter than the sitter's imperious bearing. Once more he was made to hear, "Who told you this?"

Neipas only shook his head, slowly. "I heard you say it."

There was a long period of silence then, stuffed with the weight of dreams and unreality. Neipas wondered whether he really was there. "You heard me say it?"

"The night of the waltz."

The Golden Dove, posted upright and sumptuous in the middle of the vast hall, shimmered in fiery tints, with the quality of simmering flame; like a landmark in a mythical, dewy vista. The chandeliers twinkled onto the robed creatures painted upon the dome, staring intently from their hollowed hoods, listening; the silence between lines was profound. Questions were asked to Neipas, unconvinced inquiries in an interrogation devoid of purpose — maybe. And the answers were possibly given, to the effect that he was working for none but his own mingled impulses, his own sense of morality, perhaps. By then he was scarcely awake. And, being awake still, he dreamt vivid memories: as if his consciousness plunged direct into the unsailable waters of the great river of time which, once past, cannot reflow. He saw again, as if she were again living, Magpie throwing herself to the pit from the very end of those Gardens, and Magpie at his side, about those immense windows, watching the nascent storm as it overtook the western horizon and the dying sun. And he saw again, as if he/she were again there, the Midget standing at the bottommost terrace of the Pigeon Gardens, at the bottom of their sloped abyss, that very night the tempest began; and the Midget pointing to the gathered clouds with her/his staff, directing Neipas toward the path round the tower's edge, by which the fumes seethed. He lived again the tempestuous tragedy of his childhood as the clouds regressed and collapsed into a storm of earth; and as they rose into the heavens again he saw the wildfires and he heard the yelling of the mountains in his mother's frozen semblance, in his father's hollow visage, in Orenda's grievous expression, and especially, in the burnt man's purulent face (*how long ago had it been now! that he beheld it upon the hospital bed*) through all of which he saw, he saw the eighty Oyate who had perished a few days ago in the flames, eighty people, whom he had never seen.

Before Neipas now, sat the culprit, the true arsonist. "Mary —" the Gardener mumbled. "I'm getting careless."

Neipas, seething with scorn, only shrugged, defiantly, all the while staring at the floor. His head pended unstably downward.

"Why do you care?" posed the Gardener, and Neipas then, raising his head with an effort, asked from an unconscious, rambling impulse, "How can you not care?" — and then, out of a strenuous effort to uplift his soul from the smothering circumstances, above his weighing head, he added with feeling, "Why would you do something like that?"

"Why? We needed more land to farm our meat. We need to feed people, that's why."

Neipas chuckled sourly, struck mad by the irony, and mumbled, "This is about feeding people!"

"It's about selling meat to whoever wants to buy it. We don't force anyone to eat it — It's a free market," the Gardener said, and he chuckled too. "If they keep buying, we need to keep producing to meet demand. We need to keep growing."

The captive, rope-bound, drooped under the weight of all his oppressions, and could do nothing but stand quivering and shake his head in disbelief. He muttered under his breath damnations of the most wrathful sort, steeped in revolt and drowning in hopelessness. He stood there between reality and dream, upon the squalor injected unto him by the food, unsure of what would become of him. The draining weakness had subsided; but still he was very tired, and somehow even more dizzy than before. He felt only hatred toward the Eagles and confusion toward the present situation. His position confused him; and he could only ask, in a mutter, "What will you do to me?"

"Don't worry," was the only answer.

His warden and keeper the Gardener, possessing full power over his fate, contemplated the downcast, defeated figure curiously, engaging Neipas in his blank stare with a kind of morbid interest. The wide latitude provided him by his comforts had trained in him a certain serenity of being; and the expansive free time bestowed him by his wealth gave him the space to develop a certain philosophical temperament. He perceived in Neipas' spirit a listening subject, in his hollowed pose an intriguing vessel. The Gardener, regardless of everything, admired his daring — besides which, he could not help but feeling a certain, impersonal affinity to him due to their common birthplace.

Activity of some sort rang in echoes around Neipas. The clanking of dishes and the hurried pace of steps upon the floor could still be heard, the frenzy of working churned yet about through the wide voids of air. It was as though those sounds emerged from the past, perhaps a past he had never left; and perhaps it really was the case that he wasn't bound by ropes, but only generally bound as he had always been, and that this was only the end of a normal working day, another long working day in which he felt himself exhausted, like any other day; so exhausted that he began to dream even as he stood. He imagined that he was reporting something before the Gardener, or serving him his lunch. For a bit, he struggled to remember what he was doing there — until a single voice cut through all the nebulous noises of the dream-horizon. "Untie him."

Neipas felt a loosening around his wrists; a sense of widening and alleviation through which he spread his arms. The mark of ropes slackened on his skin, and disappeared. The air suddenly felt lighter. His head arose on its own, slant back upon the dullness of the neck. Still, he slouched; but it was as if he had been given a little more air to breathe. He beheld the Gardener shooing Monsieur Drrawetz away from his side; and the former supervisor receding with excessive obeisances — the once-Chief Steward walked away with Neipas' *I* in his possession, cantering off in very mirth. The tycoon then arose, slowly, lazy with the weight of the meal — and as his bent nape lifted Neipas felt the urge to seize a stone and pummel it — and elevated himself against his cane, standing upright and rigid. After a while he turned and said: "Sit."

Neipas obeyed hesitantly. He stepped round the throne and next to the round table (which was still bursting with food), pulsing with the desire to grab a quick handful of that nutritious abundance — for he was again hungry — but the sense of the Bull's eyes upon him stifled the impulse. Then his body fell, collapsed, and sank into the dulling paddings of the chair, slackening into near oblivion. It was supremely comfortable and suddenly he felt like sleeping.

But the Gardener turned around to face him. He said, "You should be more thankful. I just fed you, didn't I?" and, looking down upon Neipas' stumped, stoned semblance, the meat magnate added, "Go ahead, N— Nepa, isn't it? Eat as much as you want."

(Neipas, feeling no compunction and void of sentiment, succumbed to hunger and ate). Moments passed in silence; during which the Gardener went to stand on the other side of the table (Neipas' eyes suddenly pierced dizzy into the distance spreading from the open gates. The moon hung tepidly over ocean waste).

The chair's cushions gave in to incredible depths, making him sink in a delicious torpor of comforts. When the pillows ceased, they had almost fully embraced Neipas. He closed his eyes for a moment. But, though he was extremely exhausted, and desired nothing more than to hide in slumber and forgetfulness, his consciousness was open and full, though lax and weak. He couldn't sleep. And in this dull state of awakeness, the Gardener's words sounded inside his head very clearly.

"You're right. It's not about feeding anyone. It's not even about my fiduciary duty to report growing profits every quarter, or — for me personally — even to keep the business alive. It's about making sure I keep being rich."

Neipas chuckled curtly and humorlessly. "You have enough money to last you generations," he sounded in a dull monotone.

"Do I? Maybe. It looks like that. But I also spend more than many generations. All rich folk fear losing their wealth. And I've been poor, Nepa, you know this. Imagine how much greater my anxiety is."

"Ha-ha! that's why the rich steal? that's why they kill? ha-ha! because they're anxious?"— Neipas didn't know whether he actually uttered this among the deep, thick gulps of his nostrils and the density of his famished breast, as he ate and gorged himself beyond the senses. The sound of his own voice was in his head; though perhaps he slept — but no, as he opened his ears, the Gardener still spoke, spoke over him.

"It depends. Some are real psychopaths," continued the Gardener, sighing sagely, tapping his cane, "but most are just shallow-headed. Most people in business are very simple-minded, their happiness lies in the numbers game... They never get to feel the profound sadness they have inside. Wealth measures their worth, it's how they keep score. To them, life is a competition. It's a race — to escape from themselves. How, why the numbers go up — that matters little. 'It's what it is,' suffices to appease their conscience. And indeed, it is so.

"To those born into wealth, it matters even less. They take wealth because they are made of wealth. Wealth made them. They're nothing without it. They're not stealing — they're simply taking what's theirs. Wealth is their birthright, wherever it is to be found. In some sense, all avarice fundamentally thinks that way. They're due fortune because of their genes, or their genius; because they are the beloved of God, the superior breeds and so, inherently deserving. If the money comes from theft, or from murder, let it come. 'It's what it is'...

"Unlike them, I've known poverty and now that I know wealth I can tell you, being rich is much better. But it's not only what money saves you from — it's what it buys.

"Ultimately — why do people seek wealth? I know myself, Nepa, and the answer is clear to me. Because they want *power*."

Neipas opened, languid, his viscous eyes into the bleariness of the world. For a moment it all looked flooded again, cloudless skies and muddied soil both. His gaze flamed in his suspended tears, and he clasped his eyelids in order to quell the burning (but still the tears remained suspended, unfallen upon the eye shut; simmering, cooking under the lid).

"Some say that life is a journey, and they're right. It's a journey upwards. Towards power.

"Power is *the vital impulse*. All life bears the imperative of ascendancy — and expansion. All life consumes, all life seeks to multiply. All life aspires to the heavens.

"Life is a race away from death, and towards power, which is life itself — a race run by the will. I've thought long and hard about this. We are energies, Nepa, we are wills — volitions struggling to rise, to expand, to inflict — to shape onto others," continued the Gardener, pronouncing himself with a particular tone of mystical imperiousness, profound in the zeal of its own convictions, pleased with itself, happy to find an echo in the receptiveness of a captive listener. "Life is a flame striving upward. Like the sun — running away from the sea, from the earth, and to the apex; until it has no more strength, and falls... Striving to fill the world with sunlight. This is how it wants to propagate itself. Sometimes it burns whatever lies below, though more often, it heals. There's no intent. It simply acts according to its nature. So do I. And so do you. Like the sun, we all want to propagate ourselves.

"I don't mean propagation of genes, like the scientists would have it. I don't mean the propagation of ideas either, you see, like the philosophers would have it. I don't mean to go beyond my own life. Once the flame is put out, it's gone. Still, many among the rich work for their legacy — that's what drives them. They think that's the way they'll live after they die — through their corporations, their charities, their children, their nations, or even, in the case of the most ambitious politicians, their names. These are the hardest working ones, the most desperate to extend their power. They are also the most delusional.

"I have no illusions about it. We will die one day. I will die one day. But before that day I can live to the fullest. I will have problems, but I can mull them over from the comfort of my estate, in the freshness of my gardens. And if I get tired of these gardens here in the city, I can fly to one of my mansions in the country and their gardens. I can fly to the mountains or the coast. If I get tired of those, I can live in my yacht for a while, or I can go to my private island. I possess an island far off shore, you see — it's total isolation, total freedom. I go there, and there's nobody. I can yell out to the skies, I can run around naked. Mary, I can take a shit on the side of the water if I want. Total privacy. That's one thing money can buy you nowadays, by the way, that you don't get for free anymore.

"I can be myself there, with all the space in the world. I can be whoever I want. I can be where I want, eat what I want, screw who I want, have what I want. I can live life comfortable and without care. Really live until I cannot live anymore. That's what — with some money, you can do some things. With a fortune, you can do everything.

"Some say that power corrupts, but it's not true. It just frees you up. Now that I am rich, I have power *over my own life*. I also have power over the lives of many." (Neipas felt a heavy hand on his shoulder, he started, he trembled).

"I rule an empire of millions, Nepa. I own seeds. I own livestock. I have command over the life of my subordinates. My domains are vast, and they brim with the plants whose birth I own, with the workers whose life I own, and with the beasts, whose death I own. They haven't seen my face — but I am their master. My voice commands armies, my signature moves mountains. Moving my arm or lips is enough to cause storms and make forests fall. I am almost anonymous, but I am mightier than kings. Politicians and their societies eat at my hand. I have judgment over fates, I have ownership over the existence of millions. *That — is power.*"

Neipas watched the blurry distances. The Gardener's words scintillated in his head like demonic jingles; they grew clearer as they followed one another into his ear. Tucked within that chair which eased his sores and was so comfortable that it almost massaged away every feeling of pain, he seemed to widen, even as his body shriveled; strangely, even as his body lazed into sloth, his mind, spurred up by the tycoon's speech, wakened more and more. Slowly, his expression coalesced and hardened into a frown, intensifying now in this period of silence occupied with the Gardener's sordid reflections — so Neipas mouthed, with a tinge of disdain: "What's your point."

"Anyway —" the Gardener rejoined, in a tone that simultaneously, it seemed, addressed and ignored Neipas, "did I get myself carried away there? My point, Nepa, is this: Did you ask *why* we are like this? By Mary! The answer could not be simpler.

"*Because it feels good!* Because it makes me feel alive!... that's what counts. Everything else is foolishness and abstraction.

"Power makes me feel alive, it's therefore the purpose — of all life. It *is* life, without it life does not exist. It is its ruling principle, its direction."

Neipas began to gain anew a great dread of this maniac beating his cane excitedly with chest broadened to the widespread ruins lying in waste beneath his tower. The sitter's breath thickened, his throat dense; his pace began to slow until he stopped eating altogether. Trembling into the silence he ventured to speak (careless and unaware of himself, he spoke just as the Gardener finished his sentence):

"B-but — how can you... (then he swallowed dry, withered, strangely stuffed and uncomfortably unsatiated; his tongue searched the ceiling of his mouth, among breaths; abruptly again he felt nervous) Eighty people died... Don't you feel remorse? about the fires — ?"

A lacuna of unspoken thoughts inserted itself into the solid and sudden hush. Had what he said been audible? Neipas blinked convulsively. Into his outer canthus the mirror on the table sparkled with twitches of sunlight; directly upon his blotched pupil reposed the ruined city; and between them (slanted before him, where the Gardener now stood) existed but a horrendous blur. He saw him indistinctly, and could but vaguely perceive the immobile white head, the golden corner of the proud sneer, the regal mask of cold clay, the long beard of wattles falling over the stomach, the broad back of his velvet suit and even the faint glimmer of its gold buttons, the once-muscular arm, the thumping cane... Neipas glimpsed between bizarre jump-cuts of blackness, and his torpor dwelt into and out of the remembrance of the pulsing thing beneath them, beneath the Golden Dove whose monstrous eyes peered behind him at the core of the tower; which squirmed in his ear always, audible, every so often, through his own soul's fog...

"Look, Nepa," said he with a sweeping motion of his cane. "A whole city lies destroyed below you. Can you see anyone?"

At last, after an unconscious and prolonged effort of concentration, the view became clear to his sight. The gardens sank obliquely and precipitously under his feet, spreading glamorously across the summit of the tower, until they dropped; in a drop so sheer, that his mind, on taking it, could only absorb the tremendous size of its extension with a spell of acute dizziness. His throat leadened; his heart fluttered; his mind reeled; and the moon, which hung vague over the sea, faded into the blueness of the nascent day and fell silent in the slow choking of its perpetual scream, reflecting in its gradual dimming the shrinking progress of his soul. Then, quietude — heavy and ample. An endless vista (endlessly curving into an inexpressible abyss) expanded from his eyes. The sky arched over a vast field of uncanny liquidness, at once familiar and unrecognizable, like a landscape long unbeheld and deeply transformed — Axiac was revealed to him like an infernal, remote abstraction, fluid and indistinct in the already-moribund day. Ostrich was a despondent blotch, it looked as if it had melted into the ooze of its own structure; only the cranes and spires of its machinery could be distinguished, vaguely hauled over the bog. On the opposite side, the Diamond Hills tucked up at the end of suburban rooftop archipelagos, inconspicuous and indefinite; beyond its fluffy crest yawned immense alien pools of stagnant liquid. Directly in front of him, the Financial District tottered hastily into the widespread flood. The Via Magna, stretching powerfully below him, was now a river blown out of the ocean. Vestiges of adverts formed its ghastly banks; and the Aventine Hill was an island upon one of its main tributaries, the Capitola Mall a nest of glassy isolation over the glacial tenebrosity of that vision. The ocean swamped everything. Babylon rose out of the waters, its skyscrapers rooted into the waters as naturally and willingly as though nothing had changed, as if they were weeds originating in some Atlantis of sewers. All was placid and seemed resigned to the dead water. Everything looked menacingly serene. Everything was too far. Nothing moved.

The sky arched, vaulted above it all... calmly beholding the spectacle with a reverent and cloudless indifference, overhanging broadly, descending, finally, into the outer band of white haze upon which the ocean ended. Under it, the entire world bore an appearance of recent tragedy — and everything in it was as if shocked into the most complete silence Neipas had ever perceived.

All of it — the whole view was revealed to him in high resolution; and still it was entirely bereft of detail. Everything was too far...

There were no bodies or voices to populate the flooded wasteland. The soundlessness was oppressive; the sight unbearably barren; the sense of widespread helplessness, overwhelming. Neipas shuttered his flaming gaze; and when his eyes opened, the view appeared blurred again. Still, he strained to look —

"Do you really care?" pursued the Gardener.

— but he simply could not focus.

Soon he could take it no more; and again, the flood lifted to his eyes and blurred them through its waters. One eye involuntarily pivoted toward the sunlit mirror at the edge of the table, and saw his own hand moving inside it, over the little feast (though Neipas had eaten much, nothing, it seemed, had been taken), its fingers harping strangely; he sought to control them and bring them to his bosom. The Gardener had disappeared again — but his voice presently sounded:

"The meek and the wounded, what are they to me? I was a shepherd once, and I too have dwelt among carcasses in my time. Blood's flown down my knife and between my fingers. And if I once had a few sheep under my hands, now whole nations lie at my feet.

"Civilizations are moving mountains. They are walking giants, progressing or regressing, ascending, or descending through time. By climbing to its head I too, have become that giant. Must I worry if I step on ants on the way to progress? This is the way of the world. This is the way of nature. Isn't the sun the head of the sky? The sky itself," said he, pointing with his cane, "is full of gradations. A divine hierarchy — you see?...

"By climbing to the top I have become the summit. Civilization must stand tall. And my role is to *lift the head* — as far away from the feet as possible. Far away from the earth. How could civilization progress otherwise? how could we walk forward if we don't stand straight?" exclaimed the Gardener with a sneer of upturned chin — "Man's role is to *reach the sun*. Our role is to *overcome nature*. Do you understand? We can and must remake nature to our liking, and how could we remake without first destroying? Birth begets life — but death feeds it. That's the essential lesson of the shepherd...

"Realities demand sacrifice, such is the way of the world. Such is nature. Such is capitalism, which is like nature, which is *our* nature — an ever rising tide, from which we, constantly escaping, must sometimes yield into. Those at the back drown, those in the front are lifted. That tide is blood, that tide is fire, it is the mirror of the sun. Those at the peak have no choice but to stir the waters on our way forth — and upward. No choice but to make the hands plunge knives into the Earth, every so often — to harvest life."

The apocalyptic imagery of raving tides of blood and fire which the Gardener's speech conveyed to Neipas' mind as he listened made him remember that there were, probably, many corpses down there, many lives lost, many people dead, killed in the flood — though he could not yet clearly grasp what that meant. Some vague horror roused in him by the Gardener's tone of voice, the cruel words, made his mind wind up with his soul to the experience of his ruptured childhood, the mountain collapsing in poisons and the flat wasteland left in its muddied, radioactive wake. Again the noises came, again the palpitations sounded, again the sun dissolved; and the ash rained across his spirit; its tree bloomed over the decay.

"All of us aspire to life, to power — all of us aspire to the freedom that power gives to life," concluded the Gardener then, with a vaguer, more despondent tone. Suddenly he seemed tired and withdrawn. "And none of those things can be found except away from the crowd, away at the top — where it's possible to breathe vastly. Wealth, profit — that's what it affords.

"If I need to burn every forest in the world for it... so be it. Through destruction we create ourselves."

Neipas bleared himself toward the oceanic abyss. His teeth gnashed.

"You'd destroy the world for profit?"

"The world?" spoke the Gardener, with a sigh, as he contemplated the vague horizon. "The world ends when I die."

For the time that quietude reigned over the immeasurable soundscape Neipas' own deep and spacious breath grew quite loud. The sunshine sizzled, twinkled inside the bead of sweat pending upon the nape of the sitting waiter as he, with pixelated gazes, watched the ruined city; as he, with mum lips, chewed unfeelingly and ruminated on an empty mouth.

"We're not monsters... Just businessmen. We create value. There are costs, sure. There are externalities... Life is sometimes taken, as it must end. But we, we give life — all things flow through the head."

...suddenly it seemed to Neipas (at the culmination of a long, gradual sensation just realized) that the Anubel was boiling. The sun pierced scalding into the insulated dome of its weatherless altitude. He felt the sun sweltering into the back of his head; the sweat dissolving into his skin, pasty, with the molten wax. His head throbbed along oscillations of starry fervor. Something pulsed hideously underneath his feet. Amid the two motionless bells, the Pearl shone fiery; and its glinting seemed to spread over the hedges of the gardens, over the boulevards of the wreckage, into the mazes of the mind, into the secrets of the soul — and burn. Orenda's anger and bereavement returned to him in sunlit tears. He recalled the gored face of the burnt Oyate at the hospital, moribund in the bed next to his own; and in his image he saw them all, the victims of the fire. "But..." Neipas was too dazed in squalor to feel the brunt of the Gardener's honesty, to feel shock. But in the dimness of his consciousness an unbelief sprouted the whisper:

"Eighty dead!"

The Gardener replied coolly: "That's just a sentence. And the first part's just a number — the second, just a word."

"It doesn't matter." A beak clicked into shivering lip; and trembling sigh. Neipas didn't speak, but merely blurted gasps of disbelief, of crushed, meek feeling. Even his efforts to rise from the chair failed; its comfort trapped him, and he was too tired, too tired. The Head Gardener meanwhile passed across his eyes, like glitter over the shadow of the west, over the vast necropolis, standing beside him on the other side of the chair, by the food table; and his voice sounded through the opposite ear:

"This is just the way people are," explained the Gardener, beating his cane lightly against the back of his hand (Neipas shuddered). "You would do the same in my place. Have the strength to accept it.

"And in fact, haven't you sought my place, by doing what you did? Didn't you record our meetings to injure us? Didn't you sneak into the vaults — to find our riches?"

Neipas snickered without smiling, deadened (one, two, one two...) "I was hungry."

"There was still food in the market. Why didn't you steal there?"

Neipas simply shrugged through his foggyheadedness. Faintly he tried to get up from the chair, and again could not.

"People follow what gives them meaning — or settle where they can. Most seek comfort," continued the magnate, inhaling deep, austere satisfaction, "some seek happiness, and others few, seek power. They are not necessarily exclusive but one way will be taken to the detriment of the rest.

"Those who succeed in the way of power mold all other paths. You are a photographer and you, like all artists, are part of this group.

"You sought revenge, thus you sought power. You sought vengeance, and so did I. I resented being poor. I thought it was the fault of the rich. Like you, I sought justice, *retribution* — but not change, because nothing can ever change... It is not the fault of the rich, it is simply the way things are. They couldn't be otherwise."

The Gardener spoke, and his voice, stern and sure, was suffused with the inauspicious tone of inspired madness. Was there truth to his drivel? Neipas began to roam in mental crannies of doubt and delirium; lost of spirit; and he felt feverish. For a moment he thought that perhaps the food had been poisoned, but it couldn't be, for the Gardener had eaten of it, too. He tried to rise again and could not. Framed by tiny silvery eyeless faces, the mirror shuffled with the motion of his rumpled body swaying back into the cushions. The sunlight yelled and pulsed out of it. "Why are telling me all this — what's all this for," he whispered from the chasm at the bottom of the yawning throne.

"You were risking prison — you are risking death, Nepa! You are a criminal — like Kasim.

"That lawyer's speech was interesting. But she forgets that those who write the law must necessarily be *above* the law, if they are to write it. To those who stand *beneath* the law, to them what's left is to understand it... and to follow the instructions. I was born beneath, and I had to transgress to rise over it... So I understand you, Nepa. The essential difference between our positions is — I wasn't caught. Mary, frankly, I admire your daring, and if we weren't enemies I would take you under my wing.

"That lawyer — she forgets that this is the natural order of things — things simply are as they always have been. At the top rule the few; and those at the bottom obey. The distances change, but the distance remains. It's the law of the universe that the strong survive, and the weak fall along the way. And the weak cannot live unless through the will of the strong.

"How could it be otherwise? If I didn't feed you, how would you eat? Don't you consume our meat? Don't you use our energy? How would you live without our gifts? Without us, the world would be full of brute hands without a brain to guide them... Civilizations would split, it would be chaos. How could a body hold without a head? All things flow down from it... The most that the head can permit is to stoop a little, to share a little light — but then, the body risks tripping altogether.

"Civilization could not hold without us. We give those below us *direction*."

From the depths of the sofa Neipas felt the world moving. The whole scene shifted slowly before his eyes, the voice of the Gardener circled round him, his overbearing influence fenced him within a great spell of weariness. "We give you *purpose*."

He faced now the mirror. Neipas couldn't discern whether it was just himself who had rotated or the whole universe before him; but the mirror, which had been in the corner of his gaze, filled it full now. It stood before him immanent. He saw in it himself, donned in the pigeon mask disfigured by shock, fire, and time. His eyes stared into him from within the mush, the pasty defacement of his identity. "Without us, you would be nothing."

Neipas felt a cold touch. The Gardener's voice hissed low in his mind, lone among a vast emptiness. The Gardener's fingers crawled up his neck and entered his jaw, his cheeks, his ears, eyes, his head; and pushed out. His fingers penetrated the wax and pulled it painfully, slowly out of Neipas' innermost skin; until the mask was fully off, with but pieces of wax sticking and hanging in bits upon the countenance now revealed.

Once more he confronted the image of his real self. Once more he beheld that vision which had haunted him since the day he woke at the hospital, between an empty bed and a dying man.

He gazed upon the reflection of his face. There was nothing there.

Nothing.

It was merely a shadow — a deep shadow, a dark pit. He gazed out of an eyeless void into the depths of its own reflection. Nothing. A surface of darkness, an abyss. There was absolutely nothing. Neipas contemplated the truth of it with the petrified horror of a soul staring down its own corpse. Sunlight shone on the edges of the glass as if from the hollow silver countenances clustering its frame; sunshine rimmed his throbbing facelessness, shedding his mind in pulsating branches scattering and sinking into the black chasm without features. Neipas felt himself drained; seep entire into the chasm of his faceless head. Time itself dissolved into it. All coalesced finally into unreality realized.

And Neipas sat immobile, unable to react, unexisting.

"Without the mask we give you," voiced the Gardener, voice of Neipas' universe, "you are nobody."

Again the tycoon's fingers coursed slowly down his face, gripping between them the molted wax, flowing in reverse; and again Neipas' facelessness was enveloped in it. The Gardener's fingers pierced it and molded it, sharpened the beak, protruded the jaw, uplifted the cheek, forced open the eye; curved the lip into a smile. Neipas stared at himself. The pigeon mask looked intact, and he looked as before.

What happened next succeeded in a confusion of progressions. Neipas was made to rise, his paralyzed body lifted by the Bull's hand. He went without resistance. By him passed the blurred figures of Drrawetz, the Chief Supervisor, the peacocks and their attendants, all of whom went on unperturbed; by him floated also the Gardener's voice, the language of which he no longer understood. The feeling of the voice lingered like a half-remembered dream. But Neipas understood nothing any longer.

At some point his blinds were placed over his eyes. They descended many steps, passed through many elevators. Neipas couldn't locate anything, had no frame of reference, no anchor to the world. His mind and soul were loose, like flapping sails, drowned wings in a muted storm.

A door opened slowly, somberly — moaning a prolonged creak.

The blinds were removed, the blackness panned away. In Neipas' eyes materialized now, beyond the door, an immensity of whiteness; a boundless expanse of unspace; an absurd and absolute infinity of nothing. Neipas' being descended into oblivion. For a moment, as the sight of that place penetrated his glare, he saw nothing, heard nothing, felt nothing... Nothing, nothing at all.

"Step forward."

Neipas stepped forward, into the infinitude.

("...")

The door closed.

END OF BOOK II

72

2nd Interlude

Neipas turned off the floodlight.

The sun yielded peacefully to the horizon, succumbing to the ever-ascending tilt of the far limits of the ocean; drew into the nether, into the spheric abyss of the world in its patient routine, its unending quest to bring the gift of light to all dwellers upon the earth. Land and sea were sheathed in the horizon's shade, and the moon blossomed clear over the cloudless, windless expanse; citylights boomed open and flooded the skies, entering softly through the drawn curtains of Eva's bedroom where the couple lay, naked, staring at the vagueness of the ceiling. For moments they lay watching the motion of languid glows shifting and intermixing as cars rumbled and blew by on the quiet street. The camera perched upon the tripod at their side, gazing inert the two silent lovers through the deep lens which mirrored, in dormant sheens, the reds and whites cast from the panning outdoors. A faint shine, motionless, appeared in it then as it nudged softly the corner of Neipas' eye. He blinked indifferently.

Eva and Neipas rested on opposite ends of the bed; lying apart, lulling in the numb twilight, reposing separately upon the physical and mental lassitude which settles in the wake of orgasms. He lingered in thoughtlessness, often dipping below sleep, melting tender into the pillow before incarnating imperceptibly back to the vacant contemplation of the lazy ceiling. She navigated the Webwork in an absentminded flight through changing colors, scrolling letters, morphing landscapes, mutating faces, myriad smiles. Their panting had died off into the ambient whirr of room and road; the sweat had cooled off their bodies. A gap of ruffled emptiness stretched between them.

They were, perhaps, never farther apart than in the moments after sex. What he most desired then was the freedom of space, to loosen himself from all contact and float, as much as possible, in the solitude of his own sensations; somehow the touch and weight of skin became uncomfortable for him in the aftermath, even mildly repellent — and though Eva craved embraces and the affection of physical proximity, she sensed his wish, and left him alone. A mysterious rift opened up between the two. There settled an awkward vibe, a discomfort of mutual alienation. They became drifters in waves of sheets; islands in a pond of gloom. Across the mattress, their minds wandered and lost themselves. "What is it?" asked Eva to the beacon alight, the *I* in the darkness — as she perceived some body breathing abreast, on the far horizon of her vast bed, invisible and alien.

Gradually Neipas would be roused from his vaguely pleasant torpor and become aware of the silence's remorseful weight. He would look to the side and perceive Eva's shape, the curve of her hip faint in the thickening gloom, like a ghost with back turned. Then she would turn to face the ceiling once more and the light of the *I* would emerge; her eyes fixated on it, immersed.

She seemed unaware of Neipas' presence. She, herself, wasn't there. And he began to feel lonely, very lonely... Watching the sight of her blur in his eyes he ruminated upon his many sorrows, with feeling but without thought; and then, almost involuntarily he stretched his arm across the immense gap separating them and touched her shoulder. Her big gaze rolled to grip his, a bit melancholy. The *I* would then vanish and she would shuffle delicately, coyly to him, and finally nestle in feline rubs and a sigh upon his chest.

He felt Eva's body shudder as her mind faded to sleep. Her breathing rose and fell in a harmonious, deep cadence, serene in the coziness of slumber. Neipas was by then fully awake. He lay still, yet nursing that terrible sense of loneliness in his breast. He lay in the dark with eyes open, feeling it seeping inside at the rhythm of Eva's gentle cooing, feeling it encroaching to the base of his throat like a misty, acrid substance. He lay, unable to sleep now, and sometimes his sorrow became so unnerving that he sought to drown it in the refuge of his own *I*, to whom he whispered with his longing eyes, listening to the phantom voices somewhere in the fathoms beyond the glass, seeking their company, finding none in the endless search. He lay musing; nursing sleepless dreams. Neipas felt very much like a prisoner of some sort, to whom the whole purpose of his existence was to get out — he dreamt and thought only of getting out, away from debt, servitude, squalor, want, out of that hole that kept deepening and sucking him in. He forced his eyes shut, and for some reason — perhaps drowsiness was infiltrating his mind then — reminiscences of childhood came to him, a vague, long forgotten memory of lying down like this, imagining himself flying away as he descended to somnolence, and listening to the crackling of fire on the homely hearth; no, it was droplets tapping the windowpane, soothing and distant... — a tranquil sound, of mom cradling him into slumber, and it seemed to Neipas for a moment, as he closed his stare round the camera lens and the curtained window of Eva's bedroom, that it floated from the stream of the canals nearby, and the steady ebb and heave of the calm, giant sea beyond...

Its waters stretched over the vastness of the deep toward him; extended from regions far remote, journeying under the shimmer of the crawling sun and the velvet of the sparkling night, to come sigh, at the end of a long pilgrimage between continents, with relief upon the tender land. Very tame, very docile, they arrived as if paying homage to the earth, bending their heads in wave and spray, their fingers of spume clutching the shore in the manner of a caress, and exhaling solemnly, like a tired messenger relaying arcane tidings from one horizon to the other, the far ends of the sea to the summits of the mountain. Between them arose the megalopolis, full of noise: and the message spirited through, unheard but in the most sensible ears, the most perceptible souls. Orenda, standing in the summit horizon, contemplated the ocean prospect and tried to decipher its meaning among the deep quietude of the air.

She had gone up to the mountain to join an Oyate encampment, assembled there to mourn the wildfire dead. People from all the villages of the Reserve had come. They had sung prayers of the Spirit, to the Spirit, from the Spirit, in solemn tones of reverence and grief, amid tears of patient suffering as they tried, in the solace of kinship and solidarity, to ease the inherited burden of cruel centuries weighing upon their noble shoulders. A few days later, Orenda walked — she trekked for hours — to a wood-crowded ridge on the limits of the Reserve which overlooked the megalopolis. She came to behold the devastation wrought by the great flood; and she beheld with grave awe. A spell of stupefaction infiltrated her senses.

Darkness covered the great city. It existed — all its towers, all its roads, all its factories and ports — in the same silvery obscurity as did the primordial night of humanity; its sky was as black, as close and as lusterless as the cupped domes of the caves sheltering the first civilizations. Only the Pearl, that soaring beacon of industry, monument attesting to humankind's achievements, shone in the terrible desolation of a city broken in a vastness of floating shards. It shone above it, suspended, floating in angelic motionlessness, like a divine sign bequeathed by a consoling deity, very far above. Yet it shone much too high to alight the flooded depths; though high enough to render the heavens starless to the eyes of the populace surviving among the dark tide in terror and quietude. The moon gaped; though none there could see it. Its black oceans hung suspended above the lightless earth. Glints of moonshine revealed the irregular motion of the sea, which was born in the distant reaches and seemed to die all the way in the foot of the mountain, washing it with refuse and soulless flesh.

Orenda watched the impenetrable gloom shrouding all the mute tragedies that Axiac contained. No sound yet pierced the air. Soon, she would hear the wail of ambulances as civilization staggered to revive; soon she would spot their flash upon the veins of wet asphalt. But for an eternal moment, not the faintest murmur, not the vaguest whisper perturbed the supreme stillness of the universe. As she observed from her quiet outpost Orenda ruminated thoughts soothed in the wind noiseless and cold. Oshana had spoken to a congregation, gathered in a sacred grove that first night, and her words affected Orenda's spirit with the gravity of reflection. She nursed and mulled over those words now, lulling against the bark in the coming chill, the frigid breath of night's great maw salivating, open over the city at its mercy, sighing ethereally from its distant black gullet...

Oshana spoke to those gathered round the fire in these terms:

"Humankind hasn't yet decided what it wants to become. It hasn't set for itself a goal.

"'Where is humankind going?' — here's a question many are afraid to ask. 'What do we *want* humanity to be?' In truth, few have imagined answers to these questions.

"The powerful whisper their answers. And though the marginalized clamor from the margins, their responses are muted at the frontiers of power.

"What do the mighty and the powerless say? My kin, in truth we cannot know where we're going without knowing where we are, and unless we know who we are, neither can we know who we can become.

"But how can we understand who we are — without deducing who we've been?

"Has anyone ever understood a picture without a frame? Can text have meaning without context? Every moment is a letter, or a word, or whole paragraphs and tales impressed on the page of current existence, my kin — the past is either written or erased and it is the context and often the pretext of the present and the future — and the future, drafted but not yet written, is the context, and often the pretext, of present and past."

Her eyes tilted downward slow, deliberate, to meet the soil — damp, the earth palpitated and glimmered under the firelight, absorbing Oshana's fingers in the dewy tranquility of complete stillness, in the essential immutability of an eternal principle; with the profound quietude of primordial truths resting forever beneath the turmoils of change and time. And as her hand spread upon the ground, and her concentration fixed upon the sense of it — its pervading influence whispering into her soul without sound — her words floated almost unconsciously toward the bonfire. "Where have we come from?..." Her eyes lifted (and scintillated brighter and brighter in the glimmer of the flame) together with the palm of her hand, blanketed yet with the fresh soil as it faced inward; Oshana left her fingers reposed upon the earth, erected, as if sprouting from earth's bosom, as she continued — "There's a question that animated curiosities throughout the ages.

"Some have said, 'we've been fashioned from earth and water and given life by wind and song.' And this was well — there was some truth to it.

"Now they still say — 'we came from the ocean deep, but we were not yet humans then. Our ancestors roamed the land for millions of years, fighting to become who we are today.' And today, it is said, 'humanity began when we lifted our hands away from the earth. We began,' they say, 'when we stood — and lifted our eyes to the sky.'

"'We became human when our hands were freed from the Earth.' — This, they say, was our birth into who we are."

Into the momentary silence a breeze mumbled, stirring Oshana's feather earring upon the edge of her motionless pose.

"They say humanity became humanity the moment our hands lifted from the Earth, and our eyes to the Heavens," she pursued serene. "It'd be truer, however, it'd be truer to say that humanity was born when our chins rested upon our hands, and we looked back down to the Earth — so we could gaze inward.

"But some would maybe say, that it was when we looked back upon the Waters, and recognized ourselves.

"Yet others would still say, that we became human when we looked at others — and recognized ourselves."

On the opposite side of the wide circle of people Orenda sat, and beheld with aching eyes her aunt speaking across the bonfire. The crackling of its flames seemed to pitch syllables, spiking the cadence of Oshana's successive words, and delivering them to the breeze in sharp tones of tenderness — in embers, sparks ascending to the quiet sky which slept still, gravely mum, deep, after its effort of strained fury. It arched above their heads quietly, mysterious, profound, like a somber dome capping the reach of their grievous musings, folding them in its caressing mantle of secrecy. They were all alone there, in the holy solitude of the mountain. The darkness seemed desolate. Orenda felt vividly the impression that the rim of firelight marked the very borders of existence. Visages emerged at the edges of long shadows all about her; their hollow flickering stares enveloped the little lady wearing the feather earring across the fire. Her face appeared to them, and to Orenda, as a cryptic symbol of inexpressible mysteries, manifesting themselves through a curtain of heat, with contours indistinct amid the swaying shimmer, rippling mystic in the charged air drafting along the sparks; a vision intimating to her heart the refracting subtleties of simple truths. It seemed to affect the air with the substance of water, and the very veil cast by the fire resembled the surface of a lake troubled by wind, as a whisper at once concealing — and insinuating — the secrets of its mirroring depths. Orenda lulled in sublimations for as long as the silence lasted, soothed into the void of the air and the consubstantial presence of her companions, dissolving together across the mute softness of essences.

Still, she remained very awake all the while, finding herself very aware of the grief hurting her body and the tears in her eyes, very conscious in the unconsciousness of shade and light passing over her as the flames moved. "All things emanate our reflection," Oshana said. "In the same way we can see ourselves in the water, so we can see ourselves in the fire, and in the light, and even in the darkness we can find ourselves. The canopies rustle and echo our voice — clouds hold in them our thoughts — the gaze of beasts contain our souls — all nature is a mirror, and an abyss. We recognize ourselves in stone, in paint, even in ink we recognize ourselves. Everywhere in the Earth we recognize ourselves, and every time we behold another, we contemplate ourselves. This is not merely because we project ourselves on to all things, though this is also true. It's because we hold all things within ourselves already — in our innermost deep.

"The truth rests there — through our selves, beyond our selves. Beyond our selves rests the All — beyond our selves we find all others, and in all others we find ourselves. A common essence binds all things beyond every difference.

"Many have found humanity's common essence throughout the ages. But we haven't yet found humanity's common purpose.

"How could we? The fates of humankind are shaped by those with power, who say, 'there can be no common purpose, humanity's a mess of incompatible wills. There can only be one purpose — *domination* — and this can never be common.'

"'How could we have anything in common with the Earth? And how could we have anything in common with others? They are down there — we are up here,' they say. In truth, they've never seen their own kin as fully human.

"In truth, they've never been fully content with being human. It'd be preferable to be gods — and that's why they've been donning masks since the beginning.

"They've hated humanity for being still too earthly. Those who've said, 'humanity began when we freed our hands from the Earth,' are the ones who say, 'we will only be whole when we remove our feet from the Earth also.'

"This is why the future was first foretold in the flight of birds. And this is why now, the future is foretold in the trajectory of charts.

"It hasn't yet been foretold by humankind's purpose."

Oshana spoke over the valley at the heart of their land. The river at the bottom of the precipice had swollen with the rains; and the sound of its rush breathed up the lustrous slopes of rock and peeping grass, watching as the torrent lapped and barreled into the bosom of the mountain, into the yawning gloom of caverns patiently molded, over centuries, by the very waters thundering down their gullet, shaped, as the valley had been shaped, in the divine graces and the whims of nature's copious fingers.

Eva entered the deep closet, over hesitant steps she went. It was in reality a separate room, a kind of pantry housing her parents' (mostly her mother's) costumes, and the darkness inside was so thick and stretched so far from the bedroom's lamplight (her parents had for some reason never installed lamps here) that Eva was forced to use the flashlight on her *I* to see. Here, between files of jackets hovering heavily above the floor, she sought the scarf which her mom had once wore. It was shaped like a serpent (here it is).

When she was little, Eva thought it was a real snake and always feared she'd be bitten whenever her mom came close. Now she touched it, she saw it *wasn't* real; though there was something to the texture of it that made her wonder if the fake withered scales had ever enveloped a living beast.

It was like a vast cape, the night sky — out from which surfaced the head of the Moon, having just shed its cover of shadow, the black blanket cast by Earth and Sun where the Moon swam and which the Moon molted. Arcane, inscrutable, its face gaped at the waters and hovered over Axiac its luminescence; in silence it conducted the languid swing of the tides, and marked, in its stillness, the rhythm of unstoppable time.

[...] The storm had swamped all but the hillocks which arose from the low-lying streets and boulevards of Axiac. The ocean had coursed Via Magna easily: Most shop windows had broken and their shards disgorged to the Belab's immense square; mannequins mingled with corpses in the lingering tides still, flesh and plastic confusing themselves in their garmented lifelessness. The very facade of the great tower had been severely battered, and its former glassed glory now rose in a series of sinister gapes, like a mouth full of broken teeth. The waters had proceeded north through Via Sacra also, reaching the suburbs — even the Crystal Palace had flooded, though the Diamond Hills remained above the waters. Indeed much of the affluent part of the megalopolis had been scathed, invaded from all directions; though its inhabitants had all gone away. Some of the mansions suspended on the hill along the northbound freeway had collapsed on their pillars and tumbled to the road, to be then washed away by the ocean, drawn in and scattered leisurely by its tremendous force.

By Golden WestBeach, the concrete edges of the manufactured canals and even the bridges were completely submerged (under the moon the tides swayed, back, forth — over the fields of concrete).

Neipas winced, and kept descending. Floating in the reversed subworld of his slumbering mind, he descended. Descending, drifting in endless obscurities, along deep currents of inwardly inverted shades, he descended among faded remembrances, memories grainy beyond recognition, splattered with the gloom of unfathomable spiritual abysses, tarnished windows where but glimpses of fragments flashed in anemic undertones; blurred mirrors into which dark wavy surfaces he swayed, swayed slowly, as he had once gently swayed across the air, lulled upon his mother's soft round back, where he leaned his ear, and from which he discerned the drum of her heart; drumming like her steps through the flowers, at the pulse of the herbal aromas and the sprinkle-chant of the nearing river, drumming as he had heard it drum inside her round womb, in the sway of her caress, the profound silence of her sanctum, the pulsing touch of her soul; when he floated in the deep waters of her being, and he was she, and they were one.

The recollection of his floating above the field, carried on his mother's back, was one of the very few Neipas kept of her — among the very few that the current of time hadn't drawn away from him. Sometimes it surfaced in his dreams. Rarer were the times he recalled it, when awake — but there was a remote vestige of its caressing motion in the turmoil of Neipas' spirit, as he carried on from day to day; and it was particularly present when, a few weeks before the flood, Neipas and Eva walked along the artificial canals, and across the bridges atop which he beheld his reflection and she listened to the music of a shell. The murky waters unveiled in his mirrored image the memory of his father, which seemed to glance up wide-eyed at him through the staring eyes underneath, through the feathery mask. But his mother was there too. Much more subtle, much more uncomprehended, faded and misremembered, much longer gone, but she, too, was there... His father was the reflection; she the floating waters —

(They oscillated and lapped gentle against the edge of the tray, glimmering dark, red lights. Eva — the image of her — formed upon the submerged print, swinging mystical and seductive, materializing through an occult sort of magic act... Neipas gazed very attentively, very studiously) yet Eva touched his shoulder and they faced the teenager holding the conch, who was about to perform once again.

Eva contemplated the flow swirling into the faucet drain, disappearing spiral-wise, round, round into the core — till it vanished.

For a while she stood listening to its gurgling sound receding into the pipes; disappearing into unimaginable depths beyond the walls and floors of her house. She stood listening long after the sound had faded away; for a long time it persisted in her ear — like the strange echo of a far cry. Like the plea of a ghost.

Inside the bathroom cabinet (she had opened it; it was behind the mirror, and abruptly she realized her reflection was no longer there) lay already the pregnancy test kit. In less than a week she would use it...—

*

Said Oshana to those congregated round the fire, "Beautiful futures have been dreamt in the past. But these dreams have always been crushed and the dreamers, murdered.

"Those who've lost hope learned to say, 'such dreams can't be fulfilled on Earth, only in sleep'. And this slumber they called 'Heaven'.

"It is good to dream, but be careful — keep one eye open always. The slumbering eye can contemplate the dream in the depths of the soul — but the open eye should observe reality very carefully. See to it that dreams aren't worn like furs to cloak unpleasant realities.

"Watch that dreams do not veil reality, for dreams must lie beyond reality — not before. Reality must be brought to the dream, and not the dream to reality. Remember that."

Orenda contemplated the wakening megalopolis — waking in the dark, as though into a further nightmare — and squinted tensely against the wind on her eyes, the breeze spinning in her ear: there was something of a faint voice in it. There was a certain hum to it. Yonder, from the hovering beacon, the motionless Pearl aloft, sounded the toll of bells, echoing in waves through the propagating air and reaching Orenda's placid notice distant, stern, indifferent, sounding as punctual, in that early hour of the night, as it had ever sounded; as punctual as ever, as if nothing had happened. But the bells sounded to her as though they, too, were marking the pulse of time. They sounded as though they knelled for the myriad pulseless floating underneath in the waters of the ocean and across all the winds whispering in the immensitude of the world.

Inbetween and through the beats, Orenda recalled placidly her aunt's words — her warnings, as she faced the devastation:

"Regarding Nature, the pundits and courtiers of our days agree: 'It will end,'" continued Oshana. "They agree still on something else: that it doesn't matter. This they may not say clearly — but how could they speak clearly, and still dominate? Power only grows old in the fog.

"The only thing they don't agree on is, how it'll happen. This is what animates their discussions. Who will bring the end of the Nature about? We will, of course — they agree on this point. But who are *we*?

"The optimists say, we are machines. The pessimists say we are animals.

But where are the ones who speak about humanity?"

Having discharged its fury upon the bay, the firmament stretched above them, yawning becalmed, and the bonfire in their midst glimmered tranquil toward the stars and the moon arching forth.

"Machines or animals is what we are, they say. When they say animals, though, they don't mean," Oshana continued, "they don't mean the exuberance, and diversity of wandering life — they don't mean the beautiful variety of beings with whom we share the Earth. They don't mean our siblings and relatives who prowl the sea, the land, and the sky," and shaking her head despondently she said, "nor do they mean the species of beings that we are a part of ourselves. No. They mean what is meant by words like 'irrationality', 'savagery', 'filth'... That is, their conception of Nature. And when they say things like 'regress to a state of nature', what they mean is constant fear, violence, perfidy, immorality — and all the sins they ascribe to the Earth.

"'We will go down the current path and become more and more beastly. Until it is to each one's own — and we all kill each other.' This is what the pessimists say.

"'And we will kill each other because we can't help being selfish, we can't help being greedy — our greed is such that we'll end up destroying the Earth, in our pursuit of things to buy. We can't help it. We will deplete most resources, then murder one another for whatever's left. We're self-serving like that. Father will rise against son, brother against brother,' and so on — because we are 'animals'... so the pessimists say. It is only natural that this would happen, they say.

"'There will be scarcity of resources. This is only natural and it's to be expected that we act according to our nature when it happens — and we will pillage and murder to survive. We can't help it — so we might as well embrace it. Rejoice! the end of times is nigh.' This is what the pessimists say.

"But today we live in abundance, and resource scarcity — it is no longer natural. The scarcities of today are mostly manufactured... And even what they call 'our nature' — it is mostly manufactured.

"The optimists of course," she continued, shaking her head, "they have the same notion about 'our nature'. But they also say, 'we are machines — just like all other animals'. We simply need to be better *engineered*.

"'We're still too unreasonable, too irrational, too inefficient — too stupid, just like Nature' — say the optimists. 'We must be *mastered* like Nature was. We must *upgrade* ourselves — for there is still too much wilderness in us.'

"'Ignorance is the root of all our problems. We uncovered Nature's secrets — but we don't yet know how human animals "work".'

"'The limits of machine ignorance begin at what it doesn't know. But human ignorance pervades also what it *thinks* it knows. Therefore it's much more dangerous. The truth is, whatever isn't knowable cannot exist,' say the optimists.

"'How did we conquer nature? It was by making nature knowable that we conquered it. We uncovered its patterns, we charted its behaviors, we made it predictable. We removed the *mysterious* from it. We eviscerated the sacred. How could we do otherwise?

"It was by excluding everything that could not be known, everything that cannot be measured, that we tamed Nature. Only by desacralizing — could we demystify. Only by demystifying could we control. And we can only master Human Nature and its deviousness and irrationalities the same way.

"'In the end, we overtook nature by force — and the trees did not sound a cry, and if the animals ever did, we didn't understand. But humans are more complex.

"'Science must simplify to comprehend. It was by abstracting nature that we got to know it. It was by ignoring things that are unquantifiable — like 'soul', 'spirit', and 'sacredness' — that we got to know the Earth. The soul is an unmeasurable factor; it is therefore, a nonfactor.

"'Science has determined that animals have no soul — this is the only thing our ancestors were right about. Nature has no soul. Therefore, we, as animal organisms, cannot have a soul. It cannot be observed, therefore it cannot be measured, therefore it is irrelevant — therefore, it does not exist.'

"They say, 'once, we worshiped animals, because they oppressed us, and we depended on them — then we worshiped the skies because they oppressed us, and we depended on them — now we worship humanity because it oppresses us, and we depend on each other.' Humanity will be the last fallen god.

"'The human animal will be the last to be quantified. To pursue this goal, we can only be objective — but how could we be objective without making ourselves objects? We must worship objects and remake ourselves in the image of the things we make — we must worship *machines* now, because we depend on them — yet we control them. We must become machines to control ourselves.

"We do not yet know human nature fully — because it cannot be *known*. And that afflicts them. That is why they say, 'the human is still the wildest of all animals.' We cannot know human nature, therefore we should abandon it, they say. 'Human nature is not measurable — it should be abandoned.

"'To carve ourselves out of Nature, such was our destiny. To carve ourselves out of *our* nature will be our new destiny.' Here's what they mumble from behind their screens, even if they don't use those words."

Her mask seemed shaped to every possible expression of joy and sadness, gravity and ecstasy, pensiveness and craze among the flame; her voice seemed to ensue from the spark.

"The pessimists of today were the optimists of yore — the ruling optimist is always novel. New power must cloak itself in optimism to appeal, and inevitability to numb all resistance. Because they're still emerging, still little known, listen then, to a little more of what they say:"

All listened carefully to her voice, sprouting from the silence, blooming into the soul, withering into the silence — sprouting once more:

"'What is a human being?' they ask themselves in secret.

"'Isn't a person but a series of acts? — and a body, just a sequence of motions? What is a thought but pulses of electricity? What is the mind if not a repository of information? What are human beings but the binding of all these parts? We are machines — this is what we are, therefore this is what we must aspire to be. Anything more than that is dangerous. All tragedies have their source in unwarranted illusions — in unprovable beliefs. Therefore we must suppress belief.

"'The world is made up of energies and stimuli. Of inputs and outputs. Nothing else. We are shaped by conflicting and abetting forces and steered in the way that the sail is driven by the wind. Much as the canvas bloated with wind would consider itself imbued with a soul if it could think, so does the human being consider himself imbued with spirit, when all he does is follow stimuli and impulse — like all animals...

"'Nothing is truly voluntary. There is no "volition". Only influence. There is no soul! And there is no free will — only *ignorance* of complex stimuli — a void we fill with myths. We must abandon myths like "free will", there's no such thing...' These are things the optimists say under their breath."

Oshana, snickering in contemptuous amusement and disbelief, shaking her head slowly, then added, throwing her head back, "And in truth, they still say, 'let's forsake the soul, let's forsake the will, for there is no possession daemon, there is no self, no I — they're all illusions.

"'Let us instead — fuse with the machine, where things are simple, where inputs are controlled, where behavior is monitored, where everything can be known. Everything's a little more dreary; but everything's a lot more safe.' But it is the safety of sedates, my kin.

"They want to make addicts of us, addicted to their machines, like invalids on life-support. Dependence is a more gripping power than even fear. And I already see abounding dependence.

"In truth we already see ourselves in their machines every day, at nearly every moment. But it is well known that looking too much in the mirror — will make the beholder become that mirror. We are glass facades to them —

and more than once a day we crack apart, into the fragments they make us out to be. In truth they'd prefer us fully transparent, and fully empty.

"They beguile us to their machines saying, 'life is chaos, it is unpredictable. But here the winds are under control, here we can foretell where human waters flow, here they're transparent, and not very deep. Simply give yourself up to the breeze — and you will fly.' This is what they mumble, grinning and thumbing. Don't believe them.

"We are machines and no more, they say. This is a lie, and a folly. Yet I know the extent to which human beings can be reduced... the extent to which convenience can beguile, and novelty can trick. O! my kin! There is a deep, tragic abyss dividing who we could be from who we are. In truth we'll need to descend to that abyss, even as we climb it — to seize the other side."

Oshana paused, inhaling serenely, breathing the sweetness of the wood. The rest waited, and in waiting they listened.

"They say 'nature gave us the opposable thumb — and in doing this, it gave us the tool of its own destruction. But if we hover above Nature today, it's because we built our own wings. They're made of chromium.'

"'We climb higher and higher, we climb mountains of our making — how could we do otherwise?' they ask. 'We fly from summit to summit, from triumph to triumph, from one pile to the next. Our heaps get taller and taller. We are creators,' they say.

"'We use tools, we've invented machines and that, is what makes us human,'" so is the view of the optimists. 'We extracted our machinery from nature, and with machinery we conquered nature — until, finally, nature became *our* machine. Before, the environment molded us. Now, we mold the environment.

"'Now, *we* create worlds. And the opposable thumb is the tool of our procreation. But the brain holds our creation's fertilizer — our *genius*.

"'We are creators,' claim the optimists. 'Our genius is expressed in our works, in them we glory. We cannot help but breed more and better machines. After all, aren't we machines built to reproduce ourselves?

"'We cannot help but keep innovating, we cannot but progress, we cannot but grow. And as our brains grow in knowledge, so does our genius grow in output — and they will keep growing, until they encompass all that can be known. This is inevitable.

"'As ignorance is the root of all our problems, so is knowledge the root of all our power. But as the brain grows in power, so do our machines, which are now — our brain,' they say. 'In order to know a lot, we must dissect a lot. The genius crushes natural ignorance and it can't help but destroy — nature. This is inevitable. But such power cannot be left to wild impulse.

Unfortunately the knowledge in our brain hasn't yet quelled the nature in our heart,' they lament.

"'Human nature gave us machines — and in doing this, it gave us the tools of *our* own destruction. Such power cannot be left to the whims of our wilderness. The brain is rational, therefore it is good — but our heart is irrational and unaccountable.'

"'Human nature is too unbridled, human societies too complex, the future too uncertain. We need to measure all those complexities. We need to catalogue all things. We need to be able to measure, to manipulate, to make efficient and harmless. If we're to move forward, we all need to be steered the same way. And much like one foresees the motion of the sail if weather conditions are known, so people are likewise predictable, if the stimulants are known. Knowing the input, one can foretell the output... We can engineer our destiny, we need only be predictable —' such is their wish, and in truth, they resemble those necromancers of the pessimists, who once claimed that everything is predestined by God. These optimists — they want to be that God.

"'Human nature, as is, is too dangerous,' they say. 'Human nature is still too natural — still too wild. Still too uncivilized... It must yield to the machine, which is the best part of its nature. Let's stop believing fantasies, let's be objective. It's the only way we can master ourselves — like Nature was mastered. It was with machines that we conquered nature. We must become machines to conquer our nature. It's our destiny.' They want us to stop believing in our own humanity.

"Though in truth, even Nature is not sufficiently mechanical for them. It's not yet controllable enough. 'Nature too is still not fully tamed,' they mutter. 'It still presents a danger. Nature itself too, is still too natural. We must finish transforming it into our own creation — conclude its remaking in our image. We must better tune the Earth-machine. We've gained dominion over the Earth, but the Sky lingers unconquered. We can foresee the weather... but still not control it. That is the next frontier.' Of humans they say likewise.

'Let us suppress the natural, for the manufactured is ours. Let's shackle the Earth-machine,' gloat the optimists. 'This will require innovation — which will always come inevitable... We're the masters of our fate.' Hear the arrogance of these fools! Haven't you heard, my kin, how they want to spray ferment in the seas and in the sky?" clamored Oshana with open arms, as though incredulous. "How dare they affront the Mother in this way? They'll lead us to extinction in their arrogant glee."

"'Innovation — this will entail 'creative destruction', as they call it. By which they mean, the Earth will be despoiled — perhaps destroyed. It's inevitable, this is what they admit in the end — but She will be ravaged in a more civilized manner. And they assure us, the fools — 'In its stead we'll create a simulation of Earth, just as pretty, much cleaner, and much less dangerous. It'll be a playground for our delusions... A quarantine of the senses.' This is what they want.

"Everyone who lives must die. So it's best to have a simulated life instead — that way we can live forever. Half-lives last much longer than full lives.

"Earth is alive and it — they say — it too must die sometime. Its life will power our own. But we will escape from Earth. If we cannot live here any longer — there's safety in outer space. This is what they call 'heaven'. You see? They prefer the endless desert to the exuberance of Earth.

"The barrenness of the void is their ideal. For barren is what they are.

"They speak of irrationality, they speak of illusions. But it is they who want to lock us in a dreamworld. The dreamworld in which they already live. The embodiment of their ideal. A barren future. A dead life.

"They whisper, 'We must yield to the machine. Fuse ourselves with the noise — until the voice inside is shushed.

"'We'll lose ourselves in the forgetfulness of machines. Because machines can remember a lot — and are conscious of absolutely nothing.

"'To be conscious is a hindrance — it causes too much headache. To be organic — is to be unclean. And to be mortal is to decay. So it's better to be artificial, mechanic, and unconscious...

"'We must become automatic — it'll be much more pleasant,' say the optimists.

"'Decisions are too hard to make. They shall be made for us. There will be machines that will know us so well they will know exactly what we want — our best friends will be machines, we will see ourselves in nothing else. We won't be able to speak except through machines, because only machines will be there to listen.

"'We'll be sterile... Imagination — that'll be a thing of the past. Madness — that'll be a thing of the past.

"'The past will look like madness to us. We'll behold it and laugh — to the extent we can laugh still — and the last men will arrive at last.

"'Our highest ideal will be to know everything,' they say.

"'We'll stuff our heads with a lot of data — our brains will be adorned with many facts. To look and sound smart will be paramount. We will have much knowledge and absolutely no wisdom, just like machines. We will neglect our souls — and this will be considered good.

"'By knowing everything, we can know what is good and bad, and we can tune up the good, and tune down the bad. We will know objectively who is fit to tune and who is fit to be tuned — we'll be able to measure precisely who should rule, and who should serve — and the last men will govern at last...'

"Such things are close at hand."

In the long intervals emanating from her speech, into the deepening silence — as it deepened to the valley plumbing vertiginously at their side — arose the groanings of the coursing river, mingling with the flames as they drizzled in ascending embers. Droplets of fire clicked into the night; and the circle rested in quietude between earth and air, among the breathing boughs and the cradling berth of their roots embracing, in their quietest depth, the grave mountain rock. Plunged to the nook of the valley yawned its caves, wherein a screaming horde of droplets raged then; the Oyate river gurgled aloud and with great resonance in the cavern's ample chamber, crashing against, tossing into the fattened city river and the rearing ocean — whirling salts and freshwater, the great flood had advanced as far as the mountainfoot and endeavored now to seep into its marrow. Eastern Axiac was all retreated against the tidal pressures. The fences of Wall Street stood mangled; they leaned in a criss-crossed stupor upon each other, flaccidly swaying to the whims of the gusts. Bubbles surfaced placidly from the submerged Park of Echoes' bloated lake — above which loomed, presiding over the somber devastation, the white Ivory Towers, lusterless in the moonshine revealing tumorous growths maculating their whiteness in blotches. The dust metastasized with moisture and chewed the books resting in the dark inside. Inside, there was no motion; not a sound in the brooding stillness.

From the flow of fire came her voice:

"In truth, the optimists and the pessimists are equal in their delusions. Both consider that Nature can be tamed. But Nature cannot. Only contained — for a time.

"Yet the beast that is shackled only mounts in fury. And the Earth is a Beast that is eternal, Her energies never deplete. She only waits. Though in truth, only the optimists still believe that subjugation can be total — forever managed. The pessimists think that to manage is impossible, one must destroy. But both wish to dominate.

"The pessimists say we'll be animals, the optimists say we'll be machines. But who professes the gospel of humanity?

"The pessimists say, 'God made us in His image', but the optimists say, 'Machines were made in Our image'. In their whispering manner the optimists claim that god is dead, but they whisper still lower, 'here's a new god — and while it may not be fully alive, it can't ever be truly dead. It's not made of flesh, but — minerals.' In this they resemble the pagans of old. Here are the new idolaters with their 'innovative' stone idols.

"The pessimists say, 'the body is vile'. But the optimists say, 'the body is all that matters'. The pessimists say, 'matter is an illusion' — but the optimists say, 'there's nothing but the body'. One urges you to withdraw from the Earth, the other from the Soul — for the Earth is a fantasy to one, and the Soul a fantasy to the other. They're both wrong.

"In this way they both despise life. The pessimists because it exists, and the optimists because it must end. In truth they are the same in saying, 'we will die, therefore everything is meaningless'.

"Death was once the supreme hope of the pessimists. But to the optimists, death is the biggest enemy — because it cannot be avoided and cannot be known.

"For the pessimists, life is a mistake. But for the optimists, death is a mistake. Therefore, Nature is a mistake — for both... They are two sides of the same coin. What we need to do is stop giving so much value to coins! We mistake them for what's truly valuable — in the way we mistake the symbol for the meaning. Coins, money, stocks — these are all symbols of value. But the value is in the Earth.

"No one can suppress the Earth, and no one can suppress Nature. No one can suppress human nature. Attempts to make human beings abstract, mere numbers, mere machines, mere data — this is precisely what turns humans into their so-called animals.

"Indifferent like machines and greedy like *their* animals — that, is who they are... It is by acting the part that they rise to the top of this civilization, by being savages they attain the summits of the savagery they erected. They project upon the world their mirror — it is characteristic of power to endeavor to shape everything to its image.

"Spiteful pessimists and barren optimists walk in front of us, carried upon mountainous litters. Like shepherds of the flock they lead us along the stream of life. They seem to lead us in different directions, but each is taking us toward the same god — the god of death. One intentionally, the other foolishly, but both take us there — through suicide. For to affront the Mother in this way, to try on the Mother's life while we're in Her womb — what is it but suicide? For we live in Her womb. Nothing lives outside of Her.

"In truth, their capes block the horizon. It's difficult to see past them. But we must. We must look to different horizons; we must rip open their veil.

"For they take us along the path of Mammon.

"That path leads to destruction.

"That path leads to death.

"We must walk off it — lest the human race is ended in the abyss marking the end of their road."

Oshana's voice seemed to remain suspended in the hovering mind of the listeners, lingering still with the lassitude of their tired souls as they expanded into the silence, which deepened again across the length of distances, as time breezed past. And the silence became so prolonged in its solemn reflection that even sounds from very far away had time to reach them. Through the crackling of the flame, through the roar of the river valley, the frantic cries of birds — millions of birds, millions of cries they uttered — traveled, floating in the scorch-scented, humid wind with the brittle corn leaves and their defunct seeds. The birds — hens all — whose cries were so loud inside the warehouse where they were kept, so loud as to even muffle the squeal of the nearby hogs, fluttered rabidly inside wire cages. Tiny cages: each bird was squeezed among a dense pack of her caged brethren, ten or so apiece along rows of such stacked iron meshes replicated across the depth and breadth of the huge, dark warehouse; barely able to move among the endless pressing of feathery bodies in the dozy twilight, they sustained — through their months-long lives — the sharp wires digging continuously and vicious into their brittle, fragile toes, their thin-skinned legs, their tender flesh; the push and suffocation of multitudes crowding their sanity; the eeriness of continual night punctured by sudden bursts of potent light, and sudden strange giants roaming in the fecal aisles between the mesh towers; the seeping of filth into the frantic throng of wings and blood, the buzzing flies, the screeching rats in the corners; the madness of ceaseless screams, the unconscious craving for sunlight they'd never feel, for space they'd never enjoy, for freedom they'd never have; the deliberate starvations, all so they could produce the maximum yield they were able of the primordial vessel for life's reproduction — eggs.

Their own lives were but abstractions to be ground up and digested in the insensible logic of capital and industry; their pain insignificant to the great designs of human dominance. Their births were frantic — a hot iron clipped their beaks, bare moments upon hatching — and their deaths unceremonious. From beginning to end their existence had but one purpose — to yield profit and to suffer for the benefit of modern civilization. They didn't know this; they could reason none of it, perhaps. And still they cried to those gathered quietly round the fire; from their manmade, manless caves — monument-ruins of civilization, lying in the abandoned plateau — which had for many hours been pummeled by the fury of their Great Mother. They cried to them, they cried to no one in the deep unconsciousness of prolonged suffering, from a profound essence of being holding the hidden meaning of all existence. Inchoate yells suffusing the stillness of the cornfields, hushed across the vastness, they pierced through, even to Orenda's senses standing over Axiac. As she watched, she heard them. She listened to the distant, faraway cries with the sense of touch and spirit; for to the body's ear they were barely audible; but to the soul's, they drummed, and raged. She listened as she saw the megalopolis, to the cries of those as suffocated as the enslaved builders of that city, brought from the waters in the shelves of tomb-ships, fastened to irons, had been. She listened, too, to those in warehouses nearer, the animals set for slaughter, as condemned to annihilation as those natives who had sprouted from that very land had been. And she contemplated that immense city erected upon sweat and blood, destroyed — as though flooded in its own foundations.

*

There was, in the northeast part of Ostrich, a certain stadium. The Stradom (as it was called) lay in an expansive park at the culmination of a trendy, gentrifying neighborhood, situated upon the ample paved hillocks where (on the far opposite side) Orenda lived. The stadium was usually dedicated to horse races, with a ball involved; yet now in the wake of the tempest, it had been converted into a massive refugee camp housing thousands from every corner of Ostrich and beyond, hailing mostly out of the industrial basin and other low-lying areas of town. The frightened, the sick, the destitute, the homeless, and those dispossessed by the elements all crowded inside, populating the field, seats, stairs, corridors, terraces and office rooms of the round facility, all fleeing heaven's stormy wrath in this massive place which, in normal times, would have been geared to host vast, rowdy multitudes — yet now found itself catastrophically unprepared to withstand the weather, and shelter its myriad victims. Its immensity lay dark; the very backup generators had failed. The air was stuffed with humidity, tense voices and faraway yells, and the stench of urine and feces which materialized before the soldiers' flashlights as they lighted upon the walls. Pools oozed from the clogged bathrooms, nothing worked. Many pounds of food were rotting in the unfunctioning refrigerators. The military and its technicians raced to fix the problem before a general riot erupted and shortly, they would — but before then, Martin huddled closely, trying to smother his terror upon his mother's bosom, as she whispered comforting words to him:

"This field was a lake once," murmured Edazima, containing the angst threatening to heave loose from the base of her chest. She petted his hair softly with one hand — with the other she enfolded one of his ears so he wouldn't understand the mania building up in the darkness around them — and into his uncovered ear she said, "Did you know that? Once upon a time, people could sail here, with boats."

Part of the concave roof had collapsed during the storm, breaking into a cascade of rain and making a gushing river of the descending terraces underneath. Now, with the clouds dissipating, the hole began piercing into a clear view of the nightsky, which disclosed the stars upon its velvety texture, thinly twinkling beyond the obfuscating and spilling glare of the Pearl — the hole was where Edazima was trying to focus her son's attention toward. That section of the stadium had been rendered uninhabitable, driving a very exodus of twice-dislodged folk upon the already-crowded field, where Edazima and Martin lay.

"They drained the lake, and they planted grass and trees here instead. Then they made this stadium in the center, where all the boats used to stop. Do you know why they stopped?"

Dim glows flared with shapes of roving presences, and wandering shadows floated and mingled within patchy darknesses in the corner of his eye. Martin blinked with a slight shiver. "Why, mommy?"

A variety of flashlights had been brought in; most shone the usual white kind, though a bit of every color seemed to be on display throughout the vast circular maw of the cavernous space, in-between pools of deep gloom. Fragments of bodies became delineated within, revealing broken features whose totality seemed like mysteries of the occult, enigmas writhing somewhere in the uncanny and unfathomable depths sinking beyond the dark surfaces beside the lights. Monsters — so it looked to Martin's frightened gaze — emerged from those surfaces. Horrendous, scary, scared masks of various beasts materialized out of nocturnal nothing, hungry, thirsty, desperate. The entertainer who had danced for the children in the middle of the field when they had first come the previous evening (or had it been the evening before? or before?) had his paper horse mask in tatters now, revealing — through the shreds — the hefty, cracking ox visage, whose saturated clay made him stoop; out from beneath the busker's bovine face plopped bits of melted wax as he walked by, disfiguring his neck and shoulders into apparitions of wrinkly and sudden old age. The mood was oppressive; paranoia hung upon the trembling fiber of every tucked soul, coiled into a conflation of tense joints about to spring, and snap.

Edazima had sprinkled her hand with perfume to ward the smells of defecation off her child's nose. She kept muttering. "This place is called 'Stradom' because the lake reflected the stars very clearly. The lake was just like the sky. Like a 'dome of stars', a 'star - dome', you see?"

The stadium's huge yawning contour could be made out from the field where they were. To Martin's maturing instincts, the indistinct, grainy ether expanding far beyond their ken, the immense circle surrounding their small forms and the misshapen blotches of flashlights and ghostly colors up and down the vertiginous heights to which the stadium's tiers arose, all seemed to hide numberless eyes bored with darkness — eyes watching him and his mother intently (a million secret owls). He felt, the poor child, like a small prey besieged by a band of wheeling predators, whose vestige of teeth he sometimes glimpsed in the salivating glows. ("Stop and you could see the stars under your feet all the way down to the horizon," Edazima meanwhile continued). The past many hours and perhaps few days had pressed upon his incubating psyche the mark of trauma, thrown him into the abrupt experience of the unknown, the ghastly, into a startled mode of living permeated with the taste of want and death. Now they — mother and child cuddled — were as if at the bottom of a nest opened to the ravages of a brooding sky. His little eyes glowed with the trembling sighs of melting masks — and his heart billowed with dread. "Mom, I'm scared..."

"It's ok baby, it's ok, mommy's here ok?" comforted Edazima. "Come here — why don't you close your eyes for a minute?" (Martin shut his eyes; she pressed him tighter upon her breast). "It's ok... Close your eyes and imagine this place, long ago... Close your eyes... Just imagine we're sailing over the lake... From the middle of the lake we stand among the stars, the stars move under us all night. We're floating and flying among the stars... We're entering the moon... We're in the middle of the moon... We're — swimming in the moon... Hush, my love... The sky and the water are like one thing and we can fly... Can you hear?..."

Her stare was fixed upward still, on the gap across the roof into which the moonrise slowly stole and discreetly filled. The moonshine dressed the leaking water in silver. Gradually, its radiance came to glisten upon the stream which was now thinning down the seats and stairs, flowing down into a pool on the field round which many sad, drained faces gathered — some of them, bereft of energy but with some spirit extant in their gazes, seemed to contemplate the cascading glimmer with some hint of enchantment.

"Things have a way of coming back to themselves," Edazima muttered in a hopeful tone as she watched — though she knew not what she meant, and indeed was barely conscious of the words as they flowed out of her heavy, sleepy, exhausted spirit.

A confusion of miscellanea surrounded them: blankets and plastic containers mostly, forming a sort of woolen sea undulating with motionless pollution surfacing all over the ground; but there were all manner of things — *I*s, flashlights, lamps, cans, clothes, pillows and magazines; a couple of guns peeked out at times, even a fishing pole made an appearance in the midst. A scarab, batting its wings in quick buzzes, landed in the general confusion of stuff, resting its ebony feet upon a soiled piece of paper dotted with inked inscriptions of some kind. Though the scarab couldn't have known it, it was a book, and the page over which the beetle spread had these very same words printed on it.

The child peeked with one eye and noticed the insect's huge carapace inching toward his fingers.

"Mom!" he yelled, flinging his hand away and burrowing himself deeper into his mother's bosom.

"It's ok! it's ok baby —" Edazima flicked the beetle away, and both her and the beetle shuddered momentarily. "Don't be scared. I'm here."

Amid the mountaintops, Orenda's solitary figure faced the direction of her own neighborhood and that of the Stradom, though she couldn't discern the big house of weekend veneration and athletic ritual, now turned makeshift shelter, clearly among the overall impressions of Ostrich's wobbling dark landscape. The imposing stadium was but a vague shape among blurry trees and the vast incomprehensibility of things. Down from the hillock, the park opened to neighborhoods of century-old houses slanting into the floodwaters; and from there, the Ostrich basin progressed mostly underwater, with many little archipelagos of roofs solid amid the waste and large islands of housefronts emerging here and there, all along the huge bleary extent of the crippled zone, from the southern beach woods to the industrial towers of steel across the shore. These rested in perfect motionlessness; refineries, chemical plants, and power facilities inoperable, the entire area lay empty and absolutely soundless. The cavalcade of pumpjacks had slowed to a halt everywhere. The chimneys spouted nothing, breathless... All manner of toxic foams coated the moribund tide, putrid and teeming with disease as they bubbled and gathered out of the silent silhouettes of metal spires and geometric blocks. The industrial swamp stretched very far, even as far as the core of Axiac and the colossal tower soaring from its depths. The Belab — and the glaring Pearl at its summit — remained within sight wherever she looked on the plain. It penetrated her consciousness deep and insinuated itself into the very marrow of her soul; something of it lodged there. From time to time, without noticing it herself, she would shift uncomfortably with the feeling of it. That massive structure of glass and steel seemed to hum, it seemed to hum even more resonantly in the lingering wake of the bells; it seemed to hum, titan and intimate, forceful and conniving, with all the clamorous noises and whispering pleas of the plateau behind her and the plain before her — with all the cries of the ailing, which she could not hear, but felt. The meat and egg farms, the charred forests, the sports stadium and all the homes sprawling across, seemed to circle quietly round the godly tower, the thickest of all shadows in that abominable darkness of mute sufferings, from the very dark depths of which there issued a void sort of sound, beyond the bells, beyond the hum, beyond all things in the drowned megalopolis — as if the profoundity of that monster called to her, as if its hollowed eyes of broken glass could see her standing there. A throb, a pulse; it was the beating of a heart... And it contained all things alive and dead, for it pumped their blood from the very bottom of the Earth into its enlightened peak. The Belab drew from every life its vigor. The farms, refineries, pipelines, docks, electric grids, roads and buildings, and all existence subsisting on them existed within it — chickens, broilers, pigeons, cattle... people. All cried mutedly...

All of it entered Orenda's consciousness.

She inhaled the windless air with a frown [...]

Albumen scattered and the yolk blotched upon the sizzling pan (Neipas?)

She sprinkled ham on top.

"Hm?"

A soft thud of ceramic clattered from the table. "Sorry — I was distracted." Steam ascended to his eyes.

Neipas observed her through the screen of omelet vapors. Her wavy locks of hair fell across her back, her arms and shoulders moved vigorously and stopped. She turned around and away from the stove, holding her plate (suddenly he realized the gas-blown fire had ceased, suddenly he became aware of an uncanny quietness — and he saw her glamorously painted pigeon mask, her finely-shaped beak and lustrously exuberant plume; he saw Eva as he surfaced from the deep sight of his own reflection in the kitchen knife.

But his father's dead eyes still pressed on his own).

(You tired? Didn't sleep well? asked Eva in a hesitant, worried tone.)

(Bit tired, he mumbled, petting the omelet, making it burst into cooked meat.)

Eva would take the pregnancy test in a couple of weeks. A vague anxiety arose in him, in the even way that floodwater rises in a closed space.

Could she be a mother? he wondered.

The silence prolonged.

2ND INTERLUDE

(...Wanna walk on the
beach today?)

*

The silence was perfect and absolute over the beach at night. Even the ample waters of the ocean — reaching forth, swinging back, languid — made no sound in the storm's wake. To listening hearts alone did the ocean play its mystic melody, lingering yet soundless in the spiral ears of the seashells strewn about. The lingering spirits of the mollusks still whispered the music of their ken. They sang yet the dancing currents of the swinging deep. And the ocean oscillated, it progressed, it receded... Through the winding of the inner shells one finds the voice of ghostly remembrance humming still and for all time, with words that sprout, and strike a tone, in the hearing heart — coiling deep into the spiral shell it goes...

Toward the ocean floor.

(Neipas?)

"You sure you're ok, baby?" probed Eva as she pulled him by the hand, and he turned up his eyes enveloped in mist, drawing in the flaxen stretch of shore glimmering in sunlight toward him. Her glance was candid, her concern before his sunken demeanor sincere — though it was momentary, and easily appeased by Neipas' feigned smile (his feathers bristled as the beak ends rose). He kissed her forehead ("don't worry, sweetie") and embraced her.

They turned away from the pier, its enormous wheel and mazes of rollercoasters impressing like stamps upon the soot horizon of factory blocks and chimney flames, and roved along the breathing water line — of foaming fingers tickling their naked feet, their sinking feet of toes mashing wet sand between them in the way that the fingers of creation molded the clay of humanity — unconsciously. Unconsciously did life surface from the ocean, unconsciously does life carry onward. Bubbling spume entered their clay footsteps, and Neipas trod beneath the humid sunlight, dallying in metaphysical half reflections, because he was so tired that he couldn't help but dream while half awake, and unconsciously ruminated on Eva's worried eyes, analyzed her eyes with his sleepy stare, as if he saw them, though she walked in front of him, with her curly nape waving with the pace of the sea, covering her eyes. Swinging back, pushing forth... And her eyes stared into him too, when her photograph materialized in the swinging water of the tray in the darkroom; stared at him as true and as real as they had upon the misty beach that day. There she was in the paper, as material as she had ever been in the consciousness of the eye — beautiful, magnificent, seductive, implacable. Feathery cushions piled about her pose. A serpent coiled around her body...

And the water swung in, and receded... swung in, and receded...

Over the canal — whither the ocean had been brought and framed — was an arched bridge, and upon the bridge a nest-shaped alms basket; it wound before two naked hoofs. A few coins lay in its hollow. Eva and Neipas had been returning from their walk on the beach when they saw the teenager to whom it belonged, a boy with hefty downward horns and a stoic demeanor, whose hands gripped a large conch ("look, baby!"). They joined the little crowd of intrigued pigeon masks, presently gathering their plumes before the cattle boy as he prepared to blow the conch.

As his lips touched the conch's spire there ensued a very deep, very solemn sound; a very dense tone which filled them with a sudden awareness of gravity. There was something unexpected in it that forced toward it all attentions, and during the initial moments in which it blew upon them none around the boy muttered a sound, none stirred in the utter absorption of the tone which sounded like something born of depths very distant, as of a well penetrating to the center of the Earth or a ear canal leading to the most secretive chambers of their own minds. Eva wound her arms around Neipas' and glared with a smile faintly drawn at the corner of her lip, listening to the profound tone, absolutely transfixed upon the perfectly wounded spiral — twisting in many rounds, something unusual — of the beautiful conch. It had a strangely hypnotic effect. Her stare was drawn to the very core of it, which was vacant, like a sort of ivory aperture which mysteriously sucked in the vitality of her breath for a moment (she nodded and giggled out the unsettling feeling in her chest).

Eva pulled out her *I* and joined the others in filming the performance.

The adolescent played the conch in tones of trumpet — for a minute or so after this initial burst (Neipas and Eva withdrew as the humble applause faded, and meanwhile some of the pigeons neared the alms basket with pecking glares. Eva's own fogged up with the surfacing of an elusive, disagreeable feeling suddenly troubling her heart).

A teardrop grew under her lower lid as it rose out onto the red eye (Eva blinked) from which it slid unexpectedly, flowing down her disheveled cheek and stopping at the jaw above the faucet. The droplet then fell. The little translucent bubble had been bled out of somewhere under her mask, out of some turmoil deep beyond it, and it contained in its small space all the concentrated angst of unconscious hours, wherein Neipas floated also, as a vague warmth accompanying her through the passing of days. Inside the tear he floated... Roaming adrift through half-conscious years, Neipas plumbed into buried fathoms, among snows of spectral grain, among flashes of flying shadows. He (something in him inside him) flew down the inscrutable waters where logic disintegrates and discernment ceases to exist. He was dredged to the bottom of his ocean-dream; and along the way as his mining beak moved — his subconscious body dissolved in specks of crumb, and propagated in the ebb of receding thought — through remembrance... In the very midst of the atom brume into which he rained there were falling vapors of spices, there were drizzling herbs — they were being peppered from myriad soft, maternal, saintly good hands suspended at the end of a thin pulse and a dim sense of presence — being sown to the bubbling ocean floor. There were a great many shards and shell bits lodged in there. His own hand (suddenly Neipas felt amazement at having hands) emerged before his phantasm's eyeless gaze, touched the shifting sands; and his fingers elongated weirdly in the maddened flow of the ground.

Neipas flinched in bed.

Going along the hilly path to the house of worship (the gates had already been passed) he found, inside the deep conch wail besetting him on all sides, voices that he recognized. Perhaps they came from the balloons fastened to the soil by rope, perhaps from the vibration of the ropes themselves. Violent winds stirred them and lifted the dust into cackling veils of earth. A giant shape loomed behind him. Neipas had a vague intention to flee from it but ran backwards instead as he conversed cheerfully with the gust that sounded at first like Eva ——————— (but baby * I ** it's

positive *

*

* just take pill * relax)

The voices flowed like
chaff in the breeze. Glows flashed and groaned.
"Why are you lagging, baby?" asked Neipas to the grave (for he stood in a graveyard), "you're right in front of me."

Again he flinched abruptly — and was startled out of slumber, heavy of breath, bleary of sight, crowded of mind, with dreams tingling yet his senses even as he plummeted back against the mattress, exhaling thick ("Mary," mumbled he in a stuffy sigh) — his arm coursed over Eva's own as she lay on her side, and his bent legs glued to hers, they fitted together like two puzzle pieces or cogs (the thought occurred to him as he sank back to the dream):

The tides of dirt had subsided. And though there was still incomprehensible babble around him he no longer paid attention.

Now the balloons were held by standing shadows, who uttered the choppy voices (the giant looming shape had broken into many equal shadows, and they spoke syllables which made up words that contained meaning individually, but which collectively braided up murders with pretty decorations) But Neipas feared them no more. He, too, held a balloon, and he gripped its cord in the same way he did when he first visited his mother's grave — he stood before it now.

Still there were egg shards peppering the earth. He stood with his balloon aright, in silence. Existence kept receding into the conch's motionless tone.

Insects carried the shards to and fro — in and out of the soil — for there was no wind.

*

His mother's grave was but a stone drawer in a mausoleum cabinet. For a while he stood with his face aslant, as if embarrassed, and refused to look at it; his neck contorted exaggeratedly in his supreme evasion and endeavor not to look, and indeed he felt very much ashamed for some reason. Then he lay down on the little mound of lifted earth (suddenly there was one at his feet) and, embracing it, he wept sourly. Neipas could still perceive that the air was made of flakes and that wet dirt and ashes suffused the breath of sounds, which made wisps and sparks as they retreated fast into some primordial quietude. The snow of film grain thickened all around him; and with dirt in his eyes everything looked like static and visual noise. In it he couldn't help but seeing the tombstone, it didn't matter how much he tried to avoid it, his eyes nevertheless leaned very close to it; he stood now with his neck extremely stretched, so as to match his sight with the height of the tomb where his mother's photograph was engraved; meanwhile he was very aware of torches palpitating on all sides, though they kept their distance.

The image of his mother zoomed into the totality of his perception and only ceased growing when it reached the edges of his dream-sight. He could hear his own breath shudder — this was the last peep before total silence. The mother stared at him, fixed, unreal. She was as if staring from beyond the surface of ice, trapped forever in that single pose: because the grave itself was bodiless (her corpse had never been found and Neipas was keenly aware of this in the dream) it seemed to him like she was frozen in the stone, inside the rock, beyond the photograph. For a moment he mused aloud about carving her out of the slab but a different development steered his attention away. The choppy voices were still clicking from the shadows standing upright on the thin atmosphere without walls (but the wall of the mausoleum standing alone in the dust), and held torches with flames which, as they crackled, made them sway right and left like drunkards. Things pulsed with the impression of flashing — the very sky was black and textured, a dark sun with thin golden edges ripped a single abyss in it. Insects writhed and scampered by the millions across the sands (they had become the sands and every grain was alive with legs) carrying shards, and all sounds kept receding and unwinding electric and mechanical in the noisy, grainy, subterranean aether which at this point was as oppressive as galloping nightmares, and took Neipas quite to the threshold of awakening — but from these furiously ebbing sounds flashed the choppy voices, which he assumed, with a measured calculation, to be coming from the umbras erect upon wallless space; Neipas took one step forward and, shrugging but once, yelled, "Why do you sound like vultures? Actually, go fuck yourselves. It's your fault things are like this!" — and as he hurled the balloon at them, he realized one of the shadows had grown into the form of a huge pigeon with human legs and arms, that it moved just like he, that it was himself. Realizing this made him erupt into a fit of laughter, though he never ceased crying and screaming. But where was his balloon? and with this he was swimming up the misty air. The sparks of flame crackling with choppy syllables lifted with him as he flapped his arms in the direction of the ground.

*

Embers danced calmly into the night, charting fanciful courses before being engulfed by the soft darkness. The fire burned in their midst, and they were quiet still, waiting for Oshana to continue. The faraway noises of the valley, the plateau and the plain had reached their senses by then, mingling their contemplations with the impression of suffering present, and past, and yet to come; the very feeling of the air upon their skins and inside their bodies imbued in them a fitful unease, which they bore sad, tragic, stoic. It was too much for some — and those that wept, the rest waited upon in silence and embrace.

Oshana recommenced thus:

"Humanity hasn't yet chosen its common purpose. It hasn't set for itself a goal.

"To serve, and to strive — here's left foot, and right foot upon which — we march. We strive toward our gods in hope — or serve them in fear of their anger.

"Gods are immanent, and transcendent. They are everywhere, but they are beyond. They are destinies to aspire toward: and because they transcend our existence, they can never be reached. But they are everywhere, therefore they are something to be *possessed* — or, as they say, be possessed by...

"In truth I tell you, all gods are symbols — symbols of power. Where does human power lie? In the embodiment of a promise, my kin.

"Such promises as inspire hope and fear, my kin. Will the harvest be fruitful, or will I hunger? Will I achieve salvation, or perdition? Will I gain wealth — or suffer wants? Will I be happy or unhappy? Will I live or die? These are questions that have troubled different generations in different degrees. But the question is always the same. It is: will the gods punish — or reward me?

"Gods were once powers of Nature. There were gods of wind, gods of rain, river gods and sun gods, gods and goddesses of the wood and of the crops, divinities of weather and land. And those who claimed, 'we know the gods — we have something of their divinity, and we can appease their fury and win their grace, we can steer their power' — if they convinced the rest by the *grace* — that is, divine charisma — and could organize the rest so as to shape Nature to serve a common prosperity, then the power was theirs to seize, and hold. To know Nature, to win Nature's favor, was the ideal, the access to life. In the same manner, to those who derived life not from the harvest, but from the hunt, to those the craftiness and the force of their animal gods were paramount — and whomever best mastered those ideals, to them belonged power over the rest."

In Orenda's stare shimmered the flame. The embers were delivered up to the heavens like spores, to be absorbed in the inscrutable nothingness of the waiting, quiet aether.

Her gaze passed in a lagging shudder over the Belab as it swept the ravaged landscape, from the wooded peninsula in the south to (— over the tower, the Pearl-lit shape of which, sticking to the surface of her orbs, materialized, multiplied and dissolved in phantom vestiges of vapor across the motion) to the Diamond Hills in the north, with its manicured shrubbery well lined up (hiding the sumptuous mansions of the Eagles) in the area most shadowed by the Pearl's glare, that light drawing all attention and devotion as the loftiest symbol of hope concentrating the horizons of a fearful million eyes. Its phantom vestige, lingering in Orenda's stare, palpitated in a spectral representation of itself at every blink, even as she attempted to discern beyond the discreet, low hilltop crowning without flair all the hidden wealth tucked in its slopes. There in the ravines and fissures of the descending canyons and in the great plains hollowed out from old clay quarries hid the various military bases forming the buttress of the nation, housing latent forces of destructive chaos between orderly, flat, diagonal walls of austere aspect, full of unassuming lights blinking professionally in a sort of ecclesiastical gloom, suffused with the air of discipline and hierarchy. Squares of light emanated abstracted visions of far places in the world; grayed out, gridded, populated with nondescript dots moving in barren, alien landscapes.

Orenda's vision still flew across the elegant sea mansions — which remained unseen behind the water-facing cliffs — as she stretched her neck and erected her posture, in the almost unconscious motion of the unconscious need to see better, see beyond what her eyes could perceive, what her ears could hear, her nose sense, her fingers touch; her gaze, fixed firm on her panning head, crossed again the mighty radiance of the Pearl and the haloed titan cascading to the black from its height. There was at once a subtle straining of her tired lids as she cast her scrutiny outward, beyond the great mountain cliff, the great extent of flooded city glinting under moonlit breezes, beyond the specter of towers erected lifelessly and mute over the wreck, and through, into, beyond the Pearl, its hum and beat, to the far, farthest distance — and a relaxation into herself, as if retreating into some profound silence, a quietude of inner confines, so as to listen better to sounds from farther away, to the voices beyond the noise. And as her stare reposed upon the horizon — the silver maw which had but a while before ingested the sun — her spirit felt for lights shining far and dim.

"Gods were once powers of Nature, then they became powers of Man — thus were born the various gods of war, to bless conquest — and the many gods of wisdom, to aid in governance. Here were the gods of human power — power before Nature, power over the rest.

"Then came the one God, God of gods, King of kings, symbol of absolute power and perfect dominion over Nature, such as tyrants had possessed over men. And those who gained power then were God's elect, imbued with God's grace, and thus, best able to lead the flock to his eternal glory, in the path prescribed to dodge his malice.

"The nearer you are to god — the ideal, the promise — the more of god you embody: the more might you gather. This, my kin, is the secret of power.

"Who are the patron-gods of our days? Money, Market and Enterprise are but the Father, the Son and the Holy Spirit of a single essence called 'Mammon' — here's the chief deity of our time. Mammon promises respect, prestige, comfort, luxury, sex, power. Mammon threatens indignity, destitution, insignificance. Mammon is the path, Mammon is the gate through which to avoid the punishments and seize the rewards of wealth. And in our days, those who possess Mammon possess power — those who can promise the rest toward Mammon, possess power.

"Mammon is everywhere, but also beyond. So we keep marching relentless toward him, who is absolute power and *independence* from the Earth — without ever reaching him. This, my kin, is the nature of greed, which has no bounds, never settles.

"My kin, we must cease walking toward Mammon. We must stop this 'progress', which is the progress toward Mammon. Progress toward destruction and away from life."

Afore the mountains, under the hushed limits of the waters — in the farthest distance of the deepest night yonder — which had sometime before extinguished the fire of the sun — the Earth curled under Her aquatic cape flapping gently with Her gentle movement, in Her gracious journey around the Universe and toward Herself — along the silent wheel of the Milky Path winding into its own center, in the great loneliness of immensity and mystery, with but a few astral glitters there in the horizon of infinitude, shining like beacons of mirage and proof of abstract existences. Inside Earth the Universe, inside Earth the Planet, over Earth the Soil, there was a city, a megalopolis of concrete and glass, of name "Axiac" — a variation of the aboriginal "Ooxor", sound by which the natives referred to the basin sieged by mountain and sea, and which after all simply meant, in their ancient idiom, "land"; land this that frothed between the fury of two oceans, amid ruins; shattered by their weight and might.

From the deluge now becalmed — swinging against the mountainfoot — the flood spuming in wreckage across shivering roads between towers and in wide craggy lakes, stagnant, slurping the edges of roofs and floating debris, the ocean broke forth, out of the shattered, splintered docks, and disappeared beneath the horizon's fold, rolling over the deep Earth.

(Orenda then closed her eyes. For an instant, an interminable moment of profound focus and vast perception, the Earth stopped).

The place where the glare of the Pearl vanished in the skyline, directly west of Axiac's coast, would have presented to the observing eye a perfect encapsulation of the sublime. A serenity, as of the rest after creation, reigned here. The sunlight had already passed over these waters and there remained only dark windlessness in its wake; a band of crimson, emitting a faint orange nimbus as of a dying fire, still lingered in the west, and meanwhile numberless clusters of stars sprouted in sweeps of dust upon the sky, like sparkling dandelions; the air was as clear and pure as in the very beginning of days. Nor was there, indeed, a single breath to ruffle its absolute stillness, nor eyes but those of the distant stars — the hovering moon — to watch the ocean uninterrupted by land and untroubled by motion. The Universe observed from its infinite inscrutability the inscrutable mantle blanketing, masking whole galaxies of life in its vast bosom. Under the vast, moonlit surface of the watery tunic, and above Earth's sandy back, there tucked vast constellations of microscopic beings and roaming planets with fins and maws, gliding giants materializing between the swaying shadows of the sea. Here was concealed an alien world of floating beings; a strange world of strange sonority, where the air, perpetually close and pressing, perpetually seemed to voice grave winds blowing very far away; winds carrying the liminal whisperings of phantoms, echoing perpetual the eternal word from which all existence blossomed. Here, in the dead silence of primordial sounds — where the leaden thickness of the waters lets ring only the deepest cry — here, it is said, is where all life began.

Its deepest fathoms are as tenebrous as the confines of outermost space. Marine snow glides across the flux of it, as cosmic dust floats through the void, falling — rising, perhaps — loosened from the shimmer of stars to the distant shadow of the abyss. Under the farthest reach of lunar twilight, beyond the grasping rim of visibility, the seas pitch into utter blackness, into a frigid netherworld, an immense swath uncharted by eye and mind. Unknown, unmapped, and undiscovered, covered yet by the elemental forces of the deep, its secrets are kept protected from the curiosity of civilization. But there, too, the beam of human rationality begins to crack the dense and dark crust of ignorance.

There, too, dwell slow twinkling lights. Mysterious beasts roam over its obscure, universal soil, they drift the fugue darkness; unbothered, for millennia, by the noisy tumults and depredations of humankind above; living beyond the frontier of human scrutiny, the beings of the deep flap their marine wings with the languor of occult divinities. Among the volcanic exhalations of Earth's heart, spouting between the primordial navel stones of the deepest valleys, life glides on. Yet already in those days, gloating at the apex of human folly, the erstwhile chiefs of human destiny cast rapacious solar glares to the nadir, directing their Eagle eyes toward the vast hidden womb of the ocean, which throbs secretly; licking their mandibles, anxious to penetrate the remotest bowels of the Earth without delay, salivating for the endless mineral wealth stored inside, they conjured up long numbers in their dreams, filled their imaginations with the bulk of entire continents; already they planned the plunder of these continents entombed underneath the waves with little care or thought for the vibrancy of arcane life living there in the bottom, waiting only for the hallowed machines to which they pinned their faiths to evolve resistance to those cold ocean-buried wastelands; and so progressed the Lord Eagles, wrapped in wings of flag and tie, with unconscious steps of giant in their cupidity, and an insatiable wish of dominion, even as the bases of the summits upon which they had built their houses had begun to chip away.

And if the spirit were to float out of those opaque obscurities to gaze yonder, with incorporeal stares, to where the sunshine seeps through the depths in the form of dancing serpents, It would see, materializing through jungles of spore and coral, titanic cliffs rising to view, dramatic ascents of submerged rock mounting from those magical vales at ocean-bottom. Upon the summit, amid the plankton mists, hiding behind strips of seaweed, the mollusks crawled and struggled in their smallness to craft their shells: an occult practice involving the amassing of mineral particles, the very building blocks of form, with which they sculpt their homes and shields, their refuge — sliding fortresses, and armor in which to tuck. They depend on the very make of the aquatic air, these tailors of molecular rock, to make their pods. But what air there is to breathe beneath — is poisoned. More and more venom gathers in the water, inhaled from the air of the firmament aloft over the surface; the same overload of pollution spewed from the chimneys and tailpipes of civilization infecting the globe. The submerged jungles here, as the immersed jungles above, draw in sun and carbon to make life.

The mollusk's pearly eye gazed through the crack upon its unfinished carapace. The hull of a ship glided across the mantled skies, carrying in its bosom fossils of sun and carbon, rivers of pitch and perpetual night, meant to pump life into the dead mounts of concrete ashore; where the young feed off the old, and the dead kill the unborn.

Then, hovering over the kelp forests and dunes of algae, there sprawl giant nets, resembling towers of diamond-shaped windows through which a million heads of fish peep out frantically. Huge swarms are snared as the tower drags along. As in a giant stack of prison cells, the fish rattle their bars of cloth in a mass, flapping desperately among ophidians of spectral sunlight, blowing bubbles of acid ocean. By the time the motored pulleys hoist the whole frenzied lot up to the airless atmosphere — the mesh choking them all into gasping crowds — the tremendous pipes of an oil rig are already in view, connecting the floating factory to the Earth like parasitic umbilical cords; thrusting into the underwater soil beside anaemic sponges and bleached reefs of coral...

In long flows of dead and moribund slime, the fish are finally disemboweled into the frozen belly of titanic ships, gliding islands of iron, chain and rigging; and then disgorged in rows and stacks of crates out in sunlit docks where laboring cattle haul freight alongside machines of burden. The sky's obscure appearance shed, the ocean seemed peppered with crystal, vast before the solitary archipelagos stretched out in the middle of its waters where the great ships stop, unload, and recharge before resuming their voyage across the great tidal amplitude circling Earth's flank, across waters of dimension immense, prolonged over innumerable horizons and spanning the very light of day from end to end. Indeed, the crimson and golden tinge of the coming sun was just flowering over the skyline of that great continent — opposite Axiac across the giant seas — to whose docks the tankers, the great fishing trawlers and all the neptunian vessels of commerce now afloat would soon moor with monstrous bellows of horn; the night floated over its landmass yet. Lights of electric colors blinked orderly on the paved, shod coast... commerce never slept. Those continental ports never empty.

"My kin, I said that gods are symbols of power, but all power comes from the Earth. 'Nature' is the deep meaning of the symbol — gods are expressions of Nature. To the sun, to the moon, to the ocean, to thunder and rain, to the woods and the fields, and even to animals they gave human form, so that they could be understood. They clothed the gods in human personas, they bestowed them human flesh. Such is the tendency to make all things our mirror.

"But gods are faces of Nature — yet, if upon all the gods human masks were placed, what god, then, has stood for that face of Nature called human nature?

"The god who was born human, and died a human — that god of the settlers, of the hunters, herders and miners of men — what did he die of? Don't they say he took upon himself our pains? That he bore our sufferings? He died for us all, they say... But my kin, isn't that the truest, the most profound expression of human nature? Beyond all the greed, envy, hatred, beyond all the prejudices and resentments of our faults, aren't we empathetic, compassionate, loving, kind — beyond all differences, aren't we each other? My kin — was that prophet not ourselves?

"Was it not when he died for the sake of humankind — that he was reborn a god?

"In truth I tell you, the deepest one is within one's humanity, the closest one is to divinity. The most profound in oneself, and the farthest beyond oneself in kinship — so closest to the divinity of Mother Earth, that exists in all and embraces All.

"Here's a symbol of our deeper nature. And in truth, we will have to suffer torments upon the tree of life, and die many times in our life to bring about the next world — for there is no birth without pain."

With very respect Oshana inhaled the scent of the firewood, with profound affinity she drew the firelight into her sad eyes.

"I am the way, he said... And if this were the way, then I would follow him. But he still spoke of sin and more sin. This human god is a symbol, and the biggest sin of their followers has been to mistake the symbol for the meaning. They *misunderstood* — on purpose, of course. And still he spoke of celestial rewards and unearthly retributions, and only to those things his followers listened, because it gave the most powerful among them their power, and to the rest, respite, and fear. But to whatever else he said, they just covered their ears. Those teachings of humility, they gave to the poor, that they may remain humble. To themselves they gave *grace*, to the rest, mercy...

"My kin, a crown of thorns rims the prophet's nest. Take care not to plant our seed in its hollow. We'll be enmeshed."

The fish carcasses (like all priced commodities) are shipped from the ports into the various markets of those oriental coasts and beyond. Dawn emerges with the bustle of merchants and murmurs of anticipation for the many who would soon stream the warehouses where the fish lie dead upon ice, to give life by feeding; and throughout those markets, connected to one another across the sprawling network of commerce spanning the whole world, humble eyes roamed in search of their daily sustenance, reproduced in deed and linked by need everywhere; and everywhere they commented as they beheld the fish, *Things are getting worse and worse*, in various languages and with distinct meanings, all coming under the influence of a sort of resigned fatalism affecting the hearts of humankind in those days. Some of them, who came everyday to buy fish, sensed that the animals were shrinking somehow, ever smaller and more feeble, with less life in their dead bodies — they, experienced, were the first to sense that perhaps the fish had less to eat, because the fish those fish ate fed upon mollusks, which were becoming smaller, weaker, and scarcer, because they fed on the submarine air inhaled by the plants from the sky, and the sky was brooding with venom thicker by the moment; and they, the merchants and buyers of like warehouses throughout the global sprawl of threaded economies, sensed that the fish were becoming overwhelmed by the relentless pace of their hunters, such that they hadn't time to secure their lineage and ensure the progression of their kind — extinction assailed the seas, evermore bereft; and all of them setting up the markets at dawn bore a vague presentiment of famine upon their unconscious brows.

Out of the loading docks of those immense commercial harbors, and beyond the coastal markets of the newfound megalopolises of the Orient whose summits strained upward in great flares of light, the fish — and many other labeled and priced extracts of Nature — are taken, in long and spacious arks that float upon wheels, along rivers of bitumen. Through here flow the composite pieces of capitalist societies. Its paths trembled, hummed, blasted without cease, at all times, back and forth across land and sea. The hubs connecting them sweated with the toil of slaves, unseen and uncared for in their own hidden arks, hidden people who supplied the flow with their hands; myriad hands of a single brutal atlas, profoundly shouldering the very foundations of civilization — which was called 'economy' then. Things were such in those days that not only food, not only fuel, not only whatever was deemed essential, but all manner of useless stuff was needed to replenish the immense and unquenchable hunger that supported these modern societies; the lightest clog in the flow sufficed to make them burst in panicked heaves.

Parades of rubber wheels and steel boxes stream fast across the bitumen, coursing the tar veins of civilization, pumping the petroleum that is its lifeblood into the scarlet sky indifferently overlooking this paved shore, towering with colossal cities that are the simulacra of Axiac popping all across the Earth. A zest of poison and putrid smells lingering in the soul rouse their activity day and night, day and night, day and —

"And Mammon? Mammon, too, is part of our nature. He is the pull to greed... Indeed, poisonous fruit grow in the branches of our soul. Mammon too is fruit of the human spirit, a fruit weighing down all our boughs.

"Fruits of the soul are mirrors of diamond, my kin. They are prisms that show — or hide our deeper nature, the deepest seed of ourselves. Mammon, like all gods, are veils to a mystery.

"In truth, we would do well to learn from the tree. Like all the Earth, it mirrors ourselves, as we mirror the Earth — as progenitors and progeny mirror one another.

"It is by pruning that the tree flourishes. Some branches make it wilt — an overabundance of boughs make it barren. Those must be cut off, so that healthier fruit may blossom. But it matters to know where to cut.

"From where does Mammon sprout? It sprouts from greed, which grows from the essential experience called 'fear'. Fear of hunger, fear of cold, fear of being bare and alone, fear of being abandoned to the elements, fear of fragility, fear of others. Fear is common to all beings, it is a pulse of life. It is natural. Fear tempers unruly passions, it brings us in accord with ourselves. But the overabundance of fear that spawns Mammon, is no longer simply fear — it is cowardice.

"Mammon grows also in the desire to propagate — the aspiration to power, the hope to sow oneself upon the rest, the will to flourish without restraint, independent of other's wishes — and satisfy every whim and every urge without reprimand or punishment. The will to freedom total, liberty *over* the rest — the will to godliness... My kin, 'fear' and 'desire' extend from the depth of our selves. Left unchecked, left to grow in the proper air, they intertwine into 'greed' — Mammon's bough, crux, and DNA.

"Indeed, the tree flourishes by pruning, my kin. Some branches must be cut off — but I'm not speaking of castration. My kin, if your eye makes you stumble, don't gouge it out. Instead look closer, pay more attention. To be willingly blind is unhelpful, we have enough of those stumbling around. We must learn to *see*, even inside ourselves, and in truth, we must learn *when* to be scandalized by what we see... It matters to know what to contain in ourselves and what to let flow, but in truth, nothing in human nature can be annihilated, nothing.

"The type of fear and desire that grows to greed, even that is natural and must be allowed to flex — in the proper time and within limits, lest it consumes you, as it is consuming our days. Our demons are part of us — we must see them, and use their energy.

"It will take courage, fortitude, patience and much honesty to learn this. We prune not to mutilate, but to grow back *healthier*... remember that. And those branches we prune off ourselves are meant to be burned, indeed — but not in some pit away from sight, and not as punishment, but as a reminder that they live, and can grow in us. We will tell the history of our days round the fire, in the fire we'll see the mirror of our mistakes. And we will hold the branches as torches, to guide us into the future — in the darkness, the flame shows us less where to go, than where *not* to go.

"In the darkness that awaits us yet, the direction must come from ourselves and the light of our spirit."

Oshana beheld smilingly those listening countenances, those faces swaying in the glow of the flames, beholding her with devotion, with love.

"We've stuffed our souls with the poisonous fruits of Mammon," she said, "gorged ourselves with consumer products, searched for fulfillment in all the wrong places. We must dim Mammon's flare — it is blinding us, we cannot see the abyss just ahead. We must turn to a new future. We must journey toward the new ideal. And we must begin now.

"We will be walking through some paths long deserted, others altogether new. And we'll have to walk through many a night, my kin. There will be many pits awaiting us, dark mirrors of today... I tell you my kin, that unless we sever Mammon from our selves, his vines will keep on twining round our hearts, making us drunk. And we won't be able to see further than our left foot — we'll fall, my kin."

The beasts of steel that feed on petroleum and fire drive onward, always somewhere; like wind over the swamps they rush. They wheel toward every direction the Market reaches; round and round Mammon's centerless circle, Mammon's sprawling roots seeping into all quarters, these motorized chariots (horned chimaeras running fuming horses) rage on, carrying in their bosoms food to be consumed, minerals to be morphed, fuel to be burnt, limbs of the Earth, to be stacked and shaped — and then shipped throughout again. Tons and tons of it all poured across these essential arteries of industry, these perennial pathways of trade.

They drive on into the night spread over the western reaches, flowing as in a pipeline without ceiling under a sky without stars.

(On the coastal stretch opposite Columbia's west, across the titan ocean)... Already at dawn, the fresh glow of pregnant horizons sighed a mollifying warmth, preluding the airless chokehold of heat that was to stuff the remaining hours of the day. The mantle of night overhung the coast yet, nevertheless, as it receded westward before the crawling sun; though its dark cloak was perforated nearly everywhere it floated in those days.

The masked charioteers of cargo-bearing trucks and ships, driving at night, could scarcely see stars if they looked out their windows. City lights, road lights, the lights of the chimaeric vessels, all crowded them. But the stars, in their ebony keep aloft, could see the blazing veins of civilization well. And through the magic of photography and the satellite, human eyes could, already then, see what the heavens saw. These satellites, mechanical fish of the eternal night, scoured the deep as they fluxed, and swam the universal currents of the firmament; drawing in the image of the rounding Earth.

What they saw and showed was worthy of awe.

In the deep void wound the Earth; and the black skin of the land was scarred and inflamed. Incandescent bitumen rivers sprawled and flooded the land. It was crusted with stars; strange stars, tremendous clusters of light breaking out like fissures spilling in lava across the holy face of the Earth; stamping the Earth with the mark of conflagrations. Galaxies of industrial humankind — here was Mammon superimposed over the Earth... Framing, mapping, walling, fracturing the Earth with pulsing roads, grids, lines, borders — a vision of grand cities twitching under the moon, consuming the land. They defied the skies in their dazzle and the soil in their spread; and sought to bleed into all things with their pulsing veins and arteries of wealth and all the bewitching splendor of their glare.

And panning over that mapped Orient, flooded in light — over some of the world's oldest nations, who now revitalized their power in a pact with Mammon — the satellite's eye hovers indifferently over the land of the first civilizations. The lights there are sparser; a great blackness of desert banishing luminous galaxies to the edges, admitting only dim nebulae in its great midst; and twitches of industrial flame. Here lie the blood-drenched fields of the East, where, it is said, History was born. The fields are fertile no longer; the glorious cities of old have long been razed to the barren ground, and craters fill the land. The soil, being so ancient, rests upon layers and layers of the dead, buried by all ages of human history and all the unsung epochs prior. And it was the dead that modern civilizations sought. Those days, gazing ever to the past with hazy eyes, fed upon the deepest, most stygian graves — the earth here, veiling whole oceans of petroleum (that great amalgam of primordial corpses) under its extent, was cause for the wanton murder of millions of its living children. Battle upon battle was waged between the great political and economic powers here, of which the greatest was Columbia. Here, fulgent stars blink fiery, as the colonizing Columbidae and their vassals offer the molten bodies of the primeval dead to the fire — and the machines sing the honors of their living God Mammon.

Somewhere in this region there is a little village, which harbors a very small, very humble graveyard. The satellite cannot see it. It can see nothing in the immense mechanical indifference through which everything it beholds is rendered level and anonymous. There are, however, eyes watching the graveyard from nearer above; cold hovering eyes, close enough to discern individual bodies — and far enough to make them faceless. Here beneath those eyes now, is the facelessness of a hunched figure, kneeling before what could be assumed to be a tombstone.

It is the figure of a mother. Veiled, faint, she weeps discreetly. With the quietude of a modest soul, and the restraint of a working life, the mother grieves for her dearest beloved, her little daughter, gone so young; and hears the air hissing the sibilations of the demon who had killed the child, disturbing the solemn immobility of her mourning. They called that demon a 'drone' — but it, too, was Columbidae. It stirred the atmosphere with its mechanical fins, it respected nothing. The feverish breeze blown from the flame stacks across the desert plain — the sacrilegious temples of Mammon — infuses the sky with infernal colors. The drone, too, whirrs by the force of stygian oil; it spits hellfire, suspended fruit of zaqqum's perverse branch...

The child's magic tree rests near; so does the miraculous wellspring beneath it. The mother didn't know why the drone had struck the child; she would never know. She had no choice but to accept the arbitrariness of that murdering machine, that judge and executor of unjust laws, that death angel of fake sun-gods. She merely prays, praising her God through mantras of adoration and grief. Finally she stands; and leaves, gushing tears among the drowning facelessness underneath her veil.

The child remains. Forever mute, forever unknowable. No elegies will be written for her, and she shall forever remain nameless to the minds of the wider world.

"The path will be long. It will be strenuous. And there will be much stumbling indeed, before we get anywhere. In truth, the path won't be linear.

"Again we must learn from the tree, who grows as it deepens, who forms wings and spreads into the Earth. We cannot journey outward without rooting deep into our selves, and through our selves into all others. In truth we cannot spread the new ideal without embodying it — how could we spread the seeds of the future without becoming fruit of life's tree?

"Trees take long to grow — we must learn from their patience. But there is also little time... O, my kin! this contrast will be the source of much agony and shivering teeth! But we must learn to bear even in that tension, we must learn to be steadfast, we must learn to prevail. In truth we must grow the fortitude to hold, we must grow root in our strength, grow root in our common strength and in each other — as we build ourselves up, and blossom the fruit that is the new world.

"In the same way that the tree grows through the shadow of the canopies to find the fire of sunlight, and through the darkness of the soil to find the water of the deep, so we must grow out of the blinding light of Mammon, as we deepen into the deep reaches of our common selves. And indeed, it will be like roaming the brightest of glooms — but we'll never be lost, so long as we see the destination in ourselves. In truth, we must use *honesty* as our compass — it will demand of us much humility and discipline, much fortitude of spirit. Only by being honest with ourselves can we be clear-eyed in the fog of power — only with honesty can we discern a path beyond Mammon's curtains. We cannot spread the new ideal without embodying it, my kin. But we must learn how to embody it even as we spread it, for time thins — and the Earth's fury mounts before our senses.

"And to those of you who have been long upon the path, I implore you — don't give up!"

Oshana looked round and saw, saw dearly and mournfully through the fire, the glinting of tears pending in the cheeks of her grievous companions; many could not contain their flow and the strength of their emotion, many shook in their sorrows.

"In truth," said Oshana, "we must learn to see the destiny in ourselves as we listen for it along the path. Our work will be long, our wait will be long. We must be suspicious of easy victories... and learn to guess the crouching genies lying beyond their veil. My kin, we must learn from the Earth, to be patient as we seek — so as to not lose ourselves. There will be much that we cannot save — indeed, much will be lost. And there will be many among us who will see the new world inside them, without seeing it outside."

The woman sitting by Oshana, who had lost her daughter to the conflagrations, began to tremble — her jaw stiffened — and the tears began to flow out of her eyes as Oshana seized her shoulder and looked at her with a gaze firm, exuding a primeval strength of being whose force, however, wallowed too in contained tears — in contained anger. Oshana embraced her, and for a while there was no sound but the subdued weeping of the mourners round the flame, the crackling.

"My kin!" clamored Oshana then. "We will need all of those who've gone, still with us on the march. And we will need those who are still to come — we will need many, many. For in truth, we can see the new world if we look deep within ourselves, even individually — but we cannot build that world alone.

"Procreation pleases the senses, and we can imagine as many futures as we wish, at our good leisure. Indeed we must, and we should rejoice in doing it. Life holds many wonders and pleasures, and the pleasure of dreaming awake — is one of the most refined and profound... to find the future in our selves, to find it in one another, should be enjoyable.

"But *creation* — creation requires pain, my kin. Every mother knows it. There is no life without pain, and if we are to beget the future, we too must bear the pains of labor — all that ensures the future takes suffering, and we mustn't shirk away from it."

The drone looped slowly over the graveyard and the village near. It troubled the sleep of its inhabitants with the threat of sudden death, its menacing murmur ripped the quiet of nighttime; it established a tyranny of unpredictable whims, it infused the air with paranoia. It hovered in slow loops, like a spectral nightwatcher; though it was a soulless thing in itself, commanded by the will of a possessing daemon, who looked intently through its eyes of glass from very far away — from across the land, across the blazing coast, across the sunlit ocean, across the heavens and through the orbiting satellites — then back down the shining deep, across the black sea, across the hollowed clay mounts of the Axiac shore and through the palpitating screens of the gloomy military base tucked in its crevices. The parabolic antennas yawned to the skies, gulped the waving signs of the air, and fed them to the eyes behind the eyes of the drone. The operator seating here (whose eyes they were) sat among oracular machines, among seers arranged in circles, over magical crystals; myriad rectangles flashed about their twilit heads. The 'feed' entered their blank and inexpressive stares. Their minds were perfectly fused with the machine. Some felt the deterioration of their souls, and suffered; others felt nothing in the immense numbing of human feeling consuming civilizations. All were compelled to embody the drone, incarnate the angel of death, and murder through the aerial eyes of their mechanical avatars — peering through an undead god's eye view to that abstracted reality of living bodies, as if they were partaking in a simulation; as if they were playing a game. But though the eye of the machine was theirs, the eyes in their heads weren't their own. They had others looking through them — commanding them. Behind them were the image and data analysts who determined whom to kill, and behind them the commanding officer who gave the execution order, and behind him many others... — behind whom gazed one or many generals, behind whom looked the politicians and the president, behind whom were the lobbyists of ArmsCorps and their competing fiefdoms, behind whom were the executives and other masters who made their fortunes from weapons of war, sowers of death — weapons such as the drone hovering above the graveyard and the village, which those executives surveilled and ravaged through politicians and generals and commanding officers down the towering hierarchy through the eyes of the operators sitting in that dim, blinking room, embodying the machine watching the tombstones from above.

They all watched the distant graveyard without emotion.

"We find ourselves upon the most critical of crossroads. Humankind possesses a power that has never before been known. With this power we can fashion from Earth a paradise, and create prosperity for ourselves and all generations to come — or we can plummet into a hell of our making and bring about our own destruction.

"What will it be? My kin, it will depend on what purpose that power is applied towards. It cannot be toward Mammon. The priests and worshipers of Mammon now hold that power — we must take it away from them.

"I see ahead of us horizons vast. I see an undead sun staggering toward one edge, I see the way to it abundantly clear. All of humankind's eyes are pointed in that direction. I see through them. I see well the pit and the putrid fire of that sun upon it — I see our feet walking to its brink. Mammon's priests are urging us onward, onward to the death of that last sun.

"And I see the opposite side in darkness. It's cloaked full of veils, only the moonlight sheds some transparency. Mammon blocks the way with his endless curtains, he wishes us not to see that way — for there, mysterious and half-forsaken, long untrodden and mostly unknown, is the way of the Earth. And through the veils I see the contours of a new world — a human world, a natural world. A world where it is *life* that reigns, where the guiding voice is the Earth's — not Mammon's. And I hear the Earth's voice guiding us there.

"On one side there is life, on the other it is death that awaits. In between there are many gradations and possibilities — there are many bare survivals and half-deaths in between these opposites. There are many paths leading in those directions, and in truth many lead to these in-betweens, where life for some and destruction for others coexist — where death for all drags on a little slower. We must allow it no more, my kin! No more! The destruction of one is the demise of all, for we all are that one. Let us trod the moonlit path, let us pierce the curtains of Mammon, let us follow the voice of the Earth speaking in our intimate bosom.

"The Earth's voice speaks in our souls, my kin. Have you the ears to hear it? There is power in that voice. It is the silence in the noise, the flame in the darkness, the shade in the swelter, it is a strength in desolation, a comfort in our struggle. It is the power of the Spirit, Earth in us — we'll need such powers to fight the might of Mammon.

"It begins with knowing the power in ourselves. It begins with seeking the fire with which to alight the shaded path. We have the power to control that fire — but for this we must respect the fire. Lo — the arrogance of our days is presiding over a conflagration, the illusion of total control veils our senses to the fact that all things are spiraling out of our control.

"Unless our power respects *life*, unless our power respects the *Earth* — for the Earth *is* Life — unless our power respects life and the Earth, it is death that our power will spawn. It is death that human power and foolishness has unburied, it is death that it's spreading, and unless we stop the foolishness of this power all will soon be buried. There will be no humanity to speak of. My kin, I speak the truth when I say that unless we learn to see the sacred in the Earth again we will not be able to see who we are and where we're going. Unless we plant our feet upon the Earth, our heads will be doomed to be submerged by the Earth. Unless we take root upon the Earth, my kin, we will never soar to our highest heights; unless we take root upon the Earth, we will take flight from ourselves, and be lost to the winds, vanished without a trace — the Earth will eat every trace of us, and humankind will be forgotten in the great indifference of passing age."

On the opposite side of the wide circle, beyond the palpitations of the fire, Orenda lowered her head and contemplated, melancholy, her two hands.

"I say 'we', my kin — but you who know me know, that I mean to say humankind and its power, which is not wielded by us," said Oshana. "Mammon commands it — and unless we steer humankind away from Mammon, it is his path and the end of his path that awaits us."

Orenda blinked as she beheld her hands; she felt in her breast the cadences of the air, in her ears the sounds carried by the wind and the void. She mulled with great aches about her eighty brothers and sisters whom the rabid flames had taken. The river kept flowing, the skies kept turning, the trees kept still. In some form, all would keep on. It was they, fragile shapes in the firelight, downtrodden, meek, that stared through blank eyes upon the prospect of annihilation. Oshana's words gave her strength; but she felt in an almost tearful shape of desolation that she was too weak to find any strength of her own, too fearful to seek it in herself, too fearful of finding nothing. It was too difficult, too difficult... The burden was too heavy, the stakes too high. She felt herself but a mere speck before the enormity and the great power of her enemies.

Orenda could find no strength in herself then; yet she followed Oshana's words in her search: "Unless we relearn the holiness of existence, Mammon will prevail. Unless we relearn the sanctity of life, my kin, we will perish. We must know that Earth gives life, Earth sustains life, Earth takes life. Earth is life — She bounds within Herself all things that can be known and lived.

"And there is in truth, my kin, much yet to be known and lived. And unless we want to know the pit beyond which nothing can be known, in which life is no longer — unless we want to live the end of Mammon's way, which is the death of humanity — then we must take the other path. Yet Mammon's path is sunlit and clear — while the other is shrouded in gloom. Here's where we must carry our fires — here's where we must learn to sustain the swelter. Here's where we must learn to sustain the pains and labors of creation.

"What awaits on the other side of this gloom? What awaits on the other side of this uncertainty? What awaits us on the other side of ourselves? In truth, there is much potential in ourselves yet to be aspired.

"My kin!" Oshana clamored then, casting powerfully her voice, lifting her head; supreme, she placed her hands, one burnt, one hale, open on either side of her face. Her expression was set, serious.

There was no mask. "My kin, the future holds the Paradise we've often imagined our pasts to be. Already it exists in the Earth — but we have to create it.

"We must create a society modeled on the new ideal — on the values of kinship, of generosity, of decency, of respect, of solidarity. We must create humane civilizations — and flourish. We must create cities that are in accord with nature and ourselves. Cities that foster communities, where neighbors are like families. It begins in seeing a family in each other, my kin — here, in the bosom of the moment, is where we create the family that will extend to all humankind." Oshana parted her arms away and held them open. "And I tell you that unless we are family to one another, unless we are brethren, we will not succeed.

"Cities that bring people together in harmony — here's what we'll create. Civilizations that grant dignity for the elderly, freedom for the children, purpose for the adults, joy for all — here's what we'll create. We will create cities that are pleasing to the senses and befitting of our common dignity.

"We will create cities made for people and not for machines, as are the megalopolises of our days. In truth, we will have machines — for we will need to measure what we have, so we know how to distribute. But enough with the folly of measuring who we are, my kin. In truth, that cannot be measured.

"No longer will the poet be enemy to the scientist — no longer will the body be enemy of the soul. We will cherish all as sacred, we'll be a society that knows Nature and worships the Earth — a civilization of knowledge and wisdom both.

"Drawing away from Nature was the rulers' biggest folly. They talk about dominating the Earth — in truth, they can't even dominate themselves!" she clamored, widening her arms wider still; her brow tightened, her nostrils flared, her eyes deepened. She beheld the fire, her gaze was fire, there was wrath and compassion in her voice. There was no mask. "Let's not follow these inebriates. They know nothing, they understand nothing, they listen to nothing but their egos, over which Mammon is sovereign complete.

"We will listen, we will know the language of the Earth in our minds and in our souls. The arrogance of civilization over having deciphered some of Her words has exceeded the awe of Her powers, and that arrogance will doom us. We must learn to respect the Earth as humankind. We will recognize that without Her we cannot live, from Her comes our life.

"No one will hunger, no one will be without shelter — the Earth provides for all. There will be croplands for every city. In every square there will be a garden, in every garden a forum. To the extent possible every city ought to be able to support itself, every city should be centered in the Earth — and whenever that isn't possible, we will distribute the surplus of other cities to those in need. There will be none of today's fictional borders between the cities of the Earth.

"In truth, the Earth is abundant enough for all of us to live like *humans*, if we share — but not abundant enough for some of us to live like hoarding gods.

"No longer will the city separate us, no longer will the city entrap us. We'll have cities that bring people together in harmony. There will be *space* — there will be space for ample parks filled with banquets and laughter — there will be space for woods within and without the cities in which to hear silence. There will be space for solitude — no longer will anyone be forced to be lonely.

"There will be *time*. No longer will the imperative for speed be the ruler of our lives. No longer will the chase of profit force us to race against ourselves. No longer will time be defiled, no longer will money be time.

"There will be *life*. We will design our cities with the dignity and sanctity of life and the holiness of the Earth at their core. We will generate cities that are attuned to the rhythms of Nature, and do not impose upon them — cities whose cycles are in accord with Nature's tempo, through which the Earth's songs of peace and fulfillment may be heard — through which Her omens and menaces can be heeded.

"We'll create *Cities of Nature*. We will worship the Earth, we will worship life — for She brings life into being at every moment, every moment is a birth and a wonder. The tree of life will sprout from the very center of such cities, our cities will spread from it — our fruit be abundant. My kin, there will be peace, happiness and fulfillment in these cities. In truth, all these things are within common reach.

"Then, my kin, then we will know humanity."

The child's grave hid a casket without a body. It had been torn apart in the explosion, fragmented in lifeless bits of flesh across the air; and the soul, so spread, lost its life, and vanished in a moment forever... A universe of vitality, of joys and possibilities, of life, gone in a moment! No eye could see it in that unsettling calm of whirring machine and factory pyres afar, no ear could listen it in that ample quiet of unrest, none but the most attuned sensibility — but lo, how the Earth squirms in rage! with the fury of a million maggots suffusing the land and flies swarming in plagues round the branches of the tree and in the darkness of the well; how the Earth quivers, boils in the blood of countless children lodged in Her grievous bosom! From the very surface of the grave She trembles, through the empty tomb She shivers, into Her depths the Spirit flounders, furious, through mountains of soil, through oceans of petroleum and primordial rock, through to the very core of the Earth — a motionless, blazing sphere, as hot as the surface of the sun; round which all things on Earth spin in their progression. All steps upon the soil of existence vibrate toward it; it senses all the little hands tearing ore from rock, all the little fingers hammering machines into being, all the little arms pressing against the great fences of nations, all the toiling souls suffering for the gluttony of a greedy few; all the blasts and the wasted lives upon the surface. All of it is carved into the inner sun; perhaps remembered.

And the Spirit going through it, again through layers of primeval rock, through oceans of primordial graves, through the wealth of the underground, swam out through the grave of Neipas' mother at the bottom of a toxic sea, up which he floated in his dreams. It was dark. Flashes burst in vague palpitations all round him and out of him in his mirroring gaze. Balloons burst in puffs of ash, sprawling and vanishing like trampled sand throughout the deep waters; balloons popping into bubbles that mirrored his hallucinated image, and spoke in the ear of his dreaming mind. From the hollow bangs quivered electric vibrations carrying the choppy voices of his father, fluttering in lacunae... *I*

      don't   ....

         know   ....

           said he,

               I   .....

            don't   .... (There were many

other voices besides,

    some of which

    he knew, most of which he'd   never

heard.)

          know   ....

          ...repeated he.

And there were shreds of plastic all about from the popped balloons, shining in iridescent glows the underwater sunlight... cabinets of drawers, towering stacks of drawers, drawers upon drawers pulsated in and out of view, near and afar in the water; and niches stuffed with feathers... He neared the surface. Flapping his wings leisurely, he approached heavens' vault. It was very bright, very glassy — made of mirror — made of ice. He could see his mother's face photographed into it.

The sun framed her unreal hovering head, like a nimbus. (Yonder there was the impression of the pier among the frothy clouds, upon it spun the vague recollection of the watermill creaking upon the river...) *** Eva floated to the siren song of her beacon. Again her eyes filled with luminosity; it had been, perhaps, the thick gloom of the closet which had drawn her there. Inside the deep wardrobe of her parents — she had entered it to seek the serpent scarf and for a moment she either could not find it or forgot about it — her wirings meshed into the Webwork, her wax face smeared the beaming glass. She flew... In the bright digital temples of titillation she indulged, wavering through feelings of jealousy, amusement, craving — all feeble. Among the motionless seaweeds of her parents' hanging clothes she flew, through their threads into the spreading form of a thousand fragments of herself.

Suddenly she looked up and found her mother's scarf; she wrapped the serpent round her neck, and before she headed to the bedroom to be photographed, she still went to the bathroom where (in that same moment perhaps, or some time later, or before) she contemplated thoughtlessly the misery of a faucet drain swirling toward enigmatic voids and listened to the mumbling water pleading to her as it disappeared down hidden pipes, after she had done her makeup. A tear fell up to the great gape of the sink. Orenda, mirroring her, watched the gaping calamity of the flooded city over the seething land. She perceived the ghostly circular rhythms detaching from the pulsing Belab and the foaming seas over the vibrating Earth quaking in stillness, motionless within the latent chaos. All writhed, driveled in wrath, and screamed in the arcane idioms of the Earth which only the most sensitive ears can understand, which they alone can sense. Orenda listened to it; she felt it... oceanic cascades coursed down her naked cheeks, dropping breathless into the vast silence of the mountain floor. Panicking and about to drown, Neipas' stare swallowed his mother's image on the icy surface of the skies, and imperious currents assailed him as they melted. There were clarions of conches, a great rumble mounting from the depths. The ice cracked; the face of his mother split. (Eva trembled before the sink. Her tear

burst)...

The sun poured unto him in aweful torrents of fire.

****

Neipas awoke.

*

989

"All that ensures the future comes through suffering — this is common knowledge among progenitors, artists, gods and every type of creator. My kin, as the fruit swells in the flower and the child in the womb, so does the future swell in our bosom, and to bear it inside us hurts — the burden is heavy, all too heavy. We will need many to share the burden, to make it light — if we are to take it to the end of the way.

"But it will hurt even more to birth the future, for it will be a process long, full of pangs, full of throes... We cannot beget it alone — nothing can be begotten alone. No one can germinate anything on one's own, not even the mightiest of creators. In truth, even the Earth — needs the Sun.

"We will need many, my kin — in truth we will need all our kin... In truth I tell you, not unless we spread the seeds of the future will we be able to take root across the Earth. They will need to sprout in many — for power resides in many, and even the power that the most powerful *possesses* is the power of the many.

"Not even the most powerful among the powerful holds power on his own. Though in truth, there is still much power yet untapped and still unknown in your innermost — in you, my kin, there live gods. You will need the power of such gods — we will need their strength to spread the seeds of the future.

"It is said that it was by the word that the world was created. Be like the wind, my kin, that spreads that word. Be the voice upon which the imagination of the unborn takes flight. Be the fruit of the future, my kin."

Dawn had by then commenced; night was dissipating into the day's slow wakening. Around her arm Oshana held the mother, whose child was consumed by the flames, whose life was taken by an Earth intoxicated with the greed of blasphemous men, powerful over civilizations; and she bore her tears and her fatigue in her bosom. The other pressed her ear to Oshana's chest; and heard her words pulsing out of her heart. Straight into her own heart, such words were whispered.

"My kin, our voice must be the wind that spreads the seed, the breath that clears the dust from the eyes. But watch that you spread the seed of the new world carefully — watch that you don't throw too much seed at the rock.

"Our tongues must be the flame that reveals the way. Watch that it does not become a conflagration that burns indiscriminately! Let us not drown our light in the chaos of screams.

"Our hearts must be living founts. We must be the wellspring of each other's strength, in each other we must be able to satiate our thirsts. We must each be the common fount, whence all others spring, whence all others bloom.

"Our souls must be one Spirit, the Spirit of the Earth that gives life. Let the Spirit fill you abundantly and spill with the force of your waters, the brightness of your flame, the softness of your breath.

"My kin! We will need many, many — yet we should not herd anybody. We must resist the temptation to fish people. In truth, many are today snared in nets, uprooted from the oceans of their spirit, confused, looking in all directions at once. They see the world in fragments, their own souls are sliced by the mesh. We ought rather to want to care for people the way the good tiller cares for the land.

"We must show them the path, and have them come along with us, walk it with us. We must teach them to see the sacred in the Earth. Their soil is ready, in truth. Many feel barren, they long for the seed that will make their lives sprout, they long for the world to enter their lives and waken their slumbers, they long for the air to fill their lungs and resurrect them from their living deaths. The time will soon come for us to sow, my kin, it has been coming again and again, in our confused days without season — and when it does come, *we* must be ready.

"But indeed, we should not be tempted into herding or fishing people. We should not be tempted into reducing people, so they are more docile — we need to foster ears and understandings, not blindness and the nodding of open mouths. And much less should we be tempted into violence, my kin — not only because it won't work, but also because it defiles our purpose and our destiny. We must be who we aspire to be.

"Beware of those who speak the words I speak, words of the new ideal, to wage war or cause suffering upon others. For words are malleable, and one can shape them to different meanings. We must remain moored to the Earth even as we walk — we must be moored to reality. Watch that abstractions lead you toward reality, and never complicate what is simple, or simplify what is complex. Violence is intolerable — it's as simple as this. It's an abomination. We shall not seek it.

"Great injustices were done to us, and within us there is great ire. My own breast nurtures heavy furies. It can't be helped. It is well. Anger lends strength, and anger is a force we must tame — so we can use it. Not toward vengeance, for revenge is lowly and the impulse of the weak, it defiles the memory of our departed kin. We must rather seize the strength of anger to achieve our destiny, and honor our departed kin. It is by honoring life that we honor the dead, and in truth we bring dishonor to the dead whenever we wish to multiply their death. In truth, we must make life flourish so the dead finally stop dying."

Oshana leaned her forehead against the forehead of the grievous mother at her side, whom she embraced with compassion; and she placed her hand upon her bosom, and whispered a word that only the mother heard, as the others watched, as the others wept along. "Courage, courage!" she then said to all. And seizing the hand of the grieving woman, the shaking hand of that orphan of her lineage, widow of her legacy, Oshana raised it to the sky yawning in clearing hues, as the eyelid of the Earth opened languidly toward the Sun — and in a wild clamor she spoke "Honor to the dead! Justice to the living!" through the powerful boom of her powerful voice, and a myriad clamors arose to echo her own, a myriad tears gushed round the fire. Fingers were lifted to brows and hands raised to the heavens and arms pressed round shivering shoulders, there were sobbing prayers and a myriad utterances of grief. Oshana remained with visage set, straining in its sorrowful expression, breathless in her strength.

There was no mask covering her face. And when the cries of the circle subsided, she retook the word once more, and said, "Bloodlust will not guide us. In truth — don't let it shock you, my kin — but even the Wechuge, those blood eaters — even the powerful of today will join us in our pilgrimage to the new world — for they too, are human, possessed as they are with the spirit of Mammon — even they need saving from their own foolishness and inequity. They too will be liberated. But they will be the last — we will not bend to their will. Not until they are cleansed of Mammon and healed of their greed can they partake in the pleasures of Paradise, which are far profounder and far more joyful than that filth they call 'success'. We will make bloom the humanity in these living zombies. We will make them human at last, we will make them see life.

"And no longer will we live under the whims of death merchants! My kin, we need a civilization that embodies new ideals, and we need ideals which affirm life — even in its sorrows. For life bears pain, it is true. Life begins with pain, and the very prospect of its ending is painful. But there are pains that are manufactured and cruel, pains born of the wiles of powerful men and their greed. To those who are restrained to enjoy life — by artifice or nature — we help. If one is oppressed by human power, we all are oppressed. For in truth, we are not simply ourselves." In the firmament above, the dawn was blooming into morning; in the valley below, the river flowered with dawn's gentle flow.

"Let your life be defined by the will to live, and not by the fear of death — natural as that fear might be, let it not possess you. It is a natural and necessary fear, for life contains all that can be known — and whatever lies beyond life is unknowable. Before the unknowable, it is well to be fearful — it is still better to also be in awe, and in reverence. Before the unknowable, it is still best to also be *strong*. And in you resides — hidden or apparent, ebbing or flowing, unknown or otherwise — there resides the strength of gods, my kin."

Then Oshana laid one hand spread upon the ground and leaned forward, her other hand gripping the hand of the ailing mother still; fiercely she arched toward the fire, and her eyes widened and seemed to blaze. Very open, her gaze seemed to see nothing, it seemed to transcend sight in its shimmer, as in a profound mystical trance; and her utterance, upon emerging from her trance, was deeper than usual, resounding from all sides as though the wind and the wood moved with her voice. Through her uncovered lips she spoke softly, and for moments the silence was absolute round her maskless words.

"Lo..." spoke Oshana. "Will to live — the *will to love life and to give life* — that is the supreme instinct. The will to power, the will to meaning — all these are the same, all manifestations of the same principle.

"Let us walk by the force of our will, my kin. Let us walk by the force of our strength. Let us walk by the force of humankind's purpose, let's be humanity at last!" her voice rising in volume, rising to a thunderous pitch, Oshana spoke now with the ecstasy of rapture. The sky had cleared and the fire palpitated in the colors of dawn; the sun was about to rise — and it was as though the world boomed with the vibrations of her tongue.

"Honor to the dead, glory to the living! Let us vanquish death my kin, let us establish the kingdom of Life upon this Earth!" leaning forward still more and pressing harder upon the ground with her one burnt hand, Oshana then, with wonderful suppleness, sprung to her feet and stood upright, and moved in spirited gestures as she said "Come! Rise!" and all around the circle stood on its feet, at varied speeds and various degrees of power and debility, hands of the stronger lifting the bodies of the meeker, all rising in strength together. "Be the waters of the Earth, be the winds of the Earth, be the fire! Let's set upon the journey, let us vanquish Mammon!"

And there was great uproar and emotion round the bonfire. "No more hunger! No more destitution! No more war! No more hopelessness!

"No more! No more! No more! Let humankind fulfill its destiny!

"Paradise is upon the Earth. We've only to seize it! Come!

"Let us walk, my kin! Claim human destiny at last!"

Here and there all arose, amid cries of song, amid chants praising the Earth and praising the Sun as one revolved and the other rose, filling them with light and the breath of life — the woods inhaled with glow — as the day was born, and they fell all to singing and dancing together in an ecstasy of mournful and cathartic and exultant feeling; they danced the circle and praised the fire which their eyes beheld reverently and praised the soil their feet touched reverently. They danced round Oshana, the clamors around her grew. Among them was Orenda, emerging yet from her hesitation and despondency, caught up by the swooping rapture of her brethren; motionless among the motion, she beheld the horizon with lingering difficulty, but with the newfound hope that the words made sprout from her — her strength would flow back, she knew, she knew.

A memory of the first time they had stood together over this valley came to Orenda as she contemplated with much feeling the Earth about her. It gave her courage. Slowly, slowly, slowly — she realized wonder. After all, if life was possible — what was impossible? And gazing tearfully upon her aunt, her mother, her devoted Oshana, she smiled.

Oshana, Oshana... She wore no mask. The sun beamed soft, breathed light unto her — and tears flowed in glistening runnels down the cheek of her mighty visage.

A freshness of dawn permeated the jade sea. The immense extending swath of saltwater glimmered with dabs of ruby, like ethereal mirages of rolling hills crowned in jewels. The air was nevertheless motionless, unstirred but for the tepid sighs of the sea upon the sand; not a peep otherwise to be discerned in the whole extension of the coast. There was no one there. The shore was shattered in a chaos of splinters, beams, twisted metals and broken seashells — the beach made a fragmented soil of shards, grains, debris, dead fish...

The glare of Belab's Pearl vanished.

Over the towering mountains of the east had peeked the morning light, covering warmly the dazed megalopolis in its tremendous quietude. It found the wreckage of a great city. Axiac's once-triumphant roads seemed to have been clawed by terrible fingers which, by their apocalyptic power, revealed the underbelly of their asphalt surface; much was upturned in sludge, from which cattle-masked workers extracted lifeless bodies, staggering between bits of glass and jarring blocks of concrete — and morticians with long pelican noses and black mantles blessed with gestures the maskless dead, all across the zigzagging extent of the straight ways. The whole megalopolis yawned thus to the carmine-brushed sky; as if swooning from a vicious gash, attacked by an unexpected wild beast. Wounded, the city mumbled softly and pleaded to the rising sun; cries emerged from its great anonymous mass of private pains. There was much weeping and suffering untold among the living; and though the tempest had gone its clouds would forever fog the blameless spirits of all who had witnessed its fury. Yet nothing attained the perfectly silent beach.

Much of Axiac's shattered remnants had been dragged in mud to the mulched coast; the pier lay strewn about the sands, the huge wheel half-submerged. Multitudes of things — clothes, furniture, doors, random appliances, even cars were to be found here — crowded the seaside. The sand resembled a stranded field of rubble in havoc's aftermath, smothered by the sheer profusion of nondescript stuff, its purity maculated.

No footprints marked its surface now.

Nothing chronicled the presence of humanity upon the shore but for the ruins of its works.

The sun rose behind Orenda; it shone soft through the dew and fog of the mountain wood. She looked back at the mists glowing gold; she looked back to the first time she had stood over that valley, Oshana at her side. Her eyes filled with the gentle sunlight.

"My niece," Oshana said to her, speaking in their language, in the language of the land from which they had been exiled. "My precious Orenda."

Overlooking the valley, the sun sprouted tender in Oshana's glare. Little Orenda looked up at her as she spoke. "All of this," she said, "is alive. All of it sacred."

Little Orenda asked — she too in the dialect of their distant valley, so tragically dispossessed of speakers — "What is sacred?"

"Everything that embodies the divinity is sacred," replied Oshana. "The sacred is a passage, and a mirror. Through it you can reach the farthest beyond and the deepest innermost. Through it you can reach the divinity within you.

"The Sun is sacred. The Earth is sacred. Life is sacred." The sunshine of yawning morn, peeking from the other end of the valley, bloomed sidelong upon Oshana's eyes; the river beneath them sparkled and blazed, all the verdant slopes of the mountain gaped in glorious color.

Oshana said still: "A life is a universe — a fragile universe of infinite extent, containing endless other universes of infinite reflections. Life is a wonder. A miracle, a miracle...

"Look, Orenda — all things in our eyes — it's all alive." And little Orenda, opening her mouth wide with much surprise, grasping in her innocent mind the tremendous significance of what she was told, immediately discerned the existence of an infinitude of universes filling every inch of the vastness around her.

"The Earth lives..." So Oshana told — she wore no mask.

Hers was a human countenance.

Her face radiated light.

*

Night's thick shadow grew lighter, retreating toward the hills of the east as the sun bloomed upon the mountaintops. Orenda was no longer there.

On the opposite side of the basin, the ocean, growing bluer, tugged at the detritus along the coastline, swinging back and forth, back and forth, gently as if tired after a great exertion and already in the womb of sleep; the waters swung calmly, as had swung the waters inside the tray held by Neipas' hands a few days before the storm, in the darkroom.

The darkroom rested in the basement of the Ivory Tower. Neipas had gone there after visiting Orenda at her porch; later, he would look for Oshana at the campus-side bookshop and find her already gone. Under him lay a large sheet of photo-paper, on which the contours of an image were emerging in the motion of the waters. He had subjected it to the gaze of an enlarger, pressing invisibly upon it the writings of light cast from the film. The yet-unborn picture lodged waiting in the tiny silver crystals coating the paper; and materialized, as if by magic, when bathed in the water.

Neipas stood over it in the crimson-lit darkroom, oscillating the tray with one hand, handling the print with the other's pincers, as solemn as a cleric in the act of baptism. Thoughts buoyed vacuously in his head — all manner of trifles journeyed across his mind, vague remembrances and perennial worries, as, for instance, how expensive the huge paper had been — but none touched his soul, he cared for nothing in the immersing mystique of the place. He beheld, carefully, his Eva emerging.

Caustic red lights upon Eva's photo divided her in luscious bits. There she was: propped royally between feathery pillows, amid rose petals — reposed triumphantly in the imitation of opulence, painted from the monochrome brushes of immemorial beauty, masked with the mask of divinity exposed, astonishing, irresistible, transcendent, supreme. The very background seemed to melt of its own in silently fervent grain. The very sight of her hip, emerging in a voluptuous curve of lustrous skin, bathed in the white glow of the white-and-black print, made his chest flutter; the hinted salience of her breast underneath the scarf, and her peeping cleavage, was enough to rouse his lust. Wavy locks of hair framed deliciously the plumage of her chiseled face; a strand of it crossed her pouting, slightly opened beak in the most attracting manner. Her stare seemed to glint even in its motionlessness, imperiously beautiful over the coiled serpent...

The photograph was perfect; it matched the perfection with which Neipas had first idealized her... and made him, for a moment, love her again (for the first time). It was so lifelike as to be uncanny. It was a copied Eva — a small sprite, a little self. Perhaps it was its size, or the sharpness of its definition. But it was the character of mystery with which Neipas had first gazed her figure, as well as the blunt sincerity of the photograph, that were most prominent among his initial impressions; as if this were the true icon of her veiled self, the symbol to correspond with the essence of Eva. It was, in fact, a true Eva — Eva in truth manifested.

For a moment, he considered it to be his masterpiece. And as he stood over the photograph ruminating, staring over the lifelike eyes staring up to him, he felt that he discerned a profound secret being revealed to him, something of Eva made clear as the waters were clear under the light. Neipas couldn't articulate it to himself; but her eyes spoke it to him in the wordless dialect of human gesture. Her eyes told him that, far more than merely being seen, she wanted to be *guessed*; thought about, mulled over. The face was a canvas, and like a canvas, it was an enigma suggesting the desire to reveal itself in the splendorous infinitude of its complexities.

He found Eva before the dressing table, with the mirror risen in the horizon of her cosmetics — her own particular shrine. She received the gift with tremendous bliss, as the idol of a goddess coming to bless her victories and quell her unrests. She stared at the photograph with an immense smile, a smile sincerely elated. And in her eyes was the emotion of a sweet revelation too, as that of a true icon unveiling — to the deep reflection of a faithfully watching devotee — the magic mysteries behind its gaze. Neipas watched her happiness and her admiration of his work — the Eva in the paper, the Eva of his make — with a feeling of joy profound.

She would tell him she was pregnant the very next day; in that same day she would swallow the abortion pill, and a week later he would step into the Anubel —

A few days before that, however, Neipas had woken from unsettling dreams.

It was with a slight twitch that he came to. Eva lay upon his chest no more, but her back was turned to him. Peeking over her slightly, he saw, without seeing her face, that she slept; the *I* lay flat upon the palm of her hand, yet lit.

Dawn stole upon the window glass; it was still very early and he didn't have to work that day. For a while he wondered in the throes of drowsy insomnia, in a sort of a sleep-deprived fugue. For indeed, he felt like he had slept little, as though he had somehow toiled through the night; and for a while imagined that he was still working nightshifts in the Belab's underground slaughterhouses. A type of latent agony leadened his heart and made it beat suspended, hard, struggling. Fragmented thoughts broke upon his mind; about how he longed to live a better life, how he longed to live without worry, how he longed to live free, how he longed sometimes to escape his own head.

How he longed to live! (and at the thought of this a suppressed sob quivered upon his nostrils). He thought that perhaps the Eagles' Nest would be the solution to his ails somehow; he thought this without reflection, and thinking this he finally succumbed to dreamless slumber.

*

Outside Eva's window (which she used to shut because she feared bugs would crawl and fly in), the fig tree shed the moonlight from its tangled boughs and its scattered roots. Its trunk was soaked; its leaves strewn. All year it had spread full of such leaves and it bore their weight — yet nothing flowered upon its branches all year. It gave no fruit.

III

BOOK OF FACES

A vast flock of birds flies across a grainy monochromatic sky and into a giant net. The web tightens in a single pull; eyes sewn shut tremble over a hushed beak, over paws strapped to a stool. "And that's how the passenger pigeon became —" a digital voice was speaking over the image; it was abruptly cut off by the blackness lidding the frantic wings.

Upon the darkness of the glass appeared a mask. In the darkness underneath it, nothing was felt; emptiness filled it.

The face lifted blindly toward the window.

73 - Hall of Lights (Nexus)

The Bull shut the door behind him, and when Neipas turned, the door was no longer there.

Neipas beheld his hand through the two refracting layers of plastic and the laving water they enclosed. The bottle was all he had been given. There was no food, no sustenance; no avail. He was on his own in that immense hollow, site of his imprisonment, knowing not what would happen, having not a clue, not a hint, as to what his fate would be. He had no idea as to whether the Gardener's intent was to make him wait in torment or make him languish and die before he got him out of that place. The angst of uncertainty seized him from the very start.

The Bull had shut the door behind him; and by the moment Neipas turned, the door was no longer there.

It had somehow vanished in the vast emptiness of the place in which he was now being held. Before him stretched an indefinite uniformity of colorless spacelessness; an unreal, featureless void. It was as if he had been swallowed by a strange light that suffused everything but didn't burn; it must've been everywhere for he could see himself (his torso, his arms, his legs) in it — and yet there was no shadow. It confounded his glare at once his eyes blotched into it. Suddenly all points of reference were lost. Directions were confused; it was impossible to distinguish, in the glaring blankness of it, whether it all ended an inch from his face or continued forever; it was impossible to tell whether the ground was level, or slanted, or dropped to an indefinite infinitude.

It was quite hot in that strange prison of boundless nothing; so Neipas eventually removed his woolen jacket, which Eva had (so long ago now, in what seemed to be a different life now) bought him; and in doing this he felt a stiffer shape inside the fabric. He looked in its inner breast-pocket... — and he found the little black notebook which Orenda had offered him in her porch, the morning after the protest. Its white pages were as white and devoid of ink as they had been the moment they were presented to him. Half the pages were still missing — half the pages were hers.

He nodded in an empty, slow gesture of recognition, as though contemplating a photograph from long ago... And he placed the pages on the side, notebook atop the jacket.

There were moments he felt like writing in the notebook, to take his mind off the boredom, the disquiet, the uncertainty and the heat, the gnawing of anxiety. [But he had no pen and] All he could do was walk around, which he did, in many circles. He wasted away slowly. Gradually it got too hot and he was damped in sweat under his shirt, so he took it off; then under his trousers and his socks, so he took the trousers, the shoes, and the socks off, and placed them all in a heap by the jacket and the notebook. He walked in circles, his naked feet flapping almost soundlessly on the warm floor.

Neipas beheld his hand.

(There was goo under his nails). Its fingers were outstretched, the skin tightly wrapped round the flesh. Rugged lines cleaved across the surface of the palm; the surface resembled bark, the lines like tree rings, cleaves expanding from a core lying silent in the beginnings of the universe; a galaxy within galaxies, inheritance of all life. It was a human hand, his — perennial tool of the human soul. Twitchy gestures of his fingers recollected the feel and weight of — what? A camera...? In his heart twitched snaps, murmurs of past moments vaguely recollected. Gradually his fingers, as though shriveling, involuntarily closed upon themselves. They no longer possessed strength; the phantom weight of unending dishes bore upon their contracting palm. He contemplated his hands both. Were these the tools of *his* soul? Were they his own?

They clawed like spiders into the muscle of his heart. How long had it been now? (*Neipas asked himself, in the pit of his breast*)

After a long spell of thirst Neipas drank the water angrily; bubbles ascended to the upturned bottom of the bottle with a fury that mirrored the water's growing rage down Neipas' throat; and the rage became such that the plastic burst as the flush sped and gushed into him in an overwhelming torrent that bloated and choked him —

(he woke up with a start)

Fingers found his face besmirched with sweated wax and tear-drenched feathers.

To satisfy his bodily necessities he would travel a good few paces away, taking different directions every time — taking care to not lose sight of his belongings in that neverending nothingness — so that after some indeterminate time there formed a wide circle of filth, by which he was eventually besieged. Somehow he didn't dare — as if the ring was magical —

to cross it and thenceforth he walked only between the heap of his clothes and the wheel of his waste. He wheeled round and round and spun himself onto the floor (which he was often not sure it really existed) and spread himself lying down before he found that he was, in fact, standing. Which was ceiling and which was floor if one could discern neither (*mulled Neipas from the chinks of his pouring frown*) ? The slowness of perception, weakness of body, languishing of vitality, the entrapment in a prolonged, odd sort of anxiety — the hunger made it impossible to think. Everything seemed to pulse and twitch in his body and everything outside of him was so unbearably still.

Often (?) he would break the circular trek and return to his clothes to search his trouser's pocket for his *I* (there was a single large key there; he no longer remembered where he got it from). Perhaps he wanted to check the time; but the concept of time seemed like a mistake and a folly in that barren, featureless nonplace.

He laughed and yelled for the sheer sake of dispelling his gathering fears away — for the most part, he couldn't help but feel, to obsess over the idea that death could take him suddenly at any moment. He had to keep moving lest life spirited away from his body. Relentlessly on the verge of dying, Neipas thus strained and suffered. Motion was the only continued assurance of existence here (his body too was still visible under his yet-open eyes).

To whose volition did his fingers belong?

It struck him hazily then that power means the reach of one's grasp. But to where he could fly? There was nothing in the distance because there were no distances (space had been abolished,

lights glinted on the plastic's surface as it rounded; the liquid shone crystalline for a moment. There was something about the packaging that inspired confidence, suggesting the purity of the insulated product inside)

He walked in circles upon circles upon circles upon circles (round his clothes). There were times he would have liked to write in the notebook, but he had no pen. Sometimes he laid face torso and legs on the floor.

Neipas' mind spiraled slowly into madness... It had already been (at least perhaps) a couple of days without eating, and longer than that without a proper meal. The spells of dizziness stretched longer and were becoming almost constant, consuming his existence; a bilious feeling of bubbling vomit munched acidly in the base of his throat and a slurping ache drained his brain from the core of his skull. The lack of showering made him feel itchy. And the itch bit and tore at his skin like a million little teeth, ants, spiders scratching the surface and undersurface of it and Neipas became desperate to kill it; and with his nails he stabbed and gashed and gored his skin everywhere, even under the dense feathers and wax of his face. And he bled, and his skin became irritated and even more itchy and biting. Neipas started doing little hopping dances and laughing hysterically, casting his booming voice into the inscrutable horizons, and — he would stop and thrust forward his head with bulging eyes and peeled ears — trying to hear an echo; but none came. Nothing answered him, nothing but the incessant nothingness, and he was all alone.

As he awoke panting he noticed his legs sprinting back and forth. He had once beheld verdant pastures which seemed to him neverending. The wind blew against his running joy and he laughed, laughed with the air of flowers in his lungs, with the voice of a child free. ... But here, it was windless. There was no reference. Nothing moved, for nothing was.

Eventually it became so hot as to become clammy even under his underwear, which he took off in a frantic movement full of ants, and hurled it with a yell somewhere afar (the fabric stretched horribly into — blending itself into — what seemed to a shaft of infinite proportion, reaching into a horizon without depth) He kept on walking round in circles upon circles upon circles upon circles upon circles upon circles upon circles upon circles and scratching his face madly, convulsively, trying to dig bloody into the core of his brains; in a sudden fit he tore away handfuls of his feathers, provoking explosions of pain in his head and his face so excruciating that it made him stop (!) — though it relieved his itch in the moment, the itch only returned in force to torture him along with the agony of his wounds. He sat, trembling and weeping uncontrollably. A sudden burst of itching in his head piercing through all other sensations, Neipas plucked out a single feather of it in grunting and slobbering frustration. A pang of hurt punched into his brain (flowing furiously upon him and ebbing numb and nauseating in his dizziness); the shaft had [been?] penetrated so far deep into the essence of his being as to become a part of it, and it tore part of it away as it was yanked out bleeding.

But a lethargy overcame Neipas. His body slackened, and the physical pain seemed relieved by a sort of spreading anesthesia. A long sigh released from his chapped lips — he closed his eyes.

Swaddled in his jacket he found a lump of flesh and skin; horrified, buggy-eyed, Neipas inhaled with mouth wide open and muttered through his nostrils his bewildered dismay. It was a baby.

It bore an uncanny resemblance to Martin — but this was not the bubbly newborn, so full of life's wonder, that he remembered. Its eyes, barely ever opened, were already glassy. Its mouth stammered, unable to cry out. Its malformed little visage swayed from side to side and it appeared to be unable to breathe. Enormous abscesses burgeoned from the tumorous body, whose heads looked bloated and intensely hued on one side, and withered and strangely discolored on the other. Ash covered its body.

(for a long time he stared...) in the dismal, barren slowness of perception, a pervasive weakness of body, a languishing mind, unable to think. He was all entrapped in an odd anxiety. He was hungry. He stared.

There it was, writhing amidst the wool.

After opening his eyes (after much time indeterminate), Neipas observed the feather he had torn from his head. It was a long, plump shaft of protruding and lustrous plume; at the tip of the shaft his blood dripped, oozed out viscous, dense, and black. By and by, almost unconsciously, he picked up the notebook, and leant the tip of the feather against it. His dripping blood blotted the page thick. And Neipas made with it letters, and shaped it into words, and wrote. He wrote here and there, he wrote his soul black onto the white pages of Orenda's notebook. And it calmed him down — though he tired of it sometimes, and he jumped up in a frenzy, and hopped about in a crazy dance of convulsions and shouts thrown into the distances of the vast prison, expecting vaguely to hear an echo; but none came. Sometimes he walked away from his clothes (he had lost the fear of his feces and stepped over the stenching circle of his waste) trying to find the edge of the prison — there was no edge — it was boundless. He yelled, but no answer came. He wrote in the absolute loneliness of his imprisonment. He kept writing, and he kept calling and shouting and crying; he wrote, which too was a calling, it too was a shouting; he cried also through his letters (after long treks he would invariably return to his heap of clothes which were his center, but he kept naked)...

But one day he shouted for so long that the veins of his neck and the nerves of his brain came to the brink of bursting. He tumbled back, overcome by dizziness; and he thought he heard something then, thin. He heard something. Yes — he heard something... He heard an echo, there was an echo. Neipas wrote about it amid pangs of heart and physical pain. He could sense his own acrid stench, the layers of soot upon his teeth were hard under his tongue.

And one day he saw something — way, way in the distance. He wrote, and he no longer hopped in delirium; he watched that something with narrow wide eyes and tense brows...

One day he walked toward it.

*

```
I realized something.
I realized that the mask, unless it's destroyed, cannot be
glued off from the face.
```

```
Earlier I tried to scream for help, but the scream never
even left my body. Instead it went inside and rippled all over.
I think I heard many things crack.
```

```
lol    now I'm lying down
```

```
What was I even thinking? I knew that plenty of people
would yell their concern but no one would actually come.
```

```
Is that someone there?
```

```
I think I'm seeing things. There's nothing around me, but
still I swear I saw something out there. I don't know what, but
it's something very far
```

```
I feel weak hungry
```

BOOK OF FACES

|||||||||||||||||||||||||||||||||||||||||||||||||||||||||||||||||||||||
|||||||||||||||||||||||||||||||||||||||| **[random drawings and
doodles and shapes, masks?]**

Eva

Or__

Just now I walked for a long long time in the direction of
that something but still its not getting closer

I'm worried that it's something in my eyes

I can see nothing around me and to make sure I'm not blind
I stare at my hands for hours and I write here

Goerhtuigtriu

Neipas Neipas Neipas Neipas Neipas Neipas is my name Neipas
Neipas Neipas Neipas Neipas Neipas Neipas Neipas Neipas Neipas

What if this something starts filling up my eyes?

Because if everything else is lights, this must contrast
with it if I can see it so it must be dark.

~~ness so what if it fills my eyes and I become blind?~~ maybe
I'm already

I was lying down on the ground. A psychedelic bug crawled
over my hand. A scarab (I think that's what they're called). It
was

[scribbles]

It was was shimmering with ~~strange~~ colors. ~~Like it was made of heatwaves or like a gem.~~ The bug crawled away in this emptiness, in the direction of that something over there. I've been following it for days. Maybe for years. WHo knows. I lost all sense of time. How long had I been here? I miss —— **[scrawlings]** ? ? ? ?

I kept walking. I swear to god I jumped out of my skin when I felt something hit my face like a cloth or a spider web or something. I can't see it. I sat here.

~~My father.~~

He's here. My father is here standing.

I walked a little more, now he's ~~sitting in front of me~~ (I sat down again) sitting in front in front of me. I passed cloth after cloth after cloth afer and here I see him. But he's covered in tar and feathers.

A while ago he opened his beak, and inside it a glistening dark maw

I feel like I'm fighting my way through falling trees   leaves everywhere

His voice is touching my face and somehow it's my mother's breath that I hear. It feels like a type riverside breeze I hadn't felt since I died that day. I don't think I ever really lived again **[teardrop blotching the ink, blotches some of words on either side, so it reads 'lived ag   ther's**

body was buried......] my mother's body was buried and so was
my father's soul,   maybe I was too. I didn't have the chance
to be born **[last sentence coils and descends obliquely, c a r e e n s]**

    I write this for the past. there's no more future for me
here.   all   my   children   are   born   poisoned

    is that someone there? SPEAK AND ILL FOLLOW

a
    broken
        mirror.   A pigeon

The mask gazed inside too   and it pecked into my heart

*

He sat for a very long time.
The sitting spanned the passing of millennia, stretching into the past and into the future.
And when he rose, time stopped and coalesced into the present, in the anticipating manner of an implosion.
He reached**[s]** his hand for the veil.
He touched**[s]** it.

Beyond the veil he sees me/you — much closer now.

But there was yet another veil before you/me, and another veil and still another. And he had to pass through many veils before he reached me/you.

And every time he swung open the invisible cloak you/I was/were suddenly closer

(as though) he peered into the mystery of life, made dense by the conjugation of many soft veils.

Until he was here.

And he saw I/you were/was himself, or the same as himself.

He recognized himself in the reflected figure standing before him. Though you/I looked different.

I/you had the plump face of a pigeon, a visage emanating luster

and the body of a [human being], fully feathered.

You/I bore mighty wings beside the torso.

I/you replicate**[d]** his movements. As he reaches**[d]** his hand toward me/you, so do**[id]** you/I toward him — until we touch**[ed]** hands.

Our fingers penetrate the chasms between fingers.

He pressed forth and found, it opened.

He stood facing a shape of black, such as a chasm of unknown depths. Round him, expanding to the infinitude of the very last confines of existence, an emptiness of white and nothing else.

And somewhere in it was him.

And before him, the gate to the chasm.

He saw nothing but nothing in the abyss. And yet there was the vestige of all things. He listened to it in the whisperings and breathings emanating from it.

He sat contemplating it. And again the sitting spanned millennia, stretching into the future and into the past.

Until again he rose, and entered.

(...)

You had been following the distant echo of your own scream, and at last you found it.

You swallowed your voice. "What's this?" you said inward.

Glass stood before you.

Was it a mirror? (in the other side you were). Was it a window? (in the other side your father — your mother? — both were; and...)

You touched the glass, you pressed it with your finger, it cracked under your skin. Light shone tepid from the broken surface; your reflection broke into multiple disfigurements and slight gradations of distance. There was dissonance between you and your reflection, it didn't accord with your motions (there were slight gradations of moment).

"Hello?" you uttered, and you heard yourself speak as if in a dream; it seemed to you enormously uncanny to see, in the reflecting glass opposite, those lips open and close, the cheeks alongside lifting and dimpling, that jaw extending and contracting along the motions of your own voice; the expression in it involuntarily formed into a gesture of disgust and bewilderment.

The light grew in intensity, the glass shards multiplied, your fragments drew farther apart. Your finger kept pressing the shattering finger. Your eye, nearing the surface, saw in itself the consistency of ash waltzing round the iris. Perfectly reflected, you saw in the shrinking pupil the whole earth uplift in a great blooming of fumes and fire. And a paralyzing fear overcame you, choked your muscles, squeezed your bones; and your mouth, opening very widely, let emerge the flesh of your throat in its soundless agony. The light flashed and blazed so that it swallowed your naked shape. The iris contracted in haste.

The pupil split.

It grew to envelop all things (the light was inhaled by the eye).

(...)

We walked in the darkness. Our feet touched no ground; and our eyes saw nothing. We concluded that we mustn't have feet nor eyes any longer, for even when we beheld our hands we could no longer discern them. We were without a body. Nor were we with a mind. It was a journey of sensation, a pilgrimage beyond the mind. All thoughts had been held, and we were now transcending reflection; to a realm of spirit, and a dimension of silence. In the course of our walkless trek we perceived being inside a cave, the walls of which, separated from us by boundless distances in the beginning, neared and closed upon us as we advanced; or perhaps it was that we hadn't advanced in the slightest, and had been still all along; and the walls themselves moved toward us. We began to sense a dampness in the airless space, and as we realized the pace of our own breath we regained slowly a sense of our bodies. With our hand we touched the wet wall, of warm, rugged flesh. It led us forth to a door, which we opened.

It creaked with the sound of ages — and we stepped out into a flood of light.

[Before us] We saw a vision of the ample sky enormous above us. The heavens possessed a milky white color, and they were mirrored perfectly in the waters expanding just a step from our feet. The surface of the waters was perfectly still; not a rustle, not a stir affected it in the whole entirety of its cosmic magnitude. We stood on an islet, from which these waters propagated to infinity. Behind us rose the mill of childhood, from whose door we had come, and whose wheel was motionless. Before our feet moored a boat. A duck poised upon one paw at the bow, and whereas its body faced the distance, its enigmatic head turned backward toward us; its eyes were closed, the chin tucked in fluff, motionless. Afar, very, very far away in the most distant of horizons, the tree of ash reared its canopy against the milky hue of the skies, its fumes, as all else, stilled. There was not a sound. Even the shifting of our feet in the sand begot nothing. All was quiet. We pushed the boat onto the waters, perturbing its absolute peacefulness. The duck flew. Small ripples spread from the wooden flanks of the boat and dissipated only beyond the range of our perception. We stepped in and gripped the oars at either side, and rowed. Slowly, we rowed. The surface of the water was transformed into a giant rippling mantle in the airless and silent universe. Looking over the side we saw our own visage[s?] distorted in the motion, and the reflection of the heavens defaced and misunderstood. The wheel aside the cabin began spinning with the movement of the waters as we rowed farther and farther under the ample dome of sky. All concentric was the seascape, and nothing arose under the heavens save for the influx, the islet, the mill, the ashen tree at the end of things, and ourselves. Eons might have passed. We hadn't the conscience of whether we traversed forward or backward in time, or even if we were still within time or ever were. All things were called into doubt as the waters were shaped anew. But a gradual realization came upon us then, and at once it struck us that we weren't oaring away from the islet at all; yet simultaneously the acrid and heavy breath of the fumes had neared us. The tree of ash was upon us, and we were upon its roots. As we entered the stuffiness of its dust we wondered whether the tree had propagated its size to engulf us; or whether we had pulled it to us by the motion of the sea.

And all at once our thoughts returned to our minds and we gained a greater sense of our bodies. Time compressed back into the present.

Ash coated the air and made it thick with toxin, spread wide by the action of a foul, persistent wind. The sky and everything under it was tainted with a deep and dark red, the color of blood coagulating into gashes of menacing cloud. The noise of the gust pushed upon the drum of our ear. We beheld the distances and we saw, in the windy mist, people walking upon the surface of the water here and there. These people wore the masks of birds upon their faces — the masks of eagles — and they were leashed by red ties and bound by black and white suits. Seeing this we thought of ridding ourselves of the boat, which rocked uncomfortably. But this was a mistake. Our feet sank at once into the waters, followed by our head[s?] and of a sudden our bodies were submerged in the depths. There we beheld a vision of myriad horrors.

In the bloodwaters we looked down upon the very depths of the world, whence emerged the whole extent of the earth. And from the earth rose a world of ruins; whole cities sunken, towers stilled and festering with rust, monuments left to rot and disappear in the advancement of epochs. Corpses of the dead everywhere, floating up from the ruins by the billions, all faceless, ascending along with all their possessions and everything they had ever done. Inside the waters we saw it — that the men with eagle masks walked not on the surface of the sea, but upon long, precarious stilts; and one by one they fell, too, and one by one they joined the society of extinct humankind.

Full of dread in our heart[**s?**] we struggled to emerge into the open air. We climbed back into the boat, soaked in all the blood of humanity upon which a few eagle-men waddled yet. The dust blew strong upon us, and it was as though the very wind was intent on choking us out of life. We took shelter within the boat's shell. The storm rushed through the dead air in increasing fury. The waters assumed the shape of a spiral coalescing into a core, a whirlpool upon which the boat sailed unguided. Huddled in the hollow of the crib we saw the heavens shift violently, the wrath of all the gods ever devised by humankind raging and spurning in great churnings of fume — our eyes gripped the sun blackened by ash, from it fell torrents of black snows — and we heard a roar of a trillion voices, uttered from the open mouths of all the corpses of all the people who had ever lived floating among the ruins of all the civilizations which had ever existed.

The boat rammed against an islet, whence emerged a gazebo. This gazebo stood at the very core of the tree of ash, and an old trunk, spreading into branches bereft of petal and leaf, sprouted from its midst, forming its ghastly canopy. Fish circled the islet over the boughs, mirroring the motion of the gale, mirrored also by the birds winding round the land under the roots. From the gazebo one could well behold all the devastation (the waters raged with hues of lava). Under its canopy we found a number of men sitting then, and they were all wearing the masks of great men, with plumes pending from their jaws and gathering round their lips, and all manner of raiment underneath. They rested upon the stuffed skins of many animals, lions most of all — all so vivid in their expressions that they seemed indeed asleep. There were cows and oxen lain; upon the tree, a sighing vulture. Immediately we recognized the men of the sarcophagi, the colors of the peacock, and the lips of the pelican bare in their midst. But on our approach the men rose all at once, startled, and began yelling at each other in a great uproar and calling one another 'false prophet!' in thunderous proclamations. We watched them for a period. Hanging from the tree branch was a serpent, and the serpent watched too, as it chewed calmly the tree's last fruit (the fruit was made of flame, this was once a tree which was covered in fire and whose bark never burned, told one of the clamoring men). Then we left, knowing in our hearts that these false prophets would be the last ones to drown along with the last eagle on stilts.

The seething tide pushed us away, spinning itself outward from the core islet where the men observed us leave, fighting one another yet. We came upon the edge of the fumes with a tremendous rumbling.

And all at once, all was quiet again. Silence absolute in the immensity of a motionless world. Time stretched into the confines of the past and the depths of the future, and once more the surface of the waters was stilled. The skies were as the waters, of a pure, deep blue. Not a breath of wind stirred it in the whole extent of its infinitude; so that it assumed perfectly the aspect of the firmament. The boat was as motionless as a stone blooming from deep below the earth.

There was no stop to the sea's extension and (though it is impossible to conceive) there was no horizon either.

As I looked up over the shell I saw the Midget in robes, standing upon the bow, holding in his/her hands the staff wound with two cords. And the root of the staff spread into the waters, and we rowed forth with it. My gaze turned up into the skies and down into the waters; one reflecting the other, the other penetrating the one. And she/he was beside me.

Once again his eyes confronted the horrendous, yawning facelessness sinking into depths upon the surface of the waters, and we, stepping beside the semblance of Neipas gliding over the waters, clutched the edges of the empty, and drew it off to reveal the truth which that persona veiled — for such facelessness, too, is mask. And through his gaze we saw our true face; and in his countenance, and through the flowing waters we saw, the face of Neipas' father, the face of Neipas' mother, the face of his sister and ancestors, and we saw the face of Magpie, Cesar and Kasim, Janu and Osir, Edazima and Martin, Oshana and Orenda, we saw the face of Eva and their unborn child and all future generations, through our gaze passed the faces of all the dead and all yet unborn, and those who yet lived, young and old, rich and poor, subject and tyrant. We saw the reverse of those maskless countenances, behind the golden beaks and the sodden stares, under the faces smeared by destitution, and those powdered in opulence. We saw all faces, stretching onward along the motionless river course. We beheld now the truth — we saw that beyond all the masks were the faces of all the people, flowing in the quiet waters, in a torrent of being traveling the span of existence. We gazed beyond all pairs of opposites, we discerned a primordial trace of the silence under every sound, we perceived the trace of the mystery before the creation and after the ultimate. And we sensed...

We sensed something intangible, beyond reason and feeling, beyond all gods; something nowhere and everywhere, within and without. The formless form of all forms.

In the beginning was the word, we heard said. **In the end will be the meaning.**

When we raised our eyes from this vision we saw we were mooring on the islet shore. The still tide had carried us there and now the mill wheel, which spun as we approached, ceased as the boat penetrated the sands. Beholding the vastness once more, we opened the door to the mill and walked the humid, carnal darkness; and once again we moved in the darkness without a body and without a mind — until we found the light, and all senses at once rushed back inside.

*

And when the shaped darkness behind Neipas, drawn out of nowhere, suspended in an infinity of white light, closed — the darkness abruptly overtook everything. Of a flash, all became black. Only yonder could be seen the glimmer of a hovering flame, and faint glittering letters; and the vague trace of water sounding, as of a cascade.

Neipas felt a hand from below gripping his own.

He staggered toward the flame now, as though through open air; and the more its palpitating sway neared his senses, the louder the rush of cataracts became with the buzz of flies.

1015

74 - Inner Sanctum

Out of the boom of copiously pouring water would sometimes emerge a type of cooing. The cascade ebbed into eerie, foreboding rumblings in the straddle between reality and dream, and just as it seemed to draw away out of reach — that soft cry gurgled, like a tender whisper out of a constricted throat, out of a voice, meek, vulnerable, released from the torment of prolonged throes. A faded moment after, the rumble diffused into the splattering of a myriad flies; raising a grainy buzz, a low din so spectral — the sensation it caused was of an army of vermin squirming their way into every pore — that Neipas would wholly twitch himself back into a fuller awareness of the waterfall's noise, which would abruptly flow and overwhelm the hovering swarm.

Discomfiting as it was, to part his eyelids and rouse his body against the heft of gravity required of him such a tremendous effort that a long, long time must have passed before the light of the hall first entered his blotched, rheumy vision. He groaned faintly. Then, setting his teeth, he strained out of a sort of very prolonged, thick wailing bubbling with gushing spit. Drool flowed down his cheek — increasingly he realized how sore it was, the ache as if gained consciousness with him — to the strange soil against which it pressed.

Neipas gained awareness of his startled heart, then of his dense, deep, troubled breathing. The brims of his nostrils touched in great intakes of air. There was a strangely pleasant scent in it. Again his eyelids pushed against the weight of their own fatigue, and again through the affected orb entered the contours of the hall. A confusion of a whitish wavy ground, black liquid, and multicolored feathers strewn throughout mixed under the palpitation of reflected light cast by the waterfall, a sort of rolling phantasmagorical film spilling over the floor, and somehow infused with the softness of candlelight. Mentally grasping for his forearm at the opposite end of the universe — his sense of physicality being so widespread in its recovering drowsiness as to cover all existence — he pushed it against the unctuous soil, whence his cheek lifted at the outermost edge of a sprinkly head, dizzy, straining to gather his wild-scattered self into the safe confines of his body. Part of his face glued to the ground as it lifted and black goo oozed from the corner of his mouth, connecting his jaw to the swampy floor.

Still deep and hard of breathing, densely sleepy, and throbbing in all manner of aches, Neipas was finally able to grasp with sufficient definition the elements of the view before him: haughty round, veiny marble walls erected, curving into an abruptly shut inscrutability of darkness; at the dim depths shone a sort of oval window; up there somewhere. To his left (the muscles of his neck tightened in protest to the motion) ran the waterfall, looping in bands beyond a portentous arch. To his right rose a gigantic candle — full of cuts.

In the silences between heavy exhalations — which filled his head with echoes — he heard a faint, angelic hum, an ethereal tune and a sort of melody familiar to him...

(Lock, and release... The slow convulsions of a heartbeat enveloped the world.)

Neipas grimaced. The vague warmth of some presence grew at his side. He strained, and turned hesitantly; frightfully, with the trace of living nightmares still vagrant about his soul. But his heart becalmed. For it was the Midget who had snuck up; ever without a sound, nearly always mute, the sage had either materialized out of nothing or she/he had floated in. Neipas hadn't perceived the merest hint of steps; maybe there were no feet under the robes, he considered.

Neipas greeted the Midget with a silent nod. He/she did the same, standing now at his height — for Neipas had sat up.

"Where am I?" croaked he.

The Midget said nothing; her/his mask of despondent crescents, old symbol of cathartic tragedy, leaned toward Neipas' as if to check he was really awake — and in the act of it, Neipas suddenly and uncannily discerned a unique opportunity. Meeting a sudden impulse, he somehow found himself endeavoring to look inside the Midget's mask, to pierce his sight beyond it, to unbury the enigma under it — but he/she

was already distant, already inscrutable again as she/he glided toward the wide round form of the wax candle, with back turned. The warm glow of the flame shone through the gashes; it enveloped his/her robes in as many streaks of light — a mysterious, multicolored light — as sunlit rivers cast upon their margins.

Neipas had been here once before — and he had seen this towering candle already a few times. It was the Candle of Man, whose wounds spelled the commandment THOU SHALT; in every language repeated, in every dialect carved, drawn into its wax body. Before it (Neipas distinguished what it was clearly now, as he staggered to his feet and listened to the Midget, who had begun to speak) on the wall, stood affixed the colossal effigy of a Dragon.

Here was the object of the Candle's worship.

Its body of serpent was entirely composed of masks glistening with the Candle's immemorial pronouncement and command — each mask was a scale upon the sculpture's reptilian skin. They were masks of all kinds, of all colors, of every stripe and preference, as suit the day's needs; ready to be shed when no longer useful.

The Dragon's wings were carved in relief off the sumptuous marble wall. So was the face of the deity, well up high; a face of closed eyes, inexpressive, nondescript, serene, mighty in size and character, a character which rested mainly on its strange universality and anonymity, on its impossibility of identification.

"Here," the Midget was saying, *"is the face of Mammon.*

"Rulers of all ages have issued commandments," he/she continued, with a slow, sweeping gesture of the staff — the lamp still fixed on top glimmered mesmerizingly with the glowing words, as if spelling them out in silence — *"yet all the commandments of Hist'ry have but a single command underwrit; and that command is 'Obey'.*

"Lo. The human flame shines narrow through the bounds of its direction."

The two voices of the sage rang mystically in Neipas' outspread mind, which lagged beyond the motion of his body standing now imperceptibly beside the Midget. In his ears lulled the melody and the soothing suffusion of the hum. His eyes glided softly round the hall, altogether unattached from their head, perusing the arcane vastness of Mammon's shrine. Fumes puffed blank from the entryway, down the marble steps of the farthest Temple chamber, the last octagonal bathhouse, by which fount Neipas had heard Magpie's voice before it was shushed into her ultimate, horrible fate. Facing North, the waterfall behind the arch curtained the clear view of flooded suburbia, the Diamond Hills floating unscathed over the deluge, and the wide desert of pools stagnant amid the waste of military bunkers beyond the hilltop; the cascade veiled the resting sea, lounged upon the moribund aftermath of its rampage, and the muscular mountains standing watch above the vast ruin. The sculpture of Mammon hovering upon a body of scales and wings of feather — upon composite layers of mask — rose opposite the falling waters, the Candle between them, at the very core of the ample hall. Circling them, the Sanctum wound into a deep corner made of darkness, which faced the passage from the Temple Bathhouse and the wider white wall expanding from its portal. In this darkness there was but a window — up there, afloat in nothing; a speck of light indiscernibly growing and shrinking.

Neipas' gaze neared it. The ground vibrated and soothed into a stop under his feet; as though a giant were walking toward him from a distance, or as if the Belab itself was the colossus moving, in deliberate march...

Faraway bells swelled dimly at every shake. The hum, the melody sheltered under and emerged from their resounding bronze heads. A heart beating beyond...

Neipas recognized the window in the darkness. The End of History was on the other side; he could see the massive hourglass — sandless. That was the frosty window to the Serpent's left, its 2nd ear.

"*The soil lives. This tower won't survive it,*" said the Midget —

"*The spear will rust, and the hand that holds it will decay, before the flesh it pierces ever dies. Here's Hist'ry's pen. — made of Earth's marrow.*

"*The human story's writ in blood, life of the living, and crafted in wealth, blood of the dead. Much water's been applied to its washing, and much fire to unwanted pages.*

"*The story of the past, 't has been drafted for one purpose: to foreclose paths to the future. Much have the curators of Hist'ry kept hidden from view, or buried under lights — veiled, or ironized...*

"*Its purpose is to say, 'we've been this, we can only be this.' They've hidden away and oft destroyed better ways of living: these we must unveil, exhume, and look to.*"

Neipas experienced the sensation of being watched as his gaze returned to himself from its flight. Mammon's scaly plumes, towering over them, seemed to laugh in the scintillation of candle glow. Somewhere deep in that glint was reflected the window at the End of History and some kind of stare observing from the other side, as Neipas had himself, once, contemplated.

...THOU —— SHALT, whispered the Candle of Man in the multitudinous shimmers of the Dragon, through the synchronized beat of the toll and the throb, and the percolation of the melody...

For some time they watched the mesmerizing glow; after which Neipas asked:

"Can the Candle of Man ever burn out? The flame, I mean?..."

— to which the Midget, after a period of silence and reflection, answered:

"*How long the flame of existence has been burning, We cannot say — We are only human, and We exist within time; thus We know nothing concerning eternity, except that it is outside of time, and therefore outside the senses.*

"*But those with knowledge say the Universe's sparked nearly 14,000,000,000 years ago.*

"*And this Earth, 4,500,000,000 years, or thereabout.*

"*And the Human, 315,000 years of age, the Human has.*

"*And History — the learned say — 6,000 years.*

"*In the 14 Billion years of the Universe, entire cities, entire nations, entire species and entire continents, entire planets and entire stars and whole constellations have come, and vanished.*

"*So yes.*"

Her/his words vanished in the crushing indifference of the marble, imposing in its towering presence. They remained quiet in their wake; again for a very long time. The remembrance of Orenda's words, spoken under the dusk, lit up vaguely in Neipas' mind as he observed the Candle, its ethereal shine and the glowing dark haze spinning out of it, its brazen mark upon the great white and black stones, upon the armor of the sculpture; and its solid wax which never seemed to wane.

"She said to me once [...] that someday we will all be gone and the Universe will never know the Sumerians wrote the Gilgamesh, or we the Webwork [...] But it doesn't have to be now. We can still flourish to our full potential. Many children can still watch the many sunrises yet to come, and bask in the moonlight, and witness the beauty of the world [...] to live. There's still a lot of life to be lived."

"There's still a lot of life to be lived. It doesn't have to be now," Neipas repeated in his soundless lips.

The Midget stood before him now. *"The flame's been brought here, where there is no air.*

"'Tis trapped within these heights. Seize it.

"Remove it from this tower." Neipas must have sat again, because the Midget's mask hovered right before him. And meanwhile the sage brandished the lamp clinking atop his/her staff, which was now

two high stilts, and the staff rested beside him.

"Where did you get those?" asked Neipas, unfazed.

"Neipas," so ensued the Midget's two voices, male and female, from the downturned crescents of the tragic visage, *"you brought them here."*

(Oh —) and he recalled the Giant Historian upon whose legs he had already once soared. But now Neipas held the stilts he was afraid. He knew (in his other hand now he seized the lamp and the two cords that had enveloped the Midget's staff) that he was to ascend over the height of the Candle of Man, presently rising colossally above his eyes; and he knew that he would have to stand upon the stilts' precipitous perches, and with freely hanging arms lower the lamp into the wide pit of the Candle, and alight it with the holy flame. Yet his heart was troubled. He doubted he could perform such an feat of jugglery, and rather feared his brain would spill out into the bleak ground when he fell.

The bells had stopped. The melody thinned outward, the hum ebbed before the swelling of his heart. It beat; it yielded (a gasping fish in the parchedness of the body). The Midget held his hand.

"Worry not."

At once the whole gigantic hall swooped down and ran in noxious gusts by his ears, against his eyes, into his nostrils, rocking his heart with abandon. His breath faltered and his every limb shook as he found himself suspended at dizzying heights, over the yawning chasm of the colossal Candle hollow. He found himself reeling aloft, his head swam as the vertiginous vision of a giant, twitching basin of fire and fluids presented itself beneath him. His toes jutted off the salience of the stilt. For —

(in gasping his eyes opened) he stood absolutely immobilized, petrified by fear, and the only movement in his body were the myriad involuntary twitches of his muscles. His mind spiraled slowly in revolutions of dreams into realities and realities into dreams, and they mingled like the rotating coffee and milk of morning in a single distant existence. Rendered unfathomable through the great chaos of the senses, the Candle was interpreted by his confusion as a chalice of baptismal fire, with its thin circular brink promptly sliding down to a yawning lake of molten wax, from the monstrous core of which emerged, like a lone island, the tallow, and the flame. It was something of a baptismal fount for giants; and the waters glinted darkly, like pools of black oil, underneath the pale multicolored glow. It was over this that Neipas unfastened his hands from the poles (his heart staggered; his head rippled; his body quaked all over) and, squinting with a great concentration of shallow quivering breaths, he lowered the lamp, whose handle was secured with the two cords. He did it slowly, carefully. His legs stood astride, half-liquid over the yawning void, lifted perilously over the heights, and it seemed to him they might falter at any moment, collapse and toss him into that vast slobbering maw and its pentecostal flame tongue. Dark fumes lapped about him; dark incantations coughed into his mind. The angelic hum suffused his shivers, his panting nervousness, to the point of making him nearly swoon — as the cords and the lamp descended, descended, descended, into the deep abyss, out of which the flame shone feeble, besieged by the dissolving, mounting tallow...

The flame enveloped the lamp. The fluids glistened and silence was made. The wick flared.

...Steps sounded faint in the echoing tune; a little flame waved without sound upon the tip of the lamp, a silent lamp, gliding out of the tip of a human hand. The Midget's robes went before the gaze. The melody, and the mystifying hum, hadn't ceased nor lowered. But every other sound had somehow shushed as they drew near Mammon, away from the cascade whose buzzing droplets seemed to die in the purifying clearness of melodious air. Their steps produced no ring; and only the echo of a slow, long pulse, of a beating heart, survived the spellbinding aroma of music bewitching his senses. He arrived, as though out of nowhere, before the mosaic body of the deity rising before the Candle. A great and intricate hive of masks spread all over his sight.

"Have you the Historian's key?" asked the Midget who stood now, as though out of nowhere, facing him. He read her/his words somehow under the mask, unexpressed in sound now, left soundless in the ethereal air; but how could he understand if the Midget had no mouth?

Neipas remembered the key in his pocket; the key of the Museum Giant. It was a very old, very rusty, bronze-like thing, the intricateness of its design made thin and feeble by age. The Midget seized one of the masks on the wall — the mask hanging at his/her height, resembling the smiling, comedic mask of the Giant — and pulled it; revealing a keyhole on a bare surface. Here Neipas inserted the ancient key; holding it with one hand low, and holding high, with the other, the lamp supporting the holy flame, burning steady the olive oil inside. It took 12 turns to unlock. During the successive revolutions, each drumming a heartbeat, Neipas stared forth at the wall; and it was only midway that he realized he was staring at an aperture, a little glass tucked between the masks. He could see the other side. He had gazed upon where he was now from the other side. He could see the final chamber of the darkrooms, the final stop of the trail of visions, where an immense, split head of Mammon produced and consumed a rising scroll. Out of the gloomy ground came that scroll, arising between barrels, out the petroleum-soaked floor upon which spread a great matrix of plump tubes, wires, pipes. The two halves of the head of Mammon he could glimpse through the corners of the aperture — and he could feel, as he gazed, the gaze of some other stare observing him from the window at the End of History, through the corner, up there, on the deep of the mysterious gloom.

12 turns it took to unlock — to unbolt — and a passage was made under a cluster of 80 masks.

The passage was little taller than the Midget, though it was quite wide — it was revealed as the mosaic of huddled masks dropped onto the waxy ground, which spread in the manner of waves, or roots, from the very base of Mammon. Neipas could now see, as he crouched down to the hole with some befuddlement, that the masks had been hanging on nothing.

He crawled inside, following the Midget, who didn't even have to stoop. The key he had placed back in his pocket; the lamp he held over his head, so as to not touch the various tars soaking the ground. In another moment — he stood again.

Once more, he stood between the head of Mammon. Aloft on one side, the chin overhanging and corbeling the obscure space. The lipless mouth slurped the rising photo-scroll. It flashed with the emanations of light coming from the opposite side, flashing from the cleft parting the top of Mammon's head, whose upper half occupied the entirety of the wall, rounding itself into the floor, which the nose sniffed. The metallic surface of each half sheened in smooth undertones, as their arcane operation progressed untroubled. Before and behind Neipas, there rose the great busts of the cherubim, each with 4 animal heads — the Midget and he had emerged from the yawning throat of the Pelican.

They moved through the light vibrations of the electricity generator, rippling among the intensifying throb and the tender musical hum, toward the core of the space; from which the scroll — which the Midget had called *Book of Numbers* last time they were here — was ejected. It lifted out of a slit on the floor, which cut at the edge of an inconspicuous hatch. It seemed possible to pull the slit in order to open it; yet Neipas' attempt didn't even make it budge. Then, as he turned (being upon one knee) he spotted the Midget again facing his sight directly, mysterious, inscrutable, indecipherable. Again he tried to construe the enigma of her/his visage — but it was impossible, in that mechanical twilight. Perhaps if he saw him/her by the lampshine...

The Midget was tapping the center of the supposed trapdoor with her/his staff. Neipas looked closer — another keyhole.

The Giant's key turned 9 times; and at the conclusion of the 9th turn, there occurred a shift in the vibrations of the air, a reaction of intensification in the rearing pulse, made stronger, slower now; the melody and the hum became louder — became ominous.

The hatch was pulled open.

They then were in a tunnel, the ceiling of which jagged full of entangled wires and pipes; the floor was covered with the Book of Numbers' blank paper sliding continuously under their feet, like a rolling carpet, rolling in the direction opposite their march (his soiled footsteps marked the scroll and he wondered if they would muddle the numbers to be printed). In the uncertain distance there glimmered a light; between it and them, nothing was, and darkness dominated the span. Neipas' lamp was for a while the only immediate source of illumination. With the mystic Midget he walked, and walked, and walked. He scarcely felt anything. Sometimes he wondered if he had slept, but if he dreamt it was only dreams of an endless quest — for what? They seemed to be making for the very core of the Belab, through its 12, or 80, or 10,000 layers. The pulse, the melody, and the march lulled him into such spiritual half-ruminations as to make him inexistent in that dim sleepy light the holy flame afforded him. Meanwhile, the glimmer yonder palpitated.

Imperceptibly they neared two columns; each spun on its axis in a serene and efficient manner on either side of the approachers. The glimmer, meanwhile, had grown larger. It had grown much larger. Its light blazed upon them fiercely, lapping in dreadful leaps of scarlet dazzle, like clamors of warning. The glimmer had evolved into a colossal fire, sparkling, blowing, bellowing and raging in a sort of monstrous, incomprehensible open furnace yawning at the end of the tunnel — it was hard to tell what it was with the absolutely impersonal, dispassionate, and frightful fury of the conflagration's expelling glare. It was possessed of an unnatural hue, blood-red, indeed as if it were bleeding and spilling ichor from unending ruby stones. The soundscape, too, had grown to envelop them, and raged all about them in fierce frothing sparks, ascending restlessly in a single uninterrupted gale of fire, like a scream ejected from that horrendous, ghoulish maw of metal; and all throughout it built into an immense pulse, pumping heart of some sinister giant. Neipas found himself sitting; he realized that though the fire raged quite near he felt none of its heat, and if he felt anything at all, it was a mild, pernicious chill gnawing somewhere in the deep roots of his heartstrings. The Midget stood at his height, again his/her mask of despondent tragedy faced him, looking almost theatrical in the extreme allegoratization of sadness and grief. It was exceedingly loud and Neipas couldn't have heard her/his voice — therefore the voice spoke directly inside his head.

(*The flame and the fire*, it said, *burns yonder — most of it lives here, in this tower, at this age... Behold — the fire that hardens clay; the fire that softens wax. The fire that molds. Anointing water.*

It alights not. It purifies not. It distorts. It immolates.)

The tall columns erected on either side of them rotated... Scroll paper wrapped round them, and out of each it stretched. The one, rotating clockwise, cast the scroll in their direction; its paper, made of cellulose and silver, swooped in a flourish to the floor and progressed along the tunnel-tube before it ascended to the light and vapors of Mammon's Sanctum and Temple, to be imprinted with the digits of the Book of Numbers. The other, rotating counterclockwise, drove its scroll toward the fire; the paper being made of vellum, with characters — letters — already inscribed upon the surface. Neipas stretched his neck and the hand holding the lamp to try to make out what the letters spelled, being careful, however, not to cross the space between the columns. It took a moment for him to see — for these were initially somewhat foreign to his knowledge — that they were names; tens, hundreds, thousands, millions of names filling the height and the ceaseless length of the scroll.

What is this, Neipas asked.

(*'Tis what you see,* so rang the double-voiced chorus into his mind, *the Book of Names.*)

He realized that the columns ran very deep under, and that the vellum spun obliquely up the unimaginable height of its column to emerge here, to float yonder, and be consumed by the fire. He seemed to see the ink melting in the conflagration's hellish crux as it blazed with unfettered violence; and shed the names in drips of sable blood.

What names, Neipas asked.

(*Names given to be forgotten. Names taken...*)

Neipas arched forth a little to look at the pipe through which the column and the scroll ascended, being yet cautious, however, to not enter the line between the two poles; for over that line, there was a sign that arched from the top of one column to the other, connecting them. And upon it was engraved the aphorism, **FACTUM CARO VERBUM EST**.

Neipas wondered, but he asked not what it meant — for he feared its meaning.

(*Come. We walk.*)

There opened, just before the columns, a downward set of stars which he hadn't noticed before.

Down they went, and many passageways they seemed to traverse on their indefinite march. Through tunnels and pipes, up steps and down steps they walked, turning a series of right angles until, finally, at the bottom of a small staircase behind an altar, the space suddenly widened enormously.

The throbbing sound — which had been rattling the passageways and shrieking in mighty, painful contractions across every surface — broadened immensely. In releasing itself from the bounds of constricted space, the sound acquired an ethereal quality; all of a sudden the profane and demonic were morphed into ecclesiastical, beatific tones. The angelic hum and melody mingled transcendentally with the reverberating echo of the pulse. Their combined effect upon Neipas' benumbed senses was to lull him out of his body, into a momentary sort of oblivion; so that a long moment was necessary to interpret what he was seeing.

The Midget said, *"Hist'ry possesses strange ears. It listens only to those who make most noise — and to those wise whisperers who whisper at just the proper frequency, the poets."*

Ushered by unconscious impulses, Neipas raised the holy flame burning upon the lamp in an attempt to see; albeit a much larger, much brighter fire radiated above him already.

He and the Midget stood in a sort of balcony, over an immense void.

Naught but one thing existed in it. At the brink, Neipas overlooked the abyss, wide and ample, deep and profound; its edges could not be (yet) discerned. But the abomination suspended in the center of the hollow made him recoil, with mouth parted and eyes large, into his every contracted muscle and the closing breast, stung by an injection of dread climbing darkly into the heart.

"Where are we?" he asked the Midget.

"We stand," replied she/he — *"upon the core of the tower."*

*

The core of the Belab — Neipas beheld it hollow.

Suspended in the hollow vast and deep, the abomination throbbed convulsively before his awed gaze. It was of a viscous white and black substance, viscous and bloody, gangrenous, resembling a sort of leech; colossal, the abomination was covered in wide patches of crust, it seemed in this way mostly made of rock. The whole of its open surface was covered with eyes; and with mouths, out of which left unending veins, or wires and cords, and pipes, and tubes, and threads to sink into the shadow of the edges, out to the succeeding layers of the tower and beyond. Out of the various clefts, something like petroleum oozed. A rancid stench hardened upon the reverse of his face. Now lacking the fragrant concealments strewn across its storeys, Neipas felt the tower's malodor unabashed — did it fester out of that thing? Perhaps; but it was evident that the pulsing sound that inoculated every moment of his existence, in and out of consciousness, inside and away from the tower, beyond the walls, within himself, emanated from the abomination; it *beat* in that thing.

"Behold the heart," said the Midget, *"abstract Babylon of eternal exile, where we take refuge from ourselves and the world."*

To Neipas it resembled the head of a mountainous spider, out of which ensued an infinitude of legs. The melody suffused all things tender, played perhaps on the tangle of strings shot out of that abominable heart. Out from the atria at the top climbed a great, bulbous sac, oval in shape, the luminosity of which made it appear like a giant flower of closed petals or a lightbulb flooded with fire. Its golden light palpitated and swelled calmly into the vastness, diffused the invisible verge, made visible the great and distant surrounding walls. It was like a lone pharos hanging in a towering sea. Its wall curved upward with many inflamed capillaries and pores: a strange, ghastly surface of skin; thoroughly dilated in the beat of the abominable swelling and contraction of the thing beneath it.

The vision was so horrendous, so unbearable; that, were it not for its being distant across the chasm, Neipas would have died on the spot from the shock of perceiving it alone.

"*The heart of these days, the seed of Mammon — called 'greed'.*

"*Mammon is their highest ideal, the aim of all their hopes, their most exalted sun!*" pronounced the Midget toward the golden radiance. "*The god dispels all darknesses with the might of its brilliance.*

"*Behold the heart of Mammon. 'Tis a spider of unending legs. It weaves veils to cloud your eyes. In reality, its eggs hatch inside your ears; its venom courses your veins.*

"*And it's a good venom. It tastes sweetly. It dissolves like sugar. You take of it daily, and bit by bit you fall asleep.*

"*Behold its fangs; they are the hooks of eagles' beaks; the anchor piercing your soul. But the poison dulls, and tastes sweetly. It's painless. It makes you sleep when you're awake and die when you're asleep.*

"*Behold, Mammon's legs run the human race.*"

Inside the closed petals (wings?) of the lightbulb stemming from that heart of stone and ulcers, there shot — out of the rocky summit of the heart that was the flower's stigma — tremendous jets of fire, a towering, continuous flame tongue emitting light which passed golden through the filtering wall of the petal closing like wings toward the end of the tower. Glitter twinkled therein in the manner of pollen in sunlight. The crumbs of gold-dust spread and ascended continuously, unceasingly coalescing toward the summit of the petals. There, in the aperture where they met, Neipas could just make out the fiery shimmering of the Golden Dove — and the Pearl above it, propagating the heart's bloodlight across the vastness of the world outside. Neipas had the impression of a tremendous distance deepening underneath his chin. The heart's glare, being heavy, pended downwards in the manner of a spotlight blurring at the edges, and it pierced the depths unimpeded until the sight lost them in the distances beyond reach. It was clear that the Belab's hollowness fell from the peaks to the ends of the abyss; Neipas conjectured that the height it spanned was infinite. There before, above and below his despondent gaze, the great profusion of venous threads of every type proliferated in massive trajectories, cleaving to the shadows and injecting themselves into the roots of civilization. Amidst their entanglement he saw (at first he thought they were suspended in mid-air yet soon realized his mistake) arms, legs, human forms shifting between the gold light and the shadow of the arteries; limbs moving in a solemnity of ritual, there under a baton, there over a drum, there round a trumpet, wailing long, long, low like a rumbling foreboding the storm. Someone singing, someone humming; he visualized the sound of ethereal glass ringing from up there... He saw it. Cups of crystal above the hanging pipes, filled with (what? tar, coffee, honey, yolk, milk, blood, water, wine... and fingers rubbing the edges).

Their feet clutched the roundness of the threads like avian paws. The Orchestra — they inhabited perhaps the chambers of the heart (which were perceived, by some instinctual faculty of the spirit, to be hollow too). The melody rippled soft, heavenly in the great void; the throb reverberated within it, percolating it celestially. Its effect was, as ever, mesmerizing...

It was then he realized that some of the heart's veins, or arteries, or limbs moved and were weaving. They were growing and reproducing themselves. They moved ever forth.

"The light obscures. Within it there's rot," said the Midget —

"It began a small seed (whence this tower sprouted). Behold it now. Its branches spread far and wide, and they pierce, and seep even now into the hearts of humankind... so that its rot may fester.

"At once fed and feeding, puppet and puppeteer, greed; 'tis the impulse that craves Mammon, whom Mammon makes flourish. Though it seems to feed all it feeds off all — 'tis a parasite. During the night it leeches, under the sun it spits venom into your veins.

"Beware those who merely seek to reduce it. For its imperative, its obsession, its sole aspiration is to **grow***. And if one attains its reduction, one did not conquer it, one still did not tame it, but only postponed its dominance; it will always find a way to expand back and beyond what it was.*

"Behold the core of today's civilization. They safeguard it amid their hoard. It underlies all things.

"Round us spread the Temple, the Darkrooms, the Vaults and the Museum. Mirrors of Hist'ry, whence human action sprouts. And the seed they have sowed — is greed.

"It bred this Mammon, this possessing spirit."

The Orchestra — source of the melody. The music beyond the music, the tune beneath every sound. Its players dotted inconspicuously the hanging pathways, perching upon the branches of that ignoble, ever-bursting cocoon, in the manner of goblins in some demonic tree. Squatting in horrid contortions, the musician yonder let his buttocks hang precipitously over the pit; the tail of his suit flowed into it long and was tended to by two of the heart's shorter, sewing arms. With the golden pallor flooding between shadows upon him, the man unsettlingly resembled a mechanical wax figure. Under his stooping head without a face aligned the cups of the glass harmonica — they seemed embossed into the very flesh of the bough upon which he perched — which edges he rubbed with delicate fingers. From there emerged the pervading element of the haunting melody.... It was hypnotizing; its notes of hypnotic glass lulled the spirit with their wails of sea-creature, sad, solemn, profound... Light and shade flickered over the solemn trumpeter, who stood upright nearly out of view, aloft. The bow of the violinist slid tenderly upon the very flesh of thin strings protruding from the heart, and upon the webbed threads unraveling out of its tattered, gem-embroidered cloth coverings; and upon the violin itself held under two arms. There were, indeed, many bows, and Neipas could behold now with amazement and shock the myriad arms protruding out of the violinist's torso afar... The organist presented a similar marvel. He was difficult to spot where he was, tucked between arteries close to the heart; but through close attention it was possible to discern the multitude of slow moving hands tapping their somber notes. The organ itself was encrusted into the rock of the heart, and over the instrument and the player oozed thick, sluggish blankets of bitumen. Beneath the instrument, numberless paws pumped frantically at the pedals — this was done only as the heart was halted, and stopped when the heart contracted and its beat swelled... as if it were pumping life into that umbilical monster suspended in flight. The soil shook in reverb anew. The metronome atop the organ swung at ease from side to side. Its tempo matched the heart's; and the organ notes sounded in mollifying punctures of harmony among the absorbing reverberation of the all-encompassing throb growing to meet the symphonic glass... Finally (though there must have been more elements of the band he couldn't spot at present) Neipas saw the Conductor; imperiously high he stood. He perched upon one of the main arteries, thick, colossal, undulating dramatically with waves recurring at each beat — as the poison of the heart thrust through its many boughs — at which moment he soared with his gentle motions of flapping wing, like a cherub ascending breezily toward the celestial light; and the tail of his suit serpentined in ripples of fold down the long depths like a neverending curtain. The hum came from him. Out of his faceless summit emanated the angelic song, sung as he swayed the long baton of command, twig for crawlers, perch for flies swarming upon the supple arms of the charmer of tempo and time. The melody breathed, and cast, and waved, and insinuated in delicate tones, as Neipas watched the musicians between wonder and horror, as he watched intently; before turning to the placid Midget standing aside the staff who (looking unto him then) pronounced:

"*Mammon casts its spell from the deep.*

"*Today all live in Mammon's head. This We have said.*

"*Yet there's danger even greater in letting its heart live in ours. Its vessels root down to our very depths, pumping venom. The parasite seeks to consume the essence of its host; and make the host its shell. So it is with Mammon.*

"*Behold how it spreads. Everything it touches turns chill... It distorts... It hollows all things. It profanes by labeling the holy with a price. The heart grinds all things, recycles all things, and returns to all things degraded. It takes from the Earth wealth, and returns waste — it takes from the human blood and returns poison. All things are suffocated into its image.*

"*It turns all into machine... Its dominance is a sacrilege to our nature.*

"*Behold — the motor of the system...*"

The hovering heart flinched powerfully and pumped its ichor into every corner of the world. Its aspect of convulsing cocoon absolutely seethed in the twitching motion of its vessels and the firelight raging inside, licking the gaps savagely and thrusting out of the peak in great heaves of oil; which Neipas' widening stare now faced upturned...

"*Mammon shall grow to consume all things... to absorb all things to its unsatiable need. Everything you love — and all that sustains life. It will eat up Hist'ry until no future remains. It wishes to grow beyond the limits of nature, beyond itself, beyond the Earth, where even Mammon can no longer breathe... A suicidal deity.*

"*Behold, the human flame burns now in a heart of stone. What you are taking is but a shard. It must be kindled anew — outside these confines. It must grow into a new sun and a new moon outside this kiln of toxins.*"

The closed wings of the lightbulb swelled and shrunk with the contractions of the heart and the great spewing of its flame, and through its transparent throbbing walls Neipas gazed in awe the great swarms of ascending petals, vermin, and banknotes before the widened orbs of the wrathful Golden Dove, whose talons rooted in the hearttop, twining round the pillar, encircling the flaming stone like a crown. He'd been there before. Like a repressed nightmare the recent memory billowed up to consciousness at the sight of its setting. In the bulbing of golden light he contemplated again the horde of insects, flower petals and money, the inscribed stone above the writhing mass, the monstrous conflagration beneath the ogling statue of the Dove, the overwhelming glare that had flooded his senses and the screams, the screams, the horrendous screams pouring into his soul...

Trembling with great fright now, he stammered out, "In the vaults. What — what was it I heard... What voices were those?..."

— to which the Midget simply responded:

"*The time approaches. You will see.*"

With his/her cord-wound staff she/he pointed to the side: the balcony where they stood protruded in the shape of its round facade, and continued, leaner, through a passage along the wide circle of the Belab's innermost ring. Neipas began to walk — his eyes faced forth, attrited by prolonged shock and agony — circumventing that circus of horrors, slanting down spiral-wise; the smell and the noise affected him ever more, turned him more and more stunned and dizzy (he felt not the heat though he was drenched in sweat); eventually he realized the Midget was no longer at his side.

An unbearable dread forced his stop. The Midget wasn't there and a terrible loneliness sank in with the fright; into his bulging stare and receding senses then plunged the shadowy image of another robed figure standing before him, a figure his own height. The push of heartlight did not reveal its visage — for a hood covered it in shadow. Hesitating greatly for fear of eying again the facelessness he'd once seen in the mirror, Neipas at last stretched the shivering lamp; the glow of which alighted a familiar mask.

Between the frame of the hood was the smiling beak and the eyes of Ms. Sunai.

It was her Eagle form. She extended him an apple.

The heart contracted. The gold permeated. Amid a sort of delirium Neipas reflected on the things he had witnessed here, in the Eagles' Nest. He had parted bread with the overlords of the age, and had beheld up-close the sheen of their gilded masks, their words he had sensed flown directly from their diamond lips. He had seen the core of the realm — and saw that all the foulness, all the rot infesting this empire of the meek and the addict, flowed first from here, from the top. It was poison which trickled down from the golden summits into the putrid vales. Evil, in the form of greed, flowed from here; and Neipas stood by its source.

Neipas shook his head slowly... and walked past Sunai, keeping his gaze fixed upon the little flame trembling under him.

Somehow he had gone around her in that narrow passage. Looking back he saw her again, turned to him, observing him, consuming him completely with giant owl eyes, now — Neipas rushed along.

Rounding the path across to the opposite side, he found a similar balcony to the one he had just been at; and found too the Midget, arriving at the very same moment, upon the very same steps, through the exact same movements, as if he/she had experienced the same hesitations and tribulations Neipas had endured on that arching unconscious trek.

Before them, likewise, was a gateway.

Inside it was an elevator without doors. It shook rustily, old, as it commenced

the descent. "Where are we going?" Neipas whispered.

The Midget took a moment to respond.

"To the bottommost floor."

75 - The Bottommost Floor

The stench hung around his nostrils and would penetrate them now and then, extremely pungent, sickly; it made him nauseous, it made his insides roil. Everything trembled and shuffled around him, within him. Various sounds intercepted his descent: the floating melody of the hovering orchestra; the booming gurgle of the contracting heart; the tempestuous flush of rivers roaring through the pipeveins as he sank by — brimming his mind with sudden torrents of childhood trauma, flooding him, in a mere flash, with the dejects of drowned villages — and the elevator's metallic rattling as it stumbled down the abyss. The brow tightened, the nostrils dilated, all body grimaced in torments through the dizzying bumpy ride. Caged in that elevator without doors, Neipas didn't even have bars to hold on to and nothing in that metal float to ease his vertigo, no security to be found in the very walls which, remote and obscure, shivered in the dim flamelight with buoying rust and writhing vermin.

But the Midget, who stood motionless and occult by his side, perhaps sensing his distress, held his hand; and Neipas becalmed.

In her/his serene presence and affect, he contemplated with abstracted tranquility the golden light drawing away; panned over by the shadowy heart that fed it, until it became a disc of fervent gleam bursting from a black sun, a macabre eclipse spectrally looming over his gaze. He fell slowly alongside taut ropes and cords — cords like those wrapped round the staff, held by the Midget upright and still — ropes moving in vertical paths, that held suspended in their fortitude, and which Neipas assumed operated the numberless elevators of the infinite Belab. This particular elevator now holding him had no doors in front, through which gaped the unmeasurable void of the tower's inner layer; and only one door and a gap in the back. Glints of form slid up across it sometimes. Desks, counters, screens, ripped curtains, corridors strewn with garbage and doors unhinged and ajar materialized in slivers of sunlight between the deepening layers of rope, glimmering here and there into Neipas' turned eye. The one-way mirrors lining the walls of the Anubel, it seemed, also plastered the circling rows of the Belab's lower floors; and in them he caught glimpses of the ruination the tempest had wrought through shattered windows. Calmly and almost unconsciously Neipas watched it all pass by, as though it were clouds vanishing in a dream; and by and by he found himself looking tenderly upon the Midget, thankful for his/her company. And in a tone almost tearful, suffused only with emotion and paying no mind to what it unconsciously uttered, his voice spoke thus, "You said you're a voice from the voiceless.

"Tell me —" pleaded Neipas with gratitude, "who are they?"

Replied the Midget, slowly — and in her/his speaking every other sound gradually fell quiet as if the universe itself, too, wished to hear: *"You are still among their number.*

"All exist within you, and each outside of you. And though you may not know them you too, exist in them. Their histories pass unrecorded. Multitudes, unsung, rejoicing in silence, suffering in silence, striving in silence, living in the quietude of the great noise, dying in the namelessness of common oblivion. Their joys were less than a flicker and their agonies passed unheard. Many of them died without ever having lived; and many of them alive today die every day without a sound. No rock was imprinted with their voices, their words were scattered to the winds. Yet they dwell in the Earth forever — and even the most acute ear can listen to but fragments."

Flickers of rumbling metal sparked in Neipas' consciousness in the quiet wake of his/her words; and the space rocking unattached and dull, Neipas let himself be lulled into stealthy slumber...

The vague and distant presence of a fuzzy glow, and of a swaying universe, jumped to proximity and startled him with a vigorous shake and a clap to the heart. Roused eyes opened to the same darkness encircling the same warm glow, though the latter became more vivid; flinching ears yawned in the screeching jerk of straining rust. With a bang and a wail the world stopped. All became still for a moment.

Naught but a frightened heartbeat somewhere underneath him and a flamelight somewhere before existed for a moment — until the fast clip thumping in the uncertain void was subsumed in a slower, larger, mightier resonance stirring the very ground, and the sensation of a cavity returned to envelop Neipas' little heart; the sensation of feet too, and the sensation of two hands, one warm in the touch of terracotta and flame, and the other cold, guided by another, smaller hand... The Midget led him out of the elevator into the wider gloom. Slowly they went. Neipas could only induce a plenitude of empty space through the dreadful shush, a quietness very restive and fidgety, as though a colossal noise had halted just moments before, and had left a trace of itself, thickening the air. Soon it came back, just as Neipas' stare was broadening in the flamelight and he gained a fuller possession of himself — it came, an unearthly, dull boom swelling onto the walls of the world in obscurity, a huge sound that expanded in his ears and filled his head double, once, then twice — like a monstrous heart beating out of the chest of some primeval titan... And then; that deadly silence — leaving the space enormous and empty.

Neipas had been here before.

WALTZ AT THE EAGLES' NEST

Whereas he had followed the Midget here last time, now the Midget had been at his side all throughout the journey; and whereas he had previously commenced in the inferno of a slaughterhouse underground, now he had begun in the nightmare of a meatmarket set about the summits. And if his *I* had failed to pierce the gloom when he last stepped here, the darkness now yielded willingly to the human flame. In a few steps the image of hanging cloths drew to its light. On his fingers he sensed the fabric that once brushed his face as he drew away the coarse tattered curtains, which palpitated in shadows of oil staining their vellum; they dried round thick clotheslines crossing web-like over the dirt, he could now see, as he pushed them over his head. The floor became strewn with gravel. Defunct moths, scarabs lay still among the pebbles. And a crepuscular gleam intensified, as before, through the succeeding veils of skin as they approached the center. The Midget kept holding his hand as they progressed steadfast, walking through the echo of pulses, the growing chill, the thickening odor...

At last, they arrived upon the clearing. The well rose beneath the creaky leafless tree as before. Again over him, there hung the throbbing dark sun, the black hole emanating golden rays of light out its porous circumference; such rays as wound and serpentined along obscure clefts, and swelled sickly as the sun-heart contracted in successive convulsions, in violent seizures, in booming reverberations deepening in volume — on its immense writhing toll Neipas had to close his eyes and tuck his head away from the feverish intensity of glare and resonance, for he stood directly under the convulsing abomination — it flashed into his soul with horrible, monstrous, titanic jerks of inhuman haste. The noise it wrought was agonizingly constricting. His muscles contracted with resurgent traumas, wrapping yet closer round the Midget's steadying hand and her/his infallibly tranquilizing influence. Becalming in long, shuddering breaths, Neipas endeavored to look forth.

Now he could see plainly. There stood by the tree root the figurine, the discreet idol of an old goddess; and on the jutting, uplifted root still hung, like the vestment of an altar, the sloughed snake skin. Faded, half-erased though it was, the message the Midget had drawn upon the ground could well be read under the light of the human flame:

WE CANNOT BREATHE
WE NEED AIR ————————————————

—————————————————————————————— [the line stretched and faded in stains]

Already soaked in the numbness of stench and cold, and wallowing in vague uncertainties, in the buoyancy of dream and inconscience, Neipas instinctively avoided the well, by which the air was coldest and smelliest. He took the few steps away from it to the statuesque; and never letting go the Midget's hand he asked:

"Whose statue is this?"

The Midget bowed solemnly before answering, *"She is the natural mother of all things — mistress and governess of all the elements, the initial progeny of worlds, chief of the powers divine, manifested alone and under one form of all the gods and goddesses. Her name, her divinity is adored throughout the world, in diverse manners, in variable customs, and by many names. She has been Gaia, Diana, Minerva, Juno, Hecate, Ramnusie, Mut, Isis, Parvati, Kali, Coatlicue, Eve, Mary — her name is uttered in many tongues, but in yours, the most accurate of names is* **Earth**.

"She is the ultimate. The impenetrable. None has lifted her veil."

Neipas stood before the idol, perplexed and mystified, and for a long time — forgetting the noise, the vibration of the air, its rancidness, its biting chill — beheld the defaced form of the sculpture.

"But," said he, "it's broken." And he said it with much desolation, as if he spoke of the Earth Herself.

"No... 'Tis but an amulet. An old symbol. The meaning survives — ever outlasting. She was before us, and will be after us."

Having said this, the Midget abruptly turned up by the well, by which Neipas now stood too, swaying. The leafless old tree and the broken figurine showed behind at a distance, as if they had dashed a few steps-length in the blank of a heartbeat. The Midget stirred the bulky lock on the well with his/her staff, pronouncing:

"Days of wrath loom ahead. The fate of the human race hangs in the balance; the fate of life, all life on this Earth, hangs in the balance; upon the agora of human decision."

And as she/he spoke it seemed as though the pulsating reverberation of quaking sound got swallowed up in the Midget's mystic double voice.

"We stand at a crossroads. The path will be arduous nonetheless; yet the choice is trivial. Prosperity or barbarism. Merriment or misery. Life or death.

"Take the flame, Neipas. 'Tis holy. Draw it faraway from this tower."

The robed sage stood facing Neipas at the end of two linked, outstretched arms, for Neipas endeavored to be as distant from the well's reek as he could; and with his visage half-turned and his body leaning back upon his heels, he muttered between the clenched beak, "But why?" — almost involuntarily he brought the tip of the lamp to his eyes, which glistened more calmly (he straightened his pose then) with the shimmer of the little flame.

"So that humankind may remember... Who they are; and who they were; and who they

can be. The flame you carry, 'tis holy. It alights beyond all masks, it strips out deceptions, it leaves intentions bare, it unveils meanings concealed. The tower no longer holds the flame prisoner."

The Midget tapped the well lock twice, as he/she had last time; though she/he must've applied more force, for the clank was louder now.

Neipas' stare was yet affixed upon the flame. He felt more silent inside himself. "So how do we get out of here?"

Through the flame he looked at the Midget, who seemed alight in cherubic glow and the haze of heat. Neipas no longer felt cold. He no longer felt the stench either. From his memory surfaced the thought of last time he was here: a representation of himself stepping back to leave, and finding no exit. Instinctively he knew that once one stepped upon this hallowed place, all doors would disappear — which prompted his question.

The Midget's answer was contained in his/her repeated gesture. The staff tapped the well-lock — twice — and the clank sounded in sparks (someway, Neipas already knew).

"The path must begin," she/he added, enigmatically, *"by looking back. You cannot know where you are, and you cannot know where to go, unless you know whence you came."*

Slowly then, Neipas lowered the flame slightly (he felt his brows furrowing; the flame dimmed timidly) and through the thin distorting air cast by the flame's breath, he beheld the Midget in doubt. A vague resurgence of frigidness, carrying a strange smell, tickled his countenance. The well jutted hauntingly at the sage's side.

"What's down there?" — his voice coarse and weak.

"The foundations of the tower," the Midget replied. *"Where all is sent to be forgotten.*

"It is upon it that the tower stands and it is it that holds the tower aloft."

Twice again the Midget's staff tapped the welllock — and its enormous clanking ring (!) [!] blocked all other sounds.

"The Historian's key," he/she said, *"opens the passage."*

The key lodged in Neipas' pocket; and the well, below him, loomed menacingly in its implied, towering depths. He was afraid, but he felt compelled to follow the Midget's request and obey his own heart's command. It whispered — the soft palpitations of the flame murmured. Gently letting go the sage's hand and putting down the lamp, he gripped the lock (a carbuncular old thing) and inserted the sinuous key. He turned it — once. The shank unlatched from the body; and just as soon as it slid out and the stocky old lock dropped, the cover upon the well topped off somehow, as if on its own, and Neipas was in the same instant facing the well's black mouth, and being seized by a tremendous blast of foul odor, unimaginably (for no imagination could ever approximate the tactile sensation) piercing and intense. His brain likely dissolved in putrefaction and all his innards seemed to rise in revulsion and disgust up his throat. Once he caught hold of himself, he found his hands and knees hard upon the gravel, and in his mouth torrents of vomit poured from his draining skull — swooning, breathless, retching and straining at the rough end of a great flight of dizziness.

His existence had somehow been ruptured, the air rendered in tatters of spasmic sound and vibration, along the motion of which his whole body trembled, his whole body, which felt at once like an emptied vessel and a cage in which he remained feverishly trapped. He was freezing, his teeth clattered violently and spurts of blood soaked his taste. The same ghastly smell filled his nose and noodled at will and whim throughout his vanquished senses. He was annihilated. Never before had he felt so ravaged, so tormented, so bereft of vitality, so torn apart from life, so close to death; and he sensed himself upon a thin thread hanging under one and hovering over the other. It was as if his soul intended to drain off with his bowels.

Slowly, slowly, relief came to fill the excruciating void in his shrunken being. The Midget's hand rested upon his head. It comforted him. It was a safety in his ails, a consolation in his final moments. Lain upon pebbles, he thought of his nursing mother, of his protecting father, and all the people and places of his life, he saw them all through closed eyes.

"You shan't die yet," spoke the Midget, as if she/he had read his spirit. And then, extending one hand out the wide sleeve, he/she offered him a fruit. *"Eat."*

Neipas gripped it between shivering fingers. It was very small — a type of berry, perhaps — and could be taken in a single bite. And the one bite replenished him, somehow, as he found himself able to stand; his mind, though empty, was no longer gripped by hollowness, but simply rested in serenity. He took the lamp and the flame from the ground where he had placed them. The tree, the well, and the effigy shone in gracious light.

"Place this about your nose," said then the Midget, extending again her/his hand, on the tip of which fingers gathered some sort of pasty herbs. From his/hers to his own fingers Neipas took them, and from there to his face. He perceived with some desolation that his mask, sodden, disheveled in messy plumage and disformed hardened wax, was still upon it. His fingers touched, pressed into the surface; and penetrating further into the airy cavity of the beak, tucked the herbs therein. They perfumed his senses — and made him relax yet more. He felt plenitude and some sorrow.

"Worry not," allayed the Midget. *"By emptying yourself you found the empty in your self, and went beyond. You now know that the emptiness you saw — is but a mask.*

"Go, Neipas," continued her/his two voices, as the hand which held the staff pointed to the well. *"Follow the tower's roots to find its exit. Yet beware.*

"Remember this you've lived here. They will try to seduce you, they will try to hypnotize you, they will speak good words, they will promise good deeds and use the whole power of their charm. Yet those are but other masks. Beyond all the glitter of their speech will throb the same aberration, the same cancer that is greed. And they will tell you pretty tales so you can better sleep at night.

"Heed this as you resurface. Emptiness is the mask they placed upon you. 'Tis the veil that hides them. 'Tis the well, by which they extract your vitality and steal your life — without your noticing the life they're taking, and all lives wherein.

"They dwell like thieves in **our** *night, Neipas. Watch that the flame glows in your darkness — so that you might see your self."*

With these words the Midget sent him off into his final inaugural journey, and Neipas, alighting the well with the holy flame, gazed into his path, and though he stretched his arm to the limit he could not see the bottom of the deep. There was but a ladder going down its old moldy stones.

"Are you not coming with me?"

This he asked, but he was no longer afraid. All fear had been washed away in the emptying torrent. And he felt cold no longer; the stench no longer assailed his senses, filled now with the aroma of mollifying herbs.

And the Midget's chorus replied him in a still more tranquil, more delicate tone than that to which Neipas was already accustomed:

"Where you are going, We cannot follow. But as long as You are, We will be with you."

Neipas climbed over the edge of the well.

But before he turned into the descent, he still asked:

"What's your name? Who are you really?"

And the Midget, upon hearing this, seemed to reflect; and then he heard him/her laugh for the very first time; a laughter serene, profound, resonant:

"Sunt Como Deus, Neipas," she/he said, *"therefore We are nameless. That We were, We are, and will Be."*

Neipas smiled. Bidding the sage farewell, he commenced his descent.

The world still shook with the echo of pulsing beat — but the Midget overlooked Neipas' passage from the welltop, and he felt no fear. Sound and sight followed him, though they became progressively dimmer — the noise meeker in its vibration, the Midget's tragic visage tinier in size. Neipas climbed down slowly, and as he could only avail himself of one hand — the other clutching the lamp — he tended to firm two feet upon each rung before proceeding to the next. Like this he went for insensible hours, the ladder kept on plunging into darknesses thick and depths unknown, and

Neipas kept his vertical progress against the faint, frigid breeze softly blowing, carrying the sickly scents from which his olfaction was now protected. The air was tight and the walls close, the space being so narrow that his back rubbed the wall opposite as it lowered. There was something comforting about the touch of a surface accompanying him, rough as it was; it felt vaguely like an encouragement, especially with the circularly framed portrait of the Midget, unyielding in its presence, watching over him benevolently — but the chilling air ascending the well strengthened the deeper he descended. It started to become terrible. His skin shook from cold again, shrinking his mind to a squeeze of physical disorientation and panting loss. He could see his enigmatic companion watching over him no longer — there was no light but the little light of the little flame. Freezing... In the growing tremble he seemed to quake off his very consciousness. He kept downward in looping, automatic motions, battling against a quickly emerging urge to give up. A mysterious force moved his body — he kept going. But he came to shiver in such fits of trepidation that the very rungs vibrated along their succession, noisy, clunky, and the ladder seemed on the verge of breaking out of the crumbling well stones; he was like one under the effect of hallucinogenics. The flame flickered — nearly out. All time had hushed and gone. How long had he been perched and fastened on that ladder? For the (?) time he lowered his foot —

but there was no rung.

(nausea) The foot hung in the air, irresolute. With a shudder of vertigo Neipas placed it back upon the safety of the last rung. Carefully then, he lowered the lamp in an attempt to see; but couldn't spot anything except darkness beyond the flame. Fearful, suspicious of his eyes, he still let his foot down to search — perhaps the next rung was merely a rung missing from the series — but he found nothing; the ladder ended there. In this strained position he caught a glimpse, however, of some strange luster reflecting the flamelight in dark glimmers yonder. A suspicion that a floor was near secreted in his troubled soul. Was it? (I dunno, I dunno...) — whispers and mutters in his head — (was it silent or loud? empty or full?) at the same time a great drop extended under him. He knew nothing. He sensed only that he was tired, so tired... And it was so cold...

His foot safely upon the rung again, he contemplated the flame shining serene by his eyes. He could perceive the scent of olive it fed on. He watched its sacred light standing at the tip of the humble lamp, glowing its uncanny holy color, wherein all colors pulsed in subtle breaths. He held it aloft, toward the mouth of the well so unbearably distant now; and he perceived himself to see, so far it was, as if the lamp had shortened all distances by its inhaling flicker, the Midget watching his progress still, not over him but *before* him, and at his side — something of the two voices lulled in his spirit... Neipas knew what its fragmentary whispers said, though he could not hope to decipher the language in which they were expressed.

The path lay at the bottom of the well — through there he must pass.

"Follow the tower's root," the Midget had instructed his soul, though the Midget had not spoken it.

Again a sole foot detached from ground and hung in the infinite air.

Silence fell absolute upon him.

One foot slid, his fingers parted onto a great reeling sensation. His heart was seized by the air, all his organs thrust upward and mind vanished in the ascent of the universe through him, his body fell through space.

*

Yet — it'd been but an intense instant of supreme disorientation — in a moment his feet met solid matter in an abrupt shock of contact. He fell in the dark; his head traveled eons until it found itself beside the elbows. A vague light shone over there somewhere through the sonorous thumping of his breast. The surface under his fingers was rugged, of moist rock making little creviced trails against his side. Soft tissue brushed his cheek, tapping silky across patches of his naked skin; he imagined himself in a fuzzy cob welter, and sensed that the place was very dusty, very old; ancient and primitive. Though he could not smell it anymore he could still perceive the mustiness and decay of forgotten things about his blinking eyes, permeating his mouth dry. Waving his hand over himself — so as to disfigure the imagined dense web (but at this he felt nothing) — Neipas got up stiffly, dull with confusion, and with his heart still palpitating behind his ears as he moved to the vague light just there — he found the lamp and the holy flame.

He raised them. A strange sort of snow fluffed the air across the lamplight. It took him a moment to identify the flakes as feathers, falling silently, silently covering the old ground, softening the stone. With the flame's aid Neipas soon realized he stood on a raised platform of some kind, a square, from which sides descended slopes, sinking into more darkness — though the feathers seemed to float in this darkness, and as Neipas extended the flame a bit closer, the darkness gained sheen, and glowed the light, broodingly, in return.

Only one of the sides was tiered in little steps. Checking the ladder over his head, he saw that it faced the same direction, and knew that he meant to go down those steps to follow the Midget's instructed direction — but he saw too how the well from which he came emerged from the same ancient stone upon which he stood, and which likewise extended into a bigger square, from which sides then rose sloped walls, lifting to the darkness above as under Neipas those walls descended... He perceived himself upon the top of a very old ruin of a very ancient temple, reflected in the brooding skies through which the tower lifted — he stood between two obscure pyramids whose peaks faced each other. Directly under the well hole a crater sank the platform a little, where Neipas had landed; and raising the flame toward the long pit above him, he felt — though he could no longer see — the Midget still overlooking in her/his enigmatic humanity.

Neipas declined across the steps; until his toes touched the darkness. All the ground there was covered in glossy, black sludge, a type of tar. He waited a while; with his ankle already submerged in bitumen he lingered, and let the sense of his own presence seep out of him. Plumes chaffed at his ears, and beat uncannily in the (he realized it now) the total absence of sound. A strange, palpable (tactile yet while sentience left his body slowly — then no more) sensation of quietude which he had never felt before impregnated his perceptions and rendered them altogether null. He stepped vacantly into the viscous substance, sinking his leg knee-deep (the ground, brittle, moist, leveled).

He was now in the bottommost floor of the tower.

The mud reacted with a gurgling moan, and then a faint squish as Neipas dragged his legs through it: sounds which yet reached his ears before the gloom buried them completely...

But he could yet see through the sacred flamelight — and he could still hear through it, though he used neither ear nor eye; and as he progressed the innermost, most secretive sensitivities grew more acute. This is what he saw: an upheaval of garbage in a vast pool of muck, pressed under a darkness nigh hermetic, and stuffed with such miscellanea of junk as broken sugarcanes, bits of cotton, rope, fronds and entire tree trunks, a lot of deflated plastic, half-submerged houses, used commodities of all types, even money — a near-impenetrable bog of discarded stuff.

Moments later — but perhaps it was all the same incompressible moment — he saw the first of them, jutting out of the dead ground where he waded.

His eyes had by then sunk into the back of his own head; but he could no longer feel the swirling nausea right behind them, nor the dismay that made the underlid twitch, nor his senses grimace into gradual shock at what lay there before him. Already he had sensed it under the mire — but here it emerged, over the surface.

The holy flame unveiled a bone. Then the darkness yawned to reveal another. Then another. Then another.

Shivering in the immense emptiness of things, Neipas alighted upon a head (a skull) — its mouth almost entirely bereft of teeth, it gaped enormously. A bubble of pitch held swollen in it; and tied round the dislodged vertebra (the remaining spine floated out across the tar, like an ivory serpent with innumerable dorsal fins) was a cord, a cord lifting into the highs, to lose itself in tenebrae; a cord like the cords which fastened balloons over the hanging gardens; like the cords winding round the Midget's staff.

"It is upon it that the tower stands ... it is it that holds the tower aloft."

They were human bones, these...

A flood of horrors seeped into his heart as he discerned the death about him. Amid the garbage, dead men, women, children, humans piled onward without limit, half-buried in the tar — from the elderly to the infant, all were reduced to bone, the oil embalming them in expressions of perpetual terror and lunacy. In the clefts between their macabre grins, and in the creases of besmirched limbs, there proliferated swarms of insects, stirring frantically over the corpses and the filth; the sight inspired gagging in the throat.

Feathers made the cord (strapped to the skeleton) vibrate and tingle all quietly. A balloon pushed it toward heaven — was it there that the skull's yell was locked? Neipas would witness still many such bones — from their gaping mouths came the same cords, ropes tied to their throats. Strings holding up the ground, parts of people all mixed, strewn without cohesion, bereft of the unity of life. Animal bones peeped in their midst, nigh indistinguishable. For miles and miles he would behold the dead. He would behold the skulls, skull after skull after skull, as himself in a dark mirror. He would behold the hollow under all eyes, the pits behind all noses, the grin beyond all lips; the skull beneath all faces. All looked as he looked behind the carnal mask. Men, women, children, all like he; he like all.

He would even find babies in there, unmistakably mauled, ripped out of a chance of life — tossed cruelly into the unknown and unfeeling beyond. Bones of people broken, crushed, deformed, all in an unfathomable evenness of oblivion.

He trembled, but he did not feel it. He stared, but he did not see. He heard nothing; he felt not the tumult in his being. Agonies gripped unknown... It was impossible, impossible to absorb such visions as that which he saw, in its abysmal immensity of tragedy and loss.

Now he stared at that skull; he felt somehow the life which had once animated it still lingering inside. Its mouth opened under eyeless sockets — two inscrutable abysses. He gazed long upon that scream without a face, long stripped of skin and feature; after which, lifting slowly the lamp, Neipas confronted the vast plain of facelessness and anonymity...

The cacophony of all multitudes had perished in the vast enigma of widespread death.

The most complete quietude befell him. Not a vibration could be sensed in the dead air; not even of his body moving. There wasn't, even, what one would call the sound of silence: which is the perception of soundlessness; no — not even perception existed here.

Neipas ceased to exist during the course of the march.

*

Words are inadequate to render certain orders of experience. Perhaps no language devised by the human spirit could approximate the perception beyond feeling, the sensations beyond the senses which suffused Neipas and of which he was made throughout the passage. Texts are but symbols; and there is no combination of words that can convey the experience of dwelling outside the bounds of time, those bounds beyond which none among the living can ever transgress. Naught but the soul — which bears no eyes, no ears, no lips, which is bereft of nose and of fingers — can sense its truths. Dwelling in the soul, Neipas wandered it without knowing; without feeling; without being; he wandered somewhere (nowhere) beyond that veil, which no tongue has soiled, nor eye drawn, nor mind captured...

............delineations of stalagmites became perceptible by and by: a motionless thunderstorm of rock embalmed in a dim rosy glow which yawned, very slowly, into the wakefulness of a dazzling maw, opened to the sun such that it resembled a divine portal to its light. Feathers snowed across it like flying shadows. Neipas stepped up to it; and his senses, being so long steeped in gloom, were viciously attacked by the ensuing glare. For a long time he remained seated upon the entrance of the grotto, regaining sensibility, the capacity of sight, the ability to hear. Violent frothing waves barreled down the rift beneath him. Spray fell upon him; the taste of salt permeated his lips; the smell of ocean filled his nose, and as the roar of the sea grew clearer in his ears he realized that the tide was picking up. Floating plumage scattered about him as he opened his eyes; he saw them swaying in dense numbers upon the growing water below, abandoned, inanimate and defeated. A gold-lined horizon glimpsed from the end of an ocean afar, framed by the ragged rock.

The holy flame burned still upon the tip of the lamp, and Neipas took great care to protect it as he trod out of the sea cave, away from the deep round crevice gaping to a watchful, bright, deliriously blue sky, stumbling his way through a path down the wide cleft's wall, across the jagged rock — he'd removed his shoes and socks, both thoroughly soaked, to better walk — the socks he kept in his pocket, the shoes he simply left between two stones. The grotesque sea tumbled and wrenched under him in successive charges of buoyant wing and liquid flap. Upon his bare feet he turned the narrow wallway and, leaving the crevice's shadow to face the big sea and the scorching sun, trod first across a large, flat stone jutting from the base of the bluffs at the level of the tide. Waves sloughed off the shimmering rock and returned, caressing the cliff like a nursing mother, or shoving into it like an intemperate parent at turns; washing over his toes and climbing in spume to his ankles, and knocking against his knees in vicious attempts to make him topple, making him hold on to the cliffwall; and as he endured the treacherous force of the waters, the whole wide emptiness of their ocean was presented to him as suffused with an almost infantile, primordial presence, as of a moody child unaware of intrinsic divine powers; with the sun hanging obliquely over the horizon, the expanse took on the form of a highly abstract baby-cyclops laying down his vigilance, entering into the nightmares of his own watery body whose slumbering rage could be felt picking up. The wind was yet uncertain — devious, perhaps, in its almost playful motions, swaying between grace and anger — but for the moment Neipas paid it no heed. He went with purpose. Stepping diminutive over crags and broken rock gathered at the bottom of the cliffs, huge cliffs dashing up the escarpment slantwise and towering steeply over him, Neipas advanced like a traditional paragon of progress with his hand held high, holding a vulnerable flame above the frothing waters. The sunlight infused them with a ghostly jade tinge as they swung in and out in magical, musical oscillations. Its song intimated arcane syllables, words cyphered between the broken waves; sybillations of an occult nature. Gasps and sighs and seething regressions and furious blasts sounded the arcane forms imbued in Neipas' spirit and concealed by his memory. Each swell of wave brimmed out of his spirit the images that his mind could not retain: here by the monochrome pallor of the flame, gaping skulls and broken limbs thickly strewn and stripped of flesh, life and identity; fields of remnants mixed in the great obscurity of oblivion, stewing in an unending and everlasting bog of tar. Orifices in the limestone (where the mollusks lodged) gurgled crudely something of its dismal bubbles, puffing up under the apprehensive flame like the aggrieved sighs of voiceless specters — and each crash of foam sprayed the images away again. Wet, salty, empty, Neipas carried on along the curving bluff, striving to escape the horizon's closing eye, and as the wind tantalized and lulled the ocean into agitated dreams he strained to keep the flame away from its lash, tucking the lamp under an enveloping arm, lifting it to the wind's briny drunken delight only when the inebriated sea came slithering between his legs. Dabs of shimmering golden crimson upon the mantle of ocean, the marine belly of the primordial beast falling in dream-exhalations of murder and feasts. Neipas discerned in its clipping shriek within himself the palpitations of that netherworld whence he'd emerged somehow alive; in the rush and gurgle of the froth about him he felt the ghastly stillness of the tar inside him; he waded through the dense substance, and pushed his leg through it, and anchored his foot, and crushed a brittle, suffocated soil, and straining black lather bubbled up as he plod on in the inanimate thickness, as if stomping unceasing grapes bursting blood mires tall; burbling languid, soundless mutters at his waist, venomous grapes, intoxicating him into complete forgetfulness and physical insensibility, into a spiritual numbness of incorporeal unfeeling. The tar had yielded to the day and the sea veered now. Menace, warned the holy flame, while the murmuring sirens of the gust massaged Neipas' shoulder with promises of eternal rest as he strained past his forces, flexing atrophied muscles across the cutting rock hurting his feet, bruising his elbows, through the gust attacking his lungs, confiding into his instincts the sea's wish to eat him entire, soul and all, palpitating unto his fluttering heart the intractable quietude of the deep he'd trudged. Its vibrations dwelt in his spirit. They roamed wildly, they roved free. He stepped over chinks and pivoted upon saliences, he hugged the cliffrock, he carved his toes into the jagged surfaces as he strained to escape the tide bombarding under him. His soul recollected as the waters slurped, the unsounding noise of pipelines down there in the abyss under the tower, under the city, arteries pumping the lifeblood of civilization to all the domesticated corners of the Earth, to all the gorging centers of industry extracting and consuming the very substances of life. He had heard nothing, for he had discerned nothing during that grim passage of nonexistence. But his throbbing spirit retained the unphysical impression of thundering skies under the asphalt plains of the megalopolis — muscles of ducts and pipelines in the unfelt ceiling, hanging in the blackness, running athwart the pitch storminess with tremendous euphorias of energy overlooking that immense stasis, feeding off the unending tomb. They were giant things, as thick as buildings, teetering invisibly. All the metal affluents of the great river of affluence roared without being heard; all drawn from this aquifer of doom, rot and forsakenness. And vast shoots drooped from their tenebrous celestial midst to pour sludge and the waste of societies upon that landfill of History, where the dead languish without peace, wallowing — in wait, perhaps — in molten tombstones, all dissolved in a great admixture of anonymity and neglect; all to keep the great box-machine running, all fuel for Axiac's artificial life, kept alive by the blood and sweat extracted from the pores of the dead and the barely living. Midway through the southward pilgrimage, Neipas had passed under the basin tucking the demon's industrial lungs — betwixt the kidney-factories and intestinal facilities of its misconstructed body, he had sensed beyond the senses the raging cauldron of Iblis, boiling in the fury of oceans, the roar of its gaseous veins, the mad, soundless trumpet of its spires marking the unbridled tempo and time of humankind's doomed march. Like armies sleepwalking upon the pavements he sensed them, unsensing, trampling subterranean heavens toward the dreaming deep, dreaming sleepless. These impressions Neipas bore many layers underneath his skin, and all those remote tragedies which he sensed but could not grasp moaned in the echoes of his heartbeat and the quiet palpitations of the human flame, flaring feebly away from the waves of the coast as Neipas climbed the vanishing cliff. The sky began to assume a red, sleep-deprived hue over the panting sea, and the world brooded in the likeness of a titanic maw salivating blood and bloodthirsty cravings. And the great diabolical waters throed before the incoming night; huffing, puffing and blowing in growing delirium, plumbing into dreams unsettling, frothing like frustrated wings, featherless wings weighed down by the pressing night, as down weighed the floating feathers falling upon the bottommost floor, snowing upon the graves of uncounted millions, uncounted billions whose individual lives had perished in the great totalizing and leveling force of civilization; feathers flown from shoots like the discarded dreams of fallen angels, landing softly upon the mass grave for which such civilizations are destined. Bones yelled their final and eternal desperation in a supreme silence of frozen motion and obliterated futures on all sides of Neipas and the little hopeful flame; and as he beheld without seeing all those people sacrificed to the maws of Tophet and the whims of Mammon, he knew the truth — he knew then that all possible hells existed within lived experience on this Earth... The ocean frothed and seethed and panted these ruminations beneath him as he climbed toward the falling clouds and the cliff turned flatter and more perilous. But he could see the beach just yonder, peeking into his eyes. He held steadfast to the rock, sticking his toes into fading cavities, stabbing over ever smaller saliences with his nails, struggling and sheltering the holy flame, careful and hurried, growing in the sensation of vertigo with the waves beneath his meek body and the tar dead wallowing in his nauseated soul. A single tree erected atop the promontory there, like an unlit beacon on the other side of the beach, flailed before the winds as if trying to escape the rising moon. The sun dipped and faded; the day's eye closed. The horizon bled nightmares. The sea, intent on eating all the annihilated dreams locked inside the cliff shell and extended under the bituminous shield of urban streets and buildings, kept pushing, heaving, blasting volleys in a tireless onslaught against the rock wall and the small, famished body and flame there precipitously perched. But he was almost there! strained he with hope, keeping the teary lamp near his breast as he rounded the final stretch — one leap more to the platform jutting there, and the way to the beach, but two meters under it, would be clear — and he spotted, yonder far in the core of emerging Axiac, the Belab tower intact, invincible, infinite, immortal, immaterial almost in its unfathomable global expression and significance. There the symbol of might and sovereignty over the subjects rose from the great deep and towered above all things — the next moment the Pearl at the summit clapped open its blinding glare — a chunk of protruding stone fled under thin grasping fingers — the dead screamed all together, his toes slipped, his body was again taken by the air — swept by water. All sounds ceased in the sudden flush of tidal groans in a blood pool. All cords plunged into the flood. Over the crimson heaven washed the foam of waves in the form of dust spraying the vanquished sky... and the tree of ash bloomed in fire over him, erupted into him, ravaged his senses and scattered his body into powder —

    ...

*

...flying under the crest of a rising wave [...] was lifted to flamelit skies, dispersed in scattering lunar dust, among the stars blown; through the gust of arid universes [...] floated. [...] spirit, [...] mind expanded to the confines of cosmic altitudes in the uppermost limit of existence, passing in [...] flight languid lights and pale fires flashing in great fathomless voids. And at the limits of existence [...] saw a mirror, darkly and without luster.

    [...] knocked, and someone [...] had known in the distant past floated on the other side. Mirror or mirage, [...] asked what existed in the farthest future, contemplating the remote and absolutely inscrutable reaches. Yet no voice emerged, but out of [...] a balloon rippled out and floated. Crowds were manifested on all sides of her, looking yonder somewhere, always with the same look of longing. [...] Mother smiled sadly and tears trickled into the wider substance where existence continued afloat. [...] finger touched the ultimate glass; transcending the [...]; and the journey was again commenced.

The balloon burst — its bosom ruptured, its wings spread, [sound]

Sounds ascended from the absolute silence, noises of voices and vermin buzzing out, amid great jets of light born from the empty; a rain of herbs in the ensuing tide; dim bubbles as [...?] attempted to scream in [Neipas]'s great panic. A hand reached into his reaching hand, across the glass — thrust in a furious ablution of awakening.

Neipas emerged. Out of the dying sun he came rippling — a tremendous dose of air rushed into his lungs the next moment. The wind blew frigid against his naked face. He gasped between swells of wave and submerged and popping sounds as the universe teetered, tipped about him, stumbling across a confusion of water. There was much panting, close, on his side of the blur. He toppled, the earth arose and crashed unto him. There he lay on the sand, his wet cheek clammy upon it, the taste of it in his mouth. Coughing pierced through the saltwater inundating his eartubes; and grew rapidly in volume as his wits returned to him.

His lungs drummed in inflamed bursts, his throat flared. Neipas shook vehemently with the cold in his marrow and the vibration of his coughs and his confusion. He got up and stumbled about, teary-eyed, completely disoriented, clamoring moans. All gravity seemed to be stepping on him, he arched his back so low and was so short of breath as to feel altogether decrepit. The sun died in the west beyond the sea, culminating in still, dead froth where the lamp lay without flame. Neipas found himself on the ground again, absorbing the fading crimson of heaven, besmirched with the wet sand and holding on to his knees, his face contorted in anguish and awash in many tears.

Eventually he found the strength to rise to his knees, and for a while so remained, with hands spread, pressed into the pasty soil, water dripping out his hair and plume drying in the chill as the night cloaked him. By the shoreline, by the resting waves, in across the beach, whole moribund colonies of those long-winged flies that materialize after the rains languished, perished into the sand. Iridescent wings stirred weakly here and there along the crystallizing tide. Full moons rose within them.

It took him a while to realize he was in the Southern Shore, in the beach where, long ago, he had parted bread with Orenda.

Watching the blur clear from the calm sway of an appeased ocean, it seemed to Neipas as if feeble plumes gasped their last breaths, too exhausted to attempt the skies again, too leadened by the world's weight. The whole extent of water, accepting the comforts of the night, seemed to him then like an immense face without eyes, a reflection of his soul, of a spirit shod, trampling among the vastness between flightless wings and sighing tar, wandering under banishing heavens as the day's fire died.

Two hands remained impressed in the sand; their fingers stretched toward the ocean — parched tributaries bereft of source and destination — reaching for something forever beyond their grasp (perhaps saluting or worshiping) — extending under the shadow of the hill covering foot by foot and blackening, finally, the sighing froth by which Neipas and the lamp were. Between his floating hands he cupped it. But there was no flame.

He still opened the little lid to see if the fire had survived wherein. But no. There was no flame.

There was but dirt and the liquid in which it had dissolved. Neipas peered into its profoundities; yet the darkness reflected in its depth was too unfathomable to grasp. In an unconscious motion, he dipped his fingers — and sprinkled his brow with the water and the flameoil before walking into the land, into the woods.

76 - Styx Ebbed

By the shoreline, by the sleeping waves, a whole moribund colony of those long-winged flies that materialize after the rains languished, perished into the sand; others yet tottered on the verge of collapse. Neipas, holding the lamp underneath his blurry stare — sensing the extinguished flame in the ebbing waters, drowned by the night — reflected that he had never seen these insects fly.

Overtaken by a nauseating feeling, he scampered away, and kept on stumbling out of the sands until he was well inside the woods.

He spent that very night in the forest. His head was gradually pushed to the ground by exhaustion both of body and of mind; and on the ground he laid himself, among the crackling of fallen leaves under his ear, among the strange noises of the darkness, among the opaque shapes of towering canopies and against the glint of stars peeking dim between the leaves. He was assailed by many fears, fueled by the ghostly rumblings and mumblings of the forest, and felt at once watched by ill spirits and hopelessly alone; all in an agony of loneliness and a febrile delirium of half-wakened nightmares, for his nerves, stimulated by the mutters around him, paranoid and afraid, would not let him sleep. There was a cool chill from the ocean, but still he felt balmy and feverish and was covered in sweat. For a while he huddled with his forehead against his knees, bearing pangs of hunger in his stomach and whirls of dizziness in his head, by the strong roots of a tree, encompassed by stooping foliage; resembling a sickly fetus in the mother womb, oscillating between birth and death. Finally, the extreme exhaustion which made his whole body numb and impotent spread to his mind, deadening the immediate distress gnawing at him restless, and overwhelming his senses; so that the entirety of his being succumbed to it, sunk heavy under the fatigue. He slept a dreamless sleep.

And he slept for a long time, waking only when the heat of the sun grew so intense as to rouse him out of it. His eyes opened for the first time to the daylight of open air, and gradually saw the destruction all around him, the damage wrought by the storm's unrelenting fury. The forest had been leveled by the winds; razed, its trees lain in disarray. The very bark and leafage that had sheltered his slumber had fallen across the bed of mud soft; in reality, there was nothing to cover the aggressive nakedness of the sky, sweaty and searing and mad, above him. His body, unprotected, was curled round the holy lamp; and through bleary disoriented blinks he seized it, and got up — and fell — and got up again. Neipas stumbled through the desolation, feeling hollow and weak. Every oscillation of body was a trial. The strain made him numb, his head ached with a feeling of vacuity, he felt sapped. Yet he kept walking. The guiding force of his being was reduced to instinct, he was reduced to the condition of beast struggling to survive. His mind was so far suffocated and frail that it couldn't produce a single coherent thought — it was all fragments and a jumble of sensation — he knew only he had to find water to drink and food to eat, it was as though that was all he had ever known. At times his mind slipped into hallucinations, and pondered in delirious flashes about profound matters, matters of the soul, the nature of the universe, what happens after death. But these were but hazy remembrances of thoughts he had already had; and so he would sway feverishly between maddened deliberations upon the quiet spirit and the immediate necessities of the moaning body. Sometimes he wavered on whether to eat of the little shrubs which he saw jutting out of the dirt here and there; but he hadn't the slightest idea what they were, their names, whether they were edible; and he feared these plants would poison him. He reflected vaguely, in his dizzy mood, about how unmoored he was from the type of knowledge passed across generations which had long been the fundament of their survival.

Deep in the fallen woods, his eyes found — he had unconsciously been following its sound — the brook which he had so long ago now (lifetimes ago now, perhaps) followed, with Edazima and Martin, to find Oshana, Orenda and the gathering. No longer was its cry a melody in the wind, dancing between the breathing trunks and flowing leaves. Its tenderness was no more; across the bare air the waters now raged, imperious and angry, in blasts tangled with blasts of cascades battering against rocks. Now the mellow brook was a stormy river; the waterfall had monstrously transformed from the gracious tongue of a singing muse to the blare of a screaming demon vomiting its fury across an ample bog. Standing at its edge, Neipas recalled how he had stopped to sit in this clearing once, when the land was yet gentle; how the blooming senses of Edazima's child had twinkled with recognition here. On the other side and across the mire now were scattered many large, quarried stones, which had once composed the facade of a building. These, Oshana had told him, were the ruins of an old temple — the first that the settlers had built upon mooring on these shores, in their effort to conceal their rapacious savagery under the guise of a civilizing mission.

"Here the settlers first built their church. Here they founded the megalopolis," Oshana had said, as they strolled about one day (this had been shortly after Neipas parted bread with Orenda). "But there is nothing that is settled upon the ground. There is nothing that Nature cannot envelop — there is nothing that Nature cannot uproot."

Though overgrown with vine and leaf then, the stones still stood — but now the ruin was ruined and meshed with the undifferentiated effect of Nature's molding powers.

Neipas went around, carefully — for he only had socks on — over the fallen trunks, the disheveled grounds devastated and suffused with the nauseous glow of morn, the land growing fevered, pressed under the ascent of a scornful sun. He limped weary into the edge of the city. As the forest ended, the old industrial districts of Ostrich began. First he saw a dilapidated warehouse withering away in a clearing, covered in vines and graffiti, every single one of its many windows smashed. A short distance beyond it rose a razor-wired fence, and beyond the fence small edifices of concrete in advanced stages of decay, which were being slowly eaten up by the forest — remnants of the old port and factory belt.

The fence sagged with signs warning invaders to keep out or be shot on sight, and Neipas, clutching on to the wire mesh, wondered vaguely what sort of treasures they could be safeguarding there still. He hobbled alongside it until he found its corner, jutting out of the woods into a neighborhood of shacks and broken houses. The insides of those houses (those few which had not been felled by the storm) were pitch dark, and from them came drowsy sighs and the stench of unclean bodies, hints of abject destitution flowing out in quiet, coughing spurts. On the fractured roads and shattered sidewalks, already crackling under the growing heat of the zenithward sun, he saw nobody. Traces — rags, needles, trash — but no one to be seen. Mud extended with scraps of boughs and foliage all around, as if the forest had been dragged here by force, and scattered among the general vista of neglect and debris. It was a while going through these forsaken ramshackle streets — until at last he found a bus stop. This bus passed by a station on the northeast-bound train line, through which he could get into town and back to his apartment, where he could collect a pair of shoes and a change of clothes. But he had no money for the fare; and he shivered full of manic trepidation as he waited for the bus, ruminating on whether the driver would let him enter — was the driver nice enough, did Neipas look shabby enough, would the driver take pity? He feared being trapped in that sunny derelict ruin, that suburban prison of tins and cardboards where no sustenance was to be found, and dying there; and he realized with despair that he still wore the fashionable jacket Eva had bought him, he still wore the refined shirt and trousers from the Eagles' Nest (so far in the heavens it was now!). He looked up suddenly then. There it was, far, far in the distance — the gigantic Belab rose from the core of Babylon, from amidst the towers quiet under the scorching sun, without luster now, without splendor — full of broken glass, mirthless.

In his agitation Neipas didn't realize how wretched he looked — whatever luxury his clothing had once displayed was buried under grime and grease from the sewers and dirt from the wild — and he still thought of going back and dressing some rags he had seen on the ground, so that he would look more miserable. But he was too tired, and his body protested against any exertion that wasn't indispensable for survival. Eventually the bus came, and Neipas peered inside with the face of a forlorn wretch, teary-eyed, tattered. The driver looked at him casually and said "come on in chief," with an air of being used to seeing such fellows daily. He let Neipas in, free of charge — and Neipas was so full of gratitude that he wept, silently, in the back of the bus.

He tucked into the hard seat, holding dearly to the little lamp. For a while he contemplated the bleariness fading from his eyes; then he watched the destruction panning by the window. The waters were slowly retreating, removing the gargantuan bulk of their extent. In their wake they left long and ample gashes of mud, debris and refuse torn, hauled and strewn with the aspect of violated things. Everything looked pitilessly mistreated. It was a mess of toppled trees atop crushed cars and blasted houses, structures dragged and smashed asunder, splinters everywhere. It resembled a war zone; the sort of thing Neipas had seen in movies or in pictures he had glimpsed right through on the Webwork. Whole blocks completely razed by the wrath of the wind, fields of scrap extending disjointedly by the side of the bumpy road: to see such a sight without the dulling filter of a shining screen made it still more unreal somehow; the feeling of fiction pervaded everything and a dozing sense of unreality padded things with a sharp anesthetic.

Transparent, faded over the passing wreckage, his mask meanwhile hovered (in the windowpane) briny, baked, melted, disfigured; as ravaged as the landscape — too horrid to behold... And as he avoided the sight of it (trying to gaze beyond it — he could not entirely look away) he seemed to see vague shapes recurring. He seemed to glimpse skulls beneath the rubble. He seemed to glimpse skulls beneath the masks. He seemed to glimpse skulls beneath the transparent face in the windowpane, he seemed to see skulls everywhere glimpsing.

(Madly he held the little lamp) "Excuse me, driver," Neipas began humbly, in a low tone, approaching the front end of the bus. "Are you still stopping at Blue Rock station?" — for he had just realized the bus was going a different route than usual (this was announced on the headsign over the windshield; in his flustered unease he hadn't noticed it).

"They're still repairing the bridge there," replied the driver with a deep, sage voice. "That got hit pretty bad. We're stopping at Industrial District more down the line though."

"I see — thank you."

"No problem."

And — simply because of the respectful tone with which the driver addressed him, and the dignity which it imparted — Neipas' eyes burned again gently with contained tears.

Neipas had been alone with the driver then, but soon more folk would enter the bus. The floods had receded in the shallower parts of the megalopolis, repairs were underway wherever repairs could be made, and the citizens of Axiac lumbered back to their normal lives as best they could. Those boarding the bus now, those from the deep blocks of Ostrich, were headed to the north — where the economic wheel was faster to recommence its spin — to retake their routines at the cafes, restaurants, and clothing stores where the rich would shop. Many of them were newly homeless now. Beneath the pigeon mask of the woman who had just entered, worn atop a barista outfit, Neipas could clearly see the strain of anxiety for the immediate future and the wrench of trauma from the recent past (and the trembling skull). But Neipas didn't look too much; mostly he coiled in his seat in the back of the bus, wishing to speak to no one.

The bus was still, however, mostly — and unusually — empty when Neipas left it. He sneaked to the front shyly as the bus neared his exit, just so he could say "thanks so much" to the driver as he stepped out.

"Have a good day," said the driver in a candidly collected and tranquil tone of voice.

Most went out the bus on that stop. Across the street was the train station; its rails stretched northward down an immense boulevard flanked by battered factory buildings and run-down shops. Big trucks clogged the road — dotted with warning triangles bordering the shattered asphalt, shaping a sort of obstacle course through which the vehicles trudged — hauling loads of heavy cargo; and the economic machine was back on here already too, ever unyielding, ever ceaseless, running here on rubber wheels. Peeking behind the low buildings, Neipas saw the oil pumpjacks spinning, hammering their ostrich heads at the earth with the urgency of someone with no time to lose.

In a corner of the station was one of those newspaper vending machines one would see peppered all over Axiac. Standing belly-high, the meager stack of gazettes rested in a box, protected by a glass facade. Neipas noticed, first, that the glass wasn't properly attached: it could be lifted up. Then he saw and recognized the newspaper brand.

Here was the newspaper for which his former teacher at the Ivory Tower, professor Moldura, was the Editor.

It was that day's edition. (Front page news related how a Columbidae missile had struck a convoy in Mesopotamia which killed, among 10 others, the head of the Persian armed forces; a general sense of mobilization transpired from the drama of the sheet, the trumpets of war panted excitedly out the headlines, through the very gritted, bloody teeth of the font) ...a tingling, premonitory sentiment rumbled in his breast. Had anything been published about the recordings? Discreetly, Neipas raised the glass cover and slipped one of the bundles out. Taking a few steps away, molding his mask to appear as casual as possible, he leaned against a pole near, and, crossing his legs (to appear more casual still), he laid his eyes and the bristled feathers atop the page of cheap paper make as he leafed through and scanned the contents. He scanned long, and as carefully as he could in his frazzled state of mind. He rolled through the paper and back through more than once. Perhaps there had been no time yet to process all the information contained in the recordings; perhaps the intrepid journalists were yet studying the best way to convey the damning revelations, Neipas pondered as he browsed through one last time.

Finally he found it.

There was a mention of the recordings. He read it several times — it wasn't very long (meanwhile he had removed one of the double spreads and placed it atop his head to protect him from the exaggerated sunshine and the balmy heat). He read it several times in the attempt to comprehend what it said; indeed, he had understood it the first time, and by the tenth he no longer read it so much as attempted to reconcile the contents of it with his own expectations. This mention of the recordings — the recordings Neipas had risked himself for, which provided evidence of abundant malfeasance, widespread corruption, generalized criminality and entrenched wickedness festering in the upper echelons of power — occupied but a thin column in the corner of a back page, tucked shyly in the depths of the newspaper.

Its title read: LEAKED ANUBEL RECORDINGS PERSIAN DISINFORMATION, INTELLIGENCE OFFICIALS SAY. The short article echoed claims by the intelligence service agencies that the leaks had been the work of Persian spies; and assurances by state diplomatic corps that every purported revelation disclosed by the Eagles talking unmasked in those recordings (objectionable as they might seem) were all entirely legal. There was a vague summary of what the recordings (part of which, it seemed, had been published by other outlets by then) were about, but the dismissals constituted the bulk of the article. Never was it claimed that the recordings were fake; not once were their contents scrutinized or investigated.

And so were the licit briberies and legalized thefts — the murders gone unpunished — casually papered over. Neipas lifted his head and directed blurry, confused eyes at the confusedly blurred landscape.

The train picked him up, and rolled northward — slower than usual today. Neipas entered without paying. Normally he would spend the ride in mortal fear of the prospective official boarding to check tickets — yet the existence of a ticket inspector in that apocalypse was inconceivable to him then, and anyway he was too exhausted to think about anything and too hungry to feel anything but his deepening hunger. Turning his head emptily to the window, he gazed a little street breaking off from the main boulevard, descending toward a little urban valley between rows of shanty houses; and he saw, down there, that everything was still flooded. A wide lake rested under the rooftops, lapping at the eaves; in it floated appliances, commodities, trash, the lifelong belongings of ruined households.

But suddenly a thought struck Neipas and he nearly jumped up his seat with anxiety. It occurred to him (indeed it kept occurring to him, it shocked him out of the daze every now and then) that he was starving, and he also had no money. What could he do? He hadn't the nerve to steal — he would, perhaps, perhaps he would, but the mere thought of it produced wrenching shivers in his mind, fears of imprisonment — so he had to find money some other way. The nervous weight and disconcertion in his chest pinned his heart to the seat. It took a formidable effort, an epic strain to lift himself out of it, and raise his lowered head above the sitting folk. He looked very meek, very diminished as he held the little dead lamp. Gravity seemed suddenly very heavy. It was a gravity laden with shame; into his mind flashed the memory of his bowing his head the exact same way, but at the top of the world, to the most powerful in the world, and for good money (which, in the end, he would never even get) — like a dignified beggar. Yet now he wore the mask and circumstance of an actual beggar, someone with nothing, stooping to those who had little more than he. It was humiliating to approach anyone in such a posture of lowered head; and the dismissive waves of hand and shakes of head punctured the innermost reaches of his soul with a pain he hadn't known before. He was dazed, but not enough to not feel — and he carried this painful procession (upon filthy socks) through the train-car at the verge of tears the whole way through. Finally, after asking what seemed a whole multitude, someone gave him a dollar, handing it over as one feeds a vending machine, emotionless and without a word.

It was a dollar made up of two coins — the hand had dropped them in the fuel chamber of the little lamp, which yawned open; the lamp which Neipas held in supplication, unconsciously. At first he took the dollar gratefully and rushed humbly back to his seat, thinking of the pack of five small bread rolls he could buy with it. But now, shrinking beside the window, his wallowing spirit considered somewhat remorsefully the coins floating in the olive oil and seawater buoying inside the lamp — inside the holy lamp. The train and the world bobbed and shuffled around his body, inside his mind, with the vibrations of blasphemous guilt. There grew a hesitant and confused sense of debasement in his heart. Was he not defiling the lamp by using it to store money? He didn't mean to do that (he rubbed his eyes violently). Muttering apologies, he took to the lamp his fingers, wet them with oil and salt, and carefully extracted the rusty coins.

Intent on going by the supermarket in his neighborhood right away, Neipas drifted out of the train, which halted several stops before Ostrich at the last station aboveground — the rest of the line, which sunk into the tunnels, was yet submerged under the flood — and he boarded another bus, to which everyone sprinted and which everyone crammed in such a way that no tickets were checked. So squeezed, Neipas endured the ride with physical hurt and abashment, looking down all the time, thinking all the time of how the others around had to sustain his smell and how disgusted they must all be. He left in a hurry when the supermarket got sufficiently near and walked the rest of the way, panting in his meager, choked chest.

He saw the familiar sights he was so used to walking by destroyed, the easily recognized places unrecognizable, as in a dream. Everything was a dream, everything was uncanny in the vast trauma of the shattered megalopolis, in the intimate anguish of Neipas' crumbling mind. His eyes wavered dizzy whenever he looked up, and it was as though the air and the sky were augmented, bigger somehow, distorted; he found the surroundings more oppressive than usual, the scald of the sun lethal; so he kept his gaze down, keeping in the shade as much as he could.

Neipas trod with rushed steps into the supermarket. The pastry section was right by the automatic doors, separate from the main section of shelves; a glass pane displayed the various pastries, and behind the shopkeeper there was a row of a variety of bread loafs. Or there should have been — for the pastry shelf was completely empty, and there wasn't much bread at all. The type Neipas was looking for was there — but he saw with a shock that it cost triple as much now! He gulped, desperately. The shopkeeper, a mid-aged lady bearing an apron and an impatiently raised brow, looked at him.

Neipas approached the counter shyly.

"Good morning," he said in a feeble moan. "Excuse me... That bread, hum... It used to be one dollar a pack of five, wasn't it?"

"Used to. All price's been going up since the storm now."

Neipas nodded meekly. "How much for each one? Do you sell them individually?..." he asked. His voice was shaky and timid, thin, so fragile as to resemble the voice of a child.

"Only sellin' them together."

Neipas didn't understand this, and seeing those raised prices after trekking all the way from the southernmost borders of Axiac provoked in him embarrassment and a type of secret outrage. He didn't know the extent to which the storm had crippled roads and means of transportation, that it had swept with wind and plummeted with rain the silos and crops of wheat, rye and corn in the fields and farms to the distant northeast, where grains were stored and from which the bread was made; cutting yields by as much as a quarter. The suppliers took the cue and, moved by the potent forces of the Market, raised the prices in triple to mitigate losses (and even up profits); assuming rightly that folk would buy in, not stopping to think of wretches like Neipas who, damaged by the storm like the fields were damaged by the storm, hadn't the means to buy such bread. The next few weeks would deliver them handsome earnings (to their already towering money would be added still much more money).

But Neipas knew nothing of this. He simply stood there, dumb, trembling slightly. A strange chill coursed up his spine.

"You want five?" asked the shopkeeper. Neipas detected an intimidating tone of impatience, but he could have imagined it. His head buoyed in the confusion between reality and fiction; his senses were in turmoil, gnawed by dizziness, every inch of his body starving.

"I only have a dollar..." Neipas whimpered, almost without a voice.

The silence extended for a very long time, it seemed; and then it passed. Neipas, staring down at the empty glass pane, didn't notice the shopkeeper handing him a little plastic bag with five rolls over the counter.

Shaken, Neipas mumbled "thank you, thank you..." with his trembling lips only, without a voice; for all the strength of his being was devoted to pushing in the tears surfacing again upon his eyes. He put his hand in his pocket, to grab the dollar; but the shopkeeper said: "It's ok, son. Keep it."

Neipas took the bread, averting his eyes from the good shopkeeper, for they welled with water and embarrassed him. He sniffled, struggling, and let out a very feeble "thank you, thank you," with his chin shivering uncontrollably, his mask disfigured by the signs of misery and destitution.

"It's all right, son."

The first bite he took still inside the supermarket, as he was walking out. A feeling of relief immediately coursed his entire body; his mind seemed to rejuvenate, to gain strength, at once. He chewed it slowly — and immediately after, gaining a fuller presence of himself, he began devouring the bread rolls one by one in large and rushed mouthfuls. He stopped at the middle of the third roll, wishing to preserve what he had for later.

He stood outside the supermarket's rolling doors for a hazy while; then he walked to his apartment, hastening between a very gauntlet of the immiserated dying against the margins of the street — they extended hands even to his shabby, shoeless figure, so desperate they were.

When Neipas turned the block into his street he saw, yonder, the entrance to his apartment building and the dilapidated shape of the Landlord wobbling about it in slippers. Neipas neared slowly and hesitantly. The Landlord wiggled his arms frantically to someone inside; like always, he wore a greased white tank and puffy shorts, his meager chest arching over a protruding beer belly bobbing lightly below the thin mustachios pending long on either side of his lipless beak — the thin degenerate mask more cavernous than ever Neipas had seen it. He looked very angry about something. Throwing his hand in an arch from his waist to the earside, he abruptly walked away along the street, nodding his pigeon head indignantly. Neipas took the opportunity and sped to the entrance of the building.

Inside, he saw two oxen donning work overalls, muttering to each other and looking around with arms akimbo. The entrance hall bore potent marks of the flooding; things were discolored, the Landlord's office, in the corner with the door open, looking damp and desolate; the walls were cracked, pale, chipped, with signs of wanting to collapse. Neipas swallowed down the novelty and shock of this vision and went right up to the elevator. He pressed the button, which gave no feedback; it seemed dead.

"Hey — ain't workin', my friend," said one of the oxen in overalls.

"Gonna have to use the stairs," said the other (in an odd driveling voice).

Neipas undertook the journey up the flight of stairs, trudging up through the many floors of the building, alongside walls that sprouted with demonic blooms, as if affected by a plague; observing with both detachment and horror that the waterline had reached as high as the third floor, where the marks of black mold and the damp stench finally eased.

Emerging from the stairwell, he spotted a heifer standing, looking about the place. She seemed to be scanning the damage; she wore overalls like the oxen on the entrance floor.

"What are you doing here?" she asked.

"I live here."

"You live here?"

"Yeah," replied Neipas tiredly, distant.

The heifer sighed (there were palpitations of fissured lung in her sigh). "Sure," she said.

Neipas walked the corridor toward his apartment. It was surreal... It felt like he had been there last an entire lifetime ago; he felt like a moribund reincarnation of his own self. There was a sense of oddity all around, he even thought he knew the oxen and the heifer from somewhere.

Here was the door. He didn't have the key — something which occurred to him only as he reached for his pocket — so he rang the bell. No answer came, so he rang again. He heard a sound coming from inside — he knew his roommate was in. So he rang thrice and four times and frantically. The heifer in overalls stared at him from the deep of the corridor with a brooding mask and mystified pose, head tilted. She took a step in Neipas' direction. Neipas rang the bell repeatedly and with increased haste.

"Open up! It's Neipas!"

His voice sprang out of him unexpectedly loud and powerful, resounding echo-like in his own ears. The heifer neared him. In frustration he began the motion leading to furious banging on the door; but as his fist was about to pound sidelong onto it he stopped. The door was slightly ajar. He simply pushed it open.

Before he stepped in he looked quickly to the side. The heifer was no longer there...

The apartment was a catastrophic mess. First step Neipas took, and he kicked a pan lying on the floor. All manner of things were spread across the floor; it was as though the cupboards, drawers, all the furniture had willingly and jubilantly vomited all the contents kept inside them; all lay strewn, and looked ransacked. The interior was gloomy; pamphlets of various types were distributed across the table, all about some march (March? was it the third month now? it could not be; to march across all the marshes of the year would require the space and time presently dissolving). In the gloom he saw the roommate. He lounged on the one item not toppled over in the place, which was the sofa; and he watched the shiny glass rising from his belly, eating chips off a plastic bag — the crumbs dripped from his crunching and munching beak onto the wrinkled chest of his shirt like slobbered snow.

The roommate lifted his eyes from his profound sloth, as though by a herculean exertion — above the disarray of litter his body even seemed to stir a little, amid the greased couch paddings — so he could say, dully: "Hey."

Neipas felt like he could choke him. The monotonic sound of his voice touched his ear like a sudden rash, a tickling irritation; the image of the roommate's deep pigeon mask, swollen with amassed layers of wax, staring stupidly at the flashing glass — it offended Neipas' every sensibility. With a shuddering of contained rage, Neipas passed on, hastening to his bedroom, saying nothing.

"Oh god! Mary..." Neipas nearly fell to his knees upon the sight.

The door of his bedroom already stood flung wide; his hand found support in the frame. The window there had been swung open and the glass pane of it scattered in shards across the space. The wind's fury had rushed the torrent into the small cube of a room, precipitating the flood even to the inside of this apartment so detached from the ground, a good few floors up. Everything was wet, seeped thick with humidity. The squall's raging force had battered walls and toppled everything. The AC unit was broken on the floor; the table slouched without a leg; the bed was twisted, the flimsy mattress slumped under the framework. But what had horrified Neipas the most was the image of his wardrobe face-flat against the floor, all its contents strewn disorderly all over the place.

His father's old camera was smashed across the leprous ground; in dismay he distinguished the little pieces among the mess. He could see across his failing eyes his clothes disjointed, sodden, cast about like rags. There were his second pair of shoes (the only consoling sight in the wreckage, and he picked them up, glad that he had kept the old footwear, even with its holes at the toes bare) — but there were also the photographs he stored in the back of the closet. They were dispersed and confused amid the litter, ravished without scruple, profaned; in the dampness they lay wet, irredeemably soaked — ruined! Neipas saw them fly off the depths of the wardrobe as it collapsed. With unfathomable horror he froze. And then, in a pull, all at once he scrambled to retrieve the prints, glimpsing with agonized eyes the vanishing images, the heirlooms of his past bleeding ink, gaining mold. He lifted the heavy wardrobe with a swooning struggle and searched every corner of that bedroom.

The wall against which the wardrobe had stood was teeming with ants; it seemed fluid and constantly fluxing in their collective, wavy motion. The corners of the ceiling were thick with cobweb; all manner of insects were caught dead in it. Moths flew perplexed in the soggy daylight.

There were several things in the debris that he did not recognize. All things were mixed, like houses entering houses; there was mud and splinters of wood, there were leaves and whole branches, as if Nature had hailed from afar and burst in with the intent of establishing dominion by laying waste upon his possessions. But though her fury was blind and without justice, She was beyond guilt — he knew that well now.

Imperceptibly he raised his stare from the upheaval that was his bedroom floor and set it upon the shattered window. Across the alley there was another window in pieces; a family had lived beyond it once. Neipas saw it deserted; all things in shambles, all fragments — undecipherable testimonies to a life.

He only stopped extracting prints from the ruins when he found a corner of his most cherished photograph, the only photograph that had survived the tragedy of his childhood. It was glued to a lump of other prints, so that he could not entirely see it; he feared trying to extricate it, he could ruin it further. With despairing eyes he feared that the landscape of childhood, lost to reality forever, would now be lost to memory too — but no, no; perhaps it was still salvageable. He saw the soft prickly leaves, shaded black, which he now knew to be the leaves of rosemary; and he guessed the contours of his mill and the jolly figures of his mother and father. The picture on top of the glued lump was completely blotched, but a blur of black and white, a haze of grays — of what it was, he did not know. Most of his photographs were irrecoverable.

Suddenly then, it occurred to him — much of his work was still at Eva's place.

Eva. It was strange — it seemed like a long time since he had last thought of her. An accelerated worry surged in him; he didn't know what had become of her, didn't know if she was ok. The hurried craving to see her made the sight of his destroyed room, his destroyed life, all the more unbearable. He tossed himself out of there at wide steps, leaving his possessions to rot in the ruins; he couldn't bear the effort of salvaging anything else then, and gave it all up for lost. With the lump of photographs in the inner pocket of the jacket Eva had given him, and holding the little bag of bread and the holy lamp firm in his hands, he darted past the loafing roommate, past the deserted corridor and the oxen on the ground floor, past the slimy landlord at the entrance — all but whizzing blurs to his perception, who made buzzing whispers.

Neipas made the trip to Eva's neighborhood, not quite knowing how. He was distinctly aware of the prints in his inner pocket and the bag of bread and the lamp in his hands. Everything else was little more than irreality and dream.

He staggered to her street, through a crossing avenue full of jumbled destruction. He turned a corner — and there it was. Eva's house.

(...? he gasped faintly). The vision in his eyes absorbed all the breath from his body. The air of the world seemed to perish and evanesce. All the flashes of catastrophe, the very sight of his annihilated possessions and everything he had witnessed until that moment did not prepare him for the shock of what he saw now.

77 - Eva

The ways of the mind are often inscrutable, unpredictable. Roused by shock, the mind recedes uncontrollably into curious paths, like a wild and independent thing, taking the soul in a rabid flight of fancy and abandoning the body to its most primitive functions; so that the being, made up of matter, thought, and that mysterious animating essence underlying all of it, seems to vanish in the parting, and become no more.

So it was for Neipas — in that moment it was as if he ceased to properly exist. And his mind, taking flight from him, plunged into the recesses of dislodged memory, as though powering through many layers of glass and taking note, flash by flash, of the mirroring in the scattering shards. His mind saw much, very quickly: and what it saw most, successively, repeatedly, stabbed sharply by the vision in between an infinitude of disparate and infinite fragments of images, were the vestiges of a short moment in Eva's bed.

His finger traced slowly the outline of her visage: her brow, her eyelids, her nostrils, her lips. Her closed eyes twitched vulnerably, as if frightened. But her mouth was calm, still; smiling seductively.

Eva opened her eyes.

The mirror revealed to them the aspect of her mask. Behind it lay the bed and the enclosing walls of her empty bedroom, which had but three openings: one window; one door; and one picture, her own portrait coiled in serpent scales, luscious and exuberant, immense, powerful; the photograph Neipas had taken and which hung framed above the headboard.

Sunshine held patiently behind the drawn curtains. The window was closed as always.

Taking a snapshot from the looking-glass, she peered at her *I* distractedly. Neipas wasn't responding to her messages — he had relayed not a word since he entered the Eagles' Nest. It made her insecurities brought to flower, and she was presently engaged in paving them over with makeup. Lonesome, she anticipated the red blink beside the *I*'s lens — an increasingly grinding anticipation, a wait more lonely the more it was prolonged. From among the tidy rows of makeup kits and palettes arose a tall bottle, which she seized; from it wine poured into the tall glass.

Eva took the glass with her to the end of her bed, settling deeply into the propped pillows; huddling with her whole body, as if taking shelter, as if cold. Yet outside (without noticing it she looked at the window fixedly, before returning her stare to the *I*), beyond the curtain and the glass, the sunshine yet shone, though a bit of wind had begun to rouse the sleepy palm fronds.

She looked up, distant, vague; as though returning from a long dream. Almost without being aware of it she gazed the mirror fixedly, drowned her sights into its depths and merged like a wayward spirit back into the body inside the glass; into the painted face staring widely beneath the painted mask framed above it. No red flash had emerged from her palm and the red drink had vanished from her other hand. Beyond the curtain, the day had darkened a little; the horizon behind the blocks of low-lying houses and the nearby ocean soured into the wine bottle's tint.

[...]

From the mirror her own stare turned to her, replicating, inside each pair of wide eyes, the deepening reflection to infinity. Suddenly it seemed to her benumbed senses that she was gazing some sort of plastered phantom. In a flash her lucidity gripped the vision of a face deadpan, with all muscles slack, as if dead, all features broad, monstrous and inhuman; at the shaking of her head that very instant she thought she heard the ruffling of feathers all about her. With an unconscious jolt out of bed she sat before the mirror once more; and for a few more minutes automatically contrived to redo her makeup. Her hands, brushes and pencils swiftly revised the sculptured, planned features; disguised every imperfection, brought out all that was flattering. Eva remade herself. Looking at the mirror, she found the whole extent of her self. A smudge on the skin was, to her, rot to the very core of her soul.

Obsessively then, after she was done, she sunk into bed and surveyed the unending catalogue of souls and perfections of the Book of Masks, feeling little urge to get out, feeling a bit sickly; ever since the pregnancy test she had been feeling a bit sickly. Weird, mysterious vibrations had been gnawing inside her of late. Reserved aspirations and unconscious desires had bloomed out to the very surface of skin, making the tiny hairs of her arm soar in a very existential dread she would never have imagined possible before. Suddenly Eva found herself reviewing the course of her life and glancing with confused eyes at its future: dreaming dreams she had never dreamt before. The hollow in her chest and the thump in her womb mixed in nauseous convolutions; and her head roiled in a confusion of mind.

Eva wanted the child. Yes — part of her wanted a child, and this newfound desire, born of an ancient instinct, made her falter at the crucial moment. She had lied to Neipas about the abortion; she never took any pills.

They rested inside their pack in the corner of her bedside drawer, untouched. Eva reasoned uneasily that she still had some time to really think about it, though indeed no force of reason kept her hand from reaching into the back of the drawer, no reasonable prospect opened up before her foreseeing thoughts; only a strange tug, wrench, and weighing of the heart in her breast. It wasn't preemptive remorse or anything of that nature. But the little seed in her womb made her turn inward to it, and made her glance, if for a moment, the rocky foundations of the being nestled deep behind the pigmented mask — her unborn child's; and her own. It awakened in her dormant soul dreams of familial life, opened to her consciousness a glimpse of the secret need and desire for constancy, for support, for stability. It uprooted her feet from vague clouds and planted them into solid ground, as it were; and made her feel that only in the firmness of shared life could she find stable footing. She felt intensely the primordial need for companionship, community, and continuity which pulses in the living fiber of every human being — and makes up the essential grounds for the various purposes animating life.

But the impossibility of it manifested itself clearly even within the sway of her buoyant thoughts and drunken senses (she had refilled the tall glass on the nightstand and, propped up against the pillows under the picture frame, consumed the wine in four full gulps). Eva liked Neipas — even loved him, perhaps, with that unsteady mode of love that is ceaselessly subsumed by weaknesses of the mind and the soul. Yet — to start a family with him? He was very gentle, caressing, and made her feel comfortable; but he was also distant and fidgety, and his generally aloof, capricious (and suddenly irritable) moods showed to her plainly that he did not want her as such. A girlfriend, a friend, temporary sharer of pleasures and intimate affections; not a wife. Often when she lay on his chest, ruminating a terrible feeling of loneliness, she realized how very difficult it was for her to talk to him, and tried to bear down the sensation that her words landed always on uninterested ears; which made her all the more loquacious and inclined to blabber as she tried to express herself in hopeless attempts to air out her secret anxieties; half-secret even to her self. An unconscious fear of time made her rushed — in particular, a dread of old age. Without knowing why herself she tacitly felt the ground running away from her all the time; and in her insecure heart beat a sort of constant angst. So she strove for the vitality of beauty, the vitality of youth; and sought relentlessly to freeze them in photographs which, unlike her own youth, and her own beauty (as she implicitly understood, but would never explicitly admit), were not subject to the corrosion of time. On the other hand, the adulation of those photographs (by strangers and acquaintances alike), the appreciation of her beauty was to her the only solid confirmation of her continued existence and worth.

And Neipas gave her that — he made her feel beautiful. The picture on the wall hanging above her now attested to the flattery of his gaze. Beholding the print through the mirror (with eyes already becoming heavy) she realized that she was wrong to call Neipas a failed photographer (he merely had a failed career). Neipas was actually pretty good. Or, at least, the lenses he had rented were pretty good: he/they was/were able to capture that ideal of beauty which gives life its voluptuous form and distracts from its substance.

Eva was more profound, and could probe deeper, than anyone, including herself, gave her credit: like all of us, perhaps, in our most intimate and secretive, our truest moments. And in the half-unconscious reflections she bore as she lay in bed with her flickering *I* she perceived between her and Neipas no shared commitment of purpose or the profound love which assure the longevity of cohesion a family requires. Neipas finding her beautiful was not enough. It was not enough to love the mask. He had to love *her* — but he, she felt with aimless affliction, a veiled tightening of the breast — he didn't. In reality, in the truth of his innermost, he didn't. He barely knew her.

Yet he looked at her with such adoring eyes... The very lenses of his gaze glimmered with admiring fascination whenever he studied her face. Maybe, maybe it could work. Maybe he would come to love her. But how would she break it out to him if she chose to keep the baby? His reaction had been so... — And what if she chose to keep the baby — what after? The prospect of daunting heavy months, of her own body bloated and disfigured — it discouraged and frightened her profoundly. Eva herself loved but the mask in her; the rest she despised and knew not.

"Mary — I shouldn't be drinking," she whispered suddenly with her fingers spread over her belly, and put down the empty glass.

Across the surface of her eye scrolled the extensive pantheon of voluptuous dreams; a catalogue of envies: pictures of models, images of flawless bodies, of perfect semblances, of unspoilt idylls, of smiling parrots in paradise, of shining bird goddesses shaped to divinity in the aeries of the digital etherworld, abstractions. All lived atop a mountain of endless crystal summits, the glass-encased deities; showcased beyond the pane of Eva's particular shrine; role-models to emulate, body-scripts to follow, souls to possess and embody, fleeting and undying, forever young in their ephemerality. Eva glared the *I* like a vague devout praying to vague heavens; like a vague phantom dreaming. And yet Neipas, whose gaze hovered permanently over her dreams upon the wall, said nothing. Eva could not know that Neipas, leaning then very high above her, very far upon the balustrade of the Ballroom on top of the world, watching dark clouds corral the red horizon, could not hear her.

The waltz was about to commence. Neipas felt his hope swim in the immensity of his unease, for he thought that night would be his last in the

Eagles' Nest. Eva pervaded that unease: and in but a few hours his head would be full of her as he sat in line to call her; but by then it would be too late.

Meanwhile Eva's words hung unsubstantial upon the glossy void, soundless within the vast immaterial indifference of the Webwork, unresponded. Neipas would not see them until next morning. Eva would never see his reply.

She felt much discomfort in her loneliness. It seemed to her to encompass the whole universe growing dark outside; she sought the aid of her gods beyond the glass to no avail. Suddenly overcome, she propped herself up on her pillows and again glared at the mirror, with eyes weighty and livid, and stared into it intensely as though begging for its company. It showed her her face — her smeared makeup disfiguring its perfection, as though the pillow had ripped strips of skin away from her lip — and in fear of her ugliness she looked away to the picture over her, the image, the icon of her self perfected; apotheosized.

Then she lay back down. She merged softly, sadly into the pillows. She let her arm hang from the edge of the bed, and very slowly opened the drawer on the nightstand. The wine bottle stood upon the top (she couldn't remember bringing it over) and she saw herself wrapping round its liquid. Horrendous. Horribly stretched. She looked bloated in it, she looked pregnant. She shuddered as her brow drooped, and it occurred to her that the mask was no mere disguise. It was protection: from alien things that lurk inside.

Beneath the wine bottle, the bedside drawer kept open. Still Eva didn't reach into it. She would decide tomorrow. She turned down the volume of the music blaring into her ears; and as the buds contracted her consciousness dimmed to a shivering insensibility, a benumbed restlessness, a heavy fatigue. She closed her eyes.

Meanwhile, the storm gathered; it blanketed the skies outside the draped window.

It began softly. The pattering of droplets lulled Eva to sleep.

*

Hovering lone upon the velvet extent of a starless firmament, the Moon, lady of tides, cast her shimmering gaze across the undulating ocean; her stare ever shocked, it perished even before the last sigh of the waves upon the shore, swallowed in the blaring lights of mighty, giant Axiac. Among all that deafening noise of lights the Moon appeared startled and dismayed, as if a great offense had been committed upon the sacredness of her lofty realm of snuffed stars.

To the keener observer, however, Her expression would seem rather like a warning: a horrified, muted scream into that immense vastness of noisy roads, of palpitating glass, paltry wires, and drunken masses tottering over the buried earth, into all that unsuspecting presumption of power and dominion laid defiantly before the overarching skies, erected arrogantly over the looming seas. The celestial yell of heed lost itself hopelessly in the great, paved confusion of the senses... None heard it. And the inscrutable face of divinity was soon veiled by a pall slipping quietly over the night.

It stole over the sand, quietly, preceded only by an unusual wind which had been gathering strength through the afternoon. Eva, sunk in the embrace of music drowning all other sounds into its gulping earbud, did not notice the changed air rattling the hinges of the window. And she was falling too quickly into sleep to be sufficiently stirred by the tumult already amassing outdoors. As to the rest — official warnings streaming into her *I*, the overly punctuated messages of her friends (but letters on a screen, abstractions in a jungle of voices) and all — the wine did the remaining work of dulling her perception and making her unaware; so that throughout it all, so absorbed, she remained buried in sound slumber, and knew nothing.

She knew not about how the waves already lapped and swung menacingly upon the pillars of Westbeach's pier, and how the waters assumed a strange, livid, foreboding aspect — as though of a great monster slowly awakening from the deep seabed; how the tide thrust with mounting fury further and further into the sands, erasing all footsteps and every trace of humanity upon the coast, and bringing the seashells back afloat over the graveyards of their makers; she knew not about the increasingly frantic cooing building up across the inland as it was assimilated that the storm was indeed coming and last-minute attempts were made to flee or buttress.

Clouds rolled, swiveled, and sobbed over the earth. Heaven's tears dripped — and amassed as the clouds frowned and choked. The canals began to swell.

Eva dreamt of paradisaical orchards, intensely glittering waterfalls, and lakes with babies swimming in them, nurturing in slumber the affliction of her dilemmas, mingling in her sleep various cropped pictures of faraway arcadias where the characters of the Book migrated to pose, and had but the most tenuous notion of the cascade flushing thunderously down her windowpane. The glass trembled behind the drawn curtain — she was very busy and very intent among the low canopies and upon the waterbank, however, for she was looking for her ID which she needed to cross over to the lake's opposite shore (though the lake looked small and the other side faintly discernible very nearby). "I had my picture on it," she explained to the silent landscape apologetically, as one would tell a ferry conductor demanding tickets. The flowers waved, flapping their petals as if to detach themselves from their roots, as if to delicately wing over to the folds in a sky made of silk. It swung, tender; much as did the waters of the lake, undulating in serpentine motions along the soothing tilt of the world. Babies swam like frogs under the surface and suddenly Neipas appeared, naked, from among the orchard's placid trees. "I need it," Eva told him, though indeed he had said nothing. Neipas leapt headlong and pierced seamlessly into the waters (you can't do that, she said to him and laughed). His bare buttocks alone appeared above the waterline, and then something like hair, or feathers, bobbed afloat — she had the amusing impression that something had changed, whatever it was, and bubbles surfaced all about the lake from the babies' sudden uncontrollable laughter. Standing on an islet something ancient and wooden, resembling a faun, blew on a conch, and perfumed the flowery air with a melodious sea-like sound. Culling a bunch of grapes from the wooden bracelet twined round her limbs and neck she sat down and watched the swimmer approach the waterfall in very deft motions, with muscular strokes deeper into the lake's far edge, and ate pleasantly, until the swimmer reached the fall and took flight, soaring up through and against the cascading waters; and as he did a fierce lunar shine bloomed from them, and their tumultuous sound, like that of an unceasing thunderstorm boiling in the gushing splash, grew louder and louder as Eva, closing her eyes (like a sheath over a blade, a hood over a crystal ball, a rotund belly over a womb, stretched flesh over a newborn), leaned back and sighed through her lips whose corners extended outward across her cheeks, exposing her teeth to the air tattering away in droplets, and her wet tongue licked across the flashing row of them while the rocking lake and the wavy heaven soothed her descending head... Lying on her side, breathing deep, she observed passively the sheen looping upon the motionless curtain from the window, the strange cascading film washing over it; she stared at it raining for a long time before she realized she was awake. Without moving, Eva rolled her gaze to the corner of her eyes. The lower edge of the dressing table hung above her line of sight, and her rolling eyes, stopping at the mirror, saw in it only the framed photo suspended, imposing, magnificent, formidable, lush, queenly — beautiful. The little row of lightbulbs affixed to the top of the mirror frame cast an uncannily pale glow onto the phantasmagorical room, nestling it deeper in its sleepy twilight of insensibility. Ethereal sounds of rainfall flowered through the earbuds. Numbed against the extent of the mattress and the soft elevation of the pillows, Eva blinked; languid, she saw herself wrapped in the tender coils of a snake and eased into the regal splendor of velvet cushions. Her skin retained a lingering sensation of sand grainy and crowded between the emerging roots of winged flowers. Again she passed her tongue over the lipstick... tasted the sweetness of the wine. The whole space cradled to the orchestral guidance of the soft rain, the mellow showers washing in glow her sleepy countenance; and the droplets weighed upon her eyelashes which, as they merged and embraced, seemed to withdraw further in their lulling melody — she blinked. Everything seemed so far away[...] On the edge of the distant mirror twinkled the windowpane, she should just see it; and it seemed somehow to sway more quickly, vibrate more intensely, shiver with more violence than the soothing and nauseating coherence of motion rocking the bedroom back and forth. The vacant thumping in her head dulled a little, and sleep was again stealing over her senses when a pang thrust into her heart suddenly and she jolted — the buds fell off her ears — with a dreadful shudder, ramming herself upward across the headboard.

"Oh my god —" All sounds broke open in an instant. A great yell as of a million flapping bullets struck her senses at once, storming from the utter madness of the convulsing window. It shook like a frothing mouth in the rabidness of arctic wrath, in the likeness of devilishly gnashed teeth. Throwing her disoriented glance all round Eva, abruptly very awake, directly spotted her bedroom floor melting and swinging in fluids and she gasped deep, with enormous and terrorized eyes; promptly she hid beneath the sheets and curled into herself as tightly as she could. Through a great tangle of panicked breaths the *I* found her eyes and beamed into them deep its tremulous glow; her shivering fingers acted upon it with difficulty athwart the bobbing neck, the jittery throat, the drooping lip, and in terror they panted to the light:

EVA: omg

The next instant her head peeped out from under the sheets irrational, frenetic, as if struggling against rushing seas of cotton. Still half buried and densely wound Eva pointed her *I* lens to the deranged window rattling against the howl of a wind possessed, holding against the brute force of the drunken air, straining against the intoxication of nature endeavoring to impose its immense fury upon every cranny of existence. It whistled like crazy through every tiny slit. It forced itself against the house in its vast indiscriminate push through the space taken up by the megalopolis, its structures of iron and glass and all the souls which populated them. To Eva, awed and lost, wits all scattered in the dissolution of sleep, it was as if she had awoken in a different place altogether, as if she had been transported to the raging gates of some alien hell along with the entire house in her slumber; indeed she was half-convinced she had wakened upon a nightmare in full career — only the vigorous heaving of her heart gave proof to the actuality of her experience. But it was dreamlike; she felt almost immaterial in the utter absorption of novel sensations, altogether suffused with a sullen imprint of fiction.

The storm, however, was still outside.

EVA: where are you right now
EVA: pls reply asap!!

This can't be happening, she whispered soundlessly to the noise as she rose straight upon her knees and stared incomprehendingly at the tremendous violence directed at her window. The floodwaters had rushed under the door and sped across the bedroom. Bewildered, stunned, she watched her slippers floating on casually atop the moving ground. All the shifting scape under her assumed the lurid colors of the mirror's lightbulbs, waved frothy, dirty and feverish like otherworldly refuse, the stuff of sickly imaginations. Then the lights went off.

[...]

A drop in every sound accompanied the disappearance of the visible world, somehow: perhaps because every organ in Eva's body and every particle within her leapt suddenly and crowded her headspace in their scare. Her heart beat sharper, the shiver of her breath ebbed more acute upon her hearing; and the sudden darkness had the effect of enhancing simultaneously the dream and the reality of her being. Dropped into the blackness of ancestral night as if dragged by an invisible hand to the first of ages, all she perceived outside of her seemed to recede suddenly very far, and all she had inside to come much, much closer. For a moment, in that first frightened jolt, she felt every bit of herself in intimate detail: the shudder in her chin, the recoil in her throat, the flexing in her stomach, the reeling of every muscle, the halt of blood in its course and the spasm in her heart, the revolution inside her womb — yet gradually, all that keenness of sensation dulled, and the outpour of noise and calamity returned to fill her sense of awareness. The rectangle on the wall lighted up through the returning sounds: the flash outside made her sight plunge through the quivering glass and affixed to her eyes the vision, gone in an instant, of ferociously swirling air, tidal gales racing through the street, furious winds made of water, trees flailing their branches before nature's wrathful scream, Earth's trumpeting howl blown from the open maw of heaven and horizon; the palms bent and flailed like seaweeds at the mercy of a rushing current, supple in the chaos of elements, while the fig on the neighbor's lawn across the road strained taut and helpless, and suffered the inexorable loss of its limbs to the weather as they were torn and tossed in all directions of the shattered air. There was a strange human shape there too... Eva only blinked: and her opening eyes cut back to the gloom of a primal universe, infinite and intimately near, loud and distant, incomprehensible and instinctual, mysterious, and all too easy to understand. All but the noise had vanished.

She sought the familiar comfort of her pillows. The chaotic universe had begun to insinuate itself into her very bones, and, burdened with its thickening weight of infinitude and emptiness, she lowered herself towards the clutching fingers swollen with feathery cushions (everything seemed to tilt in her still, rock gentle: the wine in her veins, in her brain had the mollifying consequence of making the crazed jitters assailing the walls seem like a vague thing, as the wine thumped and swayed along the ebb and push of the inundating waters below) and she laid her ear hard, she pressed it as deep as she could against the mountainous bed. Eva pulled all sheets and blankets up — slowly; with the laggardness of dreamy unfeeling — until her body was shrouded to the top of her head; then she placed the palm of her hand upon the upward-facing ear. It pushed against the eardrum in a choking effort, it pressed to insulate the senses from the crazy rain pouring outside, foaming in the struggle to break in. It pressed to the brain, as if to push it in, to make it listen only to the hesitating veins and the bulging, nervous heart — as if to bury it closer to the unsung rhythms of the soul. The storm grew distant. Over it played a rumbling, deep roll of sound, a constant, grave hum, a profound chorus of monastic voices, low and steadfast — flowing from the deepest waters. She descended into the calm of the deep; and still her eyes, veiled to the shapes of reality by the darkness of an all-consuming night, and the denser gloom of gnashed eyelids — still they saw the window with perfect clarity. The storm palpitated through the glass in all its ghastly contours: the outpour, the rivery road, the bending palm trees, the shivering, straining fig; and the woman under it... That vision, broached by lightning, was seared on her eyeballs, seeped into memory. There was a woman, or something shaped like a woman, standing there, standing very still, quite motionless in the ravaging thrust of the rain. It was her neighbor, something in her thought — the vague neighbor across the street, whom she'd never spoken to — a faint dress and a hat, and nestled in the apparel something like a void, a horrifying nothingness. All parts of the motionless body were covered except the face, but there was no face — it was a living scarecrow, a woman without a face...

Eva took refuge in the lassitude of the mattress, sheltered deeper in the cover of blankets; and tried to sleep. She shut her eyes very close and pressed her hand to her ear very hard — an overwhelming craving for sleep filled her entirely. It was all she wanted, all she wanted now, was some sleep!

Was she hallucinating? — the consideration floated above her. What was all this — but there was little time to decipher the meaning of it, for her long reverie was savagely interrupted by the clap of thunder coming down upon her like the beginnings of an avalanche.

A bit frightened, and half delirious with alcohol and a confusion of vague apprehensions, Eva seized the *I* and cast its light at the window melting away in a fury of droplets, and with faraway fingers close to her eyes she pecked the glass.

Some more time passed.

The fig tree lashed vigorously and yielded to the irresistible strength of the gale as one of its bigger branches, a burly old thing of many arms, unlatched and was thrown with indiscriminate violence in a sudden pitch, flying over the road toward Eva's hazy stare. It crashed into the house, shattered her window — Eva screamed — and the storm plunged into the bedroom like a vengeful horde driving yelling gales of rain. The drape billowed and flung madly, like a malevolent spirit abruptly there, and all things came much nearer in a moment, everything assailed the room and was spewed and poured upon Eva. Stumped completely by the unexpected disclosure of nature's power, tossed suddenly into the primordial experience of elemental forces, she could barely breathe. The mad onslaught of water produced in her shocked imagination the sensation of drowning, and for a second she stumbled in absolute disorientation and found herself only when she rammed against the wall. She was out of bed and standing almost knee-deep in the flood — her sight took another beat to realize the *I* was still in her hand and lighted the assailed bedroom. It was a vision as of a mob driving endless knives all across space — and she was in the thick of it. Shielding her visage from the torrent with raised arms, searching for breath in the liquid air, she made a quick, instinctual survey of her room while, at the same time, her *I*-less hand sprung toward the door. Her mind left her. Eva existed only in the act of each successive motion, moved by something other than reason, or even the will to survive — something raw, bare, and fundamental, animalesque, savage. One pull of the door and nothing gave. The light flashed erratic across the flush of invading drops and landed upon the portrait, which flapped madly at the hurl of rain and wind within its framed bounds, looking precipitously wet in the wheeling light. No glass cover protected the paper; so Eva pulled herself on to the bed and yanked it off the wall.

Even in the utter calamitous roar of the weather there was something in her, something unconscious in the ample unconsciousness where her being floated then, that was still unconvinced of the reality and seriousness of the moment. She was yet drenched in sleep; perhaps it was all a dream. It was all but a dream or a fleeting freak accident — Eva nearly tumbled as she landed and then waded through the flood, arms full round the wide frame, to the trembling door. Carefully, she propped it on the dressing table against the mirror — some cosmetics fell to the water, the chair floated — and, latching to the door handle, pulled with all her might. Gushes sped and beat against her body and as she drank the rain something heavy crashed against the wall behind her — Eva pulled, struggling against the weight of the flood at her legs, the pressure of the airborne ocean foaming at her eyes, her nostrils, her mouth, hearing the savage whizzing of the wind growing through the cracks, growing to boiling pitch. Leaves and wet papery debris clammed to her cheek — and finally, the door being open and spasming against the wall, Eva turned, grabbed the portrait, and thrust; but amidst the bedlam streaming in and filling the darkness she miscalculated the angle of the portrait, and as she stepped forth its edges collided against the door's own frame: her shove was met with the corner of the wall and she, pushed back, fell backward into the bog.

[...]

(!) She gurgled out, red-eyed and swallowing in sputters, pulling in air in panicked attempts to recover her breath — her heart drummed in sharp and steady bulges at the bottom of her throat. Her ears and nostrils were stuffed with sand, or something grainy. Moist substances slipped down her cheeks, slithered down her fingers (Is that) — something like blood, something black splattered, and seeped, into the water like ink; her hand dove and squeezed into her pocket, pulling out the *I* inside with difficulty. Light beamed out the glass, and the *I*, miracle of science, impervious to weather, cast forth electric flashes; Eva saw the filthy water spuming at her waist, strewn with plumage, under the plumage-stuffed air — and looked close beneath her. With a shriek of horror she saw what lay under the surface of the flood.

Eva, wrapped in serpents, stared up at her. Eva stared up at her, stared with eyes still, transfixed to the paper, rendered colorless, shrunken in size, a small sprite, a little self, reduced and barren in her immobility; looking very eerie, very uncanny — unnerving to truly contemplate. Trapped in a photograph, Eva stared; the undulation over her confident glance betrayed the profound neurosis in the bottom of the eye's well: the shivering darkness inside. Some form of scales had fallen from the eyes of the beholder standing over the lapping, sibilant floodwaters, and feathers fell from her face like leafs from an autumn tree, succumbing to the frigid impiousness of winter. She placed her hand outstretched upon her stomach and felt her heart beat. Bound in dimensionlessness, Eva stared at her, frozen in the dead stillness of the water, the inebriated swinging of the surface imbuing her eyes with a vital shimmer; and she seemed to be blinking in the motion of the flood...

The photograph seemed imbued with a spirit, and at the same time less alive — more *lifelike*; something supernatural, in the true sense of the word. Icon, idol, simulacrum, fetish — it made the one beholding over the waters shudder with the suspicion of incubi lurking in that fixed smile, those dead eyes so animated with the vigor of the living. And so she fled from the sight of her idealized reflection, returning at once to the sensory experience of the storm with a great scattering of feathers. The crazed weather continued to assail the house, without mercy and without rest. The flood crept up the walls in swings and the wind lashed at her dissolving features ruthlessly as she strained out of the bedroom into the foyer. She made for the stairs. Wax dripped in plops from her face, she stumbled on heavy things swooshing underwater, fists punching her calves, hands pulling her down, and everything seemed to wobble and spasm in the gale's outburst shoving her about. Furniture tottered, windows beat, doors convulsed, the whole house shook. The wind seemed invested in pushing the walls away from the floor with a viciousness that infused it with human character — as if it were someone bent on revenge against the woman fleeing in despair.

She stopped for a moment atop the stairs to recover her breath. The steps emerged from the clapping waves, all strewn with feathers and tarry wax. Below, the flood belched like a monstrous swamp, and the gale whistled and roared all around.

Having set some distance between her deflating lungs and the bulging waters, she looked up and down the dark corridor, all rickety and unfamiliar — the ceiling itself rattled — then rushed to open the door closest.

Once inside her parents' old bedroom she crouched fast, dizzy, and pressed her back forcefully against the door to stop its trembling. Right in front, the two mannequins she so hated jutted in dense shadow from the fainter gloom. Glints of dawn sparkled erratically in the heavily shuttered window, with the paleness of infant day, wailing, besetting the darkness, rattling the slats apart and whizzing through the spasming crevices; already the impeccably arranged sheets lay disheveled on the floor. Taken up by the unbearable spookiness of the dark, twitching space with the two haunting silhouettes, almost immediately she held up her *I* and spilled its glow upon the bed, at the foot of which, all about the tossed bedding, were scattered a bunch of open-eyed dolls; only a few remained upon the mattress with their cotton toes pointing upward. The mannequins, standing on either side of the bed, glared with their plastic, eyeless faces of stern and unchanging expression, donning fashionably trendy apparel whose dust had been sprinkled and soaked through in the brutal drizzle whistling through the cracks. She shut her eyes to the eerie vision of the room all foggy with powder and moisture, bearing a general decrepit aspect suffused by all those numberless lifeless stares evaluating the crouched figure at the shivering door; and with her eyelids shrouding her gaze she sank into the queasy vibrations of the helpless structure, the weatherworn house, and sensed all the more acutely the clapper of the door upon her back, as if she were swimming atop it, as if it were a solid plank amid a stormy tide. Her very sense of perspective was warped in the worldly wobbling and she felt for a while that she was lying down, and that the window (which flashed the dawn through her squint) was above and lodged in the ceiling. Against her the door shuffled, struggled, strained uncontrollably and wrenched upon its hinges like a chained, possessed beast fighting to break free of its shackles. It was absolutely overbearing.

The door would surely stomp on her at any moment. She tried to master her fears, she tried to find firmness among the nauseating sense of non-selfness in which she roiled, fluid and runny; she tried to find solidity, and in trying to return to her body and seize command of herself she found herself and an acute sense of her presence ("get up Eva, get up!") With a surge of courage, a hastening of blood in her heart, Eva mustered to open her eyes to the spectral bedroom and panned the flashlight around. She noticed the hyperventilation of her fluttering chest, heard it among the noises as one hears something afar and alien to oneself. She perceived her mom's deep closet by her side — it would be the first thing to see upon entering the room — and she launched into it by instinct, lunged, barely sensing her shoulder ramming violently against the half-open door which she immediately slid shut upon turning; and merged in a swoon into the lianas of hanging cloth swinging in the utter blackness.

([...], the storm, once more, receded). Things trembled more faintly here, and the push and whistle of the blowing rain sounded farther away. Dense about her, coats, dresses, blouses and delicate trousers, descended long and heavy, and oscillated, hung in obscure shoulders, marrowless bones of sleepy phantoms. Silk and woolen breezes caressed her face. The darkness was total — Eva had dropped the *I* as she ran in — and for a suspended moment, she stood still, listening to this new, deeper gloom made of textiles which, in its diminished teetering and muffled sound, seemed to whisper vaguely; a vaguely female whisper. A little rim of light lay on the floor, framing a rectangular black shape; Eva seized it. She had found the *I*, and directed its glow to reveal the muted colors of the musty apparel pending in its various forms. A few of the father's suits levitated here and there in the corners, but the space was mostly stuffed with the stylish adornments of the mother. Here, a coat of furs; there, a scarf of exuberant plume — all very neat, immaculately ironed. Mom was always very elegant. How long had it been since Eva saw her? (— wondered she fleetingly and involuntarily as she moved inward). Since childhood, perhaps... Completely out of breath, and still recovering from the nagging vagueness of drowning, Eva settled in the deep of the closet.

She tried to calm herself.

[...]

Her breath replenished, her mind sagged into the lull of bodily fatigue, yielding to the oscillations of the earth. The subtle movement of the peopleless limbs waving all around suddenly struck her as eerie and disturbing, and she turned off the *I* light. Maybe she would try to sleep.

Out of the fathoms above, the heavens stooped to gaze closely upon the land; they gathered and stooped with eye wide open, nearing by a slow, slow dance, as though lullabied by some secret chant whispered out of the earth, fathoms below. Mustered thus, the heavens cradled round, round, round... in a drowsy frolic — spinning a serene, millenar waltz; winding in an infinitude of circles that never closed, except upon the center, round which the circles revolved — the open Eye, wheeling hushed over the nations. Like most which are birthed into the realm of Time, this Eye possessed a double nature, and, while one, it could behold two scapes. Above It or, as it were, inward, there stretched the surface of the deep universe, taut and boundless across the breadth of existence, blinking, breathing, pulsing in a cadence of quiet gleams, as profound as it was silent, as still as it was ample. Yet, under It — under all that great immensitude of quiet — and outward from the dance around It poured a ruckus and a tumult of motion so frenzied that all things were overtaken in its course, until the world had entirely dissolved in a fog of rain and naught but sound remained — the sound of howling, a chorus of screams, a crescendo of crying wails infusing the billows of foaming crests, lifted by the maddened winds blowing over the oceans, driving tides deep into the land with such violent force as to topple the poles and the wires carrying electric power; driving rain in wrathful droves, feeding it to the rivers that swelled jubilantly and proliferated in screams over the asphalt lands. The clamorous spectacle entered Axiac like god's legion, a beastly swarm plummeting bullets from the clouds and carrying bombs in the winds. An awesome clamor of brute might, it was — the megalopolis, whose foundations held decrepit after ages of neglect and wanton exploitation, had but to bow and crumble in the face of the onslaught; and sink in shards of mirror and tatters of concrete down toward the rot making up its sordid plinth. Great Axiac, house and refuge of civilization, hearth of its hopes, song of its triumphs, was being hushed, quelled, and demolished by the demonic orchestra of Nature's wrath, come to splinter in its tempestuous tempo the grand monument to that age.

Thunder blazed away the darkness; tornadoes laughed in the flash, sucking fragments of the great city into the skies in their intoxicated revel; the ocean heaved against the bluffs of Golden WestBeach and attempted to climb them to the roads atop in a drunkenness of wind and rain; the pier, blown to shreds — and the canals in Eva's neighborhood had risen away from their banks and spread out in a hysteria of leaping drops, invading the houses; all soon to be overwhelmed by the raging fury of the surge which would drag through those low-lying streets...

Though she ached all over, all over, as time passed away Eva became weirdly insubstantial, bodiless, detached in the midst of that overbearing noise thrashing ceaselessly in her, routing her spirit, as it were, through the berserk pressure of the drafts. Under her, the swell caroled in resonating groans of wash and bubble, underlying the grand frenzy of dins rocking the house, and emanating a pungent smell that soaked out of the musty walls. She cooped up as if struggling to keep herself collected, so as to not let her shaking body be dispersed into the shaking world shaken brutally by a drunken Atlas: her mind, by then so scattered, so beyond muster, was but a blurry welter of fragments; her senses giddy, empty, and unbelieving. Her eyes arched wide, blank, unwrapped by the glassy light of the *I*; seeing nothing. Again the darkness flowed upon her and shushed the dead twinkle of her dead gaze; and again the *I* lit up upon the orb; and again she saw nothing. The textured crowd of ghosts hiding with her in the closet shivered more vigorously than ever now, slapping her softly, fleeing back and forth in dreadful attempts at escape, to and fro a pivot, conjuring a real sensation of being in the midst of a runaway stampede among a great throng of panicked bodies. The whole experience was very scary. Never before could she have guessed the unsuspectable fragility of the world's foundations; never before had she doubted the undoubtable steadiness of the ground; and never before had those unconscious, unshakable assumptions she held in common with the common lot of our kind been so thoroughly shaken — which was why these moments never ceased to retain the character of vacant dreams, the sense of fiction which pervades shocking unprecedented situations and removes them from the sense of continuity and time. Thus she felt much; and she felt nothing. Thus the hyper acuteness of her very real circumstances made her feel that nothing was real — and so she stared on, blankly, from the depths of a closet, among hanging clothes sprinting into the alternating dark and lit contours of a crumbling world, a reality tottering on the verge of collapse, unfeeling — remaining ignorant of Nature's might, its capacity for destruction, its power to wither and to annihilate, until the very last.

*

Bellowing, the depths of the closet seemed to ebb fast into still deeper fathoms. Suddenly the aggression of the wind appeared more violent, the ferocity of the elements more wild, the wrath of Nature more unimpeded. The darkness rattled and groaned, shook rabidly, shuffled all around her as she hugged her knees closer and hid her breathlessness between them, contracting every muscle tighter in the strain against disintegration. In thumps of drum and warlike cries of inhuman bravado and agony was the dark house invaded, and every invisible surface seemed to crack in sound and begin to come apart — sleet chaffed the humid gloom — everything bulged and tipped, everything widened vertiginously, and in the thrusting yell of all these thunders everything seemed to recede and recede endlessly as though into the dizzy well of backward-arching horizons. Clothes were shaken off their hangers and dropped heavily all about her as in a multitude tumbling into itself in its frenzied and unhinged run; and amidst this Eva herself seemed to fall, even though she sat still — her elbow landing upon the floor with a grunt, her head soaring — and the ceiling gaped vast in an abrupt, intense burst of clarity.

She could not sleep. She felt the million mild susurrations of rubbing cloth about her ear and was disturbed at length by a queasy whirl in some nook of her internal organs; a nauseating stir. By and by the palpitations of a beating heart, fluttering small in the core of her womb, reached perception upon the surface of her belly; and certain thoughts, certain flights of imagination crept up to her inhaling mind, and her gaze, shuttered by eyelids, was breathed out of her parting lips in a sigh of receding consciousness. She made plans for the future in the deep closet of her parents' bedroom. She wanted the baby.

Eva wanted the baby — she would find (she thought to her heart) some way to manage. In whispers she gazed her finger descending, lowering to touch the diminutive hand outspread, fledgling, like two little wings trying ineptly to scoop up the wind; and the little fingers gripping her own for refuge in the darkness. She heard laughter, and she sensed smiles which in this vision of the future were really remembrances of a past long forgotten and long abandoned: but when had it become so quiet? her own fingers outspread upon the (wet?) floor, and her knees pushing through the puddle (why is the ground so soaked up here?) and the tips of her wavy hair, extending from the pending tips of the limbs of cloth, wading toward the light on the seam there, were suddenly steeped in quietude. Myriad limbs oscillated, and bits of (plaster? dirt?) fell upon her upturned cheek as it turned, like the kiss of an unformed thing, grainy in its haziness; like the kiss of her unborn child lying upon her drooping back. She saw trees rising as lightning out of the earth somewhere afar, as she rose herself among swinging roots disturbing the compactness and integrity of the ground over her nape. Her fingers left the floor like plucked roots — and leaves dropped with bits of resin from her face, which, deepening in its negritude, spotted the other side of a lake somewhere afar; her toes penetrated into what must have been the edge of its banks deep inside the grotto. A cave, a cry — echoes. Was everything trembling — or just she? 'Mid roots of silk brought from Manchuria and wool out of Kashmir she walked, to the end of the closet-cave yonder; just yonder there. Clay teemed and wiggled between her toes. A moth flapped soundless across her sighing gaze. Were all things fluttering — or just her? Sunlight glittered bright down the end of the grotto there, where the cascade fell in curtains of the most pristine water, falling in tattered hems upon the middle of the lake — one half of which, it seemed like, yawned beyond the waterfall under sunshine, while another half cupped in gloom before it. Vague notions of motherhood warmed and troubled her heart as he wrapped her fingers round her arms, as her shoulders huddled round the serene pacing of a becalmed breath. She sensed Neipas in the darkness — like a star flashing its lens distantly — and the darkness, growing to fit the universe, she sensed without bounds. Acutely she sensed the queasiness of unsound foundations and the nausea of spirit upon which her own rested without rest; and with an almost mystical presentiment she thought that, perhaps, only through the seed of her womb could she grow roots through which to fasten herself to life — and sprout out of her own personal gloom. Through the new life in her she envisioned a way to a new life for herself — the loneliness tired her. No longer could it be the only thing to nurse upon her bosom at night; she could bear that no longer. She wanted for purpose — and here it was, inside her; and so she lowered herself within, and scooped down into the clay, and out of the clay she lifted up the little baby.

She whispered — and he laughed. Look at him. O! big eyes gazing so tenderly, so curiously, so anew, upon the world: a sight so cute and comforting that tears emerged in her gaze, which effected a similar expression in the child's wide, gleaming eyes — till they were a mirroring puddle of melted hearts. Her toes rustled through toward the twinkling light over yonder — there, beyond the seam, beyond the veil, on the other side of the lake. There was someone there lying upon the sands, with head upturned, in a relaxed pose of languid nakedness; her skin glossed under wet sunlight and the rippling of the waterfall; she ate (grapes?). She cried tears of purple joy over her child's dewy eyes deep inside the grotto (closet?).

"Tut, tut; hush, hush, little baby..." whispered she in song.

Swing, swing, swung the roots of textile around her, and drizzle of feather and dirt landed on her hair, her arms, her baby — but she covered him. She coveted him. What? She coveted peace; the joys of simple living — and no more mess and tangle in her head, no more dizziness. Swung the limbs of bark, pendulums on a clock. She held her baby all swaddled in the wraps of his own gleaming wings, his own soft, little wings, as she waded — already knee-deep now — toward the shine there, toward the opposite shore.

Someone lay under the fronds of a garden on the other side of the lake, eating some fruit (grapes?), drinking (water? wine?) blood from bloody fingertips — she'd cut herself in glass. And under her baby's nape her hand bled; when had she wounded it? Or was it her face (she took the other hand to her face) that was bleeding? No matter — the waterfall, the veil, the light was but steps away. Clay slithered between her toes, across her feet. The hanging vines susurrated. The (woman?) on the lake's other bank grinned to the beaming sky and her dewy-eyed baby tucked shushed in the petals of his cherub wings. Drops from the (cascade? the ground? the beams over the closet?) sleeted into her nostrils, and suddenly the tip of her toes sank and bent, and bit deep into the silt so as to not topple over (feathers flew from her, chunks of wax plopped onto the drenched floor) — her heart bulged and stopped; the iris of her eyes grew to envelop her countenance as her hand pushed the closet slider open.

Eva faced the bedroom.

Leaning over, she saw her parents' room, on the top floor of her (parents') house, shining. The whole space shone intensely. Everything had toppled lain, or leant, like her, about to topple; everything — all the dolls and the mannequins among the drenched debris — tilted. And all their eyes — all, all without exception — stared straight into hers.

("Mum? Dad?") The roof had flown off and sunshine blasted between the walls. Everything shone — beneath her, her baby's large eyes, the waters of the floor (the surface of the lake); above her, the absent roof, the open sky, the titanic eye of the storm; the rippling sun. The sun hovered in a cloudless sea, floated in the placid depths of the zenith of heaven whose vault held serene the waters of the firmament. Carefully moving so as not to hurt the child, Eva climbed atop her parents' long haunted bed; legs dripping, she stood on her toes against the headboard and her eyes lifted over the edge of the wall. The view expanded: she saw over the rooftops.

It was as though her whole neighborhood and (she looked around) all of Axiac had drifted straight into the ocean. The beach sands were gone. There was no longer pavement upon the road, no longer concrete on the sidewalks; but all the ground was made of water and fragments of its shattered former make. Palm trees rose weirdly from the mire; and the elusive neighbor's fig lay collapsed and leafless in its net of branches within the flood, with only a trapped welter of brittle, mutilated wooden veins uncannily suspended over the flooded street, all tangled with the felled electricity polls and wires. Hers (the neighbor's) was the only house standing intact — strangely; all the others seemed irredeemably battered. Some, (unless Eva was hallucinating or the shimmer producing mirages), were gone. And then the horizon...

The vision was surreal and unbelievable. Dreams have been represented by some in the pictorial arts as hazy vignettes framed by a sort of cloud — and that was how the scene here appeared to her, though augmented to a massive scale and a sharpness of reality much too acute. All the horizons had as though dissipated in smoke and closed in menacingly in the form of an immense, colossal, calmly circling ring — a vast pit gurgling, a circus of horrors: an abysmal stadium teeming with leering eyes. The mighty megalopolis seemed to shrink in fright, its multiple heads seemed to lower before rising Nature. A whole consortium of demons seemed to spy from the unreal cloud whirling round the world-arena; presided by the godly noon eye which they rounded in their slow dance.

The sun hovered in the center of a cloudless lake, observing through the fathoms of the clear atmosphere; divine pupil enclosed by a celestial iris — all things shining, in a stillness absolute, under its exacting watch.

She rotated slowly; very slowly. She might have taken epochs to reach the opposite side of the bed. Clay pasted her feet, slosh puddled about them thick; some dolls yet strewn about the mattress, most lying ruggedly in the water beneath; the two mannequins framing her cryptically with plastic eyes. Toes hanging over the edge at last, she saw (what is that at the bottom?) her reflection clear on the surface of the (lake).

She knelt down, pressing the child closer to her breast, and lowered her head over the edge of the bed. Sheets rumpled in waves of rippling liquid before her receding feet...

[...]

Concentric rings spread — over the shivering gasps overhanging, they spread — from the spot the first tear fell on, fading gradual into the placid flood. Then another fell; and another; and their echoes perturbed one another and stirred the deluge in their course.

[...]

Eva gazed herself in the lake — and she saw the absence of her self. The great void inside her had widened into expression and encompassed all her being; revealing a face that was no longer a face. It was a thing horrid, monstrous as she saw it. Where was her mask? Where her photograph? Her *I*? Yes there — underwater by the bed-pier (she grabbed it) with the screen cracked; and battery dead. Its unlit, black mirror only deepened and multiplied in deformities the abysmal ugliness and horror of her visage... Horror! Horror!... She wept; fear, angst and desolation streamed from the hollow in gusts of cascade, winds of moaning and tears shed. The lens of the *I* flashed the sun. Pressing her thumb against the cracked glass (the cracks extended and the center pussed wine under the bleeding thumb) she let it drop into the water (blackening it thicker), inside which her image rippled and scattered, showing from its turbid deep the wheeling heights staring down without motion.

("Tut, tut, hush, hush") Breathless, she watched her reflection gathering again upon the surface of the flooded bedroom.

Its floor, made a sky, seemed to mirror the truth of her substance; her roof, made a lake, extending the limitless depth of her desolation. But there was in that faceless well a manner of completeness, and there was herself, but a fragment in that completeness — perched upon the edge of her emptiness, tiny in its vastness, she peeked over the brim in the same manner as she peeked over the edge of the bed, staring into an abyss or some thing she could not understand. Upon her knees and hands at the verge of the suspended grotto — had she never left it? — in the middle of the lake, looking down at a trickle of tears and a breeze of breaths dropping among an unfathomable silence, she existed diminutive and without feature, bearing in herself but a little fragment of herself which bore another emptiness and another fragment... each held a bundle of wings in succession; each a little baby.

Her baby! she glanced down at her baby. Who was he? What was this in her arms? A blanket — a shroud? A bunch of rags fallen from the heights of the closet. Nothing but.

She unwrapped them slowly... her frown creased. Her facelessness inhaled. The infinitely deepening shards of her all arose at the same time

until the wraps unveiled their core. There was a face (a mask?)
here.

A grin.

A beak.

Feathers strewn. Two oval meshes delineating the shape of her gaze. Dust scattered and wax melting in a dark ooze: a countenance compressed, bloodless, uncanny and discomfiting; dizzying to behold. The mouth was wide open, mindless; no luster but the inhuman shine of the heavens existed in it. Even the normally iridescent pigeon plumes lay shagged and lifeless as Eva held in cloth her own dead face.

("Ah!" she laughed. What kind of a joke was this? All upside down! All insane!). Time peeled in soundless flakes, anticipating the coming outpour — for soon the eye of the storm would close — though it sat still for an extended moment, sat upon her shoulders resting against the gaping sky. She drooped her shoulders; and gazed upon her reflection again. There was nothing

there (here?). But no one can conceive the notion "nothing", for as soon as it is conceived it is nothing no longer; and hers, or someone else's conception of nothingness as a pit opaque or of uncertain depths reared across the surface of the flood until it covered the sun.

Facing her — peering from the deep — was the zenith. The vast yawn of the eye amplified from the void of her facelessness. And out of the rim of that facelessness radiated, mystic, incomprehensible, senseless, loosened rays of gold, like the flying branches or the roots of some unearthly tree; the negritude of those opaque depths that were her empty being veiling the light in eclipse — eclipsing what? Down in the heights there, beneath the island-grotto where she floated (that she was) peering out of the nothingness — beneath it circled a serpent. She had noticed it spiraling in the motions of the water round the lake before. A serpent coiling in the abyss at the center of the sky neared her, assuming in the eerie shimmer the scaly aspect of a conch and the ridged whorls of a goat's horn; which she, knotting about herself with darting tongue, licked and blew. A sound of trumpet ensued out of the quietude rippling now across the waters — everything vibrated momentarily in a soft shudder — and the sound mounted up in a fast swell of strong shivers.

The other side of the lake, where she wanted to be, was covered in fog, and she could see herself no longer. Kneeling in the middle, trapped in the flood, she saw and did not comprehend; as the fog came in foam, quelling the glow, spread her emptiness across existence entire, and noon turned to night. Waves stirred in spume and noise the stillness of the firmament, and loosened its waters, which again washed in furious roves upon the land. The storm returned with added vigor, as though seething for vengeance, charged with a wrath absolute, insatiable, intent on consuming all things in its path. The house, the earth, the heavens shook more terrifyingly than ever. And Eva, blinking and gasping long, looking round for shelter, pressing her womb where her child slowly yawned out of her seed, and feeling her heart beating still, sensed in the labors of the gale the power of divine action, the inscrutable will of some spiteful god that had come personally for her to enact his vendetta...

Eva still jumped out of bed, with dread and a will to live. It would pass over, the storm would pass — hopes for the future throbbed energetically in her being. It opened bright before her. She would live, she would.

The waters above and below plunged upon the house in an onslaught of oceans; all lakes plummeted into thunderous chasms; all the earth took flight in wings of fragment; all things torn and lifted in the wind; all things shattered.

The eye had closed. She fell into the fathoms.

Shapeless, her soul merged with the storm. Her body thundered into it violently. And she was gone — Eva was gone.

*

The ruins were coated with ashen dust.

It looked like the house had been bombed. How could the mere weather hold such power?... — but Neipas was incapable of such thoughts. The question flashed to mind and, ebbing, lingered in his innermost, in the one small parcel of his being that still pulsed, barely living. The rest of him was paralyzed by the shock of seeing Eva's house demolished, fallen and peppered with many shards of shining glass across the rubble — remnants of her many mirrors, her wine bottles, tatters from the fabric of her clothes, pieces of shoe.

And in the middle of it, a limp hand emerging clearly from the wreckage; the rest of her body was partially seen beneath, mangled, in horrible contortions...

Did he search for it? in any case he spotted it at last. And even as he felt the sight unbearable, still he could not take his eyes off of it.

He saw Eva's countenance.

Neipas saw her face. It was a human face... crushed, disfigured, defaced, with a cheek battered in and the mouth twisted (the jaw snapped) and cavernously open, very open in a rigid, horrified expression. Her eyes were shut; the horrible immobility of her expression fixing (for all time, in Neipas' memory) the horror of her last moment.

An immense grief filled him like a stone, stilling his every movement solid;

swallowing everything empty, so that he could not even weep — so that he could but stand there, void, void, completely empty, dead.

Neipas had sometimes caught glimpses of her face, beyond the many layers of mask she wore everyday. It was a kind face, expressive of a good heart, a heart laden with the weight of all the masks and expectations and intimate oppressions of her smothered being. Now her mask was off, torn off by the ruthless violence of the elements. She wore it no more; but whatever had been beyond the face was no longer there...

Eva — full of dreams of living — died.

END OF BOOK III

POSTLUDE

78 - Days of Silence

[...]

he held the lamp[.......]he did not speak...

"Ave! *AVE!* Ave! *AVE!* Ave! *AVE!* Ave! *AVE!*"

*

Horror and the muting brunt of shock drove Neipas away from the shore, and, since the tempest had rendered uninhabitable his ravaged apartment, he wandered to the place he instinctively understood as his only remaining refuge — the Ivory Tower grounds, that he had yore called home and to which he had once pinned his dreams. He was too afraid to seek Edazima — his delirious ruminations, boxed in by the shaking metal frame of some train, bus or cage, were all astir with remembrances or premonitions of clattering teeth, lifeless faces, flesh, meat in the rubble (the mountains, arising on the other side of the lake, seemed to him like diabolical fangs about to bite into the sky and ingest him at once); he would surely tip over to inescapable madness, were he to behold in Edazima what he saw in Eva. He could not bear it — the image was imprinted into his innermost eyes, vessels as helpless to brutal memory as paper was to the photo; he could never, he would never unsee what he saw.

No jet shot from the lake. It sat stagnant amid the Park of Echoes, barely recognizable; clogged full of junk, it was but one of the many mud pits cratering the soil of Axiac. A crew of workers bowed their horns over its bank with long nets, as though they were leaning over the pools of seaside mansions. Machinery would soon show up to aid them; meanwhile, the street vendors were already set up along the rim of the park, and the smell of grilled food Neipas could not buy titillated his nostrils as he dozed off on the bench (he had spent his one remaining dollar on some morsels and he would eat the last roll of bread by the end of the day). Some people strolled the gravel pathway, taking leashed pets for their walks; the mask of normality had begun to seep into the regular course of existence once more. Crunchy steps roamed in and out of consciousness as his head dipped, and flinched, dipped, and flinched... The bench had an armrest jutting right out of the middle, so that he could not lie down; he grabbed on to it for safety (the other hand held the flameless terracotta lamp) and thus strained he thickened into unsteady, sleepless naps and snapped out of them at turns.

Perhaps owing to his bedraggled appearance, he was chased off by the authorities before long. Then, in a restive stupor, half delirious, he climbed the steps to the Ivory Tower area and spent a couple of hours roaming the campus, looking in very desperation for Oshana's library. But he could not find it (Oshana, he surmised, could not be there; could she too have perished? he fled from the thought of it). Finally, he laid his leadened body down on a grassy corner hemmed under some wall and the shadow of the Ivory Tower as the sun set; and the next moment he opened his startled eyes to the night, a night of wet feverish lamps, deliriously cold; he awoke sniffling, his nose altogether stuffed. A boot tapped at his shoulder, a strange moon of ivory horns and clenched maws snarled over him, slobbering the dew of wrath onto him, and he stumbled up among threats of violence proffered from the heavens, banished by shoves and waving batons in a choreographed dance he would soon come to know well. He wandered toward the beacons of Babylon, as if unconsciously drawn; rising there over the park, the towers, with the Belab's Pearl, highest of all, like a victorious fist in their core, offered the only prospect of shelter and hideout in the vast wasteland of humid streets. The towers were manifested to his buried mind as the only mercy of wild urban habitats — the cracks between them formed many seething labyrinths to which the wretched could slink. Neipas lumbered over the Axiac River on his psychedelic way downtown. He had never seen more than a trickle of water between its margins of concrete — and yet now it roared the copious fury of screaming nature (Neipas halted his step midway over the bridge — sensing the oceanic rage beneath — suddenly paralyzed with fear). Suggestions of dead bodies flushed under the bridge occurred to his traumatized imagination, and an overpowering nausea almost led him to surrender himself to the ground, an overwhelming dread nearly made him coil into the death waiting inside him, yield to the womb of despair, and lay fetal within it; but, forcing himself, he ran like mad, as fast as he could out of there, moaning, muttering through the liverish city night; panting. Had he, in his distraction, not become aware of the river's noise only halfway through the bridge — he would've been too frightened to cross.

He had dared look over the edge but once; and the hint of raging foams in the night looked to him like the wools of a myriad blearing lambs (when he was sufficiently far away from the end of the bridge he clutched his pummeling breast, over which was Eva's jacket, inside which was the glued lump of prints amid which the photograph of his parents crumbled slowly). Then he roamed the boulevards and thoroughfares of Babylon, and the tent cities slouching in the alleyways and narrow streets under its towers, under its febrile lampposts, under its bridges, among the lowly, the meek, the miserable, the vagabonds on the shades of society, shadows without body, bodies without spirit, roving the sprawl like accursed, half-material phantoms; at the end of the night Neipas sat, bewildered and exhausted, next to a very blur of scraggly plumes who lent him a piece of cardboard to lie on. In the most serene of tones he advised the newcomer not to seek a shelter because the mattresses there were riddled with bedbugs; he would regret it. Save up for a tent or a sleeping-bag at least, even motels are too expensive nowadays in this town, and they might not even take him. What could he do then, what should he do? The old man by him became more and more definite as he told him (the severely unwashed beard, the jacket, teeming with fleas, the mouth, missing teeth, ear infested with boils, eyes very alert, all came into focus, and told him —) various things — but it was difficult to comprehend what he was saying, the fellow mumbled so much, and Neipas was so very tired. The continuous, deranged muttering completely defeated him with its suggestions of latent insanity and danger, and his mind, straining in an anguish of incapacity, was buried under the overbearing exhaustion of his body. "Caged pigeons are fed. The rest have to scavenge," kept mumbling the pixelated blotch of panting dark feathers as Neipas succumbed to the plumb of slumber.

It was a sleep unnerving, tottering always between two nightmares, two hallucinations: sounds from the outside kept plunging into his half-wakened dreams: the blare of horns and passing ambulances, random shouts, random screams, running steps right by his head threw themselves into his drowning consciousness and manifested in his half-dozing mind through all manner of elusive forms. Itches suffused every cell of his skin, he convulsed sick with gnawings, all over him he felt insects crawling, nibbling, corroding him. His mother's grave, writhing maggots under the earth, under his skin, tormented him; her stony photograph stared unto him and watched permanently. Eva's cadaver, her swollen face, her ghastly open mouth, her horrendously gaping eyes, widened so amply as to swallow him into twitching pits full of bones — he kept being pulled back from the edge of slumber by such images, his heart kept leaping; and as feeble, and exhausted, as he was, he never really slept, being always enmeshed in a fidgety daze — until he was yanked fully out of half-consciousness, wakening among coughs (it was still night but the darkness had diluted a little; dawn sparkled upon the hidden horizon) blasting from his flaming throat — roaches scuttled away from his startled heart, as if they, startled themselves, were shocked that this corpse they were salivating over still moved, as surprised as anyone would be if their steak jumped from the plate and gasped. Neipas got up quickly, all begrimed and confused upon seeing the vermin fleeing across the tar-blotched ground that'd been his bed; he scratched his hair maniacally and thought he found many spiders; and as he recovered his wits he became absolutely repulsed by his companion's smell, which he had somehow not noticed at night, and slunk away from his rag-cloaked body without saying a word, disoriented, and hastened through that street. It reeked of urine and marijuana; the sidewalks brimmed with tents, much trash: broken bottles, piles of plastic, shopping carts, discarded wheelchairs. He saw one man — his nape filthy, his torso bare through the many holes in his soiled shirt, his skin bruised, sored, gangrenous, his trousers pulled halfway down — lying face-down on the hard floor, among the waste... The smell was unbearable.

Up on the block corner he observed the name of the cross-street, which he recognized: and followed northward through it, heading alongside Via Sacra's boulevard toward Via Magna and Belab Square. All throughout, he held on to the little lamp — he clutched it fiercely, as if it were his sole remaining link to life. Somehow he felt that the object, flameless though it was, held a significance beyond his comprehension, a religious importance, and that to lose it would be to profane, and would evoke bad spirits, or bring forth some type of otherworldly punishment. Besides, it soothed him; traces of the Midget's soothing grip remained in the lamp's warm terracotta surface. Already on the Via Magna, after an hour or so approaching early commuters to ask for change and watching everyone sidestep him in the same manner they sidestepped the puddles still lingering in mud on the pavement (he was too grimy, too disheveled, too haggard and strange to stir sympathies; the sight of him at that early hour, seen mostly at first by workers dreading the incoming day, annoyed and repelled; besides which, the newly outcast were simply too many, and there is nary a compassion which can outlast the stresses of widespread pain and the restless demands of self-sustenance) he would place the lamp right before him as he sat to beg for alms; having no other vessel, he was forced to open the lamp's fuel chamber, which would eventually clatter with a stray coin here and there, for the purpose. To use the lamp as an alms nest felt to him like blasphemy — yet he had no purse, no basket, no nest, nothing in which to retain the scraps he would have to gather throughout that day to survive; he possessed nothing with which to collect his own scattering remains. It injured his soul; but how could the soul exist except through the nourishment of the body? Indeed, it was characteristic of those days to defile the soul in order to ensure the survival of the body. There was no choice for most then. Prostrating, humiliating himself, Neipas would thus languish on the Via Magna until noon crowned the ruthless firmament. Still on his way there now however, at the break of dawn, he moved past all the cripples and the beggars sleeping, and coughed along — coughing alone alleviated the itchy bulge in his throat — and accelerated into the waking day with the frigid alertness of a cornered animal and a ripping briskness of morning, a chill pulling his consciousness asunder to the edges of his body, opening it onto the surface of things, to the immediacy of his precarious situation; he was moved entirely by instinct, famished into a single thoughtless will, common to all beasts, to survive. (The faraway bells of the Belab pealed dreamily. There was someone behind him, someone followed him, step matching his step, steps matching the toll of the bells. Was it someone trying to steal from him? trying to kill him? Was it the Collector lurking, was it the Conductor singing? It was perhaps sickness and scurvy and the plague after him). He clutched the lamp. He rushed on.

At noon he got up. He had mustered sufficient change to buy a bit of bread; and so dragged himself to the burger establishment across the promenade. The sun pummeled without mercy this husk of physical discomfort, this void of mild trepidations, hollow of mind, sore of muscle, whose will to live pushed up against the last remaining weight in his body; gravity sat heavily upon his heart, pushing downward his pitifully meager breast. Slowly he crossed the crowded width of the boulevard. Via Magna: the great thoroughfare of amusements and pleasures, of recreation; of beggars stooping day in and day out, buskers dancing day in and day out, circling themselves with the cycles of sun and moon, between the glassy facades of storefronts, among the bubbles blown by clueless children, mixed in with endless bags floating through, brimming with clothes, vanities, and aspirations, full of empty vessels, full of faceless masks, full of unachievable dreams and powerful illusions, all together performing the procession of capital in the magnificent delirium and intoxication of those neverending days. The beat of Mammon's heart coursed in the steps of the thickening crowds, poor Neipas felt it. He felt it in the thickness of his own coughs. The synthetic boom he had danced to with Eva fastened in sinews round his tired brain — the dance club she had taken him to was close-by, he could spot the entrance — and the feathered throngs of smiling masks, eager to rush blindly into normality, inevitably conjured up the memory of her final visage, the horrifying vision of mortality beyond the mask of life.

So downcast and bent, Neipas lumbered through the crowd streaming the Via. He bought a couple of discount burgers, two of those small one-units easily digestible and half made of plastic. The mechanical celerity with which he was dispatched implied that the heifer beyond the counter was used to such miserable-looking tramps as he (meanwhile, waiting for his order, Neipas took the chance to relieve himself in the bathroom and wash his hands, trying with all his meager might to avoid the face whose glimpses flashed in the mirror). His teeth carved through the bun, ketchup, meat, ketchup and bun, and his tongue dissolved them all in a melting of relative succor. He was starving, and so overcame without difficulty the repulsion he had unconsciously developed for meat since he had entered the Belab's vaults; hunger being the great leveler of experience, the opiate of moral sensibility, the great vacuum of scruple. Thus he chewed very, very slowly, as he walked back to his spot on the other side of the promenade. Nibbling every last crumb, grinding every little morsel, savoring every vestige of sauce, as he neared the vitrine of the apparel shop by which he had parked, he beheld his reflection upon the glass, beyond which, at the same height (though sprightlier and more material), stood a mannequin. Upon its blank visage hovered the ghost of Neipas' defaced mask.

He noticed with some alarm now — it looked *old*. But he couldn't be — he had left the Ivory Tower only a few years back. Surely he couldn't have aged so much. Could he? Yet it's an axiom that the years get on and one grows older by the moment. Neipas was suddenly acutely, painfully aware of his own mortality; he felt keenly the passing of the age and his flushing along with it, cascading nearer time's last destination; and with time he flowed as he must...

He reflected, before his reflection, with a continuous stream of bodies in the background. The bread, at last, ended too quickly. Imperceptibly Neipas let himself be drawn with the tide of pedestrians, languishing into the crowd a while, casting his eyes, lustrous with vague longings, to the shimmering ends of the teeming boulevard, which extended itself past the Aventine Hill all the way to Golden WestBeach. And though he did not look back he could feel the presence of the Belab, towering, as ever, over them all. Its imperious shadow had arisen, had emerged into the titanic splendor of its standing form, had left the grand way uncloaked; and all in it glittered, endless heads, under the baking sunlight. Neipas ruminated his food long, and his thoughts sparse; softening the cud with sips of the free water he'd gotten, in attempts to alleviate his aching throat as he trudged down the flowing masquerade. The water flowed down his gullet and the throng oozed through his arteries; and he glimpsed the wavy mouth of the crowd-river yonder, to his eye he drew all the blurry shine sprinkled from margin to margin in a wondrous gash of civilization. Already over the riverbanks atop the colorful buildings, standing like the embodiment of deities overlooking the progress of their creation, huge billboards had been lifted; all in paper they were, for the screens of the digital facades, so characteristic of this boulevard, had not yet been realighted. There was a particular image that roused his imaginative memory: it was an ad for the newest model of the *I*.

The grand canvas swelled over them the image of a face, behind which proliferated a wide range of snowy mountain peaks, among and under which clouds scattered. The model bore a faint smile and a flushed hue atop the icy landscape, in a slightly strained expression, suggesting the glorious culmination of a supreme physical effort; as if the summit of the tallest mountain had just been conquered. Fur lined the hood like a nimbus. Wide oval, dark goggles pressed the forehead. A red nose and discolored lips, drawn in a curve of hard-won victory, were disclosed by the oxygen mask which hinged away against the cheek. It was a picture of endurance and triumph, an illustration of singular achievement amidst extreme adversity; an expression of humankind's grit before the vicissitudes of an hostile wilderness. Fingers (thumb and index) flanked both sides of the frame in a circular fashion, to make it look like the model held the billboard itself, as if it were a huge *I*; making it thus unclear whether the camera was pointed at self or another. The top of one thumb touched the corner of the lip, as if it pulled it up (the face was closer to one edge than the other; the opposite side showed the model's glory over the mountains). And across the middle a vast slogan read, **THE WORLD IN YOUR HANDS**; whereas, more discreet in the corner, the brand slogan underneath the logo spelled, *FUTURE OF VISION*. Neipas observed the white tops bathed in light, and the range of mountains, the whole shy world, seemed to hunch in subservience to this muse which bested them, who tamed them as one would tame an ox, who mounted them as one would mount a horse, who made use of them, as one would use sheep. But now that Neipas could better see through illusions, he saw better what the photograph was — the face was a mask and the mountaintops a vast field of broken glass, a world of shards and mirroring and transfiguring fragments extending endlessly, deepening into the cresting eyes of the muse within which those shards were reflected, myriad shards in which the model itself was reflected, and so on forever, unendingly deep and unfathomably hollow; the crisp blue sky under which it all extended was on the imminence of crushing them with the fury of all universes, like waters released from an unending aquarium, wherein all the vengeful gods of nature had hitherto swum in their dormant vigilance of humankind; and the clouds dispersing among the mountains were themselves, humankind deepening toward the valleys in a disheveled flight of smoke, froth, and plumes cascading and breaking in the haste for refuge. It seemed to him like a fair embodiment of the age; an age of tatters, age of shreds, epoch of fragments separated from context, and thus drained from meaning; an age of vast meaninglessness and separation, from nature, from others, from self, of diffusion without anchor, of parceling into ever smaller boxes, of propagating into ever tinier particles, until one vanished; a refracted age, a puzzled age, an age of puzzles without solution, an age of parts without unity, an age of machines and automatons, of bodies without soul, of fictions without reality, of realities without expression; of symbols without significance; of masks without face. It was an age of unsatiable thirsts, of perpetual longings, of unending searches, of promises without redress. Of spectacle and emptiness. Of aspirations and disappointments. Images of happiness, of achievement, of fulfillment, of triumph, of the victory over the vicissitudes of life smiled accusingly on either margin; titan billboards looming and towering as the sculptures of deities might have once topped ancient Roman thoroughfares or flanked the gates of primordial Babylon, pictures of aspiration and objects of devotion, coaxing, judging... The endless horizon was hemmed in by their frames. Consumers strolled through their frames and between their banks on all sides and seemed to totter on the verge of crumbling, collapsing and rearraging as they went like relentlessly renovating ruins. Scraps of reality spread all about him. Fleeting etches glinted through the daylight — the multitude flowing down the boulevard, toward the sunny ends of the world, besieged by promises and ambitions, by culminations over adversity. Up there was he — grinning, triumphal, vast — as he had once imagined himself to be; as he *should have become* by then. And it seemed to Neipas, as he faced the crowded reaches, among the multitude of downcast glares and gleaming rectangles, as if their whole lives had been so many trials, a process of ceaseless judgments and tests of their worth.

But it was too hard... it was impossible. They were doomed to fail. They were meant to. Their dreams had been dangled before them with the allure of powerful mirages — nothing but traps in the quicksand of receding horizons...

Defeated, Neipas waded through the crowd and reflected that the gap between expectation and actuality is the measure of one's own personal despair. Here he was, trapped in the vast middle, in a tar pit from which it was impossible to emerge. He had dreamed himself an expert gazer, a piercing connoisseur, a crafter of truths, a liver of life, documenting and collecting the masks of humankind, the beauties and wonders of the Earth, the accumulation of enriching personal experience; most of all, he had dreamed himself a free man, dreaming, perhaps, of recovering the freedom and awe of his childhood — yet, here he was; a homeless beggar. Without a home he had been since he was little: rendered a wanderer without anchor in spirit, he was now also a bodily vagrant without roof. He had to contend with the wretched truth of it. Reality and dream framed him — coughing meekly, dragging his feet across the promenade, he advanced into the successive nudges of commerce's wayward march, chipping at him with every evading touch as the procession of sleepwalkers shopped through, tearing him little by little with the dormant vitality of faded dreams, as he attempted to break himself from their flow — he stood firmly on neither margin; he had been half-buried underneath the river, chunks of him had been dragging along its sodden flow. Perhaps the Eagles' Nest, standing invincibly fathoms above him, had consumed whatever else remained and had been healed since then. Such was the predatory character of the age's progress — it took from each, bit by bit, and sometimes it sundered, without repose or redress, until there was nothing left. Looking up into the billboard as his back yielded its fatigue to the hard wall, he imagined that there must be rivers underneath those icy peaks, avalanches of mud buried under the snows of the photograph, like the cascades of dust under whose memory he was buried. How he wished to fly out, to transcend all these things! To be free! to live! But he was not allowed to. He had been given the mask — but not the wings. He could never detach himself from that river, which flew from his childhood and from the very origin of all things to this very place where he stood and this very being who he was. It was helpless. The horizon was death; there was no other. O, ageless age! made of ages, that completely subsumed all past, brutally negated all future, and forever postponed all present; when everything mattered, and nothing mattered; when one was everyone and no one. It consumed him utterly. Here was an age at once impervious to the corrosiveness of time, and already lost to it. Full of existential agony and material pain, with a want of meaning, a want of comprehension, a want of feeling, and most of all, a want of food and a need for life, Neipas finally sat down, hunching under those giant metaphorical depictions of his frustrated hopes; reprieving his anguish with the pragmatism of a desperate being. He leaned against a fungous wall or pillar — it seemed to breathe with the moribund scraps of living things... Again he extended his hand and the yawning dead lamp.

For hours and perhaps days he begged; he'd been begging, perhaps, for years now. He sheltered beside a window and pleaded to the stream passing by.

"Excuse me..."

Imperious, indifferent masks towered well above him... He watched their frothy stream, plumy heat waves of scraps streaming down the long, long path... watching the parallax and its glints as if he himself were gliding through a forest, a forest of silk-covered legs with far canopies of feather, gliding slowly, very slowly, listening to the ruffle of leaves through the scorching wind... (excuse me, sir) the wind carrying undulating whispers through that jungle of insubstantial algae blooms, whispers from very far away... (pardon me — ma'am?) Neipas stretched his pleading hands and it was in those moments that he realized that he really was faceless, definitely soundless, and perhaps completely invisible, as he had many times suspected (do you have a bit of change to spare?). The sun had commenced, by then, to decline...like the hand of a clock; the executioner's hand plunging the torch, the axe; and his pleas, ever louder, ever more desperate (sir ma'am I'm recently unhoused and) were met with overwhelming silence. The noises boomed across the street in roaring streams and lulled in his head, stewing in the heat of the sun dulling his increasingly exhilarated senses. He felt a sickness coming on...a presage of fevers. Sometimes his exhaustion buried any possibility of dream; other times dreams emerged, awful, from the dregs of his weeping soul. Rootless trees passed him by in a swoon, gliding through a marsh of tar and bones, in a landslide across the river of time — toward the mouth of the void yawning yonder, awaiting. Toward the bottom... Neipas kept mumbling (I'm hungry...) in and out of feverish dozes and as his eyes closed the bottommost floor of the Belab opened in his mind like a pit; in the bottom of it, among the rubble of bones, Eva's lips yawned monstrously among her waxy, rotting skin; her eyes lifeless; and his marred beak parted and mumbled through all of it (I'm hungry...) — but they understood nothing. They strolled by as if it were nothing, carrying death in their bags. Their shopping vessels yawned with the inaudible mutters of the dead and those worked to death in alien shores. Neipas could hear them. He wasn't alone. He knew, even as he murmured, that he wasn't the only one unheard. At last he was conscious of how fraught the air was with the inaudible cries of suffering billions... He had become aware of the monstrous silence on the other side of the great noise, that tortuously booming shush underneath the grand bellows of civilization, surrounding and pervading its tumult like an unnoticed and unacknowledged presence; a presence of presences, of weeping billions, weeping in silence; it was unbearable, unbearable, unbearable... Neipas became fully plunged in the despair of the consciousness of the endless hecatomb developing before the mute laughter of God Mammon. He was all feeling. He was captive to it. He never really slept, though his mind felt buried by an overwhelming fatigue, and his eyes, though intensely blurry, were always wide open. He saw Eva, he saw Eva; he saw passerbies as skeletons moving through his continuous waking dream, beings made of wax, all already somewhat dead and all without having really been born, all oozing from the nest of evils at the apex of power and all melting and debouching into the great unending flood of conflagrations below; trees of bone planted in the tar graveyard which made the foundations of those days and all their preceding days, growing at the span of aimless footsteps toward the white burning horizon, blindingly flying from roots twined between the chords of the dead, cords which now, in Neipas' crowded head, snapped ! —

"Please sir, madam, I'm hungry, I'm hungry..."

Through this his breathing was but faint moans; and he vibrated meekly with exhausted coughs; all the tears that brimmed in him shrunk and vanished upon his parched skin. A pitiful figure, he was... On occasion he was roused by a twinkle of compassion in the anonymous form of casual change; but these wordless clanks of encouragement were sparse — heartwarming manifestations of goodwill and human truth in a gripping nest of greed — and it took him the whole afternoon to gather enough for a decent meal. At the moment that happened he closed the lamp's chamber and hurriedly arose to find some food and some bench to rest on properly. His body ached all over. By then he had faintly perceived a shift in the character of the unending boulevard parade and became alarmed once — already deep amongst the mob — he realized what that shift was. The paraders were no longer shoppers, but protesters in a political demonstration. They held plastic torches (without flame, hoping, perhaps, for the light of day's end to kindle them); and marched west from Belab Square through the Via Magna, toward the Aventine and toward the Capitola, toward the horizon and the sun — under the liverish hue of decaying daylight. It was a maddened rabble wearing faux eagle masks and blinders on either side of their frowning eyes, as was so often seen at rallies. Their placards and their songs, Neipas readily perceived, expressed resentment and hatred, and over the shuffle and stomp of rabid boots and from snarling lips frothing with ire they chanted "Ave! Ave! AVE! GLORY TO THE NATION, LOVE TO THE NATION, COLUMBIA!! COME DOMINION! COLUMBIA AVE, AVE, AVE!" — a squall of parrots fluttered and perched upon their stiff shoulders, twittering and screaming the chant into their ears; slithering undergrowths of ducks quaked jubilantly between their angry feet; Pelican ministers goaded the marchers on. With the Sun yawning blazingly in front and the Belab lifting titan behind, the whole scene of pumping hands trailing the billboarded promenade made for a vast apocalyptic sight, which Neipas, in his rush and despair, neglected to contemplate in full. He pushed frightened through the motley procession under the plastic torches, past a rabid crew of fascists and religious fanatics clamoring the end of times; stumbling against them as though swimming against a tide. In his haze he discerned tar pools through the shadows of this populace marching toward the sun; and behind them and beyond all shards of glass in the snowy mountain paper and the rising city facades there glared googol eagle eyes, watching from everywhere, from beyond the surfaces, from behind the walls, around every corner, inside himself... and under their din, at each pummel of leadened steps, more and more cords snapped underground and were released into the air, with an effect of sundering the soil and launching the senses aloft and afloat; Neipas' mind seemed to break in two between the great noise all around and the great silence underneath. In the fury and disorientation of the crowd, in their chants he saw the yawning lips of Eva, her horrible face flashed before his eyes without stop, tortured him in throbbing punches of clamor, ripped into his heart and violated him unsparingly. Eva! Eva! he cried madly, without knowing it, with the mouth cavernous and the gaping eyes of a lunatic, flitting from one face to the next, trying to avoid them all, sky and ground ramming into his sight at every second, everywhere rained masks of frenzy, through which seeped the disquiet in their spirits; and in that pandemonium, strange to say, but he thought he saw — in a moment, he was sure — he saw the countenance of his roommate there; which made him stop for an instant. Then his toes swelled in pain and shouted into his brain; many feet plummeted unto him, and his eyes upon turning up met with infinite demented glares, hateful gullets yelling "MAGGOT! MAGGOT!" and in urgent lunges he strained to surface out, overwhelmed with the fear of drowning in that wrathful deluge.

Neipas fled through a narrower sidestreet. Holding the lamp fiercely, never loosening his grip, he looked back as he ran and saw the security line of irate bulls framing the procession (one by one they merged into the flow, and one by one they were replaced by those in it) and drew back a couple of blocks before turning the corner to make his way round to Via Sacra. It had been bizarre to glimpse his roommate in that protest — was he homeless too Neipas wondered, and why was he there; no mere passerby, the roommate flowed with the march, sought refuge in it, relished in it, his shining *I* sparkled with pride, Neipas thought. It tossed further confusion into his unbalanced state of mind. He reeled through the long Axiacan shadows, spotting in everything the horrors his eyes had drawn beneath the megalopolis and underneath Eva's demolished house, careening for a long time between labyrinthine linear byways under a pouncing head. Finally there yawned the big boulevard running north-south, the Via Sacra; again before he turned the corner to it, he saw the Belab cleaving out of the surrounding skyscrapers into its height of dominant behemoth, looming, here, over a different crowd: another protest unfolding, which looked much more friendly than the first. He saw signs of many gleeful colors, masks with diverse forms, hands held together in waves, clamoring for justice... The expressions of hatred were replaced by those of compassionate distress, of concern and of care. In this sight Neipas found some encouragement; he thought he could beg there, or perhaps someone would be so kind as to give him a bit of food. At the margins of the demonstration he found a kind soul who asked him, in earnest, what he needed; and was offering to go with him somewhere a meal could be bought — to which Neipas was meekly and gratefully nodding — when they were interrupted by a sudden uproar. The kind soul turned round to see what was happening, and before Neipas realized it himself the altruist had joined the disarray, shouting, sneering, turning his nose up to the thickening throng.

Fingers were pointed to someone in the middle, who had been talking to everyone smilingly but then disappeared in a chagrined droop toward the floor; then, with scarcely any transition, a million fingers were pointing to all other faces amongst an abrupt profusion of flashing *I*s, struggling all in a mayhem of incomprehensible fits that had stilled the forward motion of the purging crowd, making it whirl in self-circular, abortive motions of ruffled feather. Caught in this, Neipas looked about without knowing what was going on — when he saw his roommate again... Strange — it seemed to him for an uncannily clear and lucid moment that his roommate was somehow in this crowd too, pointing, yelling, flaunting his *I* which glinted with indulgence; like everyone else, angry and accusatory, or contrite and ashamed at turns. Shaking his head in utter disbelief Neipas turned in a hurry to the kind soul once more, half in fear of losing the charity and half in fear of losing his own runaway sanity. But with the ongoing passion of denunciations the activist had become inattentive to Neipas' suffering, and the next moment he had lost his benefactor to the mob's swirling tides. For a while he, in his extreme confusion, still tried to appeal to the erstwhile benevolent mass, stretching his flameless old lamp like the speculator who hopes to find gold in the bottom of the river; but all he got was mud. His searching eyes found cynicism where he hoped to find empathy, apathy where he hoped to find earnestness, opportunism where he hoped to find fidelity, vanity where he hoped to find selflessness; all rapidly uncovered under the moniker of justice. They spoke all at once and Neipas could no longer understand anything; the very scattered words his fraught senses managed to pick up sounded to him awfully like the type of lingo — weaved with loopy strings of long hyphened polysyllables — common in the wayward activist groups of those days and to which everyone but those in their circles was averse.

The incoherence of their babble fairly drove him away with nausea. He searched the urban nooks and crannies of central Babylon for shelter. He searched for hours. His eyes glided relentless against the sun, tingling, irritated. The cripples had taken all the good scarce spots (they too had signs which no one understood). He found nothing. The benches, hard as concrete, were slanted, wavy, or studded with metal so that he could not lie there; the grounds were spiked under all awnings and bridges, lifted in warnings of unwelcoming authority; the hiss of sprinkles banished him from whatever tiny corners of minimal comfort were left. He became well aware of the hardness of every surface, of the griminess of the pavement, of the hostile angularity of every corner, jutting like knives between walls... Every inch of the city seemed to conspire to hurt his body and kill his soul, there was not a welcome bit of space anywhere, nowhere could he rest... And as he sought and roamed he grew in his delirium. Often he was forced to stop in an effort of concentration, forgetting where he was and what he was doing. Windows gaped at him over heaps of broken glass, he passed through shadows of concrete like a succession of black mirrors, and in them he beheld the faces grinning behind the soil; he could not look up, he could not look up, he could not bear see the masks above the myriad feet stomping past him; and he could not unsee what he saw under those grounds. The Pearl tolled, the bells pulsed, the floor screamed, he crumbled, he melted with the sunlight! For miles and miles he had seen the dead which made up the dark foundation of those shiny surfaces and they seeped up now in blotches of tar (everything seemed to boil and bubble about his feet!). For ages he had beheld the hollow under all eyes, the pits behind all noses, the grin beyond all lips; the skull beneath all faces. All looked as he looked beneath the carnal mask, men, women, children... And now Eva! He could not look up, he feared seeing himself in the facades yet standing in the streets, he felt like all the walls of the hunching city watched him through glass eyes, that all the myriad soaring pedestrians watched him through mirroring eyes, and he feared seeing himself and Eva in them if he looked up. But he could not unsee himself out of the ground... He had found even babies in there, even babies, ripped out of a chance of life and tossed cruelly into the unknown and unfeeling beyond. Bones and bones of people crushed, minced, deformed, all in an unfathomable evenness of nothing... His coughs shook his frame wholly in fevers. He couldn't bear it, he fought the heaviness of his body and cast his head to the sky in pleas — the night had fallen and the arching sky sunken in a type of sulphur; plunging the chaotic tides of people in its burning pallor. Eva! even in the heights he saw her! What sin had she committed? What debt had she owed the heavens? Why had they crushed her so mercilessly, even as they spared the Eagles near who, among all, were most to blame? Why do they kill the innocents and absolve the profane? But Nature has no notion of justice. Her violence is indiscriminate. She sees all and is in all things blind. She is wanton in the exercise of Her might; the most capricious of Judges. Neipas glimpsed Eva in repetitions, and in her he saw also Magpie, he saw

Cesar, he saw Kasim, he saw the ravages of fire and water, of violence and greed. Neipas searched and searched as the lights buzzed into the deepening gloom — but he knew no longer what he searched for. All surrounded by indomitable noises he ran away toward the station, in a flurry, unconscious, wanting only to get away. But the world resounded and convulsed in the screams of the lost! how could he get away? Cords snapped, grounds dropped, winds arose. And he had a nightmare, of reproducing himself as a series of ghosts into the depths of some glass; at the surfacing end there there arose his own face, his own skull, and the skull of Eva and all others (I dunno! I dunno! murmured the father, and ash snowed upon the windowsill)... He had a nightmare of keys trembling under some apartment building, and a lock that would not open. He had a nightmare of crowds destitute and dispossessed and myriad hands groaning voices. He had a nightmare of petroleum and fire and dust bubbling out of the sidewalks and flooding all the roads. He saw the sky falling upon his cowering body. All the world convulsed in tides of black and plunged into the ocean. Eva! he embraced her on the ground. Some surface soared against his back. He stared at the bleary world, incomprehensible. Abundant shouting arose from the crypts, the sepulchers at the base of civilization shook, and the whole megalopolis convulsed in panting, and the whole sky collapsed in shattered yells. To think that Eva had died after they had fought; why had it been? — a memory of a baby emerged through his delusions. It was Edazima's son; he heard his voice. "Mom! Mom!" it yelled. Next he saw Martin's baby eyes staring widely from the crib, full of a sentiment Neipas couldn't quite tell what it was. Eva had carried their baby in her womb (his poisoned seed)... And now she was dead! Dead! Dead! The pain was too much to bear and tears spilled freely from his eyes, and it gurgled up to his throat in sounds of gasping. Martin's baby hands clasped his finger and he also began to weep. How does one deal with the fact of death? Eva died! She was no more... (The full oeuvre of literature fails in conveying the reality of death. Masks, masks, masks...) Martin's baby fingers gripped his heart and wrenched it.

(Neipas? Neipas?)

The air was cut out of the world.

Neipas reached for it and he fell.

1103

79 - Days of Fire

[...] Neipas awoke from strange and unsettling dreams, slowly he opened his blurred eyes to the world. Walls of cloth rose around him — lifted concavely, in a crescent wave — and coalesced into a small circle at the top. Carved into this circle, which was made of wood, was the inner side of an expressionless face, minuscule; its eyes were looking away from Neipas into something beyond the circle, which he could not see.

He sensed a stirring at his side, a vibration in the soft cushion where he lay. "You're awake," said a voice.

It was the voice of Orenda. Her smiling face leaned in, into Neipas' sight. "How are you feeling?"

She bent down over his lying figure, directing her head from side to side as she inspected him. Neipas was stumped for a moment, overcome by a dull confusion; though his heart was calm, and his body relaxed.

"Good..." he mumbled finally, with some difficulty; the small exertion of talking made him aware of his feeble condition. "Where am I?"

Orenda chuckled. "You still look terrible... But a little better than when you were brought in. Here —"

She panned out of his range of vision. Slightly dizzy, he kept looking straight up, and heard at his side the sound of liquid landing in a cup.

"Drink this — you should sit up." He felt her hand at the back of his neck and then her whole arm enveloping his back as she helped him ease up into a pillow. A steam of herbal scent floated up to his nostrils, the cozy warmth of tea brought to his lips. He drank of it; the beverage gave a jolt to his palate, and he spilled it back out in violent coughs.

"Easy... Drink slowly," said Orenda in a reassuring tone, adjusting softly her arm round his shoulders. She placed the rim of the cup upon his lip again, slower now; he took a sip of the bitter drink with difficulty, and as its warmth spread throughout his body, his muscles slackened into it, and the flavor of it appeared to become sweeter.

"Where —" Neipas attempted to speak; finding his throat clogged and dense, he cleared it, and retook the word: "Where am I?"

"You're in the mountain," Orenda said, taking the cup to his mouth.

"The mountain?"

"In the land of the Oyate."

Neipas drank the medicinal nectar and emerged lucid from the doze. A regained sense of presence pervaded his mind and his mind filled his body, so that, by and by, he gripped control of himself in a manner he hadn't in a very long time.

"What is this?" he asked in the tranquil fullness of his voice; the very way it coursed out of his throat was strange, and strangely familiar, emerging with a sensation — a strength — a vitality he had not felt in many, many years.

"Secret recipe! You'd have to ask the doc here, not sure what's in it," she said, laughing. "Speaking of which, I should probably call them..."

She held him until the last drop was consumed; then, easing him carefully onto the pillow, she rose, placed away the earthen cup, and walked out of the tent. She would return shortly, followed by a stout man with a streak of white paint across his eyes, a small tuft of feathers pending from the tip of his ear, and a simple shirt and jeans. Close behind him entered, hand in hand, Edazima and her child.

"Hey!" Edazima greeted joyfully, voice full of emotion, approaching.

"Edazima!—"

"How you feeling?"

"Much better, thank you. Did —" suddenly a welling up of feeling and remembrance assailed Neipas, and his chin contracted, reining it in. "Did you bring me here?"

"I dropped by a hospital first but — God, it's hell down in the city right now. Everything's super full," explained Edazima. "I called up Orenda, told me to bring you here."

"Thank you... You know, you didn't have to —"

"Oh c'mon. Of course I had to. Don't worry about it," she said.

Neipas nodded gratefully, avoiding their stares so as to conceal the emotion in his eyes. Edazima's eyes too, held tears suspended, she too seemed to be struggling against the force of her sentiments. She held little Martin's hand, who watched things a little shyly, hesitantly, perhaps intimidated by the presence of the imposing man with the feathery earring. He looked at Neipas' gaunt aspect with curiosity and indecision. And Neipas, wiping his eyes and rubbing his brow, looked at him with a smiling gaze, and with laughing lips he said to the little boy, "What's up man! It's been a while."

The boy, in his shyness, said nothing — but merely let go of Edazima's hand and, approaching Neipas, embraced him. It was difficult, very difficult for him then — he had to muster all his strength not to break out in sobs.

"Edazima did the right thing bringing you here, you were pretty beat up when I first saw you." It was the man — with the white streak of paint on his brown face — who had spoken. He introduced himself as "the doc", and inquired into Neipas' general state. Neipas told him he felt much better; the doc listened with grave, slow nods of his head.

"Let's see you get up."

Edazima and Orenda helped him up. A dizzy spell passed through his head as it was elevated. He stood reeling a little, feeling much wearier.

"How's that?" asked the doc.

"Ok... Just feeling a little weak."

"Maybe some fresh air will do him good?" suggested Orenda.

"Yeah, I think so too. Get some fresh air, eat warm foods — in small bites, and slowly. We don't have much, but what we have we share. Go to the chef, he'll give you everything you need," the doc said, peering into Neipas' eyes and analyzing his visage; then, slapping his shoulder energetically — which sent a jolt into Neipas' brain — he said with a laugh, "You'll be fine!"

They went out after the doctor left, Neipas stooping under a blanket. As he bent under the tent's entrance the hot air graced his cheek and the scent of charred wood floated under his nostrils. A profusion of naked sticks rose tall before his eyes, rearing themselves hopelessly to the heights, black and decapitated, like feeble specters in a silent effort to reach the light. The dark ground ceded tenderly under the soft sole of his foot; and just then, as though suddenly, he seemed to come before the presence of a mystifying silence. Everyone stopped. He had heard — or he thought he had heard — the general buzz of activity sounding outside the hide cloth, and assumed the murmur came from people moving about and speaking to each other; but that must have been his imagination. In reality this village of people stood quite still, and there was no sound; the quietude in which they were engulfed and immersed was quietude absolute. He gazed. The folk stood upright. People with paint on their faces and feathers sprouting from halos round their heads — in their hands they had each a bit of earth, that charred earth which was spreading under their feet into the utmost confines of the planet. They turned their heads in the windless air; they seemed to look at Neipas. A ghostly stir vibrated in the opening of his ear, something like a whisper. It was strange —

For the first time Neipas had the impression of witnessing a multitude without masks. And yet, he wondered how he could know that. Many of those faces were unknown to his memory. Nevertheless the impression was distinct — those were faces. Visages without mask; countenances with uncovered eyes, exposed to the open air in the sincere expression of the souls inside.

He looked at his own feet. The earth emerged between his toes, his weight pressed into its embracing texture. It was charred, black as coal; which is also the earth. It seemed to speak; every speck of the ground seemed to whisper a sage tune just beyond the reach of the ear. Neipas grimaced with a heavy heart, straining to hear it, to catch a little of its meaning. The tune was — was it mournful? Perhaps; at any rate indifferent. But it was sweet also, and loving. It had many voices [...] it sang all things.

(Yes; it spoke to his ear...)

A movement of the air, stirring the hot windlessness, roused him out of the reverie. Orenda was saying, "Here. Put on these shoes."

In that same moment the quietude was dispelled softly, as if by a breath of wind; and people were treading about and talking to one another, busy among the tents and the burnt trees. Edazima held him stable as he put on the shoes — a comfortable pair of soft leather, embracing his feet like cozy slippers. "Your foot's not ready to walk bare, the sole's not hard enough," explained Orenda.

"Thank you."

A couple of children ran up, both smaller than Martin, and asked him if he wanted to go somewhere or other. They ran down and Martin followed them merrily. Neipas observed this, thinking it quite unusual.

"Be careful all right?" yelled Edazima after him.

"Making friends fast," observed Neipas, curious.

"Doesn't seem like him right? It was just like last year... He was all shy the first day — didn't recognize many of the kids, you know how fast they grow — but by night they were all friends again. The second day they were all running around together," she laughed.

Neipas curved his lip into a smile and contemplated, distractedly, the joyful figures of children sprinting and hopping about the dirt and swinging round the tree trunks with pure careless mirth. "That's nice..." he said; but after a moment he started, suddenly: "Wait — what? What do you mean first day, second day?... How long have we been here?"

"Dude," began Edazima. "We've been here four days."

"Four days!" Neipas exclaimed incredulously. "I was lying down for four days?"

Orenda said: "You were messed up when Edazima brought you here you know — high fever, delirious, mumbling all sorts of things, shouting even, sometimes... It's like the doc said, you were in a pretty bad shape. Really bad —" a short fellow with an austere shape of body and a noble countenance of brown hue, wearing a collar and a skullcap of feathers, approached her as she spoke. "— but he helped you bring you back up. Took a while, but here you are — one piece. We were all pretty worried about you man."

The fellow stepped up and, introducing himself into their midst with a nod, shook Neipas' hand vigorously, with a strong grip, and asked him how he felt. Neipas told him he felt better, and thanked him with tones of much gratitude. The man was introduced as one of the Chiefs, though Neipas' instincts had already vaguely guessed it; the sure manner of his set face, the firmness of the creases in his rugged visage, the sagacity of his slow nods, and somehow also the humility of his listening pose, all made apparent the authority of his character. Neipas shook his hand again reverentially and thanked him for being such a kind host; to which the Chief answered:

"Thank the doc and the Great Mother who gave him your medicine and the air we breathe. And thank Edazima too — she's a good friend."

"And thank the car too, ran like mad to get you here," commented Edazima.

"Yes. It is as I said, good friend. Thank the Great Mother, for even the car comes from Her."

The Chief said Orenda was needed and beckoned her to come with him. Again he shook hands with Neipas and told him to make himself at home — for, the Chief said, he was home indeed.

"I'll catch you a bit later," said Orenda as she was walking away. "Go say hi to Oshana and everybody when you can."

"Where is Oshana?"

"Around — not sure. But she's not hard to find."

Neipas and Edazima were left by themselves at the mouth of the tent. She turned to him, and he saw that her face was changed. It was papered with a misty concern, an inquiring sort of perplexity.

"You were mumbling a lot in your sleep, you know," she said, chuckling in an apparent effort to dispel the graveness which had set on her face.

"Mary... What was I saying?"

"All sorts of things... You kept calling out for Eva. I dunno — most of the time you were pretty incoherent to be honest. You said Magpie's name a bunch too..."

Neipas avoided her searching stare. Numbness reigned in his head, the fogginess of his mind enveloped the sharpness of painful feeling which those names summoned in his soul.

"Look... I found you in a really messed up state, you know... You were wearing rags or something, you were all dirty, and — damn, I hope you don't mind I say this, but you smelled *horrible*. Literally like shit," Edazima said gravely and Neipas chuckled embarrassedly in response; she didn't perceive the embarrassment in it and shook her head, saying, "I wish it was funny but it wasn't. Dude — you were literally shouting in the middle of the street, you looked crazy. I didn't even recognize you. It was Martin that saw you, otherwise I would've passed you by."

She paused to contain the shuddering in her breath. Then she said: "What happened to you?"

Neipas stared at the ground with vacant orbs, watching the black earth blur from the distance of his deep, reminiscent, cold and shivering mind. Magpie died again; again he saw her nape and her upright back disappearing beyond the edge of the tower. Kasim's screaming and the flames, the trampling of hoofs over Cesar's body, resounded in his ears. Eva's beautiful face parted its lips cavernously, hideously, until her skull snapped and was battered in by the crumbling ruins of the megalopolis in the furious rush of her mute yell.

He felt the impression of a heavy hand upon his chest, squeezing his heart into a reduced pulp beating in haste and in despair; a heavy hand preventing him from speaking. He bit his lip shut, overwhelmed with trembling airs; he sighed with a shiver. Though he didn't realize it his breathing had deepened and his chest swelled and shrank in great oscillations, encompassing his meager thorax and the whole, corpse-littered infraskeleton of the Belab Tower.

Edazima's hand touched his arm. He twitched.

"You can take your time. You don't have to tell me anything now," she said caressingly.

"No, no..." whispered Neipas, shaking his head slowly, with eyes yet blank. "There are things I should tell you —" and, sharpening his hearing — staring downward still — to perceive the voices in the air and the many feet shuffling across the earth all about them, he asked, "do you think we can go someplace quiet?"

"Yeah. Yeah definitely," Edazima said, nodding and looking at Neipas with worry.

The good, faithful friend took Neipas to the edges of the camp of tents, where, close-by, there was a larger clearing, with a felled tree of thick trunk in the middle; it overlooked a slope ending in a cliff, beyond which was a deep valley in which the river coursed full and to interminable distances. From up there, Neipas, huddled dormant, abashed and unreal beneath the blanket, could see the extent of the range and how the landscape, smothered recently by fire, was already beginning to revive in short spurs of green here and there, seedlings rising from the ashes of the soil and the settling of the rainwaters underneath with opening, growing wings of leaf.

They sat on the fallen trunk and slowly, painfully, and with much pause, Neipas told Edazima of what had happened in the Eagles' Nest, at some length; omitting the existence of the Midget and that of the Belab's bottommost floor for fear of not being believed, he would tell her about his indigent wanderings across Axiac after his escape.

In his lips Magpie was again revived and killed, in his lips Eva was again revived and killed — over the span of many minutes, or perhaps many hours. He said he did not know what had become of Janu, and indeed it would be a long time before he found out, and wrote the letter to the grieving, deported mother, and before he met his sister. The others, whom Edazima had not met, he didn't mention; yet their memories stirred in his soul. Many times through the telling Edazima curled back her lips and held them with her teeth, staring at Neipas with very wide, wet eyes. Tears slid down her cheeks and she sniffled all atremble when the death of Magpie was recounted to her, and rubbed her knees and her face nervously as she learned the fates of the others. Neipas never looked at her — he gazed the blinding blue horizon with an increasingly lifeless glare, increasingly unpresent, and shrunk into the throbbing hollows of his inner spirit; opening and closing his mouth and barely feeling the words leaving it.

After he finished, they sat together in silence for a very long time. Then Edazima told her story — the affliction and the panic of the multitudes before the presaged violence of the storm, the refuge in the stadium and the crowded squalor, the inconceivable rage of the tempest as it battered against the dome, the sounds, the smells, the fear — and Neipas listened. After that, too, they sat in silence. And they remained thus nearly until dusk, when Edazima, suddenly anxious, rose to check up on her child; walking away quivering, with her face glossed full of dried tears.

Neipas sat alone. The gorge of the deep valley breathed a breeze unto him, and through the quietude of the air whispered softly, almost imperceptibly, the sound of the waters in its bosom. Contemplating the immensity succumbing to the darkness slow, the world seemed to him immeasurably desolate, boundlessly forlorn, and profoundly dismal, dismal, full of sorrow. His heart sank slowly into hopelessness and a miring depression. And in it he lingered a while, as though wallowing in a numbing ache.

He watched as nightfall smothered the embers of the sun and the last trace of its light was shushed. Fires were lit behind him, beyond the enclosure of naked trees. He kept sitting, mellow, vaguely thinking, faintly feeling. He let the night submerge him and he submerged himself into the night, all the while trying, meekly, to make sense of everything. Time whispered by and enveloped him in its quietude, until he was deaf to all aspects of existence.

He sensed... and did not understand.

In his frustrated attempt to grasp the world's significance it seemed to him at last bereft of significance. And as he meditated upon all he had lived, the valley and the sky closed upon him and into a limitless void without meaning, without the possibility of comprehension; a horrible, senseless, indifferent universe arched over — an enormous aquarium of dripping lights. Neipas let the night envelop him, he let it hide his anguish, let it cushion his sorrow. Thus freed into the darkness, he wept; he wept, he wept uncontrollably, with all the despair of grief and a breathlessness without hope. Over the valley and the river stream he wept for that cosmic body of aspirations and potentialities, the human being; being divine among all divine creatures, among them the most shallow and the lowliest, and the deepest and most high. He wept for Cesar who, lonely poet, was trampled by the hysteria of despairing multitudes. He wept for Kasim, Kasim the good tiller, whom Cesar had loved, who had loved Cesar. He wept for Magpie, who had delivered herself to the fury of the skies in her horizonless despair. And he wept especially for Eva, that kind soul buried in masks, genuine self smothered in the inanity of the age, whom Nature's revenge had caught in its furious wanton sweep. He wept — deep into the night.

A shuffling of earth (minutes — hours? — later) closer to him made him turn his head. It was Oshana. Her face was lit by the fire of a torch she held up, and she gazed at Neipas with her own tender, matriarchal smile, full of sagacity and wisdom; to which Neipas could only return a visage flushed with pallor, and a bleary gaze, drained of vitality, drained of all tears.

"Good evening," said she. "May I?"

"Good evening," breathed Neipas weakly, feeling dried and sapped. "Of course."

Oshana stepped a few meters before him and, bending with surprising agility, planted the torch deep into the earth. Now the valley danced above the flame, in the wavy heat emanating from the flame among embers, spark raining upward to the heavens. The twilit rivers and the gorge snaked tremulously and in a tranquil vibrancy, alive.

Oshana then approached to sit on the trunk next to Neipas. She cradled in her burnt hand the sacred lamp, he realized; its surface glinted timid waves of torchlight. She gave Neipas the precious relic with depths of reverence and tranquility, as with all her gestures; then sat at length.

They remained silent for a while. She contemplated the flame's gleam upon the trees; he, the holy vessel with which he had been entrusted.

Oshana waited until he spoke.

"I don't get it," Neipas began finally, after some time battling himself, pondering, drumming his toes repeatedly with an anchored heel. The meek intonation of his voice ushered sonorously into the deep — into the gap of silence which his feet (now motionless) had left. Then, equally meek in volume, Neipas shrugged, and breathed somberly, "What's the meaning of it?..."

Stillness shut over them once more.

He sighed, continuing, "I dunno... If we're all gonna die anyway... then — what? I dunno...

"Sorry I — I don't even know what I'm saying.

"I'm all...—" and his speech extended into a hesitation of quietude, ending in the abrupt motion of his shaking head.

The same silence that absorbed his words embraced their vanished sound upon his lips and in his body; his mind yielded into its warm lassitude. They said nothing else, and Neipas stared at the dancing flame through its glow on the terracotta, listening to the crackle and flow of its motion. Thoughtlessly, he felt in retroactive throes the futility of his struggles and the general barrenness of all life.

"That lamp — " Oshana said quietly, "what kind of genie were you holding inside?"

And Neipas, passing his finger across the rim of the fuel chamber (seeing that there were still some coins inside), sighing longly, with a forlorn shrug, half-inanimate in his acquiescing to wide hopelessness, mumbled, "I let the fire die.

"Look," (this he expressed almost inaudibly), "Nothing makes sense to me anymore..."

Much time seemed to pass. Hours (centuries?) loosened without bound across an omnipresent quietude.

Finally finding Oshana's silence somewhat odd (the notion of his being here alone suddenly occurred to him and startled him) Neipas turned to her; and found her gazing him. She gazed him penetratingly, soft; she seemed to be trying to read the arcane language of his hidden soul. The effect was at once discomfiting and reassuring. He averted his eyes from her own, chuckling a little out of surprise and timidity; but then setting into a grave expression once more.

"Life is flame, though it's a fire born from water. What of it?"

Neipas turned to her; then numbed into the contemplation of the lamp once more. And after another, brief period of stillness, Oshana spoke:

"Beneath us extends the realm of the salmon," she said, pointing to the valley.

"It is born high in this mountain — it is born with the river. And it is the river womb that cradles it, till it is ready for the pilgrimage.

"Down the river then," continued Oshana, "the salmon descends. Down the mountain the salmon goes, by the river carried — until it dives into the great ocean. The salmon emerges into the deep, and it is in the deep that the salmon lives and grows.

"To the far north the salmon makes its journey, feeding, growing in the cold summits of the deep. For years it lives, for years it feasts, making ready once again — to return. Once ready, the salmon stops eating. And it will never eat again. All its life becomes focused on its deep purpose, the deep purpose which the depths taught it all the years of its maturing life.

"Then finally, the final pilgrimage begins. The salmon courses the sea toward its own natal spring, its place of birth. The salmon struggles against the stream, against the cascades, against the heights, against all dangers, against its own path, against itself. Once again in the peak of its altitude, the source of itself, the salmon spawns — and dies."

Wind, laden with the sweetness of river chants, floated up the valley to kiss their senses and permeate the silent mountain air in glimmers of whisper; which Oshana, absorbing into her lips, spoke quietly back into the ether in the form of a question:

"Why does the salmon do this?"

Neipas raised his eyes from the lamp and directed them toward Oshana, whose gaze reflected the brilliance of the flame, the still depth of the stars, the quiet motion of the river.

"What does it seek in the depths?"

Neipas awaited in silence for the answer.

"What is the deep purpose?"

He waited.

Then, after submerging into quietude again, Oshana surfaced once more, with the words, "Nothing that I can say, Neipas — none of my words can alleviate your grief. Time is the only cure for it. And only time can make you comprehend.

"Time is a river into the soul, and words are but seeds — listening alone can make the spawning grounds at the river source. Do you understand?"

Neipas nodded slowly — he listened intently. His heart, parched with hardships, thirsted for the solace of one who knew life and such words as might abound in it; in such words as might embody its profound and sweet wonders; for he longed for life, even in his despair. Oshana had heard its hoarse cry, and knew. In truth, though his intellect did not yet understand Oshana's words, his spirit, collecting itself out of its anguished scatterment, understood well her sagacious, divinely serene tone as it was breathed out of her imperturbable and reassuring presence.

She began thus:

"Every life is a pilgrimage." Slowly she began.

"Its paths are dangerous. Death shadows every step.

"Many are the salmon that perish in their path. To complete the path is to perish. And yet, none refuse the way.

"The salmon must know where they are going and where they have come from. Surely they must know — that the destiny of their journey is their dissolution.

"And yet none refuse the way. How can this be?"

Then slowly, she said: "The salmon searches the ocean because it wants to live. And it searches its place of birth because it wants to give life.

"Perhaps it would live much longer if it stayed in the ocean. But it passes through countless dangers — because it wants to give its life. Only that way can the salmon perpetuate itself, because the salmon is more than itself, and we, we too, are more than ourselves. The measure of a full life is attained far beyond ourselves, because it is beyond ourselves that we fulfill ourselves, it is beyond ourselves that we become ourselves — in the other. For we are far more than just ourselves, Neipas. The life lived in the ego is a little life, a life to be pitied. What would be of a sun with nothing to give its light to? What would be of a life that couldn't give itself? That sun would have no purpose, and that life would have no purpose."

For a moment they were again quiet; Neipas had raised his head from the lamp a little, and contemplated the inscrutable horizons framed by mountaintops, from which rivers slid in distant, quiet fury.

"But I believe all things are compelled toward their source," said Oshana. "In truth, if we were to march across the Earth as far away as possible from this grove, we would end up back here, where we began — though we would bring the whole world back with us. And such is the experience of the salmon.

"Having gone into their future, the salmon must return to their past — mirroring their own life and the life of its forbears.

"It is like the sun which, having sunk to the darkness of the waters, must return to the summits of the sky every day. In truth, it is around the Sun that the Earth revolves, and all things within Her describe in their lifetimes the Sun's daily motion. Having gone into the depths of the ocean, the salmon too must return to the summits of its natal river."

Silence. At last, elongating one finger toward the river below — the waters sliding and slithering across the valley through the mesmerizing sway of the torchflame — she said, "The salmon, too, carries a fire.

"The salmon, who is born in the heights by the sun, is born a little flame — red like the rising star. But that flame seems to extinguish toward the depths. The salmon is then covered in silver, it wears the moonskin — as befits the darkness of the deep, moon's domain. It is in the deep that the salmon feeds, in the depth that the salmon grows — and in the end, when it returns to the summits, to the sun, the salmon's flame bursts again, and the salmon is again colored like the sun. But it brings in it the shadow wherein it had dwelt.

"The salmon's flame is then shed, and made new — and it is into the shadow it brought that the salmon finally yields.

"The new sun takes its parents' flame back to the deep — and the journey repeats."

Voiceless, Neipas contemplated the horizon and the mountain range huddling about the valley, and the summits looked to him like a series of jagged teeth or beaks in an upward flight; he felt as though he were inside the maw of the Earth, pitifully at the mercy of Her whims. Again he turned his eyes to the lamp.

Oshana then said, "What has the deep taught the salmon? That death is birth's mirror, and that from which we came, is that to which we must return. The shadow it sought lived already inside itself, its surface learned what its depths already knew. The salmon became what the salmon is.

"The sun had but gone inward — so that it could be born into another. Its light retreated into the salmon's own depths, and the shadow of the future wrote upon its heart the vitality of life."

The breeze which sometimes rose from the valley made the branches round them creak, and the feathers in them tingle, replicating in their whisper the breath of the river beneath. The torchflame trembled into the lull of his eyes.

"But we live in such times as rivers are dried and poisoned, and links to the past are severed without a thought. So what of the salmon without a river to return to? What would become of the sun without an horizon?"

From this Oshana, calmly drawing in the scent of plants yet-to-bloom, yet tucked all around them throughout the charred wood, answered, "Your river is no longer there for you to return to. You were uprooted. You're adrift.

"You were left to the vagaries of time, left to the mercy of tidal winds, lost in life. Rootless, roaming without control, toward the cascade — isn't that the source of your despair? Lack of control, direction, purpose — lack of source? Without continuity, without narrative, you change from day to day and know not who you are — you know not why you are."

Neipas' despondent, downcast visage nodded in blurs over a wrenching, tormented, recoiling heart. He sniffled, though no tears yet returned to his eyes.

"You were," continued Oshana, "tossed to the depths of life before you were ready — and now you find no respite and no surface to return to.

"But there is much to be learned from the depths as long as you learn to breathe in them, Neipas. And there are new surfaces to be created. It's possible to emerge from the deep — so the salmon knows."

Sighing the mountain breeze and the whispers of the river and the flapping tree leaves, Oshana then said: "In truth, we are running out of rivers and horizons are shrinking fast. It takes enormous strength to find new rivers, and broaden one's horizons, Neipas.

"But that's a strength you can find, that's a strength you can muster."

Silence.

"Where do I find that strength...?" Neipas muttered, meek, into the quietude.

At length then, with a voice tender, maternal — Oshana replied: "Your strength is to be found in the depths of yourself, Neipas. Yet, you — like so many in our days — you are not in your self."

Again, silence; the silence of the wood inhaled and sighed with every slow contraction and expansion of their hearts. Neipas contemplated the earth extending somber from his feet; the naked roots jutting hard out of the soil seemed to him like uncovered bones.

"We are a synthesis, Neipas — a certain philosopher once wrote this, and I think he wrote it well. We are individuals. But we are also much more. In truth, who we are contains everyone we ever were — they lie inside, asleep. Who we are contains everyone we can ever be — they lie inside, unborn. Who we are contains everyone that is, everyone that was, and everyone that will be.

"But many today stand over the surface of their being, at the margins of their being. When we look inside — everything beneath us seems shallow. Everything above us seems empty. Behind us we see all the people we've ever been, littered about the waters, dead. Before us we can only see darkness, and inside that darkness we sense the cadavers of all the people we ever wished to be. Underneath us, we see our reflection — and do not recognize it. Everything inside seems strange, everything inside seems empty, everything inside seems dead."

Silence. "There are many today who don't know themselves... And therefore hate themselves. Better not to behold oneself, they think, better not to be oneself, better to wear a mask. Better, oftentimes, not to be..."

Neipas listened mellow, sadly to her cryptic words, spoken all with great authority — as from the mouth of one who beholds things profoundly, who discerns clearly the transparency of opaque surfaces. Sadly he caressed the lamp and its terracotta make, staring mystically at the water glimmering inside the chamber, at the coin glinting inside the liquid.

"We can't help but dwell in the ocean of our being. Yet we live in such times as many a soul is in turmoil. Sometimes we feel full of confusion, as if in the turbulent waters, without weight — and we can barely sense ourselves. Sometimes we feel full of nothing, the ocean of the soul feels more like a muddy swamp making our feet plod, and our own body feels too heavy. In truth, our being feels more like a fishbowl nowadays, everywhere we look we see glass, we feel at once too crowded and too lonely. Everywhere we look we see our reflection in the darkness — and we cannot recognize ourselves. Everything inside seems empty — everything inside, seems dead.

"But who put those glass walls and those dead bodies in there? Who put that emptiness there? Powerful enemies have come into our lives masked in darkness — they're everywhere, they've become our very shadow. They've shone their myriad fake suns upon us and lo, we've sunken into *their* many shadows. They've cut us into fragments, they've divided us from ourselves — to make us powerless, unresistant, and pliable. But shadows of ourselves... In truth, we feel empty because our spirits have been flayed, our spirits have been mined. Mined for power — for one cannot be powerful unless through the power of others. All our waters, all our rivers, all our seabeds — drained. Everyday they hollow our souls so they can better control our minds and our bodies.

"Watch — we look inside, and we see a wasteland too painful to contemplate, too strange and empty. Then we look outside, and we see the very world reflecting that strangeness and that void. And all other beings stand around us, behind walls of glass, staring with eyes of glass — and in their eyes we can only see the reflection of our dead selves — if we ever dare to look. When we speak, we speak to walls — the walls of a pit, a well without water, where we feel ourselves drown a little each day and die a little each day."

Neipas shuddered; he swallowed. The words were barely filtered by his brain, the intellect did not mill them. They seemed to be whispered directly into the heart, and though his mind scarcely comprehended them his breast fluttered like a trembling mirror wanting to break. He scarcely understood the reaction of his body to the sound of her voice. It was odd — but it was as though Oshana spoke to the essential void in the experience of his own being, and her words bounded in the form of echoes from the dismaying bottomlessness of his sense of self.

"In truth, Neipas — the Earth is our mirror and we are mirrors of the Earth. And look at how these powerful men have molded the Earth... Look at how they desecrated and blasphemed the Earth. In doing so they blasphemed our very Nature, and by their greed they have estranged us from our common essence.

"Look at the world they have made. They've polluted the rivers and poisoned the salmon, they've exhumed the dead from the shadow, they've made toxic fire out of sunlight — they've contaminated the very sun and made its heat venomous. They've unleashed death and it is dead things we see all around us. They've separated us from one another. Is it any wonder, then, that we feel the way we do? Sick, half-dead, separated from our selves? Is it any wonder that in the hollowing of the Earth is the hollowing of our soul?

"It is necessary to change this world if we are to be made entire once more. It is by reconnecting to the Earth, by healing the Earth, that we can heal ourselves. We can only do this through much strength, through a strength profound. In truth, we can only do it together.

"You've asked, 'where do I find the strength?' And I said, 'in the depths of your self'. But where do you find your self? In truth, your self can be found in others. And those others — your kin, Neipas — they are to be found in the *struggle*, in the journey — in the pilgrimage. The pilgrimage of life, the journey across the Earth, the struggle to shape the world such as befits our dignity. And it is in the hope of the destination — and in the destination itself, in our *destiny* — that we are, and that we will, at last, become."

Again Oshana pointed through the fire into the shimmering, palpitating river of the valley deep. "In its search for itself, the salmon doesn't traverse the pilgrimage alone. Thousands go with it — all bear the strength in common, all bear the flame in common. Inside every inhabits the self of every other. And you — you have *us*, Neipas, you are not alone." Neipas' chest fluttered again upon hearing these words. Staring yet at the holy lamp, he nodded (slowly, bleary), incapable of uttering a single word. His chin trembled; his lip withdrew.

Oshana's voice filled his soul, it made up the totality of his existence, as the words arose from his depth. "And yet it matters still, child, that you have an abode ready to welcome and shelter our strength. In truth your heart mustn't be rickety, otherwise that strength will make it crumble — and you will want to retrieve to your loneliness and your emptiness, and in receiving love you will feel hatred, and in perceiving care you will feel resentment. Affection will seem like injury to you. It matters that you are not affected by a sense of dependency, even though we are all dependent on each other — it matters that you retain the unity of individuality, even as you come to realize that you are much more than a mere individual. The *strength must be found within you*, otherwise it cannot be found in others — in truth, the others must be found inside you even as you find them outside."

Neipas snickered, a sad laugh without energy, as he petted the terracotta, the holy lamp. "I have no strength of my own, Oshana. I'm too tired," he whispered.

It was as if she made him turn his head by the mere force of her stare; somehow Neipas knew that Oshana observed him as he turned his eyes shy to her, and with a smile meek and abstracted he removed them again and placed his glance upon the ground. But again he looked at her — and her eyes stared still with that particular, sage intensity of hers; he saw that she too smiled her astute, profoundly calm smile.

"The strength is yours, Neipas. You did not lose it. In truth you lost yourself, and your eyes tell me that you are not in your self. I see in them a longing — a fatigue of the search. Since I saw you on that train that day when the forests began to burn and your mask began to melt" (! Neipas turned his startled gaze to her) "that I have dwelt in the mists of remembrance and traced back my steps along the rivers of the past — and slowly I became aware of your shape. It was years ago, when you first came to me. You had just then arrived in Axiac."

Astonished, he stared at her lips moving round the shape of her words. Had he only noticed it now? he wondered from himself, to himself. He realized that Oshana had no mask. "I saw your eyes as they were then. And I behold them before me," she said, turning her eyes, and her perpetual, mystical smile toward him. At once suddenly and slowly, everything beyond the contours of her form seemed to draw very far away. "You had hope where now fear resides.

"I see ash where I once beheld fire. What happened to the fire in you? Though in truth, even then your flame was fed by noxious fuels, even then your drive to live was chased by your drive to escape. And haven't there been times, Neipas, where one has caught the other? Your luck, in truth, is that you respect death too much to desire it.

"And so it was that you've succumbed to a half-life. You've let yourself be drawn away from your self — to faraway places, places strange to you. And now you are a stranger to yourself. And now you are lost.

"You are lost in your emptiness and your lack of hope. The course of your life has drawn the life away from you; the ocean of your soul has quelled the flame of your being. You were drawn away from the self — you are lost.

"Isn't that how you feel? Sunken — in the abyss of your emptiness?"

Neipas sniffled; he passed his fingers over his lips. He was struck by the recondite accuracy of her description. A tear filled up his eye and, so held up, it kept his vision blurry; he saw Oshana and her mystic smile as though under the waters. He tried blinking and averting his stare, but he couldn't anymore.

"You have guessed me," he said. "You can see through me? How?" and here fell the teardrop; he wiped it off upon his cheek.

"Your mask is nearly vanished, Neipas," Oshana said, narrowing her eyes between her smiling features. "I can see under it."

At this Neipas felt much shame and fear, and he hid his face with both hands and with the lamp; with the surge of these sentiments he drew away his eyes. His lower lip trembled profusely.

"Don't fear," she told him. "Your emptiness is holy ground. In truth, foundations cannot be built except on a pit."

"I have no foundations, Oshana," he whispered, overcome by fatigue and desolation, hands yet upon his face. "Not anymore."

Oshana's voice breathed through his fingers. "When the salmon dives into the ocean, it is into its own emptiness that it dives. It seeks its own foundations — its own seed. It is out of the ocean and out of the deep that it builds itself, out of the deep that it grows. It is out of the deep that the salmon becomes who the salmon is.

"Did not the salmon venture to the deep to find its own strength, its own self? In the deep the salmon finds its own seed and its own source. In truth, the tallest heights mirror the deepest depths, from which they sprout — and the fullest totalities mirror the barest nothings, from which they sprout.

"The salmon descends to its own emptiness and the depths of its own ocean — to find its own *center*. Here's where the self resides.

"Lo —" said Oshana, embracing the horizon, "the whole universe expands from you. Behold how the forest, the valley, the sky, the stars — look at how all draws away from your eyes. You see how the world describes a circle around you? Notice how you stand at the very center." (slowly, Neipas shifted his hands so as to see — one hand covered the mouth and the nose, another covered the forehead, only his eyes peeked out) "You can see all things — except *yourself*. All except your head and the base of your head, all except your face and the eyes through which you see, the nose through which you smell, the mouth through which you speak, the ears through which you hear. The center resides in that which you cannot behold — your emptiness...

"That emptiness fills the center. That emptiness is the center round which all revolves — all inside us, all that is our being — that great mixture of pasts and possibilities, of all the fragments composing every moment, of every version and every facet of ourselves, of the world around us, of all others around us... And that center — is the self. It's the seat of command: the throne, and the nest. It is control — it is power.

"The self, the center, is *unity*. The self is where opposites join and becalm. To stray away from it is to mingle in the fog of crowds that populate our soul — for we are a soul of souls that mesh, and do battle upon the battlefields that we are. To plunge into those thickets is to lose oneself," said Oshana, vigorous, arcane — once again she raised her arm in a sweep. "Behold, Neipas. *Here* is where you are, in body — from you the world expands. *Self* is who you are in spirit — from the self your being expands. The body is your presence in the world — as the self, which is within the body, is your presence within yourself. Outside of them, you are less than fully present.

"In the self — that is where you **are**. It is from it, therefore, that you become."

Silence... The Earth, reality, their magic — insinuated themselves in whispers about their senses, manifested themselves differently to each of the beholders there, by the torch and the valley, by the forest of the mountain, sitting side by side.

POSTLUDE

"The self is holy ground, Neipas. And in truth, one cannot see it with the eyes lest one learn how to feel with the spirit. Turn to it, plant the seed of the spirit in the void of your soul, Neipas. Here's how you create yourself anew... In the self is the spring from which rivers grow, and horizons are revealed.

"Plant there the seed of life — the seed of the flame."

"...seed?" Neipas voiced soundlessly through his finger-draped lips; he stared out between two hands, as if afraid of what might be lurking in his intimate ken.

"The human flame, Neipas. Plant its seed — and watch grow within you a tree enveloped in flames, whose fire, always burning, never consumes its bark, its leaves, flowers, or fruit. It's the divine tree — the tree of life.

"Watch the tree grow and the light of the fire expand in a circle around it — so that you see beyond the dead bodies near you, so that you see far away from the self into the various possibilities of your being. Nurture it, grow it within you, until it reaches the very summit of your being, which is your consciousness — your I. Your consciousness — your I will then perch upon the highest bough of the tree of life sprouted from your self, and you will say then, with truth, 'I am my self'.

"Watch the tree take root and deepen; and you will see how a spring bubbles up from the pierced holy ground, and how a sea expands over the shallowness of the empty. An ocean will wash away the dead bodies and you will see that all things will flow around you — all the souls of which you are made will circle round your self. And you will be the breath that steers the waters, and you will bring to you that which is the best in you, that whom you wish to become.

"And you will contemplate the depth of the waters. Watch your spirit take root and deepen into the spring and source of life, and you will see within you those others, of whom you are a part, and who are part of you. First those closest to you — then those farther and farther, deepening across endless branching roots to the beginnings and to the ends of time, touching all who have ever lived and all who will ever live. All, Neipas, live within you. You will see them by the light of the fire, and you will see yourself in them all as in a mirror. Beneath the self you will see the great Self, from which all selves flow.

"Then you will gain consciousness — that all our destinies are inextricable, that all are one, and you will see that all those others are you, and you will see that you are them." She seemed to lean very near his uncovered ear; indeed her voice seemed to sprout from inside him:

"All this is to realize the wonder of life, Neipas. It is to partake in divinity. It is to *live* — in the profound substance of life."

The flame of the torch danced over the winding river and sang in

Oshana's quietude; and the waning moon rose over the valley, already horned, already smiling upon its nocturnal cloak of stars. Neipas respired hard, he swallowed his sorrows thick; sadness cloaked his gaze and mantled his heart.

"Yet the very Earth moves about you, Neipas," spoke she. "The world revolves turbulently and time itself is shaped to a myriad events and many prolonged silences. The very course of your life will toss you about, there is no avoiding it. You will lose your bearing every now and then — so that the flame will be quelled and your inner sight dimmed. Indeed, the flame will die time and time again... But it is characteristic of human beings to traverse the salmon path many times in a lifetime, and in order to seek the depth of life one must first die many times. All things describe within their life the Earth's trajectory, and much as the Earth faces the Sun to shed Her darkness, and turns again from the Sun to Her darkness, so will you, turn again to your darkness and your void — and back once more.

"Indeed, to be reborn — to create ourselves anew — takes much self-sacrifice. But deepen your roots into the self and beyond the self, and even in your darkness you will be able to see, even in the noise you will hear the silence, even in weakness you will be strong. To stand still in the real self is to sustain the vicissitudes of time, and remain one's own. To let pain come and overcome it, and to let pain go — to let joy come, and to let joy go, and overcome — this, is strength."

Neipas could well feel Oshana's smiling eyes upon his sorrowful hands. He no longer knew what effect her words had in him; they worked deep beneath his own awareness. And though the words dropped like so many seeds upon his spirit, still they did not sprout into their meaning, and all was yet desolation upon the surface of his being.

"Plant the seed of life in the holy ground of your emptiness, Neipas," she said. "— be patient, let life bloom within you. Take root in the nothingness in you, beyond which everything *is*. Create yourself in it, it is from it that you flow. Become yourself, Neipas.

"For, from the self, and only from the self, can you propagate without scattering. Therefore sow the seed of life in your center, in the center of the deep, where you *become* — and you will perceive the world, and realize that all things are within you. In the deep center of your being you will realize that each of us is the center — that the universe is an unfathomable circle where the circumference is nowhere, and the center is everywhere... You will realize that the Earth is holy.

"To deepen from the self this way is to expand into the world, within, and without... It is to know we are substance and mirror of the Earth, mirror and substance of all there is."

POSTLUDE

Silence — calm. The night enveloped them with its breaths of fragrant wind; the branches of the trees creaked overhead. Neipas thought it distantly strange how he somehow understood, increasingly clearly, the occult language of Oshana's allegories. He had taken his hands away from his own visage; though he still felt shame and did not gaze upon Oshana. Holding the lamp, beholding the lamp without flame, he placed it slowly upon the soil — he let it rest by the torch near, crackling yet. "And where do I find this seed?"

Oshana answered: "It's already in you, it's already yours — but your life can only be truly found in the lives of others and in the Earth from which life springs. Through the struggle for the lives of others, by giving yourself to the lives of others, and to the Earth, life itself — so it is that you see the depths of others, and thus your own as in a mirror. Only thus can you contemplate that which is your own and hidden from you — through mirrors that reflect the deep.

"It is like this that your emptiness becomes fertile ground. Yet you must be willing — willing to live, and make life your purpose — lest the seed of fire burns your soil and your tree."

Quiet, with a rising, shivering feeling, Neipas reflected in his soul that it had been the search for a seed that had provoked the death of his early life. A seed not of fire, but of ash — it was the lust for its power, buried under the Earth, that made sprout the curses of the mountain and contaminated the valley; its holy grounds forever barren, forever empty. He reflected with a rising feeling that he could not restrain — to his mind gushed his crippled father and his dead mother, his dead lover and their aborted child; the river of his childhood flooded his heart with toxins. "My seed is poisoned — my ground is dead, I have no ground, Oshana!" he cried between convulsive lips and a trembling chin, whispering meek and overcome; and his chest panting and heaving, his throat straining in breathlessness, he let out a wail, and began sobbing uncontrollably. Teardrops rained from his flooded eyes, his breaths shook panicky, his breast convulsed, he rocked back and forth, he shivered all over, he wailed, he wailed, he wailed, inconsolable... In his disorientation he found his head upon Oshana's shoulder, he found himself crying out amid the deluge of choking tears, "I'm sorry! I'm sorry!" Shame mixed painfully with his grief. He hid his face again as Oshana held him.

She fell into contemplation as she soothed the poor boy spilling his tears upon her bosom; and she too trembled a little within the firmness of her strength, filled with compassion for the grievous soul leaning on her, whose tears flowed from that common wellspring of humanity's tragedies and shames, called history. Her burnt fingers rose to the height of her barren womb; and sadly, unconsciously, she whispered to him, with maternal affection: "Don't fear... In truth, there are many ways to sow one's seed."

Her eyes were then directed deep to the soil, upon which, lustering tepid the motions of torchlight, rested the little holy lamp. Oshana seized it carefully. Holding it in her hands with much respect, she contemplated it for a few moments. Deliberately she removed the lid of the fuel chamber; and glancing into its hollow, she saw the coins languishing inside the water made of sea and olive oil, glinting fiery yet, like snapping tongues. And she extracted them with her fingers and laid them upon the palm of her hand. "They've imbued these pebbles with divine power," she said. "Were it so, a single beach would suffice to feed the hungers of humankind, so abundant is the wealth of our Mother.

"In truth, they have sown our souls with the seeds of Mammon, but lo, nothing grows out of these pebbles, and the empty remains empty. We've made Mammon the center — the core of our beings and our societies — here's why everyone feels hollow. Here's why everyone feels lost — the center round which we revolve, is a false center. Mammon made us lose our bearings, and our mirrors are like so many broken compasses.

"The disciples and the priests of Mammon promised us good harvests — but indeed, even those who reap plenty have to contend with poisoned fruit and eat of the part of their harvest that is poisoned. Our holy ground is degraded and made sterile. Who among us has never felt it?

"They've told us to fill our emptiness with money and other such icons and breeds of Mammon. Weren't they, however, warned against idols and false gods? The more we try to fill it with falsities and things strange to our nature, the more bottomless the pit will seem, and the more shallow we will become. Look, our beings are buried under these things, under the need of these things and the dream of these things.

"They've made collecting as many things as possible the highest aim — and lo, here's that we ourselves become many things without becoming anything. Here's that we become nothing, our soul is filled with nothing, our ground is made barren with trash. It's littered with stones. The highest aim has been to collect as many pieces of Mammon as possible and now we're surrounded by fragments of Mammon, we're besieged by Mammon's stale fruit. In truth, this pebble is but a fragment of Mammon. But these little stones and those small curtains they call money — they can't be eaten.

"They can't be eaten and they've become, nevertheless, tokens of life. Without them, one can no longer eat. Without them, one can no longer have garment or take shelter. So it is that we've filled ourselves with these fragments of Mammon. And we become smothered, smothered under these fragments, under the accumulation of needs and desires, short-lived sighs of relief and fleeting joys, petty conveniences and soulless inanities, fears or facts of destitution, and dreams of wealth... and the more our beings are paved with the substance of Mammon, the farther we stray from ourselves, the more unlike our selves we become — the more we lose ourselves.

"In truth, Mammon's art consists of making us search under all his fragments, all his masks, as we wonder, 'am I here?' and, 'is this me?'. And sometimes we say, 'here's a little of my mirth' and 'here's a small distraction' and 'here is, maybe, a piece of my soul', but more often we find that everything we find turns to nothing in a moment, and every mask conceals nothing but sordidness, destruction and a great emptiness... This is what Mammon's seed yields — and our bosoms are filled with it. In our pith, in truth, hide many stillbirths. In our beings hatch many moribund cravings that we come to pet dearly. But behind those cravings hides the parasite Mammon — feeding off our essence, sapping our spirits dry. Our souls are littered with his eggshells, his fragments and his hollow masks.

"Everything has become a mask of Mammon within us. And masks... they do not merely conceal — they also represent, and embody. Everything came to represent a 'resource', everything also conceals a 'price'. And we, too, have become commodities with a price. Mammon has made a carnival of our souls, all things in us have become a market. How many times have we bargained with ourselves, exchanging conveniences for humiliations and bartering necessities with abasement? In truth, our souls have been stolen and sold to the devil Mammon...

"Outside the vitrine he assembled round the circle of our soul he placed all the objects of our necessity and desire — in truth, he placed our selves beyond the glass. Lo, in their mirrors we see ourselves — in endless faces and promises rising before us, in a confusion of brightness and many pretty lights. And through the translucence of their mirrors there beholds the mask of Mammon, whispering, '*fly, fly to my summit!*' — but the shallowness and the void will rise with you, no matter how high you reach — and you will always be an island, never a mountain.

"And yet — because his mask is what we see in the mirrors, his face is what we came to wear." Oshana glanced at the minted pebble mournfully, glinting in the night; and then, lifting her head, directing her gaze far and deep into the valley, fixing her eyes upon the flow of the long stream beneath, she said: "In truth the salmon too, hatches amidst the stones of the riverbed. But from Mammon, nothing grows, nothing except emptiness, an emptiness encased in glass and in mirrors and in a myriad colors that multiply and hide our own void — an emptiness covered in masks. Forgeries... And here's that our souls are dry, dry — poisoned.

"We've become smothered, smothered..." She spoke all these things to herself in her meditations, as Neipas sobbed in her bosom; and even as she spoke and he cried, Oshana stood up, and stepped, slowly, up to the torch overlooking the valley; and through the fire of the torch she beheld the waters of the river. And even as she meditated and Neipas sobbed, Oshana seized the torch, and, arching reverently toward the holy lamp resting dim among her burnt fingers, she tapped it with the flaming head of the torch; and even as she pondered, and Neipas cried, the holy lamp flared in a light of all colors and out of the night sprouted a strange luminosity — out of the river, out of the slopes and the stones of the valley, out of the trees and bushes of the wood, out of the glinting of the stars and the darkness of the sky and out of the smile of the moon there ensued a soft, ethereal, breathing radiance; and the radiance was immanent in all things, it exuded from every fragment of existence. And in this miraculous resplendence — a light that was at once light and darkness — even as she contemplated, and even as Neipas cried in her bosom, Oshana went to Neipas, and knelt before his sitting figure, and she looked into his wide eyes with her own giant, resplendent eyes; and even as she reflected and Neipas wept, Oshana seized the back of his hands; and he took his fingers to his face, at which she (he?) pulled —

and the remainder of his mask came off in a breeze of feathers.

Silence... Silence... Silence... Silence... The world fell quiet. Only the breeze of his breath was upon his senses. His spirit hovered over the water — and between the valley, and under the trees. It was in the flame, he stood within it — and the flame did not consume him. Under the skies he opened his eyes wide, exhaled; gazed and saw. To his soul came the murmur of the stream, and the boughs above him, branching in jagged directions, were skyward rivers, through which the radiance coursed; the leaves appeared like so many river mouths and springs, opening softly to the oceans of the air. Above them, in them, round the dim firmament, the birds winded and the birds circled, floating like the loosened leafs from those endless branches or droplets rained out of those rivers of bark, to darken the twilit, radiant sky in whirling clouds dispersing from the holy flame, barely formed, dispersing from his being in sparks released to the heights and swimming like voices released from the clutch of memory. The wind made the nascent leaves sing like glinting salmon and crackle like flapping wings; and his scattering feathers were fixed upon the trees and upon the glinting waters and upon the abyssal mountains and upon the vastness of the land, they scattered about the moon in the form of stars — and they undulated, they danced, every soul of his soul, with the voice of the Earth.

Silence... There were no shadows anywhere. There no representations, no refractions and no illusions. Everything simply was; and the magic and the miracle of reality became manifest.

He gazed upon Oshana before him — and he saw her visage in the sacred resplendence.

She wore no mask. Hers was a human countenance...

And in her eyes, too — he saw his own face.

*

They smiled; but the notion that it could all end still troubled his spirit. Indeed, he still felt the weight of their neverending absence, and of his own absence within them, within himself, waiting. Afterwards, he sensed returning to him, again, the sense of time.

"But — aren't you afraid?"

"Of dying? [...] I'm at peace with life — and I'm at peace with death. When the time comes, the time comes — and it will be all right. [...] I too am descending toward my last sunset. But the horizon must be faced."

"What do you think happens?"

[...] "Indeed, that's the great mystery..."

"Do you think it's just — nothing?"

"What makes you think that? That we are, that existence is — if that is possible, who is to say? Perhaps it is nothing. Perhaps we'll be reborn another time, perhaps in another Earth — perhaps somewhere near those stars hovering distant, deep above and below — infinite around us."

"[...] Maybe that's where they are... You think?..."

"[...] I cannot know, for I can't remember ever dying. Though in truth, I can't remember ever coming into being either — and yet, here I Am."

"I wish I knew. I wish I knew."

"We must accept — we will see [...] But I suspect you will no longer be Neipas, and I, no longer Oshana."

[...]

"Don't despair. Don't fear. The limits of the future rest in death — so is the dominant way of thinking in our days, and that is why it causes anguish to think about the future. But doesn't most of the past lie beyond our birth? Our life is a cry — our life is a song — a voice between two great silences, Neipas. Our life is a word between two infinite pauses, a word where many tales fit; it's a sacred word. We must honor it deeply.

"Someday the Earth will consume all our works, or the Sun the Earth upon which they persist: and perhaps the Galaxy will one day swallow the Sun and the Universe the Galaxy. What happens then? I do not know, child. I cannot know. But we all have a right to this gift that is the present, the gift of past and future, the gift of life.

*"We are one, we are multiple, and the One binds all things. Inside each of us is a river, and everyone else's river is the tributary of our own, as our own spreads into a tributary of everyone else's. Your parents, they flow in you still... Honor them — let your inner river flow forth. Burst through the dams. **Live!**"*

80 - Days of Hope

Oshana took him to the middle of camp, where a large pile of firewood had been kindled. Beyond black trees draped in shadow Neipas saw the enormous flame rising from the wide clearing, reaching its dancing hands toward the night sky, spiriting up its glitter of embers to the stars like some zealous devotee. Round the fire sat the tribe. It was a tribe of many tribes — for the camp had taken in its midst Oyate of different clans, who had fled the mountain's widespread conflagrations; Ostrich refugees and refugees from Axiac and the surrounding areas, including some migrants who, in the confusion of the incoming tempest, managed to overcome the barricades of Wall Street, and seek shelter in the mountains; there were activists and organizers from the coalition and scattered, wayward workers from the surrounding farms — all took refuge here. A few hundred they numbered now; concentric, quiet, they assembled round the crackling light and among the palpitating shades.

Tenderly, the sage matriarch parted from Neipas, retiring to her tent. She needed to reap strength from slumber, she had said, because the march tomorrow would be long; but sit by the fire a bit, she told him, let warmth and conversation lull you into rest — and she pointed to Orenda sitting there in the circle, before placing her hand on his arm and gazing into his eyes profoundly, with a smiling stare that reflected the people and the flame burning in their midst, fluttering over lips that drew quietly a trace of hidden, mysterious divinity. Neipas watched her disappear into the darkness of the wood and watched her form growing arcane amid the shadows; thus she vanished into the depth of the wood, and from the depth of his own soothed heart flowed a gratitude that made him smile.

Neipas went and sat next to Orenda. She introduced him to the people around her, with whom she had been speaking; he was greeted with a sincere, tranquil and warm eagerness that moved him, made him feel welcome, included. In a few days, Neipas would have met everyone in the camp, and begun to forge a bond of deep kinship with them, begun to see the members of the tribe — which, in its universal extent, encompassed the whole world — as his own brethren.

After the introductions, Orenda brought Neipas into the intimacy of private dialogue.

"Oshana tell you about the march, by the way?" she began.

Neipas nodded. "Yeah, she did."

"Are you coming?"

He kept still for a moment, deepening into himself in reflection. And then, smiling, a bit melancholy, a bit tired, he said, "Yeah... I'll go."

They shared a moment of silence together. Neipas stared down at his feet and, by them, the soil palpitating in the firelight; but he knew Orenda watched him carefully, considered him, tried, perhaps, to read him.

"What you did was really brave, you know," she said after a while.

Neipas looked up at her and faced her tender, her beautiful glimmering eyes.

"What."

"At the Eagles' Nest."

"Oh."

His sight blurred in the comfy warmth and tilted back to the ground; his chin returned to the back of his hands, whose fingers folded over his knee.

"I dunno about that," Neipas mumbled, shrugging. "Doesn't matter..."

His tears had drained him of energy and sapped him of discernment. Oshana's words had had the effect of mollifying him and planting the seed of hope and strength in him, but that hope and that strength slept still under his dormant being. And though their talk had been cathartic, though it made him feel content, a certain hopelessness yet lingered in him, remaining in vestiges of meekness and in the exhaustion of his body. Mostly he felt his fatigue; it left little space for anything else.

"You think that what you did doesn't matter?" asked Orenda.

"I guess... I mean, what did it do?" He shrugged again. "Nothing."

"You think it did nothing?" repeated Orenda — tilting her head (he could see it through the corner of his eye), as if trying to see the shine of his downcast glare.

For the third time he shrugged. "Well — yeah. No? They're still going around as if nothing happened. I dunno."

And, sighing out of the quietude into which they had profounded together for moments, Neipas looked at her, and blinked despondent. "You know, I..." he swallowed dry, swallowing down the words marshaling in his throat as he sought better ones in his mind ("um..." he scratched his tired eyelids, exhaled his listless spirit. She waited). "I didn't record it but — I know who ordered the... the wildfires. I heard it — there. At the Eagles' Nest."

Silence.

"Who?"

Again he scratched his brow, again his eyes fixed the soil. "Penaguiar's chair."

There followed another quietude, through which the crackling of the fire bled into the long cadence of his breaths, the languid beats of his heart. He seemed to mull long, but his head, indeed, slept. Out of that sleep and out of the visceral sentiment that arose from it he spoke: "But I can't prove it... And what I did record — looks like it's just being dismissed. Ignored... Nobody's gonna pay attention, probably.

"So yeah — what I did was nothing." He sighed a feeling of emptiness cleaved by despair, he exhaled the void remnant in his tiredness. "I dunno, just feels like... we're too fucking small. Too fucking small..."

Again they descended into the crackling and murmuring silence — even those that sat close to them seemed distant, the two were complete in their intimacy — and after a while Neipas hesitantly looked up again. He saw Orenda's eyes distant now; she beheld the fire. He had had a sense of his cheek growing colder somehow, as if he had sensed Orenda no longer contemplating it.

At length, she began to speak. "What you've just told me I've heard from many people. I've seen the feeling in many people — I've seen it in myself, many times. I've heard myself saying your words. We feel that we're too small. That we don't matter. That nothing matters.

"Well, yeah. We *are* small — but what does that have to do with mattering? Being small is fantastic — we can contemplate the vastness of the world and feel awe and wonder. To be a giant — to fill up all things — to be everything — is to be nothing."

Then she looked at him. "We are small — but we are many. The potential of our collective force is endless... you know? It's scattered now, while the force of our enemies is concentrated — but we'll have the bigger power so long as we can gather our power. As we're building that though, it might feel like we're not progressing — like we're going around in the dark, right?

"It's like we're under the ground, and need to dig up to find the surface, the soil, the sun... And you chip, chip, chip at it... Crumbs fall, they keep falling, and it feels like we're not getting any closer — until eventually, suddenly, the ceiling caves and we can climb out. Into the vastness of the world... And the sunlight is on us, and we can finally see each other, we can finally see who we are and where we need to go — we can see that we're together and that we can go together."

Neipas smiled, chuckled a little. He was fond of Orenda's figures of speech, her ways were endearing to him. "Wouldn't the ceiling fall on us?"

"It will — if we dig enough. But we gotta sustain that if we want to see the other side."

Neipas nodded as he ruminated her words; but in this, then, he felt suddenly despondent — though the association between her metaphor and his experiences arrived late, it touched his consciousness tragically now — and he muttered, "Some will never leave the underground, though."

Into the overall haze of his awareness — suddenly populated with the giant demonic masks of the Eagles, and with the bodies of the victims whom those masks concealed — he heard a sigh seeping slowly; the muffled presage of tears too, sounded in a sorrowful note: "Marlene told me what happened at the Eagles' Nest," said Orenda. "Cesar — he..."

A silence of grief ensued, a silence that doesn't know how to choose words; a silence imbued with such things as have no words to represent them. Neipas' sight alternated between dry and wet blurs, it saw through the slumber of fiery blinks. After a long time he looked at Orenda and saw that she, too, contemplated the fire. And as if she were awaiting for him to awake from his reverie, Orenda spoke shortly after he turned his eyes to her, though she kept her own gaze steady upon the flame.

She said, "You honor the dead by honoring life." And, turning her eyes to him again, Neipas felt in her stare the profound affinity of experience and sensibility which they held between them; as she looked at him he sensed himself deep in her melodious eyes, and he sensed, mystically, his heart pulsing her words; he sensed his soul breathing with the sound of her shimmering voice, enchanted entirely in the nocturnal motion of her lips, as he gazed upon her gaze, and listened. "We must carry on for their sake also. We honor the dead by killing the death that killed them. You know...? Your parents, my parents, Cesar, Kasim — they were all victims of Mammon. We ought to remember them, honor them, fight for them. But don't let grief be the thing that glues the old mask to your face...

"You honor life by fighting for life — you honor life by *living*, Neipas. *You*. Not Neipas the waiter. You. So you should live, and honor those who left, and keep them alive in you. And you should live for those who will come, so that they may live too. You've realized by now that your life isn't just your own, and that the best way to live is to live for others. You wouldn't have risked yourself like that if you hadn't realized that. It wasn't just revenge, it wasn't just anger."

"How do you know?" he asked, softly, sad.

She smiled contemplatively. "I can tell. If it weren't for the kindness and the strength in your heart, Neipas, you wouldn't have done it. When you committed yourself to doing what you did, you committed yourself to being *who you are*. You committed yourself to *life*, Neipas. *You* did. You. Not Neipas the waiter, not Neipas the Columbidae, not Neipas the child, not Neipas the trauma. You.

"Those masks have fallen — can't you see?" and so she put her hand upon his cheek; and he sensed it upon his bare skin, unveiled, unmasked — in that moment he felt the touch of another upon him true for the very first time. The universe seemed to still and quiet in its boundless immensitude; the very fire seemed to fall silent, and all disappeared but its brilliance, and the two of them shined upon in it — in a whirl of emotion he quivered, and gazed into her with dewy eyes as she spoke thus the words:

"You can be you in the fullness of yourself, you understand? Be who you're meant to be. Do what you're meant to do. Are you a photographer? Photograph. Are you a sculptor? Sculpt. Are you a writer? Write. Do you have a voice? Speak. Do you have your senses? Use them for the betterment of the world — for the creation of the new society, where everyone alive has a chance to live, has the *right* to *live*. And you — live, too...

"Because we're doing this for life, all life. The life of those who have been, the life of those who are, and the life of those who will be."

*

They began the march at sunrise. With tents and provisions packed, they set off from the depth of the mountain range toward the megalopolis. The trek through the scorched woods would be arduous; for the path was long, and they were many. Neipas walked among multitudes, and along the way he learned a myriad names. By and by he seemed to pass the time more at ease; he seemed to grip time with meaning, feeling, by and by, more and more fulfilled within his own skin.

On the morning of the first day, Orenda returned to him the jacket which he had been wearing when he arrived, delirious and ill. It was Eva's jacket. It had been washed; Orenda asked him if he would like it mended. Wordlessly Neipas shook his head. Better to let the holes and tears be; better to be true to what he lived inside that jacket, wear it and cherish it as it was, until the end of his days — he felt somehow that it would be the best way to honor Eva's memory and the pain of her departing.

Inside that heritage of her munificence — that memento of her kind heart — he found (in the inner breastpocket) the lump of glued prints. They had been separated and whatever was recoverable had been restored. Much had been lost to blurs; yet much had been retained. As to the precious photograph of his parents, almost everything had been washed away in tidal grays — except for the face of his father and that of his mother near, which emerged from the misty nothings and laughed yet among the landscape vanishing in a sweep of inks all about them.

The notebook that Orenda had given him — upon which he had bled his madness — was nowhere to be found. Orenda, however, was there.

Alongside her much of the time, Neipas observed the expanse of charred hills, the spectral beauty of the burnt trees, the folk who settled reverentially among them, friends laughing together, children playing together, brethren eating, drinking, praying together, as they journeyed; people loving each other, people being people. There was a raw joy in that observation without filter, a spiritual comfort in those people without mask. By degrees Neipas felt his heart beat alive again in his chest. By degrees he felt himself emerged out of the stupor — it felt something like being born again.

By degrees he felt life again, and on the afternoon of the second day of marching the tribe arrived upon a wide plateau, wherein the Axiac Zoo had been built. Nothing but its ruins had been left standing. It had been gradually left to abandon, with the mountain fires being so near to it; closing in on it quickly, scaring goers away — though indeed, it had been bleeding money ever since its chaotic opening. The lack of profit translated to a lack of care; and many animals had nearly been left to starve as the project was phased down. The fury of the storm ended it — and what happened to the complex after that, no one knew. So a small group was sent to find out, in an expedition of which Neipas was a part.

The facilities were rusting, and growing nature already worked to overtake the compounds. Sunlight blasted through their windows and there were trees and undergrowth already proliferating as far as the last speck of glow allowed within the shadows of the cave. Among the moss, upon the lichens, many of the animals were found dead, disregarded and untreated. But those who were not found dead had simply disappeared. Their cages were empty, the glass enclosing them broken. The wild beasts had escaped to prowl the wilderness, to roam it freely.

The tribe took care from then on to watch for the animals on the loose. Martin and his friends spoke excitedly about seeing the lions; Edazima and every mother watched them closely and protected them near. Yet the unshackled creatures must have gone very far, for no one saw them; not the scouts, not anybody. "Truly," said Oshana when she saw the caverns which had once housed the zoo, "no one can tame the Earth." That night they camped at the mouth of the cave, once a prison of beasts, now a ruin of men.

In the morning they set out to traverse the plateau and entered the thickening forests uphill. At the close of the third day, toward dusk, Neipas and Orenda went for a short walk outside camp, after it was set. Drizzle fell, and a mist descended upon the forest. Heard in the wideness of space was only the sound of their steps, ringing invisibly out of the dense shower soft as air, as though the air itself had dissolved into droplets of water. From the watery fog only the somber forms of trees could be made out, spectral and giant in their mysterious quietude. If they stood still their ear could, perhaps, pick up the faint wavering of the branches overhead upon the wind, blown very soft from the distant ocean. They walked in silence. Orenda simply looked up and about from time to time, mesmerized, before curving her eyes back onto the ground and into deep reflection. She seemed to be enjoying the intimate mystique of the evening, somewhat bewitched under the momentary illusion that there was nothing beyond the thick veil of drizzle, nothing beyond the two of them and the sound of their steps ringing quietly into an infinite nothingness. Neipas, too, imagined. The warm breath of the earth whispered itself into his contemplation, infusing him with a calm so profound as to still his heart in immaculate quietude. The ghostly outlines of the trees would have perturbed his musings, perhaps, were it not for Orenda's company; as it was, the phantom grays didn't stop him from imagining this must have been the aspect of the world when it first started: Nothing but a veil of soft rain and a singular pulse of steps, of steps sounding side by side into the void.

The fourth day dawned cloudless and clear. The march began early. They were already at the foot of the last ascent when the sun broke free above the mountain peaks behind them. The tribe, its members of every age, of every ability, of every clan, climbed up the last of the hill, rose the strenuous march toward the rocky summit. All about them the valleys sank and the cliffs arose; the sunlight shone upon the dew, the dampened earth bloomed patiently into blades of green, seeds of flower lifted their gentle arms toward the morning star. When they stepped upon the top, it was noon — the sun rested in its zenith. Beneath them was the megalopolis.

The titanic extent of the plain of concrete and glass unfolded along the mountain range to far norths and souths, and deepened into the distant west where it shored upon the edge of an infinite ocean. It was vast in its might — but even Axiac, they saw, was enclosed by the rocks and the waters. It lay ruined by the elements — its sham of invulnerability exposed to the running breeze. The glass of the towers lay prostrate across the grounds, shining yet — but toward the heavens now, as though pleading for divine aid. Only the light of the sun shone upon the heads of its citizens. "We must be released from our concrete cage. We must be delivered from this transparent box." Even the great height of the Belab was no taller than them.

Stepping atop a stone, Orenda sounded the horn into the vastness to announce the new ideal to the peoples below.

Atop the mountain peak they sat for a while, partaking of food and drink amid the sound of music and the jubilant cries of running children, observing the flourishing valleys beside them, and the ruins of the great city beneath.

Then, they began their descent.

Milton Keynes UK
Ingram Content Group UK Ltd.
UKHW020857061224
452240UK00013B/755

9 789893 368882